LISA GARD
Three Great Novels
The Thrillers

Lisa Gardner sold her first novel when she was twenty years old and has since been published in over a dozen countries. In 1993 she graduated *magna cum laude* from the University of Pennsylvania with a degree in international relations. Now living in the New England area with her husband, she spends her time writing, travelling and hiking.

Also by Lisa Gardner

The Perfect Husband
The Other Daughter
The Third Victim

Lisa Gardner

Three Great Novels: The Thrillers

The Next Accident
The Survivors Club
The Killing Hour

ORION

First published in Great Britain in 2004 by
Orion
An imprint of Orion Books Ltd
Orion House, 5 Upper St Martin's Lane, London WC2H 9EA

ISBN 0 75286 736 9

A CIP catalogue record for this book is available
from the British Library

Printed and bound in Great Britain by Clays Ltd, St Ives plc

www.orionbooks.co.uk

Contents

The Next Accident

Acknowledgements

For most of my career as a suspense author, I've been repeatedly greeted by the comment, "Wow, you look so nice for someone who writes such twisted books." For once I'd like to agree. I really am a dull, ordinary person leading a dull, ordinary life. The only real background I have is as a business consultant, and while I suppose characters could die from process reengineering efforts gone horribly awry, I'm not sure anyone other than Dilbert enthusiasts would appreciate that.

Thus I have enlisted the help of the following experts to give my plot especially devious twists and my characters especially evil deaths. Please bear in mind that these people patiently and accurately answered all my questions. That does not mean, however, that I used their information in a patient or accurate way. I am a firm believer in artistic license, plus I possess a warped mind. We all have our talents.

That said, my deepest gratitude and appreciation to:

Dr. Greg Moffatt, Ph.D., Professor of Psychology, Atlanta Christian College, for generously answering my steady stream of questions and offering such fabulous insights into the criminal mind.

Phil Agrue, Private Investigator, Agrue & Associates, Portland, OR, who in three hours convinced me that I want to be a defense investigator when I grow up.

Gary Vencill, Consultant-Legal Investigation, Johnson, Clifton, Larson & Corson, P.C., whose delight in creating an auto accident/murder scenario was equaled only by his diligence in personally showing me how to tamper with seat belts.

Dr. Stan Stojkovic, Professor of Criminal Justice, University of Wisconsin-Milwaukee, for his insights on prison protocol and communication.

Dr. Robert Johnson, American University, who was gracious enough to allow me to use his honest academic study as a model for conducting various forms of criminal mayhem.

Larry Jachrimo, custom pistolsmith, whose ongoing assistance with firearm details and ballistics techniques enables me to be more diabolical than I ever hoped. He provides me with wonderful information; I do make some mistakes.

Mark Bouton, former FBI firearms instructor and fellow writer, for helping bring my FBI agents into the new millennium.

Celia MacDonell and Margaret Charpentier, pharmacists extraordinaire, who also have a very promising future as poisoners. Nothing personal, but from here on out, I'm bringing my own food.

Mark Smerznak, chemical engineer, great friend, and extraordinary cook.

Heather Sharer, wonderful friend, jazz enthusiast, and general shoulder to cry on.

Rob, Julie, and Mom for the tour of the Pearl District and steady stream of café mochas.

Kate Miciak, editor extraordinaire, who definitely made this a better book.

Damaris Rowland and Steve Axelrod, agents extraordinaire, who encourage me to always write the book of my heart, and even better, allow me to pay my mortgage while doing so.

And finally to my husband, Anthony, for the supply of homemade chocolate champagne truffles and chocolate mousse cake. You know how to keep a writer motivated, and I love you.

THE NEXT ACCIDENT

PLAN A

Prologue

Virginia

His mouth grazed the side of her neck. She liked the feel of his kiss, whisper-light, teasing. Her head fell back. She heard herself giggle. He drew her earlobe between his lips, and the giggle turned to a moan.

God, she loved it when he touched her.

His fingers lifted her heavy hair. They danced across the nape of her neck, then slid down her bare shoulders.

"Beautiful, Mandy," he whispered. "Sexy, sexy, Mandy."

She giggled again. She laughed, then she tasted salt on her lips and knew that she cried. He turned her belly-down on the bed. She didn't protest.

His hands traced the line of her spine before settling in at her waist.

"I like this curve right here," he murmured, dipping one finger into the concave curve at the small of her back. "Perfect for sipping champagne. Other men can have breasts and thighs. I just want this spot here. Can I have it, Mandy? Will you give that to me?"

Maybe she said yes. Maybe she just moaned. She didn't know anymore. One bottle of champagne empty on the bed. Another half gone. Her mouth tingled with the forbidden flavor, and she kept telling herself it would be okay. It was just champagne, and they were celebrating, weren't they? He had a new job, the BIG job, and oops, it was far away. But there would be weekend visits, maybe some letters, long-distance phone calls …

They were celebrating, they were mourning. It was a farewell fuck, and either way champagne sex shouldn't count with the nice folks at AA.

He tilted the open bottle of bubbly over her shoulders. Cool, sparkling fluid cascaded down her neck, pooling on the white satin sheet. She lapped it up helplessly.

"That's my girl," he whispered. "My sweet, sexy, girl … Open for me, baby. Let me in."

Her legs parted. She arched her back, the whole of her focusing down, down, down, to the spot between her legs where the ache had built and now only he could ease the pain. Only he could save her.

Fill me up. Make me whole.

"Beautiful, Mandy. Sexy, sexy, Mandy."

"Pl-pl-please …"

He pushed inside her. Her hips went back. Her spine seemed to melt and she gave herself over to him.

Fill me up. Make me whole.

Salt on her cheeks. Champagne on her tongue. Why couldn't she stop

7

crying? She tilted her head down to the sheets and sipped champagne as the room spun sickeningly.

Suddenly the bed was gone. They were outside. In the driveway. Clothes on, cheeks dry. Champagne gone, but not the thirst. Six months she'd been dry. Now she craved another drink horribly. One bottle of champagne still unopened. Maybe she could get him to give it to her for the drive home. One for the road.

Don't go …

"You okay, baby?"

"I'm okay," she mumbled.

"Maybe you shouldn't be driving. Maybe you should stay the night …"

"I'm okay," she murmured again. She couldn't stay, and they both knew it. Beautiful things came, beautiful things went. If she tried to hold on now, it would just make it worse.

He was hesitating, though. Looking at her with those deep, concerned eyes. They crinkled at the corners. She had loved that when she first met him. The way his eyes creased as if he was studying her intently, really, truly seeing her. Then he'd smiled a split second later, as if merely finding her had made him so very happy.

She'd never had a man smile at her like that before. As if she were someone special.

Oh God, don't go …

And then: *Third bottle of champagne. All full. One more for old times' sake. One more for the road.*

Her lover took her face between his hands. He stroked her cheeks with his thumbs. "Mandy …" he whispered tenderly. "The small of your back …"

She couldn't answer anymore. She was choking on her tears.

"Wait, baby," he said suddenly. "I have an idea."

Driving. Thinking really hard because the narrow road curved like a snake and it was dark and it was so strange how early she could have a thought, and how late her body would be in responding. He sat beside her in the passenger's seat. He wanted to make sure she got home safe; then he'd take a cab. *Maybe she should take a cab. Maybe she was in no shape to drive. As long as he was coming with her, why was she the one at the wheel?*

She couldn't hold on to that thought long enough to make it work.

"Slow down," he cautioned. "The road is tricky here."

She nodded, furrowing her brow and struggling to concentrate. *Wheel felt funny in her hand. Round. Huh.* Pressed on the brakes. Hit the gas instead. The SUV lurched forward.

"Sorry," she muttered. World was beginning to spin again. She didn't feel well. Like she was going to throw up, or pass out. Maybe both. *If she could just close her eyes …*

Road moved on her again. Vehicle jerked.

Seat belt. Needed a seat belt. She groped for the strap, got the clasp. Pulled. Seat belt spun out toothlessly. *That's right. Broken. Must get that fixed. Someday. Today. May day. Stars spinning away, sky starting to lighten. Sun going to come up. Now she just needed a little girl singing,*

"Tomorrow, tomorrow, there's always tomorrow—"

"Slow down," he repeated from the passenger's seat. "There's a sharp turn ahead."

She looked at him numbly. He had a strange gleam in his eyes. Excitement. She didn't understand.

"I love you," she heard herself say.

"I know," he replied. He reached for her kindly. His hand settled on the wheel. "Sweet, sexy, Mandy. You're never going to get over me."

She nodded. The dam broke, and tears poured down her cheeks. She sobbed hopelessly as the Ford Explorer swerved across the road, and the gleam built in his eyes.

"I'm as good as it gets," he continued relentlessly. "Without me, Mandy, you'll be lost."

"I know, I know."

"Your own father left you. Now, I'm doing the same. The weekend visits will stop, then the phone calls. And then it will just be you, Mandy, all alone night after night after night."

She sobbed harder. Salt on her cheeks, champagne on her lips. *So alone. The black abyss. Alone, alone, alone.*

"Face it, Mandy," he said gently. "You're not good enough to keep a man. You're nothing but a drunk. Christ, I'm breaking up with you, and all you can think about is that third bottle of champagne. That's the truth, isn't it? *Isn't it?*"

She tried to shake her head. She ended up nodding.

"Mandy," he whispered. "Speed up."

"Why didn't Daddy come home for my birthday? But I want Daddy!"

"Sweet, sexy Mandy."

Fill me up. Make me whole.

So alone …

"You hurt, Mandy. I know you hurt. But I'll help you, baby. Speed up."

Salt on her cheeks. Champagne on her lips. Her foot settling on the gas …

"One little push of the accelerator, and you'll never be lonely again. You'll never have to miss me."

Her foot …The approaching curve in the road. *So alone. God, I'm tired.*

"Come on, Mandy. Speed up."

Her foot pressing down …

At the last minute, she saw him. A man on the narrow shoulder of the country road. Walking his dog, looking startled to see a vehicle at this time of the morning, then even more surprised to have it bearing down on him.

Turn! Turn! Must turn! Amanda Jane Quincy jerked frantically at the wheel …

And it remained pointed straight ahead. Her lover still gripped it, and he held it tight.

Time suspended. Mandy looked up without comprehension at the face she had grown to love. She saw the rushing dark through the window behind him. She saw the seat belt strapped tight across his strong, broad chest. And she heard him say, "Bye-bye, sweet Mandy. When you get to hell, be sure to give your father my regards."

The Explorer hit the man. Thump bump. A short-circuited cry. The vehicle plowed ahead. And just as she was thinking it would be okay, she was still in one piece, they were still in one piece, the telephone pole reared out of the darkness.

Mandy never had time to scream. The Explorer hit the thick wooden pole at thirty-five miles per hour. The front bumper drove down, the back end came up. And her unsecured body vaulted from the driver's seat into the windshield, where the hard metal frame crushed the top of her skull.

The passenger had no such problems. The seat belt caught his chest, pushing him back into his seat even as the front end of the Explorer crumpled. His neck snapped forward. His internal organs rushed up in his chest, momentarily cutting off his air. He gasped, blinked his eyes, and seconds later, the pressure was gone. The SUV settled in. He settled in. He was fine.

He unfastened his seat belt with his bare hands. He had done his homework and he wasn't worried about prints. Nor was he concerned about time. A rural road in the early hours of dawn. It would be ten, twenty, thirty minutes before someone happened by.

He inspected beautiful, sexy Mandy. She still had a faint pulse, but she was now missing most of the top of her head. Even if her body was putting up a last-ditch fight, her brain would never recover.

A year and a half of planning later, he was satisfied. Amanda Jane Quincy had died scared, died confused, died heartbroken.

He and Pierce Quincy were still not even, the man thought, but it was a start.

1

Fourteen months later
Portland, Oregon

Monday afternoon, private investigator Lorraine Conner sat hunched over her paper-swamped desk, punched a few more numbers into her old, cagey laptop, then scowled at the results shown on the screen. She tried the numbers again, got the same dismal results, and gave them the same dark look. The Quicken-generated budget, however, refused to be intimidated.

Damn file, she thought. Damn budget, damn heat. And damn circular fan that she'd purchased just last week and was already refusing to work unless she whacked it twice in the head. She stopped now to give it the requisite double-smack and was finally rewarded with a feeble breeze. Christ, this weather was killing her.

It was three in the afternoon on Monday. Outside the sun was shining, the heat about to crest for another record-breaking July day in downtown Portland, Oregon. Technically speaking, Portland didn't get as ridiculously hot as the East Coast. Nor, in theory, did it get as humid as the South. These days, unfortunately, the climate didn't seem to realize that. Rainie had long since traded in her T-shirt for a white cotton tank top. It was now plastered to her skin, while her elbows left rings of condensation on the one clear spot on her desk. If it got any hotter, she was taking her laptop into the shower.

Rainie's loft offered central air, but as part of her "belt-tightening" program, she was cooling her vast, one-room condo the old-fashioned way—she'd opened the windows and turned on a small desk fan. Unfortunately, that little matter of heat rising was conspiring against her. The eighth-floor condo wasn't magically getting any cooler, while the smog content had increased tenfold.

Bad day for belt-tightening programs. Especially in Portland's trendy Pearl District, where iced coffee was served on practically every street corner, and all the little cafés prided themselves on their gourmet ice cream. God knows the majority of her upwardly mobile neighbors were probably sitting in Starbucks right now, basking in air-conditioned glory while trying to choose between an iced Chai or nonfat mocha latte.

Not Rainie. No, the new and improved Lorraine Conner was sitting in her trendy loft in this trendy little neighborhood, trying to decide which was more important—money for the Laundromat, or a new carburetor for her fifteen-year-old clunker. On the one hand, clean clothes always made a good impression when meeting a new client. On the other hand, it didn't do her any good to land new cases if she had no means of carrying them out. Details, details.

She tried a fresh round of numbers in her Quicken file. Showing a gross lack of imagination, the file spit back the same red results. She sighed. Rainie had just passed the Oregon Board of Investigators' test to receive her license. In the good news department, this meant she could start working for defense lawyers as a defense investigator, à la Paul Drake to their Perry Mason. In the bad news department, the two-year license cost her seven hundred bucks. Then came the hundred dollars for the standard five-thousand-dollar bond to protect her against complaints. Finally, she got to fork over eight hundred dollars for a million dollars in errors-and-omissions insurance, more CYA infrastructure. All in all, Conner Investigations was moving up—except she was now out sixteen hundred dollars and feeling the crunch.

"But I like eating," she tried to tell her computerized business records. They didn't seem to care.

A buzzer sounded. Rainie sat up, dragging a hand discouragingly through her hair, while she blinked twice in surprise. She wasn't expecting any clients today. She peered into the family room, where her TV was tuned in to the building's security cameras and now broadcasted the view from the main entrance. A well-dressed man with salt-and-pepper hair stood patiently outside the locked front doors. As she watched, he buzzed her loft again. Then he glanced up at the camera.

Rainie couldn't help herself. Her breath caught. Maybe her heart even stopped. She looked at him, the last person she expected to see these days, and everything inside her went topsy-turvy.

She ran a hand through her newly shorn hair again. She was still getting used to the look, and the heat made it flip out like a dark, chestnut dish mop. Then there was her tank top—old and sweat-soaked. Her denim shorts, ripped up, frayed, and hardly professional. She was just doing paperwork today, no need to dress up, and oh God had she put on deodorant this morning, because it was really hot in here and she could no longer tell.

Supervisory Special Agent Pierce Quincy remained gazing up at the security camera, and even through the grainy image, she could see the intent look in his deep blue eyes.

Rainie's scattered thoughts slowed. Her hand settled at the hollow of her throat. And she studied Quincy, nearly eight months since she'd last seen him and six months since even the phone calls had stopped.

His eyes still crinkled in the corners. His forehead still carried deep, furrowed lines. He had the hard, lean features of a man who spent too much time dealing with death, and damn if she hadn't liked that about him. Same impeccably tailored suit. Same hard-to-read face. There was no one quite like SupSpAg Quincy.

He pressed the ringer for a third time. He wasn't going away. Once he made up his mind about something, Quincy rarely let it go. *Except her ...*

Rainie shook her head in disgust. She didn't want to think that way. They'd tried, they'd failed. Shit happened. Whatever Quincy wanted now, she doubted it was personal. She buzzed him in.

Eight floors later, he knocked at her front door. She'd had time for deodorant, but nothing in the world could save her hair. She swung open the door, balanced one hand on her denim-clad hip, and said, "Hey."

"Hello, Rainie."

She waited. The pause drew out, and to her satisfaction, Quincy broke first.

"I was beginning to worry that you were out on a case," he said.

"Yeah well, even the good guys can't be working all the time."

Quincy raised a brow. His dry tone made her positively nostalgic as he said, "I wouldn't know anything about that."

She smiled in spite of herself. Then she swung the door open a bit wider, and truly let him in.

Quincy didn't speak right away. He walked around her loft casually, but Rainie wasn't fooled. She'd blown the majority of her savings on the loft just four months ago and she knew the kind of impression it made. The eleven-foot ceilings of a converted warehouse space. The open, sunny layout with nothing but a kitchen counter and eight giant support columns to carve out four simple spaces: kitchen, bedroom, family room, and study. The huge expanse of windows, filling the entire outer wall with original 1925 paned glass.

The woman who had owned the condo before Rainie had finished the entranceway with warm red brick and painted the living space with rustic shades of adobe and tan. The result was the shabby chic look Rainie had read about in magazines, but knew better than to try on her own.

The loft had nearly bankrupted her, but the minute Rainie had seen it, she couldn't have gone without it. It was fashionable, it was upscale, it was beautiful. And maybe if the new and improved Lorraine Conner lived in this kind of place, she could be that kind of person.

"It's nice," Quincy said finally.

Rainie scrutinized his face. He seemed sincere. She grunted a reply.

"I didn't know you did sponge painting," Quincy commented.

"Don't. The previous owner."

"Ahh, she did a nice job. New hairdo?"

"I cut off the length and sold it to buy the loft, of course."

"You always were clever. Not organized, as I can tell by looking at the desk, but clever."

"Why are you here?"

Quincy paused, then smiled grudgingly. "I see you still know how to cut to the chase."

"And you still know how to dodge a question."

"Touché."

She arched a brow, signaling that, too, wasn't an answer. Then she propped up her hip on the edge of her desk, and knowing Quincy as well as she did, she waited.

Supervisory Special Agent Pierce Quincy had started his career as an FBI profiler, back in the days when that division was called the Investigative Support Unit and he was known as one of the best of the best. Six years ago, after a particularly brutal case, he'd moved to the Behavioral Science Unit, where he focused on researching future homicidal practices and teaching classes at Quantico. Rainie had met him a year ago, in her hometown of Bakersville, Oregon, when a mass murder had ravaged her quaint community and garnered Quincy's attention. As the primary officer, she had walked that crime scene with him, having met him just an hour before and already impressed by how impassive he could keep his face, even when looking at the chalk outlines of little girls.

She hadn't had his composure in the beginning. She had earned hers the hard way, over the following days of the investigation, when things in her town had gone from bad to worse, and she'd realized just how much she had to fear. Quincy had started as her ally. He'd become her anchor. By the end of the case, there'd been the hint of more.

Then Rainie had lost her job with the sheriff's department. Then the DA had charged her with man one for a fourteen-year-old homicide, and she'd spent four months waiting for her day in court. Eight months ago, without warning or explanation, the charges against her were dropped. It was over.

Rainie's lawyer had the impression that someone might have intervened on her behalf. Someone with clout. Rainie had never brought it up, but she'd always suspected that person was Quincy. And far from drawing them together, it was one more thing cluttering the space between.

He was Supervisory Special Agent Pierce Quincy, the man who'd brought down Jim Beckett, the man who'd discovered Henry Hawkins, the man who probably did know what had happened to Jimmy Hoffa.

She was simply Lorraine Conner, and she still had a lot to do to get her life on track.

Quincy said, "I have a job for you."

Rainie nearly snorted. "What? The Bureau's no longer good enough for you?"

He hesitated. "It's … personal."

"The Bureau's your life, Quincy. It's *all* personal for you."

"But this more so than most. Could I have a glass of water?"

Rainie furrowed her brow. Quincy with a personal mission. She was hopelessly intrigued.

She went into the kitchen, fixed two glasses of water with plenty of ice, then joined him in the family room. Quincy had already taken a seat on her overstuffed blue-striped sofa. The couch was old and threadbare, one of the few remnants of her life in Bakersville. There, she'd lived in a tiny ranch-style house with a back deck surrounded by soaring pine trees and air filled with the mournful cries of hoot owls. No sounds of sirens or late-night partyers. Just endless evenings crammed full of memories—her mother drunk, her mother raising her fist. Her mother, missing most of her head.

Not all of the recent changes in Rainie's life were bad.

Quincy took a long sip of water. Then he removed his jacket and carefully draped it over the arm of the sofa. His shoulder holster stood out darkly against his white dress shirt.

"My daughter—we buried Mandy last month."

"Oh Quincy, I'm sorry," Rainie responded instinctively, then fisted her hands before she did something awkward such as reaching out to him. She knew the story behind Mandy's automobile accident. Last April, Quincy's twenty-three-year-old daughter had collided head-on with a telephone pole in Virginia, causing permanent brain damage as well as shattering her face. At the hospital, she'd immediately been put on life support, though that had only been intended to sustain her organs long enough to gain permission for harvest. Unfortunately, Quincy's ex-wife, Bethie, had confused life support with life, and refused to have the machines turned off. Quincy and Bethie had argued. Finally, Quincy had left the bedside vigil to return to work, a decision that had alienated his ex-wife even more.

"Bethie finally gave permission," Rainie supplied.

Quincy nodded. "I didn't think … In my mind, Mandy has been dead for well over a year. I didn't think it would be this hard."

"She was your daughter. It would be strange if it were easy."

"Rainie …" He appeared on the verge of saying something more, maybe caught up in this moment when they seemed like old friends again. Then the moment passed. He shook his head. He said, "I want to hire you."

"Why?"

"I want you to look into my daughter's accident. I want you to make sure that it *was* an accident." Rainie was too flabbergasted to speak. Quincy read her doubt and rushed on firmly: "Some things have come up. I want you to investigate them."

"I thought she was drunk," Rainie said, still trying to get her bearings. "Drunk, hit a man, a dog, and a telephone pole. End of story."

"She was drunk. The hospital confirmed that she had a blood alcohol level of twice the legal limit, but it's how she came to be drunk that has me concerned. I met a few of her friends at the funeral, and one of them, Mary Olsen, claims that Amanda spent most of the evening at Mary's house, playing cards and drinking Diet Coke. Now, I hadn't spoken with Mandy in a bit. You … you know I haven't had the closest relationship with her. But apparently, Amanda had joined AA six months before her accident and was doing very well. Her friends were very proud of her."

In spite of herself, Rainie frowned. "Did something happen during the card game? Get her upset, make her drive straight to a bar?"

"Not according to Mary Olsen. And Amanda didn't leave until nearly two-thirty in the morning, after the bars were closed."

"Was she alone?"

"Yes."

"Maybe she drove home and got drunk."

"And then got back into her car to drive where?"

Rainie chewed her bottom lip. "Okay, maybe she had liquor stashed in her car and started drinking the minute she left the party."

"No containers were found in her vehicle or in her apartment. Plus, the liquor stores would all be closed, so she couldn't have purchased it that night."

"Maybe she'd bought it before arriving at her friend's, then she threw away the empty containers on her way home. You know, to cover her tracks."

"Amanda crashed fifteen miles from her apartment, on some back road that bears no direct relationship to Mary Olsen's house or hers."

"As if she was just out driving …"

"Drunk, at five-thirty in the morning, with no obvious supply of alcohol," Quincy finished for her. "Rainie, I'm concerned."

Rainie didn't answer right away. She was still turning the facts over in her mind, trying to make the pieces fit. "She could have gone to someone else's house after leaving Mary's."

"It's possible. Mary said Amanda had met a man a few months before. None of Amanda's friends had met him yet, but he was supposedly a very nice man, very supportive. My daughter … Amanda told Mary that she thought she might be in love."

"But you never met this guy?"

"No."

She cocked her head to the side. "What about at the funeral? Surely he attended the funeral?"

"He didn't attend the funeral. No one knew his name or how to contact him."

Rainie gave Quincy a look. "If he's that great, he would've found *you* by now. Surely Mandy mentioned her father, and given the amount of press you've received on various cases …"

"I've thought of that."

"But no sign of Mr. Wonderful."

"No."

Rainie finally got it. "You don't think this was an accident, do you? You think it is Mr. Wonderful's fault. He got your little girl drunk, then let her drive home."

"I don't know what he did," Quincy replied quietly, "but somehow, Amanda got access to alcohol between two-thirty and five-thirty in the morning, and it cost her her life. She was troubled. She had a history of drinking … Yes, I would like to hear his side of things."

"Quincy, this isn't a case. This is one of the five stages of grief. You know—denial."

Rainie tried to utter the words gently, but they came out bald, and almost immediately, Quincy was pissed off. His lips thinned. His eyes grew darker, his features harsher. For the most part, Quincy was an academic, prone to approaching the world as a puzzle to be analyzed and solved. But he was also a hunter; Rainie had seen that side of him, too. Once—their final evening together—she had fingered the scars on his chest.

"I want to know what happened the last night of my daughter's life," Quincy uttered firmly, precisely. "I'm asking you to look into it. I'm willing to pay your fees. Now, will you take the case or not?"

"Oh for God's sake." Rainie bolted out of her chair. She paced the room a few times so he wouldn't see how mad he'd just made her, then said sourly, "You know I'll help you, and know I won't take your damn money."

"It's a case, Rainie. A simple case, and you don't owe me anything."

"Bullshit! It's another bread crumb you're tossing my way and we both know it. You're an FBI agent. You have access to your own crime lab; you have one hundred times the number of contacts I do."

"All of whom will want to know why I'm asking questions. All of whom will pry into my family's life and will sit in judgment of my concerns, even if *they* are too polite to accuse me of denial."

"I'm only saying—"

"I know I'm in denial! I'm her father, for God's sake. Of course I'm in denial. But I'm also a trained investigator, just like you, Rainie, and something about this stinks. Look me in the eye and tell me it doesn't stink."

Rainie stopped. She mutinously looked him in the eye. Then she wished she hadn't, because his jaw was tight and his hands were clenched into fists, and dammit she liked him when he was like this. The rest of the world could have composed, professional Pierce Quincy. She wanted this man. At least she had.

"Did you ask the DA to drop the charges against me?" she demanded.

"What?"

"Did you ask the DA to drop the charges against me?"

"No." He shook his head in bewilderment. "Rainie, I'm the one who told you to go through with the trial, that it was probably the best way to put the past behind you. Why would I then interfere?"

"Fine, I'll take your case."

"What?"

"I'll take your case! Four hundred dollars a day, plus expenses. And I don't know beans about Virginia or motor vehicle accident investigation, so no accusing me later of not having enough experience. I'm telling you now, I'm inexperienced, and it's still going to cost you four hundred dollars a day."

"There you go with that charm again."

"I'm a fast learner. We both know I'm a fast learner." She said that more savagely than she'd intended. Quincy's face nearly softened, then he caught himself.

"Deal," he said crisply. He picked up his jacket, drew out a manila envelope and dropped it on her glass coffee table. "There's the accident report. It includes the name of the investigating officer. I'm sure you'll want to start with him."

"Jesus, Quincy, you shouldn't be reading that."

"She's my daughter, Rainie; it's the only thing I can do for her anymore. Now, come on, I'm buying."

"Buying what?"

"Dinner. It's too damn hot in here, Rainie, and you really need to put on some clothes."

"Just for that, I'm wearing the tank top to dinner. And as long as you're buying, we're going to Oba's."

2

One night out on the town, and it was easy to slip into old roles. Quincy sweeping into town and taking her out to an extravagant restaurant. Eating great food, tropical shrimp ceviche, rare ahi tuna, butternut squash enchiladas. Quincy drank two world-famous marionberry daiquiris, served in chilled martini glasses. Rainie stuck to water, because in a place like Oba's she was too embarrassed to conduct her little ritual of ordering—but not drinking—a Bud Light.

They talked a little. They talked a lot. God it was good to see him again.

"So how is the investigative business?" Quincy asked halfway through dessert, when they had exhausted small talk and settled in.

"Good. Just got my license. Number five hundred and twenty-one, that's me."

"Doing private work?"

"Some. I got in with a few defense attorneys; they're the ones who convinced me to get licensed. Now I can do more work for them—background checks on witnesses, crime-scene reconstruction, police report analysis. Still a lot of sitting at the desk, but it beats chasing down the cheating husband or wife."

"Sounds interesting."

Rainie laughed. "Sounds dull! I spend my time logged on to the Oregon Judicial Information Network. On a really exciting day, I might access my Oregon State Police account to peruse criminal history. It takes intelligence, but we're not talking adrenaline rush."

"I read lots of reports, too," Quincy said, sounding mildly defensive.

"You fly places. You talk to people. You get there while the blood's still fresh."

"You miss it that much, Rainie?"

She avoided his gaze to keep from answering, wished she did have a bottle of Bud Light, and switched topics. "How's Kimberly?"

"I don't know."

Rainie arched a brow. "I thought she was the daughter who liked you."

Quincy grimaced. "Tact, Rainie. Tact."

"I strive to be consistent."

"Kimberly needs some space. I think her sister's accident hit her harder than the rest of us. She's angry, and I don't think she's comfortable with that yet."

"Angry with Amanda, or angry with you and Bethie?"

"To be honest, I'm not sure."

Rainie nodded. "I always wanted a sister. I figured that must be something special, to have a genetic ally in the world. Someone to play with. Someone to fight with. Someone who had your parents, too, so she could tell you if your mom really was nuts, or if it was all in your head. But it doesn't sound like Mandy has been much of an ally for Kimberly. Instead, she's been the major source of family stress."

"The rebellious older sister, getting all the attention," Quincy agreed.

"While Kimberly behaves as the model child, the born diplomat."

"Bethie hates for me to say it, but Kim will make a terrific agent someday."

"She's still pursuing criminology?"

"Psychology for her B.A. Now she's looking at submatriculating into a master's program for criminology." The lines in Quincy's forehead momentarily smoothed away. He was very proud of his younger daughter, and it showed on his face. "How's Bakersville?" he asked presently.

"Okay. Moving on the best you can after these things."

"Shep and Sandy?"

"Still together." Rainie shook her head as if to say, who understood. "Shep's working for a security company in Salem. Sandy's gotten active in revamping juvenile law."

"Good for her. And Luke Hayes?"

"Making a fine new sheriff, or so he tells me. I visited five, six months ago. The town's in good hands."

"I'm surprised you went back."

"Luke had some business for me."

Quincy gazed at her curiously; she finally gave up the information with a shrug. "He was getting inquiries about my mom."

"Your mom?" Quincy was surprised. Rainie's mother had been dead for fifteen years, murdered by a shotgun blast to the head. Most of the people in Bakersville figured Rainie had pulled the trigger. That's what happens when you leave a house with brains dripping down your hair.

"Some guy was calling around town, trying to find her. Luke thought I should know about it."

"Why after all this time?"

Rainie grinned; she couldn't help herself. "The guy had just gotten out of prison. Released after serving thirty years for aggravated murder. Yeah, my mom knew how to pick 'em."

"And apparently she knew how to make an impression," Quincy added drolly, "if the man was still thinking about her thirty years later."

"Luke gave him the score. Ran a background check to be sure nothing was funny. Passed it along to me, and that's that."

Quincy had that strange look on his face again. Rainie thought he might be about to say more, then he apparently changed his mind.

The waiter came with the bill. Quincy paid it. And just like old times, Rainie pretended it didn't bother her.

The sensible thing would've been to end the night there. Quincy had flown in, handed her some desperately needed business, and taken her out on the town. She should quit while she was ahead. But it was only seven o'clock, the temperature was just beginning to cool, and her ego still felt raw.

Rainie walked him through the Pearl District. Look at this gorgeous antique store, complete with a Porsche illegally parked out front. Here's another coffeehouse, here's an art gallery, here's a showroom for unique, hand-made furniture. She led him by rows of recently converted warehouses, their facades now redone in creamy yellows and warm brick reds, modest exteriors for half-a-million-dollar condos and luxurious penthouse suites. People sat in tiny square gardens that dotted each front door. More than a few J. Crew-clad couples walked their prized black Labs down well-manicured streets.

Look at this place, Rainie thought. Look at me. Not bad for a small-town Bakersville girl.

Then she glanced down at her ripped-up shorts and ratty tank top, and that quickly, the euphoria left her. She wanted this world, with its pretty, pretty things. She hated this world, with its pretty, pretty things. She was thirty-two years old, and she still didn't know who she was or what she wanted out of life. It made her angry, but mostly with herself.

She made an abrupt about-face, and headed for the hills. After a confused moment, Quincy followed.

Touché was a local place. It had stood when poor college students were the only ones who found the declining warehouse district inhabitable. It would stand long after the SUV crowd got tired of cavernous lofts and fled for greener pastures. The downstairs of the building was a restaurant. Not bad. The upstairs was a pool hall. Much better.

Rainie handed over her driver's license and a wad of cash at the bar. In return, she got a rack of billiard balls, two cue sticks, and two Bud Lights. Quincy arched a brow, then took off his jacket. He wore the only suit in a dimly lit room filled with half a dozen bikers and two dozen college kids. He was now the fish out of water, and he knew it.

"Eight ball," Rainie said. "Junk balls count the same as a scratch. Hit the eight in first and you die."

"I know the game," he said evenly.

"I bet you do." She racked up the balls, then handed him the cue stick to break. He offered her the first pleasant surprise by rolling the stick on the table to test for warp.

"Not bad," he commented.

"They run a good show here. Now stop stalling and break."

He was good. She'd expected that. In their time together, she hadn't found his weak spot yet, something that both irritated her and held her attention. But Rainie had been living in the Pearl District for four months now, and Touché was still the only place that felt like home. The tables were scuffed from use, the carpet well worn, the bar beat up. The place had taken its lickings, just like her.

Quincy hit two balls in on the break and went on a six-ball run before missing. Leonard, the bartender, stopped by long enough to watch, then shrugged indifferently. Touché attracted its fair share of pool sharks and he'd seen better.

Rainie took over with a swagger. She felt good now. Adrenaline in her veins, a pleasant hum in her ears. She was smiling. She could feel it on her face. A light was beginning to burn in Quincy's eyes. She could feel it on her bare arms as she bent over the table. His shirt collar was open, his sleeves rolled up. He had chalk on his hands and another light blue smudge on his cheek.

They were on dangerous ground now. She liked it.

"Corner pocket," she said, and the game truly began.

They played for three hours. He won the first game when she got cute and tried to hop the cue ball over the eight. She missed. He won the second game when she got aggressive and tried a triple bank shot to close out the table. She missed again. Then she won the third, fourth, and fifth games by nailing those same shots and giving Quincy's meticulous nature something to consider.

"Give up yet?" she asked him.

"Just warming up, Rainie. Just warming up."

She gave him a huge grin and returned to the table. Game six, he surprised her by exchanging some of his finesse for power. So he'd been holding out on her. It only made things more interesting.

He got her game six; they settled in for game seven.

"You've been playing a lot," he observed halfway through a four-ball run. His tone was mild, but his brow was covered with a sheen of sweat and he was taking more time to line up his shots than he had in the beginning.

"I like it here."

"It's a nice place," he agreed. "But for real pool, you need to go to Chicago."

He went after the eight ball and missed. Rainie took the cue stick from him.

"Fuck Chicago," she told him and cleared the felt-lined table.

"What now?" Quincy asked. He was breathing hard. She was, too. The room had grown hot. The hour was late. She was not so naïve that she missed the nuances in his question. She looked around inside, at the poor, beat-up room. She looked outside, where streetlights glowed charmingly. She thought of her beautiful, overpriced loft. She thought of her old fifties-style rancher in Bakersville and the soaring pine trees she still missed.

She looked at Quincy then, and ...

"I should go home now," she said.

"I thought as much."

"I got a big job in the morning."

"Rainie ..."

"Nothing's really changed, has it? We can fool ourselves for a bit, but nothing's changed."

"I don't know if anything changed, Rainie. I never knew what was wrong to begin with."

"Not here."

"Yes here! I understand what happened that last night. I know I didn't handle it as well as I could've. But I was willing to try again. Except next thing I knew, you were too busy to see me when I came into town, then you were so busy you couldn't even return a phone call. For God's sake, I know what you're going through, Rainie. I know it's not easy—"

"There you go again. Pity."

"Understanding is not pity!"

"It's close enough!"

He closed his eyes. She could tell he was counting to ten so he wouldn't give in to impulse and strangle her. There was irony in that, because physical abuse was something she would have understood better and they both knew it.

"I miss you," he said finally, quietly. "Eight months later, I still miss you. And yes, I probably came here and offered you a job for that reason as much as anything—"

"I knew it!"

"Rainie, I won't miss you forever."

The words hung in the air. She didn't pretend to misunderstand them. She thought of Bakersville again, the house she grew up in, that big back deck, those gorgeous towering pine trees. She thought of that one day fifteen years ago, then that one night, fifteen years ago, and she knew he must be thinking of them, too. Quincy had told her once that getting the truth out would set her free.

One year later, she wasn't so sure. She lived with the truth these days, and all she could think was that there were still so many things cluttering the space between.

"I should go home now," she said again.

And he repeated, "I thought as much."

Rainie walked home alone. She turned on the lights of her cavernous loft alone. She took a cool shower, brushed her teeth, and climbed into bed alone.

She had a bad dream.

She was in a desert in Africa. She knew the place from some wildlife show she'd watched one night on the Discovery Channel. In her dream, she half recognized the scenes as part of that TV program, and half felt they were unfolding in real time in front of her.

The desert plains. A horrible drought. A baby elephant born to a sick, exhausted mother. He rose shakily to his feet, covered in goo. His mother sighed and passed away.

Sitting too far away to help, Rainie heard herself cry, "Run little guy, run." Though she didn't know yet why she was afraid.

The hour-old baby leaned against his mother, trying to nurse a corpse. Finally, he staggered away.

Rainie followed him through the desert. The air shimmered with heat, the hard-baked earth cracked beneath their feet. The orphaned elephant uttered little moans as he searched for food, for companionship. He came to a grove of sagging trees and rubbed his body against the thick trunks.

"The newborn pachyderm mistakes the tree trunks for his mother's legs," Rainie heard an unseen narrator report. *"He rubs against them to announce his presence and seek comfort. When none comes, the exhausted creature continues his search for badly needed water in the midst of this savage drought."*

"Run little guy, run," Rainie whispered again.

The baby lurched forward. Hours passed. The baby began to stumble more. Collapsing into the unforgiving ground. Heaving himself back up and continuing on.

"*He must find water,*" the narrator droned. "*In desert life, water means the difference between life and death.*"

Suddenly, a herd of elephants appeared on the horizon. As they neared, Rainie could see other young calves running protectively in the shade of their mothers' bulk. When the herd paused, the babies stopped to nurse, and the mothers stroked them with their trunks.

She was relieved. Other elephants had arrived, the orphan would be saved.

The herd came closer. The baby ran to them, bleating his joy. And the head bull elephant stepped forward, picked up the infant with his trunk, and hurtled him away. The nine-hour-old baby landed hard. He didn't move.

The narrator commented again. "*It is not uncommon for a herd of elephants to adopt an orphan into its midst. The aggressive behaviour you see here is indicative of the severity of the drought. The herd is already under stress trying to sustain its own members, and thus is not willing to add to their group. Indeed, the bull elephant sees the newborn as a threat to his herd's survival and acts accordingly.*"

Rainie was trying to run to the downed infant. The desert grew broader, vaster. She couldn't get there. "Run little guy, run."

The baby finally stirred. He shook his head, climbed unsteadily to his feet. His legs trembled. She thought he was going to go down again, then he bowed his head, pulled himself together, and the shaking stopped.

The passing herd was still in sight. The baby ran after them.

A younger bull elephant turned, paused, then kicked the tiny form in the head. The baby fell back. Cried. Tried again. Two other male elephants turned. He ran to them. They slammed him to the ground. He staggered back up. They slammed him back down. The baby kept coming, crying, crying, crying. And they pummeled him into the hard, cracked earth. Then they turned and ponderously moved on.

"Run little guy, run," Rainie whispered. She had tears on her cheeks.

The infant crawled wearily to his feet. There was blood on his head. Flies buzzed around the torn flesh. One of his eyes had swollen shut. Nine hours of life, all of it cruel, and still he fought to live another.

He took a step. Then one more. Step-by-step, he followed the main elephant herd, no longer bothering to cry and no longer getting near enough to be charged.

Three hours later, the sun sank low and the herd found a shallow pool of water. One by one, the elephants went into the water. According to the narrator, the newborn orphan was waiting for them to be done, then he would have his turn.

Rainie finally breathed easier. It was going to be all right now. The animals had found water, they would feel less threatened, they would help the orphan. He had persisted, and now everything would be all right. That's the way it works. You bear the unbearable. You earn the happily-ever-after.

She thought that right up to the moment when the jackals appeared and in front of the uncaring bull elephants, jumped on the overwhelmed newborn and methodically ripped him to shreds.

Rainie awoke with a start. The plaintive sounds of the dying baby's cries were still ringing in her ears. Tears washed down her cheeks.

She got out of bed unsteadily. She walked through her darkened loft to the kitchen, where she poured herself a glass of water and took a long, long drink.

There was no sound in her loft. Three A.M., still, dark, empty. Her hands were trembling. Her body didn't feel as if it belonged to her.

And she wished ...

She wished Quincy was here.

3

Elizabeth Ann Quincy had aged well.

She'd been raised being told that a woman should always take care of herself. Plucked brows, coiffed hair, moisturized face. Then there was flossing, twice a day. Nothing aged you as fast as bacteria trapped in the gums.

Elizabeth had done as she was told. She plucked and coiffed and moisturized. She put on a dress to run errands. Off the tennis court, she never wore tennis shoes.

Elizabeth prided herself on playing by the rules. She'd grown up in an affluent family outside of Pittsburgh, riding English-style every weekend and practicing her jumps. By the age of eighteen, she could dance *Swan Lake* and crochet a tea cozy. She also knew how to use beer to set her dark brown hair in curlers and how to use a flatiron to straighten it out again. Girls today considered her generation frivolous. Let them stick their heads on ironing boards first thing every morning, and see if they still thought the same.

She had a tough streak. It had taken her to college when her mother had disapproved. While there, it had drawn her to a man quite outside of her family's experience—enigmatic Pierce Quincy. He was from New England originally. Her mother had liked that. (*Mayflower* maybe? Does he still have ties to the motherland? He didn't. His father ran a farm in Rhode Island, owning hundreds of acres of land, and apparently few words or sentiments.) Quincy was pursuing a doctorate in psychology. Her mother had liked that, too. (An academic then, nothing wrong with that. Dr. Quincy, yes very good. He'll settle down, open a private practice. There's a lot of money to be had in troubled minds, you know.)

Quincy had been drawn to troubled minds. In fact, it was his years on the Chicago police force that had convinced him to pursue dual degrees in criminology and psychology. Apparently, even more than the guns and testosterone inherent in police work, he was fascinated by the criminal mind. What made a deviant personality? When would the person first kill? How could he be stopped?

She and Pierce had had long talks on the subject. Elizabeth had been mesmerized by the clarity of his thoughts, the passion in his voice. He was a quiet, well-educated man and positively shocking in his ability to step into the shoes of a killer and assume his path.

The darkness of his work gave her a secret thrill. Watching his hands as he talked of psychopaths and sadists, picturing his fingers holding a gun … He was a thinker, but he was also a doer, and she had genuinely loved that.

In the beginning, when she had still thought they'd marry, settle down, and lead a normal life. In the beginning, before she'd realized that for a man like Pierce, there was no such thing as normal. He needed his work, he breathed his work, and she and their two little girls were the ones who became out of place in his world.

Elizabeth was the only member of her family to get a divorce, be a single mom. Her mother had not liked it, had told her to stick it out, but Elizabeth had found her tough streak again. She had Amanda and Kimberly to think about, and her daughters needed stability, some sort of sane suburban life where their father was not buzzed away from soccer games to look at corpses. Amanda, in particular, had had difficulties with her father's career. She never did understand why she only saw her dad when the homicidal maniacs were through for the day.

Elizabeth had done right by her children. She told herself that often these days. She'd done right by her children.

Even when she'd pulled the plug?

At the age of forty-seven, Elizabeth Ann Quincy was a beautiful woman. Cultured, sophisticated, and lonely.

This Monday evening she walked down South Street in Philadelphia, ignoring the laughing throngs of people who were enjoying the quirky mix of high-end boutiques and sex-toy shops. She bypassed three heavily tattooed teens, then sidestepped a long black limo. The horse-drawn carriages were out in full force tonight, adding the strong scent of horse manure to South Street's already distinct odor of human sweat and deep-fried food.

Bethie resolutely ignored the smell, while simultaneously refusing to make eye contact with any of her fellow Philadelphians. She just wanted to get back to her Society Hill town house, where she could retreat into a comforting shell of ecru-colored walls and silk-covered sofas. Another night alone with cable TV. Trying not to watch the phone. Trying not to wish too badly for it to ring.

She jostled against the man unexpectedly. He was walking out of the gourmet grocery store just as she was passing and knocked her square in the shoulder. One moment she was striding forward. The next she was falling sideways.

He grabbed her arm just before she hit the manure-splattered street.

"Oh, I'm so sorry. Clumsy, clumsy me. Here you go. Up again. Right as rain. You are okay, aren't you? I would hate to think I'd knocked the stuffing out of you."

Elizabeth shook her head in a daze. She started the obligatory *I'm okay,* then actually saw the man who'd collided with her, and felt the words die in her throat. His face … Strong European features with merry blue eyes, while a generous dollop of silver capped the dark hair at his temples. Older, forties or fifties, she would guess. Well-to-do. The fine linen shirt, unbuttoned enough to reveal the distinctive column of his throat and a light smattering of graying chest hairs. The well-tailored tan slacks, belted by Gucci and finished with Armani loafers. He looked … He was gorgeous.

She was suddenly much more aware of his hand still on her arm. She started to babble. "I wasn't looking …lost in my own little world … ran right into you. Not your fault, no apology necessary."

"Elizabeth! Elizabeth Quincy."

"What?" She peered up at him again, feeling even more flustered and not at all like herself. He was tall, very tall, broad shoulders, handsome. And an absolute stranger. She was sure of it.

"I'm sorry," he said immediately. "Here I go again, making a mess of things. I know you, but you don't me."

"I don't know you," Bethie told him honestly. Her gaze fell to his hand, still on her arm. He belatedly released her, and to her surprise, he blushed.

"This is awkward now," he stammered, obviously disconcerted and somehow all the more charming for it. "I don't know quite what to say. Maybe I should never have mentioned your name, never brought it up. Well, in for a penny, in for a pound. I've seen you before, you see. Had you pointed out to me. Last month. In Virginia. At the hospital."

It took Elizabeth a moment to put those facts together. When she did, her whole body stilled. Her face paled. Her arms wrapped around her waist defensively. If he'd been at the hospital, had her pointed out … She thought she knew where this was going now, and something inside her felt ice cold. She closed her eyes. She swallowed thickly. She said, "Maybe, maybe you'd better tell me your name."

"Tristan. Tristan Shandling."

"And how do you know me, Mr. Shandling?"

His answer was as she feared. He didn't say a word. He simply pulled his finely woven shirt from the waistband of his slacks, and bared his right side to her.

The scar wasn't too big, just a few inches. It was still a raw, angry red, fresh out of surgery. Give it another month or two, however, and it would fade, the swelling would go down. It would become a fine white line on a broad, tanned torso.

She reached out a trembling hand without ever realizing what she was doing, and touched the incision.

A sharp gasp brought her back to reality. She blinked her eyes, then realized her hand was on a stranger's stomach and he was still holding up his shirt for her and now people were stopping to stare.

And she was crying. She hadn't realized it, but there were tears on her cheeks.

"Your daughter saved my life," Tristan Shandling said quietly.

Elizabeth Quincy broke down. She wrapped her arms around his waist; she pressed herself against the man who carried Mandy's kidney. And she held him as tight as she'd ever held her daughter, held him as if finding him would bring Mandy back to her. A mother should never have to bury her own child. She had pulled the plug. Oh God, she had given permission and they had taken her baby from her …

Tristan Shandling's arms went around her. In the middle of bustling South Street, he patted her shoulders awkwardly, then with more assurance. He let her cry against his chest and he said, "Shhhh, it's all right. I'm here now, Bethie, and I'll take care of you. I promise."

4

Rainie crawled out of bed at five a.m Tuesday morning. To satisfy her masochistic streak for the day, she proceeded to run six miles in 90 percent humidity. Interestingly enough, she didn't die.

Upon returning home forty minutes later, she went straight into an ice cold shower where she wondered idly what Virginia would be like.

She'd never left the state of Oregon. Every now and then, she'd thought of taking a trip to Seattle, but it never quite happened, so now at the age of thirty-two she was a complete neophyte to the broader United States. She wasn't the only Oregonian like that either. Oregon was a big state. It offered beaches, mountains, deserts, lakes, upscale cities, and small frontier towns. You could gamble, windsurf, rock climb, ski, hike, sunbathe, shop, golf, sail, fish, race, white-water raft, and horseback ride, sometimes almost all at the same resort. So sure you could visit other states, but what would be the point?

She toweled off, chose loose-fitting cotton clothes for the plane, then officially kicked off her new assignment by coughing up two thousand dollars for a last-minute flight across the country. The car rental agency had even more fun with her credit card. Thank God for AmEx.

Her next issue was how to conduct business out of state. As a private investigator, she didn't technically have jurisdictional boundaries. Most state agencies, however, required a local PI license number on all requests for information. Thus, if she wanted to pull DMV records, conduct a title search, anything in Virginia, she'd be out of luck. On the other hand, this was hardly a new problem in the business, and PIs had worked out a way around it.

Rainie pulled out her *Private Investigator Digest*, located a PI in Virginia and gave the guy a call. Fifteen minutes later, after providing her Oregon license number for credibility and explaining her mission, Rainie had a pseudo-partner. She'd pass along her information requests to Virginian PI Phil de Beers, who'd pull the records in return for a nominal fee. The sixteen hundred dollars it had cost her to be licensed had now paid off.

Rainie packed three days' worth of clothes and, given her last case with Quincy, threw in her stainless-steel Glock. She headed out the door.

Three hours later, airborne and finally relaxed enough to let go of the armrests, Rainie read the official report of Amanda Jane Quincy's death.

The first officer at the scene was a Virginia state trooper, responding to a call made from the cell phone of a passing trucker. The call was logged at

5:52 A.M., and the caller, who was very shaken, reported seeing a body along the side of the road. When he'd stopped, he found an older man whom he thought was dead, a small dog that was definitely dead, and deeper in the underbrush, a Ford Explorer crumpled against a telephone pole. Steam still poured out of the smashed hood. The caller said he'd tried to verbally rouse the driver without success. He didn't attempt to touch or move her, however, as he thought that was a bad thing to do in a car accident—might cause further injury.

The trucker was still at the scene when the state trooper arrived. He led the officer straight to the pedestrian, whom the state trooper agreed was DOA. They moved on to the Explorer, where the state trooper was able to force open the driver-side door and check the female motorist for a pulse. He found signs of life, which he passed along to dispatch, while the trucker, having finally seen the full extent of damage to the woman's head, turned around and threw up.

In the good news department, the report provided a great number of details, mostly thanks to the state trooper beating EMS to the scene. As Rainie knew from her own experience, no one ruined a crime scene faster than EMTs, except maybe firemen.

She studied the Polaroids, as well as a small diagram indicating where the pedestrian and dog were found, and then the position of the vehicle against the utility pole. Records showed the vehicle to be a green 1994 Ford Explorer, registered to Amanda Jane Quincy, and purchased used three years earlier. It was a no-frills model, lacking automatic transmission, and more unfortunately for Mandy, a driver-side airbag.

At the time of the crash, the driver was not wearing her seat belt. According to a note made by the trooper, it was found to be "nonoperative." Rainie didn't know what that meant and when she flipped through the pages, she didn't find any follow-up notes.

A designated auto-accident investigator had not been called, which disappointed her. In Oregon, the state police had a separate unit that specialized in analyzing and reconstructing motor vehicle accidents (MVAs). Either Virginia didn't have one, or they didn't feel it was necessary in this case. At least the trooper had run through the basics. No sign of skid marks going into the curve, indicating that the driver never made an attempt to brake. No signs of damage or paint on the rear or side of the Explorer, which would've signaled the involvement of another vehicle. No signs of other tire tracks or impressions at the scene.

The trooper's conclusion was blunt: Single-car accident, at-fault driver lost control of vehicle, check for drugs and alcohol.

At the emergency room, the trooper got to add to his summary: Blood tests confirm blood alcohol level of .20. At-fault driver sustained massive head injury, not expected to live.

The file contained no more notes. The at-fault driver had never regained consciousness to be presented with criminal charges. Over a year later, she'd died. Case closed.

Rainie felt a chill.

She put away the notes, though the photos remained in her hands.

Pictures of that poor man, out walking his dog. Pictures of the poor fox terrier who hadn't had a long enough leash. Pictures of the twisted front end of a massive vehicle, which had crumpled like paper upon impact.

The EMTs had whisked Mandy to the emergency room, sparing everyone those images. The state trooper had captured the front windshield, however, including the shattered upper left quadrant, which bore a macabre mold of Amanda Quincy's face.

Quincy had studied these photos. Rainie wondered how long it had taken him to look away.

She sighed. The report didn't give her much hope. No evidence of any other vehicles involved. The lack of braking, which might bother an untrained investigator, was also consistent with DUI incidents. Also, no evidence of anyone else at the scene. The state trooper had written up a straightforward report, and at this juncture, Rainie had to agree.

But there was the issue of how Mandy came to be drunk at five-thirty in the morning when her friends had seen her sober just three hours before. And there was the "nonoperative" seat belt that had turned what should have been a survivable crash into tragedy. Finally, there was the mystery man, the supposed love of Amanda Quincy's life, whom no one had ever met.

"Still not much of a case," she murmured. But Quincy must be getting to her, because she no longer sounded convinced.

Greenwich Village, New York City

Kimberly August Quincy was having one of those spells again. She stood on the corner of Washington Square in the heart of New York University's campus. The sun was shining brightly. The sky gleamed a vast, vast blue. The grass around the square's signature arch was a deep, deep green. Residents strolled by, tidy in trendy suits and tiny John Lennon sunglasses. Summer students clad in ripped denim shorts and shrink-wrapped tank tops lay out on the green, ostensibly doing homework, but half of them sound asleep.

A nice July afternoon. A safe, charming place, even by New York City standards.

Kimberly was breathing too hard. Panting. She had a bag, once slung over her shoulder, now in a death grip in her hands. She had been on her way somewhere. She couldn't remember where. Sweat poured down her face.

A man in a business suit walked briskly down the sidewalk. He glanced casually at her, then came to a halt.

"Are you all right?"

"Go ... away."

"Miss—"

"Go away!"

The man hurried away, shaking his head and no doubt sorry he'd tried to do a good deed in New York when everyone knew the city was full of nuts.

Kimberly wasn't nuts. Not yet at least. The logical part of her mind, which had taken enough psych classes to know, understood that. She was having an anxiety attack. Had been having them, in fact, for months now.

She'd go days, even weeks, when everything was perfectly normal. She'd just wrapped up her junior year at NYU and with two summer courses, an internship with her criminology professor, and volunteer work at a homeless shelter, she had places to go and people to see. Out the door at six forty-five A.M. Rarely home before ten P.M. She liked things that way.

And then …

A strange sensation at first. A tingle running up her spine. A prickle at the nape of her neck. She'd find herself stopping abruptly, halfway down a street. Or whirling around sharply in the middle of a crowded subway. She'd look for … She didn't know what she looked for. She'd just suffer the acute sensation that someone was watching. Someone she couldn't see.

Then it would go away as swiftly as it had come. Her pulse would calm, her breathing ease. She'd be fine again. For a few days, a few weeks, and then …

It had been worse since the funeral. At times almost hourly, then she'd get two or three days to catch her breath before bam, she'd step onto the subway and the world would close in on her again.

Logically she supposed it made sense. She'd lost her sister, was battling with her mother, and God knows what was going on with her father. She'd consulted Dr. Marcus Andrews, her criminology professor, and he'd assured her it was probably stress related.

"Ease up a little," he'd advised her. "Give yourself some time to rest. What you don't accomplish at twenty-one, you can always accomplish at twenty-two."

They both knew she wouldn't slow down, though. It wasn't her style. As her mother loved to tell her, Kimberly was too much like her father. And in many ways that made the anxiety attacks even worse, because just like her dad, Kimberly had never been afraid of anything.

She remembered being eight years old and going to some local fair with her father and her older sister. She and Mandy had been so excited. A whole afternoon alone with Daddy, plus cotton candy and rides. They could barely contain themselves.

They'd gone on the Tilt-A-Whirl, and the spider, and the Ferris wheel. They'd eaten caramel apples, two bags of popcorn and washed it down with well-iced Coke. Then, positively buzzing with sugar and caffeine, they'd rounded up their dad to continue the adventure.

Except their father wasn't paying attention to them anymore. He was studying some man who stood off to the side by the kiddy rides. The man wore a long, grubby overcoat and Kimberly vividly remembered Mandy crinkling her nose and saying, "Oooh, what smells?"

Their father gestured for them to be quiet. They took one look at the intent expression on his face and didn't dare disobey.

The strange man had a camera around his neck. As they all watched, he took picture after picture of little kids on the rides.

"He's a pedophile," their father murmured. "This is how he starts. With photos, lots of photos of what he wants but can't have. He's still fighting it, or he'd have his own stash of porn by now and not be into fully dressed targets. He's fighting it, but he's losing the war. So he's setting himself up to be a situational offender. Going places where there are lots of children. Then when he finally gives in to his depravity, he'll tell himself it was their fault. The kids made him do it."

Standing beside Kimberly, Mandy faltered. She looked at the strange man, snapping away furiously, and her lower lip began to tremble.

Their father continued, "If you ever see someone like him, girls, don't be afraid to leave the area. Always trust your instincts. Head straight to the nearest security booth, or if you feel that's too far away, duck in behind a woman walking with children. He'll assume she's your mother, too, and give up the chase."

"What are you going to do?" Kimberly asked him breathlessly.

"I'm going to pass along his description to security. Then I'm going to come back here tomorrow and the day after that and the day after that. If he's still coming around, we'll find an excuse to arrest him. That'll at least give him pause."

"I want to go home!" Mandy wailed and started to cry.

Kimberly looked at her older sister without comprehension. Then she turned back to her father, who was sighing at having set off good old Mandy again. Kimmy didn't blame him. Mandy always got upset. Mandy always cried. But not Kimberly.

She gazed up at her father proudly, and in September, when her new teacher asked each child what her parents did for a living, Kimberly declared that her daddy was Superman. The other kids teased her for months. She never did recant.

Her father protected happy children from horrible strange men. Someday, she wanted to do that, too.

Except for this afternoon, when she merely wanted her pulse to slow and her breathing to ease and the bright spots in front of her eyes to disappear. Dr. Andrews had suggested trying biofeedback. She did that now, focusing on her hands and imagining them getting warm, warmer, hot.

The world slowly opened up. The sky became blue again, the grass green, the streets bustling. The hair was no longer standing up at the nape of her neck. The sweat cooled on her brow.

Kimberly finally relaxed her grip on her book bag. She let herself conduct a slow, sweeping circle of everything around her.

"See now," she murmured to herself. "Everyone's just going about their business, having a perfectly usual day. There's no one watching, there's nothing to fear. It's all in your head, Kimmy. It's all in your head."

She resumed walking, but at the intersection she hesitated again. She paused. She turned. She felt that chill. And even though it was a hot July day. Even though she was smart and rational and the strong member of the Quincy family, she started running and she didn't stop for a long, long time.

5

Driving through Quantico, Quincy approached the FBI Academy's guard post, located behind the Marines' facilities, and finally slowed his car. He waited for the young security officer to spot his identifying window sticker, then nodded when the officer signaled for him to proceed. Quincy waved his thanks, but didn't take it personally when the security officer remained grim. It was the guard's job to appear intimidating at all times, he knew. On the other hand, it made an interesting start of work each day.

Not much of a sleeper, Quincy had risen at three A.M. to drive to Seattle and catch a direct flight to DC. He'd spent so many years flying all over the country that layovers had become unbearable to him and he'd do just about anything to hasten the trip. Cars, he liked and his new thing was to avoid planes altogether and drive. He'd thought that might change after Mandy's accident. It hadn't.

Reaching the outdoor lot next to the firing ranges, Quincy parked his car, then walked across the street to the back entrance of the building. He swiped his security card through the electronic reader. It graciously let him in.

Taking the stairs down two flights to the BSU offices, he passed a fellow agent. Quincy nodded in greeting. Special Agent Deacon nodded back while judiciously avoiding his gaze. It had been like that for the last four weeks; Quincy barely noticed anymore. His daughter had died tragically, which was awkward in the best of circumstances, let alone when you worked with people who made their living trying to thwart, and thus control, untimely death. Quincy now stood as a reminder that bad things could happen close to home, that crime-scene photos weren't always of some stranger's daughter. How rude of him to show his face in the office and rock their carefully compartmentalized worlds. Quincy had even heard rumblings that he was wrong to have gone from Mandy's funeral straight to work. What kind of father could be so cold?

He didn't bother addressing those comments. When their own children died, they could figure it out for themselves.

Quincy opened the metal fire door and walked into the BSU offices.

Contrary to Hollywood images, the offices at the FBI Academy were purely functional, and the BSU offices even more so than most. Located in the second sublevel below the facility's indoor firing range, the walls were comprised of cinder blocks painted an appropriate bone-white. As the offices were carved deep into the earth, there were no windows.

The office of the Special Agent in Charge sat in the middle; the remaining offices formed a square perimeter around it. The floor plan reminded Quincy of most major prisons—central control office surrounded by maximum-security cells. Maybe the powers-that-be figured the ambience would help them enter the criminal mind.

The BSU boasted one impressive feature. Its state-of-the-art technology room, closely resembling a TV studio, enabled the agents to do teleconferencing as well as make major presentations with as many bells and whistles as the individual agent could dream up. It always amused Quincy that his working space could be so dull, and his speaking space so sleek. The Bureau did have its priorities.

Quincy hadn't always worked with the BSU. He was one of the rare agents who'd crossed an unspoken line by going from the Child Abduction/Serial Killer Unit (CASKU) to the BSU years ago. It made him something of a novelty in both worlds. An academic who'd entered the glamorous world of profiling, to a glamorous profiler who'd entered the academic world of behavioral science. Both sides used his work. Neither side knew what to make of him.

He hadn't told anyone yet, not even Rainie, but he was considering rocking the boat once more. A month ago, he'd been approached about switching again. He would join what was now called the National Center for Analysis of Violent Crime (NCAVC) as a profiler. At nearly the age of fifty, he would resume working active cases and return to the field.

Honestly, he'd missed it.

When Quincy had first joined the Bureau, he'd told himself he was doing it for the greater good. He'd spent two years as a private-practice psychologist, and while the money was good (Bethie's concern) and the work was interesting (his concern), it left him feeling restless. He'd quit policing to pursue an advanced degree because he felt it was psychology that held his primary interest. Now, he discovered that he genuinely missed detecting. The thrill of the chase, the camaraderie of fellow police officers, the comforting weight of his gun. When a friend in the Bureau approached him later that year, it wasn't a hard sale.

The next thing Quincy knew, he was working one hundred and twenty cases a year. He routinely traveled to four cities in five days. He carried a briefcase filled with photographs of the most savage crimes imaginable. He gave advice that saved lives, and sometimes, he missed clues that cost lives.

While his girls grew up. And his marriage fell apart. And the man who'd once testified in custody hearings was so knee-deep in dead bodies he was the last one to see it coming.

By the time Jim Beckett broke out of a Massachusetts prison by slaughtering two prison guards, Quincy was already a walking advertisement for burnout. By the end of that case, when he was done burying the bodies of various law enforcement officers he'd known and respected, he knew it was time for a change.

He'd transferred to the BSU where he could scale back his travel schedule and make more time for his daughters. He'd missed their childhood. Now, he belatedly tried to catch their high school years.

He designed and taught classes at Quantico while watching soccer games and school plays. He took up researching past cases, including the notorious child killer Russell Lee Holmes, for entry into the FBI's database. He attended Mandy's graduation from high school. He revisited the cold case files, examining records of serial killers who had never been caught. He helped Kimberly select the right college. He created a checklist for identifying potential mass murderers. He got a call to come to a hospital in Virginia, where he watched his older daughter die.

Time had given Quincy regrets. It had also taught him honesty. He understood now that he no longer did what he did to save the world. He worked as an agent for the same reason people worked as accountants and lawyers and corporate clerks. Because he was good at it. Because he liked the challenge. Because when the job was done right, he felt good about himself.

He had not been the husband he had wanted to be. He had not been the father he had hoped to be. Last year, however, he'd connected three mass murders that local officials had thought were one-off crimes.

He was a damn good agent. And year by year, he was working on becoming a better person. He had honestly tried connecting with Mandy not long before the accident. He was definitely trying to connect with Kimberly now, though she seemed hell-bent on ignoring his calls. Last month, he'd even gone to the Rhode Island nursing home and spent an afternoon with his eighty-year-old father, who was so stricken with Alzheimer's that he didn't recognize Quincy anymore and had started the visit by ordering Quincy to go away. Quincy had stayed. Eventually, Abraham Quincy had stopped yelling. Then, they sat in silence, and Quincy worked on remembering the other moments that they had shared, because he knew his father could not.

Quincy was learning the hard way that isolation was not protection, that no number of crime scenes ever prepared you for the death of your own child, and that no matter how many nights passed, it was never any easier to sleep alone.

Rainie had once accused him of being too polite. He had told her that there was enough ugliness in the world without him having to add to it, and he'd meant it.

He had genuinely loved Mandy.

And he was so sorry now that she never knew.

Virginia

When Rainie's plane touched down at Ronald Reagan National Airport, she felt a little giddy. She grabbed her bag from the overhead compartment, collected the small suitcase containing her Glock .40 from baggage claim, and proceeded straight to the car rental agency where she secured the world's tiniest economy car without a hitch. Not bad for her first trip—Dirty Harry, eat your heart out.

Her stomach was rumbling; she hadn't trusted the mystery meat they'd tried to serve her on the plane. It was already four o'clock however, rush hour traffic would be a bear, and she didn't want to miss the change of shifts at the state police barracks. Dinner would have to wait.

She headed straight for the Virginia state police station that had handled Mandy's case, and hoped she got lucky.

An hour and a half of cursing and swearing later, she found state trooper Vince Amity just striding out the door.

"Officer Amity?" she called out, as the desk sergeant waved vaguely in his direction, then went back to reading the latest edition of the *FBI Law Enforcement Bulletin*.

The officer in question paused, realized he was being waved down by an attractive young woman, and halted with more interest.

Rainie seized the opportunity to give him her most charming smile. The smile didn't get much practice, but it must have been good enough because Officer Amity walked back toward her. At six five, he was a big boy with broad shoulders, thick neck, and a jaw line only Jay Leno would love. Rainie was guessing Swedish ancestors and football. Lots of football.

"Can I help you, ma'am?" Big Boy had a southern drawl. Damn, she liked that. Before things got all warm and cuddly, however, Rainie flashed her PI's license. Officer Amity's face promptly fell. Another fine romance nipped in the bud.

"I have some questions regarding an MVA homicide," she started off. "You worked the case about a year ago."

No response.

"The case is closed now—driver died at the hospital, but I'm clarifying some of the details for the family."

Officer Amity said, "I gotta go on patrol now."

"Great. I'll go with you."

"No, ma'am. Civilians can't accompany officers on patrol. Too much liability."

"I won't sue."

"Ma'am—"

"Officer. Look, I flew all the way here from Portland, Oregon, to get answers to my questions. The sooner you start talking, the sooner we can both move on with our lives."

Officer Amity scowled. Given his size, the look really worked for him. Rainie figured the minute he stepped out of his patrol car, most perps dropped obediently to the pavement and held out their wrists for the bracelets. As a woman, she'd never had his advantage. She'd had to wrestle most of her hostiles to the ground. The thing about that, however, was it meant she'd built her career by always being ready for a fight.

Officer Amity was still working the scowl. She folded her arms. Waited. Waited. Big Boy caved with a sigh.

"Let me check in with dispatch," he said. "Then I'll meet you at my desk."

Rainie nodded. Not being a dummy, she followed him to dispatch—police stations had back doors. Five minutes later, they sat across from each other at a beat-up desk, both armed with hot cups of coffee, and got into it.

"April twenty-eight," Rainie said. "Last year. Single-car accident. SUV versus man walking a dog versus a telephone pole. The SUV got the man and dog. The telephone pole got the SUV. Kind of like an obscene version of rock, paper, scissors."

"Female driver?"

"Yep, Amanda Jane Quincy. The accident put her in a coma. Last month, her family pulled the plug. I have a copy of the police report right here."

Officer Amity closed his eyes. "Her father's the fed, right?"

"There you go."

"I should have known," he muttered, and sighed again, a rumbling sound deep in his chest. He opened his desk, drew out a spiral notebook bearing last year's date, and began flipping through the pages.

Rainie waited for him to refresh his memory with his personal notations, then plunged in. "You were the only officer at the scene?"

"Yes, ma'am."

"Why?"

"Everybody was pretty much dead. There's not a whole lot police officers can do about that."

"The driver wasn't dead. Plus, you have at least one fatality and preliminary signs that the driver was operating a vehicle while impaired. In Oregon, that's already the makings of neg homicide if not manslaughter. Surely that's worth calling out a traffic investigation team."

Officer Amity shook his head. "Ma'am, with all due respect, the driver wasn't wearing a seat belt. She'd hit the rim of the windshield and lost half her brain. While she might not have been DOA, even I could tell it was only a matter of time. Now I don't know how it is in Oregon, but in Virginia it doesn't do us any good to build the case when we got no one left alive to charge with the crime."

Rainie eyed him shrewdly. She said two words. "Budget cuts."

Amity's eyes widened in surprise. He nodded slowly, studying her with fresh interest. In most states, the minute an accident involves a fatality, particularly a pedestrian fatality, an accident investigation team will be called out regardless of the condition of the driver. But in the wonderful world of policing, accident investigation teams were the first to feel the sting of budget cuts, even though police officers spent the majority of their time dealing with MVAs and not homicides. Apparently, society couldn't stand the thought of death by stranger, but demise by automobile was okay. Merely the cost of living in the modern age.

"Tell me about the seat belt." Rainie switched gears.

"She wasn't wearing one."

"In the report, it says the strap was 'nonoperative.' What does that mean?"

Amity frowned, scratched his head, and flipped through his notes. "When I was checking for a pulse, I brushed against the seat belt and it pooled out onto the floor. No tension. Gears probably busted."

"The seat belt was defective?"

"It was nonoperative."

"No kidding." Rainie's voice gained an edge. "*Why* was it nonoperative?"

"I haven't the foggiest idea," Amity drawled evenly.

"You didn't examine it, disassemble it? Come on, Officer, if that seat belt had been working, it might have saved the driver's life. That ought to make it worth some attention."

"A defective seat belt is a civil, not criminal, matter, ma'am. Being underworked cops with an unlimited budget, we would love to focus on things outside of our jurisdiction, of course, but that would entail spitting in the face of standard investigative procedures."

Rainie blinked twice, then scowled when she finally detected the sarcasm underlining his amiable drawl. Here was the difference between formal and informal police practices, she thought not for the first time. If she'd come across an accident like Mandy's when she'd been a small-town cop, she would've checked out the seat belt. But small sheriff's departments didn't rigidly follow things like standard investigative procedures. Hell, half of their volunteer staff probably couldn't spell investigative, let alone procedures.

"I made a phone call," Officer Amity said abruptly. His face remained expressionless, but his voice dropped, as if he were about to confess a sin.

"About the seat belt?" As long as they were being coconspirators, Rainie lowered her voice, too.

"I didn't like the fact that lack of seat belt made it a fatality," Amity said, "and it just so happened that the seat belt was broken. So I called the garage that serviced the Explorer. Seems that the broken seat belt wasn't new; it happened a month before. The driver called about having it replaced. Even made an appointment. But she never came in."

"When was the appointment?"

"A week before the crash."

"Did the garage know why she canceled?"

"She called to say something had come up, she'd reschedule shortly." He shrugged. "So now we got a driver running around for four weeks without a proper harness system. Then she crawls behind the wheel dead drunk. I don't know about suspicious, ma'am, but in my book the accident is looking stupider all the time."

Rainie chewed her bottom lip. "I still don't like the *nonoperative* seat belt."

"Makes Daddy nervous," Officer Amity shrewdly guessed.

"Something like that. What about the pedestrian victim, the old man?"

"Oliver Jenkins. Lived one mile from the crash site. According to his wife, he always walked his dog along the road and she always told him it was dangerous."

"Any chance this had something to do with him?"

"Mr. Jenkins was a retired Korean War vet. He lived on a small pension from the state and loved butter pecan ice cream. No, I don't think he did anything to deserve being run over by a Ford Explorer. The dog, on the other hand, had a long history of eating shoes."

Big Boy's face remained so impassive; Rainie almost missed the sarcasm again. Were all Southern boys so charming, or was she just in for a special treat?

"No sign of braking," she tried, still working the suspicious angle.

"Never met a drunk who did."

"Could've gotten tapped by a second vehicle," she rallied.

"No fresh scratches, dents, or paint chips on the SUV. No marks on the tire walls. No additional sets of tire tracks. Look at your photos, *ma'am*."

Rainie scowled. Competent policemen could be such a pain in the ass.

"What about a second person in the vehicle? A passenger?"

"I didn't see one."

"Did you look?"

"I looked in the passenger's seat. There was no one there."

"Did you dust for prints?"

Amity rolled his eyes. "What the hell would you gain by printing a car? First off, the dashboards and most side panels are too rough to yield a print. Second, the smooth surfaces that would work, such as seat belt clasps, door handles, or steering wheels, have been handled by so many Tom, Dick, and Harrys, you'd never get clean ridges. Again, I refer you to standard investigative procedures—"

"I get the point. You're the greatest police officer that ever lived and there is no evidence of a second person at the scene."

"Why, yes ma'am, I think we're finally in agreement."

Rainie smiled thinly at him. Then she leaned forward. "Did you happen to try the passenger-side door?"

Amity's eyes narrowed. She knew he followed her train of thought, because he started to nod. "As a matter of fact ..."

"The door was operable, wasn't it?"

"Yes ma'am."

"And you looked down for footprints?"

"Too much undergrowth. Couldn't get a sign of anything."

"But you were looking, Officer. Why were you looking?"

Officer Amity grew silent. He said finally, "I don't know."

"Off the record."

"I don't know."

"Way off the record. You followed up on this case, Officer, even after you knew the driver was dying. As you kindly pointed out, you state boys are much too overworked to randomly do such a thing. Something bothered you. Something's still bothering you. I'm even willing to bet that you're not that surprised I'm here."

Officer Amity remained silent. Just when she thought he was going to continue to play hard to get, he said suddenly, "I didn't think I was alone."

"What?"

His lips thinned. He continued in a rush. "I was standing at the vehicle staring at that poor, poor girl and this guy is puking out his guts behind me and I swore ... I swore to God I heard someone laughing."

"*What?*"

"Maybe it was all in my head. Jesus, the sun wasn't all the way up yet and it gets kind of hinky on those rural routes. All the trees and brush, half of it hasn't been cleared in the last fifty years. Million and a half places for someone to hide, if they had the mind to. I looked around, checked things out. Never saw a thing. Probably was all in my head. The puking Samaritan didn't help much either. He almost got my leg."

"I want to see the car."

"Good luck."

"Come on, just a quick peek in the impound lot."

Amity shook his head. "It's been fourteen months. Sure the vehicle started in our lot, but only until the insurance company settled. They took it away months ago, probably towed it to some salvage yard where it's already been broken down for parts."

"Shit," Rainie muttered. She worried her lower lip again, not expecting this and trying to think of more options. "I thought there was some rule that seat belts from a wrecked vehicle couldn't be resold as parts. They're no longer guaranteed after the first accident."

"Yes, ma'am."

"So in theory, the salvage yard should at least still have the seat belts."

He shrugged. "If they haven't tossed them into a dumpster by now."

"I'll take my chances. Name of the salvage yard?"

"Hell if I know. The insurance company handles all that."

"Officer ..."

She gave him an intent look. He sighed heavily. "I suppose I could make a call ..."

Rainie summoned her charming smile again. Officer Amity was a smart boy, though, because this time he merely grunted and shook his head.

"You should've opened with that, you know," he told her.

"With what?"

"That you used to be a cop."

"I was just a local. I'm surprised you could even tell."

"I got a good head for these things."

She nodded grimly. "Yeah, that's what I'm afraid of."

6

Bethie was nervous. She shouldn't be doing this. She liked her solitary lifestyle; she was comfortable spending her evenings alone. What had she been thinking? And did these earrings go with this dress? Maybe the earrings were too nice. Maybe the dress was too nice. Oh God, she was going to have to start over again and she was already five minutes late.

She changed from her little black dress to a below-the-knees black skirt with an electric blue satin top. More coverage; she liked that. But she kept the same tall, strappy heels. At her age she was proud of her calves and figured it didn't hurt to show them off. God knows she had a few extra pounds tucked in other locations, let alone what gravity had done to her butt. She had aged well, but on the eve of her first date in over two years, she still felt bitter about Father Time. How is it that men fill out with age, while women fall down?

Earrings. Which pair of earrings? Come on, Bethie, it's just a date. She grabbed the first gold pair she came to, told herself firmly that they were perfect and headed for the door.

She had not expected to have dinner with Mr. Shandling. It had started out as coffee yesterday evening. He felt so bad at having upset her, and she was too topsy-turvy to resist. So he took her to one of South Street's little cafés, plied her with cappuccino, and told her stories until the tears dried on her cheeks and she began to smile.

She stopped looking at his side so much. She started listening to his words more. Tales of travel to Ireland, England, Austria. Scuba diving off the coral reefs of Australia, shopping for precious gems in Hong Kong. He had a rich baritone voice, perfect for spinning fabulous tales and in the end, while she wasn't sure if one man could have really done all those things, she found that she didn't care. She liked listening to him talk. She liked watching the corner of his sparkling blue eyes crinkle every time he grinned. She liked the way he looked at her, as if his sole purpose in life was to make her happy.

He'd asked her to dinner the very next night. She hemmed and hawed. It was moving so fast, she really didn't know …

He was only in town for a week. Surely one dinner couldn't hurt … She'd caved in with a yes. He'd chosen Zanzibar Blue, a renowned jazz club and one of her favorite restaurants. She'd promised to meet him there.

Bethie was not a complete neophyte to dating; she read *Cosmo*. On a first date, always arrive on your own, therefore you can leave anytime you choose. Don't give out too much personal information, such as your home address, right away. Get to know the person first. Just because a man was well dressed and charming didn't mean he was safe. Just ask her ex-husband, Pierce.

Bethie flagged down a taxi, and took the short ride up to Zanzibar's.

Tristan Shandling was waiting for her outside the club. Tonight he wore black pleated slacks with a plum-colored shirt and strikingly patterned silver and turquoise tie. In deference to the hot, muggy weather, he'd eschewed a jacket. With his hands tucked comfortably into his pockets, one foot crossed over the other, he looked dignified, handsome, and totally in control. Bethie took one look at him and promptly wished she'd gone with the little black dress. This man shouldn't be dating some middle-aged mother. A man like him should be meeting some bubble-gum blonde, some little bit of arm candy.

She got out of the cab, self-consciously fingering her matronly skirt. Tristan turned, spotted her, and promptly beamed. "Elizabeth! I'm so happy you made it."

For the life of her, she couldn't think of a thing to say. She stood there silently, clutching her small black purse while his eyes crinkled and he held out his arm to her. Her breath had caught in her chest.

He was still smiling, his blue eyes patient and kind. He knew, she realized abruptly. He understood that she was nervous and by grinning so effusively, he was trying to make things easier for her.

"I'm sorry I'm late," she managed.

He waved away her apology, taking her hand and tucking it into the crook of his elbow. He patted her fingers, which she knew must feel like ice. "Jazz is my favorite," he told her amiably as he escorted her to the doors and the first notes of bluesy horns washed over them. "I hope you don't mind."

"I love jazz," she volunteered. "It's always been my favorite as well."

"Really? Davis or Coltrane?"

"Davis."

" ' 'Round Midnight' or 'Kind of Blue'?"

" ' 'Round Midnight,' of course."

"Ahh, I knew from the first moment I saw you that you were a woman of impeccable taste. Of course, then you agreed to go out with me and cast my whole theory in doubt." He winked.

She found herself finally smiling back. "Well, there's no rule that says you can't enjoy water as well as wine," she said more gamely.

"Dear heavens, have I just been insulted?"

"I don't know. Depends if you're water or wine. I guess I have the whole evening to find out."

"Elizabeth," he said heartily, "we are going to have a smashing good evening!"

And she said with the first real emotion she'd felt in months, "Honestly, I would like that."

Later, over plates of steaming mussels and vegetarian pasta, and a bottle of a very fine Bordeaux, she asked the question that was burning in her mind.

"Does it hurt?" Her eyes drifted to his right side. She didn't have to say more for him to understand.

Slowly, he nodded. "Not as bad as it did, though. Just no more jumping jacks for a while."

"But you're feeling better?"

He smiled at her. "I was born with two bad kidneys, love. The first one failed when I was eighteen. The second one started going last year. I spent sixteen long months on dialysis. That felt bad. Now, as far as I am concerned, things can only feel good."

"Is there ... is there still a chance of rejection?"

"In life, love, and organ transplants. But I take my truckload of meds like a good dooby and say my prayers at night. I don't know why God gives second chances to old rascals like me, but as long as I have one, I hate to complain."

"Your family must be very relieved."

He smiled again, but this time she caught a trace of sorrow in his gaze. "I don't have much family, Bethie. One older brother. He went away a long time ago and I haven't seen him since. There was a woman once. She said she carried my child. I was young though, and I'm afraid I didn't take it too well. When I learned I needed a kidney— well, that hardly seemed the time to call. I don't have patience for fair-weather friends, let alone fair-weather fathers."

"I'm sorry," she said honestly. "I didn't mean to dredge up bad times."

"Not to worry. I've made my mistakes and taken my licks and I still think a quiet life is overrated. I'm going to die with my boots on." He grimaced. "Probably once again hooked to a dialysis machine."

"Don't say that. You've come this far. Besides, you still have plenty of things to do. Like finding your child."

"You think I'm going to find my long-lost child?"

"Yes."

"Why?"

"Because you brought it up in a conversation with a woman you've just met, so obviously you've been thinking about it."

He grew silent. His fingers thrummed the curve of his wineglass. He said seriously, "You're an extremely astute woman, Elizabeth Quincy."

"No, I'm just a parent, too."

"Ah, I don't know ..." He backed off from the conversation, picking up his glass and taking a sip. "I don't even know if the child is a boy or girl, let alone if it's mine. And even at my age ... I'm running around the world most of the time. Hardly father-of-the-year material."

"What is it you do?"

"I specialize in doohickeys."

"Doohickeys?"

"Doohickeys," he chuckled. "I scour the globe for the cute, the strange, the interesting, and most of all, the cheap. Wooden boxes from Thailand, black lacquer from Singapore, paper kites from China. You go into a gift shop, fall in love with some hopelessly overpriced, crudely carved figurine, and that's me, Bethie. I found that just for you. At a hundred percent markup, of course."

She shook her head in mock protest. "And you can make a living at this?"

"I make a very fine living at this. Bring things in by the container loads. Volume is the key."

"You must have a fine eye."

"No, just lots of experience as an impulse shopper." He grinned at her. "And yourself?"

He'd meant the question kindly. He had just volunteered more than a little about himself. Still she flinched, and the instant she did, the smile faded from his face.

"I apologize," he said immediately. "I'm sorry, Bethie. I have this habit of speaking before thinking. I swear I've been meaning to quit—"

"No, no. It's a logical question and you've been very generous about sharing your life—"

"But things are difficult for you, now. I know and I shouldn't have pried."

"It's not … it's not that," she ventured.

He nodded for her to continue, his expression patient, his crinkling blue eyes sincere. It was easy to talk to him, she discovered. Much easier than she would've thought.

"I was raised to be a wife," she told him. "A high-society wife. To create a beautiful home, throw lovely parties, always wear a smile when my husband is at my side. And be a good mother, of course. Raise the next generation of high-society wives."

Tristan nodded gravely.

"And then … then I got divorced. It's funny, I didn't notice it right away. I had Kimberly and Amanda to think about, and in all honesty, things had been rough for them. They needed attention. I needed to give it. I guess I went from being an extension of my husband to being an extension of my daughters. It seemed so natural at the time."

"Except little girls don't stay little girls forever," Tristan filled in.

"Kimberly went away to college three years ago," Bethie said quietly. "Things haven't been the same since."

She looked down at her lap. She couldn't help it. The music was blues jazz tonight, some older woman belting out the aching strains of "At last, my love has come along …" and Bethie felt the melancholy all the way down to her bones.

Her beautiful, empty brick town house. Room after room of so much silence. Four separate phones that rarely rang. Hallways lined with framed photographs that were all she had left of the people she loved.

And standing on that hillside a month ago, staring at that freshly dug, gaping black grave. *Ashes to ashes, dust to dust.*

She was forty-seven years old, and she didn't know who she was anymore. She was forty-seven years old, no longer a wife, no longer Mandy's mother, and she didn't know where she belonged.

Tristan's hand reached over, tangled with her own. He drew her gaze up and she saw he wasn't grinning anymore. Instead he wore a somber expression, not unlike her own. For an uncanny moment she had an image of him, waking up in the hospital after his transplant surgery, and discovering no one at his side. No wife or children to hold his hand. He knew, she thought. He knew.

Her fingers curled around his. The woman continued to sing, "My love has come along ..." and the moment went on and on.

"Bethie," he said gently, "let's take a walk."

Outside, the air was heavy and hot, but the sun was beginning to set and Bethie had always loved this time of day. The world became muted, velvety, offering less color but also fewer sharp lines and hard objects. It comforted her.

They walked in silence, not heading anywhere in particular, but by some mutual understanding of the city, working their way toward Rittenhouse Square.

"My turn to ask a question," Tristan said abruptly. He had loosened his tie and rolled up his shirtsleeves in deference to the wet-wool humidity. He still looked elegant, and Bethie was aware of other people casting them covert glances.

"Ask," she prodded, becoming aware that Tristan was still studying her.

"You promise not to be insulted?"

"After two glasses of wine, you have to work very hard to get me insulted."

He stopped walking in the middle of the block, then turned her so she'd have to face him. "It's not just the kidney, is it?"

"What?"

"This. It's not only about me having your daughter's kidney, is it? I know it's a rude question, and I don't want to upset you, but this evening is going even better than I imagined, and well, I need to know. Some people think when you get someone's organ, you get a piece of her soul as well. Is that what this evening is about? Am I just a proxy for your daughter?" He added in a rush, "Because I'm seriously considering kissing you, Elizabeth Quincy, and I don't think a proxy for your daughter should be doing that."

Bethie felt dazed. Her hand fell free of his, fluttered at the base of her throat, toyed with the collar of her satin shirt. "I don't ... Of course not! That's ... that's foolishness. An old wives' tale. Silly superstition."

Tristan nodded with satisfaction. He seemed ready to resume walking, when she ruined her own argument by saying. "You don't ... You don't feel any differently, do you?"

"Pardon?"

"We did run into each other by chance," she continued hastily, "and yet you knew who I was right away, even though I'd been pointed out to you only once before. That's a little odd, don't you think? God knows when I go to parties I have to meet someone three or four times before I can put a name to a face."

"You helped save my life. That's a bit more significant than some stuffed suit at a black-and-white soiree."

"There's something else."

"What?" He looked genuinely concerned now. The evening had been so beautiful. It pained her to say what she had to say next.

She whispered, "You know my nickname."

"What nickname?"

"Bethie. You've called me Bethie. Many times. Always Bethie, never Liz or Beth. I never told you that was my nickname, Tristan. And how many Elizabeths do you know who go by Bethie instead?"

The blood drained out of his face. His eyes widened, and for a moment, he appeared so horror-struck she wished she could recall her words. Simultaneously, both of their gazes slid to his side, where the scar still puckered pink and raw beneath the protective cover of his shirt.

"Blimey," he breathed.

Bethie had a chill. The night was hot, the humidity oppressive, and still she rubbed her arms for warmth.

"This was a bad idea," she said abruptly.

"No—"

"Yes!"

"Dammit, no!" He reclaimed her arm, his grip firm but not painful. "I'm not your daughter."

"I know that."

"I'm fifty-two years old, Bethie … Elizabeth. My favorite food is steak, my favorite drink Glenfiddich straight up. I run my own business. I enjoy fast cars, fast boats. Lord be praised, I have a deep and abiding love for *Playboy*, and it's not for the articles. Does any of that sound like a twenty-three-year-old girl to you?"

"How did you know Amanda's age?"

"Because the doctors told me!"

"You asked questions about her?"

"Bethie … love, of course I asked questions. Someone had to die for me to live. I think about that. Hell, half my nights I lie awake thinking of nothing but that. I am not your daughter; I swear I'm not even the ghost of your daughter. But I am a man who's grateful."

Bethie was silent. She needed to think about this. Then, she nodded. "It's possible," she offered, "that someone once referred to me as Bethie. You know, in the hospital."

His grip loosened on her arm. "Yes, probably that's how it happened."

She had to know. "Did they tell you about the crash?"

"I know she was drunk, if that's what you mean."

"She'd being doing so well," Bethie said softly. "She'd joined AA just six months before the accident. I had such hopes for her."

He didn't say anything, but his expression gentled. He tucked a strand of her hair behind her ear, his fingers lingering on the curve of her cheek. His thumb stroked her jawline.

"She was so sensitive," Bethie murmured. "Even as a little girl. Nothing fazed Kimberly, nothing scared Kimberly, but my Mandy was always different. Shy. Timid. Bugs scared her. Thanks to Hitchcock, birds scared her. One year, she was terrified of the slide at the school playground. We never knew why. She slept with a night-light on until she was twelve."

"You must have worried about her a great deal."

"I wanted her to feel safe. I wanted her to see herself as strong, independent, and capable. I wanted her to be able to dream bigger than I ever did."

"What happened to her isn't your fault," Tristan said.

"That's what I try telling myself." She gave him a halfhearted smile. "I blame my ex-husband instead."

"Why?"

"His job. He joined the FBI when the girls were little, became a profiler, and for all intents and purposes, disappeared. Granted, he did important work, but I've always been a bit biased—I thought our children should come first. Silly me." She heard the bitterness in her voice and grimaced. "Sorry. You didn't need to hear all that."

"Hear what?"

She smiled again, with none of the gaiety of before when the evening was new, but still a smile. "You're very kind to listen to me," she murmured.

"Ah Bethie, I stand by what I said before. This is the nicest evening I've had in ages. Good things can come from bad, you know. It's taken me fifty-two years and one extremely dangerous surgical procedure to learn that, but I did."

"Are you really only here for a week?"

"This time. But I could arrange to return."

"For business?"

"If that's what you'd like to call it."

She ducked her head, a slow blush creeping up her cheeks. The telltale warmth betrayed her, and his thumb slowly tilted her chin back up. He had moved closer to her. She could feel the heat of his body just an inch away. He was going to kiss her, she realized. He was going to kiss her. She leaned forward.

"Bethie," he murmured right before his lips touched hers, "let me take you for a drive."

7

Quincy's House, Virginia

It was after ten p.m. before Quincy finally returned to his darkened home. He juggled his black leather computer case, a cardboard box of manila files, and his cell phone as he fought with his key. The moment he opened the door, his security system sounded its warning beeps.

He crossed the threshold quickly and in movements born of years of habit, he punched in the entry code without ever having to look at the keys. A minute later, when the front door was closed and locked again, he rearmed the outside sensors while leaving the internal motion detectors disabled. Welcome home.

Quincy valued his security system. Ironically enough, it was probably the only object in his house worth real money.

He went into the kitchen, dropping his computer case and box of files on the counter, then opening his refrigerator for no good reason. It remained empty, having not magically grown any food from the last time he checked. He closed the door, drew himself a glass of tap water, and leaned against the counter.

The kitchen was sizable, modern. It had hardwood floors, a massive stainless steel stove with an impressive stainless steel hood. The refrigerator was industrial-sized and stainless steel. The cabinets were made of cherry wood, the countertops fashioned from black granite. Five years ago, the real estate agent had assured him that this was a kitchen perfectly suited for entertaining. Now Quincy looked at the yawning bay windows of the empty breakfast nook, which still didn't contain a kitchen table.

He traveled a lot. His place looked it.

He pushed away from the counter and roamed the space restlessly. Another long day completed. Another homecoming to ... what?

Maybe he should get a pet. Fish, parakeet, cat, something that didn't take too much care but would at least greet him at the end of the day with cheerful noise or even howling racket. He was not someone who needed a lot of creature comforts. He could handle the absence of furniture, the lack of artwork on his walls. His mother had died when he was very young, and most of his life had been lacking in softer touches. But silence ... Silence still got to him.

He found himself thinking of dinnertime with his father, two people sitting at a scarred pine table, sharing a simple meal, and never saying a word. The farm had required a lot of physical effort. Abraham would be up and out at the break of day. He'd return at sunset. They'd eat. Watch a little TV. Read. Each night, the two of them in separate patched-up recliners, plowing their way through separate novels.

Quincy shook his head. His father had raised his only child the best way he knew how. Abraham had worked hard, put food on the table, and given his son an appreciation for the written word. Quincy could respect that now. He considered himself at peace with things. At least he had until a month ago. Grief played horrible tricks on the mind, and not even he knew what sort of demons were going to leap out of his subconscious next.

He was rattled these days, self-doubt stoked by lunchtimes no one knew of, when he went to Arlington and stood by his daughter's grave; nerve endings eroded by weeks spent working with people who would no longer meet his eye.

He wasn't used to feeling like this, as if the world were an uncertain place and he needed to feel his way carefully or risk plunging into an unknown abyss. Some nights he jerked awake, his heart hammering in his chest with the frantic need to call Kimberly and make sure she was okay, that he still had one daughter left. Ironically enough, some evenings he was consumed by the desire to call Bethie, because while his ex-wife hated his guts, she was someone who had loved Mandy. She was a connection to his daughter, and with each day that went by, there were fewer and fewer of those connections left.

Quincy had not thought it would be this hard. He was an academic, a Ph.D. who'd studied the five stages of grief and the resulting physical and emotional turmoil. You should eat plenty of fresh fruits and vegetables, engage in some sort of vigorous exercise, and avoid alcohol—it never helps. He was a professional, an FBI agent who'd been present numerous times when the word came down that some wife, husband, brother, sister, child would not be coming home again. You should maintain focus, revisit the last days of your loved one's life as objectively as possible and avoid hysterics—they never help.

He was a man after all, an arrogant father who'd assumed tragedy would strike someone else's family and never his. He was not eating plenty of fruits and vegetables. He was not objective about the last few days of Mandy's life. Some days he desperately craved alcohol. And some nights he knew he was dangerously close to hysterics.

The great Supervisory Special Agent Pierce Quincy. Quantico's best of the best. How low the mighty have fallen, he thought, and it disturbed him to find himself still so egocentric, even when dealing with his daughter's death.

He wished Rainie would call. He had thought that he would've heard from her by now, and it bothered him that he hadn't. He rubbed his temples wearily, feeling the low beat of a headache that never really went away these days. And as if on cue, the cordless phone on his kitchen counter began to ring.

"Finally," Quincy muttered and scooped it up. "Hello."

Silence. Strange background noises, like metal clanging against metal.

"Well, well, well," a voice said. "If it ain't the man himself."

Quincy frowned. The voice stirred memories, something in the back of his head. "Who is this?"

"You don't remember me? Aw, and here I thought I was your *loco simpatico*. You fed boys break my heart."

All at once, the voice clicked with a name. "How did you get this number?" Quincy asked sternly, while his palms began to sweat and his gaze flew to his security system to assure himself that it was still armed.

"You mean you don't know yet?"

"How did you get this number?"

"*Amigo,* relax. I just wanna talk. Revisit old times on this fine Tuesday evening."

"Fuck you," Quincy said without thinking. He hardly ever swore, and a moment later he wished he hadn't done so now, because the caller simply began to laugh.

"Ah, Quincy, *mi amigo,* you even swear like a suit. Shit, man, we're hardened criminals here, you gotta do better than that. Fuck your mother, maybe. Fuck your mother up her mother-fucking ass. Yeah, that's a good one. Or maybe," the voice turned silky, "fuck your dead daughter in her dead-fucking grave with a white fucking cross. Yeah, I'd like that."

Quincy gripped the phone harder as the words penetrated, and the first wave of anger washed over him like a tidal wave. He wanted to smash the phone. He wanted to smash it against his bare hardwood floor or black granite countertop. He wanted to smash it over and over again and then he wanted to fly to California just so he could beat the crap out of Miguel Sanchez, thirty-four years old and already sentenced to death, and he had never felt himself this angry, the rage throbbing in his temples and his whole body rigid with the need to lash out.

Then he saw his answering machine. The red blinking light indicating that there were messages. And the red digital display screen giving him the new-message count: 56. Fifty-six new messages on what should've been his unlisted telephone line.

He amazed himself with how calm he could keep his voice. "One call from me, Sanchez, and you'll be sent straight to solitary. And remember, I'm the one who knows how much you hate to be alone."

"That mean you don't like talking about your daughter? Pretty, pretty girl, Quincy. How nice you gave her my favorite name."

"—weeks in the hole. No one to brag to, no one to boost your ego, no one to rape when you realize you're never ever going to even touch a woman again."

"Do me a favor, fed. Next time you listen to my tape, picture your daughter's face for me. Oh, and give your second daughter a kiss. Because someday, I'm gonna find a way out of this joint, and it makes me *real* happy to know that you've still got one daughter left."

"One last time," Quincy said tightly, his gaze locked on his blinking security system, "how did you get my unlisted number?"

And Sanchez drawled, "Unlisted? Not anymore."

Quincy had no sooner set down his phone, than it rang again. He snatched it back up.

"What?" he demanded harshly.

There was a moment of silence, then his ex-wife's uncertain voice. "Pierce?"

Quincy closed his eyes. He was unraveling. He would not unravel. He would not permit himself to do such a thing. "Elizabeth."

"I was wondering if you could do me a small favor," Bethie murmured. "Nothing major. Simply run a background check. You know, as you did before."

"Your father hiring more contractors?" Quincy worked on loosening his grip on the phone and taking a deep breath. His father-in-law had built an addition on his home last year. He'd made his only daughter call her ex-husband to request background checks on the entire crew. According to his former father-in-law, it was the least Quincy could do.

"The name is Shandling. Tristan Shandling."

Quincy found a piece of paper and wrote down the name. His heart was finally beginning to slow, the darkness receding at the edge of his vision. He felt more and more like his former self, and not some beast about to burst its chains. The red digital counter still glowed on his answering machine. Fifty-six messages. Something had gone wrong. He would deal with it, however, as he'd dealt with everything before. All in good time.

"Time frame?" he asked his ex-wife.

"Ummm, no rush. But soon. I think he has a place in Virginia if that helps."

"All right, Bethie. Give me a few days."

"Thank you, Pierce," she said, and for once it sounded as if she meant it.

Quincy didn't hang up the phone right away. Neither did she.

"Have you ... have you heard from Kimberly lately?" he found himself asking.

Bethie seemed surprised. "No, but I'd assumed that you had."

"Ah, so we're equally shunned."

"Maybe she tried to call you when you were gone ..." Bethie's voice trailed off. She seemed to realize how that sounded and added hastily, "I tried to reach you earlier in the week, but you weren't home and I didn't feel like leaving a message."

"I was in Portland visiting someone. An old friend." He wasn't sure why he offered the information, and the minute he did, he wished he could call it back. An old friend? Who was he trying to kid? When Bethie spoke, however, she didn't sound angry or tense, which surprised him.

"Maybe I should pay Kimberly a visit," she said. "She's just an hour away, I could tell her I was in the area. It's been a month."

Quincy almost said no, then caught himself. Once, Rainie had accused him of taking his job too far. Even in his personal life, he showed up, gave his expert opinion, and left.

"Perhaps Kimberly just needs some space," he tried neutrally.

"I don't know why. We're the only family she has left. Frankly, I thought she'd strive to be closer to us, not further away."

Quincy rubbed his temples. "Bethie, I know that you're sad. I'm sad, too."

"Pierce, you're speaking to me as if I were five."

"We tried so hard for her. I know we don't always agree on each other's role as a parent, but we both loved Mandy. We wanted the best for her. We would've ...We would've given her the world if such a thing were possible. Instead she got drunk, crawled behind the wheel of her vehicle and killed two people. I love her. I miss her. And some days ... Some days, I'm just so *angry.*"

He was thinking of Sanchez's call again, and the way his hands had fisted and his body had gone rigid. He was still angry, he realized. He was furious in places way down deep where it would take years to weed it all out and begin to feel normal again.

"Bethie," he tried one last time, "don't you get angry, too?"

His ex-wife didn't speak right away. Then she asked quietly, in a strange tone, "Pierce, do you think if someone gets an organ transplant, that maybe they get more than just the other person's tissue? Maybe ...maybe they also get part of the other person's being, some part of her soul?"

"An organ transplant is a medical procedure, nothing more."

"I thought you would say that."

"Returning to Kimberly for a moment—"

"She's angry, she needs space. I got it, Pierce. I'm not as dumb as you think."

"Bethie—"

The phone clicked off. His ex-wife had hung up on him.

Quincy slowly recradled the cordless phone on its base. And that, he thought tiredly, concluded one of the more civil conversations of his day.

Five minutes later, Quincy sat down at the kitchen counter. The scrap of paper with Tristan Shandling's name had been pushed aside. Now, he had out a fresh spiral notebook and three black ink pens. He pressed the play button on his answering machine.

Then he began the two-page list of all the nice felons who'd called his unlisted telephone number simply to wish him dead.

The light on his security panel indicated his system was fully operational and armed. He watched it for a long time, thinking of Kimberly, remembering Mandy.

Shortly, he went into the front room he used as an office. He dug through a stack of cardboard boxes marked Criminology: Basic Theories, until he found a small cassette tape labeled "Miguel Sanchez: Victim Eight." The original tape sat in an evidence storage locker in California. This was Quincy's personal copy, used in several of his classes.

He placed the tape in an old cassette recorder. He hit play. He sat alone in the dark, while his office filled with sounds of a young girl's pleading wails.

Amanda Johnson, fifteen years old and eight long hours from death.

"*Nooooooooooo,*" she cried. "*Oh God, nooooooooooooo.*"

Quincy put his head in his hands. And he knew he was in trouble, because one month after his daughter's funeral, he still couldn't weep.

8

"Who is Miguel Sanchez?" Rainie asked an hour later. She was propped up against the headboard of her mud-brown motel room, having just treated herself to a late dinner of blueberry pancakes at the nearby Waffle House. The Motel 6 had been highly visible from the highway and seemed as good a stopping point as any. Besides, at fifty dollars a night, no one could question her expense account.

She'd found the motel. She'd found the neighboring Waffle House. She'd eaten her blueberry pancakes alone, thinking of Officer Amity's take on the accident scene and wishing she didn't have a chill. Then she'd wasted ten minutes watching other diners, burly, working-class men out with their girls. In some cases, tables crowded with entire families. She was three thousand miles away from home. Funny how nothing seemed that different.

She'd walked back to the motel knowing she should call Quincy and deliver a report on her day. Instead, she'd turned on the TV and perused the modern miracle of fifty-seven channels and still nothing to see. She told herself she didn't have much to report, anyway. Besides, she didn't want to seem anxious to hear Quincy's voice. She wanted to ensure that she was treating this as business, purely business. Quincy the client.

There had been nothing good on TV. She had spent the day in a strange state thinking, this is where Quincy lives, and she had been anxious to hear his voice. She'd called. And it had taken her all of one second to realize that she should've called sooner. Quincy sounded tired, nearly flat, as if he had no emotions left. She had never heard him sound like that before.

"Miguel Sanchez was my first case," he told her now. "Worked out of California in the mid-eighties, with his cousin, Richie Millos. They specialized in sadistic rape-murders of young prostitutes. Eight total. Sanchez liked to tape his work."

"Nice guy," Rainie commented. She turned off the TV and set down the remote. "So you were instrumental in catching Sanchez?"

"I formulated the strategy used by the police for Sanchez's arrest. A witness had reported seeing two men dragging the eighth victim into a white van twenty-four hours before her corpse was found mutilated alongside 1-5. At this point, we already knew we were dealing with an organized killer. As I explained to the LAPD, partnerships are rare for psychopaths, but in the few occasions we've encountered them, the partner has generally been subservient—a weak sidekick who merely fulfills the psychopath's desire for an audience. My advice, therefore, once the police had identified two likely suspects, was that they focus their attention on the weaker member of the pair. Turn Richie to give up Miguel, who was the real instigator and threat."

"I'm guessing this was easier said than done."

"Yes. Richie idolized his older cousin. He was also terrified of him. For good reason. Six months after Richie handed over Miguel in return for a reduced sentence, he was found in the prison showers with his penis cut off and shoved down his throat. Miguel never believed in being subtle."

"Ah. So this fine piece of humanity called your personal line tonight?"

"Him, and forty-seven of his fellow deviants. Then I had eight calls from various prison officials, who thought I should know that my unlisted telephone number is currently being circulated in prison yards in everything from scraps of paper to packs of cigarettes. Oh, and in one prison, my number is now scratched into the shower wall."

"Quincy—"

"By my count, the forty-eight inmates represent twenty-one different correctional facilities, so I imagine I will be hearing from more prison officials in the morning."

"Quincy—"

"But don't worry," he continued, his voice no longer flat, but gaining an edge, "most corrections departments have the right to monitor an inmate's calls, so I'm sure the new members of my fan club will be suitably punished. Maybe have a disciplinary ticket written up or receive ad seg—administrative segregation. You know, penalties I'm sure more than compensate for the sheer thrill a bunch of psychopathic lifers can get by toying with a federal agent."

"Change your number."

"Not yet."

"Quincy, don't be an ass!"

"I'm not. I'm being patient."

Rainie grew silent, then she got it. "You want to keep everyone calling in case you can trick one of them into revealing the original source of your phone number."

"In the morning, I will report the incident to my SAC. The Bureau takes the protection of its agents very seriously. I'm sure my line will be tapped and monitored in no time at all. Calls will be going out to the various prisons. Perhaps even a personal visit to one Miguel Sanchez. I would like that."

"Do you have a theory of who did this? It has to be somebody who knows you."

"Maybe. Then again, it could be some bored college flunkie who hacked into the telephone company's records in order to have a little fun."

"But you don't think so."

"No. I think it's personal. And I think the mysterious practical joker gave out more than just my private number, Rainie. Think of what Mr. Sanchez said. That he wanted to fuck my daughter in her fucking grave with a white fucking cross. Why a white cross? What's the first thing you think of when you picture a white cross?"

Rainie closed her eyes. She pictured a white cross, and her stomach went hollow. She shouldn't be at this stupid motel, she realized. She shouldn't be sitting here pretending that business was just business. She should be at Quincy's home. She should be holding him the way he had once so kindly held her. And she should be putting her hands over his ears to spare him from what she knew he would say next. He had always been too brutally clever.

"Arlington," Quincy continued relentlessly. "The instigator didn't just give out my home telephone number. He told at least one convicted sadist where to find my daughter's grave. The son of a bitch." His voice finally cracked. "He gave away Mandy."

Rainie waited. On the other end of the phone, the sound of Quincy's breathing grew less ragged. She could feel him pulling himself back together, becoming once more the cool, composed federal agent he so prided himself on being. He needed his masks, she thought, just as she needed hers. It surprised her how much that realization hurt her.

For no good reason, she was thinking about the baby elephant again, his desperate run across the desert. Kicked down, getting back up. And still the jackals shredded him in the end.

"Do you think they're connected?" she asked him shortly.

"What?"

"The phone calls. With Mandy's accident. Seems rather interesting that you've no sooner hired someone to investigate Mandy's death, than you're getting a bunch of threatening calls."

"I don't know, Rainie. It could simply be opportunity. There are enough people out there who have nothing better to do than hate me. Maybe they heard about my daughter's funeral and decided it was their chance to have some fun. We've had incidents in the past where someone has gotten an agent's personal information. Nothing on this big of a scale, but then again, we're now in the computer age."

"I don't like it," Rainie said flatly. "Plus the fact that Sanchez evoked Mandy in the phone call … Seems a rather pointed message."

"I … I don't know." Quincy sounded tired again. "I think they must be connected. Then I think I'm paranoid. Then I think I'm merely being diligent. I don't … I'm not myself at the moment."

Rainie fell silent. She kept thinking there was something comforting she should say. She had not grown up in a house big on comfort. Thirty-two years old. It was kind of funny all the things she didn't know how to do.

"I spoke with the investigating officer," she said, since like Quincy, business was what she handled best. "He did a good job at the scene. I couldn't find anything he'd overlooked."

"What about the seat belt?"

"The driver …" She stuttered immediately, shocked by her coldness at using that impersonal word.

Quincy didn't say anything and the silence loomed huge this time, a giant black void between them. They couldn't get this right, Rainie thought suddenly, desperately. Even when they were trying, they couldn't get this right.

"Mandy reported the seat belt broken a month before the accident," she tried again, her voice meek now, humbled by her mistake. "She made an appointment with the garage that serviced her vehicle, then canceled at the last minute."

"She'd been driving without a working seat belt for a month?"

"It would appear so."

"Why didn't someone pull her over? I thought there were seat belt laws in this state!"

Rainie didn't reply to his outburst. She knew he didn't expect her to.

"What had happened to the seat belt?" he redirected his line of questioning. "How did it break?"

"We don't know yet. Officer Amity is helping me locate the vehicle so I can examine it, but fourteen months later makes things difficult. Most likely the Explorer has already been broken down for parts at some salvage yard."

"I want to know what happened to the seat belt."

"I'll find it, Quincy. You know I'll find it."

"And the man, the one she was supposedly seeing?"

"First thing tomorrow morning, I meet with Mary Olsen. Hopefully she can point me in his direction. I'll also check in with Mandy's local AA group. They probably know more about her personal life."

"AA has policies about giving out information."

"Then I'll just have to turn on my charm again."

"Rainie—"

"I'm on top of the case, Quincy. Things are beginning to happen and I know you need answers. I'll get them."

His silence was subdued now, a long soft spell where they both sat not too many miles apart and yet still too far away. She wondered if he was sitting in a darkened room. She wondered if he'd skipped dinner again, the way he'd probably skipped lunch before that and breakfast before that. She wondered how many hours he'd pace before finally falling in a restless, exhausted sleep. And then she wondered how they could know each other so well, and still have this chasm between them.

"I should go," Quincy said. "I want to speak to Everett first thing in the morning."

"Everett?"

"Special Agent in Charge. He'll want to know about the phone calls, assuming he doesn't already. Plus, I need to type up this list of names."

Rainie glanced at the clock. It was now after midnight.

"Quincy," she began.

"I'm fine."

"I'm not that far away. One hour tops, I can be at your front door."

"And then what, Rainie? Then everything's all right, because now I'm *your* charity case?"

"Hey, it's not like that at all!"

"Yes? And what do you think it is I've been trying to say? Understanding is not pity. Oh, but excuse me, in your world it is."

"Quincy ..."

"Thank you for the update, Investigator Conner. Good night."

The phone punctuated his sharp sentence with a click. Rainie thinned her lips, shook her head, and replaced her own receiver much more slowly.

"But my case was different," she muttered.

Her motel room remained silent. She figured that was an appropriate enough reply.

Later, six hours later, the motel alarm clock beeped to life and Rainie crawled blearily out of bed. Jet lag had caught up with her. She gulped down twelve ounces of Coke for breakfast and still felt half dead.

She hit the four-lane street, running for thirty minutes through the concrete maze of a seemingly endless strip mall tucked conveniently off Interstate 95. Middle-aged men in rumpled suits poured out of the motel. A line of cars sat impatiently at a McDonald's drive-through.

Rainie ran through parking lot after parking lot, dodging reckless cars and people already fed up with their morning commute. Tall maple trees and dark waxy magnolias beckoned lushly in the distance. Wild honeysuckle grabbed at cement barriers lining the parking lots as if the vine would reclaim the urban jungle as its own. Rainie coughed on diesel fumes from spewing trucks and fought her way back to Motel 6, wishing the green landscape didn't make her think of Bakersville again and long for the feel of salty ocean air upon her face.

She took a five-minute shower, towel-dried her hair, and combed in mousse. Expecting another long day, she donned a pair of worn jeans and a clean white T-shirt, the official uniform of the aspiring PI. She checked her phone messages on her home answering machine while lacing up her shoes. The weather was already brutally hot outside. Man, what she would give to wear sandals and shorts.

She blew the thought aside while hearing that she had six new messages, a personal record. She grabbed the motel pen and pad of paper.

First two messages were from clients wanting updates. She really should do that. The next three messages were all hang ups, received in hourly intervals. If the person couldn't be bothered to leave a message, she decided, she couldn't be bothered to wonder about who they were. The final message was from some lawyer she'd never heard of, requesting a basic information packet.

She eyed the clock, judged it to be four A.M. Pacific Coast time, and shrewdly called back the law firm to tell the lawyer that her secretary would send him something in the mail. Then she left her number at Motel 6, just in case the lawyer wanted a more immediate reply. She now felt industrious and exceedingly clever and it was not even noon.

Rainie finished lacing her shoes. After a moment's hesitation, she slid her Glock .40 into a shoulder holster. A simple black jacket covered the bulge.

Seven A.M., she picked up her notes and headed out the door. The sun glared harsh white, causing her to blink. Her tiny rental car felt like it was two hundred degrees inside. Damn, she thought. It was going to be a killer of a day.

9

"The first call arrived at two thirty-two p.m., Tuesday afternoon." Back in the bowels of the earth, Quincy reported last night's events in his crispest voice to Special Agent in Charge Chad Everett, while the SAC nodded attentively and a fluorescent bulb buzzed ominously overhead. "At ten-eighteen p.m., I personally handled a call from Miguel Sanchez. There have been more calls since; given the circumstances, I've been letting the machine pick up." Quincy handed over copies of the freshly made case file to the assembled agents. They accepted the information while continuing to regard him gravely.

"Enclosed you will find a complete list of caller activity and the corrections departments currently involved in the situation," he continued. "Eight officers checked in with me, which you will see noted. In some cases, they reported my personal information being passed along from inmate to inmate in the yard. More interesting, however, is the last two officers, who identified the source of the information as being an ad currently running in their local prison newsletters. In one newsletter, I'm a producer looking to interview inmates for an upcoming documentary on prison life. Interested parties are encouraged to contact me directly at the number listed below. In another newsletter, I'm eagerly seeking a prison pen pal, again, please contact me at the number listed below."

Quincy smiled tightly. "I'm still waiting to hear back from a few sources, but it would appear that similar ads just appeared in at least six other newsletters, including *Cellpals, Freedom Now,* and my personal favorite, *Prison Legal News,* which has a monthly circulation of over three thousand. Then there are the Web sites, such as PrisonPenPals.com, which apparently has been paid to e-mail my ad to dozens of prisoners 'seeking a new friend.' Look at me. I'm a groupie."

Quincy shut the case file and sat down grimly. All eyes were still on him, but he had nothing more to add. This was his life. Now it had been violated. Phone call after phone call, message after message promising a slow, tortured death. He could not remember the last time he had slept.

At least the Bureau was taking the situation seriously. A small case team had been assembled in Everett's office. A younger man with a mop of sandy brown hair, Special Agent Randy Jackson, represented the Technical Services Division, in charge of wiretapping. From NCAVC were Special Agent Glenda Rodman, an older woman with a penchant for severe gray suits, and

Special Agent Albert Montgomery, whose bloodshot eyes and hound-dog face already made Quincy uncomfortable. The agent had either taken a red-eye flight last night, or he'd been drinking heavily. Perhaps both. Then again, who was Quincy, with his own wan features, to judge?

"For the record, who has access to your personal telephone number?" Everett asked, while Special Agent Rodman sat up straighter and positioned her pen over her yellow legal pad of notes.

"My family," Quincy replied immediately. "Some professionals, including fellow agents and members of law enforcement. Some friends. I've included as complete a list as possible in my notes. In all honesty, I've had that number for the past five years, and even I was surprised by how many people now have it."

"You've worked over two hundred and ninety-six active cases," Glenda spoke up.

Quincy nodded. Frankly, he was surprised the number was not higher. As profilers served a consulting role, each routinely juggled over one hundred cases at a time.

"That's a lot of people who may feel they have the right to be unhappy with you."

"Assuming they ever knew I was involved." Quincy shrugged. "Be honest, Glenda. For a fair amount of our cases, we receive a request by phone, get the case file by mail, and return our report via fax or FedEx. In those incidents, I have a hard time believing the perpetrator's focus ever leaves the local homicide detectives who actively work the case."

"So weeding out those cases ..." she prodded.

Quincy did the math in his head. "Maybe fifty-six convicted inmates."

"What about open cases?"

Quincy shook his head. "I haven't worked an active case in six years."

"Last year," she began.

He said quietly, "Henry Hawkins is dead."

Montgomery leaned forward, his elbows resting on the knees of his rumpled pants. The fluorescent light flickered, jaundicing his jowls, and Quincy found himself pondering the agent's presence once again. Montgomery's expression was sullen, almost as if he was here against his will, and yet what kind of agent begrudged helping a fellow agent in trouble? That hardly boded well.

"Aren't we putting the cart before the horse?" Montgomery grumbled. "You got a bunch of calls. Whoopdee doo."

Special Agent in Charge Everett replied sternly, "The fact that an agent's personal telephone number was disseminated to over twenty correctional facilities *is* whoopdee doo. We don't need any more whoopdee doo than that."

Montgomery turned to the SAC. Quincy thought the disheveled agent would quit while he was ahead; he was wrong. "Bullshit," Montgomery snapped, making them all blink. "If this was something personal, if this was someone *serious*, the instigator would do more than pass along a private number to a bunch of schmucks behind bars. He'd visit the house. Or he'd arrange for someone else to visit the house. Phone calls? This is fucking child's play."

Everett's face darkened. A thirty-year veteran of the Bureau, he was a throwback to the days when an FBI agent dressed, spoke, and carried himself a certain way. Agents were the good guys, the last bastion of protection against gangsters, bank robbers, and child molesters. Agents did not arrive on the job in wrinkled suits and they did not go around saying things like "fucking child's play."

"Special Agent Montgomery—"

"Wait a minute." Quincy surprised them all by raising his hand and saving Montgomery from a lecture that wouldn't be career-building. "Say that one more time."

"Phone calls," Montgomery drawled as if they were all daft. "The question is not who, but *why* phone calls."

Glenda Rodman sat back. She was nodding her head now. Randy Jackson yawned.

"Montgomery's right," the techie agreed. "If it's a hacker, guy could get your home address from the phone company just as easily as your unlisted number. If it's just some person who happened to snag your number, they could still call information and get your street address from a reverse directory. Either way, home phone number equals home address."

"Wonderful," Quincy said. Somehow, he hadn't put those pieces together, another sure sign he was not himself these days. The dull ache was back in his temples. Morning, noon, and night. Grief was like a hangover he couldn't shake.

Why phone calls? The obvious answer was that someone was out to get him. Probably someone from an old case. Psychopaths were like sharks. They probably viewed his daughter's death as blood in the water and now they were moving in for the kill. So why not keep it simple? Move in. Attack. Finish him off. Hell, he definitely wasn't in any kind of shape for a fight.

Was that why he had gone to Rainie? Because he knew he was becoming too isolated? Or because he wanted to remember how to fight the good fight? Rainie never gave an inch, not even when backed into a corner. Not even when she should.

Focus, Quincy. Why phone calls?

"This is serious," Everett pronounced. "I want an immediate follow-up with the newsletters and Web sites involved to determine the origin of these ads. Furthermore, we need to figure out just how many inmates now have this information. We ought to be able to trace something."

Quincy closed his eyes. "So many grassroots newsletters," he murmured. "Big ones, little ones, and for all we know, he placed ads in all of them, which is a lot of work. So why ..." His eyes popped open. He had it. Dammit, he should've thought of this last night. "Cover," he said.

"What's that, Agent?"

"Cover," Montgomery repeated for him, then grunted. He stared at Quincy with red-rimmed eyes that appeared reluctantly impressed. "Yeah, probably. Let's say this guy has your home address right now—which, by the way, he probably does. He goes after you tomorrow, we can hunt him down through process of elimination. But he spreads that info to dozens of prisons where the inmates will pass it along to dozens more ... Now we gotta look at superfelons A, B, and C, their pals on the outside, and the pals of their pals on the outside. It's like a fucking criminal spider web. We'll be tracking down nasties for years after your funeral."

"Why thank you," Quincy said evenly.

"It's true," Glenda chimed in, though she had the courtesy to look at him with more concern than Montgomery. "If something had happened to you yesterday, standard procedure would have been to investigate personal acquaintances as well as people from prior cases. Not an easy feat, but certainly a manageable one. Now, however, entire prison populations have your personal information. You could be targeted by any neo-Nazi who hates federal agents, any gangster looking to build a rep, or any psychopath who's simply bored. If something should happen to you now ... The playing field is wide open. No matter how many agents were assigned to the task, we'd never wrap our arms around a suspect list this big. Frankly, it's a brilliant strategy."

"This is serious," Everett pronounced again.

As the one who was being targeted by some unknown stalker, Quincy thought he already knew that.

Glenda flipped through the file Quincy had put together. "In the good news department," she reported, "some of these newsletters are more reputable than others. If they ran an ad, it was because they received specs and payment by mail. If they've kept the original letter and envelope, we're in luck. We can trace the postmark back to city of origin, test the envelope for DNA and fingerprints, plus test the whole package for chemical residues, dirt, debris. On the other hand ..." She hesitated, glancing at Quincy apologetically. "Prison newsletters are mostly grassroots journalism. It could take us weeks simply to track down every publication carrying the ad. And even then ..."

She didn't have to say the rest. They all knew. Not all prison newsletters were really about journalism and not all were reputable. In the sixties, information was smuggled into prisons in packs of cigarettes. When the drug problem grew too big, however, correction departments across the country cracked down on all contraband by universally banning outside packages, including ones bearing tobacco products. Prisoners were allowed to receive only money, which they could then use to purchase cigarettes from the prison commissary. While it was unknown if this policy truly limited the drug problem, it did cut off the information flow.

Which brought the underground information network into the nineties and the miracles of constitutionally protected free speech. Prisons got computers, complete with desktop publishing software, and prison newsletters sprang up across the country. While some were small, many garnered national distribution. And the coded ad was born. Got some information you want to disseminate? Disguise it as a request for a pen pal, and pay five, ten, one hundred bucks to bring your message to the masses. Financially constrained? Some Web sites would now run pen pal ads and even build personal Web sites for inmates, free of charge. Just because you murdered eight people doesn't mean you shouldn't have a voice in society. Or a pretty blond writing correspondent named Candi.

"A lot of these newsletters probably didn't require much in the way of payment," Quincy filled in for Glenda. "And most of them probably did destroy the original letter of request, as a matter of protocol."

"*Prison Legal News* is a good one," she offered. "We can focus our efforts there."

"Good." Everett nodded approvingly.

"I can call the phone company," Jackson volunteered. "See if Verizon has had any breaches of security lately. You know, that they'll admit to."

Everett nodded again, looking pleased. Quincy, however, rubbed his temples. "I doubt you'll find the original letter and envelope," he said quietly. "And even if we do, there won't be any DNA evidence. There won't be fingerprints. Nobody takes the time to think of such an elaborate ruse, then forgets something as simple as fingerprints on the envelope and saliva on the seal. Whoever we're looking for, he's smarter than that."

"You think it's personal," Glenda said.

Quincy gave her a look. "What kind of stranger would bother?"

"We got another strategy," Montgomery spoke up. He threw out baldly, "Monitor the grave."

"No!" Immediately, Quincy was out of his chair.

"It's standard procedure—" Montgomery began.

"Fuck procedure!" Quincy told him coldly, the second time in as many days he'd been driven to swear. "It's my daughter. You are not using my daughter!"

Montgomery lumbered to his feet. His eyes were small and dark in the folds of his face. They reminded Quincy of the eyes of a bird, and he suddenly wondered if this was how he, too, appeared to victims' families. Not as a man, but as some bird of prey, swooping down after the kill.

"You said Sanchez implied he knew where your daughter was buried," Montgomery said flatly.

"I was wrong."

"Wrong my ass. He *knew*. Which means the UNSUB thought to look up where your daughter was buried, which means he's been considering her grave for quite some time. Guy's gotta know by now we'll be watching your house. So if he wants to feel close to you ... have a private little laugh ..."

"I do not want cameras at my daughter's grave. I do not give permission!"

But Glenda was nodding now, Jackson, as well. Quincy turned slowly toward Everett. The SAC's face was kind, sympathetic. But he was nodding, too.

Time spun away from Quincy. He was remembering an afternoon he hadn't thought of in years. At the state fair, Mandy and Kimberly in tow. Father-daughter day, he'd promised them, and taken them on as many rides as their young stomachs could handle. Then, right after buying them cotton candy, he'd turned and seen a man snapping photo after photo of children on the kiddy rides.

He remembered the smile fading from his face, a chill seeping into his body. He watched a pedophile capture rolls of film of laughing little children and all he could think was that his girls were only a few feet away. His sweet, beautiful, healthy little girls with their mother's striking dark blond hair.

He had spoken to them urgently, angrily. Look at that man, he had instructed them, his heart hammering wildly in his chest. Know what he is, he had told them. And don't be afraid to run.

Kimberly had nodded solemnly, absorbing his words with fierce concentration. Mandy, however, had started to cry. Weeks later, she still had nightmares about a man in a smelly overcoat who came with a camera to take her away.

"No," he said hoarsely now. "I won't allow cameras. Try and I swear I'll move Mandy's grave."

The other agents were looking at him curiously. Everett said, "Maybe it's time to think about taking a few sick days …"

"I'm fine!" Quincy tried again, but his voice still sounded odd, not like him. He sounded desperate, he realized. He sounded like a desperate father. And then he had a strange thought. It came to him as instinct, something he understood better than truth. *This is what the stalker wanted.* The UNSUB had set up this first wave of attack not just to make his identity harder to pinpoint, but to have some fun. To identify Quincy's deepest wound and rip at it savagely.

Quincy licked his lips and sought once more for control. "Listen to me. This is not about my daughter. The UNSUB could care less about my daughter. He gave out that information just to get a cheap thrill."

"So you know who it is then?" Glenda Rodman seemed intent on pinning him down.

"No, I don't know who it is. I'm simply theorizing based upon the company I keep."

"In other words, you don't know shit," Montgomery declared.

"Agent, you are not turning my daughter's grave into some obscene stakeout."

"Why?" Montgomery pushed. "It's not like it's something you haven't asked of other families."

"You son of a bitch—"

"Quincy!" Everett interrupted sharply. Quincy stilled as they all drew up short. He was slightly surprised to find that his hand was raised in midair, his index finger jabbing at Montgomery as if he would do the man harm.

"I know this is difficult," the SAC said quietly, "but you're still a federal agent, Quincy, and breaches of security are a threat to all of us. Take a few days. The case team will monitor your house and apprise you of any new developments. In the meantime, you can make yourself comfortable in a nearby hotel or perhaps take a visit to see family."

"Sir, listen to me—"

"Agent, how long has it been since you've slept?"

Quincy fell silent. He knew he had bags beneath his eyes, he knew he had lost weight. When Mandy had died, he had told himself that he was too smart to let it eat away at him. He'd lied.

The other agents were still staring at them. He could read their judgments on their faces. *Quincy's losing it. Quincy's strung too tight. Told you he shouldn't have returned to work so soon after the funeral …*

The FBI and animals in the wild, he thought: all culled the weak from their herd.

"I'll … I'll find a hotel," he said brusquely. "I just need to pack a few things."

"Excellent. Glenda, you and Albert will be in charge of setting up surveillance of Quincy's house."

Glenda nodded. "I'll send you daily reports," she offered Quincy, her tone even, but her eyes kind.

"I'd appreciate that," he said stiffly.

"We're on top of things," Everett concluded firmly, and nodded at the group. "You'll see, Quincy. It'll be all right."

Quincy simply shook his head. He walked back to his office in silence. He watched the play of stale fluorescent light over industrial-cream cinder block. He wondered again what kind of man chose a job that denied him daylight.

When he was inside his office, he closed the door. Then he called the one person who might be able to help him now, who might still be able to protect Mandy's grave.

He called Bethie, but somewhere in Philadelphia the phone merely rang and rang and rang.

10

Greenwich Village, New York City

Kimberly left her apartment walking fast. She'd gotten up early—Wednesday was her weekly shooting lesson—and lately she'd come to really need her time on the firing range. She'd donned jeans and a casual T-shirt, stuck her fine long hair into a ponytail, then headed out to catch the commuter train to Jersey. Just like clockwork, she told herself. Wednesday morning just like any other Wednesday morning. Breathe deep. Inhale the smog.

It wasn't like any other Wednesday morning. For starters, she no longer had to show up for work. She had been so pale and jumpy yesterday afternoon, Dr. Andrews had grumpily ordered her to take the rest of the week off, her first vacation since Mandy's funeral. She could take her time today. Stop and smell the roses. Ease up a little, as her professor had instructed her to do.

Her footsteps remained compulsively quick, more of a run than a walk. She glanced over her shoulder more than any normal person should. And even though she absolutely, positively knew better, she was carrying her Glock .40 fully loaded and with the safety off. *Don't be this freaky,* she kept telling herself.

She was doing it anyway.

Funny thing was, she didn't even feel that bad at the moment. No hairs standing up at the nape of her neck. No cold chills creeping down her spine. No sense of doom, which almost always preceded the anxiety attacks. The weather was balmy. The streets possessed enough people so that she was not isolated, while also being few enough people for her to maintain a large safety zone around herself. And even if someone did try to attack her, she found herself thinking, she was fully trained in self-defense as well as heavily armed. Kimberly Quincy a victim? Not likely.

Yet she was grateful to arrive at Penn Station. She took a seat on the commuter train, scrutinized her fellow passengers, and finally concluded that none of them appeared the slightest bit interested in her. People read magazines. People watched the scenery go by. People ignored her in favor of their own lives. Who would've thought?

"You're a fucking psycho," she murmured, which finally did earn her a look from the guy sitting next to her. She thought of telling him that she was carrying a loaded gun, but given that he was heading into Jersey, he was probably carrying one, too. As Dr. Andrews liked to say, normality was a relative term.

The train slowed for her stop. Just for the hell of it, she gave the guy next to her a big huge grin. He immediately broke eye contact and assumed the submissive position. That made her feel better for the first time in days.

She got off the train with a lighter step and was immediately assaulted by 100 percent humidity. Ah, another lovely Jersey day.

Reaching into her shoulder bag, she adjusted the Glock's safety to the on position, and started walking at a much more normal pace. New York City was behind her. The shooting range was only a few blocks away. New Jersey was hardly safer than Greenwich Village, but she did feel better here. Lighter. Free from some burden she couldn't name.

Kimberly had loved shooting from the first moment she'd cajoled her parents into letting her go. She'd started begging at eight. Her father had done the expected thing and told her to talk to her mother. Her mother had done the expected thing and said, absolutely not. Kimberly, however, had been possessed. Every time her father headed for the practice range, she started badgering. Four years later, on her twelfth birthday, her mother finally caved.

"Guns are loud, guns are violent, guns are evil. But if you won't take my word for it, fine! Go shoot yourself silly."

Mandy had wanted to go, too, but for a change their parents both agreed that handling guns would not be in Mandy's best interest. That suited Kimberly just fine. Mandy cried. Mandy got upset. Mandy was a big baby, and Kimberly was more than delighted to have an afternoon with her father all to herself.

She wasn't sure what her father thought. It was always hard to know what her father thought.

At the firing range, he carefully explained the basic rules for gun handling and firearms safety. She learned how to take apart a .38 Chief's Special, name all the parts, clean all the parts, and then put them back together again. Then came lectures on always keeping the gun pointed at a safe target. Always keep the gun unloaded until ready to fire. Always keep the safety on until ready to fire. Always wear earplugs and eye protection. Always listen to the range officer. Load when he says load, fire when he says fire, and cease firing when he says cease fire.

Then at long last, her father let her aim the .38 Chief's Special at a paper target and practice dry firing, while he stood behind her and adjusted her aim. She remembered the muffled sound of his voice next to her ear, more like a deep rumble than words. She remembered being anxious to get to live ammunition after two hours of straight lectures, and her father, exhibiting his typical, maddening calm.

"A gun is not a toy. On its own, a gun is not even a weapon. It's an inanimate object. It is up to you to bring it to life and use it responsibly. Whose job is it to use it responsibly?"

"Mine!"

"Very good. Now let's go through it one more time ..."

It had taken four trips to the firing range before he let her fire live rounds. He placed the target at fifteen feet. She hit it with a respectable six shots, four clustered in the middle. She promptly dropped her pistol, jerked off her goggles, and threw her arms around her father's neck.

"I did it, I did it, I did it! Daddy, I did it!"

And her father said, "Don't ever throw down your firearm like that! It could go off and hit someone. First put on the safety, then set down the gun and step away from the firing line. Remember, you must treat your pistol responsibly."

She had been deflated. Maybe even tears flooded her eyes. She didn't remember anymore. She just recalled the curious change that came over her father's face. He looked at her crestfallen expression and perhaps he finally heard his own words, because his features suddenly shifted.

He said quietly, "You know what, Kimmy? That was great shooting. You did a wonderful job. And sometimes …sometimes your father is a real ass."

She had never heard her father call himself an ass before. She was pretty sure that was one of the words she was never supposed to repeat. And she liked that. That made it special. Their first real father-daughter moment. She could shoot a gun. And sometimes Daddy was a real ass.

She went with him to the firing range from then on out, and under his patient tutelage she graduated from a .38 Chief's Special to a .357 Magnum to a 9mm semiauto. As a form of silent protest, her mother enrolled her in ballet. Kimberly attended two lessons before coming home and announcing, "Fuck ballet! I want a rifle."

That got her mouth washed out with soap and no TV for a week, but was still worth every syllable. Even Mandy had been impressed. In a rare show of support, she'd spent the next few weeks saying fuck everything, and together they went through two bars of Ivory soap. A curious, delirious month, back in the days when the four of them had been a family.

Funny the things she hadn't thought about in a while. Funny the way the memory made her breathe hard now, like someone had socked her in the stomach, like someone was slowly squeezing her chest.

Dammit, Mandy. You couldn't stay out of the driver's seat? Sure, quitting drinking is hard, but you could've at least stayed off the roads!

No more fucking ballet. No more fucking anything. Just a white cross in beautiful, prestigious Arlington cemetery because her mother's family was loaded with military connections and had somehow earned Bethie and her children the honor. Mandy and war heroes. Who would've thought?

Kimberly had barely been able to make it through the funeral. She had thought the irony might drive her mad, and she didn't think her mother could take it if she had started laughing hysterically, so Kimberly had spent the whole service with her lips pressed into a bloodless line. And her father? Once again, it was so hard to know what her father thought.

He'd been calling her lately. Leaving gently inquiring messages because she wouldn't pick up the phone. She didn't return his calls. Not his calls, not her mother's calls. Not anyone's calls. Not now. Not yet. She didn't know when. Maybe soon?

She didn't like the anxiety attacks. They shamed her and she didn't want to speak to her overly perceptive father when he might catch the fear in her voice.

Guess what, Dad? I couldn't teach Mandy to be strong, but apparently she's inspired me to be a flake. Whoo-hoo! Lucky you. Two fucked-up daughters.

She arrived at the shooting club. She pushed through the wooden door into the dimly lit lounge area, and the cooler air swept over her like a welcoming breeze. The club boasted a small, utilitarian lounge, empty this early in the morning, then the door leading to the cavernous shooting range. Kimberly didn't look at the threadbare sofa or the tall display case filled with shooting medals or the line of animal-head trophies mounted on the wall. She was looking for him. Even as she told herself that wasn't why she'd been so excited to get here first thing this morning, she was looking for the new gun pro, Doug James.

Thick brown hair, sprinkled with silver at the temples. Deep blue eyes, crinkled with laugh lines at the corners. A tall, well-toned body. A broad, hard-muscled chest. Doug James had started at the rifle association six months ago, and Kimberly wasn't the only female who was suddenly very interested in lessons.

Not that she thought about him that way. She wasn't like Mandy, always on the lookout for a man. She wasn't like her mom, incapable of defining herself except through a man's eyes. Anyway, Doug James was almost as old as her father. A happily married man, besides. And he was a terrific shot, of course. Had won a lot of shooting competitions, or so the rumors went.

All in all, he was a highly capable instructor, who was working wonders with her stance.

And a patient man. Kind. Had a way of looking at her, as if he was genuinely interested in what she was saying. Had a way of greeting her, as if he was made happier by her simply entering the room. Had a way of talking to her, as if he understood all the things she didn't say ... the nightmares she still had of her sister where she was in the car with Mandy, grabbing desperately at the wheel ... the sense of isolation that would sweep down upon her suddenly, with her sister gone, her parents fragmented, until she felt like a speck of sand in a vast, uncaring universe.

The need she had today, to come here and fire a mammoth stainless steel firearm at a puny paper target as if that would bring her world back together again. As if that would make her strong.

She walked up to the counter, where the head of the rifle association, Fred Eagen, was bent over a stack of paperwork.

"I'm ready for Doug," she said.

"Doug's not here today. Called in sick." Fred flipped over the next document, signed the bottom. "He was going to try you at your apartment. You must've already left."

Kimberly blinked. "But ... but ..."

"I guess it came on quick."

"But ..." She sounded like an idiot.

Fred finally looked up. "If a guy gets sick, a guy gets sick. He'll see you next week."

"Next week. Of course, next week," she murmured and struggled to recover her bearings. Sick. It happened. Why should she feel this bereft? He was just a gun instructor, for God's sake. She didn't need him. She didn't need anyone. Why oh why were her hands suddenly shaking so badly. And why, oh why, did she suddenly feel so desperately, keenly alone?

She took her gun. She went out to the firing range and set up. Earplugs and protective eye gear. Box of ammunition. Smell of cordite in the air. The fragrance of her youth, the comforting weight of her stainless steel Glock, loose in her hand.

She set up targets fifty feet back. She annihilated paper hearts, she shredded paper heads. But she already knew now, that it wouldn't be enough. She had not come here for the practice. She had come here for a man.

And more than anything else that had happened in the last month, that proved to her that something wasn't right anymore. Strong, logical Kimberly wasn't the person she had always thought herself to be.

When she left, she was walking too fast again, and even though it was ninety-five degrees out, she fought a chill.

Society Hill, Philadelphia

Bethie was nervous. No, she was giddy. No, she was nervous. Okay, she was both.

Standing outside her stately brick town house in Society Hill on a sunny Wednesday morning, she ran a quick hand over her sundress and picked imaginary lint from the tiny purple flowers that patterned the gold silk. Next she inspected her freshly painted toenails, now colored Winsome Wine, whatever that meant, and peeking out from strappy gold sandals. She didn't detect any signs of smudging. She glanced at her hands. Fine, as well.

She'd risen at five A.M.; for the first time in months, anticipation of good things had brought her instantly awake and eager to start the day. With Tristan not due to arrive for another two hours, she'd celebrated her morning with a long overdue bubble bath followed by an impromptu pedicure. She'd even done her fingernails, and it still shocked her to look down and see two well-groomed hands. It had been a while, longer than she wanted to think.

Now she had a large wicker picnic basket slung over her left arm. She'd bought it years ago on a whim, one of those impulse buys based more upon the life she wished she was leading than the life she truly led. She had thought of it immediately when Tristan had suggested they go for a drive, and had dedicated twenty minutes of her morning to locating the basket in the back of her kitchen pantry. She'd then stocked it with crackers and Brie, grapes and caviar, a fresh French baguette and a bottle of La Grande Dame champagne. Tristan struck her as a man of refined tastes, and yes, she was definitely trying to impress.

She glanced at her watch. Ten past seven. She grew nervous again. What if he didn't show? She was leaping to conclusions. After all, last night she'd been nearly twenty minutes late, but she'd still kept their date.

She wanted him to arrive. She wanted to go on a drive, far away from this house that was too big and this city that held too many memories. She wanted one afternoon when she stepped out of a middle-aged, divorced woman's skin and lived with the sun on her face.

Last night, coming home from her first date in years, she had realized that it was time to move forward again. Not easy, but time.

A short beep-beep broke into her thoughts. Bethie looked down the narrow street to see a little red convertible with New York plates dart around the corner and come flying down the lane.

"My goodness, what is this?" she asked as Tristan came to a screeching halt, ran a hand through his hair, and beamed.

"Your carriage, my lady."

"Yes, but what *is* it?"

"The Audi TT Roadster two twenty-five Quattro," he announced with pride, "based loosely on the 1950s Porsche Boxter. Cute, isn't she?"

He swung open the driver-side door and came bounding around the front, looking somehow flushed, windblown, and dashing all at once.

Bethie held out her basket, thinking now would be a good time to say something clever, but distracted by the bright, burning light in his eyes, the impact of his smile. "I fixed a picnic lunch," she stated and instantly felt foolish for the obvious comment.

"Wonderful."

She nodded, still feeling self-conscious. She returned her attention to the picnic basket. "Champagne, caviar, Brie. I didn't know what you liked."

"I like champagne, caviar, and Brie." He reached for the basket, and his hands lingered on hers. He stood very close, handsome this morning in tan slacks and a deep blue cable-knit sweater. Sandalwood and lemon, she thought and wondered if she'd given herself away by inhaling too deeply.

"Did you sleep well?" he asked, his fingers lightly brushing hers.

"Yes. And you?"

"I didn't sleep a wink. I was too busy looking forward to seeing you."

She flushed, but couldn't repress her smile. "Very smooth," she conceded.

"Is it? I practiced all the way over." He grinned. Then, without warning, he leaned over and kissed her full on the mouth. She was still reeling when he straightened again and took the picnic basket from her arm.

"In all seriousness," he said as he popped the trunk, "I have not looked forward to a day as much as I've been looking forward to this one in a very long time. We are going to go someplace marvelous, Bethie. We are going to have an ungodly amount of fun. Are you with me?"

"I could do ungodly amounts of fun."

"Perfect!"

He closed the trunk, then returned to get her door. The little red roadster really was commanding. Beautiful rounded lines on the outside. A striking black-and-chrome color scheme on the inside. It looked like something a movie star should drive, say Marilyn Monroe or James Dean. Bethie was almost afraid to touch it. Tristan, however, took her hand and without hesitation, helped lower her into the low-slung black leather seat.

"You know what?" he said suddenly. "You should drive."

"Oh, no. I couldn't—"

"Yes, yes, absolutely. Everyone needs to drive a sports car once in her life and today, it's your turn."

He helped her back out of the car. She was still protesting when she found herself in the driver's seat, holding a small, rectangular key fob and wearing a very silly grin. The sleek chrome gauges winked at her. The rounded chrome gear stick felt warm and smooth beneath her palm. Tristan climbed into the passenger's seat. She barely looked at him. She hadn't even pulled away from the curb, and she was already in love with this car.

"See the little silver button?" He pointed to a small button on the corner of the key fob in her hand. "Push it."

She did and the tiny silver key shot out of the side of the box like a switch-blade. She startled, almost dropped the key, then laughed. "Oh my goodness, who thought of that?"

"Probably somebody in marketing. Pure gimmick, but highly effective. Now love, put it in the old ignition. Here's the lights, here's the windshield wipers, and here's the hand brake. Give it a whirl."

She stalled the car in first. Jerked them into second as she tried to get a feel for the clutch, then finally spluttered down the road. It had been years since she'd driven a standard, not since her college days. But she quickly dis-covered that some part of her had missed the feel of a gear stick in her hand, the sense of controlling the vehicle as if it were a high-spirited horse, the surge of power as she felt the zippy car respond. She went around the block, grinding the gears painfully, but Tristan didn't seem to care and she found herself laughing breathlessly. She liked this car. She liked this man. She could do this.

"Listen to this, Bethie," Tristan said. "I got it just for you."

He pushed a silver panel on the dash. It rose to reveal a myriad of stereo buttons. Two more jabs with his finger, and Miles Davis's " 'Round Midnight" poured out of discreet Bose speakers and flowed all around her.

"You remembered."

"Bethie, of course."

Miles Davis's trumpet began to wail. She found the proper rhythm for the gears, and the roadster began to purr. Tristan was right, she thought. Everyone should drive a little red sports car once in her life, and this car drove like a dream.

She took the on-ramp to I-76, feeling the roadster gather beneath her feet. First, second, third, pushing the tachometer all the way up into the red zone. The second turbo kicking in and pressing her back against her seat. Twenty, forty, eighty miles per hour, and still as smooth as silk.

"There you go," Tristan said approvingly. "That's how you drive, Bethie. Go after the road like a speed racer, don't let anything hold you back."

She smiled. She pressed on the gas. She hit one hundred miles per hour and let the wind gather up her dark blond hair and the sun beat down on her upturned face.

"We're off like a herd of turtles!" Tristan roared over the rushing air.

She laughed, she drove faster, and she never bothered to mention that that was one of Mandy's favorite expressions. *I love you*, she thought. *God, I am so happy!*

Tristan was still watching her with that intent look in his eyes. He had pulled on a pair of black leather driving gloves. He ran one gloved finger down her cheek.

"Bethie," he said after a moment. "Tell me about your second daughter. Tell me about Kimberly."

11

It took Rainie four tries to find Mary Olsen's house. The first time, she didn't even notice the narrow driveway off the heavily wooded road. The second time, she spotted the driveway, but couldn't see any sign of a house through the trees. The third time, knowing she had to be close, she drove halfway up the driveway, saw a freaking mansion perched on top of a circular drive, and hurriedly backed down before some butler loosed the Dobermans on her. The fourth time, she parked alongside the road, got out of her car, and went over to the discreet black mailbox on its ornate wrought-iron post to read the house number.

"You're kidding me," she said to no one in particular, then flipped open the file of background information she had gathered on Mary Olsen, and scanned the material one last time. "Huh. Who the hell is a twenty-five-year-old unemployed waitress sleeping with to get a house like that? And does he want a mistress?"

Who, turned out to be a neurosurgeon, which Rainie learned when she drove back up the driveway and made it to the front door. Dr. Olsen had already left for the day, but an oil portrait of his grandfather was the first thing she was shown when the butler—yes, the butler—led her into the cavernous marble foyer. He left her to stare while he went to fetch Mrs. Olsen.

Rainie amused herself by price-checking the interior. One gigantic round crystal table, centered in the middle of the foyer, bearing a Lalique stamp. She figured twenty grand. One highly polished side table constructed from bird's-eye maple with black walnut trim and legs straight out of a Louis XIV wet dream—probably fifteen grand. Sixteen-foot draperies of peach velvet with gold satin lining and miles of gold cord. Twenty thousand, maybe even thirty; custom window dressings weren't her strong suit.

At any rate, the room seemed to have a fifteen-grand minimum, which put Rainie way out of her league, as the last she knew her entire body was worth a whopping buck eighty-two, or something like that.

"Would you like some coffee?"

Mary Olsen stood at the top of the circular staircase, looking down into the foyer. As she was half-expecting Scarlett O'Hara at this point, Rainie found her first impression of Mary disappointing. No hoop skirt. No big hair. Just a frightfully young-looking girl in a blue-and-yellow flowered Laura Ashley dress, leaning over the gilded railing and looking at Rainie expectantly.

"I could handle coffee," Rainie said at last, her voice booming off the marble.

"Decaf or regular?"

"Never saw the point to decaf."

Mary Olsen smiled. Rainie thought the expression appeared tight on her face. She was nervous, Rainie realized. Little Mrs. Doctor Olsen was frightened of her.

Wow, she felt good for the first time in days.

Mary descended the stairs. She held on to the railing with both hands, which Rainie found interesting. So the former waitress was now living in a mansion, but obviously still not comfortable about it. When Mary hit floor level, Rainie got her second surprise. The woman was three inches taller than Rainie and had the dark eyes and sultry features of a Supermodel. That explained Dr. Olsen's interest, but he was dressing her all wrong. Screw Laura Ashley. Mary should be running around in V-neck dresses colored deep, sinner's red. Then again, the Olsens would probably go through a lot more butlers that way.

"We'll go into the front parlor," Mary said, her features carefully blank. "Follow me."

Rainie dutifully followed. The front parlor turned out to be bigger than her whole loft, crowded with white-painted French antiques, and decorated with more pale colors, this time blue and cream. When Mary sat on the delicate loveseat, her dress blended right into the silk-covered cushions. One minute Rainie was with a person, next minute it looked like she was interviewing a sofa with a head.

"As I mentioned on the phone," Rainie said, "I have a few simple questions about Amanda Quincy."

Mary held up a hand. "The coffee, please."

Rainie blinked, feeling gauche. Then she realized that good old Jeeves was hovering with a silver tray bearing an antique coffee urn and two tiny china cups. He set the serving tray down on a side table and did the honors of pouring the first dose. Rainie accepted hers with genuine trepidation. The paper-thin china looked old, rare, and highly fragile. She was guessing that it held approximately three sips of coffee, at which time she'd be forced to refill the cup herself from the heavy silver pot. Maybe she'd just nurse this batch.

"Nice place," Rainie tried, attempting to balance the teacup on her knee while still trying to figure out why Mandy's best friend appeared so nervous.

"It's been in my husband's family for generations."

"He's a doctor?"

"Yes."

"Works lots of hours?"

"Of course. He's one of the best neurosurgeons in the country and his patients need him."

Rainie was getting a few things now. "Older?"

"In his forties."

"Met him where you used to work, huh? Went from best tipper to permanent meal ticket. Not bad."

Mary flushed. "I suppose you could look at it that way."

"Oh no, trust me, I admire you. Wouldn't mind meeting a neurosurgeon, myself."

"Mark's a wonderful husband." Mary was still in defensive mode.

"Mark and Mary. Oh yeah, those Christmas cards have got to be killers."

"I thought you said you were working on Mandy's accident."

"You're right; I'm getting off track. So about the night in question—"

"What about that night?" Mary interrupted. "I'm afraid I don't understand the reason for this interview. The accident happened over a year ago. Mandy got drunk, she drove. She did that sometimes, you know. I don't see any point in you being here."

"Well, I heard about the coffee, thought I'd stop by." Rainie sighed at the confused look on Mary's face. Sarcasm was definitely lost on the woman. "So, about that night. You told Mandy's father that she had come over to play cards."

"That's right. We always played cards on Wednesday night. At least we did."

"Who's we?"

"Mandy, myself, Tommy, and Sue."

"You knew each other from ..."

"We used to work together, at the restaurant, before I met Mark. Why is this relevant?" Mary had that tight look on her face again.

"Just asking," Rainie replied lightly. "So the four of you are playing cards."

"Hi-low-jack," Mary supplied.

"Great. Hi-low-jack. Party starts at ..."

"I wouldn't call it a party," Mary said immediately. "We were drinking soda, you know. I told Mr. Quincy that we were drinking Coke."

"I got that. Playing cards, drinking Coke. You started at?"

"Nine, maybe ten. Sue's still a waitress and she had the dinner shift."

"You guys started that late on a weeknight?"

"Sue and Mandy waitressed, Tommy's a bartender. So they don't have to be at work until noon at the earliest. And I ...well, hours don't really matter much for me anymore."

Rainie thought she detected a trace of bitterness there. All was not well with Cinderella and Prince Charming. "You played cards until?"

"Two-thirty."

"Drinking soda the whole time."

"Yes," Mary said quickly. Too quickly. She looked down at her lap, where her fingers were now intertwined. Here we go, Rainie thought.

"You told Mandy's father that she didn't have anything to drink other than Diet Coke."

"I said I didn't *see* her drink anything other than Diet Coke."

"You didn't see?"

"I didn't see."

Rainie stood up. She put her cup back on the silver tray, happy to be rid of breakable objects. Then she turned back on Mary, and this time her gaze was hard. "Didn't see, Mary? *Didn't see?* Now why does that seem to imply that Mandy might have been drinking after all, but you don't want to admit it?"

Mary's gaze had become fixated on her lap. She untangled her fingers, twisted the three-carat rock on her left hand, then tangled her fingers back up again.

"I swear I didn't know," she whispered.

"Do us both a favor, Mary. Spit it out."

Mary's head jerked up. Her eyes were growing darker; maybe Mrs. Doctor Olsen had some fire in her after all. "She carried the Diet Coke can with her everywhere, okay? I didn't think much of it at the time, but Mandy kept the can with her everywhere. You know, even when she went into the bathroom."

"You think she might have been mixing her own drink on the side. Looks like Diet Coke, smells like Diet Coke, oops so I added a little rum."

"It wouldn't have been the first time."

"Alcoholics do learn some good tricks," Rainie agreed, though personally she'd never been one for mixed drinks. For her, it would always be beer. "Well, let's think about this, Mary. Amanda is doing a little bartending of her own. You say she got here ten at the latest, and didn't leave until two-thirty. That's at least four and a half hours of spiked Diet Coke. Couldn't you tell?"

"No," Mary said immediately. There was a clarity to her voice now, certainty that had been previously lacking. Interesting. "That was the thing with Mandy," Mary continued earnestly. "No matter how much she had to drink, she always seemed fine. Functional. Back when we were working, she used to brag about her tolerance. We all believed her. We never thought ... never would've thought, that she had a problem."

"So her joining AA was news to you?"

"Yes. Though later, when we all looked back on things, it made sense. There were some nights after closing that she'd sit in the bar and down eight drinks before heading home. Even if she seemed all right, how right could she be? She wasn't much bigger than me and alcohol doesn't exactly evaporate from your bloodstream."

"So she could've been sneaking drinks that night and you wouldn't have known?"

"Yes." Mary nodded her head emphatically. "That's true."

"What about this mystery man?"

"Mystery man?" Mary blinked.

"At the funeral, you implied to Quincy that Mandy had met someone. The new love of her life."

"No, I didn't."

"You didn't?"

"No. I'm not sure where Mr. Quincy got that idea. I don't remember saying any such thing. Why would I say such a thing?" Mary spoke in a rush.

Rainie cocked her head to the side. She regarded Mary intently. "Maybe Quincy misunderstood you."

"Maybe." Mary nodded vigorously. "It was a funeral. He wasn't in the best shape. None of us ..." Her voice choked for the first time, her head bobbed back down. "None of us were."

"Mary, are you sure you want to stick with this story? That your best friend got loaded on her own. Drove home on her own. Mowed down an old pedestrian on her own."

"I'm telling you what I know to the best of my knowledge—"

"It's not what you said four weeks ago at the funeral."

"It is, too! Mr. Quincy got it all wrong! I don't know, maybe he's even more grief stricken than we thought so now he's grasping at straws and twisting what I said. Who knows what grief-crazed fathers do!"

"Grief-crazed?" Rainie echoed skeptically.

Mary finally flushed. She looked away. On her lap, however, her fingers were tangling and untangling furiously. Rainie figured it would be a miracle if they didn't end up with whiplash. Rainie took a deep breath. She nodded at Mary thoughtfully. She took her time and paced the room.

"Beautiful furniture," she commented.

Mary didn't say anything. She looked now as if she would cry.

"Must have cost your husband a lot of money."

"Mark inherited most of it," she murmured.

"Still makes quite an impression. Must have blown you away the first time you saw all this. Cinderella, entering the castle."

"Please, I'm telling you the truth about Mandy."

"Fine. All right, you're telling the truth. I haven't denied it. I mean, I wasn't around a year ago. How do I know what your best friend drank on your last night together? How do I know if she laughed honestly while playing cards with you, or if it was some kind of drunken stupor? Hey, I don't even know if she hugged you before she left, thanked you for a great evening and for keeping her busy on the long nights when she was doing her best not to drink. Quitting cold turkey is tough. I've been there. It's tough and good friends make all the difference."

Mary bowed her head again. Her shoulders had started to shake.

"You're pretty lonely, aren't you, Mary?" Rainie said bluntly. "You're sitting in the house you always thought you wanted, and it's a prison cell. The proverbial gilded cage."

"I don't think I want to talk to you anymore."

"Your best friend's dead, your husband works all the time. Yeah, if I were you and I met the right man, someone who told me I looked pretty, someone who complimented my smile, I'd pretty much do whatever he wanted."

"This is crazy! I don't know what it is you think you're doing, but we're through. I mean that." Her head came up. She said sternly, "Get out."

And Rainie replied with the same artlessness Mary had employed before: "You mean you're not looking for a new best friend, Mary? You're not looking for anyone new to betray?"

"Damn you!" Mary sprang to her feet. "Harold!" she yelled. "Harold!"

The butler came scurrying into the room, his eyes wide at the hysteria percolating through his mistress's call. Rainie feigned a yawn, while Mary stabbed a shaking finger in her direction and screeched, "Get her out. Out, out, *out!*"

The butler looked at Rainie. He was middle aged, and his bald head and gaunt features really didn't make him the intimidating type. Rainie, on the other hand, lounged against yet another side table with her right hand positioned strategically on a heavy gold candelabrum. Poor Harold didn't know what to do.

"Do you miss her?" Rainie asked Mary. "When Wednesday night rolls around, do you miss Mandy at all?"

"Get out!"

"The irony is," Rainie persisted softly, "that Mandy was the drunk, but I'm willing to bet she would've missed you. If your positions had been reversed, she would've missed you badly."

"Harrrrrooooold!"

The butler finally edged his way over to Rainie and put a hand on her arm. His touch was light, but firm, and she gave him credit. He managed to hold himself with regal dignity, when God knows the rest of the situation had clearly moved beyond that.

Rainie gave in to the light pull of his hand, and let him lead her back into the foyer toward the door.

Mary, oddly enough, followed right behind them, her features still distorted and her right hand pressed protectively against her belly.

"Thank you for the coffee," Rainie said politely to Harold. "I'm sure I'll be in touch," she added to Mary, before heading down the broad steps.

Her last view, as she opened the door of her rent-a-wreck, was Mary Olsen standing in the grand entrance of her enormous mansion, screaming, "You have no idea what you're talking about, lady. You have no fucking idea!"

Two miles from the Olsen residence, Rainie pulled over her car and killed the ignition. Despite her earlier composure, her hands had started trembling. The adrenaline was ebbing from her bloodstream, leaving her lightheaded in its wake.

"Well," she murmured, all alone in her tiny car, "that wasn't what I expected."

She thought of Mary Olsen's furious features and final taunting remark. She thought of Quincy, and the host of phone calls he'd received last night. She heard an all-too-familiar ringing in her ears.

Rainie leaned forward and rested her forehead against the steering wheel. She was suddenly very tired. Last time she'd heard ringing in her ears, small children had died. And things had gotten even worse from there.

She took a moment. Then two and three. Okay, she had a plan. She pulled back onto the windy country road and since she hadn't had the funds to buy a cell phone yet, she drove until she found a gas station with a pay phone. From there, she called her new partner in crime, Virginia PI Phil de Beers. She was lucky that he was in. She was even luckier that he was currently in between cases, and if she was willing to pay his rate to tail Mary Olsen, he was more than willing to do the work. That took care of merry Mary for a bit.

Hoping her luck would hold out, Rainie tried Officer Amity next. The officer on duty informed her that Big Boy was on patrol. Rainie asked to be switched to dispatch, whom she sweet-talked into transferring her to Amity's car. Dispatch did her the honor of introducing her, and Officer Amity picked up the radio receiver already sounding unhappy.

"What d'you want?"

"Officer Amity! How's my favorite state trooper?"

"What d'you want?"

"Oh, just thought I'd see if you'd had any luck locating that vehicle we spoke of."

"You mean in the twelve hours since we talked?"

"That would be what I'm going for."

"I have a job, ma'am."

"So the answer is no? Officer, you're breaking my heart."

"I sincerely doubt that," Amity said dryly.

"What are the chances of getting that information sometime today?"

"I don't know. Ask the broader civilian and criminal community. If enough drivers promise not to rear-end each other and enough reprobates cease breaking and entering, I may have a shot."

"So if I douse the entire state in Valium ..."

"I like the way you think."

Rainie sighed heavily. Apparently that was the right tactic; Officer Amity sighed heavily as well.

"Thursdays are my day off," he told her. "If it doesn't happen today, I'll make sure I get to it tomorrow."

"Officer Amity, you're super!"

"Wonderful," he grumbled. "I finally impress a woman and she lives three thousand miles away. Talk to you later, ma'am."

He clicked off before Rainie had a chance to reply, which also saved her from dealing with that last statement.

She returned to her car. She got out the police reports of Mandy's crash. Then she got out her newly purchased Virginia state map.

Forty minutes later, she found the bend in the road where the accident had happened. Quincy had been right. This wasn't on any direct route from Mary Olsen's mansion and it wasn't on any direct route from Mandy's apartment. In fact, this place wasn't any direct route to anywhere. It was a narrow country road leading from nowhere and going to nowhere with lots of twists and turns in between.

The bend in question was deep and arching, forming a sixty-degree curve complete with dense brush, thick trees, and a single telephone pole. Off to one side there was a small unpainted cross. Recently decorated with plastic flowers, probably by Oliver Jenkins's widow.

Rainie parked her car. She got out and for a long time, she simply stood there, feeling the wind on her face. The road was quiet, no other cars in sight. The trees rustled overhead, and in her current frame of mind, the sound reminded her of dry, clicking bones.

She had to walk seventy feet to the telephone pole. A long enough distance to stop a car, she thought, or at least start to brake. She put her hand on the telephone pole. Then she ran her fingers down the violent scar slashing into the wood. Splinters stood straight out, the raw wood of the wound still lighter than the weathered exterior. She pressed the shards of wood gently back into place, as if that would somehow make things right.

The wind rose. The trees rustled and for a moment, it was very easy to believe she'd just heard someone laugh.

Rainie's heart was thumping loudly. She was suddenly keenly aware of how alone she was in this place. And just how thick the underbrush, and just how dark the depths of the wood.

Five in the morning, Mandy had hit this post. Five in the morning, the trees barely kissed by sun, and the wind still cool. Five in the morning, dark, isolated, and terribly, terribly deserted.

Rainie had to get back to her car. She got in the driver's side and locked the doors with shaking hands. Her shoulders were hunched. She could feel her heart loud and insistent in her chest.

She sat there. She wondered how many times Quincy had come to this mournful place. And then she started to drive because she didn't care what anyone said. Standing next to that telephone pole, she'd been certain she was not alone.

12

Bethie was having a marvelous time. The sun was bright, the sky was blue, the wind was cool against her neck. She loved the feel of the car beneath her hands. She loved the sound of Tristan's voice as he regaled her with story after story. And she liked telling him her stories, of her mother, her daughter, even her ex-husband, Pierce, whom she now suspected had a girlfriend in Portland, Oregon.

Time rolled by as easily as the miles. They headed west at first, no location in mind, then, on a whim, shifted south and drove into southern Pennsylvania with its lush expanse of verdant fields and the beautiful old farmhouses. They spotted women walking down dusty roads wearing quaint white bonnets. They passed horse-drawn carriages. They saw a man in his stone barnyard, bent over a woodpile and raising a blunt ax.

Tristan told her the histories of the various Germanic religious groups who'd settled here. She nodded, inhaling the scent of fresh mowed hay and thinking this was the most alive she'd felt in years.

They came to a narrow, twisty road shooting off into the fields.

"Let's take it!" Tristan declared. So she did.

The road turned to gravel, then dirt. It grew narrower and the crop grew taller. A mile later, sheafs of wheat flowed along the side of the bright red car like a golden river.

"Keep going," Tristan urged her eagerly. So she did.

The tide of wheat broke. They emerged into the low grass of a riverbank and Bethie hit the brakes right before they hit the water. She laughed breathlessly. Tristan clambered out of the car.

"Get out," he told her. So she did.

"Come on, we're going to have our picnic," he informed her. "Look, I also brought champagne."

They drank champagne. They ate caviar. They devoured the rich old cheese. Bethie sat in the curve of his body, with her arm pressed against his right side and the scar she thought of so protectively. He brushed bread crumbs from her knee. Then he lowered her down into the sweet-smelling grass, and covered her mouth with his as his fingers found her breast.

Afterwards, she stroked his right side tenderly. Then they both got up and without speaking, got dressed.

"Isn't it wonderful out here?" she murmured. "So peaceful and isolated. I wonder how many cars must whiz by on the highway without ever thinking of taking this turn. There's probably not anyone around for miles. Think of it: it's our own special little place."

Tristan turned back toward her. In the aftermath of making love, his blue eyes seemed especially fierce.

"Let's go for a walk," he told her. So she did.

13

Rainie was in trouble. She was thinking dangerous thoughts. And she was in the middle of doing a very dangerous thing. She wasn't heading back to the Motel 6. Instead, she was driving to Quincy's.

He would want a full report of her investigation, and she had news at this point, or maybe not really news, more of a feeling that she didn't want to deliver by phone. He would want to analyze everything. That was his way. And she did not want to picture him sitting in the dark again, contemplating horrible things all alone like his daughter's murder.

Then there were all the questions. Maybe Mary Olsen was simply a little batty, a high-strung gold-digger desperate for attention. Perhaps the torrent of phone calls to Quincy's house were purely coincidence, a bunch of bored felons looking for sick entertainment. And maybe Mandy's accident was still an accident, and everyone else was merely seizing the opportunity to mess with a reputable FBI agent's mind.

Or maybe there was a mystery man. Maybe he'd helped Mandy get drunk that night, guessing from her past behavior where that would lead. And maybe he understood what Mandy's subsequent death would do to Quincy. Leave him feeling off balance, distracted, alone. Leave him vulnerable as the real plan began to unfold, the real threat to emerge ...

There had been a time when Rainie would have dismissed such a theory as outlandish. Too cold, too callous to be possible. But that was before what had happened in Bakersville last year. Now she had the same fundamental training Quincy did. She understood the worst men could do, and she no longer considered anything to be too cruel to happen. Most people thought murderers killed out of some sort of necessity. Those were the easy cases. Far worse were psychopaths who considered murder to be not only a hobby, but a recreational sport.

Quincy had been there for her once. She planned on returning the favor.

Rainie consulted her map again, blew by her turnoff, and after thirty-six hours of practice, executed a perfectly brilliant and highly illegal U-turn. She went down the desired street.

The road was wide here, boasting a gracefully curving sidewalk and tons of freshly planted magnolia trees. New neighborhood, she decided. New money. She turned into a cul-de-sac and tried to keep her eyes from popping out of her head. Huge brick colonials sat up on vast expanses of emerald lawn. Big houses. Big yards. Fenced-in properties and gated drives.

She had figured Quincy's security-conscious nature would place him in some type of gated community, but she hadn't planned on this. She followed the house numbers down to the end, where a smaller, more discreet brick house was tucked back from the road. Rainie knew it was Quincy's without having to check the address; it was the only home where every single bush had been removed, eliminating places for the discriminating intruder to hide.

She looked at his denuded lot and sighed. "Quincy, Quincy, Quincy," she murmured. "You have got to take a vacation."

She pulled up to the black, wrought-iron gate and pushed the intercom button. It was only four P.M. and she really didn't expect Quincy to be home, so she was surprised when someone answered her buzz. She was even more surprised that it was a woman's voice.

"Name and business," the woman asked evenly.

"Uhhhh, Lorraine Conner. I work with Quincy." Not quite a lie.

"Please look into the camera and show your ID."

Run now, Rainie thought, or forever hold your peace. Gamely, she stared into the mounted camera and flashed her PI's license.

Moments later, the gate began to rumble, then slide slowly back. Rainie drove up the sweeping drive to find the front door open and a woman standing there. Rainie got out of her car, feeling not nearly so good about things.

The woman in question was middle-aged. Probably forty, but maybe thirty—the severe hairstyle and stern gray suit didn't do her any favors. She stood stiffly, her arms folded over her chest and her feet clad in sensible black shoes.

Didn't look like a housekeeper, Rainie decided. Not Quincy's type so she couldn't be his ex-wife. On the other hand, she'd make one hell of a governess.

Shoulders back, head up, Rainie marched up to the entrance.

"Who are you?" she asked Dour Chic.

"The question is, who are you?"

"I already gave at the camera. Plus, I asked you first."

Dour Chic smiled, but it came out as a grim line. "Maybe, honey, but my ID is bigger than yours." Dour Chic flashed her creds. The FBI emblem did carry a bit more weight than Rainie's puny PI's license. Rainie scowled and tried to figure out what was going on.

"I'm here to see Quincy," she said.

"Why?"

"That would be Quincy's business, not yours."

"At the moment, his business is my business."

"Are you sleeping with him?"

Dour Chic blinked. "I believe you misunderstand the nature of my business—"

"So you're not sleeping with him. Then my business and his business isn't your business."

Rainie let the female agent sort that out. She knew the instant the woman had arrived at the implied conclusion, because she blushed.

"I thought you said you were a private investigator," Dour Chic said with a scowl.

"Yeah, well, I thought you might be his ex-wife," Rainie lied. "Now, if you don't mind, I've given my name and I've traded IDs, so where's Quincy?"

The woman seemed to be debating with herself. "You might be able to find him at Quantico," she allowed brusquely. "That's all I'm at liberty to say."

"You don't expect him to come home tonight?"

"That's all I'm at liberty to say."

"Oh, I get it," Rainie said. "The phone calls. You're the cavalry."

The agent didn't answer right away. Then she gave a slow nod. Rainie nodded back. She looked at the woman with new interest, and what she saw now made her feel small and more than a bit bad. Not a stern suit, but a professional suit fashioned to hide a handgun. Not a severe hairstyle, but one suitable for running down master criminals. Not a dour face, but the intelligent face of a smart, successful woman. In short, a genuine, certified one hundred percent well-trained federal agent. And then there was Rainie, a freshly hatched PI who had been fired from the policing job she'd loved because she'd once been driven to kill.

This was Quincy's world. And that quickly, Rainie was sorry that she'd intruded.

"Well, I'll be going now," she said.

"I'll tell him you came."

Rainie bit her lower lip. Of course the agent would tell him. That was her job, and Dour Chic obviously lived for her job.

"You do that. In the meantime, I'll try him at his office—"

"Quantico."

"Yeah, Quantico—"

"It's a Marine base."

"I know it's a Marine base!"

Dour Chic formed another thin-lipped smile. She was giving Rainie a fresh perusal as well, and her first impression was clearly sliding downhill.

Fuck it. Rainie didn't bother with good-bye. She turned around, climbed back into her car and tried not to let the gate hit her ass on the way out.

"Goddamn know-it-all," she muttered a moment later, but she was driving too fast. She was thinking again of nights much too long ago to change. And she was thinking again that admitting to your past still didn't allow you to escape it. Some people grew up to be federal agents. And other people?

"Fuck it," she said again.

Rainie should've quit while she was ahead. She found the turnoff to Quantico, then drove for fifteen minutes through a heavily wooded road where Marines jogged in formation along the edge of the blacktop and the air was repeatedly split by the crack of gunfire. She passed a number of indistinguishable buildings, heading deeper into the Marine base and feeling more and more like an interloper at Uncle Sam's private club. No one stopped her. No one asked for ID. She wasn't sure whether to be grateful or worried.

She had just started to relax when the Marine base ended, and a guard post abruptly loomed ahead. Apparently, someone had decided that the Marines could take care of themselves. The FBI Academy, however, required a great deal of protection. She halted at the guard post, where a stony-faced security officer took her name, studied her PI's license and told her she was not permitted to enter. She gave her name again. She flashed her ID. He told her that she was not permitted to enter.

"Look, I'm an associate of SupSpAg—er, Supervisory Special Agent Pierce Quincy," she tried.

The grim guard was not impressed.

"I don't need full access or anything," she attempted next. "Don't you guys offer a visitor's pass?"

She learned she could indeed be a visitor. If her name had been given to him ahead of time. With appropriate clearance.

"So what the hell do I do now? Wait, wait," she held up a hand upon seeing the firm expression on his chiseled face. "I remember: I am not permitted to enter."

After a little more wrangling, she finally agreed to wait in her car under the officer's tight scrutiny. In turn, he agreed to contact the BSU office and inquire if Supervisory Special Agent Pierce Quincy would like to come out and see a guest.

Fifteen minutes later, Quincy's car appeared. He looked tired, stressed, and not at all happy to see her. So much for the reunion scene where they ran to each other with open arms. Instead, she meekly followed his car off the Marine base into the nearby little town where he pulled into the parking lot of a restaurant.

"I want some coffee," he said as he climbed out of his car.

"Hello to you, too," she replied.

"You crash government facilities often?"

"I didn't realize it would be so hard."

"Rainie, it's the *FBI* Academy. We have procedures and protocol. If just anyone could walk in, it would ruin the point."

"Fine. Next time I'll wear my best cocktail dress."

"Christ," he said. "You really can be childish."

He headed for the restaurant. She stood rooted in the parking lot, stunned by the coldness in his voice. Then the shock wore off, and she went after him.

"What the hell is with you?" Rainie demanded, catching up with Quincy as he approached the cashier and grabbing his arm.

"Two coffees," he ordered. "One black, one with way too much cream and sugar."

"I don't need coffee. I want an explanation."

"Coffee's easier," he told her, and wouldn't say another word until the amused cashier delivered both cups. Then he made Rainie follow him back outside, to a picnic table in a grove of trees she hadn't noticed before. The walk was long and didn't do a thing to calm her temper.

"Okay," she announced the instant he sat at the table. "What the hell is going on, Quincy? And you'd better start talking or you'll be wearing this coffee with 'way too much cream and sugar.' "

Quincy blew on his black, steaming brew. She could see now that the shadows had deepened under his eyes and his cheeks had gained the hollowed look of a man not sleeping at night. It was funny, she thought. Last year, she had been the one looking like walking death, and Quincy had been the one lecturing her to eat and sleep anyway. Stress is an even better reason to take care of yourself, he'd told her. Taking care of the body helps take care of the mind. If she repeated his own lecture back to him now, she wondered, how childish would *that* be?

"Have you heard of something called identity theft?" Quincy asked tersely.

Rainie sat down. She sipped her coffee. She nodded.

"A person steals someone's identity. Not too hard to do in this day and age. Gets the person's Social Security number and mother's maiden name, then uses that information to get a copy of the birth certificate and voilà, becomes the new person. It's amazing all the things you can do once you have basic documentation. Get a valid driver's license. Open a bank account or apply for a credit card. Buy a car, a red Audi TT roadster, I take it, registered and financed in the unwitting victim's name."

"Someone used your name to buy a sports car?"

"In New York. Two weeks ago. In theory, I currently owe a Westchester dealership forty thousand dollars, payable in convenient monthly installments of eight hundred and eleven dollars over the next five years."

"Someone stole an *FBI agent's* identity?"

"Why not? He's already given out my personal information to half the hardened criminals in the country. After that, what's one high-performance vehicle?" Quincy paused. He added grudgingly, "At least the man has good taste."

Rainie still couldn't believe it. "Identity theft …Doesn't the Bureau have specialists in this area?"

"The Bureau has specialists in every area," Quincy told her, but didn't sound encouraged. He set down his coffee cup, and Rainie was shocked to see that his hands were shaking.

"They took over my house, Rainie," he said quietly. "This afternoon fellow agents set up cameras on my daughter's grave. It's ironic. I'm an expert. In fact, I'm an expert in precisely these kinds of cases, and as of seven oh-five this morning, no one cares about my opinion anymore. As of seven oh-five this morning, I became a victim, and I have never hated anything more."

"They're idiots, Quince. I've told you that before. If FBI agents were so smart, they wouldn't still be running around in such god-awful suits after the rest of the world has gone business casual. What kind of man starts his day by tying a noose around his neck anyway?"

Quincy glanced down at his burgundy tie, today's choice offering tiny navy blue and dark green geometric patterns and looking suspiciously close to the tie he wore the day before that and the day before that.

"I can't stand this," he said baldly. "Someone is taking over my life. I don't even know why."

"Sure you do. You're the good guy. By definition, all the bad guys hate you."

"Agents Rodman and Montgomery are working on the phone calls. They're staking out my house, and trying to trace ads placed in various prison newsletters, as if that will amount to anything. They're also working on tracking the Audi. I don't know what that has to do with anything, unless it's simply one more way for the UNSUB to thumb his nose at me—I'm still stuck in basic investigative strategies while he's shopping for luxury automobiles. He may have a point."

Quincy sighed. He dragged a hand through his hair. "Today, I amused myself by pulling all my old case files and building a database of anyone I've ever ticked off. The bad news is that there's a lot of them. The good news is that an amazing number of them are either in jail or dead."

"That's what I like about you, Quincy. Your ability to network."

He nodded absently. "I'm eighty percent sure I'm a target, Rainie. I have no idea whose. I can't even be sure why. Revenge is the obvious answer. Why not? But for whatever reason, someone has started weaving a very complex web, and no matter what I do, I think I'm already stuck right smack in the middle of it."

"You have friends, Quincy," she said quietly. "We'll help you. *I'll* help you."

"Will you?" He looked her in the eye. "Rainie," he said softly, "tell me what you learned about Mandy. Tell me what we both already know in our gut."

Rainie looked away. She finished her coffee. She set the empty paper cup on the picnic table, then spun it between her hands. She didn't want to answer his request, and they both knew it. She also understood, however, that she couldn't soft-pedal the news. One more thing she and Quincy had in common—they preferred their bad news direct. Get it out. Get it over. Get it done.

"You're right," she said shortly, "something's rotten in Denmark."

"It was murder?"

"I don't know that," she countered immediately, her voice firm. "What's the number one rule of investigating—no jumping to conclusions. At the moment, we have no physical evidence that suggests murder."

"On the other hand ..." he said for her.

"On the other hand, something's up with Mary Olsen."

"Really?" Quincy seemed genuinely surprised. He frowned, rubbed his temples, and she could tell he'd gone straight to self-doubt about his impression of sweet little Mrs. Doctor Olsen because he already appeared dazed.

"I spoke with her this morning, Quince, and Mary recanted everything. Mandy *looked* like she was drinking Diet Coke all night, but *maybe* she was spiking it with rum. You might have gotten the impression from Mary that Mandy had a boyfriend, but Mary now says that wasn't the case at all. Furthermore, Mandy had been known to drink and drive before, so it probably was as simple as that."

"Mandy spiked her own Coke at a friend's house, then made it all the way to the middle of nowhere before suddenly being so drunk that she crashed?"

"I didn't say Mary had a good story, I just said she had a new story."

"Why? She was my daughter's best friend. *Why?*"

Rainie could hear the deeper question behind those words. Why was this happening, to Mandy, to him? Why would someone hurt his daughter? Why wouldn't the world stay controlled and rational, the way all behavioral scientists wanted it to be?

"I think Mary's a lonely little princess," Rainie answered softly. "I think for the right kind of attention, she could be manipulated very easily."

"The UNSUB got to her? Made her change her story?"

"Or the UNSUB got to her and had her make up the story in the first place. We don't really know that someone hurt Mandy. We do know that Mary said things at the funeral, however, that made you *think* someone hurt Mandy."

"I'm being played," Quincy filled in slowly. "Harassing phone calls, illegal automobile purchases, rumors about my daughter ..." He sat up a little straighter. "Shit, I'm being played like a fucking violin!"

Rainie blinked. "Since when did you take up swearing?"

"Yesterday. I'm finding it highly addictive. Like nicotine."

"You're *smoking*, too?"

"No, but I haven't lost my deep and abiding love for metaphors."

"I'm serious, Quince, you're letting yourself fall apart."

"And apparently, you haven't lost your deep and abiding love for understatement."

"Quincy—"

"What's wrong, Rainie?" he quizzed with that new edge in his voice. "Can't stand for me to be so *human?*"

She was up from the picnic table before she knew what she was doing, her hands fisted at her side and her heart hammering in her chest. "What is that supposed to mean?"

"It means ... it means I'm tired," Quincy said more quietly, his voice already conciliatory. "It means I'm under pressure. It means probably, that I'm looking for a fight. But you're not the person for me to fight with. So let's not do this now. Let's forget I said anything, and simply not do this now."

"Too late."

"You looking for a fight, too, Rainie?"

She knew she shouldn't say it. She knew he was right and they were both stressed and now was not the time. Six long months without even one damn phone call. She brought up her chin and said, "Maybe."

Quincy got up from the picnic table. He dusted off his hands. He stared at her, and his gaze appeared a lot more composed than she felt. He'd always been so good at remaining in control.

"You want to know where we went wrong?" he said crisply. "You want to know why it started out seeming so right, and then the world ended, not with a bang, but a whimper? I can tell you why, Rainie. It ended because you have no faith. Because one year later, the new, improved Lorraine Conner still doesn't believe. Not in me. And most certainly not in yourself."

"I don't have faith?" she countered. "*I* don't have faith? This from the man whose only way of coming to terms with his daughter's death is to turn it into murder."

Quincy recoiled sharply. "Strike one to the woman in blue jeans," he murmured, his expression growing hidden, growing hard.

Rainie wouldn't back down, though, couldn't back down. She'd only learned one way to deal with life, and that was to fight. "No hiding behind your wry observations, Quincy. You want me to see you as human? Then act human. For God's sake, we're not even having a real argument yet, because you're still too busy lecturing me!"

"I'm simply saying you have no faith—"

"Stop psychoanalyzing me! Be less therapist, more man—"

"Man? Last time I tried being a man, you looked at me as if I was going to hit you. You don't need a man, Rainie. You need either a blow-up doll or a damn saint!"

"Son of a bitch!" Rainie opened her mouth to yell further, then suddenly froze. She knew what he was talking about. That night, their last night together nearly eight months ago in Portland. Going to Pioneer Square. Sitting outside at Starbucks and listening to some a capella group perform. Talking, relaxing, having a nice time. And afterwards, going to his hotel because she still had the dingy apartment. She'd been thinking that she'd been so lonely. She'd been thinking that it was so good to see him again.

She'd moved closer. Inhaled the scent of his cologne. How much she loved that fragrance. And she'd felt him grow still, his body nearly breathless as if he understood that even exhaling might frighten her away. He'd gone still, so she'd kept approaching. She'd smelled the skin at his throat. Explored the curve of his ear. And then, something had taken hold of her. Desire maybe—she had so little experience with the real thing. She'd just wanted to touch him, more and more, if he'd stay, just like that, not moving, not breathing. She'd unbuttoned his shirt. She'd smoothed it from his shoulders. He had a hard chest, sculpted by a lifetime of running. The whorls of chest hair felt spongy against her palm. She placed her hand over his heart and felt it race against her touch.

On his collarbone and upper arm. Three small scars. Souvenirs of a shotgun blast, not all of which had been absorbed by his vest. Tracing those scars with her fingertips. Quincy, the super agent. Quincy, the superhero. Marveling ...

His hand had suddenly snapped around her wrist. Her gaze jerked up. For the first time she saw his expression, dark and glittery with lust.

And the moment flew away from her. Her body froze, her mind rocketed back and she was thinking of yellow-flowered fields and smooth-flowing streams. She remained touching his body, but it was harsh now, a sick imitation of the real thing. The way she'd been taught in the very beginning.

Quincy had pushed her away. He'd told her to give him a minute. But she hadn't. She'd been humiliated, embarrassed, ashamed. And being Rainie, she'd told him it was all his fault, then left without saying another word. In the following months, it had been easier for her to simply let the phone ring. If he did catch her at home, she was always too busy to talk.

He was right; she was the one who'd stopped returning his calls. But he was supposed to know better. He was supposed to understand and still come after her. Except he hadn't.

"I'm supposed to be patient," Quincy said, as if reading her mind. "I'm supposed to be persistent. I'm supposed to be tolerant of your mood swings, your temper, your troubled past. I'm supposed to be everything, Rainie, but frustrated and angry—"

"Hey, I'm dealing with a lot of things—"

"And so am I! We're all dealing with things. Unfortunately, you seem to think you're the only person who's allowed to be petty. Well, I have news for you. I buried my daughter last month. My coworkers are now conducting surveillance on her grave. And no matter what I do, I can't reach my ex-wife, whose family connections might have enough power to call it off. I'm not just mad, Rainie. I'm pretty damn pissed off."

"Well, there's your problem, Quincy—you're mimicking me when we both know I should be mimicking you."

"I can't be perfect for you right now, Rainie."

"Dammit, I am not that needy!" Rainie scowled at him. Quincy merely shook his head.

"You have to have faith," he said quietly. "I know it's hard, but at some point, you have to believe. Some people are evil, some people will hurt you, but not everyone will. And trying to stay safe by going at it alone doesn't work in the end. Isolation is *not* protection. I know. I thought it would be easier if I never opened up to my family, if I never got too close. Then I lost my daughter, and it hasn't been any easier at all. I am falling apart."

"Quincy—"

"But I am going to put myself back together," he continued as if he hadn't heard her. "I am going to find the son of a bitch who did this. And if I have to be angry to do that, I'll be angry. And if I have to stop sleeping and start swearing and behave like an utter jerk, I'll do that, too. I'm coping, Rainie, and nobody ever said coping had to be pretty. Now if you'll excuse me, I need to try to reach Bethie again."

Quincy turned away. He started walking back to his car. Rainie knew she should say something, but what came out didn't make much sense.

"Just because you survive, doesn't mean you'll end up happily-ever-after," she yelled at him. "Just because you cope, doesn't mean you'll win. Bad things can still happen. There's the jackals, you know. And, and ... jackals everywhere ..."

"Good night, Rainie."

He wasn't going to stop. It was her turn to make the effort; fair was fair. Funny, she'd never thought about it until now, but in her family, no one was ever encouraged to stay.

"It's hard to teach an old dog new tricks," she muttered in her own defense. But Quincy was already gone and there wasn't anyone else left to hear. The hour was growing late, dusk beginning to fall. In his car, Quincy used his cell phone to call his ex-wife. But once more he got the machine.

Rainie didn't have a cell phone. She went into the restaurant and used the pay phone in the lobby.

"Hey, Big Boy," she said a moment later. "Let me buy you a drink."

14

By nine p.m., Rainie was edgy and tense. She'd returned to her motel for a quick shower before meeting Officer Amity—who was now suggesting she call him Vince. In her room, she discovered a phone message from the lawyer who'd called that morning. Some attorney named Carl Mitz was all hot and bothered to get in touch with her. He'd left numbers for his pager and cell phone. Rainie studied the numbers without calling any of them.

Prospective clients were never this eager. Prospective clients made it their business to make you find them.

Rainie put the message aside. She showered. She washed her hair. She stood for a long, long time with the hot water beating down on her neck and shoulders. Then she put on the same old clothes and headed for the bar.

Officer Vince Amity was already there. He'd also showered and now wore a black western dress shirt tucked into a faded pair of jeans and finished with a pair of scuffed-up boots. The shirt stretched across broad shoulders. When he stood, the jeans barely contained the bulge of his thighs. A fine specimen of a man. The proverbial hunk of burning love.

Rainie ordered her bottle of Bud Light and told herself she did not miss Quincy.

"Ribs here are really good," Vince said.

"Okay."

"And the sweet potato fries. Ever had sweet potato fries? Worth every minute of the ensuing open-heart surgery."

"Okay." The waitress came by. They placed their twin orders for ribs and sweet potato fries and the minute the waitress was gone, Vince gamely tried again.

"So how long do you think you'll be in Virginia?"

"Don't know. Right now, I have more questions than answers, so at this rate it could be a while."

"Where are you staying?"

"Motel Six."

"Virginia has more to offer than Motel Six, you know. Ever have some free time, feel like seeing any of the sights ..."

He let the invitation trail off politely. She nodded with equal politeness. Then he surprised her by saying quietly, "I ran a background check, Rainie. You don't have to pretend for me."

She stiffened. She couldn't help herself, even if she was supposedly now at peace with her past. Old habits died hard; she found she was relentlessly stroking the icy cold bottle of unconsumed beer.

"You run background checks on all your dates?" she asked finally.

"Man can't be too careful."

She gave his muscle-bound build a meaningful look and he rewarded her with a grin.

"You found me at work, asked a lot of questions, and kept following up," he told her. "Call me old-fashioned, but I like to know more about the women chasing me. Besides, your friend Sheriff Hayes sang your praises from here to the Mississippi—"

"He tell you I was indicted for man one?"

"Charged but never tried."

"Not everyone sees the difference."

"I'm from Georgia, honey. We consider all women dangerous; it's part of their charm."

"The open-minded men of the South. Who would've thought?"

Officer Amity grinned again. He leaned over the old wood table and planted his thick forearms. "I like you," he said bluntly, "but don't play me for dumb."

"I don't know what you mean—"

"I'm not who you want to have dinner with tonight."

"Luke," Rainie declared grimly, "has a big mouth!"

"Sheriff Hayes is a good friend. It's nice to see they grow them right in Oregon, too. By the end of this evening, however, I'm gonna be even a bigger friend for you."

"Oh yeah?"

The waitress interrupted them with heaping platters of food. The minute she was gone, Vince said, "Eat your ribs, ma'am. Then I'll take you to Amanda Quincy's car."

Society Hill, Pennsylvania

Bethie was humming when they finally pulled up to her darkened town house. It was nearly ten o'clock; the moon was full and the humidity a soft, fragrant caress against her wind-burned cheeks. It had been a wonderful day, a glorious day, and while the hour was growing late, she still wasn't ready for it to end.

"What a fabulous evening," she said gaily.

Tristan smiled at her. Three hours ago, as the day cooled and slid into a purple-hued dusk, he'd taken off his sweater and tucked it around her shoulders. Now she snuggled in soft, cable-knit cotton, inhaling the scent of his cologne and finding it as poignant as his touch earlier in the afternoon. He'd retrieved a navy-blue blazer from the trunk for his own warmth. The jacket was finely cut but there was something about it that nagged at her. Giggling, she'd finally gotten it. He looked like an FBI agent, she teased him. He'd become a G-man. Fortunately, the comment seemed to amuse him.

"What now?" she asked.

"I believe that's your call, love."

"Are you playing hard to get?"

"I thought it would be an interesting change of pace."

Bethie giggled. She was probably still feeling the effects of the champagne, she decided, because she'd never been the giggling schoolgirl type, not even when she'd been a giggling schoolgirl. Today, however, they'd had one bottle of champagne in Pennsylvania Dutch country, then another bottle back in Philadelphia, sitting down at the waterfront after a superb lobster dinner at Bookbinder's. She'd been worried about driving home, but fortunately the champagne didn't seem to affect Tristan at all. He was a solidly built man, and one who could apparently hold his liquor.

Interesting, she thought absently, but should a man who'd just had a kidney transplant be able to hold his liquor? She wondered when he took all his pills.

"I don't think we're alone anymore," Tristan murmured.

"What? Where?" She looked around her quiet street wide-eyed. Tristan had his arm draped casually around the back of her seat. She leaned her head closer to him.

"I don't see anyone," she said in an exaggerated stage whisper.

"Your neighbor. Through the lace curtains."

"Ah, good old Betty Wilson. Old bat. She's always watching me. About time I had something good to show her." Bethie draped her arms around Tristan's neck and kissed him full on the mouth. He complied readily, his other arm curling around her back and trying to draw her closer only to have the gearshift get in the way. They broke apart breathlessly, thwarted by bucket seats, and she was struck once more by the taste of him on her lips, and her own desperate hunger for more.

His eyes had grown dark again. She loved it when they held that intense, burning gleam.

"Bethie ..." he said thickly.

"Oh God, come inside!"

He smiled. "I thought you'd never ask."

Virginia

The salvage yard was dark and deserted, but Officer Amity had come well equipped. He handed out two high-powered flashlights, then strapped a fanny pack filled with tools around his waist. Rainie was impressed.

"I didn't take you for the breaking and entering type," she told him.

Amity shrugged. "When I called earlier, the owner wasn't big on cooperation. Salvage yards can be that way. They've paid for the vehicles and they're afraid to have their newfound property seized as part of a police case. Understandable maybe, but why should you and I keep beating our heads against a wall, when we're both so capable of scaling a chain-link fence?"

"I can do fences," Rainie assured him. "Dobermans have me a little more concerned."

"No dogs. I drove by earlier."

"No dogs? What kind of self-respecting salvage-yard owner doesn't have a dog?"

"The kind who's been turned in to the humane society twice and could no longer afford the cruelty-toward-animal fines. Now he has a security company that drives around in hourly intervals. You see headlights, duck."

"Cool," Rainie said and started whistling "We're off to see the Wizard, the wonderful Wizard of Oz."

Five minutes later, they'd scaled the eight-foot-high fence and were making their way through the final resting place for thousands of cars. Compacted cubes of metal were piled into rusted-out heaps. Back ends, front ends, bumpers were scattered about like dismembered limbs. The newer acquisitions sat quietly in long lines, fully formed skeletons still awaiting their fate.

"Sheee—it." Amity whistled, looking out at two football fields' worth of wrecked vehicles and untold numbers of tires.

"I'd say look for an SUV," Rainie murmured, "but that doesn't exactly limit our options."

"America's love for the big automobile," he agreed. "Kind of ironic that we're about to compare a Ford Explorer with the proverbial needle."

"Split up?"

"No."

Rainie nodded and pretended not to hear the concern in his voice. The moon was full, visibility great for a nighttime rendezvous. Still she was conscious of the total hush, the unnatural still of a cemetery-like place. In the dark, abandoned metal took on lifelike shapes, and it was hard not to turn shadowy corners and feel the hairs prickle at the nape of her neck.

They walked in silence, flashlights slicing through the twisted heaps. Every few feet they'd come to an SUV, check for make and model, then keep on moving. One dozen down, five hundred to go. They stumbled upon one particularly crushed compact car and Rainie recoiled at the stench of dried blood.

"Jesus!" she cried, then stuffed a fist into her mouth to keep from saying more.

Vince swept his flashlight over a four-door sedan that had forcefully become a convertible. The cloth seats had once been blue; now they were stained with ugly splotches of brown.

"I'm guessing car versus semi," he said.

"I'm guessing decapitation," Rainie moaned and quickly moved on.

The sound of an approaching engine rumbled through the silence. Rent-a-Cop. They ducked swiftly behind a mountain of twisted chassis, still too close to the bloody convertible and Rainie pinched her nose with her fingers to block out the smell. She was thinking of the medical report now, the one Quincy had no doubt read time after time after time. How Amanda Quincy had struck the telephone pole at approximately 35 miles per hour. How the force of that impact pushed the front bumper down and the rear bumper up, launching her unsecured body into the air. Her body had hit the steering wheel first. The column had crumpled as it was designed to do, sparing her internal organs but doing nothing to halt her flight. Next had come the dashboard, bending her body like a rag doll at the waist. Finally came the metal frame of the windshield, not designed to crumple on impact, and now driving deep into Mandy's brain while the unyielding glass crushed all the bones in her face.

The security guard finally moved on. Amity and Rainie stood. She said, "I know how to find the Explorer."

"The windshield?"

"Yeah." And maybe it was horrible, but things moved much faster from there.

They finally found the dark green remnant at the very edge of the salvage yard; Rainie called it a remnant because it certainly didn't resemble a vehicle anymore. The entire back end had been clipped off, no doubt soldered together with some rear-ended SUV's front end by the auto world's equivalent of Dr. Frankenstein. The runners were gone. Both doors and the front seats stripped. The tires shed. What was left looked like a gutted fish head, lying on the gaping back hole where its body used to be while its crushed bumper smiled obscenely in the dark.

"Spooky," Amity muttered.

"Let's not linger."

"I'll second that."

Officer Amity opened up his fanny pack and spread out his wares. He was the proud owner of two pairs of latex gloves—a little late to protect the evidence now, Rainie thought, but what the hell. He'd also brought a penknife, a screwdriver, a wrench, four Baggies, and interestingly enough, a magnifying glass.

He handed her the screwdriver, and wordlessly they went to work. First they took off the trim piece of the B-pillar, exposing the plastic casing around the driver-side seat belt. Rainie tested the strap with her hand, and true to Amity's report, it spooled toothlessly onto the floor. He held up the flashlight to provide better lighting and before they went any farther, she got out the magnifying glass. She held it up to the casing. Then she looked somberly at Amity. The plastic casing bore deep scratch marks: they were not the first to pry it open.

"I hereby do solemnly swear," he murmured, "to disassemble all 'non-operative' seat belts in all auto accidents to come."

Rainie exchanged the magnifying glass for the penknife and cracked the mechanism open. Inside was a giant white plastic gear, with one main white plastic paw and one small back-up lever in case the primary failed. In theory, when the seat belt was pulled forward, it turned the gear, which then caught on the lever and froze. Except that in this case, the main paw had been filed down and the back-up lever clipped off. Rainie pulled on the seat belt again, and they both watched the white gear spin around and around and around.

"If she'd taken it in," Amity said after a moment, "the mechanic guy would've caught it."

"So our guy had to make sure she didn't have the vehicle serviced."

"Isn't that risky, though? If you're going to tamper with a seat belt, why do it a whole month before? Seems like you'd do it day of, or maybe I've just been watching too much *Murder, She Wrote.*"

"Prejudices," Rainie said. "Yours, mine, any cop's. She knows the seat belt is broken, so she doesn't even put it on. And when you arrive at a scene where the driver is drunk and hasn't even bothered to strap in ..."

"You think she's pretty stupid," Amity said quietly. "You think, whether you mean to or not, that she got what she deserved. And then you don't ask too many questions."

"Nobody looks too closely," Rainie agreed. She was frowning though, chewing on her bottom lip. "It still seems risky. I mean, if you wanted to kill someone and have it look like an accident, would you simply tamper with a seat belt and hope fate sooner or later takes its course?"

"Victim has a history of drinking and driving. Perp provides the alcohol, then lets her get behind the wheel. Chances are she won't make it home."

"Are they? A shocking number of people drink and drive every day without crashing. Look at Mandy, she'd already done it dozens of times before."

"Maybe he wanted an out. Think of it this way: even if we'd caught on right away, how are you going to prove who tampered with the seat belt weeks before a collision? That just leaves us with looking at who got her drunk. Victim was of age. Serving her isn't a crime, and letting her drive is back to being a civil matter, not criminal."

"Someone who wanted to plan a murder, but wanted to be cautious," Rainie murmured, then firmly determined, "no, I don't buy it. If you're going to go to this much trouble to kill someone, you're going to see it through. You're going to make sure you got the job done. Oh shit, we're idiots!"

She grabbed the magnifying glass and before Amity could react she was around the mutilated hunk of metal to the passenger's side. She pulled on the seat belt. It caught and held. Perfectly good, of course. It would need to be.

"You son of a bitch," Rainie said. And then Amity was holding the flashlight and she was running over the tight weave of the strap with the magnifying glass. "There! Right there!"

The fabric buckled and warped, a two-inch span where the fibers had been stretched as the SUV hit the pole, the seat belt caught, and a body flew against the strap.

"Meet passenger number two!" Rainie cried triumphantly, and then a heartbeat later, "Oh, Quincy, I am so sorry."

15

The minute Bethie opened her front door, her security system sounded a warning beep. She crossed the threshold and worked the keypad. As was her custom, she entered in the disarm code first, then requested a survey of the various security zones. All quiet on the western front.

Tristan shut the front door behind her. Then locked it.

"Nice system," he commented.

"Believe it or not, as part of our divorce decree, my ex-husband must provide basic security for the girls and me for the rest of our lives. Not that he minds. Quincy has been at his job a little too long; he sees homicidal maniacs everywhere."

"You can never be too sure," Tristan said.

"Perhaps." Bethie set down the picnic basket next to the entry table. It needed to be cleaned out, but that could wait until morning. She started humming, thinking about waking up with Tristan and the various possibilities for breakfast in bed. When was the last time she'd made omelets or biscuits or crêpes suzette? When was the last time she'd started her day with anything more than black coffee and a boring piece of toast? She was so happy she'd gone out with Tristan today. And she was even happier that she'd taken these first few baby steps back into the land of the living.

She glanced absently at her answering machine and was surprised to see that she had eight new messages.

"Do you mind?" she asked, nodding her head toward the digital display. "It will only take a minute."

"By all means. Do you have some sherry? I can pour us each a glass while I wait."

Bethie directed him toward the small wet bar in her dining room, hoping her cleaning woman had been conscientious about checking the crystal decanter for dust; Bethie had last had a glass of sherry five years ago. Well, this was a night for new beginnings.

She picked up a little spiral notepad and hit play.

The first message was a hang up, from seven-ten that morning. The caller had just missed her: she'd left with Tristan only moments before. Then came another hang up. Then another. Finally, a person: Pierce calling shortly after noon. "We need to talk," her ex-husband said in that crisp manner of his. "It's about Mandy."

Bethie frowned. She felt the first prickle of unease. Another hang up.

97

Another hang up. Then another one. The muscles in her abdomen tightened. She realized now that she was steeling herself for something bad, preparing her body for the blow.

It came at precisely 8:02 P.M. Pierce, once more on the machine. "Elizabeth, I've been trying to reach you all day. I'll be honest, I'm very worried. When you get this message, please call me immediately on my cell phone, regardless of time. Some things have come up. And Bethie—maybe we need to talk about Tristan Shandling because I tried to run a background check on him today and no such person exists. Call me."

Bethie's gaze came up. She fumbled with the volume switch on her answering machine but it was already too late. Tristan stood in the doorway, holding two tiny glasses of sherry and gazing at her curiously.

"You asked Pierce to run a background check on me?"

She nodded dumbly. The blood had drained out of her face. She felt suddenly light-headed, unsteady on her feet.

"Why, Elizabeth Quincy, you have finally surprised me."

Tristan set down the two glasses on a side table. *Run,* Bethie thought. But she was in her own house, she didn't know where to go. And then she was thinking of all those textbooks Pierce used to have in his office. The day she'd come home and found her girls staring wide-eyed at a pile they'd pulled down from the bookshelf, color photo after color photo of mutilated female flesh, naked, tortured bodies with hacked-off breasts.

"Who ... who are you?"

"Supervisory Special Agent Pierce Quincy, of course. I have a driver's license that says so."

"But ... but you have the scar. I touched it, I know!" Her voice was rising.

In comparison, he sounded increasingly serene. "Did it myself, the day you pulled the plug on Mandy. A sterile knife, a steady hand with the needle. There are certain things you should never leave to chance."

"Mandy ... You knew Mandy... Her expressions, my nickname ..."

"Have you seen me take any pills, Bethie? Haven't you wondered if a man with a brand-new kidney should drink two bottles of champagne? My cover is never perfect, you know. I like to leave the person a sporting chance. But you women insist on seeing only what you want to see—at least while you're falling in love. We all know it changes after that."

"I don't understand."

"Your understanding is not important to me."

"Pierce is a high-ranking FBI agent. You won't get away with this!"

He smiled thinly. Then he reached into his pocket and pulled out his black leather gloves. "That's what I'm counting on. You know, I wasn't going to do this so soon. I was going to wait until the night you came to me, hysterical about what had happened to Kimberly. And then I was going to tell you how much she always hated you. Kimberly and Mandy. It was never their father who traumatized them, Bethie. It was you, weak, overprotective, unforgiving you."

"Don't hurt my daughter. Don't you touch Kimberly!"

"Too late." He pulled on the gloves. "Run, Bethie," he murmured. *"Run!"*

Greenwich Village, New York City

In the middle of the night, Kimberly bolted awake. Her breathing was harsh and sweat had glued her T-shirt to her skin. She was shivering. Bad dream. She didn't remember of what.

She waited, focusing on breathing again until her heart finally slowed in her chest. Then she turned on her bedside light and padded silently into the kitchen. The door of her roommate's bedroom was closed. She could just make out the low undertones of Bobby's rhythmic snores. The sound soothed her. Bobby had a new girlfriend and hadn't been around much lately. That was his business, of course, but tonight she was glad that he was here. Someone else shared the tiny apartment. She was not alone.

She sat down at the kitchen table. She knew from prior experience that it would be a while before she would go back to sleep. Even then, she could not be sure that she wouldn't dream. Sometimes it was Mandy driving her Explorer while Kimberly tried desperately to grab the steering wheel. Sometimes it was herself, running through a long dark tunnel, seeing her father far ahead but never able to catch up with him. Once she dreamed of her mother. Bethie was dancing ballet in a beautiful white tutu and no matter what Kimberly did, she could not get Bethie's attention. Then a rift opened up in the floor, and Kimberly watched her mom dance right over the edge.

Anxious dreams from an anxious subconscious. Kimberly glanced at the phone. She should just pick it up. Call her mother. Call her father. Get over whatever it was she needed to get over.

But she didn't do it. She sat at the kitchen table. She listened to the deep sound of silence that exists only after midnight. And then, after minutes turned into an hour, she made her way back to bed.

Motel 6, Virginia

Rainie had just returned from her salvage-yard rendezvous, when the phone in her motel room shrieked to life. She glanced at the clock. Three A.M. She looked back at the phone. She wondered if the caller was Quincy or the hotshot lawyer Carl Mitz. Then she wondered which would be worse. She picked up the phone.

It was Quincy. "I'm in Philadelphia. At Bethie's house. She's dead."

Rainie said, "I'll be right there."

16

Rainie made the nighttime drive to Philly in just over two hours. She ignored speed limits, rules of the road, and most standard courtesy. And she arrived in full-warrior mode.

Elizabeth Quincy's elite town house was not hard to find. Rainie simply drove into Society Hill and followed the garish display of flashing lights. A white medical examiner's van was illegally parked up on the sidewalk. A cluster of three police cruisers represented the ground troops. One older unmarked sedan would be the pair of homicide detectives; they'd had the decency to also park up on the sidewalk, trying to leave enough room for traffic to squeeze by on the narrow lane. Three larger, dark sedans, however, lined up as a single clog in the space the detectives had tried to leave. They would be the feds. Too many chiefs, not enough Indians, Rainie thought immediately, and wondered how Quincy was faring.

She parked a block back and walked up as the sky was just beginning to lighten with the first tinge of dawn. Half a dozen neighbors hovered in over-priced doorways, wearing silk dressing robes and Burberry overcoats and gazing at Rainie cautiously as she passed. The neighbors looked scared. The tall, narrow town houses sat shoulder to shoulder, and for all their impression of discreet wealth, they weren't that different from one long apartment complex. Now, a very bad thing had happened down the hall, and not all the money in the world could put enough distance between that and them.

Rainie arrived at Bethie's residence. Inside the hastily roped off perimeter, a young officer was guarding the scene, sipping coffee from Wawa's and yawning every two or three seconds. Rainie flashed her PI's license.

"Nope," he said.

"I'm working for FBI Agent Pierce Quincy," she countered.

"And I'm working for Mayor John F. Street. Fuck off."

"You kiss your mother with that mouth?" She arched a brow, then dropped her voice to deadly serious. "Hey rookie, go inside. Find Supervisory Special Agent Quincy and tell him Lorraine Conner is here."

"Why?"

"Because I work with him, because he personally called me to this scene, and because you don't want to start your day getting your ass kicked by a girl."

"Like I'm going to start my day taking orders from one—"

"Officer."

Both Rainie and the young officer jerked their attention to the open doorway. Of all people, Special Agent Glenda Rodman stood there, wearing the same stark gray suit from the day before, except as she'd also been dragged out of bed in the middle of the night, her dark hair was a bit more mussed around her face. Rainie thought the hairstyle was kinder, but mostly she was mortified at being caught in yet another losing battle.

"Special Agent Quincy has requested Ms. Conner's presence," Glenda informed the officer. "Do allow her in, and don't mind what she says. I understand that she's not a morning person."

"Oh, I like mornings just fine. It's people I can't stand."

"If you will follow me …"

Officer I'm-in-Charge grudgingly raised the police tape. In turn, Rainie flashed him a gloating smile, then immediately blanked her features before entering the scene. She had no sooner followed Special Agent Rodman into the foyer, when she was assaulted with the stench of blood.

She recoiled, caught herself, and for a moment, simply had to stand her ground. Special Agent Rodman had stopped as well. Her expression was patient, perhaps even kind. At that moment, Rainie understood just how bad it was going to get.

Blood was everywhere. Streaked across ecru-colored walls, splattered onto oil canvases, pooled on parquet floors and century-old silk carpets. In the foyer, the table had been toppled, the phone yanked out of its socket, and the answering machine dashed against a massive gold-framed mirror. Shards of glass riddled the floor, and the sweet smell of alcohol mingled with bodily fluids.

Jesus, Rainie thought. She couldn't get beyond that. *Jesus.*

Special Agent Rodman was moving. She led Rainie into the dining room, where crime-scene technicians were now dusting a gleaming cherrywood table for prints, while another pair of officers were rolling up the oriental rug to be shipped to the lab. Glenda paused again. She was providing a tour of the scene, Rainie realized. Giving discreet but effective highlights of events.

It would appear that the attack started in the foyer. Given the spray pattern, the weapon was maybe a knife or blunt object. Elizabeth is ambushed. Elizabeth fights back. Elizabeth runs into the dining room. A gilded French lamp. Rainie saw it ripped out of the wall and flung across the room. The base bore a small round mark of blood and hair. His? Hers? She supposed it depended on who grabbed the lamp first. More spray patterns on the far wall. Someone had taken another solid hit, probably Elizabeth.

Bloody footprints on the oak parquet floor. Rainie and Glenda followed them into the Spanish-style kitchen, where a large butcher's block of knives had been overturned on the tiled counter. The smaller knives, paring knives, steak knives, had been knocked on the floor as someone—again him, her, who got here first?—reached frantically for the butcher blades. It had not gone well. More blood, smeared along the vast expanse of deep blue tiles, a larger print on the floor.

Rainie could see it now. Quiet, refined Elizabeth Quincy attacked, wounded, already dizzy from terror and blood loss, racing into the kitchen.

Knowing she was overpowered and outmaneuvered. Desperate to even the odds. Then seeing her collection of knives. And making a desperate gamble.

Poor, poor, Elizabeth. Knives were always a bad choice for a woman. Blades required skill, strength, and reach, attributes better suited to a man. It was one of those things police officers got to analyze in case studies. Women who ran into the kitchen for a knife, almost always had it used on them instead. Bethie should have gone after a cast iron skillet. Something big and heavy that could punish an opponent without a great deal of accuracy.

Had she realized that as he caught her at the end of the counter? Had she considered her other options as she went down on the hardwoods, her bloody fingers scrabbling at the cupboard handles, desperate for support?

On the floor was a clear imprint of her hip and her thigh as she'd fallen on her side. But somehow she'd managed to fight him off, because the blood trail kept going. She had been tough. Or he simply hadn't wanted it to end.

"It's trickier in here," Special Agent Rodman murmured. "Follow the tape."

For the first time, Rainie noticed the masking tape forming a thin, zig-zagging line through the debris field. Smart, she decided, having once worked a large, complicated crime scene herself. By the time all was said and done, dozens of people would have walked through this house, searching for evidence and providing their individual areas of expertise. It would take weeks to sort it all out, and months to write it all up. Best to try and corral the intrusion from the very start, versus trying to sort out all the sources of contamination later, as she had needed to do.

Rainie tiptoed along the masking tape, following it into the hallway, where the burgundy runner carried wet splotches and the walls bore a cacophony of bloody handprints. The prints ran the length of the tight, claustrophobic space, an obscene version of sponge painting. *Jesus*, Rainie thought again.

"We think he did this postmortem," Glenda said.

"But the palm prints are too small to be his."

"They're not his."

"Quincy walked through all this?" Rainie asked sharply.

"Many times. At his own request."

They came to the master bedroom. Rainie didn't look at the bed right away. The ME and his assistant were standing over there and she did not want to see what they were studying that had already caused the assistant to turn an unnatural shade of green. She looked at the perimeter first. More shattered mirrors. Two lamps ripped from the wall. Another phone jerked from a nightstand. Pillows had been gutted, strewing feathers across the deep-pile rug. Perfume bottles had been shattered, leaving the horrible, cloying scent of flowers in a blood-ravaged room.

"Somebody had to have heard something," Rainie said, her voice no longer quite sounding like her own. "How could all of this go on without someone calling the police?"

"The previous owner was a concert pianist," Glenda said. "When he had the town house redone twenty years ago, he soundproofed the walls so he wouldn't disturb his neighbors."

"Who ... who finally called the police?"

"Quincy."

"He was here?"

"He claims he drove here shortly after midnight, when he still couldn't reach his ex-wife by phone. He was worried about her safety, so he took a ride."

"He claims?" Rainie didn't like that phrase. "He *claims?*"

Special Agent Rodman wouldn't meet her gaze anymore. "There is a stained-glass window broken in the master bathroom," she murmured. "One theory is that the UNSUB broke into the house earlier in the evening, and surprised Mrs. Quincy when she came home."

"One theory?"

"This house is equipped with a state-of-the-art alarm system. It never went off."

"Was it armed?"

"We are working with the security company now to determine that information. They should be able to provide us with a record of the system's most recent activity."

"So one theory is that a stranger broke in and ambushed her. The second would be that the attacker was someone she knew and trusted." Rainie could no longer contain herself. "You're looking at Quincy, aren't you? Goddammit, you suspect him!"

"No, I don't!" Special Agent Rodman spoke up in a low hush. Her gaze darted toward the ME, then she quickly bent closer. "Listen to me, Ms. Conner. It is not in my nature to share information about a case. And it is certainly not in my nature to needlessly provide details to some out-of-state pseudo-cop. But it would appear that you and Special Agent Quincy are friends, and he's going to need friends. We—meaning the Bureau—are behind him right now. Personally, I have spent all day listening to various sexual sadists leave not-very-subtle messages on his answering machine. We understand that there is more to this situation than meets the eye. We cannot, however, say the same for the locals."

"You're the feds, pull rank!"

"Can't."

"Bullshit!"

"Honey, there's this thing called law. Look it up sometime."

Rainie scowled. "Where is he? Can I talk to him?"

"Detectives willing, you can try."

"I want to see him."

"Then follow me."

Glenda headed back toward the hallway. Passing through the doorway, Rainie made the mistake this time of looking at the bed. She could not quite contain the gasp that rose up in her throat.

Glenda glanced at her grimly. She said once more, "Quincy needs friends."

Two plainclothes detectives had Quincy sequestered off in the one room that appeared spared in the attack. At any other time, Rainie might have laughed at the incongruous sight. This room had obviously been one of the girls', the walls papered in a soft yellow with tiny pink and lilac flowers, the twin bed covered in a matching comforter, and the canopy top draped with yards of dreamy white gauze. A white wicker makeup table sat against one wall, topped by an oval mirror and still bearing small photos marking a young girl's major passages in life—leaping in cheerleading practice, arms wrapped around a best friend, attending the prom. A dried corsage hung from a ribbon on the mirror, and a collection of brightly colored stuffed animals sat on the dresser top.

The room offered only a dainty, lilac-covered wicker bench, now occupied by one burly detective whose chin was nearly resting upon his knees. The other detective stood, while Quincy sat on the gauze-draped bed with a ruffled yellow pillow tucked against his thigh. *The Gestapo does Laura Ashley,* Rainie thought, and wished the sight of Quincy's pale, tightly shuttered face didn't twist her heart painfully in her chest.

"What time did you say you arrived again?" the seated detective was asking. He had a single fierce, bushy brow that overshadowed his eyes—Cro-Magnon man in a cheap gray suit.

"A little after midnight. I did not glance at my watch."

"The neighbor, Mrs. Betty Wilson, claims she saw the victim return home with a man fitting your description shortly after ten P.M."

"I was not here at ten P.M. As I've stated already, I did not arrive here until after midnight."

"Where were you at ten?"

"By definition, Detective, I was in my *car* at ten P.M., driving here, so I could arrive after twelve."

"Got any witnesses to that?"

"I drove here alone."

"What about toll receipts?"

"I never asked for any receipts. At the time, I didn't realize that I would need an alibi."

The two detectives exchanged glances. Victim's ex-husband appears evasive and unnecessarily hostile. Let's get the thumbscrews and brass knuckles.

Rainie figured now was a good time to interrupt. "Detectives," she said quietly.

Three pairs of eyes swung toward her. The two detectives scowled, obviously assuming she was a lawyer—who else would turn up at this time of night/morning? Quincy, on the other hand, registered no reaction at all. He had obviously seen his ex-wife's remains on her feather-strewn bed. After that, any further emotion would be superfluous.

"Who the hell are you?" Cro-Magnon did the honors.

"Who do you think? Name is Conner, Lorraine Conner."

She held out her hand authoritatively, and with the long-suffering sigh policemen reserve just for lawyers, Cro-Magnon conceded to shake her hand—with a crushing grip. "Detective Kincaid," he muttered. Rainie turned to his partner, a slightly built man with intense blue eyes. "Albright," he supplied and shook her hand as well while giving her a more appraising assessment. Rainie pegged him as the brains behind the operation. Cro-Magnon rattled the beehive. Smaller, less threatening guy took excellent notes.

"Where are we?" Rainie asked, plopping down on the bed as if she had every right to be here. In the doorway, Special Agent Rodman wore a small smile.

"Trying to establish an alibi—"

"Are you saying that an FBI agent is a *suspect?*" Rainie gave smaller, less threatening guy an imperious stare.

"He is the ex-husband."

Rainie turned to Quincy. "How long have you been divorced?"

"Eight years."

"Do you have any current legal proceedings against your ex-wife?"

"No."

"Do you stand to gain any money upon her death?"

"No."

Rainie turned back to the detectives. "Is it just me, or is there a total lack of motive here?"

"Is it true that you purchased a red Audi TT coupe two weeks ago in New York?" Detective Albright asked Quincy.

"No," Rainie answered for him.

"Counselor, we have a record of the vehicle's registration, bearing the agent's name."

"Fraudulent purchase. A man *posing* as Supervisory Special Agent Quincy made that purchase, as the FBI is already aware of and actively investigating. Isn't that correct, Special Agent Rodman?"

"We are actively investigating," Glenda provided dutifully from the doorway.

Rainie addressed the detectives once more. She took a page out of Quincy's book, keeping her voice crisp and manner perfectly relentless. "Are you aware that someone is currently stalking Supervisory Special Agent Quincy? Are you aware that his personal telephone number has been made available to prisoners all across the country? In addition, someone has used his name to make a series of purchases"—slight lie, but it sounded better—"all of which is currently being investigated by reputable agents at the Bureau. Perhaps you should consider that before you proceed."

"And are you aware," Detective Albright replied in her same cadence, "that Agent Quincy has logged eight calls to his ex-wife's house in the last twenty-four hours?"

"As he said, he was worried about her."

"Why? They've been divorced eight years."

Oh, score one for the homicide detective.

"Elizabeth had asked me to run a background check." Quincy spoke up quietly. Rainie wished he wouldn't. He sounded too composed, too professional, like someone who had walked through such scenes hundreds of times and made his living by reviewing them hundreds more. She understood his detachment. She even heard the subtle, more dangerous thread of anger beneath his words, while noticing that his right hand was clenched too tightly on his lap and his left hand clutched the edge of the mattress as if he was trying to keep himself from spinning away. She wished she could touch him. She was afraid of how savage his reaction might be. So she merely sat behind him, pretending to be his lawyer so she could stay at his side, and wishing he'd trust her more, because his FBI composure was only going to sink him further with the local boys.

"However," Quincy was continuing, "I could find no record of the name Bethie gave me. Coupled with the incidents going on in my own life, I grew concerned about who this person was and what he might do."

"Name?"

"Tristan Shandling."

"How did she meet Shandling?"

"I don't know."

"When did she meet him?"

"I don't know."

Detective Albright arched a brow. "So, let me get this straight. You're conscientious enough to run a background check, but you didn't ask your ex-wife any questions?"

"As you said, Detective, we'd been divorced eight years. Her personal life is not my business anymore."

"Personal life? So you suspected he was a new love interest—"

"I didn't say that," Quincy interjected sharply. But it was too late. Detective Albright was already making fresh notes. And now, Rainie thought with a sigh, they had motive—the ever-classic, ever-popular, jealous ex.

"Detectives," she said crisply. "While I'm sure we all have nothing better to do at five in the morning than continue this conversation, aren't you missing the obvious?"

Detective Albright cocked his head and regarded her curiously. Cro-Magnon went with the more obvious, "Huh?"

"Look at this house. Look at this scene. There is blood everywhere; there are indications of a savage fight. Now behold Supervisory Special Agent Quincy: His suit is immaculate, his shoes are polished, and his hands and face don't bear a single mark. Doesn't that tell you anything?"

"He took lessons from O. J. Simpson," Cro-Magnon declared.

Rainie sighed. She appealed to Albright, who seemed to have more common sense. She was honestly surprised to realize that even smaller, less threatening guy was not convinced. What the ... ?

Her gaze flew to Quincy. He would not return her stare, his gaze locked somewhere on the far wall where flowers bloomed pink and lilac amid a sea of yellow. She turned to Glenda Rodman, and that agent, too, glanced away.

The feds knew something. At least Quincy and Glenda did, but they were not yet volunteering it to the locals, which could only mean one thing. How bad could one night get? And what would Quincy do, when she told him that the same person who had murdered Bethie tonight, had most likely started by killing his daughter fourteen months ago?

A tall, thin man appeared in the doorway. He was wearing a white doctor's coat. The medical examiner's assistant. "I ... uh. We thought you should see this."

With gloved hands, the man held up a plastic bag. Glenda didn't take it. Instead, Detective Albright accepted the marked evidence bag, held it up to the light, and promptly said, "Jesus Christ!" He dropped the bag on the lilac-colored rug, where it resembled a fresh pool of blood.

"It was ..." The medical assistant wasn't doing so well. His face still carried a tinge of green and he was staring at the plastic bag with the horrified fascination of someone who knew he really should look away. "We found it ... abdominal cavity ..."

Cro-Magnon wasn't moving. On the bed, Quincy's hand was gripping the floral comforter so tight, tendons stood out like ridges. Very slowly, Rainie reached down. Very slowly, she picked up the bag. She held it by the corner gingerly, as if it were a snake with the power to strike.

It looked like a piece of Christmas wrapping paper. Bright red with swirls of white. Shiny veneer. Except ...

It was paper, she realized dizzily. At least it had been. Cheap, white paper, probably like the kind used in any copy machine. Except now it was soaked bloody red. And those were not pretty swirls. They were letters, forming words, written in some kind of white wax, in order to come to light as it sat, according to the assistant, in Elizabeth Quincy's insides.

"It's a note," she said.

"Read it," Quincy whispered.

"No."

"*Read it!*"

Rainie closed her eyes. She had already made out the words. "It says ... it says, 'You'd better hurry up, Pierce. There's only one left.' "

"Kimberly," Glenda Rodman said from the doorway.

A strange sound came from the bed. Quincy was finally moving. His body rocked back and forth. His shoulders started to shake. And then a low, dreadful sound came from his lips. Laughter. A dry, bone-chilling chuckle spewing from his lips.

"A message in a bottle," he singsonged. "A message in a fucking bottle!"

His shoulders broke. He bowed his head. The laughter turned to sobs.

"Kimberly ... Rainie, get me out of here."

She did.

17

Greenwich Village, New York

They drove toward New York City in silence, Rainie at the wheel, Quincy leaning against the passenger-side window. His eyes were closed, but she knew he wasn't asleep. They would arrive at his daughter's apartment in about an hour. She didn't like to think about how that conversation would go. Poor Kimberly, who had just buried her older sister. Poor Kimberly, who would now learn that her mother had been savagely murdered, and that most likely, she was next in line.

Quincy needed to regain his composure, Rainie thought, for the clock was ticking now and in this kind of game you couldn't afford a time-out.

"Talk," he said shortly.

"We found Mandy's SUV. I was going to call you in the morning with the news."

"The seat belt was tampered with."

"Yes. And someone else was in the vehicle at the time of the crash. We found warping on the passenger's seat belt that proves it. In the good news department, Officer Amity recovered hairs from the cloth visor on the passenger's side. If we can find the man, we can use the hairs to tie him to the crime."

"What crime? Sitting in the passenger's seat of a sports-utility vehicle?"

"We'll work on it, Quincy. Officer Amity is a good guy; he can build a case. Now tell me this: Why did you go to your ex-wife's house on tonight of all nights?"

"I was worried. Elizabeth ... Bethie never went out much. It was unusual not to be able to reach her all day."

"I wonder if he knew that."

"Probably." Quincy finally turned in his seat. His face bore the stamp of freshly etched lines. In a matter of hours, his dark pepper hair seemed to have gained more salt at the temples. He was an experienced FBI agent, a man who made his living seeing the most horrible of horrors. Rainie wondered if that helped at a time like now, when he was desperate to save his remaining daughter, or if the intimate knowledge of what men could do only made things worse.

"It's obvious this Tristan Shandling is trying to frame you," she said quietly. "The car purchase in your name. Disguising himself to look like you when he showed up at Bethie's house. And there's more, isn't there? Things you and Dour Chic have already picked up on, but aren't volunteering to the local boys."

"The scene was staged. When the crime-scene techs examine the broken bathroom window, they'll discover it was broken from the inside out."

"But the broken glass was on the inside of the house, on the bathroom floor."

"True. But if you fit one of the broken shards back into the window, the angle of the break reveals the blow came from the inside. Moving glass is easy. You can't, however, disguise the fragments. The UNSUB was already inside the house when he broke the window. And I'm sure when the police get the report back from the alarm company, they'll find it was properly disarmed."

"He entered with Elizabeth," Rainie murmured. "The man fitting your description the neighbor saw at ten."

"That would be my guess. Then there is the crime scene itself. The level of destruction is out of proportion with the crime. Each room appears destroyed, but the blood trail is actually extremely contained. My guess is the initial struggle was fast, focused. The rest of the damage occurred postmortem."

"He wanted it to look bad?"

"He wanted it to look horrific, terrifying, demoralizing. He's very good at what he does."

"The body," Rainie whispered.

"The body," Quincy repeated, his voice detached again, overly analytical. "When the medical examiner finishes with the autopsy, he'll know the victim was killed fairly quickly—at least on a relative scale. There won't be any evidence of rape, despite how he posed the body. There aren't any abrasions on the wrists and ankles, indicating that hog-tying occurred postmortem. I suspect the disembowelment and other mutilation occurred postmortem as well."

"But why?"

"To make it look like a sexual-sadist attack. But a *posed* sexual-sadist attack. Such as what an expert in violent crimes might do to try and cover the cold-blooded murder of his ex-wife."

"Parlor tricks," Rainie said. "The police will see through them soon enough."

"I wouldn't be so sure about that."

"There's still the fact the police saw you hours after the murder without a trace of blood or bruising on your body."

"They'll simply argue that the crime was more controlled than it originally appeared to be. They'll find traces of blood in the sink pipes, indicating the murderer cleaned up afterwards. As knowledgeable as our UNSUB has been, I wouldn't be surprised if he didn't follow washing his hands by pouring a sample of blood that is the same type as mine into the sink. Or maybe he has the same blood type as me. At this point, how would I know?" His voice started out cool, but ended bitter.

"There's still the note," Rainie persisted. "That proves it was done by somebody out to get you."

"The note's not going to help me."

"Sure it will."

"No." Quincy shook his head. An odd smile curved his lips. "The note ... the handwriting. Rainie, it's mine. I don't know how, but it's as if this man ... it's as if he's really me."

Kimberly was sitting at the battered kitchen table, sipping a cup of coffee and trying to figure out what to do with her second day off, when the buzzer rang. Her roommate, Bobby, after announcing that he would stay tonight at his girlfriend's, had left for work. That left Kimberly with a whole day to kill and a whole apartment to kill it in. She should take a long nap. Exercise. Eat lots of fresh fruits and vegetables. Screw her head on straight.

Kimberly sipped black coffee, felt the weight of another sleepless night on her shoulders, and wondered how many city blocks she'd have to run to feel human again.

The buzzer repeated its whine. She finally got up and pressed the intercom button. "What?"

"Kimberly, it's your dad."

Oh no, she thought instantly. She hit the front-door button and let him in.

The old, eight-story apartment building didn't offer an elevator. It would take her father a few minutes to mount the stairs. She should do something. Gain ten pounds. Sleep four days straight. Down a bottle of vitamins to get some luster back in her too-long, too-dirty blond hair. Her old FBI sweats bagged on her frame. Her threadbare T-shirt hung low enough to reveal the gaunt line of her collarbone.

She stood trapped in the middle of the tiny kitchen until her father finally rapped on the door. She didn't want to answer it. She couldn't explain why. But she didn't want to open that door.

A second round of knocking. Her heart was pounding too hard in her chest. She slowly crossed the kitchen. She slowly opened her apartment door. Her father stood gravely in front of her, accompanied by some woman Kimberly had never seen before.

"I'm so sorry," he said hoarsely.

He took her in his arms. She started to cry and she didn't even know what bad thing had happened yet.

Thirty minutes later they sat in the TV room, Kimberly Indian-style on the floor, her father and his friend, Rainie Conner, on the sofa. Kimberly had gone through the first box of Kleenex. Somewhere in the middle of her crying jag, things had gone from unbearable to horrible to simply numb. Now she sat, staring at the worn blue berber carpet and struggling to get the words to make sense in her head.

Your mother is dead.

Your mother has been murdered.

Someone is stalking our family. He's killed Mandy. He's killed Bethie. He will most likely come after you next.

"You don't ... you don't know who's doing this?" she asked finally, working on forming the words, working on getting herself to think, working on keeping herself from splintering apart. She was the strong one. Her mother had always said so.

Your mother is dead.

Your mother has been murdered.

Someone is stalking our family. He's killed Mandy. He's killed Bethie. He will most likely come after you next.

"No," her father answered quietly. "But we're working on it."

"It's probably someone from an old case, right? Someone you caught, or nearly caught, or you caught his dad, his son, his brother."

"Probably."

"Then you build a database! You build a database and you fill it with all the old names, and then … then you figure out who got out from jail when and you arrest his ass! Process of elimination, then arrest his ass!" Her voice was high, she didn't sound anything like herself.

Her father repeated, "We're working on it."

"I don't understand." Her voice broke. She was close to weeping again. "Mandy … Mandy was always attracted to the wrong sort of men. But Mom … Mom was careful. She didn't talk to strangers, she wouldn't let some guy sweet-talk her into entering her home. She was too smart for that."

"Had you spoken to your mother recently?"

"No. I've been … busy." Kimberly bowed her head.

"She called me two days ago. She was worried about you."

"I know."

"I've been worried about you, too."

"I know."

He waited. An expert pause, she'd always thought. But she'd been studying and learning things, too. That was the hard part of following in her father's footsteps. Once he'd seemed almost God-like to her. Lately, however, no longer a neophyte, she watched him perform the old tricks and could see him pulling the strings. The first time it had happened, she'd been proud of her new insight. After Mandy's funeral, however, it only left her feeling empty.

He got off the sofa. Paced the room the way he did when he was tense or working on a particularly baffling case. He was pale, she realized. Thinner, nearly gaunt. Then it hit her. He looked like her. She nearly started crying again.

Her mother, yelling: "You're just like your father!"

Herself, yelling back: "I know, Mom, and Mandy's just like you!"

"Why don't we walk through this from the beginning," the chestnut-haired woman said from the sofa. Her father turned and frowned at her, his favorite intimidating look. The woman, however, wasn't impressed. "Quincy, she's part of this now. She might as well know as much as we know. Information may be the only defense we have left."

"I don't—"

"Yes!" Kimberly interrupted from the floor. "I am part of this. I need to know … There has to be something we can do."

"Dammit, you're my daughter—"

"And I'm his target."

"You're only twenty-one—"

"I've been trained in martial arts and firearms. I am not helpless!"

"I never wanted this. If there was anything I could do ..."

"I know." Her voice quieted. She said more sincerely, "I know. But here we are. There must be something I can do."

Her father closed his eyes. For a moment, she thought she might have glimpsed tears in them. Then he sighed, returned to the sofa, and sat down. When he spoke again, he sounded cool, composed, like an FBI agent instead of a father. She wasn't sure why that comforted her.

"We'll start at the beginning," Quincy said. "It would appear that someone is seeking revenge against me for some perceived wrong. We don't know who, but as you suggested, Kimberly, process of elimination should be able to tell us more. For now, what we do know is that this person has been planning this for a long time. At least a year and a half, more likely two years."

"Eighteen to twenty-four months?" Kimberly was genuinely shocked.

"We think he started with Mandy," Rainie said. "Maybe targeted her through an AA meeting. Things progressed from there."

"Her new boyfriend," Kimberly filled in. "She mentioned something once, but I didn't pay much attention. Boyfriends ... There were a lot of them."

"It would seem that he positioned himself to be someone very special," Quincy agreed. "They dated for months. Mandy trusted him. Maybe she even fell in love."

"But the accident," Kimberly protested. "She'd been drinking, she was behind the wheel. She'd done that kind of thing before. What did it have to do with him?"

Rainie spoke up. "We think he was with her that night. According to one friend, Mandy may have started drinking early in the evening. I'm not sure I trust the 'friend,' however, so Mandy may have still been sober when she met up with her boyfriend, and he was the one who got her intoxicated. Either way, our mystery man tampered with her seat belt so it wouldn't work. Then, he got in the vehicle with her, strapped himself in so he'd be all right, and ... and either let nature run its course or physically helped her hit the telephone pole."

"He was with her when she crashed?"

"Yes."

"Oh my God, he killed that old man!" Kimberly slapped a hand over her mouth in horror. She didn't know why, but somehow that was worse. Mandy was Mandy. She'd built an entire lifestyle on poor decisions and high-risk behavior. When her mother had called her the morning after the accident, Kimberly hadn't even been surprised. Instead, she remembered thinking, *finally,* as if part of her had been waiting for that phone call for years. Mandy was always on a course for heartbreak and disaster. That poor old man, however, had just been out walking his dog.

"She didn't die, though," Kimberly said after a moment, pulling herself together. "Mandy didn't actually die. Not then. Shouldn't that have panicked him?"

"Even if she came out of the coma, what would she know? What would she remember?" Rainie shrugged. "Her body might have recovered, but her brain ..."

"So he was safe."

"I think things pretty much went as he planned."

"But what about Mom? I can see Mandy being sweet-talked, but not Mom. Definitely not Mom."

"Think of the circumstances," Rainie countered. "Bethie's just buried her older daughter. She's feeling lonely, struggling to cope. Then we have this man, Tristan Shandling, who dated your sister for months. Consider all the things he could have learned about your mother from Mandy in that amount of time. Her taste in music, food, clothes. Likes, dislikes. It becomes a pretty simple equation. Vulnerable, grieving mother. Well-informed, charming man. I doubt she had a chance."

"I think he went a step further to gain Bethie's trust," Quincy said. "I think ...I think he might have pretended to have received an organ transplant. From Mandy."

"What?" Both Rainie and Kimberly stared at him.

"The last time I spoke with Bethie, she asked me about organ donation. Was there any chance the recipient received more than just tissue? Couldn't he maybe get some of the person's habits or feelings or soul? At the time, I dismissed it. It was only today when I had to wonder why she asked."

"My God," Rainie murmured. "Elizabeth gave permission to terminate her daughter's life just weeks ago, and now here comes this man, claiming to have part of Mandy inside of him."

"It's very clever," Quincy said.

"It's the domino theory," Kimberly declared. "He started with the weakest one—Mandy. Got to her, then used the trauma of her death to get to Mother and now ... now—" She looked at her father and knew his grim face was a match for her own.

"Shit!" Rainie abruptly bolted off the sofa, staring at them both wildly. "The frame-up, Quincy. What we were talking about earlier. Even if it's not perfect, it doesn't matter—it still gets the job done. Think about it! Bethie's been murdered. As her ex-husband, you're already on the cops' radar screen, give them a few more lab results and you'll be their number one man. There you go. Mandy's death to access Bethie, Bethie's murder to lead to your arrest, and then boom—Kimberly's all alone. It's perfect!"

"But ...but you can make bail, right?" Kimberly asked desperately.

Quincy was staring at Rainie. He looked stunned. "It doesn't matter," he whispered to his daughter. "Rainie's right. The minute I become a lead suspect, they'll notify the Bureau. And following standard protocol, the Bureau will place me on desk duty, ask for my creds and confiscate my weapon. Even if I stay out of jail, what will I be able to do to protect you? My God, he's done his homework."

"*Who the fuck is this person?*" Kimberly screamed.

Nobody had an answer.

18

Things got worse. Quincy wanted his daughter shipped to Europe. Kimberly yelled that she wouldn't go. Quincy told her now was not the time to be arrogant. Kimberly started laughing, accused the pot of calling the kettle black, then her laughter dissolved into tears, which seemed to hurt Quincy more. He stood in the middle of the dingy TV room, looking stiff and uncomfortable while his daughter wept.

Finally, Rainie sent Quincy to bed. In the past forty-eight hours, he'd had four hours of sleep and he was no longer close to fully functional. Then she brewed a fresh pot of coffee and sat with Kimberly at the kitchen table. The girl was a chip off the old block; she took her caffeine jet black. Rainie found skim milk in the fridge, then a bowl of sugar.

"Don't laugh," she told Kimberly, as she added scoop after heaping scoop to the brew. "I hate for the caffeine to be alone in my bloodstream."

"Has my father seen you do that?"

"Couple of times."

"How disparaging were his remarks?"

"On a scale of one to ten, I'd rate them a twelve."

"Oh that's not bad. My grandfather's comments would've hit fifteen."

"Your grandfather's still alive?" Rainie was surprised. Quincy never spoke of his father. For that matter, he never mentioned his mother, though Rainie had a vague memory of him saying once that she'd died when he was young.

Kimberly was blowing clouds of steam off the top of her coffee. "He's still alive. At least technically. Alzheimer's. He was hospitalized when I was ten or eleven. We used to visit him several times a year, but we haven't even done that in a while. He doesn't recognize any of us anymore, not even Dad, and well … Let's just say Grandpa isn't that fond of strangers."

"That's gotta be hard. What was he like before?"

"Tough. Quiet. Funny in his own way. We used to drive up to Rhode Island to visit his farm. He had chickens and cows, horses, an apple orchard. Mandy and I loved it. Plenty of space to run around, plenty of things to get into."

"And your mother was okay with this?" Rainie asked skeptically.

Kimberly smiled. "I wouldn't say that. I remember one day this hot air balloon comes crashing down from the sky. Some tourist outing or something. And this little guy is yelling at the passengers to grab the branches to help brake as the balloon plows through the apple trees then plunks down in the middle of my grandfather's field. Mom comes rushing out, all excited. 'Oh my goodness, did you see that? Oh my goodness.' Then Grandpa comes out of the chicken coop, stands in front of the balloon holding five embarrassed people and gives them the complete up and down, never saying a word. The guide gets nervous. He holds out this bottle, going on and on about how sorry he is and the tracking vehicle will be here any minute and oh yeah, here's a bottle of wine for his trouble. Grandpa just looks at the guy. Finally, he says, 'It's God's country.' Then he walks back to the chicken coop. That's Grandpa."

"I like him." Rainie said it sincerely.

"He was a wonderful grandfather," Kimberly said. She added more astutely, "But I wouldn't have cared for him as a father."

They both returned to their coffee.

"Are you and Dad dating?" Kimberly asked after the silence had stretched on too long.

"That's it, start with the easy questions." Rainie sipped her coffee more earnestly.

Kimberly, however, had also inherited her father's probing stare. "You're pretty young," she said.

"I'm aware of that."

"How old?"

"Thirty-two."

"Mandy was twenty-four when she died."

"All the more reason not to let a silly thing like age hold you back."

"So you are dating?"

Rainie sighed. "In the past, we have dated. What we are now ... I don't know. When Quincy wakes up, do me a favor and ask him."

"How did you meet?"

"Last year. The Bakersville case."

"Oh," Kimberly said with feeling. "That was a bad one."

"You could say that."

"You're the one who lost her job."

"That would be me."

Kimberly nodded with a freshly minted psych major's knowing confidence. "I see the problem."

"Great. Want to explain it to me?"

"Age alone wouldn't be reason enough, but now you two are at different phases of the life cycle, which makes the gap even more extreme. You have to rebuild, which puts you back at infancy. He's established, keeping him middle-aged. That's a tough gulf to bridge. I think figuring out how to have a successful relationship in the face of such complex career issues will be the challenge of the new, dual-income generation."

"You're working on your thesis, aren't you?"

"My thesis is on 'Challenges of Modernity: The Growth of Urbanization and Its Impact on Disrupted Personalities,' thank you very much."

"Oh. Mine was on attachment disorder. You know, why good families can still breed little fucking psychopaths."

Kimberly blinked. "Attachment disorder. That's one of my favorite subjects." She looked at Rainie more appraisingly. "I didn't realize you were a psych major."

"B.A. I never went back for my master's."

"Still, that's pretty cool."

"Thanks."

They both returned to their coffee. After a moment, Kimberly said softly, "Rainie, could you keep talking? In all honesty, it's easier to dissect your life than to think about my own."

"I'm really sorry, Kimberly."

"Who's going to help me plan my wedding? Who will I call when I'm expecting my first child? Who will hold my hand, when I give birth to a baby girl and see Mandy and my mother in every curve of her face?"

"We'll find out who's doing this. We'll find him, and we'll make him pay."

"And will that make things better? Look at you and what happened last year. You found the guy who did it. You and my father killed him. Are you better off?"

Rainie didn't say anything. After a moment, Kimberly said, "I thought as much."

Quincy dreamed. In his dream he was back in Philadelphia, walking through Bethie's beautiful, ravaged town house. He held a pillowcase in one hand. He was trying to capture all the feathers and stuff them back in. Then he was standing over the bed, his hands now holding Bethie's intestines, and trying frantically to pile them back in her body.

Don't, his subconscious told him in his dream. *Don't let him win by remembering her the way he intended.*

His dream spiraled backwards, his mind seeking happier times. Bethie, mussed hair, sweating face. No makeup, no pearls, but a smile that could light up a city as she lay in the white hospital bed and held out their first-born child. Himself, touching their baby girl delicately. Marveling at the ten perfect fingers, ten perfect toes. Then touching his wife's cheek. Telling her how beautiful she looked. And vowing that he would be a better father than his own dad had been. Fresh family. Fresh start. His heart, so big in his chest.

Bethie sixteen years later, coming into the family room with a dazed look on her face. She'd been cutting up carrots in the kitchen. The knife had slipped. She now carried her finger in her other hand. Himself, fresh from a California crime scene, twenty-five corpses found in a hillside, fifteen of them young women, two of them babies. Telling his wife, "Oh honey, it's just a scratch."

Bethie yelling, "I can't take it anymore! How did I end up married to a man who is so goddamn *cold?*"

Time fast-forwarding. He was in Massachusetts, keeping watch on human bait, Tess Williams returning to her old house in the hopes that it would lure her homicidal ex-husband out of hiding. Everything going wrong. Himself now inside the house as shots erupted down the street. Telling Tess not to go near the door. Promising he would keep her safe. Jim Beckett appearing, and blasting him back with a close-range spray from his double-barrel shotgun.

Himself thinking, *Wow, I feel so hot, for someone who is so cold.* Later, out of the hospital, paring back his work hours, trying to find some balance, picking up the girls for a weekend visit.

"How are you?" he asked Bethie.

"Better."

"I miss you."

"No you don't."

"Bethie ..."

"Go back to work, Pierce. Who needs to be a mere husband, when you can play at being God?"

In his daughter's two-bedroom apartment, Quincy jerked awake. He lay in the darkened room, watching threads of light from the closed blinds dance with dust in the air, listening to the sounds of the huge city below. "I'm sorry, Elizabeth," he said.

Then he got up and went to the TV room, where the last living member of his family sat watching *M*A*S*H*. Rainie was by her side. Her short, reddish-brown hair contrasted with his daughter's long, dusky blond locks. Her big gray eyes and wide cheekbones rebuffed Kimberly's own finely patrician face. Yin and yang, he thought, and both so beautiful the sight of them nearly broke his heart. For a moment, he simply stood there, wishing he could stop time, wishing he could take this moment and hold it safe forever in his hand.

"Ladies," he said. "I have a plan."

19

Quincy's House, Virginia

It was early evening on Thursday, and Special Agent Glenda Rodman had yet to return to bed from the night before when she looked at the security monitor and saw Quincy standing outside his front gate. She had slept two hours before receiving the call to come to Philadelphia last night, but that now seemed a lifetime ago. The two hours of sleep were the aberration. The rest of the time, touring the Philadelphia crime scene, then returning to Quincy's home to listen to message after message promising sick, perverse death, was the norm.

They were up to three hundred and fifty-nine callers. Some Quincy had personally put in jail. Others simply hated feds. Still others were merely bored. Either way, word was definitely out that the thinly disguised ad circulating in so many prison newsletters contained an FBI profiler's home number. Everyone felt compelled to call. Some, she had to admit, were more imaginative than most. One artistic soul had gone so far as to compose a death rap. It wasn't half bad.

Glenda hit the button and let Quincy into his own property. The agent wore the same suit from the night before. His features were pale. On the camera, they were also hard to read. Whether he knew it or not, Pierce Quincy was a legend around the Bureau. These days, Glenda felt sorry for the agent. But she felt even more curious about what would happen next.

He knocked on his front door. She kindly let him in.

"I need to gather a few things," he said.

"Certainly."

"I'll check in with Everett next, then I'm leaving town."

"The Philadelphia P.D. aren't going to like that."

"My daughter comes first." He disappeared into the master bedroom. Moments later, Glenda heard the sound of closet doors opening, as he began to pack a bag.

She wandered into his home office, not sure what to do with herself. It was interesting, she'd been in this house two days now and there wasn't much here to give a sense of the man who technically occupied the space. Several of the rooms were completely empty. The majority of the walls were bare; the kitchen couldn't feed a rat. The only room with any atmosphere was this room, the office, and she found herself coming here again and again, if only to escape the starkness of a vast, overwhelmingly white space.

Here was an old sound system that offered mediocre comfort in the shape of classical jazz tapes. A state-of-the-art fax dominated the corner of a beautiful, antique cherry desk. Gold-framed diplomas and academic certificates leaned against one wall, still not hung, but at least unearthed, while cardboard boxes were piled in each corner. The desk chair, black leather, was supple and distinctly expensive. Quincy obviously spent time in this room. Sometimes she caught a whiff of his cologne.

She sat in his chair, feeling like an intruder, as the phone once more began to ring. Following protocol, she let the answering machine pick it up.

"Hey baby," a voice crooned. "Heard you were trying a new policy of accessibility. I dig that. God knows there isn't anyone interesting to talk to in here. Bad break about your luscious daughter. Not so sorry about the frigid ex, though. Word on the street is that somebody's got your number. The hunter has become the hunted. Don't worry, Quince baby, I got my money on you in the prison pool. Hundred to one odds is just my style. You go, girl. Life hasn't been this entertaining in ages."

The caller hung up. It was a good call, Glenda thought, probably long enough to trace. Not that wire-tapping had helped them much; it only proved that lots of prisoners read their local newsletters. For that matter, half the callers were only too happy to leave their names and prison facility.

She left the office and spotted Quincy standing in his kitchen, holding a small black travel bag, and staring at the answering machine.

"We're taping them all," she said by way of explanation.

"One hundred to one odds." He gave her a sideways glance. "Considering how many of them I put in prison, I think I deserve better than that."

"I have a copy of the ad if you would like to see it," Glenda said, feeling the need to sound professional. She went to fetch it from the office. When she returned, Quincy had set down the traveling bag. He was standing in front of the empty refrigerator with the look of a man who'd opened it many times before and still kept expecting something different. She understood. Her own fridge held only water and low-fat yogurt and yet she continuously checked it for a fried-chicken dinner.

She handed Quincy the fax.

The ad was already typeset, a simple four-by-four square. It read, *Reporter from BSU Productions seeks inside information on life at death's door. Interested inmates should contact head agent, Pierce Quincy, at daytime number printed below. Or, contact his assistant, Amanda Quincy, at the following address.*

"Not very subtle," Quincy commented with that same unnerving calm. "BSU Productions. Head agent. Life at death's door."

"Codes can be more elaborate. From what I understand, the inmates generally disguise their communications as ads for pen pals. Then they play around with the letters. You know, instead of SWM/L for Single White Male/Lifer, they do things like BPO/M, which stands for Black Power Organization/Message. Members of the gang then know to piece through the ad for relevant information."

"Ah, the power of grassroots journalism. And people with too much time on their hands."

"From what we can tell, this ad ran in four major publications: *Prison*

Legal News, National Prison Project Newsletter, Prison Fellowship, and *Freedom Now*. Combined circulation reaches over five thousand subscribers. That number isn't high given total prison population, but the four newsletters basically account for at least one ad reaching every major corrections department. We think word of mouth took over from there."

"Quilting bees have nothing on the average prison for sheer amount of gossip," Quincy murmured. "I take it what we theorized before still stands. My phone number, and thus access to my address, has been spread so far and wide we'll never be able to pare it down. Who knows where I live? Who doesn't?"

"The *National Prison Project Newsletter* has the original hard copy of the ad," Glenda said. "We're having it couriered to the crime lab now. The Document Section should have more information for us in a matter of days. Also, Randy Jackson is still working on how the UNSUB got your unlisted number. I'm sure he'll have something shortly."

"The UNSUB got my phone number from Mandy. He used my daughter." Quincy set down the fax. For the first time, he turned and fully met her gaze. She was immediately shocked by the hardness in his eyes, the cool expression on his face. Dissociation, the professional part of her deduced. Events of the past eighteen hours had left him in a state of shock, and his mind was coping by keeping him detached. The rest of her felt an unexpected tingle at the back of her neck. She had seen that remote gaze before. Old photos of Ted Bundy. Some people believed there was only a thin line between profilers and their prey. At this moment, in Quincy, that line didn't exist. The tingle on the back of her neck grew into a shiver.

"My daughter's death wasn't an accident," he said. "Rainie Conner has evidence that the UNSUB tampered with her seat belt."

"Oh no," Glenda said immediately, and meant it.

"We believe he befriended her, gained her trust. There is no telling what all he knows. Hobbies, likes, dislikes, personal habits, personal quirks. Friends of mine, where they live. He most certainly has the address and phone number of this house. You shouldn't be here alone."

"I'm not," she said automatically, for the Bureau would never send an agent alone in the field. "There's Special Agent Montgomery ..."

Quincy merely looked at her. Then he let his gaze roam the empty rooms.

"Montgomery's been busy," she said defensively.

"Why is he on this case? He doesn't exactly seem the cavalry type."

"He requested it. You're one of us. It's important to get to the bottom of this, so we can all be safe."

Quincy looked at her again. She was beginning to understand his reputation now. That direct, probing stare. Those hard, compelling eyes. She broke, her gaze skittering away.

"Montgomery ... Montgomery was on the Sanchez case. First." She didn't have to say anything more. It was common knowledge that the first agent had botched the Sanchez case fifteen years ago. He'd insisted that they were looking for a single, charismatic sociopath, à la Ted Bundy, when the police already had evidence that more than one killer was involved. Further, the presence of cement dust had the LAPD wanting to check out blue-collar workers, not the local law schools. The police had finally thrown a fit. Montgomery had been removed. Quincy had come in. The rest was now law enforcement history.

"That would explain his language and dress in front of Everett," Quincy commented.

She smiled thinly. "No point in auditioning for the Bureau fast track when your career has already been derailed."

"His mistake. Apparently he's made a few. Don't let the next one involve you."

"I'm fine here. You have a wonderful security system, plus we've taken the liberty of upgrading. Let me show you." She led Quincy to the front door, where a new security box had been installed next to his doorbell. His old system had been a simple four-by-four keypad inside the entry. Now the system entailed a significantly sized plastic case boasting a keypad, scanner, and multicolor digital display located outside the front door.

"It combines a pin code with fingerprint technology," Glenda explained. "Instead of unlocking the front door, then rushing in to enter the security code, this box controls the front door. You enter in your personal pin number twice, then hold your index finger over the scanner to be read. If you match the print on file, the system automatically disarms and allows you into the house. The minute you close the door, it automatically resets for the next guest. In other words, the house is always protected and it now takes more than a simple sequence of numbers to gain access."

"It's set up for multiple people?"

"Yes. We've entered your fingerprints, Montgomery's, and mine into the system. More can be added as necessary. This way, we can come and go as we please. Plus, it eliminates having a key, which frankly poses another security risk as keys can be stolen or copied."

Quincy nodded. "What about lifting someone's fingerprint? The UNSUB has already stolen my name. Perhaps he got my fingerprints off a piece of mail I sent to my daughter."

"No good," Glenda said. "The scanner not only looks at ridges, but also analyzes the fingerprint for temperature and electrical properties. A lifted print wouldn't register the right temperature or have electrical properties." She smiled tightly. "Nor for that matter, would a severed digit."

Quincy nodded again. She could tell that he liked that. "What about override protection? There must be ways to circumvent the scanner. After all, a homeowner might end up with his hand in a cast, or cut his finger, temporarily altering his own fingerprint. The security company must also consider those things."

"The security company has thought of them, and is even more devious than you are, Quincy. All ten digits are on file. As long as the homeowner has one available finger, he can enter his home."

Quincy rocked back on his heels. He finally looked impressed. "Why didn't I buy this before?" he murmured.

"You weren't a corporation. It's just now becoming available for private residences." Glenda punched in her pin number twice, placed her index finger on the scanner, and opened the front door. Walking back into the house, she said, "So we have a state-of-the-art security system, cameras monitoring most rooms, and wiretaps on your phone lines. And if by some chance our mysterious UNSUB makes it through all that, I always have this." She patted her trusty 10mm, snug in its shoulder holster.

"Fair enough. But bear in mind that my ex-wife also believed her security system would keep her safe, she had taken night classes in self-defense, and she was most certainly nobody's fool."

"She didn't know to expect trouble. I do. Don't underestimate me."

"I won't underestimate you, if you promise not to underestimate him." Quincy offered her a half smile. Instead of lightening the mood, however, the twist of his lips made him look sad. He was worried, she realized for the first time. Worried and truly hurting. She wondered if even he knew how badly.

"Where are you going?" she asked more gently.

"Out of town. My daughter is wrapping up her affairs now. Rainie is attending to a last few details. First thing tomorrow morning, we'll depart. He knows too much about us here. Our homes, our family, our friends. In a fresh location, I hope to negate that advantage."

"That's not a bad idea."

"Well, I am an expert. Just ask Bethie. Or Mandy."

"Quincy—"

"I need to get going."

"What should we tell the Philadelphia P.D.?"

"Tell them I'm tending to my daughter, but that I'll be in touch."

"The crime scene," she tried again. "You know there are issues."

He didn't say a word.

"Quincy, it's staged. You know it's staged, I know it's staged, but the homicide detectives ... They're going to interpret that fact as yet another indication that you did it. After all, who better to stage a crime scene than a federal agent?"

"I know."

"And that note ... Left in the victim's abdominal cavity. That's cold, Quincy. It's also very personal, and that won't help you."

"You have word on the note?" he asked sharply.

She shook her head. "No, it's too soon. I mean simply that I don't think it convinces them that you're a target. At least it doesn't convince them enough. You are the ex-husband, after all; it's easier to make you their primary suspect."

"I didn't kill Elizabeth."

"Of course not!"

"I mean that, Glenda. You're a good agent. And I didn't murder my wife."

She faltered. She would have to be dense not to catch the undercurrents in his voice and she had not advanced so far in the Bureau by being dumb. "There's more, isn't there?"

"This person"—Quincy's voice sounded almost far away—"he's very, very good."

"He may be good, but we've gone up against good before. We'll find him."

"Really? Because I've been going through my old cases and I haven't seen a hint of him yet. Glenda, for the last time, don't stay here alone."

"I'll be fine."

"I don't think you understand. I'm removing my daughter from the playing field. With her out of reach, it's anybody guess where he'll strike next."

20

"I can't believe she's dead."

Kimberly sat in Professor Andrews's office as the last rays of daylight gave way to a slinky gray dusk. Day One, Kimberly called this Thursday. Day One without her mother. She gripped the edge of the old maple seat harder, as if that would keep this day from ending. Day One would only be followed by Days Two, Three, and Four, then Months One, Two, and Three, then Years …Tears slid down her cheeks.

She had come here with the intention of being professional. She had to leave town. She would provide a rough sketch of the last few days for her professor. She would end by calmly stating that circumstances now warranted the resignation of her coveted internship position. Dignified. Firm. In control. Those were her goals. She was nearly a master's student, for heaven's sake. She had buried her sister and had now lost her mother. If she had been a young woman once, she wasn't anymore.

She had stepped into the warm, crowded office with its hodgepodge mix of precariously stacked papers and dying plants and her composure had instantly dropped like a rock. Her eyes welled up. She stood in front of a man she respected almost as much as her father, and bits and pieces of the last few days burst out of her mouth before her throat finally closed up on her.

Dr. Andrews had led her to the chair. He had brought her a glass of water. Then he had sat patiently on the other side of his cluttered desk, his hands folded and his expression steady while he waited for her to recover. He didn't offer any platitudes or comforting noises. It wasn't his style.

In his ten years at NYU, Dr. Marcus Andrews had garnered a reputation for reducing even the most brilliant Ph.D. candidates to tears with his unwavering blue stare. Speculation placed his age anywhere between sixty and older than dirt. He had thinning gray hair, a perpetual scowl, and a penchant for tweed. While in reality he was an average-sized man, trim from a lifelong devotion to yoga, he had an uncanny ability to seem four times his natural size as he stood at a podium and railed at his students to try harder, think broader, and for heaven's sake, be *smarter*.

According to the grapevine, he'd started his career as a psychiatrist assigned to the fabled San Quentin prison. The work had intrigued him so much, he'd gotten a Ph.D. in criminology and made a name for himself doing groundbreaking work on the institutionalization of criminals, and how the very nature of prisons guaranteed further acts of brutality when hardened inmates were released back into society.

He was hard, gruff, and demanding. He was also brilliant, and Kimberly respected him immensely.

"Maybe you should start at the beginning," he told her.

"No. I don't want to go through it again. It's painful, and I can't afford to be in pain right now. It's funny, I never understood how my father could come home from his job and look so composed. All the cops on TV, they came back from crime scenes and they drank, or smoked, or cursed, or raged. My sister and I, we understood that. It made sense to us. Then my father would come home again, and it was ...He was like a pool of still water. No matter how long you studied his face, you never saw a thing beneath the surface. I get that now. The job is war. And you can't afford any emotion. It's your enemy."

"What do you think your father would feel right now if he could hear you?" Dr. Andrews asked.

"He would be hurt."

"And this person who is targeting your father, what is his goal?"

"To hurt him," she replied, then bowed her head as she saw his point.

Dr. Andrews gave her his lecturer's stare. "If this is war, Miss Quincy, which side is currently winning?"

"My mother hated his job."

"Law enforcement has a disproportionately high rate of divorce."

"No, she *hated* his job. The violence. The grit. The way he seemed to belong more to it than to us. She created a beautiful home. She produced two beautiful daughters. And still he'd rather live in the shadows."

"It's a calling. You understand that."

"But that's my whole point. My mother is dead and I'm sad and I'm furious but I'm also ... motivated. For the first time in months, I feel awake. One moment I was existing in some sort of fugue state, and now ... I want to *find* the bastard. I want to read the crime-scene reports. I want to trace this monster's steps, I want to tear apart every little facet of his personality and unmask him. And I am thinking about him more than I'm grieving for my mother. Dr. Andrews, what is *wrong* with us?"

Dr. Andrews finally smiled, an unheard-of softening of his hard-lined face. "Ah, Miss Quincy. Haven't you ever noticed that criminologists never do a study on criminologists?"

"We're sick, aren't we?"

"We're intellectualists. Our desire to understand why things happen outweighs our rage at the events."

"Rage is purer," she said bitterly.

"Rage lacks constructiveness. Think of it this way: Cops are doers. They get angry at what they encounter. They make arrests. In that way, they help control crime, but their intervention is always after the fact. Criminologists, sociologists, criminal behaviorists, are thinkers. We get curious. We do studies. We come up with things like profiling, which enables law enforcement to prevent future atrocities."

"When I was growing up," Kimberly said, "I used to think of my father as a general, off fighting in some foreign land. It made me proud. Even when my feelings were hurt, even when I was mad because he missed my soccer game or my birthday, I was proud."

Dr. Andrews leaned forward. He said gently, "You say you're proud of your father, Miss Quincy, and I believe that you are. But lately, you've also been distancing yourself from him. Why is that?"

She stiffened. "I don't know what you mean."

"The anxiety attacks. You've mentioned them to me, but I get the impression you haven't mentioned them to him."

Kimberly bowed her head again. Her fingers fidgeted in her lap. "I didn't …I don't know. I tell myself I don't want to worry him. But I don't think that's it. I think … I don't want to seem high-strung. You know—like Mandy."

Dr. Andrews winced. He sat back, and for the first time, Kimberly noticed how troubled he appeared. The lines were deeper in his face, his eyes didn't have that stern stare she'd grown accustomed to. For a moment, he almost appeared human. "I have a confession to make, Miss Quincy. I think I might have led you astray."

"What do you mean?" She sat up straighter. Her heart began to pound again.

No, she thought. *No mistakes from you.* No mere mortality from NYU's most-feared professor. Her world was falling apart and even if it was immature of her, she needed the gods in her life to remain gods.

"I'm the one who originally attributed your anxiety attacks to stress," Dr. Andrews said.

"My sister had died, it made sense."

"But now we have additional data points. Think of what your father said. Someone has targeted your family. That someone has been at this for at least two years."

"Yes." She looked at him quizzically, then it suddenly clicked. The blood drained out of her face. Oh no. Oh no, oh no, oh no. "My feeling of being watched. You think … you think it's him."

"We can't rule it out," Dr. Andrews said quietly. He added with the most kindness she'd ever heard from him, "I am truly sorry, Miss Quincy. I rushed to the most obvious conclusion. Perhaps it's time to listen to my own lectures."

"He's stalking me." She couldn't get over that idea. The concept was a curious one. It made her feel at once violated, yet relieved. Violated because some unknown predator had invaded her life and hunted her down like cattle. Relieved because the violation was real, not just in her head. All those times. The goose bumps, the cold chills creeping up her spine. She hadn't gone mental. Strong, logical Kimberly was still strong, logical Kimberly. Oh thank God …

"It fits his MO," Dr. Andrews was saying.

"Goddammit, he's been stalking me!" She was mad now. The rage brought desperately needed color to her cheeks, and stiffened her spine for the first time in weeks. Hunted? She would not be hunted.

Dr. Andrews was studying her. He must have liked what he saw, because he nodded encouragingly. "Remember what we were saying. Get curious. Put yourself in the predator's shoes. What makes him tick?"

She took a deep breath. "Games," she said after a moment. "He likes playing games."

"That is consistent with what we know. What else?"

"He doesn't want a quick kill. It's not about the murder, it's about the *process*. Personal. He wants it to be personal. Intimate."

"He won't be a stranger to you."

"But I might not have met him yet," Kimberly said slowly. "That feeling of being watched ... If I had already met him, he wouldn't have to monitor me from a distance; he'd already be part of my life."

"Reconnaissance," Dr. Andrews theorized. "When did the sensation begin?"

"A few months ago. So he's been doing his homework. Looking for an opening."

"New boyfriend," Dr. Andrews offered.

"Too obvious. He's done that ploy, first with Mandy, and then with my mother. Though he upped the ante with my mother—we think he also posed as someone who received one of Mandy's organs."

Dr. Andrews blinked. "Brilliant."

"I'm supposedly the smart one," Kimberly murmured softly, still thinking out loud. "That's what Mandy and my mom would have told him. I'm the serious one, the one who's always wanted to join law enforcement. The one who started taking martial arts at the age of eight, who likes tackle football and guns ..." Her voice trailed off, her mind already forming a connection with one new person in her life. A charming gun pro who just happened to join her rifle association six months earlier. Doug James.

"You have an idea?"

"I don't want to jump to conclusions."

"Better to be safe than sorry, Miss Quincy."

She smiled. "That's the first platitude I've ever heard from you. I didn't know that you knew any. Then again, duly noted."

Dr. Andrews smiled. "You're leaving, yes? I assume that is what you're here to tell me. Strategic retreat is a perfectly valid option."

"I don't know how long I'll be gone."

"Understandable."

"I can't tell you where I'm going."

"Did you hear me asking?"

"You ... you should probably find another intern. I mean, I would understand ..."

"At this late date? Bah. I can read my own notes for a change. Might do me a world of good. Jumping to obvious conclusions. Next thing you know I'll be dreaming of the Washington Monument and blaming everything on my toilet training."

"Dr. Andrews ... Thank you."

"Miss Quincy, it has been a pleasure."

There was nothing left to say. Kimberly rose. Held out her hand. Across the desk, Dr. Andrews also stood and extended his hand. Kimberly was touched by how grave he appeared.

"One last piece of advice?" he asked solemnly.

"Of course."

"Law enforcement, Miss Quincy. This man, he seems to specialize in identifying his victim's vulnerability, the thing she thinks she needs or admires most. For you, it's law enforcement. You have an inherent trust and respect for anyone wearing a badge."

"Point taken." Kimberly hesitated. It was silly to say what she was going to say next. But then, she felt that she must. *Day One,* she thought. *My sister is gone, my mother is dead, and I am learning to question everything.* Her gaze went to the window, now robbed of the light of day. Outside, a car backfired, sounding like a gunshot on the crowded streets.

"Dr. Andrews," she said quietly. "If anything should happen, can you tell my father something for me? Tell him the last person I saw this evening was a newly hired instructor at my gun club. Tell him I met a man named Doug James."

21

"I want a name."

"Anonymity is the spiritual foundation of AA; we don't give out that kind of information."

"Fine. Screw the name; it's probably just an alias anyway. I want a description."

"And one more time, anonymity is the spiritual foundation of AA. We don't give out that kind of information."

"Mr. Zane, this is a homicide investigation. You give me information now, quietly, or to the police later as part of an official investigation that will be reported to the press. Now, do you want to provide one man's description as a private exchange between you and me, or do you want word to get out that some psychopathic killer is using AA meetings to select his victims?"

William Zane, president of Mandy's AA chapter, finally hesitated. He was a big guy. Six one, two hundred and forty pounds. He wore a suit that screamed investment banker and carried himself in a way that suggested he was accustomed to people doing exactly what he said. Rainie figured he had at least three ex-wives and one helluva cocaine habit somewhere in his past. In theory, he was clean now and did an impeccable job of running the AA meetings. Someday, she'd be sure to send him a Hallmark card congratulating him on being such a nicely reformed human being. At the moment, however, she simply wanted the name and description of Amanda's "friend" at the AA meetings.

It was six P.M. Thursday, nearly twelve hours until departure to the relative safety of Portland, and for no good reason, Rainie was increasingly worried about Kimberly. In other words, she didn't feel like dicking around.

William Zane sighed. He'd agreed to see Rainie upon hearing that Amanda Quincy's car accident had been reopened as a murder investigation. Now, he clearly regretted that decision. He got up from his chair in his posh office, moved his impressively clad bulk to the door and shut it firmly.

"You have to understand what you're asking," he said. "The key to AA's effectiveness is its simple operating principle—we provide confidential support to anyone willing to stop drinking. We aren't beholden to the courts, or to the police, or to anyone. We're an equal-opportunity support organization. And for a lot of people, we're the only lifeline they've got."

"Amanda doesn't need a lifeline anymore."

"You're not asking about Amanda. You're asking about current members."

It was Rainie's turn to sigh. "Here's the kicker, Mr. Zane. I'm a member of AA. I confess that I wouldn't have walked into my first meeting if it hadn't been anonymous and I wouldn't have continued to attend meetings after I became a police officer if it hadn't been anonymous. So as a matter of fact, I see your point. But this man *murdered* Amanda Quincy. He set up a scenario that sent her face crashing into a windshield at thirty-five miles per hour. And then there's what he did to her mother. Would you like to see the crime-scene photos?"

"No, no, no, no." Mr. Zane shook his lily-white hands emphatically and managed to go another shade of pale. To the image of the three ex-wives, Rainie added the picture of him pacing *outside* the delivery room with a box of Cuban cigars. She wondered if he ever did manage to change a diaper.

"I'm looking for a killer, Mr. Zane," she pressed. "You want to be a lifeline, be a lifeline for the other women who are doomed to die unless you help me stop this guy. Be a lifeline for the future victims. Because at this moment, you're the only chance of finding this guy that I've got."

"Perhaps," Mr. Zane said finally. "Off the record. *Way* off the record—"

"Deal. Sit, Mr. Zane; let's talk."

Mr. Zane sat behind his big desk. She got out her notebook.

"Do you remember Amanda Quincy?" Rainie asked.

"Yes, she joined our meetings nearly a year and a half ago."

"Did she have a sponsor?"

"She had a sponsor. I don't see the need to give out his name unless absolutely necessary."

"Yeah, and here's a photo of what happens to the human skull when it hits the rim of a windshield—"

"Larry Tanz," Mr. Zane said. "Nice guy."

"How did Amanda know Larry Tanz?"

"He owned the restaurant where she worked. Larry's been an AA member for ten years and has sponsored a fair amount of his staff in that time." Mr. Zane slid her a look. "It's amazing how many bartenders are drunks. And then there're the cooks ..."

Rainie rolled her eyes, then jotted down a quick note. Larry Tanz, manager where Mandy used to work, which meant by definition, manager where Mary Olsen used to work. Interesting.

"Did Mandy and Mr. Tanz seem to have any other kind of relationship? You know, beyond the sponsor-sponsee kind of thing?"

"Our chapter suggests that people wait at least a year before dating," Mr. Zane said promptly. "As I'm sure you know, quitting cold turkey is very hard. You don't want to risk the additional stress of having a serious relationship end—it might send even the strongest person back to the bottle. We don't recommend dating until the initiate celebrates his or her one-year anniversary."

"Sounds romantic. So was Mandy fucking Larry or what?"

Mr. Zane said stiffly, "I don't think so."

"Why not?"

"One, Larry is a good guy. And two, while he felt sad and disappointed by Amanda's accident—perhaps even guilty—I wouldn't call him crushed. Her death was tragic, but certainly not deeply personal for him."

"How nice for Larry. What about someone else? Someone she might have befriended at the meetings?"

"She befriended lots of people—"

"New members who may have joined around the time she did who seemed like particularly close friends."

Mr. Zane hesitated. Rainie stared at him. He picked up a laser-etched paperweight, a souvenir from some exotic vacation. She stared harder.

"Well, there was one guy ..."

"Name."

"Ben. Ben Zikka."

"Description."

"I don't know. Older. Late forties or early fifties, I would say. Not tall, five ten, maybe. Thinning brown hair. Soft around the middle. Not good taste in suits—definitely off the rack." Mr. Zane ran a hand down his own tailored jacket with authority. "I think he said he was a police officer or something like that. I could believe he'd eaten a lot of doughnuts."

Rainie scowled, then began chewing on her lower lip. This wasn't what she'd expected. "Older, kind of frumpy-looking guy? You're sure he was with Mandy?"

"Fairly sure. They started leaving the meetings together. At one point, I noticed they now came in the same car."

"And we're talking about the same Amanda Quincy, right? Twenty-three, slender, blond hair, big blue eyes? If the star quarterback hadn't dated her in high school, it wasn't from lack of trying."

"She was pretty," Mr. Zane said with more enthusiasm.

Rainie was getting a headache. "You're sure Zikka and Amanda were an item?"

"I don't know. You asked about new members she'd befriended. He was the new member she'd befriended. To tell you the truth, however, he only came the first few months. Then he stopped coming. She showed up a few more times, but each time was farther apart. Larry Tanz was going to call her about it, when she had the accident."

"So she comes to AA, meets this guy, and slowly trails off."

"Yes." Mr. Zane shrugged. He said, "It's often like that in the beginning. Admitting you're an alcoholic is tough. Staying sober is even tougher. Most of our members end up starting and stopping a few times before it sticks."

"Was there anyone else at this meeting who seemed to know Mandy? Say, someone six feet tall, well dressed, trim build, late forties, early fifties?" Rainie was working off Bethie's neighbor's statement to the police that she'd seen someone resembling Quincy enter the townhouse. But Mr. Zane shook his head.

"Are you sure?" she persisted.

"You haven't been to an AA meeting lately, have you, Ms. Conner? You spend half your life overindulging in alcohol and drugs and you're rarely the well-dressed, trim-build type. Maybe a Hollywood star can pull it off, but the rest of us, we've abused ourselves and we look it. Even Amanda Quincy was becoming harsh around the edges."

Rainie scowled again. One name and description later, she was more confused than when she'd started. She studied good old William Zane. His gaze was clear. He met her eye. Dammit, just when you were hoping someone was feeding you a lie, he went and told the truth.

She glanced at her watch. T-minus ten and still two stops to go. She rose, shook Zane's hand, and tried not to take his obvious relief at her departure too personally.

At the door, however, she was struck by one last question. "At your meetings," she said, "you talk about some very personal things, right?"

"Yes."

"What did Mandy talk about?"

He hesitated.

"Crime-scene photos, Mr. Zane. Crime. Scene. Photos."

"Mandy had self-esteem issues. Mandy ... had *a lot* of self-esteem issues. She talked about how famous her father was. She talked about how beautiful her mother was. She talked about how smart her sister was. And she talked about— Let's put it this way, she often categorized herself as a disposable blonde."

"A 'disposable blonde'?"

"Mandy had this obsession with violence, Ms. Conner. She liked to see slasher movies, to read true-crime novels. She told the group that when she was younger, she used to sneak into her father's office and look through his homicide textbooks, even read his case files. They terrified her, but she still came back for more. It wasn't a healthy thing. It wasn't a face-your-fear kind of thing. She did it to punish herself. You see, most of us identify with the crime solver when we watch slasher movies or read mystery novels. Not Mandy. She identified with the pretty, blue-eyed, blond victims. Disposable blondes, Ms. Conner. Beautiful women who exist simply for the deranged killer to savage first."

Rainie was still shaken by the time she pulled into the tiny commercial real estate building that housed Phil de Beers's office. Clouds had rolled in. The air crackled with electricity. A nearly full moon had to be up there somewhere, but the night had taken on a dense, suffocated feeling. Even the crickets had gone quiet.

She got out of her car hunch-shouldered and skittish, ready to shoot first, question later. Nine P.M. Kimberly should be back in the relative safety of her apartment. Quincy had probably wrapped things up with his boss at Quantico and was now returning to New York City. Rainie just needed to finish up two last chores, then it would be her turn.

Instead, she stopped in the middle of the empty parking lot and searched the inky black depths for something she couldn't name. Beyond her line of sight, she could hear cars humming by on the distant freeway. Four streetlamps bounced puddles of light off shiny black asphalt. The scent of honeysuckles and blackberries came to her, cloying and thick.

"Howdy, ma'am."

She startled, then whirled, her right hand already reaching for her Glock.

Phil de Beers stood in the doorway of the building, the spitting image of his Internet photo as he gazed at her curiously. "Want to come in?" he asked politely.

She shivered violently and nodded.

"Brewed some coffee," he said a moment later as he gestured her inside the building. "Don't know what it is about thunderstorms, God knows they generate enough humidity to drown a rat, but they always make me feel in need of a good hot drink. Or whiskey. But on account of this being a professional visit, I thought I'd stick with coffee."

"Bummer," Rainie said, and earned a wide, flashing smile from the small, neatly dressed black man.

"You caught me. I do have some good ol' sour mash …"

"Yeah," she said gloomily, "but I'm an alcoholic. I only get the coffee."

"Bummer," he echoed solemnly, and she decided that she liked him very much.

They went first to the tiny kitchenette shared by all the clients in the building. Phil splashed a delicate mist of whiskey into his brew. Rainie poured in cream and sugar until the private investigator began to laugh.

"I see some dependency issues," he commented.

"Sugar and fat are socially acceptable drugs."

"And you carry them well," he assured her, conducting an unabashed sweep of her figure before leading her into his office. He took a seat behind his desk in a positively sinful red leather chair. That left a hard, spindly old kitchen chair that she figured was designed to discourage lengthy visits.

Phil held up a small glass dish. "M&M's?" Rainie shook her head. He took a large handful. "I got some dependency issues, too," he admitted cheerfully and munched on the candy while she finished taking inventory of his office.

The space wasn't large but it was adequate. One wall contained two rows of bookshelves bearing thick volumes of *Virginia State Law* as well as piles of magazines. The other wall contained a gallery of framed prints. A diploma from the Virginia police academy. A variety of black and white photos showing de Beers with various men in suits. Probably important men in suits, Rainie thought, but now she was merely showing off her powers of deductive reasoning.

"Important person?" she asked, picking one photo at random.

"Director Freeh," he said.

"Director Freeh?"

De Beers flashed her that wide grin. "Head of the FBI."

"Oh yeah, *that* Director Freeh." Rainie shut up and drank her coffee. It would've been better with whiskey.

"So," de Beers said. "I've been watching Mary Olsen as you requested. Damn boring woman, Mrs. Mary Olsen. Didn't leave her house yesterday or today."

"That's not very helpful."

"No, but I got a contact at the phone company. I'll pull her records, give 'em a whirl. If you rattled the woman, she's probably not passing the time merely watching TV."

"She's checking in with people."

"There you go. I can get names, numbers, and addresses. Then what do you want me to do?"

"Fax me the phone numbers and names of whomever she's called the most. I know a state trooper who can check them out."

"I don't mind doing it."

"I want you to stay on Mary, in case phone calls are no longer enough. Oh, and here's a new name for you. Larry Tanz. He supposedly owns the restaurant where Mary Olsen used to work, and where Amanda Quincy worked up until the time of her death. I'd be curious to know if he suddenly paid his former employee a personal visit."

"Frightened women can be consoled long distance for only so long …"

"Absolutely." Rainie hesitated. "You carry, right? All the time? Heavily?"

De Beers gave her a look. "Uh oh. Now is when I get that not-so-fresh feeling anymore."

"We have evidence that my client's daughter didn't die in an automobile accident as originally reported," Rainie told him. "It was murder. Then last night in Philadelphia … Most likely the same man murdered my client's ex-wife. Brutally."

De Beers arched a brow. He got up. He found a folded newspaper on the side bookshelf. He tossed it on top of the desk so Rainie could see the head-line. "High Society House of Horrors." Some enterprising photographer had managed to snag a crime-scene photo of the hallway and its endless rows of bloody handprints.

"I'd call this brutal," de Beers said.

"That would be the one."

"Says here she was the former wife of an FBI agent. Which would make your client—"

"I can see how you've succeeded as a private investigator."

De Beers sat down again and studied her face. "Let me recap, darlin'. You want me to tail a woman who will hopefully meet a man whose current hobby is taking on the Federal Bureau of Intimidation and murdering the ones they love?"

"Just one man's loved ones. It's personal."

"Personal?" His gaze strayed to the gruesome newspaper photo. "Hell, you're talking a psychopath with balls of steel."

"Before you kick him, make sure you put on combat boots."

De Beers sighed. "I wished you would've told me yesterday that I should be carrying around kryptonite."

She shrugged. "I've been busy."

De Beers sighed again. "Okay. Looks like I'm breaking out my TEC-DC9 and leaving my thirty-eight Special for backup. Anything else you can tell me about the biggest badass in town? Name, age, description?"

Rainie got out her notebook. "We have record of two aliases. Tristan Shandling, used recently in Philadephia to approach Elizabeth Quincy. Then the name Ben Zikka, used approximately twenty months ago here in Virginia, to approach Amanda Quincy. I haven't gotten to run down Ben Zikka yet, but the name Tristan Shandling wasn't backed up. We knew it was an alias the minute we tried to run it through the system."

"You'd think a man taking on a Feebie would be more careful."

"He uses the aliases to approach women outside of law enforcement. What normal woman bothers with something like a routine security check?"

De Beers nodded his agreement. "Makes my life easier. I'll get a list of names from the phone records and find out which ones stand up to scrutiny. Then you sic your state trooper on the ones that don't."

Rainie was struck by another thought. "Actually, to get an account with the phone company, the man will have to document the name, and we do know one ID that's fleshed out."

"That name?"

"FBI agent, Pierce Quincy."

De Beers gave her a look. She smiled tightly. "He stole my client's identity. No one realized it until two days ago. The Bureau has a whole case team on it now, but given the murder in Phildelphia ... The fraud investigation is probably slipping through the cracks at the moment."

"Balls of steel," de Beers muttered. "Balls of steel. Well, let's return to what we do know. Subject's description?"

"I have two. They don't match."

"Of course."

"As Ben Zikka, recovering drunk twenty months ago, our guy was described as being five ten, overweight, balding, and frumpy. According to members of AA, Zikka claimed to have some sort of tie with law enforcement. This information is only two hours old, so I haven't gotten very far with it."

"Other descript?"

"In Philly, he used the name Tristan Shandling. According to a witness, he's tall, well-built, and sharply dressed. In fact, he looks very much like an FBI agent. At least the age is the same. Mid-forties to early fifties."

"So I'm looking for a middle-aged white male. That's what you have for me?"

Rainie thought about it. "Yep," she agreed. "That's about it."

"Well, there you go. At the first sight of a middle-aged white male, I'll shoot to kill. Darlin', you've just made my day."

"I try. Listen, I have to leave town. You can reach me at this number on my business card, but I'm going to be three thousand miles away so don't consider me the cavalry. You get into real trouble, call state trooper Vince Amity. He's handling the investigation of Amanda Quincy's MVA. He's a good guy. And Phil—don't put yourself on the line, okay? Just watch, take notes. If Mary meets this guy in person, feel free to keep a very low profile. I went into the house in Philadelphia. That picture is not the half of what this man did."

"What are you going to do?"

Rainie smiled. "My client has one daughter left. I plan on keeping it that way."

Two minutes later, de Beers watched from the doorway as she got into her rent-a-wreck and started the engine. She appreciated his diligence. But then she was out of the parking lot, onto the freeway, heading for her motel. The sky broke. The rain poured down in sheets as thunder rumbled off in the distance. Rainie drove alone through the torrent, listening to the rhythmic sound of her windshield wipers, and periodically tugging on her seat belt. The tension held.

Ten-fifteen P.M. Eight hours until departure and still, at the moment, safe.

22

"I'm here to see Doug James."

"He's with a student."

"He's an instructor of mine. I just need to speak with him for a second ..."

"Would you like to leave a message?"

"Can't. Needs to be in person. I swear it will only take a moment."

The teenage boy working the front desk gave Kimberly a long-suffering sigh. He was new here, or he would have recognized her as a regular and given her less hassle. Instead he was trying to be diligent new employee of the month. Kimberly's hands were shaking. She was on the verge of losing her nerve. She wished Diligent New Employee would diligently do what she asked. Otherwise she might be forced to reach across the desk and wring his new-employee neck.

Maybe her thoughts showed on her face, because he started to look at her nervously.

"PMS," she told him curtly.

Geek boy turned bright red and quickly scurried off. She'd have to remember this strategy for the future. *Day One,* she thought again, advancing her mental notes. *I realize that even I can be a homicidal maniac.*

Four minutes later, Doug James walked from the shooting gallery into the gun club's lobby. He looked right at her and Kimberly had to catch her breath all over again. Doug James was handsome. And not in that slick, preppy sort of way. She would've been able to see through that. Instead he was older, gray hairs blatantly sharing space with sun-bleached brown. His face was weathered. He had the squinted, deeply peering eyes of a man who'd spent his life outdoors, staring into the sun. Some days he was clean-shaven, but by evening he almost always sported a five o'clock shadow and even with the gray stubble mixed in with the dark, he looked good.

He wasn't too tall, but he possessed a solid, broad-shouldered build. And he was well muscled. She'd felt the rippling band of his arms around hers as he'd adjusted her aim. She'd felt the hard plane of his chest as he'd shifted her stance. She'd felt the heat of his body, standing mere inches from hers.

He also wore a gold wedding band on his left ring finger. She'd thought of that often when he'd first started as her instructor. She'd thought of him as older, married, and way out of her league. And it had made her even more aware of each and every touch.

"He won't be a stranger to you."

Kimberly thought of Dr. Andrews's warning and her stomach churned. She looked at Doug James, ruggedly handsome Doug James, and she felt desire sweep over her again, even as her body was swamped with fear. Was this how her mother had felt about the man who had butchered her? And poor Mandy?

"Kimberly, how can I help you?"

She gazed at Doug blankly. Her mouth opened, but no words came out.

He smiled. "I'm sorry, I didn't mean to startle you."

"I have to cancel all my lessons," she said.

He stilled, then frowned. She searched his gaze for anything sinister. He simply appeared concerned, and somehow that frightened her more. *He makes himself into what the victim wants*, Dr. Andrews had theorized. Kindness. That's what all women wanted. Someone who was kind.

"I'm sorry to hear that, Kimberly. Is everything all right?"

"Where were you yesterday?"

"I was sick. I'm sorry. I tried to reach you at your apartment, but apparently you had already left."

"And last night?"

"I was at home with my wife. Why are you asking?"

"I thought I saw you. Somewhere. At a restaurant."

"I don't think so. I did come here briefly to pick up some paperwork, but then I went straight home."

"To your wife?"

"Yes."

"What is her name again?"

"Laurie. Kimberly—"

"You don't have any kids, do you?"

"Not yet."

"How long have you been married?"

"I don't like this conversation, Kimberly. I'm not sure what is going on, but I don't think this is appropriate."

"I thought we were friends. Friends can ask questions, can't they? Friends can talk."

"We are friends. But I don't feel that you're asking these questions in a friendly way."

"Does that make you nervous?"

"Yes."

"Am I asking too many questions?"

"I think so."

"Why? What are you trying to hide?"

Doug James didn't say anything right away. He stared at her, his peering eyes impossible to read. She returned his look inch for inch, though her pulse was fluttery and her hands had fisted at her side.

He said slowly, "I'm going to return to my student now."

"I'm not coming back."

"I'm sorry—"

"I'm leaving this state. You won't be able to find me."

"Okay, Kimberly."

"I'm not as easy as my mother."

"This other student *really* needs my attention."

"She was a lovely woman, did you know that? Maybe she was raised out of step with the women's revolution. Maybe she should have tried harder in her marriage. But she loved us, and she did her best and she never stopped trying to be happy. Even when it was hard, she never stopped trying to be happy—"

Her voice broke off. She was crying. She stood in the middle of the threadbare lobby with its trophy case, stuffed animal heads, and sagging couch, weeping while other gun club members began to stare. Doug James slowly backed away, his hand fumbling behind him for the door connecting to the shooting gallery.

"I miss my mother," Kimberly said, and this time her voice held as her tears stopped. She stood there dry-eyed, which she knew must be worse. The other members looked away. Doug James fairly bolted out of the lobby.

After a moment, she turned back to the front desk where the new, diligent employee of the month was regarding her with unabashed terror.

"What time did Doug stop by last night?" Kimberly asked.

"Eight P.M.," the boy squawked. "Stopped in the office, grabbed paperwork and left. His wife was waiting outside for him."

"You saw her?"

"Yes."

"What does she look like?"

"Not nearly as pretty as you," the boy said hastily, still not understanding the situation.

Kimberly slowly nodded. Her mind was still trying to make the pieces fit. What had the witness said about her mother last night? Her mother and the strange man had pulled up together at ten P.M. in a fancy red car. According to the neighbor, her mother had been out all day.

"Was the woman a blonde? Mid-forties, slender, nicely dressed?" she asked.

The boy frowned. "No. Doug's wife is a brunette and she's kind of big right now. I think they're expecting a baby."

"Oh." It definitely wasn't her mother who'd come here at eight. Which meant it might indeed be Doug James's wife. And hey, he might be telling the truth and he might be an actual gun instructor, happily married and now expecting his first child.

Day One, I don't know what to believe anymore. Day One, I've grown so afraid. Day One ... Mandy, I'm so sorry I never realized before how life must feel to you.

Kimberly walked out the door. The air was black as pitch outside and just about as heavy. Nine-thirty P.M. She thought there was going to be a storm.

Quantico, Virginia

Quincy left Quantico shortly after ten P.M., as the first fat drops of rain hit his windshield. He peered up at clouds so thick they obliterated the moon. The wind was whipping. It was going to be a good, old-fashioned thunderstorm. He turned toward 1-95 as the first bolt of lightning lit up the sky.

Not much longer, he kept telling himself. Not much longer.

Everett didn't like Quincy's decision to leave town. He demanded full accountability—where Quincy would be staying and who he would be with at all times. It did not give Quincy the level of security that he would've liked, but he couldn't very well tell the Special Agent in Charge that he didn't trust him, not when the man was going out of his way to help Quincy salvage his family and career. Both of them gave up what they had to. Neither of them was happy. It was the usual sort of compromise.

Quincy had packed up his laptop. He'd put a box of old case files in his trunk. He still had his FBI-issued 10mm, which he planned on keeping until the bitter end. He did not feel ready, but he was as prepared as he was ever going to get.

Not much longer.

Wind howling fiercer now. Trees starting to bend. He had to slow the car, but he did not get off the road. Ten-thirty P.M. His daughter needed him.

Not much longer.

He stared in his rearview mirror at the approaching headlights and he felt an incredible sense of doom.

Motel 6, Virginia

Ten forty-five P.M. Rainie dashed from her car to the entrance of her motel. The rain was coming down in sheets and the four-second sprint left her soaked. The night manager looked up as she bolted through the door, spraying raindrops and bits of tree leaves that had gotten stuck in her hair.

"Ugly night," he commented.

"F-ugly night," she amended. She stalked down the hall, shivering as the blast from the motel's air conditioner cut her to the bone. She needed to grab her things and check out. A hot shower could wait. Dinner could wait. All attention was focused on making it to New York. T minus seven.

In her room, the message waiting light was blinking. She glanced at it apprehensively. Then she sighed, sat down, and prepared to take notes.

Six calls. Not bad considering hardly anyone knew this number. Four were hang ups. The fifth was Carl Mitz. "I'm still trying to reach Lorraine Conner. We need to talk." She gave anxious Carl the credit for the hang ups as well, though she could be wrong. The sixth call surprised her the most. It was from her former fellow Bakersville officer, Luke Hayes.

"Rainie, some lawyer is calling all over town with all sorts of questions about you and your mom. Name is Carl Mitz. I thought you should know."

Rainie glanced at her watch. She didn't have time for this now. Mr. Mitz, on the other hand, didn't seem inclined to back off. Asking questions about her and her mother. All these years later, and the memory still gave her a chill.

She called Luke at his home, but got his machine. "It's Rainie," she informed the digital recorder. "Thanks for the heads-up. I'm out of town, but I'll be back in the morning. Do me a favor, Luke. Set up a meeting with Mitz. Just you and him. Then let me know when and where so I can crash the party. The man has spent the last three days hunting me down like vermin. It's time he and I had a chat."

She hung up the phone. Rain ran off her short hair and splattered onto her T-shirt. She caught her reflection across the room, and was startled by the broad, pale lines of her face, the deep shadows hollowing out her rain-dampened cheeks. Her lips appeared bloodless. Her chestnut hair was spiky and wild. She looked like a punk rocker, she thought. Or maybe a vampire's latest victim. She gazed at her own reflection, felt no kinship with that beat-up woman, and was nearly struck dumb by sheer exhaustion.

Bethie had fought in the end. She'd seen her attacker and she'd tried desperately to escape. What did a woman feel in those last moments? Did the mind give you the luxury of feeling betrayed? Or was the terror only physical? Adrenaline and testosterone. Pure animal instinct to fight, to live, to breathe?

When she was younger, she'd watched wild cats stalk field mice. The cat would catch the mouse in its mouth, then let it go. Then scoop it up, then let it go. And the mouse would squeak and squeak and squeak, first shrill, then, as the game wore on, with less and less volume. Until finally, even after being released, the mouse rolled over on its back and very clearly surrendered. Dying had become preferable to living. Maybe that was nature's way of taking pity on the smaller members of the food chain.

She thought of Mandy, willing to get drunk again even after those hard-fought months of AA, then willing to get behind the wheel without a working seat belt. She thought of Bethie and how after years of isolation she'd agreed to allow a strange man through her front door.

Dying becomes preferable to living.

Rainie got off the bed. She threw the last of the toiletries in her bag. Eleven P.M. Seven hours until liftoff, and two hours left to drive. Life's a battle, she thought. Time to rejoin the war.

Quincy's House, Virginia

Special Agent Glenda Rodman was curled up on the floor in a corner of the cologne-smelling office. Outside the wind howled. Rain scoured the windows. Trees beat against fellow trees. Thunder still growled ominously, but the lightning struck further and further apart.

The alarm had shrieked five times, power punching in and out. Apparently, the backup system had not been properly wired. Every time the power failed, so did the alarm. She had the security company on speed dial now. Special Agent Montgomery was still nowhere to be found.

While in the kitchen, the phone began to ring again and the answering machine picked up.

"Death, death, death, kill, kill, kill, murder, murder, murder," a voice sang. "Death, death, death, kill, kill, kill, murder, murder, murder. Hey Quincy, check your mailbox. I disemboweled that puppy, just for you. Death, death, death, kill, kill, kill, murder, murder, murder. Death, death, death, kill, kill, kill, murder, murder, murder. Death, death, death …"

Glenda wrapped her arms around her knees. On the floor of the office, she rocked back and forth as the power went out again, and the state-of-the-art alarm system once more began to shriek.

23

"Mace."

"Mace."

"Firearms?" Quincy asked.

"I carry a Glock forty," Rainie replied. "I have to check it, though. Private investigators don't qualify to carry onboard."

Quincy nodded, then turned toward his daughter who was standing over her open suitcase, having just handed her father her canister of Mace.

"I have a Glock, too," Kimberly said, which caused her father to do a double take.

"You have what?"

"As long as you're armed, you might as well be well-armed," she replied seriously. "What can you really accomplish with a twenty-two?"

Quincy raised a brow. He brought out his own pistol, a stainless steel 10mm Smith & Wesson, standard FBI issue. The Smith & Wesson held nine .40 caliber cartridges in the magazine and one in the chamber. Clipped to his belt in a brown leather holder, he carried two additional magazines, giving him total access to thirty rounds. Firepower would not be a problem.

"As the only person in this room qualified to carry on a plane," he said, "I'll cover us during transit. I'll also take the Mace. Otherwise, pack up, Thelma and Louise. Upon arrival in Portland, I want you carrying at all times."

"I have to meet with Luke Hayes once we get to Portland," Rainie said. "I can ask him if any of the deputies would like to moonlight as bodyguards. That would give us more coverage."

Kimberly's face brightened at this suggestion, but Quincy shook his head. "Too conspicuous. Plus, I don't think bodyguards will do us any good. He's not going to strike long distance. Drive-by shootings, sniper fire, isn't his style. He'll create an elaborate ruse, something to get up close and personal. Bodyguards can't protect you when you're the one letting the UNSUB through the front door."

"Dr. Andrews said he'll be someone I know," Kimberly said quietly. "The man ... the UNSUB, works on identifying what the victim needs or wants. Mandy always wanted someone to take care of her. Mom wanted Mandy. Me ... I have an instinctive trust of anyone wearing a badge."

Quincy had been folding one of his daughter's shirts. Now his hands stilled. He looked down at the blue-and-white-striped top as if he didn't see it.

"Kimberly …"

"It's not your fault, Dad. It's not your fault."

Quincy finally nodded, though both Rainie and Kimberly could tell he didn't believe her. He finished placing the shirt in the single duffel bag. It was a little after one in the morning. None of them had slept much in the last two days and they were working off a list to keep their minds functioning through a sleep-deprived haze.

"What's next?" Quincy asked.

"Toiletries," Kimberly announced. She went into her bathroom, and a moment later, they heard the clatter of the medicine cabinet as she started throwing things into a waterproof bag.

"Did you meet with the private investigator?" Quincy asked Rainie under his breath, his gaze on the open bathroom door.

"Yes. Nothing. You?"

"They don't know about the note yet. It's a big crime scene; it will take the technicians several days to process everything. If I'm lucky, they'll get to the note last."

"How can it be your handwriting? You didn't write it!"

"I don't know, but that's my handwriting. The loops, the slant, the dot over the I's … He's obviously been practicing."

"Isn't there a way of telling that it's forgery? Hesitation marks, something like that?"

"Depends on how good he is. Depends on how good the handwriting analyst is. In all honesty, I doubt the forgery is perfect, but I also doubt that will help me in the end. All the UNSUB needs is an initial report that the handwriting *appears* to be mine. The Bureau will follow up, but by then I will also have been arrested, disarmed and discredited. This UNSUB is not only clever, but efficient. He knows just how half-assed he can be, and still get the job done. In a perverse way, I admire that."

Kimberly walked back into the bedroom. She tossed the plastic bag into the suitcase. "What's next?"

They didn't have any items left on the list. They zipped up the small collection of bags and piled them by the door. In three hours, Rainie would drive them all to JFK airport where they would return her rental car and board the six A.M. flight to Portland. Outside the storm still raged and from time to time Quincy glanced nervously at the window. Rainie knew he didn't care about thunder and lightning. He was extremely concerned, however, about their flight possibly being delayed.

They huddled around the small kitchen table. Kimberly poured fresh cups of coffee, though they were already twitchy from too much caffeine. The roommate Bobby was gone. Quincy had suggested it might not be safe for him to be in the apartment either. Given the option between being terrified of every sound in his apartment or having unlimited sex at his girlfriend's place, Bobby had decided to stay at his girlfriend's. Bobby was a smart guy.

Rainie drank more coffee, her hands wrapped around the steaming mug.

She'd gotten a chill running around in wet clothes, and now nothing she did made her warm.

"So what else did Dr. Andrews say?" she asked Kimberly at last.

The young girl shrugged. She was holding up remarkably well, Rainie thought. Pale, jumpy, but functional. Rainie supposed they'd all hit the edge where you either kept moving or completely collapsed. Dying was not preferable to living at this point, so they kept moving.

"He ... he told me I should tell you something," Kimberly said abruptly. Her gaze flicked to her father, before becoming locked once more on her coffee mug. "I um ... a few months ago, I started having what I thought were anxiety attacks. I felt as if someone was watching me. I'd get goose bumps, find it hard to breathe. The hair would stand up on the back of my neck."

Quincy set down his mug hard on the old table. Hot coffee sloshed over the edges. "Why didn't you tell me?"

"At the time, I thought it was stress related. The situation with Mandy, I've been carrying a heavy course load plus the internship ... It doesn't matter. What's important is that I'm telling you now and that maybe it wasn't all in my head. Maybe it wasn't stress induced—"

"He's been watching you," Quincy said flatly. "Some man has been stalking my daughter and you didn't even tell me!"

"I carry Mace! I pay attention to the people around me. I make eye contact. You can't hold my hand, Dad, and you can't always protect me—"

"Like hell! It's my job and what's the purpose of all these years of training if I can't protect my own family?"

"No father can protect his family. All children grow up. It's what we do."

"I'm a professional—"

"You're human, just like all other fathers."

"You should have told me—"

"So, I'm human, just like all other daughters."

"Dammit, I'm sick of this!" Quincy roared.

"Good, I am, too!" his daughter yelled back. "So let's catch this son of a bitch, so I can return to my classes and finish up my degree. Then I'll join law enforcement, neglect my own family, and the cycle will be complete!"

Quincy pressed his lips into a thin line. He opened his mouth, shut it. Opened his mouth, then shut it again. Finally, he picked up his mug of coffee and stared at the rain-splattered window.

"You know," Rainie said, "these family moments are very touching."

"I may have a lead," Quincy said thirty minutes later. The clock had now struck two. By some unspoken agreement, it appeared that none of them were going to bed. Quincy's 10mm sat on the kitchen table for easy access. They'd drawn all the blinds, then dimmed the overhead lights to prevent their silhouettes from standing out against the shades. The storm still raged. They'd tried the Weather Channel once, which told them things should clear up by morning. In their current mood, Rainie wasn't sure any of them believed that.

"What did you learn?" she asked Quincy. Kimberly was no longer making eye contact with her father. Rainie decided they could all use some rest.

"An agent working this case, Albert Montgomery, has a bone to pick with me. He worked the Sanchez case first. He screwed up, however, and the Bureau gave the case to me."

"What was the Sanchez case?" Kimberly asked.

"Fifteen years ago, California. Sanchez and his cousin were murdering young prostitutes. Eight of them. Sometimes ... they held the girls for a while."

"Oh," Kimberly said. "The cassette tapes."

"You listened to them?"

Kimberly shrugged. "Mandy did. She had an obsession with your work. When you were gone ..."

"Oh for God's sake—"

"So," Rainie interjected, in her new role as peacekeeper. "Montgomery is on the case, but not in your corner."

Quincy turned back toward her. His gaze was blazing, his face gaunt. "In Montgomery's view, my success with the Sanchez case made his own failings even more glaring. Let's just say that when the supposed 'evidence' reports finally come in from Philadelphia, I wouldn't count on his support. In fact, I'm relatively sure he'll be the first to lead the lynching."

"Not much time," Kimberly whispered.

"No," Quincy said bluntly. "I give it three days. Then the first wave of lab reports will arrive and Everett will call me in. That's that."

"Well," Rainie said briskly. "Let's keep focused then. I also managed to make progress today. I met with the president of Mandy's AA chapter, William Zane. He confirms that she befriended someone at the meetings, but the man doesn't sound anything like what I expected—he's described as being five ten, balding, overweight, and prone to rumpled suits."

"I thought Mom's neighbor reported a guy who was tall, well-dressed, and handsome," Kimberly interjected.

"Exactly. But the sightings were twenty months apart, which could mean the man has the ability to dramatically change his appearance."

"Ted Bundy was notorious for changing his look," Quincy reported. "His weight often fluctuated more than fifty pounds, changing impressions of his face, and also of his height—heavier people are often perceived to be shorter. Then we have Jim Beckett, who pursued his victims and eluded police for over a year by significantly altering his appearance. He would wear padding, stuff his cheeks, things of that nature, to change the contours of his build."

"So one implication is that this guy is a master of disguise," Rainie said. "The second is that he's patient. Twenty months apart ... that's not someone who is committing a rash or random act."

"He's planned this for quite some time," Quincy agreed.

"When we get to Portland, I'm putting you two into a hotel room under aliases. And then we go on the offensive. I have Officer Amity reopening the investigation of Mandy's crash. Investigator Phil de Beers is tailing Mary Olsen and should have word for us shortly. Even if we don't trust Montgomery, Everett seems to be on your side, Quincy, and Special Agent Rodman appears to know what she's doing. She may be able to help connect the dots from the inside."

"We sit," Kimberly murmured. "We wait. We wonder where he'll strike next."

"We're ahead now," Rainie rebutted firmly. "He had the advantage with Mandy because she was his first victim. He continued his advantage with Bethie, because we didn't know any better. We know now. And in exactly"—she glanced at her watch—"three hours, we'll be out of strike zone. We'll finally be ahead of his game."

Kimberly and Quincy nodded tensely. Rainie returned to her notes. "Now then, I have another person for us to pursue. According to the AA president, Mandy's sponsor at the meetings was her boss. Larry Tanz owned the restaurant where she and Mary both worked. Now, I don't know a thing about Mr. Tanz, but given Mary's strange behavior and the fact that Mr. Tanz knows both Mary and Mandy ..."

"He's worth considering," Quincy said.

"I told my new best friend Phil de Beers to work on it. You know," she added seriously, "he makes his coffee with sour mash. I think my cream-and-sugar habit is now looking quite respectable."

As a unit, Quincy and Kimberly rolled their eyes. They looked just like father and daughter when they did that. Huh.

Rainie flipped the page of her notebook. "Finally, I have the two aliases that the UNSUB has used thus far. He used Tristan Shandling in Philadelphia—we should run that through a database of names from your past cases, Quince, to see if it rings any bells. Then, twenty months ago in Virginia, he used the name Ben Zikka to approach Mandy at her AA meeting."

"What?" Quincy spoke up sharply.

"Ben Zikka," Rainie repeated. "The name Ben Zik—"

"No! *Son of a bitch. No, no, no!*"

Quincy bolted from the table. He grabbed the cordless phone, fumbled it for a moment, then got a hard grip. His knuckles were white. Rainie didn't even recognize his face. Something bad had happened. She didn't understand what. She glanced at Kimberly and saw the girl's face turn the color of bone.

"Grandpa," Kimberly whispered.

"Oh no." Rainie closed her eyes. None of them had even thought about Quincy's father. He was a sick old man, stricken with Alzheimer's, tucked away in a retirement home. "Oh no ..."

"Shady Acres Elder Care," Quincy barked into the phone. "Put me through!" And a moment after that, "Abraham Quincy, please. What do you mean he's not there? Of course he's there; he requires full-time medical attention. His son picked him up? His son, Pierce Quincy, picked him up earlier this afternoon. Of course you made him show ID. Of course he had a driver's license. His son, Pierce Quincy ..."

A horrible stillness had come over Quincy's face. Rainie couldn't move. *Go to him,* she thought. *Touch him.* But she knew she couldn't. She knew Kimberly couldn't. Because they were watching a man in the throes of something terrible and it had only just begun.

He punched off the phone. He lowered it, cradling it against his neck as if the plastic receiver were something special.

"Ben Zikka was my father's best friend," Quincy murmured. "They grew up together, went to war together. He used to tell stories ..."

Kimberly and Rainie remained silent.

"He's an old man," Quincy whispered. "Seventy-five years old, can't even remember to piss in a toilet, for God's sake. He's sick, he's easily frightened. He doesn't recognize his own reflection, doesn't know he has a son. He doesn't even remember the name Pierce Quincy."

Kimberly and Rainie didn't say a word.

"He worked hard his whole life. Built a farm, raised a son, helped pay my way through college when money was tight. Never even wanted a thank-you. He did it because that's what he did. Seventy-five years old. At the stage where he deserves to die with dignity."

"Quincy ..."

"He's doesn't even know he has a son! How can the man kill him? He doesn't even remember I exist. Goddammit, goddammit, GODDAMMIT*!"*

He hurtled the phone receiver to the floor. It shattered into bits but it wasn't enough. He grabbed a chair and smashed it into the stove. He hurtled the coffeepot into the sink. He flipped over the table with a roar.

"Dad ..."

"I can't go I have to stay he might be alive you never know. I can't leave him he's my father and he doesn't even know he has a son. He's going to be tortured and murdered and oh God did you see what that monster did to Bethie and he's just a sick old man he doesn't even know he has a son. Jesus Christ, Rainie, he doesn't even know he has a son ..."

"You're coming to Portland."

"NO!"

"You're coming to Portland, Quincy. We won't let you stay. It's exactly what this sicko wants."

"My father—"

"Quincy, he's dead. I am so sorry, but he's dead. You know he's dead. I am so sorry ..."

Quincy's knees buckled. He went down on the floor, surrounded by glass and wood and fragments of plastic phone. He went down on the floor and he looked at Rainie with an expression she hoped she would never have to see again.

"My father," he whispered. "My father ..."

"Daddy, I'm scared. Please Daddy, I need you."

Quincy turned toward his daughter. She had begun to cry. A heartbeat passed. Rainie didn't know what he was thinking. Looking at his daughter and seeing traces of his rapidly vanishing past? Or looking at his scared, stricken little girl, and seeing a future that could still happen?

Quincy held open his arms. Kimberly flew into his embrace.

"It's going to be all right, Kimmy," Quincy murmured. "I promise you, it's going to be all right."

Then he closed his eyes, and Rainie knew why. He didn't want any of them to see that he had just told a lie.

24

Friday morning, five thirty-five, eastern standard time, they boarded the first flight for Portland, Oregon, proud owners of three tickets purchased with cash the day before. They had shown ID to pick up the tickets, then Quincy had used the power of his FBI creds to get the woman at the counter to change their names to aliases so there would be no record of their flight. The attendant had looked secretly excited to be involved in some sort of covert law enforcement operation. The three of them had remained pale and drawn, exhaustion making them sway on their feet.

The thunderstorms had finally passed, though the sky was still dark and the runway slick with rain. Ground crews in yellow windbreakers ran around the plane, loading bags. Onboard, Rainie watched them shout orders at each other, but could not hear their words.

Kimberly sat next to the window. She had taken her seat and almost immediately fallen asleep, her head slumped against the bulkhead. Rainie had the middle. She'd passed the threshold where sleep was still possible and now she was too awake, unbearably aware of the world around her. Quincy sat on her right. His face had become a mask. Once, she'd touched the back of his hand. He had moved it away from her. She had not tried again since.

"When my mother died, I hated my father," he said.

"What caused her death?"

"Heart attack. She was only thirty-four. No one saw it coming."

"Doesn't sound like it was your father's fault."

"I was a boy. My father had the power to make everything right, ergo he was also responsible for everything that went wrong. I used to ask him why she died. He always gave me the same answer. 'Because she did.' "

"Shit happens," Rainie said.

"Yes, the swamp Yankee version of shit happens. It took me years to realize it was the best answer he could give. Sometimes there's simply no reason for why things happen. What is karma to a little boy? What is the divine wisdom of God? What is the fecklessness of fate? Why did my mother die? Because she did. In his own way, my father was teaching me a very important lesson."

Rainie didn't say anything.

"Mandy didn't deserve to die," Quincy said. "Bethie didn't deserve to die, and my father didn't deserve to die. Shit didn't happen. One man did."

"We'll find him, Quincy."

"I'm going to kill him, Rainie. I spent four years being trained to heal as a psychologist, and the thought doesn't bother me. I'm going to find him and kill him. What does that make me?"

She hesitated. "Vengeful," she said at last.

He nodded as the plane finally powered up and prepared for ascent. He said, "I can live with that."

THE NEXT ACCIDENT

PLAN B

25

Sheriff Luke Hayes lounged against his patrol car outside of Martha's Diner, looking deceptively sleepy in the midday heat. Standing at five nine, with rapidly thinning hair and a featherweight's wiry frame, he didn't possess the kind of physical presence that immediately struck fear in a suspect's heart. It wasn't a problem, however. For one thing, he hit harder than most timbermen. For another thing, he moved three times as fast. Word generally spread pretty quick. See that bald guy? Don't go after him or he'll whip your ass. Hey, it was bad enough to go down in a bar brawl, let alone to be publicly dropped by a guy roughly half your body weight and possessing only a tenth of your hair.

By far, Luke's best feature was his eyes. He possessed a pair of riveting baby blues that soothed enraged housewives, calmed rifle-toting drunks, and pacified screaming kids. A suspect had once accused him of practicing major mojo with his gaze. Luke didn't think he possessed any special magic. He was just a naturally calm guy with a solid, even temperament. You'd be surprised how many women dug that.

His eyes weren't visible at the moment. They were closed against the white-hot sun, his face turned up slightly as if seeking a cooling breeze. The coastal air was flat today, however. Stagnant. He sighed heavily.

His head came down. He opened his eyes. And found Rainie standing in front of him.

"Another busy day in Bakersville," she said dryly.

"Gonna be a fight by six. Probably two fights if this heat keeps up."

"Maybe you should give up law enforcement. Sell air-conditioning units instead."

"It's not half-bad an idea. I could start by giving myself one. Hello, Rainie. Good to see you again."

He held out his hand. She clasped it warmly and didn't immediately let go. He thought she looked tired. Her cheeks had that gaunt look she always got when she was pushing herself too hard. She was a beautiful woman, always had been in a striking sort of way. Wide cheekbones, full lips, soft gray eyes. But her body was slimmer now, rangy like a fighter's. And she'd cut off all her rich, chestnut hair, giving herself some spiky city do when he could've told her that half the men in Bakersville dreamed about that long, lush hair. The feel of it in their hands. The look of it, pooled on their pillows. Pipe dreams, of course. But nice ones during the gray Oregon winters.

"Sheriff uniform suits you," Rainie said.

Luke puffed out his chest. "I'm a stud."

She laughed. "All the nice Protestant ladies are lining up their daughters just for you?"

"Tough to be a hero, but somebody's got to do it."

"God, I miss this place."

"Yeah, Rainie. We've missed you, too."

They went into the diner. Carl Mitz wasn't due to show up for another hour. By mutual agreement, they slid into their old booth and ordered a late lunch/early dinner.

"How's Chuckie?" Rainie asked after ordering the Friday special— chicken-fried steak with extra gravy and garlic-mashed potatoes. Guaranteed to add an inch to your waistline, or your money back.

"Cunningham has settled down," Luke answered. "Bit more confident these days. Plus, I think we've gone a whole month without him drawing down on some poor civvie whose only mistake was daring to run a red light during Chuckie's shift."

"He's stopped attacking the taxpayers? That *is* progress. And the rest of the town?"

"One-year anniversary was tough," Luke said softly. "Still a lot of paranoia, some bad blood. I hate to say it, but it's probably a good thing Shep and Sandy moved away. I'm not sure folks could've handled it otherwise."

"What a shame."

"It's human nature, Rainie. We're all looking for something to believe in, and someone to blame."

"Still—"

"We're okay, Rainie. That's the joy of small towns—even when we change, we don't change. Now how about you?"

She didn't say anything right away, which he had expected. She had always been a private person, even when it had been just her, him, and Shep, a three-man sheriff's department united against the world. But then, that's what Luke liked about Rainie. She could be moody. She possessed one hell of a temper. But you knew she'd get the job done. She showed up, she delivered, and when things had gotten rocky, Luke had been proud to have her in charge.

He'd been sad—no, he'd been angry—when the narrow-minded town council had demanded that she go. He had thought she'd put up more of a fight, and like a lot of folks in Bakersville, he'd been surprised, maybe even hurt, when she hadn't.

"Quincy's in trouble," she said abruptly.

"I gathered that."

"It's ... bad, Luke. Very bad."

"Accident wasn't an accident?"

She nodded. "Amanda was murdered by somebody out to get Quincy. Except it didn't end there. The man then used her death to target Quincy's ex-wife. Befriended her, romanced her, and slaughtered her, Luke. Absolutely butchered her. That crime scene was barely twenty-four hours old, before he kidnapped Quincy's father."

Luke arched a brow. "Bureau's got to be involved," he said tightly. He liked Quincy, seemed like a good guy. At least for a fed.

"Sure, the Bureau's involved. Any day now, we think they'll arrest Quincy."

"What?"

"He's been framed for the murder of his ex-wife. Did I mention that?"

"When G-men make enemies, they make enemies." Luke was frowning. "How's he holding up?"

"I don't know."

Luke's frown deepened. "I thought you'd know better than most. Or has something changed?"

"For God's sake, Luke, the man's family is being hunted. We're living Agatha Christie's *And Then There Were None*. Now is not exactly the time to put him on a sofa and say, Hey, Quince, tell me how you *really* feel."

"That's convenient."

"And what the hell is that supposed to mean?" Her voice had picked up. Color stained her cheeks. This was supposed to intimidate him. Instead it simply made him feel better. Rainie needed some color in her cheeks. He only wished that he'd brought a box of #2 pencils for her to snap. For old times' sake.

"I'm just saying—" he began mildly.

"Oh I heard what you were saying. Now I'm sorry I brought this up."

"I would've brought it up if you didn't," he assured her. "That's what friends are for."

"Speaking of which, thanks for telling some Virginia cop that I have the hots for a fed."

"You have the hots for a fed?"

"Luke Hayes—"

He was grinning and the sight of his amusement sent her temper spluttering. But then his grin faded, and he said a bit more honestly, a bit more gently, "Face it, you and Quincy have a genuine meeting of the minds. That's serious shit, Rainie. You can go an entire lifetime without finding anyone who matches like that. I know I have."

"Harumph," Rainie said. She scowled, but Luke wasn't fooled. He saw something in those wide gray eyes. Gratitude maybe. Or relief. Someone else thought she and Quincy could work out. Someone else believed the scrappy home-town girl was worthy of a fed.

You were bigger than this town, Luke wanted to tell her. *You were too smart to spend your career patrolling Friday-night football games. Damn, I'm proud of you.* But he didn't say those words because he understood that she wouldn't know how to take them.

The waitress came over with two Cokes. Luke accepted his with a smile. Rainie set hers on the table and proceeded to spin it absently between her hands.

"It's ... it's insane," she murmured. "There's someone out there, Luke. We don't know his name. We don't have a clear description. We don't even know how he ties in with Quincy. We just know he's smart. Methodical. And at least twelve steps ahead of us."

"Plan of attack?" Luke asked quietly.

"Attack is a strong word. We have a plan of retreat. We fled here with Quincy's surviving daughter, Kimberly. The man knows too much about their lives on the East Coast."

"You need manpower?"

Rainie shook her head. Then she ran a hand through her short-cropped hair. "It's hard to explain. This man … his system. He's not hit-and-run. This guy, it isn't just about the kill, it's all about the game. We know he's still coming. We know he'll follow us here. But he won't strike out of the blue. Somehow, someway, he'll convince one of us to open the door."

"Carl Mitz," Luke filled in.

"You have to admit, the timing is suspicious."

"I see your point." Luke sighed. He spread out his hands on the table. "Well, I don't know what to tell you, Rainie. Mitz started calling four days ago. I checked with the law offices of Avery & Abbott in Portland and they confirm having him on staff. He's also on record with the Oregon State Bar. I don't like his timing either, but at this point …"

"Mitz checks out."

"Mitz appears to be a genuine vermin, er, lawyer."

"What about his client?"

Luke frowned. "His client?"

Rainie nodded. She leaned forward. "This guy—Tristan Shandling, for lack of a better name—he's been using each family member to learn about the other family members. Mandy tells him about Bethie who tells him about Kimberly. Shandling plays his game and conducts his recon all at once. Except Amanda, Elizabeth, and Kimberly don't know a thing about me."

Luke got it. "So assuming he's learned that Quincy has a friend in Portland—"

"Not a big assumption. He seems to know everything about Quincy's life, plus he's stolen Quincy's identity. All you need to check anyone's phone bill is a name and Social Security number."

"Then Shandling needs a source of information about you."

"He can't come himself." Rainie thought out loud. "He's been too busy with Bethie in Philadelphia."

"So he hires someone."

"Someone reputable. Just in case we get suspicious and check the person out."

Luke nodded thoughtfully. "You're right, he's smart and methodical. So how do you want to play it?"

"I'm thinking we stick to the basics. I sit in the booth behind this one with a newspaper in front of my face so Mitz doesn't see me when he walks in. You greet him, make him comfortable, and pretend to be willing to cooperate."

"Good cop," Luke filled in dryly.

"Exactly. I wait here, eavesdrop, and let you pour on the charm. Then, when he's nicely entrenched in his, 'we don't give out information on our clients' speech, I pounce and tear him to shreds."

"Bad cop."

"Yeah." She smiled wolfishly.

Luke shook his head, "Rainie," he said, "damn, it's good to have you home."

At exactly five P.M. Carl Mitz strolled through the doors of Martha's Diner. In a crowd of plaid western shirts and field-stained jeans, he stood out conspicuously wearing a tan linen suit and carting a behemoth brown briefcase. He identified Luke easily enough—maybe the sheriff's star gave him away—and proceeded straight to the booth.

Rainie opened the newspaper and ducked down against the red vinyl seat. The newspaper easily obscured her face, but she still felt vulnerable. Not that she had much to fear. Her first impression of Mitz was an oversized accountant with bad taste in glasses. Mussed-up hair, ill-fitting suit, pinched white features. Whatever kind of law he did, it wasn't criminal because there wasn't a jury in the world who would take that face seriously. He probably did taxes or corporate deals. Something with really big spreadsheets.

Luke shook the man's hand. Mitz winced.

Oh boy, Rainie thought. When your stalker cares enough to send the very best …

Mitz sat down. He slid his briefcase onto the seat beside him. It took up half of the booth, but he seemed determined not to let it go.

"Thank you for seeing me," he told Luke crisply.

"No problem at all," Luke drawled, his voice magically two octaves lower and eight beats slower. "You seemed like an earnest fellow. I figured it would be easiest to meet in person, shake your hand, and address all your questions at once."

"Well yes, of course. Face-to-face is always nice. I only hate to intrude …"

"Oh you know how it is in small towns. We got plenty of time and we're always happy to meet new folks."

Rainie rolled her eyes. She thought the Andy Griffith routine was laying it on a bit thick, but Mitz seemed to relax a fraction more, his spine actually making contact with the back of the booth.

"It's a simple matter really," Mitz said briskly. "I'm running a routine background check on someone who used to live in this town. Lorraine Conner. I understand she was a police officer here."

"Yes sir. I believe she was."

"She lived here?"

"Yes sir. I believe she did."

"For how long?"

"Oh … for a long time. Years. Yeah, definitely years."

"Mmmm, yes. And her mother was Molly Conner?"

"Yes sir. I believe that is correct."

"Do you know how old Lorraine is?"

"Oh no, sir. I'm much too smart to ask a woman her age."

"You must have it in the files, though. Personnel records, something like that."

"We might. But she left with our previous sheriff, Shep O'Grady. You'd have to ask him. He's not here anymore, of course. Lives somewhere else now."

"Shep O'Grady." Mitz made a note.

Luke said, "So what's this all about, sir? We don't often get lawyers asking about our former officers."

"It's a routine background check."

"She's applying for a job?"

"Uh ... no."

"She's applying for a credit card?"

"I'm a lawyer, Sheriff. I assure you I don't get involved with credit card applications."

"Of course, pardon me. So when do you get involved?"

"That's confidential. Something I will share with Ms. Conner when the occasion arises."

"Fair enough. I would never ask a man to compromise his principles. Say, just out of curiosity, what is your specialty?"

Mitz, however, was no dummy. "That would also be something for me to share with her when the occasion arises. So Lorraine Conner served as a police officer for how many years?"

"Several," Luke obliged.

"I understand she resigned last year."

"Yes sir."

"A bit of scandal or something? About a fifteen-year-old incident?"

Luke shrugged. "Officer Conner resigned in good standing, Mr. Mitz. We're all real proud of her."

"Well," Mitz said briskly. "That's good to hear. Of course, as long as I'm in town, you won't be offended if I ask others the same question?"

"Ask away," Luke said graciously.

"Yes, well. What about the rest of her family?"

"What about them?"

"She has other family?" Mitz sounded surprised. For the first time, Luke hesitated, clearly caught off guard.

"Not that I know of," Luke said hastily, abandoning the drawl. "But you asked the question."

"So she doesn't have an ex-husband, half-siblings, children?"

"Not that I know of. Why do you ask?"

"Line on the form," Mitz said curtly. He began to make a note again, but Luke caught his hand. The Andy Griffith routine had vanished. Luke's face was hard set, and his voice had grown stern.

"These are very personal questions for a routine background check, sir, and even if Rainie doesn't live here anymore, she's a good friend of mine. Now I'm asking you one more time, what is this all about?"

"And I'm telling you one last time," Mitz said stiffly. "I'm not at liberty to say."

Rainie decided that was her cue. The conversation was going no place, plus good cop was about to beat the crap out of Mr. Mitz, which would give her role a tough act to follow. She came around the booth. She gave the lawyer a big smile. "Hey, Mitz," she said. "Surprise." Then she slid into the booth and effectively trapped the man between her and Luke.

"What … what is going on?" Mitz had started stuttering. Perspiration dotted his upper brow and Rainie figured in the last ten seconds, he'd sweat through his tan linen suit. She scooted in a little closer, letting her hand fall to his prized briefcase and stroking the leather almost lovingly.

"You've been trying very hard to meet me, Mr. Mitz," she said.

"Well, yes. I left several messages in Virginia. I didn't know … When did you get back in town?"

"Make you uncomfortable?"

"Well, yes. But, but, it's not bad either!" The lawyer perked up. "I mean, I wish you would've called first. I would've brought the whole file, been better prepared. But you are here now and I have wanted to talk to you."

"About my past," Rainie said knowingly.

"Oh, in all honesty, we know all details about your past. Even the, well, 'incident.' I assure you, he's not concerned about that. Doesn't bother him a bit."

"What?" Now it was Rainie's turn to feel confused. She glanced at Luke. He was shaking his head slightly, equally baffled. Shit.

"You've spoken to him, correct?" Mitz was saying in a merry rush. "I gave him your number in Virginia and he promised to call. After all, it seemed more appropriate for him to personally give you the news."

The hang ups, Rainie thought. Two days of hang ups she'd naively assumed were Mitz. Why is it wrong to assume? Because it makes an ass out of u and me.

"What news?" she heard herself ask.

"The estate, Ms. Conner. The will. That's what I do, you know. Estate planning. I'm his attorney."

"Whose attorney?"

"Ooooooooh deeeaaaaarrrr." Mitz drew up short. He blinked behind his glasses. "He didn't call you, did he? He said he would, but he didn't. It's the wild card, you know. Estate planning, it is an intense, personal experience. You never know how your client is going to react."

"Mr. Mitz, you start explaining now or I swear I'm going to break every bone in your overly educated body."

Mr. Mitz ducked his head. He blinked again. And he said in a small voice, "I work for Ronald Dawson. Ronnie thinks—we think—that he's your father. Which would make you, Ms. Conner, his sole surviving heir."

26

"You have a father?"

"Not bloody likely."

"You don't seem very happy about it."

"Happy about it? *Happy about it!*" Four hours later, Rainie stood in the middle of the one-bedroom deluxe hotel suite in downtown Portland and whirled on Kimberly Quincy as if the girl didn't have a brain in her head. Rainie had made the two-hour drive back to the city in one hour and thirty minutes. She'd cut off two semi's, flashed half a dozen cars, and nearly rear-ended a police cruiser. Only the fact that the state trooper was a personal friend of Luke's had saved her from a speeding ticket or worse. She should've taken a deep breath then. She hadn't.

Now she started pacing the living room of the suite, where Quincy and his daughter were registered as Larry and Barbara Jones. Quincy was catching a badly needed nap in the bedroom. Kimberly had been staring blindly at some network's TGIF TV-lineup before Rainie had burst through the door. Far from being wary of Rainie's mood, the aspiring psych student seemed grateful for the distraction. Rainie now understood how guinea pigs felt. If Kimberly gave her that deep, probing stare one more time, Rainie was going to start pushing brightly colored buttons in return for pellets. Then she was going to bounce said pellets off of Kimberly's blond head.

Rainie held up her hand. "One," she ticked off crisply. "Let's consider the father-to-be. Ronald Dawson, aka Ronnie. He's a thug. Better yet, a convicted thug. The man has spent the last thirty years incarcerated for aggravated murder. He was only paroled last year because at the age of sixty-eight, he's too arthritic to be considered a menace to society. In his thirties, however, he gutted two men in a bar fight with a hunting knife. Oh wait, I'm sorry. According to his lawyer, Carl Mitz, there were mitigating circumstances. Good ol' Ronnie was so damn drunk, he didn't know what he was doing at the time. Hellooooooooo, Dad!"

"Still, he hired a lawyer to find you," Kimberly said mildly.

Rainie scowled at her. "Two," she continued. "Ronnie claims to be looking for an heir to his estate, but it's not like he did anything to earn the estate. His father had a hundred-acre farm in Beaverton. Ronnie didn't help on the farm. He drank, gutted, then went to jail. His father worked the farm. His father built the farm. And when the real estate boom hit Beaverton in the early nineties, his father sold the farm to a real estate developer for ten million dollars. Praise be to Grandpa Dawson. Ronnie still sucks."

Kimberly smiled sweetly. "As they say, you can't choose your family."

"To hell with Tristan Shandling," Rainie said seriously. "Keep talking, girl, and I will kill you myself."

"Come on, Rainie. This is exciting news. Your mother is gone. You don't have any aunts, uncles, brothers, or sisters. But think about it. You might have a dad! A real, live, anxious-to-meet-you dad!"

"There's no proof he's my father," Rainie snapped. "So he slept with my mother thirty-two years ago. Who didn't?"

"But you'll take the blood test, right?"

"I don't know."

"Rainie …"

"I don't know!" Rainie threw her hands in the air. "You want to know the truth? I don't like it. I just plain don't like it."

"Because he's a convict."

"Of course he's a convict. My mother didn't hang out with aspiring astrophysicists. Hell, I'm not surprised my potential sire was in jail. I'm just shocked he was ever paroled."

Kimberly frowned. "So … it's the money you don't like? Becoming an heiress to ten million dollars? You're right, that's tough."

"Kimberly, think about it for a moment. What do all children who don't have parents do? They dream about their missing parents, right? They make up exotic stories. 'My mommy and daddy are secretly eastern European royalty, forced into hiding to flee the communists. When it's safe, they'll come back for me.' Or, 'my father was a Nobel prize-winning scientist, killed by evil government agents who wanted to halt his impending discovery of world peace.' Kids create fables, caricatures of real life. No one's absent father is ever a thug, or drunken white trash who simply didn't want to own up to his responsibility. He's always handsome, dashing, and frankly, rich."

It took Kimberly a moment, then she got it. "You think this is all fake. It's *too good* to be true."

Rainie finally grew still. She looked at Kimberly and demanded bluntly, "What does Tristan Shandling do? He *identifies* who the victim wants more than anything in the world. *And then he becomes that person.* I've been without a family for fifteen years, Kimberly. As you said, no aunts, uncles, brothers, sisters. There's a loneliness in that I don't think other people can understand."

"Rainie, you don't know that it's a ruse."

"Think about the timing."

"Just because you don't like coincidences, doesn't mean they don't happen."

"And just because it walks like a duck and talks like a duck, doesn't mean it *isn't* Tristan Shandling in disguise." Rainie plopped down on the sofa, then hit a cushion. Hard.

"You're scared," Kimberly said softly.

"Don't psychoanalyze me."

"I'm not trying to. It's just … You're scared."

"I was so sure he'd go with law enforcement," Rainie murmured. "Or maybe a fellow PI. Even knowing how he works, I didn't see this coming. God, he's good. I'm sitting here now, and half of me is warning, Don't fall for it, you're too smart for this. And the other half of me ... Christ, the other half of me is already picking out Father's Day cards."

Kimberly took a seat next to her on the sofa. Her long blond hair was pulled back from her face in a rubber band. She'd slept through the long plane ride and she looked better than she had in days. Rested. More composed. It was interesting to Rainie that as their situation grew more dire, Kimberly seemed to actually grow stronger. Young, but rising up to the challenge. Inexperienced, but definitely determined.

"Let's think about this," Kimberly said. "What's the next step?"

"Blood testing. Mitz gave me the name of a lab. They'll take a blood sample from me and ostensibly test for a DNA match with Ronald Dawson's."

"That sounds reasonable."

Rainie smiled grimly. "Do you know how long it takes for DNA testing? We're talking at least four weeks, or more probably, a few months. If this is all a scam, it will be over long before then."

"We can do some checking first," Kimberly countered firmly. "You said that Dawson's father sold a farm in Beaverton. Real estate transactions are public records. We can also search for the arrest record of Ronald Dawson."

"One step ahead of you. Luke already pulled Dawson's rap sheet. That checks out. Now he's working on the real estate records."

"Well, there you go!" Kimberly clapped her hands. She seemed genuinely excited. Rainie shook her head. She wished she could share the girl's enthusiasm. There was a numbness inside her, though. A sense of dread she couldn't shake. Or maybe it was simply the stunning realization that she was more vulnerable than she'd ever realized. And even as she told herself she knew better, there was something new and soft growing in her belly. Not numbness. Hope.

Thirty-two years old. The last fifteen years with no plans for Thanksgiving, Christmas, Easter. Always working the holiday shifts because what else was she going to do? Always watching other people go home to their families at the end of the day, moaning about their in-laws, bellyaching about the demands of another family gathering, joking about the bad presents on Father's Day. Sometimes the whole concept of a family seemed like an exclusive club to her. Other people were members. She was the perennial outsider, the guest who got the pity invite, but never really belonged at the table.

She wished Quincy was awake. She wished ... She would like to talk to him right now. Maybe, she'd even like to lean her head against his shoulder and have him tell her it was going to be okay. You have to have faith, he'd told her. She wished it were really that simple.

"Eight months ago," Rainie told Kimberly softly, "a man started calling around Bakersville, trying to find my mother. Luke told me about it a few months later, but never gave me the man's name as it didn't seem important. The man was Ronald Dawson. Luke still had the name listed in his notes. A few weeks after Ronnie's first call, the assistant district attorney dropped the criminal charges against me. At the time, I thought Quincy had intervened.

In fact, I was really angry with him for it. But I called the ADA after meeting Mitz this afternoon. Quincy never talked to him. The district attorney himself was the one who asked for the charges to be dropped. He's about to run for office again. And according to the ADA, his campaign recently received a healthy donation from a local citizen—otherwise known as Ronald Dawson."

"Well there you go, Rainie. The timing isn't coincidental at all. Ronald Dawson started looking for you nearly a year ago, and you have proof."

"Tristan Shandling's been active for at least twenty months. He could still be part of this."

"But he was focused on Mandy then, and after that, my mother. He can't be on both sides of the country at once."

"Sure you can. The magic of the telephone, Internet, cable. Plus, it's just an eight-hour plane ride. You can visit the West Coast for a day. It's not fun, but it's feasible."

"There are cheaper and simpler ways of targeting you than paying off a DA," Kimberly countered, "not to mention meddling in a criminal case."

"I don't think cheap or simple are particular concerns of Mr. Shandling right now. He's on the warpath. So what if he runs up the ol' Visa?"

Kimberly frowned. "Do you, or don't you, want this man to be your father?"

"I don't know. I just … I don't know."

Kimberly was silent for a moment. Then she said, "Rainie, I never realized you were so pessimistic."

"Oh God, we have to get you back to college."

"It's true! You may be on the verge of something wonderful, but you'd rather steel yourself for the downside than inspire yourself with the good. Oh …" Kimberly blinked. "You and my father, I get it."

"Oh, no. Don't you go there right now. I *really* don't need this right now."

She might as well have not spoken. "I was so sure my father was the holdout in your relationship," Kimberly declared. "I mean, given his distant relationship with his father, his reserve with his own children, his fears of intimacy with my mother. But this time around, it's not Dad, is it? It's you. You're the one who doesn't trust the relationship."

"Why do you people insist on speaking of trust as if life were a Disney movie? Kimberly, my mother beat me as a hobby. My father was basically a sperm donor, who fucked the town whore and moved on. Seventeen years later, my mother's current boyfriend decided she wasn't good enough and turned his attention on me. I have trouble trusting people? Hell yes, I have trouble trusting people. My mother was a mean, ill-tempered drunk. And I still loved her. That's not Disney; that's a complicated world."

"My father doesn't drink."

"Give him a few days," Rainie said sourly. "He also didn't curse or plot revenge until three days ago, and he's doing a fine job of that now."

"He would never hurt you," Kimberly said seriously.

Rainie groaned. "God save me from psych majors. Kimberly, look … I know your father is a good guy. I know he's different from the others. But knowing isn't always knowing, if that makes any sense. I mean, it's one thing to grasp something intellectually. To tell myself that Quincy's different, that he's okay, that he won't hurt me. It's another thing to change a lifetime way of thinking. To emotionally, really … believe. To genuinely feel safe."

"I tell myself logically that my mother is dead," Kimberly said abruptly. "But emotionally, I don't believe it yet."

Rainie nodded slowly. Her voice softened. "Yeah, it's kind of like that."

"I tell myself it's not my mother's fault, or Mandy's fault, or my father's fault," Kimberly said. "But I'm mad at all of them. They left me. I'm the strong one and I'm supposed to take it, but I don't want to be this strong. I'm angry at them for that."

"I keep having this dream," Rainie said. "Two or three times a week, always the same dream. This baby elephant is running across the desert. His mother is dead; he's all alone and desperate for water. Then these other elephants come, except instead of helping him, they beat him into the ground because he's a threat to their own survival. He gets up though. He fights to live and staggers after them. Finally they find water. I relax. In my dream, I think the baby is going to be all right. His struggle has now paid off. He will live happily ever after. Then the jackals come and tear him apart. And I wake up with little baby screams still echoing in my head. I don't know why I can't stop dreaming it."

"We read this study last year," Kimberly said, "about how children go through phases when they will want to hear the same story over and over again. According to the scientists, there is an issue or theme in the story that the children identify with. When they have resolved the issue, they don't need to hear the story anymore. But until then, night after night, they'll request the same tale."

"I'm a four-year-old?"

"You identify with something in your dream. Probably the baby elephant."

"The baby elephant dies."

"But he fights to live."

"Nobody helps him. He's desperate to join the herd. He would've been better off alone."

"He's following instinct. It's everyone's instinct to be part of something. In evolutionary terms, we are stronger together than alone."

"But not in my story. In my story, the baby elephant's desire to be with other elephants kills him."

"No, Rainie. In your story, the baby elephant's desire for companionship keeps him alive. What's he running across the desert for? Why does he get up each and every time? He's not fighting to live simply to live. He's a herd animal. He's fighting to join the other elephants, he's living off the hope that if he keeps on fighting, he will get to belong. The drought will end and they will accept him. Or he'll prove his mettle and they will accept him. Either way, he'll end up with his herd. You did the same, Rainie. Your mother hit you, but you still kept believing it would get better. Otherwise you would've succumbed to alcoholism by now, or even committed suicide. You didn't. Why didn't you?"

"I'm stubborn," Rainie muttered. "And stupid."

Kimberly smiled. "But in your own way, you're also hopeful. You're just not comfortable with that part of yourself. I understand. I'm hopeful I will kill Tristan Shandling. I'm not comfortable with that yet either, but I figure I have a few days."

"Kimberly," Rainie said gently. "Word of advice—don't go there. Tristan Shandling is a piece of shit. You play by his rules, and you won't ever get yourself back. He will have molded the start of your career, and you'll never get to know the kind of officer or agent you would have become. You'll simply be what he made you."

"You don't know that."

"Yes I do. I'm a murderer, Kimberly. Thanks to Ronnie Dawson, I'm free and clear in the eyes of the law, but years ago I killed someone. I'm a murderer. And I'll never know what else I could've been. Yeah, I pretty much hate that. Then again, the other person's dead. That's gotta suck, too."

"I didn't ... I didn't know."

Rainie shrugged. "Life's about baggage. Think twice before you hang a boulder around your neck."

"But he's going to keep coming," Kimberly insisted. "You know Shandling is going to keep coming and coming until either he, or us, winds up dead. The shark is in the water, Rainie. Now, we need a bigger boat."

Thirty minutes later, Kimberly was asleep on the sofa, her long blond hair pooled around her. The sun was beginning to wane, the white walls of the hotel room becoming washed in shades of gray. Outside the air was probably stifling. Inside it was cool and for a while Rainie simply leaned against the windowsill, six stories above, looking out at nothing in particular. Jet lag was catching up with them. Kimberly was probably down for the night. No sound came from Quincy in the bedroom.

The room was quiet. It hadn't occurred to Rainie until now how much she both craved and abhorred silence.

Maybe she had a father. It was hard to imagine. Her mother had told her once, with Molly's stunning indifference, that her dad could be any one of over a dozen men, and that she'd already forgotten all of their names. Men came, men went, Molly said. Don't be a fool and expect something more.

Thirty-two years later, Rainie's father remained a perfect blank in her mind. He had no eye color, no hairstyle, no distinguishing features. He was a black silhouette, like the mystery person with a white question mark in the middle they showed in magazines. *I gave you life. Do you know who I am?*

No, she didn't.

Maybe she had a father. Or maybe it was a lie and this was all Tristan Shandling. She had to have faith. Cynicism was more likely to keep her alive.

Rainie pushed away from the windowsill. She crossed the room and opened the door to the bedroom. The blinds were drawn. The room was swathed in black intersected by faint beams of fading light. Quincy sprawled in the middle of the bed, his left arm flung across the dark floral bedspread, his right arm crooked over his head. He'd taken off his shoes and tie. His firearm and shoulder holster were positioned within easy reach on the nightstand. Otherwise he'd fallen asleep fully dressed.

Rainie entered the room. She closed the door behind her. Then finally, fully clothed herself, she crawled onto the bed. Quincy didn't stir.

The collar of his white dress shirt was unbuttoned. She could just make out the first whorls of dark, springy chest hair. She had once run her fingers through that light matting of hair. She had pressed her palm over his breast and felt the strong rhythm of his heart.

"Quincy," she murmured, so he wouldn't startle awake and try to shoot her, "it's me."

He sighed heavily in his sleep. Then he rolled over on his right side, away from her.

She sat beside him. She inhaled the faint, soapy scent of his cologne. A year later she still didn't know its name and she wondered why she'd never asked him. Back when they'd tried dating, she would return home with that scent still lingering in her nostrils. She'd fall asleep smelling Quincy, and burrow deeper into the covers like a contented cat. When she woke up the next morning, alone, fragrance gone, she'd always felt a stab of disappointment.

She reached out now and lightly touched his shoulder. His cotton shirt was soft beneath her fingers, his arm warm. He didn't jerk away.

Rainie lay down at his side. She kept waiting for something. Fear. Discomfort. Yellow-flowered fields. Smooth-flowing streams. The places she'd learned to escape to in her mind. Mostly she was aware of the heat of Quincy's body, pressed against her side. And she remembered now what she'd felt that final evening with him. Desire. Real, honest to goodness desire. She hadn't known she was capable of such a thing.

Quincy would never hurt you, Kimberly had said. Rainie knew that. She probably even truly *knew* that. Maybe it was herself she still didn't understand.

People could hurt you. They could beat you with their fists and they could do worse; they could die and leave you all alone with no hope of ever making things right. And people could attack you. They could inflict great physical and emotional harm. And you could attack back. You could even kill them, inflicting its own kind of great physical and emotional harm.

And you could punish yourself then, because your mother was dead and someone had to play the role of the abuser. So you could punish yourself day after day, creating the very lifestyle that got you into this mess because you didn't know any other way to live.

You could do all that, or maybe you could try to change. You could give up drinking. You could stop sleeping around. You could try treating yourself better, even respecting yourself. Except sooner or later, you also had to try believing in yourself, and maybe she still wasn't so good at that. She'd always figured it was better to be hostile and belligerent first, then no one could ever accuse her of hiding her true colors. Truth in advertising, that was her policy.

Dying in the desert. Struggling to survive, desperate to belong, but still not figuring out how to live.

She rolled over on the bed. She pressed her cheek against the curve of Quincy's back. She could hear his heartbeat here, too. It sounded slow, and steady, and strong. She wrapped her arm around his lean waist. He murmured in his sleep. And then his hand came up and clasped hers.

She waited for the fear to strike. Images of yellow-flowered fields and smooth-running streams. Nothing.

She inhaled his cologne. She felt the warmth of his hand. And she thought ... She thought this spooning business felt very nice.

Rainie closed her eyes. She held Quincy and finally fell asleep.

27

"Where have you been?"

A little after six-thirty Saturday morning, Glenda Rodman stood blurry-eyed in Quincy's foyer, watching Special Agent Albert Montgomery finally walk through the front door. It had been forty-eight hours since she'd last seen her fellow agent. Her gray suit was hopelessly rumpled from sleeping fitfully in Quincy's desk chair. Her face looked like death warmed over. Multiple days of listening to threatening phone call after threatening phone call did take its toll on a person.

Now, the gifts had started. Yesterday morning, a disemboweled puppy in Quincy's mailbox. Yesterday afternoon, four rattlesnakes released outside the gate. Two had made it onto Quincy's property. Two had gone to the neighbors, where they had garnered the attention of a pet cat and two-year-old boy. Fortunately, the child's mother had snatched him away and called animal control before anyone got hurt. Last night, Glenda had gotten to listen to a voice cackle with glee on the answering machine, telling Quincy that when the rattlesnakes were done with him, he'd personally come skin the agent and make him into a belt.

When Glenda slept, she did not have pleasant dreams.

Now, she glared at Montgomery, who had managed to shower and change since she'd last seen him. Her resentment felt an awful lot like a wronged wife's.

"I've been in Philly, of course." Montgomery scowled at her, coming through the door and kicking it shut behind him. He shrugged off his stained overcoat.

"Your assignment was to help me stake out Quincy's house."

"Yeah, but that was before he turned his ex-wife into a shish kebab. You think the local yokels know how to handle a scene like that? Christ, I had to teach 'em how to analyze the glass shards myself. They really thought the window was broken from the outside. Dipshits."

"Agent, your assignment—"

"Hey, fuck assignment. The action isn't here anymore, Rodman. It's in Philadelphia. If we want to know what's going on, we gotta focus our attention there."

"There are still things happening here!"

"What, a bunch of harassing phone calls? Dead pets? Oh you're right, we've learned so much by being here the last three days." Montgomery gave her a dubious look. Glenda shifted uncomfortably.

Nothing much had happened here. Poor Bethie had been attacked and brutalized in Philadelphia. Yesterday, Glenda had received word from Everett that Quincy's ailing father had been kidnapped from a Rhode Island nursing home. Three agents had immediately been assigned to look for Abraham Quincy; after seeing what had happened to Pierce's ex-wife, however, no one was hopeful.

So yes, there was action. But none of it was here. Glenda simply sat. She listened to horrible, horrible phone threats. And she felt her nerves fray inch-by-inch, hour-by-hour. Still, this was her task. She believed in her assignment. And it bothered her that Montgomery hadn't had the decency to even consult with her, though he apparently knew as much about what was going on in Quincy's house as she did.

"It's important to learn the source of the information leak," she told Montgomery. "And the person might still show up. We can't rule that out."

"What person? Quincy's phantom stalker? Come on, don't tell me you're still buying his little fairy tale."

"What do you mean?"

"Look, I'll do you a favor. As the agent who's spent the last forty-eight hours in Philadelphia, I'll give it to you straight. That was no break-in. That was no stranger-to-stranger crime. The whole fucking thing is so staged it could open as a Broadway show. Take the bathroom window, the supposed mode of entry. It was broken from the inside out and the glass shards moved to disguise the fact. Then we have the state-of-the-art home security system—deactivated with proper code a little after ten P.M., same time the neighbor swears she saw Elizabeth Quincy enter the home with a man matching Quincy's description. Even the crime scene—it was a fast, brutal attack, no rape, no torture. Posing of the body, postmortem mutilation, all done for show. All done to make it *look* like a sexual sadist predator."

"You think Quincy did it."

"I *know* Quincy did it. But hey, I have no career track left in the Bureau, so I can afford to look honestly at the reigning golden boy. On the other hand, I'm sure the very notion makes you real uncomfortable. I mean, taking on the best-of-the-best and all—"

"Shut up." Glenda stalked away from him into the kitchen. Montgomery, however, followed.

"I know you don't like me," he persisted. "I know I dress wrong. I know I don't do politics well or play all the little reindeer games. I'm a fat, wrinkled slob. That doesn't mean I'm an idiot."

"True, your state of dress does not mean you're incompetent—your conduct on the Sanchez case does."

"Oh." He drew up short, his hands clasping self-consciously in front of him. "Figured it was only a matter of time before you heard about that."

Glenda felt better now, as if she were gaining the upper hand. She had known there were problems with the Society Hill crime scene. Quincy had all but told her that he would end up as the prime suspect. It was still difficult to hear her own doubts pouring from Montgomery's lips. She went on the offensive instead.

"You screwed up the Sanchez case—"

"I made a mistake."

"Quincy saved the day."

"I never said he was a bad profiler."

"Oh come on, everyone knows you blame him. It's bad enough to choke, let alone have another agent come along, get it right, and grab all the credit. How many times do you replay that in your head at night, Albert? How many times do you revisit every little nuance of that case, and feel your hatred for Quincy grow a little bit more?" She stared hard at Montgomery. The agent bowed his head.

"You wanted this, didn't you?" she challenged. "The perfect opportunity to come in and torpedo Quincy's career."

"No."

"Yes!"

"No! Dammit!" Montgomery glowered. He looked trapped and cornered, shifting around his heavy bulk until he finally seemed to realize there was no place left to run. Then he planted his feet. "You want to know the truth?" he spat back. "Fine, I'll tell you the truth. Not that you'll believe me, not that anyone will believe me, but I took this goddamn case to save Quincy's butt. I took it 'cause I thought, hey, if you can't be the hero, you might as well *save* the hero. That's gotta count for something."

"What?"

"Do I have to put this on a Hallmark card? I figured I could help Quincy. And yeah, I kind of thought that might jumpstart my career. Altruistic, I ain't. But I'm not a total jackass either. My career is in the toilet. Do a good deed, however, and I might escape the eternal flush. I'm fifty-two years old, Glenda. My ex-wife hates me and so do my kids. I got nine hundred dollars in the bank. What the fuck am I going to do if I'm no longer an agent?"

Glenda frowned, wanting to refute Montgomery's argument, but coming up empty. She didn't know what to think anymore. She didn't like Montgomery. His ill-kept appearance did bother her. So did his disappearing act. But he had a point. In the patriotic world of the Bureau, there was no greater currency than saving a fellow agent's hide. If he did find Quincy's stalker, Montgomery's career would get a second chance. Probably, its only chance.

"But now you think Quincy murdered his ex-wife," she said.

"You bet I do."

"Because the scene is staged?"

Montgomery shrugged. "Because of a lot of things. Frankly, the phone calls bother me. If you were out to get someone and you had his private telephone number, would you fool around with prank calls, or would you just go out and kill the man? I mean, we're saying this guy has some connection with Quincy's career. So we're talking about a psychopath. Now, what kind of psychopath wants to talk about killing an agent, when he can attack the agent?"

"We discussed this. It's a ruse, a way of disguising the UNSUB's true identity by creating hundreds of other suspects with opportunity and motive."

"But it also alerts the victim," Montgomery countered. "Seems like a massive downside to me. Especially when you consider that in this day and age, the UNSUB can simply read articles on-line about how to conceal evidence. He has the element of surprise, then has all night to cover his tracks."

"Maybe the UNSUB didn't want an easy murder. Assuming vengeance is the motive, maybe he wanted to make sure Quincy suffered first."

"Maybe. Or maybe we're making this all too complicated. Look, from where I sit, there is another plausible theory to everything that's happened: Quincy made this whole thing up. Ran the ad in the prison newsletters himself. Then showed up in Everett's office with his, 'The sky is falling, the sky is falling!' routine, knowing that Everett will follow protocol and assemble a case team. Now Quincy has four federal agents swearing to the Philadelphia police that someone is stalking him, and that mysterious person probably murdered his ex-wife and kidnapped his old man. But *is* someone stalking him? Or was this all a cover-up, so that he could kill his ex?"

"Listen to yourself, Albert. You're saying Pierce was willing to dupe the Bureau and harm his own father, simply to cover up an attack on his wife."

"We don't know that Quincy harmed his father."

"Abraham Quincy is a bedridden Alzheimer's patient. He's now been missing from the nursing home for over twenty-four hours. That's not good."

"Papa Quincy was checked out by Pierce Quincy, bearing proper ID."

"Anyone can get a fake driver's license."

"Yeah, and anyone can use a real one. Glenda, we got no body. For all we know, Abraham is tucked away at some nice posh resort, courtesy of his son. When the police buy Quincy's story of the phantom stalker, Abraham will promptly reappear, having magically escaped his evil captor. Or maybe Quincy will phone in an anonymous tip and the searching agents can rescue his dad. Either way, no harm, no foul, and Quincy's story is better all the time."

"It's too far-fetched!" Glenda protested. "Three *more* reasons: One, you saw Pierce in Philadelphia and there wasn't a mark on him."

"Quick kill. Plus, police have found blood in the drainpipes. Killer cleaned up at the scene."

"Two, you still have no motive. Quincy and his wife have been divorced for years. You're talking about a long, complicated scheme leading up to a particularly brutal murder. Why? The marriage is old business."

"I don't know that part," Montgomery conceded. "But it's still early. Maybe she never took him off her life insurance. Maybe he blames her for the daughter's death. Give me time. I'll work on it."

"Ah-hah," Glenda announced triumphantly. "Three, the daughter's death—Quincy has evidence that it wasn't an accident. She was murdered. Probably the stalker's first victim."

"What?" That brought Montgomery up short. "I thought the daughter was an MVA. Drunk driving. How does a DUI become murder?"

"Someone tampered with the driver's seat belt, rendering it useless. And there's evidence that someone else was sitting in the passenger's seat. The Virginia state police are investigating it now."

"Maybe the daughter tampered with the seat belt. Maybe it was suicide."

"Why tamper with the seat belt?" Glenda asked dryly. "Why not simply not wear it?"

"Oh." Montgomery was flummoxed. He shifted around his bulk, then grimaced. "I don't know," he said at last. "Have to think about it."

"It's a complicated case," Glenda said softly. "Three family members of a fellow agent are now dead or missing. We shouldn't be rushing to conclusions about Quincy, or anyone else."

"That's not what Everett said."

"You already presented this to Everett?" Glenda's voice raised a notch.

"Sure, I called him last night. If Quincy really is our killer, the Bureau is going to have a little bit of egg on its face."

"You shouldn't have done that. Dammit!"

"I can't speak to Everett? Christ, you really do hate my guts." Montgomery wandered over to the refrigerator.

Glenda remained poised in the middle of the kitchen. Her hands were clenched into fists at her side. Her heart was beating too fast. She was angrier than she'd ever been, angrier than she probably should've been. Except . . . Except Everett would now call Quincy back. The SAC would have no choice. He'd bring Quincy back and if there really was someone out to get him . . .

You asshole, Montgomery. Why couldn't you wait? What's one more afternoon, one more day of due diligence? Stupid son of a bitch.

The phone rang; the answering machine clicked on. Glenda raised a hand, and began to slowly and methodically rub her temples. It didn't ease the ache. She didn't know what to believe anymore. Montgomery raised interesting points, and if Quincy had committed the murder then it was her job to track him down.

And yet, if he hadn't. If he'd told the truth . . .

Then they were doing exactly what the UNSUB wanted. Three highly skilled federal agents were dancing to a killer's tune. And Quincy, what could he do if Everett ordered him to come in? The minute he walked through Bureau doors, he would be forced to surrender his creds and his gun. He wouldn't be much help to his daughter then. But what was his other option? Become an outlaw to protect Kimberly? It would never work. The Bureau had long arms, particularly when faced with embarrassing situations such as policing its own.

Two scenarios and neither showing much promise. Jesus, she thought. Quincy was either the most brilliant criminal the Bureau had ever faced, or one truly unlucky son of a bitch.

The fax line rang in the office. A moment later, a faint whir sounded as the machine picked up. Glenda went to retrieve the message, leaving Montgomery alone in the kitchen.

The preliminary report on the hard copy of the ad that had run in the *National Prison Project Newsletter* was coming over the wire. The report was four pages long. Glenda scanned each page as it came through.

Latent found five fingerprints on the typeset ad, all of which matched with various staff members of the *National Prison Project Newsletter*. Serology found no hairs and fibers, but some dust residue that, again, was traced to the *National Prison Project Newsletter*. To complete the evidence-less trifecta, the DNA unit had also been unable to recover any samples from the paper or envelope.

At least the Document Examination Unit had had some fun. Their findings comprised the last three pages of the report, and were a welcome change from N/A, N/A, inconclusive. The ink on the paper was traced to a standard black laser-print cartridge commonly used in HP printers. That narrowed it down to millions of possible printers. Never fear, they were able to trace the font and graphics of the typeset ad. The UNSUB had used PowerPoint. Oh, the magic of desktop publishing.

Glenda sighed. Investigating crimes had been so much easier when people had no other choice but to write notes by hand. How the hell were you supposed to analyze a computer font? Where were the hesitation marks or angrily slanted T's in a typewritten ransom demand? And how the hell did you narrow the field when even serial killers were using Microsoft Office?

On the last page, she finally found some news. The paper was distinct. Not cheap grade white, but heavy-duty cream stationery, handmade with a watermark. According to the Document Examination Unit, the paper came from Britain where it was sold exclusively by a small store on Old Bond Street. Approximately two thousand boxes were sold worldwide each year. And it retailed for nearly one hundred dollars per twenty-five sheets.

Glenda set down the report. So, they had an UNSUB with computer access, PowerPoint savvy, and extremely expensive taste in stationery. Who in the world sent an ad to a prison newsletter on hundred-dollar stationery? It probably came in some kind of fancy gift box with pressed flowers and silk ribbons tied around the top. Maybe a gift. What a wife might give to a husband, or a boss to a colleague, or a daughter to a dad.

Glenda looked at Quincy's desk. His beautiful, richly finished desk with the state-of-the-art fax machine, the fine leather chair. Everything perfectly matched, such as what a well-bred wife might select for her workaholic husband back when they were still married ...

She grabbed the first desk drawer. Ripped it open. Pens, pencil, a Louis Vuitton cheque holder. She tried the drawer beneath that, then the one beneath that. Finally, in the bottom drawer, the location of a man who didn't write much, three boxes of stationery, all hardly touched.

She'd been wrong about the dried flowers and silk ribbons. The stationery came in a beautiful sandalwood box, tied with a leather thong. Geppetto's Stationery, imported from Italy, beautiful to behold, and now down to nineteen sheets.

"Oh Quincy," Glenda whispered, box in hand. "Oh Quincy, how could you?"

28

When Rainie woke up, Quincy was gone. She glanced at the red-glowing alarm clock next to the bed. Seven a.m., making it ten eastern standard time. Quincy and Kimberly had probably been up for hours. She dragged a hand through her hair, caught her reflection in the mirror above the bureau and winced. She looked like she'd stuck her hand in a light socket. Then again, her mouth tasted like old socks.

Ah, another beautiful Saturday morning.

She rolled out of bed and into the adjoining bathroom. Toothpaste helped. So did a quick shower. She donned her three-day-old jeans and white T-shirt, wrinkled her nose with distaste, and bravely left the bedroom.

Quincy and his daughter sat at the brown circular table in the tiny kitchenette that comprised the front half of the living room. Quincy was hunched over his laptop computer, while Kimberly leaned against his shoulder to get a better look at the screen. Both held cups of Starbucks coffee, and both were arguing vigorously. Rainie identified a third cup of coffee, probably hers. She scooped it up, while trying to come up to speed on their squabble.

They seemed to be working on the database. Kimberly wanted to focus more on Miguel Sanchez, Quincy thought it was a dead end—the man couldn't exactly do much from the confines of San Quentin. Well what about family, Kimberly argued. What family? Quincy countered. Sanchez's only living relative was a seventy-year-old oxygen-dependent mother, hardly a likely candidate for psycho of the week.

"Touché," Rainie murmured.

They finally paused, Quincy glancing up from the computer. Something passed over his face, an expression she couldn't read. Then he said evenly, "Good morning, Rainie. There are croissants in the bag if you'd like."

She shook her head. "Been up long?"

"A few hours." Quincy was avoiding her gaze. That was okay; she couldn't seem to meet his eye either. Had he been surprised to wake up and find her pressed against him on the bed? Pleased? Or had he considered it purely practical—Kimberly already had the sofa. Rainie studiously memorized the Starbucks logo on her cup of coffee.

"Where are you with things?" she asked.

"Working the database."

Kimberly chimed in, "I think we need to reexamine the Sanchez case.

Miguel's the one who reached Dad by phone, plus, his treatment of his cousin, Richie Millos, proves that he's big on revenge. Then there's the Montgomery factor—that Albert Montgomery also worked that case and happens to hate Dad because of it."

"That I personally took Sanchez's call was a random event," Quincy countered. "There were fifty-six other convicts on the answering machine, whose calls I could just as easily have caught in person. And while the 'Montgomery factor' is interesting, coincidence does not equal conspiracy. Bottom line: Miguel is securely behind bars in California. He has no opportunity, and frankly, I don't think he's that smart."

"What about the cousin?" Rainie asked.

"Millos? What about him?"

Rainie took a seat. Safe on the comforting topic of homicidal maniacs, she could face Quincy again. "Think of it this way: Your assessment of Richie and Miguel's partnership led the police to focus on Richie. And by focusing on Richie, the police guaranteed his death at the hands of Miguel. Ergo, someone could argue that you were responsible for Richie's death."

"Ergo, I killed Richie," Quincy murmured. "Not bad."

"Does Richie have surviving family?" Kimberly asked.

"I don't know. Grab the case file."

Kimberly began digging in the box next to Quincy's feet. Apparently, they'd been through this drill a few times already, because she came up with the manila file in four seconds flat. "Millos, Richie. Let's see what kind of nuts are hanging from the family tree." She flipped it open, turned three pages, and began to briskly scan the background report. "Okay, we got a mother—fifty-nine years old and listed as a housewife. We have a father—sixty-three years old, former janitor, now on disability. Oh, condition is listed as rheumatoid arthritis. That probably rules him out."

"Any siblings?" Quincy asked.

"Two younger brothers and one younger sister. Jose is thirty-five and comes with his own rap sheet. A B&E guy, but not currently incarcerated. That's food for thought. Mitchell 'Mickie' Millos is thirty-three, and hey, no rap sheet. In fact, he's an engineer with a degree from the University of Texas in Austin. So apparently one of the men in the family made good. Finally we have Rosa Millos, the baby daughter, who is twenty-eight. We have no info on her, why is that?"

"Chauvinism," Rainie replied. "The feds have a history of underestimating women."

"I'm not going to comment on that," Quincy murmured, "given that I'm outnumbered, and outgunned, in this room. Now, for no good reason at all, tell me more about Mickie."

Kimberly flipped back through the background report. "I don't have anything more on Mickie. Once the investigating agent determined he had no criminal history, he seemed to have lost interest."

"Figures." Quincy frowned, mulling something over in his mind. Then his gaze rose to meet Rainie's. She'd been staring at the column of his throat, admiring his dark blue polo shirt and wondering why she hadn't gotten him out of a suit more often. The soft cotton fabric draped nicely over his chest, accentuating the hard planes of his runner's body, the deep color of his piercing eyes.

Why hadn't he woken her this morning? He could've taken at least one moment to brush her cheek and say ... anything.

Belatedly she realized he was looking at her. A fresh flood of color rose in her cheeks. She looked away hastily, feeling not at all like herself.

"Rainie?" he asked softly.

"Ummm, the youngest brother. Yes, let's look harder at him."

Kimberly frowned. "Why Mickie? He's not even the right age. Our guy's much older."

"Age can be faked," Quincy said, his gaze still on Rainie. "Plus, people are notoriously bad at estimating age. You put a man in T-shirt and jeans and people will say he's early twenties. You put the same man in a dark suit, and people will say he's early thirties. While eyewitness testimonies remain the number one way of catching suspects, they are very easy to manipulate, especially by someone who's done any reading on the subject."

"But Mickie's an engineer," Kimberly protested. "Educated, no history of crime."

"Exactly," Rainie spoke up. "The UNSUB we're looking for is sophisticated. He has a complex plan, a gift for manipulation, confidence in approaching both a beautiful young woman—your sister—and a sophisticated older woman—your mother. Most likely he is educated, fairly worldly, and with a knack for problem solving."

"And he has money," Quincy added. "At the current pace of development, our UNSUB's most likely engaged in this pursuit full-time. So he must have a nest egg to live off of. He's also been traveling, demanding additional resources. Then there's this new development with you, Rainie. Kimberly told me about your meeting with Carl Mitz. If, as you suspect, your 'father' really is Tristan Shandling, then our UNSUB has paid off a DA and hired a lawyer as part of his plan, both actions requiring significant financial resources.

"Now, does a thirty-three-year-old engineer such as Mickie have that kind of money? Generally, I'd say no. But in this day and age of software millionaires and dot-com billionaires, who knows? Mickie could be a very wealthy young man."

Kimberly nodded slowly. "I hadn't thought of that. Okay, so we run a complete background check of youngest brother Millos, including his financial assets. One name down." She looked at the box of files. She sighed. "Fifty more names to go."

"With all due respect," Rainie spoke up, "I don't think this database project is going to get us anywhere." Quincy immediately frowned. He and his daughter swiveled to look at her. Rainie shrugged. "Think about it, Quincy. Is this guy's name somewhere in that box or in this database or in FBI files? Probably. Is it going to help us? No. Why not? Because he knows his name is in there, too."

She leaned forward, speaking intently. "What is the UNSUB's major vulnerability? Process of elimination. It's a personal case, not stranger to stranger, so given enough time and resources, he knows you'll be able to identify him. What's his strategy then? In the beginning, it's secrecy. He selects Mandy, the family member in the least amount of contact with the rest of the family. He disguises his appearance, he uses an alias, and he conceals her murder as an accident. And in the beginning, that works. He understands, however, that he can't hide his actions forever. The minute he attacks Bethie, you'll start connecting the dots. You'll start looking for him. And he prepares for that as well.

Fourteen months after Mandy's accident, he starts a fresh wave of maneuvers. First tactic: Diversion. He spreads around your address and telephone number to every psycho in the continental U.S. Next tactic: Confusion. He steals your identity, assumes your appearance, and begins to plant evidence that will get your fellow agents off his trail and on to you. Final tactic: *Speed*."

"Everything is now happening at once," Quincy said.

"Wednesday, Mom is murdered," Kimberly whispered. "Thursday, Grandpa is kidnapped. Friday, we're all on the run and Rainie is approached by some lawyer about her father. He's not going to give us time to think, anymore. He's not going to give any of us time to stop and consider and analyze. Because the minute we do, he knows he's in trouble."

Rainie was looking at Quincy. "This guy ... he's a black hole, Quincy. We don't know who, why, how, when. He's not giving you any information. He's not making the mistake of underestimating you. Why?"

"Because I definitely know him."

She smiled. "Because he definitely knows you. You thrive on information, puzzles, games. It's your whole life. So step one was to keep his actions hidden for as long as possible. And step two is to keep you moving, instead of thinking. As long as you're reacting to him, you can't get ahead. Keeping you reacting is keeping you vulnerable. We have to break that cycle, Quince. We need an active game plan, a way of going on the offensive. And hiding out in Portland playing with databases isn't it. He'll find us here—probably a lot sooner than you think."

Quincy grew silent. Then his gaze rose slowly to meet hers. "What do you think of Carl Mitz's allegation that you have a father?" he asked.

"I don't know."

"Just because it's coincidence, doesn't mean ..."

"I got that!" Rainie took a deep breath, then let it out. "I just ... I have to be careful. Mitz seems legit. There are aspects of Ronald Dawson's background that also appear genuine. He was in prison for most of my life, we may very well find public record of the real estate deal that made his father a millionaire. On the other hand ... Tristan Shandling's MO is to disguise himself as the person his victim wants most. And yeah, I am interested in Ronald Dawson. I'm desperately interested in Ronald Dawson, and frankly, that scares me to death."

"What if Mitz could arrange for you to meet Mr. Dawson in person?"

"No way." She shook her head adamantly.

That intent look was back in Quincy's eyes, and not his slow sexy look, but his all-knowing professional stare. "Active game plan," he murmured.

Rainie closed her eyes. She knew what he wanted. It hurt her, it killed her, but it didn't change the fact that once more, he was right. "Fine! I'll meet with Ronnie. I'll put my achy, breaky heart at risk. Never say I didn't do anything for you."

"But you can't meet with him," Kimberly blurted out. "If he's the UNSUB, he could attack you, or kidnap you, or worse."

"I don't think your father intends for me to meet with Ronnie alone," Rainie said dryly. "Not that he's opposed to offering me as some juicy little bait."

"I never—"

"Oh shut up, Quince. For God's sake, I'm the one who just said we needed to be proactive. If Dawson is our favorite stalker, then let's turn the tables on him. I'll contact Mitz and set up a lunch date, with Luke and the boys singing backup. I can drill Ronnie for additional information about his paternity claim. At the very least, I can get yet another description to add to our files. Tristan Shandling, the man of many faces."

"What if he tries something?" Kimberly protested.

"He won't," Rainie said.

"How can you be sure?"

"Because it's his MO," Rainie said flatly. "If Ronald Dawson is Tristan Shandling, he's not going to come out of the gate swinging. Oh no. Quite the opposite. He's going to sit across from me telling me how much he's always wanted a daughter. He's going to dazzle me with stories of what I could do with a ten-million-dollar inheritance. He's going to tell me that finding me is the single best thing that's ever happened to him." Her voice cracked. She caught it. "And I'm going to get to doubt every word he says. I'm going to sit there thinking this man is either the world's most perfect long-lost father, or someone who wants me dead. Hey, all in a day's work."

"Rainie—"

"I'll do it, Quincy."

"I've changed my mind. I don't want you to do it. I was wrong."

"You were right," she snapped crisply. "Don't grow soft on me now."

He fell silent. So did she. His eyes locked on hers. The moment drew out, grew long.

"This is very hard," Kimberly said at last.

Quincy nodded, his gaze not leaving Rainie's. "This is very hard."

"I mean, we don't even know who this man is, and look what he's doing to you. Mom is gone, and Mandy's gone, and now you have to fear for Rainie and me."

"I've always feared for the people I care about."

"But not like this. Not this active, immediate, horrible kind of worry."

"I always worry," Quincy said quietly. "It's the nature of my job. I know what can happen, and I do think about it late at night."

"We're going to be okay," Kimberly said fiercely. "We know what's going on now and information is power! We're going to be okay."

"We'll delve deeper into Mitchell Millos," Quincy said softly. "I'll try to come up with a list of five or ten other names. Then I'll check in with Everett, see if he has any new developments. Perhaps, my father ..." His voice grew too wistful. He caught himself and said more firmly, "And we'll move on Ronald Dawson. One way or another, we're going to get a fix on him."

"We have one last ace in the hole," Rainie spoke up. "Phil de Beers in Virginia. He's still tailing Mary Olsen. Think about it. She's alone. She's betrayed her best friend, and she has no self-esteem or she never would've gotten into this mess in the first place. She's probably already reaching out to the guy. And as each day passes, she's only going to get more demanding about meeting him in person. When she does ..."

"I want photos," Quincy said immediately. "Best quality Mr. de Beers can get. It's time we develop a better physical description."

"But he uses so many disguises," Kimberly protested. "The two descriptions we have don't match. How will a third help us?"

"He only *seems* to be good at disguise, because we're relying on accounts from laymen," Rainie pointed out. "Everyday people get bogged down with eye color, hairstyle, facial hair, clothing—all easily altered elements. What people should look at are standard features such as the amount of space between the eyes, the location of the ears on the head, the shape of the jawline. Those features can't be changed, they're unique. If we can get a photo, then we could have it analyzed by a forensics artist for those elements and *then* we'd finally have something to work with."

"You'll contact de Beers?" Quincy asked.

"I'll call him this minute," Rainie promised. She smiled thinly. "And then I'll call Mitz about setting up lunch with Daddy. We gotta get moving— thirty-six hours since Señor Psycho's last strike; I doubt we have much time left."

29

The Olsen Residence, Virginia

Curled up in the deepest corner of her walk-in closet, Mary Olsen cradled the cordless phone to her ear. Her dark hair was snarled. Mascara streaked her face. On her left shoulder was a fresh bruise she didn't want to talk about. Her icy blue silk robe hid the remains of many more. Her husband had come home this morning from an emergency surgery that had not gone well. Ten minutes after he tore back out of the driveway in his Jag convertible, she had grabbed the phone.

"I know I'm not supposed to call," she said in a rush, "but I can't take this anymore. You don't understand how bad things have been. I need to see you. Please, baby, please …"

"Shhh, take a deep breath. Everything will be all right."

"No it won't. No it *won't!*" Her voice rose to a frenzied pitch, then dissolved in a flood of tears. Her ribs hurt. She was going to have bruises between her thighs. Who ever would have thought that a man who looked so soft could hit so hard? "I'm lonely," she sobbed. "It's been weeks of nonstop torment, and now I don't even have you to look forward to. I can't keep living like this!"

"I know, baby. I know it's been hard." In contrast to her high-pitched pain, he sounded calm, gentle, kind. She let the words wash over her bruised thoughts and strained emotions. She held the phone closer to her mascara-stained cheek.

She had always loved the sound of his voice. Mandy once had commented on his eyes, that it was the power of his gaze that drew her in. For Mary, however, not allowed to see him much, it had always been the sound of his voice. How he could seem to know her anguish from hundreds of miles away. How he could whisper in her ear across the telephone lines and lend her his strength in the middle of the night when her husband had finally fallen asleep but she knew it was only a matter of hours before he awoke and it would start all over again.

"He tells me what to say, what to do, what to wear," she whispered brokenly. "I didn't know it would be like this. Why did he want to marry me, if he hates me so much?"

"You're a beautiful woman, Mary. Not all men can handle that."

"But I never gave him anything to worry about!" she cried. "I mean … well, you know, not before. God, I'm tired! I miss you. I *need* you. I'd give anything just … just to hold your hand, see your smile. Make me feel beautiful again."

"I wish I could, honey," he said apologetically. "I really do."

"Why not? It's been days since the Conner woman showed up. Surely it's safe by now. We can meet anyplace you want. I'll take the precautions you showed me. Please, it'll be all right."

"But love, it's not all right. Don't you know? You're being watched."

"What?" She gasped, genuinely surprised.

"I tried to get a note to you two days ago," he explained. "But then I saw a small silver hatchback tucked inside the bushes with a clear view of anyone entering or exiting your property. I watched the car for hours, and it never moved. I'm sorry, baby, but I think your husband is having you followed."

"No! The goddamn jealous prick. I've never given him any reason … I mean not before. Oh, fuck him! What are we going to do?"

"What can we do? If he gets even one picture of us together … I know you don't want that to happen. Not after everything you've been through."

"I won't give him the satisfaction!" Mary vowed. "By God, when I leave the son of a bitch he's going to pay me every dime he's worth. I should leave him today, this instant. I'll just … I'll just do it!"

"The shorter the marriage, the less likely you are to receive half his assets," he said gently.

She started to cry again. "What am I going to do? I miss you. I am *going insane!*"

He didn't say anything right away. There probably wasn't anything to say, and she knew that even if she didn't want to admit it. She was a married woman. She did need her husband's money. Oh God, her shoulder hurt. So did her ribs. Some mornings she wasn't sure how she made it out of bed. The more her husband beat her, the angrier he seemed to be. Was it himself he hated for hitting her, or herself for never saying no?

How did my life come to this? I don't know, I don't know, I don't know …

"I have an idea," her lover said.

"Yes. Anything. Please."

"This afternoon, a box of chocolates will arrive. Godiva, I think. The brand doesn't matter. Are you listening?"

"Yes." Her voice was breathless.

"I want you to take the box and walk down the road until you see the silver car. A black man will be sitting behind the wheel."

"Oh my God!"

"He's not going to hurt you, baby. He's a private investigator, no doubt the best your husband's money can buy. Tap on the window. Smile charmingly. Then, tell him you know what he's doing. He'll be chagrined, embarrassed about being caught. You become even more charming. Invite yourself to join him, tell him you just want to talk. Then pour out your heart about your evil husband, and while you're at it, offer him a chocolate. If he refuses, take one yourself. Eat it in front of him. Then offer him more. Make sure he eats two or three. That will do it."

"Are they poisoned?" she asked. A shiver ran down her spine.

"You think I would ask you to eat poisoned chocolates? What has your husband done to you?"

"I'm sorry, it's just—"

"The candies are doctored, love. A chocolate-flavored laxative, that's all, melted down and injected with a syringe. One truffle will have a minor impact on your system. Two or three, however, should, well, give the private investigator more pressing things to do with his time than watch you. When he drives off in search of proper facilities, you can get away."

"To meet you!"

"I've missed you, too, love."

"Tell me I'm beautiful."

His voice was generous. "You are beautiful beyond compare, particularly in black lace."

"I'll wear the garters," she said breathlessly.

"Perfect. I'll wear nothing at all."

"Oh God, I can't wait to see you!"

"One box of chocolates later, I'll be at your side."

She smiled for the first time all morning. But then she remembered how she looked, and she hesitated. "I'm a little ... sore," she said softly.

He understood instantly. "Then when I see you, baby, I will kiss all your pains away."

She started to cry again, quietly this time, genuinely. He would make her feel better. He always did. The first time she'd arrived with black-and-blue ribs, she'd told him that she'd fallen down the stairs. But he'd known. And instead of turning away, instead of looking at her with disgust, he had taken her in his arms and held her tenderly.

"You poor thing," he had said. "You are much too precious for this."

She had cried that night for hours. The whole time, he simply held her and stroked her hair. In her entire life, she had never had anyone touch her as gently as he did. In her entire life, no one had ever made her feel so special.

Briefly, for one instant, she thought of Amanda. Amanda who had never hurt her. Amanda who had been a good friend. Amanda who had been so excited to introduce her new man ...

But you kept drinking, Mandy, she thought. *You had the world's most perfect beau, and still you hit the bottle. After that, you deserved what happened. Besides, you always had plenty of men. And I ... I* needed *him.*

She replaced the phone, using the sleeve of her robe to wipe away the streaks of mascara and tears. One box of chocolates later on she would be with him again, she thought. One box of chocolates later. She hoped they came quick.

30

A little after eleven a.m., Quincy followed Rainie into her downtown loft. She flicked on the lights out of habit, though daylight streamed through the front bank of windows and the space was bright. The air carried the musty scent of a home that had been empty too long. Quincy knew that fragrance—it was how his own residence always greeted him.

"I should check on a few things," Rainie said nervously. He nodded, walking into the living area while she flitted about the open space. She had been like this all morning. Rarely meeting his eye, skittering away if he moved too close. Soft and still one moment. Nearly frantic the next. He thought he knew what was going on. Then again, his instincts weren't the best these days.

Shortly after their discussion that morning, Rainie had left a message on Carl Mitz's cell phone. She couldn't leave the number for Quincy's cell phone without revealing that he was with her, and she couldn't give the phone number of the hotel room without compromising that location, so she provided the number Mitz already knew—her loft in the Pearl District. Kimberly had opted to stay in the hotel room, where she was using Rainie's PI license number to access various law enforcement databases for background reports. Quincy and Rainie would wait for Mitz's response at her place. The division of labor made practical sense. If there were other motives, no one was mentioning them.

Quincy walked around the sofa, pausing in various sunbeams. He liked the feel of light and heat washing over his face. He closed his eyes and felt knotted muscles unclench. He took a deep breath and reminded himself that this, too, shall pass. He held on to that thought fiercely these days.

He had called Everett about his father. No news yet, and Quincy knew better than most what that meant. Each hour that passed without finding Abraham decreased the probability of ever seeing him alive. It had been thirty-six hours now. One moment, Abraham had been sleeping peacefully in his antiseptic-smelling bed. The next he was gone, checked out by a stranger posing as his son, not that Abraham would know the difference. A janitor reported seeing Quincy's father being led to a little red sports car, probably the same Audi TT the UNSUB had used to pick up Bethie.

No sign of the car since. No sign of Abraham. No big break in the case to ease the pain steadily building in Quincy's chest. His father's kidnapping was the ultimate failure, worse somehow than Amanda's and Elizabeth's murders, because they had been independent adults. His father, on the other hand, had been vulnerable and utterly helpless. Once a proud man who had single-handedly raised his son, now a dependent. Quincy should've done more to keep him safe.

The realization left him in a strange place. At once bottomed out, yet fiercely enraged. Empty of all emotion, yet desperate to feel alive. Defeated. Determined. Unbelievably angry. Unbearably sad. The academic searching for a reason. The man, knowing there was no such thing.

Why is my father gone? Because he is. Isolation is not protection. No amount of distance numbs the pain.

And then Quincy had a strange memory, a moment he hadn't thought about in years. Little Kimmy coming home from her fourth ballet lesson, walking into the living room where the family was gathered, and with her feet planted and her hands balled on her hips, announcing in her loudest voice, "Fuck ballet!"

Quincy remembered Bethie's stunned gasp, Mandy's awed expression, and his own desperate attempt to fight a smile. Fuck ballet. Such attitude. Such confidence. Such fearlessness. He had felt so proud.

Had he ever told his father that story? Abraham would've liked that. He wouldn't have said anything, but he would've smiled. And he also would've been proud. Each generation takes the next step forward. From a stoic swamp Yankee to a reserved federal agent to a brash aspiring criminologist, who obviously knew her own mind.

Isolation was not protection. He had lost his father, but maybe, just maybe, he was getting an opportunity to rediscover Kimberly.

"I'm going to grab some clothes," Rainie called from the walk-in closet. "If the phone rings, let me answer it."

"I am not here," Quincy promised her.

"Do you think Kimberly needs anything?"

He smiled faintly. "I think you would know that better than me."

"That's not true. You're not a total idiot savant."

"Coming from you, I take that as a compliment."

Rainie exited the closet. He could tell she was happy to be home because there was an extra bounce in her step, a spark of energy that had previously been missing. She'd changed from her T-shirt into a blue chambray button-down. As she walked toward the kitchen, he found himself studying how the soft, well-worn cotton flowed over the curve of her hips.

She is beautiful, he thought, and this time around, the realization stunned him. She was not just good-looking or attractive or sexy. She was beautiful. Beautiful in jeans and a cotton shirt. Beautiful in the way she burst past two homicide detectives at a Philadelphia crime scene simply because she knew that he needed her. Beautiful in the way she stood up to his fellow FBI agents even though she felt uncomfortable and outclassed. Beautiful in the way she was still beside him, when God knows that his life was disintegrating quickly and it would be so much easier to walk away.

She'd told him once that she didn't know anything about relationships or commitment. She was the most loyal, trustworthy person he knew.

"Rainie," he said quietly, "I messed up this morning."

That grabbed her attention. She froze with one foot in the kitchen, and the other in the bedroom. "I don't know what you're talking about," she said.

"I was having the best dream, probably the first good dream I've had in months. We were together, on a beach, curled up on white-hot sand. I remember I was playing with your hair. We weren't saying anything. We were simply ... happy."

"That had to be a dream."

"Then I woke up and you really were beside me."

"Was I snoring?"

"You weren't snoring."

"Phew." She made an exaggerated motion with her hand as if wiping sweat from her brow. "Here I was sure that I'd been snoring so loud, you'd had to run for your life."

"You had your head on my shoulder," he said softly. "And your arm around my waist. And your leg ... it was curved over my thigh."

"I get cold when I sleep."

"It was ... it was one of the nicest things anyone has ever done for me."

"Oh, fuck you, too, Quince." He blinked his eyes in shock. Rainie stalked toward him. Her cheeks were flushed, her finger making dangerous, jabbing motions in the air. Somewhere along the way, his little speech had obviously pushed the wrong button because she was definitely pissed off. Run, he thought immediately. Where? The place had no walls.

"I am not nice!" she spit out. "Can we get this straight? *I* am *never* nice."

He watched her finger warily. "Okay."

"I did not crawl into your bed to be nice. I did not curl up beside you to be *nice*. And I did not fall asleep to be *nice*. Got it?"

"I didn't mean—"

"Yes you did. I reached out to you. I made a *huge* leap forward for me. And you not only took the coward's way out this morning, but you're taking the coward's way out now, by reducing my act of caring to an act of pity."

"Are you going to stab me with that thing?"

"With what?"

"Your finger!"

"Quincy!" she yelled, throwing both hands into the air. "Stop being a smartass. For God's sake, you're acting like *me*! Snap out of it!"

He fell silent. After a moment, so did she. "I might have panicked this morning," he admitted.

"There you go."

"You could be gracious about this."

"No, I couldn't. Keep talking."

"It's possible," he said softly, "that I fell back on old habits. I woke up, saw you there, liked having you there, and ... Rainie, now is not a great time to be someone I care about. People I care about are suffering notoriously short life spans."

"Quincy, boyfriends apologize, shrinks analyze. Which are you?"

He blinked. "Damn, you're getting good at this."

"Come on. Mitz could call at any time and then we'll have to get going. So apologize and make it snappy."

"I'm sorry," he said dutifully.

She wiggled her fingers. "For … ?"

"For sneaking out of bed like a thief in the night. For not waking you up first. For pretending it didn't happen, when spending the night with me was a monumental step for you and I appreciate your growth—"

"Okay." She held up a hand. "Quit while you're ahead. Any moment now, they'll be giving you your own talk show."

"Rainie, I liked waking up with you by my side."

Her hands finally came to rest in front of her. She gave him a sideways glance. "I kind of … I kind of liked it, too."

"I didn't snore?" He couldn't help himself. He took a step forward. She didn't move back.

"You didn't snore," she said.

"No tossing and turning, stealing covers, keeping you awake all night?" He kept approaching. She still didn't move back.

"Actually, you were rather cuddly. For a fed."

He was now only an inch away from her. His nerve endings had flared to life. He could smell the faint scent of her soap, the apple-ish fragrance of her shampoo. He could see every nuance of her face, the direct line of her gaze, the firm resolve of her lips, the way her chin was up as if preparing for a fight. Now was not the time, he reminded himself. Carl Mitz could call at any moment. The world could end.

He wanted to touch her so badly, his fingertips burned. She challenged him. She pushed him. And more than all that … She made him dream of white-hot sands when for so long he'd been a shell of a man, methodically analyzing humanity and sacrificing his own somewhere along the way.

"I don't want to hurt you," he whispered.

"Bad things happen, Quince. Someone I respect explained it to me once. We can't stop all the bad things in the world. We can simply try to enjoy the good."

"If I lost you …"

"You would get on with life," she said bluntly. "So would I. We're practical people, Quincy. And we're tough, and we're going to make it through this. Now stop talking. Stop thinking, stop analyzing, dammit, and *kiss me*."

He obliged.

His first touch was light. In spite of her bold words, he knew she was nervous. He could feel the tension in her spine as his hand settled on the small of her back. He could feel the finite hesitation as she tilted back her head and offered her lips. She expected him to dive right in, and she had steeled herself for the attack. He wasn't interested in a stoic or a martyr, however. He understood her history. Sex for Rainie had been about pain and punishment. Even if she thought it would be easier that way, he wasn't going to rush.

He brushed the corner of her mouth with his lips. He raised his left hand, and feathered back her hair. Her eyes were squeezed shut. He ran the ball of his thumb over her silky eyelashes.

"That tickles," she murmured.

He smiled. "Open your eyes, Rainie. Look at me. Trust me. I won't hurt you."

She opened her eyes. The gray depths were wide, translucent. He had never seen eyes quite like hers, the color of smoky, midnight skies. He bent lower, his gaze still locked on hers, and kissed her left cheekbone.

"Have I ever told you how much I love your profile?" he murmured. "Such a stubborn jaw and then these dramatic cheekbones ..."

"I look like a Picasso painting," she said.

"Rainie, you're the most beautiful woman I know." His lips came down and found her mouth. This time her gasp was unmistakable. Her spine relented. Her hands curved round his head. Her hips connected with his.

She had full lips, he'd appreciated that the first time he'd seen her. And he'd been struck by the dichotomy of her hard-boned face coupled with an undeniably sinful mouth. Men dreamed about lips like these. Men paid money, wrote sonnets, and sold their souls for lips like these. She should never have gone thirty-two years without appreciating her own sexuality, he thought. And he was honored that she trusted him with it now.

She shifted restlessly. He felt the faint gyration of her body through his hand on her waist. He took that as a signal to move lower, his lips feathering across her jawline, then down the long, smooth column of her throat. Her breathing quickened. He felt her pulse flutter beneath the tip of his tongue.

"Tell me a story," he whispered as he dipped his head into the V of her soft chambray shirt and inhaled the fragrance of her skin.

"I can't ... talk."

"I don't want you remembering, Rainie. I want you in this moment with me." He picked up her left hand and placed her palm on his chest, where he knew his heart was racing. "Talk to me about anything you wish. You talk. I'll touch." His lips returned to her throat.

"Mmmmm, when I was a little girl"—her voice was husky—"I was ... going to be ... a gymnast. An Olympic athlete. Mmmm hmmmm."

"You have an athlete's body." He ran his hand down her side, appreciating the taut feel of her form. She was a runner, like him. He had a sudden image of their long, naked limbs intertwined on white cotton sheets and had to catch himself. Breathe deep. Take it slow.

"Did you take lessons?" he asked softly, his fingers finding the first button of her shirt and slipping it free.

"Lessons?"

"Gymnastics."

"Mmmmm ..."

He kissed the base of her throat.

"No ..."

"Watch competitions?" His lips whispered across her collarbone while his leg slipped between hers, supporting her weight and simultaneously making her gasp.

"I watched ... the Olympics ..."

"The Olympics are good," he said. He undid the final button on her shirt. The sides fell open. She shivered as the cooler air hit her skin, but didn't protest.

"Nadia Comaneci is my favorite," he said casually. He slid his hands inside her shirt. Her skin was warm and silky, stretched taut over her abdomen, tight around her waist. He stroked her sides, and she shifted restlessly against him.

"Favorite what?" she mumbled.

"Gymnast."

"Oh yeah ... that. Mmmmm."

He didn't take off her shirt. Instead, he resumed kissing her mouth, which was opening now, meeting his own advance, and beginning to counter. He trailed more kisses along her jaw, then nuzzled the curve of her ear. Her head turned. She drew him back to her lips, her hips moving faster against his leg, her tongue finally, tentatively, wrapping around his own.

His hands stroked up her spine. They found the clasp of her simple white bra. He let it go, and the undergarment sagged forward.

"I thought you were supposed to do that with one hand," Rainie whispered against his lips.

"I'm out of practice. Remind me next time, and I'll show off."

"Quincy?" she said softly. "Maybe ... maybe we should move to the bed."

He didn't need a second invitation. He scooped her up in his arms and headed for the queen-sized bed. At the last moment, he tripped over her shoes. They went down in a tangle of limbs, but managed to land on the down-covered bed. The comforter puffed up. The pillows went poof. Rainie laughed breathlessly. And Quincy found his face between her half-covered breasts. He had to kiss one, then the other. Then his mouth was on her nipple and far from pushing him away, her hands were urging him closer.

"Gymnastics," she was murmuring. "In this moment. Gymnastics, floor routines, balance beams. Quincy ..."

Her sigh undid him all over again. He wanted bare skin against bare skin, moan meeting moan. No rush, take it slow. If he didn't get his shirt off now, he was going to die.

He got his shirt off. He stripped off her loose top and dangling bra, then somehow he was on his back and she was on top of him, her pale white breasts pressed against the tanned expanse of his chest.

"I'm not thinking about the Olympics anymore," she whispered.

"What?" he muttered thickly.

"Exactly." She'd found the scar on his left shoulder. She kissed it. Then the small pucker down his arm. The other above his collarbone. "Who did this?"

"Jim Beckett."

"Did you kill him?"

"His ex-wife did."

"I like her." Her head trailed down. She rained tiny kisses across his rib cage, down to his abdomen, and he sucked in his breath sharply. Her hair tickled him. The good kind of tickle. God, she was killing him.

"Quincy," she said solemnly, "I don't want to be like my mother."

"You're not like your mother."

"Night after night. Guy after guy."

"If there's a new guy tomorrow night, I'll shoot him."

"All right then."

"Rainie?"

She placed a finger over his lips. "Don't say it," she murmured. "Save something for afterwards."

She slid off her jeans. She helped him shimmy out of his pants. Then she was on her back and he was poised above her. Her legs parted. Her hips lifted. He couldn't take his eyes off her face, filled with both delicate hope and grim resolution.

"Rainie," he whispered. "It's all right to enjoy life."

"I don't know how."

"Neither do I. We'll learn together."

Her legs wrapped around his. He gritted his teeth and eased in slowly. He tried to be gentle, but immediately, her body stiffened. A spasm moved across her features. He stilled, wanting so badly for it to be good for her, trying so hard to make it good for her. Breathe deep. Don't rush. And then a heartbeat later, her expression changed. Her body eased, adjusted. Wonder lit up her face. She shifted beneath him. Then again, then again.

"Easy …"

"Please … Now. Please!"

He bowed his head. He gave himself over to her and the feel of her hands urging his body. No more control. No more thoughts in his head. Rainie's cries. Rainie's body. Rainie's trusting gaze.

She cried out. Surprised. Ecstatic. He took one moment to enjoy the expression on her face. Then it was too much; he joined her in the dark, shuddering abyss.

Afterwards, Rainie fell asleep first. Quincy thought he would also doze, but found himself wide awake. The white down comforter was tangled around them. Sun streamed through the bank of windows. He lay on his back with Rainie's head resting upon his shoulder and her arm across his stomach. From time to time, he trailed his fingers down the bare curve of her shoulder and enjoyed the feel of her snuggling close.

He marveled at the sight of her sleeping. Her dark mahogany hair tousled around her pale face. Her long eyelashes like dark smudges against her cheeks. Her shell-pink lips slightly parted, as they uttered small, whispery breaths. Half woman, half child. All his.

His fingers brushed her arm again. She murmured something softly in her sleep.

"I'll never hurt you, Rainie," Quincy said quietly. Then his gaze went to the phone, which he knew would ring shortly. Back to the hunt, back to a psychopath's killing game.

He thought of his daughter, young and proud, sitting in a hotel room right now, diligently scouring financial records. He thought of Rainie, the tilt of her chin, the way she sparked a room just by sauntering through the door. He thought of himself, older, wiser, and determined to learn from his mistakes.

He reached a conclusion. Time to stop mourning the things he had lost. Time to start fighting for what he had left.

31

The Olsen Residence, Virginia

The chocolates arrived shortly after 3 p.m., marked for special Saturday delivery and borne up the steps by a bouncing, brown-suited UPS man with gorgeous hazel eyes. Mary signed for the chocolates, gave the man a wink, and felt even better when he blushed. She took the plain delivery box inside and eagerly opened it. A small dark green box sat nestled in a sea of gold foil paper. Not Godiva; she didn't recognize the name on the label.

She opened the inside box, and was immediately struck by the scent of bittersweet chocolate and almonds. Twelve truffles, she saw, four rows of three. Each one dusted in cocoa powder and topped with a candied nut. Beautiful box, beautiful truffles. She wondered if PIs got the munchies.

She put the lid back on while consulting her reflection in the mirror. The dark shadows beneath her eyes were now coated with a heavy layer of makeup. A pink silk cardigan covered her bruised arms. Hot rollers had done wonders with her hair. She looked fine, better than fine, actually. She looked lovely. The perfect doctor's wife, swathed in layers of Pepto-Bismol pink.

"Here goes nothing," she told her reflection. Then she grabbed the box of chocolates and headed out the door.

True to her lover's word, she found a silver hatchback two driveways down with a well-dressed black man sitting in the front. He appeared to be studying a road map. The minute he made eye contact with Mary, however, his gaze dashed frantically from side to side. She marched right up to the driver's side and rapped on the window.

"Howdy, darlin'," he said immediately, rolling down the glass. "I was hoping someone like you would come along. I have no idea where I am and could sure use some help." He held up the wrinkled map and flashed a helpless grin. She noticed, however, that his left foot was furiously kicking something beneath the driver's seat. Probably his surveillance camera.

"I know you're a private investigator," she said.

"I'm telling you, ma'am, you get on these windy back roads and suddenly everything looks alike—"

"Especially when you're seeing the same road for the second day in a row. May I?"

She gestured to the empty passenger seat. He blanched. "Now darlin', if you could just point out the quickest way to 1-95 ..."

"Fine, I'll show it to you on the map." She came around the front and climbed into the car before he could utter further protest.

Inside, the air was stifling. The cloth-covered seat pressed her dress uncomfortably against her skin; the dash was warm to the touch. Belatedly, she realized that she should've brought iced tea or lemonade. God knows who'd want candy in the middle of this kind of heat. Live and learn, she thought, and resolutely held up the green-wrapped box.

"I thought you might want a snack," she said, "so I brought you something."

"Ma'am—"

"I'm not an idiot. Please don't treat me like one. And for God's sake, it's only a box of chocolates."

"Chocolates?" The investigator's voice picked up in spite of himself. He shot her another wary look, then took the box from her hands. The minute he opened it, however, the odor of chocolate and almonds overwhelmed the tiny space. Too sweet, too strong for this kind of heat. He closed up the box immediately. Even she was grateful.

"Thank you, ma'am," he said politely. "I confess I have a bit of a sweet tooth, but maybe I'll pass for now. I had a big lunch." He stuck the green-wrapped box on the dashboard. They both stared at it.

"I'm Mary Olsen," she said finally, sticking out her hand, "but then, you must know that."

The man didn't seem to know what to do. "Phil de Beers."

"You work for my husband."

"Darlin', I'm just a man having a very bad day." He sighed heavily.

"My husband doesn't like me much," Mary volunteered. "When we first met, I was a lowly waitress, and boy was I flattered to meet him. He's a world-renowned neurosurgeon, you know. He saves lives, he helps young children. I'm very proud of his job."

Phil de Beers nodded miserably.

"When he asked me to marry him," she continued, "I thought I was the luckiest girl in the world. I didn't understand then, what it was he wanted. I didn't understand that he didn't like the way I dressed or talked or acted. I guess I was a little naïve, Mr. de Beers. I thought my husband asked me to marry him because he loved me."

"I am so lost," de Beers said, and this time, he might have been telling the truth.

"He thinks I'm cheating on him, doesn't he?" Mary said. She turned in her seat, looking the man in the eye. "He thinks I'm sneaking around, dating other men behind his back. Why? Because he leaves me alone all the time? Because he's cut me off from my family and friends? I have no job, sir. No life, no hobbies, nothing to do but flit around some big ol' empty house waitin' for my big ol' doctor husband to come home. Or did he tell you everything?"

She let the pink silk cardigan slip from her shoulder. De Beers's gaze fell immediately to the darkening bruise. His lips tightened, a muscle twitched in his jaw. Surely he felt sorry for her now. They could be allies. She, not her husband, would win. De Beers didn't say anything, though. The silence dragged out, then grew unbearable. Mary turned away, feeling suddenly desolate and overexposed. She pulled back up her cardigan and buttoned it around her neck.

"Maybe... maybe I'll have one of those chocolates now," she said in a small voice.

He handed her the box. She took it without looking at him. And then she knew she had him.

"You must have a chocolate, too," she said briskly. "I won't feel so guilty if I'm sharing the box with you." She handed him a truffle, took one for herself, and then returned the box to the dash. He couldn't back out now. Welcome to southern courtesy. She held up her truffle. He had no choice but to do the same. "Cheers," she told him. She popped the chocolate into her mouth. A moment later, Phil de Beers reluctantly followed suit.

She steeled herself for the taste of chemicals or something related to laxatives. It never came. The chocolate was nice—soft and freshly made, melting on her tongue. It was definitely flavored, some kind of liquor maybe, mixed with dark chocolate and almonds. Not bad. She swallowed the candy down, feeling encouraged.

De Beers had also eaten his, but now he was frowning. "Who makes these?"

"They're good, aren't they? Want another?"

"It's ... strong."

She nodded brightly, reaching for the box again, when she became aware of a slight burning sensation on her tongue. Her heartbeat tripled, her cheeks flushed. Suddenly, the car spun sickeningly, and she grabbed the dash for balance.

Across from her, Phil de Beers began to pant. As she watched, sweat burst from his pores. His dark eyes dilated, grew huge.

"Jesus, woman, what's in these things?"

She tried to answer, but her throat had caught on fire and she could feel moisture flecking across her face. Oh God, she was foaming at the mouth. Why? How? So dizzy. Not good. Not good.

"Hot," she whispered. "Hot ..."

She fumbled for the door handle. Popped it open. And he was standing there.

No, she cried, but the word remained in her head instead of uttering from her spittle-spewed lips. She tried to wave him away with her hand. *You mustn't be here. He'll see you and I already got him to eat a chocolate. Another hour, we'll be together. You'll kiss all my bruises away. You'll make me feel beautiful. Please ...*

Her lover didn't move, however. He was looking at her strangely. As if he'd never seen her before. As if he'd never held her in his arms or whispered sweet words of encouragement. His lips wore an icy smile. What had happened to his thick, dark hair?

She tried to speak again. She couldn't catch her breath. "Help," she tried to say this time. "Help." She reached out her hand to him.

Her lover turned away. She slowly followed his line of sight back into the car, where Phil de Beers now lay gasping over the steering wheel. He was looking at the man in horror while his right hand fumbled beneath the seat.

"Al—" the private investigator muttered. "Stupid bastard ... Almonds ... I gotta ..."

His hand reappeared, his arm trembling convulsively. And then Mary saw ... a gun. He held a gun.

No, Mary tried to yell to her lover, but couldn't. *Move, run, get away.* The warning never left her mouth. Her throat burned, burned, burned, the car spun, spun, spun. God, she had never felt such pain. *Help me, help me.*

Her hands wrapping around her stomach. *I'm sorry, I'm sorry, I'm sorry.*

Phil de Beers raised his shaking arm. His finger fumbled with the safety. He couldn't get it. He couldn't get it. His arm began to fall ...

Mary stared at him, and in the spinning, churning, burning car, their gazes finally locked. Funny, how he looked so apologetic, as if he had somehow let her down. An odd gargling sound came from his throat. His eyes rolled back. He slumped over the steering wheel, his gun tumbling to the floor as a wave of white foam gushed from his mouth.

Mary stared at the gun. Stared at the gun. And ...

Car ... spinning. *Hot. Can't breathe. Heart too fast.* Her hands clenching her stomach. *Almonds, almonds, why almonds? Hot. Makeup melting. Don't look at me. Don't look ...* Fading into the seat.

Her gaze rose to her lover's face. She stared at him, with his strange thinning hair, stared at him standing there and not making any move to help.

"It will be over soon." He checked his watch. "Another sixty seconds, I'd say. In all honesty, I'm surprised you've lasted this long. Then again, everyone reacts a bit differently."

Almonds, almonds, almonds ...

"Oh, did I forget to mention it on the phone? I changed my mind about the laxative. I injected one hundred fifty milligrams of hydrocyanic acid into the center of each chocolate instead. The smell is a bit much, but boy is it quick."

Her lips moved. He leaned down closer to hear. "Praying? *Praying?* Why Mary Margaret Olsen, did you forget? You betrayed your best friend. God's not going to have anything to do with you."

He straightened, the bright sunshine blazing behind him and turning him from a glorious man into an even more glorious avenging angel.

I loved you, she thought as her lungs froze up. And a heartbeat later, *I should've known. What other kind of man would have loved me?*

One last thought. The only thought she had left as her body began to convulse and her lungs fought for air.

"Yours," she whispered. "Y-y-yours."

He frowned. Then he followed the spasm of her hands around her belly and his eyes widened in stunned surprise. "No! No, no, no ..."

"Yours," Mary Olsen whispered one last time. And then her eyes rolled back into her head.

The man jumped forward. He dragged her out of the car. Down on the hot asphalt, he shook her shoulders and slapped her face. "Wake up! Goddammit, wake up! Don't you do this to me!"

Mary's arms fell limply to her sides. Her pulse was gone, her heart silent in her chest. Cyanide induced a horrible death, but, as he'd promised, it was swift. The man stared at the tiny mound of her belly. Something she would have told him about that afternoon when they were finally together again. She would've looked at him earnestly, so meek and desperate for reassurance. And he would've felt …

After all this time. Years of being alone, decades of having no family left.

"Son of a bitch," he whispered. And then more gutturally, "*Pierce Quincy, goddamn son of a bitch! Look at what you made me do! You'll pay! You'll pay … Now, now,* NOW!"

32

Kimberly reread the Miguel Sanchez file for the fourth time in two hours. Strands of fine blond hair kept working themselves loose from her hastily constructed ponytail and falling over her eyes. She impatiently brushed the strands back with her left hand. She should shower and change now that she had the hotel room to herself. She kept reading the file. Something was in here. She understood her father's point that his personal conversation with Sanchez was purely random. She understood that Special Agent Albert Montgomery's assignment to the case was most likely coincidental. But something was in here. She had her own instincts, and they were screaming at her to revisit Miguel Sanchez.

An odd sound came from the hallway outside her room. Slow, squeaking wheels laboriously rolling down the hall. Most likely some rusted-out metal cart. Kimberly frowned. She continued to read the file.

As a death row inmate in San Quentin, Sanchez now lived alone in a six-by-ten-foot cell. That ruled out the possibility of him having a roommate who might have been released and taken up efforts on his behalf. On the other hand, some condemned prisoners spent up to four hours a day in the rec yard with sixty other inmates, lifting weights, shooting hoops, and doing God knows what.

Kimberly delved deeper into Sanchez's file. According to San Quentin corrections officers, prisoners were classified as two types: Grade A or Grade B. Grade A covered prisoners who had assimilated well to prison life. They followed the rules, didn't give the guards any hassles, and were seen as successfully "programming." These inmates were eligible for privileges such as daily rec time with their fellow deviants.

Grade B inmates, on the other hand, were men who hadn't taken to their cells like hens to a chicken coop. They threatened corrections officers, they threatened each other, they actually inflicted physical harm. These men spent lots of quality time in ad seg—administrative segregation, according to the staff, or the hole according to the inmates. Miguel Sanchez was familiar with the hole. According to his file, he'd started out as a Grade B inmate, managed to calm down to Grade A status for about six months in 1997, then went back to his Grade B ways. In other words, Miguel should not have had the opportunity to make many friends in San Quentin. Then again, Richard Millos wound up dead while Sanchez was ad seg, which seemed to indicate that even the most severe type of incarceration had not rendered Sanchez powerless.

That damn squeaking was driving her nuts. Room service should oil the wheels of its carts. Something. Sheesh.

In the good news department, she had found tons of press on the convicted serial killer. Partnerships for psychopaths were unusual, and Sanchez had carved out quite a niche as a professional guinea pig for criminologists writing case studies on famous homicidal duos. The interviews probably helped Sanchez ease the boredom of his now tedious existence. They also allowed him to gloat, reliving the glory of the kill under the guise of an academic exercise.

As Kimberly learned, there had been a couple of male-female sexual-sadist killing teams, but in those cases, the female was completely subservient, more of a live-in victim than a live-in partner. Most psychopaths were loners with no genuine ability to relate to others and thus little need for any kind of relationship. In Miguel and Richie's case, experts theorized that the partnership was based on Miguel's interest in having an audience for his actions and Richie's complete willingness to do as he was told. Plus, Richie Millos genuinely feared his cousin. Most likely, Miguel fed off that, perhaps even found that element even more appealing than an extra pair of hands.

One criminologist had written that Richie represented Miguel's latent homosexual desires. When that criminologist had tried to interview Miguel again, the convicted murderer waited until he was locked in the visitor's room with his shackles removed, then dove at the researcher over the table and tried to strangle the man with his bare hands. Miguel had to be forcibly dragged out of the room by four prison guards. Apparently, Miguel didn't care to be labeled a latent homosexual.

One thing was clear: Miguel Sanchez was not a nice man. Kimberly had found a photo of him on-line. He had dark, wild hair only Charles Manson would love. His eyes were deeply sunk into his forehead, his cheekbones craggy. Tattoos riddled his shoulders, and according to one report, he continued to add to his body art while incarcerated with the aid of a needle and a ballpoint pen. He claimed to be a walking monument to his victims. Kimberly had stared at his photo three times before she realized what the elaborately scrolled design on his shoulder said. Then she had gone cold.

Amanda.

He had the name Amanda permanently etched into his body. Kimberly had to work on easing her heart rate again. She knew Miguel Sanchez's Amanda. A long time ago, she and Mandy had listened to the tape. One more link, however. One more link between a stone-cold psychopath and Kimberly's rapidly disintegrating family.

The squeaking was growing closer. Fuck, she couldn't think.

She got out of her chair, scowling at the door and the noise that was now right behind it. She didn't need this kind of distraction. She had a job to do. And as long as she kept focused, kept determined, she felt like her old self again. Capable, strong, self-possessed.

Funny how Mandy's death had sent her drifting, filled with too many conflicting emotions of rage and grief and fear. And ironic how her mother's murder had anchored her again, taking all of those same emotions and giving them a purpose. She was going to find this bastard. And she didn't care what Rainie said. She was going to kill him. Frankly, if he was anything like Miguel Sanchez, she wasn't going to feel bad about it either.

Darwinism, she thought. *Survival of the fittest. You take on me and my family, you'd better be prepared for the consequences. Because I've been training for this day since I was twelve, you son of a bitch. I won't go down easy.*

A knock sounded on the door. Standing just three feet away in the kitchenette, Kimberly froze. And that quickly, her confidence left her. The color leeched from her face, her heart ratcheted up to one hundred and fifty beats per minute, and sweat burst from her pores.

"Room service," a high squeaky male voice called out.

Room service. Oldest trick in the book. Kimberly ran into the bedroom. She fumbled through her bag, pulled out her stainless steel Glock, and sprinted back to the living area where she leveled her semiautomatic at the cheap wooden door.

"You got the wrong room, buddy," she yelled. "Back away from my door!"

There was a pause. Her hands were trembling so badly, she couldn't sight her gun. She was thinking: *Wednesday, my mom. Thursday, my grandpa. Friday, we're all on the run, and today? Not me! I won't go down easy!*

"Uh, I got an order here for your room—"

"Get the fuck away from my door!"

"Okey dokey. I'll be going now. You want your, uh, champagne and strawberries, you can come downstairs yourself, ma'am. Sheesh."

Kimberly heard squeaking again. Then a moment later, the same high-pitched voice muttering, "Gotta be a fucking full moon tonight or something. Sheesh."

She slowly lowered her gun. Her body was still shaking. Sweat had plastered her T-shirt to her skin. Her heart hammered fast, as if she'd been running a marathon.

She took a deep breath. Then another. Then another.

And then, still not feeling good about things, she got down on her hands and knees and peered beneath the door. No dark shadow of feet standing outside her door. She collapsed into a sitting position on the carpet, her Glock cradled in her lap.

"Oh yeah," she murmured darkly in the empty room, "I'm doing just fine."

"I'm thinking, no sickening-sweet pet names. Phrases that have been used on nighttime soaps do not belong in the home. Plus, if it's been used on a Hallmark card, I don't really think it applies to me. I'm not a Hallmark sort of gal. Though, for the record, I could probably learn to like flowers now and then. Pink roses. Or that champagne color. Yeah, I'm pretty sure I would like that. Of course, that raises the whole issue of chocolates and other special-delivery sweets. I'm going to say yes to the chocolates, no on the heart-shaped box. Things that involve red velvet also do not belong in the home. What do you think?"

Rainie was sprawled next to Quincy in the deep-pile comfort of her bed. They hadn't bothered getting dressed yet. It was a little after twelve, the sun was high in the sky and at any minute, her phone was bound to ring. Screw it.

Her head was on his shoulder and she was doodling little designs on his chest with her index finger. She liked the feel of his chest hairs, crisp but silky. She liked the way he smelled, aftershave mixed with sex. She liked the way he looked, his broad, well-toned chest like a vast plane beneath her hand. She was thinking she'd soon be ready for more talk of Olympic-medal events.

"Green-light flowers and square boxes of chocolate," Quincy dutifully repeated. "Red-light sickening-sweet pet names." His hand was stroking her hair; he was obviously in no rush to get up either. He tilted his head down to see her better. "For the sake of argument, what qualifies as a sickening-sweet pet name? I'd hate to think I was being cute and adorable, only to wind up dead."

"Sweetheart, cupcake, sugar pie, honey bunch," Rainie rattled off. "Sweetie pie, cutie pie ... You know, the kind of names that when other people use them, you want to give them a whopping dose of insulin ... or a smack on the head."

"No terms of endearment that owe their origin to the glucose family?"

"That's my stance. You don't call me sweet cheeks and I won't call you stud muffin."

"I don't know," Quincy said mildly. "I kind of like stud muffin ..."

She hit him on the chest. He pretended to be mortally wounded. She was just leaning over to kiss him back to life when the phone rang. She groaned.

"Carl Mitz," Quincy murmured.

"Gymnastics!" she countered.

"Later, I'm afraid."

"Spoilsport." Rainie reached over and grabbed the cordless phone off her nightstand. "Hello," she declared grumpily.

"Lorraine Conner. How nice to speak with you."

Rainie frowned. She didn't recognize the voice. Not at all. "Who is this?"

"You know who this is. I want to speak with Pierce."

Rainie looked questioningly at Quincy. If the caller wanted him, that ruled out Carl Mitz or her long-lost father. But hardly anyone called Quincy Pierce. So who ...

Shit. She bolted upright, covers falling away as her heart began to thud furiously. She knew who this was. "How the hell did you get this number?"

"Directory assistance, of course. Hand the phone to Pierce."

"Fuck you, asshole. I'm not doing anything you want."

"How marvelously childish. Hand the phone to Pierce."

"Hey, you call my number, you get to speak with *me*. So if you have something to say, I suggest you start talking or I'm hanging up." Her words ended in a screech; Quincy had grabbed the phone out of her hands. She was ready to battle him for it, but then she saw the steely look in his eyes.

He put the receiver to his ear. "Hello," he said evenly. "Who is this?"

"Pierce Quincy, of course. Would you like to see my driver's license? Or perhaps a sample of my handwriting?"

"Delusional disorder, subtype grandiose," Quincy said.

The man laughed. "As if to be Pierce Quincy is such a grand thing. Your daughter is dead, your wife is dead, and your father is no place to be found. You don't seem so powerful to me."

"I don't have a wife," Quincy said.

"Ex-wife then," the man granted graciously. "Still demoting her even after she's gone. You are a cold fish."

"What do you want?" Quincy shifted the phone to his other ear. He caught Rainie's eye and made a circular motion with his hand. She nodded immediately, and slid off the bed naked in search of a tape recorder.

"It's not what I want, Pierce, it's *who* I want. But all in good time. Would you like to speak with your father?"

"We both know he's dead."

"You don't know that. You're assuming he's dead so you won't feel guilty. I understand he raised you all by himself, served as both mother and father. And yet how quickly you let him go. 'My father has been checked out of his nursing home? Goodness gracious, let me run away and hide!' I expected more from you."

"I doubt it."

Rainie arrived with the tape recorder. Quincy held the phone out for better audio as she fumbled with the buttons, then began to tape.

"He's alive," the man said. "Well hidden from federal minions and quite querulous, but very much alive."

Quincy didn't answer.

"Maybe we can arrange a swap. You can exchange your daughter for your father. She's younger, but in his current state he's more of a child."

Quincy didn't say anything.

"Or maybe we should bring the lovely Lorraine into the mix. You can swap your lover for your father. Sure she has a nice ass, but we both know you don't keep women around for long. Does she moan for you, Pierce? Your wife moaned for me. So did your daughter."

"How is the weather in Texas?" Quincy asked. Rainie looked at him in confusion. Then she remembered. Mickie Millos lived in Texas. Quincy was fishing.

"Texas? You aren't on the right track."

"And what track would that be? The one where I ruined your career, destroyed your life? Interesting, that I could have such an impact on your life and not remember you at all. Guess it was all in a day's work. I have met so many incompetent criminals over the years." Quincy's voice was light, goading.

In contrast, the man's voice gained an ugly edge. "Don't fuck with me, Pierce. There are plenty of people in your life left to kill, and I can make it better for them, or worse."

Quincy feigned a yawn. "Now you're boring me."

"Will I be boring when I touch your daughter? Will I be boring when I rip off her shirt and run my hands over her tomboy breasts? I'm much closer than you know."

"You won't touch my daughter."

"Going to protect her, proud papa?"

"I won't have to. Get within four feet, and she'll kick your balls into your throat."

The man laughed. "Funny," he said. "That's not what Bethie or Mandy did."

For the first time, Quincy's grip tightened on the phone.

"Pierce," the man said, "intermission is over. If you won't go back home for your father, I'll just have to find somebody else to kill. You have one hour to get on a plane headed to Virginia."

"I don't think so."

"Then I will make her death very long and excruciatingly painful."

"You can't touch my daughter—"

"It's not Kimberly I'm going to punish. Get to the airport, Supervisory Special Agent Quincy—you don't have many friends left. Oh, and please tell Ms. Conner that next time she hires a private investigator, she should find one who doesn't like chocolate."

The line clicked off. Quincy stared at Rainie. There was a fierceness in his expression she had seen only once before—the night Henry Hawkins had tried to kill her.

"He's coming after you," he said.

She shook her head. "No, not me. Think about his words, Quincy. He wants you home. He's obviously gotten to de Beers. That means East Coast. He's still somewhere around Virginia."

"But who ..."

They got it together. "Glenda!" Quincy swore.

"We have one hour."

Quincy picked up the phone and dialed furiously.

33

"Get out of the house."

"Pierce? I don't think—"

"Glenda, listen to me. The UNSUB just called. He wants me back on the East Coast and he's prepared to kill someone to force me to return. He's targeting you. I'm almost sure of it. Now, please get out of the house."

Glenda's grip tightened on the phone. Alone in the middle of Quincy's office, she stared at the incriminating box of stationery—one sheet already sent to the document section of the science-crime lab—and she wished... She wished she had never taken this goddamn case.

"I don't think I should be speaking with you," she said quietly.

"Is Montgomery there?"

"That's none of your business."

"You're alone, aren't you? Dammit, how did he even qualify to be an agent? Glenda, the UNSUB knows where I live. He understands Bureau protocol, so he knows someone is manning my residence. Hell, for all I know, he also has knowledge of the layout of my home, the best way of scaling the fence, accessing the grounds ... You cannot underestimate him."

"Your phantom stalker," she said.

Quincy fell silent. *Good,* she thought. *Be surprised. I have lived in this house for three days, listening to nothing but hate, and now I have to wonder if it hasn't all been some horrible, twisted game. Are you the hunter or the hunted, Pierce? I don't know anymore, and I'm tired!*

"What's wrong, Glenda?" Quincy asked. He sounded wary now, uncertain. She took pride in that.

"There's no such thing as a perfect crime, Quincy. You should know that better than most. For every little detail that is considered, there is always one or two more that slips through the cracks."

"The police report came back from Philadelphia, didn't it? They know the note found at the scene matches my handwriting."

"What?"

He fell silent again. She could practically feel his confusion across the phone line. It was nothing, however, compared to the sudden acceleration of her heart. She'd still maintained some small residue of doubt about Quincy's guilt. But now ... That note, that dreadful note stuffed in Elizabeth Quincy's abdominal cavity, soaked in blood. He had written it. Pierce Quincy, a fellow agent, the best of the best. *Oh sweet mother of God ...*

"You're a monster," she breathed. "Montgomery is right. You're a monster!"

"Glenda—"

She snapped her cell phone shut. She let it fall to the floor where she eyed it as if it were a coiled snake. She had goose bumps running up and down her arms. She had gone nights without sleep and she could now feel it all crashing down on her. She was cold, she was horrified. She had believed in this man. Oh God, she was never going to feel clean.

On the floor, her flip phone started to chime.

She didn't answer it. She wasn't going to let him manipulate her like this. The musical ringing went on for ten seconds, then voice messaging took over and the noise stopped. She had just started to relax, when it started again. And went on and on and on.

Dammit! She snatched back up the phone.

"I don't believe you!" she cried. "You're making this up. And I am armed, Quincy, so you just stay the fuck away from me."

"I am in Oregon. I can't hurt you," he said.

"I don't know that!"

"Listen to me. We don't have much time, Glenda. I did not write that note. I know it looks bad, but I did *not* write that note."

"Of course you did. You just said so."

"*I know my own handwriting!* For God's sake, I recognized it the minute the ME's assistant brought the note into the room. But I did not write it, Glenda. This man, he got copies of my handwriting, he studied it, he did one hell of a superb impression. I don't know exactly how he did it. But *he* did it, not me."

"Listen to yourself, Quincy. 'It's my writing, but I didn't do it.' Things are unraveling and you're not even lying very well anymore."

"Glenda, *why* would I use my own script? I am a professional. I've taken classes on how to analyze handwriting. If I'm so smart, why would I be so dumb?"

"Maybe you're not dumb. Maybe you're arrogant. Besides, it's not just that note. We've also traced the original newsletter ad. We know it was sent on your stationery."

"The bottom drawer," he murmured. "Christ, it's been years ..." And then, "Dammit, then he's definitely been in my house. Glenda, I beg you, get out of there."

"I'm not listening to you." Her voice was rising hysterically. In spite of herself, her gaze had gone to the uncovered windows. She felt suddenly vulnerable, a lone woman standing in a fishbowl. What if Quincy was already out there? Or the phantom stalker or maybe more rattlesnakes? God knows. She was tired. She was so tired. Where was Montgomery? She was not herself.

"Think, Glenda," Quincy was saying relentlessly. "You are a bright agent, you are a brilliant agent. And so am I. So why would I create such an elaborate stalking story, then use my own stationery for the newsletter ads? Why would I stage such a brutal murder in Philadelphia, then use my own handwriting? Why would I even commit these crimes? What would I have to gain?"

"Showing off. Cracking up. Maybe the job has finally done you in."

"I haven't been out in the field in years."

"Maybe you resent that."

"So I butchered my own family? Fifteen minutes, Glenda. Please get out of the house. I'm begging you, *get out of the house*."

"I can't," she whispered.

"Why not?"

"I … I think someone may already be out there."

"Oh Glenda …" She heard him take a shaky breath. He was murmuring to someone at the other end of the line. She caught the distinct tones of a female reply. Lorraine Conner. So they were in this together.

For the first time, Glenda frowned. They were in this together? What together? Murdering his family? Threatening a fellow agent? It didn't make much sense. And who sent an ad on hundred-dollar stationery anyway? A criminal mastermind who was provocatively stupid?

Holding the phone, Glenda moved out of the office, into the kitchen where she had a better view of the entrance and was framed by fewer windows. She unsnapped her shoulder holster. Then she reached down to her ankle and checked on her backup piece. Quincy returned to the line.

"You're going to be okay, Glenda," he said firmly. "I'm going to get you through this. First, I'm going to play a tape for you. Rainie made this recording just twenty minutes ago, sitting beside me in her loft in Portland. This is the UNSUB, Glenda. If you still don't believe me, hear for yourself what he has to say."

Glenda heard a click. Then a fuzzy recording filled her ear. She needed about three minutes of the conversation. Somewhere about the time the man said, *Then I will make her death very long and excruciatingly painful*, she had had enough. Quincy was right, the evidence against him was *too* perfect and they had still uncovered no good reason for a highly respected federal agent to suddenly begin butchering his entire family.

Which meant the stalker did exist. A man who thought nothing of killing an agent's young daughter. A man who had viciously slaughtered the agent's ex-wife. And a man who had topped it all off by kidnapping, and probably murdering, the agent's sick, Alzheimer's-stricken father. Oh God …

"All right," she said quietly. "What do we do?"

"Do you have a car outside?"

"Not on the driveway. Down the street."

"How far away?"

"Three to four minutes."

"You can do this, Glenda. Think of it as a training exercise in Hogan's Alley. Take out your Smith & Wesson, undo the safety, and run like hell. You'll make it."

"No."

"Glenda—"

"There's no cover, Quincy. He could be out there anywhere, behind a neighbor's bush, up a tree. Your property offers nothing. The minute I'm out of the front door, he has me. No, I'm safer in here than out there."

"Glenda, he *knows* the house. Inside you're trapped. Outside you have options."

"Outside he can pick me off. Inside I can at least see him coming. Besides, we changed the security system of your home. He has to have a fingerprint and an access code now. That will hold him up, buy me some time." Her eyes were on the kitchen window. She had her 10mm out. Working on the safety. Her hands were sweating badly. She fumbled the piece.

"He'll have a plan for the security system. He's had a plan for everything thus far."

Glenda finally got her pistol secure in her grasp. She forced herself to take a deep breath and steady her nerves. "Remember his MO," she told Quincy briskly. "The UNSUB relies on his gift for manipulating people. Well, the computerized system could care less. It has no deep dark secrets to exploit and it will not accept a severed digit."

"Call for backup." Quincy remained urgent.

"Fair enough."

"How long before they arrive?"

"Five to ten minutes. No more."

"If he gets there first ... Remember his strengths. Do not let him talk. Shoot first, question later. Promise me, Glenda."

Glenda nodded into the phone as she reached for the radio to summon her fellow agents. Just as she was about to click it on, however, Quincy's home line began to ring. Another admirer, she thought. Just what her nerves needed at a time like this. But then the machine picked up, and the voice was not a stranger's. It was Albert Montgomery and he did not sound like himself at all.

"Jesus Christ, Glenda," he wailed. "Pick up the goddamn phone. I've been trying to reach you on your cellular ... I was wrong. Not a phantom stalker. He's here, he's here, he's here. Oh God, he has a knife!"

She heard Quincy screaming something in her ear. She wasn't paying attention anymore. She dropped her flip phone on the marble countertop. She reached over with her right hand. She grabbed Quincy's white cordless phone and ...

The pain was instantaneous and intense. Deep, searing heat as if someone had branded her hand with a red-hot iron. She cried out. She dropped the cordless phone on the floor. And in the next moment, she heard the *beep beep* of someone disarming the security system, followed by a click as the front door swung open.

She looked over at her 10mm, within easy reach. She looked down at her right hand, seared by some sort of acid, now bubbling up with blisters, her fingers impossible to move.

"I'm sorry, Quincy," she murmured.

Then she watched Special Agent Albert Montgomery walk into the kitchen holding his cell phone in one hand and his 10mm in the other.

"Surprise, baby! It's me!"

The last sound Quincy heard was gunfire. And then nothing but his own desperate voice, "Glenda, Glenda! Talk to me. *Talk to me!*"

Quincy hung his head. His breath came in ragged gasps. The disconnected phone had fallen from his fingertips and now lay on Rainie's bed. *He must stay in control*, he thought. Now more than ever ... Rainie's arms were around his shoulder. She had not spoken, but there were tears on her cheeks.

"I should call Everett," he murmured. "Get agents over there. Maybe ..."

Rainie didn't say anything. Like him, she didn't really believe that Glenda was still alive.

Quincy took a deep breath, and reached for the phone just as it began to ring. He picked it up slowly, figuring he knew who this would be, and already steeling himself for the man's mocking tone.

"I shot Special Agent Montgomery," Glenda Rodman said without preamble.

"Glenda? Oh thank God!"

"He put ... something on the phone. Last time he was here, I suppose. He thought it would disable me. Stupid bastard. He should have read my file more closely. My father was a cop—he believed strongly in being able to shoot ambidextrously. You never know which hand will wind up free under fire."

"You're okay?"

"Albert's shooting skills are equal to the rest of him," she said dryly. "My right hand needs immediate medical attention. Other than that, I'll live."

"And Special Agent Montgomery?"

"I aimed to kill."

"Glenda—"

"I disabled him with shots to his kneecap and his right hand instead; I know you need answers. Quincy, he says he'll only speak with you. He says he knows where your father is. You need to get back here ASAP. At least, before I change my mind and start shooting again."

"Glenda," he tried again.

"You're welcome," she said. And hung up the phone.

34

Back at the hotel, Quincy swiftly threw his clothes into his travel bag. Rainie was in the living room, talking to Virginia state trooper Vince Amity on the phone. Kimberly, on the other hand, stood watching him from the doorway, her shoulders hunched as if preparing for a blow. She'd had a run-in with room service while he and Rainie had been gone. Apparently, an over-worked bellhop had transposed two numbers and tried to deliver someone else's anniversary surprise to Kimberly's room. The bellhop had hoped for a good tip. Instead, he'd encountered a screaming woman who—fortunately unknown to him—was brandishing a loaded semiautomatic.

The hotel had explained the mixup to Quincy upon his return. He'd relayed the story to Kimberly. She'd smiled in an attempt to find humor in the situation, but Quincy could tell the incident had left her shaken, and news of Glenda's attack had only further frayed her nerves.

"So Special Agent Rodman is all right?" Kimberly asked for the third time. Her voice had taken on the anxious edge he remembered from two days ago. Nothing he'd offered in the last ten minutes seemed to change it.

"Special Agent Rodman is an extremely capable woman," Quincy said, trying a new tack as he rounded up his socks. "She took her training seriously, and when the moment came, that training paid off. She not only met the threat, but she took out Montgomery with two clean shots."

"She must be an excellent marksman."

"I believe she's won a few medals."

"I'm a good shot," Kimberly said. "I practice three times a week."

Quincy raised his head and met his daughter's eyes. He said firmly, "You're going to be fine, Kimberly. Rainie is staying here with you, and you're a capable young woman. You'll be safe."

Kimberly's gaze fell to the floor. She was gnawing on her bottom lip; he couldn't tell if he had reached her or not.

"What about Special Agent Rodman's hand?" she asked.

"I don't know. Montgomery confessed that he sprayed the phone with Teflon to protect the plastic, then applied hydrofluoric acid, which is an extremely corrosive chemical. The acid reacted with the moisture of Glenda's hand, burning her fingers and part of her palm. I'm not sure of the long-term prognosis."

"It's her right hand. She could be permanently damaged, or scarred."

"She's receiving the best medical attention you can get. I'm sure she'll recover."

"But you don't know—"

"Kimberly!" he said sharply. "Albert was going to kill her. You know that, I know that, she knows that. Instead, she controlled her fear and pain and disabled her attacker. This is a triumph. This is a lesson in the value of hard work and proper training. Don't give this victory away. Don't demoralize yourself like that."

"I don't want you to go," she whispered.

Quincy closed his eyes. The irritation drained from his body. He felt simply rotten instead. "I know," he said softly.

"It's just ... So you have Albert in custody. So he went after Glenda. There's still something wrong ... something else going on. If Albert looks the way you say he does, I can't see him getting anywhere near Mom. Plus, there's the matter of brainpower. If Albert was this clever, he wouldn't have had problems at the Bureau in the first place. Don't you think?"

"He fits the description of the man in Mandy's AA group," Quincy said, though he knew that wasn't really an answer.

His daughter knew it too. She gazed at him miserably, obviously needing more than he was giving. He wished he knew what to do at times like this. He wished he knew how to make his daughter feel safe and confident and strong. And then he really did miss his ex-wife, because Bethie had always been better at these moments than him. He held a doctorate in psychology. Bethie, on the other hand, had been a mom.

"I love you, Kimberly," he said.

"Dad—"

"I don't want to go. Maybe sometimes it seems that I do. Maybe we both mistake my sense of duty for desire. But it is duty. Montgomery has information about Grandpa that I need to know and he claims he'll only give that information to me. It's been forty-eight hours, Kimberly. If we don't find Grandpa soon ..." His voice trailed off. His daughter had taken law enforcement classes; he knew that she understood as well as he did how the probability of finding Abraham alive decreased with each passing hour. The UNSUB had claimed that Abraham was tucked away safely. Quincy, however, had subsequently learned a new detail. He'd called Everett after he'd gotten off the phone with Glenda. The red Audi TT convertible had been found by Virginia state police at four that morning. It had been left parked in the exact spot where Mandy had hit a telephone pole fourteen months before. Forensic technicians found traces of urine in the passenger's seat, probably from Abraham. Extra personnel had now been brought in to scour the surrounding woods. They were also using dogs—cadaver dogs.

"There's a good chance that Montgomery planned this whole thing," Quincy said now, his voice purposefully firm. "He hated me because of the Sanchez case, he plotted revenge. If that's the case, then it's over, Kimberly. You're safe now. Everything will be all right."

"Then why won't you let us go with you?" she protested.

"Because I'm not one hundred percent certain, and I'm not going to risk you without being completely sure! Until we know everything, you're safer here than there."

"But what about you? You're returning to the East Coast, where some man knows all about you."

"I've also had a lot of training."

"Mom is *gone!*" Kimberly exclaimed. "Mandy is gone! Grandpa is gone! And now you're leaving, and, and, and ..."

Quincy finally got it. His daughter wasn't seeking reassurance for her own safety. She was terrified for *him.* She'd already lost most of her family and now her good old dad was once again walking out the front door into the face of danger. Christ, sometimes he was an idiot about the most basic things.

Quincy came around the bed. He took Kimberly into his arms, and for once, his stubborn, independent daughter did not protest. "I'm not going to let anything happen to me," he whispered against the top of her head. "I promise you that."

"You can't make that promise."

"I am Quantico's best of the best. I can, too."

"Dad—"

"Listen to me, Kimberly." He pulled back enough to look her in the eye, to let her see how serious he was. "I'm a good agent. I take my training seriously; I do not underestimate my opponent. This is a game, but it's a game where the stakes are life or death. I never forget that. And because I never forget that, I'm better at this than most."

Her blue eyes were still watery. He could tell she was on the brink of crying, but she sniffed back her tears. "You won't let down your guard?" she pressed. "You won't be fooled by anything this Albert guy says?"

"I am going to keep myself safe so I can come home to my daughter. And you are going to take good care of yourself and Rainie, so I can come home to you."

"We'll look out for each other."

"Kimberly, thank you."

From the doorway, Rainie cleared her throat. Quincy looked up, and knew instantly from the expression on her face that she had bad news. He took a deep breath. Then slowly, reluctantly, he let his daughter go.

"I have an update from Virginia," Rainie said as Quincy and Kimberly turned to face her.

Quincy nodded. "Go ahead."

"Phil de Beers and Mary Olsen are dead. The police found their bodies an hour ago in a car just down the road from Mary's house. The car was registered in Phil's name. We'll need the medical examiner's report to be sure, but the police are guessing poison. The bodies have white foam around the mouth. There's a strong smell of almonds ..."

"Cyanide," Quincy deduced.

She nodded grimly. "They found a box of chocolates in the car. Two are gone. The rest have that same bitter almond scent. According to the butler, Mary accepted a delivery shortly before leaving the house. He found the empty shipping box in the foyer, no return address."

"So someone sent Mary a box of poisoned chocolates and she took them to de Beers? But why did she eat one, too? That doesn't make any sense." Kimberly looked baffled.

"For the sake of argument," Quincy said slowly, "let's assume Montgomery spotted de Beers conducting surveillance on Mary. Mary probably knew Montgomery through Amanda, so now Albert has two loose ends. An accomplice who can connect him with the murders and a private investigator watching the accomplice. He doesn't have a lot of time, but he must do something."

"He poisons the box of chocolates," Rainie murmured, "sends them to Mary, and makes up some story that convinces her to share them with de Beers. Not bad really. Eliminates two people without burning a lot of time or resources. You're right, Quincy, this guy is an efficiency freak."

"Death by UPS," Kimberly said. Her shoulders sagged.

Rainie shot her a look. "Hey, Kimberly, if Montgomery is so good, why is he the one in FBI custody? He might be efficient, but we're the ones who won the war."

"Tell that to Phil de Beers."

Rainie's lips tightened. She turned on her heels and marched back into the living room. A second later, Quincy heard the sound of wood snapping. She had finally found his stash of #2 pencils in his computer case. From here on out, he would apparently be taking notes in pen.

"I guess I shouldn't have said that," Kimberly murmured after a moment.

"No, you shouldn't have."

"I'm sorry—"

"I'm not the one to whom you should be apologizing." His voice came out too harsh. Kimberly instantly looked stricken. Quincy repressed a sigh. He wasn't used to Kimberly being this sensitive. Then again, she had never lived under the threat of immediate death before.

"Kimberly," he said more patiently, "Rainie hired Phil de Beers. She met with the man. She gave him an important assignment, which means she trusted and liked him. She is not going to cry into her coffee right now because she knows the situation is still live and she can't afford that luxury. But don't think she doesn't have feelings. And don't lash out at her, just because you feel helpless."

"I'm sorry. I'm just … I don't know myself anymore!" Kimberly's voice rose, the full force of her anxiety now flooding to the surface. She stepped away from him, rubbing her arms compulsively and shaking her head. "I'm tense, I'm moody. One moment I feel strong and in control. I can meet this challenge, I can take this man! The next moment I'm shaking in my boots, drawing down on room service and mistrusting every noise I hear. I can't stand this level of uncertainty. I hate doubting myself, I hate worrying about what's going to happen next. I'm not supposed to fall apart like this, Dad. I'm supposed to be *strong!*"

"Are you having panic attacks again?" Quincy asked immediately. "Do you feel as if you're being watched?"

She drew up short. "No …" she said slowly. "In fact, I haven't felt that prickly sensation since we came here."

"Good." Quincy started breathing again. "You are strong, Kimberly," he said evenly. "You are doing remarkably well for everything you've been through."

"Do you feel like you're falling apart?" she demanded. "Are you swamped by anxiety, do you jump at shadows, are you tempted to open fire on room service waiters?"

"No, but I've been doing this kind of work for over fifteen years."

"Dad, does it frighten you?"

"What?"

"To feel so comfortable in the face of so much death?"

He bent down and kissed her cheek. "Yes, Kimberly. Sometimes it frightens me to death." He moved back to his duffel bag. "Help me pack, sweetheart. The only way out of this is to keep moving forward. So let's keep moving, one step at a time and then one step beyond that."

Kimberly nodded. She uncrossed her arms. She took a deep breath and picked up one of his shirts. And she looked so determined, it made Quincy's heart ache all over again. He lowered his head so she could not see his eyes.

He had lied to his daughter. He didn't think Albert Montgomery had masterminded this elaborate plan. He didn't think it was safe to head back East. Instead, he was absolutely certain he was once again being manipulated, but he didn't know what else he could do. Damned if he did, damned if he didn't. Fifteen years of being the best of the best and now he was being played like a toy violin.

There had to be another option. There was always another option …

"I couldn't uncover anything interesting on Millos," Kimberly spoke up. "He doesn't even have that much money in the bank. Most of the searches I did just kept bringing up Miguel Sanchez. The man has spawned even more case studies than Bundy."

"His partnership was unusual," Quincy said.

"Maybe not anymore," Kimberly murmured.

He didn't pretend to misunderstand her. His bag was full. He zipped it up, then finally met his daughter's waiting gaze.

"Maybe you could do me a favor," he said casually. "You have a good memory. Perhaps you could make a list of everyone you knew in your childhood, friends of yours, friends of the family. You know, the people we knew when your mother and I were still married."

Kimberly looked at him. He hadn't fooled her. After a moment, she nodded wordlessly.

"Hey Kimberly," he called softly. "Fuck ballet."

Her gaze remained somber, but then finally, slowly, she smiled.

Minutes later, Rainie and Quincy rode the elevator down to the lobby to hail a cab for the airport. Kimberly had tactfully agreed to stay upstairs in the room, seeming to understand that they might want a moment alone. Quincy figured there was something profound he should say to Rainie. All he could think was no sickening-sweet pet names.

In the lobby, Rainie glanced at her watch. "Two hours," she said, "not one."

"And yet I'm heading home."

"Intermission is over," she agreed.

"Rainie—"

"I won't let anything happen to Kimberly," she interjected quietly. "You have my word."

He nodded. He had figured that Rainie also realized that Montgomery was a long shot for a lone gunman.

Say something. Do something. Learn from your mistakes. Quincy heard himself murmur weakly, "Take care of yourself."

"I'm not the one walking into the lion's den." Rainie jerked her head toward a cab that had just appeared on the street. Quincy flagged it down, and before he was really ready, the driver was out of the car and taking his bag.

"I'll call you," he said.

"At my loft, not here. Just to be safe."

"Agreed." The cab driver had the back door open. He looked at Quincy impatiently. Quincy, however, was still gazing at Rainie. His chest felt tight. He knew now what he needed to say, then realized he couldn't utter the words. They would make the moment too final. They would reveal too much of his fear.

Rainie seemed to understand. She leaned forward and before he could react, she kissed him quick and hard on the mouth.

"Hey Quince. See you soon." She walked back into the hotel. A moment later, Quincy got into the cab.

"Airport," he told the driver.

Then, alone in the backseat ... "Hey Rainie," he whispered. "I love you, too."

At three P.M., Rainie finally heard back from Carl Mitz on her home answering machine. She listened to it from the hotel room as she called in to check messages. Kimberly sat at the table in the kitchenette, hunched over Quincy's laptop and rereading some report on Miguel Sanchez that was making her scowl. Rainie occupied the sofa in the adjoining living room, restless since Quincy's departure, feeling not at all like herself.

Mitz informed her answering machine that he'd just gotten her message on his cell phone. He would be available for the next few hours if she wanted to call back. Rainie hung up, then glanced at Kimberly.

"What would you think if I arranged a meeting with Ronald Dawson for tomorrow?" Rainie asked quietly.

Kimberly looked up from the computer. "I think Special Agent Albert Montgomery is a putz," she said.

"Me, too."

"I think he couldn't have reached my mother with a ten-foot pole, which means while he might be an Indian, he's definitely not Chief."

"Agreed."

"And I think ... I think if Ronald Dawson *is* the head honcho, well, if you invite him here, then he can't be there in Virginia."

"My thoughts exactly."

"Set up lunch," Kimberly said firmly. "Then call your sheriff friend and get out your gun."

Rainie grinned. "Girl," she said, "I like your style."

Three-thirty P.M., Rainie reached Carl Mitz. Three-forty P.M., Quincy arrived at the Portland International Airport. Three forty-five P.M., Sheriff Luke Hayes received a phone call. He spoke for approximately fifteen minutes, then hung up the phone, told Cunningham he was leaving him in charge, and got into his car.

It wasn't perfect, but it was a plan.

35

"Here's what you need to know, Quincy." Glenda snapped open a manila file, stuck a pen behind her ear, then resumed pacing the eight-foot length of the narrow conference room. He watched her restless movements without commenting. It was nearly 3 p.m. Sunday afternoon, almost twenty-four hours since Montgomery's attack, and they were still denied access to the disgruntled agent. First Montgomery claimed he needed immediate medical attention. Given the state of his kneecap and right hand, that was hard to dispute. The trip to the emergency room had been followed by surgery to repair the damage to his leg. The doctors had then said he needed time to recover from the anesthesia. The anesthesia, however, had been followed by large amounts of morphine personally requested by Montgomery. He was in a significant amount of pain, he claimed. He needed drugs, he needed medical assistance, he needed rest.

He couldn't be properly interviewed while under the influence of medication and they all knew it. Even if they forced the issue, the first judge who heard the case would toss his comments out of court.

Albert Montgomery had an aptitude after all. He could stall like nobody's business. And as each hour passed, they grew increasingly nervous. Something big was brewing. They could feel it.

"Stop fidgeting," Glenda said.

He looked down to find himself methodically twisting the top button of his suit jacket, and instantly jerked his hand away. Glenda had met him with fresh clothes first thing this morning. As a general rule, wearing a nicely tailored suit made him feel polished, more in control. Not today. As hour grew into hour, he could've sworn the necktie was conspiring to strangle him.

He wondered how Rainie was doing. He wished it felt safe to call.

Glenda had returned her attention to the manila file. Her right hand was heavily bandaged. Late last night, she'd been treated for third-degree burns, then released. She couldn't move her fingers yet, and the doctors had warned her that the deep-searing acid might have caused permanent nerve damage. Time would tell and at this stage of the game, she didn't seem to want to talk about it.

"Albert first crossed paths with you fifteen years ago on the Sanchez case," she said briskly. "For the record, he'd already received a less-than-stellar review for his prior work, but it was his inept profile of Sanchez that officially torpedoed his career. He fought with the locals, pegged Sanchez as a

213

lone gunman, then lost all credibility when you came aboard, identified the work as part of a killing team, and cracked the case. Albert's wife left him three weeks later, taking the two kids with her. Doesn't look like they were big fans of weekend visitation either."

"He fits the profile," he said hoarsely.

"The *circumstances* fit the profile," Glenda said. "Now let's look at the man. According to Albert's file, his IQ is a respectable one hundred thirty. The problem seems to be in execution. What do they call that these days? Why an idiot can build a successful business while a genius can't even find his socks?"

"EQ—emotional intelligence." His voice was still rough.

"Emotional intelligence." Glenda rolled her eyes. "That's it. Albert has none. According to four different case reviews, he lacks focus, diligence, and basic organizational skills. In his twenty-year career at the Bureau, he's been written up six times. In each case, he's written a counter opinion stating that he's not incompetent after all, Supervisor So-and-So is simply out to get him."

"Albert Montgomery, a walking advertisement for government downsizing."

Glenda finally smiled. "If you can get that made into a bumper sticker, I'll put it on his car." Her expression sobered. "Before we write off Albert completely," she said, "there is another factor to consider: While Albert may not be the sharpest tool in the shed, he has had plenty of free time on his hands. The estimated time of death for Elizabeth is ten-thirty P.M., Wednesday. Albert has no alibi for that time. Furthermore, he claims he spent Thursday and Friday in Philadelphia assisting the local detectives. Not true. I followed up with the detectives—they only saw him Friday morning. The rest of his time—basically Wednesday afternoon through Saturday morning—is an open question. Which means he could've visited Mary Olsen in Virginia or shown up at a Rhode Island nursing home, or flown to the West Coast for a Portland rendezvous. We simply don't know."

"Travel records, plane tickets, hotel stays?"

"Checked with his credit cards—nothing. Checked with the local airport, nothing. Of course, there are roughly half a dozen airports within a three-hour drive of here. He could've left from any one of those, paying cash and/or using an assumed name." Glenda smiled. "Welcome to the convenience of the Eastern Corridor."

"And even if he lacks focus, seventy-two hours provides plenty of time for misdeeds." He grimaced, then caught himself and said more crisply, "What about financial resources?"

"Albert is currently proud owner of nine hundred dollars in his bank account, so while he's had time to run around the country, financially I'm not sure how he could've pulled it off. On the other hand, if he has been traveling he's been paying in cash, so it's possible a second person has funded his venture with a briefcase of money. Without access to the second person's accounts, it's impossible to know."

"Smart, but lazy. Poor, but possibly funded by vengeful deviants-R-us. Wonderful."

"At the very least," Glenda said, "we know Albert has been actively involved in positioning you as a suspect. He called Everett Friday night, saying that he's convinced you killed your ex-wife. Then he made a point of visiting me first thing Saturday morning to let me know all his doubts about the Philadelphia crime scene."

"Poisoning the well."

"He was extremely persuasive," Glenda said quietly. "Everett was strongly considering calling you in. In fact, the only reason he didn't is that Albert's credibility is an issue. That wouldn't have mattered much longer, however. Albert got me wondering, which is what he intended. I found the stationery in your desk, messengered a sheet over to the lab ...That report should come back any time now, confirming the original ad was sent on your stationery. Once that report arrived, Everett would have no choice but to ask you to turn yourself in. Plus, Albert's accusation and the subsequent finding of your stationery made me seriously doubt you, which set everything up for act two."

"You turning up dead."

"In your home, protected by a state-of-the-art security system to which you have access. And, if that wasn't damning enough, the casings from the two shots Albert fired both bear your fingerprints. It would appear Albert helped himself to your ammo during one of his visits to the house."

"What?" He was so startled, he momentarily forgot himself and exclaimed, "Son of a bitch!"

Glenda frowned. "You can't say that," she said sternly.

"I'm sorry," he said immediately.

"Stop fidgeting."

The button was getting to him again. He forced his hand away, then caught his reflection in the room's long mirror and felt even more discouraged. He looked tense and uncomfortable, not at all like a ruthlessly competent federal agent. When word came down that he could finally interview Montgomery, he needed to walk into that room appearing 100 percent calm and in control. *You messed with us, Montgomery, now let me mess with you.*

He did not look calm and in control. He looked like someone who hadn't slept. He looked like someone who was deeply worried. He looked like someone who was, for the first time in his life, out of his league.

Albert Montgomery is nothing, he reminded himself firmly. Not even the real deal. Just a hired hand.

"He wants to talk," Glenda said softly, as if reading his mind. "Don't forget, Albert is driven by his need to prove himself smarter than you. All you have to do is sound skeptical, and he'll hand you the keys to the city simply to prove he can. You hate him. You want to lean over the table and kill him. But other than that, Quincy, this interview shouldn't be too hard."

He nodded, then glanced once more at his watch. Three thirty-two P.M. Twenty-four and a half hours since the attack on Glenda ...Enough time for someone to cross the country. Enough time for someone to assume any manner of disguises. He wished once more he could talk to Rainie. Goddammit he had to leave this button alone!

The door opened. A young agent poked his head into the room. "They're escorting Special Agent Montgomery to the interview room," he reported.

Glenda nodded. The agent closed the door.

He took a deep breath. Then, he squared his shoulders and ran a hand down his jacket. "Well," he said, "how do I look?"

Portland, Oregon

Twelve-eighteen P.M., Pacific standard time, Rainie and Kimberly were sitting side by side on the tiny sofa. From this vantage point, they could see into the adjoining bedroom on their right, or through the kitchenette area to the front door of the small suite on their left. They weren't doing anything. They weren't saying anything. They both simply stared at the phone.

"Why doesn't he call?" Kimberly asked.

"He must not have anything to say."

"I thought something would've happened by now!"

Rainie glanced at the hotel-room door. "So did I," she murmured. "So did I."

Virginia

Sitting in the dimly lit interrogation room, Special Agent Albert Montgomery looked pretty good for a man who'd been shot. He wore light-blue surgical scrubs in lieu of his customary rumpled suit. His mussed hair was combed, his face freshly scrubbed and slightly less jaundiced. His right hand, heavily bandaged, rested on the table. His left leg, with its recently repaired kneecap, was encased in a cast and propped up on a chair. All in all, he appeared quite comfortable and at ease.

They eyed each other steadily for the first thirty seconds, neither one of them wanting to blink first.

"You look like crap," Montgomery said.

"Thank you, I worked on it all night." He walked up to the table, but didn't sit. From this vantage point, he could look down on Albert Montgomery. He could cross his arms over his chest and stare at this man as if he were the lowest form of life on earth. Albert simply smiled up at him. He'd also attended interrogation classes and knew the tricks.

"You sound like shit, too," Albert said. "Catch a cold on the airplane, Quince? Those things are nothing but petri dishes with wings. And you've had plenty of time to incubate. East Coast, West Coast, East Coast. Tell me, Quincy, how does it feel to be a puppet on a string?"

His hands clenched. He almost rose to the bait, then remembered what Glenda had said. He couldn't afford to kill Albert. Too much depended on what the man had to say.

He pulled out a chair and took a seat. "You wanted me here: I'm here. Now speak."

"Still arrogant, huh Quincy? I wonder how arrogant you're gonna be when the Philly detectives get through with you. Have you checked out their prison system yet? Maybe you can get a tour of your future home."

"I'm not worried about the PPD."

Albert stared at him. He stared back. Albert broke first. "Son of a bitch," he rasped.

"What's his name, Albert?"

Albert didn't answer right away. His gaze flickered to the clock on the wall. "I don't know what you're talking about."

"You acted alone?"

"Sure I did. You don't think that I hated you enough? You fucked my career, Quincy. You took my family, you ruined my life. Well hey, guess who has the last laugh. Where's your beautiful daughter, Quince? Where's the mother of your children? Where's your own dear old dad who desperately depended upon you? And I don't care what you say, when that report from Philly comes in, where's your precious fucking career? The bigger they are, the harder they fall."

"You didn't do this."

"Like hell."

"You don't have the brains."

Albert's face turned red. "You think you're so smart, Quincy, consider this: Revenge. Fifteen long years of desperately wanting revenge. I could try to get the same case as you, set you up to fail, but that would be risky. I could try to get on the same case as you and shoot you in the back, but that would be no fun. So one night it comes to me—"

"Comes to him."

"Comes to *me*. Why go for the direct attack? On the job is where you're in your element, where you do good. But you don't do everything right, Quincy. Hell no, you're not perfect. In fact, when it comes to being a husband, being a father, being a son, you pretty much suck. Once I realized this, I knew I had you."

"You approached Mandy at her AA meeting."

"I started looking up your father, your ex-wife and daughters. Didn't take me too long to figure out Mandy was the weak link. Shit, you must've done quite a head job on that kid, Quincy. She's a drunk, she's promiscuous. She's the perfect, insecure wreck. What do you have your Ph.D. in again?"

He thinned his lips. Montgomery smiled, happy to feel he had the upper hand and as Glenda predicted, now expansively verbose.

"Yeah, I approached Mandy, pretended to be the son of an old acquaintance of your dad's, Ben Zikka, Jr. That's the nice thing about AA meetings. They build a sense of camaraderie, allow even perfect strangers to bond. Three meetings later, I had her."

"You introduced her to him."

"I *had* her."

"Mandy had standards. You never so much as held her hand."

Albert scowled, so he'd struck a nerve. But the disgruntled agent quickly scrambled to make up lost ground. "Your daughter was a real friendly girl, Quince. Lunches, dinners, breakfasts. Didn't take any time at all to learn all about the rest of the family. And so many fascinating details about you, Pierce. Your habits, your home security system, your pathetic letters trying to keep in touch with your oldest daughter and build some kind of relationship."

"Handwriting samples," he deduced. "Material to copy as the UNSUB prepared the note for Philadelphia. For that matter, stationery."

Albert merely smiled. His gaze flicked once again to the wall clock.

"I was at Mandy's one night when you called," Albert said. "Got to hear one helluva stilted conversation, that was for sure. Really, Quince, you never did understand your own daughter. You ought to be ashamed of yourself."

"He milked her for information," he said softly. "And then he killed her."

"*I* came up with the idea. Get her drunk and behind the wheel of the car. It was a little risky. Maybe she didn't die right away. Maybe she regained consciousness. In the end, who cared? She was so damn drunk, she'd never remember what really happened, and we could always arrange a little accident in the hospital."

"We?"

"I," Albert said hastily. "*I* could arrange a little accident. I considered her murder a little test, Quince. Would you catch on? How good was Quantico's best of the best? But, true to form, when it comes to your family your instincts are a complete zero. Hell, you didn't even stay at her bedside. Just showed up and agreed to pull the plug. You helped kill your daughter, Quince. Not that I mind, but how do you feel about that?"

He ignored the question. "You used her to approach Bethie."

"Sure. Mandy told us ... me! all about her mom. Favorite restaurants, favorite music, favorite food. It's not rocket science after that. And I do have my charm."

"Bethie hates charm. He approached her as an organ recipient. He disguised himself as part of Mandy."

Albert's eyes widened. He clearly hadn't known they knew that much. His gaze dashed to the clock. The time seemed to soothe him. He took a deep breath and eyed his interrogator more warily.

"When I'm brilliant, Quincy, I'm brilliant," Albert tried.

Quincy merely shook his head. "He had to wait over a year for Mandy to die. Did that make him anxious? That couldn't have been part of his plan."

"Patience is a virtue," Albert said.

"No, he got nervous. He needed my attention for the game to be interesting. So he used Mary Olsen to raise my suspicion."

"I didn't want destroying you to be too easy," Albert said. "After fifteen years of planning, a guy's gotta have a little fun."

"Mary Olsen is dead."

That shocked him. Albert's gaze widened again and this time, he distinctly paled. "Ummm, yeah."

"How'd you kill her, Albert?"

"I ... uh ..."

"Gun, knife?"

"I shot her!"

"You poisoned her, asshole!" He felt a spark of anger, then checked himself, and said more sternly, "She received a care package in the mail, chocolates from her lover, laced with cyanide. Horrible way to die."

"Stupid bitch," Albert muttered. He was definitely uncomfortable now. His fingers drummed on the table.

"How do you think he'll kill you?"

"Shut up!" His eyes shot to the clock.

"Poison? Or something more personal? You're a liability, Albert. A big, fat liability who, thanks to Glenda, is in no shape to run and hide."

"Shut up, shut up, shut up!"

"Or did you forget that from the Sanchez case? Psychopaths can have partners, but partners are never equal. Miguel Sanchez lived. His partner, Richie, died on a prison floor with his balls crammed down his throat."

Albert shot up from his chair. The movement jarred the supporting chair from beneath his injured leg and his cast fell heavily to the floor, making him yelp. Albert gripped the edge of the table to keep himself from falling, then glared at him with a face mottled with rage.

"You just fucking blew it!" he roared. "I was gonna tell you where your father is. I was gonna take pity on the pathetic old man. But not now. Now he can rot where he is, tied up, starving, shitting in his own pants and getting bedsores from his piss. How do you like them apples, you arrogant prick!"

"My father is dead," he said quietly, though he really didn't know that and his heart had begun to beat hard in his chest. This was the big risk. The life-or-death gamble. If he was wrong ... *I'm sorry. Lord have mercy, because I cannot.* "My father is dead," he repeated more forcefully. "We already found his body."

"Impossible!"

"Would you like to go to the morgue to see him?"

"But he shouldn't have washed up for days, not after all the weights we put on him." Albert suddenly heard his own words. He drew up short, then burst out, "You tricked me. *Goddammit, you ice-cold son of a bitch*, you gave up on your own dad!"

"All in a day's work," he murmured, though his throat felt tight now. He had an ache in his chest. Montgomery was a monster. The UNSUB was a monster. God, he was sick of all of this.

"It's over, Albert," he said hoarsely. "You're nothing but a liability now. You either talk to us, or you die for him."

"You don't know shit!"

"Tell that to Mary Olsen."

"Dammit, *I'm* the one in charge here."

"Then prove it! Tell us something we don't know. Dazzle me!"

Albert froze. He suddenly smiled. He drew himself up straight. His gaze was on the wall clock again, but this time he made no attempt to hide it.

"Hey Quincy," he said. "Here's something interesting. Mandy wasn't the first target. Mandy didn't give up her family. Kimberly did."

"What?"

"Oh, look at the time. Four-fourteen P.M. Why don't you call your daughter's hotel room, Quincy? Reach out and chastise Kimberly who's staying right where Everett told me she would be. Oh wait, I'm sorry, you won't be able to reach your daughter anymore. Four-fifteen P.M. Time's up, Agent. And your daughter is *dead.*"

36

When the phone on the coffee table finally rang, Rainie nearly jumped out of her skin.

"Shit," she said, then glanced hastily over at Kimberly.

"Shit," Kimberly agreed. One P.M. Much later than they had thought and they were both now wound too tight. Rainie scooped up the phone before it could ring again.

"Hello."

"Rainie? It's Luke. I got a problem."

"What problem?" she said without thinking. Then her eyes widened and she motioned furiously to Kimberly. The girl got the hint and ran for her Glock.

"I'm not convinced this afternoon's meeting is the way to go, Rainie," the man was saying. "Maybe too risky. Can we meet ahead of time and talk about it?"

"My God, you're a perfect mimic," Rainie murmured. "If I didn't know any better …"

"What's that?" He sounded friendly and still so much like Luke Hayes that even knowing better, one part of her kept thinking it was him. But it wasn't. He was simply a person with a superb aptitude for mimicry and an extremely cruel sense of humor.

"How did you get this number?" she asked.

"I looked up the hotel."

"I never told you where we were staying, *Luke.*"

"Sure you did. When we met with Mitz."

"No, I didn't. And Luke knew better than to ask where I would be. Nice try, Super Freak. Wanna try again?"

The voice changed instantly, from an almost dead-on impression of Luke Hayes to the silky, smooth voice Rainie remembered from yesterday on the phone. "Why Ms. Conner, you don't trust your own friends. How interesting. You know Bethie surprised me, too. She actually requested a background check on me. What do you suppose it means that all the women in Quincy's life are so suspicious?"

"That he values common sense. Where are you?"

"Now Rainie," the caller chided. "After all this time you wouldn't take this fun from me, would you? I truly deserve an A for effort."

"You did deserve an A for effort. But Glenda Rodman lived, and I got you pegged."

"Glenda Rodman was supposed to live."

"What, you got a weakness for stern gray suits?"

He laughed. "Come now, we both know Albert Montgomery is incompetent. You were a police officer, Rainie, you know the importance of understanding your fellow officers' strengths and weaknesses. I let Albert have Glenda. He really has such a deep-seated rage for anyone in law enforcement. I think it goes back to his father, a washed-up security guard. A little too strict, Albert's father. He produced a son who desperately needed to prove himself better than his own dad, and yet despised himself all the more for following in his father's footsteps. But that's neither here nor there. Albert's conflicted, Albert's incompetent. Therefore, it stood to reason, Albert would fail."

"You bet against your own pawn," Rainie said.

"Of course, although it hardly matters. If Albert succeeded, Pierce would stand accused of Glenda's shooting and would have to return to Virginia. If Albert failed, Pierce would need to question Albert and he'd have to return to Virginia for that. Either way, I win my game."

"You lured Quincy back home so you could kill him."

"No, I lured Quincy *away,* so I could kill *you.*"

"Oops, I'm sorry. But now that I've given it some thought, I don't feel like dying today." Rainie made another motion to Kimberly. The girl nodded, and headed straight for each window, cautiously raising the sash and inspecting the outdoor fire escape. Kimberly looked both up and down. When she was done, she left the windows open as they had planned, nodded to Rainie that the fire escape was clear, and headed for the bedroom to do the same with those windows there.

"Are you afraid of hell, Rainie?" the man asked. Rainie could hear static now. He was definitely calling from a cell phone, which meant he could be anywhere. Riding up the elevator. Creeping down the hall. He thought keeping her talking would keep her distracted. He would learn soon enough that talking was his mistake.

"I'm not afraid of hell," she answered. "I pretty much figure that's what life is for."

"Suffering here on earth? Come now, surely you have some notion of spiritual reward and punishment. Given everything you've done, that must make you wonder where you will spend your end of days."

"You're one to talk. Your whole life is about punishing Quincy. To do that you've killed how many people? It *therefore stands to reason,*" she mocked him, "that you're not one for religion, since your eternal punishment is gonna be one helluva long suntan session."

Kimberly returned from the bedroom, shaking her head. So far, nothing on the fire escape. She started toward the door, but Rainie hastily waved her away. She'd read of people getting shot as they peered through the peephole. She didn't know if that could really happen, and she didn't want to find out. She gestured to the carpet. Kimberly got the hint and peered beneath the door instead. No sign of feet.

"Are you going to kill me, Rainie?" the man asked.

"I'm thinking about it."

"Oh, thinking's not good enough. You have to commit to the act, Rainie. Visualize the goal, imagine yourself as the victor."

"Wonderful, *Chicken Soup for the Serial Killer*. Just once, I'd like to be attacked by a mute."

Kimberly was looking at Rainie for new instructions. The girl was clearly nervous. Despite her cavalier tone, Rainie was increasingly nervous, too. He was close. He craved intimacy with his victims. He liked to be there for the kill.

"Is Kimberly with you?" the man asked.

"Why? I'm not good enough for you?" Rainie was desperately looking around the room. The fire escape was clear, the hotel-room door clear. Where else could he come from? What had they missed?

And then she got it. Simultaneously, she and Kimberly both looked up. Jesus Christ, there was the tip of a drill bit coming through their ceiling. How the hell had he done that?

"Go!" Rainie yelled. Kimberly dashed for the front door just as the man said, "Thank you, Rainie. I'd love to come in."

Too late, she realized her mistake. If he'd been actively drilling, they would've heard it, so it had to have been sometime earlier. And peering beneath the door was never foolproof. All the person had to do was stand to one side. Rainie shot to her feet.

But Kimberly had already flung open the door and his gun was already pointed at her chest.

"Carl Mitz," Rainie snarled.

And Kimberly whispered shakily, "Oh my God—Dr. Andrews."

"I'll take your guns, please," Dr. Andrews announced, stepping into the hotel room and kicking the door shut behind him. He was dressed plainly today. Tan chinos, white-collared shirt. He looked like anyone walking down the street, except that in addition to a large black canvas bag slung over his left shoulder, he also carried a 9mm semiautomatic. The barrel was now four inches from Kimberly's heart. The girl couldn't take her eyes off of it. Her face had gone bone-white.

"You don't surrender your weapon," Kimberly told him in an unnatural tone of voice. "An officer should never surrender her weapon!"

"Hand over the gun, Kimberly," Rainie told her tersely. "For Christ's sake, this isn't the police academy's final exam and you're not bullet-proof!"

"One of us will live," Kimberly insisted in that same tone of voice. "He'll fire, but he can't kill us both."

"Kimberly—"

"It's all my fault. Look at him. Don't you get it? *It's all my fault!*"

Dr. Andrews smiled. He let the large canvas bag slide from his shoulder. It landed heavily on the floor. "Very good, Kimberly. I was wondering when you were going to figure that out. After all, I did tell you that I wouldn't be a stranger."

"But my anxiety attacks—"

"I tailed you. Just because I was willing to confess that you would know your own killer, didn't mean I wanted you to know that you'd already met him. Frankly, didn't it ever occur to you that you hardly saw me after your sister's funeral? You thought I was giving you time off to recover. But I was really buying myself time to destroy your family. We all have our priorities." He gestured to his sharply pressed pants and white linen shirt. "What do you think of my new look, by the way? The right wig, nicely tailored clothes, contact lenses … I wasn't always such a wreck as a professor, you know. I just thought you'd find me more comforting in tweed. So over the years, I became more and more dowdy, and you became more and more trusting. Interesting that for your mom and Mandy, I had to reverse the process. Now drop your gun and kick it over to me slowly."

"*I thought you were my friend!* My mentor! I told you so much about my family. My father, my mother, my sister … And all along … All along …" Kimberly's body convulsed. She looked like she was going to be physically ill, yet she still didn't lower her Glock.

"Kimberly," Rainie growled. She was sweating profusely, reluctant to let go of her own pistol and feeling the situation spinning dangerously out of control.

Andrews looked at her. Kimberly noticed the change in his gaze and followed his eyes toward Rainie. *No,* Rainie started to yell, but she was too late. The instant Kimberly's focus left Andrews, he chopped his left hand down hard on her right forearm. The girl cried out, her gun slipping from nerveless fingers onto the floor. Rainie jerked up her own pistol, but found Andrews's weapon already trained at her body.

"I trust you'll be more reasonable," he said, twisting Kimberly's arm behind her back and positioning her as a human shield.

Rainie nodded. Slowly, she lowered her gun to the carpet, her gaze falling on the black canvas bag. Why such a big bag? What would he bring with him?

"Now, kick the firearm toward me."

Rainie complied, jabbing at her Glock .40 with her toe but not putting much effort into it. The heavy pistol stopped three feet away, under the glass coffee table. She made a show of shrugging helplessly, and waited to see if Andrews would push the issue. He frowned at her, but with his hands already full with one female, seemed content to let it go.

Rainie took a deep breath. *Remain calm,* she instructed herself, though her hands had begun to shake and her heart hammered in her chest. She'd kept him on the phone for a decent interval. Now if she and Kimberly could stall him just a minute or two more. The open windows. The unwatched fire escape with easy access to their room. Come on, cavalry …

What was in that bag?

Kimberly was weeping. Trapped against Andrews, her shoulders had slumped, her spine was bowed. She didn't seem to have much fight left.

"Perfect," Andrews said. "Now that everyone is feeling more agreeable, we have a lot of work to do, ladies. Bombs to build, detonating devices to wire to telephones. Your father is going to call at precisely one-fifteen, Kimberly. I don't want to miss the opportunity for him to blow his own daughter and his lady love into tiny little bits."

Oh shit, that was what was in that bag. Rainie closed her eyes. Andrews had brought all the ingredients for a homemade bomb. God knows it wouldn't take much to blow up a room this size and who cares if Andrews took out a fair portion of the hotel and other unsuspecting guests with him? It would be the ultimate triumph for him. Restraining Kimberly and Rainie. Then rigging a bomb to the telephone, so that the first ring triggered the blast. Quincy would not only lose the only family he had left, but when the first forensics report came in, he'd get to learn that he'd basically pulled the trigger. He'd killed his own daughter. He'd murdered Rainie. Oh, Quincy. Oh, poor, poor Quincy.

Rainie's eyes came open. She felt the breeze from the open window on her face, but she no longer knew if they had enough time to wait. She and Kimberly could not let Andrews build that bomb. Under no circumstances could they let Andrews take out half a hotel simply to spite Quincy.

Rainie looked at Kimberly, trying to catch the girl's gaze. They needed some kind of plan. Maybe Kimberly could get the professor talking, keep him focused on exchanging banalities with his former student so Rainie might ease her way toward her Glock. Three feet. That wasn't much. Right?

Kimberly, however, had her head down. Her slender figure appearing despondent. She was so young, after all. And under such terrible stress.

"I blamed my father," Kimberly whispered, maybe to herself, maybe to Andrews. "All along, I blamed my father, but in reality, I'm the one who betrayed my family." Another thought seemed to strike her. Her head jolted up, her eyes suddenly growing wide. "Oh my God, the Sanchez case. I've been going over it and over it, thinking there was more of a connection. Of course. Dr. Andrews's research work at San Quentin." She twisted toward Andrews, straining to see his face. "You knew Sanchez! You're the connection! How could I be so blind? *Dammit!*"

"You failed to ask the right question in the very beginning," Andrews said matter-of-factly, yanking Kimberly's arm more savagely to quell her movements. Rainie saw her chance. She eased forward an inch.

"If this was revenge, why now?" Andrews postulated for his former student. "You could theorize that it was a felon who finally got out of prison, but I trust you already explored that option and found it to be a dead end. Then you could look at family of felons but again, why, after all this time? Interestingly enough, I think Quincy was finally getting on the right track, that it wasn't a past FBI case at all. So if it was from his pre-FBI days, then truly, why *now?*"

"Because you found me!" Kimberly spat at her captor.

"Because you fell into my fucking lap!" Andrews roared. "Nearly twenty years after that man took my own daughters from me, and here you are! Beautiful, smart, poised to become everything a father could want for his girl. Why should he be so lucky? Why should he have everything that I deserved? Goddamn interfering *shrink!*"

His gaze suddenly shot back to Rainie. She froze, having made it two steps closer to her gun, and wanting that to be progress, while knowing it wasn't enough. Andrews was frowning at her. Had he figured out that she'd cut the distance to her discarded handgun? He studied her hard.

"You were one of Quincy's patients," Rainie said quickly, seeking to distract him again, and holding perfectly still now that his attention was back upon her.

"I was not!" Andrews replied indignantly. "My stupid ex-wife was. She went to him for help. She had all sorts of outlandish stories that I was an unfit father and that my children were terrified of me."

"You abused your kids?" *Your turn, Kimberly,* she thought frantically. *I'll keep him talking, you think of something brilliant.*

"I did not, I did not, I did not. They were my girls! I *loved* them, I wanted what was best for them. It was their mother who could not appreciate their potential. She wanted to coddle them, give them time to play, give them time to grow. For God's sake, you do not get anywhere in life by playing!"

"Quincy testified against you in the custody hearing, didn't he?" Rainie persisted. "His opinion helped sway the judge." *Come on, Kimberly. We have to do something here. Fast.*

"He told the judge that I suffered from severe personality disorder! He told people that in his professional opinion I was manipulative, egocentric, and totally lacking in genuine ability to empathize. In short, I exhibited psychopathic tendencies, I used my children as pawns to get what I wanted, and should they ever try to exert their own personalities, he couldn't vouch for their safety. And I never saw my children again. Do you realize what that does to someone? One day, I'm a highly respected family man. The next, I'm a name on a restraining order! If I so much as said boo, they would've taken my license from me. I would've been totally ruined!"

"You haven't done too badly since then." Rainie shrugged dismissively, working on prolonging Andrews's diatribe.

"After I moved from California to New York and started all over again," Andrews countered. "All alone. With no one. Having nothing. You know, I might have had a second chance with Mary Olsen. She was pregnant with my child, maybe we could've been happy. But Pierce fucked even that up for me. Forced me to kill her before I ever knew." Andrews's voice changed. "Son of a bitch. Everything I ever wanted, he's taken from me. No more! I'm the one calling the shots, I'm the one in control. He wants an expert opinion? I'll give him an expert opinion. An expert in explosives. Goddammit, it's *time!*" He suddenly yanked on Kimberly's right arm. The girl had just raised her foot to stomp down on his instep. Now her foot fell to the floor harmlessly as he jerked her off balance. She grimaced and sagged despondently against him. Rainie grimaced along with her, her gaze going longingly to her Glock, so visible beneath the glass tabletop, and yet still so far out of reach.

They had to do something. No more time. Think, think. Come on, come on …

"Oh thank God! Luke!"

Rainie jerked her eyes to the space behind Andrews. It was a desperate act, a stupid gamble. Andrews twisted around, feeling the breeze for the first time and thinking he'd left himself vulnerable to a flank attack. No time for digging around under the coffee table for a gun. Rainie darted left and grabbed the best weapon she could find. One of the metal kitchen chairs.

"What the …?"

"Kimberly, *now!*"

The girl dug her elbow into Andrews's exposed side and lashed out with her foot. Twisted and off balance, Andrews released his hold on her instinctively, struggling to bring his gun up and around. Rainie whipped the metal chair into Andrews's neck and shoulder. He howled as his gun and the chair both went flying and he realized too late he'd been duped by the oldest trick in the book.

"*Bitch!*" he roared.

"Kimberly," Rainie cried out again. "Gun, now!" They needed to find a weapon. Now, now, now.

Her Glock, under the coffee table. Rainie scurried over on all fours. Andrews saw her movement, and cut her off with a brutal kick to her chin. Her jaw cracked. She collapsed on her back, seeing stars. Dimly she was aware of Kimberly diving across the room reaching for Andrews's fallen gun. Andrews saw her. He had the chair. Raising it over his head, towering above Kimberly.

The chair slammed down. Kimberly made a heavy, wet sound Rainie had never heard before.

Andrews smiled in triumph. Then he flung down the chair and crouched for the 9mm Rainie could now see it lying just inches from Kimberly's body. The girl had been so close ...

One last chance. Rainie flipped onto her side, looking, looking, looking. The Glock, there against the brass leg of the table. Come on, Rainie. Dying is not preferable to living. Dying is not preferable to living! Damn, she'd be an optimist in the end. *Reach!*

The startling sound of a cartridge being ratcheted into a gun chamber. The sound of death.

"Bye-bye, Rainie," Andrews said.

And Quincy said, "Hey Andrews. Get your fucking hands off my daughter."

Virginia

Albert Montgomery was still feeling calm and controlled fifteen minutes later when Quincy returned to the dimly lit interrogation room. Four thirty-one P.M. The agent probably had just confirmed his daughter's death. Albert wondered if he'd get to see him cry. He would like that.

His interrogator stopped in front of him.

"Howdy Albert," the man said in a crystal-clear voice Albert had never heard before. "It's my turn to tell you some things *you* don't know. One, I'm sure Kimberly is just fine. And two, I'm not Pierce Quincy." The man reached up and ripped off the salt-and-pepper wig it had taken Glenda and an FBI makeup expert two hours to apply. Then he stepped out of special shoes with two-inch lifts. And he removed his navy blue suit jacket, custom-tailored to mirror Quincy's taller, broad-shouldered build. "The name is Luke Hayes," the stranger said calmly. "And I'm a friend of Rainie's."

Andrews's face paled. He snapped around toward the bedroom door, the gun in his right hand dipping down toward the carpet, but his left hand still on Kimberly's shoulder. "Who? How? But you're in Virginia!"

Quincy stepped into the living room from the adjoining bedroom. He had his 10mm out, but down at his side. His gaze was locked on Andrews. He'd wasted fifteen minutes relentlessly searching the lobby for a man talking on a cell phone before he'd realized his mistake. The man was already upstairs. The man was already in his daughter's room. Plan B had always been the fire escape. Six floors up, rung over rung. Quincy should be tired. He should be exhausted.

He stood looking at this man who was heavily armed and crouched over his daughter, and he felt unbelievably calm. Time had slowed. All was manageable. The UNSUB finally had a face. And like so many killers before, the face wasn't even that impressive. He was just a man after all, average height, average weight, average age.

"You killed Mandy," Quincy said. He kept approaching. Andrews still hadn't brought his gun back up. He hadn't shot any of his other victims. Chances were that he wasn't that comfortable with guns, Quincy decided. An ambush was one thing. A genuine face-off, another.

"Easy pickings," Andrews snarled. But his voice wobbled. Behind him, Rainie was slowly extending her arm again, reaching for a pistol Quincy could just make out beneath the glass table. Quincy quickly looked away, not wanting Andrews to follow his line of sight. He focused his gaze on Kimberly instead, who was beginning to moan at Andrews's feet.

"You killed Bethie," Quincy said.

"More easy pickings." Andrews shifted suddenly, wrapping his arm around Kimberly's neck and dragging her up against him. Kimberly's eyes fluttered open. She looked disoriented, bewildered. Then her gaze met her father's and she simply looked heartbroken.

"It's okay," Quincy told her automatically. He wanted to comfort his daughter, erase the pain from her gaze. He wanted to reach out to her. He kept his hands at his sides. Kimberly was strong. He would trust her strength to carry her through, just as he hoped she trusted his strength now. *Believe in me*, he willed his daughter. *I will always take care of you.*

Andrews smiled cruelly, and jerked Kimberly closer. "On your feet, Sleeping Beauty. Time to say bye-bye to Daddy."

Andrews jerked them both upright. Quincy didn't make any move to stop them.

Out of the corner of his eye, he discerned another movement in the background, but once again he resisted the temptation to look. He homed in on Andrews, focusing now on narrowing the man's universe. There was just Andrews, Kimberly, and Quincy. Just one vicious predator, one daughter, and one father determined to keep his child safe. If he had eyes only for Andrews, Andrews would have eyes only for him. Rainie ... The rest must be a leap of faith.

"How does it feel, Quincy?" Andrews demanded, twisting Kimberly's arm savagely and bringing her even closer against him. "How does it *feel* to lose everything and never even understand why!"

"You're not a real person," Quincy said conversationally, moving slightly to the left, away from the living room, and drawing Andrews's gaze with him. "You're a shell of a man, lacking genuine feelings, connections, compassion. You've spent your whole life acting at being a human being, molding yourself into other people's images because otherwise you don't know how to be. You don't know *who* to be. The greatest justice in life was that your little girls never had to see you again."

Andrews jerked up his pistol. He pointed it at Quincy's head. "Fuck you," he screamed, causing Kimberly to flinch. "I'm going to kill you! I'm going to blow out your goddamn brains!"

"You can't," Quincy said, his voice as calm as Andrews's was angry. He looked at his daughter, willing her to remain strong, willing her to be all right. *Trust me, trust me, trust me.*

"Yes I can!"

"You can't. Without me, your life has no purpose. When I'm gone, who will you be, Andrews? What will you do? What will you dream about at night? As much as you hate me, you *need* me even more. Without me, the game ends."

Andrews's face grew red. His eyes dashed from side to side. The rage was building inside him, the implosion imminent. From rational act to crazy reaction. This was what Quincy needed. For Andrews to finally lose control. For Andrews to unleash the monster he kept locked inside.

Andrews's finger wrapped around the trigger. Quincy kept his eyes on Kimberly. He tried to tell his daughter how much he loved her, and he tried to apologize for what she would have to watch next. Rainie. Kimberly. Rainie.

God give them both strength.

A movement out of the corner of his eye …

"Kimberly," Quincy murmured. "Fuck ballet."

On cue, she sagged heavily in her captor's arms. Andrews howled in surprise and pulled the trigger, but her unexpected movement had rocked him off balance. Gunfire spit low across the wall. Quincy dashed left. He brought up his 10mm to return fire but Andrews and Kimberly were too tangled together. He didn't have a shot. He didn't have a shot.

"Kimberly," he yelled, though he didn't know why.

"Daddy!"

"Hey Andrews," Rainie called. "Look here."

The man jerked around. Kimberly broke free and dove to the floor just as Rainie racked back her Glock.

"No!" Andrews howled. He pointed his gun at her—

And Quincy very calmly, very coolly shot the man point blank in the chest. Andrews dropped to the floor. He did not move again.

"Is it over?" Kimberly asked when the echoes of the gunshot faded away. She was trying to raise herself off the floor. Her left arm wouldn't bear her weight. Blood and gray matter streaked down her long, fine hair.

Quincy went over to her. He took his injured daughter into his arms, feeling the tremors rocking her slender body. He cradled her against his chest, holding her as gently as he had when she was a newborn. Oh God, she was infinitely precious to him. He had saved her, but he had also hurt her, and he knew it would take them both years to sort out the difference between the two. All he could do was try. Isolation was not protection. No amount of distance kept you safe in the end.

His gaze went to Rainie, now bent over Andrews.

"He's dead," Rainie said quietly.

Kimberly clutched his shoulders more tightly. And then she began to cry. Quincy rocked his daughter against him. He stroked her blood-splattered hair.

"It's over," he said to Kimberly, to Rainie. And then more firmly, to all of them, "The game is over."

A loud knocking on the door. "Hotel security," a voice barked.

And the aftermath began.

Epilogue

Six weeks later, Rainie Conner sat hunched over her desk in her downtown loft, ostensibly trying to make her budget love her, but really eyeing the phone. Damn thing wasn't making a sound. Hadn't made a sound for days. She was really starting to hate that.

She picked up the receiver. "Well, what do you know, dial tone."

She set down the receiver. She went back to studying her Quicken file. It didn't do a thing to improve her mood.

Quincy had paid her. She'd yelled and screamed and put up a fuss. When they were both satisfied that she'd made all the appropriate noise, she'd accepted his check. A girl had to eat, and all those cross-country plane tickets had just showed up on her AmEx card. Conner Investigations got to have a profit. For about seven days. Then she started flying to Virginia again. She kept telling herself it was all for good reason.

First she had to join Quincy to finish picking Albert Montgomery's brain. The agent had finally admitted that the esteemed Dr. Marcus Andrews had approached him two and a half years ago. Andrews had wanted revenge against Quincy. His wife, Emily, had hired Quincy as an expert witness in the bitter child-custody hearing between her and her ex-husband. Quincy's testimony had been pivotal in the judge's decision to deny Andrews access to his children permanently. While the case had been important at the time, Quincy hadn't thought about it now in years and the name Andrews had been too common to make Quincy think twice when Kimberly began talking about her highly respected professor.

Funny how Bethie had always thought it was his career at the Bureau that would put Quincy's family in jeopardy. None of them had considered that mental health professionals also faced dangers in the form of unbalanced patients and disgruntled families.

Andrews had interviewed Miguel Sanchez as part of his prison research study. As he became familiar with the killing spree and the officers involved in the Sanchez investigation, he'd identified Montgomery's role and realized here was someone else who probably hated Quincy as much as Andrews did. Dr. Andrews tracked down Montgomery in Virginia, introduced his cause over dinner, and a few beers later, had enlisted Montgomery in a joint quest for revenge.

Montgomery had been playing the inside man ever since. First he helped Andrews understand how the Bureau worked. What would happen if an agent seemed in jeopardy? What if an agent's family was in jeopardy? How fast could the Bureau review past case files? What if an agent was suspected of a crime? From there, Montgomery had simply sunk in deeper. From introducing Mandy to Andrews to confiscating Quincy's stationery to attacking Glenda because his hatred had festered and grown that insane.

Nine months ago, Montgomery had searched the Oregon corrections department data banks to find a good candidate for Rainie's father. Yes, Ronnie Dawson existed. He went to jail at the right time, he was paroled at the right time. And upon personal investigation, he was a five-foot-two aging redhead, who'd never heard of Molly Conner and was as shocked as anyone to hear that a fat donation had been made to a county DA in his name.

Easy come, easy go. Rainie dedicated three days to feeling kind of funky. Then she surprised herself by getting over it. It was hard to miss something you never had, and she hadn't even truly lost her dream. She did have a father. He was somewhere out there. You never knew.

Attorney-at-law Carl Mitz existed, too. A good lawyer, and as Rainie had learned over lunch, a genuinely nice guy. Just one more person who had the right credentials, so Montgomery got his Social Security number, mother's maiden name, and date of birth. Andrews took over from there.

Rainie was not feeling so good anymore about the electronic age. She'd ordered a copy of her credit report the other day. She found herself checking it compulsively.

Special Agent Albert Montgomery wasn't going to stand trial. Apparently, Andrews had left one last present for him: Cyanide in his blood-pressure medication, which some kindly agent retrieved for him from home. Shortly after Quincy's final interview with him, Albert opened the bottle. Both he and his guard smelled the odor of bitter almonds immediately. The guard dived forward. Albert downed half the bottle. Sixty seconds later, Albert didn't have to worry anymore about how he was going to live with himself.

For Quincy and Kimberly it wasn't quite that easy. Kimberly spent forty-eight hours in the hospital with a broken arm and severe concussion. Fortunately, she was young and strong and recovered quickly from her wounds. The physical ones, that is. Quincy tried to get her to return to Virginia with him. She insisted on going to New York, however. She wanted her apartment back. Her classes, her routine, her life. Rainie and Quincy called her every day for the first week. Kimberly liked that so much she took her phone off the hook. She was an independent girl and as Rainie understood from personal experience, she needed to deal with things in her own way, in her own time.

Two weeks after Albert committed suicide, the Philadelphia police got the handwriting analysis back from their crime lab and tried to arrest Quincy for his ex-wife's brutal murder. Rainie definitely had to return to Virginia for that. She'd yelled at the detectives, yelled at the district attorney, and made a general nuisance of herself. Glenda, on the other hand, finally convinced the DA to send the incriminating note to the FBI lab, which promptly verified the presence of numerous hesitation marks—a classic sign of forgery. Quincy thanked Rainie for coming. Glenda got a promotion.

Rainie returned once again to Portland. She had her business, Quincy had the case to wrap up and his daughter to think about. Of course they spoke by phone. Rainie told him she understood he had a lot going on. She practiced being sympathetic, supportive, and all around undemanding. He couldn't be there for her, but she could be there for him. This is what relationships were about. Real, adult, mature relationships. If she became any more well adjusted, she was going to have to beat someone.

Two weeks before, a fishing vessel off the coast of Maryland pulled up Abraham Quincy's body in its nets. Montgomery had already revealed that Andrews had ordered the body heavily weighted and dumped in such deep water that it would never be found. He wanted Quincy to never know what happened to Abraham, to always have to wonder if his father was still out there, maybe still alive, maybe still waiting for his son ... Not even Andrews could control fate. A fishing vessel happened to be active in the area. The fish happened to eat through the ropes bearing the weights. Abraham Quincy was found.

Rainie heard the news from Kimberly, who called her sounding quiet and much too old. They were going to have a small family ceremony for Abraham later in the week. Perhaps Rainie could come?

Rainie bought a third ticket to Virginia. Then she waited to hear from Quincy and waited to hear from Quincy and waited to hear from Quincy. Finally, she picked up the phone. He didn't return her call.

Rainie had had enough. She drove to the airport, flashed a ticket that wasn't valid for another two days, told them she had a family emergency and boarded the plane. Eight hours later, she knocked on Quincy's door. He opened it, looking tense, then shocked, then genuinely grateful. She jumped his bones before he ever made it to the bed. She decided she was getting pretty good at this sex thing.

Later, they went out to Arlington and simply sat next to Mandy's and Bethie's graves. Didn't talk. Didn't do anything. Just sat until the sun had sunk low and the air had grown cold. On the way back to the car, Quincy held her hand. Funny, she was thirty-two years old and she'd never walked hand-in-hand before. Then he opened her door for her, and by the time he got around to the other side she had this strange ache in her chest. She wanted to touch him again. She wanted to take him into her body and wrap her legs around his flanks and hold on tight.

Instead, when they were back at his house, she put his exhausted body to bed. Then she stayed awake for a long time afterwards, stroking the lines on his face, the ones that didn't go away, not even when he slept. She fingered the salt in his pepper hair, the scars on his chest. And she finally got it. All of it. The enormity of it. Why people sought each other out and formed families. Why baby elephants stumbled relentlessly through drought-stricken deserts. Why people fought and laughed and raged and loved. Why people, at the end of it all, *stayed*.

Because even when it hurt, it felt better to hurt with him, and when she was angry it was better to be angry with him, and when she was sad it was far, far better to be sad with him. And damn, she didn't want to get back on that plane. So silly. They were two adults, they had independent lives and demanding jobs, and it's not like there wasn't the telephone, and damn she didn't want to get back on that plane.

She stayed through the funeral. She held Quincy's hand. She patted Kimberly's shoulder as the young girl wept. She met extended family and played nice with everyone. Then she went back to Quincy's house where they came together as if they'd never touched before and would never touch again.

Monday morning he drove her to the airport. She had that tight feeling back in her chest. When she tried to speak, nothing came out.

Quincy said, *"I'll call you."* She nodded. Quincy said, *"Soon."* She nodded. Quincy said, *"I'm sorry, Rainie."* And she nodded, though she wasn't really sure what he was sorry for.

She got back to Portland. Five days, six hours, and thirty-two minutes ago. Her phone did ring. But when she picked it up, Quincy was never there.

"I can't be this well adjusted forever," she told her computer screen. "You know this isn't my style. Are women supposed to change everything for men? I mean, I was hostile, insecure, and stubborn before and he wanted to get to know me better. Now I'm honestly trying to be a mature, productive member of society, and I haven't heard from him since. On the one hand, the man is under enormous amounts of stress. On the other hand, that's just plain rude."

Her computer screen didn't reply. She scowled. "Do you think it was the sickening-sweet pet names? Maybe if I had called him stud muffin …"

Her buzzer sounded. Her head bobbed up, her gaze going to her TV/security monitor. A man was standing in front of the outside doors. He wore normal clothes, but she would've known that salt-and-pepper hair anywhere.

"Shit!" Rainie yelled. "Why doesn't he ever give me a chance to shower!"

Screw the shower. She buzzed him up, ran to the kitchen sink, and hastily splashed water on her face. Two sniffs. Hey, at least this time she'd done deodorant. He rang the doorbell of her loft just as she dragged on a clean white shirt. One last hand through the hair, and she was at the door.

"Hello, Rainie," he said.

She just stood there. He looked good in his Quincy-like way. A little uptight, a little too smart, a little too much weight of the world resting upon his shoulders. But he was wearing slim khaki pants with a navy blue open-collar shirt, the first time in weeks she'd seen him out of a suit.

"Hey," she said. She opened the door a little wider.

"Can I come in?"

"It's been known to happen."

She let him in. SupSpAg had something on his mind. He walked all the way to her family room where he promptly paced back and forth while she gnawed her lower lip. Six days ago they'd been so close. Why did they suddenly feel like strangers?

"I've been meaning to call," he said.

"Uh-huh."

"I didn't, though. I'm sorry." He hesitated. "I didn't know what to say."

" 'Hello' is always a good start. Some people like to follow that with, 'And how are you?' I find that works better than, 'Drop dead.' " She smiled.

He winced. "You're mad."

"Getting there."

"You've been very understanding."

"Oh God, are you breaking up with me?"

He finally stopped pacing, looking genuinely startled. "I didn't think so."

"You didn't *think* so? What does that mean? I asked if you were breaking up with me. If you're not, for God's sake say no, with authority!"

"No, with authority!" he said.

"Five days, six hours, and thirty-seven minutes!"

"What's that?"

"How long since you promised to call. Not that I'm counting or anything." Her hands flew up into the air. "Oh God, I've become one of those women who waits by the phone. I swore I would never be one of those poor saps waiting by the phone. Look at what you've done to me. You ought to be ashamed of yourself!"

"Rainie, I swear I haven't been trying to torture you. I swear, last week when you arrived, I've never been so happy to see anyone. I've never ... *needed* anyone the way I needed you. When I drove you to the airport, all I could think was that I didn't want you to go. Then I had this image of us— driving to and from airports, the high of getting together, the low of splitting apart, trying to be a couple, but still leading separate lives and ...And in all honesty, then I thought that I was much too old for this shit. There are so few things that make me happy, Rainie. There is so little I have left. So why was I driving you to the airport?"

"I had a ticket?"

He sighed. She could see the tightness around his eyes. He stood too far away, half of the loft looming between them, but she couldn't bring herself to close the gap. He had more to say. That was the problem. He'd said the good stuff, so if he still had more ...

"I'm no longer an FBI agent," he told her quietly. "I tendered my resignation to the Bureau two days ago."

"No way." She rocked back on her heels; she couldn't have been more surprised if he'd suddenly announced that he could fly.

"I've decided to reinvent my life. Kimberly has returned to school and is saying she's perfectly fine, so we know she's going to need help. Even if she's too stubborn to let me hold her hand, I think it would mean a lot to her to know that I'm really there for her this time. Not out in the field where I could get hurt. Not running back to the job as I've always done. But close. Say in New York, somewhere by NYU, where she could drop in for dinner if she liked or simply show up to chat. I'm thinking I'll get a loft, put up a shingle and work as an independent consultant for law enforcement agencies."

"Profiler for Hire?"

He smiled. "You'd be surprised how many profilers retire to become consultants. You get to pick your cases, choose your hours, and best of all, ignore all the politics because they're no longer your problem. It's a good setup. Of course, there is one problem."

Rainie eyed him warily. "I'll bite. What problem?"

"I'd like to have a partner."

"You came all the way here to tell me that you're offering Glenda a job?"

He rolled his eyes. "No Rainie, I came all the way here to offer you a job. With full benefits I might add."

"What?" Far from being calmed, she became incensed. "Five days, six hours, and thirty-seven minutes later, this is what you're offering me? *A dental plan?*"

He finally appeared uneasy. "Well, maybe not dental. The company is a start-up."

Rainie stalked toward him. Her eyes had narrowed into slits. Her finger jabbed the air. "What are you doing, Quincy?"

"Apparently once again dodging your finger."

"You fly across the country, you come to my home, and you offer me employment? Do I look like a woman who needs a boss?"

"Not boss," he said immediately. "Oh no, I am not that dumb. I said partner, and I meant partner."

"*It's a professional arrangement!* Five days, six hours, and thirty-seven minutes later, I do not want a professional arrangement. I have not flown across the country three times in six weeks looking for a professional arrangement. I did not jump your bones just last week, looking for a professional arrangement. So help me God, Quincy—"

"I love you."

"What?" She drew up short. Her finger froze in midair.

"Rainie, I love you. You don't know how many times I've already said that because it was always after you'd fallen asleep or left the room. I didn't know if you were ready, or maybe I didn't know if I was ready. But I love you, Rainie. And while I need to stay on the East Coast for my daughter, I don't want to drive you to airports anymore."

"Oh."

"Now would be a good time for you to say something more than, oh."

"I get that."

"You're making me nervous."

"I have a mean streak. And you made me wait five days."

"All the casework you can handle," he offered quietly. "Never easy, nothing boring. You know how it is in my world. I've waited so long to be happy, Rainie. I've made so many mistakes. I want to do better this time. And I want to learn to do better with you."

She sighed. She had that tight feeling back in her chest. So that was what this was about. So this is what everything was about.

She leaned forward. She wrapped her arms around his neck. "Hey Quince," she murmured. "I love you, too."

The Survivors Club

Acknowledgements

As a general rule, I enjoy researching all of my novels. Murder, mayhem, investigative procedures, it's all good stuff. This time around, however, I had a particularly wonderful experience, and for that I'm deeply indebted to the Rhode Island State Police. Not only are they one of the best law enforcement agencies in the country, but they are also helpful, generous and patient people. From explaining the proper protocol for rendering a salute to demonstrating the new AFIS technology, the officers went out of their way to answer my questions and impress upon me the pride they have in their organization. It worked. I'm very impressed by the RI State Police, and I have even started following the speed limit. Well, okay, so the latter half only lasted for a bit. I tried and that says something about their powers of persuasion right there.

Of course, as with all novels, I promptly warped most of the information they graciously provided. In this novel you'll find police procedure and forensics testing happening at approximately the speed of light. Also, my police detectives are perhaps a tad rougher around the edges and a bit more familiar with murder suspects than their real-life counterparts. Remember, the RI State Police detectives have real jobs. I, on the other hand, am a fiction writer who makes things up.

I would like to thank the following members of the RI State Police for their assistance: former Superintendent Colonel Edmond S. Culhane, Jr. (ret.); Superintendent Colonel Steven M. Pare; Major Michael Quinn; Inspector John J. Leyden, Jr.; Lieutenant John Virgilio; Lieutenant Mark Bilodeau; Corporal Eric L. Croce; and Detective James Dougherty.

From the Providence Police Department I would like to thank Lieutenant Paul Kennedy and Sergeant Napoleon Brito. They also gave me the warmest reception, as well as a wonderful collection of gory anecdotes. Let's just say I never fully appreciated the history of dismemberment in the Ocean State before visiting the PPD.

Finally, I owe the following people my deepest gratitude for assisting me in the development of this novel:

Dr. Gregory K. Moffatt, Ph.D., Professor of Psychology, Atlanta Christian College, a wonderful friend and a very wise man.

Albert A. Bucci, Assistant to the Director, State of Rhode Island Department of Corrections, who provided a highly enthusiastic overview of prison life.

Margaret Charpentier, pharmacist and general shoulder to cry on, as well as her fellow pharmacist/partner in crime, Kate Strong.

Monique Lemoine, speech language pathologist and very kind soul.

Kathy Hammond, phlebotomist, Rhode Island Blood Center, and my bloodsucker of choice.

Jim Martin, Public Information Officer, Department of the Attorney General, Rhode Island.

The Providence Preservation Society.

Kathleen Walsh, executive assistant and overall savior of my sanity.

And finally, my very tolerant husband, Anthony. This time around, it was his Ghirardelli double-chocolate brownies that saved the day.

Once again, all mistakes in the novel are mine. Anything you think is particularly brilliant I'll take responsibility for as well.

Happy reading!
Lisa Gardner

Prologue

Eddie

It started as a conversation:

"The scientists are the problem—not the cops. Cops are just cops. Some got a nose for jelly doughnuts; others got a nose for pensions. The scientists, though . . . I read about this case where they nailed a guy by matching the inside seam of his blue jeans with a bloody print left at the murder scene. I'm not kidding. Some expert testified that the wear pattern of denim is so individual there's something like a one-in-a-billion chance that another pair of jeans would leave the same print, yada, yada, yada. Fuckin' unreal."

"Don't wear blue jeans," the second man said.

The first man, a kid really, rolled his eyes. "That's fuckin' brilliant."

The second man shrugged. "Before you lecture me about Calvin's sending someone to the big house, perhaps we should start with the basics. Fingerprints."

"Gloves," the kid said immediately.

"Gloves?" The man frowned. "And here I expected something much more innovative coming from you."

"Hey, gloves are a pain in the ass, but then again, so is serving time. What else are you gonna do?"

"I don't know. But I don't want to wear gloves if I don't have to. Let's think about it."

"You could wipe down everything," the kid said shortly. "Ammonia dissolves fingerprint oil, you know. You could prepare a solution, ammonia and water. Afterwards, you could spray it on, wipe stuff down. You know, including . . ." The kid's voice trailed off. He didn't seem quite able to say the word, which the man thought was pretty funny, given everything this "kid" had done.

The man nodded. "Yes. Including. With ammonia, of course. Otherwise they might be able to print the woman's skin using Alternate Light Source or fumigation. Instead of spritzing, the other option is to put the woman in a tub. To ensure that you're being thorough."

"Yeah." The kid nodded his head, contemplating. "Still might miss a spot. And it involves a lot of maneuvering. Remember what the textbook said: 'The more contact with the victim, the more evidence left behind.'"

"True. Other ideas?"

"You could leave fake prints. I once met this guy from New York. His gang liked to cut off the hands of their rivals, and use them to leave false prints at their own crime scenes."

"Did it work?"

"Well, half the gang was in Rikers at the time . . ."

"So it didn't work."

"Probably not."

The man pursed his lips. "It's an interesting thought, though. Creative. The police hate creativity. We should find out where those people went wrong."

"I'll ask around."

"A fingerprint is nothing but a ridge pattern," the man thought out loud. "Fill in the valleys between the ridges and there's no more print. Seems like there's gotta be a way of doing that. Maybe smearing the fingertips with superglue? I've heard of it, but I don't know if it works."

"Wouldn't that interfere with feel, though? I mean, if you're going to lose sensation, you might as well return to gloves which you know will do the trick."

"There's scarring. Repeated cutting of the fingertips with a razor to obscure the print."

"No thank you!"

"No pain, no gain," the man said mildly.

"Yeah, and no pleasure, no point. What do you think scar tissue is gonna do to the nerve endings of your fingertips? Might as well hack 'em off and be done with it. Keep it simple, remember? Another thing the textbook pointed out—simple is good."

The man shrugged. "Fine, then it's gloves. Thinnest latex possible. That resolves the matter of fingerprints. Next issue: DNA."

"Shit," the kid said.

"DNA is the kicker," the man agreed. "With fingerprints you can watch what you touch. But with DNA . . . Now you have to consider your hair, your blood, your semen, your spit. Oh, and bite marks. Let's not forget about the power of dental matches."

"Jesus, you are a sick son of a bitch." The kid rolled his eyes again. "Look, don't bite anything or anyone. It's too risky. They've nailed thieves by matching their teeth to indentations left in a hunk of cheddar in the fridge. After that, God knows what they can do with a human breast."

"Fair enough. Now back to DNA."

"Pull an O.J.," the kid said grumpily. "Let the lawyers deal with it."

"You really think lawyers are that good, all things considered . . ." The man's tone was droll.

The kid got hostile. "Hey, what the fuck is a guy supposed to do? Wear a goddamn condom? Hell, man, might as well fuck a garden hose."

"Then we need a better idea. Blaming the cops is no kind of defense. They don't handle the DNA anyway. The hospital sends it straight to the Department of Health via a courier. Or don't you read the paper?"

"I read—"

"And a bath won't help there either," the man continued relentlessly. "Just

look at Motyka. He stuck the woman in a tub and t
now facing life in prison. The semen goes up into the bo
thing more, some kind of flush action, I don't know. Plus
Hair can also yield DNA, if they get a root, or they can simply m
the scene to hair on your head. Bathtub won't help with hair, eith
anal-retentive crime tech will retrieve your hair from the drainpipes—
can retrieve blood samples from there too, you know. You can't approac
this half-assed."

"Shave."

"Everywhere?"

"Yes." The kid's tone was grudging. "Yeah, shit. Everywhere. Tell people
you're into swimming. What the fuck."

"Shaving is good," the man conceded. "That resolves the hair. What else?
They'll swab the woman's mouth. Remember that."

"Yeah, yeah, yeah, I read the same book you did."

"No touching anything with your bare hands—not even an eyeball."

"I read about that case, too."

"No blue jeans, I guess."

"Wear dust covers over your shoes to limit soil and fiber," the kid added.
"And, whenever possible, resort to social engineering. Breaking and entering
leaves behind tool marks, and tool marks can also be matched."

The man nodded: "That covers most of the trace evidence except for
DNA then. We still need to figure out DNA. They get one little sample of
semen, send it to the DNA database . . ."

"I know, I know." The kid closed his eyes. He appeared to be thinking.
Hard. He finally opened them again. "You could try confusing the issue.
There was that guy who was arrested as a serial rapist based on DNA, then
while he was in prison, another rape was reported with the same kind of
DNA found on the girl's panties."

"What happened?"

The kid sighed. "They busted the guy in prison for that, too. Perpetrating
fraud, something like that."

"He raped the other girl while he was behind bars?"

"No, man, he jacked off into a ketchup packet while he was behind bars,
then mailed it to a friend who paid a girl fifty bucks to smear the stuff on
her underwear and cry rape. You know, so it would appear like there was
another guy running around with the same DNA, who was actually the
rapist."

"There is no such thing as two guys with the same DNA. Not even identical twins have the same DNA."

"Yeah, and that would be the problem with the plan. The scientists knew
that and the prosecution knew that, so they pressured the girl until she confessed what really happened."

"Is there a moral to this story?"

"Pay the girl more than fifty bucks!"

The man sighed. "That is not a good plan."

"Hey, you wanted an idea, I gave you an idea."

"I wanted a good idea."

ything. The kid lapsed into silence as well.

muttered after a bit.

an agreed.

hn Thomas," the kid mocked from Monty

lp anyway. Condoms leak, condoms break.
at tracing the lubricants and spermicide. That
ey start checking stores and next thing you know
ust happened to notice some guy buying some

"Yeah. ts. Any little thing you introduce into the scene . . ."
The kid suddenly rked up. "Hey," he said. "I have an idea."

1

Jersey

The blonde caught in the sights of the Leupold Vari-X III 1.5–5 x 20mm Matte Duplex Illuminated Reticle scope didn't seem to fear for her life. At the moment, in fact, she was doing her hair. Now she had out a black compact and was checking her lipstick, a light, pearly pink. Jersey adjusted the Leupold scope as the reporter pursed her lips for her own reflection and practiced an alluring pout. Next to her, her cameraman let his heavy video equipment fall from his shoulder to the ground and rolled his eyes. Apparently, he recognized this drill and knew it would be a while.

Ten feet away from the blonde, another reporter, this one male—WNAC-TV, home of the Fox *Futurecast,* because heaven forbid anyone call it a *forecast* anymore—was meticulously picking pieces of lint off of his mud-brown suit. His cameraman sat in the grass, sipping Dunkin' Donuts coffee and blinking sleepily. On the other side of the stone pillar that dominated the sprawling World War Memorial Park, a dozen other reporters were scattered about, double-checking their copy, double-checking their appearance, yawning tiredly, then double-checking the street.

Eight-oh-one A.M., Monday morning. At least twenty-nine minutes until the blue van from Adult Correctional Institutions (ACI) was due to arrive at the Licht Judicial Complex in downtown Providence and everyone was bored. Hell, Jersey was bored. He'd been camped out on the roof of the sprawling brick courthouse since midnight last night. And damn, it got *cold* at night this early in May. Three Army blankets, a black coverall, and black leather Bob Allen shooting gloves and he still shivered until the sun came up. That was a little before six, meaning he'd had two and a half more hours to kill and not even the chance to stand up and stretch without giving his position away.

Jersey had spent the night—and now the morning—hunkered behind a two-foot-high decorative-brick trim piece that lined this section of the courthouse's roof. The faux railing afforded him just enough cover to remain invisible to people in the courtyard below, and more importantly, to the reporters camped in the grassy memorial park across the street. The railing also offered the perfect rifle stand, for when the moment came.

Sometime between 8:30 and 9:00 A.M., the blue ACI van would pull up. The eight-foot-high wrought-iron gate that surrounded the inner courtyard of the judicial complex would open up. The van would pull in. The gate would swing shut. The van doors would open. And then . . .

Jersey's finger twitched on the trigger of the heavy barrel AR15. He caught himself, then eased his grip on the assault rifle, slightly surprised by his antsiness. It wasn't like him to rush. Calm and controlled, he told himself. Easy does it. Nothing here he hadn't done before. Nothing here he couldn't handle.

Jersey had been hunting since the time he could walk, the scent of gunpowder as reassuring to him as talcum. Following in his father's footsteps, he'd joined the Army at the age of eighteen, then spent eight years honing his abilities with an M16. Not to brag, but Jersey could take out targets at five hundred yards most guys couldn't hit at one hundred. He was also a member of the Quarter Inch Club—at two hundred yards, he could cluster three shots within a quarter-inch triangulation of one another. His father had been an American sniper in 'Nam, so Jersey figured that shooting was in his genes.

Five years ago, seeking a better lifestyle than the Army could afford him, he'd opened shop. He used a double-blind policy. The clients never knew his name, he never knew theirs. A first middleman contacted a second middleman who contacted Jersey. Money was wired to appropriate accounts. Dossiers bearing pertinent information were sent to temporary P.O. boxes opened at various MAIL BOXES ETC. stores under various aliases. Jersey had a rule about not hitting women or children. Some days he thought that made him a good person. Other days he thought that made him worse, because he used that policy to try to prove to himself that he did have a conscience when the bottom line was, well, you know—he killed people for money.

If his father knew, he definitely wouldn't approve.

This gig had come along five months ago. Jersey had been instantly intrigued. For one thing, the target was a genuine, bona fide rapist, so Jersey didn't have to worry about his conscience. For another thing, the job was in Providence, and Jersey had always wanted to visit the Ocean State. He'd made four separate trips to the city to scope out the job, and thus far, he liked what he saw.

Providence was a small city, bisected by the Providence River, where, no kidding, they ran gondola rides on select Friday and Saturday nights. The slick black boats looked straight out of Venice, and the mayor even had a bunch of good ol' Italian boys manning the vessels in black-striped shirts and red-banded strawhats. Then there was this thing called WaterFire, where they lit bonfires in the middle of the river. You could sit out at your favorite restaurant and watch the river burn while tourists bounced around the flames in gondolas. Jersey had been secretly hoping someone would catch on fire, but hey, that was just him.

The city was pretty. This courthouse, on the east side of the river, was an impressive red-brick structure with a soaring white clock tower that dominated an entire city block. Old world colonial meets new world grandeur. The front of the courthouse sat on Benefit Street, which seemed to be a mile-long advertisement for old money—huge historical homes featuring everything from Victorian turrets to Gothic stone, interspersed with green lawns and neatly constructed brick walls. The back of the courthouse, where Jersey was, overlooked the sprawling memorial park, the grassy expanse littered with dignified bronze sculptures of soldiers and significantly less dignified pieces of modern art. The modern art carried over to the Rhode Island School of Design (RISD), with its urban campus stretching alongside the courthouse.

Rhode Island didn't have much in the way of violent crime. Thirty homicides a year, something like that. Of course, that would change today. The state was better known for its long history of financial crimes, Mafia connections and political corruption. As the locals liked to say, in Rhode Island it isn't what you know, but who you know. And in all honesty, everyone did seem to know one another in this state. Frankly, it freaked Jersey out.

Jersey started to yawn again, caught it this time and forced himself to snap to attention. Eight twenty-one A.M. now. Not much longer. On the grass across the street, the various news teams were beginning to stir.

Last night, before coming to the courthouse, Jersey had sat in his hotel room and flipped back and forth between all the local news shows, trying to learn the various media personalities. He didn't recognize the pretty blonde down below, though her cameraman's shirt indicated that they were with WJAR, News Team 10, the local NBC affiliate. Network news. That was respectable. Jersey was happy for her.

Then he wondered if the woman had any idea just how big her morning was about to become. His target, Eddie Como, aka the College Hill Rapist, was major news in the Ocean State. Everyone was here to cover the start of the trial. Everyone was here to capture shots of slightly built, hunch-shouldered Eddie, or maybe get a glimpse of one of his three beautiful victims.

These reporters didn't know anything yet. About Jersey. About his client. About what was really going to happen this sunny Monday morning in May. It made Jersey feel benevolent toward all the bored, overhyped, over-groomed individuals gathered on the grass below. He had a treat for them. He was about to make one of them, some of them, very special.

Take this pretty little blonde with the pearly pink lips. She was up first thing this morning, armed with canned copy and thinking that at best, she'd get a shot of the blue ACI van for the morning news at her station. Of course, the other twenty reporters would shoot the same visual with pretty much the same copy, nobody being any better than anyone else, and nobody being any worse. Just another day on the job, covering what needed to be covered for all the enquiring minds that wanted to know.

Except that someone down in that park, sitting on the grass, surrounded by war memorials and freakish exhibits of modern art, was going to get a scoop this morning. Someone, maybe that pretty little blonde, was going to show up to get a routine clip of a blue ACI van, and come away with a picture of a hired gun instead.

There was no way around it. The only time Jersey would have access to Eddie Como was when the alleged rapist was moved from the ACI to the Licht Judicial Complex on the opening day of his trial. And the only time

Jersey would have access at the Licht Judicial Complex was when Eddie was unloaded from the ACI van within a fenced-off drop-off roughly the size of a two-car garage. And the only way Jersey could shoot into a drop-off zone enclosed by an eight-foot-high fence was to shoot down at the target.

The massive red-brick courthouse took up an entire city block. Soaring up to sixteen stories high with swooping red-brick wings, it towered above its fellow buildings and zealously protected its back courtyard and the all-important drop-off zone. So Jersey's options had been clear from the beginning. He would have to access the courthouse itself, easily done in the cover of night once he learned the routine of the Capital Security guards.

He would have to take up position on the sixth-story roofline immediately overlooking the drop-off point to have a clean shot down into the fenced-off area. He would have to line up the shot in the cover of darkness. And then, when the van finally arrived sometime between 8:30 and 9:00 A.M., he would have five seconds to stand, blow off the top of Eddie Como's head and start running.

Because while the state marshals who escorted the inmates probably wouldn't be able to see him—the angle would be too steep—and while the prisoners themselves wouldn't be able to see him—they would probably be too busy screaming at all the brains now sprayed in their hair—the reporters, every single greedy, desperate-for-a-scoop reporter camped across the street—they would have a clear view of Jersey standing six stories up. Jersey firing a rifle six stories up. Jersey running across the vast roofline six stories up.

The shot itself was going to be easy. A mere seventy feet. Straight down. Hell, Jersey should forget the assault rifle and drop an anvil on the guy's head. Yeah, the shot itself was downright boring. But the moments afterward . . . The moments afterward were going to be really entertaining.

A disturbance down the street. Jersey flicked back to the pretty blonde in time to see her drop her lipstick and scramble forward. Show time.

He glanced at his watch. Eight thirty-five A.M. Apparently, the state marshals didn't want to keep the reporters waiting.

Jersey brought his rifle back down against him. He adjusted the scope to 1.5, all he would need for a seventy-foot head shot. He checked the twenty-cartridge magazine, then chambered the first round. He was using Winchester's .223 Remington, a 55-grain soft-point bullet, which according to the box was best for shooting prairie dogs, coyotes and woodchucks.

And now, the College Hill Rapist.

Jersey got on his knees. He positioned the rifle along the top of the rail, then placed his eye against the scope. He could just make out the street through the stone archways lining the outer courtyard. He heard, more than saw, the black wrought-iron fence of the inner courtyard swing open. Calm and controlled. Easy does it. Nothing here he hadn't done before. Nothing here he couldn't handle.

He flexed his fingers. He listened to the reassuring crinkle of his black leather shooting gloves . . .

The prisoners would be shackled together like a chain gang. Most would be in khaki or blue prison overalls. But Eddie Como would be different.

Facing the first day of trial, Eddie Como would arrive in a suit.

Jersey waited for the barking sound of a state marshal ordering the unloading of the van. He felt the first prick of sweat. But he didn't pop up. He still didn't squeeze the trigger.

Twenty reporters and cameramen across the street. Twenty journalists just waiting for their big break . . .

"Courtyard secure! Door open!"

Jersey heard the rasp of metal as the van door slid back. He heard the slap of the first rubber-soled shoe hitting the flagstone patio . . .

One, two, three, four, five . . .

Jersey rocketed up from his knees and angled the AR15 twenty-two degrees from vertical. Searching, searching . . .

The dark head of Eddie Como emerged from the van. He was gazing forward, looking at the door of the courthouse. His shoulders were down. He took three shuffling steps forward—

And Jersey blew off the top of his head. One moment Eddie Como was standing shackled between two guys. The next he was folding up silently and plummeting to the hard, slate-covered ground.

Jersey let the black-market rifle fall to the roof. Then he began to run.

He was aware of so many things at once. The feel of the sun on his face. The smell of cordite in the air. The noise of a city about to start a busy work-week, cars roaring, cars screeching. And then, almost as an afterthought, people beginning to scream.

"Gun, gun, gun!"

"Get down, get down!"

"Look! Up there. On the roof!"

Jersey was smiling. Jersey was feeling good. He clambered across the courthouse roof, the gummy soles of his rock-climbing shoes finding perfect traction. He turned the corner and rounded the center clock tower, which rose another several stories. *Now you see me. Now you don't.*

Shots fired. Some overpumped state marshals shooting their wad at an enemy they couldn't see.

Jersey's smile grew. He hummed now as he stripped off his gloves and cast them behind him. Almost at the rooftop door. He grabbed the front of his black coveralls with his left hand and popped open the snaps. Three seconds later, the black coveralls joined his discarded rifle and gloves on the rooftop. Five seconds after that, Jersey had replaced his rock climber's shoes with highly polished Italian loafers. Then it was a simple matter of reclaiming the black leather briefcase he'd left by the rooftop door. Last night, the briefcase had contained the dismantled parts of an AR15. This morning, it held only business papers.

From world-class sniper to just one more guy in a suit in five minutes or less.

Jersey pulled open the rooftop door. He'd jammed the lock with wire last night so it would be ready for him. Moments later, he was down the stairs and joining the main traffic flow, just another harried lawyer too busy to look anyone in the eye.

Capital Security guards and state marshals rushed by. People inside the courthouse were looking around, becoming increasingly aware that something had happened but not sure what. Jersey, following their example, pasted a slightly puzzled expression on his face as he journeyed forth.

Another gray-clad marshal sprinted by him, voices screaming from the radio at the man's waist. He hit Jersey's shoulder, knocking him back. Jersey spluttered, "Excuse me!" The state marshal kept running for the stairs leading to the roof.

"What happened?" a lady walking next to Jersey asked.

"I'm not sure," he said. "Must be something bad."

They exchanged vigorous nods. And thirty-two seconds later, Jersey was out the front door, taking a left and heading back down steeply pitched College Street toward the memorial park. He resumed humming now, in the homestretch. Even if some police officer stopped him, what would the officer find? Jersey had no weapons, no trace of gunpowder on his hands or clothes. He was just a businessman, and he always carried valid ID.

The screech of sirens abruptly split the air. The city wasn't big and the Providence Police had their headquarters downtown. Cops would be streaming in from all over, roadblocks just a matter of time. Jersey picked up his step but remained calm. His thoughtful client, no doubt familiar with the parking crunch in downtown Providence, had sent Jersey a RISD visitor's pass for the parking lot just across the street. The cops would be here in two minutes. Jersey would be gone in one.

The sirens roared closer. Jersey arrived at the tiny college parking lot at the base of College Street and South Main. Found his key for the blue rental car. Unlocked the doors, threw in his briefcase, slid into the seat.

Calm and controlled. Easy does it. Nothing here he hadn't done before. Nothing here he couldn't handle.

Jersey turned the key in the ignition. And then, he heard the *click*.

One frozen instant in time. His eyes widening, his bewilderment honest. But, but, the double-blind policy. Nobody knew his name. He never knew theirs. How could, how could . . .

And then his eyes went to the red visitor's parking pass hanging from his rental-car mirror, the lone visitor's pass in a minuscule city parking lot of only twenty vehicles.

His client's thoughtfulness . . .

Calm and controlled, Jersey thought helplessly. Easy does it. Nothing here he hadn't done before. Nothing here he couldn't handle . . .

The current from the car's starter box hit the electrical ignition switch of the custom-made bomb, and Jersey's rental car exploded into the bright morning sky.

A dozen city blocks away, on Hope Street, the well-groomed patrons of the trendy restaurant rue de l'espoir—made even trendier by its all-lowercase name—looked up from their decadent business breakfasts of eggs Benedict and inch-thick slices of French toast. Sitting in comfy booths, they now gazed around the rich, earthy interior where the walls were the same color as aged copper pots and the booths were decorated in hues of red, green, brown and eggplant. The tremor, though slight, had been unmistakable.

Even the waitresses had stopped in their tracks.

"Did you feel that?" one of the servers asked.

The people in the chic little restaurant looked at each other. They had just started to shrug away the minor disturbance when the harsh sound of screaming sirens cut the air. Two cop cars went flying down the street. An ambulance roared by in their wake.

"Something must have happened," someone said.

"Something big," another patron echoed.

Sitting at a small table tucked alone in the far corner, three women finally looked up from their oversized mugs of spiced chai. Two were older, one was younger. All three had caused a minor stir when they had walked through the door. Now the women looked at one another. Then, simultaneously, they looked away.

"I wonder," said one.

"Don't," said another.

And that was all they said.

Until the cops came.

2

Griffin

At 8:31 a.m. Monday morning, Rhode Island State Police Detective Sergeant Roan Griffin was already late for his 8:30 briefing. This was not a good thing. It was his first day back on the job in eighteen months. He should probably be on time. Hell, he should probably be early. Show up at headquarters at 8:15 a.m., pumped up, sharply pressed, crisply saluting. Here I am, I am ready.

And then . . . ?

"Welcome back," they would greet him. (Hopefully.)

"Thanks," he would say. (Probably.)

"How are you feeling?" they'd ask. (Suspiciously.)

"Good," he'd reply. (Too easily.)

Ah, shit. Good *was* a stupid answer. Too often said to be often believed. He'd say good, and they'd stare at him harder, trying to read between the lines. Good like you're ready to crack open a case file, or good like we can trust you with a loaded firearm? It was an interesting question.

He drummed his fingers on the steering wheel and tried again.

"Welcome back," they'd say.

"It's good to be back," he'd say.

"How are you doing?" they'd ask.

"My anxiety is operating within normal parameters," he'd reply.

No. Absolutely not. That kind of psychobabble made even him want to whoop his ass. Forget it. He should've gone with his father's recommendation and walked in wearing a T-shirt that read "You're only Jealous Because the Voices are Talking to *Me*."

At least they all could've had a good laugh.

Griffin had joined the Rhode Island State Police force sixteen years ago. He'd started with four months in a rigorous boot camp, learning everything from evasive driving maneuvers to engaging in hand-to-hand combat after being stung with pepper spray. (You want to know pain? Having pepper spray in your eyes is pain. You want to know self-control? Standing there willingly to be sprayed for the *second* time, that is self-control.) Following boot camp, Griffin had spent eight years in uniform. He'd boosted the state coffers writing his share of speeding tickets. He'd helped motorists change tires. He'd attended dozens of motor vehicle accidents, including way too many involving children. Then he'd joined the Detective Bureau, starting in Intelligence, where he'd earned a stellar reputation for his efforts on a major FBI case. Following that, he worked some money laundering, gunrunning, art forgery, homicide. Rhode Island may not have a large quantity of crime, but as the detectives liked to say, they got quality crime.

Griffin had been a good detective. Bright. Hardheaded. Stubborn. Ferocious at times. Funny at others. This stuff was in his blood. His grandfather had been a beat cop in New York. His father had served as sheriff in North Kingstown. Two of his brothers were now state marshals. Years ago, when Griffin had first met Cindy on a hiking trip in New Hampshire, first looked into her eyes and felt her smile like a thunderbolt in his chest, he'd blurted out, before his name, before even hello, "I'm a cop." Fortunately for him, Cindy had understood.

Griffin had been a good detective. Guys liked working with him. The brass liked giving him cases. The media liked following his career. He went on the Dave Letterman show when the Rhode Island State Police won a nationwide award for best uniform. He led Operation Pinto, which shut down a major auto-theft ring in a blaze of front-page *Providence Journal* headlines. He even got appointed to the governor's task force on community policing, probably because the little old ladies had been asking for him since he'd strutted across Letterman's sound stage. (Officer Blue Eyes, the *ProJo* had dubbed him. Oh yeah, his fellow detectives had definitely had that made into a T-shirt.)

Two and a half years ago, when the third kid vanished from Wakefield and the pattern of a locally operating child predator became clear, there had never been any doubt that Griffin would head the investigation. He remembered being excited when he'd walked out of that briefing. He remembered the thrum of adrenaline in his veins, the flex of his muscles, the heady sense that he had once again begun a chase.

Two days before Cindy went for a routine checkup. Six months before everything went from bad to worse. Eleven months before he learned the true nature of the black abyss.

For the record, he'd nailed that son of a bitch. For the record.

Griffin made the left-hand fork on Route 6, headed into North Scituate. Five minutes from headquarters now. He drove by the giant reservoir as the landscape opened up to reveal a vast expanse of water on his right and rolling green hills on his left. Soon he'd see joggers, guys grabbing a morning run. Then would come the state police compound. First, the flat, ugly 1960s brown building that housed Investigative Support Services. Then, the huge old gray barn in the back, a remnant of what the property used to be. Finally, the beautiful old white semimansion that now served as state police headquarters, complete with a gracefully curving staircase and bay windows overlooking more rolling green hills. The White House, the rookies called it. Where the big boys lived.

Damn, he'd missed this place. Damn.

"Welcome back, Griffin," they'd say.

"Thanks," he'd say.

"How are you feeling?" they'd ask.

And he'd answer—

In the left-hand lane, a blue Ford Taurus roared past, red lights flashing behind the grille. Then came two more unmarked police cars, sirens also screaming. What the hell?

Griffin turned into the parking lot of state police headquarters just in time to see detectives pour out of ISSB and race for their state steels. He recognized two guys from the Criminal Identification Unit (CIU), Jack Cappelli and Jack Needham, aka Jack-n-Jack, climbing into the big gray crime-scene-investigation van. Then they had flipped on the lights and were peeling out of the lot.

Griffin swung in front of the ISS building. He hadn't even cut the motor before Lieutenant Marcey Morelli of Major Crimes was banging on his window.

"Lieutenant." He started to salute. Morelli cut him off.

"Providence just called in reports of rifle fire and a major explosion at the Licht Judicial Complex. ATF and the state fire marshal get the explosion. We get the shooting. All units respond."

"A shooting at the *courthouse?*" His eyebrows shot up. No friggin' way.

"You been following the Como case? Sounds like somebody got tired of waiting for the trial. Better yet, the media's already there, catching the before and the after. Can you say 'Film at eleven'?"

"Somebody up there hates you, Lieutenant."

"No kidding. Look, whatever just happened, we know it's going to be big. I've already asked the detective commander for additional resources, plus I want all of Major Crimes down there ASAP. The uniforms can handle the canvassing, but I want you guys on initial interviews. Find out when, where, why, how, radio it to every uniform in the area so they can be on the lookout for the shooter, and hey, catch this guy yesterday. You know the drill." Morelli paused long enough to take a breath, then narrowed her eyes as, for the first time, she truly saw his seated form. "Jesus Christ, Griffin, I thought you'd spent the time fishing or something like that."

"Well yeah. And some weights." He shrugged modestly.

"Uh huh."

"And some running."

"Uh huh."

"Okay, boxing, too."

The lieutenant rolled her eyes. Griffin had spent the last year of his eighteen-month medical leave mastering the art of sublimation—funneling nonproductive tension into a productive outlet. He'd gotten pretty good at it. He could sustain a five-minute mile for nearly ten miles. He could box sixteen rounds. He could bench-press a Volvo.

His body was good. His face was still a little too harsh—a man not sleeping well at night. But physically . . . Griffin was a lean, mean machine.

The lieutenant straightened. "Well," she said briskly, "The Boss is on his way. So get moving, Sergeant. And remember, there are only a hundred cameras about to document every step we take."

Lieutenant Morelli resumed running. Griffin sat there for one more moment, honestly a little dazed. *My anxiety is operating within normal parameters,* he thought stupidly. Ah fuck it. Back is back. He flipped on his lights and joined his fellow officers, roaring toward Providence.

3

Jillian

She is driving to her sister's apartment. Work has held her up, she is running an hour late. Traffic is miserable, of course. Another accident on 195, when isn't there an accident? She is thinking about all the things she still has to get done. Cash-flow analysis of the first six months. Cash-flow projection of the next six months. Storyboards for Roger. Copy proofs for Claire.

Toppi called her at work to say that Libby was having a bad day. Please don't stay out too late.

She is driving to her sister's apartment, but she is not thinking about her sister. She is not looking forward to dinner with Trish. It has become one more thing to do on a long list of things to do, and part of her suspects that this is bad. She has lost perspective. She has let her life get away from her. The rest of her is too busy to care.

She has her responsibilities. She is the responsible one.

Trisha is off to college. Trisha has her first apartment, tiny, cramped, but beautiful because it is all hers. Trisha has new friends, new life, new goals. She wants to be a playwright, she told Jillian excitedly last week. Before that she had wanted to study communications. Before that it had been English. Trish is young, beautiful, bright. The world is her oyster, and Jillian does not doubt that Trish will become exactly who she wants to become, doing exactly what she wants to do.

And this pains her in a way she doesn't understand. Lifts her up, pushes her down. She is the surrogate mother, proud of her child's accomplishments. She is the tired older sister, feeling a nagging twinge of jealousy when she has nothing to be jealous of. Yes, her path was harder. No, she was never nineteen and carefree. No, she has never gotten to live on her own, not even now. But she went to college, earned a business degree. At thirty-six she runs a successful ad agency, calling all the shots. She didn't sacrifice everything for her mother and sister. She carved out her own life, too.

And yet . . .

Visiting Trish is hard for her these days. She does not do it nearly as often as she should.

Now, she drives around Thayer Street, looking for a place to park. The third week in May, the sun is just starting to set and the sidewalks are crowded with Brown University summer students, milling outside of Starbucks, the Gap store, Abercrombie & Fitch. Jillian still gets a twinge of unease over Trisha living in the city. Especially after the recent reports of two rapes, the second of which was only two weeks ago. One was over at Providence College, however, and the other was some woman in her home.

Trisha knows about the attacks. They even talked about it last week. Some of the girls have started carrying pepper spray. Trish bought a canister as well. Plus she inspected the locks on her apartment. Her apartment is really very secure. A little basement studio, with only tiny windows set high in the wall and not big enough for a grown man to crawl through. Trisha had also installed a bolt lock when she signed her lease last spring. It's a key in, key out kind of lock; supposedly one of the best money can buy.

"I'll be fine," Trish told Jillian in that exasperated way only a teenager can manage. "For heaven's sake, I've taken two courses in self-defense!"

Jillian finally finds a parking spot deep down on Angell Street. She has a bit of a hike now to Trisha's apartment, but that's not unusual given the state of Providence's parking. Plus, it's a balmy, dusky evening and she could use the exercise.

Jillian doesn't have pepper spray. She contemplates this as she locks the door of her gold Lexus. She does what she's seen on TV—she carries her car keys in her fist, with the biggest key sticking out between two fingers like a weapon. She also keeps her head up and her footsteps brisk. Of course, this comes naturally to her. She has never been the shrinking violet type. She likes to think that Trish got her independent spirit from her.

Trisha lives at the edge of the Brown campus. Generally, they meet at her apartment, then walk to Thayer Street with its host of ethnic restaurants and upscale coffee shops. Jillian could go for some Pad Thai. Or maybe grilled lamb.

For the first time, her footsteps pick up. Thayer Street has such great restaurants; it's nice to be out and about on College Hill, with its youth and vitality. And the night is lovely, not too hot, not too cold. After dinner they can go for some ice cream. Trisha can tell her all about her summer internship at Trinity Theater, whether the set guy—Joe, Josh, Jon—has asked her out yet. There would be fresh gossip on her group of friends, of course, The Girls. Tales of adventure from their recent trip to Providence Place Mall, ladies' night out in Newport, etc., etc.

Jillian could relax, sit back, and let Trisha go. Tell me about *every hour, minute, day*. Tell me *everything*.

For this is where the proud surrogate mother and tired older sister come together: they both love to listen to Trish. They love her enthusiasm. They cherish her excitement. They marvel at her wonder, a nineteen-year-old woman-girl, still learning about the world, still convinced she can make it a better place.

Jillian arrives at Trisha's apartment complex. Once, it was a grand old home. Now, the building is subdivided into eight units for the college crowd. As the basement renter, Trisha has her own entrance around back.

Jillian rounds the house as the sun sinks lower on the horizon and casts the narrow alleyway into gloom. Trisha has a powerful outdoor spotlight above the back door. Jillian is slightly surprised, given the rapidly falling night, that Trish has not turned it on. She'll mention it to her.

At the door, Jillian raises her hand, she lets her knuckles fall. And then she *catches her breath as the door soundlessly swings in to reveal the darkened stairs.*

"Trisha? Trish?"

Jillian moves cautiously down the steps, having to use the handrail to guide her way. Had Trisha grown tired of waiting for her? Maybe she'd decided to start her laundry and had run down the street to the Laundromat. That had happened once before.

At the bottom of the stairs is another door, this one wooden, simple. An inside bedroom door. Jillian puts her hand on the shiny brass-colored knob. She turns. The door sweeps open and Jillian is face-to-face with a deep-shadowed room.

"Trisha?"

She takes three steps in. She glances at the tiny kitchenette. She turns toward the bed, and—

A force slams into her from behind. She cries out, her hands popping open, her car keys flying across the room, as she goes down hard. She catches herself with her left palm and promptly hears something crack.

"Trish?" Her voice high-pitched, reedy, not at all like herself. The bed, the bed, that poor woman on the bed.

"Goddamn bitch!"

A weight is pressing against her back. Rough hands tangle in her hair. Her head is jerked back. She gasps for air. Then her head is slammed against the floor.

Stars. She sees stars, and her scattered senses try to understand what is happening. It's not a cartoon. There is no Coyote or Road Runner. This is her, in her sister's apartment, and oh my God, she is under attack. That is not a store mannequin tied naked and spread-eagled to the bed. Trish, Trish, Trish!

All of a sudden, Jillian is pissed off.

"No!" she cries.

"Fucking, fucking, fucking," the man says. He has her hair again. Her head goes up. Her head goes down. Her nose explodes and blood and tears pour down her face. She whimpers, but then her rage grows even hotter. She must get this man! She must hurt this man! Because even in pain, even in shock, she has a deeper, instinctive understanding of what has just happened here. Of what this man just did to her sister.

Her hands come out from beneath her, flailing wildly, trying to whack at the weight on her back. But her arms don't bend that way, and he's still beating her face and the world is now starting to spin. Her head goes back, her head goes forward. Her head goes back, her head goes forward . . .

He is sliding down her back. He is rubbing against her and there is no mistaking his arousal. "I'm going to fuck you good," the man says. He laughs and laughs and laughs.

Jillian finally twists beneath his body. She beats at his thighs. She knits together the fingers on her right hand and tries to jab them into his ribs. And he whips her head from side to side to side until she can no longer feel the sting. She is in a dark, black place with a weight crushing her body and a voice stuck in her head and he is going to fuck her good.

His left hand curls around her throat. It starts to squeeze. She tries to claw at his wrist, but encounters only latex.

Oh no. Trish. Oh no.

She must get him off. She can't get him off. Her lungs are burning. She wants to fight. She wants to save her sister. Oh please stop, please.

Somebody. Help us.

The lights grow brighter behind her eyes. Her body slowly, surely, goes limp. The man finally loosens the grip his legs have on her ribs. His weight comes up off her body slightly.

And she jabs her hand forward as hard as she can and nails him between the legs.

The man howls. Rolls to the side. Clutches his balls. Jillian twists her shoulders, grabs at the floor, and tries to find something to pull herself free.

And then the weight is completely gone. The man is gone. He is curled up on the floor and she's gotta move. Phone, phone, phone. The kitchen counter. It's on the kitchen counter. If she can just get to the phone, dial 911.

Jillian pulls herself across the hardwood floor. Gotta move, gotta move. Trisha needs her. She needs her.

Come on, Jillian.

And then, before she even feels him, she hears him coming again.

"No," she whimpers, but she's already too late.

"Goddamn, fucking bitch! I'm gonna KILL *you! I'm gonna* SNAP *your goddamn neck, I'm gonna pop out your fucking eyes. Goddamn . . ."*

He slams down upon her back and grabs her throat with his steely hands. Squeeze, squeeze, squeeze. Can't swallow. Can't breathe.

Her chest, growing so tight. Her hands, plucking at his gloved hands. No, no, no.

Come on, Jillian. Come on, Jillian.

But he is too strong. She realizes this as the world begins to spin and her lungs start to burst. She is proud. She is smart. She is a woman who believes she controls her own life.

But he is brute strength. And she is no match for him.

She is sinking down. She wants to say something. She wants to reach out to her sister. She is so sorry. Oh Trish, oh Trish, oh Trish.

And then, all of a sudden, the hands are gone.

"Fuck!" Fast footsteps run across the room. Footsteps pounding up the stairs. A distant boom as the external door bursts open.

Jillian draws a ragged, gasping breath of air. Like a drowning victim bursting free from water, she bolts upright, desperately dragging more oxygen into her lungs.

He's gone. He just . . . gone.

The room is empty. It is over. She's alive, she's alive. She is not stronger. She is not more capable. But she is lucky.

Jillian pulls herself unsteadily to her feet. She staggers across the room. She falls onto the bed next to her sister's form.

"Trish!" she cries out.

And then, in the unending silence of the room, she realizes that she is not lucky at all.

Seven A.M. Monday morning, Jillian Hayes remained prostrate on her bed.

She stared up at the ceiling. She listened to the sound of her mother's muffled snoring down the hall, then the faint *beep, beep, beep* of Toppi's alarm clock going off for the first time. The adult-care specialist hit snooze right away. It would take three or four more alarms before Toppi actually got out of bed.

Jillian finally turned her head. She looked out the window of her East Greenwich home, where the sun was shining bright. Then she looked at her dresser, where the manila envelope still lay in plain sight.

Seven A.M. Monday morning. The Monday morning.

The phone next to her bed bleated shrilly. Jillian immediately froze. It might be another reporter demanding a quote. Worse, it might be *him*. He probably hadn't even started the ride to the courthouse yet. What did he wake up thinking about on a day like today?

The phone rang again, loud and demanding. Jillian had no choice but to snatch it up; she didn't want it to disturb her mother.

"Did I wake you?" Carol asked in her ear.

Jillian started breathing again. Of course it was Carol. Good ol' Dan was probably up and out already. Heaven forbid that even on a day as important as this day, he stay at home with his wife. Jillian said, "No."

"I couldn't sleep," Carol said.

"I now know every pattern on my ceiling."

"It's funny. I feel so nervous. My stomach is tied in knots, my hands are shaking. I haven't felt like this since, well"—Carol's laugh was brittle—"I haven't felt like this since my wedding day."

"It will be over soon," Jillian said quietly. "Do you think we should call Meg?"

"She knows about breakfast."

"All right."

"What are you going to wear?"

"A camel-colored pantsuit with a white linen vest. I laid it out last night."

"I went shopping. Nothing in my closet felt right. Then again, what do you wear for this sort of thing? I don't know. I found this butter-yellow Chanel suit at Nordstrom. It was nine hundred dollars. I'm going to burn it when the day is done."

Jillian thought about her camel suit, then the coming day. "I'll join you," she said.

Carol's voice grew soft. "What did you do with the clothes you were wearing that day?"

"When the police finally gave them back, I took them to the dry cleaners. And I've never . . . I've never picked them up."

"We'll be thinking about Trisha today."

Jillian's throat grew a little tight. "Carol . . . Thank you."

And then, of course, the most important question, the question the whole phone call had been about.

"Do you know . . . Do you know what will happen?" Carol asked.

Jillian's gaze went back to the manila envelope on top of her dresser. Then she glanced at the clock. Seven-ten A.M. At least one hour to go.

"No," she said honestly. "But I guess we're about to find out."

4

Waters

Nine-oh-five a.m. Downtown, the scene was pretty much what Griffin had expected. Lots and lots of flashing lights. Very little organization. Even with an official vehicle and blaring horn, it took Griffin thirteen minutes to fight his way through the last three blocks around the courthouse. Almost immediately, he saw the problem. The media wasn't just there. They were *there*.

White media vans choked off the main artery of South Main Street. Choppers flooded the air. He'd already figured that most of the local news stations had sent reporters to cover the opening day of Eddie Como's trial. Apparently, at the first sound of rifle fire, the reporters had yelled a collective yippee and called in every station resource they could muster. Now if only the police could manage such great coverage of the scene.

Griffin drove his car up onto the curb, parking on cobblestones that technically formed a courtyard around one of the RISD buildings. Three students hastily scrambled out of his way, cursing. About four dozen more remained rooted in place, staring awestruck at the unfolding drama.

Climbing out of his Taurus, Griffin was immediately assaulted by the acrid stench of burning gas and scorched metal. Thick black smoke poured out of the parking lot just across the street, where men were frantically shouting orders and shooting four streams of water onto a mangled heap of flame-covered autos. The state fire marshal was already there, along with a collection of rescue vehicles and illegally parked police cars. A slew of Providence detectives stood alongside the fire marshal, waiting for the firemen to squelch the flames so they could move in to secure the scene.

"Jesus," Griffin muttered, coughing twice, then wishing he hadn't because it sucked more of the smoke into his lungs. Plus, this close, he caught another, richer smell underlying the odor of gasoline.

Griffin turned toward the courthouse on his right and found more chaos. Reporters, hastily contained on the grassy lawn of the memorial park, strained against blue police barricades and shouted questions in the ears of the poor Providence cops assigned to stand guard. Across from them, an ambulance was perched on the courthouse curb, along with the ME's van and more police cars than Griffin could count. Providence, state, marked, unmarked, even one belonging to Brown University's campus police. Apparently if you wore a badge, you were now part of this party.

Griffin shook his head. He pushed his way through the swelling crowd of city gawkers as a young officer in a Providence uniform and slicked-back black hair spotted him from across the street and jogged over to meet him.

"Sergeant!"

"Hey, Bentley. Imagine meeting you here." Bentley played softball with Griffin's younger brother, Jon. For the record, the state's team had creamed their corn three years in a row.

Bentley pulled up in front of Griffin, looking a little jazzed. Griffin didn't blame him. In all his years, he hadn't seen anything like this. He kept thinking he'd stepped out of his car into LA. All they needed now was a movie producer hawking film rights on the nearest street corner.

"I'm first responder," Bentley said in a rush. "I was across the river on patrol. Heard the rifle crack myself and stepped on the gas. My God, you shoulda seen the press. I thought they were gonna scale the courtyard fence to get more photos. We spent the first five minutes just getting them under control, never mind looking for the shooter."

"No kidding?" First responder. Griffin was suitably impressed. "You'll be the stuff of legends," he assured the young Providence cop as he headed across the street with Bentley in tow. "So what do we got?"

"One down, Eddie Como, DOA at the scene. Shot was fired shortly after eight-thirty A.M. as he was unloaded from the ACI van. According to initial reports, it was a rifle shot from the roof. Five, ten minutes later, an explosion came from the RISD parking lot."

"Car bomb?"

"Fire marshal isn't saying anything yet, but between you and me, five cars are wrecked, so I'm guessing that's a safe bet."

"Fatalities?"

"Don't know. Scene's too hot. I saw what looked like an arm, though, so there's at least one victim. Plus there's the, well . . ."

"Smell," Griffin filled in for him.

"Yeah." Bentley swallowed heavily.

"Uniforms searching the area?"

"Yes, sir."

"Stopping anyone with an overcoat?"

"Yes, sir."

"Any luck?"

"No, sir."

Griffin nodded. "Yeah, your arm probably belongs to a guy who used to be good with a rifle. Didn't anyone ever tell him there's no honor among thieves?"

"Sounds like the Mafia," Bentley volunteered.

Griffin shrugged. "What does the Mafia care about the College Hill Rapist? Dunno. One thing at a time. I gotta go here. Keep us posted on the search, okay?"

Griffin had arrived at the yellow crime-scene tape. Across the street, several of the reporters spotted him and a fresh shout went up.

"Sergeant, Sergeant—"

"Hey, Griffin!"

Griffin ignored them, focusing instead on the state uniform posted outside the yellow tape. Griffin didn't recognize the female officer, who was now asking his name, rank and badge number for the crime-scene logbook. Of course, in eighteen months, some things were bound to change. He told himself that was all right, though the thought left him feeling uncomfortable. Work was work. Just like riding a bike. He ducked beneath the tape.

Inside the enclosed courtyard, he saw several things at once. The blue ACI van pulled over to the left, doors still open and the interior emptied out. Three gray-clad state marshals standing to the right, talking to another Major Crimes detective. A strung-out row of blue- and khaki-suited prisoners still shackled together and now seated on the ground. In the middle was a really big pool of blood, topped by what was left of Eddie Como's body. The guy shackled to the left of Como's body was covered in blood and brains and sat in stunned silence. The guy to the right was also covered in blood and brains, but he wouldn't shut up.

"No way. No fuckin' way. Not happening. Really, really not happening. Why are we still tied up, man? I mean, like we're really going to run off right now. Because of course this isn't happening. Really not happening. *Get these fucking things off me!*"

The state marshals ignored him. So did Jack-n-Jack, the crime techs from CIU. Both were already moving around the flagstone courtyard with a digital camera, capturing the scene. Deeper in, the two death investigators from the ME's office were also diligently recording their findings. At the moment, they were standing over what might have been a man's jaw.

"Hey, Griffin," Jack Cappelli said, finally looking up.

"Look at you," Jack Needham said, also looking up. "Ooooh, that's gotta be Italian."

Griffin obligingly ran a hand down the silk-wool blend of his blue-gray sports coat. Cindy had picked it out for him. It had been one of her favorites. "Of course. Nothing but the best for this job. Now tell me the truth. Did you miss me?"

"Absolutely," they said in unison.

"Jack killed your plant, Griffin," the first Jack piped up.

"Can't prove it," the second Jack said.

"Bet I can. I shot a round of black-and-whites documenting the scene."

"In other words," Griffin deduced, "it's been a little slow lately."

They both nodded glumly. Then the first Jack perked up again. "But not anymore. Hey, do us a favor. Kill those choppers, Griff."

"Yeah, they're messing with our scene, Griff."

Griffin obligingly looked up at the swarm of media helicopters buzzing the sky, then grimaced. Media choppers were such a pain in the ass. If it wasn't bad enough to have to worry about an overly aggressive photographer capturing some sensational image of the victim, the wash from the rotor blades ruined half the evidence. He picked up his radio to contact the State Aeronautics Department just as the guy shackled to the left of Como's body raised his hand to his blood-spattered face.

"Stop!" Jack-n-Jack ordered as a single unit. "No touching! Remember, you are part of the crime scene. We need your face to analyze spray."

"Ahhhhhhh," the guy said.

Jack-n-Jack looked at him and snapped a fresh photo.

Griffin suppressed a grin. Yeah, just like old times. You know, other than the fact that they'd never had an assassination at the state courthouse before. He finished securing the airspace above the judicial complex, then returned his attention to Jack-n-Jack.

"What do we got?"

"Single head shot. Entrance wound top of the skull. Exit wound beneath the chin. No sign of powder burns. We're guessing a rifle with a soft-point slug, which would provide enough force to penetrate the skull and enough spread to do . . . well, to do *that*."

Jack-n-Jack pointed to the body. It was a good thing Griffin had seen Eddie Como's face on TV, because he definitely couldn't see it now. Soft-point bullets expanded on impact, creating a wonderful mushrooming effect.

"So a steeply vertical rifle shot." Griffin looked up. A rooftop sniper would be consistent with initial reports. Unfortunately, from this angle inside the courtyard, he couldn't see anything tucked back from the roofline six stories up. That didn't bode well for witnesses. On the other hand, that's why they paid him the big bucks. He pulled out his Norelco mini-recorder and focused on the five shackled prisoners.

"Anybody," he said. "I'm pretty sure all of you could use the brownie points."

None of the guys looked particularly impressed. Finally, the first guy shook his head.

"Man, we don't know nothin'. We were just climbing out of the van and then boom! We hear this crack like fuckin' lightning overhead and the next instant, we all get yanked off our feet. Look back and Eddie's on the ground, state marshals are yelling gun, gun, and Jazz here"—the first guy gave the kid shackled to the right of Eddie's body a derisive glance—"is already scream-ing, 'I've been hit, I've been hit.' 'Course he ain't been hit. He's just wearing most of Eddie's brains."

Griffin looked down the inmate line. They all nodded. This seemed to be the official summary of events. He glanced back up at the roofline, trying to figure out if he should separate them all and push the issue. Not worth it, he decided. Even knowing there were two crime-scene techs on the roof, he couldn't see a damn thing from this angle. Across the street, on the other hand . . .

A voice came over the radios secured to Jack-n-Jack's waists.

"*We got a gun,*" a crime-scene tech reported from the roof. "*AR15 assault rifle with a Leupold scope, two-twenty-three Remingtons in the magazine. Also have three Army blankets, black coveralls, a pair of shooting gloves, and a pair of shoes. Oh, and three empty wrappers from snack-sized packages of Fig Newtons. Apparently our guy didn't just want ordinary cookies, but fruit and cake.*"

"Cigarette butts?" one Jack asked hopefully.

"*No cigarette butts,*" the tech reported back. "*Sorry, Jack.*"

"Bummer." The first Jack looked at the second Jack morosely. Cigarette butts contained such a wealth of information, from brand specifics to DNA-yielding saliva.

"Cheer up," Griffin said supportively. "You have shoes. Think of everything you can get from shoes."

The Jacks brightened again. "We like shoes," they agreed. "We can do things with shoes."

Griffin gave the pair another encouraging nod, then walked over to the state marshals. Detective Mike Waters had the three men huddled around his Norelco Pocket Memo, making official statements.

"Griffin!" the first marshal said. He pulled back from the recorder long enough to vigorously pump Griffin's hand.

"Hey, Jerry. How are you?" Heavyset with thinning gray hair, Jerry was an old-timer with the state marshals. He'd helped train Griffin's older brother, Frank. Then again, Jerry had helped train just about everyone in the gray uniform.

"Fine, fine," Jerry was saying. "Well, okay, could be better. Jesus, I heard you were coming back but I didn't realize it would be today of all days. You always could pick 'em, Griff. Hey, you actin' as ringleader of this circus?"

"Nah, just another working stiff. Hey, George. Hey, Tom." Griffin shook the other two men's hands as well. Beside him, Detective Waters cleared his throat. Griffin belatedly turned toward his fellow officer. Mike Waters was five years Griffin's junior. He was tall and lanky, with a penchant for navy blue suits that made him look like an aspiring FBI agent. He was smart though, deceptively strong and thoughtfully quiet. A lot of suspects underestimated him. They never got a chance to make that same mistake twice.

There had been a time when Griffin would have greeted Mike with a hearty "Cousin Stinky!" And there had been a time when Waters would have responded with a booming "Cousin Ugly!" That time was gone now. One of the open questions in Griffin's life was would that time come again.

"Sergeant," Waters said, nodding in greeting.

"Detective," Griffin replied. The three state marshals perked up, gaze going from officer to officer. They had probably heard the story. For that matter, they had probably helped spread the story. Griffin tried but couldn't quite keep his gaze from going to Waters's nose. That was okay. Waters's gaze had gone to Griffin's fist.

Both men jerked their eyes back to the marshals. The silence had gone on too long, grown awkward. Griffin thought, *Shit.*

Waters cleared his throat again. "So as you guys were saying . . ."

"Oh yeah." Jerry picked up the story. "We secured the courtyard."

"We opened the van doors," George supplied.

"We took up position," Tom filled in. "Started the unloading—"

"Boom!"

"Ka-boom!" George amended.

"Definitely a high-powered rifle. Nice sharp crack. I honestly thought for a second that someone was shooting deer."

"Then I saw red. Literally. Stuff sprayed everywhere."

"Kid dropped straight down. Dead before he hit the ground. You hear about this stuff, but I've never seen anything like it."

"I yelled 'gun.' "

"He did. Jerry yelled 'gun,' we all dropped into a crouch. You know, with the sun coming up behind the roof like that, you just can't see a damn thing. Scariest goddamn moment of my life."

"I thought I saw movement. Maybe somebody running. That's it, though."

"Then we could hear all the reporters yelling across the street. 'On the roof,' they were shouting. 'There he goes, there he goes.' "

"Distinguishing features?" Waters prodded. "Height, weight?"

"Couldn't even make out if it was a man or woman," Jerry said bluntly. "I'm telling you, it was more like catching the flash of a silhouette. Moved fast though. Definitely one well-conditioned sniper."

Waters gave the marshal a look. " 'One well-conditioned sniper,' huh? Well, let me run straight to my lieutenant with that. I mean, by God, Jerry, let's get out the APB."

The three marshals squirmed. "Sorry, guys," Jerry finally said with a shrug, "but from here . . . Look up yourself. You can't see a damn thing."

"Try the reporters, though," George spoke up. "They had a much better vantage point. Hey, they might have even gotten the guy on film."

The three marshals, not above getting a little revenge after they'd been put in the hot seat, smiled at them. While they'd been talking, the roar from the reporters had grown even louder outside the courthouse. Now they sounded kind of like King Kong—right before he burst his chains.

Waters sighed. Looked miserable. Then morosely hung his head. He hated the press. Last time he and Griffin had worked together, he'd let a statement slip within a reporter's earshot and paid for that mistake for weeks. Besides, as he'd later confided to Griffin, his butt looked even bonier on camera. Two fine citizens had written letters to the editor requesting that somebody in the Rhode Island police department start feeding him.

"Are you sure you didn't see anything?" he prodded the state marshals one last time.

The state marshals shook their heads, this time a bit gleefully. But then, Jerry, kind-hearted bastard that he was, took pity on him.

"If you don't want to mess with the press, you can always go straight to the women," Jerry said.

"The women?" Griffin spoke up.

"Yeah, the three women Eddie attacked. Haven't you seen them on the news?"

"Oh, those women," Griffin said, though in fact he hadn't watched the news in months and knew very little about the College Hill rape case.

"Let's face it," Jerry was saying. "If anyone has reason to turn Eddie into liver pâté, it's the three ladies. My money's on the last one, the business one, what's her name? Jillian Hayes. Yeah, she's a cool one, could kill a man with her eyes alone. Plus, after what Eddie did to her sister . . ."

"No, no, no," George interrupted. "The Hayes woman wasn't even raped. You want to know who did it, it was the second one, Carol Rosen, the high-society wife from the East Side. My brother's wife works in the ER at Women & Infants and she was there the night they brought in Mrs. Rosen. Man, the things Eddie had done to her. It's a miracle she didn't need plastic surgery to repair her face. Twenty to one, the shooter wore pearls."

"You're both wrong," Tom spoke up. "One, no way some woman made this shot. Like an ad executive or rich socialite is going to go climbing all over the courthouse roof with an assault rifle. Key to this shooting is the first victim. The pretty young coed, Pesaturo—"

"Oh, leave the girl alone." Jerry looked stern. "Meg Pesaturo doesn't even remember anything. 'Sides, she's just a kid."

"She *says* she doesn't remember anything. But that always sounded pretty fishy to me. Maybe she just wanted to keep it private. A family matter. And you know who her family is." Tom gave them all an expectant look. They obligingly leaned forward, even Griffin. Law enforcement officers were never above a bit of juicy gossip.

"Vinnie Pesaturo," Tom said, in the waiting hush. "Yeah, the Carlone family's favorite bookie. If Vinnie wanted something done, you can be sure it got done. So maybe pretty little Meg doesn't remember anything. Or maybe she's adopting the party line, while Vinnie sets everything in motion. A rooftop sniper, a nearby explosion. Oh yeah, this has got the Carlone family written all over it. Mark my words, Meg Pesaturo is the one."

5

Meg

She is laughing. She doesn't know why. The police are here. Some girl, her roommate, she is told, is crying. But Meg is standing outside. She is looking up at the dark night sky, where the stars gleam like tiny pinpricks of light, where the breeze is cool against her cheeks, and she is hugging herself and laughing giddily.

The police want to take her to the hospital. They are looking at her strangely.

"It's a beautiful night," she tells them. "Look, it's a gorgeous night!"

The concerned officers put her in the back of a police cruiser. She hums to herself. She touches her cheek, and she has a first glimmer of memory.

A touch, whisper light, impossibly gentle. Eyes, rich chocolate, peering into her own. The beginning of a slow, sweet smile.

"Who am I?" she asks the officers up front.

"Why don't you wait until we get to the hospital."

So she waits until they get to the hospital. It's all right with her. She's singing some tune she can't get out of her head. She is daydreaming of whisper-light touches. She is shivering in anticipation of a lover's kiss.

At the hospital, she is whisked through the emergency room doors, led to a tiny exam room where a special nurse, a sexual assault examiner, comes bustling in. She seems to know the officers, which is fine by Meg, because she doesn't know anyone at all.

"How bad?" the nurse asks briskly.

"You tell us. The roommate came home and found her tied to the bed. She claims she doesn't remember a thing, including her name—"

"What's my name?" Meg speaks up.

They ignore her. "She claims she doesn't remember her roommate either," the police officer says, "not anyone, not anything. The roommate gave us contact information, so the parents are on the way."

The nurse jerks her head toward Meg. "Original clothes?"

"No, the roommate released her from the bindings and dressed her before calling us." The police officer sounds disgusted. "Someone's gotta teach these people to know better. We found a ripped T-shirt on the floor, plus a pair of panties. They're already on their way to the lab."

"I'll bag these clothes as well, just in case any hair or fiber has rubbed off inside them. I'll mark them as second-set clothing. That work for you?"

The officers shrug. "We're just the limo drivers; what the hell do we care?"

"Hey," Meg says again. "Isn't it a beautiful night?"

The officers roll their eyes. The nurse dismisses them and comes over to Meg. The nurse has blue eyes. The eyes look at her kindly, but they are also sharp.

"What is your name?" she asks as she snaps on a pair of gloves.

"I don't know. That's what I was asking them. That girl called me Meg. Maybe I'm Meg."

"I see. And how old are you, Meg?"

Meg has to think about it. A number pops into her mind. "Nineteen?"

The nurse nods as if this is an acceptable answer. "And what day is today?"

This is easier. "Wednesday," Meg says immediately. "April eleventh."

"All right. I just need to check a few things, Meg. I know this may feel uncomfortable, but I'm not going to hurt you. Please understand we're all here to help you. Even if it seems that we're asking too much, we have your best interests at heart."

The nurse reaches out. She takes Meg's wrist with her gloved fingers. Immediately, Meg recoils. She yanks back her hand.

"No," Meg says, though she doesn't know why. She is shaking her head. The night is not so beautiful anymore. "No," she says again. "No, no."

"Your wrist is bleeding," the nurse says patiently. "I just need to look at it, see if it needs treatment." She reaches out again with her gloved hand and takes Meg's wrist.

"No!" This time Meg flies off the table. She clutches her bleeding wrist against her chest, feeling her heart pound as she searches frantically for some means of escape. The door is closed. She is trapped in the tiny exam room with this woman and those gloves. The gloves smell. Can't the woman smell them? They have a horrible, horrible smell.

Meg turns around and around. No place to go. No way to escape. She shrinks down onto the cold, white floor. She cradles her bleeding wrists against her, and for reasons she can't explain, she whimpers.

The nurse is looking at her. Her face has not changed. Her expression is set, unreadable, but at least she doesn't come any closer.

"Does your wrist hurt?" the nurse asks quietly.

Meg has not thought about it. But now that the woman mentions it . . . Meg looks down at her wrists. Big, huge welts circle the tiny forms. She can see fresh blood and dark purple bruises marring her skin.

"They . . . they sting," Meg says. Her voice holds a trace of wonder.

The nurse squats down until she is eye level.

"Meg, I'm here to help you. If you let me, I will treat your wrists and help them feel better. I also want to help you another way, Meg. My job is to assist in catching the person who did this to you, who made your wrists sting. To do that, I need to take some pictures. And I need to examine the rest of you as well. I know this isn't easy right now. But if you will trust me, I promise I won't hurt you."

Slowly, Meg nods her head. She isn't afraid of this woman. In fact, she has come to like her stern face and unwavering gaze. This woman seems strong, in control. Meg rises back up. She holds out her raw, torn wrists.

But the moment the woman touches her again, places those latex-covered *fingers against her skin . . .*

"*I'm going to be sick,*" *Meg says, and just barely makes it to the stainless steel sink.*

The door opens, then closes as the nurse leaves the room. Meg runs the water for a bit. She rinses off her face, which she had already done twice before the police came, another thing that made them growl in disapproval.

Meg's mouth hurts. She finds a mirror and studies her face for a long time. The corners of her mouth are bleeding slightly. The flesh there is torn.

Meg is honestly confused. She searches her memory for some kind of hint, but all she can recall is a faraway sensation of whisper-light touches against her skin. Soft, teasing caresses. And she is holding her breath, hoping he will come closer, closer.

Please, kiss me.

She shivers. And a moment later, she realizes that for the first time all night, she is afraid.

From outside comes the sound of voices. The nurse and the police officers are once more talking about her.

"*Latex? She was tied up with strips of* latex? *For God's sake, gentlemen, that's the kind of detail you might want to mention to me. I just approached her all gloved up and she about climbed the walls. No wonder she was scared out of her mind.*"

"*So you think she was raped?*"

"*Of course she was raped. Have you looked at her mouth? Consensual lovers don't generally gag their partners.*"

"*Yeah, yeah, but . . . listen to her. 'Isn't it a beautiful night.' And she's humming all the time and smiling to herself. What's that about?*"

"*It's called euphoria, Officer. Because even if Miss Pesaturo doesn't consciously remember being raped yet, her subconscious knows damn well what happened and it's telling her she's grateful to be alive.*"

The officers don't say anything more. A moment later, the door bursts open and the nurse comes bustling back in. Meg stares at the woman's hands, but they are bare now. The woman opens a cabinet, pulls out a separate box. She hands the box to Meg.

"*Are these okay with you?*"

Meg looks into the box. It also contains gloves, but these are different. She takes one out, holds it in her hand. It is thin and smells of rubber. The box says it is a vinyl glove. She sniffs again. She has an instant memory of dish soap and sudsy water. That's all.

She hands the box back to the nurse. "Okay," she says and her voice is now equally grave.

The nurse spreads a white drop cloth on the floor. Meg stands on the drop cloth and takes off her clothes, including her bra and panties. The nurse puts each item in a separately marked bag. Meg holds out her arms. The nurse shoots Polaroids of her naked body, including her mouth, wrists and ankles. The nurse runs a comb through her pubic hair. The results go into another bag.

Then Meg must lie back on the table. Her feet go into stirrups. Her heart is pounding again. She tries not to think about it. She tries to remember she must trust this woman, because something horrible has happened even if Meg can only recall rich chocolate eyes and a gentle lover's kiss.

Meg shivers. The room is too cold. She is frightened by the swabs the nurse is taking. Frightened by the things they might know that she doesn't. She is overexposed, and even when the nurse hands her a pink hospital gown, it is not enough.

There is evidence of vaginal penetration, the nurse tells her. Traces of fluid in the cervix. Is Meg on birth-control pills?

This sounds right to Meg. She nods. It is only the beginning, however. She doesn't have to take the morning-after pill unless she really wants to, but there is still the risk of sexually transmitted disease. Herpes. Gonorrhea. AIDS. She will give blood samples today, and more in the coming weeks as they continue to look for signs of infection. For example, it can take up to six months to detect the first sign of AIDS after initial exposure.

Meg nods again. Her euphoria is gone. She is tired. More tired than she has ever felt. Her mouth hurts. Her ankles, her wrists. She sits with her legs tightly crossed and she hopes, somewhere way down deep, that no one will ever touch her again.

A knock on the door. An officer sticks in his head. Meg's parents are here. A Providence detective is here. They need to ask her some more questions . . .

"You're going to be all right," the nurse tells Meg.

Meg just looks at the woman. She finally understands that this kind, stern woman is paid to lie. Meg has been raped. Meg has lost her mind. Meg does not recognize the man and woman now rushing into the room sobbing her name.

Meg will be many things in the days, weeks, months to come. But she will not be all right. That will be a much longer-term project. It will take years. Most likely, it will take the rest of her life.

Monday morning, 7:10 A.M., Meg finally crawled out of bed. She hadn't slept well last night, though she wasn't sure why. Today might be the big day, but it would be a bigger day for everyone other than her. The prosecutor, Ned D'Amato, wasn't even going to call her to testify. As D'Amato so bluntly put it, what could she contribute? She still didn't know anything about that night. During cross-examination, the defense would eat her alive.

Kind, gentle Meg. Sweet, lucky Meg, who still didn't remember a thing.

From downstairs came the distant clang and clatter of pans. Her mother must already be in the kitchen, whipping up breakfast. Then came a high-pitched giggle, followed by a shrill demand for "Pancakes, pancakes, pancakes!" Meg's little sister, Molly, liked to get up at six.

Meg's lack of memory didn't bother her so much anymore. About four months ago, she realized she possessed a deeper, instinctive knowledge of things if she was just willing to listen to her inner voice. For example, she couldn't remember her mother's name, age or general description. But the minute her mother had burst into the hospital exam room and wrapped her arms around Meg's trembling shoulders, Meg had known that this woman loved her. She felt the same way about her father and Molly. And when they brought her back here she'd definitely had a sense of coming home, even if she couldn't have given a street address.

Sometimes, little things got her going. A song on the radio would shake the cobwebs in her mind. She would feel a memory stirring, rising up, like a word stuck on the tip of her tongue. If she tried too hard, however, strained her mind, the thought would disappear almost immediately. She'd have to wait for the song to air once more, or the scent to ride the wind, or the déjà vu to return.

Lately, she'd been working on not working so hard. She focused on her inner voice more. She let the moments of semiclarity linger like a fog in front of her eyes. She spent long periods of time thinking of nothing and everything. Post-traumatic amnesia was the mind's way of coping, the doctors had told her. Forcing the issue only created more trauma. Instead she should rest, eat healthily, and get plenty of exercise. In other words, take good care of herself.

Meg took good care of herself. These days, she didn't have anything else to do.

Now she heard the sound of voices, closer, down the hall. Hushed voices, the way people spoke when they were fighting and didn't want others to hear. Her parents, again. She'd gone to sleep listening to the same sound.

Her Uncle Vinnie kept coming by. Yesterday he'd been here until almost ten at night, speaking low and furiously with her father. Her mom didn't approve of Uncle Vinnie. Her mom didn't like him coming over so much, and obviously didn't like whatever he and her father had been talking about.

Meg herself didn't get it. Uncle Vinnie had a loud, booming laugh. He smelled of whiskey and stale cigars. His head was nearly bald, his stomach bursting huge. He looked to her like Kojak crossed with Santa Claus. How could you not like Kojak crossed with Santa Claus?

Meg waited on the other side of her door until her parents' voices finally faded away. Molly was still downstairs. Probably now decorating the floor with bits of pancakes. Her mother had probably returned to her. Her father had to get ready for work. Meg crossed the hall unnoticed and crept into the upstairs bathroom, where she took a long, steaming shower.

She needed to get moving if she was going to be at the rue de l'espoir by eight.

Twenty minutes later, clad in jeans and a T-shirt, her long, damp brown hair pulled back in a ponytail, her face freshly scrubbed, she went galloping downstairs. By now her father had probably left for work, which made it easier for her, easier for him. One year later, he couldn't look at her without seeing a rape victim. And Meg couldn't look at him without seeing him look at her as someone who had been raped.

Her mother was easier. She had cried, she had raged and she had been so damn happy the day the police had arrested Eddie Como. But she was also happy to have Meg home again, plus she had her hands full with Molly, and there were so many things to be done. Life was busy. Life went on. She also probably understood better than Meg's father that women were stronger than they looked.

Now, Meg threw her arms around her mother's trim, efficient form and squeezed her good.

"I gotta meet Carol and Jillian downtown," she said, kissing her mom on the cheek. This was the kind of thing she could tell her mother. Her father didn't approve of the Survivors Club meetings. Why should his little girl sit around with two older women talking about rape? For God's sake, what was the world coming to?

Meg didn't mind the discussions. Frankly, she had been a little surprised and a little pleased that Jillian had invited her to join. After all, Meg didn't know anything. She hadn't turned militant like Jillian. She hadn't gone half-crazed like Carol. Meg was still Meg. She talked about her family, about the people she was learning to love all over again, while Jillian coolly discussed topics such as victims' rights and Carol railed against the injustices of a world created by men.

"Pancakes?" her mom asked hopefully.

"Meg!" Molly screamed. "Good morning, Meg!" Molly was a morning person.

Meg let go of her mother and crossed the kitchen to plant four wet kisses on Molly's syrup-smeared face. "Molly! Good morning, Molly!" Meg wailed back.

Her five-year-old sister, her parents' little midlife oops, but a happy oops, giggled at her. "Are you going to eat pancakes?"

"Nah, I'm going to drink chai."

"No chai. Eat pancakes with me."

"Can't, got a hot date. But I'll see you this afternoon."

She kissed Molly's syrupy cheek again, then tickled the little girl until she squealed and squirmed in her chair.

"You're leaving already?" her mother asked from the stove.

"Sorry, I'm running late. I'm supposed to be at rue de l'espoir by eight."

"You'll call." Meaning if Meg heard anything from the courthouse, from Ned D'Amato.

"I'll call."

Her mom finally stepped away from the stove in the tiny kitchen. She held the flipper in one hand, wore an oven mitt on the other. She looked at Meg for a long time.

"I love you," her mother said abruptly.

"I love you, too."

"You'll call me?"

"I'll call you."

"All right then." Meg's mother nodded, returned to the stove and dished out a fresh plate of pancakes in a kitchen where there was no one left to feed.

Meg headed out the door. The sun was bright, the morning cool but already warming with the promise of heat. A beautiful day, but that didn't mean anything. After all, one year ago, it had been a beautiful night.

Meg climbed into her little brown Nissan, parked on the street. She tried not to notice the expired parking sticker for Providence College still stuck on her window. Her father no longer felt college was safe enough for his little girl. If he had his way, she would never go back.

And Meg? What did Meg want? She was the lucky one. Everyone told her that. Detective Fitzpatrick, Ned D'Amato, Carol, even Jillian. Sure she had been raped, but that had been it. No broken bones, no scars, no burial plots.

She had been the College Hill Rapist's first victim and after her, he'd definitely done worse.

Meg started the engine of her car. Meg drove down the street. Meg felt once more the eyes that followed her so often these days. Meg did not turn around.

But she shivered.

It had been four months now. She didn't know what was going on. But one thing was clear. Somehow, someway, sweet lucky Meg was no longer alone.

6

Maureen

In downtown Providence, Griffin and Waters walked together out of the courtyard. Griffin thought he should say something.

"Tell me about the Eddie Como case." Okay, he probably should have said something more personal than that.

Waters shrugged. "I don't know much. Providence handled the case."

"Give me the headlines."

"Four women were attacked, one was killed. The first was a student at Providence College, Meg Pesaturo. Guess her family is connected, though that's news to me. The next victim, the Rosen woman, lives in one of those big, historical homes near Brown, which you can believe got the whole East Side screaming for better police protection. The third attack was at Brown, another college student, except the woman's sister walked in during the rape. He beat up the older sister pretty badly, and the younger wound up dead. Anaphylactic reaction to latex, something like that."

"The guy was wearing gloves?"

"Yeah, plus he tied them up with latex tourniquets. You know, the kind they use in the hospital when they're drawing blood. That's how the Providence police caught him in the end. Turns out the victims had donated blood at a campus blood drive prior to the attack. Police did a little digging . . . Eddie Como was a phlebotomist with the Rhode Island Blood Center. Theory is he used the blood drives to identify potential targets, then looked up their home addresses in the blood donor database."

Griffin waved his head from side to side, working out a kink in his neck. "Circumstantial case?"

"No, they had DNA. Perfect match, all three victims. Como's the guy."

"Going to get buried at trial?"

Waters nodded vigorously. "Going to get *buried* at trial."

"Interesting. So on the one hand, Eddie's probably going away for life. On the other hand, according to the state marshals, three women still wanted him dead."

"You haven't seen the crime-scene photos," Waters said. And then they arrived in front of the press.

"Sergeant, Sergeant, Sergeant!" The roar went up, followed by an immediate hail of questions.

"Is Eddie Como dead?"

"What about the state marshals?"

"Are there other fatalities?"

"What about the explosion? Was that a car bomb?"

"Who's going to be leading the case? Providence? State? When will we get a briefing, when will we get a briefing?"

Griffin held up his hand. Bulbs immediately flashed. He grimaced, suffered a spasm of bad memory, then got it under control.

"Okay. This is the deal. We're not answering any of your questions."

Collective groan.

"We're here to ask you our questions."

A fresh pique of interest.

"I know, I know," Griffin said dryly, "we're excited about it, too. In case any of you haven't noticed, you're all witnesses to a shooting."

"It's Eddie Como, isn't it? Someone killed the College Hill Rapist!"

The rest of the reporters started in again, kids turned loose in the candy store. "When do we get a briefing? When do we get a briefing?"

"Who's going to handle the case?"

"What can you tell us about the explosion?"

"Has anyone interviewed the women yet? What do the victims have to say?"

Griffin sighed. Reasoning with the press was such a waste of breath. But in this job, you had to do what you had to do. He and Waters squared their shoulders, shoved aside two of the blue police barricades and waded bravely into the fray. Four microphones promptly appeared in front of Griffin's face. He pushed them back, homed in on one reporter in particular, and stabbed at the man with his finger.

"You. You and your cameraman can start. Over here."

He and Waters pulled the two away from the group. The pair weren't very happy, but then Waters and Griffin didn't much care. Griffin made the reporter review his notes, while Waters had the cameraman play back his tape. At the last minute, they were rewarded with a grainy image of the back of a man running across the courthouse roof. The focus was all wrong, though. The cameraman had been zoomed in on a close-up shot of his reporter talking in front of the courtyard. When he yanked up the camera after hearing the gunfire, the shooter was too far away to yield a good image.

"He was wearing all black," the reporter provided. "With something on his head. Maybe a stocking. You know, like bank robbers do in the movies."

Griffin grunted. Waters noted the names and news affiliate for the twosome, then they moved on. Their second subjects were even better. This cameraman liked gunshots so well, he dropped his five-thousand-dollar piece of hardware onto the lawn.

"I don't do well with loud noises," he said sheepishly.

"For God's sake, Gus," his reporter snapped, "what happens if they send us to Afghanistan?"

"We work for the UPN affiliate in the smallest state in the nation, Sally. When the fuck are we going to be sent to Afghanistan?"

"Did you at least look up?" Griffin intervened in this lovefest.

"Yeah," Gus said. "Saw a person, running across the roof."

"Person?" Waters pressed.

Gus shrugged. "All I could see was the back. Could be a man, could be a woman. In this day and age, who the hell knows?"

"Real observant, Gus, real observant."

Griffin turned toward Sally. "And you?"

The hard-faced brunette gave Griffin an appraising stare. "I thought it was a man. Broad shoulders. Short, dark hair. Dressed in black coveralls, like the kind mechanics wear. Now then. You're looking good after your little vacation, Griffin. A sergeant of Major Crimes, light caseload from being gone so long. Twenty to one they're going to put you in charge of this baby. So why don't you give me an interview? Five minutes on the record. My boss will clear it with your boss. What do you say?"

Waters was looking at him strangely. He probably hadn't given any thought to who would be assigned as the primary case officer yet. The decision generally wasn't made right away. Sally was correct, however. Griffin was a sergeant, he had lead case experience and at the moment he had a remarkably light caseload.

"I'm sure the detective commander will be giving a statement to all of the reporters shortly," Griffin told Sally. Then he walked back to the crowd. "Next!"

It took him and Waters two hours to make it through the nest of reporters. In the end, they had a description of a white male who was between five and six feet tall, who might have brown hair, blond hair or black hair, who was either heavyset or rail-thin, who was wearing a ski mask, a Zorro-like mask, a stocking mask or nothing at all, and who may or may not bear a striking resemblance to James Gandolfini's character on *The Sopranos*.

"That's it, I think we can arrange for a lineup right now," Waters said.

"Absolutely. And here I thought it would take all day to learn that nobody saw nothing. Instead it's been what, two and a half hours?"

"The Boss will be pleased," Waters agreed.

They both sighed heavily. They wandered away from the reporters, who had spotted the major arriving at the courtyard across the street, and were now resuming their manic cries for a briefing.

"What do you think?" Waters asked quietly, looking around to make sure no gung-ho reporter had spotted their break from the crowd. Acrid smoke from the car explosion still wafted through the air. It gave their voices a raspy edge.

"We're pissing in the wind," Griffin said. "Single head shot, so most likely the guy was a pro. Left everything on the rooftop, so most likely he knew the assault rifle, etc., was untraceable. I'm betting the minute he finished shooting, he stripped down to civilian threads and headed into the courthouse where he blended into the rest of the pedestrian traffic."

"He simply strolled down the street to his getaway vehicle," Waters filled in.

"Where he made an even bigger exit than he planned."

"A description's not going to help much, except down at the morgue," Waters agreed.

"We're still going to have to know who he is to confirm his occupation, then figure out who hired him."

"I don't know. Based on what we've heard, Uncle Vinnie's looking better all the time. Has a grudge, has the connections to hire a gun. Seems to me that Tom was onto something. Or"—Waters's voice grew more thoughtful—"the East Side wife obviously has money. Maybe she arranged for the hit. Or maybe all the women conspired together—I heard that they formed some kind of support group. Of course, I'm not sure why they'd kill the hired gun. Then again, once you've decided to kill one felon, what's one more?"

Griffin merely grunted. He didn't like to rush to conclusions when working a case. He flipped through his spiral notebook. "Hey, Mike, what happened to NBC?"

"I don't know. *Seinfeld* ended, *ER* lost Clooney?"

"No, no, I mean, we haven't interviewed anyone from WJAR. You really believe Channel Ten didn't send a news team?"

Waters frowned. He looked around the memorial park. And then his eyes widened. "There, at the end of the block. Doesn't that white van say News Team Ten?"

"Well, what do you know. Two reporters have actually left the herd and are holed up on their own. Now, why would two reporters run away from the pack?"

"They have something."

"No, no, Mike, *we* have something. Let's get 'em."

Sixty seconds later, Griffin rapped on the van's sliding metal door. It didn't magically open. He knocked louder. Immediately, the voices inside shut up.

"Come on, guys," he called out. "This is Sergeant Griffin of the state police. Now open up, or I'll huff and I'll puff and I'll blow your van down."

Another long pause. Finally, a click, then the door slid meekly back. Perched inside, Maureen Haverill gave both detectives her best reporter's smile.

"Griffin!" she said warmly. "I heard you were returning to the fold."

Maureen Haverill had been working at the local NBC affiliate for five years. A petite blonde, she was perky enough for one of those national morning news shows and probably figured it was only a matter of time. At the moment, her blue eyes were particularly bright. She looked like an addict who'd just gotten a fix. Or a reporter who'd just landed a scoop. Her cameraman was out of sight. Probably frantically dubbing the tape. Damn.

"Both of you, out, now." Griffin's voice was harsh.

"Griffin—"

"Out!"

Maureen scowled. She made a big show of carefully maneuvering out of the van, the helpless blonde in a too-short, too-tight pale green skirt. She probably bought her cameraman another thirty seconds.

"So help me God, Maureen," Griffin informed her, "you dub that tape and I will nail you for tampering with evidence."

"I don't know what you're talking about."

"Jimmy," he called out. "You, too. *Now.*"

A big head of rumpled red hair reluctantly appeared. "We were just making some notes," Jimmy said sulkily. "Can't two reporters get a little work done?" The hulking redhead climbed out onto the sidewalk. He kept his eyes carefully averted. There was a fresh sheen of sweat glistening across his forehead.

"I want the tape," Griffin said.

"What tape?" Maureen tried again.

"The tape you're frantically copying for your lead story, which will probably be airing at any moment. It would be a shame, Maureen, if some junior reporter had to provide the vocals for the piece because you were detained behind bars."

"You can't arrest me! On what grounds?"

"Obstruction of justice."

"Oh please. That's horseshit and you know it."

"It's been eighteen months. My grasp of the law is a little rusty. I'll arrest you first, then let the courts sort it out."

Maureen started to look pissed. "Dammit, I have Fourth Amendment protection against illegal search and seizure!"

"Then it's a good thing we're standing next to a courthouse. I'll stay with you. Detective Waters can run across the street and get a subpoena. Thirty minutes later not only will we still seize the tape, but I promise you that when we're done, we'll provide copies of the visual to every single news organization in this state. You understand? Every single one."

"No way. That's my scoop!"

"Yes way. That's our evidence and once we seize it, we can do whatever we see fit."

"Goddammit, Griffin! I liked you so much better before—" Maureen's protest ended abruptly. She seemed to realize what she was about to say, then even she had the good grace to blush.

Griffin said nothing. He just stared at her. He'd gotten good at this stare over the last year. Sometimes, especially in the first few months after the Big Boom, he'd find himself standing in front of a mirror just staring like this. Like he was trying to look into his own eyes and get some sense of the man living there.

"I want the tape," he repeated. "It's evidence. And anything you do to it, including developing it or copying it, would be considered tampering with evidence. We got sixty state detectives crawling all over this one city block, Maureen, not to mention well over a hundred uniforms. Do you really think the attorney general is going to take kindly to hearing how some local reporter tampered with a potentially critical piece of evidence?"

Maureen gnawed her lower lip, looked a great deal less certain. "I want a deal," she said abruptly.

"Why, Maureen, are you confessing to a crime?"

"We cooperate, hand over the tape—"

"You mean we seize it."

"We *hand* it over. In return for some kind of consideration. An exclusive interview with the colonel."

Griffin laughed.

"The major," she amended.

Griffin laughed harder.

"The detective commander. Come on, Griffin. This is *exclusive* footage you're taking from me. Best damn visual of my career. We deserve at least an interview. Plus, exclusive rights to the copy of the tape. No releasing it to the general population. If they didn't look up, it's their own fucking problem."

"Your compassion touches me."

"Yeah, yeah, yeah. What do you say? Five minutes with the detective commander, exclusive tape rights."

"Thirty seconds, primary case officer, exclusive tape rights."

"Three minutes."

"One, with approval in advance of the questions. Otherwise, you're only going to get no comment."

Maureen scowled. She shot him a sideways glance. "Are you going to be the lead investigator, Griffin?"

"A lead investigator will be assigned when a lead investigator is assigned."

"Because that would be a good story, you know. Rhode Island's golden boy returning to the war. A lot of people didn't think you'd come back after the Candy Man case. A lot of people weren't sure you'd have the interest, and others weren't sure you'd have the guts. Do you love the job that much, Griffin, or is it one of those things that simply gets under the skin?" She changed tactics. "I understand that he still sends you letters."

"One minute with the primary case officer. Yes or no, Maureen. The deal is off the table in five, four, three, two—"

"Okay," she said hastily. "Okay. One minute with the primary case officer. We'll take it." She sighed, devoted another moment to looking forlorn as she saw her dream of a lead five o'clock news piece go up in smoke, then got over it. "That'll teach us not to shoot live," she muttered. "Well, you might as well come inside. You're going to want to see this."

In the back of the van, Jimmy had his huge camera hooked up to an external monitor. He and Maureen hadn't developed the tape yet, but had been running it over and over again, looking for the best cut. Now Jimmy hit play one last time. The visual lasted seventy-five seconds, and it showed everything. Absolutely everything.

"How the hell did you get this?" Griffin demanded immediately, angrily. He took two steps forward before Waters could stop him, and had Maureen pressed against the control panel running along the side of the van. "Are you toying with us?"

"No, no, I swear—"

"Did you get an anonymous tip? A Deep Throat telling you something big was going down, but you just didn't feel like sharing it with us?"

"Griffin, Griffin, you have it all wrong—"

"You never taped the ACI van! That entire footage is of the *rooftop*! There are eleven other news teams out on that lawn, Maureen. All of them were looking at the van, all of them were shooting the van. So why were you looking up? What the hell did you know that they didn't?"

"I don't know!" she cried. Her chin came up, her shoulder squared against the control panel. "I just . . . The whole morning I kept thinking someone was watching me. I'm not kidding. I had shivers down my spine, hairs going up on the nape of my neck. No matter where I went, what I did, I could just feel . . . something. Then, I heard a shout that the van was coming, so I started to adjust my mike and I . . . I looked up. One last time. At the roof. I swore I saw a movement. So I hit Jimmy on the arm and told him to shoot the roof. Now."

"I thought she was nuts," Jimmy spoke up from the rear. "But hey, it's not like a shot of the outside of a blue van is anything special. So I focused on the roof of the courthouse and well, what do you know? This guy pops up and opens fire. Really damn freaky. I figure we could get national coverage out of this."

"Awards," Maureen spoke up. "Definitely awards." The light in her eyes had gone full glow again. Pressed against the side of the van, she shivered.

Very slowly, Griffin stepped back. His hands were still fisted at his sides. He worked now on letting his fingers go, forcing his shoulders to come down and his breathing to relax. He felt suddenly disgusted. And he was aware for the first time that Waters was watching him nervously. Maureen and Jimmy, too. Everyone was probably thinking about that damn basement. Maybe they should.

He took another deep breath, focused on his racing pulse and slowly counted to ten.

"Tape," he prodded once he trusted himself to speak. Reluctantly, Jimmy opened his camera and popped out the digital cassette. Waters provided the evidence bag. Jimmy gave the tape one last, lingering look, then dropped it in.

"You'll remember our deal," Maureen said.

"Yeah, yeah, yeah."

"If we can get a copy before four," she said seriously, "we can still make the five o'clock news."

"I'll be sure to tell CIU." Copy before four. She'd be lucky to get a copy in six months.

Maureen leaned against the side of the van. She'd lost this round, but he could tell she was already plotting her next battle. "Hey, Griffin, be honest. That guy's dead now, isn't he? Blown up in that parking lot after assassinating Eddie Como?"

"No comment."

"That's what I thought. You'll be talking to the vics now? The three women?"

"No comment."

"Maybe they'll hold a press conference. That would be nice. Over the last year we've certainly scored some serious ratings off those three and their little club." Maureen bit her lower lip. "I wonder if there's a way I could get them to do an exclusive this time . . ."

"The rape vics like to hold press conferences?" Griffin looked at Waters in confusion.

Maureen, however, did the honors. "Jesus Christ, Griffin, where have you been? Right after the death of Trisha Hayes those women practically owned the five o'clock news. The sister, Jillian, got them united in some sort of group. The Survivors Club, they call it. Then they started sending out the press releases. Worked like a charm. Before they went public, people knew about the attacks, but weren't losing a lot of sleep over it. You know how people are—violent crimes happen to someone else. Especially rape. That definitely happens to other women—you know, poor women, minority women, women living in high-risk areas or leading high-risk lives. Except one day, the general public turned on the TV and there were the three victims—beautiful, white, well-educated and well-to-do. Two aren't even sweet young things but respectable, middle-aged women, leading respectable, middle-class lives.

"People went nuts," Maureen said bluntly. " 'Look at these poor women, so tragically victimized in their own homes. Arrest someone, arrest anyone, but by God, get us justice before that becomes my daughter, my sister, my mother, my wife. What the hell have the police been doing anyway?' I understand after their first appearance, the AG's phone didn't stop ringing for a week."

"They gave the crimes a face," Griffin filled in.

"The Survivors Club gave the crimes three extremely attractive faces. Ever take Psych 101? People really do judge a book by its cover. Ugly people get what they deserve. Pretty people, on the other hand . . ."

Griffin nodded. He understood. "They hold a lot of press conferences?" he asked curiously.

"I don't know. Five or six."

"Always all three women?"

"*Always* all three women. No individual interviews, they made that clear in the beginning."

"What about their families?"

Maureen shrugged. "Sometimes you saw Carol Rosen's husband or Meg Pesaturo's mother in the background, but the press conferences were very clearly the women's show. After all, they were the ones viciously attacked while the Providence cops sat on their asses for six weeks."

"They're bitter?"

"My words, not theirs."

"Emotional?"

"Sometimes. Not often. More like . . . focused. For each venue, the Survivors Club had clear demands. For example, when they held a press conference in front of the PPD, they were asking for more foot patrols in College Hill. When they were in front of the mayor's office, they launched an appeal for community policing. In front of the AG's office, they wanted a more aggressive investigation, get a suspect and get him off the streets, now, now, now. We're talking a serial rapist, after all, and we all know serial rapists don't magically stop on their own."

"In other words, they whipped the public into a frenzy," Griffin mused. Oh yeah, he could see that. The Providence detectives had to love those afternoons. Nothing like a public flogging by the very people you were trying to help, to make you feel good about the job. Of course, if it had been the state's case, they would've nailed the guy day one. That went without saying.

"Eddie Como attacked four women in six weeks," Maureen said firmly. "He killed one of them. How do you think it must feel to be Jillian Hayes right now, knowing that if the Providence detectives had been paying more attention after the second attack, maybe the third attack never would've happened? Maybe her sister would still be alive."

"She say that?"

"She never had to. Just by standing up there, she reminded the public of what happened to her sister and in turn, what could happen to one of their sisters as long as the rapist remained at large. The public responded to that. Hell, the public ate it up. I'll bet you the women could hold a press conference this afternoon announcing that they'd shot Eddie Como, and no one would bat an eye."

"They're that attractive?" Griffin asked dryly.

"No!" Maureen rolled her eyes. "They're that . . . compelling. Think about it. You got Jillian Hayes, the hardworking older sister who runs her own business while taking care of her invalid mother. She's polished, she's poised, plus she's always holding a bright, smiling photo of her younger sister, who was only nineteen when Eddie Como killed her. Then, you have Meg Pesaturo, looking like Bambi, with her big brown eyes and trembling shoulders. Trust me, there's not a man in this city who can look at her and not want to kill Eddie Como himself. And finally, we have Carol Rosen, a blue-eyed blonde, the socialite wife who on the one hand lives in a mansion, but on the other hand spends her time doing work for local charities. You couldn't cast a better group if you tried."

"A business woman, a college coed and an upper-crust wife. In other words, a little something for everyone."

"Exactly."

"Each taking turns on the mike," Griffin murmured.

"Oh no. Jillian Hayes serves as the spokesperson for the group. She does all the talking."

"All the time?"

"All the time. I'm guessing they have an agreement. Plus, she has a marketing background, and the other two never appeared very comfortable on camera."

"So *they* never made demands," Griffin said slowly. "Jillian Hayes made demands."

"She was speaking for all of them. For God's sake, Carol and Meg were standing right there."

"But Jillian's the ringleader of this so-called Survivors Club?"

"Why, Griffin, you make it sound like she's plotting something."

"Just thinking out loud."

Maureen was quiet for a moment. Her blue eyes had taken on that feral look again. "We have some footage you might like to see."

Griffin and Waters exchanged glances. "Sounds like everyone has footage," Griffin said neutrally. "That's the nature of a press conference."

"We have better footage."

"More gazing up at rooftops, Maureen?"

"Something like that."

"Come on." Griffin was growing tired of this conversation. He made a waggling motion with his fingertips. "Spill it, Maureen. You've already aired whatever you got, that makes it public property. So let's just cut to the chase and your cooperation will be duly noted."

"How duly noted?"

"Next time we meet, I promise not to growl at you as much as I'm going to growl at you now."

"Funny, I would've thought that vacation would have improved your temper, Sergeant Griffin."

"And I would've thought that covering three women who had been brutally attacked would've taught you some compassion. Guess we're both wrong."

Maureen thinned her lips. Behind her, Jimmy turned away before she could glimpse his smile.

"We have this footage of Carol Rosen," Maureen said abruptly.

"The socialite wife."

"Yeah, it's the third or fourth press conference. I don't even remember for what. But Jillian's talking away at the mike, and Carol and Meg are doing what they do best, standing beside her, when Carol's husband appears. He walks up behind his wife, and I guess she never heard him coming, because the next moment he puts his hand on her shoulder and she about jumps out of her skin. Jimmy happened to have the camera on her when it happened, and the look on her face . . . You could just tell—even in broad daylight, even surrounded by a roomful of people, that woman was terrified. She didn't feel safe. And *that's* what it means to be a rape survivor. It's a powerful TV moment. And, for the record, we're the only ones who got it on tape."

Maureen sounded so proud about that, Griffin could only stare at her. Waters must've been doing the same, because after a second, Maureen snorted and waved her hand at both of them. "Oh, come on. You're big boys, you've been around the block. You know how this game is played."

"You're telling us," Griffin said slowly, "that you think Carol Rosen killed Eddie Como. And you believe this, because you happened to catch a moment on camera, when she was experiencing abject terror?"

Maureen narrowed her eyes. "Do you know what he did to her, Griffin? Have you read the police report from that attack? My God, when Eddie Como was done, Carol Rosen couldn't walk for five days. Jillian Hayes may have lost her sister. Meg Pesaturo may have lost her memory. But from what I've seen, Carol Rosen's pretty much lost her *mind*. I'd kill someone for doing that to me. Wouldn't you?"

It was a loaded question and they all knew it. Griffin didn't say anything. After another moment, Maureen impatiently shook her head.

"Look, we both know what you're going to do next. You're going to find the three victims. You're going to ask which one pulled the trigger. And the minute one of them so much as blinks, you're going to haul her ass to jail. So don't lecture me about compassion, Sergeant. This is a game. And you wouldn't have come back if you hadn't missed playing it."

"Poor me," Griffin murmured.

Maureen shook her head again. "No. Poor Carol Rosen."

7

Carol

She is watching The Ten O'Clock News *on* Fox. *Her eyes keep drifting shut. An early riser, she has been up since five, and ten o'clock is pushing things a bit. She should turn off the TV. She should go to bed.*

The house is big and silent. The grandfather clock has finished tolling in the foyer, but she can still feel the deep vibrations working their way through the nooks and crannies of her hundred-fifty-year-old Victorian home. There had been a time when she had found that sound comforting. When she had run her hand up the gleaming cherry banister of the central staircase with pride. When she had sought out each tiny room in the attic, in the old wood-shingled tower, like a hunter in search of treasure.

Those days are gone now. More and more she looks at this house she has so painstakingly refurbished and sees her own prison.

"Must you always work so late?" she has asked her husband, Dan.

"Jesus Christ, Carol, someone has to pay for all this. New plumbing isn't exactly cheap, you know."

She doesn't remember him being like this in the beginning. He's the one who actually found the house, who came running through the door of their rental one afternoon and announced excitedly that he'd just seen their future home. An East Side address is a big step up. This is where the great families of Providence once lived. The bankers, the shipping magnates, the jewelry manufacturers. Dan used to talk about one day having a Benefit Street address, but there is no way they could afford those huge, well-pedigreed homes.

This house, however—old, neglected, tragically subdivided into rental units—was different. The purchase price was cheap. The long-term obligation, on the other hand . . .

To be honest, Carol had fallen in love with the home, too. The three-story turret, the wraparound porch, the exquisite gingerbread trim. Yes, it needed a new roof, new wiring, new plumbing. It needed new walls torn down and old walls built back up. It needed carpentry work, it needed masonry work. It needed power washing, it needed sanding, it needed painting.

It needed them. That's what she had thought in the beginning. It needed a nice, young, upwardly mobile couple, with growing financial resources, and lots of tender loving care. They would slowly but surely restore this home to its former glory. And they would fill its five bedrooms with a new generation of happy, bouncing children. That's what old homes need, you know. Not just new wiring, but a fresh injection of life.

They had been so hopeful in those days. Dan's law practice was growing and while she was currently working as his legal secretary, they were certain it was only a matter of time before she'd be a stay-at-home mom with two-point-two children, and what the hell, an extremely well-mannered small dog.

Carol rises off the sofa now. She turns off the TV. She listens to the silence, the absolute, total silence of a four-thousand-square-foot home that remains too empty. And she thinks about how much she hates this sound.

"Jesus Christ, Carol, someone has to pay for all this . . ."

Upstairs, the air is hot and stuffy. The temperature hit almost ninety today, freakish for this early in May but that's New England for you. If you don't like the weather, just wait a minute. Unfortunately, the house has no air-conditioning and the bedroom is unbearably warm. Carol opens a window to cool the room. She can still arm the security system with a window open, but that involves lining up the window connector with the second set higher on the windowsill to complete the circuit. The security company is proud of this innovation. Carol, however, thinks it's stupid. If she lines up the connectors, she can only open the window three inches, which doesn't give her much of a breeze. She needs cooler air to sleep; she opens the window all the way.

It's 10:08, after all. Dan will be home soon.

She strips off her clothes without turning on the light. Outside she can hear cars going by, plus the distant murmur of voices. Lots of college students live in this area, and it seems to Carol that they never sleep.

Carol pulls the down comforter to the foot of the bed. Clad in a silky pink nightgown, she finally slides between the sheets. She sighs, the three-hundred-forty-thread-count cotton cool against her skin.

In a minute, she is asleep.

A sound wakes her. She doesn't know what. She blinks her eyes, disoriented, then sees a figure at the foot of her bed.

"Dan?" *she murmurs sleepily.* "What time is it, honey?"

The figure doesn't say anything.

"Dan?" *she asks again.*

And then, suddenly, she knows.

Carol scrambles out of bed. She makes it two feet, then the man grabs her by the hair. Her neck snaps back. She cries out, but the sound is muffled, choked, not at all like her. Scream, she thinks. Scream!

But she can't. Her throat won't work. There is not enough spit in her mouth. All that comes out is a gasp.

As the man pulls her by her hair, back to the bed.

Dan, she is thinking. DAN!

The man throws her down on the bed. She tries kicking out her feet, but somehow he has her ankles in his hand. Frantically, she beats at his head, but her futile efforts don't seem to bother him at all. Then he draws back his other hand. He smacks it across her face.

Her head whips to the side. Her cheekbone explodes, her eye wells up. Before she can recover, he smacks her again. Her lip splits. She tastes the salt of her own blood as tears roll down her face.

He has something looped around her wrist. She tries to yank her arm back, but the sudden motion only snaps the tourniquet into her flesh. Then he is straddling her body, and though she is sure she is struggling, she must be struggling, he has her hands, then her feet, tied to her wrought-iron bedposts.

She is crying openly now, horrible, heaving sobs. Her body strains against the ties. She twists, she heaves. But she can't do anything. She is caught, her shoulders aching, her legs spread wide, revealing . . . everything.

She is vulnerable. She is helpless. And even as she begs, she knows what he will do next.

Abruptly, he unrolls a strip of material and forces it into her mouth as a gag. Latex, her shocked brain registers. He has bound her with strips of latex, the tough, rubbery substance pinching her skin.

A fresh strip over her eyes. She can't see what will happen next, and that makes it even worse.

Her nightgown yanked from her body. The clink of metal in the silent room as he unfastens his belt. The rasp of metal as he undoes his zipper. Then the soft thud of his pants hitting the floor, his heavy breathing as he comes closer and closer . . .

The bed sagging, his weight descending . . .

Dan, please Dan . . .

And then the man's hand, suddenly, brutally snapping around her neck.

She does not clearly recall the things that come next.

She retreats somewhere inside herself. The room is a black void, a place where someone else, a mannequin, a Barbie doll, an unfeeling woman, exists. She is a tiny, tiny girl, curled up in her head, where her arms are wrapped tight around her bent knees and she is whispering over and over again, "Dan, Dan, Dan."

Then the weight is gone. It takes her a moment to notice. She feels his hands at her ankles. The right noose goes. Then the left. The blood flow has been cut off. She can no longer feel her feet.

He moves up the bed. Her left hand sags free. Then her right.

Her body is beaten and tired and sore. She can't think. She can't move. But it's over, she tells herself, and feels the beginning of hysteria. It's over and she is still alive!

Then the man flips her over. Then the man climbs back on the bed. Then the man does stuff she has only ever read about, and this time she is sure she is screaming. She is screaming, screaming, screaming.

But the gag is in her mouth. The mattress absorbs the sound.

She is screaming and nobody hears a sound.

Time is gone. Reality has suspended. Her eyes glaze over. Saliva pools around the gag and drips onto her lovely Egyptian cotton sheets.

When he is finally done, she is beyond noticing, beyond caring. The man comes back. Sticks something in her unmoving body. Cold liquid gushes everywhere.

He rolls her back over, renews the ties at her hands and feet, then stares down at her face. Finally, almost tenderly, he reaches down and pulls the gag from her mouth.

"It's over," he whispers. "Go ahead and scream. Call your neighbors. Call the police."

The man disappears out her open window. At last, she is alone.

Carol does not scream. She is tied naked and spread-eagle to her own bed. She will not call out for her neighbors. She will not call out for the police. The man knew that, and now so does she.

She lies there instead, feeling the moisture run down her thighs. She lies there, with another man's semen running down her legs and she waits . . .

She waits for her husband to finally come home.

Six A.M. Monday morning, Carol Rosen prepared for her day. The day. Dan was already gone. He claimed that he wanted to get to work early so he could take the afternoon off if she was called to testify. They both knew that he lied. The state prosecutor, Ned D'Amato, has assured them that nothing happens the opening day of trial. The defense uses up the morning with last-minute motions to dismiss, then jury selection takes up the afternoon.

But Dan had insisted. You never know, he said. You never know.

Dan now came home by seven most nights. But even when he was here, he was gone, and it seemed to Carol that he got up earlier all the time. As if by five in the morning, he could no longer stand being alone with her in this house.

Carol hated him for that. But maybe she hated the house even more.

She went upstairs, showered forever with the curtain open, the bathroom door open. She needed lots of space these days. Had to see what was coming. Had to know where she'd been. The security system was always on. She had not turned off the TV in ten months. More often than not, she slept on the sofa in front of its babbling voices and multicolored screen.

After showering, she took out her new butter-cream suit. Dan didn't know about the suit yet. Lately, he'd been obsessed with money. Last month, she'd overheard him liquidating their brokerage account. She hadn't said anything; neither had he.

It was odd. In some ways he was more attentive than ever. Coming home for dinner, asking her what she needed. Right after that night, when she'd still been in the hospital, he had stayed glued to her side. Four days, four nights, probably the most time they'd spent together since their honeymoon ten years before.

When she had finally returned home, he'd already moved them into a different bedroom, one of the round turret rooms far from the scene of the attack. He had bought a new bed, new mattress, new sheets. He'd had elaborate, wrought-iron bars placed over each window.

She had taken one look at the round, shuttered room and collapsed in a fresh wave of tears. He had held her awkwardly, patting her back, though it was difficult for him to touch her and difficult for her to be touched. He didn't understand her despair, and she couldn't explain it.

For a week, he brought her a fresh bouquet of flowers each night and takeout from her favorite restaurants. Guilt, she decided, smelled like red roses and veal piccata.

The house held a deeper silence now. Dan didn't hear it, but she did.

Carol put on her suit. She stood in front of the mirror and gazed at the woman reflected there.

Most days, she still did not feel like she belonged to herself. That woman with the high cheekbones and stubborn chin could not be her. That woman with the pearl drop earrings and Chanel suit looked like she should be at a garden party, or a museum opening. Or perhaps another social sponsored by the Providence Preservation Society. In other words, the things that Carol used to do.

That woman in the mirror looked too normal to be her.

She took off the suit. When the hour was more civilized, say 7:00 A.M., she would call Jillian and ask her what she was going to wear. Jillian was the expert on these things. She always looked cool, calm, composed. Even at her sister's funeral, she had seemed to know exactly what to say and do.

Now, Carol put on a pair of gray sweatpants and a baggy T-shirt. Then she went downstairs to the gourmet kitchen, where at six-thirty in the morning, she got out a pint of Ben & Jerry's Chunky Monkey ice cream. The morning news anchor babbled away in the family room. The grandfather clock sounded the half-hour gong in the foyer.

Six-thirty Monday morning. The Monday morning.

Carol Rosen looked down at her wrists, pale, delicate and still marred by faint white scars. She looked around her kitchen, with its cherry cabinets and marble countertops, still so goddamn empty. And she thought about her body, her supposedly beautiful, supposedly attractive body that now hadn't been touched in nearly a year. And then she was glad for today. She was extremely happy for today. She couldn't fucking wait for today!

"It's still too good for you, you son of a bitch!" she exclaimed hoarsely in the silent room.

Then Carol put her head in her hands and wept.

8

Fitz

Griffin and Waters exited the World War Memorial Park in time to spot Lieutenant Morelli, Captain Dodge and Major Walsh huddled together in the middle of the crowd of illegally parked police cars. Lieutenant Morelli looked up, caught their eye and hastily waved them over.

"Oh boy," Waters said. Lieutenant Morelli's appearance was hardly unusual. The lieutenant of the Major Crimes Unit in the Detective Bureau, she generally attended a new crime scene if it involved a homicide. The detective commander, Captain Dodge, also wasn't too unexpected. He generally appeared if the case was considered high profile. The arrival of the Major of Field Operations, Major Walsh, the number-two man in the organization, aka the Boss, on the other hand, signified big-guns time. Headline case. High-pressure stakes. The kind of investigation that makes careers or breaks careers. The last time Waters and Griffin had seen this much brass at a crime scene . . .

Waters went back to studiously avoiding Griffin's fist. Griffin went back to pointedly not looking at Waters's nose.

"Major," Griffin said, clicking his heels together and rendering the proper salute. "Captain. Lieutenant." He saluted them, too, then waited as Waters did the same. Waters only saluted the major and captain, however, as he'd already officially greeted Lieutenant Morelli earlier in the day.

"Do we have a description of the shooter yet?" the major asked immediately. He was looking photo-op ready, decked out in a sharply pressed Rhode Island trooper's uniform. The dark gray fabric was edged with deep red piping, and a buff-colored Stetson was pulled low to the ridge of his brow, while dark brown boots were laced up to his knees. Best damn uniform in the nation. Just ask Letterman.

Waters did the honors of holding up the evidence bag. "Better. We have video footage of the sniper, courtesy of News Team Ten. Shows everything down to the nervous tic on the shooter's face."

"Outstanding. Let's deliver this to the crime lab ASAP. Get the tape developed, and print out a visual of the shooter's face to be distributed to all uniforms, Detective." The major looked at Waters expectantly.

"Yes, sir," Waters said crisply, already turning away. Waters was no dummy. A uniform could just as easily serve as evidence courier to the crime lab. The powers-that-be obviously wanted to speak with Griffin alone.

The minute Waters was out of earshot, the major, captain and lieutenant turned their attention to Griffin.

"Sergeant," the major said.

"Yes, sir," Griffin said. In spite of himself, he could feel his stomach tense, as if steeling for a blow.

"You look good," the major said.

"Thank you, sir."

"Assessment?"

"What?" For a moment, he was confused. *My anxiety is operating within normal parameters. No. Wait. Ah, shit.*

"The situation, Sergeant. Tell me what you think."

Griffin's shoulders came down. His stomach unclenched. Talking about the job, he could finally relax. "Professional hit. Shooter camps out on the courthouse roof. Nails his target, Eddie Como, aka the College Hill Rapist, as he exits the ACI van shortly after eight-thirty this morning. Shooter then returns to his car to make a quick getaway, except his client left him one last payment in the form of a bomb."

"Confirmation from the state fire marshal?"

"No, sir. My understanding is that the scene is too hot to approach. It will probably be another hour or so."

"But you're sure the shooter is DOA?"

Griffin shrugged. "We know we have one DOA in the RISD parking lot. Given that the parking lot explosion happened within ten minutes of the shooting, I think it's a safe bet that the two incidents are related. Now, one possibility is that our shooter actually performed two hits—the first being Eddie Como, the second being some unidentified person in the parking lot. But in my opinion, that's a low probability scenario. For one thing, it's uncommon to change MO's—going from sniper to explosives expert. For another, we know the shooter left his assault rifle and a full magazine of two-twenty-threes up on the roof. Why leave the gun if he still had work to do? No, I think it's more probable that the sniper felt he'd completed his task, abandoned his tools in order to make a clean getaway, then ran into an unexpected complication when he got into his car. Ergo, the shooter is now one extracrispy DOA."

The major grunted. Lieutenant Morelli suppressed a smile.

"Next steps?" Captain Dodge spoke up. Griffin turned his attention toward him, forcing himself to remain patient even though he was being grilled like an FNG, a fucking new guy.

"Assuming it's a professional," Griffin said briskly, "we need to identify the shooter, establish that he did kill Eddie Como—which will be pretty easy thanks to the videotape—then find a connection between the shooter and his client. Identifying the shooter shouldn't be too hard. We have a visual of his face. The state fire marshal will retrieve the VIN of his car. The ME will get prints. Bada-bing, bada-boom."

"But that could take days," the captain said pointedly. His gaze swept toward the park, where the media churned up the grass and strained against the police barricades.

"Well then, consider this. The RISD parking lot. It's permit only, right? And we know the shooter must have been parked there for a while, because he was camped out on the roof. Assuming he didn't want to call attention to himself by getting a parking ticket, or worse, lose his getaway by being towed, that means he probably had a parking pass. We contact RISD, obtain a list of names, run the names through the system and get a big head start on names to go with the face."

"Not bad," the captain said.

"Cross-reference the names of people with RISD parking passes, with the rape victims and families," Griffin added.

"Even better," the major concurred.

Griffin, however, had started to frown.

"Uh-oh," Lieutenant Morelli said. "I know that look."

"Ah, I don't know . . ."

"Humor us, Sergeant. At the rate things are going, we could use a good laugh today."

Griffin had to think it through. "We're getting a long list of assumptions here. Assumption one is that we have a sniper hired to kill alleged College Hill Rapist, Eddie Como. Assumption two is that the obvious motive for hiring the shooter is revenge, meaning the obvious suspects are the rape vics and/or their families. The only good rapist is a dead rapist, etc., etc. But how many vengeance cases do you know that involve a hired gun? Your typical distraught father, irate husband, shattered victim, they show up at the courthouse, pull out the family pistol and take care of business up close and personal. They're not concerned with getting caught or covering their tracks. They're obsessed with revenge. They're angry, mad, sad. It's an emotional act. A hired assassin on the other hand . . . That's pretty cold."

"It's been a while," the lieutenant said. "Maybe the person's had time to calm down."

"Which would be my second problem," Griffin said immediately. "It's been what, a year since the attacks? Sounds to me like the vics have been doing pretty well. They formed some sort of survivors club, took their mission to the press, became activists. By all accounts, Eddie Como's arrest was a victory for them. And now they're in the homestretch. The actual trial's about to start. Two weeks from now it would end, and most likely Como would be sentenced to life behind bars once and for all. The women, their Survivors Club, whatever, would have justice. Now, it would be one thing if there was doubt about the outcome of the trial, but from what I've heard they had Como dead to rights—DNA evidence."

"They had DNA on O.J., too," the captain spoke up dryly.

"But Como isn't packing the legal dream team. We're talking public defender. In other words, this kid was toast and we're a mere two weeks from his public toasting. So why shoot him now? If you're really angry, and you want to spare yourself or your loved one the agony of the criminal justice system, shouldn't you have shot Eddie Como when he was collared one year ago?"

"Better late than never?"

"Yeah, I suppose." Griffin was still frowning. "I don't know. A rooftop sniper is cold. Calculated. It feels wrong."

"How much do you know about the Como case?" the major asked.

"Not much," Griffin answered honestly. He looked the major in the eye. "I took a break from watching TV."

"And now?"

"I can watch a little telly. I doubt I'll have the time in the foreseeable future, but I can watch."

"Good," the major said brusquely. He cleared his throat. "So, Providence wants in on the case."

"No kidding."

"Como's their catch. They know him, the rape case, and the victims the best."

"Yeah, well, if they know everyone so well, how did 'their catch' just wind up dead?"

Lieutenant Morelli was biting back another smile. She stopped looking at Griffin, and made a big show of examining her shoes.

"We're going to need their cooperation," the major was saying, "to get information on the explosion. Specifically, Providence would like the lead investigator of the College Hill Rapist case to join our case team looking into the shooting."

"Who was the lead investigator on the rape case?" Griffin narrowed his eyes suspiciously.

"Detective Joseph Fitzpatrick from Sex Crimes."

"Ah, nuts." Griffin only knew Detective "Fitz" Fitzpatrick by reputation, but by reputation, Fitz was a third-generation Providence cop who didn't care much for Rhode Island's Detective Bureau. According to him (as well as some other members of the PPD), the state should stick to doing what it did best—patrolling the highways—while the city cops did what they did best—investigating real crimes.

"Can't we just copy them on our reports?" Griffin asked, already feeling cranky.

"No. Besides, you're going to need to interview the victims next, and Detective Fitzpatrick has a relationship with them that could be quite useful. Plus, he's been in on the Como case since the first attack. He can bring you up to speed."

"Shouldn't he be bringing the primary case officer up to speed?"

The major smiled at him. "Exactly."

"We assume that's all right with you," Lieutenant Morelli spoke up. She gazed at him intently now. The major and the captain did the same. This was it. The closest anyone would come to asking the real question. Griffin understood. Last week, he had passed the fitness-for-duty diagnostic. According to rules and regs, he was back in. That was the system and everyone would honor it. If he was wrong, however, if he wasn't ready, if he couldn't do this job with the full attention and diligence it deserved, it was on Griffin to bring it up. Speak now or forever hold your peace, as the saying went.

"Where do I find Providence's best and brightest?" Griffin asked Morelli.

"Over at the parking lot, mopping up smoke."

"Anything else I should know?"

"The AG doesn't like having a homicide in his backyard. Oh, and the mayor feels major explosions are bad for tourism."

"In other words, no pressure?"

Morelli, the captain and the major all smiled at him. "You got it."

Griffin raised a dubious brow. He nodded his good-bye, then walked down the block toward the smoking parking lot, passing in front of the press again and inspiring a fresh round of screaming questions. For a moment, he got to feel like a rock star, and the adrenaline went straight to his brain. Lead investigator. The thrill of the hunt, the excitement of the chase. Oh, yeah. He did a little two-step, caught the motion, decided maybe he was crazy and felt the best he had all year.

Hot damn, whoever would've thought a high-profile assassination would be just what Sergeant Psycho needed?

Arriving at the smoldering parking lot, he immediately spotted Detective Fitzpatrick in one corner. The heavyset Providence cop wore an ill-fitting gray suit over a pale blue shirt and 1980s navy blue tie. He looked like he was taking fashion direction from *NYPD Blue,* down to his palette of thinning brown hair. Judging by what Griffin had heard, Fitz was a detective from the "old school." Ate doughnuts for breakfast and informants for lunch. Spent his after-hours down at the seedy FOP club in Olneyville, drinking Killians. Not a lot of guys like that around anymore. The new breed of cop was too health-conscious for doughnuts, and too fitness-oriented to go anyplace after work other than the gym. Times were changing, even in law enforcement. Griffin doubted Fitz liked those changes much.

And then suddenly, out of the blue, Griffin missed his wife. He shook his head, wishing he could control his own emotions better and even more frightened that someday he would. Cindy had been fascinated by police work. An engineer herself, she had a wonderfully analytic mind. She'd go over tough cases with him, fretting over pieces of the puzzle, helping him hammer out riddles. She'd love a case like this one. She'd want to know all about Eddie Como, his victims, the hired gun. Frankly, the thought of a female victim turning on her attacker probably would've thrilled her to death. Why settle for simple castration if you could kill the man instead?

Cindy hadn't exactly been a damsel-in-distress kind of girl.

Then, as still happened too often these days, Griffin's thoughts turned. He stopped thinking about Cindy. He started thinking about David. And his fists clenched reflexively while a muscle leapt in his jaw. The tension was there again. Would be for a long time. It was his job now to manage it, to learn better coping skills. Like going running. Like finding a punching bag. Like seeing how many rounds he could go before he finally took the edge off his rage.

A week after the Big Boom, before he understood it was the Big Boom, his brother had come looking for him and found him out in his garage still working the heavy bag. His hands were bleeding. Giant blisters had welled up and burst on his feet. He was still going at it, four fingers broken and the buzzing worse than ever in his head. Frank had had to wrestle him to the ground. It cost him two black eyes and a swollen lip.

Griffin had collapsed shortly thereafter. He had not eaten or slept in over five days. He had a last impression of Frank standing over him. Frank looking at Griffin's bloody hands. Frank with tears on his cheeks.

He had made his older brother cry. He remembered being stunned, being appalled, being ashamed. And then he'd sunk, down, down, down into the great black abyss. He'd sunk down, down, down, whispering his dead wife's name.

Griffin turned away from the parking lot. He didn't want to approach Fitz in this kind of mood, so he practiced his even-breathing techniques while locating the state fire marshal. An ATF agent was standing next to the marshal, a two-for-one sale in information shopping.

"Marshal." Griffin shook the man's hand, then waited a moment as Marshal Grayson introduced him to Special Agent Neilson from ATF. More handshaking and head bobbing. Both the fire marshal and the ATF agent had faces smeared with black soot and sweat. The men looked at once tired and angry, so Bentley had been right about the DOA.

"I heard you were back," Grayson commented.

"Can't fish forever," Griffin said.

Grayson smiled thinly. "On a day like this, I wouldn't mind trying. No, on a day like this I wouldn't mind trying at all."

All three men turned toward the smoking ruins. "What can you tell me?" Griffin asked.

"Not much yet. We're just now getting into the scene."

"One dead?"

"One dead."

"Cause of the explosion?"

The marshal nodded his head toward the pile of five vehicles. "See how the one to the left is almost entirely burnt out? Upholstery's gone, all six windows are blown? That would be the primary scene of the explosion. The other cars bear peripheral damage."

"But that car is off to one side."

"The force of the explosion lifted the vehicle up and carried it through the air. Whoever did this wasn't fooling around."

"So we're talking a car bomb."

"The scene is consistent with some sort of incendiary device. More than that, I don't know yet. The thing about an explosion of this size and nature is that it sets off secondary explosions as well. Several gas tanks went, so we have burn patterns consistent with the use of an accelerant. The seat on the driver's side bears shrapnel, which could either be from a packed pipe bomb, or be fragments from the site of the main explosion, gas tanks, etc. Until I have a chance to take it all apart and put it back together, I won't know what's what."

"I'm going to need to know what kind of bomb," Griffin said. "Are we talking a sophisticated device, something that uses unusual parts, or is it a homemade concoction even a Boy Scout could whip up out in the garage? Oh, and is there a timer, etc.?"

Grayson gave him a look. "When I'm done, Sergeant, you'll know exactly what kind of wires were used to build this baby and if those wires came from a spool used in wiring any other bombs in the United States. But you're not going to know that until I'm done, and I'm not going to be done with this for at least a week or ten days."

"I'm told that the AG doesn't like a homicide in his backyard and that the mayor feels explosions are bad for tourism," Griffin said. "Just so you know."

The state fire marshal sighed. "I gotta get a new job," he muttered. "Or a new pacemaker. All right. Give me five days. I'll try to have something for you then."

Detective Fitzpatrick chose that opportunity to walk over. "Sergeant Griffin?"

"Detective." Griffin held out his hand. Fitz accepted the handshake, and for the next few seconds they both amused themselves by squeezing too hard. Neither one of them blinked. Having set the tone, they excused themselves from the state fire marshal and walked off to one corner where they could eye each other for weakness in peace.

"Any news on the shooter?" Fitz asked.

"He liked Fig Newtons. Any news on the identity of the owner of the vehicle?"

"It's a rental."

"Ran the VIN?"

"Looked at the plate. Do you have a description?"

"We have several. Where's the body?"

"At the morgue. You got the weapon?"

"We got a rifle. Can the ME get prints?"

"Ask the ME. Got a name?"

"No. But we're guessing he had a RISD parking permit."

Fitz grunted. His breathing had accelerated. So had Griffin's. "These free flows of information are very helpful," Fitz said. He ran a hand through his thinning hair, then chewed on a toothpick dangling from the corner of his mouth.

"That's what I always think."

"You got a body," Fitz said after another moment. "I got a body. Now what we both need is a link."

"That sums it up."

"You're thinking the women or their families."

"I would like to talk to the women and their families."

"I know these women," Fitz said seriously.

"Okay."

"I've spent a year interviewing them, reassuring them, preparing them for today. You know what that's like."

"I still get some Christmas cards."

"Then you understand why I want to take the lead in questioning them."

"You can start," Griffin said, a phrase that didn't fool either of them.

Fitz narrowed his eyes. He opened his mouth, started to say something harsh, then seemed to think better of it. He shut his trap. He regarded Griffin stonily.

Rhode Island law enforcement was a small, incestuous community, much like the rest of the state. Everyone knew everyone, promoted each other's brother, gave other family members a break. Fitz had probably heard about Griffin, the basement, the Big Boom. He was probably now wondering how much of those stories was true. And he was probably wondering, looking at Griffin's thickly muscled chest and hard-planed face, if pushing Sergeant Psycho was really very safe.

At this stage of the game, Griffin didn't feel a need to comment either way.

Abruptly, Fitz shrugged. "All right. Let's go speak to the women."

"They're all together?"

"Yep."

"A Survivors Club meeting?" Griffin guessed.

"So you've heard."

"I understand they have a penchant for press conferences."

"They take a hands-on approach," Fitz said. Far from sounding bitter, however, the older detective merely shrugged. "Last year, they're the ones who identified the key break in the case. In all honesty, without the Survivors Club, I'm not sure we ever would've nailed Eddie Como."

9

The Survivors Club

"Jillian Hayes is the de facto leader of the group," Fitz explained as he drove through the maze of narrow one-way streets that comprised East Side Providence. "Her sister was the third rape victim, a nineteen-year-old sophomore at Brown. She died during the attack of an anaphylactic reaction to latex."

"I thought the victims were blood donors."

Fitz slid him a sideways glance, obviously surprised Griffin knew that much. "One link discovered in the course of the investigation was that both the first victim, Meg Pesaturo, and the third victim, Trisha Hayes, had donated at campus blood drives in the weeks prior to the attacks."

"So Trisha Hayes gave blood, even though she was allergic to latex?"

"Sure. According to Kathy Hammond, the phlebotomist who assisted Miss Hayes, Trisha informed her that she was latex-sensitive and Mrs. Hammond switched to vinyl gloves, following the Rhode Island Blood Center's policy and procedures. Latex allergies are becoming more common, you know. Most hospitals, blood-donor centers, visiting nurse associations, etc., stock other kinds of gloves as well."

"Do they note latex-sensitivity on the blood-donor card?"

Fitz understood where Griffin was going with this and regretfully shook his head. "No. Too bad, too. If we could've proven that Como had prior knowledge of Miss Hayes's allergy, we could've gone after him for murder. Instead, we had to settle for manslaughter."

"Too bad," Griffin agreed. He glanced idly at the side-view mirror, caught a glimpse of white and narrowed his eyes for closer scrutiny just as Fitz lurched the car forward.

"So," Fitz was saying. "Jillian Hayes was supposed to meet her younger sister at seven for dinner, but was running late. She showed up around eight, entered the basement apartment and was promptly jumped from behind. Eddie beat the living shit out of her. Choked her with his bare hands. God knows how far he would've gone, except an upstairs neighbor was alerted by the noise and called the police. Eddie took off at the sound of sirens. Jillian dragged herself over to the bed, where she found her sister's body tied up with latex tourniquets."

"That was his signature?"

"Yep, latex tourniquets, all three victims. He used ten ties, one for a gag, one for a blindfold, then two each for the wrists and ankles, forming a double noose that actually grew tighter when the victim struggled. If they relaxed, on the other hand . . . Let's just say Eddie had a keen sense of irony."

"I assume after the neighbor's call, uniforms responded from all over and immediately canvassed the neighborhood. They never stumbled across a guy running from the scene?"

"Nope. But to be fair to the uniforms, we had no description. The only victim who caught a glimpse of the attacker was number two, Carol Rosen, and she says her room was too dark to get a good look. The first girl, Meg Pesaturo, doesn't even remember the attack, so she couldn't help. Trisha Hayes may have seen Eddie, but she never regained consciousness to give a statement. And her sister, Jillian, was attacked in a gloomy basement apartment, so she couldn't provide any details either. In other words, sure, we poured all sorts of manpower into the streets that night, but Eddie either holed up, or played it cool. No one ever stopped him."

"Eddie Como sounds either very lucky or very smart," Griffin muttered. He turned to Fitz. "Hey, see that white van four vehicles back? You know, the one with the satellite dish up top."

Fitz glanced in the rearview mirror. "Yep."

"I'm thinking that's the Channel Ten News van."

Fitz studied it for a moment. "Oooooh," he drawled. "I think you're right. Bringing your admirers with you, Sergeant Griffin?"

"Oh, I don't think it's me they're admiring. You were the one who led the College Hill Rapist case. Ergo, you're the one most likely to know where to find the women."

"Ah shit. Little bloodsucking leeches. You'd think two corpses would be enough to keep them occupied. But no, you're probably right. They want to find one of the victims. Then they can stick a mike beneath her nose and say, 'Hey, Victim Number Two, your rapist was just splattered all over the sidewalk. What are you going to do now? Fly to Disneyland?' Fuck."

Without warning, Fitz flung the vehicle right. The Ford Taurus, technically the same vehicle Griffin drove but in Fitz's case considerably more abused, groaned in protest. Fitz ignored the creaking steering, shuddering shocks and his entire suspension system, gunning the engine as he shot up onto the curb, cut across the corner and landed hard on the cross street.

Griffin grabbed the dash for support, then glanced in the mirror. "Still got 'em."

"That's what you think." Fitz came to a narrow alleyway, jerked left, came to a parking lot, jerked right, then came back to a side street and shot left again. Impressive, Griffin thought. But then, like a great white shark, the van appeared again.

"Maureen, Maureen, Maureen," Griffin murmured. "Feeling a little vindictive over the loss of your videotape?"

"I'm not leading any fuckin' reporter to my women," Fitz growled. "No way, not on my watch."

Griffin took that as a hint to grab the handle protruding from the roof. Good thing. Fitz hit the sirens, shot through a red light without the customary tap on the brake and about plowed into a garbage truck. Apparently not one to sweat near misses, he merely accelerated faster, rocketed through another red light, hung a left, sped four blocks, then hung a right before finally ducking into a parking space between two cars.

"That's gotta do it," he said, breathing hard and fast. Both hands still gripped the wheel. He had a savage gleam in his eye.

For no reason at all, Griffin decided *not* to let go of the safety handle. "I don't see them anymore," he commented.

"Keep looking."

"Aye, aye, Kimosabe."

"I *hate* reporters," Fitz growled.

"Hey, isn't this *People* magazine?"

The magazine had slid out from underneath Griffin's seat. Fitz reached over, snatched it off the floor and flung it into the back.

"I know, I know," Griffin filled in for him. "You only buy it for the pictures."

"Not the pictures," Fitz said grumpily. "The crossword."

They waited a few more minutes. When the news van still hadn't appeared, Fitz slowly pulled back into the street. Traffic was light here, the neighborhood quiet. In the good news department, they had left most of the madness of the downtown scene behind. In the bad news department, it would take them that much longer to get to their destination. Ah well. Quality time for bonding, Griffin was sure. He flexed his biceps, then rolled his neck.

"Now, where were we?" Fitz asked, finally relaxing at the wheel and picking up the threads of their earlier conversation.

"One amnesic victim, two others who couldn't see the rapist in the dark," Griffin cued up. He turned toward Fitz curiously. "If you never had a physical description, how did you determine it was Como?"

"We didn't right away. You have to understand, this wasn't your typical investigation of a serial crime. Our first victim, Meg, was no help at all thanks to trauma-induced amnesia. She doesn't recall the attack, the day of the attack, or for that matter most of her life leading up to the attack—"

"Most of her life?" Griffin interrupted, baffled. "I thought trauma-induced amnesia was forgetting the trauma. How did she leap from blanking one bad night to blanking her whole entire life?"

Fitz shrugged. "How the hell do I know? Maybe Meg didn't like her whole life and this provided a good opportunity. Maybe her brain doesn't like to differentiate. Beats me. But her doctor swears her amnesia is legit, her parents say her amnesia is legit and she seems to think her amnesia is legit. God knows I've interviewed Meg about two dozen times over the last year and she hasn't slipped up yet. So if she's faking it, she's a damn good actress."

"Huh," Griffin said.

"Huh," Fitz agreed. "Either way, Meg's condition made investigating the initial rape complaint difficult. We tried her roommate, Vickie, but all she knew was that when she came home at two A.M., Meg was mysteriously bound to her bed. Then we turned to trace evidence, which was equally unenlightening—no tool marks, no hair, no fiber, no fingerprints. In fact, at the end of attack number one, all we had was one confused college coed, one traumatized roommate, ten strips of latex and one DNA sample that yielded no hits in the sex-offenders database."

"You follow up on the latex?"

"Of course I followed up on the latex. Only damn lead I had. I made the lab analyze chemical compositions, do brand comparisons, batch comparisons, look at the amount of latex powder used on each strip. Frankly, I learned way too fucking much about latex. And none of it did us any good. The way it's manufactured, there is no way to narrow down a batch or shipment number based on a handful of strips. Three weeks after the first attack, we had hit the wall. Case was dead, dead, and deader."

"Oh yeah? What did Meg's Uncle Vinnie have to say about that?"

Fitz promptly laughed. "So you've heard about him. Uncle Vinnie's a funny guy. He came to my office one day. Wanted to know if I was holding back any information from the family. For example, I might already have a name in mind. And for instance, if I already had a name in mind, then he might have a name in mind, and his name might be able to take care of my name, without any taxpayer expense."

"In his own way, Vinnie's a helpful guy."

"Yeah," Fitz agreed, then promptly sighed. "We probably need to pay Uncle Vinnie a visit. In all honesty, I didn't think of him as an advocate of sharpshooting. Rooftop snipers and courthouse assassinations attract a lot of attention, and I don't think Uncle Vinnie likes to attract attention. Personally, I was betting that someday, Eddie would enter the prison showers and suffer a little incident. You know, one involving someone else's prison shank and Eddie's liver. But hey, live and learn."

"Live and learn," Griffin agreed. He returned to the initial string of rapes, still trying to get a sense of that investigation and how they'd gone from one victim with amnesia to an arrest two months later. "Okay," he said. "So after the first rape, you didn't have Eddie Como in mind. You didn't have anyone in mind."

"After the first rape, we were chasing our tails. We went through the drill. Looked at past boyfriends, rattled the sex-offender tree—who had been recently released from the ACI, who might live in the area, etc., etc. Frankly, Meg didn't date much, and all the known perverts were doing other perversions at the time. Probably watching *Sex and the City* on HBO. None of them go out as much now that they have cable."

"But then came the attack on the East Side."

"Right. Four weeks after the Pesaturo rape came the attack on the East Side."

"Quite a different neighborhood," Griffin observed.

"It's also a college area," Fitz said, but then shook his head. "Yeah, attack number two had some key differences. Carol Rosen's a forty-two-year-old housewife, not a college coed. She lives with her husband in an old Victorian house, which isn't exactly the same as a college apartment. Finally, and this is probably the most significant difference, the level of violence was way up. According to the sexual assault nurse, Meg Pesaturo suffered only vaginal penetration, with minor lacerations on her wrists, ankles and mouth from the tourniquets. No sign of beating, and more importantly, no bruising around her throat. With Meg, Eddie apparently got in, got it done and got out.

"Carol Rosen, on the other hand, suffered vaginal and anal penetration. She had bruises on her breasts and buttocks, multiple contusions on her face, multiple lacerations on the inside of her thighs, plus he started flirting with asphyxiation, squeezing her throat so hard he left bruises from his fingertips. He also tied her up so tightly that she still has scars on her wrists and ankles. On a relative scale of things, Meg was lucky. Carol was not."

"But you're sure it's the same guy?"

"Ten latex strips," Fitz said. "One DNA sample. Oh yeah, it was Eddie again."

"And where was the husband through all this?"

"Dan Rosen works as an attorney, corporate stuff. He just opened his own practice a few years ago and keeps long hours. He didn't get home until after midnight, which was when he discovered his wife tied to their bed. We called in uniforms, we tried a canvass, but once again we had no description and once again we had no luck."

Griffin frowned. "Wait a minute. The first victim has a roommate who just happens to work that night, second victim has a husband who also happens to work late. Does this mean what I think it means?"

"We think he watched the victims beforehand," Fitz agreed. "He targeted them at the blood drives, then he spent some time doing his homework, hence the lapse of time between when he first saw them and when he attacked. Now, this theory works well when we look at Meg and Trish, who were blood donors. We get in trouble with Carol Rosen, however, because she didn't actually participate in any blood drives. In her case, we think she was a last-minute substitute. A pretty brunette college student who fits Eddie's 'type' lived just one block away. She'd donated blood during the campus drive, and she remembers someone ringing the buzzer of her apartment that night. She wasn't expecting anyone, though, so she refused to open the door. Good news for her. Not so good for Carol."

"That doesn't explain the husband being gone," Griffin pressed.

"Hey, you think I have all the answers to life? Maybe in the course of watching the brunette, Eddie also noticed that Carol Rosen pretty much lived alone. Maybe he simply saw Carol's open bedroom window, conveniently located above the wraparound porch, and decided to go for it. He was hungry. He'd psyched himself up for a big meal and then lo and behold, he'd been denied service. Besides, Eddie was capable of lifting two hundred pounds. Climbing onto a porch overhang was probably nothing to him. And if the woman's husband was also at home . . . Eddie probably figured he could handle it. After all, it's late at night, and he's got a little bit of adrenaline firing through his veins . . ."

"Which he then took out on Mrs. Rosen. So maybe Como was very unhappy at having to change plans. Or maybe he was building to something more."

"Maybe." Fitz slanted Griffin a look. "Jillian Hayes was also beaten very badly. Not her sister, but then again, Jillian interrupted that party. I don't know. It seemed to me after Carol Rosen's attack that we had a sexual predator with a rapidly escalating penchant for violence. And I thought . . . I thought if we didn't catch the guy soon, we'd end up with someone dead. Unfortunately, that day came before even I expected. Eddie Como attacked Trisha Hayes just two weeks later. The guy took hardly any time off at all."

Griffin nodded grimly. "Too bad."

"Yeah," the Providence detective said gruffly. "Too bad."

"So how did you finally determine the perpetrator was Eddie Como?"

"Process of elimination. Once we homed in on the blood-donor angle, we got a list of names from the Rhode Island Blood Center of who worked the relevant blood drives. Lucky for us, the majority of phlebotomists are female. So once we focused on the males we were looking at only ten suspects. Then we started pushing." Fitz rattled off on his fingers. "One, Eddie had access to two of the victims' home addresses, plus plenty of latex tourniquets. Two, while Eddie's not the biggest guy you'll ever meet, he's shockingly strong. Used to be a champion wrestler in high school and still likes to work out with weights. Eddie is . . . was . . . five eight and one hundred fifty pounds, but he could bench-press over two hundred. Let's face it, that's someone with some muscle. Of course, once we got a DNA sample from him, that cinched it."

"How'd you get the sample?"

"We asked."

Griffin stared at him. "You asked, and he just gave it to you? No lawyering up? No pleading the fifth? No claiming illegal search and seizure?"

From behind the steering wheel, Fitz smiled. It was a predator's smile. "Let me tell you something else about the rapes that very few people know. Eddie thought he was smart. In fact, Eddie thought he was so smart that in fact he was dumb, but now I'm getting ahead of myself. See, Eddie had a book on forensics. Apparently, he'd bought it on-line and thought it made him a bit of an expert. He was pretty good at a lot of it. Three rapes later, we had no hair, no fiber, no fingerprints. Not even tool marks. We think he used social engineering, because in none of the attacks did we find any evidence of breaking and entering. So okay, the kid did all right. But he made one mistake."

"No condom?"

"No condom. He thought he had a better idea. Berkely and Johnson's Disposable Douche with Country Flowers."

"What?"

"Yeah, exactly. See, Eddie had been following the Motyka case—we found newspaper articles of that trial in his apartment. Do you remember the Motyka case?"

Griffin had to think about it. "Tiverton, right? Some handyman who had been doing work on a woman's house broke back in, raped her, murdered her, then put her body in a bathtub."

"Yeah. During the trial, the prosecutor argued that Motyka thought immersing the body in water would wash away the semen. Of course it didn't, they matched the sample to him, and now he's spending the rest of his life behind bars. Because semen goes *up* in the body. Because you need more than simple bathwater to wash it out."

"Something like a douche," Griffin filled in.

"That's what Eddie believed. But he wasn't thinking straight. Sure, a douche can wash out a lot of the semen, but it's just rinsing it onto the sheet. And when we process a rape case, we don't just collect samples from the victim, we also collect samples from the sheet. A couple of lab tests later . . ."

"So Como thinks he's come up with the perfect way of beating DNA, hence he's not worried about providing a sample, but oops, he's not so good after all."

Fitz nodded. "There you have it."

"That's not a bad plan," Griffin said honestly. "He have any priors?"

"Nope."

"History of violence with girlfriends?"

"Nope. In fact, his girlfriend was going to be the primary witness for the defense. She claims Eddie's really a kindhearted, sensitive guy who wouldn't hurt a flea, plus she was with him the nights there were attacks."

"He had an alibi?" Griffin asked with surprise.

Fitz rolled his eyes. "No, he had a pregnant girlfriend who wasn't interested in the father of her child ending up behind bars. Trust me, we looked into it. We never found another witness who could corroborate seeing Eddie at home those nights. Plus, we still had the DNA. If Eddie was really watching *Who Wants to Be a Millionaire?*, then how did his DNA end up at not one, or two, but three crime scenes?"

Griffin bobbed his head from side to side. Fitz had a point. "So the big break came when you made the connection with the blood drives?"

"Yeah, pretty much."

Griffin narrowed his eyes. Okay, now he had it. "And this club, the Survivors Club, they helped you with that."

"Jillian Hayes knew her sister had donated two weeks before the attack. She mentioned it because of the latex strips. We went back to check, and sure enough, good ol' amnesiac Meg had also donated one month prior to being raped. That was the first link we had between the victims. And yeah, everything finally fell into place after that."

Fitz pulled the car over and parked next to the curb. "We're here," he said.

Griffin looked out the window. They had arrived at the rue de l'espoir, a chic little café on Hope Street. Cindy had liked rue de l'espoir. Griffin, on the other hand, preferred its next-door neighbor, Big Alice's, which served the city's best ice cream.

Fitz cut the engine. Now that they were here, he was back to looking uptight, a territorial detective claiming his turf. "Here are the ground rules," he announced. "As the youngest and quietest, Meg's the weakest member of the group. She also knows the least, so pressuring her doesn't do any good. Carol's the most prone to outbursts. I don't think she's dealing so well with the attack, and I get the impression it hasn't done wonders for her marriage. If we play our cards right, we might get something out of her. But here's the kicker. Jillian runs this show. She organized the group, she dictates the agenda. And she—if you'll pardon the phrase—has balls of steel. Piss her off, and the interview's done. She'll clam up, they'll clam up and we'll all end up wasting our time. So the name of the game is prodding just enough to make Carol say something before Jillian gets fed up and sends us packing."

"You're anticipating an antagonistic interview." Which was interesting, because Fitz supposedly had a rapport with these women. After a year of working their cases, he was their police guardian, protector, friend.

"I think these women won't be losing any sleep over Eddie Como's murder," Fitz said carefully. "And I think, even if they are *completely* innocent, they won't care for any investigation into the events surrounding his death. Eddie Como . . . he was scum. Now he's dead scum. How much are any of us supposed to care?"

"Do you think one of them hired the shooter?" Griffin asked bluntly.

Fitz sighed. "None of them are proficient with firearms," he said finally. "If they wanted Eddie dead, they would require outside help."

"But do you think they are *capable* of ordering a hit?"

Fitz hesitated again. "I think they're rape survivors. And as rape survivors, they are capable of many things they never thought of before."

"Even killing a man?"

"Wouldn't you? Come on." Fitz popped open his door. "Let's get moving while we're still one step ahead of the press."

10

The Survivors Club, cont'd

Inside the restaurant, it was easy to spot the women. They sat alone in a corner, huddled over gigantic red mugs, trying to ignore other people's curious stares. Taking in the three, Griffin had several impressions at once. First, Como had good taste in women. They were a startlingly attractive group: two older, one younger, as if two former models were having lunch with the next generation of talent. Second, all three women were clutching their oversized mugs much harder than necessary. Third, and most interesting, none of the women seemed surprised that Fitz was there.

Fitz walked over to the table. The other patrons had started to whisper. He didn't pay them any attention.

"Jillian. Carol. Meg." He nodded at each of the women in turn. Much more slowly, they nodded back. Fitz didn't say anything more. Neither did the women, and the silence immediately stretched long. Griffin had to admit he was impressed by everyone's composure. He let them engage in their staring contest while he did his own sizing up.

Meg Pesaturo looked almost exactly as he'd pictured her. Pesaturo was an old Italian name, and she looked it, with her golden skin, long brown hair and dark gleaming eyes. She was dressed casually this morning, jeans and a brown T-shirt. Definitely the youngster of the group. She was also the first to break eye contact.

In contrast, victim number two, Carol Rosen, looked like middle-aged money. Upswept blond hair, heavily painted blue eyes, pale designer suit. She sat stiffly, back straight, shoulders square. She'd probably gone to some kind of finishing school where girls learned how to drink tea with their pinkies in the air and never let their husbands see them cry. She returned Fitz's stare with overbright eyes, her lips pressed into a bloodless line and her body quivering with tension.

Griffin had to suppress the urge to take her jogging with him. Or throw her into the boxing ring. He was probably oversensitive, given his own state, but Fitz had been right about this one. She wasn't coping well. Maybe she thought she was, but take it from an expert. Carol Rosen was heading for a Big Boom of her own, and when it came, she was going down hard.

He wondered if her husband could read the signs. And if he could, had he been willing to trade Eddie Como's life for his wife's peace of mind?

He turned his gaze to the last member of the group. Jillian Hayes. Never actually raped, but beaten and otherwise victimized. Ad hoc leader. Grieving sister. And at the moment, as cool as a crisp fall day.

She was much older than he'd anticipated, given the young age of her sister. He'd thought she would be mid-twenties, but she looked closer to mid-thirties, a mature woman comfortable in her own skin. She sat loosely, wearing a tan pants suit with a white linen vest. Her thick brown hair was pulled back in a clip at the nape of her neck. She wore simple gold hoops in her ears, and a chain bearing some kind of medallion around her neck. No rings on her fingers. Short, manicured nails.

Stupid thought for the day—he found himself thinking that Cindy would like that suit.

Man, he wanted to go running now. And then he realized that Jillian Hayes was no longer looking at Fitz. Instead, her brown/gold/green eyes were staring straight at him.

"You're from the state," she said. A statement, not a question.

"Detective Sergeant Roan Griffin," he supplied. Fitz shot him a dark look. Maybe he'd wanted the pleasure of making the introductions. Fuck him. It was now out of their hands.

"Tell us what happened," she said. An order, not a statement.

"We have a few questions," Fitz began.

"Tell us what happened."

"What makes you think something happened?" Griffin spoke up, earning another scowl from Fitz.

"Why else would you be here?"

Good point. Griffin glanced at Fitz, understanding now that this really was going to be fun, so hey, here you go, Fitz. Run the show. Fitz did not look amused.

"We need to know where you were around eight-thirty this morning," Fitz said.

Jillian shrugged. Actually, she raised one shoulder in a cool gesture that was as dismissive as it was submissive. Fitz was right—she was clearly the spokesperson of this group. The other two women didn't even open their mouths but simply waited for her to address the question.

"We were here," she said. "Together. The three of us. As most of this restaurant can attest. Now, Detective, please tell us what has happened."

"There was an incident," Fitz said carefully. "Eddie Como is dead."

Griffin and Fitz simultaneously tensed, waiting for the coming reactions. Griffin homed in on Meg: she'd be the most likely to give something away. But if she was a co-conspirator, she was a damn good one. Because at the moment she appeared mostly confused. She cocked her head to the side, as if listening to something inside her brain.

Carol, on the other hand, released her pent-up breath as a sharp hiss. She leaned forward and grabbed the edge of the table in a white-knuckled grip.

"Are you sure?" she demanded.

"What do you mean?" Fitz asked.

"Have you seen his body?"

"Yeah," Griffin replied. "I've seen the body."

She turned on him fiercely. "Tell me. I want every detail. How he looked. How long it took. Was he in pain? Was it horrible? Was it bloody? I want every detail."

"We're not at liberty to discuss the case—" Fitz began.

"*I want every detail!*"

The other patrons turned to stare again. Griffin didn't blame them. Carol was definitely wound a wee bit tight. Not enough blood in the world to satiate her lust. And probably not enough justice to right her wrong.

"It was quick," Griffin said.

"Fuck!" Carol cried.

Okay, maybe Maureen had a point about her. Griffin amused himself by waiting to see who would do what next. Jillian Hayes simply raised her mug and took a sip of chai, her expression carefully blank. Meg Pesaturo still had her head cocked, listening to something only she could hear. Only Carol appeared agitated. She remained breathing too hard, her hands gripping the edge of the table while she waited for something, anything, to make her feel better about things. Maybe Griffin should've lied and told her that Eddie Como had been shot to pieces one limb at a time. She would probably sleep better at night.

And maybe pay the shooter a bonus? Oh wait, he'd already received one.

Jillian or Meg must have kicked Carol under the table, because she finally sat back and seemed to work on regaining some measure of control.

Fitz cleared his throat. "We think it would be best if you all came with us," he told them.

"Why should we go with you?" Jillian set down her mug. She gestured with her hand to include her fellow Survivors Club members. "We've been here all morning. If Eddie Como's dead, we obviously didn't do it."

"There are a few things we'd like to discuss with you—" Fitz tried again.

"I don't understand," Carol interrupted. "He's dead. It's over. We don't need to talk to you anymore. The case, the trial, everything, it's done."

"The detective is fishing," Jillian told her calmly. "While we didn't shoot Eddie Como, he's thinking we might have arranged for whoever did."

"How did you know he was shot?" Fitz asked sharply. "I didn't say he was shot."

"Detective, haven't you seen the morning news?" Jillian paraphrased softly: " 'Shortly after eight-thirty this morning, shots broke out at the Providence County Courthouse. According to initial reports, it is believed that the alleged College Hill Rapist, Eddie Como, was gunned down as he was being unloaded from the prison van. Sources close to the investigation believe an unidentified man fired the fatal shot from the rooftop of the courthouse. Also, an explosion in a nearby parking lot has left one dead.' Isn't that about right? I think that's about right."

She smiled, cool and undaunted, while Fitz muttered something harsh under his breath. Griffin could only shrug. Of course the press had gone ahead with the story even without confirmation of Eddie Como's identity. The College Hill Rapist was big news. Real big news. And why act responsibly when you could further fuck up a murder investigation?

Maureen, Maureen, Maureen, he thought again, and suddenly had a bad feeling about that tape.

"All right," Fitz said grudgingly. "Eddie Como was shot. He's dead. But I don't think this is the place to have a discussion about that. I think it would be best if all of you accompanied us down to the station."

"No," Jillian said firmly. "But thanks for asking."

"Now, ladies—"

"We don't have to go with them," Jillian cut in. She turned her gaze to Meg and Carol, and once more Griffin was impressed by her composure. "We don't have to answer any questions. Without probable cause, Detective Fitzpatrick and Sergeant Griffin can't make us do or say anything. I would keep this in mind, because Detective Fitzpatrick didn't come here to pay us a friendly visit. This is a big day for us, ladies. Eddie Como was shot, and we've just graduated from rape victims to murder suspects."

"She's right, you know," Griffin spoke up.

"What?" Jillian Hayes zoomed in on him with narrow eyes. Fitz was scowling at him.

"Well, aren't you going to tell them the rest of it?" he asked innocently.

"The rest of it?"

"Absolutely. The rest of it. These women are your friends, right? Surely you want them to understand everything. For example, if you ladies don't want to speak with us, then we'll just have to move on down the list. Contact your friends, your family. Husbands, fathers, uncles, mothers, sisters, aunts. Coworkers. Subject them all to police scrutiny. Oh, and we'll subpoena your financial records, of course." All three women sat up straighter. Griffin shrugged. "You have motive and opportunity, that gives us probable cause. We'll pull your bank records, the bank records of every member of your family. Maybe even your uncle's business." He gazed serenely at Meg. "Or maybe a husband's law practice." He gazed at Carol. "Any recent payments that can't be accounted for . . ." He gave another helpless shrug. "A murder is a murder, ladies. Cooperate now, and maybe we can work out a deal where you don't serve life."

Meg and Carol didn't look as certain anymore. Jillian, on the other hand . . . Jillian was looking at him as if she'd just noticed an unpleasantly buzzing fly in the room, and was now about to squash the bug with her bare hand.

"Diminished capacity," she challenged.

"Not for a hired gun. Requires premeditation. If you were going for a plea, you should've showed up in the courthouse and shot Como yourself."

"Not necessarily. Diminished capacity simply means outside influences made you commit an act you otherwise wouldn't have done—that you were not operating in your proper mind, so to speak. You could argue the trauma of being raped, the fear of being attacked again, drove you to employ a hired gun."

"Sounds like you've been thinking this over."

"You never know what you'll need to know until you need to know it."

"Do you have a legal background, Mrs. Hayes?"

"Ms. Hayes. I have a marketing background. But I know how to read."

"Defense statutes?"

"You're not asking the right question yet, Sergeant."

"And what question is that?"

Jillian Hayes leaned forward. "Did we have reason to be afraid? Did we have probable cause to fear for our lives?"

"I don't know. Did you?"

"He called us, Sergeant. Did Detective Fitzpatrick tell you about that? For the last year, Eddie Como has been phoning and mailing us constantly. Do you know what it's like to get a shiver down your spine every time the phone rings?"

"I've suffered through my fair share of telemarketers," Griffin said. But he was looking at Fitz questioningly.

"He shouldn't have been able to call them," Fitz supplied. "In theory, inmates have to enter a pin number into the pay phones to get a dial tone, and each pin number has only so many numbers approved for calling. Trust me, none of the women were ever approved, but then again, this is prison. For every rule the officials impose, the inmates find a way around the rule. Probably with outside help."

"You can ask to censor outgoing mail," Griffin said with a frown. "Impose a no-contact order."

"If an inmate is threatening. Eddie never threatened them, so we couldn't deny access. Basically, they changed their phone numbers, he went to mail. They put a hold on prison mail, he got someone to mail his letters from a different location. Eddie was persistent, I'll give him that."

"And what was he so persistently trying to say?"

"That he was innocent," Jillian said dryly. "That we had made a huge mistake. He never meant to hurt anyone. This was all some big misunderstanding. And then, toward the end, of course, he was demanding to know why we were ruining his life, why we were taking him away from his child. He murdered my sister, Sergeant, and then he's asking *me* how come I'm denying him access to a child?"

"He wouldn't leave us alone," Carol interjected vehemently. "For God's sake, he even contacted my husband at work! He asked him for a list of recommended attorneys! My rapist, consulting my husband for a good legal defense! And when that didn't yield results, he started mailing us countless letters with all the free stamps available to inmates. Think about that. My rapist, harassing me, with stamps I provide as a taxpayer. The man was a fucking monster!"

Griffin looked at Meg. She merely shrugged. "My parents don't let me answer the phone or get the mail."

"The point is," Jillian spoke up, pulling attention back to her, "you're barking up the wrong tree, Sergeant. So someone blew away Eddie Como. We don't care who did it. And we don't need to know who did it. Frankly, we are damn grateful that he's dead."

11

Jillian

Detective Fitzpatrick and Sergeant Griffin stuck around the restaurant for another five minutes. They thrust, Jillian parried. They punched, she counterpunched. The two cops grew frustrated. Jillian didn't much care. She'd been telling Meg and Carol the truth. They didn't have to say anything or go anywhere. As of this moment, they were still merely Eddie Como's victims. They might as well enjoy that advantage while it lasted.

One year ago, when Jillian had first thought up the Survivors Club, she'd had no illusions about the road ahead. She'd woken up that morning with the crushing realization that Trisha was still dead and she was still not. She'd lain there, terrified of each noise in her own home, painfully aware of just how physically weak and inadequate she was, and then she'd gotten mad again. No—she'd gotten furious. She didn't want more police questions. She didn't want DA's walking through her hospital room, cops grilling her about what she had done and said the night her little sister was viciously raped and murdered. She didn't want to get out of bed knowing that the man was still out there. He had killed Trish. He had attacked two other women. And the police hadn't done a damn thing about it.

Jillian had gotten out of bed then. And she had picked up the phone.

Perhaps Meg and Carol had joined the group looking for comfort. Maybe, these days, it even was a source of comfort. But Jillian wasn't ready for soft things yet. First and foremost, she had needed action for Trish, for herself, for all of them. She had formed this group, then honed this group to be their sword.

"We are not the Victims Club," she had told them at their inaugural meeting. "We are the Survivors Club, and while we may have lost control once, we aren't ever going to lose control again. These attacks are our attacks. That rapist is our rapist. And we're going after him. The three of us are going to use the press, we're going to use the attorney general's office, we're going to use the police and we're going to find the man who did this to us. And then we're going to teach him what it means to have messed with us. I promise you that. From the bottom of my heart, I promise you we will get this man and we will make him pay."

And in a matter of three short weeks, they watched the police lead Eddie Como away. What Providence detectives hadn't been able to do for nearly two months, the Survivors Club had accomplished in half that time.

Detective Fitzpatrick and Sergeant Griffin left. A waitress came by. Her look was both curious and sympathetic.

"More chai?"

They shook their heads.

"Stay as long as you'd like, girls. Oh, and don't fret the bill. After everything you've been through, this is on the house."

The waitress bustled away. Jillian looked at Carol and Meg. No one seemed to know what to do next.

"Free breakfast," Carol murmured at last. "Who said being raped didn't have its advantages?"

"We didn't get free breakfast for being raped," Jillian countered. "We received free breakfast for killing Eddie Como. Quick, let's run to Federal Hill. There's no telling how much free food we can get there."

Federal Hill was Providence's Italian section, famous for its restaurants, pastry shops and Mafia connections. Maybe they could get toasted by various mob bosses or receive free cannolis from made men. It was a thought.

Meg spun her now empty mug between her hands. She looked up at Carol, then Jillian. Then she shocked them both, probably even herself, by speaking of serious matters first.

"Maybe you should've told them," she said to Jillian. "You know, about the disk."

"Why? Eddie has contacted us before without the police doing anything about it."

"But this time was different."

" 'Sticks and stones may break my bones,' " Jillian quoted, " 'but words will never hurt me.' "

"He sent the tape to your *house*." Carol now, clearly agreeing with Meg. Carol hated the fact that Eddie Como could access their private residences. As she had told Detective Fitzpatrick six months ago, when the first phone call had come, it was like letting a murderer return to the scene of the crime. Eddie had been charged with three counts of first-degree sexual assault, one count of manslaughter and one count of assault with the intent to commit first-degree sexual assault. After all that, how was it that he still had the freedom to make phone calls and send mail? Eddie Como might have been the one behind bars, but most of the time, they agreed, they were the ones who felt as if they were in prison.

"He's contacted all of us at our homes," Jillian said. "Face it—he likes to play games. He likes trying to mess with our minds. This was just his latest effort."

"But he threatened to kill you," Meg argued. "Detective Fitzpatrick told us he could do something if Eddie became threatening. And that video file"— Meg shuddered delicately—"that was definitely threatening."

The computer disk had been sent to Jillian's house on Friday. The return address had been Jillian's business—yes, Eddie was very smart in his own way. So she'd opened the manila envelope, thoughtlessly popped in the disk, figuring it was from Roger or Claire, and then . . . Then Eddie Como's face had been staring back at her from her own computer screen. And as she fumbled for the eject button or the mouse, or the escape button, or for God's sake, some kind of button, he had begun to speak.

"You fucking bitch," Eddie Como told her as she sat in her own home, ten feet away from her ailing mother, fifteen feet away from her mother's live-in assistant, two feet away from a photo of Trisha, smiling and happy and still so full of life. "You fucking bitch, you've ruined my life. You've ruined my kid's life, my mother's life and my girlfriend's life. Why? Because I'm a spic? Or just because I'm a man? It doesn't matter anymore. I'm gonna get you, even if it takes me the rest of my life. I'm gonna get you even if it's from beyond the grave."

Jillian had gotten the disk out then. She had flung it back into the manila envelope and quickly resealed it, as if it were a poisonous spider that might try to escape. Then she'd sat there a long time, breathing too hard, shaking like a leaf, and in all honesty, very near tears.

Jillian hated being near tears. Crying never helped. Crying never changed the world. Crying certainly didn't fend off the likes of Eddie Como.

"If I was going to contact Detective Fitzpatrick, I would have done it Friday night," she told the group now. "I didn't. So there you go."

"You should've told him," Carol said, voice still disapproving. Carol was very good at disapproving. "Maybe he could've done something."

Jillian rolled her eyes. "It was after eight by the time I opened the envelope. Detective Fitzpatrick was already gone for the day. And . . . and it seemed juvenile at the time. A last-minute scare tactic by Eddie with the trial about to start on Monday. Besides, he's sent this thing out, he's probably already waiting for the police to come or the prison guards to come, or someone to come and give him a bad time. Then he could sit back and amuse himself with how much he rattled my cage. But if I say nothing . . . Then he spends all weekend waiting. Wondering. Not knowing. I liked that."

"Punishing him with silence," Meg said softly. "It's not half bad."

Jillian shrugged modestly. "But it doesn't matter anymore, does it? Whatever Eddie has done, whatever he's threatened to do . . . It doesn't matter anymore. He's dead."

A strange silence descended over the group. For the first time, alone with confirmation that Eddie Como had indeed been fatally shot, the words began to penetrate, grow real, become the new state of the universe. They looked at each other. No one knew what to say. No more Eddie Como. It defied the imagination. For the last year he had been the center of their world. Everything they hated, despised, feared. Weekly they met simply to talk about how mad he had made them, or how determined, how confused, how heartbroken, defenseless, shattered. Was there a thought that went through any of their heads that did not connect back to Eddie Como? A resolution that did not start with him? A good day, a bad day, a good episode, a bad episode that wasn't directly attributed to him? Meg could not remember her life. Carol couldn't turn off her TV. Jillian couldn't relax, and one way or another it all had to do with Eddie Como. Except now he was gone and the world kept turning and the other patrons kept eating and . . .

"I don't think we can talk about it," Jillian said shortly.

"We need to talk about it," Meg said quietly.

"We have to talk about it!" Carol seconded more vehemently. "We'd better talk about it! I for one—"

"We can't," Jillian interrupted forcefully. "We're suspects. If we talk about the shooting, or the fact that he's dead, later someone—hell, maybe Ned D'Amato—could construe that as conspiracy."

"Oh for the love of God!" Carol cried. "The College Hill Rapist is dead and you're still making up rules and setting agendas. Give it a rest, Jillian! We have spent the last twelve months gearing up for a trial that will suddenly never happen. Oh my God, I don't know where to begin."

"We can't—"

"Let's vote." Carol was emphatic. "All in favor of dancing around Eddie Como's grave, raise their hands."

Carol raised her hand. After a second, Meg's hand also went into the air. She gazed at Jillian apologetically. "When the news report came on, I was so sure they were wrong," she said quietly. "How could someone as evil as Eddie actually die? Did the shooter use a silver bullet? But then the cops came, so I guess this is all really happening, and well . . . I think I'm a little confused. He's dead, but in my mind, he can't be dead. Everything's different, but everything's the same. It's . . . surreal."

Jillian frowned. She still smarted from Carol's agenda comment. But then . . .

Her skin felt funny, too tight for her bones. The air felt strange, too cool upon her cheeks. Meg was right. Everything was different, yet everything was the same, and had there been a night in the last twelve months when Jillian had not gone to bed wishing for Eddie Como's death, praying for Eddie Como's death, *willing* Eddie Como's death with every fiber of her being?

She had won. The Survivors Club had won. And then she finally understood what was wrong. Eddie Como was dead. But she didn't feel victorious.

"Perhaps . . . perhaps we can talk about how we feel," Jillian said slowly. "But no getting into specifics of the shooting. Agreed?"

Meg nodded. More reluctantly, Carol followed suit.

"Well, I for one am happy!" Carol stated immediately. "I'm bursting! Hell, yes. This is a great day in America. The bastard finally got what he deserved! You know what we need? We need champagne. We need to celebrate this properly, that will put it in perspective. Where is that waitress? We're going to get ourselves some champagne, and why not, that piece of chocolate cake."

The waitress magically materialized. Carol ordered a bottle of Dom Pérignon, then the entire chocolate cake.

"Don't worry, we'll pay for it," she told the waitress. "We're not trying to abuse anyone's generosity, we just need a good toast. Do you have any strawberries, honey? Put a strawberry in each glass. That'll be perfect. And then the cake. Don't forget the cake. My God, that looks luscious."

Carol was waving her hands about enthusiastically. Her blue eyes were overbright again, her expression at once glowing and brittle. Meg and Jillian exchanged looks across the table.

"Now then," Carol said in her overloud voice. "Bubbly is on the way. In the meantime, let's tick off all the ways our lives will be better. I'll start. One, we no longer have to worry about testifying at trial. No horrible recaps, no vicious cross-examination, no showing crime-scene photos of our own bodies to complete strangers. Survey says, no trial is a good trial. Thank you, Dead Eddie. Oh look, here's the champagne."

The waitress was back. She had the Dom Pérignon and yes, glasses with fresh strawberries. She popped the cork, poured the three glasses and began dishing out the cake.

Jillian accepted her glass, already picturing the headline. *Eddie Como Is Shot, The Women Eat Cake.* But then, in the next instant, Carol's mood infected her as well. What the hell were they supposed to do? Cry in their coffee? Wring their hands? Maybe this wasn't sane and maybe it wasn't socially acceptable, but they'd had lots of moments less sane than this one. And they had endured plenty of things that should not be socially acceptable.

Trisha tied up, stripped naked, then viciously assaulted as her throat swelled shut, as her lungs gasped for air. Trisha struggling furiously. Trisha trying to scream. Trisha, dying, with her last conscious moments being a strange man looming over her body . . .

"Okay," Jillian said. She held up her champagne flute. "My turn. Here's to no more phone calls in the middle of the day, no more notes in the mail, no more twisted video displays. Thank you, Dead Eddie."

"Here's to no halting our lives every ten years for parole hearings," Meg said. "No worrying that if we don't halt our lives and relive our rapes for some parole board, he will end up back on the streets. Thank you, Dead Eddie."

"No more fear that somehow he'll get out and attack someone else," Carol continued.

"No more fear that somehow he'll get out and attack one of *us*," Jillian amended.

"No more fear!" Meg said.

They drank. The champagne tasted startlingly good. Brought color to their cheeks. What the hell. Jillian poured another round while Carol dug into her cake.

"Good thing the cops left," Meg said somewhere around the third glass. She had barely eaten a bite for breakfast, and the champagne was going straight to her head.

"Oh they'll be back," Carol said. She'd stopped drinking champagne after the first glass and instead gone after the cake. Her lips were chocolate stained. She had a smear of frosting on her cheek, two more smudges on her hands.

"The new one is cute," Meg declared. "Those deep blue eyes. And that chest! Did you see his chest? Now there is a man who looks like he knows how to serve and protect."

"You said that about Fitz, and Fitz is not cute. You just like uniforms." Carol finished off her piece of cake, and immediately dished up another.

"I thought he looked familiar," Jillian mused.

"In this state, everyone looks familiar," Carol said.

"Not to me!" Meg cried gaily and held out her empty glass for more champagne.

"Maybe you should slow down a little," Jillian cautioned her.

"Sensible Jillian. Always in control. You know what this group needs? We need a party. With a male stripper!"

"I don't think a rape survivors group should hire a stripper."

"Why not? Man as an object. It might do us some good. Come on, Jillian, you've had us read all the traditional books and discuss the traditional methods. Why not go off the beaten path for a bit? It's been a year. Let's go wild!"

Meg looked at Carol for support. This was the problem with a three-member support group, Jillian had realized in the beginning. Two people could always gang up against one. In the beginning, it had been Jillian and Carol determining things for Meg. But lately . . .

Now, however, Carol merely shrugged. Apparently, she was more interested in chocolate cake than some male beefcake. Of course, Carol had little use for men these days. Not that any of them were doing great, but Carol, in particular, loathed any thought of sex.

"I'm serious about Sergeant Griffin," Jillian said, trying to regain focus. "I know him from somewhere. I'd swear I could picture his face on TV. Maybe I'll look him up."

"No wedding ring." Meg waggled a brow.

"For heaven's sake, Meg. He's an investigating officer, not a contestant on *The Dating Game*."

"Why not? You're very pretty, Jillian. And you can't punish yourself forever."

That ground the conversation to a halt. Even Carol paused with her fork suspended in midair.

"I don't think we should talk about this now," Jillian said quietly.

"I'm just saying—"

"And I don't want to talk about it now. It's been a big morning. Let's just drink our champagne and let it go at that."

Carol resumed eating her chocolate cake. Meg, however, had gotten a far-away look in her eye. She was definitely drunk. Of course, even sober, she generally said more than Jillian or Carol dared. They were older, more wedded to their privacy and carefully erected walls. Not Meg. Never Meg.

Now she said suddenly, "I'm angry. Eddie Como's dead, but I'm still angry. Why is that?"

Jillian picked up her empty champagne flute, twirled it between her fingers. "It's too new," she said softly. "You're going to need time to absorb, we're all going to need time to absorb, that he's truly gone."

Meg shook her head. "No. I don't think that's it. I think that maybe it doesn't matter. No, I'm *afraid* that it doesn't matter. Eddie Como is dead. *And so what?* Are you going to magically move on with your life, Jillian? Will I magically remember my past? Will Carol finally turn off her TV? I don't think so." Her voice picked up a notch. "Oh my God, it's the thing we've wanted most, *and nothing's different!*"

"Meg . . ."

Jillian tried reaching out a hand. Meg, however, pulled away, hitting the nearly empty champagne bottle, knocking it over. Jillian grabbed the bottle. Carol grabbed a napkin. Meg kept talking.

"Think about it. We hated him. All of us. Even me. And he gave our anger a focus. Why did you form this group, Jillian? To catch Eddie Como. And why did we stay together? To fight Eddie Como. Everything, for the last twelve months, has been about him. And it's *easier* that way. When we wake up mad or disoriented or afraid, we know why: Eddie Como. When the police are invading our privacy by asking more questions, or our friends or family are looking at us funny, we know why: Eddie Como. But . . . but now . . ."

Her voice trailed off. Jillian and Carol didn't say anything. Couldn't say anything.

"I'm so angry," Meg whispered. "I don't know who I am. I still have to take AIDS tests and sometimes late at night . . . I just lie there wondering. This man knows more about my body than I do. He did things, he invaded places. He took me away from me. And even if he's dead, I'm still *mad* about that."

"I doubt I'll sleep tonight," Carol said abruptly. "Meg's right. It's not really him. I mean, yes, I'm afraid of Eddie. But I'm also afraid of . . . everything. I'm afraid of the dark, I'm afraid of the quiet, I'm afraid of my house, I'm afraid of my bedroom window. I'm afraid of my husband, you know. We never talk about it, but he knows sometimes I wake up in the middle of the night, look at him and see only Eddie. I like the couch. Bedrooms aren't safe anymore. It's best to sleep on the sofa. Even, even now. It's better to be on the sofa."

They both looked at Jillian. Her turn. That's the way the group worked. One shared, they all shared.

"At least we have some sense of closure now," she tried.

Carol nodded immediately. "Closure. That's good."

Meg, however, shook her head. "You're avoiding again."

"I'm not avoiding," Jillian protested, as she always protested. "I don't have an answer yet."

Carol and Meg simply looked at her. Waited. Lately, they had grown tough.

"My loss is different," Jillian said finally. "My sister is dead. No matter what happened to Eddie . . . nothing is going to bring Trisha back. I've always known that."

"It's easier for you." A trace of bitterness crept into Carol's voice. "You fended him off. You won."

"I didn't win."

"You did."

"I got *lucky,* all right? You think I don't know that? I got lucky!"

"Well, I'm not picky, I would've taken luck!"

"And I would've preferred my sister's life!" Jillian's voice had risen sharply, catching other patrons' attention once more. She caught herself, pressing her lips into a thin line in an effort at control, although her breathing was harsh now, her face red, her nerves shockingly raw. She sat back. She picked

up her flute of champagne. Set it down. Picked it up again.

"That was good," Meg said, nodding. "Honest. I think you're making real progress."

Jillian just barely repressed the urge to throttle the girl. Meg's intentions were good, of course. She should appreciate that. But Jillian was *not* an amnesic twenty-year-old. She was thirty-six, she had responsibilities and she remembered everything. Absolutely everything. Goddammit . . .

She picked up the flute, set it back down, picked it back up and fought the desire to send it smashing to the floor. One year later . . . Oh God, look at them.

Carol finally broke the silence. "It's still better, right? Life has been unbearable with Eddie Como alive. Surely it must be better with him dead."

"Closure," Jillian said crisply.

"Closure," Meg repeated.

"Closure," Carol echoed.

"Life will get better," Jillian insisted.

Meg finally smiled. "Think of it this way. It can't get any worse."

12

Tawnya

"Well, they certainly have their act together."

"Jillian, Carol and Meg?" Fitz was once more navigating his battered Ford Taurus through narrow city streets. He glanced over at Griffin from behind the steering wheel. "Don't let them fool you. It's been a rough year. I've seen them all break down a time or two."

"Even Jillian Hayes?"

"Well"—Fitz had to think about it—"maybe not Jillian."

"The sister was quite a bit younger than her. Fifteen, sixteen years? Seems like they might have had less of a sibling relationship and more of a parent-child."

"Possibly. The mother, Olivia, isn't well. Had a stroke several years back and has been wheelchair-bound ever since. Jillian takes care of her with the help of a live-in aide."

"So Jillian's been the head of the family?"

Fitz shrugged. "She's thirty-six, you know. It's not that tragic."

"No. I'm just thinking . . . It's hard enough to lose a sibling. But thanks to Eddie, Jillian lost both her sister and her surrogate child. That's gotta be hard." Griffin thought about Cindy. "That's gotta make you mad," he added gruffly. "Truly, royally pissed off."

Fitz was looking at him strangely. "Guess I hadn't thought about that."

"She was dressed nicely," Griffin said, more neutrally. "What does she do?"

"She owns a small marketing firm. It's fairly successful, but she also has some other assets. You follow blues music at all? Her mom, Olivia Hayes, was a fairly well known singer in her day. She banked hundreds of thousands, and Jillian has turned it into millions."

Griffin's eyes widened. "That would certainly buy an assassin or two."

"It would."

"She's cool enough." Griffin's tone was goading. He knew Fitz hated this topic.

Fitz didn't say anything.

"In her own words, she's grateful," Griffin pressed.

Fitz flexed his hands on the steering wheel, remained quiet.

"She's also got the most powerful motive, and apparently she's been studying her best defense."

"She doesn't outsource," Fitz said abruptly. "All right? I've spent a year with the woman. Hell, she didn't even trust *us* to catch her sister's killer without her. Ask D'Amato how many phone calls he received from her each day. Ask my lieutenant how often she personally stopped by. Why do you think she formed the Survivors Club? Why do you think she spent so much time in front of the press? What Jillian wants, Jillian goes out and gets."

"Why, Fitz, it almost sounds like you like her."

Fitz growled behind the steering wheel. "Don't make me kill you, Griffin."

Griffin had to smile at that. Even if Fitz managed to land a blow, he'd probably just break his hand. "So personally, you're not betting on Jillian Hayes?"

"If Jillian really wanted Eddie Como dead, she would've pulled the trigger herself."

"Even if she wasn't proficient in firearms?"

"She'd hire a teacher and learn. First day she came into my office, she was carrying a crime-scene textbook, and Robert Ressler's book on sex offenders. After we learned of the DNA match on Eddie Como, she asked our BCI sergeant for a recommended reading list on DNA testing. I'm pretty sure she now knows more than most of our crime-scene techs. The woman can be annoying, but she's never dumb."

"So who do you like for the shooting?"

Fitz thinned his lips. He definitely didn't want to have this conversation. Griffin understood. After the last year, suspecting one of the women was, for Fitz, like suspecting a fellow cop.

"Uncle Vinnie," Fitz said grudgingly.

"An enraged uncle with Mafia ties. I can see that. Though personally, I'm still interested in Meg. That amnesia thing. Something about that bugs me."

"A girl can't forget?"

"Her entire life?"

"Rape is a powerful trauma."

"Yeah, but it also happened a year ago, and trauma-induced amnesia is supposed to get better with time."

"Whose idea of time? I know vets still suffering from post-traumatic stress syndrome and it's been thirty years since the Vietnam War. You need as long as you need, simple as that." Fitz was looking at him sideways again. Griffin wasn't an idiot.

"Personally," he said lightly, "I don't think anyone should need more than eighteen months."

Fitz rolled his eyes, but apparently decided not to pursue the subject. "Dan Rosen," he said abruptly.

"Carol's husband?"

"Yeah. I've interviewed the guy half a dozen times and I don't know . . . There's something about him I don't like. He thinks too much before he speaks. You can practically see the wheels turning in his head as he picks each word, weighs each syllable. For God's sake, I know the man's a lawyer, but his wife was raped in their bedroom. It's bad enough he didn't come home to help her. The least he could do now is stop mincing words."

"They have money?"

"Nah, they got a house that bleeds them dry. At least that's how it looked a year ago when we pulled financials. Back then the practice was pretty new and the house freshly renovated. In other words, they had plenty of assets and not a dime to spare. Maybe his practice is doing better by now, maybe not."

"And assets can always be turned to cash," Griffin pointed out.

"True."

"What about Jillian Hayes's family?"

"What family?" Fitz shrugged. "She's got an ailing mother and a live-in adult-care aide. That's it."

"That's it? No father?"

"Nope. I get the impression that her mom only rented men, never bought."

"She and Trisha were half sisters then?"

"Yep."

"And what about the men in Jillian's life? Was she seeing anyone seriously at the time of the attack?"

"Not that she mentioned."

"And now?"

Fitz slid him another look. "Getting awfully personal, aren't you, Griff?"

"Just making conversation." Griffin drummed his fingertips on the dash. "Hey, Fitz, where are we going?"

"As long as I have backup, we're paying a visit to Eddie's mom."

Ten minutes later Fitz and Griffin arrived at the Como residence. This time, they hadn't beaten the press. Two oversized news vans were already clogging the tiny street of the rundown residential neighborhood. A bank of microphones dominated the postage-stamp-sized yard. Fitz and Griffin didn't see any members of Eddie Como's family outside yet, but that didn't mean anything. Either they'd just finished giving a statement or they were about to speak to the press. Either way, it didn't bode well for Griffin or Fitz.

"Eddie's mother hates me," Fitz announced, parking his Taurus up on the crumbling curb. "Eddie's father died when he was a kid, or he would probably hate me, too. Now, however, it's just his mom, his girlfriend and his baby. Oh, and the girlfriend, Tawnya, she bites."

Griffin, who was about to pop open the car door, stopped and stared at Fitz.

"Bites?"

"Yeah. And sometimes she scratches, too. She's got these nails. They're about three inches long. She likes to paint them with little palm trees and flamingos. Then she sharpens them into points, so that you're thinking about Key West right before she goes for your eyes."

"Is there a back door?"

"A kitchen door."

"Good, because we absolutely, positively, can't have that kind of reunion scene in front of the press."

Fitz looked down the street at the news vans. "Good point. No wonder they pay you state boys the big bucks."

Griffin opened his door. "We also get better cars."

He and Fitz had no sooner headed down the quiet street than the doors of the news vans slid back and two reporters, armed with cameramen, poured out. Griffin and Fitz said no comment a dozen times each before they finally reached shelter behind the tiny white house. There they paused, exchanged grimaces, then knocked on the back door. After a moment, a faded yellow curtain covering the window on the top half was drawn back. They found themselves face-to-face with a small Hispanic woman who regarded them somberly with deep black eyes.

"Mrs. Como." Fitz gave a little wave, a nervous smile. "I'm sorry, ma'am, but I'm afraid we need to speak with you."

Mrs. Como made no move to open the door. "I know what happened," she said from behind the glass. "Tawnya, she was there. At the courthouse. She told me."

"We are very sorry for your loss," Fitz said.

Mrs. Como snorted.

"We're here now to investigate what happened to Eddie," Fitz continued bravely. "I know we've had our differences in the past, but . . . I'm here about your son, Mrs. Como. Surely you could give us just a moment of your time—"

"My Eddie is dead. Go away, Mr. Detective. You have hurt my family and I don't have to talk to you anymore."

Right about then, a strikingly beautiful girl rounded the back corner of the house. Griffin had one moment to think, *Whoa—she looks just like Meg Pesaturo,* before the young lady was hurling herself at Fitz with neon pink nails unsheathed and white teeth flashing.

"Hijo de puta!" Tawnya cried.

"Ahhhhhh!" Fitz said.

He threw his arm up to defend his face just as Griffin snaked out one hand and caught the girl around the waist. He hefted her into air, where she kicked out her legs and beat at his forearm with her puny fists.

"What do you weigh, about ninety-five pounds?" Griffin asked conversationally.

"Son of a bitch! Miserable shit-eating pig—"

"I got a good hundred and ten pounds on you," Griffin continued. "That means I can pretty much hold you like this all day. So if you want to get down anytime soon, maybe you should take a deep breath. Cool the language. We're just here to talk."

Tawnya whacked his arm again. Then she lashed out with her leg. When he still didn't flinch, she finally eased her struggling, though her dark eyes remained locked on Fitz, who was now huddled against the house with his hand cupped protectively around his cheek. Mrs. Como stood behind the closed door, watching it all with an impassive face.

"Ready to play nice?" Griffin asked when a full minute elapsed without Tawnya trying to kill anyone.

She nodded grudgingly.

He released his hold.

She bolted for Fitz, who managed to grab one of her attacking arms this time, twist it behind her back and slap on a pair of handcuffs.

"That's it!" Fitz exclaimed, breathing heavily. "You're in bracelets until I leave. Just be happy that I don't charge you with assaulting a police officer."

"It's not a crime to kill a swine," Tawnya spat at him.

"Jesus, girl, the father of your child just died. Haven't you had enough violence for one day?"

The bruising words did the trick. Tawnya's shoulders sagged. Her chin came down. For just one moment, it looked to Griffin like Eddie's little spitfire was going to cry. She didn't, though. She pulled it together, then nodded at Mrs. Como, who finally opened the door.

Inside, the house was pretty much as Griffin had expected. Cramped kitchen with a ripped-up vinyl floor and stacked-up flats of baby food. A living room with threadbare gold carpet and a sagging brown sofa. The most expensive item in the room was easily the powder-blue playpen, positioned in front of the window. Tawnya headed for it immediately, then turned and glared at Fitz when she realized she couldn't pick up her son. She rattled the handcuffs.

"Hey, next time think before you scratch," Fitz called back from the kitchen.

Griffin, who had a soft spot for babies—he really loved their smell—crossed over to inspect the playpen himself. Tawnya's son—and Eddie's too, he presumed—was sleeping soundly on his stomach, his diapered butt stuck up in the air as little bubbles blew contentedly out of his mouth.

"Name?" he asked Tawnya.

"Eddie, Jr.," she said grudgingly.

"How old?"

"Nine months."

"He's a cutie. Sergeant Griffin, by the way. State police." Griffin flashed a smile.

"Have you arrested those bitches for killing my Eddie?"

Griffin took bitches to mean Meg Pesaturo, Carol Rosen and Jillian Hayes. "No."

"Then fuck you." Tawnya turned and stormed down the hall. So much for playing good cop. Griffin returned to the kitchen, where Mrs. Como was banging around pans, probably to have something to do. Now sitting at the worn kitchen table and obviously not sure how to proceed, Fitz was chewing on his lower lip.

"Hey, state boy." Tawnya again, yelling from the other end of the house. "Come here. There's something I want to show you."

"Watch the nails," Fitz muttered. "And the teeth."

Griffin walked warily down the narrow hallway. But it seemed that Tawnya no longer had death and destruction on her mind. Instead, she was gesturing awkwardly with her cuffed hands at a brown-and-gold photo album sticking out from a sagging bookshelf.

"Get that. There's something I want you to see."

Griffin inspected the rickety bookshelf. Seeing no sign of booby traps, he gingerly removed the album. When Tawnya still didn't bite him, he followed her back to the kitchen, where she informed him where to place the album, how to open the album and what photos to look at. Griffin was beginning to wonder if Eddie hadn't gone to prison in order to escape.

"Look!" Tawnya told him when he'd finally turned to the desired page. "See that. That's Eddie and me. Look at that face. That the face of a rapist?"

"They don't come with stamps on their forehead," Griffin said mildly, though he got her point. Eddie was a good-looking guy. Small, but trim, neatly dressed in tan khakis and a dark-blue shirt. Clean-cut features, tidy black hair. If you passed him on the street, you wouldn't think twice.

"Now look at me," Tawnya ordered, jerking her chin toward the photo, where she posed in a skimpy black dress, draped luxuriously over Eddie's arm. "I'm hot. Plain and simple. Been beating away the boys since I was twelve. And I *know* how to make my man happy. A guy has a girl like me, you can be sure he comes home for his meals."

"How much cooking were you doing six months pregnant?" Fitz spoke up.

Tawnya shot him a look of pure venom. "I made Eddie happy. I made Eddie *fucking* delirious." She glanced at the stove. "No offense, Mrs. C."

Mrs. Como didn't say anything. Her expression had scarcely changed the entire time they'd been here. No grief, no rage, no denial, no fear. Now she stirred something in a giant metal pot. It smelled to Griffin like bleach. Then he got it. She was preparing to wash diapers by boiling them on the stove. He looked around the kitchen, the cramped quarters filled with baby food, baby clothes, baby toys. And he got the rest of it. For Mrs. Como, Eddie had already been gone for nearly a year. Now her life was about her grandson.

Two Como males gone, one left to go. Did she wonder about that late at night? Did she cry when no one was looking? Or was it simply a fact of life for a woman like her, in a place like this? Seemed like too much of Griffin's job was spent dealing with these kinds of scenes. He felt suddenly, unexpectedly, sad, and that bothered him even more. You needed walls for this kind of business. You needed to compartmentalize if you were going to be a cop and maintain your peace of mind.

He should go for a run soon. Find a punching bag. Beat at the heavy leather until all the tension was drained from him and he had no emotions left. Then he could pretend that sad old ladies didn't twist his conscience and that two years later he didn't desperately miss his wife.

"You were with Eddie the nights the women were attacked?" Griffin asked Tawnya.

"Yeah. I was. Not that Detective Dickwad believed me." She gave Fitz another dark look. Fitz smiled sweetly. "We had an apartment then," Tawnya went on. "A decent place, over in Warwick. Eddie, he made good money with the Blood Center. That's not easy, you know. He had to get special training, take some courses. Eddie was smart. He had plans. And he really liked what he did. Helping people and all that. We were doing all right."

"No one saw you two together those nights."

"*Mierde!* You sound just like him." Chin angled toward Fitz. "Come on, Eddie had a tough job. He was on his feet six, eight hours a shift. He got home, he was tired. He wanted to relax. You know what Eddie liked to do best? He liked to stretch out on the sofa, watch a rented movie and place his hand on my belly so he could feel his baby kick. Yeah, that's your College Hill Rapist. Hanging out with his pregnant girlfriend and telling stories to his baby. And now . . . now. Ah, fuck you all."

Tawnya turned away. In front of the stove, Mrs. Como picked up a pile of cloth diapers and threw them into the pot. Round and round she went with a big metal spoon. The kitchen filled with the smell of bleach and baby powder and urine.

"You know he called the women," Griffin said quietly.

Tawnya whirled back around. "Of course he called them! They fucking ruined his life. Railroaded the police into his arrest. Worked the public into a frenzy talking on the news about this horrible, horrible rapist, gonna kill your daughter next. You know we got death threats, thanks to those women? Even Mrs. C. here, and what'd she do? One day, some guy called a radio station saying that if there was any justice in this world, Eddie, Jr.'s, little penis would fall off before he could turn into his father. Jesus Christ! Someone should lock that man up, threatening a baby like that. I couldn't bring Eddie, Jr., to the courthouse 'cause I was too afraid of what people might do. What the fuck is up with that?"

"You don't think Eddie did it."

"I *know* Eddie didn't do it. He was just a poor dumb spic working in the wrong place at the wrong time. That's the way the world works. White girls get hurt, some yellow or black man loses his ass."

"The state found Eddie's DNA at the crime scenes."

"Bah! Cops fake DNA all the time. Everyone knows that."

"Cops fake DNA?" Griffin glanced over at Fitz as if to ask if such a thing could be true. Fitz shrugged.

"Cops don't handle the DNA," Fitz said. "And in this case, we had two different nurses and one medical examiner handing evidence over to three different couriers to be sent to the Department of Health. That's a lot of people for conspiracy, but hey, I'm just the poor dumb cop who gets accused of corruption anytime I do my job. You know—that's the way the world works." He looked at Tawnya, his voice dripping sarcasm.

"Why would the cops tamper with evidence?" Griffin asked Tawnya more reasonably.

"The pressure, of course! Come on—three white women, attacked in their homes. One in a big fancy house on the East Side. Cops can't ignore that kind of thing. Then one dies and the whole state goes apeshit. Cops gotta arrest someone then. Next thing you know, cops are looking at blood drives and there you go. Young Hispanic male. Can't even afford an attorney. Eddie was guilty before they ever asked him a question. Cops got their arrest, mayor got his headline, and hey, who gives a fuck about the rest of us?"

"Eddie was victimized by the state?"

"Damn right."

"Because he was a minority?"

"Damn right."

"So if the state already had him on the rapes, who do you think shot him this morning?"

Tawnya finally drew up short. She inhaled deeply, held the breath in her lungs, then blew it out all at once. "Everybody thinks Eddie's a rapist. Everybody wants a rapist dead."

"The threats on the radio station?"

"Yeah. And in the newspaper. And in prison." She added hotly, "Tell me the truth, you really gonna do something about this?"

Griffin thought of the bank of microphones outside. He said honestly, "As of this morning, we had every state detective working this case."

Tawnya narrowed her eyes. She wasn't dumb. "It's 'cause he was shot at the courthouse, isn't it? If they'd got him in prison, you wouldn't even be here right now. But they shot him in public. In front of cameras. That makes you guys look bad."

"Murder is murder. We're on the case. I'm on the case."

Tawnya snorted again, unimpressed. She did know how the world worked.

"Do you have any specific names?" Griffin asked. "People you know of who threatened Eddie? People you heard say they wanted him dead?"

"Nah. Check the papers. Talk to the prison guards. They should know. If they can be bothered to tell you."

"Anyone else we should consider?"

"The fucking women, of course."

"The three victims?"

"Victims, my ass. Those bitches are the ones who picked Eddie. They pushed for his arrest, harassed the cops all the time. Maybe they wanted to make sure it was done all the way. Eddie can't defend himself now. And hey, they don't have to worry about anything unpleasant coming out at trial."

"Was something unpleasant going to come out at trial?" Griffin asked sharply.

"You never know."

"Tawnya," Fitz began warningly. He leaned forward, elbows on his knees, but Tawnya shook her mass of dark hair.

"I'm not doing your job for you, Dickwad. You wanna know what was gonna happen, you figure out what was gonna happen. Now come on. I gotta feed my kid." She turned around, gesturing at the handcuffs with her fingers. When Fitz still hesitated, she shot out, "I'll call the ACLU!"

Fitz grudgingly undid the bracelets, though Griffin noticed the Providence detective now leaned farther away, mindful of his face. Tawnya flashed her teeth at him, then smiled when he flinched.

"I don't care what you guys think," Tawnya said right before she left the room. "I was with Eddie those nights. I *know* he didn't hurt those women. And you wanna hear something else? You guys are screwed. 'Cause that dude's still out there. And now Eddie's gone. No one to blame anymore. No one to hide behind. It's a full moon tonight. Perfect weather for when the College Hill Rapist rides again."

Fitz and Griffin didn't speak until they were back on the street, climbing into Fitz's beat-up detective's car.

"Is it just me," Griffin said, "or is Tawnya the spitting image of Meg Pesaturo?"

"Wait 'til you see a photo of Trisha Hayes. Oh yeah, Eddie definitely had a type."

"She would've made a good witness for the defense," Griffin commented.

"Yes and no. Eddie's phone calls to the women . . . One way it could've been done was if someone on his approved calling list, say his girlfriend, had a phone feature, say call forwarding, and, ignoring the recorded warning which specifically says do not forward this call, did it anyway."

"Ah, so pretty little Tawnya takes her girlfriend duties seriously."

"ACI has tapes of the calls if you want to listen."

"Anything good?"

"Only if you buy into conspiracy theories. Eddie seemed convinced that the women were out to get him. Of course, the inmates know their calls are taped, so it might have merely been window dressing for the trial."

"That was going to be his defense? That three strange women were picking on poor little innocent him?"

"The perpetrator as victim. It's a classic."

"And unfortunately, it seems there's always someone in the jury box who buys it."

"Damn juries," Fitz muttered.

"Yeah, whatever happened to good old-fashioned mob justice? String 'em up, cut 'em down. Saves a ton of money on appeal."

Fitz eyed Griffin suspiciously, probably trying to figure out if he was toying with him or not. Griffin kind of was, kind of wasn't. The jury system was a royal pain in the ass.

Fitz glanced at his watch. "It's three o'clock now. Somehow, I don't think we're going to have this wrapped up in time for the five o'clock news."

"Doesn't look it."

"In fact, given that nobody seems to want to magically confess, I'm guessing this might take a bit."

"It might."

"That gonna be a problem?" Fitz's gaze went to Griffin's overpumped chest and hard-lined face. Griffin understood what he was asking.

"Not for me," he said.

"I was just wondering—"

"I'm back. When you're back on the job, you're back on the job. You can't do policing halfway."

"I never thought so." Fitz's eyes were still narrowed, appraising. "Look, I'm just going to lay it on the table. If we're going to work together on this, I think I have the right to know a few things."

"Such as?"

"I heard about that Candy Man case, that it went on a little too long, then got a little too personal. Did you really beat up two detectives in the kid's house? Nearly put one of them in the hospital?"

Griffin was silent for a moment. "That's what I'm told," he said at last.

"You don't remember?"

"It's a bit of a blur. I wasn't aiming for Detective Waters or O'Reilly anyway. They were simply doing the honorable thing and throwing themselves in the way."

"You were going after Price."

"Something like that."

"And if you'd gotten to him?"

"We'll never know, will we?"

Fitz grunted at that. "You on Prozac?"

"I don't take any meds."

"Why not?"

Griffin smiled. "Not that kind of crazy."

"Just wear my hockey mask?"

Griffin's smile grew. "You could try, Detective, but I don't make any promises."

"Hey now—"

"Look," Griffin said, his tone serious because they weren't going to get this wrapped up by five so they might as well clear the air. "I'm not going to attack you. Two years ago, when my wife died . . . I let too many things go. Personally. Professionally. Life, this job . . . You gotta take care of things. We all learn, one way or the other. Last year was my lesson. I got it. I'm on top of things now."

Fitz remained silent, so maybe he had his own opinions on that subject.

"I'm sorry about your wife," Fitz said at last.

"I'm sorry, too."

"I know a lot of the guys who went to the service. She sounded like a really neat lady."

"She was the best," Griffin said honestly, and then, because two years wasn't nearly long enough, he had to look away. He fidgeted with the door handle. Fitz put the car in gear. They both cleared their throats.

"So what are you going to do now?" Fitz asked as he pulled away from the curb. "About the case."

"Return to headquarters and set up command central. Then, I'll probably go for a run."

"I'll follow up with the crispy corpse. With any luck, we got enough skin to print."

"Hey, Detective, as long as you're returning home, get me a copy of the College Hill Rapist file."

Fitz stopped immediately, his foot hitting the brake and stalling the car in the middle of the street. Griffin kind of thought that might happen.

"Come on!" Fitz exclaimed. "Don't let Tawnya get to you. The College Hill case was a good investigation. We had MO, we had opportunity, we had DNA. Took us six months to put it all together, and I'm telling you now, we did just fine. Eddie Como raped those women. End of story."

"Didn't say he didn't."

"I don't need the state reviewing my work! That's bullshit."

"Life sucks and then you die."

Fitz scowled at him.

Griffin returned the look calmly. "I want the file. The shooting is connected to the case, ergo, I need to learn the case."

"I told you about the case."

"You told me your opinions."

"I'm the lead investigator! I built the goddamn theory of the case, I am the opinion!"

"Then explain this to me: You found Eddie once you started looking at blood drives. And you started looking at blood drives because of the latex strips."

"Yeah, absolutely."

"So why did Eddie, who left behind no hair, no fiber, and no fingerprints, leave behind ten latex strips? Why did he on the one hand learn how to cover his tracks, and then on the other hand leave you a virtual calling card?"

"Because criminals are stupid. It's what I like best about them."

"It's inconsistent."

"Oh Jesus H. Christ. We didn't plant DNA evidence! We did *not* frame Eddie Como!"

"Yeah," Griffin said. "And frankly, Detective, that's what worries me."

13

Griffin

In spite of his words, Griffin didn't head immediately back to police head-quarters in North Scituate. Instead, operating on a hunch, he returned to the rue de l'espoir restaurant in downtown Providence. It was 3:30. The three women definitely had had plenty of time to finish their mugs of chai and head out.

Except then he started thinking. Where would they go? They were obvi-ously well experienced in the ways of the media. Surely they realized that as of 9:00 that morning, news teams had descended upon their front lawns, climbed up their front steps, started banging on their front doors. Let alone the number of white news vans trolling the streets, looking for leads, any leads, to give that station the advantage in the evening news race.

If it were him, he decided, he'd simply stay right where he was. With his fellow club members. That way if some earnest reporter did track them down, they'd at least all be together. Safety in numbers. According to Maureen, the Survivors Club had rules about that.

So Griffin returned to Hope Street. And then, operating on another hunch, he checked the license plates in the tiny parking lot. He found Jillian's car in less than a minute. Gold Lexus with license plate TH 18.

"Damn," he murmured, and for a moment, he simply stood there, feeling a rush of sadness that struck too close to home.

Rhode Islanders had a thing about license plates. He didn't know how it had started. Maybe the original colonists had had a thing about horse brands. But Rhode Island was a small state, so its plates had literally started with one letter, plus a one- or two-digit number. Then the state had gone to two letters with a two-digit number. Now, the state did a straight five num-bers, but only cultural outsiders settled for those. A true Rhode Islander, wanting to show off his long-standing ties to his state, personally went to the plate room of the DMV and requested the lowest letter/number combina-tion possible, or, since highly prestigious plates such as A 20 or J 28 were mostly doled out to well-connected insiders, he requested his initials with a low two-digit number. Then he held on to those plates for life. Literally.

TH 18. Trisha Hayes, probably eighteenth birthday. Someone, Jillian most likely, had gone to a lot of trouble to get her little sister the special plates. Had Trisha been excited at the time? Had the plates gone with a new car, just what Trisha had always wanted? Maybe she'd thrown her arms around her sister's neck. Maybe she'd kissed her mother on the cheek. Eighteen-year-old Trisha Hayes, celebrating a new car. Eighteen-year-old Trisha Hayes, about to embark on a whole, brand-new college life.

Griffin doubted that cool, composed Jillian Hayes would ever say much about that day. She'd probably sold the car by now, at the same time she was sorting through her sister's clothes, closing up her sister's apartment, sifting through her sister's things. He could picture exactly what she'd had to do, because not that long ago, he'd done the same. The bureaucracy of death had surprised him. Nearly broken his heart all over again. But you did what you had to do. Get it done, people always advised. Then you can get on with your life.

Driving a car, he supposed, bearing your dead sister's license plates.

"What are you doing?"

Griffin whirled around. Jillian Hayes stood four feet from him, her car keys clutched in her fist and her hazel eyes already starting to blaze. Quick, say something clever, he thought.

He said, "Huh?"

"What the hell do you think you are doing?" She enunciated each word clearly, like steel nails she was hammering into a coffin. He wondered if he should clutch his chest theatrically.

"Would you believe I was in the neighborhood?"

"No."

"Well then, let's not bother with the small talk." He leaned against the side of her car and crossed his arms over his chest. Oh yeah, that definitely pissed her off.

"Get away from my car."

"Nice plates."

"Fuck you."

"Already been told that once or twice today. Apparently, it's time for me to contemplate a new aftershave."

"You really think you're cute, don't you?"

"In all honesty, I hate to think of myself as being cute, but that's just the male ego for you. Handsome, riveting, intimidating, compelling, charming, intelligent, threatening even, all good. Cute . . . Cute, bad."

"I don't really like you much," Jillian Hayes said.

"Is it the aftershave?"

"I'm serious. And I'm not answering any of your questions without a lawyer present."

"So you're taking the Fifth in regards to my cologne?"

Jillian sighed, crossed her own arms and gave him a stern look. "I've had a long day, Sergeant. Don't you have any other women you can go harass?"

"Not really."

"A girlfriend, a sister, a wife?"

"I never had a sister, and I'm not married anymore."

"Let me guess—she stopped thinking you were cute?"

"No. She died."

Jillian finally shut up. He'd caught her off guard. She looked troubled and perhaps fleetingly sad. Then she looked angry again. Jillian Hayes really did-n't like being caught off guard.

"I don't think this is an appropriate conversation," she said curtly.

"I'm not the one who started it."

"Yes, you did. You showed up again after we'd already chased you off today."

"Yeah, but tell me honestly—would you really sleep well at night know-ing the state police sergeant working your case could be chased off by three women?"

She scowled and appeared even more flustered. Interesting, he thought. Her eyes went gold when she was angry, and brown when she was troubled. What about when she was sad? Or when she was plotting revenge against the man who'd killed her little sister?

"You miss her, don't you?" he asked more softly.

Her voice was stiff, but at least she answered. "I think that's obvious."

"I lost my wife two years ago. Cancer. I still miss her."

"Cancer is hard," Jillian said quietly. She wrapped her arms around her middle, looked away. She did hurt. He could see it in every line of her body, whether she meant him to or not.

"I hated the disease," he continued. "Then I hated the doctors who could-n't make her better. I hated the chemo that robbed her strength. I hated the hospitals that smelled like antiseptic death. I hated God, who gave me some-one to love, then took her away from me."

Jillian finally looked at him. "And if you had a high-powered rifle," she said, "you would've tried to kill the disease, too, isn't that what you mean?"

Fitz had been right. She was no dummy.

"Something like that," Griffin said lightly.

She shook her head. "I'm sorry you lost your wife. I'm sorry anyone loses someone they love. But don't try to play me, Sergeant. Don't think that because you've also known loss, you can climb inside my head."

"Your grief is special?"

"Everyone's grief is special."

It was Griffin's turn to look away. She was right, and that shamed him.

"Are you sure it was Eddie Como who attacked you and your sister?" he asked.

"Yes."

"Never had a moment's doubt?"

"Never."

"Why not?" He looked her in the eye. "Everyone has doubts."

"Voice," she said crisply.

"Voice?"

"When I was attacked, the man spoke. So while I couldn't see his face, I definitely heard his voice. And that voice was consistent with Eddie Como's."

"Consistent?" Griffin raised a brow. He caught that nuance right away. "Did they do a voice line-up with Eddie?"

Jillian scowled. "Of course."

"Just you?"

"Carol, as well." More grudging.

"What went wrong, Ms. Hayes?"

"I'm telling you, it was consistent. That means nothing went wrong."

"Bullshit. Consistent is not a positive ID. You couldn't make him, could you?"

"We could narrow it down to him and one other guy."

"Yeah, in other words, not a positive ID." Griffin rocked back on his heels. That was interesting.

Jillian, however, was vehemently shaking her head. "Positive ID is a legal phrase. It's law-enforcement fine print. As far as Carol and I are concerned, we stood in a darkened room, we heard six guys speak and we could pick Eddie out of that bunch. Think of it this way. Four of the guys we were certain *weren't* the College Hill Rapist. And Eddie wasn't one of those."

"A legal breakeven," Griffin mused. "You can't use the voice ID at trial because you didn't really make an ID, but the defense can't afford to bring it up either, because then as you point out, you can argue that you did home in on Eddie. And once again we're back to DNA to break the tie."

She regarded him curiously, her face less obstinate for a change. "You make it sound like that is a bad thing. Last I knew, DNA evidence was a very, very good thing."

"Yeah, generally."

"*Generally?*"

"Have you ever met Eddie's girlfriend?" Griffin switched gears. "Ever personally spoken to Tawnya Clemente?"

Jillian hesitated a fraction too long. "I . . . I'm not sure."

"You're not sure?"

She sighed. "Did Fitz tell you his theory that Tawnya forwarded Eddie's calls to our homes?" Griffin nodded. "I've also gotten some other calls," she continued. "Someone on the line, just *being* there. I don't know why, but I think the caller might be Tawnya."

"She's very convincing about Eddie's innocence."

"She's a woman with a child to protect. A woman with a child to protect can be very convincing about anything she needs to be."

"Do you like her?"

"I don't know her."

"You sympathize, though." Griffin was sure of this, and it surprised him. Once again there was more to cool, composed Ms. Hayes than met the eye.

"She has an infant son, Sergeant Griffin. Whatever Eddie did or didn't do, it's not her crime, nor the baby's crime."

"But she forwarded his calls to you. Helped harass you. Maybe even called you on her own."

Jillian smiled dryly. "Women in love, Sergeant, have done far worse."

"Call me Griffin."

"No offense, but I think I'll stick to Sergeant."

Now it was Griffin's turn to smile. "Hey, Jillian," he said lightly. "Do us both a favor. Look me in the eye, and tell me you weren't involved in Eddie Como's murder."

Her chin came back up. She looked him in the eye. And she said, "I won't tell you any such thing."

"You understand that we have a second corpse, from the RISD parking lot. Now the bodies are piling up. We can't ignore that, Jillian. The state is in charge of this investigation, and we're manning it with every detective we have. Whatever we learn, whomever we zero in on, we're going to come down on that person very, very hard."

Jillian snorted. Her eyes had gone gold again, about the only warning he got. "Is that supposed to scare me, Sergeant? Is that supposed to terrify my weak little female mind? Because I'm not exactly quaking in my boots. Let's get this straight once and for all. My sister wasn't Eddie's first victim. She was his *third* victim. *Third* victim, Sergeant! And six whole weeks after the first attack. That's how well Providence's 'serious police investigation' was going. And even then, my sister is dead, I'm beaten within an inch of my life and the Providence detectives still didn't have jack shit until we, three *women,* three *civilian women,* got involved in the case. So fuck you, Sergeant. If you cops are so good at your job, you should've been good at it a year ago, when it might have still saved my sister's life!"

She ended harshly, her face red, her breathing coming out in ragged gasps. In the next instant, the full extent of her outburst must have penetrated because she immediately turned away, wrapping her arms tightly around her waist. For a long time, they both simply stood there. Griffin looking at her back, the fallen line of her shoulders, the bowed curve of her neck. Griffin, hearing all her grief and rage still boiling so close to the surface. Calm, controlled Jillian Hayes. Accustomed to single-handedly running her own company while simultaneously raising her little sister and taking care of her invalid mother. Calm, controlled Jillian Hayes, who had probably never felt powerless before in her life.

And then for the first time, Griffin got it. Carol wasn't the member of the Survivors Club closest to falling apart. Jillian was. She merely hid it better than the rest.

"I remember who you are," Jillian said abruptly. She turned around.

Immediately, Griffin's stomach tensed. He forced himself to remain leaning casually against Jillian's car, arms folded over his chest, hands hidden beneath his elbows where she couldn't see his fingers clench. "And who am I?" he asked lightly.

"You led the case. Against that pedophile in Cranston. The Candy Man? Young children kept disappearing, month after month after month. And you were on the nightly news talking about how you were going to find them all. I guess you did, in the end. In your neighbor's dirt basement."

Griffin forced his hands to open, relax. Breathe deep, count to ten.

"Your wife was dying," Jillian said softly. Her voice had changed, not so hard anymore, maybe even sympathetic. Perversely, he found that worse. "Your wife was sick, that's right. I think she had even died—"

"The cancer got her quick."

"And still kids were disappearing and there got to be a bit of a hubbub about whether you were paying enough attention to the case—"

"I did nothing but work that goddamn case. It was all I had left."

"And then"—her eyes were locked on his—"then the police finally found all those poor missing kids. Buried in the basement right next door to your home. The Candy Man was your next-door neighbor."

"It took eleven months, but I caught him."

"You were the one who figured out that it was him?"

"Yeah."

"Why didn't you see it sooner? Were you distracted because your wife died?"

"Maybe. Mostly I think it was because he was my friend."

"Oh." Jillian stopped, blinked her eyes. "I hadn't heard that."

"It wasn't relevant to the case."

"You arrested him?"

"Yes." After he tried to rip him from limb to limb. Down in that base-ment, with the acrid smell of lime and the deeper stench of death. Down in that basement, with those poor, poor kids. Down in that dark, dark base-ment, from which he'd been clawing his way back up ever since.

"I learned something that day," Griffin said abruptly.

"Not to have friends?"

He had to smile at that. "Maybe. But that's not true. I'll tell you some-thing, Jillian. I'll tell you something about only a dozen other people offi-cially know. For everyone else, it's merely a rumor."

She hesitated, chewed her lower lip, then worried the gold medallion hanging around her neck. He understood her dilemma. Accepting a confi-dence was like accepting a gift. If she took it, they wouldn't be strangers any-more. Maybe they'd even have a bit of a bond. And he doubted that right now, for a variety of reasons, Jillian Hayes wanted to bond with a cop.

Her curiosity won out. "What?" she asked.

"When I figured out it was David Price, my friend, my neighbor, it was bad. But when I went down to that basement, when I saw what he'd done to those kids, it was even worse. I went a little nuts that day. I went after David, and if I could've gotten my hands on him, I would've killed him. I would've ripped off his head with my bare hands, I would've pummeled him into a bleeding mass of bruised flesh. And I would've felt good about it. I didn't though. Two other detectives got in my way. They took his beating, and they did it because they were professionals who didn't want that son of a bitch to get off on charges of police brutality, and they did it because they were my friends and they understood. It's because of them he's now in prison for the rest of his life. And it's because of them that I still have a job. One friend betrayed me. But two other friends saved me. When all is said and done, it's still very good to have friends."

Jillian didn't say anything. Whether she knew it or not, she was leaning forward slightly, a strange look on her face. Yearning, maybe? Had she trusted anyone since the day her sister died? Even the Survivors Club, did she really trust them?

"But that's not the lesson I learned that day," he said.

"It's not?"

"No. What I really learned is that it's arrogant to be certain of anything. The world is a complex place and only idiots or assholes think they know it all."

Jillian recoiled just as a back door opened and Carol Rosen came walking out of the restaurant into the parking lot.

"Jillian, there you are—" Carol spotted Griffin and suddenly drew up short. Her gaze dashed between the two of them, standing alone together in the parking lot, and it was clear she didn't like what she saw.

"Yes?" Jillian belatedly turned around to face Carol. Her movements were jerky.

"Ummm, Meg . . . We, uh . . . Can I see you inside for a moment?"

"I don't know." Jillian still seemed distracted, but she recovered her bearings quickly, turning back to Griffin. "Are you done accusing me of murder, Sergeant?"

"For now."

"Well then"—she gave him a thin smile—"I think I'll be on my way."

She headed back to Carol, chin up, shoulders square. But then at the last minute, halfway through the restaurant's back door, she turned again.

"You're wrong, Sergeant," she called out to him.

"About Eddie?"

"About the world. You have to be certain of some things. Otherwise you'd go crazy."

It was Griffin's turn to smile. "I wouldn't be so sure of that," he said lightly as she disappeared through the doorway. "I wouldn't be so sure of that at all."

14

Price

Griffin swung by his house a little after 4:30. At the rate things were going, the workday was going to stretch deep into night. Not the ideal first day back for a man who'd gone bonkers just eighteen months ago, but what could you do? As he'd told Fitz, back was back.

Besides, he was increasingly intrigued by this case. Puzzled, confused, fascinated. In other words, in that perverse sort of way homicide detectives had, he was enjoying himself immensely.

Griffin parked outside the little waterfront shack he'd recently purchased in North Kingstown, and went inside to prepare the working homicide detective's Big Case Kit. In other words, a duffel bag containing two fresh shirts, two ties and lots of clean underwear. You could never have too much clean underwear. Oh yeah, he also added a toothbrush and an electric razor—never as good as a blade, but handy in a pinch.

He stopped in the kitchen for a glass of water as he idly went through his mail. Bill, bill, grocery store flyer. Ooooh, oranges for ninety-nine cents a pound. God bless the USA.

He got to the last item, a plain white envelope, and then his heart accelerated in spite of himself. *To: Good Neighbor Griffin.* At Griffin's new address. *From: Your Buddy Dave.* No return address.

David Price never could stand being bored.

Little psychopathic shit.

David had written many times before, mostly to the old house in Cranston, where Griffin had stayed for nearly a year after the Big Boom. He probably should have put it up for sale immediately after he took his medical leave, but who was going to buy the home next to the home where the Candy Man had brutally murdered ten kids? Who was going to buy the home of the dumb fuck detective who'd lived twenty feet away and never suspected a thing?

David Price, who used to pop over and mow their lawn when Griffin and Cindy got too busy. Small, boyish David Price, who looked seventeen even though he was twenty-eight, who could barely lift a forty-pound bag of potting soil but was hell on wheels with electrical wires. Easygoing, neighborly David Price, who helped Griffin lay the pipes for his irrigation system one summer, who liked to come over for barbecued hamburgers and beer, who fixed the light over the sink when the buzzing threatened to drive Cindy mad, who had no family of his own and over the course of three years somehow became part of theirs.

When Cindy had first learned of her cancer, a mere two days after Griffin had landed the Candy Man case, she'd told David about the disease herself. Griffin had an important case, she'd explained. Griffin was going to be very busy. It was so reassuring to her then that David lived right next door.

David had cried that night. All of them had. In the small family room Cindy had painted butter yellow and decorated with pictures of birds in flight. And then David had held Cindy's hand and promised her he'd do whatever she needed. They were going to beat this thing! They were going to win!

Six months later, Cindy was dead.

And five months after that, Griffin was talking to a little girl who had managed to escape from a man who'd tried to pick her up on the school playground. The stranger had been there when Summer Marie Nicholas had first come out, playing on the swings, but when he'd offered to give her a push, she'd gotten nervous.

His pants were "too full," she had said. The little girl had noticed that the man had an erection.

She had run straight back into the school, where she had found a janitor cleaning the gym. And he'd been wise enough to call the police. The man was gone from the playground by the time Griffin had arrived, of course, but seven-year-old Summer Marie had been brilliant.

She announced without hesitation that the man looked exactly the same as the boy in that big eighties movie *Back to the Future*. She liked that movie. That mad professor made her laugh so hard! Plus, when she was old enough to get a car, she wanted one just like that, with the funny doors.

Griffin had stared at little Summer Marie. And through the haze of depression and grief and exhaustion that had kept him half-functioning for months, he had a memory as clear as day: Cindy, Griffin and David sitting on the back porch the first time David had come over. Cindy laughing, saying, "Hey, Dave, anyone ever tell you that you look exactly like Michael J. Fox?"

David, an independent contractor with flexible hours. David, whose electrical jobs took him to different neighborhoods all over the state. David, whose small build, boyish face and easy smile would seem completely nonthreatening to a child. At least until it was much too late.

The girl's description earned them a search warrant. Two hours later Griffin was back in his own neighborhood, leading a small posse of detectives that included Mike Waters into David's home, while his next-door neighbor stood by silently, a strange smile fixed upon his face.

Fifteen minutes later, the first detective opened the door to the basement. The initial waft of odor was so overwhelmingly floral the detective had actually sneezed. And then they'd all caught the smell beneath the smell. The incredibly hard to conceal odor of death.

Down into that basement, with the hard-packed dirt floor and soundproofed ceiling. Down into that basement, with its three harshly glaring bare bulbs. Down into that basement, with a stained mattress and an old workbench covered in handcuffs, dildos and porn. Down in that basement with another corner where the dirt wasn't hard-packed at all. Where instead the dark, loamy soil undulated in ten tiny lime-topped waves.

Ten heartbreaking little white-flecked waves.

David had brought each child down here, down to the odor of death. And he had done unspeakable things to them while they had inhaled the stench of death. Had it made him even more excited?

Or had that come later, when he'd gone next door to mow a state police sergeant's lawn?

Griffin should've killed David Price that day. Most nights, when he awoke drenched in sweat and choking back screams, he still wished that he had. Sometimes when people did the right thing, it was still much too wrong. He'd spent eighteen months in therapy, when frankly, he probably could've cured himself that day with one properly landed punch.

Shrinks just didn't know shit about this job.

Now Griffin looked down at the envelope in his hand. He should throw it away, toss it in the bin like so much garbage. But he didn't. In all honesty, he'd come to consider these little notes the very best in home sanity tests. The state had its fitness-for-duty diagnostic; Griffin had this.

He opened the envelope. It was short by David's standards. Generally he included several pages about his life in maximum-security prison. The carpentry classes he was taking. His newfound love of yoga—good for the body and the mind. Rumors that the ACI might win a contract soon to have inmates make American flags and wouldn't that be a heck of a lotta fun? Oh, and by the way, here's a sketch of a rose to put on Cindy's grave. *I still miss her, buddy.*

In contrast, this letter contained only two lines. It read: *Best wishes with the new case. It's going to be a good one.*

Griffin's blood went cold. He grabbed the envelope, flipped it over. Postmarked Saturday, the eighteenth of May. But that was before Griffin had gone back to work, before Eddie Como had been shot. How could David . . . ? What did David . . . ?

The ringing building in his ears. Heart starting to race, blood starting to pump, sweat bursting from pores.

Griffin took a shaky breath, counted to ten, closed his eyes, and in the next moment, the anxiety attack passed. His breathing calmed. His powers of reason returned.

David was simply fucking with him. He'd probably learned of Griffin's first day back on the job the same way he'd learned Griffin's new address. The power of the prison rumor mill, coupled with way too many big mouths on TV.

And when Griffin returned to work, of course he was assigned a new case. He was a detective, after all. That's what he did. To read any more than that into the note was like giving a psychic all the credit for predicting that "soon, your luck will change."

David Price didn't deserve that kind of credit. And he certainly didn't deserve that kind of power.

Griffin stepped on the foot pedal of the kitchen's white trash bin. The lid popped open and he dropped David Price's letter into the pile of used Kleenexes and sticky eggshells.

"Fuck you, too," he murmured. Then for good measure, he looked at his hands. Not a tremor in sight. Yeah, eighteen months later, he was doing just fine. Eighteen months later, he was fucking fabulous.

Griffin grabbed his Big Case Kit and hit the road.

15

Carol

Carol left the rue de l'espoir shortly after 4:00 but didn't return home until nearly 6:30. First, she spent some quality time at Nordstrom. Dan would scream when he got the bill, but let him scream. It was four in the afternoon on the opening day of her rape trial, which was no longer the opening day of her rape trial, and by God, she would shop if she damn well wanted to shop.

So Carol went to Nordstrom, where a petite young thing helped her select a multitude of designer suits while trying hard not to stare. Carol didn't mind the staring. She'd gotten used to it by now. In the beginning, when Jillian had first proposed the Survivors Club, she had spelled out the side effects of going public. On the one hand, never underestimate the power of three beautiful women standing in front of a crowd of TV cameras demanding that the police ratchet up their investigation and do more to protect the female population of the great Ocean State.

On the other hand, never underestimate the power of the press to descend on three bruised and battered women like vultures on roadkill. *Did they have any idea who was behind these vicious attacks? What about the slow progress of the ongoing investigation? Did they still suffer nightmares? What about their husbands, fathers, sisters, brothers? Did they have any advice for other women out there?*

Jillian fielded all the questions, of course. Jillian was good at that sort of thing. Crisp, professional, never giving too much away.

Now, Carol, if she'd gotten her hands on the mike . . . *Of course I have fucking nightmares! Women, you want to protect yourselves, buy a gun. Shoot first, question later. Fuck 'em all, ladies. It's the only way.*

So, yes, I have nightmares . . . When I sleep . . . Which hasn't been for months . . . And by the way, when I look at my husband I see a rapist's face and when my husband touches me I feel a rapist's hands. And I hate Eddie Como, and open windows and houses that grow too quiet at night. But most of all I hate the fact that when I do fall asleep, I dream of blood and slaughtered lambs, and when I wake up I am so angry I have to press my eyeballs into my sockets to keep them from bursting out of my head.

Other than that, esteemed members of the fourth estate, I am coping just fine.

340

Carol dropped two thousand bucks. Dan would go ballistic. Good for him. Yes, she was definitely in a mood.

Maybe she should've stayed with Jillian and Meg. Jillian was going to drive Meg home, providing backup in case Meg's father was there and saw his little girl under the influence of not one, but two bottles of champagne. Carol wasn't even sure how Meg had gotten her hands on the second bottle. She'd gone to the restroom, and next thing she knew, a fresh bottle was on the table and half consumed. At least she'd been able to catch Jillian out in the parking lot. Of course, that had been weird, too. Jillian talking to Sergeant Blue Eyes. The two of them standing so close together, so deep in conversation . . . Then the way Jillian had jerked back. Startled. Guilty.

Carol had a strange feeling in the pit of her stomach. Betrayal, though she didn't know why. Suspicion, though she had no proof.

As she and Jillian walked back into the restaurant, Carol had asked her what she had been talking to Sergeant Griffin about. Nothing, Jillian had said. And Carol had wondered what kind of nothing took fifteen minutes to cover in a restaurant parking lot.

Once Jillian was inside, she'd appraised the situation, as Carol had known she would. She'd come up with a plan of attack, as Carol had known she would. Carol could go on her way. Jillian would handle Meg, and by extension, her father, Tom Pesaturo. Go, Jillian.

Personally, Carol didn't like Tom. Based on things Meg said, he sounded overbearing, brutish and chauvinistic to the core. Making his daughter drop out of college. As if denying his child higher education was the secret to keeping her safe. For heaven's sake, was there anything of value in the Y chromosome? One ounce of intelligence to go with all that raging testosterone?

Of course, that made her think of Dan, and the scent of red roses and veal piccata. And that thought sliced through her heady steam of rage, her frenzy of self-righteousness. She was left suddenly empty and bereft, the legs taken right out from beneath her.

She had loved him so much once. Did he ever remember those days? When just the sight of him across the room sent her heart beating rapid- fire with lust? When the thought of seeing him for dinner made her smile all day? When the scent of his cologne was the first thing she wanted to smell in the morning and the last thing she wanted to smell at night? When they used to sleep intertwined like vines, legs and arms coiling, her head planted securely on his chest?

She still remembered those days. Some nights, when she was not busy hating Eddie Como, she stayed awake replaying those first wild, wonderful moments in her mind. She was never sure which set of thoughts hurt her more.

Now she plopped down in the Nordstrom Café, where she had a heaping chicken Oriental salad, and yes, another piece of chocolate cake. Then she ordered a glass of wine. Or two or three or four.

She was still hungry afterward, but that didn't surprise her anymore. She had been hungry for well over a year.

Being raped was an interesting thing. More interesting than Carol would've imagined. Yes, she now suffered from a variety of lovely mental conditions. Post-traumatic stress syndrome that left her with nightmares, cold sweats and irrational mood swings. Generalization that left her hating not just her rapist, but pretty much all men, including her husband, Detective Fitzpatrick and Ned D'Amato. Then there was her "trigger syndrome"—she literally could not turn off the TV because turning off the TV was one of the last things she'd done before being attacked, and thus her mind associated the act with causing the rape. And finally there was good old-fashioned guilt—guilt that she'd been attacked, guilt that she'd survived. Guilt that she'd inconvenienced her husband, guilt that she'd left her window open, guilt that she'd not been able to fend off a grown man. Jillian, whether she would admit it or not, still held the prize in the guilt category, but Carol thought she should get credit for having not just one of the various syndromes they'd read about in rape survivors' handbooks, but pretty much all of them rolled up in a nice, neat, therapy-desperately-needed ball. In her own way, she was an overachiever, too.

So on the one hand, being raped was as traumatic, painful, messy and soul wrenching as Carol had ever imagined. She did not recommend it. Women really should shoot first, and question later.

On the other hand . . .

On the other hand, for lack of a better word, being raped did have its advantages. Take the Survivors Club. Carol now spent the majority of her time with two women whom before this, she probably wouldn't have given the time of day. Meg, after all, was too young for Carol to have ever considered seriously as a friend. And, if Carol was being truly honest, too working class. Assuming their paths ever did cross, it probably would've been in some swanky restaurant where Carol was the patron and Meg the waitress. Neither would have thought of it again.

Jillian was a more interesting case. She was closer to Carol's age and economic status. The type of woman Carol might have met naturally at some society event or charity fund-raiser. They would've exchanged polite chitchat, the normal cocktail party pleasantries. Most likely, Carol would've found Jillian to be too much of a career woman. And most likely, Jillian would've found Carol to be too 1950s, the socialite wife who stayed at home while her husband did the real work.

But now here they all were. Pissy sometimes, mean sometimes, awkward sometimes. Telling each other all the things normal people couldn't understand. Rallying one moment, crying the next. Holding back more confidences still. Carol was sure of this. God knows she had her own things that even a year later she could not bring herself to put into words. And as for Jillian—well, Carol and Meg were certain they hadn't even begun to scratch the surface there. So they had their secrets. But they also had this bond, one that shouldn't exist, and it was sad that it did exist, but here they were. And in all honesty, their weekly meetings were about the only thing that kept Carol going.

Normal people could not understand these things. Normal people, if they were at all lucky, would never have to understand these things.

Carol finished her glass of wine. Then, duly fortified, she finally headed home.

No reporters in sight. That was a welcome relief. They'd probably been camped out most of the day, another reason for her not to hurry home. It was after 6:00 now, however, too late to make the 5:00 news crunch. Or maybe the police were holding a briefing across town. Jillian, Carol and Meg had learned to love police briefings, when the reporters would scurry from their front lawns to police headquarters, leaving the women at least fifteen minutes to breathe. Until the police briefing ended, of course, and the hordes once more came trooping down the street, rows and rows of white news vans carrying legions of question-wielding combatants. On her good days, Carol pictured having a machine gun battened to her roof, which she would use to mow them all down. On her bad days, she cowered in the upstairs bathroom, the only room in the house with no windows, and gobbled pints of Ben & Jerry's ice cream while curled up in the empty bathtub.

Dan's car was parked in the driveway. The hood was cold to the touch; he'd been home for a bit. Not a good sign.

Five minutes later, she found Dan sitting in the family room with only the constantly chattering TV as a source of light. He started when she entered the room, and she would've sworn he made some kind of furtive motion. When she walked around for a better look, however, he was merely picking up a large, round cognac glass for one last sip. She stared at him, waiting to see who would talk first. Then she realized that he still wore a suit and his short, dark brown hair was horribly rumpled—he always ran his fingers through his hair when he was anxious.

On the TV, some blond newswoman was standing in front of the courthouse, talking into her microphone as a barrage of red and blue police lights relentlessly swirled around her head.

"Police have now confirmed that alleged rape suspect, Eddie Como, aka the College Hill Rapist, was shot and killed here earlier this morning. Sources close to the investigation say that twenty-eight-year-old Como was shot once in the head as he was being unloaded from the ACI van at the Licht Judicial Complex around eight-thirty. According to a fellow prisoner—"

"I came home as soon as I heard the news," Dan finally spoke up.

Carol didn't say anything.

"I thought you might want to see me."

Carol still didn't say anything.

"You could've at least called," he said quietly. His eyes rose to meet hers. "I do worry, you know."

"You're dressed for work."

"Dammit, Carol, I canceled three meetings today—"

"You're going back to the office."

"I don't have a choice! Clients pay me to be available at the snap of their fingers. Lawyering isn't a nine-to-five job. You know that."

She said simply, "It will be dark."

Dan's eyes fell. He opened his mouth, then closed it into a grim line and focused instead on rotating the now empty cognac glass between his fingers. He was angry. She read his tension in the tight, bunched line of his shoulders. But he didn't say another word. And the silence went on and on and on.

"I went shopping," she said at last, chin held up defiantly.

"I can see that."

"I bought three suits. Nice ones."

"All right, Carol."

"I spent two thousand dollars," she pushed.

A muscle twitched in his jaw. He spun the fine crystal goblet with even greater concentration. She decided on a new tack. The sun was going down. Dusk descending on their too big, too empty house. And he was leaving her again, proof that no matter what punishment she inflicted upon him, he was more than capable of inflicting it right back.

"The police came to see us today," she announced. "Detective Fitzpatrick crashed our meeting."

"He wanted to be the first to give you the big news?"

"No, he wanted to be the first to ask us if we killed him."

"And what did Jillian say to that?"

"She told him to fuck off. Using bigger words, of course."

"Detective Fitzpatrick should've known better." Dan finally set his glass down on the coffee table. He rose off the sofa. His movements were restless and agitated.

"It wasn't just Fitzpatrick. A state guy came as well."

"The state?" Dan's head jerked around.

"Detective Sergeant Roan Griffin. Big guy. Smart. He claims they'll subpoena our bank records next. You know, to see if they can find any mysterious cash withdrawals or money transfers, anything that might be construed as a payment to a hired gun. He seems very determined about it."

Dan walked away from her, finally halting in front of the mantel around the fireplace. He ran one finger down the scrolling woodwork. Dan had long, lean fingers. He could've been a sculptor or a musician. Or a father teaching his son how to tie his first bowknot.

"Why are they bothering with an investigation?" he asked curtly. "Eddie Como has caused enough damage. He's dead. Let it be."

"I don't care," Carol said fiercely. "Whoever shot him. I don't care."

She was holding her breath, willing her husband to turn around and look her in the eye. She had started this conversation to goad him, but now . . . Now she heard the ache in her voice. She hadn't told anyone, not even Meg or Jillian, but Carol half hoped her husband *had* shot or paid someone to shoot Eddie Como. It would be the first sign she had that he still loved her.

I know where you were that night. I've never told anyone, but I know where you were that night, and it was not working late.

Dan turned around. Dan looked her in the eye with his deep brown gaze. Ten years of marriage later, his face held new lines, darker shadows, grayer hair. The years had been rough on both of them. So many things that had not turned out quite the way they'd planned. And yet she still thought he was handsome. She still wished he would cross the room right now and take her in his arms.

If you would promise to try to touch me, I would promise to try not to pull away. If you would promise to try to reach out to me, I would promise to try not to see you as another Eddie Como. If you would promise to try to love me again, I would promise to try to forgive you. And maybe, if you did try and I did try . . .

He said, "I have to go. The meeting starts at seven and I still need to prepare."

"Dan—" She caught the rest of the sentence. Bit it back. Swallowed it down.

"You'll lock the door behind me?"

"Of course."

"And turn on the alarm?"

"I know, Dan."

"Think of it this way, Carol—the press are bound to be back soon. Then you won't be alone, after all."

He came around the sofa, glanced at her shopping bags and grimaced on his way out of the room. The next sound she heard was the front door opening, then closing behind him. A moment later, his car started up in their driveway.

Carol's gaze went outside, where the sun sank low on the horizon. Dusk falling. Night approaching. The dark coming, coming, coming to find her.

The silence, on the other hand, was already here.

On TV, the perky blond reporter said, *"Eddie Como's family announced this afternoon that they will seek to claim his body from the medical examiner's office no later than tomorrow night, in order to prepare for a Catholic funeral service first thing Wednesday morning. The family, still claiming his innocence, has also said that they would like to start a memorial fund to help other wrongfully accused men . . ."*

Carol locked the front door, armed the security system. Then she went upstairs to the main hallway. She walked down its long, shadowed length to the tightly shut door at one end. She opened the door. And she looked inside the room, the room she had once shared with her husband, the room where she had once made love to her husband, and what she saw now was merely a collection of dusty furniture held captive behind wrought-iron bars.

No open windows. No wet, blood-spattered cotton sheets. No piles of latex strips still littered with pieces of long, blond hair.

Nothing. Nothing, nothing, nothing.

Her hands started to shake. Her heart picked up its pace. He's dead, she tried to tell herself. He's dead, it's over, you're finally safe.

No good. No good, no good, no good.

Carol slammed the door shut, recoiling down the hallway, grabbing blindly at the walls with her bare hands. She had to get away. The TV was still on. Didn't matter, didn't matter. The house was too big, the silence too powerful, and God knows Dan would come home much too late. On her own. Always alone. Run, Carol, run.

She stumbled into the upstairs bathroom. She slammed the door. And then she leaned over the white porcelain sink, where she vomited until she dry-heaved.

Eddie Como's dead. Eddie Como's dead. Eddie Como's dead.

It's over, Carol. You're finally, finally safe.

But her whole body was shivering, trembling, quaking. And she couldn't stop thinking about her empty bedroom. She couldn't stop thinking about that one bedroom window. She couldn't stop thinking that she would swear, she would swear, she would swear that Dead Eddie had been standing right there.

16

Meg

"Jesus, Mary and Joseph, are you *DRUNK*?"

"I just . . . it was champagne. Only a glass. Maybe two. I swear."

"Mr. Pesaturo, if you would just calm down for a moment—"

"And you!" Mr. Pesaturo swung around on Jillian, beefy face bright red, thick finger stabbing the air. His blue electrician's uniform strained over his gut, two of the white buttons literally quaking with the force of his rage. The effect was rather comical, and now that he was safely yelling at Jillian, Meg started to giggle again. Jillian tried shooting her a warning glance. Meg had had nearly six glasses of champagne. It was hopeless.

"How dare you serve my underaged daughter alcohol!" Tom Pesaturo boomed. "For God's sake, haven't you done enough already?"

Jillian blinked. "Done enough?"

"Daddy—"

"Tom, calm down, have a seat. Meg is home now and that's what's important." Meg's mother, Laurie, intervened, placing her hand on her husband's bulging forearm. She was clearly the voice of reason in the family, thank God. Mr. Pesaturo glowered at Jillian again, but finally, reluctantly, sat.

Meg chose that moment to exclaim, "Holy Lord, I have got to pee!" and go racing from the room.

Mr. Pesaturo renewed his growl of disapproval. Jillian sighed, took her own seat on a threadbare blue recliner and realized she had a raging headache.

"Mr. Pesaturo—"

"Have you seen the news? Do you understand what happened this morning? Our phone has been ringing off the hook since nine A.M. The first news van was here by nine-fifteen. And we didn't even know where Meg was."

"We knew exactly where Meg was," Laurie interjected again, her voice firm. "I told you she was having breakfast with Jillian and Carol."

"That's what Meg *said*," Tom asserted, with just the right tone of doubt.

Jillian looked at him. "Mr. Pesaturo, do you think we were running around shooting Eddie Como this morning? Is that what you thought we were doing?"

"Hey, I'm not saying I disapprove . . ."

"We were at the restaurant, Mr. Pesaturo. All day, as a matter of fact. With

347

witnesses. Though you should know that the police stopped by. Detective Fitzpatrick and a man from the state, Sergeant Griffin, definitely have us on their radar screen."

"What did you tell them?"

"We didn't tell them anything, of course. We don't have to give them a statement, and personally, I don't want to give them a statement. As far as I'm concerned, they'll have my cooperation the day they bring my sister back from the dead."

Mr. Pesaturo finally stopped scowling. After another moment, he grunted and settled deeper into the loveseat, probably as close as she'd get to praise. "Yeah, well," he said gruffly. Sitting beside him, his wife smiled.

"They will start looking into all of us," Jillian said levelly. She'd been thinking of nothing but that for the last half hour. The state police were on the case. The state police were going to get serious. She wondered what that really meant. Big, bad Sergeant Griffin, who probably could've ripped off that pedophile's head. Big, bad Sergeant Griffin with those penetrating blue eyes. She felt herself getting angry again, then confused. Big, bad Sergeant Griffin . . . She cut off the thought, focused again on the matters at hand. "I'm told that every detective in the state is now working this case. The next order of business will be examining our financial records for any unexplained withdrawals."

Mr. Pesaturo rolled his eyes. "Good luck. I don't have any unexplained withdrawals. I got a mortgage and I got two kids. That pretty much covers it."

"I imagine they'll also want to talk to your brother," Jillian said. "You know, Uncle Vinnie."

The smile vanished from Mrs. Pesaturo's face. She jerked back, looking at her husband sharply. "Tom?"

"Oh come on. Let 'em talk to Vinnie. He don't care."

Mr. Pesaturo was looking at Jillian now. From the hallway, Jillian could hear Meg's voice, followed by a high-pitched giggle. Meg was talking to her little sister, Molly. More laughter floated down the hall.

"You care?" Tom asked Jillian abruptly. Jillian was not an idiot. She understood the nuances of the question.

"I'm all right."

" 'Cause you know, if you needed anything . . ."

Jillian smiled. In his own way, Mr. Pesaturo was a very sweet man. It made it almost tempting, but the problems she had were nothing he could help her with. Now that she'd had more time to contemplate the impact of Eddie Como's death, she figured she had twenty-four to forty-eight hours before she saw Sergeant Griffin again. Life would get tricky. Then again, had it ever been simple?

"I'm all right," she repeated. Mr. Pesaturo was smarter than she'd given him credit for, however, and she could see the open doubt on his face.

"Vinnie . . . he's got a lotta friends."

"I know. In fact, I'm not sure if you know, but I believe Vinnie and my mother have some of the same friends."

"No kiddin'?"

"Do you follow music? My mother used to literally sing the blues—"

"Wait a minute. Hayes. Olivia Hayes. *That's* your mom?"

"She'll be pleased you remember."

Tom Pesaturo was clearly impressed. He rocked back, turning to his wife. "No kidding, Olivia Hayes. You ever hear of her? Pretty little thing about a hundred pounds soaking wet. Then she'd open her mouth and blow the place away. My father used to listen to her records all the time. I probably got a vinyl or two stashed in the attic. Fine, beautiful lady." He turned back to Jillian. "What happened to her anyway? I haven't heard her name in years."

"She retired." Said she was going to finally spend time with her daughters. Had a stroke. Lost her legs. Lost her voice. At least they'd never had to worry about money.

"You tell her I said hi."

"I'll do that."

"Vinnie's gonna flip." Mr. Pesaturo suddenly smiled and sat up straighter. "My daughter is friends with Olivia Hayes's daughter. Vinnie's gonna have a fucking *cow*!"

"Tom . . ." His wife rolled her eyes at his profanity, then glanced at Jillian apologetically. Jillian smiled. She was genuinely pleased that Mr. Pesaturo was pleased. Her mother's time, Jillian's own childhood, was a bygone era not many people remembered anymore. When Trish had been little, stories from the nightclubs had been her favorite ones. The night their mother had sung for Sinatra. How later Frank had let eight-year-old Jillian sit on his knee. Jillian had done her best to tell the tales, though even for her they'd taken on a hazy quality, a life lived so long ago it now seemed more like a distant dream.

The days her mother had had a voice. Jillian had not even heard her hum in years now.

Tom Pesaturo had settled back into the sofa. His face was finally relaxed, his big hands resting comfortably on his knees. Jillian's parentage had done the trick. They were now old friends and he was happy to have her in his living room. It was funny, but during the last twelve months that Jillian's and Meg's lives had been intertwined, she'd never visited Meg's house. Not Carol's home either. By some unspoken rule, the group always met in restaurants or other public places. It was as if after everything they'd told one another, they couldn't bear to share this last little bit.

"I was worried," Mr. Pesaturo said abruptly, maybe even a little apologetically. "When I heard the news on TV, when I couldn't find Meg. I went a little nuts."

"I understand."

"You got kids?"

Jillian thought of Trish and her bright, bright eyes. She thought of her mother, wheelchair-bound since her stroke. "No."

"It's not easy. You wanna keep 'em safe, you know. I mean, you want 'em to go out in the world. Be strong. Make you proud. But mostly, mostly you want 'em to be safe. Happy. Okay."

"She's okay," Mrs. Pesaturo murmured. "They're both okay."

"If I coulda been there, that night . . . That's what kills me, you know. This Como guy," Mr. Pesaturo spat. "He's not even that big. If I'd been there that night, I would've kicked his sorry spic ass."

Jillian thought of Trisha's dark apartment. Her sister's unmoving form on the bed. Those strong, strong hands grabbing her from behind. She said, "I wish you would've been there, too."

"Yeah, well, I guess there's not much I can do about it now. At least the guy's dead. I feel better about that. Hey"—his head jerked up—"think Meg'll be all right now?"

Jillian was puzzled. "I think Meg is already all right."

"No, no. Start remembering. Get her life back. You know."

"I'm . . . I'm not sure. I really don't know that much about amnesia."

"She don't talk about it?"

"What do you mean?"

"Her amnesia. What that asshole did to her. Don't you girls talk about this stuff over coffee or something like that?"

"Mr. Pesaturo . . ." Jillian began, but Laurie Pesaturo beat her to the punch.

"Tom, shut up."

Mr. Pesaturo blinked at his wife. "What?"

"Jillian is not going to tell you about our daughter's state of mind. If you want to know what Meg is thinking, ask her yourself."

"I was just asking," Tom said defensively, but he hung his big head, suitably chastised. Jillian took some pity on him.

"For the record," she told him. "I think Meg is doing remarkably well. She's a strong young lady, Mr. Pesaturo. You should be proud of her."

"I *am* proud of her!"

"Are you? Or are you mostly afraid for her?"

"Hey now!" Mr. Pesaturo didn't like that much at all. But when he found Jillian staring at him steadily, and his own wife regarding him steadily, his shoulders hunkered again. "I'm a father," he muttered. "Fathers protect their daughters. Nothing wrong with that."

"She's twenty years old," Laurie said.

"Still young."

"Tom, it's been years . . ." Laurie said. Which Jillian didn't get. Didn't she mean one year?

Mr. Pesaturo said, "Yeah, and we've been lucky to get her this far."

"That's not fair."

"You're telling me."

Jillian was very confused now, which must have shown on her face, because suddenly both Mr. and Mrs. Pesaturo drew up short. They looked at their guest, they looked at each other, and that was the end of that conversation.

"I should get going," Jillian said at last, when the silence had gone on too long. Meg's parents didn't waste any time getting up off the couch.

"Thank you for bringing Meg home," Mrs. Pesaturo said. "We'll make arrangements to retrieve her car."

"The champagne . . . Well, it seemed like a good idea at the time."

Mrs. Pesaturo smiled kindly at her. "It's been a long, strange day, hasn't it?"

"Yes," Jillian said, and she didn't know why, but at that moment she wanted to cry. She pulled herself back together. Her nerves were rattled, had been all day, and her private conversation with Sergeant Griffin had only made things worse. But her weariness didn't matter. There were probably still cameras outside. You had to wear your game face. Besides, she would need her strength for when she returned home, to where her aphasia-stricken mother had probably already heard the news and was now sifting through her picture book, trying to find an image that could communicate *My daughter's murderer died today and I feel . . .*

Meg was back. "Come on," she told Jillian. "I'll walk you to the door."

Jillian followed her down the narrow hallway. Meg's little sister, Molly, peered out at them from around the corner, a mass of dark corkscrew curls and big doe-brown eyes. *Trish,* Jillian thought. She had to get out of this house.

When Meg opened the door, Jillian was startled to see that it was already dark outside. The night wind felt cool on her face. The street was long and empty. Not a reporter in sight, which made her both grateful and more unsettled. Where were all the flashing lights and rapid-fire questions? Where had the day gone? It was already a blur.

Meg was swaying slightly in the breeze. "Thank you," she murmured.

"For what?" Jillian was still staring into the night. On her right, something moved in the bushes.

"I'm starting to feel better already, you know. The shock's wearing off, I guess. I didn't think it would be this fast, but now . . . I feel like for the first time in twelve months, I can finally breathe."

Jillian just stared at Meg. And then she got it. Meg was talking about Eddie Como's demise. She was thanking Jillian for Eddie Como's murder.

"But you're right," Meg continued expansively. "We shouldn't talk about it. The police will probably still be coming around, at least for a few days. Then the worst will be past. The dust will settle. And we'll be . . . we'll be free."

"Meg . . ."

"Isn't it a beautiful night?"

"Oh God, Meg . . ."

"Such a lovely, lovely night."

"You've had more to drink! Why do you keep drinking?"

"I don't know. The doctors said not to push. The mind will heal itself. But it hasn't, and really, as of today, I thought it should. So I added some bourbon. But you know, it didn't work."

"Meg, you just need rest."

"No, I don't think I do. I think it's all much weirder than that. I've had rest, I've had peace and now I've had closure. But I can still feel the eyes following me. What does that mean?"

"It means you've had too much to drink."

"I want to be happy. I don't think I was. Because if I had been happy, shouldn't I be able to remember it? Shouldn't it come back to me?"

"Meg, listen to me—"

"Shhhh, the bushes."

Jillian stopped, drew up short. She looked at the bushes, still twitching on the right. She looked at Meg. This close, she could see the glassy sheen to the girl's dark eyes, the red flush of bourbon warming her cheeks.

"Whoever is hiding in the bushes, you'd better come out," Jillian called.

"Beautiful, beautiful night," Meg singsonged. "Oh, what a lovely night, just like the last night, that night."

"I'm warning you!" Jillian's voice started to rise in spite of herself as another leaf quivered and Meg rocked back and forth like a giant pendulum.

"A beautiful, beautiful night. A lovely, lovely night . . ."

"Goddammit!" Jillian strode over to the bush. She thrust in her hand as if she would drag out the interloper by his ear. She'd yank him out. And then she'd . . . she'd . . .

The gray tiger-striped cat sprang out of the bush with a hostile MEOW and Jillian staggered back, her heart hammering hard in her chest. She had to take a deep breath, then another. Her heart was still racing. The hairs had prickled up on the back on her neck. Oh God, she suddenly wanted away from this house and out of this too-empty street. She couldn't stop shivering.

On the porch, Meg had a beatific smile plastered on her face. "Gone now. He's all gone now."

"Please go inside, Meg," Jillian said tiredly.

"It won't make a difference. He's here, he's here, he's here."

"Who is here?"

And Meg whispered, "I don't know. Whoever's worse than Eddie Como."

17

Griffin

"We got a problem."

Now at the state police headquarters in North Scituate, Griffin finally paused in the middle of five piles of paper. It was a little after six-thirty, and he was trying to get the command post up and running in the vast gray-carpeted Detective Bureau meeting room. It never failed to amaze him how much paperwork could be generated by a single crime. Contact reports, witness statements, detective activity reports (DARs), financial workups and preliminary evidence reports. He was already knee-deep in paperwork and even as he pored over documents, uniformed officers, financial crimes detectives and CIU detectives were breezing through the conference center to drop even more reports on the table. Occasionally, the lieutenant or major or colonel also stopped by, wanting to know if he'd magically solved the case yet. Oh yeah, and the phone rang a lot. Reporters wanting quotes. Local businessmen wanting justice. The AG wanting to emphasize once again that he didn't like shootings in his backyard and that the mayor felt major explosions were bad for tourism.

Now he had Fitz on the phone. "Are you watching this?" Fitz was saying. "Can you fuckin' believe this?"

"I'm not watching anything."

"Then turn on the TV!"

Griffin raised a brow, sifted through the precariously stacked mounds of paper for the remote, then turned on the TV. He was instantly rewarded by a live news feed being shown on Channel 10.

"Ah, so that's where all the reporters went. I kind of wondered when they magically disappeared from the parking lot."

"This is not good," Fitz moaned. "So really not good."

Eddie Como's public defense lawyer, an earnest fellow by the name of Frank Sierra, was now explaining to the equally earnest press corps that a true tragedy had happened this morning on the steps of justice. Why, just last night, he'd gotten a fresh lead that proved once and for all his client's innocence. He'd been planning on introducing the new evidence first thing this morning to clear Eddie Como's name. Another fifteen, twenty minutes, that was all he would've needed, and Mr. Como would have been as free as a bird.

"That doesn't sound promising," Griffin informed Fitz by phone.

"I fucking hate lawyers," Fitz growled.

"Don't worry, I'm sure they hate you, too."

Griffin paused long enough to listen to Sierra's next statement. In the conference room, Waters and a bunch of other Major Crimes detectives had also halted to watch the show. Better than Barnum & Bailey, most of these press conferences.

"Late last night," public defender Frank Sierra was saying, "I made contact with a witness who can place Mr. Como halfway across town on the night and time of the second attack, offering corroboration of my client's activities on the evening in question. Ladies and gentlemen, may I please introduce Lucas Murphy."

Eddie Como's lawyer stepped aside, and a gangly kid who couldn't have been more than eighteen took his place. The kid, all arms, legs and zits, stared at the flashing cameras like a deer in headlights. For a moment, Griffin thought the kid might bolt, and Sierra must've thought so, too, because he grabbed the teenager's arm. Then he remembered his audience, and smiled brightly for all the pretty people.

"A witness," Fitz muttered on the phone. "What the hell kind of evidence is that? For fifty bucks or less even I could conjure up a witness."

Sierra announced, "Mr. Murphy works at Blockbuster Video over in Warwick."

Griffin said, "Uh oh."

"Mr. Murphy, on the night of May tenth, could you please tell these fine people where you were?"

"Oh my God!" Fitz went apoplectic. "He's treating him like a witness. Right here on the evening news, he's launching into his defense. I cannot fucking believe this!"

"I was . . . uh . . . well . . . working," the kid squeaked. "You know, um, at Blockbuster."

Sierra was getting into things now. "And did you happen to see Mr. Como that evening, the evening of May tenth, in your video store on Route Two in Warwick?"

"Um . . . yes."

The reporters obligingly gasped. Fitz swore again. Griffin simply rolled his eyes.

On TV, Eddie Como's lawyer practically rubbed his hands together with glee. "Mr. Murphy, are you certain you saw Eddie Como on the night of May tenth?"

"Um, yes."

"But, Mr. Murphy, because I know the fine members of the press will ask this next, *how* can you be so certain it was Mr. Como who came into your store that night?"

"Well . . . I saw his name. You know, on his membership card."

The press gasped again. Fitz mumbled something along the lines of "Oh my God, someone shut that kid up. Quick, get me a gun."

Griffin told him kindly, "Oh yeah, now you're in trouble."

On TV, Sierra paused, beamed for the cameras again, and prepared to move in for the kill. "Mr. Murphy, isn't it true that whenever someone rents a video at Blockbuster, there is a record of the transaction?"

"Well, yeah . . . you know. People hand over their card. We scan that in. Then, you know, we scan in the video. So the computer has um, the video, and um, who rented it, and oh yeah, at what day and at what time. You know, so we know who has what video and if it's late when they return it, in case, you know, they owe any late fees, that sort of thing. You gotta know that stuff if you're a video store." The kid nodded earnestly. "Also, we got this program now, where if you return a new release right away, like, um, in twenty-four hours, you get a dollar credit on your Blockbuster account. So people come inside for the returns to show their card. I mean, a buck's a buck."

Eddie Como's lawyer practically creamed his pants on live TV. "So," he boomed. "Not only did you *personally* see Eddie Como returning a video to your store on the night of May tenth, at ten twenty-five P.M., just five minutes before the alleged attack on Mrs. Rosen, over on the East Side, which Eddie couldn't possibly have driven to in just five minutes, you have a *record* of that transaction. A computer-generated *record!*"

"*Fucking computers!*" Fitz roared.

While on TV, Lucas Murphy, Blockbuster's new employee of the month, said, "Mmmm, yes."

The reporters started to buzz. In the conference room, Waters shook his head and sighed. Over the phone, Fitz sounded like he was moaning, then came the distinct crunch of antacid tablets.

"Come on," Griffin murmured, staring intently at the TV. "Ask him the next question. Ask him the logical next question . . ."

But Eddie Como's defense lawyer was smarter than he looked. Frank Sierra thanked the press, he thanked the Lord for giving them the truth, even if it was tragically too late, and then he yanked his young, big-eyed witness out of the line of cameras while he was still ahead. The news briefing broke up. Channel 10 cut to a shot of good old Maureen, her blue eyes brighter than ever, saying breathlessly, "Well, it has certainly been a big day in the College Hill Rapist case. New information casts doubt that Eddie Como, shot dead just this morning, was indeed the College Hill Rapist. Ladies, does that mean the real rapist could still be out there—"

Griffin shut off the TV. Waters was looking at him, while on the other end of the phone, Fitz continued chomping away on Tums.

"Sierra ambushed us," Fitz growled between mouthfuls of antacid. "Didn't give us any warning. Not even a peep about his new evidence, new witness, nada. One minute I'm down at the morgue watching the ME search for viable skin on a deep-fried John Doe, the next I got a call from my lieutenant telling me I'd better turn on the news. What the fuck is up with that? Sierra could've at least given us the courtesy of a phone call."

"Ah, but then you could've prepared a reply," Griffin said.

"This is bullshit," Fitz continued, full steam ahead. "Sierra's client is dead, so now he's carrying out his case on the evening news, where he'll never have to fear being cross-examined. The public will only hear what he wants them to hear." His voice built again. "*Forget* about three raped women. *Forget* about Trisha Hayes, tied up and asphyxiating in her own apartment. *Forget* that Eddie Como irreparably damaged four innocent lives. Let's just focus on the poor little rapist, who was probably potty-trained at gunpoint. For heaven's sake, why didn't Sierra just march over to the women's homes and personally slap them across the face!"

"It's not conclusive evidence," Griffin said, addressing both Waters and Fitz at once. "Saying he could have Eddie's name cleared by afternoon was overstating things a bit. Who's the prosecutor?"

"D'Amato," Fitz grumbled. He seemed to be working on taking deep breaths.

"Yeah, well, that's why Sierra made his case on TV instead of in the court-room. D'Amato would've eaten this kid alive. Do Blockbuster Video cards contain photo ID? No. Isn't it true that anyone could've come in with Eddie Como's card to return a movie, not necessarily Eddie Como? But he thought the guy did look like Eddie Como? Well then why didn't he come forward before now? Why did he wait a full year to share this news? That's the *real* question."

"He was scared." Fitz played devil's advocate.

"Why? The College Hill Rapist never attacked a man. And don't you have a girlfriend, mother, sister, Mr. Murphy? Didn't you think about them, worry about them? If you really thought Como wasn't the guy, then that means the rapist is still out there. So why didn't you come forward to help catch the real perpetrator and keep your girlfriend/sister/mother safe?"

"I don't know," Fitz said.

"Of course you don't know, Mr. Murphy. That's because it's now been over a year since ten May. How sure can you be after a whole year? Do you remember what you ate that morning for breakfast? What were you wear-ing? What did you do for lunch? Who did you call? Who were your other customers? What video did you watch that night at work? That's what I thought, Mr. Murphy, you don't really remember that much at all about that night, *do you*?"

"Uh oh, I think I just wet myself," Fitz intoned. "You're right, I am noth-ing but miserable scum. On the other hand, those fine, magnificent detec-tives at the Providence Police Department are geniuses, men above men. And that Detective Fitzpatrick, he's a stud. If I had a young, nubile sister, I would send her to him."

"Yeah, but since he's already given his best years to the job, I wouldn't bother."

"Ain't that the truth," Fitz murmured. He took a last deep breath and seemed to come to grips with things. "Computerized records of a rental return. Who would've thought?"

"How sure are you of the time of the rape?"

"It's not exact. Carol Rosen went to bed a little after ten. She thought she'd been asleep about a half an hour when she woke up to a sound in her bedroom. She didn't look at the clock, though."

"So even if Eddie was returning a video in Warwick, that doesn't prove he *didn't* later head into Providence."

"It's not concrete. But if you take this kid's statement and you combine it with Eddie's girlfriend, Tawnya, talking about Eddie's favorite pastime being hanging out with her and their unborn child and watching a few movies . . ."

"Eddie starts looking sympathetic. A quiet family man. Given his fetish, you never checked with Blockbuster?"

"When we asked Eddie what he'd done that night, it was already six weeks later. He thought he might have rented a movie, which was his habit, but when he checked his credit card statement he hadn't. No one thought about a *returned* movie as an alibi."

"Live and learn," Griffin said.

"The DNA evidence is still DNA evidence," Fitz muttered. "God knows, if cops comprised juries, we would send him to the chair. But of course jury boxes are filled with, well, jurors. If Eddie starts looking good . . ."

"The outcome of the trial grows doubtful," Griffin concluded for him. He was quiet for a moment. "You know, if this testimony looked really bad, D'Amato had another option. He could drop the charges pertaining to the second attack. Only try Eddie for Meg Pesaturo, Trisha Hayes and Jillian Hayes. He loses one count of first-degree sexual assault, but life in prison is still life in prison."

"Carol Rosen wouldn't like that much."

"No, she wouldn't," Griffin said meaningfully.

"Even if D'Amato dropped the charges involving Carol so Eddie's lawyer couldn't get Teen Blockbuster in court," Fitz said, "Sierra could still trot the kid out for the press like he's doing now. That makes Eddie start looking good to the public, the ACLU or anyone else who gets off on pitying rapists. And that would piss *all* the women off. Hell, it pisses me off."

"Makes things interesting. Do you think this is what Tawnya meant when she said something was going to come out at trial?"

"I don't know. She's been firm about Eddie's innocence. Seems to me that if she knew about Teen Blockbuster, she would've been shouting this evidence from the rooftop. I had the impression she was talking about something on one of the women."

"Is there something we should know about the women?" Griffin asked sharply.

"Hey, I spent a year with the women, and if there was something we should know, we would know it. Then again," Fitz admitted sulkily, "I'm 'refreshing' my report on them as we speak."

"It provides motive. Particularly for Mrs. Rosen and/or her family."

"Assuming they knew about Teen Blockbuster."

"Which gives us a starting point. How did Eddie Como's lawyer hear about this kid? And how many other people knew about him as well? Assuming, of course, that the kid is telling the truth."

Fitz sighed. "I knew this day was going to end badly. Okay, let's talk it through. Scenario A is that Eddie's lawyer finally got bright and decided to check Blockbuster just in case. Then . . ."

"Kid's probably telling the truth, and never came forward on his own because he didn't want to get involved, or was afraid to get involved, or all of the above."

"All right, so in Scenario A we do have a witness. Which doesn't mean we were *wrong* about what Eddie did after he dropped off the movie," Fitz added testily, "but does make the trial more interesting and the victims/family/friends more anxious about the outcome."

"Agreed."

"Okay, then we have Scenario B, which is that Teen Blockbuster is coming forward now with his own agenda. What might that be?"

Griffin's voice was dry. "Maybe he saw Tawnya. In her own words, she's been beating away the boys since she was twelve. Maybe she decided Eddie needed a little insurance at trial and this was the best way of getting it. Of course, that means someone, probably the kid, had to be willing to mess with Blockbuster's computer system to show a false transaction. I don't know how believable that is."

"Hey, did you see the kid's face? A teenage boy with that many pimples could probably hack into the Pentagon."

"In your own way, you're a real Sherlock, Fitz."

"I like to think so."

"All right," Griffin said. "If it was just the kid's statement, I'd buy into Scenario B. I don't like the computer record, though. That's getting pretty elaborate to be a ruse."

"So we're back at Scenario A, where the kid is legit. Of course, we'll have to pay him a visit to be sure."

"Meaning Eddie Como may have a semblance of an alibi," Griffin filled in.

"No way," Fitz said firmly. "Even if the kid is right, it's just a little confusion over time. So Eddie returned a video in Warwick before he continued on to Providence. There's no rule that says rapists can't run errands. Hell, I'll bet even Ted Bundy tended to daily chores every now and then. But Eddie did it. DNA doesn't lie, and we've got Eddie's DNA. Once, twice, three times. The kid went up to bat, and we have struck him out."

Griffin was quiet for a moment. He had a sense of déjà vu again. For the second time today, he was having a conversation where the evidence against Eddie Como appeared sketchy, *except* for the DNA. And then he finally got what was bothering him about this case. "Hey, Fitz," he said. "How *good* was the DNA match with Eddie Como?"

"Huh?"

"How many points of the DNA matched? A four-point, eight-point, twelve-point match?"

"How the hell do I know? I'm not the guy in a lab coat. The report from the health department said the samples matched. A match is a match is a match."

"Not necessarily."

"Griffin, what the hell are you talking about?"

"I'm not sure yet. But tell me this: Are you absolutely *positive* that Eddie Como didn't have a brother?"

18

Jillian

Jillian got home late. Nearly 9:00 p.m., a late end to a too-long day that had left her jumpy and anxious. She'd checked the backseat of her car four times for interlopers since leaving Meg's house. She'd walked everywhere with her car key sticking out like a weapon from her fisted hand. Once, she had even popped open her trunk, just to be sure. She was protecting herself from overly aggressive reporters, she told herself, but knew that she was lying.

Arriving home, she was grateful to see lights blazing. Since the first phone call from Eddie Como nearly a year before, she had installed motion-sensitive floodlights in the front of her residence, as well as strategically placed spotlights that illuminated each bush and shrub. There would be no skulking around her East Greenwich home. The house also featured a new state-of-the-art home security system with a panic button in every room, and a remote her wheelchair-bound mother kept in her pocket. Jillian hadn't quite convinced herself to buy a handgun yet, but had perhaps gone a little nuts procuring pepper spray. She slept with a canister beneath her pillow at night. Her mom had hers tucked in her bedside drawer. As Toppi had dryly observed, the Hayes women were ready for war.

Jillian pulled into her garage with her car lights on, closed the garage door first, then scrutinized the interior for trespassers before finally unlocking and opening her car door. She once more had her car key protruding like a blade from her fist. She would keep it that way until she entered her home and conducted a brief inspection of the kitchen.

Did you know that approximately one woman is raped every *minute* in the United States? Did you know that women are more likely to be raped in their own homes than anywhere else? Did you know that many intruders bypassed home security systems by simply ducking into the garage behind the woman's car? Did you know that fewer than ten percent of reported rapists go to jail, meaning that an overwhelming number of rapists are still walking the streets, ready, willing and able to strike again?

Jillian knew these things. She read the books. She scrutinized the statistics. Knowledge was power. Know thy enemy. And don't believe for a minute that for some special reason you are entitled to be safe.

Most nights, Jillian went to sleep with a giant knot in her chest. Most nights, around two A.M., she jerked awake with sweat pouring down her face and a scream ripe on her lips. It took some time to recover from these things. She had read that, too. In the meantime—and this was her own philosophy—that's why they invented good makeup.

In the garage, Jillian drew a deep breath, squared her shoulders, then raised her chin. Show time, she told herself, and carefully blanked her face as she walked through the door.

In the kitchen, she immediately encountered her mother's live-in assistant, Toppi, who was leaning against the kitchen counter with her arms crossed disapprovingly over her chest.

"Sorry I'm late," Jillian said. She dropped her purse on the desk in the kitchen, took off her jacket, fiddled with her keys.

"Uh huh."

"How is she doing?"

"She lost her voice, not her mind," Toppi said testily. "How do you think?"

"She saw the news?"

"Of course."

"And the press?"

"Phone's been ringing off the hook. At least until I disconnected it. Not like I was worried about *your* call getting through." The edge returned to Toppi's voice. She gave Jillian another stern look, and Jillian obediently hung her head.

At twenty-six, in a wildly colored skirt and with a mass of kinky brown hair, Toppi looked more like a traveling gypsy than a health-care professional. She was cheerful, energetic and, in theory, Jillian's employee. Toppi, however, didn't answer to anyone. Since she had started three years ago, she had turned their stale little household upside down and inside out. She knew not only what was best for Libby, but what was best for Jillian, Trish and the paperboy down the street. She always gave her opinion freely and with great enthusiasm. Jillian's mother adored her. So had Trish.

"You hurt her," Toppi said now. "I know you don't mean to. I know you have other things on your mind. But you hurt her, Jillian. She's already lost one daughter and when you disappear like this, she worries about you."

"I'm sorry."

"It's not me who deserves the apology."

"I'll tell her, too."

Toppi snorted. "Like she hasn't already heard enough sorries from you. Come on, Jillian, she's your mother. She doesn't want your apology, she wants your presence. Come home for dinner. Read her a story. Or better yet, take her to see Trish."

Jillian hung her car keys on the little hook. Then she picked up the mail and started sorting through. Bills, bills, bills. Junk mail. At least there was nothing from him. She didn't even realize that was what had her so worried, until she came up empty. She set down the stack of mail, and Toppi took that as an opportunity to continue her attack.

"That's where you've been, haven't you? You've been visiting Trish."

"I went there."

"Your mom misses her, too."

Jillian didn't say anything.

"She can't tell stories, Jillian. Surely you understand that. When someone dies, you want to relive their life, and what they meant to you. Share the moments, the laughter, keep them alive a little bit longer by talking about them. Your mom can't do that out loud, but that doesn't mean she isn't doing it in her head."

"I know."

"If you would just sit with her, hold her hand. Let her look at you and tell you everything with her eyes. She does that, you know. In her mind, she is fluent, she does have a voice. If you would just be with her, it would allow her to pretend. She could tell you everything without saying a word. And I think it would mean the world to her."

"I know, Toppi. I know." Old ground. They had been covering it for twelve months now. And Toppi was right and Jillian was wrong, and she wanted to be a better person, but right now, she simply wasn't. At work she had to function, meeting every client's demand or she would lose her business. With Carol, Meg, the press, the police, she had to be capable, always saying and doing the right thing, because she was the leader and she couldn't let anyone down. And then, when she got home . . .

When she got home, she had nothing left. She simply saw her mother, so small and frail and easy to damage. She saw Toppi, hired by Jillian so Trish wouldn't feel guilty about going off to college. And the walls came tumbling down, the barriers eroded and Jillian wasn't ready yet for the woman underneath. Eddie Como had changed her. He'd brought fear into her life, and she would've hated him for that alone. Of course, he'd also done so much worse.

"You bitch . . . I'm gonna get you, even if it takes me the rest of my life. I'm gonna get you, even if it's from beyond the grave."

Jillian opened the fridge. In spite of spending most of her day in a restaurant, she'd hardly eaten a thing. She eyed shelf after shelf crammed with food, but nothing sparked her appetite. Behind her, Toppi was frowning.

"Are you all right?" Toppi asked abruptly. "Lately . . . Jillian, are you all right?"

Jillian closed the door. She started to say, "Of course," but then she saw the look in Toppi's face and the blatant lie died on her lips. She felt her insides go hollow again. The ache, so close to the surface since her discussion with Sergeant Griffin, rose up and pressed back down on her with a heavy, heavy weight. She had lied to the sergeant this afternoon. She had told him she was certain, when in fact she hadn't been certain of anything for a whole year.

"It's been a big day," she said tersely. "I just needed some time to absorb everything. Some time to just be . . . alone."

"With Trish?"

"Something like that."

"Your mom wanted to go there today. I was worried, though, about the press."

"I'm sorry about that."

"It's okay, Jillian," Toppi said gently. "She doesn't blame you. *I* don't blame you. You reserve that right for yourself."

Jillian smiled. She'd heard this lecture before, too. Many times, really. Where was Trish? She leaned against the refrigerator, took a deep breath. "Does it feel different to you, Toppi? Him being dead. Does it feel different?"

Toppi shrugged. "I'm not losing any sleep over it, if that's what you mean. You lead a violent life, you'll come to a violent end."

"What goes around, comes around."

"Sounds good to me."

"I thought it would feel different," Jillian said quietly. "I thought I'd be . . . relieved. Vindicated maybe. Triumphant. But I just feel . . . empty. And I . . . I didn't know how to come home tonight. How to face Libby. I feel . . . I feel like I failed her."

"You failed her?"

"Yes." Jillian smiled again. "I'm in a weird mood. I've been in it all day. Not myself at all. I should go to bed."

"Jillian . . . the police were here. Two plainclothes officers. They wanted to interview Libby until I explained to them that wouldn't be happening. Is there something I should know?"

"No," Jillian said honestly, then shook her head. "Maybe that's the problem. I didn't kill Eddie. I don't know who killed Eddie. And frankly, that pisses me off. Someone else got to him before I had the chance. Someone else killed him, and in my fantasies I had reserved that honor for myself. Apparently, I'm even more bloodthirsty than I thought."

"I've dreamed of killing him, too," Toppi said.

Jillian looked up in surprise.

"Sure," Toppi said. "Guy like that. After what he did to you, to your mom, to Trish. Death isn't good enough for him. They should've hacked off his penis, then left him to live."

"Castration doesn't work with sex offenders," Jillian said immediately. "In fact, studies suggest that surgical or chemical castration leads them to commit even more violent acts, such as homicide. Because it's not about sex, it's about power. Take away a sex offender's penis, and he'll simply substitute a knife."

Toppi was looking at her strangely. "Jillian, you read too much."

"I know. I can't seem to stop."

Toppi was quiet for a moment. "I don't suppose that reading has included information on post-traumatic stress syndrome?"

"It has."

"Because . . . because that kind of thing would be expected, you know. After what you've been through."

Jillian smiled. "I've earned the right to be a little nuts?"

"Jillian, that's not what I meant—"

"I know I'm struggling, Toppi. I know I'm not quite myself. Maybe I didn't forget everything like Meg and maybe I'm not as aggressively hostile as Carol, but I am . . . wounded. There, that's an accomplishment for me right there. I hate saying that out loud. It sounds so weak. Birds get wounded. Children get wounded. I'm supposed to be above all that. Frankly, I wasn't even raped. What do I have to cry about?"

"Oh, Jillian . . ."

"I know I'm being unfair to Libby," Jillian said quietly. "I'd like to tell you

I have a good reason, but I don't know what it is. Right now . . . I just don't feel like coming home these days. Some nights I wish I could go anyplace but here. I'd like to get in my car and just drive. Drive, drive, drive." She smiled again, but it was sad. "Maybe I can work my way to Mexico."

"You're running away from us."

"No. I'm just running. It's the only time I feel safe."

"He's dead now, Jillian. You are safe."

Jillian's shoulders came down. She shook her head and said hoarsely, "But there are so many more just like him, Toppi. I've been reading the books. And you have no idea . . . The world, it is such a bad place." Her shoulders started to shake. God, she was not herself today. And then she was back in that room, that horribly dark room, with Trish needing her, Trish depending on her, and she had not got it done. Far from saving the day, she had nearly gotten raped herself. And now he was gone, and what would give her life meaning without Trisha to take care of or Eddie Como to hate?

And then she was thinking of Meg, *I don't think I was happy,* and she was thinking of Carol, *Let's have some chocolate cake,* and suddenly she knew she had failed both of them. She had turned them into warriors, but long after defeating their enemy, were they really better off? They had nailed Eddie Como, but none of them had managed to heal.

And now Eddie Como was dead and they were unraveling at the seams.

Jillian squeezed her eyes shut, covered her mouth with her hand. Pull it together, pull it together. Her mother was in the next room. And then she was thinking of Sergeant Griffin again, and that confused her even more. Men did not make things better. Just look at Eddie . . .

Toppi had crossed the kitchen. She touched Jillian's shoulder gently as Jillian drew in a ragged breath.

"I'm not an expert," Toppi said quietly. "Lord knows I couldn't have gone through everything you've been through. But I do know this. When you're really hurting, when you're really feeling low, nothing is as good as crying on your mother's shoulder. You can do that, Jillian. She would like that. And it would do you both a world of good."

Jillian drew in another deep breath. "I understand."

"Do you?"

Toppi's gaze was too penetrating. Jillian looked away. She focused on her breathing, getting to slow, steady breaths. Then she wiped her cheeks with her hands, blinked her eyes clear. She should go to bed soon. Get a good night's sleep. Tomorrow would be another day. She would feel better then. Stronger, in control, ready to take on the press, ready to take on the police because it was only a matter of time . . .

"Well, let me go see her," Jillian said briskly.

"All right," Toppi said. "All right." But it was obvious from her voice that she wasn't fooled.

Jillian went into the living room, where her mother sat in her favorite chair watching TV. At sixty-five, Olivia Hayes was still a beautiful woman. Tiny as a bird, with thick dark hair and big brown eyes. Her hair was dyed, of course, every eight weeks at her favorite salon, with six shades of brown to match her original color as closely as possible. Libby had always been vain about her hair. When Jillian was a little girl, she used to watch her mother brush out the long, thick locks when she came home at night. One hundred strokes. Then would come the saltwater gargle to preserve her vocal cords, followed by a heavy cream to protect her face.

"If you take good care of your body," Libby always said with a wink, "your body will take good care of you."

Jillian leaned over. "Hello, Mom," she murmured. "Sorry I'm late." She hugged her mother gently, careful not to squeeze too hard.

When she straightened, she saw something flash in her mother's gaze. Frustration, anger, it was hard to tell, and Libby would never say. Since her stroke ten years ago, she had limited movement in the right side of her body, as well as expressive aphasia—while she could understand communication perfectly, she could no longer speak or write back. As one of the doctors tried explaining to Jillian, in her mother's mind she could think fluently, but when she tried to get the words past her lips, her brain ran into a wall, blocking the flow.

Now Libby communicated via a "picture book," filled with images of everything from a toilet to an apple to pictures of Jillian, Toppi, Trish. When she wanted something, she would tap on the picture. Right after Trisha's funeral, Libby had stroked her daughter's photo so often, she had literally worn it out.

"You saw the news?" Jillian asked, taking a seat on the couch.

Her mother tapped her left index finger once, meaning *yes*.

"He's dead now, Mom," Jillian said quietly. "He can't hurt anyone ever again."

Her mother's chin came up. She had a fierce look on her face, but her fingers remained quiet.

"Are you happy?"

No movement.

"Sad?"

No movement.

"Frightened?"

Her mother made an impatient sound deep in her throat. Jillian paused, then she got it. "You're mad?"

One tap.

Jillian hesitated. "You wanted the trial?"

Hard tap!

"But why, Mom? This way you know he's punished. He can't get off because someone in the jury box has a guilty conscience. We'll never have to worry about parole or some kind of prison break. It's over. We won."

Her mother made another impatient sound in the back of her throat. Jillian understood. Why questions didn't work well with this system. To get the right answer, you had to ask the right question. It was Jillian's job, as the person still capable of speech, to come up with the right question.

Toppi had materialized in the doorway. "You didn't see the news conference at six-thirty, did you?"

"No."

"Eddie's lawyer says he has a witness who proves Eddie couldn't have attacked Carol. Instead, he was across town returning a movie at the time."

"You're kidding!" Jillian sat up straight. Beside her, her mother had flipped open the picture book. Her left fingers frantically skimmed away.

"That's ridiculous," Jillian announced. "Carol's not even sure what time he broke into her house. You can't have a definite alibi without a definite time."

"Some of the press is starting to talk of a miscarriage of justice. Maybe Eddie was railroaded. Maybe the police were a little too eager to have a suspect. Maybe . . ." Toppi hesitated. "Maybe you, Carol and Meg applied a little too much pressure."

"That is absurd!" Jillian was on her feet, her hands fisted at her sides. When backed into a corner, her first reaction was always anger, and now she was in a rage. Quick, someone get her a reporter. Any reporter. She wanted to slug one good. "All we did was put together the blood-donor connection between Trisha and Meg. That's it! Eddie's the one who just happened to have access to their home addresses. Eddie's the one who just happened to see two out of three rape victims within weeks of their attacks. Eddie's the one who just happened to have his semen present in their houses. How the hell does the press explain that?"

"They don't. They just flash clean-cut photos from his high school yearbook and use words like *minority, suspected* of rape, *tragically* shot down."

"Oh for the love of God!" Jillian had to sit down again. Her head was suddenly pounding. She thought she might be ill. "They're turning him into a martyr," she murmured. "Whoever shot him . . . He's making him seem innocent."

Libby thumped Jillian's arm. She had found the picture she wanted. A new one, added by Toppi just one year ago to help Libby communicate about the trial. It featured a blindfolded woman holding the scales of justice.

"I know you wanted the trial," Jillian said impatiently. "I understood that."

Her mother thinned her lips. She tapped the photo more emphatically, this time the scales.

"Justice? Not just a trial, you want justice?"

Hard tap!

"Because we don't have it yet," Jillian filled in slowly. "The press is now trying the case in absentia, and they're using Eddie's looks and ethnicity as evidence. And the only way we could counter is with Eddie himself. By actually having the trial and proving beyond a shadow of a doubt that Eddie Como *is* the College Hill Rapist."

Her mother tapped, tapped, tapped.

"You're right, Mom. I'm angry now, too. We were robbed this morning." Jillian's voice grew bitter. "As if we hadn't already lost too much."

Her mother flipped through the pages again. She came to another picture, this one also new. It looked like a child's drawing, a caricature of a monster with big yellow fangs and red bugged-out eyes. Toppi had done the honors, her rendition of Eddie, because there was no way they would permit his real photo in the picture book. They refused to give him that much presence in their lives.

Now Libby's left hand scrabbled with the page of the photo album. She got the plastic cover back. She yanked Eddie's picture from the sticky back. Then she looked at Toppi and Jillian with her chin up, her brown eyes ablaze, and her lower lip trembling with unshed tears. She crumpled up Eddie Como in her feeble left hand. Then she flung the monster across the room.

Toppi and Jillian watched the paper hit the floor. The wad rolled to a stop five feet away. Then it was still.

"You're right," Jillian said softly. "Eddie Como is gone, so once and for all let's get him out of our lives. Frankly, I'm tired of being afraid. I'm tired of being angry. I'm tired of wondering over and over again what I could've done differently." Her voice rose, gained strength. "Fuck the press, Mom. Fuck the public defender. And fuck some voyeuristic public that has nothing better to do than watch our pain get played out on the nightly news. Eddie Como has taken too much from us, and I'm not giving him anything more. It's over. That's that. We're not talking about him anymore. We're not worrying about him anymore. We're not afraid of him anymore. From here on out, Eddie Como is gone, and we are *done!*"

19

The Victims Club

Ten forty-five p.m.

Carol was not done. She had not gotten Eddie Como out of her life. Instead, she was curled up, fully dressed, in an empty bathtub. The cold porcelain sides gave her a chill, so an hour ago she had pulled down all the towels to keep her warm. It was dark in the upstairs bathroom. No windows, no source of natural light. She didn't know what time it was, but she suspected that it was late. Probably after ten. Things happened after ten.

Dan still wasn't home. The house maintained its silence. Sometimes she hummed to herself simply to make a sound. But mostly she lay in the bathtub, a grown woman who couldn't return to the womb. She rested her head on the hard, cold ledge and waited for the inevitable to happen.

I didn't turn off the TV. I didn't turn off the TV.

It wouldn't matter. It was after ten. She was all alone. And she knew, she knew way down deep, that somewhere in the house, a window was sliding open, a foot was hitting the floor, a man was ducking into her bedroom.

Bad things happened. Women got raped, people got shot, others were blown up by car bombs. Husbands deserted you, wives went crazy, children were never born. Bad things happened. Especially after 10:00 P.M. Especially to her.

Eddie Como had sent her a note. She found it in the day's mail, which Dan had left on the kitchen counter. The pink envelope looked like a Hallmark card and bore Jillian's return address. A nice little note, Dan had probably thought. So had she. Until she'd ripped it open.

I'm going to get you, Eddie had scrawled in red ink across white butcher paper. *Even if it's from beyond the grave . . .*

Carol had bolted back upstairs to the bathroom, but not before first making a stop at the home safe.

I'm going to get you . . .

Not this time, Carol decided. Not anymore, you son of a bitch. Carol reached beneath the towels and, very gently, stroked the gun.

Ten fifty-eight P.M.

Sylvia Blaire was walking home alone from the university library. She had a test tomorrow morning. Final exam for Psych 101. In theory, Sylvia enjoyed Psych 101, but she hadn't kept up on the readings quite the way she should have. Now she was cramming twelve weeks' worth of learning into two nights of studying, a feat she'd mastered in high school, but which was proving far more difficult in college.

Personally, she thought Professor Scalia should cancel the test. As if anyone could study today, with the big explosion just six blocks away, then the sirens wailing all morning long. The air still smelled acrid, a mixture of gasoline, scorched metal and melted plastic. In the student union, all anyone could talk about was the commotion. Frankly, nothing exciting ever happened in Providence. As far as the students were concerned, the school should cancel exam week and let them enjoy the buzz.

No such luck, though. Professors were such pains in the ass. So Sylvia had left the student union in favor of the library, where she'd managed to read six chapters of her textbook before falling asleep and dreaming about chickens scratching out the Pythagorean theorem in return for pellets. Screw it. She was going home to bed.

Sylvia walked down the street to her apartment. Generally there were more people out this time of night, but during finals week most of the students were sequestered away in various study labs suffering massive anxiety attacks. The street was quiet, the old shrouded houses still.

It didn't bother her. The full moon was bright, the lamps cheery. Besides, she knew the drill. Walk with your chin up, your shoulders square and your steps brisk. Perverts sought out meek women who wouldn't fight back, not former track stars like her.

Not that Providence had many perverts anymore. That rapist dude was dead. The women on campus had cheered.

Sylvia finally arrived at the old house that boasted her second-floor studio apartment. She paused on the darkened front steps, then shook her head. Stupid outdoor light had burnt out again. Thing seemed to go every three weeks and the landlord liked to wait another three before replacing it. This one Sylvia had bought with her own money. Like she could see anything tucked inside the covered patio without a light.

She dragged her backpack off her shoulder, and with a long-suffering sigh began digging for her keys. She finally found the heavy metal key chain in the bottom of her bag. The new key ring was a gift from the Rhode Island Blood Center commemorating the donation of her eighth pint of blood just two weeks ago. Way to go, Sylvia, she was now a member of the gallon club.

Sylvia drew out her keys. She flipped through the massive lot that she kept meaning to pare down but never did, until she came to the desired one. She slid her key into the front door lock.

A noise sounded on the right. Sylvia turned her head . . .

Eleven-twelve P.M.

Jillian is dreaming. In this dream, she knows that she is dreaming, but she doesn't care. This dream is filled with warm, happy colors. This dream lifts the weight off her chest and takes her, for the first time in a long time, to a place she wants to go.

Jillian is sixteen years old. She is in a hotel—most of her childhood has been spent in hotels. It is two A.M. and Libby is gone. Her gig ended hours ago, but time has never meant much to Libby. Nights are for singing, dancing, drinking, having a good time. Libby has probably met another man by now and is once more falling in love. At this stage of the game, Jillian is used to the drill. Libby falls in love and disappears even more nights of the week. Her singing grows more robust, she wears her nicest gowns and brings Jillian lots of frivolous gifts. Then the bloom goes off the rose. She dumps him, he dumps her, or maybe his wife comes home. Who knows?

Libby falls out of love. They get a new hotel and she promises to spend more time with her daughter. Until, of course, the next handsome man enters the room.

The last time was different, however. The last time had consequences. Jillian now has a baby half sister, whom she was allowed to name. Jillian chose Trisha.

Three-month-old Trisha has fat pink cheeks and big blue eyes. Her head is covered with a downy mist of soft brown hair. She likes to grip Jillian's finger in her tiny little fist. She likes to kick her tiny little feet. And she gurgles a lot, and blows bubbles a lot, and loves big wet zerberts right on her tummy. She also breaks into a wide, smacking smile every time Jillian picks her up.

Now Jillian is cradling baby Trish in her arms and watching her baby-blue eyes grow heavy with sleep. She tickles Trish's chubby cheek with her finger. She inhales the sweet scent of baby powder. She feels her chest expand with the force of her love and thinks that if she cared for Trisha any more, her heart would surely explode.

Libby has never been the perfect mother. There have been times, in fact, when Jillian has grown close to hating her and her careless ways. But as of three months ago, Jillian forgave her mother everything in return for this one, precious gift. Trisha Jane Hayes. Finally, Jillian has someone she can love with her whole heart. Finally, Jillian has someone who will never leave.

The quiet, still night. The perfect weight of Trisha in her arms. The pure beauty of her baby sister, smiling back up at her and kicking her tiny, little feet.

In the dream Jillian knows she is dreaming, she would like to hold this moment forever. She understands, in this dream she knows she is dreaming, that darkness lingers just beyond her sight. That if she turns her head, the beautiful hotel room will spin away and she will find herself in a far different, uglier place. That if she looks at baby Trisha too closely, baby Trisha will spin away and she will find herself holding her grown sister's dying form. That if she thinks too hard at all, she will realize that this moment never happened, that her baby sister cried most nights for her mother, and that Jillian was actually little more than an overwhelmed sixteen-year-old substitute. In this dream she knows she is dreaming, it is only her love for her sister that is real.

A sound intrudes. In the dream hotel room, the dream Jillian turns her head. She listens to the loud, squawking sirens racing down the street.

But then the hotel room falls away. Baby Trisha falls away. And dream Jillian and the real Jillian realize at the same time that the noise is not a siren on the street.

It is in the house. It is in Jillian's bedroom.

Someone has pressed the panic alarm.

Sound. Carol heard it again. A thud in the nether regions of her home. It was followed by a thump.

Someone was in her house. Someone was genuinely inside Carol's home. The panic that held her in its grip all night gained momentum and became suddenly, terrifyingly real.

Carol's breathing accelerated. Very slowly, she straightened legs that had grown cramped and numb while curled beneath her. Then she drew back the pile of towels and slid way down, until just her eyes peered above the rim of the bathtub. More noises down the hall. Maybe the bedroom. That bedroom. The bedroom.

Very carefully, Carol raised the barrel of her .22 and aimed it at the door.

Now the sound was in the hallway. Footsteps, definitely, coming her way.

"Dan?" she called out hoarsely. Questioningly. Hopefully.

There was no reply.

And then the footsteps stopped, two dark shadows coming to rest in the lighted crack beneath the bathroom door. He was here.

Goose bumps rippled up Carol's arms.

Steady, Carol. Steady . . .

The gun in her hand. The breath held in her chest . . .

She watched the brass doorknob slowly begin to twist.

Jillian bolted out of bed. She grabbed her bathrobe, made it to her door, then did an abrupt about-face and raced back to her bed for her pepper spray. The alarm still sounded shrilly through the house.

Running out into the hallway, she found Toppi standing in a white linen nightgown, looking sleepy-eyed and dazed.

"Did you—"

"No."

"Libby!" they both cried and went rushing for her room.

Jillian shoved through the door, leading with her pepper spray and looking around frantically. Libby was lying in her bed. Her face was stark white. She had the security remote clutched tight against her chest.

"Mom, Mom, what is it?"

Libby raised her trembling arm. She pointed to the window behind them. And very slowly, Jillian and Toppi turned.

Eleven thirty-three P.M.

Griffin was still at headquarters sifting through paperwork and rubbing the bridge of his nose tiredly when the officer on duty stuck his head into the conference room.

"Sergeant."

"Officer Girard."

"Sir, 911 just got a report of a disturbance over in East Greenwich. A home security system is going off, and apparently a woman in a bathrobe is now running through the yard. I thought you'd want to know—the house belongs to Jillian Hayes."

"Damn." A disturbance at Jillian's house tonight of all nights could not be a good thing, and he was at least twenty minutes away. Griffin started talking as he headed for the door.

"Do me a favor, Officer, and put in a call to Detective Fitz."

"He's with Providence?"

"That's the one."

"Sorry, sir, but I believe the Providence detectives are out on a call. I heard it on the scanner, though they seem to be keeping the details hush-hush. Some kind of incident on College Hill."

Griffin drew up short. "On College Hill?"

And Officer Girard repeated, "Yes, sir. College Hill."

The bathroom door swung open. Carol closed her eyes, then squeezed the trigger.

Pop, pop, pop. The tiny .22 leapt in her hand. And the dark shrouded form fell flat on the floor.

"Oh my God," the dark shrouded form moaned. "I think you just shot me."

And Carol said, "Dan?"

Jillian was running. She tore through her yard in her baby-blue bathrobe, shoving back tree limbs, pouncing on bushes. Lights were blazing, neighbors gathering, sirens roaring down the street. She was making a spectacle of herself. She didn't care.

"Come out, come out, you bastard!" she cried. She pointed her pepper spray and attacked a shuddering leaf. "You want to play a practical joke? I'll show you a joke, you cowardly son of a bitch. Come on. Show yourself!"

She ran close to the perimeter. Her neighbors shrank back. She ignored them, tears streaming down her face, her nose running from the blowback of pepper spray. He had to be out here somewhere. He couldn't have gone far. And she would find him, and she would grab him by his scruffy, probably teenage neck, and, and . . .

She needed to hurt someone. She needed to inflict violence and pain, and that scared her, too, so she kept running, trampling new budding bulbs and freshly planted pansies. She had to move. She had to fight. She was not in a dark basement anymore. She was not powerless!

There, that bush. It moved. Cowardly son of a bitch . . .

Jillian made a beeline for the trembling sand cherry, and abruptly ran into something hard. "Umph," she said, falling back a few steps, then belatedly raising her eyes to discover Sergeant Griffin's large, unrelenting form.

"Jillian," he said quietly.

"Did you see what he did?"

"The officers told me what happened."

"It was my mother's bedroom. *Do you know what that did to her?* The EMTs had to come, she's having problems breathing. If that sick bastard gave her another heart attack, I swear I'll kill him myself. I'll find him and I'll rip him from limb to limb!"

"Jillian," he said quietly.

"It was my mother's bedroom! What kind of idiot does such a thing? Today of all days. My poor mother. Oh God, my poor mother . . ."

Her shoulders convulsed, then she was swaying from side to side. She looked down to see that her bathrobe had come open and she was standing half-naked in the middle of her lawn. Sirens everyplace, police lights washing her home in violent red light. People everywhere, staring at her, staring at her home, gossiping about her pain.

Eddie Como lives. Scrawled across her mother's bedroom window in red dripping spray paint. *Eddie Como lives.*

"It's not funny," she mumbled. "It's a horrible, horrible practical joke." And then she swayed again and Sergeant Griffin had to catch her in his arms.

"I'm very sorry," he said.

"I hate this!" Her voice was muffled against his chest.

"Jillian . . ." he said gently, and something about his tone finally cut through her haze. Slowly, she raised her head. His blue eyes were somber. So somber. She stared and stared and stared. And then, for no good reason, she was thinking of his dead wife. What had it been like to love this man? To be held in these strong arms, to look up at this steady gaze, and to still feel yourself, slowly but surely, slipping away?

"What happened?" she whispered.

"I'm very sorry. I just talked to Detective Fitzpatrick . . . On College Hill. There's been another incident."

"But there can't be. Eddie . . . he's gone. It's over, it's ended. Even this . . . It's probably just some teenage jerk with a spray can. Please tell me it's just a teenage jerk with a spray can. I *need* it to be just a teenage jerk with a spray can."

Sergeant Griffin didn't say a word. His arms were still around her, supporting her half-crumpled form, shielding her from her neighbors. He wouldn't let her go until she was ready. She understood that now. He would stand here as long as she needed, support her as long as she needed. It was his job, and even back then, on the pedophile case, the reporters had said that he took his job seriously.

She studied his face, broad, hard-planed, firm. She looked into his steady blue eyes. Impulsively, she reached up a hand and touched the raspy line of his chin. She wondered what he would think to know that no one had touched her, and she had touched no one, for well over a year.

Then very slowly, she straightened up, stepped away, and belted her robe at the waist.

"Brunette?" she asked.

"Yes."

"Latex strips?"

"Yes."

"Is she . . . ?"

"Manual strangulation."

Jillian closed her eyes. "All right, Sergeant. Maybe you had better come inside."

Twelve twenty-one A.M.

The lights were out in the Pesaturo home. Tom and Laurie slept peacefully on the opposite sides of their king-sized bed. Little Molly was curled up with her head at the foot of her pink Barbie bed. While in her room, Meg began to thrash from side to side in the throes of a dream.

Rich chocolate eyes. Soft, gentle hands. A slow lover's smile. His fingers stroke her hair. His hand drifts down to her breast. She arches her back and aches for him to do more.

"We should stop," he whispers in her ear.

"No, no . . ."

"It wouldn't be right." His thumb flickers over her nipple. His fingers squeeze tight.

"Please . . ."

"This is wrong."

"Oh please . . ."

His hand moves down. She arches her hips toward him, straining. And then . . . His hand presses against her. Her whole body thrums. She throws back her head.

Rich chocolate eyes. Soft, gentle hands. A slow lover's smile.

Meg thrashed again in her sleep. She whispered, "David."

20

The Survivors Club

"I shot my husband."

"You *shot* your husband?"

"Last night, when he came home. I was scared. I'd just received another card from Eddie Como—this time bearing your address, Jillian. And . . . I swear I called out Dan's name first. But he didn't answer. So I pulled the trigger, and I . . . well, I hit him in the upper arm. Pretty good, really. The doctor was impressed."

Jillian frowned. "I thought we agreed no guns."

"No, Jillian, *you* said no guns. I, on the other hand, still reserve the right to think for myself. So how do you like that?" Carol's tone grew hot.

In contrast, Jillian's voice remained particularly cool for this first emergency meeting of the Survivors Club. "I think the real question is," she said dryly, "how did *Dan* like that?"

Meg sighed and slid down deeper in her chair. This was not going well. Carol was so agitated she couldn't even sit at the table they'd reserved in the private room of this intimate Federal Hill restaurant. Jillian, on the other hand, was wearing a navy blue power suit buttoned up to her chin and sitting stiffly enough to do the Queen of England proud. The tension was sky high. Except for Meg, of course. She never knew enough to be tense. Besides, this morning she was too busy nursing her first hangover. At least she thought it was her first hangover.

"In the words of my mother," she spoke up now, "could you two please use your inside voice?"

Carol glared at her. Jillian's look was droller.

"Little slow getting going this morning?" Jillian asked.

"You could say that."

"Did you get to worship at the porcelain God last night?"

It took Meg a moment to get it. Oh, puking. "No. At least I don't think so."

"Well, you'll live."

"Excuse me," Carol interjected curtly. "I was discussing shooting my husband. What do I have to do—kill him?—to get some attention around here?"

"I don't know," Jillian replied. "Is that why you shot him?"

"Oh for God's sake—"

"No, you listen to us for a minute—"

"There *is* no us, Jillian. There's just you. It's always been you. Meg and I are merely window dressing for your holy pursuit of justice. Survivors Club. That's a joke. This club isn't about surviving, it's about vengeance. You just can't use that word in front of the press. Well, here we are now. Eddie Como's dead, I've shot my husband, another girl has been attacked, and the press is crying miscarriage of justice. What are you going to do, Jillian? How are you going to *spin* this one?"

Jillian got up from the table. She walked a small circle, then repeated the motion two more times. Her movements were stiff and jerky. Her face was pale and impossible to read. Meg had seen her in this mood only once before. The first time Eddie Como had contacted them. Meg had honestly been a little frightened of Jillian that day.

"Someone trespassed on my property last night," Jillian said crisply. "Someone loosened all the bulbs in my motion-activated lights, then walked up to my home and spray-painted 'Eddie Como lives' on my mother's bedroom windows. Then he screwed the lights back in. For God's sake, my mom had to receive oxygen to recover from the shock. You think I don't understand fear, Carol? You think I don't know what went on in your head last night as you heard unknown footsteps coming down the hall? If I'd had a gun twelve hours ago, I would've shot someone, too. And I probably would've hit a neighborhood boy, which is why I said no guns."

"Holier-than-thou Jillian . . ."

"Goddammit. You want to have this conversation, Carol? Fine. Detective Fitz and Sergeant Griffin are going to be here in less than ten minutes, so let's get it done."

"There you go again, Jillian. I'm trying to have a conversation and *you're* setting an agenda."

Jillian thinned her lips, then switched her gaze to Meg. "Do you want out?"

"What?"

"*Do you want out?* Have you had enough? Are you sick of this group?"

"I don't . . . No," Meg said more firmly. "I don't want out."

"Why not?"

"Because . . . because we need each other. Look at us. Who else could discuss midnight vandalism and shot husbands without looking at us as if we were freaks? With other people . . . the conversations aren't real."

"But these conversations aren't real either!" Carol said impatiently. "That's my whole point. It's been a year. We're beyond polite conversation, victims' rights or legal strategy. At least we should be. If *we* are the Survivors Club, then it's time we got down to the business of surviving. Or maybe the fact that we're *not* surviving. Except you don't want to have those conversations, Jillian. You're fine about getting the police in here to give us briefings, or getting D'Amato to present legal tactics. But when it's simply us, all alone, ragged, raw, *emotional*. You shut down, Jillian. Worse, you shut us down. And that's not fair. Frankly, if I wanted to be treated like that, I'd go home to my husband."

"Armed?" Jillian asked.

"If I had a brain in my head," Carol snapped.

Jillian finally smiled. The wan expression, however, only made her look tired.

"I'm sorry," she said quietly.

Carol regarded her suspiciously. Meg yawned, wishing they would both just get on with it. Jillian's and Carol's personalities were like oil and water, but they did need each other. They all needed each other, especially now, when a new girl had been raped and murdered. Meg kept thinking it could've been her. And poor Jillian, she had to be thinking of Trish. After a night like last night, how could she not be thinking of Trish?

Jillian's chin had come down a fraction. She regarded Carol steadily. "It's possible . . ." Jillian's voice trailed off. She cleared her throat, tried again. "When I'm under stress, when I'm angry, it's easier for me to remain focused. To outline a plan of attack and implement that plan. I need to keep busy. Keep . . . moving. I suppose I might be forcing that approach onto the group."

"I can't do that," Carol said flatly. "I go home to the same house every night, to the same husband who didn't come home in time, to the same second-story room where a man crawled through a window and took away my life. You can get some distance from things. Meg can get some distance from things. I can't. That night has become like mud, and I'm just spinning my wheels in it over and over again."

"Why don't you sell the house? Why don't you move?" Meg this time. She was curious.

"Dan loves that house," Carol said immediately.

"I'm sure he loves you more."

Carol didn't say anything. The look on her face was enough.

"He shuts you out that much?" Jillian asked softly. The mood in the room shifted. Grew more subdued. And Meg was thinking again, that poor, poor girl. They were fighting with each other, but really, underneath it all, that poor, poor girl.

"Dan shuts me out so much, I don't know why he bothers coming home," Carol was saying. Her shoulders had come down, her angry expression giving way to a pain that was far worse. "He won't talk. He won't fight, grieve or even rationalize. The subject is strictly off-limits. We live in a house with a giant elephant both of us pretend not to see."

"You've never talked about the rape?"

"In the beginning we talked about what the doctors said. Then we talked about what the police said, or what D'Amato said. Sometimes we talk about what our group says. So we talk. About what other people say."

"It's got to be hard for him," Meg spoke up. "I mean, he's a guy. Look at my father. He still hates himself for not being there when Eddie attacked me, and he didn't even live in my apartment. For your husband, that's gotta feel like a hundred-pound weight around his neck. I wonder what other guys say to him."

"Other guys?"

"Well, sure, guys talk. Well, okay, not really. I mean, not like us. But he's a guy and other guys know his wife was raped in his own home. That's gotta make him feel . . . bad. Like a first-class failure. What kind of man doesn't protect the woman he loves? I know if something ever happened to my mom, my father would get out the brass knuckles. Then probably a chain saw. And then my Uncle Vinnie would . . . Well, that's a whole 'nother story."

"He had no way of knowing what was going to happen that night," Carol said.

Jillian looked at her curiously. "Have you told him that?"

Carol hesitated, then shook her head.

"Why not?"

"Because I do blame him, all right? Because I prayed for him to come home that night. I lay there while that man did unspeakable things to me *hoping* that Dan would come home. And it went on and on and on, and still, where was my husband? I *needed* him. How could he not come home?"

"He had no way of knowing . . ." Jillian tried.

"You said yourself he was always working late," Meg offered.

"*But he wasn't at work!* Goddammit . . . Goddammit." Carol sat down hard. She buried her face in her hands. And then in the next moment, her head came back up and her cheeks were covered in tears. "I'd suspected it for months. All the late nights. All his sudden 'meetings.' So I started calling his office. There was never any answer. Never. And then, that night. I called his office at nine-thirty. Nobody was there. Nobody. Face it. My husband couldn't save me from being raped because he was too busy fucking his girlfriend."

"Oh, Carol . . ."

"Oh, Carol."

"So how do you bring that topic up?" Carol demanded thickly. "Huh? Anyone? Hey, Dan, I'll apologize for being raped if you'll apologize for having an affair. Or, Dan, how about I say I'm sorry for being an emotional train wreck if you'll say you're sorry for not coming home in time to stop my attacker. Or, I'll say I'm sorry for not being able to have children if you'll say you're sorry for constantly shutting me out, for putting your job ahead of me, for ensconcing me in some four-thousand-square-foot mausoleum that only reminds me of how much I am alone. And then what happens? We grow old together, always looking at each other and knowing what big failures we are?

"That's the problem with marriage, you know. You start out wanting intimacy, and then when it happens, you remember too late that familiarity breeds contempt."

"Do you still love him?" Jillian asked.

"Oh God, yes," Carol said, and then she started to cry again. For a long time, no one said a word.

A knock sounded at the door. The waitress, an old hand with their meetings, poked her head in.

"Jillian, the police are here."

Jillian looked at Carol. "Do you want to postpone?"

It was, Meg thought, the closest Jillian had ever come to a peace offering.

Carol, however, was already pulling herself back together. She picked up a napkin, worked on blotting her face. "No. Let them in. We have to hear about this girl. We have to know."

"It's probably just a copycat," Jillian said.

"It's not," Meg spoke up.

"We don't know that."

"I do."

"Meg—"

"No, if Carol can have a nervous breakdown, then I should be able to have my feelings, too. And this feels all wrong. This girl, she was one of us. Except we learned about her too late."

Carol and Jillian frowned at her, reunited again over their shared sentiments for flaky little Meg. But Meg stuck to her guns. She was right about this. She knew. This morning the eyes had been following her again. And she had understood for the first time. Eddie Como's death. It was not an end for them, but simply a new beginning.

That poor, poor girl . . .

"Show the police in," Jillian told the waitress.

"I'm sorry, Carol," Meg murmured.

"I'm sorry, too," Jillian said.

Then they all fell silent as Detective Fitzpatrick and Sergeant Griffin walked into the room.

21

Fitz

Taking in the three women for the second time in as many days, Griffin's first thought was that none of them looked nearly as composed as yesterday. Carol Rosen, sitting across the table, bore the red cheeks and puffy eyes of someone who'd recently been crying. Jillian Hayes, standing at the head of the table, had the pale features and dark shadows of someone who hadn't gotten any sleep at night. Finally, Meg Pesaturo, sitting closest to the door, looked pasty around the edges. Hangover, he would guess. From yesterday's champagne. Maureen had included eyewitness testimonies from the rue de l'espoir as part of this morning's news report.

The women didn't know it yet, but they were rapidly becoming the center of a first-rate legal hailstorm. And all this after Eddie Como had been dead for only twenty-four hours. It made Griffin wonder what the next twenty-four might bring.

"Jillian, Carol, Meg." Fitz greeted each woman in turn. Griffin didn't know if Fitz was even aware of it, but he always greeted the women in the same order. By rank, Griffin thought dryly. Or ascending order of victimhood.

The women didn't say anything. They just stared at Fitz and Griffin with the flat eyes of people who were expecting bad news and only wanted to get it over with.

"Thank you for taking the time to meet with me," Fitz said formally, pulling out a chair and preparing to take a seat. "I'm sure you all remember Detective Sergeant Roan Griffin from yesterday. I invited Sergeant Griffin to join us as a professional courtesy—to the extent that last night's activities may be tied in with the death of Eddie Como, the sergeant is also participating in this case."

Griffin smiled at the group, careful not to let his gaze linger too long on Jillian. Professional courtesy. You had to like that. Fitz had just welcomed him to the party while simultaneously putting him firmly in his place. You couldn't get anything past these Providence boys.

"Now then," Fitz said briskly. "I understand there was some excitement at your home last night."

Carol and Jillian both said, "Yes."

Fitz's smile grew tight. "Carol, why don't you start."

"I got a note," Carol said stiffly. "In a pink envelope. The return address was Jillian's. I didn't look at the postmark. When I opened it, however, it was from Eddie."

"Do you still have it?"

Carol's chin came up. "I know the drill."

"All right. What did the note say?"

"It said, 'I'm going to get you. Even if it's from beyond the grave.' I . . . panicked a little. I was home alone and that scared me more. So I got my gun out of the safe. And then, well, unfortunately, I ended up shooting Dan when he returned."

"Taking your marital tensions a little seriously there, Carol?"

"It was an honest mistake!"

"Uh huh. So how is he?"

"He'll survive," she said stiffly. "It's going to take some time, however, for his left arm to heal. And well, probably more time before he'll feel safe walking down the halls of his own home. Of course, I already know all about that."

Fitz ignored that bitter comment and switched his gaze to Jillian. "Your turn."

"Someone spray-painted in big red letters 'Eddie Como lives' on my mother's bedroom window. Then he reactivated the motion-sensitive lights to make sure she woke up and saw it as he was running off my property. Good news, my mother will live. Bad news, graffiti boy won't. Not once I find him." Jillian spoke in clipped tones.

Fitz grunted. He'd probably already read the East Greenwich police file, which basically said the same. With photos, of course. He turned to Meg.

"And you?"

She shrugged. "Nothing. Let's face it, I'm the boring one."

"Thank God for small favors. You three generate any more paperwork, and the city's going to run out of uniforms to work the cases." Fitz's voice was harsh. He'd been up all night. Working the College Hill scene and catching snippets of the other events on his cell phone. Twenty-four hours without sleep took its toll on a man. Fitz's eyes were red rimmed, his cheeks sallow. His last few strands of graying brown hair stood up wildly on his head, while his rumpled white dress shirt strained over his gut with two new stains. Looked like mustard and ketchup. He'd probably caught dinner/breakfast on the run, grabbing something from the Haven Brothers Diner outside City Hall. Been serving the men in blue for decades, and they all had the cholesterol levels to prove it. Having only slept an hour or so himself, Griffin knew these things.

"Speaking of which," Jillian said levelly.

Carol joined her. "Did he do it? Just tell us that, Detective. Did he do it?"

Fitz leaned back until his chair was balanced on only two legs. He contemplated the room, regarding each woman in turn and taking a long time before answering. "Did he do it? That is the million-dollar question now, isn't it? If by him, you mean Eddie Como, and if by it, you mean attack a girl last night on College Hill, then the answer is no. Hell, no. Eddie Como is dead. I've seen the body. Sergeant Griffin's seen the body. Eddie Como is dead." Abruptly, Fitz slammed forward. "I even understand you ladies drank a champagne toast in his honor."

Carol startled. A moment later, all three of them had the good grace to blush.

"Jillian, Jillian, Jillian," Fitz chided softly, his gaze going to the head of the table. "I thought you were smarter than that. Did you really think the press wouldn't follow up on your whereabouts yesterday morning? Did you really think that in a whole restaurant crowded with people, at least one or two wouldn't be willing to talk?"

"It was my idea," Carol started.

"It doesn't matter," Jillian spoke up. "We all agreed to order the champagne. We all drank it. If people have a problem with that, then it's their problem. We're not public officials running for office. We're not even movie stars or local celebrities. We're just people, and our business is our business."

"Don't be naïve," Fitz said curtly. "You sought out the press on your own last year. The minute you did that, you made your problems everyone else's problems. You can't go back on that now."

"He was our rapist! He died. What the hell did they think we were going to do? Tear out our hair? Throw our bodies on his grave?"

"It would've helped!"

"Helped who? He killed my little sister. Fuck Eddie Como! *Fuck him!*"

"Fuck him, Jillian? Or *kill him*?"

Jillian blew out a breath. She walked away from the table. "Now, now, Fitz. You keep talking and I'm going to want my lawyer present."

Fitz flicked a glance at Griffin. Griffin hadn't planned on bringing this up yet, but what the hell.

"Can your lawyer explain the large cash withdrawals recently made from your savings account?" Griffin inquired.

"You've been busy, Sergeant."

"I try," he said modestly. Both Carol and Meg were staring at Jillian curiously. While Jillian didn't seem surprised by the question, they clearly were.

"I needed the money," Jillian said after a moment.

"Why?"

"Personal reasons."

"What personal reasons?"

"Personal reasons unrelated to Eddie's demise."

"You're going to have to prove that," Griffin said.

"Are you charging me with something, Sergeant?"

"No."

"Then I don't have to prove anything."

Griffin had to nod. He'd seen that coming. Jillian prided herself on appearing cool, and when under pressure, becoming even cooler. Except last night. She hadn't been the composed, corporate woman then. Her long hair had been down, wild and thick around her face. Her movements had been frenzied, her fear honest, her rage unfettered. And her hands, when they had closed upon his shoulders, had been seeking genuine support as her legs collapsed beneath the weight of those red, dripping letters scrawled upon her home. Her mother, he realized abruptly. Jillian was calm when it came to herself. But when her family was threatened . . .

Stupid thought for the day—Cindy would've liked Jillian Hayes. Really bad idea for the day—he was beginning to like her, too.

"Tell us about that attack," Jillian said.

Fitz thinned his lips. "You know I can't discuss an ongoing police investigation."

"Detective," Carol protested.

"Fitz!" Meg chimed in.

Fitz merely shook his head. He was pissed. Even Griffin could see that. If he didn't know any better, he'd guess that the women's cold front had hurt the detective's feelings.

"We could help," Jillian said.

"Drink more champagne?"

"We made a mistake." Carol's turn. "Detective, please. We have to know. Surely you understand. This new batch of mailings, then this vandalism at Jillian's home and then this attack on College Hill. We feel like we're losing our minds."

"Mailings?" Griffin interjected. "As in plural, with an 's'?"

Carol and Meg simultaneously turned to Jillian. "I got one, too. Last Friday. A computer disk, sent to my house with my business address as the return. I didn't look at the postmark, either. You would think we'd all know better by now." She smiled miserably, then got on with it. "The disk contained a video file. A leering picture of Eddie Como, who told me he'd get me for doing this, even if it was from beyond the grave. I should've told you, Detective Fitzpatrick. I know. But at the time, I wrote it off as one last prank before the trial started. He'd already mailed us so much stuff. It seemed silly to bother with one more."

"You still have the disk?"

"Envelope and all. I touched it with my bare hands, though. I should've examined it more closely first. I'm sorry."

Fitz sighed unhappily. He appeared tired and frustrated and fed up with all of them. Perpetrators were bad, but all homicide detectives could tell you that sometimes the victims were even worse. You got to know them more. You grew to care. And then, with the best of intentions, they fucked you royally and all you could do was remind yourself that it wasn't really their fault. People were people. And everyone made mistakes.

"So we got a theme," Fitz said finally. "Eddie Como wants vengeance, even if it's from beyond the grave."

"Interesting choice of words," Griffin commented.

Jillian had caught it, too. "Yes," she said slowly. "It's almost as if he knew he was going to die."

An uncomfortable silence filled the room.

"You don't suppose . . ." Carol said.

"He arranged for his own death?" Meg picked up with a frown. "Why would anyone do that?"

"Could be merely coincidence." Fitz shrugged. "Remember, real life is stranger than fiction."

"Detective." Jillian turned to him with pleading eyes. "The new incident last night. You of all people know what this is doing to us. We understand you don't owe us anything. We understand there is a police protocol . . . But this is so close to home. After everything we've been through. Please . . ."

Fitz hesitated one last time, probably for ego's sake, but the end was never in doubt. He rubbed his red-rimmed eyes, then ran a hand through his thinning hair. "Yeah. All right. You might as well know because the press is gonna come after you, too. We had another assault. A Brown University student. She was attacked in her apartment, tied up with ten latex strips, raped and then . . . strangled to death. She was pronounced DOA at the scene."

"Her name?" Meg asked.

"You really want to know that?"

"I do."

"Sylvia Blaire."

"Her age?"

"Twenty."

"What was she studying?"

"I'm not sure. Psychology, I think. We're still putting together the victim profile."

"Was she pretty?"

"Come on, Meg." Fitz gestured impatiently. "Don't do this to yourself. She's gone now. Learning all this . . . You're just going to torture yourself with it in the middle of the night."

"We need to know," Meg said quietly. "*I* need to know."

"It won't help you, Meg."

Meg smiled gently. "I'm not looking for help, Detective. I'm looking to learn about Sylvia Blaire, a young college student just like Trisha Hayes or myself. This is the Survivors Club, after all. And one of the obligations of survivors is to learn about the other victims and remember them well."

A heavy silence filled the room. Fitz didn't know where to look. Neither did Griffin. And for the first time he got something about the women, their group, this club. They had become a unit. They gave each other strength. And Sylvia Blaire, if she hadn't died . . .

Fitz looked old. Fitz looked like a detective who'd been to one too many crime scenes, and this one, this last one, would be the one he'd never get out of his head. Guys around here liked to retire to Florida, but even there, most of them would say, the images still followed. Too many sad faces staring back up from the tranquil blue waters as they cast their lines and tried to fish.

"In her photos she was very pretty. Long dark hair, big brown eyes. A former high school track star. Got good grades. Donated time to the Boys & Girls Club in Pawtucket."

"A regular blood donor," Jillian filled in.

"Yeah," Fitz said heavily. "Yeah."

"It sounds like him," Carol spoke up. Her gaze went around the room. "You have to admit . . ."

"Too soon to know." Fitz shook his head, his voice picking back up. "Sure, there are common elements, but this isn't exactly a case that's been held back from the public."

"You think it might be a copycat," Jillian filled in.

"It's a possibility. The victim profile—young, brunette, college student— is hardly rocket science. All anyone has to do is flip on the TV and see a picture of Meg or Trish. The connection with the blood drives, also on the evening news, given that Eddie worked as a phlebotomist for the Blood Center. And that latex-ties business came out shortly after Eddie's arrest. So there you have it. One rapist profile, ready to go."

"Was there sign of forced entry?" Jillian again.

"Nah."

"That wasn't in the news."

"Might not be a stranger-to-stranger crime."

Jillian frowned, then got it. "Meaning maybe someone this girl knew—an ex-boyfriend, say—staged this as one of the College Hill Rapist's attacks to cover up what he had done."

"Could be."

"Did she have an ex-boyfriend?"

"It's only been eight hours. Ask me in another two."

"What about fingerprints?"

"We took all sorts."

"DNA?"

Fitz hesitated, shot Griffin a look. Griffin didn't say anything; it was Fitz's party after all. Jillian, however, was too fast for both of them. Her eyes widened. Her face paled. Very slowly, her arms wrapped around her waist.

"No," she whispered.

"Yeah," Fitz said.

"But the douche wasn't in the news. None of the reports *ever* gave out that information."

Carol was picking up on things, looking around the room even more wildly. "Are you saying . . . Was it the same kind?"

"Berkely and Johnson's Disposable Douche with Country Flowers." Fitz sighed again, then brought up his hand and rubbed his bleary face. Griffin had done much the same when Fitz had given him the news. The douche was the kicker. You could spin the scene so many ways, until you got to the douche.

"But . . . but," Meg said. She couldn't seem to get beyond that. "But . . . but . . ."

"Let's not rush to any conclusions," Fitz warned.

"There are still other possibilities," Griffin said.

"Like what?" Jillian cried.

"Like maybe Eddie had a friend," Fitz stated flatly. "Or maybe he liked to brag all about it. Just because *we* didn't give out the details doesn't mean that he didn't."

"He always claimed he was innocent," Carol said, her eyes still dashing all about. "You don't say you're innocent, and then brag all about your crime."

"Sure you do, happens all the time."

Meg had started rocking back and forth. "It's not a friend. It's not a friend. Oh God, oh God, oh God . . ."

"Meg . . ." It was Jillian, her voice hard, trying to restore order.

But Meg was beyond reason. Carol was beyond reason. Only Jillian remained tight-lipped and determined at the head of the table. Her gaze rose to meet Fitz's, to meet Griffin's.

"Eddie Como lives," she whispered helplessly. "Oh God, Eddie Como *lives.*"

22

Griffin

Griffin and Fitz stepped outside the restaurant, and the first camera flash exploded in their faces.

"Detective, Detective, can you comment on reports that last night's victim was also tied up with latex strips—"

"Was it true that a man matching Eddie Como's description was seen running from the girl's apartment—"

"Sergeant, Sergeant, will the state police now be taking over the case—"

"What does this latest attack mean for the case against Eddie Como—"

"Detective, Detective—"

"Is it true that someone used blood to scrawl 'Eddie Como lives' on the wall of the new victim's—"

"What about rumors that the man shot yesterday wasn't really Como?"

Fitz and Griffin finally forced their way to Fitz's car. Technically, Griffin had arrived in his own vehicle, but given that it was parked another two blocks away on the crowded street, Fitz's beat-up Taurus beckoned like a godsend. Griffin used his shoulder to muscle back one particularly aggressive reporter, got the passenger-side door open and ducked inside just as a new round of flashes erupted from the herd. A cry went up. The women were now trying to leave the restaurant. The whole pack shifted right and immediately surged forward.

"Shit," Fitz said.

"Shit," Griffin agreed.

They abandoned the Taurus and grimly waded back into the fray.

"Step aside, step aside, step aside."

"Police, coming through."

On the restaurant steps, Jillian stood shell-shocked in front of Carol and Meg as more lights flashed and heated questions started peppering the tiny space. She had probably thought their little rendezvous was safe from the press. In a private room in a restaurant that she knew. She probably hadn't seen the morning news and the public flogging the local news affiliates had delivered to both the Providence Police and the so-called Survivors Club for their aggressive pursuit of Eddie Como. She probably hadn't realized just yet, that last year's press coverage had only been a warm-up. Now, as of this morning, was the real thing. She and Carol and Meg could run. But they could not hide.

Jillian's features had turned the color of ash. A moment later, however, she recovered her bearings and got her chin up. Behind her, Carol had raised a hand in a vain attempt to shield herself from the cameras. Meg simply looked dazed.

"Ms. Hayes, Ms. Hayes, how do you respond to allegations that your group pressed too hard for Eddie Como's arrest?"

"Do you believe this newest attack proves Eddie's innocence?"

"What about the defense attorney's witness? Mrs. Rosen, how sure are you of the time when you were attacked?"

"Ms. Hayes, Ms. Hayes—"

"Did you shoot Eddie?"

"Hey, step aside. State police, don't make me seize your tape."

In all honesty, Griffin couldn't legally seize any of the reporters' tapes, but evidently word of what he'd done to Maureen had gotten around, because three reporters immediately leapt back and snarled at him. He gave them his most charming smile. Then he flung out his massive arms and forced the rest of the jackals back four steps.

Not an idiot, Jillian seized the opportunity to grab Meg's and Carol's hands and bolt from the steps.

"Ms. Hayes, Ms. Hayes—"

"Did you persecute an innocent man?"

"What about his wife and baby?"

"Hey, Miss Pesaturo, remember anything yet?"

The Survivors Club disappeared around the corner and the last question dissipated into the crisp morning air. The press corps took a second to regroup. Then they went after Fitz and Griffin again.

"Who's leading the investigation?"

"What will be your next steps?"

"Is the real College Hill Rapist still out there? What is your advice for all of our young women?"

"Press briefing at four," Fitz barked. "Through official channels. For God's sake, we're just the working stiffs. Now get outta our way."

He and Griffin still had to battle their way back to Fitz's car. This time, they both managed to get inside the Taurus and slam the doors. The reporters tapped on the window. Fitz gunned the engine.

Not doubting for a moment that a Providence cop would run them over, the reporters finally dropped back. Fitz pulled away from the curb while simultaneously digging around his feet for a bottle of Tums. Griffin amused himself by picking up the newest edition of *People* magazine from the dash. Sure enough, Fitz had already inked in half of the crossword.

"You're fucked," Griffin said conversationally.

Fitz had gotten his Tums open. He started chomping. "At this rate, we're all fucked."

"I'm not fucked. I just have a dead rape suspect. Same as yesterday."

"Don't kid yourself. Eddie turns up innocent, we're all fucked. The women'll get heat for applying pressure. We'll get heat for making the arrest. DA'll get heat for building the case. State marshals will get heat for not better protecting one of their transports. And you, the lucky state, will get heat for not stepping in and keeping the rest of us from fucking up. So there."

"You're an optimist, aren't you, Fitz?"

"Tried and true. Goddamn case." Fitz's features grew more haggard. "Goddamn case . . ."

Griffin understood. He lapsed into silence, giving Fitz a chance to pull himself back together as they drove aimlessly around Federal Hill.

"Dr. No," Griffin said finally.

"Dr. No?"

"Forty-eight down. A four-letter James Bond movie. *Dr. No.*"

Fitz grunted, felt around his shirt pocket, then handed Griffin a pen.

"I'm honored," Griffin assured him, and filled in the spaces.

"You went to the Hayes residence," Fitz said. "Last night."

"I did."

"Why?"

"A uniform caught the report on the scanner and let me know. I figured anything happening at Jillian's place the same day as Como was shot couldn't be good."

Fitz looked at him. "You just called her Jillian."

"Mmmm, yes."

"I haven't met a statey yet who doesn't use formal address when working a case. For God's sake, you guys don't even refer to each other by first names. You're like a bunch of friggin' Marines."

"I'm the black sheep?"

"Don't go getting any ideas, Griffin. This case is messy enough."

"You like her that much, Fitz?"

For his answer, Fitz growled and flexed his hands on the wheel. "I am having a really bad day."

"We're both barking up the wrong tree," Griffin told him lightly. "Have you ever asked Jillian Hayes what she thinks of men in our profession? She's not exactly an aspiring groupie. In fact, from what I can tell, she pretty much considers us incompetent morons who are at least indirectly responsible for her sister's death. Hence her total openness and willingness to cooperate with us now."

Fitz grunted, which Griffin took as at least partial acknowledgment of Jillian's point.

"Serial crime is the worst," Fitz grumbled after a moment. "Longer it goes on . . . more victims the perp claims . . . Yeah, maybe I should just be happy I can still find my pants in the morning, 'cause these days I'm sure as hell not finding much else."

"You're riding the case hard," Griffin said. "It's the most a detective can do."

Fitz grunted again. "That incident at Jillian's house, you think it was a prank? Some teenage kid armed with a can of red spray paint and up to no good?"

"It's East Greenwich's call."

"Don't fuck with me, Griffin. Not after the night I've had."

Griffin was silent for a moment. "I don't know," he said finally, then held up a hand to ward off Fitz's snarl. "Honest. The spray paint, graffiti, yeah that fits with a teenage kid. But loosening the bulbs in the motion-sensor lights . . ."

"I wondered about that."

"When you were a kid going to egg someone's house, did you unscrew the outdoor lights?" Griffin shrugged. "Couldn't have done it at night either. The minute someone approached in the dark, the lights would go on. So that means it was done before, during the day, when no one would notice the lights being activated."

"Premeditation."

"Seems very thoughtful. For a kid."

"Ah shit . . ."

"My turn. Off the record, just you and I. Last night, what are you thinking?"

"Christ, I haven't had enough sleep to think." Fitz rubbed his face wearily, then belatedly grabbed the steering wheel as the car swerved across the street.

"There's still the DNA evidence."

"Yeah, that's what bothers me so much. If it had been merely a circumstantial case, just the fact that he worked for the Blood Center and knew the victims, well then . . ."

"You might have jumped too soon."

"Maybe."

"But you got DNA."

"We got *good* DNA. I went back after our little discussion yesterday evening. Grabbed the report. Given the high-profile nature of the case, we sent the samples out to an independent lab in Virginia in addition to the analysis done by the Department of Health. Both agree. DNA samples from Eddie Como match DNA samples taken from the sheets and the women in all fourteen sites tested. Meaning the likelihood of another person being responsible for the DNA present at the rape scenes is one in three hundred million times the population *of the entire earth*. That's pretty damn conclusive if you ask me."

"Sounds pretty good to me, too," Griffin agreed. "Do the women know this?"

"D'Amato knows this. He's the one who sent it out for the independent analysis, plus it was gonna be the linchpin of his case. He probably went over it with them."

"Meaning they must really, truly feel that they *know* Como was the attacker."

"Hey, I *know* Eddie was the attacker."

"Meaning we're back to a very good motive for murder."

Fitz blew out a breath. "I hate this."

"I know."

"What kind of fucking case is this, anyway? You got me doubting my own victims, and the press has me doubting my own perp. I don't like this. This is not what police work is supposed to be about. You gather the evidence, you put together a theory, you build a case, you nail the SOB. End of story. Eddie Como lives. Christ, it's like being in the middle of a freak show."

"I'm not a big fan of it either."

"I think it's an accomplice," Fitz said abruptly.

"Eddie talked?"

"Yeah. Makes the most sense. Maybe in her own way, Tawnya's right, and all she's ever seen of him is good-boy Eddie. But we know for a fact that there's also a bad-boy Eddie who was running a few more errands than returning a movie to Blockbuster's one night. Now bad-boy Eddie has a need to live on the edge, explore the wild side. And maybe bad-boy Eddie also needs to talk about it later. To some other bad-boy friends that I'm betting Tawnya doesn't even know about."

"Eddie Como led two lives."

"Wouldn't be the first time. And it fits."

Griffin nodded his head. "True."

"Now consider this. Maybe one of those bad-boy friends has spent the last year fantasizing about all those stories he heard from Eddie. Maybe he's even bought a few bondage magazines and gotten heavy into the darker side of porn. But twelve months later, none of it gives him that same secret thrill. Then one day, he turns on the news and lo and behold, Eddie Como is dead. And it comes to him. He could do it. He knows everything from Eddie, so why not? He'll become the College Hill Rapist and *nobody will suspect a thing*. The MO points to Eddie and Eddie can't deny it because he's dead. Eddie can't even say, well I told everything to so-and-so, because again, Eddie's dead. It's the perfect cover."

Griffin regarded him steadily. "Why stop there, Fitz? Maybe the other guy has been fantasizing about the rapes for a year. Maybe he's been thinking he'd like to try that. Except rather than wake up one morning and discover Eddie Como is dead, maybe he decided to ensure the perfect cover, by arranging Eddie's death."

"Shit!" Fitz pounded the steering wheel, and very nearly drove them into a streetlight. "Of course! It's *Single White Female,* except with, well, Freaking Violent Rapists. Why didn't I think of it?"

"Because it's borderline preposterous," Griffin said quietly.

"I don't care."

"I know. Which is the second problem."

"Huh?"

"Off the record. Way off the record. Between two experienced detectives. You need the College Hill Rapist to be Eddie Como."

"Hey now—"

Griffin shook his head. "I know what it's like. I've been there myself. The internal pressure, the external pressure. The media isn't wrong. At a certain point, we all have to get our man."

"You think I'm all wigged out because maybe I gave in to the public's demand for justice and screwed a major investigation?"

"No. I think you're all wigged out because maybe by rushing the investigation, you missed Sylvia Blaire's killer."

Fitz didn't say anything, which they both knew was a yes. If Eddie was innocent, if the real College Hill Rapist was still out there . . . then Fitz had screwed up, and probably the women had screwed up, and not only were two young girls dead, but Eddie Como, Jr., was orphaned for no reason, and someone, probably a victim or a family member, had been driven to murder for no reason. The cost, the carnage, grew very high.

Which was one of the fundamental problems with a long-term investigation. At a certain point, the suspect *had* to be guilty, because everyone involved in the case couldn't afford for it to be otherwise.

Fitz had finally come around the block again and located Griffin's car. He double-parked beside it, ignoring the irate honking that promptly sounded behind him.

"One in three hundred million times the population of the earth," Fitz said. "Think about that."

"I will."

"Hey, Griffin, how much money was missing from Jillian's account?"

Griffin hesitated, his hand on the door handle. "Twenty thousand."

"Enough to hire a shooter."

"Probably." Griffin hesitated again. "Fitz, she's not the only one. Dan Rosen is up to his eyebrows in hock. He took out a second mortgage on his home six months ago for a hundred thousand. Then last week, he liquidated one of his brokerage accounts. The financial guys are still trying to figure out where that money went."

Fitz closed his eyes. "And the day just keeps getting better and better."

"Nothing on the Pesaturo accounts yet," Griffin said, "but I think we all know that they wouldn't need money to hire an assassin."

"They already got Uncle Vinnie."

"Exactly."

"You really think one of them did it."

"I think it's the answer that makes the most sense."

"Yeah." Fitz nodded, sighed heavily, then went fishing for more Tums. "I like them, you know. You're never supposed to get too close, but after the last year, the shit they've been through, the way they've held up, Jillian, Carol and Meg. They're good people. I've been . . . proud . . . to work with them."

"We'll get this figured out."

"Sure." Fitz looked at him. He smiled, but it was bitter. "State's involved now. And the state always gets their man, right, Griff? Not like us hardworking city cops who are only fit for drive-by shootings and other lowbrow gangbanging hissy fits. No, state detectives never make any wrong turns in an investigation. State detectives never succumb to *pressure*."

Griffin's hand spasmed on the door handle. A muscle leapt in his jaw. The buzzing was almost immediate in his ears. Very slowly, he let go of the handle. Very slowly, he took a deep breath and counted to ten.

"You've had a rough night," Griffin said quietly when he finally trusted himself to speak. "So I'm going to do us both a favor and pretend you didn't say that."

Fitz continued to regard him steadily. His pupils were small and dark, his sagging face twisted into a stubborn scowl. For a moment, Griffin thought Fitz would push it anyway. Probably because he had had a rough night, spent at the side of a young girl who never should have died. And now the press was beating up on him, the state was beating up on him, and probably, within the next half an hour, his lieutenant would be beating up on him. And that kind of frustration could build in a man. Build and build and build, until you didn't care anymore. You thought too much about those poor young victims, all the ones that if you'd just moved faster, thought smarter, fought better . . . Until your desire to destroy was even higher than your desire to be saved.

Then you went home and held your dying wife in your arms, so weakened by cancer she couldn't speak, but only blink her eyes. Soon that would be gone, too. You would just come home, sit in an empty house and see images of missing children dance before your eyes.

"Go home and get some sleep," Griffin said.

"Fuck you, Griffin. You know, I may not be young like you. I may not be able to bench-press three times my body weight or whatever the hell it is you do in your free time. But don't underestimate me, Sergeant. I'm old. I'm bitter. I'm fat. I'm bald. And that gives me a propensity for violence you can only dream about. So don't you lecture me about procedure and don't you patronize my handling of a case. Oh, and one more thing. I know where Jillian's money went."

"Fitz—"

"Call Father Rondell of the Cranston parish. Tell him Jillian gave you his name."

"The Cranston parish?" Griffin frowned, then blinked. "Oh, no way."

"Yeah way. I *know* these women, Sergeant. I *know* them. Now get the fuck out of my car."

Griffin shrugged. Griffin got out of the car. "You know, Fitz, these cross-jurisdictional investigations continue to improve relations all the time," he said.

"Yeah, that's my thinking, too."

Fitz peeled away from the curb. Griffin headed for Cranston.

23

Jillian

The waves rolled into the beach, gentle today, peaking low with a cap of frothy foam, then fading back into the dark depths of the ocean. The sandpipers rushed into the retreating wake of low tide, searching frantically for anything good to eat. Slow day on the beach this early in May. Another dark green wave descended upon the sand, and the small white birds took flight.

Jillian continued watching the water long after she heard the car pull up, the engine turn off, the door open, then close. Footsteps in the sand. The thought reminded her of the religious poem she'd read as a child. She smiled, and the pain cut her to the bone.

She had never been good at belief. Never been one for faith. Too many nights alone as a child maybe. Too many promises broken by her mother, until she internalized, somewhere way down deep, that the only one she could depend upon was herself. Yet she had flirted with religion, talked about it with friends, found herself attending the occasional Christmas mass. She loved the sound of a choir singing. She took comfort, during the endless gray days of winter, from going to a cathedral warmed by hundreds of bodies, standing side by side in communal worship.

Trisha had joined a Congregational church when she was in high school. She'd gotten quite into things. Faith in a higher power fit her rosy outlook on life. Conducting good works suited her bubbly nature. Jillian had attended services with her several times, and even she had been struck by the glow that filled her sister's face during prayer. Faith recharged Trisha. Made her somehow even bigger, larger, more *Trisha* than she had been before.

Until the night she had truly needed God . . . or Jillian . . . or even a big, strong policeman intent on doing his job.

If there was a God, and He hadn't seen fit to save Trish, then should Jillian really feel so guilty? Or maybe there was a God, and He had turned to Jillian as His instrument, and by not being up to the task, she had failed Him and her sister both. So many thoughts she could torture herself with in the middle of the night. Or even during bright spring days in May, standing in the warm caress of the sun and watching the ocean break against the shore.

Oh God, Sylvia Blaire. That poor, poor girl. What had they done?

"Jillian."

She didn't turn around. She didn't need to, to know who it was. "Bring your thumbscrews this time?"

"Actually, we're always armed with thumbscrews. Department policy. But I'm a good old Catholic boy—I wouldn't dream of using thumbscrews on a priest."

She stiffened, then finally turned. Sergeant Griffin stood in the sand outside the deck railing. His cheeks were dark and shadowed, the line of his jaw impressively square, his eyes impressively bright. Even ten feet away, she could feel the impact of his presence. The broad shoulders, muscular arms, bulging chest. No different than any other state policeman, she thought resentfully. It was as if the department had a mold, and churned out one well-chiseled officer after another. She'd never been one for brawn anyway. She considered the size of a man's muscles directly inverse to the power of his brain.

"You should've just told me," he said now, his voice quiet but firm.

"Why? I'd already said the money had nothing to do with Eddie's death. If you weren't prepared to believe that, why should I have expected you to believe an even bigger fairy tale?"

"It's not a fairy tale."

She shrugged. "Close enough. I gave the money to Father Rondell in cash, took no receipt, ensured there were no witnesses, and made anonymity the primary condition of the donation. If you want evidence of where the money went, I have none to give you."

"A priest's word is pretty good evidence."

"Yes, but he wasn't supposed to tell you."

Griffin smiled. "I confess, all good Catholic faith aside, I kind of tricked him."

"You tricked a priest?"

"Well, it was for a good cause. I was proving a woman's innocence."

Jillian snorted. "Let's not get carried away."

"Actually, I can't take all the credit. Fitz told me to go talk to Father Rondell. So I approached him, saying that I needed confirmation that you had donated money to help Eddie Como's son. Immediately, he was quite gushing about your twenty-thousand-dollar generosity. It seems that Eddie, Jr., has a guardian angel."

"It's not his fault what his father did. He wasn't even born."

"Tawnya doesn't know?"

"Nobody knows."

"Not even the Survivors Club?"

"Not even the Survivors Club."

"Why, Jillian?"

"I don't know," she said honestly. "I just . . . Trish was gone. Carol's a mess. Meg has lost her past. And I . . . well, I have my own issues, don't I? Last year when the police finally arrested Eddie, I expected to feel better. Vindicated, satisfied, something. But I didn't. Because Trish was still gone, and Carol's still a mess and Meg still has no memory, and now we're seeing pictures of Eddie's pregnant girlfriend and all I can think is here's another victim. A baby who will grow up without his father. One more destroyed life. It seemed too much." She shook her head. "I needed . . . I just needed something good to come out of all of this. I needed to feel that someone would escape Eddie's mistakes. And God knows we never will."

"So you set up a trust fund for Eddie's child."

She shrugged. "I asked Detective Fitzpatrick for the name of someone close to the Como family. He gave me Father Rondell's name. Father Rondell took care of things from there."

"But you kept it secret."

"I didn't know if Miss Clemente would accept the money if she knew where it came from."

"And why not tell Meg and Carol?"

"I didn't think they'd like it. Besides, it's not really their business, is it? It's my money. My decision."

Griffin smiled. "You like to do that. Be a group player as long as it suits you, but revert back to an individual the minute it cramps your style."

She just looked at him. "How did you know I was here?"

"Brilliant detective work, of course."

She snorted again. He raised his right hand. "Scout's honor. Finding you is my biggest accomplishment today. Well, other than tracing your money, but Fitz is the one who connected those dots. After talking to the priest, however, I wanted to confirm the transaction with you. Being of sound mind, however, I figured you wouldn't magically take my call. So I figured I needed to see you in person. And then I started thinking, if I were Jillian Hayes, where would I be today of all days, with the press hot on my heels? I figured you wouldn't go to work, because you wouldn't want to turn your business into a media circus. Then I figured for the same reason, you couldn't go home—it would just bring the press down on your family. Then I confess, I made a wrong turn and tried your sister's gravesite. For the record, three reporters already had it staked out."

Jillian looked at him curiously. "I did try there first. After spotting the reporters, however, I turned away."

"Exactly." He nodded. "Then it occurred to me. Like any good Rhode Islander, you're bound to have a beach house. So I did a search of Narragansett property records. Nothing in your name. Then I tried your mother's. The rest, as they say, is history."

"I see your point. Positively brilliant detective work. So who killed Sylvia Blaire?"

Griffin promptly grimaced. "Touché."

"I'm not trying to be cruel. At least not yet."

"Are you beginning to doubt Eddie's guilt, Jillian?"

"I don't know."

"That's the same as a yes. May I?" He gestured to the three steps leading up to the deck. She hesitated. Nodding would invite him in. He'd take a seat, become part of her last hideaway, and she had such little privacy left. Maybe he'd even sit close to her. Maybe she'd feel the heat of his body again, find herself staring at those arms.

When her legs had given out last night . . . When he had caught her in his arms, and shielded her from her neighbors' voyeuristic stares . . . She remembered the warmth of him then. The feel of his arm, so easily supporting her weight. The steadiness of his gaze as he waited for her to pull herself together once more.

And she *hated* herself for thinking these things.

Jillian moved to the opposite side of the deck from the stairs. She was still in her navy blue suit from this morning, and it was difficult to negotiate the deck boards in heels. She took a seat on a built-in wooden bench. Then, finally, she nodded.

"It's nice here," Sergeant Griffin commented, climbing aboard. "Great view."

"My mother bought it twenty years ago, before Narragansett became, well, Narragansett." She gestured her hand to the oversized homes that now bordered the property. Not beach houses anymore, but beach castles.

"Never thought of expanding?"

"If we built out, we'd lose the beach. If we built up, we'd block the view for the house across the street. And what would we gain? A bigger kitchen, a more luxurious bedroom? My mother didn't buy this place for the kitchen or bedroom. She bought it for the beach and the ocean view."

"You have an amazingly practical perspective on things."

"I grew up with a lounge singer, remember? Nothing teaches you to respect practicality more than growing up on the New York club circuit."

"Different hotel every night?"

"Close enough." She tilted her head to the side. "And you?"

"Rhode Islander. All my life. Good Irish stock. My mother makes the best corned beef and cabbage and my father can drink a man three times his size under the table. You haven't lived until you've been to one of our family gatherings."

"Large family?"

"Three brothers. Two of them are state marshals, actually. We've probably been policing for as long as there have been cops. If you think about it, it's a natural fit for Irishmen. No one knows how to get into trouble better than we do. Ergo, we're perfect for penetrating the criminal mind." He smiled wolfishly.

Jillian felt something move in her chest. She gripped the edge of the wooden bench more tightly, then looked away.

"Jillian, you said that in the voice lineup, you and Carol could narrow it down to two men. What was it about the two?"

"I don't understand."

"Why those two men? What made you focus on them?"

"They . . . they sounded alike."

Griffin leaned forward, rested his elbows on his knees. His blue eyes were intent now. Dark, penetrating. She found herself shivering, though she didn't know why. "Think back, Jillian. Take a deep breath, open up your mind. You're in the viewing room. The mirror is blacked out, but one by one, men are stepping forward and speaking into a microphone. You are listening to their voices. One strikes close to home. Then another. Why those two voices?"

Jillian cocked her head to the side. She thought she understood now. So she closed her eyes, she tilted her face up to the warmth of the sun and she allowed her mind to go back, to that dark, claustrophobic room, where she stood with just a defense attorney and Detective Fitzpatrick, dreading hearing that voice again and knowing that she must. Two voices. Two low, resonant voices sounding strangely flat as they delivered the scripted line "I'm gonna fuck you good."

"They were both low pitched. Deep voices."

"Good."

"They . . . Accent." Her eyes popped open. "It's the way they said fuck. Not fuck, but more like foik. You know, that thick Rhode Island accent."

"Cranston," Griffin said quietly.

She nodded. "Yes. They had more of a Cranston accent."

"Como grew up in Cranston."

"So it's consistent." She was pleased.

"Jillian, *lots* of men grew up in Cranston. And most of them do butcher the English language, even by Rhode Island standards. We still can't arrest them for it."

"But . . . Well, there's still the DNA."

"Yeah," Griffin said. "There's still the DNA. What did D'Amato tell you about it?"

She shrugged. "That it was conclusive. He'd sent it out to a lab in Virginia and they confirmed that the samples taken from the crime scenes matched Eddie Como's sample by something like one in three hundred million times the population of the entire earth. I gather it's rare to have that conclusive a match. He was excited."

"He told you this. All three of you?"

Jillian brought up her chin. "Yes."

"And that convinced all three of you, the Survivors Club, that Como was the College Hill Rapist?"

"Sergeant, it convinced D'Amato and Detective Fitzpatrick that Eddie was the College Hill Rapist. And if we'd been able to go to trial, I'm sure it would've convinced a *jury* that Eddie was the College Hill Rapist."

"What about the Blockbuster kid?"

"What about him? Carol's never been sure about the time she was attacked. You'll have to forgive her, but while she was being brutally sodomized she didn't think to glance at a clock."

"Jillian . . ." Griffin hesitated. He steepled his hands in front of him. He had long, lean fingers. Rough with calluses, probably from lifting weights. His knuckles were scuffed up, too, crisscrossed with old scars and fresh scratches. Boxing, she realized suddenly. He had a pugilist's hands. Strong. Capable. Violent. "Jillian, did they get a sample from your sister?"

Her gaze fell immediately. She had to swallow simply to get moisture back into her mouth. "Yes."

"So he . . . before you came . . ."

"Yes."

"I'm sorry."

"I was late," she said for no good reason. "I was supposed to be there an hour earlier, but I'd gotten too busy . . . Something silly at work. Then traffic was bad, and I couldn't find parking. So I'm driving around the city and my sister is being . . . I was late."

Griffin didn't say anything, but then Jillian hadn't really expected a reply. What was there to say, after all? She was late, her sister was attacked. She couldn't find parking, her sister died. Running late shouldn't matter. Not being able to find parking in a congested city shouldn't cost someone her life. But sometimes, for reasons no one could explain, it did.

What silly mistake had Sylvia Blaire made last night? Waited too late to head home? Not paid enough attention to the bushes around her house? Or maybe the mistake had been earlier, falling in love with the wrong man or breaking up with the wrong man? Something that had probably seemed completely inconsequential at the time.

Which led her to wonder, of course, what mistakes the Survivors Club might have made with the best of intentions. *Had* they pressured the police too hard? *Had* they believed in Eddie's guilt too quickly? She honestly didn't know anymore, and this level of doubt was killing her. Trish was bad enough. She didn't know if she could stand any more blood on her conscience.

"You didn't see the man?" Griffin asked finally.

Jillian closed her eyes. "No," she said tiredly. "As I've told Fitz, as I've told D'Amato . . . I didn't see anything that night. My sister had a basement apartment, the lights were turned out . . . He rushed me from behind."

"But you remember his voice?"

"Yes."

"You struggled with him?"

"Yes."

"What did you feel? Did you grab his hands?"

"I tried to pull them away from my throat," she said flatly.

"Were they covered with something?"

"Yes. They felt rubbery, like he was wearing latex gloves, and that made me think of Trish . . . worry about Trish."

"What about his face? Did you go after his face, try to scratch him? Maybe he had a beard, mustache, facial hair?"

She had to think about it. "Nooooo. I don't remember hitting his face. But he laughed. He spoke. He didn't sound muffled. So I would say he didn't have anything over his head."

"Did you hit him?"

"I, uh, I got him between the legs. With my hands. I had knit my fingers together, you know, as they teach you in self-defense."

"Was he dressed?"

"Yes. He had clothes, shoes. I guess he'd already done that much."

"What was he wearing? You said you hit him between the legs, what did the material feel like?"

"Cotton," she said immediately. "When I hit him, the material was soft. Cotton, not denim. Khakis, maybe some kind of Dockers?"

"And higher?"

"I hit his ribs . . . Soft again. Cottony. A button. A button-down shirt, I guess." She nodded firmly, her head coming back up. "That would make sense, right? For that neighborhood. When he walked away he would be nicely dressed, a typical student in khakis and a button-down shirt."

"Like Eddie Como was fond of wearing?"

"Exactly." She nodded her head vigorously.

He nodded, too, though his motion was more thoughtful than hers. After a moment, he twisted around on the bench, looked out onto the water. Sun was high now. The beach quiet, the sound of the water peaceful. Just them and the sandpipers, still trolling the wet sand for food.

"Must be a great place to come on weekends, recover from the demands of owning your own business," he said presently.

"I think so."

"Does your mom still come?"

"She likes to sit on the deck. It's a nice adventure for her and Toppi, once the weather gets hot."

He looked at her sideways. "And Trisha?"

She kept her voice neutral. "She liked it, too."

"Tell me about her, Jillian. Tell me one story of her, in this place."

"Why?"

"Because memories are good. Even when they hurt."

She didn't say anything right away, couldn't think of anything, in all honesty. And that panicked her a little. It had only been a year. May twenty-fourth of last year. Surely Trisha couldn't fade away that quickly. Surely she couldn't have lost that much. But then she got her pulse to slow, her breathing to steady. She looked out at those slowly undulating waves, and it wasn't that hard after all.

"Trisha was mischievous, energetic. She would crash through the waves like an oversized puppy, then roll on the beach until her entire body was covered in sand. Then she would run over to me or Mom and threaten us with bear hugs."

"And what did you do?"

She smiled. "Made faces, of course. Trisha could tell you. I'm not into water or gritty sand. I take my beach experience on oversized towels with an oversized umbrella and a good paperback novel. That's what made it so funny."

She turned to him finally, looked him in the eye. "Tell me about your wife. If memories are so good, even when they hurt, then tell me about her."

"Her name was Cindy, she was beautiful, and I loved her."

"How did you meet?"

"Hiking up in the White Mountains. We were both members of the Appalachian Mountain Club. She was twenty-seven. I was thirty. She beat me going up Mount Washington, but I beat her coming down."

"What did she do?"

"She was an electrical engineer."

"Really?" Jillian looked back at him in surprise. Somehow, she had pictured this phantom wife as someone . . . less brainy, she supposed. Maybe a blonde, the perfect foil for Griffin's dark good looks.

"She worked for a firm in Wakefield," Griffin said. "Plus she liked to tinker on the side. In fact, she'd just come up with a new type of EKG before she got sick. Got the patent and everything. Cindy S. Griffin, granted a patent for protection under U.S. copyright laws. I still have the certificate hanging on the wall."

"She was very good?"

"Cindy sold the rights to her invention for three million dollars," Griffin said matter-of-factly. "She was very good."

Jillian stared at him. She honestly couldn't think of anything to say. "You don't . . . you don't have to work."

"I wouldn't say that."

"Three million dollars . . ."

"There are lots of reasons to work. You have money, Jillian. You still work."

"My mother has money. That's different. I want, need, my own."

Griffin smiled at her. "And my wife made money," he said gently. "Maybe I also want, need, my own. Besides"—his tone changed—"I gave it all away."

"You *gave* it all away?"

"Yeah, shortly after the Big Boom. Let me tell you, if going postal on a suspected pedophile doesn't convince people that you're nuts, giving away millions of dollars certainly does."

"You gave it all away." She was still working on this thought. Trying to come to terms with a police detective who must make, what, fifty thousand a year, giving away three million dollars. Well, okay, one point five million after taxes.

Griffin was regarding her steadily. She was surprised he was telling her all this. But then again, maybe she wasn't. He hadn't really needed to come to her home last night in person. He really didn't need to clarify her donation to Father Rondell face-to-face. Yet he kept showing up and she kept talking. They were probably both insane.

"When Cindy first signed the deal," Griffin said, "first negotiated selling the rights, it was the most amazing thing. For five years she'd been working on this widget, and then, voilà, not only did she make it work, but she sold it for more money than we ever thought we'd have. It was amazing. Exciting. Wonderful. But then she got sick. One moment she was my vibrant, happy wife, and the next she was a doctor's diagnosis. Advanced pancreatic cancer. They gave her eight months. She only made it to six."

"I'm sorry."

"When Cindy had earned the money, I liked it." He shrugged. "Hell, three million dollars, what's not to like? She took to shopping at Nordstrom, we started talking about a new home, maybe even a boat. It was kind of funny at the time. Surreal. We were two little kids who couldn't believe someone had given us all this loot. But then she got sick, and then she was gone. And the money . . . It became an albatross around my neck. Like maybe I'd made some unconscious deal with the devil. Gain a fortune. Lose my wife."

"Guilt," Jillian said softly.

"Yeah. You can't get anything by us Catholic boys. Probably a shame, too. Cindy wasn't like that. Up until the bitter end, she was thinking about me, trying to prepare me." Griffin smiled again, but this time the smile was bittersweet. "She was the one who was dying, but she understood I had the tougher burden to bear."

"You had to live after she was gone."

"I would've traded places with her in a heartbeat," Griffin said quietly. "I would've climbed gladly into that hospital bed. Taken the pain, taken the agonizing wasting away, suffered the death. I would've done . . . anything. But we don't get to choose which one of us dies and which one of us lives."

Jillian nodded silently. She understood what he was saying. She'd have given her life to save Trish.

"So here we are," she said at last. "I gave my money to a suspected rapist's son to assuage my guilt. And you gave yours to . . . ?"

"American Cancer Society."

"But of course."

He smiled at her again. "But of course."

"How long has Cindy been gone?"

"Two years."

Her voice grew softer. "Do you still miss her?"

"All of the time."

"I'm not doing a good job of getting over Trish."

"It's supposed to hurt."

"She wasn't just my sister. She was my child. I was supposed to protect her."

"Look at me, Jillian. I can bench-press my own body weight, run a five-minute mile, shoot a high-powered rifle and take out pretty much any shit-head in this state. But I couldn't save my own wife. I *didn't* save my own wife."

"You can't fight cancer."

Griffin shrugged. "What is someone like Eddie Como if not a disease?"

"I didn't stop him. I was late, so late. Then I was down in Trish's apartment, seeing her on the bed. And I knew . . . I knew what had happened, what he had done, but then he came at me. Knocked me to the floor, and I tried. I tried so hard. I thought if I could just break free, find the car keys, go after his eyes. I'm smart, I'm well-educated, I run my own business. What's the point of all that if I couldn't break free of him? What's the point if I couldn't save my sister?"

Griffin moved closer. His eyes were dark, so blue. She thought she could drown in those depths, but of course they both knew that she wouldn't. And then she thought that maybe he would touch her again, and she didn't know if that would be the nicest thing to happen to her, or the very worst.

"Jillian," he said quietly. "Your sister loves you."

Jillian put her head in her hands then. And still he didn't touch her. Of course he didn't touch her. For he was still a homicide detective and she was still a murder suspect and it was one thing to catch her as she was falling and quite another to cradle her against his chest. And then there was a new sound in the background. Another vehicle, bigger this time, more guttural, the sound made by a white news van. The press was finally as smart as Sergeant Griffin.

And Jillian cried. She wept for her sister. She wept for Sylvia Blaire. She wept for the grief it had taken her a full year to finally confront. She wept for those moments in the dark apartment, when she'd tried so hard and failed so smashingly. And then she wept for those days, not so long ago, when Trish had run happily along this beach. Days and days and days that would never come again.

And then she heard the guttural engine die. She heard the van door slide open, the sound of feet hitting her gravel drive. She raised her head. She wiped her tears. She prepared to fight the next war. And she thought . . .

Days and days and days that would never come again . . .

24

Maureen

Going around the house to the front drive, Griffin saw good ol' Maureen, already out of the van and adjusting her mike. Griffin knew immediately from the light in the reporter's eyes that they were in trouble. Maureen's gaze shot from him to Jillian and back to him.

"Hey, Jimmy," she called out. "Come out here. I need you to get a shot of this."

Griffin knew better than to rise to the bait. He found himself taking another step forward, positioning himself between the emerging cameraman and Jillian. Not that Jillian required a shield. She'd already wiped her cheeks, touched up her mascara, squared her shoulders. From mini-breakdown to pale composure in ten seconds or less. If he hadn't actually witnessed her crying, he wasn't sure he would've believed it himself. And, frankly, that worried him a little.

"What ya doing, Griff?" Maureen asked with naked speculation.

"Police business."

"Didn't know you made house calls."

"Didn't know you wanted to be arrested for trespassing on private property."

"She can't have me arrested. It's not her property. It's her mother's."

"I have power of attorney over my mother's affairs," Jillian spoke up. "So, yes, I can."

"Oh." Maureen finally faltered. But then she brought up her chin and gave them another dazzling smile. "Then I'll only take a minute of your time."

"No comment," Jillian said.

"I haven't asked the question yet."

"Whatever it is, the answer remains no comment."

"Oh, well, Mr. and Mrs. Blaire will be very sad to hear that."

"Mr. and Mrs. Blaire?"

"Yes, the parents of the slain college student? They flew in from Wisconsin this morning to claim her body. Very nice people. Apparently Mr. Blaire owns a dairy farm which supplies milk for all that wonderful Wisconsin cheese. Sylvia was their only daughter. The real apple of their eye, quote, unquote. They were so proud of her getting a scholarship to an Ivy

403

League school. The first member of their family to get a college degree and all that."

Maureen smiled again. Griffin had to fight back the urge to wring her neck.

"I don't understand what this has to do with me," Jillian said.

"Well, they want to meet you, of course."

"They want to meet me?"

"The head of the Survivors Club? Absolutely!"

"I'm not the head of the Survivors Club. There is no head of the Survivors Club."

Maureen waved her hand carelessly. "Oh, you know what I mean. You are the woman whose face has been in the news. They really do want to speak with you."

"Why?"

"To ask you why you didn't save their daughter, of course." Maureen smiled. Jillian stiffened as the arrow struck home.

"Maureen—" Griffin growled.

"You need to leave," Jillian said.

Maureen ignored them both. "Do you still believe Eddie Como was the College Hill Rapist? What about reports that Sylvia Blaire was also tied up with latex strips? What does this new attack mean for the allegations against Como? And even more importantly, *what does it mean for the safety of the women in this city?*"

Maureen stuck out her microphone greedily. Jimmy homed in with his camera. And Griffin took three steps forward, never raising a hand, never touching a hair on either reporters' head, but effectively blocking their shot with the broad expanse of his chest.

"The homeowner has asked you to leave," he said firmly. Ominously.

"Don't you mean the murder suspect?"

"Maureen . . ."

"What ya gonna do, Griffin, seize my tape?" Maureen dropped her microphone. Far from being intimidated, she stepped right up to him and jabbed her finger into his chest. "I have First Amendment rights here, Sergeant, so don't you go threatening me or my cameraman. I don't care if you think freedom of the press is the root of all evil. As far as I'm concerned, a little fourth-estate action is exactly what we need around here. For God's sake, a man was gunned down at our own courthouse yesterday morning. Now another young college student is dead. And what are you doing about it? What is *she* doing about it?" Maureen jerked her head toward Jillian. "Something about this whole case stinks and I have not only a constitutional right but a civic obligation to do something about that."

"Maureen Haverill, defender of the free world," Griffin drawled.

"Goddamn right!"

"You've been reading your own press briefings again, haven't you?"

"You son of a bitch—"

"I am sorry Sylvia Blaire is dead." Jillian spoke up quietly, unexpectedly. All heads swiveled toward her.

"What?" Maureen said.

"I'm sorry Sylvia Blaire is dead," Jillian repeated. "Her family has my deepest sympathies."

Maureen stepped back from Griffin, motioned furiously at Jimmy, and quickly adopted her most serious reporter's expression. The woman could cry on command. Griffin had seen her do it once by plucking a nose hair. "Do you believe Eddie Como was the College Hill Rapist?" she asked Jillian, thrusting her microphone forward.

"I believe the police conducted a thorough and responsible investigation."

"Ms. Hayes, another young girl is dead."

"A tragedy we should not lose sight of."

Maureen frowned. "Surely you understand there is a connection between Sylvia Blaire's attack and the College Hill Rapist."

"I wasn't aware that the police had made any such connection."

"You don't *want* the police to make any such connection, isn't that true, Ms. Hayes? Because if the police did make a connection, that would mean the police were *wrong* about Eddie Como. That would mean *you* were *wrong* about Eddie Como. *You and your friends have spent the last year persecuting an innocent man.*"

"I have spent the last year aiding the police and the district attorney with their investigation into who brutally raped and murdered my nineteen-year-old sister, Trisha Hayes. I want justice for what was done to my sister. I think anyone who has lost someone they love can understand that."

"Even at the expense of an innocent man?"

"I want the man who brutally killed my sister. No one else."

"What about allegations that you and your group, this so-called Survivors Club, contributed to a miscarriage of justice by whipping the public into a witch-hunt mentality, desperate for an arrest?"

"I think the citizens of Providence should object to being characterized as an angry mob."

Maureen scowled again. Jimmy made the mistake of choosing that moment to home in on her face with the camera. She furiously waved him off.

"Sylvia Blaire is dead," Maureen said.

Jillian was quiet.

"Eddie Como is dead."

Jillian remained silent.

"From the RISD parking lot, the police have another, unidentified body at the morgue. That's three dead people in a space of twenty-four hours."

Jillian still didn't say anything. Maureen changed tactics.

"The day the police arrested Eddie Como, you said you were pleased they had gotten their man. You stood with Meg Pesaturo and Carol Rosen on the steps of City Hall and all but publicly branded Eddie Como as the College Hill Rapist."

"The police had compelling evidence—"

"Another girl is *dead*! Raped and murdered just like your own sister!"

"And I am sorry!"

"*Sorry?*" Maureen trilled, "*Sorry* doesn't help Sylvia Blaire. *Sorry* doesn't give Mr. and Mrs. Blaire their beautiful young daughter back."

"It is not our fault—" Jillian bit back her own words, shook her head. Her composure was beginning to slip, her voice starting to rise angrily. Griffin tried to catch her with his gaze, but she would no longer look at him.

"You pushed for justice," Maureen persisted.

"We were raped! Of course we pushed for justice."

"You told the public they weren't safe until the College Hill Rapist was put behind bars."

"They weren't!"

"You held numerous press conferences, applying enormous pressure on the Providence police to make an arrest."

"Four women had been attacked. The police were already under enormous pressure!"

"You said you were happy with Eddie's arrest."

"*I was happy with Eddie's arrest!*"

"Yeah? Well, how do you feel about his *death*? Need more champagne, Ms. Hayes? It's not every day someone publicly toasts the murder of an innocent man."

Jillian drew up short. Too late she saw the trap. Too late she looked into Jimmy's camera, with her round, dazed eyes, her loose hair wild around her face, her cheeks flushed with outrage.

"Death is not justice," she replied quietly, but her words no longer mattered. Maureen had her clip, and they all knew it. The reporter smiled, genuinely this time, and motioned for Jimmy to turn off the tape.

"Thank you," she said crisply, lowering the mike.

"Do you really think you're helping things?" Jillian asked.

The reporter shrugged. "Can't fuck it up any more than you did now, can I?"

"This is my fault?"

Maureen looked at her. "Are you fucking nuts? Have you ever gone back and watched your old press conferences, Ms. Hayes? Have you ever seen yourself on camera? You spin. Hell, you spin better than most politicians. Always cool, always composed, telling the public what happened to you, what happened to Meg, what happened to Carol. Reminding the public that it might be their daughters next.

"You didn't just insert yourself into a story. You *became* the story. Even I sympathized with you and those other two women. Hell, a bunch of the reporters bought a round of drinks in your honor the day they arrested Como. But that was before Sylvia Blaire. Of course you bear a responsibility for what happened yesterday. Maybe if you hadn't kept the fire so hot, the police investigation could've been more thorough. Maybe if the police hadn't had to spend so much time reacting to your presence on the news, they could've spent more time on the case. The police are vulnerable to public pressure, you know. Just ask your good friend Sergeant Griffin."

"I love you, too, Maureen," Griffin said.

She flashed a smile at him. "That's what makes my job so meaningful."

"There is no conclusive evidence that Eddie Como's innocent," Jillian insisted.

"Tell that to Sylvia Blaire."

"It could be a copycat."

"Would you like to go on record?"

Jillian didn't say anything. Maureen nodded. "Yeah, that's what I thought."

She and Jimmy were back in the news van. They had come, they had seen, they had conquered. Maureen waved quite merrily, right before slamming the door shut.

"You shouldn't listen to her," Griffin said shortly, as the news van sped away.

Jillian merely smiled. "Oh, but I will. And Meg will and Carol will. In the middle of the night, we'll think of nothing but what she said. We're women. It's what we do." She turned and headed for her car.

"Jillian . . ." He caught her arm. The contact startled them both. They stared at his hand on her forearm until his fingers slipped away. "Fitz ran a good case. I run a good case. We're going to get to the bottom of this."

Jillian looked out at the sky. "Four hours before nightfall, Griffin. I wonder what young woman will be home alone tonight. I wonder what college student will be hitting the books or daydreaming about her boyfriend or maybe even resting in front of the TV. I wonder what girl is making what small mistake right now that will very soon cost her her life."

"You can't think that way."

"Oh, but I do. Once you've been assaulted, it's very hard to think of anything else. The world is a very dangerous place, Sergeant. And I haven't seen anything to give me any hope yet."

25

Griffin

"Good news," Detective Waters said on the other end of the cell phone. "Eddie Como's dead."

"Now there's something I haven't heard lately." Griffin passed under the Towers on Ocean Road and headed toward Providence while holding the cell phone pressed against his right ear. Traffic wasn't too bad this early in May. Give it another month, and this area of Narragansett would be turned into a tourist-crazed parking lot. Ah, the joys of summer.

"ME confirmed the fingerprints this afternoon," Waters was saying. "Our vic is definitely Eddie Como. In the even-better-news department, Providence just got a hit on the deep-fried DOA, as well."

"No kidding."

"Guy had a military record. Gus J. Ohlsson, formerly of New York. Get this—he served eight years in the Army, as a sharpshooter."

"Ah, so our detective intuitions are right again. Let's face it, the nose knows."

"Yeah, well, you can pat yourself on the back all you want. Providence is still taking the credit. As we speak, they're putting together a subpoena for Ohlsson's military records, plus bank accounts. He has a father listed as next of kin, also out of New York, so you can bet Boz and Higgins are doing the happy dance."

"Road trip," Griffin said. Boz and Higgins had worked in Providence's Detective Bureau for fifteen years. As Providence was a main way station on the I-95 corridor between New York and Boston, lots of the city's crime ended up tied to New York or Boston case files. Somehow, Boz and Higgins always got the New York trips. Always. The rumor was, they had a thing for Broadway shows.

"Given Ohlsson's military background," Waters was saying, "our hired-gun theory is looking good. Of course, Providence also wants to check out Family ties."

"With a name like Ohlsson?"

"Hey, haven't you heard? It's a global village out there. Everyone has gone multinational, including the Mafia."

"Wow, you take a year's sabbatical and the whole geopolitical landscape of crime shifts on you. Who would've thought?" Griffin came to the exit for

Route 1 North and headed up the ramp. "Anything from the state fire marshal's office yet?"

"After only two days? You *are* out of touch."

"I prefer the term optimistic. Hey, Mike, can you touch base with the financial guys for me? Tell them Jillian Hayes donated the twenty thousand missing from her accounts to a Cranston parish. The priest has confirmed the donation, but we need to keep the details under wraps."

"Since you didn't give me any details, that shouldn't be too hard. Aren't you heading back to HQ?"

"No, I'm on my way to see Dan Rosen."

"*You're* on your way to see Dan Rosen?" Waters's voice grew tight, and the silence that followed was immediately tense. Griffin understood. In theory, primary case officers didn't do much legwork. In theory, his job was to remain in headquarters, coordinating and overseeing detectives like Waters, who would handle interviews like Dan Rosen's. And in fact, if Griffin didn't appear at the command center shortly, his lieutenant was probably going to have a few words with him. He wouldn't like those words much.

"What are you doing, Griffin?" Waters asked.

"I have a theory. I need to play it out."

"Tell me your theory. I can play it out."

"You could, but I figured you'd prefer to spend your afternoon in a bar."

"*What?*"

"I need you to go to Cranston," Griffin explained patiently. "I need you to identify all the bars/pubs/watering holes in the near vicinity of Eddie Como's house. Then I want you to show the bartenders a picture of Eddie Como and find out if he spent a lot of time there, and more importantly, with whom."

More silence. Long silence. "Griffin . . ."

"I know."

"Fitz finds out about this, he's gonna be pissed."

"Fitz was born pissed. Nothing we can do about that now. Besides, that's why I need you to do it. I'm counting on your charm."

"Ah hell, Griff, nobody has that kind of charm. In a state this small, everything gets around. Providence is going to think we're sniffing at their rape case, and the next thing you know, their lieutenant will be on the phone screaming at our lieutenant. Morelli doesn't like being screamed at or haven't you noticed?"

"Look, we have a body. Our job is to find out who killed that body. Working up a victim profile, complete with names of friends and associates, is not outside the realm of our investigation."

"So you say." Waters wasn't fooled. Neither would Fitz be.

"If anyone asks, just tell them I told you to do it," Griffin said. "I'll take the heat."

"You know that's not what I meant—"

"Cranston accent, Mike. I'm looking for someone who knew Eddie well, who grew up in Cranston, and who was seen on occasion in khaki pants with a button-down shirt. Maybe I'm way off base. But maybe . . . I need you to do this."

"Ah nuts." Waters blew out a big huff of air, which meant he'd do it. "And if I find this mystery man?"

"Then I'm probably going to be even more confused than I am right now, but in a better sort of way."

"Ah nuts," Waters said again, and Griffin could practically see the gaunt detective rolling his eyes.

"I don't like the rape case," Griffin said abruptly.

"So I've heard."

"Something about this . . . I don't know. Something about this feels wrong."

"You know you've been gone awhile. The first case back . . ."

"I should play by the rules?"

"It wouldn't hurt."

"Yeah, but then how would I have any fun?"

More silence. A stranger silence. Griffin didn't like this silence.

"Griff, I got a call from Corporal Charpentier at the ACI," Waters said.

Griffin honestly didn't get it at first. And then, all of a sudden . . . "No!"

"Yeah. I'm afraid so. Good ol' David Price reached out first thing this morning. He claims to have info on Eddie Como and wants to speak with you immediately. I guess we shouldn't be surprised. Your face was on the morning news and God knows he likes to yank your chain."

"Goddammit . . ." Griffin smacked the steering wheel. Thought of his former neighbor. Thought of Cindy. Then hit the steering wheel again; this time his hand stung. He should remain calm. Little psychopathic shit. "Why the hell am I even surprised? The bastard sent me a letter just yesterday, congratulating me on the new case. Of course he wants in on the action."

"He already knew about the case? But he had to mail that letter on Saturday, Griff, *before* Eddie Como was shot."

"Yeah, yeah, yeah. He just wrote congrats on the new case, not the Eddie Como case, not the College Hill Rapist case, just *case*. This is David Price, re-member? King of head games. He's bored, he's been waiting for some enter-tainment. And now that I'm back on the job, he's trying to bluff his way into the party. What could he know about Eddie Como anyway? They were both at the ACI. So are three thousand other humps and they aren't bothering us with calls. Como was held in Intake, right?"

"Yeah."

"And Price is still stinking up Steel City, right?"

"Yeah."

"Ergo, David Price doesn't know shit."

"Roommate," Waters said.

"Son of a bitch."

"Yeah. Eddie Como's former roommate at Intake, Jimmy Woods, already had his day in court. He got sentenced to Old Max three months ago for a B&E job gone sour. Price is claiming that Jimmy Woods has been talking, and for a little *consideration,* Price'll give us the inside scoop."

"Consideration." Griffin spat out the word. "Price murdered ten kids. There is nothing he can give us *ever* that warrants consideration after that. He committed his crimes in a state without the death penalty. He got a big enough break right there."

"Nobody's disagreeing with you."

"Then why don't I feel good about this?"

Waters's tone grew more subdued. "Things are hot, Griff. You haven't been back to HQ yet, but let me tell you. Phones are ringing off the hook from the colonel on down. People are frightened. People with young daughters are freaky-scared. We know David Price. Corporal Charpentier knows David Price. Hell, the lieutenant, the major, the colonel all know David Price. The mayor and the governor, on the other hand . . ."

"First person who wants to open a serious dialogue with David Price gets full-color crime-scene photos," Griffin said coldly. "I don't care if it's the fucking governor. Are we clear?"

Another pause. "We're clear."

"Mike . . ."

"When will you be done with Dan Rosen?"

"I don't know. Six o'clock?"

"I'll be over."

"Mike, I don't need—"

"Yeah, you do. See you at six. And don't worry. This time I'll bring a face mask."

By the time Griffin arrived in the tony Providence neighborhood harboring the Rosen house, his mood had gone south. He was thinking too much. That had always been his problem. He was thinking of Meg's pale features. He was thinking of Carol's brittle smile. He was thinking of Jillian, not even allowed to properly grieve for her sister because some overeager reporter was already pulling into her drive.

And then he was thinking of Tawnya and plump-cheeked Eddie, Jr. He was thinking of lives that had no potential and the kind of people he saw every day, already knowing someplace way down deep that he'd see them again soon enough, in jail, in court, in the back of a squad car. Cycles that went round without end.

And then he was thinking of that goddamn basement, and the lives he could've saved if he hadn't been thinking so much. He thought of Cindy. He thought of David. He thought of the stuff he still hadn't told anyone, not his brothers, not his father, not the nice little therapist assigned to screw his head on straight.

Fuckin' world sometimes. Too much like a boxing ring. You just kept taking the blows, then getting back on your feet. Mike was right. He needed to move. He needed to run. He needed to beat the living shit out of something soon, or the buzzing would return in his ears. His arms and legs would start moving on their own. Instead of eating and drinking like a normal person, he'd turn into a hulking Energizer bunny, churning, churning, churning until five sleepless days passed and his pink fuzzy head blew off.

Some cops got depressed, burnt out. Griffin went to the other extreme. He had hyperanxiety disorder, meaning when he got stressed, he could no longer calm down. The pressure built and built and built until no amount of running, weight lifting, boxing or fucking *anything* did any good.

He could break all the bones in his hand without feeling it. He could go without sleep for three days and still be wired when he finally lay down in bed. His hands shook, his knees trembled and he appeared downright manic. Then six, seven days later, his body would simply give out beneath the strain. He'd come down hard, like someone who'd been mainlining cocaine.

Then he'd enter the true danger zone. Physically and emotionally he had nothing left in reserve, but the pressure was still there. His wife gone, his neighbor a baby-killer, his job intense. His family had helped out the first time. His brothers had taken turns staying at his house so he was never alone. They had got him through the worst. He'd taken over from there.

He was learning now how to manage his stress from the start. Eat well, sleep well and get a good aerobic workout four to five times a week. That way he tapped off steam every day, instead of letting it build. Not always that easy, but not really that difficult. Besides, on the bad days, he simply thought of Cindy. She had fought so damn hard to live. Even after the cancer started shutting down her internal organs, took away her voice and sapped away her flesh. Even at the bitter end, when she could communicate only by blinking her eyes and her hands had not even the strength to hold his. She had fought. How could he do any less?

Breathe deep, he told himself now. Count to twenty. You can't change the world, but you can improve a bit of it a little at a time.

He got out of his car. Shut the door. Breathed in, breathed out. Thought of reopening his door and slamming it, but got hold of the impulse. *Just breathe*. He boarded the front steps of the Victorian home and knocked on the dark-stained door slightly harder than necessary, but not too bad. No one answered, though he heard voices coming from inside.

He knocked again, counted to ten, then knocked again and made it all the way to thirty before he heard the click of someone drawing back the brass cover from the peephole. A moment later, Carol Rosen stood in front of him. She wore blue-checkered flannel pajamas buttoned up to her neck, even though it had to be nearly sixty outside. Her cheeks were flushed. Her eyes held a glassy sheen.

Drunk, he thought immediately, though when she swayed forward he couldn't catch the scent of any booze on her breath. Vodka then.

"I don't . . . talk to you," she said, gripping the door tight.

"Is your husband home?"

"Nope."

"His office said he wasn't at work."

"Well, he's not at home."

"Mrs. Rosen—"

"Try his girlfriend's." Her eyes grew brighter. She stabbed a finger at him and for the first time he saw the knuckles on her right hand. They were bleeding. He looked at her sharply, but she didn't seem to notice. "Not here. Not there. Must be at his girlfriend's."

"Your husband has a girlfriend?"

"That's what I said."

"What is her name?"

"I don't know. I betcha she was never raped. What do you think?"

Griffin was quiet for a moment. "Would you like me to call someone for you, Mrs. Rosen? Maybe a friend or relative who could come stay with you for a while?"

She waved her finger, falling forward, then getting a better grip on the door. "Not a reporter. I hate them! Phone ringing . . . all the time. Tell us about Eddie! What about that poor college student? Sylvia Blaire. Pretty Sylvia Blaire. Eddie's dead, and still the women suffer."

"How about I call Miss Pesaturo or Ms. Hayes?"

"Meg doesn't know shit. She's so young." Carol sighed. She tilted her head to the side, her long blond hair sweeping down her shoulder. "Young and sweet and innocent. Do you think I was ever that young and sweet and innocent? I don't remember. Even before Eddie . . . I don't remember."

"Ms. Hayes?" he asked hopefully. No dice.

"She hates me," Carol announced. "I'm too broken, you see. Jillian only loves people she can fix. Improve yourself! Get with the program! Take control of your life! Jillian is really Oprah Winfrey. Well, she's not black."

"Are you going to be all right, Mrs. Rosen?"

"I can't have children," she said mournfully. "I bet Dan's girlfriend can have children. I bet she can turn off the TV anytime she wants. I bet she's never slept in an empty bathtub or compulsively checked all the bars on the windows. She's probably never shot at Dan either. It's hard to compete with that."

"Mrs. Rosen . . ." She was definitely drunk. He took another deep breath, then acknowledged that it didn't matter. He still had a job to do, and frankly, her inebriation made his life easier. He said, "Does Dan ever talk to you about money?"

"No."

"A home like this must be very expensive."

She singsonged, "New plumbing isn't exactly cheap, you know."

"So things have been tight?"

"'Jesus Christ, Carol, someone has to pay for all this.'"

"Very tight."

"Meg and Jillian think we should sell this house. I picked out almost everything in it. This door, I selected this door." She stroked it with her hand. "This molding, I selected this molding." She touched the doorjamb tenderly. "So much of it was gone before. Rotted out, yanked out. Replaced with cheap pine trim. I read books. Scoured old pictures of Victorian homes, talked to experts in historical restoration. No one could have loved this house more than I did. God, I wish it would just burn to the ground."

"Mrs. Rosen, we know Dan liquidated his brokerage account. Do you know where that money went?"

She shook her head.

"We're going to have to look into that, Mrs. Rosen."

She smiled and leaned her head against the door. "You think he hired an assassin? You think he spent that money to kill my rapist?"

"I would like to ask him that question."

"Sergeant Griffin, my husband doesn't love me that much. Try the girlfriend. Maybe she also likes expensive old homes."

Griffin brought up his hand. Too late. Carol Rosen had already closed the door. He tried knocking, but she wouldn't respond. After another minute, he returned to his car, where he sat behind the steering wheel and frowned.

He didn't like leaving Carol Rosen alone in her current state of mind. Last night she'd shot her husband, and that was *before* she'd learned about Sylvia Blaire.

He picked up his cell phone and gave Meg Pesaturo a try. No answer. Next call, Jillian's beach house. Also a dead end. Then he dialed her East Greenwich residence, where he finally got a person.

"Hello," Toppi Niauru said.

Jillian wasn't in, so Griffin told Toppi about Carol Rosen. She said that she and Libby would be right over.

Carol's historic house didn't have wheelchair access, so Griffin hung out in the driveway. Forty-five minutes later, Toppi pulled up in a dark blue van. She opened the side door and operated the wheelchair lift to lower Olivia Hayes to the ground.

Jillian's mother had put on makeup for the occasion. She had her dark hair piled high on her head, and greeted Griffin with a kiss.

At 5:00 P.M., he carried Libby up the front stairs while Toppi followed with her wheelchair. At 5:01, they all knocked on the door.

At 5:10, they stopped knocking, and Griffin took down the door with his shoulder. At 5:11, they found Carol sprawled on the rug in front of the blaring TV, her hand still clutching the empty bottle of sleeping pills.

Griffin started CPR, Toppi called for an ambulance and Dan Rosen, with his usual sense of timing, finally came home.

26

Carol

Jillian arrived first. She forcefully shoved her way through the pack of reporters clogging the hospital parking lot, then bustled through the emergency room doors.

"Goddamn vultures!" she cried as the electronic doors finally slid shut, but not before some earnest reporter shouted out, "Ms. Hayes, have *you* ever thought of committing suicide?"

Meg and her family were shortly behind Jillian. A uniformed officer had located their vehicle outside Vinnie Pesaturo's home and passed along the news. Arriving in the hospital parking lot, Vinnie shouted, "Outta my way, you rat bastards," and the reporters, recognizing an armed man when they saw one, let the family through.

The moment they were inside the ER, Meg homed in on Jillian. "Where is she? Is she okay? What have you heard?"

"I don't know. We need a doctor. There. You in the white coat. What can you tell us about Carol Rosen?"

"Jillian! Over here. Jillian!"

Jillian and Meg turned in time to see Toppi waving at them from the other side of the waiting room. Next to her sat Jillian's mother. Next to Olivia, sat Sergeant Griffin.

"Why is your mother here?" Meg asked.

"Is that really *the* Olivia Hayes?" her father breathed.

"I'm going to kill Sergeant Griffin," Jillian said.

They rushed across the emergency room, where Toppi rose to meet them. "How is she? Is she going to be all right?" Jillian's hands were shaking. She didn't even realize it until Toppi reached out and clasped them in her own.

"We don't know yet."

"Oh God—"

"Her husband is talking to one of the doctors now. Maybe he'll know something soon."

"What *happened?*"

"It looks like she overdosed on sleeping pills. Maybe some alcohol as well."

"Oh no." Meg now. She had started to cry. "I didn't realize . . . I mean, I knew she was upset, but I didn't think . . ."

"No one could know," Jillian said, but the words were automatic, lacking genuine conviction. They were Carol's friends; they'd seen her just this morning. Maybe they should have known. Meg's mother put an arm around her daughter's shoulders.

"And where was the husband during all this?" Uncle Vinnie boomed.

Toppi shrugged and looked at Griffin. He said simply, "Out."

"Figures," Uncle Vinnie snorted.

"I can't take this," Jillian said. "I'm going to find a doctor."

She headed for the receptionist's desk, and wasn't surprised when Griffin followed.

"How could you?" she railed at him the moment they were out of earshot of the others. Her hands were still shaking. She felt sick to the bottom of her stomach with worry for Carol.

"How could I what?"

"Get my mom involved in all of this!"

"Oh don't you start!" Toppi had just caught up with them, and she barreled into the conversation fiercely. "Look at her! Glance over your shoulder and just look at her!"

Jillian thinned her lips mutinously, but did as she was told. Her mom now had Meg's father and uncle literally at her feet. The two men were talking animatedly. Her mother was smiling.

"She looks pretty good to me," Griffin said.

Jillian stabbed his overpumped chest with her finger. "*You* are not allowed to speak." Then she turned back on Toppi. "She's fragile—"

"She's fine."

"EMTs put her on oxygen just last night!"

"She had a shock."

"And finding Carol on the floor of her home wasn't shocking?"

"Probably, but I imagine it was still worse for Carol."

"Oh!" Jillian was so mad she yanked on her gathered hair. "I don't want her involved!"

"Too late. She's your mother. She's involved."

"She'll just worry more."

Toppi snorted. "She was already worried. This finally gave her something to do."

"Toppi!"

"Jillian!" Toppi mocked. "Look, I'm being serious now. When Sergeant Griffin called, I asked your mom what she wanted to do. She didn't hesitate for a second. Carol is your friend. Libby was delighted to help her in any way we could. And it's a damn good thing, too." Toppi's voice finally quieted. "I know she wasn't around much when you were a child, Jillian. But you're not a child anymore. You grew up. Have you ever stopped to consider that maybe she did, too?"

Toppi walked back to the group, where Meg was now leaning her head against her mother's shoulder and Libby was flipping rapidly through her picture book to the apparent delight of Tom and Uncle Vinnie. Jillian turned back to Griffin. "Don't say it," she warned.

"Haven't muttered a word."

"She's wrong, you know. Toppi's the one who doesn't get it. I know my mom has changed. But I've never had a father, and I no longer have a sister. Libby . . . She's all I have left."

At the receptionist's desk, no one would help her. She wasn't family, and in the eyes of medical protocol being a fellow rape victim didn't count. They knew who Jillian was, of course. The nurse in charge was even kind. And then for the first time, Jillian realized the full implication of where they were. Women & Infants. One of Providence's best hospitals and where each one of them had been at least once before . . . On those nights, that night, the night.

She turned away, no longer so steady on her feet. Of all the strange bonds . . . And then she suddenly realized that she couldn't lose Carol. She just couldn't. Carol had to survive and then it would be Jillian, Carol and Meg again, sitting in the back room of some restaurant, and arguing or laughing, or being petty or being genuine, but certainly helping one another cope.

She had started the Survivors Club with so much purpose, but maybe at the end of the day, the group had worked even better than Jillian had thought. Because standing here now, she couldn't imagine not seeing Carol. She couldn't imagine even a week going by without it being her, Carol and Meg.

"Sit," Griffin said quietly. "Wait."

"I can't sit. I don't know how to wait. That's my whole problem." Her fingers had closed around his sleeve. She didn't know when that had happened. "Oh God, I just want to know that Carol is all right."

A door on the left suddenly swung open; Dan Rosen walked through. His features were ashen. His dark hair stood up in a rumpled mess on top of his head, while his left arm stood out prominently in a white sling. He wore a tan jacket with a gold tie, as if he'd once been on his way to work. Now he didn't seem to know where he was.

Jillian took one look at his face and felt the world tilt again beneath her feet. "Oh no . . ."

"Mr. Rosen," Griffin said quietly.

"Huh. What?"

"Dan?" Jillian whispered more urgently.

He finally seemed to register their presence. "Oh. Hello, Jillian."

"Is she? Please, Dan?"

"They're pumping her stomach. Treating her . . . an activated charcoal slurry, I think the doctor said. She took all her Ambien. Booze, too. Not good, not good at all. Ambien plus booze equals a coma, that's what the doctor said." Dan looked at Griffin shakily. "He said . . . he said if you hadn't gotten to her so soon, she'd probably be dead."

"She's been drinking?"

"I guess. And her throat . . ." His fingers touched his own. "Her esophagus is . . . aggravated. I think that's how the doctor said it. And her back teeth show signs of erosion. From bile, he told me. When she makes herself sick."

It took Jillian a moment. "Bulimia?"

"He thinks. So my wife, it appears, spends her free time eating too much and maybe drinking too much and then making herself sick. Over and over again. I swear I didn't know." He looked at them, still dazed. "Jillian, did you know?"

"I didn't know."

"You should've, though." Meg had come over while they were speaking. Now she had her hands placed authoritatively on her jean-clad hips while she regarded Dan with an imperious stare. "We were her friends, but we only saw her once or twice a week. You *lived* with her. How could you not know what she was doing?"

"I've been . . . working."

"Meg," Jillian tried. She was too late.

"Working?" Meg said. "Or playing with your *girlfriend*?"

"What?" Dan's head popped up. "What?"

"Oh don't play innocent with us." Meg was on a roll now, and everyone, including Sergeant Griffin, was watching with great interest. "Carol told us all about it. Your pathetic excuses of late-night meetings and overburdened workload. She called your office, you know. She knew you weren't really there. That night she was raped—she knew what you were *really* doing."

"Carol thinks I'm sleeping with another woman?" Dan asked in a strangled voice.

"Oh come on—"

"I'm not. I swear I'm not. I wouldn't do that to Carol. My God, I love my wife!"

"You're never home!" Meg cried.

"I know."

"You're never at work!"

"I know."

"Then where the hell are you?"

Dan didn't answer. He simply looked stricken. And then another voice spoke up from across the hushed waiting room.

"Foxwoods," Uncle Vinnie announced. "Danny boy's not a cheater. He's a gambler. And if you don't mind me saying, he's a really bad one, too."

Next to Jillian, Dan Rosen nodded his head miserably. "I love my wife," he said again. Then he turned away and slammed his one good hand into the wall.

"You're going to have to tell me everything," Griffin said to Dan ten minutes later. He had commandeered an empty exam room in an attempt at privacy. Of course, Jillian, Meg and the rest of their entourage had immediately followed him and Dan into the room, and were now looking at them both as if they had every right to be there. Griffin considered kicking them out but figured what the hell. Vinnie Pesaturo obviously had relevant information, and Jillian and Meg seemed to be the interrogative equivalent of brass knuckles. All they had to do was look at Dan, and he gave up the store.

"I never meant to hurt Carol," Dan started off weakly.

"You know, Dan, she did shoot you."

"That was an accident! I should've announced myself the minute I got home. It was late . . . She gets nervous after dark." His lips twisted. "After what happened to her that night, can you really blame her?"

"Yes, that night. Let's talk about that night." Griffin took out his Norelco Pocket Memo, turned on the mini recorder and got serious. "You told the police you were working late."

Dan hung his head.

"I gather you told your wife the same?"

"Yes."

"But you weren't really at work?"

Dan didn't look up. Vinnie smacked his arm. "For God's sake," the bookie said. "Stop being such a whiner and stand up for your wife."

Dan shot the bookie a look, but seemed to get ahold of himself. "I, uh, I was at the Foxwoods casino."

"You lied to the police?"

"Yes."

"You do that a lot?"

"I was embarrassed! It was bad enough to be gone when my wife needed me. But then, to have to admit that I was sitting at a blackjack table while she was being viciously assaulted . . ." He groaned. "My God, what kind of husband does a thing like that?"

Griffin let the question hang, which was answer enough. "So you lied to the police, and you lied to your wife. All to cover up one night at the gaming tables. Do you gamble a lot, Mr. Rosen?"

"I don't know. Is four, five days a week a lot? Is liquidating my business a lot? Is second-mortgaging my home?" Dan's face gained some color. He looked at Griffin hotly, as if daring him to state the obvious.

"You tell me," Griffin said quietly.

That quickly, Dan folded again. His shoulders slumped. His chin sank against his chest. "I think . . . I think I have a gambling problem." And then, "Oh God, Carol is going to kill me!"

"How long has this been going on?"

"I don't know. Three years, maybe. I went to Foxwoods one night with some friends. Business associates, really. And I . . . I had a *really* good night. Seriously." Dan's features perked up again. "I quit the blackjack tables ahead ten thousand dollars. And back then, ten thousand dollars . . . Wow. I was just about to open my own law firm, and God knows the house needed some kind of something. Ten thousand bucks helped out. Felt good. Easy money."

"Uh huh," Griffin said knowingly.

Dan smiled thinly. "Exactly. So I opened my own law practice, except instead of taking with me five loyal clients, I only took three. Money was tighter than I thought, and things got off slower than I thought, and health care cost more than I thought . . ."

"You started taking on debt."

"I didn't want to tell Carol. We'd talked about me starting my own practice so many times. She wasn't as sure. That house, those mortgage payments, my God. But it was my dream. I had to have my own practice. Trust me, I told her. Trust me. So she did."

"But you got behind in payments. And then you . . . ?"

"I remembered Foxwoods. Ten thousand bucks. Easy money, right? I'm a smart man, I've read all the books on blackjack, memorized the odds tables. Hey, it's not like betting on horses. That's pure luck. Now blackjack, that takes strategy."

"Hence all the blackjack millionaires out there," Griffin observed dryly.

"I've won," Dan said immediately. His face held that flush again. "Hey, I've won a lot!"

"How much are you down, Mr. Rosen?"

The lawyer faltered. He didn't seem able to meet anyone's eye. After several moments, when the silence ran long, Vinnie raised his arm to smack the man again. Griffin waved the bookie off.

"Mr. Rosen?"

"I owed eighty thousand dollars," Dan said gruffly. He ran his right hand through his hair, leaving the brown strands standing up on end. "Only twenty now. I, uh, I liquidated my brokerage account. Otherwise, they weren't going to give me any more money. And then . . . Well, then I wouldn't have any chance of getting ahead, would I?"

"Who's they, Mr. Rosen?"

"Why don't you ask Mr. Pesaturo?" Dan said bitterly.

Griffin looked at Vinnie.

"Not with that tape on," Vinnie said.

"I'm working on a murder here—"

"Not with that tape on."

Griffin sighed, shut off the Pocket Memo. "Let's hear it."

"I might be aware of Mr. Rosen's predicament."

"You think?"

"Hey, man needed money, and I happen to know people who don't mind loaning a few bucks every now and then."

"Percentage?"

"Well, you know how it is in banking. The interest rate on the loan is dependent upon the level of risk. Look at him." Vinnie shot Dan Rosen a disparaging glance. "Eighty grand down at jack? He's high risk."

"You're charging him a hundred percent?"

"Fifty. We're not completely unsympathetic."

"Wait a minute." Jillian raised a hand, finally interjecting herself into the conversation. "You mean to tell me that you—"

"My associates," Vinnie amended.

"Fine, *your associates* are loaning Dan money for his gambling habit with an interest rate of fifty percent?"

Vinnie nodded. She turned to Dan. "And you are *taking* the money at that rate?"

"One good day," he said immediately. "That's all you need. One good day, and the loan is repaid and I can get the credit cards down, maybe even make an extra payment on the mortgage. One good day."

"Oh God," Jillian said. "Poor Carol."

Dan deflated again. Griffin turned the recorder back on. "Is it correct to say, Mr. Rosen, that you used the sixty thousand dollars you liquidated from your brokerage account to repay loan sharks?"

Dan nodded. Griffin gave him a look. "Yes," Dan said belatedly into the minirecorder.

Griffin turned to Vinnie. "And can you, Vincent Pesaturo, verify—through *sources*—that such a transaction took place?"

"Yeah. My *sources*, they say such a thing took place."

"Vinnie Pesaturo, did you order a hit on Edward Como? Did you arrange for him to come to harm in any way?"

The questions came out of left field, but Vinnie didn't blink an eye. He bent lower, so his mouth was directly above the recorder. "No, I, Vincent Pesaturo, did not order a hit on Eddie Como. If I, Vincent Pesaturo, wanted that piece of garbage dead, I would've done it myself."

"Or ordered a hit in prison," Griffin muttered. Vinnie smiled, looked at the recorder and didn't say a word.

"Tom Pesaturo," Griffin spoke up again. "Did you order a hit on your daughter's suspected rapist, Edward Como?"

Tom looked a bit more defensive. "Nah," he said slowly. "I decided against it."

"Tom!" his wife gasped.

"Daddy!" Meg seconded.

He shrugged. "Hey, I'm a father. After what that bastard did to my daughter, I'm allowed to think these things. But I didn't do anything." He shrugged again. "I don't know. Sounded like the police had a good case. That DNA and all. And I figured . . . I figured the trial might be better for Meg. She could face down her accuser and all. I, uh, I read someplace that sometimes that's better for the victim, you know. Gives her some sense of power back, control. That kind of thing."

"You read about rape victims?" Meg asked.

"Kinda. I saw this article . . . in *Cosmo*."

"*Cosmo*?" Vinnie exclaimed.

Tom Pesaturo huffed his shoulders. "Hey, she's my daughter. I want what's best for her. 'Sides, there was a long line at checkout, and you know they got all those women's magazines just sitting right there, decorated up with half-naked cover models. Of course I started looking. And then, well, I saw the title for the article. And then I kind of opened up the magazine. And hey, it was a really long line and, and . . . It was a good thing to read."

"You are a sweet man, Tommy Pesaturo," Meg's mother said. She slipped her hand into her husband's and squeezed.

"Ah well," he said. Everyone was looking at him now. He turned bright red.

A tapping sound came from the back of the room. Heads turned to Libby, who was staring at Griffin expectantly.

"Oh," he said belatedly. "Um, Olivia Hayes, did *you* hire someone to kill or harm Edward Como?"

Olivia made a motion with her hand, which he took to mean no. She was using her left hand to flip through her picture book. Toppi came closer, leaning over her shoulder as Libby tapped on one picture, flipped several more pages, then tapped on two more pictures.

"She's pointing out Jillian, Carol and Meg," Toppi said. She looked at

Libby. "The Survivors Club?"

Libby tapped once, flipped through the book, tapped again.

"The number one," Toppi said. "The Survivors Group, plus one?"

Single tap.

"That means yes," Toppi translated for the group. She knelt down. "I don't know what that means, Libby. Do you mean the other victim? Sylvia Blaire?"

No response.

"Do you mean the Survivors Club should be four people?"

Libby frowned, then tapped once. This tap was clearly reluctant, however. The statement still wasn't quite right.

"Why four people?" Meg asked.

"It can't be an open-ended question," Jillian spoke up. "She knows what she wants to say, but you have to help her find it by using yes or no questions."

She was studying her mother now as well. It was hard to read the look on her face. Some compassion, some yearning, some resignation. Then Libby looked at her as well. The softening of her features was immediate and obvious. A mother looking at her daughter. A mother, looking at the only daughter she had left.

"Yes or no question," Tom muttered.

"Four people, four people," Vinnie was saying.

"A bigger Survivors Club," Meg mused.

Then all of sudden, Jillian's eyes grew wide. "I know what she means. Oh my God, why didn't we think of it before?"

In her wheelchair, Libby leaned toward her daughter, waited for her daughter to speak the words from Libby's head.

"Sergeant Griffin asked all of us if we were involved in Eddie's death, because we're Eddie Como's victims. We have the best motive."

Tap, tap, tap.

Jillian turned toward Griffin now. Her cheeks were flushed, her eyes dazed. "But what's the other major statistic in rape cases, Griffin? That rape is a largely unreported crime. That in fact, something like only one in every four rapes is ever brought to the attention of the police."

Griffin closed his eyes. He understood now as well. "Ah, no."

And in her wheelchair, Libby went tap, tap, tap.

"Ah, yes," Jillian said softly. "Meg, Carol and I are the women who came forward, the women who called the police. But that doesn't mean we were the College Hill Rapist's only victims. It is quite feasible, it's very probable, that there's at least one other woman out there. Another woman, another family, and a whole host of other people who wanted Eddie Como dead."

27

Griffin

By 6:30, there was still no word on Carol, but Griffin had to go. Waters was waiting for him, plus he had work to do. He left the subdued group inhabiting one corner of the waiting room, an odd sort of family. Dan had started off slightly apart, but then Jillian, of all people, had moved to the seat beside him. Maybe Dan was grateful. It was hard to tell. He should be, Griffin thought. He gave Jillian one last glance, then headed out the door.

In the parking lot, he was immediately assaulted by the gathered press.

"Any word on Carol Rosen's condition?"

"Are you prepared to make an arrest?"

"Is Carol Rosen's attempted suicide connected with Eddie Como's murder?"

Griffin ignored them all and climbed into his car. In all honesty, there weren't as many reporters present as he would've thought. Then he turned on the radio and found out why.

Tawnya Clemente was holding a press conference in downtown Providence. At a law firm. Where her new attorney was announcing the fifty-million-dollar wrongful-death suit he was planning to bring against the city of Providence and the Providence Police Department on behalf of the Como family.

"As recent evidence indicates," the lawyer boomed, "Edward Como never should have been arrested by the Providence Police Department. Indeed, the premature and irresponsible indictment of Edward Como as a serial rapist set in motion the events leading to the tragic death of this young man, shot down in front of the very courthouse where he would've shortly been found innocent. Yesterday was a dark, dark day in the halls of justice. The city of Providence turned on one of its very own sons. Now the city must make restitution. The city must make amends."

On cue, Griffin's cell phone rang.

"Are you listening to this?" Fitz yelled into his ear. "Holy mother of God, I am having a heart attack. My heart is literally fucking exploding in my chest. I'm gonna die on this thankless, shitty, fucking nuts job, and then my wife is gonna sue this city for seventy-five million just so she can stay ahead of the Comos. Jesus H. Christ. I should've arrested Tawnya when I had the chance."

"You have a wife?" Griffin said.

"Eat my shorts, Sergeant!"

"I take it you had another lovely afternoon."

"Blockbuster," Fitz moaned. "Goddamn kid seems legit. Showed us the computer records of Eddie's transaction, then practically cried as he told us how he'd been too scared to come forward earlier. His sister goes to Providence College and he was so sure Eddie was guilty, he didn't want to do anything that might set the College Hill Rapist free."

"So on the one hand, the kid from Blockbuster did see Eddie that night, but even he's still convinced that Eddie is guilty?"

"The DNA. Some people really do believe in that stuff. Why the hell aren't any of them ever on juries?"

Griffin had turned onto the highway. The lack of sleep the night before was starting to catch up with him. So much information, and he couldn't seem to get his brain to process half of it.

"Is this kid the basis of Tawnya's claim?"

"Maybe. I'm guessing, though, her lawyer's mostly focusing on last night's assault on Sylvia Blaire. That case is consistent with the College Hill Rapist attacks and since that happened *after* Eddie was dead, Eddie couldn't have done it, meaning he couldn't have done any of them."

"Meaning the heat is on to resolve what happened to Sylvia Blaire."

"Would you believe the mayor just gave us carte blanche on the Blaire case?"

"Oh, you big boy you."

"Yeah, apparently you can spend a small fortune on manpower and high-priority forensic tests without coming close to the expense of a fifty-million-dollar lawsuit."

"I take it you're fast-tracking the tests on the DNA sample?"

"Oh yeah. We're trying to get results by first thing tomorrow morning. Please let it be an ex-boyfriend. About the only thing that will save our asses now is for it to be an ex-boyfriend. Oh, and when we pick him up, he's gotta confess that it was a copycat crime and he learned all the details from reading some Internet site, www.IWannaBeARapist.com, or something like that. Ex-boyfriend. Confession. Yeah, that's about what it's going to take to salvage my career."

"I think you stood a better chance of having the heart attack," Griffin said.

"Probably." Fitz sighed again. He still hadn't gotten any sleep and it showed in his voice. "Hey, Griffin, did Carol Rosen really try to commit suicide?"

"We found her passed out with an empty bottle of prescription sleeping pills. I understand that she'd probably been drinking as well."

"Ah, shit."

"I'm sorry, Fitz."

"It's the Blaire case, isn't it? Has everyone wigged out. Press is going nuts, people are phoning nine-one-one if the bush outside their house moves . . . It's a copycat. How hard is that for people to grasp? Sometimes you get copycats." Fitz sounded desperate. He knew it, too. He sighed again, then said gruffly, "It's not her fault, you know. Whatever happened, whatever mistakes we may or may not have made . . . It's not her fault, not Jillian's fault, not Meg's fault. We're big boys over here. We handled the case the way we handled the case."

"Fitz, did you guys ever try to find any additional rape victims?"

"What do you mean?"

"Jillian and her mom raised an interesting point. Rape is a largely unreported crime. Sure, we have three known victims of the College Hill Rapist. But that doesn't mean they were his only victims."

Fitz was silent for a moment. "Well, we ran the details of the case through VICAP to see if we'd get any hits. No crimes matching these descriptions came up in any other states. Of course, that's not exactly foolproof. Another victim might not have filed a police report. Or maybe she did, and the police department still hasn't gotten around to entering it into the database, etc., etc. D'Amato waited six months before going to the grand jury, just in case we could find any other women willing to come forward and add their charges to the package. That's one of the reasons he didn't mind Jillian and her group going on TV all the time. He figured if anything would influence another victim to come forward, it would be seeing Jillian, Carol and Meg standing tall."

"But no one came forward?"

"Not that we ever heard of."

"But that doesn't rule out the possibility . . ."

"Griffin, there is no way of ruling out that possibility. You could interview every woman in this state, point-blank ask her if she was ever raped, and still not rule out the possibility because one of them might lie. We're cops. We can't focus on the impossible. We have to focus on the probable."

"I can account for everyone's money," Griffin said abruptly.

Fitz was clearly stunned. "No shit."

"Yeah. I even asked Vinnie Pesaturo if he arranged for a hit. He said no. And call me crazy, but I actually believe him."

"In other words, you just ran out of suspects."

"I ran out of suspects for this theory," Griffin said.

"Meaning?"

"Meaning maybe it wasn't a vengeance case. Maybe it was about something else. You tell me, Fitz. Why else would someone want Eddie Como dead?"

Griffin had no sooner set down his cell phone from that call than it rang again.

"Sergeant Griffin," he said.

"Where the hell are you?"

"Lieutenant Morelli! My favorite LT. Have I told you how lovely you look today?"

"You wouldn't know how lovely I look today. You haven't bothered to see me today. Funny, but my memory of the primary case officer's job is to keep the higher-ups informed. To actually be at headquarters overseeing information, generating theories and keeping the ball rolling. What is your memory of the primary case officer's job, Sergeant?"

"Good news," Griffin said hastily. "We're making lots of progress."

"Oh really? Because I've been listening to the news, Sergeant, and it seems to me that this case is going to hell in a handbasket."

"It's the fifty-million-dollar lawsuit, isn't it?"

"That's one problem."

"And the fact that the public is now convinced there is a serial rapist on the loose, and they're all about to be raped and/or murdered in their sleep?"

"That would be another problem."

"The mayor is getting calls, and the colonel is getting calls and the media is having an absolute field day at our expense?"

"Very good, Sergeant. For someone who's never around, at least you're keeping up-to-date. Detective Waters taking pity on you?"

"Yes, ma'am," Griffin acknowledged.

"Well, that speaks highly of Detective Waters. Whom, I understand, you have running around Cranston looking for associates of Eddie Como. That sounds an awful lot like you're poaching on Providence's rape case. Are you poaching on Providence's rape case?"

"I'm being thorough," Griffin said carefully.

"Sergeant, don't make me kill you."

Griffin smiled. He'd always liked Lieutenant Morelli. He took a deep breath. "Here's the problem. We started out with a basic theory. Eddie Como is an alleged rapist, ergo the most likely suspects in his murder are the rape victims."

"I remember that conversation."

"Pursuant to that angle, the financial crimes detectives did a full workup on the three women and their families. That yielded two good leads: Jillian Hayes and Dan Rosen have both made substantial cash withdrawals with no identifiable recipient."

"They could've hired the gunman."

"They could've. Unfortunately they didn't. Jillian Hayes donated her money to a Cranston parish, as confirmed by the parish priest. And Dan Rosen blew his money at Foxwoods, as corroborated by Vincent Pesaturo. It appears Mr. Rosen has a gambling problem."

"Which means you now have a problem."

"Yeah. At least as it stands now, none of the known victims and their families make good suspects, not even Vinnie Pesaturo."

"Where are you going with this, Sergeant?"

Griffin laughed. It was the hollow, stressed-out laugh of a detective watching his case go down the tubes. "Well, we have two angles left. First, we hold with the vengeance theory, and pursue the possibility that there were *other* victims of the College Hill Rapist. Ones that have never come forward to the police."

The lieutenant was silent for a moment. "That's an interesting theory."

"Isn't it? Jillian Hayes and her mother came up with it. Remember, rape is a drastically underreported crime. I checked with Fitz, and they did some initial legwork. Ran the rape profile through VICAP, etc. No hits, but that doesn't mean much. If there are other victims, they may never have gone to the police at all."

"Did they try the rape hotline or a rape-crisis organization?"

"Uh, no . . ."

"Well, maybe you'd like to send out some detectives, Sergeant. A rape-crisis organization won't give you names, but they can tell you if they received calls from someone who suffered a similar attack. Then at least you'll know if you're on the right track."

"Ummm, good point."

"That's why my name starts with the initials LT. Now what's your second theory?"

"It involves the Sylvia Blaire case. Fitz is hoping it's a copycat, praying really, that it's a copycat, but there are some problems with that theory."

"The douche."

Griffin scowled. "For a neglected lieutenant, you're keeping well informed."

Morelli said, "I'll have you know, I do look very good today. Plus, it just so happens that Lieutenant Kennedy from Providence has the hots for my sister. Which is, by the way, the only thing that is keeping Detective Fitzpatrick from wringing your neck. Well, that and the fact that Detective Fitzpatrick has his own problems at the moment."

"I appreciate that," Griffin said seriously. "Well, okay. So Fitz and I had an interesting discussion on the Sylvia Blaire case this morning. One possibility is that Eddie Como led two lives, one as the loving fiancé, and the other as a sexual deviant. And maybe Sexual Deviant Eddie had some friends to whom he liked to brag."

"Drinking buddies?"

"Maybe."

"Who knew all the details of what he did, including the douche?"

"That's the thought."

"Another interesting thought," Morelli concurred. "But why just a drinking buddy? Why not an actual accomplice? We've seen rape duos before."

Griffin shrugged. "Only one semen type was ever recovered from the vics. Plus, Carol and Jillian only reported seeing one man."

Morelli was silent for a moment. "What if the second person was more of a passive partner? Maybe a lookout?"

Griffin pursed his lips. "Oh," he said. "Ooooooh."

"I'm good, aren't I, Sergeant?" she said knowingly.

"You're good," he agreed. "The times! That would explain the times. See, it would appear that the first vic, Meg Pesaturo, was a quick in and out. Like the rapist was afraid of being discovered. But he spent a lot of time with Carol, who was always considered a last-minute substitute. Why wasn't he worried about someone coming home? And it would appear that the rapist had been in Trisha Hayes's apartment for a while, too. He'd already completed the rape before Jillian arrived, but he hadn't left yet. And even though in theory Jillian walked in on him, he was aware she was coming. He hid and jumped her from behind. Now, part of his lingering at the Rosen and Hayes crime scenes probably had to do with his escalating appetite for violence. He needed more and more to get the same thrill. But maybe he also had a look-out, or gained one as he went along. Someone whose job was to give him the security to stay as long as he liked. Except in Trisha Hayes's case, when some-one did unexpectedly appear, it was a basement apartment with only one point of entry/exit. So he couldn't bolt without being spotted. His better move was to ambush her instead, which he then prepared to do."

"And now this accomplice is no longer just a lookout?" Morelli said.

"That could be. Huh, that might explain the incident last night at the Hayes residence. Someone spray-painted 'Eddie Como lives' across a bank of windows. Maybe that's what this guy thinks he's doing. Carrying on the tra-dition of Eddie Como."

"But this person would also have reason to kill Como, correct? Both to protect what he'd done in the past and what he was thinking of doing in the future."

"Yeah, maybe. When Fitz brought it up this morning, I thought he was pushing the limits. But then again . . ."

"It assumes a shift in behavior." Morelli was thinking out loud. "Perpetrator number two was willing to be just a lookout, and now has graduated to actually committing sexual assault—and murder."

"A graduating level of involvement is not uncommon in sex crimes, though," Griffin added. "Most rapists start with bondage fantasies, then commit lower-level acts of violence against women—battery, assault—before moving to rape. In this case, we have a perpetrator who's definitely interested in rape. He's hanging out with a rapist, taking some role in the crimes. To have his first solo incident involve a high level of violence, homi-cide . . ." Griffin scowled. "That doesn't fit the pattern as well, but there could be mitigating circumstances. If Sylvia Blaire was attacked by Como's partner, the guy had gone a whole year without doing anything. Maybe the tension had built too high. He saw a potential victim. He went nuts."

Lieutenant Morelli was silent. He could tell she had to think about it, too. "It's worth pursuing," she said at last. "So I can tell Lieutenant Johnson that you're searching for associates of Eddie Como as possible suspects in our murder case?"

"You can say that."

"I think I will say that. Providence has enough problems without feeling as if they're at war with us, too."

"Providence has problems," Griffin agreed.

"Speaking of which . . ."

He knew what was coming next. His grip tightened on the phone, but at least he kept his breathing steady.

"Sergeant, have you spoken with Corporal Charpentier at the ACI?"

"Not yet. I've heard of the issue, though."

"No one here is taking him seriously," she said quietly.

"I appreciate that."

"On the other hand . . ."

He didn't say anything.

"This case is growing hot," Morelli said evenly. "It's getting a life of its own. You know what happens when a case gets a life of its own."

"I'm on top of it."

"Speed, Sergeant. We need to close this one. Quick. Before the public gets more frightened. Before Tawnya Clemente's lawyer gains more ammunition. And before the press realizes there is a man in the ACI who claims to have information relevant to the case. You understand?"

Griffin closed his eyes. He understood perfectly.

He was pulling into his driveway now. Waters's blue Taurus was already parked to one side, the detective sitting behind the wheel.

"I gotta go," Griffin said.

"First thing in the morning—"

"I'll have a report on your desk."

"Damn right, you will. And in the meantime?"

"I'll put detectives on the rape-crisis organizations and others on the Cranston bars."

"Good luck, Sergeant."

"Yeah." Griffin flipped shut his phone, thought about Carol lying in the hospital and Price sitting behind bars. "Good luck."

28

Waters

Detective Mike Waters got out of his car already wearing a pair of gray sweats and a white T-shirt bearing the emblem of the Rhode Island State Police. He swung a dark blue gym bag over his shoulder, and waited for Griffin to unlock the front door. Both were parked in the driveway; Griffin had his weight set and boxing equipment set up in the single-bay garage.

"Nice place," Mike said, eyeing the small, teetering white bungalow warily.

Griffin smiled. "You see any places in the floor that look mushy, trust me. Don't step there."

He opened the door and led the way in. He'd purchased the house six months ago, needing a fresh start and finding a new hobby. The home sat on prime real estate. North Kingstown. Waterfront access. On a clear day, he could sit on the back deck and see well past the Newport Bridge. Peaceful place. Lots of birds, a few gorgeous hundred-year-old beech trees. In other words, the house itself was an absolute shack. A real person—i.e., one with money—would've bulldozed the place and started over. After his generous donation to the American Cancer Society, however, Griffin didn't have that kind of money. Besides, he liked to live dangerously.

"I heard you were fixing it up." Mike's tone was more dubious now. He stepped over the threshold with a critical look at the water-stained hardwood floor, then the plaster ceiling that was literally peeling away in foot-long sheets.

"Full-time for six months," Griffin said.

"No way."

"I started with wiring, then moved on to plumbing, then did the roof. Now I just have the kitchen, bathroom, the ceilings, the floors and three bedroom walls to go. Oh, and the back deck. Oh, I think something may have crawled in and died beneath the garage."

"So . . . sometime before the extinction of man?"

"That's my plan." Griffin directed Mike into the tiny kitchen. The floor was a dirt-brown vinyl, straight out of the seventies. The stove was olive green, also from the seventies. The refrigerator, on the other hand, was a tiny, domed icebox circa 1950. He pulled on the metal lever-handle and gave a sigh of relief when the door actually opened. "Beer? Soda?"

"Afterward."

"Suit yourself."

Griffin disappeared into the first-story bedroom, changed into sweats himself, then led Mike to the garage. He had a nice free-weight system. Not from his brief days of money, either. No, he'd been carefully acquiring these pieces since he graduated from college. His first purchase, of course, had been the Everlast heavy bag hanging from a heavy-duty swivel and chain in one corner. Next to it was a twin pair of small, leather-covered speed bags with specially inserted rubber bladders for greater recoil. If you blinked at the wrong time, those things could knock you out—or give you one helluva black eye. Don't ask Griffin how he knew.

They headed to the boxing corner first. Mike had done some lightweight work in college. He looked too skinny for the sport, but what he lacked in bulk he made up in reach and speed. First time he and Griffin had squared off, he'd nailed Griffin four times before Griffin ever saw him coming. Of course, with an extra fifty pounds behind him, Griffin only had to land a single punch to end the sparring. They'd stuck to the bag after that. Pretty much.

Waters unzipped his blue canvas tote. He took out an ump's face guard, and matter-of-factly slipped it over his head.

Griffin froze. He got the hint and wasn't sure how to respond. He finally settled on a smile. "I'll just batter the rest of you," he warned and was secretly relieved when Mike smiled back.

"I don't think so," Waters said. "I've been practicing. You know how much shit a guy gets when his best friend breaks his nose?"

"Ahhh, they all figured out that you were slow?"

"Slow? Hell, they left a Ronald McDonald nose in my locker. I even wore it one day just to make them feel guilty."

"Did it work?"

"Nah. Next day they left me his shoes. Detectives have way too much time on their hands."

Mike stood. He left his face guard on, and positioned himself behind the heavy bag.

"Any luck with the bar search?" Griffin asked.

"Not yet. But I only made it to six joints. Ask me again tomorrow."

Griffin grunted and got on with it. He started slow. Warmed his muscles and thought that for the first time back with Mike it would be good to show a little control. But the day had been long, the case hard. He was thinking too much about Eddie Como and was he or was he not perpetrator number one and then was there or was there not a perpetrator number two. Then he thought of Carol, still no news. And then he thought of Jillian Hayes, the way her eyes turned molten gold when she was mad, the way her fingers had curled around his arm just an hour before.

He pummeled the living shit out of the heavy bag. Even Waters was breathing hard when he was done. The detective didn't say a word. He motioned with his head, and they changed places.

Holding a bag for Mike wasn't too difficult. He didn't have the mass to hit that hard. But he liked to thoroughly work over the target; Griffin had watched him do it before. Turning the bag into a human proxy, then going after various points. Kidney, kidney, kidney, right uppercut. Stomach, stomach, stomach, left chin.

Griffin relaxed, let his body do the work on setting the bag, and allowed his mind to drift. It had been a while since he'd worked out with anyone else. Brought back a certain measure of comfort. The smell of chalk and sweat. The heat of bodies working hard. The silence of men who didn't need to talk.

Afterward, Griffin hit the weights while Mike amused himself with a jump rope. Then Griffin played with the speed bags while Mike used the weights. Then an hour had passed, neither one of them could move, so they grabbed two beers, a gallon of water and headed for the back deck.

Sun was down. In the distance, the lights of the Newport Bridge twinkled like stars while the breeze came in off the water and covered their sweat-dampened skin with goose bumps. Mike dug out a sweatshirt. Griffin retrieved a fleece pullover.

They still didn't speak.

Cell phone rang. Griffin went back inside to get his phone off his bed. It was the hospital calling. Carol Rosen had been moved to the ICU. Her stomach had been pumped, but she had yet to regain consciousness. The doctors wanted to keep a close eye on her.

When he came back out, Waters had finished off the H_2O and cracked open both beers. He held out the red-and-white can of Bud to Griffin as he took his seat.

"I see you still only buy the best," Mike said.

"Absolutely."

They lapsed back into silence. Finally, ten, twenty, thirty minutes later, it didn't really matter, Mike said, "You still miss her?"

"Every day."

"I miss her, too." Mike looked at him. "It was hard, you being out. It was as if I'd lost both of you."

Griffin didn't say anything. He and Mike went back fifteen years now. Mike had been there for Griffin's first promotion to detective. He'd been there when Griffin came back from a hiking trip raving about this woman he'd just met. He'd served as best man at Griffin and Cindy's wedding, and then one bright spring afternoon, he'd been a pallbearer at her funeral. It was hard sometimes for Griffin to remember that the pain was not his alone.

"David Price was a piece of shit," Waters said abruptly. "And he hid it really well, not just from you. It's over, though. He took enough. Don't give him any more."

"I know."

"Good. She'd want you to be happy, Griffin. She never wanted less for you than you wanted for her."

"It wasn't fair, you know," Griffin said.

"I know."

"That's the hardest part. If I think about that . . ." He spun the can of beer in his hands. "If I focus on that, I start to go a little nuts again."

"Then don't think about that."

Griffin sighed heavily. He went back to studying the dark depths of the ocean at night. "Yeah. Things happen as they happen. People who think they're in control of life—they're just not paying attention."

"Amen," Waters said. He went back inside and fetched them both another can of beer.

Later, Griffin said: "Did you follow up with Corporal Charpentier?"

"Yeah."

"And?"

"David Price doesn't know anything."

"You're sure?"

"Corporal Charpentier tracked down Como's former roommate Jimmy Woods, the guy now serving time in Steel City. According to Woods, Eddie Como was a first-class whiner even behind bars. All he ever did was go on and on about how he was innocent, and this was all some horrible mistake."

"This is what Woods said?"

"That's what Woods said. Just for the sake of argument, Charpentier followed up with Price. Price said Woods was lying, but Charpentier wasn't impressed. Charpentier even asked Price if he knew who had done Sylvia Blaire. You know what he said?"

"What did he say?"

"He said Eddie Como. And then he laughed."

29

The Survivors Club

Nightfall. Meg sat on the floor of her little sister's room, ostensibly braiding the hair on her sister's new Barbie doll, but really trying to pretend she didn't notice the thick darkness gathering outside the second-story window— or the sound of her parents' voices, arguing down the hall.

"The pink dress," five-year-old Molly announced. She'd been going through her shoebox of Barbie clothes for the past ten minutes, trying to pick the perfect outfit for Barbie's upcoming wedding. Molly didn't own Ken, so Barbie was going to marry Pooh Bear. Pooh seemed very excited about the whole thing. He was wearing a new pink cape for the occasion. Molly loved the color pink.

Molly handed over the long, sequined dress, more appropriate for receiving an Oscar than, say, a wedding, but Meg dutifully tugged it up over the doll's feet.

"Maybe we should tell someone," her mother was saying down the hall.

"Absolutely not!" her father's muffled voice replied.

"What about Jillian—"

"No."

"Sergeant Griffin?"

"Dammit, Laurie, this is a family matter. We've made it this long, we're not getting strangers involved now."

"Shoes," Molly declared. She looked at Meg and promptly frowned. Matching shoes were hard to come by for the real people in this house, let alone the tiny plastic pairs that went with Barbie.

"She could have a barefoot wedding," Meg said.

"No!" Molly was shocked.

"Pooh doesn't have any shoes," Meg pointed out reasonably.

Her little sister rolled her eyes. "Pooh is a bear. Bears don't wear shoes, *everyone* knows that."

"Bears wear capes?"

"Yes, pink capes 'cause pink is Barbie's favorite color and her husband has to know that her favorite color is pink."

Purple, Meg thought idly. The color of royalty. His favorite color. Who was he? How did she know that?

"I'm worried . . ." Her mother's voice was rising down the hallway.

"Now, honey—"

"No! Don't honey me! For God's sake, Tom. The doctors told us her memory would come back shortly. Trauma-induced amnesia isn't supposed to last this long or be this complete. But she doesn't seem to remember anything. *Anything.* What if she's doing worse than we thought?"

"Come on, Laurie. You've seen her. She's happy. So what if she doesn't remember anything. Hell, maybe we're all better off that she forgot."

"Or maybe she hated her life that much. You ever think of that, Tom? Maybe what we did . . . Oh my God, maybe we scarred her that badly!"

"*Shoes!*" Molly squealed. She triumphantly dumped out her box of Barbie clothes and fished out a pair of bright red platform heels that had probably come with Barbie's flower child outfit or a killer pair of jeans. Now Molly took Barbie out of Meg's hands and used the shoes to finish up Barbie's hot-pink wedding ensemble. Outfits that would not be appearing in a Mattel commercial anytime soon, Meg decided. But Molly was very pleased.

"It's time for the wedding," Molly said with a big smile. "Dum-dum-de-dum, dum-dum-de-dum . . ."

"*I'll marry you.*"

"*No . . . no . . .*"

"*It's them, isn't it? Well, fuck them! I'll take you away. I'll make you happy. Come on, Meg, sweet Meg, my precious little Meg . . .*"

"*I'm scared.*"

"*Don't be scared. I won't let anyone hurt you, Meg. Not anyone. Ever.*"

"I'm scared," her mother was saying. "What if one day it suddenly comes back to her? Bang. Just like that. What if she's not ready?"

"The docs said if she did remember, then she'd be ready."

"Oh please, the doctors also said there was no reason for her to have forgotten this much. Face it, Tom, they don't know anything. It's amnesia. A brain thing, a mental thing. They're making this up as they go along."

"Laurie, honey, what do you want?"

"I want her to be happy! I want her to be safe. Oh Tom, what if *we* were the ones who had come home today to find Meg passed out from an overdose of sleeping pills? If the trauma of being so viciously raped is too much for a grown woman, what do you think it must be doing to Meg?"

"Meg?" Molly asked.

Meg blinked her eyes. Her sister's pink-painted room came back into focus. She was sitting once more on the floor. Her little sister was beside her, peering up at her anxiously.

"Meg doesn't feel good?" Molly asked. She was still clutching Barbie in her right hand.

"I'm, uh, I'm . . ." Meg touched her cheek. Her face was covered in sweat. Her skin had grown cold and clammy. "Just a little headache, I guess." She smiled at her sister weakly, trying to get her bearings back.

"*Marry me.*"

"*I can't—*"

"*Marry me.*"

Her stomach rebelled. For a moment, she thought she might be sick. And then suddenly, in the back of her head:

"Fucking brat. Run home to your mommy and daddy. Go hide behind their narrow little minds and fucking suburban panacea. You don't want my love? Then I take it back. I hate you, I hate you, I hate you . . ."

"Meg?"

"Just . . . a minute."

And then again from down the hall. "I don't want her to end up like Carol. I couldn't stand it if she ended up like Carol. Oh Tom, what if we've failed her?"

"M-M-Meg?"

"I hate you, I hate you, I hate you . . ."

"The doctors still aren't sure Carol's even going to make it. Meg's honestly grown close to the woman. What if she dies, Tom? What will happen then? My God, what will happen then!"

Meg bolted off the floor. She stumbled out of Molly's room.

"M-M-Meg?"

She careened down the hall.

"I hate you, I hate you, I hate you."

"What if Carol dies, what if Carol dies . . ."

Meg got the toilet seat up. She leaned over . . .

Nothing. She'd never eaten lunch. She'd forgotten about dinner. Her stomach rolled and rolled and rolled, but there was nothing present to throw up. She moved over to the sink. Turned on the cold water. Stuck her head under the faucet and let the icy flow shock the distant images from her brain.

Minutes passed. Long, cool minutes while the water sluiced over her sweaty skin and dampened all the voices in her head. Cool, cool water bringing blessed nothingness back to her brain.

When she finally looked up, her parents were standing in the doorway. Her father appeared his usual stoic self. Her mother, on the other hand, had one arm wrapped tightly around her stomach, while her right hand fidgeted with the gold heart dangling around her neck.

"Meg honey?" her mother asked.

Meg straightened. Strange voices, faint rumblings returned to the back of her mind. Like faraway scenes, threatening to come closer, closer, closer.

Meg found a towel and used it to methodically blot her face.

"You okay, sweetheart?" her father asked.

"Just a little queasy. All that time in the hospital, you know." She offered a faint smile.

"I'm sure Carol will be all right," her mother said briskly. Her right hand was now furiously twisting the dangling gold heart.

"Sure." Meg turned off the faucet. Rehung the towel. Ran a comb through her long brown hair.

"If there's anything you need . . ." her father tried.

"I'm fine, Daddy."

"We love you, sweetheart." Her mother this time.

"I love you, too."

What were they doing? Saying so many words, but none of the ones that mattered. Lies. She had never realized it before, but sometimes love produced lies. Big lies. Whopping lies. Gigantic lies, all packaged prettily and offered up with the best of intentions. Protection through falsehood. That's right—a suburban panacea.

Her parents were still standing in the doorway. She was still standing at the sink. No one seemed to know what to do.

"I, uh, I have a wedding," Meg said.

"A wedding?"

"Barbie and Pooh Bear. Didn't you get the invite?"

"Oh, Molly's marrying off Barbie again." Her mother finally relaxed. Her hand stilled around her neck. "The hot-pink dress?"

"Absolutely."

"Red platform shoes?"

"The kid's got style."

"Well, by all means." Her mother moved to the side, gestured for Meg to pass. "We wouldn't want to stand in the way of true love."

"I hate you, I hate you, I hate you."

"Okay then." Meg pasted the smile back on her face. She made it down the hall, where Molly sat uncertainly in the middle of her room, still clutching Barbie on her lap.

"Let's have that wedding!" Meg said with forced cheerfulness.

Molly looked up at her and positively beamed.

Hours later, the Pesaturo family went to sleep. One by one, the tiny rooms of the tiny home went dark. Meg turned off her own light. But she didn't go to bed. She went to her window. She stood in front of her window.

"I hate you, I hate you, I hate you."

She stared at the night outside her window, and she wondered at the darkness waiting for her there.

Those rich chocolate eyes. That gentle lover's kiss.

"David," she whispered, then licked her lips and tried out the name once more. "David. Oh no. David Price."

At midnight, Jillian finally left the hospital. Carol had yet to regain consciousness. Her stomach had been pumped, her body purged. Now she lay peacefully beneath stark white hospital sheets, her long golden hair a halo around her head as a heart monitor beeped in rhythm to her pulse and a respirator pumped air into her lungs.

Coma, the doctors said. She had ingested nearly 125 mg of Ambien, or twelve times the recommended dose. Combined with the alcohol, it had shut down her system to the point where she responded only to painful stimuli. The doctors would test her again in the morning, see if she began to pull out once the levels of sleeping pills and alcohol in her bloodstream came down. In other words, they would poke and prod at her poor, peaceful body. See if they could inflict enough pain to jar her back to life.

Dan remained in the room. He had pulled up a chair next to Carol, where he had finally fallen asleep with his head on the edge of her bed, his hand cradling her wrist. From outside the ICU door, Jillian had watched a nurse drape a blanket around his shoulders. Then Jillian had turned to go.

The night was cold, a sharp slap against Jillian's cheeks. She still wore her suit from this morning, no coat, no scarf. She hunched her shoulders beneath the tailored blue jacket and shivered as she walked. The parking lot was nearly empty this time of night. Certainly no reporters anymore. In the news world, Carol's suicide attempt was already old. Been there, done that. As of six this evening, the hot story had become Tawnya Clemente's lawsuit against the city.

God, Jillian was tired.

At her car, she went through the drill. Peered through the windows at the backseat. Glanced at neighboring cars to make sure no one loitered. Unlocked her door with her left hand. Held her canister of pepper spray in her right. Preparedness was nine-tenths of the battle. If you don't want to be a victim, then you can't act like one.

She got straight into her Lexus, immediately locked all the doors, then finally started the engine. She glanced again at her backseat. Nothing but empty, shadowed space. Why did she have chills running up and down her spine?

She got her car in reverse, turned to back out and nearly screamed.

No. Eddie Como. *No.* It was all in her head, all in her head. The backseat was empty, the parking lot was empty. She turned back around, shoved her automatic in park and sat there shaking uncontrollably, the fear still rolling off her in waves.

Panic attack, she realized after a moment, trying to regain her breath. In the beginning, she'd had them all the time. It had been a bit since the last one, but then again, today had been a bad day. First Sylvia Blaire. Then Carol.

Oh God, Carol . . .

Jillian rested her head against the steering wheel, and suddenly started to cry. Second time for her in one day. Had to be a new record. She couldn't stop, though. The sobs came up from the dark pit of her, angry and hard and desolate, until her stomach hurt and her shoulders ached and still she choked out rough, bitter tears. This is why she didn't cry. Because there was nothing dainty or tragic about her grief. She cried like a trucker, and afterward she looked like a disaster, with red, blotchy cheeks and mascara-smeared eyes.

What if Sergeant Griffin saw her now? The thought made her want to weep again, though she didn't know why.

She could call him. He would probably take her call, even though it was after midnight. He'd probably even let her go on and on about her sister and the ache that wouldn't ease and the grief that knew no end. He would listen to those things. He seemed to be that kind of guy.

She didn't pick up her cell phone, though. Maybe she wasn't that kind of woman, the kind who still believed in Prince Charming. Or maybe she was, but Meg was right and she wasn't ready to stop punishing herself for her sister's death.

Or maybe it was all a bunch of psychobabble bullshit, and the bottom line was that she just wasn't ready. She did still miss her sister. She did still ache. And she did hold too much in and she did suffer too much guilt. And now she was worried about Carol, and as always she was worried about her mother, and then there was this thing with another poor dead college student and who knew what was really going on out there in that pitch-black night?

Shit. Jillian put her car back in drive. She got out of the dark parking lot.

At home, outside lights fired up her home like a suburban landing strip. She'd had three new spotlights added first thing this morning and God knows her neighbors had probably put on sunglasses just to go to bed. Good for them. May that be the worst tragedy they ever had to face.

Jillian drove by the patrol car parked down the street. The two officers sitting inside nodded at her. She waved back. So Griffin had kept his word as well.

She pulled into her garage with the normal drill. Car doors still locked. Gazing out the rearview mirror and watching the opening until the garage door had closed all the way. Checking out the shadowy depths of the garage for other signs of intruders. The coast appeared clear. She finally unlocked her car door, and entered her home.

Toppi had left her a plate covered with plastic wrap on the kitchen counter. A chicken sandwich in case she was hungry. Jillian put the plate in the refrigerator, poured a glass of water and made the rounds. Doors still locked. Windows secure. Nothing out of place.

The house was quiet this time of night. Just the ticking of the hallway clock, and the occasional fluttery snore from behind Toppi's bedroom door.

One A.M. now. Jillian should go to sleep. She kept prowling the house, driven by a compulsion she couldn't name.

Had she failed Carol? In the past, Carol and Meg had accused her of carrying too much guilt. Then, just this afternoon, Griffin had implied she took too much responsibility for things. No one could keep everyone safe.

It was her job, though. For as long as she could remember. Libby had led the wild life. Jillian held things together. Baby Trish required stability. Jillian made them a home. Her mother's health declined. Jillian took her in as well. They were her family, she loved them and with love came responsibility. So she did everything she could for them. She just never let them get too close.

Just as she had done with Carol and Meg.

For the first time, it occurred to her—was she feeling guilty that Trisha was dead, or was she feeling guilty that she had not loved her more when she was still alive? All those summers with Trisha racing along the beach and Jillian alone beneath an umbrella. Why hadn't she run out into the sand? Why hadn't she splashed through the waves with her sister? What had she been so afraid of?

Strong, responsible Jillian who had never had a serious relationship. Independent, serious Jillian who focused on work work work, all of the time. Proud, lonely Jillian who marched through life as if it were a battlefield and she didn't want anyone taking her prisoner. Not her mother. Not her sister. Not Eddie Como and not the Survivors Club.

Poor, stupid Jillian who, at the age of thirty-six, still knew so little about what was important in life. Griffin had been right before. Trisha had loved her. And it shouldn't have taken Jillian nearly a year to remember that.

Jillian moved into the hallway. She thought of Trisha again, and the days that would never be. And then she thought of her mother, and all the years still to come. Proud, fierce Libby tapping, tapping, tapping. Sad, silent Libby who so longed to visit her daughter's grave. Jillian walked down to her mother's bedroom. She pushed in the door. She spotted Libby, lying upon her bed, bathed in the icy blue glow of a night-light. Libby's eyes were wide open. She'd been watching the door and now she stared straight at Jillian.

"You've been waiting for me to come home," Jillian said softly, with genuine surprise, genuine wonder.

Her mother's finger tapped the bedspread.

"You wanted to make sure that I got home safe."

Her mother's finger, rising and falling on the bedspread.

Jillian went farther into the room. "You can rest now. I'm home, Mom. I'm . . . safe." And then, a heartbeat later, "And I love you, too, Mama."

Her mother smiled. She held out her arms. And for the first time since she was a little girl, Jillian went into her mother's embrace. And it didn't hurt so much after all. All of these years, all of these miles later, it finally felt right.

While the clock ticked down the hall. And the spotlights lit up the house. And the uniformed officers sat in their patrol car, waiting to see what would happen next.

30

Griffin

Four a.m., Wednesday morning, Detective Sergeant Roan Griffin drove to state police headquarters in North Scituate. He was early. Very early. Good thing, too. He had contact interviews to review, witness statements to consider and detective activity reports to analyze. Then he needed to prepare a time line of events. Oh, and he wanted to produce a chart, filling in the recent findings on their key suspects. That ought to make Lieutenant Morelli happy.

Yep, Griffin had gotten a whole five hours of uninterrupted sleep last night. No new rapes, no new shootings, no new lawsuits. Now he was feeling downright chipper. He should've known better.

Walking into the Investigative Support Service building, he was immediately greeted by the uniform on duty. Griffin nodded back, then proceeded down the narrow, yellow-lit hallway to Major Crimes. The ISSB, a flat, dull-brown 1960s building that could've passed as any government office, was divided into a series of wings. The Criminal Identification Unit took up the back right corner of the building, with one large office space for the five CIU detectives to share and a series of smaller rooms to house their toys—the lie detector room, the two Automatic Fingerprint Information System (AFIS) rooms, the significantly sized evidence-processing room, the photo lab.

In contrast to the CIU suite, the Major Crimes detectives were granted a small corner in the front of the building, where they had five gray cubicles crammed into one blue-carpeted space. Of course, they considered themselves to have the nicer room. The ten-foot-high drop ceiling only had a fraction of the yellow water stains found in the rest of the building. Plus, the detectives kept their tidy desks free of paperwork and openly displayed nicely framed family photos. A few detectives had brought in plants over the years, and now massive green vines draped cheerfully down the cubicle walls. All in all, the place could've been an accountant's office—if accountants had a back wall covered with "Most Wanted" photos and a front wall bearing a white board with homicide notes.

Griffin liked the Major Crimes office. Not nearly as dreary as other law enforcement facilities, say, for example, the Providence station where Fitz worked. That place ought to be condemned, and maybe would be once the new headquarters was completed across the highway. It was a thought.

Griffin stuck his head across the hall, where Lieutenant Morelli had her office. Nobody home. Perfect. He'd sit down, whip the case notes into order and know exactly what was going on in the Eddie Como homicide file by 8:00 A.M. Just like a good case officer. Hell, maybe he'd surprise them all and actually have the case solved by 9:00 A.M. Oooh, he was a cocky son of a bitch.

Griffin's optimism lasted until 7:00 A.M., when his cell phone rang. It was Fitz, and he didn't sound good.

"You gotta get down here," Fitz said without preamble.

"Where's here?"

"Providence," Fitz said tensely. "Hurry."

"Has there been another attack?"

"Just get here. Now. Before the press finds out."

Fitz hung up the phone. Griffin sat there a moment longer, staring at his silent cell phone. Ah, shit.

He grabbed his jacket and headed for the door. Halfway down the hall, he ran into Waters, who was just getting in for the day. Mike was moving a little stiffly this morning, which under other circumstances would've made Griffin proud. Now, however, he simply swapped notes.

"I gotta run to Providence. Something's up."

"Another attack?" Waters asked immediately.

"I don't know. Have you heard the morning news?"

"Drive time was quiet."

"Well, then, whatever it is, we're still one step ahead. That's worth something. Listen, can you follow up with the other detectives? See if they're making any progress with the rape-crisis groups. Oh, and take a few more bodies with you to the Cranston bars. I'm guessing we're going to need progress, mmmm, now."

"Got it. You'll let us know?"

"When I know what I know, you'll be the first I'll let know." Griffin headed down the hall.

"Hey, Griffin," Waters called out behind him. Griffin turned. "I'll call ACI. Just in case."

Griffin hesitated a fraction of an instant. "Yeah," he said more slowly. "Just in case."

He went out the door, no longer feeling so good about the day.

The Providence Police Department was located right off I-95 in downtown Providence. The rapidly aging building took its role as an active urban police station quite seriously. Ripped-up gray linoleum floors, water-stained drop ceilings, scuffed-up walls, exposed pipes. The Providence detectives liked to joke that their offices were straight out of *Barney Miller*. For interior decorating, their color options were dirt, dirty and dirtier.

Definitely a far cry from the state police's White House in North Scituate. Not that there was any resentment or anything.

Griffin arrived shortly after seven-thirty. He parked his Taurus in the tow-away zone near the front entrance. A Providence uniform would ticket him out of spite. Fitz would make it go away. Every organization had its rituals.

He walked through the exterior glass doors, passing three black youths in baggy jeans and sleeveless sweatshirts who glared at him balefully. He stared back and, by virtue of size, got them to look away first. Inside was a small dark foyer. Griffin took the door to the left into another small dark foyer, where three receptionists sat behind bulletproof glass. This room was crowded with various people pleading various cases. "Man, I gotta see so-and-so." "Hey, this parking ticket's bogus!" The receptionists didn't have the power to do anything, of course, but that didn't stop the masses from trying.

Griffin pushed to the front, flashed his shield and was promptly buzzed through the main doors, into the heart, or rather, bowels of the police station. Lucky him.

He took the stairs up. He'd tried the elevator only once and it had groaned so badly and moved so painfully he'd vowed never again. The way Griffin saw it, the Providence police would be lucky to get out before the whole building came down on their heads.

The Detective Bureau was on the second floor, adjacent to the Bureau of Criminal Identification. Griffin tried the main room, didn't see Fitz, then moved down to the locker room. Still no Fitz, but plenty of artwork; the detectives liked to hang photos of their more interesting cases on their lockers. The victim who was folded in half when hit by an oncoming train. The badly decomposed body of a victim who wasn't found for several weeks. A pair of hands, covered in marijuana leaves, found in the trunk of a car after it was pulled over for a routine traffic stop. The body, found a day later, that went with the hands . . .

Griffin continued through the labyrinth of tiny gray rooms until he came to the end of the hall. There, Providence had their evidence-processing center, basically two adjoining rooms, each the size of a coat closet, crammed full of cabinets, tables, gear and AFIS. Fitz was standing in front of the folding table, deep in hushed conversation with a sharply dressed black man whom Griffin recognized as Sergeant Napoleon, head of the BCI. Both men looked up the minute he filled the doorway.

" 'Bout time," Fitz muttered.

"You rang, I ran," Griffin said lightly. Fitz's face had an unhealthy flush. His eyes had sunk deeper into the folds of his face and his sparse hair stuck up in unusual disarray. He'd finally changed clothes since yesterday, so he'd obviously managed to make it home. Unfortunately, the break didn't seem to have done him any good.

"Griffin, Napoleon, Napoleon, Griffin." Fitz made the introductions.

"We've met," Griffin said as he and the sergeant obligingly shook hands. In contrast to Fitz, Napoleon appeared excited. He had a light in his eyes, a fervor to his face. Oh no, Griffin thought immediately. When the forensics guys got excited . . . Oh no.

"You got the reports back," Griffin said abruptly.

"Uh huh," Fitz said.

"The DNA?"

Fitz looked at the open door. He dropped his voice to nearly a whisper. "Uh huh."

Griffin leaned forward. He lowered his voice as well. "And?"

"We got a match," Fitz whispered.

"A *good* match," Napoleon emphasized.

"We know who raped Sylvia Blaire," Fitz said grimly. "According to the Department of Health, it was Eddie Como."

"This has got to be a mistake," Griffin declared five minutes later. He, Fitz and Napoleon had commandeered the lieutenant's office, shut the door and resumed their earnest huddle. They kept their heads together and their voices down. In a police station, there were eyes and ears everywhere.

"Of course it's a mistake!" Fitz snapped, then immediately dropped his voice again. "A dead man did not rape and murder Sylvia Blaire. Now do you want to tell me who did?"

Griffin turned to Napoleon. "Could it be a family member? What about an uncle, a cousin, a father? Hell, what about a long-lost brother?"

Napoleon shook his head. "We got a preliminary match in seven out of seven sample sites. We'll send it out for further analysis, but we're looking at a dead-on hit."

"Okay, a long-lost identical twin brother."

"Identical twins don't have the same DNA. It would be close, yeah, but again, seven out of seven sample sites . . ."

Griffin raked his hand through his hair. "Shit," he said.

"It is not Eddie Como," Fitz muttered. "It is not *fucking* Eddie Como."

"Okay, okay, okay." Griffin held up his hand. "Let's be logical about this. Assume for a moment that the DNA from the Blaire crime scene really does match the sample taken from Eddie Como. What if someone else had some-how saved semen from Eddie Como and smeared it at the scene?"

He and Fitz promptly stared at Napoleon, who at least seemed willing to consider the possibility.

"Swabs are first tested for semen, to see if we have something for DNA testing," Napoleon mused. "Now, spermatozoa only tests positive for seventy-two hours, so if someone had gotten a Como 'sample,' so to speak, it would have to be fresh. Otherwise the spermatozoa would be dead, the swabs would test negative for semen and nothing else would be done."

"The man's been behind bars," Fitz growled. "How do you get a fresh sample from a man in prison?"

Griffin just looked at him.

"Hey," Fitz said. "I know there's more sex in prison than in most bordellos, gimme a break. But we're not talking about someone smuggling out a stained sheet and dropping it at the scene. The match was seven out of seven sample sites, meaning they found matching DNA on the sheets, the nightgown, vagi-nal swabs, etc., etc. You wanna explain that scenario to me?"

"That makes it trickier," Griffin confessed. "Eddie could've preserved a sample somehow. I don't know, jacked off in a Dixie cup and sent it out?"

It was Fitz's turn to stare at him. "Now why the hell would he do that? This is a guy who's been swearing to anyone with a microphone that he's innocent. Wouldn't he kind of wonder about a request for, gee, seminal fluid?"

"Conjugal visits?" Napoleon tried.

"Not at Intake," Griffin said.

"This is crazy," Fitz muttered.

"This is nuts," Griffin agreed. "Okay, what if we're going about this backward? What if the swap wasn't made at the scene? What if the swap was made with Eddie Como's sample?"

"What do you mean?"

"I mean, the samples from the crime scenes are showing a match with another sample *labeled* Eddie Como. But what if *that* is where we have the mistake?"

"No way," Fitz said immediately.

"Couldn't happen," Napoleon seconded. "Standard operating procedure for executing a search warrant for DNA samples: Detective Fitzpatrick and Detective McCarthy picked up Eddie Como and brought him to the Reagan Building, where two clinicians and I were waiting. The clinicians drew two vials of blood, plucked several strands of hair from Como's head, then took additional combings from his pubic region. *I* personally packaged each sample and labeled it as evidence to preserve chain of custody. So that's what, five people who can vouch that Eddie Como was in the room—"

"I'm not saying you guys had the wrong man," Griffin interrupted.

"And four *samples,*" the BCI sergeant continued relentlessly, "all properly sealed and labeled that you would have to swap. What are the chances of that?"

"It would be difficult," Griffin said grudgingly.

"Try impossible," Fitz countered hotly. "Try fucking impossible. We know how to do our goddamn jobs!"

"Then how did we get this match?" Griffin's voice was rising.

"I don't know! Maybe it was Eddie Como. We haven't seen his body."

"Eddie Como is dead! The ME already confirmed his fingerprints. The guy is dead, deader and deadest. So once again, how the hell did his DNA wind up at another rape-murder scene?"

"I don't know!"

"Someone is fucking with us," Griffin said. "Someone is playing a game." And then, on the heels of that thought. "Shit!"

"What?" Fitz asked wildly.

"Shit! Shit! Shit! I gotta make a phone call."

"Now?"

"Yeah, now. Where's a landline? How the hell do I dial out?"

"Who are you calling?"

"The Easter Bunny, who do you think?" Griffin impatiently punched in the number. "Detective Waters," Mike said thirty seconds later.

"Mike, Griffin. You talk to ACI? What did he say?"

"Price said . . . Price said, he told you so, and he's still waiting for your visit."

He told you so . . . Who murdered Sylvia Blaire, David? Eddie Como.

Ah shit. Griffin hung his head. The room simultaneously closed in on him and fell away. Eighteen months later. Eighteen painful, careful, deliberate months later, here he was again. Knee-deep in some strange, twisted

David Price game. Griffin took a deep breath, struggled to pull it together. A dead man couldn't have killed Sylvia Blaire. Something else had to have happened. Something else that put Como's DNA at the scene.

And then he was thinking back to Monday afternoon and his conversation with Fitz: "*So why did Eddie, who left behind no hair, no fiber, and no fingerprints, leave behind ten latex strips? Why did he on the one hand, learn how to cover his tracks, and then on the other hand, leave you a virtual calling card?*"

Fitz had angrily declared that the Providence police had *not* framed Eddie Como. Now, Griffin finally, horribly, had an idea who had.

Games. Games didn't sound like Eddie's style. But Griffin knew another man, a young man with an even younger face, who loved to play games. Who also sent notes and made phone calls, except they never declared his innocence. A man who had spent two days now claiming insider knowledge and had even graciously sent Griffin a note welcoming him to the case.

And then Griffin was back to thinking about that stupid DNA, the *only* evidence that had pointed at Eddie Como. DNA that was supposed to have been washed away by Berkely and Johnson's Disposable Douche with Country Flowers . . . Except . . . What's the worst thing a detective could do? Make an assumption. And what was the major assumption they had all made? That the douche had been used in an attempt to *remove* DNA from the scene. Son of a bitch.

The final pieces started clicking into place and for a moment . . . For a moment, Griffin was so mad, he couldn't speak.

"What's going on?" Waters was asking on the other end of the phone.

"Who? Who?" Fitz was saying beside him.

"What day was the first reported rape?" Griffin asked harshly. "When was Meg Pesaturo attacked?"

"Eleven April, last year," Fitz replied. "Why? What do you know?"

April eleventh. Five months after David Price's November arrest. Five months after Griffin's little meltdown. It seemed impossible. And yet . . .

"He's playing us."

"What do you want to do?" Mike asked on the other end of the line.

"Who? What?" Fitz was still parroting wildly.

"The guy who saw this coming." Griffin closed his eyes. "The guy who somehow knows more about this case than we do."

"Who saw this coming?" Fitz pleaded.

"David," Griffin said quietly. "My good old sexual-sadist neighbor, David Price."

31

Price

Griffin was dialing his cell phone, navigating his way furiously through tiny Providence streets to the I-95 on-ramp while Fitz clutched the dashboard and continued cursing colorfully under his breath. Jillian answered the phone, and Griffin immediately started talking.

"Jillian, I need you to tell me something and I need you to be honest."

"Griffin? Good morning to you, too—"

"I know you're angry with the police," he interrupted steadily. "I know you think we failed your sister and I know you haven't had a lot of incentive to cooperate with us. But I need your help now. I need you to tell me if you ever met a man named David Price. And don't lie, Jillian. This is deadly serious."

Silence. He gripped the wheel tighter, wondering what that silence meant, and wishing that his stomach wasn't beginning to turn queasily while the ringing picked up in his ears. Breathe deep, release. Eighteen months of hard work. Don't lose sight of the ball now.

"The name sounds familiar," Jillian said finally. "Wait a minute. Wasn't he your neighbor? Griffin, what is this about?"

"Did your sister ever mention his name?"

"No, not at all."

"Ever get any correspondence? Maybe something in the mail?"

"No. Wait a minute." There was a muffled clunk as she moved the receiver from her ear. Then he heard her voice shout out, "Toppi. Have you ever received anything from someone named David Price? Check with Mom." Another muffled thunk, then Jillian was back on the line. "They both say no. Griffin, you arrested him, right? You sent him to jail . . . a long time ago. Why are you asking about him now?"

Griffin ignored her question, and instead asked one of his own. "What are your plans for the day?"

"I told Mom I would take her to see Trish. Griffin—"

"Don't."

"Don't?"

"I want you to stay close to home. Or better yet. Load up Toppi and your mom and take them to the Narragansett house. I'll arrange for a pair of uniforms to meet you there."

"Did he get out of jail?" Jillian asked quietly.

"No."

"But you're targeting him. Is he involved in all this? Did David Price somehow hurt my sister?"

"That's what I'm trying to find out. Any word on Carol?"

"I was just about to call the hospital."

"I should send uniforms there as well," he muttered out loud, then wished he hadn't.

Jillian's voice grew even more somber on the other end of the line. "Something's happened, hasn't it? Something bad."

"I'll be in touch," Griffin told her. "And Jillian. Be careful."

He flipped shut his phone. Mostly because he didn't know what else to say. Or maybe because he did know what he wanted to say, and now was not the time or place, especially with Fitz sitting red-faced and haggard beside him.

He took the on-ramp for 95 South, headed for the ACI and simultaneously tossed his cell phone to Fitz. "You're up."

Fitz dialed the Pesaturo residence. Thirty seconds later, they both heard Meg's mother pick up the phone.

"Detective Fitzpatrick here," Fitz said roughly, then cleared his throat. "I, uh, I need to speak to Miss Pesaturo, please."

"Detective Fitzpatrick!" Meg's mother said warmly. "How are you this morning?"

Fitz kept his tone gruff. "Mrs. Pesaturo, I need to speak with Meg."

Laurie Pesaturo faltered. From the driver's seat, Griffin could hear the confusion in her staticky voice as she asked Fitz to wait one moment. It was several more minutes, however, before she was back on the line. "I'm sorry," she said stiffly. "Meg seems to have stepped out."

"She's not home?"

"Not at the moment."

"Do you know where she is?"

An even stiffer reply. "Not at the moment."

Fitz cut to the chase. "Mrs. Pesaturo, have you ever heard the name David Price?"

A pause. "Detective, what is this about?"

"Please, just answer the question, ma'am. Do you know, or have you ever known, a man named David Price?"

"No."

"Meg has never mentioned his name?"

"Not that I recall."

"Has he ever sent anything to your home? Perhaps called?"

"If he had done that," Laurie Pesaturo said crisply, "then I would know the name, wouldn't I? Now I'm asking *you* again, Detective. What is this about?"

"I would like you to find Meg, Mrs. Pesaturo. I'd like you to keep her close to home today. In fact, it might not be a bad time for your husband to take a day off, spend the afternoon with his family. Perhaps you could all pay Uncle Vinnie a visit, something like that."

"Detective . . ."

"It's just a precaution," Fitz added quietly.

Another pause. And then, "All right, Detective. Thank you for calling. Will you call again?"

"I hope to touch base again this afternoon, ma'am."

"Thank you, we would appreciate that."

"Find Meg," Fitz repeated, and then they were turning into the vast facility that comprised the ACI.

Griffin found the red-brick admin building that housed the prison's Special Investigation Unit as well as the state police's ACI unit. He turned the car into a parking space, cut the ignition. He no longer looked at Fitz. He was focusing on the growing tension in his shoulders, that steadily building ringing in his ears. Breathe deep, release. Breathe deep, release.

"Hey, Griffin baby, you think this is bad? Let me tell you about your wife . . ."

Fitz got out of the car. After another moment, Griffin followed suit.

The ACI "campus" spreads out over four hundred acres of land. With brick towers and barbed-wire fence visible from the freeway, the facility is actually half a dozen buildings nestled among half a dozen other government institutions. Nearly four thousand inmates reside in the ACI at any given time, and they generate enough internal and external complaints to employ six ACI special investigators and two state detectives full time. The special investigators are the first responders, handling all inmate-to-inmate complaints. In situations, however, where there are criminal charges—serious assault, murder for hire, drug trafficking, etc.—the state police are brought in to lead the inquiry.

In between these cases, the state detectives spend their time receiving calls from various inmates looking to flip on various other inmates in return for various considerations. The detectives get plenty of calls. Very few of them, though, ever lead to anything.

That's what Griffin had been hoping for when he'd first learned of David Price's outreach. Now Griffin wasn't so sure anymore.

Corporal Charpentier met Griffin and Fitz in the lobby of the admin building, then led them down the one flight of stairs to the state's basement office. Griffin immediately wrinkled his nose at the stale air, while Fitz actually recoiled.

"I know, I know," Charpentier said. "In theory, the building is now asbestos-free. As the people actually inhaling, however . . ." He let the rest of the thought trail off. Griffin and Fitz got the picture. They were also both getting a headache.

Charpentier came to the end of the hall, opened the door and led them into a tiny office. Two desks were set up face-to-face, topped with computer terminals, manila folders and a variety of paperwork. The remainder of the cramped space was taken up by two desk chairs and a wall of gunmetal-gray filing cabinets. No cheery office plants here. Just cream-painted cinder-block walls, gray industrial carpet and dim yellow lights. Police officers led such glamorous lives.

"They're bringing him down to the rear hall," Charpentier said, taking a seat and gesturing for them to do the same. "They need another ten minutes."

"All right," Griffin said. He didn't sit. He didn't want anyone to see that his body was beginning to twitch.

"Personally, I don't think he knows jack shit," Charpentier added, then gave Griffin an appraising look.

"How is he adapting?" Griffin asked.

"Better than you'd think." Charpentier leaned back, shrugged. "He's young, he's small, he's a convicted pedophile. Frankly, he's got jail 'bitch' written all over him. But I don't know. I heard this story from one of the corrections officers. Six guys surrounded David Price in the prison showers. Were going to give him a little prison indoctrination, show him the way this place works for small, flabby-muscled baby-killers. Then David started talking. And talking and talking and talking. The guards were running to the scene, of course, expecting to find carnage, and . . . And David Price was now surrounded by six laughing guys, not hitting him, not pummeling him, but slapping him merrily on the back. Basically, in three minutes or less, he'd turned them into six gigantic, brand-new friends." Charpentier shook his head. "I don't get it myself, but in another year, he'll be running the place, the world's smallest prison warlord."

"He's good with people," Griffin said.

Charpentier nodded, then slowly leaned forward. His gaze went from Griffin to Fitz to Griffin again. "You want to hear something wild? Assaults in maximum have doubled since David was assigned there. I was just looking at the stats again this morning. Code Blue nearly every day for the last nine months. It's been open season over there. And the only new variable I can see is a man who could still buy his clothes from Garanimals."

"You think he's responsible," Fitz said bluntly.

Charpentier shrugged. "We can't prove anything. The guys always have their reasons for why they did what they did. But . . . David talks a lot. All the time. He's like some frigging politician, working the yard, passing notes along the cell block. And the next thing you know, we'll have trouble. A lot of trouble. Guys ending up in the infirmary impaled with sharp metal objects kind of trouble. I don't know what the hell Price says or does, but there's something scary about him."

"He's very good with people," Griffin said again.

"Let me tell you about your wife . . ."

The corporal's phone rang. He picked it up. "All right. They're ready for us."

ACI's maximum-security building, aka Old Max, is a singularly impressive building. Built in 1878 from thick gray stone, the three-story structure is dominated by a gigantic white-painted center dome. In the old days, a light would burn in that dome, green light if everything was okay, red light if something was wrong. The folks in Providence would then send a horse and buggy to check things out.

The prison also boasts one of the oldest working mechanical systems in the nation. Most prisons are electronic these days. Push a button to buzz open cell door A or cell block B. Old Max still has working levers for operating the thick steel doors. The inmates probably don't appreciate these things, but it lights a fire under the history buffs.

Mostly, Old Max has sheer charisma. The thick stone walls look like prison walls. The heavy, steel-constructed six-by-eight cells, stacked three tiers high and thirty-three cells long, look like prison cells. The black-painted steel doors, groaning open in front of you, snapping shut behind you, sound like prison doors. The steady assault of odors—sweat, urine, fresh paint, ammonia, BO—smell like prison odors. And the rest of the sounds—men shouting, TVs blaring, metal clinking, radios crackling, water running, men pissing—sound like prison sounds.

Tens of thousands of men have passed through these gates in the past hundred years. Rapists, murderers, drug lords, Mafiosi, thieves. If these walls could talk, it wouldn't be words at all. It would be screams.

Griffin and Fitz signed in at the reception area. Civilians were required to pass through a metal detector. As members of law enforcement, however, they got to skip that honor, and they and Corporal Charpentier were immediately buzzed through a pair of gates into the main control area. Security was still tight. They had to wait for the gate to close behind them. Then a corrections officer who sat in an enclosed booth gestured for Griffin and Fitz to drop their badges into a metal swivel tray. The officer rotated the tray around to him, inspected the IDs, nodded once, dropped in two red visitor's passes and swiveled the tray back around.

Only after Griffin and Fitz had fastened the visitor's passes to their shirts did the white-painted steel gate in front of them slowly slide back and allow them to proceed into the bullpen. There they stood again, waiting for the gate to close behind them before a new set of gates opened in front of them. Then they had finally, officially arrived into the rear hall of Old Max.

Half a dozen guards sat around the red-tiled, white-painted space. Directly to the left was the door leading to the left wing of cells. Ahead of that was the lieutenant's office, where two corrections officers were monitoring the bank of security cameras. Straight ahead was the corridor leading to the cafeteria. And to the right was a visiting room, used by corrections officers for official business. Today, David Price sat shackled inside. Two other corrections officers sat outside. They looked up at Griffin, nodded once, then made a big show of looking away.

Did they think he was going to attack the kid again? Was this their way of saying that if he did, they didn't care? It sounded like Price had been keeping the whole facility hopping, whether the officers could prove anything or not. Even in maximum, inmates got a good eight hours a day outside their cell—eating, working, seeing visitors, hanging in the yard, etc. In other words, plenty of opportunities to mingle with other inmates and plenty of time to cause trouble.

This place really was too good for Price.

Corporal Charpentier opened the door. Griffin and Fitz followed him in.

Sitting in a tan prison-issued jumpsuit, David Price didn't look like much. He never had, really. At five eight, one hundred and fifty pounds, he wouldn't stand out in a crowd. Light brown hair, deep brown eyes, a softly rounded face that made him look seventeen when he was really closer to thirty-two. He wasn't handsome, but he wasn't ugly. A nice young man, that's how women would classify him.

Maybe that's even what Cindy had said, that first day he'd stopped by: *"Hey, Griffin, come meet our new neighbor, David Price. So what's a nice young kid like you doing living in a place like this?"*

David Price was smiling at him.

"You look good," Price said. He didn't seem to notice either Corporal Charpentier or Detective Fitz. They were irrelevant to the matters at hand. Griffin understood this, probably they did, too. God, please keep him from killing David Price.

David was still smiling. A nice, friendly smile. The kind a kid might give his older brother. That was Price's thing. He never challenged directly, particularly larger men. He'd play the sidekick, the loyal student, the good friend. He'd be respectful but never gushing. Complimentary but never insincere. And at first you simply dismissed him, but then he kind of grew on you, and the next thing you knew, you were looking forward to his company, even eager for his praise. And things started to shift. Until it was never really clear anymore who was in charge and who was the sidekick, but you didn't think about it much anyway, because it seemed as if you were doing what you wanted to do, even if you didn't really remember wanting to do those kinds of things before.

Men liked David—he was the perfect unassuming friend. Women liked David—he was the ideal nonthreatening male companion. Children liked David—he was the favorite uncle they never had.

Man, Griffin should've just killed him when he had the chance.

"Have you replaced Cindy yet?" David asked conversationally. "Or is no other woman good enough? I imagine it can't be that easy to find another soul mate."

"Shut the fuck up," Fitz snarled.

"Tell us about Sylvia Blaire," Griffin said. He pulled out a chair but didn't take a seat.

David cocked his head to the side. He wasn't ready for business yet. Griffin hadn't thought that he would be. "I miss having dinners at your house, you know. I used to love watching the two of you together. Cindy-n-Griffin, Griffin-n-Cindy. Gave me faith that there was something worthwhile in life. I hope someday I get to fall in love like that, too."

"What's his name?"

"Hey now, Griff, that's sorta rude, don't you think?"

"I want the name of the man who raped and murdered Sylvia Blaire." Griffin placed his hands on the table and leaned forward pointedly.

David merely smiled again and held up his shackled hands. "Hey now, no need to get physical, Griff. I'm quite helpless. Can't you see?" Another one of those goddamn sugary smiles.

Griffin's voice rose in spite of himself. "Give me the name."

Instead, David looked at Fitz. "You don't look the type to bail a guy out," he said matter-of-factly. "Now Mike Waters, he was a guy. Leapt forward and took the hit, so to speak. And your buddy Griff here, he can pack a punch. Have you ever seen the pictures of Mike's face?" The kid let out a low whistle. "You would've thought he'd gone ten rounds with Tyson. I imagine he got some first-rate plastic surgery when all was said and done, and probably at taxpayer expense. You might want to bear that in mind, Mr. Providence Detective. You look like you could use a little plastic surgery, or at least some liposuction here and there. And there and here. Say, I don't suppose french fries are your favorite food or anything?"

"Give us the fucking name," Fitz snarled.

David sighed. Blatant hostility had always bored him. He returned to Griffin. "I thought you'd at least write."

"You're going to tell us what you know," Griffin said quietly. "We both know that you will. Otherwise, you can't have any fun."

"Did you get my letters?"

Griffin shut up. He should've done this sooner. For David to play his game, he had to have input. Take away your participation, and there was nothing left for him to manipulate. No more happy reindeer games. No more jolly schoolboy fun.

"It's not so bad in here, you know," David said, switching strategies. "Food's actually pretty good. I gather the fuckers in charge have figured out it's best to make sure the animals in the zoo are well fed. Keeps us from sharpening our fangs on one another—or maybe on them. I'm learning inner peace through quality time in a lotus position, and wouldn't you know it, I have a natural gift for carpentry. I know, I'll make you a table, Griff. Carve your initials in the base. For old times' sake. Come on, any size."

Fitz opened his mouth. Griffin shot him a look, and the detective frowned but fell silent.

"Ooooh, just like a trained seal," David said. He was smiling joyfully, all smooth round cheeks and big brown eyes. Back with his favorite kind of audience, he was happy. He was horrible. Jesus Christ, he looked like he was barely sixteen.

"Who raped and murdered Sylvia Blaire?" Griffin said quietly.

"Eddie Como."

"How did you meet?"

"Griff, buddy, I never met Eddie. That's what I keep saying. It's his roommate, Jimmy Woods. We've spent some time together here in good ol' Max."

"I'm not interested in your patsy, David. I want to know about the real College Hill Rapist. Tell me, which one of you thought of the douche?"

For the first time, Price faltered. He disguised it well, recovering swiftly and smiling again. On his lap, however, his fingers were beginning to fidget with his shackles. "You like this case, don't you, Griffin? It's complicated. Clever. You always appreciated that. Which one of the three women do you think hired Eddie Como's assassin? Or was it a member of their families? Personally, I got my money on the cold one. What's her name? Oh yeah, Jillian Hayes."

"David, you have ten seconds to say something useful, or we're all walking out that door. Ten, nine, eight, seven, six—"

"I know who the real College Hill Rapist is."

Griffin shrugged. "I don't believe you. Five, four, three—"

"Hey, hey, hey, don't be too hasty, man. Haven't all those months of therapy taught you anything? Slow it down. Take it easy. It wasn't my idea to yank your chain. He came to me."

Griffin finally paused. "The College Hill Rapist came to *you*?"

"Yeah. Sure."

Griffin already knew he was lying. "Why?"

"I don't know. Maybe he heard about my rep. Maybe he just desired a decent conversationalist. I can't read some guy's fucking mind. But he came to me, and we, uh, we talked about a few things."

"How to commit a crime?"

"We both had an interest."

"How to fuck with the police."

David Price smiled. "Oh yeah. We both had an interest."

"Congratulations, Price," Fitz spoke up. "You just became an accessory to multiple rapes and murders. Now you're going to have to keep talking just to save your dumb-ass hide."

David shot the detective a look of disdain. "Save my ass from what? The life in prison I'm already serving? Hey, buddy, haven't you heard about me? I'm the guy who befriends little kids on the playground. I hand them some candy, I push them on the swings. And then I take them home, down into my soundproofed basement, where I strip off their cute little clothes and—"

"You still haven't said anything new yet," Griffin said. "Three, two, one—"

"He puts Como's little swimmers into each douche."

"Fuck it, David. *I* told you that."

"It was my idea," David said seriously. "That DNA is troubling stuff. Hell, that's why I had to bury my pretty treats. Let decomposition do its nasty work. And then it occurred to me. DNA so likes to be up there in those deep, dark places . . . Why not let it have its way, man? Why not go with the flow? Don't hide DNA, own it. Man, bring it to the fucking game."

Griffin stood up. "Thanks for repeating my own theory back to me. You're a shithead, David. Always have been. Always will be."

Griffin headed for the door. And behind him, David Price said, "He knew Eddie Como. Eddie probably didn't know him. But he met the great Eddie Como. Met him one afternoon, probably for no more than ten minutes, just enough time for poor dumb Eddie to mention that he worked for the blood center. After that, my friend, his fate was sealed. The College Hill Rapist had his man."

Griffin turned slowly. "He stalked Eddie Como?"

"He did his homework."

"And what, stole old condoms out of Eddie's trash can?"

David had that sly look back on his face. "I won't answer that. But it is the key question, isn't it? How do you steal a man's mambo jambo? It's not like we lose track of it."

"I don't believe you."

"What's so hard to believe, Griff? That I'd help someone attack young college coeds? Or that you still can't do a thing to stop us? You got a serial rapist on the loose, Detective Sergeant Roan Griffin. Someone who looks like Eddie Como, sounds like Eddie Como and tests as Eddie Como. In other words, you have absolutely no fucking idea who he really is. So *you* sit down. And *you* listen up. Because I do know his goddamn name, and you're going to give me something for it. You're going to give me whatever I want, or you'll get to see my face on the five o'clock news, telling the frightened public how some overpumped, overranked state trooper is willfully disregarding critical evidence which could stop the bastard murdering their precious daughters. Now how do you like that?"

Griffin came forward. Then he took another step, and another step. Breathe deep, part of his mind said. The rest of him didn't give a flying fuck. His hands were fisted, his muscles were tensed and his face was mean. He should've killed David that day. He should've pounded his own friends into the ground, just so he could've gotten to David and ripped off his too-cute, too-smart, lying head.

"You're not getting out," he said harshly. "No matter what you say, you're not getting out."

"College coeds are dying—"

"Ten kids are dead!"

"I can guarantee you a new body by tonight. Count on it."

"And I can guarantee you a transfer to Super Max. No more carpentry classes, yoga or cafeteria hours. Just the rest of your life, rotting alone in a six-by-eight cell."

"Do you want to punish me, Detective Sergeant, or do you want to stop the man preying on pretty brunettes? Think carefully before you answer. The parents of all the College Hill Rapist's future victims breathlessly await your reply."

"You little fucker—" Fitz snarled.

Impatiently, David cut him off. "Six o'clock," he said crisply, eyes on Griffin's face. "Standard hardship leave for three hours. I get to have street clothes, you get to put me in shackles. I get to go into the outside world, you get to supervise. That's the deal."

"No."

"Oh yes. Or I go straight to the press and tell them that the same detective who tried to break my face eighteen months ago, now won't protect their precious little girls out of spite. Think about it, man. You don't deal with me, and another girl dies. You don't deal with me, and the public will eat you for dinner." David glanced at the overhead clock. "It's ten A.M. now. You have until noon to decide."

"We don't make deals with pedophiles."

"Sure you do. You make deals with whoever has the fucking information. Now ask the question, Griff. Come on, man. Ask me what you really need to know." David leaned forward. He stared up at Griffin with that wide beaming smile, that round choirboy face.

"You didn't hurt her," Griffin said abruptly.

David Price blinked.

"You like to think you did. But you didn't. Cindy was better than you, David. Let's face it. She was better than me."

"Ask the goddamn question!" David barked.

"Why do you want a three-hour leave, you little psychopathic shit?"

David finally sat back. For the first time since the interview started, he appeared satisfied. He glanced at Fitz, he glanced at Charpentier and then he looked at Griffin. "I want to see my daughter. No prison suits, no interview rooms. Just her and I, face-to-face. It's probably the only time I'm ever going to see her, so I want it to be good. Let's face it, man, her grandparents are never bringing her here."

"Her grandparents?"

"Tom and Laurie Pesaturo. Or didn't Meg tell you? Molly Pesaturo is my kid. See, I didn't kill all the little girls, Griff. Some I let breed."

Five minutes later, Griffin, Fitz and Charpentier were back in the parking lot. They were all taking in huge lungfuls of crisp, outside air. Later, they would shower until their skin was raw.

"He doesn't get out," Griffin said flatly. "Not at six P.M., not at any time, not for three hours, not for any hours. The man doesn't get out, period!"

Griffin's arms were moving on their own volition, his left leg twitching, ears ringing. Yeah, ringing, ringing, ringing. Fuck it all, he might as well go crackers. Insanity was probably what it took to deal with the likes of David Price. He turned on Charpentier.

"I want lists, lots of lists. Names of anyone who visited, wrote, called David Price. Names of all the inmates who could've come into contact with David in any way, shape or form. Names of all known friends, families and associates of said inmates, especially those with a criminal past. And then I want a list of which of those inmates have recently been released. Got it?"

"It's going to take some time," Charpentier said grimly.

"You have two hours. Commandeer whatever resources you need."

Charpentier nodded. He got into his car and headed for his dank basement office. That left Griffin and Fitz alone in the parking lot.

"He doesn't get out," Griffin said again.

"We'll work on it."

"He doesn't get out!"

"Then find the fucking rapist!"

"Then I fucking will!" Griffin thumped the top of his Ford Taurus. Fitz pounded it right back.

Griffin yanked open the driver's-side door. "He's got a plan."

"No shit."

"He's thought of this. Set it all in motion. Don't be deceived by those peach-fuzz cheeks. He doesn't give a rat's ass about his daughter. He has something else in mind."

"You think?"

"He doesn't get out," Griffin said again. "Not now, not ever." But as they pulled out of the maximum-security parking lot, they both saw the white Channel 10 news van roll in.

32

Molly

Fitz drove. Griffin worked the phone. He dialed Waters first.

"Here's the deal. David Price is claiming he knows who the real College Hill Rapist is, and he'll give us that information in return for a personal visit with his long-lost daughter, Molly Pesaturo. We have two hours to decide."

"Huh?"

"No kidding. Look, are you still in Cranston?"

"Trolling the bars as we speak."

"Perfect. Get a picture of Tawnya Clemente. Fuck Eddie Como. Start shopping her picture around."

"Tawnya's picture? You think the loyal girlfriend is in on this?"

"Half of everything David says is a lie, but he's right about one thing: Eddie Como was innocent. The real College Hill Rapist set him up, used him as a patsy to commit the perfect serial crime. Now, to do that, the real rapist had to get Eddie's semen from somewhere. Tawnya's the logical place to start."

"She conspired against the father of her child?"

"Fifty-million-dollar lawsuit, Mike. Think about it. All she has to do is sacrifice one guy. Then she—and Eddie, Jr.—never have to worry about anything, ever again."

"Well, when you put it that way . . ." Waters said.

"Yeah. Now, remember, you got two hours. Have fun!"

Griffin hit end, then promptly dialed the next number. Thirty seconds later, he had Sergeant Napoleon on the phone.

"Sergeant! I'm calling on behalf of Detective Fitzpatrick. He'd like you to run a few tests."

"Uh oh," Napoleon said.

Griffin pretended he hadn't heard him. "Detective Fitzpatrick has brilliantly deduced the source of the Eddie Como DNA. He believes Como's semen was injected into the rape victims via the douche. What do you think?"

There was a moment of silence. Fitz was rolling his eyes at the thick praise. Then Napoleon said, "Well, shit on a stick. That makes some sense."

"It could be done?"

"Sure. You inject the semen into the douche, give the douche a little

457

shake, then expel the contents into the body cavities. The resulting linen stains, vaginal swabs, etc., would test the same as if the douche was being used to flush the semen out. Of course, that assumes the rapist did use a condom, otherwise we'd pick up a second DNA sample as well."

"Yeah, I'm pretty sure he used a condom. You still have the douche bags in evidence?"

"Well, you know us Providence detectives. Every now and then we do practice proper evidence handling and storage."

"Really? Huh. Well, so much for that rumor. Okay, so you could test the inside contents of the bag, right? If there's a DNA sample *inside* the douche, then definitely . . ."

"Oh yeah. I'll look into it. For Detective *Fitz,* of course."

"One last question. You said the semen sample would have to be fresh for it to test positive for spermatozoa. What about if it had been frozen?"

"You mean frozen at time of ejaculation, then thawed at time of use?"

"Okay."

"Sure," Napoleon answered promptly. "As long as the semen sample was frozen within seventy-two hours, the spermatozoa would be preserved until thawed again. Sperm banks do it all the time." Then Napoleon got the full implication. "Ooooh," he said. "How interesting. And the dead come back to life."

"And the dead come back to life," Griffin agreed blackly. Then muttered, "Even from beyond the grave . . . Thanks, Sergeant. Fitz'll be in touch."

He flipped shut his phone just in time for Fitz to say, "We're in Cranston. Meg or Tawnya? Who do you want to hit first?"

"Meg," Griffin said immediately. "I want to give Detective Waters time to complete his inquiry into Tawnya's social life. With any luck, he'll provide the ammo, then we'll go in for the kill."

Fitz glanced over at him somberly. "Have I told you lately that I love you?"

"No. But just for that, I'll let you go after her first."

"Ah, I just love this job!"

"Come two hours, remember that, Fitz. Remember that."

Griffin and Fitz pulled in front of the Pesaturo house shortly before ten-thirty. Already down to an hour and a half and they'd barely made progress. Why, then, Griffin thought, was he surprised to knock on the Pesaturos' door and have Jillian Hayes answer it.

"Sergeant," she started.

He didn't give her time to finish. He shouldered past her and stormed down the tiny hall toward the back family room as Fitz followed suit. "I want to speak with Meg. Now!"

"She's not here," Jillian called out behind them, scrambling to catch up.

"Where is she?"

Griffin burst into the family room. Meg's parents, Tom and Laurie, were sitting side by side on the sofa. Tom appeared sullen, Laurie had her arms wrapped protectively around Molly and had obviously been crying. Sitting opposite them were Toppi and Libby Hayes. One big happy family. Christ, just what he and Fitz needed.

He whirled on Jillian, who was apparently the only speaking member of the party. "Where is Meg?" he demanded again.

"We don't know."

"You *lost* her?"

"She . . . We don't know."

Griffin thought of a word, remembered that Molly was in the room, and bit it back. He homed in on the Pesaturos, jerking his head at their *granddaughter*. "Get her out of the room."

"I don't really think—" Laurie started vaguely.

"Get her out of the room!"

"I'll do it." Toppi stood, crossing over to take Molly's hand, but not before giving Griffin a reproachful look. He glared right back at her. No more friendly Sergeant Griffin. Friendly Sergeant Griffin had gotten royally screwed. Now it was time to put the fear of God into these folks.

"You," he gestured at Jillian, who had her chin up and her feet planted for battle. "If you want to remain in this room—"

"I am a guest of the Pesaturos. They asked me to come here—"

"If you want to remain in this room—"

"Probably because they knew you were going to be pigheaded and hostile about this."

"I will arrest you for obstruction of justice."

She snorted. "Oh get over it. We're all worried about Meg."

"Jillian, sit down and shut up. The Pesaturos have some talking to do, and unless you're their attorney, I don't want to hear a single peep out of you."

Jillian gave him a look. But after another moment, she crossed stiffly to the wingback chair next to her mother. She sat down. She seemed to shut up. Just in time for Libby Hayes to stick out her tongue at him. Oh for heaven's sake . . .

"You." Griffin stabbed his finger at Tom, because he couldn't keep yelling while looking at Laurie Pesaturo's tearstained face. "Start talking."

"It was a long time ago. We didn't think it was relevant—"

"Your daughter had a relationship with a known pedophile, and you didn't think it was *relevant?*"

"The man's behind bars!"

"No thanks to you, and not in another few hours!"

Tom fell silent. All at once, his massive shoulders slumped. He appeared miserable. "I swear to God, Sergeant, we didn't know. We never dreamed of a connection until you called . . . Oh God, Meg . . ."

Griffin and Fitz gave him a moment. Griffin needed to count to ten anyway. So much ringing in his ears. He knew if he looked down now, his hands would be shaking. If he tried to sit, his knee would jog up and down with a mind of its own. Reel it in, reel it in. Whatever these people had done, they were suffering for it now. And he needed to play it cool a little longer.

"Maybe if you started from the beginning," Jillian spoke up quietly. She had obviously been briefed on the situation, and she was gazing at Tom and Laurie compassionately. Griffin resented that. He didn't know why, but he did.

"Meg was only thirteen," Laurie murmured. "We had no idea. None at all. Not until I found her one day, curled up weeping on the bathroom floor. She'd just taken a pregnancy test and it was positive. We didn't even know she was dating."

"How did Meg meet Price?" Fitz asked. Griffin turned toward Tom, though he already knew the answer. His former next-door neighbor, the electrician . . .

"Work," Tom said predictably. "We were on the same job, wiring a new CVS. He was such a nice kid. I remember thinking that. What a nice kid. Did good work, too. And he mentioned one day that he didn't have any family. Parents were dead, I don't remember why. And I felt kinda bad for him. He couldn't have been more than twenty-four, twenty-five. So I started inviting him over for dinner."

"He was always so polite," Laurie murmured. She couldn't seem to get over that. "Please, thank you, yes ma'am. Even helped with the dishes." She finally looked up. "I knew Meg had a crush on him. He was a nice-looking young man and of course at thirteen, she was beginning to notice that sort of thing. But I thought of it as a schoolgirl's crush. The kind you have on your father's hired hand, or the bag boy at the grocery store. She was still so young. I never imagined . . ."

"You never saw them together?" Fitz again.

Both shook their heads. "Never," Tom said. "She snuck out at night. I didn't even know she'd think of doing such a thing. I'm sure he must've suggested it to her. I'm telling you, she'd never been a problem. She was a good girl, got good grades. Oh Meg . . ."

"So you found out she was pregnant," Griffin fast-forwarded. "She tell you he was the father?"

"She was upset," Laurie said. "She told us everything."

"Did you confront him?"

Tom made a small, uncomfortable motion that led Griffin to understand there had been a confrontation, but it hadn't involved much talking. Tom's fists and David's face, however, had spent some quality time together. Griffin understood completely.

"If Meg was only thirteen," Fitz said, "that's statutory rape. Why didn't you file a report? Get the kid arrested?"

Tom and Laurie exchanged miserable glances. "We were embarrassed," Laurie said softly. "Meg was humiliated—and frightened and confused and heartbroken. She seemed to think she really loved him. According to her, he'd even proposed marriage. We just . . ." She took a deep breath, got herself together. "It all seemed a horrible mistake. We hadn't been paying enough attention. Meg didn't show good judgment. Going to the police would just bring it all out in the open and make things worse. You have to understand, we didn't know David had done this kind of thing before, or have the wildest idea what he'd go on to do next. Seducing a thirteen-year-old girl isn't right, but still . . . We never would've guessed." She looked at Griffin earnestly. "Please, you have to believe us. We never would've guessed."

"You covered it up," Griffin said bluntly, harshly. She wanted forgiveness from him? What about the ten other families David had victimized?

"I have relatives," Laurie whispered. "Upstate New York. We sent her there for the duration. I started telling people I was pregnant. And then, when the time came, I, we, had a beautiful baby girl. We love her, Sergeant." She looked up earnestly. "The circumstances were horrible, but Molly is perfect. I have been proud to have her as my daughter, and we've been saying that for so long, as far as I'm concerned, she *is* my daughter. And I will do anything in my power to protect her."

"He wants to see her," Griffin said.

"No!"

"Price has information on the College Hill Rapist. In fact, we're coming to believe that he helped create the College Hill Rapist, and set this whole thing in motion—"

"Eddie Como is dead," Jillian said firmly from across the room.

Griffin pivoted and glared at her. "Yeah, but he's not who raped and murdered your sister."

There was silence. Even Libby's hands were perfectly still on her picture book. How to absorb, what to say? Griffin and Fitz had had more time with the thought than the others, and they were still reeling themselves.

Fitz finally spoke up, "We, uh, we got DNA results back from Sylvia Blaire. They match Eddie's."

"What?" Jillian again, her face still pale, her voice bewildered. "But that's impossible!"

"We're working on the assumption that Eddie's DNA was introduced as a red herring at the rape scenes. The douches were not being used to wash semen out, but to inject semen into the body cavity." Fitz paused for a moment. He said out loud, without seeming to realize it, "Well, that would explain why Eddie was so willing to give a DNA sample. Poor bastard honestly thought he hadn't done it."

"But the notes," Jillian insisted. "All those phone calls and letters . . . He harassed us!"

"Claiming his innocence," Griffin said. "Wouldn't you, if you were behind bars for a series of crimes you knew you didn't commit?"

Her mouth worked. "But that tape!" she said finally, firmly. "The tape he sent me on Friday. *That* was threatening. And the letter to Carol's house. All that, 'I'll get you from beyond the grave.' What was that all about?"

"Do you know they came from Eddie?"

"I . . . well . . ." She frowned. "The tape that contained his picture."

"A video file, right? Of a man whose image has been broadcast all over TV for nearly twelve months." Griffin looked at her. She closed her eyes.

"It could be faked," she whispered.

"Part of the setup. In the interesting-but-true department, the first time you mentioned the tape, I thought immediately of David Price. It sounded like something he would do."

"Oh my God!" Jillian covered her mouth with her hand. "Poor Eddie Como. Oh that poor man . . ."

"I don't understand," Tom Pesaturo spoke up. "You're saying this was all done by some other guy?"

"It's the theory of the day."

"Well, who the hell is he?"

"If we knew that, Mr. Pesaturo, we wouldn't be here right now."

"But David Price is helping this guy?"

"It would appear that way."

"Why?"

"To get out of prison, Mr. Pesaturo. To return to the real world where he can rape and murder small children. Why do you think?"

"No!" Laurie's voice shot up. Her face was wild. "You can't let him. You can't let him out."

Griffin just shrugged. "He says it's the only way. We have a sexual-sadist predator running around who for all intents and purposes *is* Eddie Como. We don't have prints, we don't have DNA, we don't even have a description. And according to David Price, the real College Hill Rapist will kill another girl by tonight unless we let David have a three-hour hardship leave to visit your granddaughter."

Griffin turned abruptly on Tom. "For God's sake, Mr. Pesaturo, why didn't you and Vinnie kill the little prick when you had the chance? He impregnated your thirteen-year-old daughter. That wasn't enough for you?"

"We didn't know." Tom was positively moaning. "And Meg was so confused, believing that she really loved him, I worried about what it would do to her if he suddenly disappeared. Then after his arrest . . . when we all learned what he was really like . . . Meg locked herself in her room and cried until she was sick. Couldn't eat, couldn't sleep, had horrible nightmares. We just wanted to get her through. So we vowed never to mention his name again. We would pretend it had never happened. David was going away after all. The papers said he'd never get out, never see the light of day . . ."

"We started lying," Laurie murmured. "And in our lie, there was no David Price. There was just Molly, our new daughter. Everything was so nice that way. So much easier to believe."

"Well, welcome back to the real world, Mrs. Pesaturo. Where there is a monster named David Price. And he probably is working hand in hand with a serial rapist. Why do you think Meg was the College Hill Rapist's *first* victim?"

Tom moaned again. "David wanted revenge. After what *he* did to Meg, he wanted revenge . . ."

"Yeah, Mr. Pesaturo. And knowing Price, he's just getting started."

33

Jillian

Sergeant Griffin and Detective Fitz went upstairs to look through Meg's room for any hint of where she might have gone, while Tom and Laurie remained sitting in the family room, their bodies drained, their faces shell-shocked.

"It's going to be all right," Jillian said firmly. "The police are starting to make genuine progress now. It's going to be all right."

"Meg," Laurie whispered.

"We'll find her. She probably just ran out to do some errands, maybe grab some lunch." But that didn't sound like Meg, and Jillian knew it. Conscientious Meg always told her parents where she was going. Cautious Meg never spent much time out alone.

"He can't see Molly," Tom muttered. "Can't. Just . . . can't."

"It's going to be all right," Jillian repeated. "Everything will work out fine." She turned to her mother. "Mom, maybe you can show Tom some more pictures from your singing days. I need to go upstairs and talk to Sergeant Griffin."

Her mother tapped her left finger somberly, a soldier accepting her mission. The look on her face made Jillian's heart tighten in her chest. She gave Libby's hand a quick, reassuring squeeze. Funny how in the last twenty-four hours, Jillian felt that she had finally taken the first step forward with her life. Funny how in the last twenty-four hours, it would appear that Griffin had taken at least three steps back.

There was an air about him now. A crackle of barely concealed anger. If he stood in front of a punching bag, she thought, he would easily tear it to shreds. And then he would stomp on the torn, tortured bits while the tendons corded in his neck and the menace in him grew and grew and grew.

He'd said he'd tried to kill David Price the day of his arrest. Two fellow detectives had gotten in Griffin's way. Seeing his fury now, she wondered how they could've been so brave. And she wondered what those two men had looked like five minutes after the encounter.

She squared her shoulders and headed up the stairs.

She heard Detective Fitz's voice first. He was down the hall, apparently asking Toppi some questions in Molly's room. Jillian bypassed that door and headed to Meg's bedroom, where she found Griffin standing in front of

Meg's small, white-painted desk. His powerful shoulders filled the window, blocking the light.

In spite of herself, Jillian couldn't take another step forward. She remained in the doorway, where she cleared her throat.

He turned slowly, Meg's calendar held between his hands. "This is an official police investigation, ma'am. Get out of the room."

"I'm not in the room."

"Jillian," he growled.

"Griffin," she replied, and now she did step forward. She came right up to him, where she could see that his hands were shaking, his blue eyes had turned jet black and his jaw was set so tight, he had to be grinding his teeth.

"They were just trying to protect their family," she told him quietly. "Laurie and Tom, they never meant anyone any harm."

"Tell that to the ten other families. The mothers and fathers who had to file through the morgue, looking at videotape because the real remains of their children were too gruesome for even seasoned professionals to see. Tell that to the detectives who went through peer counseling just to get those images out of their head."

"They didn't know, Griffin. Nobody knew. Isn't that why you're so angry? Because their mistake reminds you of your own, and that just pisses you off all over again."

He literally snarled. She had never seen a human being do that before. He snarled at her, raw and savage, and in the depths of his rage, she also saw his pain. It gave her the courage to raise her hand and place it gently on his chest.

"It's different this time. It's going to be okay."

"How do you know? You've never met Price. You don't know just how much he enjoys a good game. And that's all this is to him: a game. Another way to pass the time until he gets his ass out of jail. Which I think he's going to do shortly after six this evening if I don't magically figure everything out."

Jillian didn't say anything.

"What do you know, anyway?" His tone picked up in hostility. "You and your little Survivors Club. What a joke that name turned out to be. It's the Liars Club, that's what it is. Each one of you hoarding your precious little secrets, and in the meantime real people are out there dying. Real people are getting hurt because you women won't tell the police everything."

She still didn't speak.

"What do you even know about Meg, anyway?" he went on relentlessly. "According to her own parents she once considered herself in love with a man who's a convicted serial killer. How do you know she isn't *still* in love? Ever think of that? Her rape was the least traumatic. Hardly a bruise on her. You always considered her lucky, but maybe she was simply in cahoots with Price all along. Her rape was staged, her amnesia is staged. She's part of Price's game, too, and right now, she's off doing things to help good old lover boy."

"No."

"No? You're sure? Absolutely, positively sure?"

"Yes."

"Why, Jillian, you suddenly have that much faith?"

And she replied firmly, "I do."

He closed his eyes. "Goddammit," he muttered hoarsely.

"I know," she whispered. "I know. She needs you, Griffin. I don't know where Meg is. But she's not helping David Price. She's not in cahoots with the College Hill Rapist. She's a young girl who's already had two very bad breaks in life, first being seduced by a pedophile, then being attacked by a sexual predator. And maybe her rape was the least violent, but the police have said all along that's not uncommon for the first attack. The College Hill Rapist used her as a trial run, and unfortunately for all of us, it went so well, he unfettered his anger even more. Also, based on what her parents just said, her total amnesia finally makes some sense. How is she supposed to remember the truth when her life doesn't have any? Her sister's really her daughter, her first love is a perverted killer, and her parents are also grandparents. For God's sake, I can't even keep that all straight."

He opened his eyes, peered at her curiously. "You care for her that much, Jillian?"

"Yes," she answered honestly. "I do."

He stepped away, placed the calendar back on the desk, and seemed to stare at the clean surface without seeing much. Was he thinking of David Price again? Except further back, to the days they had once been friends? It sounded as if he had genuinely liked David Price once. Maybe he had believed in him, too.

"How is Carol?" he asked abruptly.

"The doctors took her off the respirator this morning. Apparently that's a positive sign her body is starting to recover. Of course, no one will know how much she will recover until we see how much she has recovered."

"Has she regained consciousness?"

"No."

"Dan?"

"They say he hasn't left her side."

"Probably can't," Griffin muttered. "Minute he leaves the hospital, some of Vinnie's boys are due to break his legs."

"I had a conversation with Vinnie about that."

He looked at her in surprise. "Trying to save the world, Jillian?"

"I protect what's mine," she said evenly. "Though I have it from good sources that I can't protect everyone all of the time. I've decided, however, that it's still good to try. Besides, Libby asked me to."

"You bailed Dan out? Paid his debts at your mother's request?"

"No. I convinced Uncle Vinnie that my mother would consider it a huge favor if he forgave the rest of Dan's debt. Then she smiled at him, and that took care of that. Then I told him *I* would consider it a huge favor if he arranged it so Dan could never borrow money again. Vinnie thought that was cruel, so naturally he liked the idea." She hesitated. "Griffin . . ."

He looked at her.

She took a deep breath. "I know no one wants to say it, but what if . . . What if negotiating with David Price is the best idea?"

"No way!"

"Please! Hear me out. You said yourself he knows the College Hill Rapist's real identity. Are you sure of that?"

"The man is a natural-born liar and a natural-born predator. So, no, I'm not sure of anything."

"But you're taking his allegations seriously."

"He knew about the DNA," Griffin said curtly. "He knew when we got the DNA analysis back on Sylvia Blaire it would point to Eddie Como. Plus there's Meg. It's too much of a coincidence that the rapist's first victim would also be Price's first conquest. And there's me, of course, the detective who put David Price away, and who is now leading the supposed College Hill Rapist homicide investigation. Well, shit!" Griffin's eyes widened. "Of course, an assassination at the state courthouse. Hey, good news everybody, three days later, I finally know why poor Eddie Como is dead."

"Why?"

"To bring me in on the case, of course. Because if Como dies *at* the courthouse, it's automatically state police jurisdiction." Griffin smiled bitterly. "Leave it to David to send only the bloodiest invite to his party."

Jillian closed her eyes. Oh God, she had never heard of a man as evil as David Price. It pained her, then, to say what she had to say next. She opened her eyes. She peered at Griffin intently, trying to get him to see the truth, even if it hurt. "So David Price must be involved. And if he does know the name of the College Hill Rapist . . . Griffin, I know you don't want to deal with him. I know *I* would give anything to keep such a man away from Molly. But as you said, real people are dying out there. And if you're not any closer to knowing the real identity of the College Hill Rapist . . . David only wants three hours," she whispered. "Surely saving even one life is worth giving David Price three supervised hours on the outside. Won't you at least consider it?"

Griffin's hard-lined face was no longer mottled red. Instead, his expression went dangerously cold.

"The press is going to agree with you," he said softly. Menacingly.

"The press is not always wrong."

"And the public will call the mayor, and the mayor will call the governor and the governor will call my superintendent, and David Price will get his way."

"But you'll get the College Hill Rapist!"

"Do you really think so, Jillian? How will we know if the name Price gives us is the right one? How will we know it's not another patsy? And even if it is the right man, how will we build the case? We have no prints, no hair, no fiber, no DNA. We could arrest him today, only to let him go tomorrow."

"D'Amato is good. He'll come up with some sort of charge to buy you time. You can put things together. It worked before."

"When Providence arrested an innocent man?"

She lost some of her composure. Poor Eddie Como. The true impact of his innocence hadn't sunk in yet. She wasn't ready for it to sink in. She tried again. "At least an arrest will start the ball rolling."

"Price has offered us nothing," Griffin argued quietly. "It's what he does best. He gives you ashes, but makes it sound like prime rib. Face it, he's the perfect criminal for this day and age—sound-bite ready for network news and cable TV."

"Griffin, all those girls, those poor, poor girls . . ."

Griffin was silent. She thought maybe she'd finally gotten through to him, and then he started to speak.

"I'm going to tell you something, Jillian. Something very few people know. I'm going to tell you, and then I don't want you to mention it ever again. Do you agree?"

Jillian got a chill. She had a feeling she should say no. She had a feeling this is how it felt to make a deal with the devil. She nodded helplessly.

"Eighteen months ago, when we arrested David Price, I went down into the basement of his home. I saw ten tiny mounds where he buried his victims beneath the dirt floor. I saw the mattress where he raped them and I saw the paraphernalia he used to torture them. But I still didn't attack him. I called CIU to process the scene. I ordered him put into handcuffs, and I got on with the business at hand. This was a big arrest in a big case. We were all taking it very seriously."

Griffin's eyes were locked on hers. "Price started talking. Making conversation really, as he stood there cuffed between Detectives Waters and O'Reilly. How he met the kids, how he kidnapped the kids, what he did to them. It was hard. We were professionals, but what he said, and so calmly, too, it wore on you. But it was also incriminating, a bona fide confession, so we let him talk while Waters started recording him. And then, then Price switched topics. He stopped talking about the kids. He started talking about Cindy."

Griffin paused. Jillian simply stared at him. She had the horrible thought she was going to wish she had never heard what he had to say next.

"In the last two weeks of Cindy's life," Griffin said quietly, "it was obvious she wasn't going to make it. The cancer had eaten her from the inside out. She couldn't walk, couldn't sit up, couldn't even raise her hand. I brought her home as we'd agreed, set her up in a special bed in the family room, and got a hospice worker to come over and help out. Cindy could still blink her eyes, and that's how we would talk. I would ask her questions and she would blink once for yes and twice for no. Much like your mother. I, uh"—he swallowed, his voice finally growing husky—"I used to ask her if she loved me, at least ninety times a day, just so I could see her blink. Just so I would know she was still that much alive. I was working the damn Candy Man case, of course. I could make a lot of the phone calls from home, process the paperwork . . . But sometimes I'd have to go out, and sometimes the hospice worker also needed a break, and sometimes, sometimes David would come over.

"That's right." He nodded. "Our good friend and helpful neighbor, 'we're going to beat this thing' David Price, would come over and sit with Cindy. As the saying goes, it seemed like a good idea at the time.

"But now we're down in the basement, with that mattress and that workbench and those dark, tiny waves. Now we're down in the basement and David is telling me exactly what he did those afternoons he sat with Cindy. Exactly what he did to my wife."

Griffin saw the look on her face and immediately shook his head. "No, nothing like that, Jillian. Cindy was a grown woman and David's into little kids. She provided something even better for him. An audience. Yeah, a fucking audience. For over a year, see, Price has been involved in this incredible crime spree, kidnapping and murdering small children. And no one suspects a thing. Which means he has no one to talk to, no one to brag to. That kind of thing only gets you in trouble anyway, and David knows it. But now, here's Cindy. Helpless, dying, unable to speak a word. So he goes over there and tells her everything. Every tiny, terrible detail of how he finds the kids and stalks the kids and abducts the kids and hurts the kids and strangles the kids and buries the kids in his basement. On and on and on, an unending litany of depravity. And Cindy can't escape. Cindy can't repeat a word.

"You have to wonder how she must have felt, David told me, as she watched me greet him so gratefully each time I returned home. You have to wonder how desperate she must have been, he said, for me to see something in her face, or in his face. If I would just ask the right question . . . My smart, brilliant wife, he mused, knowing all about his horrible crimes, and unable to do a thing to stop them. My compassionate, gentle-hearted wife, he postulated, dying with all those murdered children on her conscience. And all the while, her husband never suspected a thing. All the while, her husband was so grateful to have David come visit . . .

"That's when I broke, started swinging my fists. I don't remember much of it after that, honestly. They tell me Waters and O'Reilly got in my way. And they tell me that David Price never stopped smiling.

"That's the kind of man we're dealing with, Jillian. He makes friends purely so he has people to betray. He seeks out children purely to have life-forms to destroy. And he is very smart, in an ingratiating, awful sort of way. He is brilliant."

Griffin bent over the desk. He picked up the plain desk pad, and from beneath it, a piece of paper fluttered to the floor. It landed by Jillian's feet, so she picked it up first. It was a page from a notepad, and written all over it in Meg's large, round script were the words: *David Price, David Price, David Price. Oh no, David Price.*

"Well," Griffin said after a moment. "Apparently Meg has finally started to remember."

Five minutes later, Griffin and Fitz were striding out of the house, their faces carefully shuttered, but the line of their mouths grim. Tom and Laurie remained inside. They couldn't seem to move, couldn't seem to digest this new, dreadful turn of events.

Jillian was the one who followed the two detectives to their car, watched them climb in, slam the doors.

At the last minute, she knocked on the driver's-side window. Griffin lowered the glass.

"Were you with your wife the day she died?" she asked him.

"Of course."

"Did you ask her if she loved you? What did she say?"

Griffin's voice softened. "She blinked yes."

Jillian nodded, stepped back. "Remember that, Griffin. If David Price does get leave from prison, if you do catch up with him, remember that. He didn't win. You did."

Griffin finally nodded. Then his window was back up, the car in gear. He and Fitz peeled away from the curb and hit the road.

34

Meg

Griffin and Fitz had made it only four blocks from the Pesaturo home when Fitz shouted, "Stop!"

Griffin obligingly slammed on the brakes, and Fitz obligingly hit the dash. "Ow, shit, Jesus, over there!" Griffin followed the detective's pointing finger to a mini-mart on their right. Three cars were gassing up at the pumps. Fitz, however, was fixed on a small brown Nissan parked in front of the mini-mart's glass doors. "That," he declared, "is Meg's car. Check out the plates."

MP 63. Griffin swung them into the parking lot.

They circled the car first. It held the usual clutter—Kleenex box, hairbrush, discarded mail, plus a variety of hair scrunchies looped over the parking brake. Griffin noted the expired Providence College parking sticker just as Fitz placed his hand on the car's hood and declared it cold.

The two men exchanged frowns. If the engine had already cooled, the car had been there a bit. They walked into the mini-mart. Two women and a clerk were in the store. The first woman, with graying hair and an oversized navy blue sweatshirt, was deep in consideration at the ice cream case. The second woman, over in the snack aisle, had bright blond hair. Definitely neither one was Meg. Fitz and Griffin exchanged more concerned looks.

They approached the cashier, a pimple-ridden teenager who could've doubled as Teen Blockbuster. Fitz badged him.

"Where's the driver of the Nissan?"

Kid gaped at Fitz's badge, swallowed audibly, gaped at the badge some more. "Don't know," kid squeaked.

"What do you mean, you don't know?"

"I mean, she's not here. Sir," the kid added belatedly.

"Did you *see* the driver of the brown Nissan?"

"Yes, sir! I mean, she was pretty, sir!"

Okay, that woman sounded like Meg. "Did she come inside, say anything to you?"

"No, sir."

"She didn't come inside?" Fitz glared at the kid.

"No, sir. I mean, I think she was going to, sir. But then her friend pulled up and she went with him."

"Him?" Griffin asked sharply.

The kid flicked a glance at Griffin for the first time, noticed the state detective's imposing size and promptly blanched. "Y-Y-Yes."

Fitz leaned on the counter. Both of the female shoppers had stopped eyeing food by now and were shamelessly eavesdropping on the conversation. Fitz ignored them. He focused his amiable tone on the kid.

"Can you describe exactly what you saw for me? Take your time. Think about it."

The kid took a deep breath. He thought about it. "Well, I saw her get out of her Nissan. And then, well, I looked again 'cause, well, she was *very* pretty."

"What was she wearing?"

"Umm, some kind of brown jacket. Suede, you know, and this big purse swung over her shoulder and jeans, I guess. I don't know. Nothin' special."

"Okay, so she's out of the car with her coat on and her purse over her shoulder. Did she close the car door?"

"Yeah. She did that."

"And then?"

"She took a step forward, like she was coming inside. But then she suddenly stopped and turned. I saw another car pull up and this man get out. He seemed kind of urgent, you know. He ran up to her, said something, then they both got into his car."

"Describe the man," Fitz ordered.

"Ummm, not too tall, I guess. Maybe your height. Brown hair. Just . . . a guy, an average guy." The kid shrugged.

Fitz looked at Griffin, who nodded slightly. An average guy. Everyone's favorite description of Eddie Como. Shit.

"Age?" Fitz asked.

"Ummm, older, I guess. I couldn't see him real well from here, but I remember thinking that he was too old for her. I don't know why I thought that."

"Did you see his car?"

"Not from here. It sounded big, though. Big engine. Old. Sputtered when he pulled out. Probably needs new plugs," the kid added helpfully.

Griffin spoke up. "Did he touch the girl?"

The kid's gaze shot toward him, then promptly plummeted to the countertop. "Umm . . ."

"Touch her arm, shoulder, anything?"

"Oh yeah! When he first came up. He put his hand on her arm. And he escorted her to his car, you know. Got the door for her. A girl like her probably has a thing about manners." The kid nodded, then sighed morosely. At his age, he probably understood how life worked, and that guys like him never won a girl like Meg.

"Was he still holding her arm when he got the car door?" Griffin pressed.

"Well, now that you mention it. He had his left hand on her arm, and he got the door with his right."

"He never let go of her?"

"I guess not."

471

Griffin and Fitz exchanged new glances. This did not sound good. Griffin glanced at his watch. Eleven forty-six A.M. Shit, they were never going to make Price's twelve o'clock deadline.

"What time did she pull up?" Fitz's gaze had followed Griffin's to the watch, and his tone held fresh urgency.

"Oh, a while ago. Wait—a big Suburban had just filled up both tanks. That was a couple of pennies. Let me check the receipts."

The kid opened his register and started slowly turning over pieces of paper. Griffin and Fitz began shifting restlessly. The clock was ticking, ticking, ticking. The kid idly turned over one receipt, said "Huh," then moved methodically to another. Then another. Then another. Just when Griffin thought he couldn't take it anymore, Fitz snapped.

The detective snaked his arm across the counter and grabbed the kid's wrist. "Listen, just estimate. Eight, nine, ten A.M., *what?*"

"Uh." The kid looked down at the detective's whitened knuckles. "Nine A.M., sir!"

"Fine, thanks. You've been great." Fitz was motioning at Griffin furiously. He said to the kid, "A uniform is going to come by shortly to take your statement. I want you to tell him everything you've told us, plus anything more you remember. Can you do that?"

"Um, yes, sir."

"This is important. We appreciate your help. Okay?"

"Okay, sir!"

"Good man. We'll be in touch." Fitz headed out the door, working to catch up with Griffin, who was already on his hands and knees beside Meg's car. Ten seconds later, Griffin spotted a silver flash and fished out a key ring from beneath the vehicle.

He and Fitz stared at the mass of keys, complete with a green plastic parrot from a Jimmy Buffet concert.

"She probably still had them in her hand," Griffin mused. "Then when the guy grabbed her arm . . ." He released his hold, and the keys dropped just about where he'd found them.

"I don't think she met a friend," Fitz said quietly.

"No."

"Why do you think he grabbed her now?"

"Because nobody can crack a case in two hours and David Price knows it." Griffin reached down to recover the keys, then glanced up at Fitz. "Price is betting he's going to get his little hardship leave at six P.M. And when he makes his break for it, he doesn't want to be alone."

"Poor Meg," Fitz murmured. "Poor Molly."

Griffin glanced at his watch. Five minutes before noon. He said, "If David Price gets out of prison, poor all of us. Let's go."

Griffin and Fitz had no sooner gotten back into the car than Griffin's cell phone chirped. It was Waters.

"My two hours are up. Sorry, Griff, I have nothing."

"How many bars?"

"We've hit two dozen and counting. You know, this entire city is nothing but one giant tavern. Several places reported knowing Tawnya, but they mostly recognized her picture from the five o'clock news. One place said she used to come in, but that was before she got pregnant."

"Get more uniforms and keep trying. Someone had to see something."

"Will do."

"Mike . . . Meg Pesaturo is missing. She was last seen being led into a car by a strange man. Whatever's going down, it's already started. We have to catch up, Mike, and we have to do it now."

"Griffin, it's already twelve—"

"I'll take care of Price's deadline. You just keep on looking for information on Tawnya Clemente. Got it?"

Griffin hit end, then started punching a fresh round of numbers.

"Calling God for a miracle?" Fitz asked glumly.

"Nah, even better. Corporal Charpentier."

Griffin got Charpentier's pager, punched in his number followed by one for urgent, and in thirty seconds had Charpentier ringing back.

"Where are you?" Griffin asked. He could hear lots of noise in the background.

"Parking lot of Max. Maureen Haverill of Channel Ten just finished up with David Price's lawyer. Now she's demanding to speak with Price. Visiting hours for his cell block officially start at noon. Sergeant, I think the jig is up."

"Got my lists?"

"Detective James is downloading names as we speak. We're talking nearly a hundred men, though. I don't see how it's going to help."

"I have a new theory. Cull out names of people David Price met when he was still at Intake, *before* he got sentenced. And of those names, guys that didn't end up going to jail. Maybe they were found innocent, or got off on a technicality, anything."

"Why those guys?"

"Because after the first rape happened, Detective Fitz says they rattled the sex-offender tree and nothing fell out. So maybe the real rapist isn't a convicted sex offender. He was arrested but not convicted."

"Meaning his DNA is in the system," Corporal Charpentier filled in slowly, "taken at the time of his arrest. The rapist himself, however, is still a free man."

"A free man in need of a new way to do things," Griffin said.

"Which David Price helped him find," Charpentier concluded. "Why not? As long as you're in jail, why not pick the brain of a master?"

There was more noise in the background. Charpentier's voice grew muffled, as if he was covering his mouth with his hand. "Sergeant, I can get you the list, but it will probably be another hour and it looks like this media circus is about to begin. The director of the department of corrections wants to examine the cameraman's equipment, but he can't keep the press out. It's visiting hours, Price's lawyer has sanctioned the interview . . . We're screwed."

"How long will examining the equipment take?"

"Fifteen minutes at most. We might stretch it to twenty."

Griffin glanced at his watch. They were almost at the Como residence, but fifteen minutes would never be enough time to break Tawnya Clemente. And once Maureen stuck her microphone in front of Price and he began his pathetic spiel . . .

"Code," Griffin said suddenly.

"Code?"

"Yeah. Code Blue or Code White, I'll settle for any color. If there's a code, they have to shut down the whole prison, right? Clear everyone out, even lawyers and aspiring news anchors?"

"That's right," Charpentier said, his voice picking up.

"And it could take a while to sort it all out and let everyone back in, right? Prisoners have to be searched and escorted back to the visiting areas. Maureen and Jimmy would have to go back through security . . ."

"It could take a while," Charpentier agreed happily. Then he hesitated. Griffin understood. A Code Blue only happened if there was a major disturbance, a guard down, a fight between two inmates. A Code White, on the other hand, was sounded in case of a medical emergency. Either way, something had to happen in the prison first. "The director isn't wild about a news team entering the prison," Charpentier said finally. "I could talk to him. Maybe now would be a good time for a drill. You know, as a favor to the state police."

"We would appreciate that favor," Griffin said.

"Hang on a sec." There was a pause, the muffled sound of footsteps, then some definitely muffled talking. Moments later, Charpentier was back. "You know what? It turns out Max hasn't had a drill in quite some time. The real thing, sure, but not a drill. And you know how it goes, if you don't practice every now and then . . ."

"You're golden, Corporal, and tell the director we always approve of good practice. One more thing—"

"Yeah?"

"If the interview does go down . . . ask the director not to return Price to his cell. Escort him anywhere else, but *not* to his cell."

"You don't want him picking up anything he might have stashed there."

"It's never too early to take precautions."

"I'm sure the director will see your point. And gee, the cell block is probably due for a surprise inspection, as well. What a wonderfully educational day for the corrections officers."

"Practice makes perfect. Work on that list, Corporal. I'll be in touch."

Griffin flipped his phone shut just in time to turn down Tawnya's street. Twelve-ten P.M. He parked his Taurus in front of her house.

"You go first," he told Fitz.

The detective positively beamed.

35

Tawnya

They went around to the back door again. Given that you never knew what bushes were hiding what kind of cameramen, it seemed the thing to do. This time Tawnya appeared after their first knock. In her normal good humor, she took one look at Fitz through the door's window and spat.

Griffin wagged a finger at her playfully. Maybe his charm was returning, because she grudgingly opened the door.

"If you pigs are here about the lawsuit," Tawnya said, "go fuck a goat. My lawyer says I'm not supposed to talk to you."

"Colorful," Griffin observed to Fitz.

"I got more. Keep talking and you'll hear them all."

"Hello, Mrs. Como." Fitz eased into the kitchen behind Griffin, keeping the state detective's larger bulk between him and Tawnya. Mrs. Como stood in front of the stove again. Today's culinary adventure seemed to be simmering black beans. The wafting odors of garlic gave the kitchen a homey touch. Not that the bleaching baby diapers had been lacking.

Eddie, Jr., was awake this time, nestled in a baby carrier on top of the kitchen table. He studied Griffin with big brown eyes, then stuck a multicolored teething ring into his mouth and drooled away. Griffin tucked his hands in his pockets before he did something stupid like tickle the baby's pudgy cheeks. He was supposed to be big bad detective here. Clock was ticking, ticking, ticking. Man, babies were cute.

"Maybe we should talk in the family room," Fitz said and jerked his head toward Eddie, Jr.

"I don't got nothin' to say to you," Tawnya said.

"Let's go into the family room," Fitz repeated, more firmly. Tawnya scowled at him, but went.

The minute they were out of the kitchen, Fitz opened fire. "We know what you did, Tawnya. Come clean now, before another girl dies, and maybe we can still work something out. Eddie, Jr., has already lost one parent. You want him to grow up completely orphaned?"

"What the fuck are you talking about?"

"Fifty million dollars. For that kind of money, people sell out their own mothers, let alone some boyfriend who's knocked you up but still not walked you down the aisle."

"Are you talking about my lawsuit? Because I'm not talking about my lawsuit. My lawyer told me I don't have to tell you pigs one damn thing. You killed my Eddie. Now it's your turn to pay!"

"There won't be any lawsuit, Tawnya," Griffin spoke up quietly.

"Not one red cent," Fitz emphasized, "not once the public knows what you really did to Eddie."

Tawnya was good. Real good. She looked at them first in bewilderment, then drew herself up for battle. She bared her teeth. She flashed those long hot-pink nails. "Get out of my house."

"You need to listen to us, Tawnya. Work with us now, and you can still salvage something for Eddie, Jr."

"Miserable, fucking, shit-eating, donkey-humping, flea-repelling, toad-hopping jackasses. *Get out of my house!*"

Fitz and Griffin didn't move a muscle. Fitz glanced at Griffin. "You're right, the language is very colorful."

"Goes with the nails."

"Think she'll attack soon?"

"That'd be nice. Then we can arrest her now, and she'll never see the light of day."

"Too bad for Eddie, Jr."

Griffin shrugged. "You know what they say. You can't pick your parents."

Tawnya foamed at the mouth. Griffin promptly went in for the kill.

"You have thirty seconds to start talking," he told her, his voice low and intense. "We know you framed your boyfriend. We know you're an accomplice to four rapes and two murders. You come clean right this moment, and Eddie, Jr., still has a chance at having a mother. You jerk us around one more second, however, and we're arresting you. We'll shackle you in front of your kid. We'll drag you out of this house and you'll never see your baby again. Thirty seconds, Tawnya. Twenty-nine, twenty-eight, twenty-seven . . ."

Tawnya wasn't into negotiating. She growled once, then launched herself at Griffin's massive form. He grabbed her raking hands, slipped his foot behind hers, and neatly face-planted her onto the worn shag carpet. Fitz produced the cuffs. They didn't have time for fooling around. They hauled her, spitting and sputtering, back onto her feet and were preparing to march her out the door when Mrs. Como stepped into the room, dried her hands on a kitchen towel and uttered a single word.

"Stop," the old woman said.

Some instincts ran deep: they froze. Griffin recovered first. "Mrs. Como," he said firmly, "we have reason to believe that Tawnya helped frame your son for rape—"

"I did not!" Tawnya screeched. She started squirming again, then kicked out at Fitz, who deftly stepped aside.

"Tawnya is a good girl," Mrs. Como said.

"Good girl, my ass!" Fitz sputtered, still dodging.

"Good girls have done far worse for fifty million dollars," Griffin reminded her tightly, and tugged Tawnya away from Fitz.

"Tawnya no do lawsuit," Mrs. Como said. "I do lawsuit. I want money. For my grandson."

"The lawsuit was your idea?"

"*Sí.*"

"But Tawnya was the one on TV," Fitz spoke up.

"I no like TV."

Fitz and Griffin exchanged troubled looks. They pulled back from Tawnya, but only slightly. She, of course, took the opportunity to spit at both of them. "I would never do anything to harm Eddie! I loved Eddie, you stupid, miserable—"

"Yeah, yeah, yeah," Fitz interrupted, holding up his hand and glancing at his watch. "We got the picture."

"My son was framed?" Mrs. Como asked from the doorway. "My Eddie no do bad things?"

Griffin looked at Fitz's watch, too. Nearly twelve-thirty now. Shit. "Mrs. Como, are you aware that another girl was attacked last night?"

Mrs. Como nodded.

"We got DNA tests back from that victim, Mrs. Como. They match samples taken from Eddie."

"But that's impossible!" Tawnya burst out. "Eddie's dead. What, you pigs are so desperate you're going after corpses now? Not even dead Latinos are safe from you. Miserable, fucking—"

This time Griffin held up a hand. He studied Tawnya's red, outraged face. He looked at Mrs. Como, and her much-harder-to-read expression. Something was wrong here, he could feel it in his bones.

And that damn clock was still ticking, ticking, ticking.

"Tawnya," he said, "are you aware that when detectives searched Eddie's and your apartment last year, they found all sorts of books on forensics and police procedure? Some clippings, too, right, Detective? News articles from another rape case that had happened in Rhode Island."

"I told the police, that stuff wasn't Eddie's!"

"Whose was it?"

"I don't know! A box came in the mail to Eddie. The note said it was from a friend. He didn't know what that meant so he stuck it in a closet. He figured someone would call about it later or something. I told that to the detectives. I *told* them."

"When did you get the box?"

"I don't know. A long time ago. Last year. Before . . ." She frowned. "Before the bad things started happening. I don't understand. How can you think Eddie killed that woman last night? Eddie's *dead*."

"Did the box have a return address?"

"I don't know. I didn't open it. It came to Eddie."

Griffin glanced at Fitz. "No," the detective told him. "It was just an old cardboard box with a mailing label on it. Frankly, it looked to us like he'd used the box for storage of the materials. When we found it, it was shoved in the back of a coat closet."

" 'Cause it wasn't his stuff!" Tawnya cried again. "Eddie didn't know why it had come in the mail!"

"Have you ever heard the name David Price?" Griffin asked Tawnya.

"Who?"

"Did Eddie ever mention the name David Price?"

"Who the fuck's David Price?"

"Have you ever heard of the Candy Man?"

"The pervert who hurt all those little kids," she said immediately. "Now there's a dude who deserves to have his little weenie whacked off—or the electric chair!"

Griffin studied her again. Her brown eyes were clear, earnest. If she was lying, she was very, very good.

"Tawnya, did Eddie have another girlfriend?"

She instantly erupted again. "Eddie loved me! Why is that so hard to believe? Eddie loved me and I loved Eddie, and we were gonna be all right. He had a good job, you know, and after Eddie, Jr., was born I was gonna go to beauty school. And then, and then . . . Ah, fuck you all!"

Her shoulders sagged, the first tear slid down her cheek and she immediately turned away. Crocodile tears? Or the saddest display Griffin had ever seen? He'd been lied to so much lately, it was getting hard to tell. But he had the suspicion he was getting a lesson in irony here. In this case, the victims and their families had lied—with the best of intentions, of course—while the prime suspect and his family may have been telling the truth.

"Tawnya," Griffin said quietly, "we're running out of time here. I need you to tell me the truth, I need to hear it now."

"I *told* the truth!"

"Tawnya, did you give someone a . . . sample, from Eddie? Maybe it seemed like you were supposed to, or it was a favor for a friend."

She stared at him in bewilderment. "A sample? You mean a *sample*? Are you fucking nuts? Who gives out a thing like that?"

"Tawnya, Eddie's semen ended up in a murder victim the day *after* he died. You tell me, how could that have happened?"

And all of a sudden, she must have figured it out, because her eyes went wide. "Oh no," she said. "Oh no, oh no, oh no . . ."

"What, Tawnya? What is oh no? What did you and Eddie do?"

Her face crumpled, her voice grew hollow. "We needed the money," she whispered. "I was pregnant, and Eddie wanted to get me something special, you know. Plus, we had to start saving more . . ."

Ah no. Griffin glanced at Fitz and saw from his face that he'd finally gotten it, too. It made so much sense, but who would've thought to ask the question? Who asks a question like that?

"Eddie was in good health," Tawnya was saying. "Gave blood every eight weeks so you know he didn't have any diseases. And he's nice-looking. They like guys who are nice-looking, you know."

"Who likes guys who are nice-looking?" Griffin prodded. She had to say it. And then she did.

"The sperm bank. Eddie donated at the Pawtucket sperm bank. A couple of times. Right after I found out I was pregnant. They pay cash, you know." Tawnya looked at them helplessly. "They pay cash."

Fitz and Griffin were out of the house and walking fast. Twelve forty-five P.M., starting to make progress but still running out of time.

"We need a couple of uniforms," Griffin said.

"Someone to keep her under lock and key until we can verify her story," Fitz agreed. They piled into Griffin's car and he picked up the radio for the request.

"Ever get the impression we're dumb as skunks?" Fitz muttered.

"I don't know, how dumb are skunks?"

Fitz finally unleashed a little, and whacked the dash with his hand. "Goddammit! Sergeant Napoleon nailed it this morning. 'Sperm banks do it all the time.' Why don't we just get the full frontal lobotomy and be done with it!"

"And miss having all this fun? Come on, clock's ticking. Let's talk it through."

"Eddie makes a donation at a sperm bank," Fitz said as Griffin pulled away from the curb.

"In theory, donors are anonymous."

"To the recipients. The sperm bank knows who they are, the sperm bank's gotta clear them first. I don't know, how much vetting do you do before you hand a guy a plastic cup and send him into a porn-filled room? Lucky bastard."

"Someone inside," Griffin prodded.

"Someone who would have access to the frozen samples."

"And Eddie's name."

"David Price said the guy had met Eddie. Eddie probably didn't remember him at all, but the guy had met him."

Griffin rolled out his neck, shrugged his shoulders. He hated to give weight to anything David Price had said, but they had to start somewhere. "Maybe he's a technician, then. Someone who worked one of the days Eddie donated, made small talk with him. Maybe he noticed that Eddie was roughly his same size and build, and had that same Cranston accent. He decided here was a good candidate."

"So he was already in the market for a patsy," Fitz said.

"Meaning he had already met David Price."

"Meaning he'd probably been to prison. At least held in Intake on some kind of charge."

"He's already in the system," Griffin said slowly. "Isn't that the key issue? He's a sex offender, he knows he's a sex offender, and even if he didn't get found guilty, he at least got caught. So now he knows his prints and DNA are in the system, just as he knows he won't stop, because sex offenders never stop. They just get more creative with their attacks."

"He knows when he gets out, if he gets out, it's still only a matter of time."

"So he befriends David Price."

"Who must've thought that was funny as hell."

"Except then Price realizes maybe he can get something out of this, too. Someone on the outside, working for him. Someone he can someday cash in for a get-out-of-jail-free card."

"And then a partnership is born."

"So who do we have?" Griffin demanded. "Someone who's at least been charged with a sex crime. Someone who's been held at Intake during the same time Price was there, so that's what, November through March. He's gotten out and gotten a job at a sperm bank."

"Unlimited access to porn," Fitz muttered. "Where else would a sex offender go?"

"Can't be a technician, though," Griffin countered. "They'd investigate someone like that, find out about his criminal past and get nervous."

"Someone lower level then, but with unlimited access. Has keys to the rooms with the freezers and doesn't look suspicious moving about at strange hours."

They got it at the same time. "Janitor!" Fitz shouted.

"Or cleaning crew," Griffin said grimly. "Something like that."

He flipped open his phone and got Waters on the line.

"Sorry, Griff—" Waters started.

"We know who it is," Griffin cut him off. "I mean, we know how it was done. We just need a name. Meet me at the Pawtucket sperm bank in ten minutes."

"Where?"

"The sperm bank. Where the College Hill Rapist works."

"All right," Waters said, but he didn't sound as excited as Griffin thought he would. And then he finally heard the sounds coming from behind Waters in the busy bar. A woman's voice talking. Maureen Haverill, introducing David Price to the general viewing public on the bar's big-screen TV. One P.M. Griffin and Fitz had just run out of time.

36

The Victims Club

It was dark. Meg kept squinting her eyes, trying to peer into the gloom. It didn't do her any good. The dark was a thick, tangible presence, as smothering as any wool blanket, as pervasive as an endless sea.

She twisted her body, straining against the ties that held her hands captive above her head. The latex bindings dug into her wrists cruelly. She felt a fresh trickle of moisture running down her arm and guessed that it was blood. At least she didn't feel much pain anymore. Her hands had gone numb hours ago, her bound feet shortly thereafter. She still had a dull ache in her shoulder blades from the awkward position. She imagined that would be gone soon, as well. And then?

She shifted her bound feet again. Tried to find leverage against the corner wall, as if she could climb her way up the vertical surface, slog her way through the ocean of black and burst out the top, gulping for air. Of course, she could do no such thing. She remained a captive twenty-year-old girl. Peering into the dark, inhaling the stomach-churning scent of latex, and feeling the blood drip down her arm.

Sound. She shifted, trying to guess the direction of the noise. Footsteps. Above her. From the right? From the left? She never realized how much the darkness echoed before she had been tied up in this musty basement.

Closer, definitely, closer. Humming now. The man, she thought, recoiling reflexively, then holding her breath.

He had called her name in the mini-mart parking lot. She had stopped on instinct, even though she hadn't recognized the car or the driver inside. Not recognizing someone was hardly new at this point, and mostly she remembered feeling faintly curious. Who was this stranger and what stories from her past would he know?

Instead, he'd told her there'd been an accident. Molly needed her right away. While she was still absorbing that shock, he'd hustled her into the passenger's side of his car. At the last moment, something inside her had balked. She'd seen him open the driver's-side door, watched his body bend down to slide inside and something had stirred in the dark pit of her mind. Not a memory, per se. But an emotion. Fear, stark and raw and instantaneous. She'd grabbed for the door handle at the same time he'd hit the lock button and flashed his gun.

She'd known him then. She'd stared at his face, and while the individual features still sparked no recognition, she had a clear image of a body laboring above hers in the dark. The grunting, the groaning, the endless noises to accompany her endless shame. How the ties, the horrible latex ties, kept her body exposed, vulnerable and there for his taking.

And just when she thought it would never end, she could take no more, and her body would be ripped in half, he had finally collapsed on top of her, heavy with sweat.

The man had laughed low in his throat. And then he'd murmured, "David said you liked it rough. Need a brother or sister for Molly, Meg? Or maybe I'll just wait a few years and give little Molly a try instead."

She had started screaming then. But the gag smothered the sound, forced it back into her lungs, where it built and built and built. A scream without end.

"David misses you, Meg. David wants you, Meg. You never should've turned him down. Now he's sitting in prison, surrounded by beasts eager to learn your name. We all get out sometime and we all know where you live."

The man rolled off of her, reached for his shirt. "Oh yeah," he said casually. "David sends his love."

The scream had grown too big then. It had exploded up her throat and ripped through her mind. It had burst out of her eyeballs and wiped out her brain. It had gone on and on and on, a sonic boom of a scream. And still she never made a sound. No one heard a thing.

And then as violently as it had started, the scream recoiled, turned in on itself, sank back into her body and took her with it into a dark, velvety abyss.

She had spent a year wanting to remember. Now, in the car with this man, Meg wished she could forget.

He had driven her to a section of town she didn't recognize. Remote. Desolate. The kind of place where only bad things happened. Pulling into a side alley, he took her hands in a surprisingly strong grasp. She smelled the latex before she saw it. Her stomach roiled. She thought she would be sick. He slid the figure-eight ties over her wrists, tightened the bindings, then placed his hand on her breast.

So this was it, she'd realized.

Absurdly, she thought of Jillian. The classes they'd taken in self-defense, the books they'd read on surviving assault.

Women do not have to be victims.

But then why did they make men with such strong grips?

"We have a few hours," he said lightly. "I have some things I need to do first. But once I've completed my chores . . . Don't worry, Meg. I remember how you like it." He flicked his thumb over her nipple. He gave her one last cruel smile, then tied a rolled black T-shirt around her head.

She had been living in darkness ever since.

More sounds now. Banging. Cupboard doors opening and closing. The rattle of pans. Her stomach growled and she suddenly knew what he was doing. He was making lunch. The monster had brought her to his lair, tied her up, captive, terrified for her life, and now he was fixing himself a goddamn cup of soup.

She jerked her arms painfully. Pulled hard on the bindings looped through a metal anchor above her head. Nothing, nothing, *nothing!* She wanted to scream in frustration.

Women are not victims! She was not a victim! Dammit, she had read the books, she had taken the courses. She had listened to Jillian and she had *believed*. How could one girl be so damn unlucky? How could she have spent the last year coming so far, just to wind up here?

She yanked on the bindings again. Felt the concrete hold strong while her own flesh tore, and her wrist once again began to bleed.

And then she just wanted to weep.

He would finish eating soon. He would open the door at the top of the stairs. He would descend into the basement with its musty smell of decay and fresh-turned earth.

And then?

Jillian had told them that they could control their own lives. Jillian had told them that if they tried hard enough, they could win. They could be confident and independent and strong.

But Meg couldn't think like Jillian anymore. She was just a twenty-year-old girl. And she was tired and she was hungry and she was terrified. And soon, very soon, something bad was going to happen. Something worse than even the College Hill Rapist.

Very soon, the man had promised her, David would be here.

In the intensive care unit, Dan sat reading a book. *Recovering from Rape: A Guide for Victims and Their Families*. He had bought the book two weeks ago. He was now on the chapter "The First Anniversary and Beyond—When You Are Not 'Over It.' "

Monitors beeped in steady rhythm to his wife's pulse. Down the hall, some other machine started to beep frantically and a nurse boomed, "Code, code, code!" The words were swiftly followed by the clatter of wheels and metal as someone raced a crash cart to the rescue.

Carol never stirred. Her chest rose and fell peacefully. Her head lay serenely on a golden pool of hair. The white sheets remained smooth and unmussed over the faint mound of her chest.

Every now and then, her right hand would twitch. In the last twenty hours, it was the closest they'd gotten to any sign of consciousness.

Dan finished the chapter from the survivor's point of view. Now he moved on to "The Significant Other—When She's Not 'Over It.' "

He read, and though he was not aware of it, sometimes he cried.

Down the hall, the doctors and nurses fought desperately to save a life. While in Carol's room her heart beat steadily, her lungs worked rhythmically, and her very peacefulness threatened to steal her away.

Dan finished the chapter. Now he gazed at his sleeping wife, his elbows planted on his knees, his head bent. His left arm still ached where Carol had shot him. He barely noticed it anymore.

Twenty hours of vigilance. Twenty hours of hoping and praying and wishing and cursing.

He thought of all the years and all the ways fate had been unkind. He thought of all the things Carol had done and he had done. He wondered why we always hurt the people we love. And then he wondered why it took an emergency room visit to understand what was really important in life.

He would turn back the clock if he could. He would forget the lure of blackjack; he would find a way to be happy at a corporate law firm. He would come home more, ignore his wife less, concentrate on all the little things that used to make her smile. He would be the perfect husband, a man who came home in time to stop the vicious attacker, a man who didn't drive his wife to bingeing, purging, booze and pills.

Of course that wasn't an option. All he could do now was slog messily on, with his injured arm and massive debts and drowning sense of guilt. Carol was broken, he was broken. According to the rape book, such feelings were natural and it would probably be a while before either one of them felt whole—if they ever felt whole. You just had to keep going, the book advised. Wade through the pain, keep looking for the other side.

There had to be another side.

"I love you," he said to Carol.

He got no response.

"Dammit, Carol, don't let him win like this!"

Still no response.

Down the hall, things took a turn for the worse. No more frantic noises. Just a far eerier silence. Then a doctor's voice penetrated the hush. "Time of death," the doctor announced.

"Fuck it!" Dan cried. He threw down the book. He climbed onto the white hospital bed. He negotiated wires and tape and tubes until he could gather up his wife. Her head lolled against his shoulder. Her long blond hair poured down his chest.

Dan got his arms around Carol. He pressed her against his body, and he held her as close as he could.

While down the hall, the crash team wearily retreated to the break room, where they turned their attention to the TV.

"Hey," someone said. "Isn't that David Price?"

Still sitting in the Pesaturos' living room, Jillian didn't know what to do. Tom was staring at the floor, as if the worn carpet held the secret to life. Laurie had disappeared into the kitchen, where, judging from the distinct smell of Pine-Sol, she was waging a holy war against dirt. That left Libby and Toppi to entertain Molly. The little girl now had Libby picking through a shoe box of Barbie clothes while Toppi was in charge of getting a hot-pink cape onto a stuffed Winnie the Pooh. Jillian couldn't begin to fathom what that was all about.

Tom stared, Laurie cleaned, Molly played, and Jillian . . . ? She didn't know what she was supposed to do. The Survivors Club was fractured. They had careened away from one another, whether they had meant to or not, and alone they definitely weren't as strong as they had been together. Bitter Carol had given in to her self-destructive rage. Flaky Meg had vanished when her family needed her the most. And Jillian? Grim, determined, holier-than-thou Jillian? She had no troops to lead into battle. She sat next to her mother, slowly twisting Trisha's gold St. Christopher pendant, and tried to rein in her scattered thoughts.

If Griffin was right, the Survivors Club had been doubly victimized. First the rapist had battered their bodies. Then he'd duped them into wreaking not their vengeance, but *his* vengeance upon some poor guy who'd tried to tell them better. Poor Eddie Como, proclaiming his innocence right up to the bitter end.

If Jillian thought about that too much, thought of the man, Eddie, them, Trish, she was afraid she would start with yelling and end with breaking every object in the room.

If she thought about it too much, she would be down in her sister's dark apartment again. The man would be squeezing her throat, calling her vile names. And while he did these things, he would be laughing on the inside, because he already knew that when she tried to seek justice later, she'd only be serving his needs once again.

While Trish died on the bed.

One year ago, she had called Meg, she had called Carol. She had told them that they had been victimized once, but it never had to happen again. She had told them they could reclaim their lives. She had told them they could win.

She had lied.

Is this what life came down to in the end? You tried and you failed, you tried and you failed. The opposition was not just physically stronger than you but smarter as well? You could struggle as hard as you knew how, but still your sister died. You could finally arrest a murdering pedophile, and the man would simply smile and tell you exactly what he had done to your wife.

David Price. David Price. It all came down to David Price. Charming, seemingly harmless, perfect neighbor, David Price.

Jillian gripped Trisha's medallion in her hand. It wasn't so hard to transfer her rage after all. She wanted David Price dead. And then, for the first time, she truly understood Griffin. And then, for the first time, she had an inkling of an idea.

The front door opened and shut. Laurie, who had gone out to get the mail, walked into the family room, sifting through the pile.

She came to the middle. Meg's mother started to scream.

37

Maureen

"This is Maureen Haverill, reporting live from the Adult Correctional Institutions, Cranston. Today, startling new revelations in the College Hill Rapist case, which gained fresh intensity last night with the brutal murder of Brown College student Sylvia Blaire. Was twenty-eight-year-old Eddie Como, tragically shot down Monday at the Licht Judicial Complex, the real College Hill Rapist, as he was charged? Or was Como merely another victim in a sadistic game? I am here with ACI inmate David Price, a convicted murderer, who claims to know the real identity of the College Hill Rapist but tells us that state police have repeatedly ignored his offers of assistance. Mr. Price, what can you tell us about the attack on Sylvia Blaire?"

"Good afternoon, Maureen. May I call you Maureen?" He kept his voice friendly, then gave her his most neighborly smile.

"If you'd like. Now, Mr. Price—"

"Please, call me David."

"David, you claim to have information on a very serious case. How is it that you know the College Hill Rapist?"

"Well, we're kind of like pen pals."

"Pen pals?"

"Yes. See, the man, the real rapist, he's been sending me letters."

"Letters? As in more than one?"

"That is correct."

"Interesting. How many letters have you received from the man alleging to be the College Hill Rapist, David?"

"I'd say six or seven."

"And when did you get the first letter?"

"Over a year ago, shortly after I was sentenced to Max. Of course, in the beginning I didn't take them very seriously. I mean, why would some rapist write to me? It wasn't until the past few days I figured out the man might be legitimate."

"Can I see these letters, David? Do you have them? Can you show them to our viewers?"

"Well, I do have them, Maureen . . ."

"Yes?"

"Well, they're evidence, aren't they, Maureen? Letters from a rapist. I don't think we should be handling something like that. I should just keep them safe for the state police. This is an important investigation. I don't want to do anything that might mess it up." He smiled at her again.

She frowned. "But you said the state police aren't taking your claims seriously, isn't that right, David?"

"The state police don't like me very much."

"Why is that?"

"Well, the head of the current investigation, Sergeant Griffin, used to be my next-door neighbor. Sergeant Griffin never liked me much. He was always working, you know—those state police detectives have very important jobs. But that meant his wife was home alone a lot. We became good friends, and I think . . . well, I think Sergeant Griffin might have been threatened by that. Not that he had any reason to be! His wife was a lovely lady, very nice. I don't have any family, and she was very sweet to keep me company. She was really a wonderful, beautiful, sexy lady."

"David, isn't it true that Sergeant Griffin was the arresting officer in your murder case?"

"Well, yeah. And that makes him mad, too. I mean, it took him nearly a year to catch me, Maureen, and I lived right next door. When you're a state police detective, I think that's a little embarrassing."

"This was the infamous Candy Man case, was it not?"

"I heard that's what they called me."

"You were found guilty of murdering ten children, isn't that correct, David?" She regarded him sternly. "The bodies of the children were found buried in your basement, and you are now serving ten consecutive life sentences with no hope of parole. Isn't that correct?"

David Price humbly bowed his head. Sitting once more in the private interview room of ACI's rear hall, he practiced looking contrite. "It shames me to say it, Maureen, but you are correct. I've done some bad things in my time. On the other hand, I think that's why the College Hill Rapist latched on to me. He seems to regard me as some kind of hero."

"The College Hill Rapist is *impressed* by you?" She looked dubious, maybe it was disgusted.

"I believe so, Maureen. He said that in the first letter. He was doing something he thought only I would understand."

"He told you about the rapes?"

"In the most recent letter. He provided very graphic detail, Maureen, including things only the real rapist could know. Which is what I've been trying to tell the police."

"Can you give us an example, David? What is something only the 'real rapist' would know?"

David switched from looking contrite to looking troubled "I don't know, Maureen . . . It's an official investigation. Maybe I should keep quiet. Sometimes the police don't like the public to know everything. It compromises the investigation. I wouldn't want to do anything like that . . ."

Maureen took the bait. "Authenticity, David," she responded instantly. "If you give us just one detail, one little thing that only the *real* College Hill Rapist would know, that would prove the authenticity of your letters. And that would be a huge break in the investigation. People would be very proud of you."

"You think?"

"One little detail, David. Just one little detail."

"Well, I can think of one. But, it's kind of graphic . . ."

Maureen leaned closer with the mike. "This is a serious crime, David. The women of Providence are scared. We need to hear what you know."

"Well, okay. He, um, well, he uses douches on the victims. That's a detail. He's used it on all of them, when he was done. The police think it's because he's trying to remove . . . well, you know. I can't say it in front of a lady."

"Semen, David?"

"Well, yes." David squirmed in the orange plastic chair, then looked right into the camera and blushed charmingly. "So he uses a douche when he is done with each woman. But the police are wrong, Maureen. He's not removing semen. Instead, according to his letters, he's . . . well, he's putting stuff *in*. He's using the douche to spray another man's sample, Eddie Como's DNA, at the scene. And that's why the police can't catch him. All the evidence points to another guy. Let's face it, four attacks later, the police are no closer to identifying the real College Hill Rapist. They haven't a clue."

Sitting across the table, Maureen was clearly breathless. "This man thinks he's invented the perfect crime, doesn't he, David?"

"Oh, absolutely. He's proud of what he's done. And he has no intention of stopping. His letters are very clear. He enjoys hurting women. Honestly *likes* it. And he's going to keep going and going and going—"

"You've told this to the state police?"

"Maureen, I've been calling the police ever since Eddie was shot, poor guy. The minute I heard he was gunned down at the courthouse, I knew the letters were for real. This guy, you see, he framed Eddie and then he killed Eddie so it would look like a dead man was attacking Providence's coeds. He's smart, Maureen. Very smart. That's what I've tried to tell the police."

"You've actually spoken with the police?"

"Sergeant Griffin finally met with me this morning. It didn't go well, though, Maureen. He threatened me with interfering with a police investigation. Then he got mad and started going on about his wife. I'm telling you, we were just friends!"

"Did you show Sergeant Griffin the letters you received?"

"He never gave me the chance. From the beginning, it was obvious he thought I was lying."

She leaned forward intently. "Are you lying, David?"

David looked straight at the camera, and deep into the eyes of the viewing public. "No, Maureen. And the fact that I know about the douches should be proof enough. Call the ME, call a Providence detective. They'll tell you that a Berkely and Johnson's Disposable Douche with Country Flowers was found at every rape scene, even this last one. Now how could I know that if I hadn't learned it from the real College Hill Rapist?"

Maureen turned toward the camera. She said somberly, "In fact, I learned just this morning from an inside source that douches are considered a signature element of the College Hill Rapist's attacks, something that has never before been revealed to the general public. Also, police found a used douche in the home of slain college student Sylvia Blaire, raising the theory that she is the College Hill Rapist's latest victim." She turned back to David, her expression grave. "David, I don't think you're lying. The viewing public doesn't think you're lying. So tell us the real name of the College Hill Rapist."

And David Price, reformed sinner for the day, said, "I'm sorry, Maureen, but I don't think I should tell you that."

"Come on, David. You want to make good. You want to help the public. Here's your chance."

"I should tell the police and only the police."

"But according to you, David, the police don't believe you."

"I know. And it's sad, very sad, Maureen, because I received a new letter just this morning. The College Hill Rapist went a whole year without attacking a woman because he wanted to kill Eddie first and wrap up his plan. Now he's done that. Now he's ready to make up for lost time. I'm pretty sure . . . No! I'm *absolutely certain* he's going to attack another girl tonight."

"He's going to strike again, *tonight?*"

"I think so, Maureen. Yes, ma'am, I'm *sure.*"

Maureen leaned across at the table.

Her blue eyes were blazing. She was gripping the microphone so tightly her knuckles had gone white. She was jazzed. Her cameraman was jazzed. In the small room, they radiated pure energy. David amused himself by picturing them both dead. "David, tell us his name. You did a horrible thing once. You kidnapped little kids, you hurt children, you damaged a lot of families out there. People still remember that. There are people watching this right now, wondering why they should believe any word spoken by a monster such as you. Tell those people the College Hill Rapist's real name. Show those people that you're ready to make amends."

"I can't."

"What do you mean you can't?" Maureen was nearly shouting now. "Do you or don't you know the name? Speak to me, David. Help us! According to your own words, another innocent college student is doomed to die!"

David finally let loose. "I know his name! I want to help!" reformed sinner David wailed. "But . . . but look at me! I'm living in maximum security, Maureen. I'm living in the middle of Steel City, surrounded by the worst of the worst. And look at me! I'm only five eight. I weigh a hundred and fifty pounds. For God's sake, do you know what it means to be so small in a place like this? Do you?"

"What are you saying, David?"

"Information is power, Maureen. In prison. In life. This is the only information I have. It's my only chance at power in a place like this. God forgive me, but I can't just give it up. I need something in return."

Maureen finally drew back. For the first time, she sounded genuinely disappointed. "You'll only give up the name of the College Hill Rapist in return for something else? That's what you're saying, isn't it, David? You'll only help us if there's something in it for you."

This was the tricky part. David bowed his head, then he sneaked a humble peek at his audience. "I'm sorry, ma'am. I'm sorry to everyone out there, too. I know it's not right. But that's how the system works, and I'm part of this system now. I have to play by these rules."

"Are you hoping to get out of prison? You raped and murdered babies, David. You buried their bodies in your basement. No matter what you know now, people are going to be uncomfortable with you getting any kind of consideration."

"I know."

"You're a murderer, David. Let's be honest. You're in maximum security for a reason, and most people are grateful that you're there."

David took a deep breath. "I'm a father."

"You're a father?" Maureen was so shocked, she actually blinked her eyes. It was probably the first genuine emotion she'd ever shown on camera.

"Yeah. I'm a father. I have a little girl. Five years old. Maureen, I've never gotten to see my little girl. Never even . . . gotten to say hi."

Maureen's face grew serious again, her tone intent. "What do you want, David?"

"I want to see my little girl, that's all. Look, I'm not denying what you say. I know I'm never getting out of prison. I've made my peace with that. After the things I did, I should be grateful just to be on God's green earth. I've seen the chaplain. I'm reading the Bible. While I can't change what I have done, Maureen, I can try to be a better man from this day forth—"

"Tell us the name of the College Hill Rapist, David."

"I have a daughter," he continued relentlessly, "and she's getting to that age where she's noticing that she doesn't have a father like other kids. I want her to know that it's not her fault. I want her to know that someone loves her. I want her to know that *I* love her."

"What do you *want,* David?"

"Three hours, Maureen. That's what I want, all I want. Three hours, fully supervised, in street clothes, to go see my daughter. For the first time. For the only time. So I can tell her that I love her. So I can tell her that she's a good girl. So I can tell her that I can't be her father, but it's not her fault."

"You want the state to release you from prison for *three hours.* To turn a convicted killer loose on the outside?"

David held up his hands. "Supervised hardship leave, Maureen. Like the corrections department does for funerals, things like that. I'd be shackled, wrists and ankles. Escorted by corrections officers at all times. The police can pick where we meet, they can pick how we get there. I'll do whatever I'm told. Greeting my daughter in leg irons with a security escort is still better than making her come here. Let's face it, no little girl belongs here."

Maureen finally sat back. She was frowning but for the first time she seemed willing to consider his proposal. And if she was willing to consider it, others would be willing . . .

"A three-hour hardship leave, fully supervised. And in return you'll provide the name of the College Hill Rapist?"

"Yes, ma'am."

"Who is your daughter, David?"

"I won't tell you."

"This daughter you love so much?"

"My daughter exists, Maureen. Just ask any prison official. But I'm not announcing her name on public TV. I wouldn't do that to my little girl."

Maureen made one last play. "Why don't you give us the rapist's name now, David, and in return I'll go to work on securing a three-hour leave as you have requested. In return for doing the city such a big favor, I'm sure something could be arranged."

"You're a nice lady, Maureen."

"Thank you, David."

"But I'm not that dumb."

"What?"

"I get my three hours. I see my little girl. And when it's done, I'll turn to the first police officer I find and tell him the College Hill Rapist's name. That's the deal. I hope it happens, and for all of our sakes, I hope it happens soon. The College Hill Rapist is a hungry man. Come nightfall, he'll strike again."

"David—"

"Oh, and Sergeant Griffin, if you're listening, I'll say it again. Your delicious wife and I, we were honestly just friends."

38

Griffin

Griffin was having a hard time controlling his rage. He leaned his massive frame across the gleaming, cherry-wood desk, homed in on the young man who had the misfortune to be the sperm bank's business manager and didn't waste any time on words.

"Janitor. Name. *Now.*"

"I'm trying to tell you, we don't have a janitor."

"Who cleans?"

"A service."

"Their name. *Now.*"

"I need to look it up."

"Then look it up, dammit!"

The man turned hastily toward a cherry file cabinet, manicured hands fumbling with the wooden handle while he sweated through his Armani suit. Apparently there was money in infertility treatments. Lots of it.

Fitz stood behind Griffin. Waters stood next to Fitz. Both were eyeing him carefully, but neither of them intervened.

"Korporate Klean," Mr. Management Money announced two minutes later.

"Address?"

The man handed over the manila file. Griffin flipped through the pages.

"There are no names of which individuals actually handle your building."

"Our contract is with Korporate Klean. They figure out the staffing."

"How often do they come?"

"Every night."

"What about daytime?"

"When they have special projects. The inside of the windows, polishing the brass railings in the elevators and stairs. Oh, and laundry. They bring in fresh loads of linens, towels, etc., a few afternoons a week. We, uh, we like to make our patrons feel like they're at home, and not in a clinical environment."

"How thoughtful of you. Who brings in the laundry?"

"I don't know."

"How big is the crew that works this building?"

"I don't know."

"Same people all the time?"

"I don't know!"

"Mr. Matthews—"

"Our contract is with Korporate Klean, Sergeant. I'm sorry, I'm honestly trying to help. But we don't worry about those details. You'll have to talk to them."

"Thanks for the file," Griffin snarled, and stalked out of the building.

In the elevator, Fitz took the folder. "I've heard of them. Korporate Klean."

"The PPD has cleaners?" Waters drawled mildly. "I never would have guessed."

Fitz shot the skinny detective an impatient glance. "No, we investigated them once. You numbnuts should've heard of them, too. Korporate Klean hires mostly ex-cons."

"What?" Griffin stopped pacing the brass-trimmed elevator and stared at Fitz.

He shrugged. "It's a 'second chance' company, you know. Run by a couple of Ben & Jerry liberals who believe people really can reform their evil ways. Guy serves his time, gets out of prison, he's gotta start somewhere. He goes to Korporate Klean and reenters polite society as a janitor. We've checked into them a few times but never found any funny business. Everyone makes good, everyone works hard, everyone plays well with others. At least that's what the owner, Sal Green, says."

"Companies are willing to be serviced by a cleaning crew of former inmates?" Waters asked.

"I don't know how much the companies know. You heard Mr. Sperm Bank. Their contract is with Korporate Klean. Korporate Klean takes care of staffing."

"Oh great," Griffin muttered darkly. "So when we ask them for a list of employees with past records, that's going to be their entire damn company."

"Yeah, but not everyone's cleaning the sperm bank."

Griffin's cell phone rang. He snatched it up as the elevator hit ground floor and dumped them into the lobby. "Griffin."

"You saw the news?" Lieutenant Morelli asked.

"I listened to the radio."

"Sergeant, we'd like you to return to headquarters—"

"We're onto him, Lieutenant. According to Tawnya, Eddie made several donations to a local sperm bank, which just happens to be serviced by a cleaning company comprised of ex-cons. We're on our way to Korporate Klean as we speak. One hour, two hours, we're going to have the perp's name."

"Sergeant, in light of David Price's involvement . . ."

"I'm fine, Lieutenant."

"We appreciate your efforts, and we think it would be best—"

Griffin thrust out his phone to Waters. "Tell the Lieutenant I'm fine." He probably shouldn't have growled when he said that. Waters took the phone while Griffin rolled out his neck.

"Afternoon, Lieutenant. Uh huh, uh huh. Yeah. Uh huh."

Waters handed the phone back to Griffin. "She doesn't like you much."

"I'm telling you, I gotta try a new cologne." Griffin tucked his phone against his ear and opened the door to his car. "Lieutenant, we're going to get him. Before six o'clock, and without David Price. We're going to nail the son of a bitch."

And Lieutenant Morelli said quietly, "We're making plans for a three-hour release."

"*What?*"

"Target time is six P.M. We're working hand in hand with the department of corrections, the state marshals and SWAT. I'll be leading the team."

"Lieutenant, don't do it. It's what he wants. Don't do it!"

"Do you think I can't handle the team, Sergeant?"

"It's not about you," Griffin said, closing his eyes. "It's not about me. It's about David Price. Listen, the rapes started over a year ago. Think about that. That means Price has been in on this for over twelve months, twelve months of thinking, planning and scheming for this day. He's got another agenda. And he's had ample opportunity to get it into play."

"Do you think I can't handle the team, Sergeant?"

"The Pesaturos will never allow it," he tried again, more desperate now. "They're not about to have their five-year-old granddaughter serve as bait."

"The Pesaturos have personally requested the meeting. It was their call to the superintendent, not the other hundreds of calls," the lieutenant added dryly, "which influenced the final decision."

"What? How? Why?"

"They found a note in their mail. If David Price doesn't see Molly, they don't get to see Meg. The note came with a picture. Do you understand now how serious this situation has become?"

"He's covering all the bases," Griffin murmured. "If the public outcry isn't enough, pressure from the victim's parents will definitely get the job done. Oh, and now we can't hurt him either. You can position all the snipers you want at this *meeting,* but none of them can take a shot. Something happens to David at any time, and we lose Meg. Think about that, Lieutenant. He has already set up a human shield, without the human even being present. It's fucking brilliant. *That's* what one year of planning can do."

The lieutenant didn't say anything right away, so she probably agreed. Sometimes, even when you knew you were being manipulated, you couldn't avoid it.

"It's three P.M. now," Morelli said quietly. "I'm starting preparations for the cover team as we speak." And then, even more quietly, "Griffin . . . we know who we're dealing with. *I* know who we're dealing with. I'm getting the best people, I'm demanding the tightest security. I don't want Price out of prison any more than you do. But if it does happen, if it comes to that, I'll make sure it goes down right."

"We're going to get the man's name," Griffin said.

"I look forward to that call. And Sergeant—if you find the College Hill Rapist first, remember what you've spent the last year learning. Remember, we still need Meg."

39

The Victims Club

The man entered the basement. Meg heard the protesting groan of the old wooden stairs, then his out-of-tune humming. He'd paid her a visit earlier. Skipped down the steps, told her to smile and turned on a bright light right before she heard the whir of an instant camera. She'd still been tilting her head up, trying to peer beneath the bottom edge of her blindfold, when he had summarily clicked the light back off and thumped back up the stairs. She was left alone in the endless dark, her arms pulled painfully over her head, the muscles in her rib cage beginning to protest.

Now she heard him approach once again and unconsciously shrank back against the concrete wall, as if that would save her.

"How is pretty, pretty Meg?" the man whispered. He cupped her cheek. She turned her head and he chuckled, running his fingers down her throat, dipping them beneath the collar of her shirt. "My, my, you've been working up a bit of a sweat."

With the latex gag cutting into her mouth, she couldn't say anything and didn't bother to try.

"Tsk, tsk," the man scolded, "I don't think David's going to like that much. Maybe before he comes, I should give you a bath. You, bound and naked in a tub. I haven't tried that before. I think I might like it."

His hands were inside her shirt, on her lace-covered breasts. He didn't squeeze, didn't stroke. Just let his hands rest on her chest as if to prove his point—he held the power to do anything he wanted to her body. And there was nothing she could do to stop him.

"Well," the man said briskly, "I have one last chore to attend to. A little present for David, one not even he's expecting. Should be lots of fun for everyone, especially me. Wish me luck, dear. If all goes as planned, I should have a few moments to come back and play."

Now his fingers did move. She pressed her cheek against the dank wall. She did her best not to vomit.

The man chuckled. "See you soon, Meg." He kissed her on the neck. Then he resumed his toneless humming as he ascended the stairs.

The moment she heard the door click shut, Meg released her pent-up breath. She sagged against the hard-packed dirt floor, her legs trembling, her arms screaming with savage pain. She cried a little, but her tears were short-lived. He hadn't given her any water since her kidnapping, and she couldn't afford the loss of moisture.

She sniffled, she took a deep breath and then she tilted her head up toward a wall anchor she couldn't see. When she pulled forward, nothing happened. But as she'd twisted away from the man's fingers, she was sure she had detected the slightest wobble. If the anchor moved a little now, then maybe, over time, it would move a lot.

It wasn't much, but it was all she had. Meg, the human pendulum.

David Price was coming. David Price was coming. Meg started swaying.

Lieutenant Morelli sat in the living room of the Pesaturo home. Toppi had whisked Molly upstairs the moment the lieutenant had arrived. Now Lieutenant Morelli spread out a map on the living room floor and went straight to business. She gazed at Tom, Laurie, Jillian and Libby somberly. She told them, "This is what we're going to do. We want the meeting in public, so we can properly monitor it, but we also want it semiprivate to reduce the risk of pedestrian interference."

"You mean hostages," Jillian murmured.

"We like this residential park." The lieutenant tapped the green square on the map. "Direct street access that can be easily monitored. We close off all the side roads, of course, and shut down the park to the general public. The park itself is an open, green space, meaning it's easy to monitor with few places to hide—"

"You mean in case the College Hill Rapist is setting up an ambush," Jillian said.

This time, the lieutenant paused long enough to give her a stern look. Apparently, in the state police officer's world, civilians were to be seen, not heard. Well, that explained Griffin. "We can also position snipers on rooftops here, here and here," the lieutenant continued curtly. "In other words, we will have a bead on David Price at all times during the three hours."

"If you shoot him, what happens to our daughter?" Tom asked.

"Given the situation, our snipers will have to radio for permission to use deadly force."

"What does that *mean*?" Laurie asked.

"It means we understand Price holds valuable information and we'll do our best to conduct the operation accordingly."

Jillian spoke up. "But under some circumstances, you would authorize use of deadly force."

"We're professionals," Lieutenant Morelli said firmly. "We know what we're doing."

Jillian, Tom, Laurie and Libby exchanged glances. They thought they knew what that meant. The snipers wouldn't kill David Price if he still appeared controllable. But if it looked like he was getting away . . . If the state police had to weigh the life of one woman against a convicted serial killer who would definitely return to his murderous ways should he ever get free . . .

"The state marshals will be in charge of transferring Price from the ACI to the park." Lieutenant Morelli resumed speaking. "Transporting prisoners is their job and they know it best. Given the extreme situation, we will provide police escort and we will follow a predetermined, secured route. Upon arrival at the park, the state marshals will turn Price over to two state detectives for the duration of the meeting."

"He'll be in street clothes?" Laurie asked.

"Price's lawyer will deliver clothes for the visit by four this afternoon. We will thoroughly inspect the articles of clothing, of course, as well as conduct a full search of David Price."

"His wrists and ankles will be shackled?" Tom asked.

"Absolutely. His ankles will be bound. His cuffed hands will be secured to his waist with a chain. His mobility will be extremely limited, I assure you. Now then, I want to talk about Molly—"

"I don't want him to touch her!" Laurie cried.

"We plan on keeping them ten feet apart at all times."

"How about the length of the park?" Tom growled.

"We may increase that distance at our discretion," the lieutenant replied.

"In other words, if David is acting hinky . . ." Jillian murmured.

"We won't let Molly anywhere near him," the lieutenant finished for her.

Tom sighed heavily. His big shoulders sagged, his face was haggard. It was obvious he hated the idea of what was to come, and it was obvious he felt he had no other choice.

"Now," Morelli said briskly. "About Molly's escort—"

"We'll take her!" Tom said instantly, head popping up.

"We would prefer that you didn't—"

"Hell, no! Not an option. This is our daughter . . . granddaughter we're talking about. Molly needs us, she depends upon us. We will be there at her side every step of the way."

"Mr. Pesaturo, we understand your concern. But this is a potentially volatile situation. We feel it would be best to minimize the number of civilians involved and maximize the number of experienced professionals."

"Too bad. I'm her father. I'm not leaving her side."

"Mr. Pesaturo, it would be my honor to escort Molly—"

"I'm her father!"

"And I have two daughters of my own!" Lieutenant Morelli's voice finally rose angrily. She caught the emotion, leveled her tone. "Mr. Pesaturo, we don't know what Price's true intentions are. We suspect, however, that they involve a great deal more than simply saying hi to his long-lost daughter. If he springs something, what are you going to do?"

"Kill the bastard." Tom saw her look and hastily added, "In self-defense, of course."

"And what about Meg?"

"I don't . . . I don't know." His shoulders sagged again. Meg had been missing nearly six hours now. Six long, uncertain, fearful hours. Tom whispered, "What would you do?"

"I don't know," the lieutenant answered gently. "I suspect none of us will know what to do until the moment it is asked of us. But the point is, there may be split-second decisions that need to be made, and as someone experienced in these matters, I'm better equipped to make them."

"This is ridiculous." Laurie again. "We're doing exactly what he wants."

Lieutenant Morelli didn't say anything.

"Isn't there something else you can do? Some way you can *force* him to tell you where Meg is? To give us the rapist's name?"

"He's in prison for life," Morelli said. "That's already the maximum penalty this state allows."

"But prisons do have punishments," Jillian spoke up. "Protocols, procedures for when prisoners get out of line."

"Inmates can be LFI—locked and fed in, meaning they must remain in their cells even during mealtimes. It's ACI's version of solitary, except the inmate remains in his original cell. Or, in cases where an inmate routinely disrupts prison life, he can be reassigned to Super Max, where inmates are confined to their cells twenty-three hours a day. In other words, they lose all the perks still offered in Old Max."

"Then threaten him with reassignment!" Tom boomed. "Tell Price you're going to send him to this Super Max place."

"Sergeant Griffin already did. Price didn't care." Morelli leaned forward. "I'll be honest with you, Mr. Pesaturo. If we had more time, we could try some different tactics, place Price in Super Max and see if the pressure got to him. But I suspect Price knows that. That's why he's given us an aggressive timetable. That's why we have only a matter of hours. If we don't do what he wants, something could happen to Meg, or something could happen to another innocent young girl. Yes, what we're doing is not ideal. But we're going to do it with the best of our abilities. I'd like to escort your granddaughter, Mr. Pesaturo. I promise you I will do my best to keep her safe."

"What will Sergeant Griffin be doing?" Jillian asked.

Morelli gave her a wary glance. "The sergeant is pursuing another avenue of the investigation."

"I would think you would want him at the scene," Jillian pressed, giving the lieutenant a steely glance of her own. "Isn't he the one who knows David Price the best?"

"Sergeant Griffin feels he has a good lead. We thought it was best to let him pursue it."

"Does he think he knows where Meg is?" Laurie spoke up hopefully.

The lieutenant didn't say anything, and then Jillian got it. "Griffin thinks he might be able to identify the real perpetrator," she said slowly. "He's trying to find the College Hill Rapist, *without* David Price."

"We are doing everything in our power to avoid granting David Price's request," the lieutenant said.

"Oh, thank God," Laurie said. Sitting next to Jillian, Libby tapped her finger.

"But," the lieutenant reminded them firmly, "the meeting Price is demanding may still happen. We need to be prepared. I would like permission to escort your granddaughter—"

"No!"

"Mr. Pesaturo—"

"No," he said again. Tom looked at his wife, then took her hand. Together, they turned toward the state lieutenant. "We've raised Molly as our daughter. She needs us now. We'll do this together. As a family."

"And if Price tries something?"

"Then we'll see how good your snipers are, won't we, Lieutenant?"

Four P.M. Griffin, Fitz and Waters finally found the Korporate Klean world headquarters. In other words, a decrepit old warehouse in south Providence, amid a bunch of even more decrepit old buildings. Apparently cleaning companies didn't make as much money as, say, sperm banks.

The front doors were locked. Griffin started punching buttons on the mounted intercom system while Waters gazed up at the security camera. It took four or five rings before a scratchy female voice crackled through the box.

"*What?*"

"We're looking for Korporate Klean," Griffin said.

"*Why?*"

"We're dirty and we need a good scrubbing, why do you think?"

"*You cops?*"

"Worse," Griffin announced. "We're IRS."

That did the trick. The doors instantly buzzed open. A bunch of ex-cons would have nothing but disdain for law enforcement. Everyone, on the other hand, fears the IRS.

Up on the fifth floor, the office "suite" of Korporate Klean was a pleasant surprise compared to the rest of the building. Sure, the gray carpet was threadbare, the bone-colored walls boring, but the place was spic-and-span. Even smelled like ammonia and Pine-Sol. This must be where the recruits practiced their new trade.

The three detectives came to an empty front desk in the tiny entryway, gazed down a long narrow hallway behind it and waited impatiently for someone to appear. Griffin's leg was starting to jiggle again. He clasped his hands behind his back so no one would see them shake. When he glanced back up, Waters was staring at him, so maybe he wasn't fooling anyone after all.

Four-oh-three P.M. Not much time. Christ . . .

A door down the hall finally opened. A girl with jet-black hair walked out, wearing way too many piercings and not nearly enough clothes.

"May I help you?" she asked, and gave them a very direct glance for someone half-naked in front of three men.

"We're looking for the owner of Korporate Klean."

"May I ask what this is regarding?"

"Taxes."

"IRS agents don't make house calls."

"How would you know?" Griffin gave up on the staring contest. He flashed his ID. "This is official business. Find the owner. Now."

The girl raised a silver-studded brow, gave them a dismissive look just so they'd know that they hadn't scared *her*, and then retreated down the hall.

Griffin's other leg got a tremor. He paced around the room while Waters and Fitz watched.

Another minute, a long, interminable minute. One of so many minutes, ticking, ticking, ticking. Didn't anyone understand the urgency of time?

The girl finally returned. Mr. Sal Green would see them now. The last doorway on the left. Try not to break anything on their way there.

Too late. They stormed down the hall, stormed into the room and arrived as a definite physical presence.

"Officers." An older, trimly built man in faded jeans and a graying ponytail greeted them as they burst into the office. He belatedly rose to his feet, then waved his hand vaguely at the two empty chairs.

"Sergeant," Griffin corrected him sharply.

Green wasn't impressed. He shrugged, then commented, "I'd say I'm surprised by your visit, but of course I'm not. What happened this time, gentlemen? A paper clip is missing from someone's lobby, and you're here to follow up with your favorite scapegoats?"

"The state police doesn't get involved in missing paper clips."

"Oh, you're right, you're right. So one of my crews was speeding instead. You know, it really is safe to hand them the ticket. Not all ex-cons bite."

Griffin's blood pressure jumped another fifty points. He turned to Waters, who got the hint.

"We need a name," Waters said.

"No kidding."

"We need to know who works the sperm bank up in Pawtucket and we need a record of their date-of-hire."

"Then I would need a subpoena."

"Then you're going to need a cast," Griffin growled.

"Oooh, good cop, bad cop." Green turned to Fitz. "What are you, the comedic sidekick?"

Fitz said, "I'm the corroborative witness who'll testify that the first two didn't really hurt you."

"Oh spare me." Green sat back down behind his desk. "Look, I run a good company, with good guys. You people run screaming through my personnel records once a month, and you haven't found anything yet. Whatever it is this time, get a subpoena. If you finally have proof someone in my employ has done bad, then you shouldn't have any trouble getting a judge to agree."

"We don't have time," Waters said tightly.

"And I don't have a million dollars. Welcome to life."

Griffin had had enough. He planted his hands on the desk, leaned in until his face was inches from Green's and held the man's stare. "It involves the College Hill Rapist, got it? Have you been watching the news? Do you understand what we're talking about?"

Green finally paused. He looked away from Griffin, then frowned. "My guys work at night—"

"Not every night."

"I vet them myself. We have no one with a history of sex crimes. The women on my crews would object—or hurt him."

"This guy was never convicted."

"Then how do you know he's one of mine? Look, Sergeant, I'm just a beleaguered small-business owner, and you're not making a very good case."

"We have our reasons. We have *compelling* reasons—"

"Then tell them to a judge," Green interrupted firmly. He picked up his phone, as if to signal that he was done.

Griffin slammed the phone back down. "If another girl is hurt—"

"Then you know where to find me, don't you, Sergeant?"

"You son of a bitch," Fitz snarled.

Green shot him a look, too. He was angry now and it showed in his face. "Gentlemen, it's called due process. You're the police, you ought to know about it. Now if I were you, I'd find a judge. Because it's getting late, and frankly I plan on going home at five."

Griffin almost went for him then. Blood pressure so high. Ringing so loud in his ears. Waters touched his arm. He reined himself back in. Breathe deep, count to ten. Count to twenty. Man was an asshole. The world was filled with them.

"We'll be back," Griffin said.

"You and Schwarzenegger," Mr. Green said dryly and picked up his phone.

They exited the building fast. Four thirty-two and counting. "We need a judge, a friendly judge," Griffin growled. "I'm out of the loop."

"I know one," Waters said immediately.

"Okay, you and I will get the warrant. You"—Griffin turned to Fitz—"watch the building. I don't want to come all the way back with paper just to find Mr. Bleeding Heart gone."

"Oooh, me and all the ex-cons. I can hardly wait."

"Neither can they. Come on, Waters. Let's roll."

Fitz went back inside the building. Waters and Griffin climbed into Waters's car. The sky was still light, dusk three hours away. But it would come, and it would come quick, and Price would be out of prison, walking toward his five-year-old daughter. While some young college student walked out of the student union, headed for her apartment.

And Meg? And Jillian? And Carol?

Griffin had failed his wife once. He had failed ten helpless children. He had failed himself. He was supposedly older and wiser now. He didn't want to fail again.

"Are you going to make it?" Waters asked tightly.

"I'm holding it together."

"Just barely."

"See?" Griffin said lightly. "I've made progress."

Four forty-six.

A corrections officer stopped outside the solitary-confinement cell where David Price had been temporarily placed.

"Hands," the guard said.

"You're going to shackle me already? Wow, you guys really aren't leaving anything to chance."

"Hands," the guard repeated.

David shrugged. He knew the drill. He stuck his hands through the slit in the cell door. The corrections officer slapped on the cuffs. David withdrew his shackled wrists, and his cell door was finally opened. The guard pulled him out by the shoulder and led him over to Processing.

"Can I stop by my cell?" David asked.

"Why?"

"I like that toilet better. You know, it's hard to relax in a new cell."

"Eat more fiber," the guard told him and pulled him down the hall. At the end was a room where three more guards waited. One saw him coming and snapped on a pair of gloves.

"Full cavity search?" David arched a brow. "Why this is just my lucky day."

The guard regarded him stonily. David shrugged.

"Oh, the price of freedom." He went into the room, where his favorite shirt and pants were stacked on the table. The clothes had probably already been searched. Now it was his turn.

David turned away from the stack of clothing, trying not to smile too brightly.

"Free at last," he murmured as he raised his hands above his head, "free at last. O Lord Almighty, free at last."

Five P.M.

David Price bent over.

Griffin and Waters pleaded their case before a judge.

Fitz stared at a half-dressed receptionist.

Tawnya fed a crying, fussy Eddie, Jr.

Meg swayed from side to side.

Carol's right hand started to twitch.

And Jillian sat in the Pesaturo home, thinking of Meg, thinking of Carol, thinking of her sister, thinking of Sylvia Blaire and then thinking of David Price's game plan. Something was wrong here, she thought, then rubbed her temples as she tried desperately, quickly, to think of what.

Molly sat on the floor of her bedroom and waited.

40

Price

"We need a subpoena—"

"We have probable cause—"

"The College Hill Rapist Case—"

"Como donated sperm to a Pawtucket sperm bank—"

"The rapist had to have access to those samples in order to plant evidence at the crime scenes—"

"We need to see some personnel records. Now!"

It wasn't the most elegant arguing Griffin and Waters had ever done before a judge, but it did the trick. At five-eleven, they received their subpoena. They promptly drove ninety miles per hour back to Korporate Klean, burnt some rubber making the hard right turn into the parking lot and squealed around to the front doors.

First thing they saw was Fitz, standing outside, hand on Mr. Green's arm, talking furiously. Green was obviously trying to make good on his threat to go home at five. Fitz was obviously making good on his vow to stand guard.

Griffin screeched to a halt directly in front of them, while Waters thrust the subpoena out his open window.

"We require access to your files, *now*!" Waters announced.

Sal Green sighed and shook his head at their persistence. Then he turned back toward the building.

Five minutes later, he kicked an old gray metal filing cabinet three times, jerked the lower drawer open, then gestured to the emerging row of files. "These are my current employees."

Griffin eyed what appeared to be forty to fifty names. They didn't have that kind of time. "People who work the sperm bank," he said curtly. "Past and present."

"I rotate the crews—it keeps everyone on their toes."

"Date of hire November through April, Mr. Green. *Move it*!"

For a moment, it looked like Green might protest. Griffin's hands started itching at his sides. He was trying to remember what Lieutenant Morelli had said. For that matter, what his therapist, his brothers and Waters had said. Mostly, however, he felt himself descending down, down, down into that dark basement with its neat rows of sad little graves.

Green started pulling files. Griffin figured it was the best decision the man had made all day.

He, Waters and Fitz began skimming. Ten minutes later, Fitz won the prize. "I know this man! Ron Viggio. I arrested him myself, several years back. A regular Peeping Tom. The woman was embarrassed though, and wouldn't press charges."

"Peeping Tom," Waters said. "That sounds like a budding rapist to me."

"Hey, all I know about was an arrest for B&E," Green protested immediately. "Viggio told me about it up front. It was all some misunderstanding, he was trying to plant a surprise in his girlfriend's apartment and a neighbor took it the wrong way."

"He was caught breaking into a woman's home?" Griffin asked sharply.

Green shrugged. "He was charged, not tried. At least that's what I was told."

Griffin was already dialing his cell phone. "Sergeant Griffin here. I need you to run a name through the system. Ronald Viggio. V-I-G-G-I-O. Yep. Uh huh." And two minutes after that. "Current address?"

"All right." He grabbed the file. "Let's go."

"Hey now!" Green started to protest again, but no one waited around to hear.

Five-thirty P.M.

The state marshals appeared and led David to the waiting transport van. Courtesy of his lawyer's timely delivery, David was wearing his own clothes for the first time in a year and a half—a pair of tan khakis, a dark blue button-down shirt and dark brown loafers. The clothes had been searched and run through the metal detector, of course. So had he.

Now his hands and ankles were shackled. A state marshal walked on either side, both heavyset faces grim. David smiled at his escorts. He smiled at the assembled corrections officers. He smiled at the waiting blue van. He was in a good mood.

They loaded him up.

"Try anything, buster," one of the state marshals said, "and we'll grind you into dust. *Capisce*?"

"I don't speak Italian, you English-challenged hump."

The marshal growled at him. David smiled back.

The van doors closed. Soon the prison gates would open.

Five thirty-five P.M. So close to freedom, David could taste it on his lips. Five, ten more minutes, and the gates would open. Five, ten more minutes, and his real journey would begin.

Thank you, Sergeant Griffin, he thought. And of course, thank you, Meg.

"Apparently, Ron Viggio didn't feel the need to tell his employer about his entire criminal history," Griffin said as he hurtled his car onto the interstate and Waters called for backup. "Turns out he wasn't arrested for B&E, but for first-degree sexual assault. He also spent three years behind bars in the mid-nineties for breaking into a woman's home."

"So first he's a Peeping Tom, then he's breaking into women's homes, then he goes for assault. Wow, he's positively textbook."

"Yeah. Unfortunately, the sexual-assault charge didn't stick. The woman had had a prior relationship with Viggio—they'd dated briefly—and since she'd slept with him willingly in the past, she got worried the jury wouldn't believe her claim. Or maybe she just got freaked out at the thought of the trial. It's not exactly a walk in the park."

"Why try the defendant when you can beat up the victim?"

"Exactly. Viggio entered Intake in December, his accuser dropped the charges in January. His probation officer can probably tell us even more stories." Griffin came to the Cranston exit, flashed his lights at the sluggish traffic, then whipped around them, cursing. Some jerk pulled out in front of him. He slammed the brakes hard and swore, and Waters grabbed the bullhorn. "*To the right. NOW!*"

That put the fear of God into the asshole. Of course the driver shot them a dirty look as they went barreling by. Civilians.

"Viggio had four weeks at Intake during the same time as David Price," Griffin said, breathing hard, his palms dampening with a combination of adrenaline and anticipation. He found the proper side street, his speedometer over eighty and his attention focused on the wheel.

"Oooh, is it just coincidence?"

"Or is it probable cause? By December, Viggio had probably figured out that it was only a matter of time until he attacked a woman again. But he also knew his DNA and prints were already in the system, so the first time he gave in to impulse, he'd have two detectives knocking on his door. Then he remembered good ol' David Price, who lived next door to a cop and still got away with killing ten kids. Good ol' David Price, who's conveniently locked up with him in Intake."

"Even rapists need role models," Waters said.

"Unfortunately for us. And now, unfortunately for Viggio. Hang on a sec, we're here." Griffin saw the street sign belatedly, hit the brakes and let the momentum of the car's back end whip them around the turn. He promptly killed the grille lights and eased up on the gas. He didn't want to spook Viggio by racing down the street, lights flashing. First, they would conduct a casual drive-by to assess the home.

They neared the address and immediately spotted a man walking out the front door, heading for his car in the driveway. The man wore dark blue pants, a light blue chambray shirt and, from the back at least, could've been a double for Eddie Como. Hello, Ron Viggio.

"Jesus Christ," Waters murmured in awe.

"He's gonna bail!" Griffin warned. He grabbed the radio. "Everyone, greenlight, greenlight, *greenlight!*"

Griffin whipped his car sideways onto the driveway, blocked Viggio's vehicle and slammed on the brakes. Viggio's head popped up. He registered the two unmarked cars and one police cruiser bearing down on him. And then he ran.

"Move, move, move." Griffin was out of his car. Up ahead, he saw Fitz swerve his Taurus into another driveway in an attempt to stop the fleeing suspect. Viggio leapt onto the Taurus's hood, jumped down the other side and kept moving.

Shouts now. Waters bellowing, "Police, stop!" Residents peering out of their homes and yelping in surprise at the commotion. Officers yelling as they tore out of their cruisers and prepared to give chase.

Griffin had the lead. He scrambled over Fitz's hood and thundered down the sidewalk. He'd show Ron Viggio what a five-minute mile meant. Vaguely he was aware of Waters racing right along beside him. Fitz panted somewhere in the distance.

Viggio glanced frantically over his shoulder and saw them closing the gap. He darted right, headed between two small houses and leapt a low wooden fence. A woman shrieked. A dog barked. Griffin heard it all from far away as he vaulted the fence, homed in on Viggio and dove for the man's legs.

At the last minute, Viggio spun left, avoiding the tackle and reaching a tall chain-link fence. Griffin went down, rolled into the fall and was back on his feet in time to see Viggio and Waters disappear over the barrier. He jumped onto the chain link and resumed pursuit.

They had arrived in someone's personal version of a salvage yard. A small white house sat forlornly in the middle of a pile of twisted, burnt-out wrecks. For a moment, Griffin couldn't see anyone at all. Then he heard a clatter as Viggio darted past a pile of rusty hubcaps, and Waters went careening around another gutted car.

Griffin watched Viggio's line, saw the obvious destination—a kid's bike by the home's front door—and raced around the other side of the house.

He burst into view twenty feet in front of Viggio. "Boo!" Griffin roared.

A startled Ron Viggio drew up short.

And Waters took him out with a flying tackle.

Ten minutes later, Ron Viggio sat handcuffed in the back of a Rhode Island police cruiser, sullenly refusing to talk. They let him be for now and descended upon his home. In the bathroom, Waters found the neatly stacked boxes of latex gloves. In the kitchen pantry, Fitz bagged and tagged three rows of Berkely and Johnson Disposable Douches, all Country Flowers. Then, of course, there were the vials they found in the freezer.

The kitchen table held an open package of model rocketry igniters and was covered with some sort of gray clay. Griffin sniffed the gray material suspiciously, then left it for Jack-n-Jack to figure out. They checked the upstairs bedrooms, the downstairs bathroom and all the closets. Still no sign of Meg.

Griffin finally found a door beneath the staircase, a door leading to the basement. He took a deep breath, motioned to Waters, and together they descended into the depths.

"Meg?" Griffin called out. Something grazed the top of his head. The end of a pull chain for an overhead light.

Still no sound in the dark.

Steeled for the worst, he yanked the chain and turned on the light.

Thirty seconds later, he and Waters had walked the entire length of the dank, empty space.

"Floor doesn't even look disturbed," Waters said. "I don't think anyone's been down here for a bit."

Griffin thought about it. "Car?" he asked with a frown.

"Gotta be."

"Shit."

They were back up the stairs and out of the house. Car wouldn't be good. Trunk of a car would be even worse. Hold it together. Remember the lessons of the past year.

The driver's-side door wasn't locked. Waters opened it with gloved hands, while Griffin ran around to the trunk. He had his firearm out, just in case. On the count of three, Waters popped the trunk.

Griffin leveled his gun.

"Hey," he said a split second later. "Isn't that a bomb?"

Carol had started to move. Dan didn't know if it was good movement or bad movement. At first, just her right hand twitched. He'd taken that as a good sign, stroking her fingers, trying to talk his wife back to life.

Then, her left leg had started to twitch, and she had developed a hitch in her breathing. He wasn't sure what that meant. The doctors had told him that the high dosage of Ambien and alcohol in her bloodstream had effectively shut down her system. In theory, however, her kidneys would do their job, removing the impurities from her bloodstream, and she would respond by waking up. At least that's what they hoped.

Was twitching the same as waking? Did people regain consciousness by first suffering labored breathing?

Dan was standing now. He patted Carol's hand, smoothed back her hair from her pale, cool forehead.

"Come on, honey," he murmured. "Come back to me, love. It's going to be all right. I promise you, this time, things are going to be better."

Her left leg twitched again. Her breathing hiccupped.

Dan leaned forward. He gazed down at his wife's quiet, peaceful face, as beautiful now as the first day he had met her.

And he realized for the first time that her chest was no longer moving. Her breathing had not returned.

A machine started to beep. Dan dropped his wife's hand. He raced into the hallway, his voice already frantic.

"Help, help! Somebody, help us, *please!*"

Five forty-five P.M.

The massive ACI gates swung open. The blue transport van pulled forward. David Price, still grinning, was on his way. In the Pesaturo home, Lieutenant Morelli finished up last-minute details of the meeting, including handing Tom and Laurie bulletproof vests.

They had told Molly they were going to play a game. They were going to a park for a police officers' picnic. They would have some punch, eat some cookies and she could watch all the police officers do their jobs. A man might come and play pretend, too. But not to worry. He was just part of the game.

Molly regarded them solemnly. Children always knew when adults were telling a lie.

They were walking out the front door, faces somber, moods grim, when Morelli's cell phone rang.

It was Griffin. "We got him, we got him, we got him! We've found boxes of latex gloves, plus the douches. Ron Viggio, former cleaner of the Pawtucket sperm bank, is definitely the College Hill Rapist."

"And Meg?" Morelli asked sharply. Tom and Laurie froze, stared at her.

"Not here."

"Where the hell is she?"

"We don't know yet. Viggio's not talking. But we can apply some pressure, retrace his steps. We'll find her, Lieutenant. It's only a matter of time."

Morelli looked at Tom and Laurie. "We have a man who may be the College Hill Rapist," she told them quietly, "but we haven't found Meg."

"Do they have any leads?" Laurie asked.

"Sergeant Griffin believes it is only a matter of time."

"How much time? Does she have food, does she have water? What if she's being held somewhere outside? We want our daughter, we need our daughter to be safe."

"Don't let him go, Lieutenant," Griffin was saying excitedly into the phone. "Don't let Price out. We can do this on our own. We don't need Price anymore."

Morelli looked again at the Pesaturos' anxious faces. She glanced at her watch. Five fifty-five P.M. She said, "I'm sorry, Sergeant. It's too late."

41

The Candy Man

Meg was frightened. Her arms and shoulders hurt seriously now, throbbed with a low keening ache. Her fingers, however, she barely felt at all. They were slow, sluggish, like a separate entity that no longer belonged to her.

Sometimes she felt moisture in her hair, a slow, steady drip. At first, she thought the ceiling had developed a leak. Now she realized it was more blood from her torn, shredded wrists.

She still swayed back and forth, slower now, with less force. Sometimes the wall anchor moved. More often than not, it remained rigidly fixed. She was slightly built, admirably thin. In other words, she didn't have the mass to get the job done. And now she was feeling tired beyond tired. She had strange spells where she couldn't tell whether she was asleep or awake. Her lips were dry and cracked. Her tongue felt glued to her mouth.

Perversely, her bladder had finally given out on her. She hadn't gone to the bathroom since first thing this morning and she simply couldn't hold it any longer. The shame was worse than the discomfort. To be a grown adult with urine-soaked pants; it wasn't right.

And now, to add insult to injury . . .

She missed her captor. She genuinely wished, way down deep, that he would return to her. Maybe, her fuzzy, fatigued mind reasoned, he would cut her down, ease the ache in her shoulders. Maybe, she fantasized, he'd give her a bath, let her feel human again.

And if he did touch her after that, if he did demand some kind of payment . . .

She wouldn't be in the dark anymore. She wouldn't be lost with wet jeans and bleeding wrists. She wouldn't be alone in a musty basement that felt too much like a grave.

These thoughts were bad, she realized in the saner corner of her mind. These thoughts let him win. She had to hold tough, be strong. She had to ignore her pain. To focus her anger, as Jillian liked to say.

We are not victims. The minute we believe that, we let the rapist win. When it boils down to brute strength, ladies, perhaps we can't protect our bodies. But we can always *control our minds.*

Oh please, oh please, oh please let her get out of this. Before her arms gave out completely. Before she did anything she'd regret. Before . . .

Before David Price arrived.

David couldn't see out of the van very well. The transport vehicle offered no side window, and there was a mesh screen between him and the two state marshals, which blurred the front windshield.

That was okay: he didn't need to know where he was or where he was going. That was not relevant to matters at hand.

David leaned forward and pretended to stretch out his back. Then he shifted restlessly from side to side, his fingers slipping along his left shirt-sleeve until he found the slim wooden shape sewn into the cuff.

The bulk was barely noticeable. The quarter-inch-thick, heavily lac-quered wooden lock pick was tucked inside the top seam of the cuff, where the heavy chambray fabric already formed a ridge. If nothing else, Viggio was very good at following instructions. Then, in a move he'd spent the past four months practicing, David leaned forward and bit the hem of his right pant leg. Inside the pant cuff, his tongue found the waiting treasure—what appeared to be crumbled bits of white chalk. Pieces of Alka-Seltzer—too small to be easily noticed, and like the wooden pick, guaranteed not to set off a metal detector.

Sometimes, the simple things truly worked the best.

David eased the pieces of tablet out of the pants cuff and into his mouth. Then, he started to chew.

Forty seconds later, he made a gurgling noise in the back of his throat.

The state marshal glanced in the rearview mirror.

"What the hell?" he said.

In the back of the transport van, David Price was foaming at the mouth.

Griffin was in Ron Viggio's face. "Where is she?"

"I don't know who you're talking about."

"Don't play dumb with me. *Where is she?*"

"My grandma's been dead for years, but thanks for asking."

"We have you, Viggio. We know all about how you stole semen samples from the sperm bank, then injected them into douches. You're already look-ing at two counts of murder, let alone four counts of first-degree sexual assault. You're a little beyond minimum time behind bars, Ronnie boy. Start talking now, and maybe you have some hope of ever seeing daylight."

Sitting in the back of the police cruiser, Viggio yawned.

"Are you trying to protect David Price? Because he's already sold you out. Three hours from now, when he's done meeting with his daughter, he's going to give your name."

Viggio laughed.

"We caught you because of him, Viggio. If he hadn't told us that you'd personally met Eddie Como, we wouldn't have thought to check personnel at the sperm bank."

Viggio frowned.

"Yeah, that's right. You were doing so well, too. You had the perfect setup, a great little plan. Except for David Price. He was your weak link. He's who got you into this mess. Here you thought he was helping you, when really he was playing you all along. You're not a brilliant criminal mastermind. You're just David Price's pawn."

Viggio thinned his lips. Despite his best intentions, he was starting to look pissed.

Griffin's turn to shrug. He straightened, crossed his arms over his chest and gave Viggio a dismissive glance. "Pawns can be sacrificed, Viggio. Guys like Price do it all the time. Why do you think we're here? Price wanted to buy his freedom, so he sold you out. Now he gets to meet his little girl, while you go to prison for the rest of your life. Hardly seems fair. Where is Meg, Viggio? Talk now, while you still have a chance."

"Go to hell."

"Come on, Viggio. David isn't going to help you. You're fucked, you're screwed. Whatever you thought you had coming, it's over. What do you still owe him?"

Viggio's gaze flickered toward his car, now cordoned off in the driveway. Griffin caught the look. He stared at Viggio's vehicle, and then he got it.

"That's another car bomb, isn't it, Viggio? Except, instead of using it on a hired gun, you were going to use it on David Price. You were going to hook it up, then watch your favorite partner-in-crime go boom. Well, I'll be damned. So there really isn't any honor among thieves. Wait a minute." Griffin's voice changed. He leaned forward intently. "That means David Price was going to get into a vehicle. What the hell do you know, Viggio? *What the hell does David Price have planned?*"

Jillian was pacing the living room of the Pesaturo home while Libby and Toppi watched. Her right hand twisted Trisha's medallion relentlessly. Her left hand was clasped behind her back.

"This isn't right," she told Libby and Toppi, though they had probably grown bored with her tirade by now. "Tom and Laurie need us. Meg needs us. We should be *doing* something!"

"Jillian," Toppi said firmly, patiently, "we're not professionals. Sometimes the right thing to do is to wait."

"But David Price is getting exactly what he wants! Surely there's got to be another way! God, why can't I think of another way?"

Libby sighed. Toppi stared at Jillian.

"How do we even know he will give up the rapist's name?" Jillian quizzed them. "Griffin is right. After meeting with Molly, Price can say anything he likes. It's too late to do anything about it then."

"They could send him to Super Max," Toppi said. "Or punish him with this LFI thing."

"Oh, like David Price cares about that. It's games he likes, getting the upper hand, controlling all the moves on the board." She stopped abruptly, frowned. "Huh."

"What?" Toppi asked.

"David likes to control everything," Jillian said slowly. "But this meeting . . . He let the police pick the place and the route for getting there. He only set the time. If he were planning something, you'd think he'd want to choose the location. Someplace he knew well, or had an opportunity to booby-trap.

Or have the College Hill Rapist booby-trap. That would make sense. David helps the College Hill Rapist come up with the perfect crime. In return, the rapist helps David get out of jail."

"Maybe he's not planning anything," Toppi said firmly. "You heard Lieutenant Morelli. The police are focusing all of their resources on this meeting. Price can hardly just exit the van and keep walking."

Jillian glared at her irritably. "Of course he's planning something! If he really wanted to see his daughter, he would've pressed the issue *before* going to jail. So this isn't about Molly. It's about getting out of prison." She paused, still thinking out loud. "And it's about revenge. Arranging things so that Meg would be the first victim, then setting up the assassination of Eddie Como so it would bring Griffin onto the case. His actions are personal, almost autobiographical—same victim, same detective. But he didn't pick the place. Why didn't he pick the place?"

And then, her eyes flew open. "Oh no!"

"What?"

"It's not going to be at the location! Don't you get it? All the snipers, the lieutenant and Molly . . . That's just a cover, something to distract the police. He didn't pick a place, *because he has no intention of getting there!* Whatever he's going to do, it's going to be en route. Quick, where's the phone, where's the phone? I've got to call Griffin!"

Driving down Route 2 in Cranston, State Marshal Jerry Atkins urgently radioed the state police cruiser in front of him. "Something's wrong with Price. He's foaming at the mouth. Jesus Christ, I think he's going into con-vulsions! What do you want us to do?"

Pause.

"Well we can't just let him die . . . He's supposed to give up the damn rapist. Wait a sec. Whooooa! He's out. He's on the floor. Jesus, I think he's choking on his tongue. He needs immediate medical attention. Quick, pull over!"

Up ahead, the police cruiser abruptly turned right, heading into a restau-rant's parking lot. This part of Route 2 was nothing but an endless strip mall, not a great place for an emergency stop with a violent felon on board. But then, from the back of the van, came another loud crash as Price's shackled ankles jerked violently.

A second police cruiser pulled in behind them and tried to fashion a bar-ricade in the back of the lot. The parking lot wasn't crowded. It was the best they could do.

Jerry jumped down from the driver's side of the van. He had a small first-aid kit, and only the faintest idea of how to proceed.

"Radio for an ambulance," he yelled.

"We're talking to the lieutenant!"

"Does she know first aid?"

"Don't unshackle him!"

"Jesus Christ, do I look like an idiot?"

Jerry threw open the side door. His partner was right behind him. Apparently, the state police did think they were idiots and their escorting officer, Ernie, shoved them both aside. He peered in first with his holster unsnapped and his hand on the butt of his firearm.

"Holy shit."

Jerry and his partner pushed past Ernie and promptly drew up short. David Price's scrawny body seemed to have folded in on itself, a jumbled tangle of shackled arms and legs that could not be natural. As the three men stared in shock, his body spasmed again and his head lolled back, giving them an eerie image of a man trying to stare out through the whites of his eyes.

Jerry was galvanized first. "Quick, quick, get him straightened out. We gotta get a stick in his mouth before he bites off his tongue." He jumped into the van, grabbing at David's shackled feet. Ernie went for his shoulders.

Jerry had a strange thought. Price's hands—they weren't where they should be. What had happened to the thick belt that should be shackling his hands to his waist? His gaze fell to the floor, he saw a small wooden sliver. Almost like a lock pick. And then . . .

Jerry's head came up.

David's magically freed hand grabbed Ernie's Beretta.

Jerry yelled, "N—"

The bullet slammed into his brain.

Crackle, confusion. In the cordoned-off park in Cranston, Lieutenant Morelli strode away from the Pesaturo family with her cell phone in one hand and her radio in the other. She was sweating heavily beneath the weight of her Kevlar vest, and her gaze kept going to the surrounding rooftops, checking on her snipers.

"What do you mean Price is having some kind of fit?

"No, don't pull over. What? You've already pulled over? Whose dumb idea was that?"

Her cell phone rang. She flipped it open first ring and while still listening to Brueger's muddled explanation on the radio, barked, "Morelli."

"He's going to do something on the way," Griffin yelled over the phone. "He was never planning on meeting Molly. It's a ruse. Viggio was going to tamper with his getaway car!"

"Griffin . . ." And then to the radio, "I know you can't let him die!"

"Lieutenant, where is the transport van? Tell me where to find the transport van."

"Dammit, Brueger, where are you? Griffin's yelling that Price has some kind of escape plan. Don't touch him. You hear me? Nobody touches David Price. Brueger?"

Shots. Sudden, sharp, coming over the airwaves. Lots of them. And then men swearing, and more gunfire, and then a gurgle. Close. In the receiver. A man choking on his own blood.

"Brueger? Brueger, do you hear me? Brueger, what is happening?"

"Where is the van, where is the van?" Griffin was yelling.

"Brueger!"

Silence. Total silence. Even Griffin had finally fallen quiet. Seconds ticked away. The sweat trickled hot from Morelli's forehead to the tip of her chin.

She turned around slowly. She stared at Tom and Laurie Pesaturo, who were watching her with shocked, frightened eyes. Her gaze fell. She looked at Molly. Pretty little Molly, who, if there was any justice in this world, would never know her real father.

And then. A voice.

"Send Griffin my love," David Price said over the radio. *"Oh, and somebody might want to send an ambulance. Wait, on second thought, I believe the coroner will do."*

Griffin swore once, stunned, as the radio clicked off.

Lieutenant Morelli hung her head.

Griffin shut his cell phone. It promptly rang again. For a moment, he simply stared at it. Waters did, too. They had heard everything coming over Morelli's radio into Griffin's phone, and now their faces were white, drained. Fitz appeared shell-shocked. The assembled officers were shattered. Sometimes life was like being submerged twenty miles beneath the sea. All sounds were muted. Your limbs felt too heavy to move. You drifted in the dark, the surface too far away, the pressure about to collapse your chest.

Griffin's phone rang again.

He flipped it open and steeled himself for Price's smirking voice.

"He's going to do something along the way!" Jillian exclaimed. "He's never going to make it to the park!"

"I know," Griffin whispered.

"Think about it," she continued excitedly. "He let the police pick the location. He never would have done that if that's where he was planning on making his escape."

"I know."

"And with the snipers and the SWAT team and all that coverage . . . It would be impossible to do something there. En route, on the other hand, when it's just him and some drivers—"

"Jillian, I know."

"You do? Well, then, stop him!"

He didn't say anything. He didn't have the words to voice what he had just heard. How many men had been involved in the escort? Four, six, eight? How many had wives? How many had children? Waters had turned away. Fitz sat down hard on Ron Viggio's driveway, staring bleakly at a streetlight. Somewhere in the neighborhood, a dog howled.

"Griffin?" Jillian said, her voice suddenly uncertain. "Did he? Is it . . ."

"It just happened."

"Oh my God. What did . . ."

"I can't."

"Meg?"

"We don't know."

"Griffin, he can't get away."

"You think I don't know that?" His body finally came alive. He kicked the tire of the police cruiser. Then kicked it again and again. Sitting in the back of the car, Viggio gazed at him balefully. The prick had probably heard it all and still didn't give a damn.

Griffin's vision started to cloud over. He could see his hands so clearly. He could envision them fastening on Viggio's neck, squeezing, squeezing, squeezing . . .

Breathe deep, exhale. Breathe deep, exhale. Don't give in. Picture yourself in a happy place. He wanted to dance on David Price's grave. Was that a happy place? Or did that simply mean that one year later, he hadn't learned a goddamn thing?

"Griffin," Jillian said, "Lieutenant Morelli claimed you had a lead on the rapist."

"Found him."

"But he doesn't have Meg?"

"Nope. And he doesn't seem to be in the mood to talk about it."

"Griffin, I know where she is."

"What?" He perked up. Waters and Fitz caught the change in his demeanor and glanced at him sharply.

"David's self-centered," Jillian said in a rush. "Self-absorbed. This has all been about him. He picked Meg to be the first victim again. He picked you to lead the case again. And now, for the grand finish . . ."

"No!" Griffin breathed.

"Yes. He has one more grave to dig, don't you see, Griffin? He started with Meg. And now he's going to do what he probably thinks he should've done six years ago. He's going to kill Meg. And he's going to bury her in the basement. He's going back to your old neighborhood, Griffin. He's going back to his old house!"

Griffin looked at Viggio. The rapist tried to blank his features, but was too late. The look of amazement on his face said enough.

"How did you get access to Price's former home?" Griffin barked.

"My mother bought it."

"*What?*"

"Price recommended it. Face it, who wants to buy a home that used to have murdered babies in the basement? The real estate agent gave up months ago, and my mother bought it cheap. She's on fixed-income, so hey, she's happy."

"You involved your *mother* in this?"

"Of course not! She's in Florida. I surprised her with a free trip."

"Son of a bitch!" Griffin motioned furiously at Waters and Fitz. "Jillian, thanks. We're on our way there."

Griffin's car was blocked by the police cruiser. They ran for Fitz's Taurus while Griffin started yelling into the radio.

David had a ten-minute head start and they were a good fifteen minutes away. Once more the clock was ticking. For Meg's sake, Griffin hoped they weren't too late.

In the Pesaturos' living room, Jillian hung up the phone, grabbed her coat, grabbed her purse and then grabbed her pepper spray.

"This is insane," Toppi said immediately. "You're not a cop!"

"It's Meg."

"Let them handle this."

"Because it's gone so well thus far?" Jillian turned to her mother. "May I have your pepper spray? I'll take as much as I can get."

Libby frowned, gazed at her reproachfully.

"I can't sit around and wait anymore, Mom! Meg needs me. I have to try." Libby didn't budge.

"Oh for heaven's sake, I'm not going to just barrel into the house! I did that once before and I know as well as anyone that it didn't work. I'll be careful. I'll . . . I'll think of something along the way."

Libby's expression started to waver. Jillian bent down and looked her mother in the eye.

"I have to do this," she said quietly, intently. "I didn't save Trisha, don't you see? You miss her terribly, I know you do. But I *failed* her, and I have to live with that every day of my life. Yes, he was stronger than me. Yes, you should blame the rapist and not the victim. It all sounds so well and good. But I was there. I saw her. And I . . . I didn't get to her in time. I didn't save her.

"I don't want to lose someone else, Mom. I don't want to lose you or Meg or Carol. So I need to do this. Maybe I can't change the world. But I'm finally learning that, for me at least, it's important to try. Please, Mom, may I have your pepper spray?"

Libby reached into her pocket. She held out the canister with a trembling, liver-spotted hand. She looked at her last daughter with open concern. Then she sighed and dropped the canister into Jillian's palm.

Jillian kissed her mother's cheek.

Then she turned and ran for the door.

42

The Survivors Club

Meg had drifted off again. She was at home, in Molly's pink-colored room. They were preparing Barbie for her big wedding day, except this time Pooh's cape was blood red. Meg was trying to get the cape off when she looked down to see that Pooh's fuzzy cheeks had morphed into David Price's smirking face.

"Daddy!" Molly cried in delight.

Meg jerked awake with a scream. Her legs had given out beneath her, and her arms screamed at the sudden impact of her dead weight. Hastily she scrambled to get her footing on the rough dirt floor. Perversely enough, her arms and shoulders ached worse.

A sound. Up above. A door opening. Footsteps moving quickly across a wooden floor.

Meg couldn't help herself. The College Hill Rapist was back, and she was grateful. Her bloody wrists stung, her bound ankles hurt. She couldn't stand the feel of her urine-soaked jeans plastered against her skin. She wanted down. She wanted out. She wished . . . she wished so badly to feel human again.

She turned her head to where she believed the staircase was, and held her breath in anticipation of his approach.

Another click, the door opening at the top of the stairs. And then, "Hi, honey," David Price's voice sang out clearly, "I'm home!"

Through her gag, Meg started to scream.

Five blocks from Griffin's old home, Fitz hit the brakes. Adrenaline demanded that they roar up to the front door and leap out, guns blazing. Prudence advised a different course. The three men gazed studiously around the neighborhood for any sign of David Price while Fitz drove a grid.

Up one street, down another. Around this block, around another. Clock ticking, tension mounting. Griffin could feel the knots bulging in his shoulders, while Waters cracked his knuckles incessantly.

The streets were quiet. The sun was beginning to sink and firing the sky bright orange and deep crimson.

They got within one block of Griffin's former home, where he had lived and loved and lost his wife. Then Fitz pulled over.

"How many points of entry?" he asked quietly.

"Three. Front door, side patio door and basement bulkhead."

"We split up," Waters murmured.

"Finesse job," Griffin said. "David's armed and he won't hesitate to use Meg as a shield. Basically, it's a hostage situation that, given the neighborhood, could rapidly grow worse."

"Contain him," Fitz muttered.

"Yeah. Meg is bad enough. We don't want him to end up in another home, with an entire family to torment."

No one asked the next logical question—at what point did they sacrifice Meg to contain Price? They had to hope it wouldn't come down to that.

"All right," Griffin said.

They got out of the car, got out their firearms, and one by one disappeared into the fiery dusk.

The doctors poured in. Kids, really, in oversized lab coats raced into Carol's room and surrounded Dan's wife. Her left leg was twitching, her right arm thrashing. The machine beeped and the doctors shouted strange codes to the nurses, who were already pushing Dan aside as they scrambled for more equipment and one helluva big syringe.

"Carol, Carol, Carol . . ."

"You need to leave, sir."

"My wife . . ."

"A doctor will be with you shortly, sir."

"Carol—"

The nurse shut him firmly out of the room. He stood outside, alone in the hallway, while the doctors yelled, the machine beeped and his wife's body convulsed on the bed.

David touched her. His fingers stroked Meg's cheek and gently feathered back her hair. She tried to turn away, but she couldn't escape. He had taken off her blindfold first thing. All the better to see you, my dear, he'd crooned. The sudden glare of the bare overhead light hurt her eyes.

"You grew up," David said now. "Pity."

He ran one finger up her arm, then raised it to his lips and sucked her blood off his fingertip.

"You've been busy, my dear. Look at the mess you've made. It didn't help you at all, but it's sweet that you tried. Did Ronnie tell you I was coming, Meg? Did you work yourself into such a state, simply for me?"

She still had the gag in her mouth, so she didn't bother to reply.

"Well, I really can't delay too long," David said briskly. "So let's get you unhooked and down to business."

Meg eyed him warily. She could see the butt of a gun sticking up from the waistband of his pants. One side of his shirt carried a red stain, and his right cheek was flecked with blood. He reeked of gunpowder and death. She had no illusions what that meant.

He slipped his hand behind his back. It emerged with an ugly, black-sheathed knife.

"Courtesy of Jerry," he told her, though she didn't understand whom he meant.

She watched him unsnap the leather sheath. She watched the large, serrated hunting knife slide into view, the overhead light caressing the menacing edge. She should've worked the wall anchor more. She should've tried harder. Who cares that her arms and shoulders had ached. Whatever David did to her now was going to hurt far, far worse.

He rested the tip of the blade against her collarbone. It felt cool and sharp against her sweat-soaked skin.

She closed her eyes, pressed her back against the wall and tried to tell herself it couldn't hurt forever. Everything, even pain, had to end. Poor Molly. Poor Mom and Dad. Poor Jillian and Carol . . . Poor Meg. She had been getting things together. Really, even without a memory, she had been looking forward to getting on with her life. And now . . . The knife moved. She whimpered helplessly . . .

And David cut her down.

Her arms fell forward abruptly, her bound hands hitting her stomach like a rock. In the next instant, blood flow returned to her strained limbs, prickling nerve endings to sudden life, and she nearly screamed at the sudden whomp of pain.

Watching her, David laughed. "Yeah, sometimes the recovery is worse than the injury. You know, I've spent the last year getting into yoga. Take it from me, if you had conditioned your muscles properly to begin with, it wouldn't hurt so much now. Jesus, Meg, did you wet your pants?"

She wanted to hit him. She couldn't move her arms. They felt strange and rubbery, as if they no longer belonged to her. And her shoulders felt different, overly loose. Parts were assembled, but someone hadn't done the wiring right.

"I had planned on playing here for a while," David announced matter-of-factly, "but the fact that Ronnie's absent leads me to believe he might have been detained, and if Ronnie's been detained, then this house is no longer safe. In the good-news department, I see he's already procured a car. What do you say, Meg? Let's go for a ride. For no reason at all, I'm going to have you start the engine first."

He stepped toward the stairs and when she didn't automatically follow, he looked back at her with a frown. "Come on, don't be shy." Then his gaze fell and he finally noticed her bound ankles. "Well, well, looks like Ronnie didn't like to leave anything to chance. Believe me when I say I know exactly how you feel. Come on, I need you to walk."

David got the knife back out. He bent and started sawing through the latex ties. The material finally snapped free. He looked up at her with a smile.

Meg smiled back. And then she drove her knee as hard as she could into the underside of his chin. His jaw cracked sharply. His face went bone-white as the pain ricocheted up to his forehead. David stumbled back, still gripping the knife.

Don't give him time to recover, their self-defense instructor had told them. Don't give your attacker time to think.

Meg lashed her foot out at David's groin; he blocked her with his thigh. She drove her foot down into his tender instep. He made a funny noise in the back of his throat. She went after the side of his kneecap and he finally went down.

She wanted his gun. She wanted his knife. She wanted to stick her fingers in his eye sockets and dig for his brain. But her fingers wouldn't move, her arms wouldn't obey.

Meg whirled toward the wooden staircase with her useless, bloody arms. She started to run.

Behind her, David yelled, "One more step, you fucking bitch, and I will blow you away!"

Meg didn't stop.

David opened fire.

Griffin was easing along the front of the house, approaching the front door, when he heard the first gunshot. It was quickly followed by many more. He ducked low, grabbed the doorknob with his left hand while holding his Beretta with his right. Twist, turn, he rolled into the front entryway and came up in time to see David Price standing at the top of the basement stairs only four feet away. David was bellowing, "I'M GONNA KILL YOU, BITCH!" and brandishing a gun that matched Griffin's own—apparently David had armed himself courtesy of his state police escorts.

Griffin squeezed the trigger just as David spotted him, dodged right and returned fire. Shit! Griffin hurtled himself into the room on the left, getting off a few wild shots while David splintered the floorboards at his feet. Another shape suddenly appeared on Griffin's left—Fitz, emerging through the side patio door.

Griffin yelled: "Down!"

David raised the barrel and squeezed off another shot as Fitz hit the ground.

Griffin fired again. David whirled around the corner into the kitchen, where he had access to the next flight of stairs.

"Damn!" Fitz swore into Griffin's ear, crawling to his feet. "I think he took out the last of my hair."

"Where's Meg?"

"I don't know, but he shot the hell out of something in the basement."

"You go down, I go up."

"And let you have all the fun?"

"You get the girl."

"Oh yeah. Enough said."

Griffin scrambled across the floor, on his hands and knees now and finding the shattered flooring the hard way. He drove four splinters into his forearms before he finally arrived at the entranceway to the kitchen. He reached in with one hand, toppled a small table onto its side and dove behind it for cover.

Then he waited, letting his eyes readjust to the gloomy interior. A light glowed from the bottom of the basement, but apparently that was the only light on in the tightly shuttered house. Griffin blinked, worked on catching his breath, then turned his gaze to the ceiling above him.

Not a sound from overhead. Not a footstep, a scuffle or a muttered curse.

Seven-oh-five P.M. The house was deathly still as the sun began its final descent, and the combatants prepared for round two.

Jillian was trying to drive and read a printout from maps.com detailing how to get to Price's former address, which she'd found listed in old news stories detailing his arrest. The first time she drove right by the street. She went to do an illegal U-turn, then realized it was better this way; she would have a better chance at surprise if she approached the house on foot.

She had one canister of pepper spray in her hand, another in her pocket. Spray worked best up close. Go for the eyes and nose, get it in the mucous membranes. For someone like her, that would require stealth. David was looking for the police, after all. He probably had his hands full battling seasoned professionals like Griffin. Maybe he was even having difficulty controlling Meg. They would be the distraction.

She thought of Trish's apartment again. The man's weight pressing her to the floor, pinning her in place while her sister suffocated and died on the bed. The man laughing at her futile efforts. The man promising to fuck her good.

But she needed to keep those memories at bay. She needed to focus on the sidewalk beneath her feet, the cool metal canister in her hand and the house looming near.

Trish had died, the man had won. You couldn't change the past. Time to move forward. Focus on Meg. Think of the lessons she had learned.

And then return home to her mother, who truly needed her.

Jillian homed in on the house. She was still trying to figure out how to approach, when she heard a low moan, then a male voice shouted, "Jesus Christ, Waters. Oh man. Oh . . . Jesus . . . Hang in there, buddy. Oh man, we need a doctor *quick!*"

Meg was breathing hard. Her body had started trembling uncontrollably and she had to remain plastered to the bedroom wall or she was afraid she'd shatter into a million pieces. As she'd raced up the basement stairs, she'd heard gunfire behind her. At first she'd ducked instinctively, dodging imaginary bullets, then she'd realized that even more gunfire came from behind David. Someone had penetrated the bulkhead. For one moment, her spirits had soared. She *was* being rescued! The cavalry *had* arrived. Then she had heard a man's sudden, sharp exclamation. A stranger's voice. Someone else, not David, had been hit.

She had run and run. And still she had heard shots, coming steadily closer and gaining fresh intensity in the foyer. Then, just as abruptly as it had started, it was over. No more shots, just David's harsh exclamation as he careened up the first-floor stairs.

If the police had come, then he'd shot them all. Because David didn't seem to be running away. Instead, from what she could tell, he was now on the second floor with her. Somewhere down that shadowed hallway, he was looking for her.

Her gaze went around the dusky bedroom, now searching for some means of escape. The blinds were pulled, casting the room into a deep gray pall that made every shadow sinister and every piece of furniture a hulking monster waiting to attack. She spotted the bed in the room's far corner. Her first temptation was to crawl underneath, push herself to the back and curl up her legs and hide. He would look under the beds, of course. And once he found her, she'd be trapped, helpless. He'd grab her by the ankles and drag her out, his knife already in hand.

She couldn't get boxed in. She needed to preserve her options. She was trying to think: *What would Jillian do?*

The bathroom. Maybe she could find a razor or hairspray. Of course, a razor didn't exactly compete with a hunting knife and hairspray hadn't been known to checkmate a gun. Halt or I'll spritz you to death!

She almost giggled, then realized she was becoming hysterical and bit her lower lip. The movement pressed the gag deeper into the corners of her parched mouth. Her eyes teared.

What if she could make it to the bedroom window? She could open it, maybe get onto the roof. Or if the house didn't have a first-story overhang, she could always just jump. It would probably hurt. She might break a leg or worse. But given the alternative . . .

She heard a sound. It was a whisper, slithering down the long dark hall.

"Oh Meg, pretty Meg," David crooned softly. "Come out, come out, wherever you are."

Fight or flight? Not much time left . . .

Poor beaten Meg made her decision.

Griffin had to get up to the second story. He wasn't sure how. As in so many small New England homes, the staircase was narrow and steep. With his build, he'd be a walking target all the way up. All Price had to do was hear him coming, turn the corner and open fire.

Then again . . .

Floorboards creaked up above. Price was on the move.

And then Griffin heard another sound. More old wood groaning, then the telltale squeak of a window finally giving way. But this noise came from the opposite corner from the first noise.

There was a second person upstairs. Oh no, Meg . . .

Griffin didn't have a choice anymore. He abandoned the cover of the table and made his move.

Jillian came around the side of the old house. The first thing she saw was Fitz on the ground, kneeling over another man. "Come on, buddy, come on, hang in there."

"Detective Fitzpatrick?" she called softly.

He jerked around sharply. It was hard to see his features in the rapidly growing dusk, but his movements appeared dazed.

"Jillian, what are you . . . Never mind. Got a cell phone? I need it now!"

"Is he . . ."

"That son of a bitch David Price shot him as he opened up the basement bulkhead. Guess David was already waiting in the cellar."

"Meg . . ." the man on the ground murmured. "Price . . . going to shoot . . . her."

"Shhhh, Griffin's got her."

"She's still in the house?" Jillian dropped down on her knees next to Fitz, then dug in her purse for her cell phone. The downed detective didn't look good. She could see the stain growing rapidly along his left side. His thin face was abnormally pale, sweat beaded his brow. He was going into shock.

"Here." She thrust her phone out to Fitz, then took off her long coat and draped it over the man's chest. He was starting to shake now. The cold grass wasn't good for him, but she didn't know if they should move him. She glanced nervously around the bare yard. They were five feet from a house with an armed killer and the damn landscaping didn't even offer a bush or tree for cover.

Fitz was on the phone. In a quiet, controlled rush he was demanding backup, demanding an ambulance, demanding assistance for an officer down. "Detective Waters has been shot," he said. "Repeat, we require immediate medical assistance."

Jillian took Waters's hand. His fingers felt cold and clammy to the touch. "M-M-Meg."

"Meg's fine," Jillian lied. "Please don't worry."

"Got up . . . basement stairs. I . . . distracted . . . Price."

"Shhhh, it's going to be all right, Detective. Relax now. You heard Fitz. Griffin's inside. Griffin will take care of Meg."

Fitz was done with the phone and was now looking from her to Waters frantically. Jillian understood his dilemma.

"I'll stay with him," she said. "You go help Griffin."

"He's a good guy," Fitz said gruffly, still torn as he looked at a downed fellow officer.

"I have Detective Waters," Jillian repeated firmly. "You help Meg."

Fitz gave Waters one last look. The detective wearily, blearily waved him off. "G-G-Go."

Fitz turned. He ran back around to the front of the house, where David Price waited with a gun, where Griffin stalked a killer and where Meg fought for her life.

Jillian sat down in the cold, damp grass. She clasped Waters's hand in hers. "Stay with me, Detective," she murmured. "We're going to get through this. I promise you, we're all going to get out of this alive."

Meg was at the window, exposed and vulnerable to the partially open doorway. She could hear movement now, creaking down the hall, growing rapidly closer. David was coming. Slowly but surely, he was checking out each small, bare room.

Not much time, not much time. Come on fingers, work!

She had her arms up, her elbows bent. Sensation was returning to her swollen fingers, and though they felt clumsy and sluggish, she finally had some movement. She'd gotten the blinds up. Now she fiddled with the metal half-moon window clasps until she finally got them turned.

Finally, the tricky part. Her arms were all wrong. Her shoulders still felt strange and disjointed. She didn't think she could push anything up, let alone an old window stuck in its casing. But there was only one way out of this house at the moment. Only one way to circumvent David.

I am not a victim. I am not a victim.

Meg was weeping. Her breath was labored, her whole body hurt. She thought of how much she loved her parents. She thought of how much she loved Molly. And then she shoved her arms beneath the window, sank her teeth into her bottom lip and pushed with all her might.

The window squeaked, her arms screamed, and then . . . The window rocketed up. She stuck her head out into the crisp night air. And found herself looking straight down at none other than Jillian.

David heard the squeak of a window opening. Meg! She was trying to bail on him. He took two quick steps down the hall, leading with his gun, then he heard another sound, also up ahead, but this time to the right. He halted immediately, straining his ears.

Griffin, he deduced, trying to sneak up the stairs. Goddammit, why couldn't he have just died in the foyer? David was running out of time for these little games. Dammit, he'd had a *plan*!

He frowned, caught the expression and forced his brow to smooth back out. Think. What could Meg really do from a second-story window? Fall? Break her back? All the easier to kill her later. Griffin posed the more immediate threat. He would deal with Griffin first.

David moved to the right side of the hallway. He pressed his back against the wall and brought his gun up to his chest in a two-handed grip. Griffin would be coming up the stairs low, trying to be less of a target. He might also be wearing a flak vest. So David would also go in low and aim for the head.

He bent his knees, sinking down to the hall floor. He felt fluid, smooth as silk, even after picking the locks of his shackles, divesting himself of his chains, and taking out a fully armed escort. In some ways, prison had been the best thing that had ever happened to him. He'd entered the ACI a physically weak man with a gift for charm. He'd emerged with a finely honed, absurdly flexible physique and a whole new understanding of human nature. Old David had preyed on kids. New David would prey on the entire world.

But first, he would kill Sergeant Griffin.

David eased steadily into the shadows.

"You can't jump," Jillian was saying, low and frantic from the yard.

Meg shook her head desperately and leaned out the window.

"Dammit, Meg, it's too high—"

Meg couldn't speak through the gag, just show her bound, bloody wrists.

"Oh, Meg . . ."

Meg took a deep breath, then threw one leg over the windowsill.

"Wait, wait, wait!" Jillian cried. "Quick, I have an idea!"

Flat on his belly, Griffin slithered his way slowly up the hardwood stairs. He held his gun just in front of his face as he peered warily into the dark void waiting at the top. He grew closer and closer, knowing that at any time Price could strike.

Five steps from the top.

Groans down the hall. Squeaky floorboards, the sound of glass vibrating. He couldn't think about those things yet. He had to keep his attention on the top of the stairs.

Four steps from the top. Three, two . . .

And then.

Suddenly, quickly, David Price's face materialized in the gloom. A burst of fire. BOOM, BOOM, BOOM.

Griffin squeezed the trigger even before he felt the first bullet graze his forehead. He rolled sideways, hitting the unforgiving wall as he fired desperately, trying to hit a man he could no longer see. Rings of light exploded in front of his eyes, the muzzle flash temporarily breaking into his dark, dusky world and blinding him.

Blood. Pain. His head.

Griffin kept firing. Then he came up the stairs with an enraged roar.

David ran across the hall. He heard Griffin still firing. Good, good, good, blow your fucking wad, shoot up the staircase. David didn't have many shots left; he certainly wasn't going to waste them.

He darted into the bedroom, already looking for Meg.

A cool breeze immediately hit his cheeks, accompanied by a relatively brighter flash of fading daylight. He forced his gaze to readjust and realized that the blinds were up and the bedroom window was open. In the next moment, he heard a thump out in the yard.

David rushed to the open window. He stuck out his head in time to see a woman's shadowy figure scramble to her feet and run across the lawn.

No, no, no. It wasn't possible. Meg should be hurt. She couldn't just get away like that. She was his, his, HIS.

David raised his gun to fire. Just as a second shape suddenly materialized from behind the closet door.

"I hate you, I hate you, I hate you!"

David whirled around. "Meg? What the—"

She caught him in the side with her shoulder and they both went smack against the wall as Griffin roared into the room.

David was tangled. He had to get to his feet, find his balance and regain control. He got one hand around Meg's neck and shoved her brutally aside. Just in time to encounter Griffin's fist.

David's left cheek exploded. He went down hard, registered the new threat in the room and rolled left. He came back up with his gun, squeezing off one wild shot before Griffin had his hand in his massive grip and started twisting his arm behind his back.

David cried out at the sudden pain. Then he grew royally pissed off. This was not according to his plan! This had not been part of his equation!

He went still, sagging forward and letting the sudden impact of his weight drag Griffin off-balance. They both fell forward. David rolled clear first and sprang up onto his feet. This time he had out the hunting knife. That was better.

He went for Griffin's ribs, just as his old friend and neighbor threw up his arm. David sliced through Griffin's shirt and had the satisfaction of drawing first blood. He danced back, watching Griffin rise thunderously to his feet. Griffin didn't appear to have a gun anymore. He had probably run out of bullets on the staircase, then thrown down his gun in disgust. Griffin always acted on impulse. All the better for David.

"I've learned a few things since we last met," David said, bouncing around on the balls of his feet, flashing his knife. He'd lost track of Meg. He decided it didn't matter. What could a girl do?

"Needlepoint?" Griffin drawled.

"I'm not going back, no fucking way. I'm going to kill you, then I'm going to take out every goddamn cop along the way. I've already racked up at least six today. What's a few more?"

"I think you should take the car in the driveway," Griffin said, circling warily. "You know, Viggio went to a lot of trouble to set it up just for you."

"Shit! He rigged it, didn't he? Well, that just curdles my cheese. I'm the one who told him where to go on-line for the bomb-making guide, you know. Without me, that low-level turd would be *nothing*."

David leapt forward, slashing at Griffin's unprotected thigh. Griffin, however, saw him coming, stepped neatly left and slammed him with a fresh uppercut to his left eye. David's head snapped back. He saw stars but didn't go down. Instead he spun away and worked to regroup. Griffin was bigger, all right. But David was smarter, and better armed.

Griffin didn't lunge again but just kept circling. He appeared strangely calm, almost curiously patient.

"Without you, Viggio could've been the College Hill Rapist forever," Griffin said. "No one could ever rat him out—like you were planning on doing."

"I wasn't necessarily going to turn him in. What do I care if he's running around this state terrifying college coeds? I sort of considered him a going-away present for you, Griff. Your job would never be boring. Now I'll just have to kill you instead."

"So you keep saying."

"What the fuck are you doing, Griffin? Where's the rage, where's the holy war? Don't you remember what I did to Cindy? Do I have to tell you again what her last moments were like?"

"Cindy died surrounded by the people who loved her. We should all be so lucky."

"I told her *every little detail*."

Griffin didn't say anything. David frowned. He didn't like this. Where the fuck was Griffin's rage? He needed his old friend's anger. He fed on Griffin's rage. Griffin's beautiful, dark, mind-fogging hate, which always lured the oversized detective into doing something stupid.

"She tried to close her eyes, Griffin. I held her eyelids open with my fingers. It's not like she could fight me."

Griffin still didn't say anything. He appeared to be looking behind David at the doorway. David whirled around sharply, saw only the shadowed hall, then had to quickly twist again before Griffin jumped him from behind.

"What you looking at?" David demanded. He was getting the heebie- jee-bies again, feeling his control of the situation slip away, though there was no logical reason why.

"I'm not looking at anything."

"There's no one left, Griffin. I shot your stupid friend, the skinny one, Waters. 'Fraid you can't break his nose anymore, Griffin. He interrupted me in the basement, so I killed him."

Griffin remained silent.

David waved his knife. "Do you hear me! You're all alone! I killed your friend, I tormented your wife. I murdered ten kids and *you didn't do a thing.* And now, my good friend, I'm *out of jail.* Yep, you helped me with that, too. Welcome, Great Sergeant Griffin. Welcome, the aspiring criminal's best friend."

"Where's Meg?"

"What?" David drew up short again. Something was wrong. None of this was going according to the usual script. He had sweat on his forehead. And he felt . . . he felt strangely tired. All this effort. He was putting on a good show. What the fuck was up with his audience?

"Where is Meg?" Griffin asked again, circling, circling, circling.

"Meg's irrelevant."

"You think?" Circling, circling, circling.

"What do you mean?"

"Well, you haven't exactly gotten away yet, David. Think about it. You went to a lot of trouble to get out of prison, only to become trapped in your former home. That's a lot of running, I would agree, but not much progress."

"Shut up."

Griffin shrugged. "If you say so."

"What the fuck is wrong with you!" David screamed. "Goddammit, *yell at me!*"

Griffin didn't say a word. Just circled, circled, circled.

And David . . . And David . . . Something went. In his head. Behind his eye. He felt a little pop, as if all of his homicidal fury had just exploded like a neutron bomb. And then his arm was above his head. And then he was running, because he had to kill Griffin. He had to kill this man with his calm face and steady voice and knowing, knowing eyes. Goddammit, after all of this planning, he deserved a better audience.

David screamed at the top of his lungs. He charged forward . . .

And Griffin pulled his gun out of the small of his back and shot him point-blank in the chest. Pop, pop, pop. David Price went down. He didn't get back up again.

Thirty seconds later, Fitz stepped into the room from where he'd been sheltering Meg in the hall. He approached David's body while Meg peered in cautiously from the doorway. The detective leaned down, discovered no pulse, and looked back up at Griffin.

"That was expertly played," Fitz said grimly.

And Griffin said, "I learned from a master."

He came out of the house, Meg and Fitz in his wake. Ambulances had arrived, their lights blazing, their sirens piercing. Funny how he had never heard their approach. In the bedroom, his world had been small, just comprised of David and the lessons of his past. Now it was lights, camera, action.

Jillian came around the house, fresh from her cameo as a fleeing Meg Pesaturo. Her cheeks were flushed, her hair was a long, tangled mess, her clothes were stained with blood. He thought she had never looked better. She glanced at him once, her chin up, her gaze curiously open and proud. Then Meg was flying into her arms and she was holding the girl close, stroking her hair.

Griffin went to the ambulance where they were loading up Waters on a stretcher. An oxygen mask was over Waters's face, but his gaze was alert, focused.

"How is he?" Griffin asked.

"Gotta get to the hospital," the EMT said.

"He gets the best."

"Men in blue always do."

"Mike . . ."

Waters tried a halfhearted thumbs-up. Then the stretcher was in the back, the doors were closing and the ambulance was pulling away.

More cruisers came screeching down the street. More lights, camera, action.

Griffin stood in the middle of the chaos of his old neighborhood, his old life. He looked at Meg. He looked at Jillian. He looked up at the bedroom where a dead David Price now lay.

And he whispered, "Cindy, I love you."

The night wind blew down the street and carried his words away.

In the intensive care waiting room, Dan sat with his elbows on his thighs and his fingers digging into his hair. Thirty minutes had passed. It might as well have been a year.

A door opened and closed. Dan finally looked up to see a white-jacketed doctor standing before him. He tried to read the man's face, tried to steel his body before he heard the words.

"Your wife would like to see you."

"What?"

"Your wife . . . She suffered an episode. But the good news is, she's now regained consciousness."

"What?"

"Would you like to see your wife, Mr. Rosen?"

"Oh, yes. I mean, *please*."

Dan went down the hall. Dan went into the room. And there was Carol, pale but conscious, lying on the bed. His feet suddenly stilled. He couldn't remember how to move.

"Honey?" he said.

"I heard your voice," she whispered.

"I thought I'd lost you."

"I heard your voice. You told me that you loved me."

"I do, Carol! Oh I do. There has never been anyone else. You have to believe me. I've made so many mistakes, but Carol, I have never stopped loving you."

"Dan?"

He finally got his feet to move. He took tiny, meek little steps toward the bed. She was awake now, capable of remembering all that he'd done, all of the ways that he had failed her. She was awake and he had not been a good husband, and . . .

Carol took his hand. "Dan," she told him quietly. "I love you, too."

Epilogue

Jillian, Carol and Meg

"What about this dresser? Coming or going?"

"Going."

"And the lamp?"

"Definitely going."

"I don't know, I kind of like it."

Carol rolled her eyes at Meg, then looked at Jillian for support. "I don't think French country quite goes with anything in a college dorm," Jillian told Meg. "Maybe it's the heavy gold fringe."

"Hey now, *anything* can coordinate with beanbag chairs and lava lamps. I believe it's called *eclectic*." But Meg dutifully tagged the lamp for Dan and Carol's upcoming furniture auction. She'd been cheerfully trying to scam items for two hours now. Fortunately, not many of Carol's heavy French antiques were small enough for Meg's soon-to-be new address—the Providence College dorms.

"Next room?" Jillian asked.

"Next room," Carol agreed.

"Are you sure?

"I'm sure."

All three of them exited the bedroom and journeyed down the hall. Passing the staircase, they could hear the voices of their families floating up the stairs. Dan and Tom were busy sorting through the toolshed, but Laurie, Toppi and Libby had staked out the kitchen. Last Jillian saw, they had Griffin retrieving all of the high objects from the cupboards. As fast as he got an item in one box, they'd want it placed in another. He kept wiggling his eyebrows at Molly, then doing as he was told. Molly thought the whole project was loads of fun, and even now they could hear her shrieks of laughter as Griffin performed his latest Herculean task.

Molly was doing extremely well these days, and had surprisingly few questions about her strange sojourn to the park six months ago. Meg, on the other hand, was looking paler, thinner. She had recovered physically from her abduction, as had Detective Waters. But with Meg's newfound memories had come nightmares, night sweats, panic attacks. She was holding up, pushing through. She had her life back, she'd told Jillian and Carol at their last Survivors Club meeting, and she was determined to get on with it. Just next month, she'd return to Providence College for her degree. Her father was still negotiating for the right to call her every night and provide armed guards, but that was to be expected. And in his own way, Tom was really sweet.

Jillian, Carol and Meg came to the closed door at the end of the hall. The last room to be tagged for auction. The room.

"Are you sure?" Jillian asked again. "Meg and I could do this."

"Dan offered as well," Carol said quietly.

"Maybe you should accept his offer."

"I thought about it. He'd like to help more."

Jillian and Meg didn't say anything.

Carol shook her head. "I'll tell you the same thing I told him. I *need* to do this. It's just a room, after all. Just a room in a house that's not even mine anymore. The new owners arrive next week. They'll fill this place with their things, their kids, their dreams. If they can handle this room, I can, too."

Jillian didn't think that was quite the same, but it wasn't for her to say. She opened the door to the musty, shadowed space, then gave Carol a moment to marshal her resources.

The master bedroom had been unused for over a year and a half. The air smelled stale, the corners were draped with long, intricate cobwebs. The hardwood floor held a fine coating of undisturbed dust. Old ghosts fit in comfortably in a space like this. Jillian could look at the dusty wrought-iron bed, and for the first time picture perfectly what Carol had gone through. A man coming through that window under cover of night. A man pouncing, hitting, gagging, tying. A woman screaming, and still not making a sound.

A woman victimized in a place where she had every right to feel safe.

Meg had unconsciously taken Jillian's hand. Then Carol walked right in, snapped on a light, and that easily the spell was broken. The room was just a room after all. One, as a matter of fact, in need of a good cleaning.

"Everything in here," Carol said briskly, "goes."

Twenty minutes later, they retired to the hallway. Carol sat on the floor with a sigh. Jillian and Meg followed suit, leaning their heads against the wall.

"Any regrets?" Jillian asked softly.

Carol opened her eyes. "Honestly? Not as many as I thought I would have."

"It's a beautiful home," Meg said. "You should be proud of what you did with it."

"I am. But you know, it is just a house. And for as much love and attention as went into renovating it, a lot of not so loving things happened here. It's good to get out. I can get a fresh start. The money will help Dan make a fresh start. And you know, our new home is nice, too. Just on a much smaller scale. But that back family room, I'm already thinking . . . Take out a wall, add a few more windows, and we'd have the perfect sunroom right off the kitchen. Put up some plants, polish the hardwood floors . . ."

She broke off. Jillian and Meg were smiling at her.

"You're hopeless," Jillian said.

"I like houses. All houses, I guess. Oh, hey. I'm a house slut!"

She beamed proudly and they laughed.

"Dan's taking to corporate life?" Jillian asked.

Carol shrugged. "As well as can be expected. Being on payroll again means less freedom, but it's also a lot less stress than running his own practice. Plus, let's be frank, we need the money."

"The auction will help," Meg said.

"Sure. Between downsizing the house, getting Dan a real job, getting me a part-time job, hey, we might actually be debt-free by the end of the year." She smiled, though it was chagrined. "Not exactly what we were expecting as we hit our mid-forties. No savings, no retirement funds. No white picket fence."

"Is he going to his Gambler's Anonymous meetings?"

"He goes to his meetings, I go to my shrink. Ah, yuppie love."

"You put the new house in your name?" Jillian checked.

"He insisted upon it himself. The car's in my name now, too, and get this, we have only one credit card, which is owned by me. Even if he does slip, there's not much damage he can do."

"He's trying very hard, Carol."

"Actually, I'm proud of him. Maybe life isn't what we were expecting. But maybe that's the way it's supposed to be. When we had everything we thought we wanted, we were miserable. Maybe by having nothing we'll finally learn to appreciate one another. Own less, but have more. I think . . . well"—her tone grew brisk again—"we have to start somewhere."

"You love him?" Meg asked.

"Absolutely."

"Then you're very lucky."

Carol smiled. She angled her head and looked directly at Meg. "Now, how about you, hon? You're still very pale."

"Too many nightmares," Meg said immediately, making a face. "You know what's strange? I keep dreaming about Eddie Como. He's the man lurking over me. I know that's not right. I know it was Ron Viggio, but somehow . . . We spent so long focused on Eddie, it's like my subconscious can't make the change."

"He's a symbol," Jillian said softly.

"Exactly."

Now they all made a face and looked away. Eddie was still a tough subject. They had spent too long hating him. Viggio seemed almost like an abstraction, whereas Eddie remained tangibly real. Poor Eddie Como, railroaded for crimes he didn't commit, framed by a psychopath and then sacrificed at a courthouse just to lure a certain state detective onto the case.

Tawnya had finally dropped her lawsuit. Because Eddie's semen was definitely found at the four rape scenes, her lawyer explained that he could no longer make the case for police negligence or corruption. Plus, the police had found the editing software that Ron Viggio had used to make the computer image file of Eddie threatening Jillian with violence, further evidence that Eddie had been deliberately framed by a madman. In the end, Eddie really hadn't done anything worse than be in the wrong place at the wrong time. Just like them, he had been a victim.

Two months ago, Jillian, Carol and Meg had gone together and put flowers on Eddie's grave. It was as much as they could do for now. After that visit, on her own, Jillian had written another check for Eddie, Jr.'s, college fund.

"At least there won't be a trial this time," Meg said now.

"Thank God," Carol echoed.

Jillian was more philosophical. "It would've been too hard for D'Amato to argue the case. Viggio's lawyer would simply keep saying Eddie, Eddie, Eddie, and the whole thing would've grown too confusing. A plea bargain was probably better all the way around."

"Cool, composed, Jillian," Carol said, but smiled.

Jillian's look was more somber. "He killed my sister, Carol. I would've liked to see him on trial. I would've liked to hear twelve jurors find him guilty. And maybe it would've helped us make a better transition, refocus our anger where it belongs."

"He's never getting out of jail," Meg spoke up.

"Yes, but if only he could've died like David Price."

No one argued that. As part of Viggio's plea bargain, he had to make a full allocution of his and Price's scheme. The details had been chilling. How Viggio had grown increasingly convinced that he needed to come up with the perfect way to commit rape. How he had approached David Price while they were both being held in ACI's Intake and worked with David to devise the perfect plan. Viggio had already heard about Korporate Klean from his last time behind bars. One of the big jokes among inmates was that when you finally get out, the only job you could get would be cleaning up after a bunch of "jerk offs"—everyone knew Korporate Klean had the contract for the sperm bank.

From there, things fell into place. Viggio spotted Eddie in the waiting room and realized they were a close physical match. He struck up a conversation with the guy, found out he worked for the Rhode Island Blood Center and needed some extra money because his girlfriend was pregnant. He started shadowing Eddie at the college blood drives and realized this was the perfect opportunity. He could attack socially conscious college coeds, and it would simply further implicate Eddie in the eyes of the police. He'd written the details to David Price, who had recommended using latex ties. That would make the frame airtight. David had also kindly suggested Meg as the first victim. A suitable "trial run," he'd called her.

Even if Viggio did screw up, they figured Meg wouldn't go to the police. She wouldn't want to have to admit her association with David Price, whose name Viggio made sure to mention during the rape. That the trauma of the attack induced amnesia wasn't part of the plan, but hardly hurt them.

Viggio scoped out the other victims in advance. Carol was a last-minute substitute but felt safe to him: he'd spent enough time in her neighborhood to figure out her husband's car was never in the driveway. Trish met his criteria of a young coed living alone. Jillian's intrusion had startled him, but it had proved irrelevant to his plan.

By this point in the allocution, Viggio's voice was cocky. In theory, he'd suffered three complications—Meg's memory loss, Carol's substitution and Jillian's unexpected arrival, and none of them had stopped him. He was invincible. Then the women had gone on TV, and not even that mattered.

The police did the sensible thing. They arrested Eddie Como, and phase two of the plan went into effect.

David's involvement hadn't been free, of course. He saw Eddie's frame-up as the perfect opportunity to get out of prison. Viggio had instructions to hire an assassin, kill the assassin, then immediately strike again, leaving Eddie's sperm at the scene. The new rape would stir the public into a panicked frenzy. And David could step to the plate with his offer to save the day. A hop, skip and jump later, and David would finally be out of prison.

Viggio, of course, had had his reservations. But once he figured out he could kill David Price the same way he'd killed the hired gun, he hadn't minded anymore. He'd followed David's instructions and inserted the wooden lock pick and Alka-Seltzer tablets into David's favorite pair of clothes, which were then dutifully retrieved by David's lawyer from David's storage area. Then Viggio had kidnapped Meg to increase police pressure to release David. Finally he'd secured a getaway vehicle, to be left at David's former home.

Of course, what David didn't know was that Viggio had taken the liberty of booby-trapping the getaway car with a bomb. For Viggio, David getting out of prison equaled David winding up dead, which equaled Viggio attacking, torturing and killing young women forever. It was the perfect plan.

Until the police pulled up in his driveway, and Detective Waters tackled him in a neighbor's salvage yard. Viggio wasn't going anyplace anymore.

And the three women . . . The three women were doing their best to heal.

Now Meg turned to Jillian. "Your turn," she said. "Carol is getting a fresh start with Dan, I'm getting a fresh look at my sordid past. Now what's new with you?"

"Not much."

Carol and Meg exchanged looks.

"I would never call Sergeant Griffin 'not much,' " Carol drawled.

Jillian promptly blushed.

"Uh huh," Carol said. "So that's the way it is."

"You have a dirty mind!"

"Damn right. Come on, Dan and I are seeing a sex therapist who has literally banned us from having sex for the next six months. I have to live through someone."

Both Jillian and Meg looked at her curiously. "Does that work?" Meg asked.

Carol's turn to blush. "Actually . . . well, yes. It . . . it takes the pressure off. Sometimes, before, when he would touch me, I would freeze up. I was already thinking, then he's going to want to touch here or touch there and I just couldn't handle that level of intrusion. I wasn't ready. Now—now I know a kiss will be just a kiss. I can focus on that. On him kissing me. And when I do that, all the other things go away. I'm not in the bedroom anymore. It's not dark, the TV's not on. I'm just a woman kissing her husband of over ten years. It's . . . nice. Honestly, we're dating again."

"I'm going to cry," Meg said thickly, and rubbed her eyes. "You're getting to fall in love all over again, and I can't even figure out if I'm ever going to have a normal relationship. Look at me! I'm almost twenty-one, my sister is really my daughter, and the total sum of my sex life boils down to one pedophile whom I thought I loved, and one rapist who was a present from the pedophile. Now that's *sick*!"

"Molly is your sister," Jillian said evenly. "You've said yourself it's better to keep it that way."

"If I'm her mother, then she must have a father. I don't want her to *ever* ask about her father."

"Then remove that from the equation. Molly is your little sister, you love her, your parents love her and she is very happy."

"Molly is very happy."

"The rest . . . Meg, you were only thirteen when David first approached you. That's much too young to know better. And you certainly can't blame yourself for being raped. So that means you've made only one mistake, as a thirteen-year-old girl. You're nearly twenty-one now. You're strong, you're resilient, you're smart. You're going to be all right."

Meg sniffled a little. "What if I meet the right guy, freeze up, and he goes away?"

"Then he's not the right guy," Carol said firmly.

But Meg was looking at Jillian. "I wasn't raped," Jillian told her.

"You were assaulted."

"I . . . I have moments."

"You think about your sister," Meg said quietly.

"I do."

"Poor guilt-ridden Jillian."

She didn't deny it. "Griffin told me something earlier, during his investigation. And it was one of the hardest, saddest, truest things I ever needed to hear: Trisha loves me."

"She does," Carol said immediately.

"She does," Meg seconded.

Jillian smiled at them. "I lost sight of that. I don't know why. But I'm remembering now. I'm . . . enjoying . . . my memories of Trish, and that feels good. And Griffin understands that Trish is a part of me, just as I understand that Cindy is a part of him. Sometimes we just talk about them. It feels right."

"He's a lucky man," Carol said seriously.

"I'm a lucky woman. Well, and Libby isn't doing so badly either. Have you seen how much she flirts with him? I swear, she hasn't taken this much care with her appearance since she discovered the UPS man was single."

"Ooh, competition!" Meg teased.

"He definitely has a soft spot for her. Next thing you know, she's going to add the word *stud* to her picture book."

Carol and Meg chortled. Jillian rolled her eyes, but she was smiling, too. She felt lucky these days. Sometimes she found herself humming at work for no good reason. Clients seemed less annoying, the days were brighter, the evenings more beautiful. When the weather was nice, she had picnic lunches with Libby and Toppi in the park. And sometimes she left work early, sometimes she came in late, and one day she brought in four giant pots of yellow mums simply because she'd seen them at the florist and thought they were beautiful. Her employees looked at her curiously a lot, but no one complained.

"Speaking of family," Jillian said.

"We should return to the fold," Carol agreed.

"Think they're done with the kitchen?" Meg asked. "We could pick up some pizzas."

Food would be good, they all agreed. They climbed up from the floor and headed downstairs. In the kitchen, Jillian spotted Griffin first. He had Molly perched on his shoulders, running a duster along the top of the kitchen cabinets.

"I'm a dust bunny!" she cried.

"Well look at you," said Meg and held out her arms for her little sister.

Griffin swooped the giggling girl down onto the ground. He was wearing jeans and a T-shirt today, with dust on his left cheek and cobwebs in his hair. Griffin looked good in jeans and a T-shirt. Libby had actually blushed when he'd pulled into their driveway and assisted her into the van.

Right now, his twinkling blue eyes were on Jillian. She felt his gaze as a warmth in her chest. Tonight, they were having Mike Waters over for dinner. Toppi had taken quite a bit of interest in the lanky detective's recovery. She'd bought a new outfit for tonight. You never knew.

Now Griffin opened his arms and wagged a brow in a look that could only be called a leer. She, of course, pretended to look coolly away. In response, he thundered across the kitchen and playfully swept her into his embrace.

Molly shrieked, Meg and Carol smiled. Libby pretended to chastise.

Jillian simply slipped her arms around Griffin's narrow waist. She leaned into the warmth of his broad chest, felt the strength of his arms around her shoulders. He didn't step back.

"Pizza!" Molly yelled, and they all prepared for dinner.

The Killing Hour

Acknowledgements

A little bit of research went into the making of this novel. In the absolutely, highly recommended, great-way-to-spend-a-weekend department, I was privileged to once again visit the FBI Academy and learn more about life amid an active Marine base. I have done my best to re-create the facilities and culture of the Academy. In regard to some of the anecdotes and traditions, however, buyer beware. The Academy is a living, breathing institution, undergoing constant change depending on the year, the class, and Bureau needs. As fast as one agent told me a story of a hallowed tradition during his Academy days, another agent would confess he'd never heard of such a thing. Being a crafty writer, I sifted through the various anecdotes, selected the ones I liked best and delivered them here as the gospel truth. That's my story and I'm sticking to it.

As much as I enjoy interviewing FBI agents, I confess I was totally blown away by the nice men and women I met via the U.S. Geological Survey team of Richmond, Virginia. I needed some experts on the great outdoors and boy, did I hit the mother lode. Not only were the team members very patient when explaining to me the intricacies of properly analyzing water samples, but they came up with a dynamite list of cool places to kill people. They also gave my husband and me a personal tour of their recommended crime scenes, which had us on good behavior for weeks.

Following is the rather extensive list of nice folks who took time away from their very busy lives just to answer my phone calls. These people gave me correct information with the best of intentions. What happened to it after that is entirely my fault.

FIRST, THE EARTH EXPERTS:

Jim Campbell, Subdistrict Chief, U.S. Geological Survey
David Nelms, Hydrologist, U.S. Geological Survey
George E. Harlow, Jr., P.G., Hydrologist, U.S. Geological Survey
Randall C. Orndorff, Geologist, U.S. Geological Survey
William C. Burton, Geologist, U.S. Geological Survey
Wil Orndorff, Karst Protection Coordinator, Virginia Department of
    Conservation and Recreation
Wendy Cass, Park Botanist, Shenandoah National Park
Ron Litwin, Palynologist, U.S. Geological Survey

SECOND, THE DRUG EXPERTS:
Margaret Charpentier
Celia MacDonnell

THIRD, THE PROCEDURE EXPERTS:
Special Agent Nidia Gamba, FBI, New York
Dr. Gregory K. Moffatt, Ph.D., Professor of Psychology, Atlanta
    Christian College
Jimmy Davis, Chief of Police, Snell Police Department, GA

FOURTH, THE SUPPORTING CAST:
Melinda Carr, Diana Chadwick, Barbara Ruddy, and Kathleen Walsh
    for their invaluable proofreading assistance
My husband, Anthony, who didn't have to make any chocolate this
    time, but was required to unpack an entire house while I tended
    to deadline. Love, let's never move again.

Also, my deepest thanks to Kathy Sampson, who generously bought her daughter, Alissa Sampson, a "cameo" appearance in this novel as part of a charity auction. I'm never sure if it's a good thing to be a character in one of my novels, but I appreciate Kathy's donation and hope Alissa enjoys the book.

And finally, in loving memory of my grandmother, Harriette Baumgartner, who supplied me with my favorite paperbacks, baked the best chocolate chip cookies in the world, and taught us all a dozen different ways to play solitaire. Here's to you, Grandma.

Happy reading,
Lisa Gardner

Prologue

The man first started noticing it in 1998. Two girls went out to a bar, never came home again. Deanna Wilson and Marlene Mason were the first set. Roommates at Georgia State U, nice girls by all accounts, their disappearance didn't even make the front pages of the *Atlanta Journal-Constitution*. People disappear. Especially in a big city.

Then, of course, the police found Marlene Mason's body along Interstate 75. That got things going a bit. The fine folks of Atlanta didn't like one of their daughters being found sprawled along an interstate. Especially a white girl from a good family. Things like that shouldn't happen around here.

Besides, the Mason case was a head-scratcher. The girl was found fully clothed and with her purse intact. No sign of sexual assault, no sign of robbery. In fact, her corpse looked so damn peaceful, the passing motorist who found her thought she was sleeping. But Mason was DOA. Drug overdose, ruled the ME (though Mason's parents vehemently denied their daughter would do such a thing). Now where was her roommate?

That was an ugly week in Atlanta. Everyone looking for a missing college coed while the mercury climbed to nearly a hundred degrees. Efforts started strong, then petered out. People got hot, got tired, got busy with other things. Besides, half the state figured Wilson had done it—offed her roommate in some dispute, probably over a boy, and that was that. People watched *Law & Order*. They knew these things.

A couple of hikers found Wilson's body in the fall. It was all the way up in the Tallulah Gorge, nearly a hundred miles away. The body was still clad in Wilson's party clothes, right down to her three-inch heels. Not so peaceful in death this time, however. For one thing, the scavengers had gotten to her first. For another, her skull was shattered into little bits. Probably from taking a header down one of the granite cliffs. Let's just say Mother Nature had no respect for Manolo Blahnik stilettos.

Another head-scratcher. When had Wilson died? Where had she been between that time and first vanishing from a downtown Atlanta bar? And had she offed her roommate first? Wilson's purse was recovered from the gorge. No sign of any drugs. But strangely enough, neither was there any sign of her vehicle or her car keys.

The Rabun County Sheriff's Office inherited that corpse, and the case once again faded from the news.

The man clipped a few articles. He didn't really know why. He just did.

In 1999, it happened again. Heat wave hit, temperatures—and tempers—

went soaring, and two young girls went out to a bar one night and never made it back. Kasey Cooper and Josie Anders from Macon, Georgia. Maybe not such nice girls this time. Both were underage and never should've been drinking except that Anders's boyfriend was a bouncer at the bar. He claimed they weren't "hardly tipsy at all" when he last saw them climbing into Cooper's white Honda Civic. Their distraught families claimed that both girls were track-and-field stars and wouldn't have gone anywhere without a fight.

People got a little more nervous this time. Wondered what was going on. Two days later, they didn't have to wonder anymore. Josie Anders's body was found along U.S. 441—ten miles from the Tallulah Gorge.

The Rabun County Sheriff's Office went into hyperdrive. Rescue teams were organized, search dogs hired, the National Guard called in. The *Atlanta Journal-Constitution* gave it front-page coverage. The strange double-disappearance so like the one the summer before. And exactly what happened when a person went missing in this kind of heat.

The man noticed something he'd missed before. It was small, really. A minor little note under letters to the editor. It read: "Clock ticking . . . planet dying . . . animals weeping . . . rivers screaming. Can't you hear it? Heat kills . . ."

Then the man knew why he'd started the scrapbook.

They never did find Kasey Cooper in the gorge. Her body didn't turn up until the November cotton harvest in Burke County. Then, three men operating a cotton picker got the surprise of their lives—a dead girl right smack in the middle of thousands of acres of cotton fields, still wearing a little black dress.

No broken bones this time. No shattered limbs. The ME ruled that nineteen-year-old Kasey Cooper had died from multiple organ failure, most likely brought on by severe heatstroke. In other words, when she'd been abandoned out in the middle of that field, she'd still been alive.

An empty gallon jug of water was discovered three miles from her mummified corpse. Her purse was another five miles away. Interestingly enough, they never did find her vehicle or her car keys.

People grew more nervous now. Particularly when someone in the ME's office let it leak that Josie Anders also had died from a drug overdose—a fatal injection of the prescription drug Ativan. Seemed sinister somehow. Two sets of girls in two different years. Each last seen in a bar. In both cases the first girl was found dead along a major road. And in both cases, the second girl seemed to suffer a fate that was far, far worse . . .

The Rabun County Sheriff's Office called in the Georgia Bureau of Investigation. The press got excited again. More banner headlines in the front pages of the *Atlanta Journal-Constitution*. GBI SEEKS POSSIBLE SERIAL KILLER. Rumors flew, articles multiplied and the man clipped each one diligently.

He had a cold feeling growing in his chest now. And he started to tremble each time the phone rang.

The GBI, however, was not nearly so sensational about the case. Investigation ongoing, a spokesperson for the state police declared. And that's all the GBI would say. Until the summer of 2000 and the very first heat wave.

It started in May. Two pretty, young Augusta State University students headed to Savannah one weekend and never returned home. Last known sighting—a bar. Vehicle—MIA.

This time, the national media descended. Frightened voters hit the streets. The man pawed furiously through stacks of newspapers while the GBI issued meaningless statements such as "We have no reason to suspect a connection at this time."

The man knew better. People knew better. And so did the letters to the editor. He found it Tuesday, May 30. Exact same words as before: "Clock ticking . . . planet dying . . . animals weeping . . . rivers screaming. Can't you hear it? Heat kills . . ."

Celia Smithers's body was found along U.S. 25 in Waynesboro, just fifteen miles from the cotton-field crime scene where Kasey Cooper had been found six months before. Smithers was fully clothed and clutching her purse. No sign of trauma, no sign of sexual assault. Just one dark bruise on her left thigh, and a smaller, red injection site on her upper left arm. Cause of death—an overdose of the prescription tranquilizer Ativan.

The public went nuts; the police immediately went into high gear. Still missing, Smithers's best friend, Tamara McDaniels. The police, however, didn't search the Burke County cotton fields. Instead, they sent volunteers straight to the muddy banks of the Savannah River. Finally, the man thought, they were starting to understand the game.

He should've picked up the phone then. Dialed the hastily established hotline. He could've been an anonymous tipster. Or maybe the crazy whacko that thinks he knows everything.

He didn't, though. He just didn't know what to say.

"We have reason to believe Ms. McDaniels is still alive," reported GBI Special Agent Michael "Mac" McCormack on the evening news. "We believe our suspect kidnaps the women in pairs, killing the first woman immediately, but abandoning the second in a remote location. In this case, we have reason to believe he has selected a portion of the Savannah River. We are now assembling over five hundred volunteers to search the river. It is our goal to bring Tamara home safe."

Then Special Agent McCormack made a startling revelation. He had also been reading the letters to the editor. He now made an appeal to speak to the author of the notes. The police were eager to listen. The police were eager to help.

By the eleven o'clock news, search-and-rescue teams had descended upon the Savannah River and the suspect finally had a name. The Eco-Killer, Fox News dubbed him. A crazed lunatic who no doubt thought that killing women really would save the planet. Jack the Ripper, he ain't.

The man wanted to yell at them. He wanted to scream that they knew nothing. But of course, what could he say? He watched the news. He obsessively clipped articles. He attended a candlelight vigil organized by the frantic parents of poor Tamara McDaniels—last seen in a tight black skirt and platform heels.

No body this time; the Savannah River rarely gives up what she has taken. But 2000 hadn't ended yet.

July. Temperatures soared above one hundred degrees in the shade. And two sisters, Mary Lynn and Nora Ray Watts, met up with friends at T.G.I. Friday's for late-night sundaes to beat the heat. The two girls disappeared somewhere along the dark, winding road leading home.

Mary Lynn was found two days later alongside U.S. 301 near the Savannah River. The temperature that day was 103 degrees. Heat index was 118. Her body contained a faintly striped brown shell crammed down her throat. Bits of grass and mud were streaked across her legs.

The police tried to bury these details, as they'd buried so many others. Once again, an ME's office insider ratted them out.

For the first time the public learned what the police had known—what the man had suspected—for the past twelve months. Why the first girl was always left, easy to discover, next to a major road. Why her death came so quickly. Why the man needed two girls at all. Because the first girl was merely a prop, a disposable tool necessary for the game. She was the map. Interpret the clues correctly, and maybe you could find the second girl still alive. If you moved quickly enough. *If* you beat the heat.

The task force descended, the press corps descended, and Special Agent McCormack went on the news to announce that given the presence of sea salt, cord grass, and the marsh periwinkle snail found on Mary Lynn's body, he was authorizing an all-out search of Georgia's 378,000 acres of salt marshes.

But which part, you idiots? the man scribbled in his scrapbook. *You should know him better than that by now. Clock is* TICKING!

"We have reason to believe that Nora Ray is still alive," Special Agent McCormack announced, as he had announced once before. "And we're going to bring her home to her family."

Don't make promises you can't keep, the man wrote. But finally, he was wrong.

The last article in an overstuffed scrapbook: July 27, 2000. Nora Ray Watts is pulled half-naked from the sucking depths of a Georgia salt marsh. The Eco-Killer's eighth victim, she's survived fifty-six hours in hundred-degree heat, burning sun, and parching salt, by chewing cord grass and coating herself in protective mud. Now, a newspaper photo shows her exuberantly, vibrantly, triumphantly alive as the Coast Guard chopper lifts her up into the blue, blue sky.

The police have finally learned the game. They have finally won.

Last page of the scrapbook now. No news articles, no photos, no evening news transcripts. In the last page of the scrapbook, the man wrote only four neatly printed words: *What if I'm wrong?*

Then, he underlined them.

The year 2000 finally ended. Nora Ray Watts lived. And the Eco-Killer never struck again. Summers came, summers went. Heat waves rolled through Georgia and lambasted the good residents with spiking temperatures and prickling fear. And nothing happened.

Three years later, the *Atlanta Journal-Constitution* ran a retrospective.

They interviewed Special Agent McCormack about the seven unsolved homicides, the three summers of crippling fear. He simply said, "Our investigation is ongoing."

The man didn't save that article. Instead, he crumpled it up and threw it into the trash. Then he drank long and heavily deep into the night.

It's over, he thought. It's over, I'm safe, and it's as simple as that.

But he already knew in his heart that he was wrong. For some things, it's never a matter of if, but only a matter of when . . .

1

Quantico, Virginia
3:59 P.M.
Temperature: 95 degrees

"God, it's hot. Cacti couldn't take this kind of heat. Desert rock couldn't take this kind of heat. I'm telling you, this is what happened right before dinosaurs disappeared from the Earth."

No response.

"You really think orange is my color?" the driver tried again.

"*Really* is a strong word."

"Well, not everyone can make a statement in purple plaid."

"True."

"Man-oh-man, is this heat *killing* me!" The driver, New Agent Alissa Sampson, had had enough. She tugged futilely on her 1970s polyester suit, smacked the steering wheel with the palm of her hand, then blew out an exasperated breath. It was ninety-five outside, probably one hundred and ten inside the Bucar. Not great weather for polyester suits. For that matter, it didn't work wonders for bulletproof vests. Alissa's suit bled bright orange stains under her arms. New Agent Kimberly Quincy's own mothball-scented pink-and-purple plaid suit didn't look much better.

Outside the car, the street was quiet. Nothing happening at Billiards; nothing happening at City Pawn; nothing happening at the Pastime Bar-Deli. Minute ticked into minute. Seconds came and went, as slowly as the bead of sweat trickling down Kimberly's cheek. Above her head, still fastened to the roof but ready to go at any minute, was her M-16.

"Here's something they never tell you about the disco age," Alissa muttered beside her. "Polyester doesn't breathe. God, is this thing going to happen or *what*?"

Alissa was definitely nervous. A forensic accountant before joining the Bureau, she was highly valued for her deep-seated love of all things spreadsheet. Give Alissa a computer and she was in hog heaven. This, however, wasn't a back-room gig. This was front-line duty.

In theory, at any time now, a black vehicle bearing a two-hundred-and-ten-pound heavily armed suspected arms dealer was going to appear. He might or might not be alone in the car. Kimberly, Alissa, and three other agents had orders to halt the vehicle and arrest everyone in sight.

Phil Lehane, a former New York cop and the one with the most street experience, was leading the operation. Tom Squire and Peter Vince were in the first of the two backup vehicles. Alissa and Kimberly were in the second backup. Kimberly and Tom, being above-average marksmen, had cover duty with the rifles. Alissa and Peter were in charge of tactical driving, plus had handguns for cover.

In consummate FBI style, they had not only planned and dressed for this arrest, but they had practiced it in advance. During the initial run-through, however, Alissa had tripped when getting out of the car and had landed on her face. Her upper lip was still swollen and there were flecks of blood on the right-hand corner of her mouth.

Her wounds were superficial. Her anxiety, however, now went bone deep.

"This is taking too long," she was muttering. "I thought he was supposed to appear at the bank at four. It's four-ten. I don't think he's coming."

"People run late."

"They do this just to mess with our minds. Aren't you boiling?"

Kimberly finally looked at her partner. When Alissa was nervous, she babbled. When Kimberly was nervous, she grew clipped and curt. These days, she was clipped and curt most of the time. "The guy will show up when the guy shows up. Now chill out!"

Alissa thinned her lips. For a second, something flared in her bright blue eyes. Anger. Hurt. Embarrassment. It was hard to be sure. Kimberly was another woman in the male-run world of the Bureau, so criticism coming from her was akin to blasphemy. They were supposed to stick together. Girl power, the Ya Ya Sisterhood, and all that crap.

Kimberly went back to gazing at the street. Now she was angry, too. Damn. Double-damn. Shit.

The radio on the dash suddenly crackled to life. Alissa swooped up the receiver without bothering to hide her relief.

Phil Lehane's voice was hushed but steady: "This is Vehicle A. Target now in sight, climbing into his vehicle. Ready, Vehicle B?"

"Ready."

"Ready, Vehicle C?"

Alissa clicked the receiver. "Ready, willing, and able."

"We go on three. One, two, THREE."

The first siren exploded across the hot, sweltering street, and even though Kimberly had been expecting the noise, she still flinched in her seat.

"Easy," Alissa said dryly, then fired the Bucar to life. A blast of hot air promptly burst from the vents into their faces, but now both were too grim to notice. Kimberly reached for her rifle. Alissa's foot hovered above the gas.

The sirens screamed closer. Not yet, not yet . . .

"FBI, stop your vehicle!" Lehane's voice blared over a bullhorn two blocks away as he drove the suspect closer to their side street. Their target had a penchant for armor-plated Mercedes and grenade launchers. In theory, they were going to arrest him while he was out running errands, hopefully catching him off guard and relatively unarmed. In theory.

"Stop your vehicle!" Lehane commanded again. Apparently, however, the target didn't feel like playing nice today. Far from hearing the screech of brakes, Alissa and Kimberly caught the sound of a gunning engine. Alissa's foot lowered farther toward the gas.

"Passing the movie theater," New Agent Lehane barked over the radio. "Suspect heading toward the pharmacy. Ready . . . *Go.*"

Alissa slammed the gas and their dark blue Bucar shot forward into the empty street. A sleek black blur appeared immediately to their left. Alissa hit the brakes, swinging the back end of their car around until they were pointed down the street at a forty-five-degree angle. Simultaneously, another Bucar appeared on their right, blocking that lane.

Kimberly now had a full view of a beautiful silver grille gunning down on them with a proud Mercedes logo. She popped open the passenger's door while simultaneously releasing her seat belt, then hefted her rifle to her shoulder and aimed for the front tire.

Her finger tightened on the trigger.

The suspect finally hit his brakes. A short screech. The smell of burning rubber. Then the car stopped just fifteen feet away.

"FBI, hands on your head! HANDS ON YOUR HEAD!"

Lehane pulled in behind the Mercedes, shouting into the bullhorn with commanding fury. He kicked open his door, fit his handgun into the opening made between the window frame and the door and drew a bead on the stopped car. No hands left for the bullhorn now. He let his voice do the work for him.

"Driver, hands on your head! Driver, reach over with your left hand and lower your windows!"

The black sedan didn't move. No doors opening, no black tinted windows rolling down. Not a good sign. Kimberly adjusted her left hand on the stock of the rifle and shrugged off the rest of her seat belt. She kept her feet in the car, as feet could become targets. She kept her head and shoulders inside the vehicle as well. On a good day, all you wanted the felon to see was the long black barrel of your gun. She didn't know if this was a good day yet.

A fresh drop of sweat teared up on Kimberly's brow and made a slow, wet path down the plane of her cheek.

"Driver, put your hands up," Lehane ordered again. "Driver, using your left hand, lower all four windows."

The driver's side window finally glided down. From this angle, Kimberly could just make out the silhouette of the driver's head as fresh daylight surrounded him in a halo. It appeared that his hands were held in the air as ordered. She eased her grip slightly on her rifle.

"Driver, using your left hand, remove the key from the ignition."

Lehane was making the guy use his left hand, simply to work the law of averages. Most people were right-handed, so they wanted to keep that arm in sight at all times. Next, the driver would be instructed to drop the car key out the open window, then open the car door, all with his left hand. Then he would be ordered to step slowly out of the car, keeping both hands up at all times. He would slowly pivot 360 degrees so they could visually inspect his form for weapons. If he was wearing a jacket, he would be asked to hold it open so they could see beneath his coat. Finally, he would be ordered to walk toward them with his hands on his head, turn, drop to his knees, cross his ankles and sit back on his heels. At that time, they would finally move forward and take their suspect into custody.

Unfortunately, the driver didn't seem to know the theories behind a proper felony vehicle stop. He still didn't lower his hands, but neither did he reach for the key in the ignition.

"Quincy?" Lehane's voice crackled over the radio.

"I can see the driver," Kimberly reported back, gazing through the rifle sight. "I can't make out the passenger side, however. Tinted windshield's too dark."

"Squire?"

Tom Squire had cover duty from Vehicle B, parked twenty feet to the right of Kimberly. "I think . . . I think there might be someone in the back. Again, hard to tell with the windows."

"Driver, using your left hand, remove the key from the ignition." Lehane repeated his command, his voice louder now, but still controlled. The goal was to remain patient. Make the driver come to you, do not relinquish control.

Was it Kimberly's imagination, or was the vehicle now slowly rocking up and down? Someone was moving around . . .

"Driver, this is the FBI! Remove the key from the ignition!"

"Shit, shit, shit," Alissa murmured beside Kimberly. She was sweating hard, streams of moisture pouring down her face. Leaning half out of the car, she had her Glock .40 positioned in the crack between the roof of their vehicle and the open door. Her right arm was visibly shaking, however. For the first time, Kimberly noticed that Alissa hadn't fully removed her seat belt. Half of it was still tangled around her left arm.

"Driver—"

The driver's left hand finally moved. Alissa exhaled forcefully. And in the next instant, everything went to shit.

Kimberly saw it first. "Gun! Backseat, driver side—"

Pop, pop, pop! Red mushroomed across their front windshield. Kimberly ducked and dove out of the vehicle for the shelter of her car door. She came up fast and spread cover fire above the top of her window. More *pop, pop, pop*.

"Reloading rifle," she yelled into the radio.

"Vince reloading handgun."

"Taking heavy fire from the right, backseat passenger window!"

"Alissa!" Kimberly called out. "Cover us!"

Kimberly turned toward her partner, frantically cramming fresh rounds into the magazine, then realized for the first time that Alissa was no longer to be seen.

"Alissa?"

She stretched across the front seats. New Agent Alissa Sampson was now on the asphalt, a dark red stain spreading across her cheap orange suit.

"Agent down, agent down," Kimberly cried. Another *pop*, and the asphalt exploded two inches from Alissa's leg.

"Damn," Alissa moaned. "Oh damn, that *hurts!*"

"Where are those rifles?" Lehane yelled.

Kimberly shot back up, saw the doors of the Mercedes were now swung open for cover and bright vivid colors were literally exploding in all directions. Oh, things had gone definitely FUBAR now.

"Rifles!" Lehane yelled again.

Kimberly hastily scrambled back to her side, and got her rifle between the crack of the car door. She was frantically trying to recall protocol. Apprehension was still the goal. But they were under heavy fire, possible loss of agent life. Fuck it. She started firing at anything that moved near the Mercedes.

Another *pop,* her car door exploded purple and she reflexively yelped and ducked. Another *pop* and the pavement mushroomed yellow one inch from her exposed feet. Shit!

Kimberly darted up, opened fire, then dropped back behind the door.

"Quincy, rifle reloading," she yelled into the radio, her hands shaking so badly now with adrenaline that she fumbled the release and had to do it twice. Come on, Kimberly. Breathe!

They needed to regain control of the situation. She couldn't get the damn rounds into the magazine. Breathe, breathe, breathe. Hold it together. A movement caught the corner of her eye. The car. The black sedan, doors still open, was now rolling forward.

She grabbed her radio, dropped it, grabbed it again, and yelled, "Get the wheels, get the wheels."

Squire and Lehane either heard her or got it on their own, because the next round of gunfire splattered the pavement and the sedan came to an awkward halt just one foot from Kimberly's car. She looked up. Caught the startled gaze of the man in the driver's seat. He bolted from the vehicle. She leapt out from behind her car door after him.

And a moment later, pain, brilliant and hot pink, exploded across her lower spine.

New Agent Kimberly Quincy went down. She did not get up again.

"Well, that was an exercise in stupidity," FBI supervisor Mark Watson exclaimed fifteen minutes later. The vehicle-stop drill was over. The five new agents had returned, paint-splattered, overheated, and technically half-dead to the gathering site on Hogan's Alley. They now had the honor of being thoroughly dressed down in front of their thirty-eight fellow classmates. "First mistake, anyone?"

"Alissa didn't get her seat belt off."

"Yeah. She unfastened the clasp, but didn't pull it back. Then when it came time for action . . ."

Alissa hung her head. "I got a little tangled, went to undo it—"

"Popped up and got shot in the shoulder. That's why we practice. Problem number two?"

"Kimberly didn't back up her partner."

Watson's eyes lit up. A former Denver cop before joining the Bureau ten years ago, this was one of his favorite topics. "Yes, Kimberly and her partner. Let's discuss that. Kimberly, why didn't *you* notice that Alissa hadn't undone her seat belt?"

"I did!" Kimberly protested. "But then the car, and the guns . . . It all happened so fast."

"Yes, it all happened so fast. Epitaph of the dead and untrained. Look—being aware of the suspect is good. Being conscious of your role is good. But you also have to be aware of what's right beside you. Your partner overlooked something. That's her mistake. But you didn't catch it for her, and that was *your* mistake. Then she got hit, now you're down a man, and that mistake is getting bigger all the time. Plus, what were you doing just leaving her there on the pavement?"

"Lehane was yelling for rifle support—"

"You left a fellow agent exposed! If she wasn't already dead, she certainly was after that! You couldn't drag her back into the car?"

Kimberly opened her mouth. Shut her mouth. Wished bitterly, selfishly, that Alissa could've taken care of herself for a change, then gave up the argument once and for all.

"Third mistake," Watson demanded crisply.

"They never controlled the car," another classmate offered up.

"Exactly. You stopped the suspect's car, but never controlled it." His gaze went to Lehane. "When things first went wrong, what should you have done?"

Lehane visibly squirmed. He fingered the collar of his brown leisure suit, cut two sizes too big and now bearing hot-pink and mustard-yellow paint on the left shoulder. The paint guns used by the actors in the drills—aka the bad guys—stained everything in sight, hence their Salvation Army wardrobe. The exploding shells also hurt like the dickens, which was why Lehane was holding his left arm protectively against his ribs. For the record, the FBI Academy trainees weren't allowed paint guns but used their real weapons loaded with blanks. The official explanation was that their instructors wanted the trainees to get a feel for their firearms. Likewise, they all wore vests to get used to the weight of body armor. That all sounded well and good, but why not have the actors shoot blanks as well?

The students had their theories. The brightly exploding paint shells made getting hit all the more embarrassing. And the pain wasn't something you forgot about anytime soon. As Steven, the class psychologist, dryly pointed out, the Hogan Alley live-action drills were basically classic shock therapy on a whole new scale.

"Shot out the tires," Lehane said now.

"Yes, at least Kimberly eventually thought of that. Which brings us to the Deadly Deed of the Day."

Watson's gaze swung to Kimberly. She met his look, knew what it meant, and stuck her chin up.

"She abandoned the cover of her vehicle," the first person said.

"Put down her weapon."

"Went after one suspect before she finished securing the scene."

"Stopped providing cover fire—"

"Got killed—"

"Maybe she missed her partner."

Laughter. Kimberly shot the commentator a thanks-for-nothing glare.

Whistler, a big burly former Marine—who sounded like he was whistling every time he breathed—smiled back. He'd won Deadly Deed of the Day yesterday when, during a bank robbery of the Bank of Hogan, he went to shoot a robber and hit the teller instead.

"I got a little lost in the moment," Kimberly said curtly.

"You got killed," Watson corrected flatly.

"Merely paralyzed!"

That earned her another droll look. "Secure the vehicle first. Control the situation. Then give pursuit."

"He'd be gone—"

"But you would have the car, which is evidence, you'd have his cohorts to flip on him, and best of all, you'd still be alive. A bird in the hand, Kimberly. A bird in the hand." Watson gave her one last stern look, then opened up his lecture to the rest of the class. "Remember, people, in the heat of the moment, you have to stay in control. That means falling back on your training and the endless drills we're making you do here. Hogan's Alley is about learning good judgment. Taking the high-risk shot in the middle of a bank holdup is not good judgment." Whistler got a look. "And leaving the cover of your vehicle, and your fellow agents, to pursue one suspect on foot is not good judgment." A fresh glance at Kimberly. Like she needed it.

"Remember your training. Be smart. Stay controlled. That will keep you alive." He glanced at his watch, then clapped his hands. "All right, people, five o'clock, that's a wrap. For God's sake, go wash all that paint off. And remember, folks—as long as it remains this hot, drink plenty of water."

2

Twenty minutes later, Kimberly stood blessedly alone in her small Washington Hall dorm room. Given this afternoon's debacle, she'd thought she'd have a good cry. She now discovered that as of week nine of the Academy's sixteen-week program, she was officially too tired for tears.

Instead, she stood naked in the middle of the tiny dorm room. She was staring at her reflection in a full-length mirror, not quite believing what she saw.

The sound of running water came from her right; her roommate, Lucy, fresh off the PT course, was showering in the bathroom they shared with two other classmates. Behind her, came the sounds of gunfire and the occasional exploding artillery. The FBI Academy and National Academy classes were done for the day, but Quantico remained a busy place. The Marines conducted basic training just down the road. The DEA ran various exercises. At any given time on the sprawling 385-acre grounds, someone was probably shooting something.

When Kimberly had first arrived here back in May, first stepped off the Dafre shuttle bus, she'd inhaled the scent of cordite mixed with fresh-cut lawn and thought she'd never smelled anything quite so nice. The Academy seemed beautiful to her. And surprisingly inconspicuous. The sprawling collection of thirteen oversized beige brick buildings looked like any kind of 1970s institution. A community college maybe. Or government offices. The buildings were ordinary.

Inside wasn't much different. A serviceable, blue-gray carpet ran as far as the eye could see. Walls were painted bone-white. Furniture was sparse and functional—low-slung orange chairs, short, easily assembled oak tables and desks. The Academy had officially opened its doors in 1972, and the joke was the decorating hadn't changed much since.

The complex, however, was inviting. The Jefferson Dormitory, where visitors checked in, boasted beautiful wood trim as well as a glass-enclosed atrium, perfect for indoor barbecues. Over a dozen long, smoked-glass corridors connected each building and made it seem as if you were walking through the lush, green grounds, instead of remaining indoors. Courtyards popped up everywhere, complete with flowering trees, wrought-iron benches, and flagstone patios. On sunny days, trainees could race woodchucks, rabbits, and squirrels to class as the animals bounded across the rolling lawns. At dusk, the glowing amber eyes of deer, foxes, and raccoons appeared in the fringes of the forest, peering at the buildings with the same intensity the students used to stare back. One day, around week three, as Kimberly was strolling down a glass-enclosed corridor, she turned her head to admire a white flowering dogwood, and a thick black snake suddenly appeared among the branches and dropped to the patio below.

In the good news department, she hadn't screamed. One of her class-mates, a former Navy man, however, had. Just startled, he told them all sheepishly. Honestly, just startled.

Of course, they had all screamed a time or two since. The instructors would've been disappointed otherwise.

Kimberly returned her attention to the full-length mirror, and the mess that was her body now reflected there. Her right shoulder was dark purple. Her left thigh yellow and green. Her rib cage was bruised, both her shins were black and blue, and the right side of her face—from yesterday's shot-gun training—looked like someone had gone after her with a meat mallet. She turned around and gazed at the fresh bruise already forming on her lower back. It would go nicely with the giant red mat burn running up the back of her right thigh.

Nine weeks ago, her five-six frame had been one hundred and fifteen pounds of muscle and sinew. As a lifelong workout junkie, she'd been fit, trim, and ready to breeze through physical training. Armed with a master's degree in criminology, shooting since she was twelve, and hanging out with FBI agents—basically her father—all of her life, she'd strode through the Academy's broad glass doors like she owned the joint. Kimberly Quincy has arrived and she's still pissed off about September 11. So all you bad people out there, drop your weapons and cower.

That had been nine weeks ago. Now, on the other hand . . .

She'd definitely lost badly needed weight. Her eyes held dark shadows, her cheeks were hollowed out, her limbs looked too thin to bear her own weight. She looked like a washed-out version of her former self. Bruises on the outside to match the bruises on the inside.

She couldn't stand the sight of her own body. She couldn't seem to look away.

Inside the bathroom, the water shut off with a rusty clank. Lucy would be out soon.

Kimberly raised her hand to the mirror. She traced the line of her bruised shoulder, the glass cool and hard against her fingertips.

And, unbidden, she remembered something she hadn't thought of for six years now. Her mother, Elizabeth Quincy. Dark, softly curling brown hair, fine patrician features, her favorite ivory silk blouse. Her mother was smil-ing at her, looking troubled, looking sad, looking torn.

"I just want you to be happy, Kimberly. Oh God, if only you weren't so much like your father . . ."

Kimberly's fingers remained on the mirrored glass. She closed her eyes, however, for there were some things that even after all these years she still could not take.

Another sound from the bathroom; Lucy raking shut the curtain. Kimberly opened her eyes. She moved hastily to the bed and grabbed her clothes. Her hands were trembling. Her shoulder ached.

She pulled on FBI-issued nylon running shorts and a light blue T-shirt.

Six o'clock. Her classmates would be going to dinner. Kimberly went to train.

Kimberly had arrived at the FBI Academy in Quantico, Virginia, the third week of May as part of NAC 03-05—meaning her class was the fifth new agent class to start in the year 2003.

Like most of her classmates, Kimberly had dreamt about becoming an FBI agent for most of her life. To say she was excited to be accepted would be a little bit of an understatement. The Academy accepted only 6 percent of applicants—a lower acceptance rate than even Harvard's—so Kimberly had been more like giddy, awestruck, thrilled, flabbergasted, nervous, fearful, and amazed all in various turns. For twenty-four hours, she'd kept the news to herself. Her own special secret, her own special day. After all the years of educating and training and trying and wanting . . .

She'd taken her acceptance letter, gone to Central Park, and just sat there, watching a parade of New Yorkers walk by while wearing a silly grin on her face.

Day two, she'd called her father. He'd said, "That's wonderful, Kimberly," in that quiet, controlled voice of his and she'd babbled, for no good reason, "I don't need anything. I'm all set to go. Really, I'm fine."

He'd invited her to dinner with him and his partner, Rainie Conner. Kimberly had declined. Instead, she'd sheared off her long, dirty-blond hair and clipped down her fingernails. Then she'd driven five hours to the Arlington National Cemetery, where she sat in silence amid the sea of white crosses.

Arlington always smelled like a freshly mowed lawn. Green, sunny and bright. Not many people knew that, but Kimberly did.

Arriving at the Academy three weeks later was a lot like arriving at summer camp. All new agents were bundled into the Jefferson Dormitory where supervisors rattled off names and crossed off lists, while the new trainees clutched their travel bags and pretended to be much cooler and calmer than they really felt.

Kimberly was summarily handed a bundle of thin white linens and an orange coverlet to serve as her bedding. She also received one threadbare white towel and one equally threadbare washcloth. New agent trainees made their own beds, she was informed, and when she wanted fresh sheets, she was to pack up the old bunch and go to the linen exchange. She was then given a student handbook detailing all the various rules governing life at the Academy. The handbook was twenty-four pages long.

Next stop the PX, where, for the bargain-basement price of $325, Kimberly purchased her new agent uniform—tan cargo pants, tan belt, and a navy blue polo shirt bearing the FBI Academy logo on the left breast. Like the rest of her classmates, Kimberly purchased an official FBI Academy lanyard, from which she hung her ID badge.

ID badges were important at the Academy, she learned. For one thing, wearing ID at all times kept students from being summarily arrested by Security and thrown out. For another thing, it entitled her to free food in the cafeteria.

New agents must be in uniform Monday through Friday from eight A.M. to four-thirty P.M., they learned. After four-thirty, however, everyone magically returned to being mere mortals and thus could wear street clothes—excluding sandals, tube tops, or tank tops. This was, after all, the Academy.

Handguns were not permitted on Academy grounds. Instead, Kimberly checked her Glock .40 into the Weapons Management Facility vault. In return, she received what the new agents fondly referred to as a "Crayola Gun" or "Red Handle"—a red plastic gun of approximately the same weight and size as a Glock. New agents were required to wear the Crayolas at all times, along with fake handcuffs. In theory, this helped them grow accustomed to the weight and feel of wearing a handgun.

Kimberly despised her Red Handle. It seemed childish and silly to her. She wanted her Glock back. On the other hand, the various accountants, lawyers, and psychologists in her class, who had zero firearms experience, loved the things. They could knock them off their belts, drop them in the halls, and sit on them without shooting themselves or anyone else in the ass. One day, Gene Yvves had been gesturing so wildly, he whacked his Crayola halfway across the room, where it hit another new agent on the head. Definitely, the first few weeks, it was a good idea that not everyone in the class was armed.

Kimberly still wanted her Glock back.

Once piled high with linens, uniforms, and toy handguns, the new agent trainees returned to the dorms to meet their roommates. Everyone started out in the Madison and Washington dormitories, two people to a room and two rooms sharing a bath. The rooms were small but functional—two single beds, two small oak desks, one big bookshelf. Each bathroom, painted vivid blue for reasons known only to the janitor, had a small sink and a shower. No tub. By week four, when everyone's bruised and battered bodies were desperate for a long, hot soak, several agents rented hotel rooms in neighboring Stafford purely for the bathtubs. Seriously.

Kimberly's roommate, Lucy Dawbers, was a thirty-six-year-old former trial lawyer who'd had her own two-thousand-dollar-a-month Boston brownstone. She'd taken one look at their spartan quarters that first day and groaned, "Oh my God, what have I done?"

Kimberly had the distinct impression that Lucy would kill for a nice glass of Chardonnay at the end of the day. She also missed her five-year-old son horribly.

In the good news department, especially for new agents who didn't share particularly well—say, perhaps, Kimberly—somewhere around week twelve, new agents became eligible for private rooms in "The Hilton"—the Jefferson Dormitory. These rooms were not only slightly bigger, but entitled you to your very own bathroom. Pure heaven.

Assuming you survived until week twelve.

Three of Kimberly's classmates already hadn't.

In theory, the FBI Academy had abandoned its earlier, boot camp ways for a kinder, gentler program. Recognizing how expensive it was to recruit good agents, the Bureau now treated the FBI Academy as the final training stage for selected agents, rather than as a last opportunity to winnow out the weak.

That was in theory. In reality, testing started week one. Can you run two miles in less than sixteen minutes? Can you do fifty push-ups in one minute? Can you do sixty sit-ups? The shuttle run must be completed in twenty-four seconds, the fifty-foot rope must be climbed in forty-five seconds.

The new agent trainees ran, they trained, they suffered through body-fat testing and they prayed to fix their individual weaknesses—whether that was the shuttle run or the rope climb or the fifty push-ups, in order to pass the three cycles of fitness tests.

Then came the academics program—classes in white-collar crime, profiling, civil rights, foreign counterintelligence, organized crime and drug cases; lessons in interrogation, arrest tactics, driving maneuvers, undercover work, and computers; lecture series on criminology, legal rights, forensic science, ethics, and FBI history. Some of it was interesting, some of it was excruciating, and all of it was tested three times over the course of the sixteen weeks. And no mundane high-school scale here—it took a score of 85 percent or higher to pass. Anything less, you failed. Fail once, you had an opportunity for a make-up test. Fail twice, you were "recycled"—dropped back to the next class.

Recycled. It sounded so innocuous. Like some PC sports program—there are no winners or losers here, you're just recycled.

Recycling mattered. New agents feared it, dreaded it, had nightmares about it. It was the ominous word whispered in the halls. It was the secret terror that kept them going up over the towering Marine training wall, even now that it was week nine and everyone was sleeping less and less while being pushed more and more and the drills were harder and the expectations higher and each day, every day, someone was going to get awarded the Deadly Deed of the Day . . .

Besides the physical training and academics, new agents worked on firearms. Kimberly had thought she'd have the advantage there. She'd been taking lessons with a Glock .40 for the past ten years. She was comfortable with guns and a damn good shot.

Except firearms training didn't involve just standing and firing at a paper target. They also practiced firing from the sitting position—as if surprised at a desk. Then there were running drills, belly-crawling drills, night-firing drills, and elaborate rituals where they started out on their bellies, then got up and ran, then dropped down, then ran more, then stood and fired. You fired right-handed. You fired left-handed. You reloaded and reloaded and reloaded.

And you didn't just use a handgun.

Kimberly got her first experience with an M-16 rifle. Then she fired over a thousand rounds from a Remington Model 870 shotgun with a recoil that nearly crushed her right cheek and shattered her shoulder. Then she expelled over a hundred rounds from a Heckler & Koch MP5/10 submachine gun, though that at least had been kind of fun.

Now they had Hogan's Alley, where they practiced elaborate scenarios and only the actors actually knew what was going to happen next. Kimberly's traditional anxiety dreams—leaving the house naked, suddenly being in a classroom taking a pop quiz—had once been in black and white. Since Hogan's Alley, they had taken on vivid, violent color. Hot-pink classrooms, mustard-yellow streets. Pop quizzes splashed with purple and green paint. Herself running, running, running down long endless tunnels of exploding orange, pink, purple, blue, yellow, black, and green.

She awoke some nights biting back weary screams. Other nights, she simply lay there and felt her right shoulder throb. Sometimes, she could tell that Lucy was awake, too. They didn't talk those nights. They just lay in the dark, and gave each other the space to hurt.

Then at six A.M. they both got up and went through it all over again.

Nine weeks down, seven to go. Show no weakness. Give no quarter. Endure.

Kimberly wanted so desperately to make it. She was strong Kimberly, with cool blue eyes just like her father's. She was smart Kimberly, with her B.A. in psychology at twenty-one and her master's in criminology at twenty-two. She was driven Kimberly, determined to get on with her life even after what happened to her mother and sister.

She was infamous Kimberly, the youngest member of her class and the one everyone whispered about in the halls. *You know who her father is, don't you? What a shame about her family. I heard the killer nearly got her, too. She gunned him down in cold blood . . .*

Kimberly's classmates took lots of notes in their eagerly awaited profiling class. Kimberly took none at all.

She arrived downstairs. Up ahead in the hall, she could see a cluster of green shirts chatting and laughing—National Academy students, done for the day and no doubt heading to the Boardroom for cold beer. Then came the cluster of blue shirts, talking up a storm. Fellow new-agent trainees, also done for the day, and now off to grab a quick bite in the cafeteria before hitting the books, or the PT course, or the gym. Maybe they were mentoring each other, swapping a former lawyer's legal expertise for a former Marine's firearms training. New agents were always willing to help one another. If you let them.

Kimberly pushed her way through the outside doors. The heat slammed into her like a blow. She made a beeline for the relative shade of the Academy's wooded PT course and started running.

Pain, Agony, Hurt, the signs read on the trees next to the path. Suck it in. Love it!

"I do, I do," Kimberly gasped.

Her aching body protested. Her chest tightened with pain. She kept on running. When all else failed, keep moving. One foot in front of another. New pain layering on top of the old.

Kimberly knew this lesson well. She had learned it six years ago, when her sister was dead, her mother was murdered and she stood in a Portland, Oregon, hotel room with the barrel of a gun pressed against her forehead like a lover's kiss.

3

Twenty-year-old Tina Krahn had just stepped out the front door of her stifling hot apartment when the phone rang. Tina sighed, doubled back into the kitchen and answered with an impatient hello while using her other hand to wipe the sweat from the back of her neck. God, this heat was unbearable. The humidity level had picked up on Sunday, and hadn't done a thing to improve since. Now, fresh out of the shower, Tina's thin green sundress was already plastered to her body, while she could feel fresh dewdrops of moisture trickle stickily down between her breasts.

She and her roommate Betsy had agreed half an hour ago to go anyplace with air-conditioning. Betsy had made it to the car. Tina had made it to the door, and now this.

Her mother was on the other end of the line. Tina promptly winced.

"Hey, Ma," she tried with forced enthusiasm. "How are you?" Her gaze went to the front door. She willed Betsy to reappear so she could signal she needed a minute longer. No such luck. Tina tapped her foot anxiously and was happy her mother was a thousand miles away in Minnesota, and couldn't see her guilty expression.

"Well, actually I'm running out the door. Yeah, it's Tuesday. Just the time zones are different, Ma, not the days." That earned her a sharp rebuke. She grabbed a napkin from the kitchen table, swiped it across her forehead, then shook her head when it immediately became soaking wet. She patted her upper lip.

"Of course I have class tomorrow. We weren't planning on drinking ourselves silly, Ma." In fact, Tina rarely drank anything stronger than ice tea. Not that her mom believed her. Tina had gone away to college—egads!—which Tina's mother seemed to equate with choosing a life of sin. There was alcohol on college campuses, you know. And fornication.

"I don't know where we're going, Ma. Just . . . out. It's like . . . a gazillion degrees this week. We gotta find someplace with air-conditioning before we spontaneously combust." Lord, did they.

Her mother was instantly concerned. Tina held up a hand, trying to cut off the tirade before it got started.

"No, I didn't mean that literally. No, really, Ma, I'm all right. It's just hot.

I can handle some heat. But summer school is going great. Work is fine—"

Her mother's voice grew sharper.

"I only work twenty hours a week. Of course I'm focusing on my studies. Really, honestly, everything's fine. I swear it." The last three words came out a smidgeon too high. Tina winced again. What was it with mothers and their internal radars? Tina should've quit while she was ahead. She grabbed another napkin and blotted her whole face. Now she was no longer sure if the moisture was solely from the heat, or from nerves.

"No, I'm not seeing anyone." That much was true.

"We broke up, Ma. Last month. I told you about it." Kind of.

"No, I'm not pining away. I'm young, I'll survive." At least that's what Betsy, Vivienne, and Karen told her.

"Ma—" She couldn't get in a word.

"Ma—" Her mother was still going strong. Men are evil. Tina was too young to date. Now was the time to focus on school. And her family, of course. You must never forget your roots.

"Ma—" Her mother was reaching her crescendo. Why don't you just come home? You don't come home enough. What are you, ashamed of me? There's nothing wrong with being a secretary, you know. Not all young ladies get the wonderful opportunity to go off to college . . .

"*Ma!* Listen, I gotta run."

Silence. Now she was in trouble. Worse than her mother's lectures was her mother's silence.

"Betsy's out in the car," Tina tried. "But I love you, Ma. I'll call you tomorrow night. I promise."

She wouldn't. They both knew it.

"Well, if anything, I'll call you by the weekend." That was more like it. On the other end of the phone, her mother sighed. Maybe she was mollified. Maybe she was still hurt. With her, it was always hard to know. Tina's father had walked out when she was three. Her mother had been going at it alone ever since. And, yeah, she was bossy and anxious and downright dictatorial on occasion, but she also worked ferociously to get her only daughter into college.

She tried hard, worked hard, loved hard. And Tina knew that more than anything in the world, her mother worried it still wouldn't be enough.

Tina cradled the phone closer to her damp ear. For a moment, in the silence, she was tempted. But then her mother sighed again, and the moment passed.

"Love you," Tina said, her voice softer than she intended. "Gotta run. Talk to you soon. Bye."

Tina dropped the phone back on the receiver before she changed her mind, grabbed her oversized canvas bag and headed out the door. Outside, Betsy sat in her cute little Saab convertible, her face also shiny with sweat and gazing at her questioningly.

"Ma," Tina explained and plunked her bag in the backseat.

"Oh. You didn't . . ."

"Not yet."

"Coward."

"Totally." Tina didn't bother opening the passenger-side door. Instead she perched her rump up on the edge of the car, then slid down into the deep, beige leather seat. Her long legs stuck up in the air. Ridiculously high brown cork sandals. Hot-pink toenails. A small red ladybug tattoo her mother didn't know about yet.

"Help me, I'm melting!" Tina told her friend in a dramatic voice as she threw the back of her hand against her forehead. Betsy finally smiled and put the car into gear.

"Tomorrow it's supposed to be even hotter. By Friday, we'll probably break one hundred."

"God, just kill me now." Tina straightened up, self-consciously checked the knot holding her heavy blond hair, and then fastened her seat belt. Ready for action. In spite of her lighthearted tone, however, her expression was too somber, the light gone out of her blue eyes and replaced now by four weeks of worry.

"Hey, Tina," Betsy said after a moment. "It's going to be all right."

Tina forced herself to turn around. She picked up Betsy's hand. "Buddy system?" she asked softly.

Betsy smiled at her. "Always."

The sun setting was one of the most beautiful sights in the world to him. The sky glowed amber, rose, and peach, firing the horizon with dying embers of sunlight. Color washed across the clouds like strokes of an artist's brush, feathering white cumulus billows with iridescent hues from gold to purple to finally—inevitably—black.

He had always liked sunsets. He remembered his mother bringing him and his brother out to the front porch of the rickety shack every evening after dinner. They would lean against the railing and watch the sun sink behind the distant rim of mountains. No words were spoken. They learned the reverent hush at an early age.

This was his mother's moment, a form of religion for her. She would stand alone, in the western corner of the porch, watching the sun descend, and for a brief moment, the lines would soften in her face. Her lips would curve into a slight smile. Her shoulders would relax. The sun would slip beneath the horizon and his mother would sigh long and deep.

Then the moment would end. His mother's shoulders would return to bunched-up tension, the worry lines adding ten years to her face. She would usher them back into the house and return to her chores. He and his brother would do their best to help her, all of them careful not to make too much noise.

It wasn't until he was much older, nearly an adult, that the man wondered about these moments with his mom. What did it say about her life that she relaxed only when the sun eased down and signaled the end of the day? What did it mean that the only time she seemed happy was when daylight drew its last gasping breath?

His mother had died before he could ask her these questions. Some things, he supposed, were for the best.

The man walked back into his hotel room. Though he'd paid for the night, he planned on leaving in the next half hour. He wouldn't miss this place. He didn't like structures built out of cement, or mass-produced rooms with only one window. These were dead places, the modern-day version of tombs, and the fact that Americans were willing to pay good money to sleep in these cheaply constructed coffins defied his imagination.

He worried sometimes that the very fakeness of a room like this, with its garish comforter, particle-board furniture, and carpet made with petroleum-based fibers would penetrate his skin, get into his bloodstream and he'd wake up one morning craving a Big Mac.

The thought frightened him; he had to take a moment to draw deep breaths. Not a good idea. The air was foul, rank with fiberglass insulation and plastic ficus trees. He rubbed his temples furiously, and knew he needed to leave more quickly.

His clothes were packed in his duffel bag. He had just one thing left to check.

He wrapped his hand in one of the bathroom towels, reached with his covered hand beneath the bed, and slowly pulled out the brown attaché case. It looked like any other business briefcase. Maybe full of spreadsheets and pocket calculators and personal electronic devices. His, however, wasn't.

His carried a dart gun, currently broken down, but easy to reassemble in the field. He checked the inside pocket of the attaché case, pulled out the metal box, and counted the darts inside. One dozen hits, preloaded with five hundred and fifty milligrams of ketamine. He had prepared each dart just this morning.

He returned the metal box and pulled out two rolls of duct tape, heavy duty, followed by a plain brown paper bag filled with nails. Beside the duct tape and nails, he kept a small glass bottle of chloral hydrate. A backup drug, which thankfully he'd never had to use. Next to the chloral hydrate, he had a special insulated water bottle he'd been keeping in the minibar freezer until just fifteen minutes ago. The outside of the container froze, helping keep the contents cool. That was important. Ativan crystallized if not kept refrigerated.

He felt the bottle again. It was ice cold. Good. This was his first time using this system and he was a little nervous. The plastic drinking bottle seemed to do the trick, though. The things you could buy for $4.99 from Wal-Mart.

The man took a deep breath. He was trying to remember if he needed anything else. It had been a while. Truth be told, he was nervous. Lately, he'd been struggling a bit with dates. Things that happened a long time ago seemed bright as day, whereas yesterday's events took on a hazy, dreamlike quality.

Yesterday, when he had arrived here, three years ago blazed in his mind with vivid, Technicolor detail. This morning, however, things already started to fade and curl at the edges. He was worried that if he waited much longer, he'd lose the memories altogether. They'd disappear into the black void with his other thoughts, his nonflaming thoughts, and he'd be left sitting at the edges again, waiting helplessly for something, anything, to float to the top.

Crackers. Saltines. And water. Gallon jugs. Several of them.

That's right, he had these things in the van. He'd gotten them yesterday, also from Wal-Mart, or maybe it had been Kmart—now see, that detail had disappeared, slipped into the pit, what was he supposed to do? Yesterday. He'd bought things. Supplies. At a very big store. Well, what could the name matter anyway? He'd paid cash, right? And burned the receipt?

Of course he had. Even if his memory played tricks on him, it was no excuse for stupidity. His father had always been adamant on that point. The world was run by dumb-fuck idiots who couldn't find their own assholes with a flashlight and two hands. His sons, on the other hand, must be better than that. Be strong. Stand tall. Take your punishment like a man.

The man finished looking around. He was thinking of fire again, the heat of flames, but it was too soon so he let that thought go, willed it into the void, though he knew it would never stay. He had his travel bag; he had his attaché case. Other supplies in the van. Room already wiped down with ammonia and water. Leave no trace of prints.

All right.

Just one last item to grab. In the corner of the room, sitting on the horrible, fake carpet. A small rectangular aquarium covered in his own yellow faded sheet.

The man slipped the strap of his duffel bag over his shoulder, followed by the strap for his attaché case. Then he used both arms to heft up the heavy glass aquarium. The sheet started to slip. From inside the yellow depths came an ominous rattle.

"Shhhh," he murmured. "Not yet, my love, not yet."

The man strode into the bloodred dusk, into the stifling, heavy heat. His brain fired to life. More pictures came to his mind. Black skirts, high heels, blond hair, blue eyes, red blouse, bound hands, dark hair, brown eyes, long legs, scratching nails, flashing white teeth.

The man loaded up his van, got behind the wheel. At the last minute, his errant memory sparked and he patted his breast pocket. Yes, he had the ID badge as well. He pulled it out and inspected it one final time. The front of the plastic rectangle was simple enough. In white letters against the blue backdrop, the badge read: Visitor.

He flipped the ID over. The back of the security card was definitely much more interesting. It read: Property of the FBI.

The man clipped the ID badge to his collar. The sun sank, the sky turned from red to purple to black.

"Clock ticking," the man murmured. He started to drive.

4

Stafford, Virginia
9:34 P.M.
Temperature: 89 degrees

"What's up, sugar? You seem restless tonight."

"Can't stand the heat."

"That's a strange comment coming from a man who lives in Hotlanta."

"I keep meaning to move."

Genny, a tight-bodied redhead with a well-weathered face but genuinely kind eyes, gazed at him speculatively through the blue haze of the smoky bar.

"How long have you lived in Georgia, Mac?" she asked over the din.

"Since I was a gleam in my daddy's eye."

She smiled, shook her head and stubbed out her cigarette in the glass ashtray. "Then you won't ever move, sugar. Take it from me. You're a Georgian. Stick a fork in you, you're done."

"You just say that because you're a Texan."

"Since I was a gleam in my great-great-great-grandpappy's eyes. Yanks move around, honey. We Southerners take root."

GBI Special Agent Mac McCormack acknowledged the point with a smile. His gaze was on the front door of the crowded bar again. He was watching the people walk in, unconsciously seeking out young girls traveling in pairs. He should know better. On days like this, when the temperature topped ninety, he didn't.

"Sugar?" Genny said again.

He caught himself, turned back to her, and managed a rueful grin. "Sorry. I swear to you my mother raised me better than this."

"Then we'll never let her know. Your meeting didn't go well today, did it?"

"How did you—"

"I'm a police officer, too, Mac. Don't dismiss me just because I'm pretty and got a great set of boobs."

He opened his mouth to protest, but she cut him off with a wave of her hand, then dug around in her purse until she found a fresh cigarette. He held up a light and she smiled her gratitude, though the lines were a bit tighter around her eyes. For a minute, neither one of them said a word.

The bar was hopping tonight, flesh pressed against flesh, with more people still pouring through the doors. Half of them, of course, were their fellow National Academy classmates—detectives, sheriffs, and even some military police enrolled in Quantico's eleven-week course. Still, Mac wouldn't have expected the bar to be this busy on a Tuesday night. People were fleeing their homes, probably trying to escape the heat.

He and Genny had arrived three hours ago, early enough to stake out hard-to-find seats. Generally the National Academy students didn't leave Quantico much. People hung out in the Boardroom after hours, drinking beer, swapping war stories, and by one or two in the morning, praying that their livers wouldn't fail them now. The big joke was that the program had to end week eleven, because no one's kidneys could survive week twelve.

People were restless tonight, though. The unbearable heat and humidity had started moving in on Sunday, and reportedly were working their way to a Friday crescendo. Walking outside was like slogging through a pile of wet towels. In five minutes your T-shirt was plastered to your torso. In ten minutes, your shorts were glued to your thighs. Inside seemed little better, with the Academy's archaic air-conditioning system groaning mightily just to cool things to eighty-five.

People started bailing from Quantico shortly after six, desperate for any sort of distraction. Genny and Mac had followed shortly thereafter.

They'd met the first week of training, eight weeks ago. Southerners had to stick together, Genny had teased him, especially in a class overrun with fast-talking Yanks. Her gaze, however, had been on his broad chest when she'd said this. Mac had merely grinned.

At the age of thirty-six, he'd figured out by now that he was a good-looking guy—six two, black hair, blue eyes, and deeply tanned skin from a lifetime spent running, cycling, fishing, hunting, hiking, canoeing, etc. You name it, he did it and he had a younger sister and nine cousins who accompanied him all the way. You could get into a lot of trouble in a state as diverse as Georgia, and the McCormacks prided themselves on learning each lesson the hard way.

The end result was a leanly muscled physique that seemed to appeal to women of all ages. Mac did his best to bear this hardship stoically. It helped a great deal that he was fond of women. A little *too* fond, according to his exasperated mother, who was dead-set on gaining a daughter-in-law and oodles of grandkids. Maybe someday, he supposed. At the moment, however, Mac was completely wedded to his job, and days like this, boy, didn't he know it.

His gaze returned to the doorway. Two young girls walked in, followed by another two. All were chatting happily. He wondered if they would leave that way. Together, alone, with newly met lovers, without. Which way would be safer? Man, he hated nights like this.

"You gotta let it go," Genny said.

"Let what go?"

"Whatever's putting lines on that handsome face."

Mac tore his gaze away from the door for the second time. He regarded Genny wryly, then picked up his beer and spun it between his fingers. "You ever have one of those cases?"

"The kind that gets beneath your skin, jumps into your brain and haunts your dreams, until five, six, ten, twenty years later you still sometimes wake up screaming? No, sugar, I wouldn't know a thing about that." She stubbed out her cigarette, then reached in her purse for another.

"Sugar," Mac mocked gently, "you're lying through your teeth." He held up a lighter again and watched how her blue eyes appraised him even as she leaned toward his hands and accepted the flame.

She sat back. She inhaled. She exhaled. She said abruptly, "All right, pretty boy. There's no dealing with you tonight, so you might as well tell me about your meeting."

"It never happened," he said readily.

"Blew you off?"

"For bigger fish. According to Dr. Ennunzio, it's now all terrorism all the time."

"Versus your five-year-old case," she filled in for him.

He grinned crookedly, leaned back, and spread out his darkly bronzed hands. "I have seven dead girls, Genny. Seven little girls who never made it home to their families. It's not their fault they were murdered by a plain-vanilla serial killer and not some imported terrorist threat."

"Battle of the budgets."

"Absolutely. The Behavioral Science Unit has only one forensic linguist— Dr. Ennunzio—but the nation has thousands of whackos writing threats. Apparently, letters to the editor are low on the list of priorities. Of course, in my world, these letters are about the only damn lead we have left. National Academy prestige aside, my department didn't send me here for continued education. I'm supposed to meet this man. Get his expert input on the only decent lead we have left. I go back to my department without so much as saying boo to the fine doctor, and I can kiss my ass good-bye."

"You don't care about your ass."

"It would be easier if I did," Mac said, with his first trace of seriousness all night.

"You ask anyone else in the BSU for help?"

"I've asked anyone who'll give me the time of day in the hall for help. Hell, Genny, I'm not proud. I just *want* this guy."

"You could go independent."

"Been there, done that. Got us nowhere."

Genny considered this while taking another drag from her cigarette. Despite what she might think, Mac hadn't let the great set of boobs fool him. Genny was a sheriff. Ran her own twelve-man office. In Texas, where girls were still encouraged to become cheerleaders or, better yet, Miss America. In other words, Genny was tough. And smart. And experienced. She probably had *many* of those cases that got under an investigator's skin. And given how hot it had become outside, how hot it would be by the end of the week, Mac would appreciate any insight she could give him.

"It's been three years," she said at last. "That's a long time for a serial pred-ator. Maybe your guy wound up in jail on some other charge. It's been known to happen."

"Could be," Mac acknowledged, though his tone said he wasn't con-vinced.

She accepted that with a nod. "Well, how about this, big boy? Maybe he's dead."

"Hallelujah and praise the Lord," Mac agreed. His voice still lacked conviction. Six months ago he'd been working on buying into that theory. Hell, he'd been looking forward to embracing that theory. Violent felons often led violent lives and came to violent ends. All the better for the taxpayers, as far as Mac was concerned.

But then, six months ago, one single letter in the mail . . .

Funny the things that could rock your world. Funny the things that could take a three-year-old frustrated task force and launch it from low-burn, cooling their heels, to high-octane, move, now, now, now in twenty-four hours or less. But he couldn't mention these things to Genny. These were details told only on a need-to-know basis.

Like why he really wanted to talk to Dr. Ennunzio. Or why he was really in the great state of Virginia.

Almost on cue, he felt the vibration at his waist. He looked down at his beeper, the sense of foreboding already gathering low in his belly. Ten numbers stared back up at him. Atlanta area code. And the other numbers . . .

Damn!

"I gotta go," he said, bolting to his feet.

"She that good-looking?" Genny drawled.

"Honey, I'm not that lucky tonight."

He threw thirty bucks on the table, enough to cover his drinks and hers. "You got a ride?" His voice was curt, the question unconscionably rude, and they both knew it.

"No man's that hard to replace."

"You cut me deep, Genny."

She smiled, her gaze lingering on his tall athletic build, her eyes sadder than she intended. "Sugar, I don't cut you at all."

Mac, however, was already striding out the door.

Outside, the heat smacked the grin off of Mac's face. Merry blue eyes immediately turned dark, his expression went from teasing to grim. It had been four weeks since he'd last received a call. He'd been beginning to wonder if that was it.

GBI Special Agent Mac McCormack flipped open his cell phone and furiously started dialing.

The person picked up after the first ring. "You are not even trying," an eerily distorted voice echoed in his ears. Male, female—hell, it could've been Mickey Mouse.

"I'm here, aren't I?" Mac replied tightly. He stopped in the Virginia parking lot, looking around the dark, empty space. The phone number always read Atlanta, but lately Mac had begun wondering about that. All a person had to do was use a cell phone with a Georgia number, then he could call from anywhere with the same effect.

"He's closer than you think."

"Then maybe you should stop speaking in riddles and tell me the truth." Mac turned right, then left. Nothing.

"I mailed you the truth," the disembodied voice intoned.

"You sent me a riddle. I deal in information, buddy, not childish games."

"You deal in death."

"You're not doing much better. Come on. It's been six months. Let's end this dance and get down to some business. You must want something. I know I want something. What do you say?"

The voice fell silent for a moment. Mac wondered if he'd finally shamed the caller, then in the next instant he worried that he'd pissed off the man/woman/mouse. His grip tightened on his phone, pressing it against the curve of his ear. He couldn't afford to lose this call. Damn, he hated this.

Six months ago, Mac had received the first "letter" in the mail. It was a newspaper clipping really, of a letter to the editor of the *Virginian-Pilot*. And the one short paragraph was horribly, hauntingly similar to other editorial notes, now three years past: planet dying . . . animals weeping . . . rivers screaming . . . can't you hear it? heat kills . . .

Three years later, the beast was stirring again. Mac didn't know what had happened in between, but he and his task force were very truly frightened about what might happen next.

"It's getting hot," the voice singsonged now.

Mac looked around the darkness frantically. No one. Nothing. Dammit! "Who are you?" he tried. "Come on, buddy, speak to me."

"He's closer than you think."

"Then give me a name. I'll go get him and no one will be hurt." He changed tack. "Are you scared? Are you frightened of him? Because trust me, we can protect you."

"He doesn't want to hurt them. I don't think he can help himself."

"If he's someone you care about, if you're worried for his safety, don't be. We have procedures for this kind of arrest, we'll take appropriate measures. Come on, this guy has killed seven girls. Give me his name. Let me solve this problem for you. You're doing the right thing."

"I don't have all the answers," the voice said, and for a moment, it sounded so plaintive, Mac nearly believed it. And then, "You should've caught him three years ago, Special Agent. Why, oh, why didn't you guys catch him?"

"Work with us and we'll get him now."

"Too late," the caller said. "He never could stand the heat."

The connection broke. Mac was left in the middle of the parking lot, gripping his impossibly tiny phone and cursing a blue streak. He punched send again. The number rang and rang and rang, but the person didn't pick up and wouldn't until Mac was contacted again.

"Damn," Mac said again. Then, "Damn, damn, damn."

He found his rental car. Inside, it was approximately two hundred degrees. He slid into the seat, leaned his forehead against the steering wheel, then banged his head against the hard plastic three times. Six phone calls now and he was no closer to knowing a single goddamn thing. And time was running out. Mac had known it, had been feeling it, since the mercury had started rising on Sunday.

Tomorrow Mac would check in with his Atlanta office, report the latest call. The task force could review, rework, reanalyze . . . and wait. After all this time, that's about all they had left—the wait.

Mac pressed his forehead against the steering wheel. Exhaled deeply. He was thinking of Nora Ray Watts again. The way her face had lit up like the sun when she had stepped from the rescue chopper and spotted her parents standing just outside of the rotor wash. The way her expression had faltered, then collapsed thirty seconds later after she'd excitedly, innocently asked, "Where is Mary Lynn?"

And then her voice with that impossible reedy wail, over and over again. "No, no, no. Oh God, please *no.*"

Her father had tried to prop her up. Nora Ray sank down on the tarmac, curling up beneath her army blanket as if that could protect her from the truth. Her parents finally collapsed with her, a huddle of green grief that would never know an end.

They won that day. They lost that day.

And now?

It was hot, it was late. And a man was writing letters to the editor once again.

Go home, little girls. Lock the doors. Turn out the lights. Don't end up like Nora Ray Watts, who ran out with her younger sister for a little ice cream one night and ended up abandoned in a desolate part of the coast, frantically burying herself deeper into the muck, while the fiddler crabs nibbled on her toes, the razor clams slashed open her palms, and the scavengers began to circle overhead.

5

Fredericksburg, Virginia
10:34 P.M.
Temperature: 89 degrees

"I'm ready," Tina said two inches from Betsy's ear. In the pounding noise of the jam-packed bar, her roommate didn't seem to hear her. They were outside Fredericksburg, at a little hole-in-the-wall joint favored by college students, biker gangs, and really loud Western bands. Even on a Tuesday night, the place was jamming, the people so thick and the bass so loud Tina didn't know how the roof stayed on over their heads.

"I'm ready," Tina tried again, shouting louder. This time, Betsy at least turned toward her.

"What?" Betsy yelled.

"Time . . . to . . . go . . . *home,*" Tina hollered back.

"Bathroom?"

"HOME!"

"Oooooh." Her roommate finally got it. She looked at Tina more closely and her brown eyes instantly softened with concern. "You okay?"

"Hot!"

"No kidding."

"Not feeling . . . so well." Actually, she was feeling horrible. Her long blond hair had come untangled from its knot and was plastered against her neck. Sweat trickled down the small of her back, over her butt, and all the way down her legs. The air was too heavy. She kept trying to draw deep, gulping breaths, but she still wasn't getting enough oxygen. She thought she might be sick.

"Let me tell the others," Betsy said immediately, and headed out to the jostling dance floor, where Viv and Karen were lost amid the sea of people.

Tina closed her eyes and promised herself she would not projectile vomit in the middle of a crowded bar.

Fifteen minutes later, they had pushed their way outside and were walking toward Betsy's Saab, Viv and Karen bringing up the rear. Tina put her hand against her face. Her forehead felt feverish to her.

"Are you going to make it?" Betsy asked her. After screaming to be heard in the bar, her voice cracked three decibels too loud in the parking lot's total silence. They all winced.

"I don't know."

571

"Girl, you had better tell me if you're going to be sick," Betsy warned seriously. "I'll hold your head over the toilet, but I draw the line at puking in my car."

Tina smiled weakly. "Thanks."

"I could go get you some club soda," Karen offered from behind her.

"Maybe we should just wait a minute," Viv said. She, Karen, and Betsy all drew up short.

Tina, however, had already climbed into Betsy's Saab. "I just want to go home," she murmured quietly. "Please, let's go home."

She closed her eyes as her head fell back against the seat. With her eyes closed, her head felt better. Her hands settled upon her stomach. The music faded away. Tina let herself drift off to desperately needed sleep.

It seemed to her that they had no sooner left the parking lot than she was awakened by a savage jerk.

"What the—" Her head popped up. The car lurched again and she grabbed the dash.

"Back tire," Betsy said in disgust. "I think I got a flat."

The car lurched right and that was enough for Tina. "Betsy," she said tightly. "Pull over. *Now!*"

"Got it!" Betsy jerked the car onto the right-hand shoulder of the road. Tina fumbled with the clasp of her seat belt, then fumbled with the door. She got out of the car and sprinted down the embankment into the nearby woods. She got her head down just in time.

Oh, this was not fun. Not fun at all. She heaved up two cranberry and tonics, then the pasta she'd had for dinner, then anything else she'd ever eaten for the last twenty years. She stood there, hands braced upon her thighs as she dry-heaved.

I'm going to die, she thought. I was bad and now I'm being punished and my mom was right all along. There is no way in the world I'm going to be able to take this. Oh God, I want to go home.

Maybe she cried. Maybe she was just sweating harder. With her head between her knees, it was hard to be sure.

But slowly her stomach relented. The cramping eased, the worst of the nausea passed. She staggered upright, put her face up to the sky, and thought she'd kill for an ice-cold shower right about now. No such luck. They were in the middle of nowhere outside of Fredericksburg. She'd just have to wait.

She sighed. And then for the first time, she heard the noise. A non-Betsy noise. A non-girls-out-on-the-town noise. It sounded high, short, metallic. Like the slide of a rifle, ratcheting back.

Tina slowly turned toward the road. In the hot, humid dark, she was no longer alone.

Kimberly never even heard a noise. She was an FBI trainee, for God's sake. A woman experienced with crime and paranoid to boot. She still never heard a thing.

She stood alone at the Academy's outdoor firing range, surrounded by 385 acres of darkness with only a small Mag flashlight. In her hands, she held an empty shotgun.

It was late. The new agents, the Marines, hell, even the National Academy "students" had long since gone to bed. The stadium lights were extinguished. The distant bank of towering trees formed an ominous barrier between her and civilization. Then there were the giant steel sidewalls, designed to segregate the various firing ranges while stopping high-velocity bullets.

No lights. No sounds. Just the unnatural hush of a night so hot and humid not even the squirrels stirred from their trees.

She was tired. That was her best excuse. She'd run, she'd pumped iron, she'd walked, she'd studied, then she'd downed three gallons of water and two PowerBars and headed out here. Her legs were shaky. Her arm muscles trembled with fatigue.

She hefted the empty shotgun to her shoulder, and went through the rhythms of firing over and over again.

Place butt firmly against right shoulder to absorb the recoil. Plant feet hip-width apart, loose in the knees. Lean slightly forward into the shot. At the last minute, as your right finger squeezes the trigger, pull forward with your left hand as if the gun were a broom handle you were trying to tear in half. Hope against hope you don't fall once more on your ass. Or smash your shoulder. Or shatter your cheek.

Live ammunition was limited to supervised drills, so Kimberly had no real way of knowing how she was doing. Still, lots of the new agents came out after hours to go through the motions. The more times you handled a weapon, the more comfortable it felt in your hands.

If you did it enough times, maybe it would become instinctive. And if it became instinctive, maybe you'd survive the next firearms test.

She leaned into her next practice "shot." Went a little too far, and her rubbery legs wobbled dangerously. She reached out a hand, had just caught herself, and then, in the pitch darkness beside her, she heard a man say, "You shouldn't be out here alone."

Kimberly acted on instinct. She whirled, spotted the hulking, threatening form, and whipped the empty shotgun at the man's face. Then she ran.

A grunt. Surprise. Pain. She didn't wait to find out. The hour was late, the surroundings remote, and she knew too well that some predators preferred it if you screamed.

Footsteps. Hard and fast behind her. In her initial panic, Kimberly had sprinted toward the trees. Bad idea. Trees were dark, and far from help. She needed to cut back toward the Academy buildings, back toward lights, population, and the FBI police. The man was already gaining on her.

Kimberly took a deep breath. Her heart was pounding, her lungs screaming. Her body was too abused for this kind of business. Good news, adrenaline was a powerful drug.

She focused on the footsteps behind her, trying to separate their staccato beat from her heart's frantic hammering. He was gaining. Fast. Of course. He was bigger and stronger than her. At the end of the day, the men always were.

Fuck him.

She homed in on his rhythm, timed it with her own. One, two, three—

The man's hand snaked out for her left wrist. Kimberly suddenly planted her foot, pirouetted right. He overshot her completely. And she took off at warp nine for the lights.

"Jesus!" she heard the man swear.

It made her smile. Grim and fierce. Then the footsteps were behind her again.

Is this how her mother had felt? She had fought bitterly to the end. Her father had tried to protect Kimberly from the details, but a year later, on her own, Kimberly had looked up all the articles in the *Philadelphia Inquirer*. HIGH SOCIETY HOUSE OF HORRORS, the first banner headline had declared. Then it had gone on to describe the trail of blood that ran from room to room.

Had her mother known then that the man had already killed Mandy? Had she guessed that he would come after Kimberly next? Or had she simply realized, in those last desperate minutes, that beneath the silk and pearls she was an animal, too? And all animals, even the lowliest field mice, fight to live in the end.

The footsteps had closed in on her again. The lights were too far away. She wasn't going to make it. It amazed her how coolly she accepted this fact.

Time's up, Kimberly. No actors here. No paint guns, no bulletproof vests. She had one last ploy.

She counted his footsteps. Timed his approach. And then, in the next heartbeat, as he was upon her, his giant form swooping down on her own, she dropped to the ground and curled her arms protectively over her head.

She saw the man's face, faintly caught by the distant lights. His eyes went wide. He tried to draw up short, his arms flailing wildly. He made one last desperate move, careening left to spin around her.

Kimberly adroitly stuck out her leg. And he went flat on his face on the ground.

Ten seconds later, she flipped him over on his back, dropped down on his chest and placed the silver blade of her serrated hunting knife against his dark throat.

"Who the fuck are you?" she asked.

The man started to laugh.

"Betsy?" Tina called nervously. No answer. "Bets?"

Still nothing. And then it hit Tina, the second thing that was wrong. There were no other sounds. Shouldn't she be hearing car doors opening or closing? Or even Betsy heaving as she dragged the spare to the ground? Surely there should be some noise. Other cars. Crickets. The wind in the trees.

But there was nothing. Absolutely nothing. The night had gone completely, deathly still.

"This isn't funny anymore," Tina said weakly.

Then she heard a twig snap. And then she saw his face.

Pale, somber, maybe even gentle above the black collar of his turtleneck. How in the world could someone wear a turtleneck in this heat? Tina thought.

Then, he hefted up the rifle and leveled it against his shoulder.

Tina stopped thinking. She bolted for the trees.

"Stop laughing. Why are you laughing? Hey, stop!"

The man laughed harder, a steady ripple of spasms moving down his large frame and tossing her from side to side as easily as if she were a small boat caught in a rough wake. "Toppled by a woman," he gasped with an unmistakable Southern accent. "Oh, please, honey . . . don't tell my sister."

His sister? What the hell?

"All right. That's it. Move one more muscle and I will slit your throat." Kimberly must've sounded more impressive this time. The man finally stopped laughing. That was better. "Name?" she asked crisply.

"Special Agent Michael McCormack. But you can call me Mac."

Kimberly's eyes widened. She had a sudden bad feeling. "FBI?" she whispered. Oh no, she'd taken out a fellow agent. Probably her future boss. She wondered who would make the call to her father. *You know, Quincy old fellow, you were a star among stars here at the Bureau; but I'm afraid your daughter is just too, er, freaky for us.*

"Georgia Bureau of Investigation," the man drawled. "State police. We've always had a soft spot for the Bureau, though, so we stole your titles."

"You little—" She was so angry she couldn't think of a word. She whacked his shoulder with her left hand, then remembered, oh yeah, she had a knife. "You're with the National Academy," she accused him, in the same tone of voice others used for addressing vermin.

"And you're a new agent . . . obviously."

"Hey, I still have a knife at your throat, mister!"

"I know." He frowned at her, his easy tone throwing her for another loop. Was it her imagination, or had he just shifted to get more comfortable beneath her? "Why are you carrying a knife?"

"They took away my Glock," she said without thinking.

"Of course." He nodded as if she were a very wise person, instead of a highly paranoid aspiring federal agent. "If I might ask a personal question, ma'am. Umm, where do you hide the blade?"

"I beg your pardon!" She could definitely feel his gaze on her body now, and she immediately blushed. It was hot. She'd been working out . . . So the nylon shorts and thin blue T-shirt didn't cover much. She was training after hours, for God's sake, not preparing for an interview. Besides, it was amazing the things you could strap to the inside of your thigh.

"Why did you chase me?" she demanded, pressing the tip of her knife deeper against his throat.

"Why did you run?"

She scowled, pursed her lips, then tried another tack. "What are you doing out here?"

"Saw the light. Thought I'd better investigate."

"Ah ha! So I'm not the only one who's paranoid."

"That's true, ma'am. It would appear that we're both equally paranoid. I can't stand the heat. What's your story?"

"I don't have a story!"

"Fair enough. You're the one with the knife after all."

He fell silent and seemed to be waiting for her to do something. Which was an interesting point. What was she going to do now? New Agent Kimberly Quincy has just made her first apprehension. Unfortunately, he was a fellow law enforcement officer whose title was already bigger than hers.

Damn. Double damn. God, she was tired.

All at once, the last of the adrenaline left her, and her body, pushed too hard too fast, simply collapsed. She slid off the man's chest and let her aching limbs sprawl in the relative comfort of the thick green grass.

"Long day?" Southern Boy asked, making no effort to get up.

"Long life," Kimberly replied flatly, then promptly wished she hadn't.

Super Cop didn't say anything more, though. He tucked his hands beneath his head and appeared to be studying the sky. Kimberly followed his gaze and for the first time noticed the clear night sky, the sea of tiny, crystal stars. It was a beautiful night, really. Other girls her age probably went for walks during nights like this. Held hands with their boyfriends. Giggled when the guy tried to steal a kiss.

Kimberly couldn't even imagine that sort of life. All she'd ever wanted was this.

She turned her head toward her companion, who seemed content with the silence. Upon closer inspection, he was a big guy. Not as big as some of the ex-Marines in her class, but he was over six feet tall and obviously very active. Dark hair, bronzed skin, very fit. She'd done good to take him out. She was proud of herself.

"You scared the shit out of me," she said at last.

"That was uncalled-for," he agreed.

"You shouldn't skulk around at night."

"Damn straight."

"How long have you been in the program?"

"Arrived in June. You?"

"Week nine. Seven to go."

"You'll do fine," he said.

"How do you know?"

"You outran me, didn't you? And trust me, honey, most of the beautiful women I've chased haven't gotten away."

"You are so full of shit!" she told him crossly.

He just laughed again. The sound was deep and rumbly, like a jungle cat's purr. She decided she didn't like Special Agent McCormack very much. She should move, get away from him. Her body hurt too much. She went back to gazing at the stars.

"It's hot out," she said.

"Yes, ma'am."

"You said you didn't like the heat."

"Yes, ma'am." He waited a heartbeat, then turned his head. "Heat kills," he said, and it took her another moment to realize that he was finally serious.

Tree branches scratched at her face. Shrubs grabbed her ankles, while the tall grass tangled around her sandals and tried to pull her down. Tina pressed forward, panting hard, heart in her throat, as she careened from tree to tree and tried frantically to get one foot in front of the other.

He wasn't running behind her. She heard no stampede of footsteps or angry commands to halt. He was quieter than that. Stealthier. And that frightened her far more.

Where was she going? She didn't know. Why was he after her? She was too afraid to find out. What had happened to Betsy? The thought filled her with pain.

And the air was hot, searing her throat. And the air was wet, burning her lungs. And it was late, and she'd run away from the road, instinctively heading downhill, and now she realized her mistake. There would be no savior for her down in these deep dark shadows. There would be no safety.

Maybe if she could get far enough ahead. She was fit. She could find a tree, climb high above his head. She could find a ravine, duck low and curl up so small and tight he'd never see her. She could find a vine, and soar away like Tarzan in the animated Disney movie. She would like to be in a movie now. She would like to be anywhere but here.

The log came out of nowhere. A dead tree probably felled by lightning decades ago. She connected first with her shin, couldn't bite back her sharp cry of pain, and went toppling down the other side. Her palms scraped savagely across a thorny shrub. Then her shoulder hit the rock-hard ground and her breath was knocked from her body.

The faint crackle of twigs behind her. Calm. Controlled. Contained.

Is this how death comes? Slowly walking through the woods?

Tina's shin throbbed. Her lungs refused to inhale. She staggered to her feet anyway and tried one more step.

A faint whistle through the dark. A short stabbing pain. She looked down and spotted the feathery dart now protruding from her left thigh. What the . . .

She tried to take a step. Her mind commanded her body, screamed with primal urgency: *Run, run, run!* Her legs buckled. She went down in the knee-high grass as a strange, fluid warmth filled her veins and her muscles simply surrendered.

The panic was receding from her consciousness. Her heart slowed. Her lungs finally unlocked, giving easily into that next soft breath. Her body started to float, the woods spinning away.

Drugs, she thought. Doomed. And then even that thought wafted out of her reach.

Footsteps, coming closer. Her last image, his face, gazing down at her patiently.

"Please," Tina murmured thickly, her hands curling instinctively around her belly. "Please . . . Don't hurt me . . . I'm pregnant."

The man simply hefted her unconscious form over his shoulder and carried her away.

Nora Ray Watts had a dream. In her dream it was blue and pink and purple. In her dream the air felt like velvet and she could spin around and around and still see the bright pinpricks of stars. In her dream, she was laughing and her dog Mumphry danced around her feet and even her worn-out parents finally wore a smile.

The only thing missing, of course, was her sister.

Then a door opened. Yawned black and gaping. It beckoned her toward it, drew her in. Nora Ray walked toward it, unafraid. She had taken this door before. Sometimes she fell asleep these days just so she could find it again.

Nora Ray stepped inside the shadowy depths——

And in the next instant, she was jerked awake. Her mother stood over her in the darkened room, her hand on her shoulder.

"You were dreaming," her mother said.

"I saw Mary Lynn," Nora Ray countered sleepily. "I think she has a friend."

"Shhh," her mother told her. "Let her go, baby. It's only the heat."

6

"Get out of bed."

"No."

"Get out of bed!"

"No."

"Kimberly, it's seven o'clock. Get up!"

"Can't make me."

The voice finally disappeared. Thank God. Kimberly sank blissfully back down into the desperately needed blackness. Then . . . a bolt of ice-cold water slapped across her face. Kimberly jerked upright in the bed, gasping for breath as she frantically wiped the deluge from her eyes.

Lucy stood beside her, holding an empty water pitcher, and looking unrepentant. "I have a five-year-old son," she said. "Don't mess with me."

Kimberly's gaze had just fallen on the bedside clock. Seven-ten A.M.

"Aaaagh!" she yelped. She jumped out of bed and looked wildly around the room. She was supposed to be . . . supposed to do . . . Okay, get dressed. She bolted for the closet.

"Late night?" Lucy asked with a raised brow as she trailed behind Kimberly. "Let me guess. Physical training or firearms training or both?"

"Both." Kimberly found her khaki pants, tore them on, then remembered she was supposed to report to the PT course first thing this morning, and ripped off her khakis in favor of a fresh pair of blue nylon shorts.

"Nice bruises," Lucy commented. "Want to see the one on my ass? Seriously, I look like a side of beef. I used to be a trial lawyer, you know. I swear I once drove something called a Mercedes."

"I thought that's what drug dealers had." Kimberly found her T-shirt, yanked it on while walking into the bathroom, then made the mistake of looking in the mirror. Oh God. Her eyes looked like they'd collapsed into sunken pits.

"I spoke to my son last night," Lucy was saying behind her. "Kid's telling everyone I'm learning to shoot people—but only the bad ones."

"That's sweet."

"You think?"

"Absolutely." Kimberly found the toothpaste, brushed furiously, spit, rinsed, then made the mistake of looking in the mirror a second time, and fled the bathroom.

"You look like hell," Lucy said cheerfully. "Is that your strategy? You're going to scare the bad guys into surrendering with your looks?"

"Remember which one of us is better with a gun," Kimberly muttered.

"Yeah, and remember which one of us is better with a pitcher of water!" Lucy brandished her weapon triumphantly, then, with a final glance at the clock, replaced the pitcher on top of her desk and headed for the door. Then she paused. "Seriously, Kimberly, maybe you should curtail the midnight sessions for a bit. You have to be conscious to graduate."

"Have fun shooting," Kimberly called after her exiting roommate while frantically lacing her sneakers. Lucy was gone. And in another second, Kimberly was also out the door.

Kimberly was a lucky girl after all. She could pinpoint the exact moment when her whole career fell apart. It happened at eight twenty-three A.M. That morning. At the FBI Academy. With only seven weeks to go.

She was tired, disoriented from too little sleep and a strange midnight chase with a Georgia special agent. She'd been pushing herself too hard. Maybe she should've listened to Lucy after all.

She thought about it a lot. Later, of course. After they'd taken away the body.

Things started out fine enough. PT training wasn't so hard. Eight A.M., they did some pushups, then some sit-ups. Then the good old jumping jacks everyone learns in grade school. They looked like a sea of blue-clad kids. All obediently standing in line. All obediently going through the motions.

Then they were sent out to run three miles, using the same course Kimberly had jogged just last night.

The PT course started in the woods. Not a difficult path. Hell, it was paved. That would be one hint of where to go. The signs were another hint. Run! Suck it in! Love it! *Endure.*

They started as a herd, then gradually thinned out as people found their individual paces. Kimberly had never been the fastest in her class. She generally wasn't the slowest either.

Except this morning. This morning she almost immediately fell behind.

Vaguely, she was aware of her classmates pulling ahead. Vaguely, she was aware of her own labored breathing as she struggled to keep up. Her left side ached. Her feet were sluggish. She stared down at the blacktop, willing one foot to land in front of the other.

She didn't feel well. The world tilted dangerously, and she thought for a moment that she was honestly going to faint. She just made it off the path and grabbed a tree for support.

God, her side hurt, the muscle stitched so tight it felt as if it had a vise-grip on her lungs. And the damn air was so hot already, filled with so much humidity that no matter how many times she inhaled, she couldn't get enough oxygen.

She headed deeper into the woods, desperately seeking shade. Green trees whirled sickeningly, while goose bumps suddenly burst out across her arms.

She started shivering uncontrollably.

Dehydration or heat sickness, she thought idly. Is that good enough for you yet, Kimberly, or would you like to take this self-destructive streak a step further?

The woods spun faster. A faint roaring filled her ears while black dots spotted in front of her eyes. Breathe, Kimberly. Come on, honey, breathe.

She couldn't do it. Her side wouldn't unlock. She couldn't draw a breath. She was going to pass out in the woods. She was going to collapse onto this hard, leaf-strewn ground and all she wanted was for the dirt to feel cool against her face.

And then the thoughts rushed her all at once.

Last night, and the genuine terror that had seized her by the throat when she'd seen a strange man standing beside her. She had thought . . . What? That it was her turn? That death had come for every other woman in her family? That she'd barely escaped six years ago, but that didn't mean death was done with her yet?

She thought that she spent too much time with crime-scene photos, and though she would never tell anyone, sometimes she saw the pictures move. Her own face appeared on those lifeless bodies. Her own head topped shattered torsos and bloodied limbs.

And sometimes she had nightmares where she saw her own death, except she never woke up the moment before dying, the way sane people did. No, she dreamt it all the way through, feeling her body plummet over the cliff and smash into the rocks below. Feeling her head slam through the windshield of the shattered car.

And never once in her dreams did she scream. She only thought, *finally.*

She couldn't breathe. More black dots danced in front of her vision. She grabbed another tree limb, and hung on tight. How had the air gotten this hot? What had happened to all the oxygen?

And then, in the last sane corner of her mind, it came to her. She was having an anxiety attack. Her body had officially bottomed out, and now she was having an anxiety attack, her first in six years.

She staggered deeper into the woods. She needed to cool down. She needed to draw a breath. She had suffered this kind of episode before. She could survive it again.

She careened through the underbrush, unmindful of the small twigs scratching her cheeks or the tree limbs snatching at her hair. She searched desperately for cooler shade.

Breathe deep, count to ten. Focus on your hands, and making them steady. You're tough. You're strong. You're well trained.

Breathe, Kimberly. Come on, honey, just breathe.

She staggered into a clearing, stuck her head between her knees and worked on sucking air, until with a final, heaving gasp, her lungs opened up and the air whooshed gratefully into her chest. Inhale. Exhale. That's it, breathe . . .

Kimberly looked down at her hands. They were quieter now, pressed against the hollow plane of her stomach. She forced them away from her body, and inspected her splayed fingers for signs of trembling.

Better. Soon she would be cool again. Then she would resume jogging. And then, because she was very good at this by now, no one would ever know a thing.

Kimberly straightened up. She took one last deep breath, then turned back in the direction of the PT course . . . and realized for the first time that she was not alone.

Five feet in front of her was a well-worn dirt path. Wide and very smooth, probably used by the Marines for their training. And right smack in the middle of that path sprawled the body of a young girl in civilian clothes. Blond hair, black sandals, and splayed tanned limbs. She wore a simple white cotton shirt and a very short, blue-flowered skirt.

Kimberly took one step forward. Then she saw the girl's face, and then she knew.

The goose bumps rippled down her arms again. A shiver snaked up her spine. And in the middle of the hot, still woods, Kimberly began to frantically look around, even as her hand flew to the inside of her leg and found her knife.

First rule of procedure, always secure the crime scene.

Second rule, call for backup.

Third rule, try hard not to think of what it means when young women aren't safe even at the Academy. For this girl was quite dead, and by all appearances, it had happened recently.

7

"One more time, Kimberly. How did you end up off the PT course?"

"I got a stitch in my side, I went off the course. I was trying to walk it out, and . . . I don't think I realized how far I had wandered."

"And you saw the body?"

"I saw something up ahead," Kimberly said without blinking. "I headed toward it, and then . . . Well, you know the rest."

Her class supervisor, Mark Watson, scowled at her, but finally leaned back. She was sitting across from him in his bright, expansive office. Mid-morning sun poured through the bank of windows. An orange monarch butterfly fluttered just outside the glass. It was such a beautiful day to be talking about death.

At Kimberly's cry, two of her classmates had come running. She'd leaned forward and taken the girl's pulse by then. Nothing, of course, but then Kimberly hadn't expected any signs of life. And it wasn't just the girl's wide, sightless brown eyes that spoke of death. It was her violently stitched-up mouth, some kind of thick black thread sealing her waxy lips in macabre imitation of Raggedy Ann. Whoever had done this had made damn well sure the girl had never screamed.

The second classmate promptly threw up. But not Kimberly.

Someone had fetched Watson. Upon seeing her grisly find, he had immediately contacted the FBI police as well as the Naval Criminal Investigative Service. Apparently, a death at the Academy's front door did not belong to the FBI, but rather to NCIS. It was their job to protect and serve the Marines, after all.

Kimberly and her classmates had been hastily led away, while young Marines in dark green camouflage and more sophisticated special agents in white dress shirts descended upon the scene. Now, somewhere in the deep woods, real work was being done—death investigators photographing, sketching, and analyzing; an ME examining a young girl's body for last desperate clues; other officers bagging and tagging evidence.

While Kimberly sat here. In an office. As far away from the discovery as a well-meaning FBI supervisor could bring her. One of her knees jogged nervously. She finally crossed her ankles beneath the chair.

"What will happen next?" she asked quietly.

"I don't know." Her supervisor paused. "I'll be honest, Kimberly, we've never had this kind of situation before."

"Well, that's a good thing," she murmured.

Watson smiled, but it was thin. "We had a tragedy a few years ago. A National Academy student dropped dead on the firearms course. He was relatively young, which led to speculation. The ME determined, however, that he had died of a sudden massive coronary. Still tragic, but not so shocking given the sheer numbers of people who pass through these grounds in any given year. This situation, on the other hand . . . A facility of this kind relies heavily on good relations with the neighboring communities. When word gets out that a local girl has been found dead . . ."

"How do you know she's local?"

"Playing the law of averages. She appears too young to be an employee, and if she were either FBI or Marine, someone at the scene would've recognized her. Ergo, she's an outsider."

"She could be someone's sweetheart," Kimberly ventured. "The mouth . . . Maybe she talked back one too many times."

"It's possible." Watson was eyeing her speculatively, so Kimberly pressed ahead.

"But you don't think so," she said.

"Why don't I think so?"

"No violence. If it were a domestic situation, a crime of passion, she would show signs of battery. Bruises, cuts, abrasion. Instead . . . I saw her arms and legs. There was hardly a scratch on her. Except for the mouth, of course."

"Maybe he only hit her where no one would see."

"Maybe," her tone was doubtful. "It still doesn't explain why he would dump the body on a secured Marine base."

"Why do you think the body was dumped?" Watson asked with a frown.

"Lack of disturbance at the scene," Kimberly answered immediately. "Ground wasn't even stirred up until I crashed in." Her brow furrowed; she looked at him quizzically. "Do you think she was alive when he brought her onto the grounds? It's not that easy to access the base. Last I saw, the Marines were operating at condition Bravo, meaning all entrances are guarded and all visitors must have proper ID. Dead or alive, not just anyone can access Academy grounds."

"I don't think we should—"

"That doesn't make sense, either, though," Kimberly persisted, her frown deepening. "If the girl's alive, then she would have to have clearance, too, and two security passes are harder to find than one. So maybe she was dead. In the trunk of the car. I've never seen the guards search a vehicle, so she wouldn't be too hard to sneak in that way. Of course, that theory implies that the man knowingly dumped a body *on* Quantico grounds." She shook her head abruptly. "That doesn't make sense. If you lived here and you killed someone, even accidentally, you wouldn't take the remains into the woods. You'd hightail it off the base, and get the evidence as far away from here as possible. Leaving the body here is just plain stupid."

"I don't think we should make any assumptions at this time," Watson said quietly.

"Do you think he's trying to make a personal statement against the Academy?" Kimberly asked. "Or against the Marines?"

At that comment, Watson's brows fired to life. Kimberly had definitely crossed some unspoken line, and his expression firmly indicated that their conversation was now over. He sat forward and said, "Listen, the NCIS will be handling the investigation from here on out. Do you know anything about the Naval Criminal Investigative Service?"

"No—"

"Well, you should. The NCIS has over eight hundred special agents, ready to be deployed anywhere around the globe at a moment's notice. They've seen murder, rape, domestic abuse, fraud, drugs, racketeering, terrorism, you name it. They have their own cold case squad, they have their own forensics experts, they even have their own crime labs. For heaven's sake, these are the agents who were called upon to investigate the bombing of the U.S.S. *Cole*. They can certainly handle one body found in the woods at a Marine base. Is that understood?"

"I didn't mean to imply—"

"You're a rookie, Kimberly. Not a special agent, but a new agent. Don't forget that difference."

"Yes, sir," she said stiffly, chin up, eyes blazing at the unexpected reprimand.

Her supervisor's voice finally softened. "Of course NCIS will have some questions for you," he allowed. "Of course you will answer to the best of your ability. Cooperation with fellow law enforcement agencies is very important. But then you're done, Kimberly. Out of the picture. Back to class. And—this should go without saying—as quiet as a church mouse."

"Don't ask, don't tell?" she asked dryly.

Watson didn't crack a smile. "There are many times in an FBI agent's career when she must be the soul of discretion. Agents who can't be prudent don't belong on the job."

Kimberly's expression finally faltered. She stared down at the carpet. Watson's tone was so stern, it seemed to border almost on threatening. She had found the body accidentally. And yet . . . He was treating her almost as if she were a troublemaker. As if she'd personally brought this upon the Academy. The safe course would be to do exactly as he said. To get up, seal her lips, and walk away.

She'd never been good at playing it safe.

She lifted her gaze and looked her supervisor in the eye. "Sir, I'd like to approach NCIS about assisting with the investigation."

"Did you just hear anything I said?"

"I have some experience in these matters—"

"You know *nothing* about these matters! Don't confuse personal with professional—"

"Why not? Violent death is violent death. I helped my father after my mother's body was found. I'm now seven weeks from becoming a full-fledged FBI agent. What would it hurt to jump the gun a little? After all, I found her." Her tone was possessive. She hadn't meant to sound that way, realized it was a misstep, but it was too late to call it back now.

Watson's face had darkened dangerously. If she thought he'd appeared stern before, he was downright intimidating now. "Kimberly . . . Let's be frank. How do you think you're doing as a new agent?"

"Hanging in there."

"Do you think that's the best goal for a new agent?"

"Some days."

He smiled grimly, then steepled his hands in front of his chin. "Some of your instructors are worried about you, Kimberly. You have an impeccable resume, of course. You consistently score ninety percent or higher on your exams. You seem to have some skills with firearms."

"But?" she gritted out.

"But you also have an attitude. Nine weeks here, Kimberly, and by all accounts you have no close friends, allies, or associates. You offer nothing to your classmates. You take nothing from them. You're an island. Law enforcement is ultimately a human system. With no connections, no friends, no support, how far do you think you're going to get? How effective do you think you can be?"

"I'll work on that," she said. Her heart was beating hard.

"Kimberly," he said, gently now, and she winced further. Anger could be deflected. Gentleness was to be feared. "You know, you're very young."

"Growing up all the time," she babbled.

"Maybe now is not the right time for you to join the Bureau—"

"No time like the present."

"I think if you gave yourself a few more years, more space between now and what happened to your family . . ."

"You mean forget about my mother and sister?"

"I'm not saying that."

"Pretend I'm just another accountant, looking for a little more excitement in my life?"

"Kimberly—"

"I found a corpse! Is that what this is about? I found a blight on the Academy's front porch and now you're kicking me out!"

"*Stop it!*" His tone was stern. It finally shocked Kimberly into silence and in the next instant she realized everything she had just said. Her cheeks flamed red. She quickly looked away.

"I would like to go back to class now," Kimberly murmured. "I promise not to say anything. I appreciate the task NCIS has before it, and I wouldn't want to do anything to compromise an ongoing investigation."

"Kimberly . . ." Her supervisor's tone was still frustrated. It appeared he might say something more, then he just shook his head. "You look like hell. You obviously haven't slept in weeks, you've lost weight. Why don't you go to your room and get some rest? Take this opportunity to recuperate. There's no shame in slowing down a little, you know. You're already one of the youngest applicants we've had. What you don't accomplish now, you can always accomplish later."

Kimberly didn't reply. She was too busy biting back a bitter smile. She had heard those words before. Also from an older man, a mentor, someone she had considered a friend. Two days later, he'd put a gun to her head.

Please don't let me tear up now. She would not cry.

"We'll talk again in a few days," Watson said in the ensuing silence. "Dismissed."

Kimberly headed out of his office. She walked down the hall, passing three groups of blue-clad students and already hearing the whispers beginning again. Were they talking about her mother and sister? Were they talking about her legendary father? Or maybe they were talking about today, and the new body she of all people had managed to find?

Her eyes stung more fiercely. She pressed the heels of her hands against her temples. She would not give in to pity now.

Kimberly marched to the front doors. She burst back into the blistering hot sun. Sweat immediately beaded across her brow. She could feel her T-shirt glue itself stickily to her skin.

But she did not return to her room. NCIS would want to talk to her. First, however, they would want to finish up at the scene. That gave her a solid hour before anyone would come looking for her.

An hour was enough.

Kimberly made a beeline for the woods.

8

Quantico, Virginia
11:33 A.M.
Temperature: 89 degrees

"Time of death?"

"Hard to tell. Body temperature reads nearly ninety-five, but the current outside temp of eighty-nine would impede cooling. Rigor mortis appears to be just starting in face and neck." The white-clad ME paused, rolled the body slightly to the left and pressed a gloved finger against the red-splotched skin, which blanched at his touch. "Lividity's not yet fixed." He straightened back up, thought of something else, and checked the girl's eyes and ears. "No blowfly larvae yet, which would happen fast in this heat. Of course, the flies prefer to start in the mouth or an open wound, so they had less opportunity here . . ." He seemed to consider the various factors one last time, then delivered his verdict. "I'm going to say four to six hours."

The other man, probably an NCIS special agent, looked up from his notes in surprise. "That fresh?"

"That's my best guess. Hard to know more until we cut her open."

"Which will be?"

"Tomorrow morning."

The special agent stared at the ME.

"Six A.M.?" the ME tried again.

The special agent stared harder.

"This afternoon," the ME amended.

The special agent finally cracked a smile. The ME sighed heavily. It was going to be one of *those* cases.

The investigating officer returned to his notes. "Probable COD?"

"That's a little trickier. No obvious knife or gunshot wounds. No petechial hemorrhages, which rules out strangulation. No bleeding in the ears, which eliminates some brain traumas. We do have a large bruise just beginning to form on the left hip. Probably occurred shortly before death." The ME lifted up the girl's blue-flowered skirt, eyed the contusion again, then shook his head. "I'm going to have to do some blood work. We'll know more then."

The investigating officer nodded. A second man, also clad in khakis and a white dress shirt, moved in to snap more shots with a digital camera, while several grim-faced Marines stood guard along the yellow-ribbon-draped scene. Even in the deep shade of the woods, the heat and humidity were impossible to escape. Both NCIS special agents had sweated through their long-sleeved shirts, while the young sentries stood with moisture rolling down their chiseled faces.

Now the second special agent, a younger man with the requisite buzz-cut hair and squared-off jaw, looked down the heavily wooded path. "I don't see drag marks," he commented.

The ME nodded and moved to the victim's black sandals. He picked up her foot and studied the heel of her shoe. "No dirt or debris here. She must've been carried in."

"Strong man," the photographer said.

The first special agent gave them both a look. "We are on a Marine base cooccupied by FBI trainees; they're all strong men." He nodded back toward the victim. "What's with the mouth?"

The ME put his hand on her cheeks, turned her head from side to side. Then suddenly, he flinched and snatched his hand away.

"What?" the older agent asked.

"I don't . . . Nothing."

"Nothing? What kind of nothing?"

"Trick of the light," the ME muttered, but he didn't put his hand back on the girl's face. "Looks like sewing thread," he said curtly. "Thick, maybe like what's used for upholstery. It's certainly not medical. The stitching is too rudimentary to be a professional's. Just small flecks of blood, so the mutilation probably occurred postmortem."

There was a green leaf caught in the girl's tangled blond hair. The ME distractedly pulled it free and let it flutter away. He moved on to her hands, flung above her head. One was curled closed. Gently, he unrolled her fingers. Inside her grip, nestled against her palm, was a jagged green-gray rock.

"Hey," he called to the younger special agent. "Want to get a picture of this?"

The kid obediently came over and snapped away. "What is it?"

"I don't know. A rock of some kind. Going to bag and tag?"

"Right." The kid fetched an evidence container. He dropped the rock in and dutifully filled out the top form.

"No obvious defensive wounds. Oh, here we go." The ME's gloved thumb moved up her left arm to a red, swollen patch high on her shoulder. "Injection mark. Just the faintest bruising, so it probably occurred right before death."

"Overdose?" the older agent asked with a frown.

"Of some kind. An intramuscular injection isn't very common for drugs; they're generally administered intravenously." The ME lifted the girl's skirt again. He inspected the inside of her thighs, then moved down to between her toes. Finally, he inspected the webbing between her index finger and thumb. "No track marks. Whatever happened, she's not a habitual user."

"Wrong place at the wrong time?"

"Possibly."

Older Special Agent sighed. "We're going to need an ID right away. Can you print her here?"

"I'd prefer to wait until the morgue, when we can test her hands for blood and skin samples. If you're in a real hurry, though, you can always check her purse."

"What?"

The ME smiled broadly, then took pity on the Naval cop. "Over there, on the rock *outside* the crime-scene tape. The black leather backpack thingy. My daughter has one just like it. It's very hip."

"Of all the stupid, miserable, incompetent . . ." Older Special Agent wasn't very happy. He got the kid to photograph the purse, then had two sentries expand the crime-scene perimeter to *include* the leather bag. Finally, with gloved hands, he retrieved the item. "Note that we need to take full inventory," he instructed his assistant. "For now, however, we'll detail the wallet."

The kid set down the camera and immediately took up paper and pencil.

"Okay, here we go. Wallet, also black leather . . . Let's see, it contains a grocery store card, a Petco card, a Blockbuster card, another grocery store card, and . . . no driver's license. There's thirty-three dollars in here, but no driver's license, no credit cards, and for that matter, no kind of any card bearing a person's name. What does that tell us?"

"He doesn't want us to know her ID," the kid said eagerly.

"Yeah." Older Special Agent was frowning. "How about that? You know what? We're missing something else. Keys." He shook the bag, but there was no telltale jingle. "What kind of person doesn't have keys?"

"Maybe he's a thief? He's got her address from the license, plus the house keys . . . It's not like she's going to come home anytime soon."

"Possibly." But the Naval officer was looking at the stitched-up mouth and frowning. From her vantage point behind a tree, Kimberly could read his thoughts: What kind of thief stitched up a woman's mouth? For that matter, what kind of thief dumped a body in the middle of a Marine base?

"I need to fetch paper bags for the hands," the ME reported. "They're back in my van."

"We'll walk with you. I want to review a few more things." The older Naval officer jerked his head toward his counterpart, and the younger man immediately fell into step. They headed off down the dirt path, leaving the sprawling corpse alone with the four sentries.

Kimberly was just considering how to make a stealthy exit herself, when a strong hand snapped around her wrist. In the next instant, a second hand smothered her mouth. She didn't bother with screaming; she bit him instead.

"Damn," a deep voice rumbled in her ear. "Do you ever talk first and shoot later? I keep running into you, I'm not gonna have any hide left."

Kimberly recognized the voice. She relaxed against his large body, but grudgingly. In return, he removed both hands.

"What are you doing here?" she whispered, casting a furtive glance at the crime-scene attendants. She turned to face Special Agent McCormack and he frowned.

"What happened to you?" He held up a silencing hand. "Wait, I don't want to see the other guy."

Kimberly touched her face. For the first time she felt the zigzag welts creasing her nose and cheeks with flecks of dried blood. Her scramble through the woods had taken its toll after all. No wonder her supervisor had tried to send her to her room.

"What are you doing here?" she asked again, voice low.

"Heard a rumor. Decided to follow it up." His gaze briefly skimmed down her body. "I heard a young new agent made the find. I take it you had the honors? Little ways off the PT course, don't you think?"

Kimberly simply glared at him. He shrugged and returned their attention to the crime scene.

"I want that leaf," his voice rumbled in her ear. "You see the one the ME pulled out of the victim's hair—"

"Not proper protocol."

"You tell him, honey. I want that leaf. And as long as you're here, you might as well help me get it."

She jerked away from him. "I will not—"

"Just distract the sentries. Strike up a conversation, bat those baby blues and in sixty seconds, I'll be in and out."

Kimberly frowned at him. "You distract the guards, I'll grab the leaf," she said.

He looked at her as if she were slightly slow. "Honey," he drawled. "You're a *girl*."

"So I can't grab a leaf?" Her voice rose unconsciously.

He covered her mouth with his palm again. "No, but you surely have a bit more natural *appeal* to young men than I do." He glanced down the wooded path at the direction the ME and two Naval investigators had gone. "Come on, sugar. We don't have the rest of our lives."

He's an idiot, she thought. Sexist, too. But she nodded anyway. The ME had been grossly negligent to pull the leaf out of the girl's hair, and it would be best if someone retrieved it.

Mac motioned to the left pair of guards and how he wanted her to draw them to the front. Then he'd go in from the back.

Thirty seconds later, taking a deep breath, Kimberly made a big production of walking from the woods right onto the dirt path. She made a sharp left and walked straight up to the pair of sentries.

"I just need to see the body for a moment," she said breezily.

"This area is restricted, ma'am." The first sentry spoke in clipped tones, his gaze fixed somewhere past her left ear.

"Oh, I'm sure it is." Kimberly waved her hand negligently and stepped forward.

The young sentry made a discreet move left and without seeming to exert any real effort, blocked her path.

"Excuse me," Kimberly said firmly. "But I don't think you understand. I have clearance. I'm part of the case. For heaven's sake, I was the first officer at the scene."

The Marine frowned at her, unimpressed. The other pair of Marines had moved closer, obviously prepared to offer backup. Kimberly flashed them a sickeningly sweet smile. And watched as Special Agent McCormack eased into the clearing behind them.

"Ma'am, I must ask you to depart," the first sentry said.

"Where's the crime-scene log?" Kimberly asked. "Just get the log and I'll show you where I'm signed in."

For the first time, the Marine hesitated. Kimberly's instincts had been right. These guys were just foot soldiers. They knew nothing about investigative procedure, or law enforcement jurisdiction.

"Seriously," she pressed, taking another step closer and getting everyone antsy now. "I'm New Agent Kimberly Quincy. At approximately oh-eight twenty-two hundred I found the victim and secured the scene for NCIS. Of course I want to follow up with this case."

Mac was halfway to the body now, moving with surprising stealth for a big guy.

"Ma'am, this area belongs to the Marines. It is restricted to the Marines. Unless you are accompanied by the appropriate officer, you may not enter this area."

"Who's the appropriate officer?"

"Ma'am—"

"Sir, I found that girl this morning. While I appreciate that you're doing your job, I'm not leaving a poor young girl like that to a bunch of camo-clad men. She needs one of her own around. Simple as that."

The Marine glared at her. She'd definitely crossed some line in his mind over to wacky. He sighed and seemed to be struggling to find his patience.

Mac was now at the area where they had both seen the leaf flutter to the ground. He was on his hands and knees, moving carefully. For the first time, Kimberly realized their problem. There were many dried-up leaves on the ground. Red, yellow, brown. What color had been in the girl's hair? Oh God, she already didn't remember.

The backup sentries had edged closer. They had their hands on the stocks of their rifles. Kimberly brought up her chin and dared them to shoot her.

"You need to leave," the first sentry repeated.

"No."

"Ma'am, you depart on your own or we will forcefully assist you."

Mac had a leaf now. He held it up, seemed to be frowning at it. Was he also wondering what color it should be? Could he remember?

"Lay a hand on me and I will sue you for sexual harassment."

The Marine blinked. Kimberly blinked, too. Really, as threats went, that was a pretty good one. Even Mac had turned toward her and appeared sincerely impressed. The leaf in his hand was green. All at once, she relaxed. That made sense. The leaves already at the scene were old, from last fall. A green leaf, on the other hand, had probably been brought in with the body. He had done it. *They* had done it.

The backup sentries were now right behind the first pair. All four sets of male gazes stared at her.

"You need to leave," the first Marine said again, but he no longer sounded as forceful.

"I'm just trying to do right by her," Kimberly said quietly.

That seemed to disarm him further. His stare broke. He glanced down at the dirt path. And Kimberly found herself still talking.

"I had a sister, you see. Not that much older than this girl here. One night, a guy got her drunk, tampered with her seat belt, and drove her straight into a telephone pole. Then he ran away, leaving her there all alone, her skull crushed against the windshield. She didn't die right away, though. She lived for a while. I've always wondered . . . Did she feel the blood trickling down her face? Did she know how alone she was? The medics would never tell me, but I wonder if she cried, if she understood what was happening to her. That's gotta be the worst thing in the world. To know that you're dying, and nobody is coming to save you. Of course, you don't have to worry about such things. You're a Marine. Someone will always come for you. We can't say the same, however, for the women of the world. I sure couldn't say the same for my sister."

Now all the Marines were looking down. That was okay. Kimberly's voice had gotten huskier than she intended. She was afraid of the expression that must be on her face.

"You're right," she said abruptly. "I should go. I'll come back later, when an investigating officer is here."

"That would be best, ma'am," the Marine said. He still would not look her in the eye.

"Thank you for your help." She hesitated, then just couldn't help herself. "Please take care of her for me."

Then Kimberly turned quickly, and before she did anything even more stupid, disappeared back down the path.

Two minutes later, she felt Mac's hand upon her arm. She took one look at his somber expression and knew he'd heard everything.

"Did you get the leaf?" she asked.

"Yes, ma'am."

"Now would you like to tell me why you're really here?"

And Mac said, "Because all these years later, I've been waiting for him."

9

"It started in nineteen ninety-eight. June fourth. Two college roommates went out to a tavern in Atlanta and never came home. Three days later, the first girl's body was found near Interstate seventy-five just south of the city. Four months later, the second girl's remains were found a hundred miles away in Tallulah Gorge State Park. Both girls were found fully clothed and with their purses; no signs of robbery or sexual assault."

Kimberly frowned. "That's different."

Mac nodded at her. They were in a corner of the Crossroads Lounge, huddled over a small table, heads together and voices low. "Next year, nineteen ninety-nine. First heat wave of the year doesn't hit until July. Two high school girls in Macon, Georgia, sneak into a local bar on July tenth. Never seen alive again. First girl's body is found two days later, this time next to U.S. four forty-one, which happens to be near the Tallulah Gorge State Park. Second girl is found . . ."

"Inside the gorge?" Kimberly tried gamely.

"Nope. Burke County cotton field. One hundred and fifty miles away from the gorge. It's the gorge that we searched, however, so nobody discovered her body until the cotton harvest in November."

"Wait a minute." Kimberly held up a hand. "It takes all the way until November to find a girl's body in a field?"

"You've never been to Burke County. We're talking eight hundred square miles of cotton. The kind of place where you can drive all day without ever hitting a paved road. There ain't *nothing* out in Burke County."

"Except a dead body." Kimberly leaned forward intently. "Both girls fully clothed again? No sign of sexual assault?"

"The best we can tell," Mac said. "It's difficult with the second girl of each pair, given the condition of their bodies. But for the most part, yes, all four girls are found wearing their party clothes and looking relatively . . . peaceful."

"Cause of death?"

"It varies. For the girls left next to roadways, an overdose of benzodiazepine, the prescription drug Ativan. He injects the lethal dose into their left shoulders."

"And the second girls?"

"We don't know. It looks like a fall may have been what killed Deanna Wilson. For Kasey Cooper, exposure, maybe, or dehydration."

"They were abandoned alive?"

"It's a theory."

She wasn't sure she liked how he said that. "You said you found their purses. What about ID?"

Mac's turn to frown. He was obviously thinking of the girl they'd found that day, and the lack of ID in her wallet. "They did have their driver's licenses," he admitted. "IDing the bodies was never an issue. No keys, though. For that matter, no cars. We've never recovered a single vehicle."

"Really?" Kimberly's scowl deepened. She was fascinated in spite of herself. "Okay, continue."

"Two thousand," Mac said crisply, then promptly rolled his eyes. "Bad year, two thousand. Brutally hot summer, no rain. May twenty-ninth, we're already in the mid-nineties. Two students from Augusta State University head to Savannah for a girls' weekend. They never come home. Tuesday morning, a motorist finds the first girl's body next to U.S. twenty-five in Waynesboro. Can you guess where Waynesboro is?"

Kimberly thought about it a minute. "The cotton field place. Burke County?"

He smiled, a flash of white against his dark skin. "You catch on quick. That's one of the rules of the game, you see: the first body of the new pair is always left near the second girl of the last pair. Maybe he likes the continuity, or maybe he's giving us a fighting chance at finding the second body in case we missed it the previous year." He paused for a second and eyed her appraisingly. "So for this new pair, where's the second girl?"

"Not in Burke County?"

"You're cheatin'."

"Well, he hasn't repeated an area. So you can assume not the gorge and not a cotton field. Process of elimination."

"Georgia has nearly sixty thousand square miles of mountains, forests, coastline, swamplands, peach orchards, tobacco fields, and cities. You're gonna need to eliminate more than that."

Kimberly acknowledged the point with a slight shrug. Unconsciously she worried her lower lip. "Well, you said it was a game. Does he leave you clues?"

His answering smile was dazzling. "Yes, ma'am. Second rule of the game—for it to be competitive, you gotta leave clues. Let's go back to the very first girl, found outside of Atlanta. Girl's laid out next to a major interstate, remember? We have no signs of violence, no sexual assault, so that means no blood, no semen, none of the normal trace evidence you might expect to collect in a homicide case. But here's something interesting. The body's clean. Very clean. Almost as if someone has washed the victim's legs, arms, and shoes. We not only lack hair and fiber, we can't even find traces of spilled beer on her shoes or a stray peanut in her hair. It's like the girl's been . . . sanitized."

"All of her?" Kimberly asked sharply. "Then you can no longer be sure of lack of sexual assault."

Mac shook his head. "Not all of her. Just the parts . . . exposed. Hair, face, limbs. My best guess? He wipes them down with a sponge. It's like . . . he's wiping a slate clean. And then he starts his work."

"Oh my God," Kimberly breathed. She was no longer sure she wanted to know what had happened next.

"They're a map," Mac said quietly. "That's why the first girl exists. That's why she's left next to a major road and easily found. Maybe why she gets a quick and relatively painless death. Because she doesn't matter to him. She's just a tool, a guide to where the real game is being played out."

Kimberly was leaning forward again. Her heart had started pounding, neurons firing to life in her brain. She could feel where this was headed now. Almost see the dark, twisted road open up before her. "What are the clues?"

"From the first girl, we found a feather in her hair, a crushed flower beneath her body, traces of rock on her shoe, and a business card in her purse. The crime lab followed protocol and took samples of everything. And then . . . nothin'."

"Nothing?"

"Nothin'. You ever been to a real crime lab, Kimberly? And by that, I don't mean the FBI lab. The Feds have money, no doubt about it. I mean what the rest of us working stiffs get to use."

Kimberly shook her head.

"We have equipment. Lots of equipment. But unless it's fingerprints or DNA—God's honest truth—it's as worthless as an unmatched sock. We don't have databases. So sure, we collect soil samples, but it's not like we can scan them into some giant computer and have a matching location magically blip across the screen the way they do in some of those crime shows. Frankly, we operate on tight budgets and tight budgets mean forensics is mostly reactionary. You take samples and someday, if you have a suspect, then you have a reference sample to work with. You take your dirt from the crime scene and hope it matches dirt from the bad guy's yard. That's as good as it gets.

"In other words, we collected the rock sample, the feather, the flower and we knew they were worthless to us. So we sent them out to real experts who might be able to make something of them. And then we waited nine months."

Kimberly closed her eyes. "Oh no," she said.

"Nobody knew," he said quietly. "You have to understand, nobody ever expected the likes of this man."

"He abandoned the second girl in the gorge, didn't he?"

"With a gallon jug of water. Wearing high heels. In nearly a hundred-degree heat."

"But if you had interpreted the clues in time . . ."

"You mean, if we'd identified the white flower as persistent trillium, a rare herb found growing only in a five-point-three-square-mile area in all of Georgia—an area inside the Tallulah Gorge? Or if we'd realized the feather belonged to the peregrine falcon, which also makes its home in the gorge? Or if we'd understood that the granite in the rocks found ground into her shoes matched samples taken from the cliffs, or that the business card found in her purse belonged to a customer service representative from Georgia Power, the company that just so happens to own and manage the gorge? Sure, if we'd known that stuff, then maybe we could've found her. But most of those reports didn't come in for months, and poor Deanna Wilson was dead and buried by then."

Kimberly hung her head. She was thinking of a poor young girl lost and bewildered in the middle of a hostile forest. Trying to hike her way out over uneven terrain in party heels and a little black dress. The burning, scorching heat. She wondered if the girl had drunk the water quickly, convinced someone would find her soon. Or if she had rationed it from the start, already fearing the worst.

"And the second pair of girls?" she asked quietly.

Mac shrugged. His eyes were dark and somber. "We still didn't know any better. The minute the first body appeared outside of the gorge, that's the connection everyone made. We have someone who kidnaps girls and likes to hide 'em in the gorge. Given the extreme heat, the Rabun County Sheriff's Office did the logical thing and threw all resources at searching the state park. It took another week to realize she wasn't there, and even then, it was hard to be sure."

"What were the clues?"

"Josie Anders had white lint on her red top, dried mud on her shoes, four kernels in her purse, and a phone number scribbled on a cocktail napkin wadded up in her front pocket."

"The lint and kernels have something to do with cotton?" Kimberly guessed.

"Upon further examination, the lint proved to be linters, made from raw cottonseed. The kernels were cotton kernels. The mud turned out to be high in organic matter. And the phone number belonged to Lyle Burke, a sixty-five-year-old retired electrician, living in Savannah, who'd never heard of the two girls, let alone Roxie's Bar, which was where they were last seen alive."

"Burke County," Kimberly said.

Mac nodded. "Cotton's not a fair clue in a state like Georgia. There's only ninety-seven counties that grow the stuff. But by throwing in the phone number . . . I think in his own way, the man considered it sporting. Now we had only eight hundred square miles to search. If we'd been paying attention—" He shrugged, his hand knotting and unknotting in a frustrated motion.

"When did you start putting it together?" Kimberly asked.

"Two months after Kasey Cooper was found in the cotton field. The last of the evidence reports came in, and we made the connections after the fact. Gee, we've had four girls disappear in pairs. In both instances, one girl is found right away, next to a major road. And in both instances, the second girl isn't found for a long time, and when she is found, it's in a remote and dangerous area. The first girls, however, have evidence that ties them to the second location. Gee, maybe if we figure out those clues sooner, we can find the second girls in time. Good golly, Miss Molly, that might make some sense." Mac blew out a breath of air. He sounded disgusted, but then he got on with it.

"We assembled a task force. Not that the public knew. We worked behind the scenes at that point, identifying some of the best experts on Georgia— biologists, botanists, geologists, entomologists, etc., and getting them thinking about this guy and where he might strike next. The goal was to be proactive. Failing that, at least we'd already have the experts in place to give us real-time answers should the man strike again."

"What happened?" Kimberly asked.

"The year two thousand," he said bluntly. "The year we'd thought we'd gotten smart. Instead, everything went to hell in a hand basket. Two more kidnappings, three girls dead." Mac glanced at his watch. He shook away the rest of what he was going to say, and startled them both by taking her hand instead. "But that was then. This is now. If this is the Eco-Killer, Kimberly, we don't have much time. The clock is ticking. Now here is what I need you to do next."

10

Special Agent Mac McCormack was going to get her kicked out of the FBI Academy. Kimberly thought about it dispassionately as she drove through Quantico's winding roads on her way to the main highway. She'd showered after talking to Mac. She'd changed into the appropriate uniform of khaki cargo pants and a navy blue FBI Academy shirt. Then she'd tucked her good ol' Crayola gun into a holster on the waistband of her pants and attached handcuffs to her belt. As long as she was going to trade in on the cachet of being a new agent, she might as well look the part.

She could've told Mac no. She thought about that, too, as she drove. She didn't really know the man. Good looks and compelling blue eyes aside, he had no claim on her. She wasn't even sure she believed his story yet. Oh sure, this Eco-Killer guy had probably ravaged the state of Georgia. But that was three years ago. In a state hundreds of miles away. Why would some Georgian nut suddenly turn up in Virginia? Better yet, why would a Georgian nut leave a dead body on the FBI's doorstep?

It didn't make sense to her. Mac saw what he needed to see. He wasn't the first cop to be obsessed by a case and he wouldn't be the last.

None of which explained why Kimberly had just blown off her afternoon classes, a violation that could get her written up. Or why she was now driving to a county ME's office, after her supervisor had explicitly told her to stay away from the case. That little act of insubordination could get her kicked out.

And yet from the minute Mac had made his request, she'd agreed. She wanted to speak to the ME. She wanted to con her way into the autopsy of a poor young girl she'd never met.

She wanted . . . She wanted to know what happened. She wanted to know the girl's name and the dreams she'd once had. She wanted to know if she'd suffered, or if it'd been quick. She wanted to know what mistakes the unidentified subject might have made, so she could use those mistakes to track him down and find justice for a young girl who deserved better than to be abandoned like garbage in the woods.

In short, Kimberly was projecting. As a former psych student, she recognized the signs. As a young woman who'd lost her sister and mother to violent deaths, she couldn't stop if she tried.

She had found the victim. She'd stood alone with her in the dark shadows of the woods. She couldn't walk away from her now if she tried.

Kimberly followed the address she'd received from the Marine base. She'd asked about the NCIS investigator while there, only to discover he'd already left to observe the victim's autopsy at the morgue.

In the good news department, Special Agent Kaplan's presence at the autopsy gave Kimberly a better excuse for insinuating herself into the procedure. She'd just come to talk to him, but hey, as long as she was there . . .

In the bad news department, an experienced special agent was probably going to be a bit savvier about a new agent trying to horn in on his investigation than an overworked ME.

That's why Mac had volunteered her for this mission after all. No one was going to let another cop into the case. A mere student, on the other hand . . . Play to your weaknesses, he'd advised her. No one ever suspects the small, bewildered rookie.

Kimberly parked her car outside the nondescript five-story building. She took a deep breath. She wondered if her father had ever felt this nervous before a case. Then again, had he ever gone off the beaten path? Risked everything to learn the truth for yet another dead girl in a world of so many murdered blondes?

Her cool remote father. She couldn't picture it. Somehow that bolstered her spirits. She squared her shoulders and got on with it.

Inside, the odor hit her at once. Too antiseptic, too sterile. The smell of a place that definitely had things to hide. She went to the glass-enclosed receptionist area, made her request, and was grateful when the woman buzzed her straight through.

Kimberly followed a long corridor with stark walls and linoleum floors all the way to the back. Here and there metal gurneys were shoved up against bone-colored walls. Steel-gray doors led off other places, security boxes demanding access codes she didn't have. The air was colder in here. Her footsteps rang out with a startling echo, while the fluorescent lights buzzed overhead.

Her hands were trembling at her sides. She could feel the first trickle of sweat slide stickily down her back. Being inside this cool place should've been a welcome relief from the stifling outdoor heat. It wasn't.

At the end of the hallway, she pushed through a wooden door into a new lobby area. This is where the ME's offices were housed. She pressed a buzzer, and wasn't horribly surprised when a door cracked open, and Special Agent Kaplan poked out his head.

"You lookin' for the ME? He's busy."

"Actually, I'm looking for you."

Special Agent Kaplan straightened in the doorway. This close Kimberly could see the faint sheen of silver mixed into his dark, buzz-cut hair. He had a weathered face, stern eyes, and thin lips that reserved judgment before smiling. Not a cruel man, but a hard one. He was the guy, after all, who kept all of the Navy plus the Marines in line.

This was not going to be easy.

"New Agent Kimberly Quincy," Kimberly said, and stuck out her hand.

He accepted the handshake. His grip was firm, his expression wary. "You had quite a ride."

"I understand you have questions for me. Given my schedule, I thought it might be easier if I found you. At the Marine base, they said you were here. So I decided to make the drive."

"Your supervisor know you left the Academy?"

"I didn't mention it to him directly. When I spoke with him this morning, however, he underscored the importance of cooperating fully with NCIS's investigation. Naturally I assured him I would do whatever I could to help."

"Uh huh," Kaplan said. And that was it. He stood, he stared, and he let the silence drag on and on and on. If this man had kids, they *never* snuck out at night.

Kimberly's fingers desperately wanted to fidget. She stuck them into her pockets and wished once more she were carrying her Glock. It was tough to project confidence when you were armed with a red-painted toy.

"I understand you visited my crime scene," Kaplan said abruptly.

"I stopped by."

"Gave the boys quite a scare."

"With all due respect, sir, your boys scare easily."

Kaplan's lips finally cracked into a ghostly semblance of a smile. "I told them the same," he said, and for a moment they were coconspirators. Then the moment passed. "Why are you crowding my case, New Agent Quincy? Hasn't your father taught you better than that?"

Kimberly's shoulders immediately went rigid. She caught the motion, then forced herself to breathe easy. "I didn't apply to the Academy because my interests ran to sewing."

"So this is an academic study to you?"

"No."

That made him frown. "I'll ask one more time: why are you here, New Agent Quincy?"

"Because I found her, sir."

"Because you found her?"

"Yes, sir. And what I start, I like to finish. My father taught me that."

"It's not your case to finish."

"No, sir. It's your case to finish. Absolutely. I'm just a student. But I'm hoping you'll be kind enough to let me watch."

"Kind? No one calls me kind."

"Letting a green rookie watch an autopsy and puke her guts out won't change your image, sir."

Now he did smile. It changed the contours of his whole face, made him handsome, even approachable. The human in him came out, and Kimberly thought she had hope yet.

"You ever see an autopsy, New Agent Quincy?"

"No, sir."

"It's not the blood that will get you. It's the smell. Or maybe the whine of the buzz saw when it hits the skull. Think you're up to it?"

"I'm pretty sure I'll be sick, sir."

"Then by all means, come on back. The things I gotta do to educate the Feebies," Kaplan muttered. He shook his head. Then he opened the door and let her into the cold, sterile room.

Tina was going to be sick. She was trying desperately to control the reflex. Her stomach was clenching, her throat tightening. Bile surged upward. Bitterly, harshly, she forced it back down.

Her mouth was duct-taped shut. If she started vomiting now, she was terrified she'd drown.

She curled up tighter in a ball. That seemed to alleviate some of the cramping in her lower abdomen. Maybe it bought her another few minutes. And then? She didn't know anymore.

She lived in a black tomb of darkness. She saw nothing. She heard very little. Her hands were behind her back, but at least not taped too tight. Her ankles seemed bound as well. If she wiggled her feet, she could get the tape to make a squishy sound, and earn herself some extra room.

The tape didn't really matter, though. She'd figured that out hours before. The real prison wasn't the duct tape around her limbs. It was the locked plastic container that held her body. It was too dark to be sure, but given the approximate size, the metal gate in the front, and the holes that marked the top—where she could press her cheek—she had a feeling that she'd been thrown into a very large animal carrier. Honest to goodness. She was trapped in a dog crate.

She'd cried a bit in the beginning. Then she'd gotten so angry she'd thrashed against the plastic, hurling herself at the metal door. All she had to show for that tantrum was a bruised shoulder and banged-up knees.

She'd slept after that. Too exhausted by fear and pain to know what to do next. When she'd woken up, the duct tape had been removed from her mouth and a gallon jug of water was in the crate with her, along with an energy bar. She'd been tempted to refuse the offering out of spite—she was no trained monkey! But then she'd thought of her unborn baby, and she'd consumed the water greedily while eating the protein bar.

She thought the water might have been drugged, though. Because no sooner had she drunk it than she fell deeply asleep. When she woke up again, the tape was back over her mouth, and the wrapper from the energy bar had been taken away.

She'd wanted to cry again. Drugs couldn't be good. Not for her. And not for her unborn child.

Funny, four weeks ago, she hadn't even been sure she wanted a baby. But then Betsy had brought home the Mayo Clinic book on child development and together they'd looked at all the pictures. Tina knew now that, at six weeks past conception, her baby was already half an inch long. It had a big head with eyes but no eyelids and it had little arms and little legs with paddlelike hands and feet. In another week, her baby would double to being one inch long and the hands and feet would develop tiny webbed fingers and teensy little toes until her baby looked like the world's cutest lima bean.

In other words, her baby was already a baby. A tiny, precious, something

Tina couldn't wait to hold one day in her arms. And Tina had better enjoy that moment because her mother would be killing her shortly thereafter.

Her mom. Oh God, even the thought of her mother made her want to weep. If anything happened to Tina . . . Life was too unfair sometimes to a grown woman who had worked so hard in the hope that her daughter would have a better life.

Tina had to be more alert. She had to pay more attention. She wasn't going to just disappear like this, dammit. She refused to be a stupid statistic. She strained her ears again. Struggled for some hint of what might be going on.

Tina was pretty sure she was in a vehicle. She could feel movement, but it confused her that she couldn't see. Maybe the crate was in the back of a covered pickup bed, or a blacked-out van. She didn't think it was night, though without being able to glance at her watch she had no idea how much time had passed. She'd slept for a long while, she thought. The drugs, then the fear, having taken their toll.

She felt isolated. The pitch black was too sterile, devoid of even the soft whisper of someone else's breath, let alone whimpers of fear. Whatever else was back here, she was pretty sure she was the only living thing. Maybe that was a good thing. Maybe she was the only person he'd kidnapped then. He'd taken just her.

But somehow, she doubted that and it made her want to weep.

She didn't know why he was doing this. Was he a pervert who kidnapped college girls to take them to his sick hideaway, where he would do unspeakable things? She was still fully clothed, however. Down to her three-inch sandals. He'd also left her her purse. She didn't think a pervert would do such a thing.

Maybe he was a slave trader. She'd heard stories. A white girl could fetch a lot of money overseas. Maybe she'd end up in a harem, or working in some sleazy bar in Bangkok. Well, wouldn't they be in for a big surprise when their pretty young thing suddenly grew big and fat. That would teach them to snatch first and talk later.

Her child born into slavery, prostitution, porn . . .

The bile rose up in her throat again. She grimly fought it back.

I can't be sick, she tried telling her tummy. You have to give me a break. We're in this together. I'll figure out a way to get out of the crate. You have to hold down all food and water. We don't have much to work with here, you know. We have to make these calories count.

Which was very important actually, because as perverse as it sounded, the less Tina had to eat, the worse her nausea became. Basically, food made her sick and lack of food made her sicker.

Belatedly, Tina was aware that the motion was decelerating. She strained her ears and detected the slight squeak of brakes. The vehicle had stopped.

Immediately her body tensed. Her hands fumbled behind her. They found her black shoulder bag, gripping it tight like a weapon. Not that it would do her any good with her hands bound behind her back. But she had to do something. Anything was better than simply waiting for what would happen next. . . .

A door suddenly rolled back. Bright sunlight penetrated the vehicle, making her blink owlishly, and in the next instant, she was aware of an intense wall of heat. Oh God, it was boiling outside. She shrank back, but couldn't avoid the scorching air.

A man stood in the open doorway. His features were a black shroud haloed by the sunlight behind him. His arm came up and a cellophane package fell between the plastic bars. Then another and another.

"Do you have water?" he asked.

She tried to speak, then remembered the tape over her mouth. She did have water, but she wanted more, so she shook her head.

"You should ration your supplies more carefully," the man scolded.

She wanted to spit at him. She shrugged instead.

"I'll give you another jug. But that's it. Understood?"

What did he mean by "that's it"? That's it before he set her free? Or that's it before he raped her, killed her, or sold her to a bunch of sick twisted men?

Her stomach was roiling again. She closed her eyes to savagely fight it back.

Next thing she felt was a prick on the arm. A damn needle. The drugs, oh no . . .

Her muscles melted as if trained. She slumped against the side of the dog crate, the world already fading away. The kennel door opened. A jug of water materialized in her crate. A hand casually ripped the tape from her mouth. Her lips stung. Blood trickled from the corner of her mouth.

"Eat, drink," the man said quietly. "By nightfall, you're going to need your strength."

The kennel door snapped shut. The van door rolled closed. No more sunlight. No more heat.

Tina slid down to the floor of the dog crate. Her legs came up. Her body curled up protectively around her belly. Then the drugs won this battle and swept her far away.

11

They hadn't gotten very far with the postmortem. Kimberly wasn't surprised. Most autopsies were scheduled for days after the recovery of the body, not hours. Either things were slow at the moment, or an NCIS investigation carried some hefty weight.

Special Agent Kaplan introduced her to the medical examiner, Dr. Corben, and then to his assistant, Gina Nitsche.

"Your first post?" Nitsche asked, wheeling in the body with quick efficiency.

Kimberly nodded.

"If you're gonna puke, don't ask, just leave," Nitsche said cheerfully. "I got enough to clean up after this." She continued talking briskly, while unzipping the body bag and folding back the plastic. "I'm called a diener. Technically speaking, Dr. Corben is the prosector. He'll handle all the protocol and I'll do what I'm told. Usual procedure is that the body arrives a day or two earlier and is logged in, in a separate area. We inventory clothes and possessions, take the weight, give the body an official tag with an ID number. Given time constraints, however," Nitsche shot Kaplan a look, "this time we're doing it all as we go. Oh, and while I'm thinking about it, there's a box of gloves on the side table. The cupboard has extra caps and gowns. Help yourself."

Kimberly glanced toward the cupboard uncertainly, and Nitsche, as if she were reading her mind, added, "You know, 'cause sometimes they splatter."

Kimberly went to the cupboard and found herself a cap to cover her short feathery hair and a gown to cover her clothes. She noticed that Special Agent Kaplan followed her over and also snagged a set of protective gear. He'd brought his own pair of gloves. She borrowed her pair from the ME's supply.

Nitsche had finished unwrapping the body now. First she'd pulled back the external layer of heavy-duty plastic. Next, she'd unfolded a plain white sheet. Finally, she unpeeled the internal layer of plastic, much like a dry cleaning bag, which was what came into contact with the corpse's skin. Nitsche folded each layer down around the base of the gurney. Then she methodically inventoried the dead girl's clothing and jewelry, while Dr. Corben prepped the autopsy table.

"I inventoried her purse before coming in," Nitsche said conversationally. "Poor thing had brochures from a travel agency for Hawaii. I've always wanted to go to Hawaii. Do you think she was going with a boyfriend? Because if she was going with a boyfriend, well then, he's available again, and God knows I need someone to take me away from here. All right. We're ready."

She wheeled the gurney over to the cutting table. She and Dr. Corben had obviously done this many times before. He moved to the head. She moved to the feet. On the count of three, they slid the now naked corpse from the gurney onto the metal slab. Then Nitsche wheeled the gurney away.

"Testing, testing," Dr. Corben said into his recording equipment. Satisfied that it was working, he got down to business.

First, the ME catalogued the victim's naked body. He described her sex, age, height, weight, and hair and eye color. He commented that she appeared in good health (other than the fact that she was dead? Kimberly thought). He also listed the presence of a tattoo, shape of a rose, approximately one inch in size, on the deceased's upper left breast.

Victim and deceased. Dr. Corben used those words a lot. Kimberly began to think this was the heart of her problem. She never thought in terms of victim or deceased. Instead, she thought in terms such as young, pretty, blond, girl. If she was supposed to be a dispassionate, world-weary death investigator, she hadn't achieved it yet.

Dr. Corben had moved on to perceived injuries. He described the large bruise on the girl's—the victim's—upper left hip, his gloved hand poking and prodding at the waxy skin. "Victim has presence of large ecchymosis, approximately four inches in diameter, on the upper left thigh. Center area is red and swollen, approximately one and a half inches around puncture site. It's an abnormal amount of bruising for an intramuscular injection. Perhaps the result of inexperience or a large-bore needle."

Special Agent Kaplan frowned at that and made a gesture with his hand. Dr. Corben snapped off the minirecorder in his hand. "What do you mean, a large-bore needle?" Kaplan asked.

"Different needle gauges have different thicknesses. For example, in the medical community, when we give injections we use an eighteen-gauge needle, which slides very easily into a vein. Administered correctly, it can be done with relatively little bruising. Now, this injection site has a great deal of bruising. And not just of the muscle area. This center spot where it's red and swollen—that's where the needle punctured the skin. The size of the aggravation leads me to believe that either it was a needle wielded with a fair amount of force, really, truly stabbed into the thigh, or it was an abnormally large needle."

Kaplan narrowed his eyes, considering the possibilities. "Why would someone use a bigger needle?"

"Different-sized needles are used for a variety of different procedures." Dr. Corben's brow furrowed. "Sometimes to inject large amounts of a substance at a faster rate, you need a larger-bore needle. Or when mixing substances, you would use a larger needle. Now, here's something interesting. The second injection site, the arm. Note the relatively small amount of aggravation we see here. Just the slightest swollen spot. That's more like what we would typically see—consistent with a standard eighteen-gauge needle. Granted, the limited amount of bruising is also due to the fact she died shortly thereafter. But either way, this injection is clearly more skillfully done. Either it's two different needles, or it's two very different approaches toward intramuscular injections."

"So first she's injected in the hip," Kaplan mused slowly. "Forcefully and/or with a very large needle. Then, later, she's injected in the arm. But more controlled, more carefully. How much time occurred between the two?"

Dr. Corben frowned. He resumed studying the first bruise with his fingers. "Given the large size, it had time to develop. But notice the coloring is all purple and dark blues? None of the green and yellow tinges that happen later. I'd say twelve to twenty-four hours between the hip puncture and the injection into the arm."

"Ambush," Kimberly murmured.

Special Agent Kaplan turned on her. He had the hard stare again. "Come again?"

"Ambush." She forced herself to speak up louder. "The first bruise . . . If it could be caused by more force, then maybe it's from an ambush. How he gains initial control. Later, when she's already subdued, he can take more time for the final injection."

She was thinking of what Mac had said about the Georgia murders. How the girls found first always had bruises on their hips, plus a fatal injection mark on their upper left arms. She'd never heard of such an MO before. What were the odds that two different killers were using it in two different states?

Dr. Corben had the recorder back on. He rolled the body onto its back, noted the absence of bruises and contusions, then finished his initial exam by narrating the condition of the mouth. Nitsche handed him some kind of standardized form, and he quickly and efficiently sketched each one of the external injuries he'd noted in the protocol.

They moved on to her hands. They had been bagged at the scene. Now Nitsche pulled off the paper bags and both prosecutor and diener leaned close. Dr. Corben scraped beneath each nail. Nitsche collected the samples. Next Dr. Corben swabbed around each nail bed with a Q-tip, testing for traces of blood. He looked up at Kaplan and shook his head. "No signs of defensive wounds," he reported. "No skin, no blood."

Kaplan sighed and resumed leaning against the wall. "Not my lucky day," he murmured.

As the victim's hands had now been examined for evidence, Nitsche brought over an inkpad for fingerprinting. The body, however, had achieved full rigor since being found and the stiff fingers refused to cooperate.

Dr. Corben moved up to assist her. He worked the first joint of the girl's index finger until with a faint popping sound, the rigor broke. Nitsche started inking, and Dr. Corben methodically worked his way through both hands, each popping sound echoing faintly in the cold tile room and bringing up bile in the back of Kimberly's throat.

I will not be sick, she promised herself. And then—Oh God, this is only the external exam.

Fingerprinting done, Dr. Corben moved down the body to between the girl's—the deceased's—legs. While the condition of her clothing had been inconsistent with rape, he still had to examine the body itself.

"No bruising of the inner thighs, no lacerations of the labia majora or labia minora," Dr. Corben reported. He combed the pubic hair and Nitsche collected the loose strands in another bag. Then he picked up three swabs.

Now Kimberly had to look away. The young girl was dead. Far beyond insult or injury. But Kimberly couldn't watch. Her fingers were knotted, her breathing shallow. She was once more aware of the strong smell of the room, and the feel of sweat on her back. She noticed out of the corner of her eye that Kaplan was now intently studying the floor.

"From the external exam," Dr. Corben concluded shortly, "there is no evidence of sexual assault. Now then, let's get her cleaned up."

Kimberly's eyes flew open. Nitsche had just moved into position and she and Dr. Corben were now hosing down the body. Kimberly's bewilderment must have shown on her face, because Dr. Corben spoke up above the spray of water: "After concluding the external exam, we wash the body before making the first incision. You don't want factors from the outside—dirt, fiber, debris—contaminating the internal organs and confusing your findings. The outside had its stories to tell. Now, it's the inside's turn."

Dr. Corben matter-of-factly turned off the hose, passed out plastic goggles, and picked up a scalpel.

Kimberly went green. She was trying hard. She had seen crime-scene photos, dammit. She wasn't a novice to violent death.

But she felt herself sway on her feet anyway. She told herself to hold it together, but then she looked at the young girl's face, and that did it completely.

"Oh my God," she gasped, "what is in her mouth?"

It was there, unmistakable now, the shadow of the thing Dr. Corben had sensed earlier. First the girl's left cheek bulged, pale and waxy. Then with dazzling speed, her right cheek went, until it looked like she was puffing up her mouth while staring at them with her dead brown eyes.

Kaplan was fumbling with his holster. Kimberly was fumbling, too. He brought out a gun. She brought out a red plastic toy. Shit, damn. She dropped down to her ankle, without ever taking her gaze off the girl's face.

"Stand back," Kaplan said.

Dr. Corben and his attendant needed no urging. Nitsche's gaze was wide and fascinated. Dr. Corben had that pale tight look from earlier in the day. "It could be gases from decomp," he tried vainly. "She was out in intense heat."

"The body just achieved full rigor. It's not that far along," Kaplan muttered tightly.

The cheeks bulged again. Moved from side to side.

"I think . . ." Kimberly's voice came out too faintly. She licked her lips, tried again. "I think there's something in there. In her mouth. That's why he stitched it shut."

"Holy shit!" Nitsche said with awe.

"Mother of God," Kaplan murmured.

Kimberly stared at Dr. Corben. His right hand was shaking badly. She was pretty sure nothing like this had ever happened in one of his postmortems before. The look on his face said he'd retire before letting it happen again. "Sir," she said as calmly as she could, "you have the scalpel. You need . . . You need to cut the stitching."

"I will not!"

"Whatever's in there has gotta come out. It's better on our terms than its."

Kaplan was nodding slowly. "She has a point. We need to do the autopsy. So whatever's there, needs to go."

Dr. Corben looked at them both wildly. He definitely was thinking of an argument. He definitely wanted to argue. But then his scientific mind seemed to reassert itself. He glanced at the body again, watched the horrible distortion of its face, and slowly, very slowly, nodded.

"Eye gear on," he said at last. "Masks, gloves. Whatever it is, I want us to be prepared." And then, almost as an afterthought, "Gina, stand next to the special agent."

Nitsche moved hastily behind Kaplan's large build. Kimberly straightened up and worked on her own composure. Knees slightly bent, legs ready to move. She put on her goggles, her Crayola long since discarded on the floor, and her favorite hunting knife now in her hand.

Dr. Corben moved gingerly. He got just close enough to be able to touch the girl's stitched-up mouth with his scalpel, without his body being in the line of fire for Kaplan's gun.

"On the count of three," Dr. Corben said tightly. "One. Two. Three."

The scalpel went slash, slash. Dr. Corben fell back from the body, his feet already scrambling. And a dark, mottled shape exploded from its unwanted prison and hurtled halfway across the tiled floor.

One moment Kimberly was alone in her corner of the room. The next, she saw the unmistakable, brown-splotched shape of a coiled rattler. The viper reared up with an ominous hiss.

Kaplan's Glock exploded in the tiny room, and Kimberly hurled her knife.

12

Quantico, Virginia
5:14 P.M.
Temperature: 97 degrees

Mac was standing outside a classroom asking Genny if she happened to know of a good botanist in the state of Virginia, when the blurred form of a blue-clad figure came roaring down the hall. The next instant, he felt a sharp pain in his left shoulder, just had time to look up in surprise, and promptly got whacked again by his favorite new agent.

"You did not say anything about *snakes*!" Kimberly Quincy swung a solid right; he barely dodged left. "You did *not* say *anything* about leaving live *vipers* in their *mouths*!" She followed with a jab to the ribs; he fell back three steps. For a tiny thing, she really could hit.

"You lying, manipulating, cold-hearted bastard!" She took a good windup and he came to his senses just in time to block the blow, twist her arm behind her back, and turn her into the solid restraint of his body. She, of course, tried to flip him over her back.

"Sugar," he murmured in her ear. "I appreciate your enthusiasm, but maybe you'd like to wait 'til we're alone."

He felt the outrage scream through her stiffened frame, but then his words must've penetrated. She seemed to become aware of their surroundings. For example, as students generally didn't assault other students in the halls of the Academy, she now had everyone's full attention. Genny's gaze was most amused. She had it locked on Mac's face with blatantly unconcealed interest.

"Just practicing a little drill," Mac drawled out loud. "You know, always happy to help out a new agent." He gingerly released Kimberly's arm. She didn't hit him, or stomp on his foot, so he figured he was making some progress. "Now then, darlin', why don't we go outside where we can discuss other ways for ambushing a possible suspect?"

He hightailed it for the double doors. After another awkward moment, Kimberly scrambled after him. She managed to make it all the way around the corner of the building to a somewhat isolated flagstone patio before she went after him again.

"Why didn't you warn me about the stitched-up mouth!" she yelled.

He threw up his hands in surrender. "Warn you about what? I still don't know what you're talking about!"

"He left a rattlesnake in her mouth. A real live rattler!"

"Well, that'll put hair on your chest. Did you hit the rattler as hard as you hit me?"

"I threw a knife at it!"

"Of course."

She scowled. "But I missed. Special Agent Kaplan shot it with his gun."

Ah, no wonder she was pissed. Her big moment, and she missed throwing a knife at a striking viper. The girl did have her standards.

"I want my Glock!" she was still raging.

"I know, honey, I know." His arms had come down. He was thinking hard. "A live snake," he said at last. "I didn't see that coming. Once he left an alligator's egg down a girl's throat. And for the last one, Mary Lynn, he used a snail. But I never . . . A live rattler. Damn, give a guy three years and he goes and gets mean."

And that frightened him. God, that frightened him all the way down to his big Southern bones.

Kimberly didn't seem to have heard him. Her hands were rubbing her arms compulsively, as if she were trying to ward off a chill in hundred-degree heat. She was also holding herself carefully, a woman made out of glass and trying not to shatter.

Shock, he realized. He belatedly pulled out one of the wrought-iron chairs and gestured to the seat. "Come on. Sit. Take a minute. Autopsy's over, honey. Nothin' can happen to you here."

"Tell that to the dead girl," Kimberly said roughly, but she accepted the chair and, for a moment, they both simply sat in silence.

Kimberly didn't know it yet, but Mac had been doing his own investigative work that afternoon. For starters, he'd inquired all about her. And boy, it had been quite an education. In the good news department, his current partner-in-solving-crime came with a genuine law enforcement pedigree. Her father had reputedly been a brilliant profiler in his day. Handled a lot of cases, put away a lot of very bad guys.

Rumor had it that his daughter had inherited his brains and aptitude for anticipating the criminal mind.

Bad news, however—the daughter was also regarded as a little bit of a head case. Didn't like authority figures. Didn't like her fellow classmates. Didn't seem to actually like much of anyone, which may explain why every time Mac ran into her, she was trying to kill him.

Of course, then there was what had happened to her family. Losing most of your relatives to a homicidal maniac was bound to make an impression on you. Perhaps Mac should just be grateful she hadn't actually inflicted bodily harm on him yet.

Mac stole another glance beneath the cover of his eyelids. Kimberly's gaze was off in the distance, her eyes unfocused. She appeared profoundly exhausted, haggard beyond measure, with deep shadows bruising her eyes and a patchwork of red scratches still welting her skin.

The girl definitely wasn't sleeping at night. And that was before she'd met him.

"Was it an overdose?" he asked at last.

She seemed to rouse herself from her daze. "I don't know the results of the tox screen. But she was hit first—and forcefully—by something in the upper left thigh. Later, probably after twelve to twenty-four hours had passed, she received the fatal injection in her upper left arm."

"Intramuscular injections?" Mac asked.

"Yes."

"All her clothes were intact? Her purse? No sexual assault?"

"Yes on all counts."

"What about defensive wounds? Blood, skin, anything?"

"Nothing."

"Shit," Mac said heavily.

She nodded.

"They have an ID?"

"Not yet. They took her prints. They'll need time to run them through the system."

"We need to know who she is," Mac murmured. "We'll need a list of her friends and family, who she was out with last night. Where they went, what was the make and model of their car . . . Jesus." He ran a hand through his hair, his mind beginning to race. "It's already been at least twelve hours . . . Jesus. Who's in charge of the case?"

"Special Agent Kaplan."

"I'd better go talk to him."

"Good luck," Kimberly snorted.

"He let you watch the autopsy."

"Only because I promised to throw up."

"Did you?"

"I was thinking about it," she admitted. "But the rattler put a damper on things. Then Kaplan exploded its head, and then we all had to debate how carefully to clean up snake guts, as you could consider them evidence."

"You had quite a first autopsy," Mac said seriously.

"Yeah," she sighed. She seemed rather surprised by the notion herself. "I think other ones will be easier after this."

"I think they will be."

They both lapsed back into silence, Kimberly probably thinking of the snake she still wished she'd killed; Mac contemplating past cases that once more loomed larger than life.

The heat settled in on them, rolling in like a heavy blanket and pressing them deep into their chairs while their clothing glued to their skin. Mac used to not mind heat like this. It was perfect for sitting next to his parents' pool. Put on a little Alan Jackson, drink a lot of homemade lemonade. And later, when dusk fell, watch the fireflies flicker and dart in the purple-tinged air.

He didn't think of idyllic summer days anymore. Summer had become the enemy, when heat waves would roll in, and girls would no longer be safe, even when traveling in pairs.

He needed to call Atlanta. He needed to figure out how to best approach this Special Agent Kaplan. And then they were going to need resources. ASAP. The best experts they could find. A botanist, biologist, a forensic geologist, an entomologist, and God knows what other kind of ologists. Was there an expert on snakes? They should find someone who knew everything about rattlers and what it signified when one burst out of a dead girl's mouth.

Then there was the rock, of course, which Mac hadn't even gotten to see. And the leaf they'd recovered this morning, but he'd had no luck tracing. And that was just the clues/evidence he knew off the top of his head.

He needed the body, that was the deal. The clothes would be good to study as well. And her purse, her hair, her sandals. This guy liked to leave clues in the damnedest places, and it sounded like he was refining his technique all the time. A live rattlesnake crammed into a body . . .

Shit. Just plain . . . shit.

Nearby doors opened. Mac heard footsteps approach, then a shadow fell across their patio. A man stood in front of them. Mac didn't recognize him, but he could tell from the look on Kimberly's face that she did.

"Kimberly," the man said quietly.

"Dad," she said with equal reserve.

Mac's eyebrows had just disappeared beneath his hairline when the man, older, trim, and very impressive looking in a deep gray suit, turned toward him.

"And you must be Special Agent McCormack. Pierce Quincy. Pleased to meet you."

Mac accepted the man's handshake. And then he knew. A funny grin came across his face. The bottom dropped out of his stomach, and he heard a faint ringing in his ears. He had been so concerned that the NCIS had done nothing in the past eight hours. But, apparently, they had done something after all.

Pierce Quincy shouldn't know his name. Former FBI Agent Pierce Quincy should have no reason to know anyone at the National Academy. Unless he had been explicitly told to look for Mac. And that could only mean . . .

"If you two would follow me, we need to have a meeting," Quincy was saying in that carefully modulated voice.

"You shouldn't be here," Kimberly said tightly.

"I was invited."

"I didn't call you!"

"I would never presume that you did."

"Dammit, did they tell you about the body?"

"Kimberly—"

"I am doing just fine!"

"Kim—"

"I don't need help, especially from you!"

"K—"

"Turn around. Go home! If you love me at all, please for God's sake just go away."

"I can't."

"Why not!"

Pierce Quincy sighed heavily. He didn't say anything right away. He simply reached out a hand and touched his daughter's battered face. She flinched. And his arm instantly dropped back to his side, as if burned.

"We need to have a meeting," Quincy said again, turning toward the front of the building. "If you'll please just follow me."

Mac finally rose. Kimberly much more grudgingly shoved back her chair. They both fell in step behind her father, Mac's arm settling lightly around her waist.

"I think we're in trouble," Mac murmured in Kimberly's ear.

And she said bitterly, "You have no idea."

13

Quincy led them to an office in the main administrative wing. The sign on the door read Supervisor Mark Watson. Inside, the man in question was leaning against the edge of his desk, facing two guests. The first person Mac recognized as being the NCIS officer from the crime scene. The second person was actually a very attractive woman. Late thirties, Mac would guess. Gorgeous long chestnut hair. A face that was startlingly angular, more arresting than classically beautiful. Definitely not FBI. For one thing, she already looked annoyed as hell with Watson.

"Kimberly!" the woman said. She stood the moment Kimberly walked in the room, and gave the girl a quick hug.

"Rainie," Kimberly acknowledged. She offered the woman a faint smile, but immediately appeared wary again as Watson pushed away from his desk. It was clearly the supervisor's show. He was now holding up his hands and awaiting everyone's attention.

He started with the introductions: Rainie turned out to be Lorraine Conner, Quincy's partner in Quincy & Conner Investigations out of New York; the NCIS officer was Special Agent Thomas Kaplan from General Crimes out of Norfolk.

Quincy & Conner Investigations, Watson announced, had been retained by NCIS to assist with the case. Given the location of the body on Marine grounds and near FBI facilities, the powers-that-be had determined the presence of independent consultants would be in everyone's best interest. Translation: Everyone was keenly aware of what it would mean if the bad guy turned out to be one of their guys and it looked like they'd tried to cover it up. Score one for the politicians.

Mac settled in next to the door, which had now been closed for privacy. He noted that Kaplan stood next to Watson, while Quincy had taken the seat next to Rainie Conner. Kimberly, on the other hand, had put as much distance between herself and her father as possible. She stood in the far corner of the room, arms crossed in front of her chest, and chin up for a fight.

So everyone had their alliances. Or lack thereof. Now they could get down to business.

Mark Watson addressed his opening comments to Kimberly. "I understand you saw Special Agent Kaplan earlier today, New Agent Quincy."

"Yes, sir."

"I thought we had reached an understanding this morning. This is NCIS's case. You are not to go near it."

"As part of my pledge to cooperate with NCIS," Kimberly replied evenly, "I found the officer in charge in order to volunteer my statement. At the time, interestingly enough, he was about to observe the autopsy of the body. I asked if I could join him. He graciously let me in." Kimberly smiled stiffly. "Thank you, Special Agent Kaplan."

Watson turned to Kaplan, who shrugged big Marine shoulders. "She told me her name. She asked permission. What the hell, I let her join us."

"I never lied," Kimberly spoke up promptly. "And I never misrepresented my interests." She scowled. "I did, however, miss the snake. For that I apologize."

"I see," Watson said. "And earlier in the day, when you directly violated my orders and attempted to revisit the crime scene, were you also thinking of the urgency of NCIS's investigation?"

"I was looking for Special Agent Kaplan—"

"Don't play me for dumb."

"I was curious," Kimberly immediately amended. "It didn't matter. The Marines obediently chased me away."

"I see. And what about *after* you harassed the Marines in the woods, New Agent Quincy? What about the *hour* you then spent talking to Special Agent McCormack, after you were explicitly told *not* to discuss your find with anyone in the Academy? How would you care to explain that?"

Kimberly stiffened. Her gaze flickered to Mac, uncertain now, while he swallowed back a fresh curse. Of course: their meeting in the Crossroads Lounge. In full view of everyone. Stupid, stupid, stupid.

This time, Watson didn't wait for Kimberly to reply. He was on a roll—or maybe he was aware of just how tense Quincy had grown in the seat opposite him.

"Imagine my surprise," Watson continued, "when I discovered that far from returning to her room as requested, my student first wandered into the woods, and then was seen in animated discussion with a National Academy student who just happens to have once worked a case bearing a startling resemblance to the homicide discovered this morning. Were you sharing information with Special Agent McCormack, Kimberly?"

"Actually, I was getting information from him."

"Really. I find that extremely interesting. Particularly since ten minutes ago, he became Special Agent Kaplan's primary suspect."

"Oh, for heaven's sake," Mac burst out. "I'm doing my best to help with a case that is only the beginning of one long, hot nightmare. Do you have any idea what you've waded into the middle of—"

"Where were you last night?" Special Agent Kaplan interrupted curtly.

"I started the night at Carlos Kelly's in Stafford. Then I returned to Quantico, where I ran into New Agent Quincy on the firing ranges. It doesn't matter—"

Kaplan's gaze had swung to Kimberly. "What time did you see him on the ranges?"

"Around eleven. I didn't look at my watch—"

"Did you see him go back to the dorms?"

"No."

"Where was he headed?"

"I don't know. I was heading back to the dorms. I didn't pay attention to him!"

"So in other words," Kaplan homed in on Mac, "no one knows where you were after eleven-thirty last night."

"Don't you think it's an awfully big coincidence," Watson spoke up, "that we should just happen to get a homicide that bears so many resemblances to one of your past cases, *while* you're staying here at the Academy?"

"It's not coincidence," Mac said. "It was planned."

"*What?*" Watson finally drew up short. He shot a glance at Kaplan, who appeared equally perplexed. Apparently, they'd both been big fans of the Georgia-cop-as-a-killer theory. Why not? Get a dead body at eight A.M., wrap up the case before six P.M. It made for good headlines. Assholes.

"Perhaps," Quincy interjected quietly, "you should let the man speak. Of course, that's only the advice of the independent consultant."

"Yes," Rainie seconded beside him. "Let him speak. This is finally getting to be good."

"Thank you." Mac shot Quincy and Rainie a grateful look, while carefully avoiding Kimberly's gaze. How must she feel right about now? Hurt, confused, betrayed? He had honestly meant none of those things, and yet there was nothing he could do about that now.

"You can verify everything I'm about to say with my supervisor, Special Agent in Charge Lee Grogen from the Atlanta office. Yes, starting in 'ninety-eight, we had a string of murders similar to the one you discovered today. After the third incident, we formed a multi-jurisdictional task force in charge of the investigation. Unfortunately, seven murders later, the man we were seeking, the so-called Eco-Killer, simply vanished. No new crimes, nothing. The task force started out with over a thousand leads. Three years later, our work was down to a trickle. Until six months ago. When things went hot again.

"We got a letter in the mail. It contained a newspaper clipping of a letter to the editor similar to the ones our guy used to send the *Atlanta Journal-Constitution*. Except this letter wasn't sent to a Georgia paper. It was sent to the *Virginian-Pilot*. And then I started getting phone calls—"

"You?" Quincy interrupted. "Or the task force?"

"Me. On my cell phone. Hell if I know why, but lucky me has received six calls now. The caller's voice is always distorted by some kind of electronic device and he/she/it always has the same message—the Eco-Killer is getting agitated again. He's going to strike. Except this time, he's picked Virginia as his favorite playground."

"So your department sent you here," Watson spoke up. "Why? To be a watchdog? To magically prevent another crime? You didn't even make anyone aware of your concerns."

Mac shot the man a look. "For the record, I told everybody who would listen about my goddamn concerns. But let's face it, around here, cold cases are a dime a dozen; everybody comes bearing that one investigation that's still keeping them up at night. Best I could do was get a preliminary meeting with a forensic linguist in the BSU—Dr. Ennunzio—and show him the letters to the editor. What he thinks, however, I don't know 'cause he's been dodging my calls ever since. And now here we are. I got a good lead a bad way, and you're barking up the wrong tree, you paranoid piece of shit."

"Well, that summarizes things nicely," Rainie said.

Watson's face had developed a red mottled look above his regulation red tie. Mac just kept staring him in the eye. He was angrier than he should be, making enemies when he needed allies. He didn't care. Another girl was dead, and Mac was tired of standing in an office, discussing a case these guys would never understand in time to make a difference.

"I still see no compelling evidence between this body and what happened in Georgia." Kaplan spoke up finally. "Did the caller tell you this so-called Eco-Killer was going to strike this week?"

"Not specifically."

"Did he tell you it would be at the FBI Academy?"

"Can't say that he did."

"Did he give you a reason why this killer has done nothing for three years?"

"Nope."

"Or why he would move from Georgia to Virginia?"

"Nope."

"In other words, the caller has told you nothing at all."

"You got me, sir. That is the major weakness of our investigation. Five years later, we still know nothin', and today hasn't changed a thing. So maybe we can wrap this up now, so I can get back out there and, you know, do something."

The former Marine ignored him, turning his attention to the rest of the suits instead. "So what we're really left with is a letter to the editor written six months before the body was found today. It's too far-fetched," he said flatly. "Some Georgian serial killer, who does nothing in three years, suddenly delivers a body to Quantico grounds, while only notifying a National Academy student. It doesn't make any sense."

"Should he have called you instead?" Rainie asked. Her voice held just the barest hint of sarcasm and Mac liked her immensely for it.

"That's not what I'm saying—"

"Or maybe he should've explained himself better in one of his notes?"

"Now that's not a half-bad thought! If this guy is leaving notes, where's the one for this body? Seems to me he likes to take credit for his crimes. So where's the ownership?"

"It's been three years," Rainie said. "Maybe he's had a change of heart."

"Listen," Mac interjected tightly. He could feel the urgency growing in his voice. Vainly, he tried to swallow it down. But he just didn't have time for this. They didn't understand; without the proper paperwork and memos, they never would understand. And maybe that's what the Eco-Killer grasped better than any of them suspected. No bureaucracy moved fast, particularly one involved in law enforcement. No, law enforcement agencies moved painfully slow, dotting i's, crossing t's, and covering asses along the way. While a lone girl was dropped off in some surreal wilderness terrain, clutching her gallon of water, wearing her party clothes, and probably wondering what was gonna get her next.

"There's more than a damn letter. The Eco-Killer has rules, Rules of the Game, we call them, and we're seeing plenty of them in this murder. At least enough to convince me." Mac ticked off his first finger, "One, he only strikes during a heat wave."

"It's July, we have plenty of heat waves," Watson objected.

Mac ignored the FBI agent. "Two, the first girl is always found with clothing and purse intact. No sign of robbery, no sign of sexual assault. Body has one bruise in the thigh or buttocks, but cause of death is an overdose of the tranquilizer Ativan, injected into the upper left arm."

Watson skewered Kimberly with a look. "Well, you really didn't spare him any of the details, did you?"

"I went and looked for myself!" Mac spoke up sharply. "Dammit, I've been waiting for this moment for three long years. Of course I paid a visit to your crime scene. New agents aren't the only people who can go skulking around in the woods—"

"You had no right—"

"I had every right! I know this man. I have studied him for five goddamn years. And I'm telling you, we don't have time for this kind of bullshit. Don't you get it yet? This girl isn't the only victim. Rule number three: he always kidnaps in pairs, because the first girl is just a map. She's a tool to help you find where the real game is going down."

"What do you mean, 'where the real game is going down'?" Rainie asked.

"I mean there's another girl out there, right now. She was traveling with this girl, maybe her sister or roommate or best friend. But she was with the first victim when they were both ambushed, and now she's been taken somewhere. He picked out the place ahead of time. It's somewhere geographically unique, but also very, very treacherous. In our state he chose a granite gorge, a vast farming county, then the banks of the Savannah River, and finally marshlands around the coast. He likes places exposed, with natural predators such as rattlesnakes and bears and bobcats. He likes places isolated, so even if the girls roam for days they still won't run into anyone who can offer them help. He likes places that are environmentally important, but no one thinks about anymore.

"Then he turns these girls loose, drugged, dazed, and confused, and waits to see what will happen next. In this kind of heat, some of them probably don't make it more than hours. But some of them—the smart ones, the tough ones—they might make it days. Maybe even a week. Long, tortured days, without food, without water, waiting for someone to come and save them."

Rainie was looking at him in rapt fascination. "How many times did he do this before?"

"Four. Eight girls kidnapped. Seven dead."

"So you got one back alive."

"Nora Ray Watts. The last girl. We found her in time."

"How?" Quincy spoke up.

Mac took a deep breath. His muscles were bunching again. He grimly fought his impatience down. "The man leaves clues on the first body. Evidence that, if you interpret correctly, will narrow down the location of the second girl."

"What kind of clues?"

"Flora and fauna, soil, sediment, rocks, insects, snails, hell, whatever he can dream up. We didn't understand the significance in the beginning. We bagged and tagged according to SOP, merrily trotted evidence off to the labs, and found only dead bodies after that. But hey, even we can be taught. By the fourth pair of kidnappings, we had a team of experienced specialists in place. Botanists, biologists, forensic geologists, you name it. Nora Ray had been traveling with her sister. Mary Lynn's body was found with a substance on her shirt, samples of vegetation on her shoes and a foreign object down her throat."

"Down her throat?" Kaplan spoke up sharply. Mac nodded his head. For the first time, the NCIS agent seemed to have gained real interest.

"The sediment on her shirt proved to be salt. The vegetation on her shoes was identified as *Spartina alterniflora*. Cord grass. And the biologist identified the foreign object as a marsh periwinkle shell. All three elements were consistent with what you would find in a salt marsh. We focused the search-and-rescue teams on the coast, and fifty-six hours later, a Coast Guard chopper spotted Nora Ray, frantically waving her bright red shirt."

"She couldn't help you identify the killer?" Rainie asked.

Mac shook his head. "Her last memory is of her tire going flat. The next she knew, she woke up ravenously thirsty in the middle of a damn marsh."

"Was she drugged?" Watson interjected.

"Bruise still fading on her left thigh."

"He ambushes them?"

"Our best guess—he scopes out bars. He looks for what he wants—young girls, no specific coloring required, traveling in pairs. I think he follows them to their car. While they get in, he drops a tack or two behind their back tire. Then he simply has to follow. Sooner or later the tire goes flat, he pulls over as if offering to help, and boom, he has them."

"Sneaks up on them with a needle?" Watson asked skeptically.

"No. He nails them with a dart gun. Like the kind a big game hunter might use."

In the quiet room came the unmistakable sound of sharply indrawn breaths. Mac regarded them all stonily. "You think we haven't done our homework? For five years, we've been hunting this man. I can tell you his profile. I can tell you how he hunts his victims. I can tell you he doesn't always get his way—after the fact, we learned about two different pairs of girls who got flat tires and had a man pull over behind them. They refused to roll down their windows, however, and they got to live another day.

"I can tell you that Mary Lynn, whose body we found the earliest, tested positive for a second drug—ketamine, which is used by vets and animal control officers for its quickly subduing effect. I can tell you ketamine is a controlled substance, but also readily available on the streets; kids use it in rave parties, calling it Kit Kat or Special K. I can tell you Ativan is also controlled, and also used by vets. But pursuing all vets got us nowhere. As did investigating members of various hunting groups, the Appalachian Mountain Club, or the Audubon Society.

"I can tell you the man is growing angrier. He went from striking once a year, which takes a tremendous amount of control in a serial killer, to striking twice in twelve weeks. And I can tell you the man's game only gets tougher. The first time, if we'd been paying attention, one of the clues was a rare herb found only in a five-mile radius in all of Georgia. Identify that herb, and we would've gotten the girl for sure. The last time, for Nora Ray Watts, the clues only led us to salt marshes. There are nearly four hundred thousand acres of salt marshes in Georgia. Quite frankly, Nora Ray was the proverbial needle in a haystack."

"And yet you found her," Kimberly said.

"She kept herself alive," Mac replied tightly.

Quincy, however, was regarding him intently. "Four hundred thousand acres is not a feasible search area. A chopper could not pick out a lone girl when covering that kind of terrain. You knew something else."

"I had a theory. Call it geographic profiling."

"The victims were related somehow? Had areas of geography in common?"

"No. The bodies did. When you put them on the map and identified the direction in which they were facing—"

"He used them as compasses," Quincy breathed.

"Maps. The guy sees the first girls as nothing but maps. So why not line up Mary Lynn's body to point to her sister? She's just a tool, after all. Anything for the sake of his game."

"Jesus," Rainie murmured. And all around the room, they were silent.

After a moment, Kaplan cleared his throat. "The victim this morning, she wasn't aligned in any particular manner. In fact, her arms and legs were spread in four different directions."

"I know."

"It's another inconsistency."

"I know."

"She did have a rock in her hand, though," Kaplan was saying, his eyes appraising Mac. "And a snake in her mouth. Can't say I've seen much of that."

"She also had a leaf in her hair," Mac said. "The ME pulled it out at the scene. I retrieved it later. I'll fetch it when we're done."

"You've destroyed chain of custody," Watson spoke up immediately.

"So paddle my behind. You want the leaf or not?"

"It just doesn't make sense," Kaplan was saying, still looking troubled. "On the one hand, the snake. Seems to indicate something off the business-as-usual map. On the other hand, all you really have in common is a letter to the editor written six months ago. Otherwise . . . it's been three years between bodies and this is the wrong state for your man. Could be related.

Or your caller could just be some asshole jerking your chain, and this body a matter of chance. You got an equal shot of going either way."

Around the room, others slowly started to nod. Watson, Quincy, Rainie. Only Kimberly remained apart. Mac was proud of her for that.

"I have a theory," he said abruptly. They looked at him, and he took that as an invitation.

"When this man started in 'ninety-eight, the first clues were obvious and easy. He ramped up pressure from there. Clues which were more difficult to find. Conditions which were harsher for the victims. A rapid escalation in time. He anticipated our own learning curve and to keep his game competitive, he remained one step ahead.

"Until the year two thousand. When we finally, seven bodies later, got it right. We saved the girl. And he quit. Because we'd finally won the game."

Mac looked at Quincy. "Serial killers don't quit," the profiler said obediently.

"Yeah, but they don't always know that, do they?"

Quincy nodded thoughtfully. "Sometimes they try. Bundy broke out of jail twice and both times he swore he'd stop attacking women. He'd quit, live a quiet life and get away scot-free. Except he couldn't. He underestimated the physiological and emotional need he had to kill. In fact, the more he tried not to kill, the worse the compulsion became. Until he attacked five girls in a single night."

"I think this guy tried to stop," Mac said, watching as Rainie and Kaplan closed their eyes. "Except the compulsion, like you said, just grew and grew and grew. Until he had to start again . . .

"It's not the old game," Mac told them grimly. "We won the old game. So now it's a new game. One where the victim's limbs will no longer serve as compass points. One where the map contains a live, lethal rattlesnake. And one where the body is left outside the FBI Academy because what point is there to inventing a game if you can't get the best to come out to play?

"In the year two thousand, this man killed three girls in twelve weeks. If this is the same man, if this is a new game, then whatever he's doing now, I promise you, it's going to be much, much worse. So sorry if I offend you ladies and gentlemen, but I can't just stand around talking about this anymore. You don't get to talk this case. You don't get to write up detective activity reports or create timelines of events. From the second that first body is found, the clock starts ticking. Now, if you want to have any chance at finding the second victim alive, then believe you me, get off your butts and get to work. 'Cause there's another girl out there, and I just hope to hell it's not already too late."

14

Virginia
7:52 P.M.
Temperature: 92 degrees

He was getting tired now. He'd been awake for close to forty-eight hours, and driving for a solid sixteen. The sun, bright and strong for most of the day, had helped keep him going. Daylight, however, was at long last beginning to fade. Behind him, the horizon was streaked with the vivid pinks and bright oranges of a dying sun. Ahead of him, in the thick wilderness into which he drove, the sun had already lost the war.

Darkness crowded under the thick canopy of trees. Shadows grew and lengthened, forming deep wells of black that swallowed up the world beyond sixty feet. Trees took on twisted, unnatural shapes, with leaves few and far between. Now, the landscape was interrupted only by double-wide trailers that squatted in the middle of fields, surrounded by the shells of burnt-out cars and old electrical appliances.

The man didn't have to worry about anyone noticing his approach.

Kids didn't play on these lawns. People didn't sit out on these front porches. Here and there he saw lone bloodhounds, scrawny dogs with drooping faces and jutting hipbones, sitting dispirited on broken-down steps. Otherwise, only the steady line of road-killed possums marked his way.

Life still existed around here. Not everyone could afford to move. And some people simply got used to the smell that constantly permeated the air. A cross between rotten eggs and burning garbage. A heavy, acrid smell that made old folks gag while bringing tears to the eyes of strangers. A smell that made even the locals wonder if the high rate of cancer among their neighbors was really so random after all.

This place was still Virginia. But technically, most of the state would like to forget this place ever existed. Virginia was supposed to be beautiful, famous for its green mountain ranges and wonderful sandy beaches. Virginia is for lovers, the tourism board liked to declare. It wasn't supposed to look like this.

The man took the right-hand fork in the road, leaving pavement behind and traveling on dirt. The van jostled and bounced noisily, the steering wheel jerking beneath his hands. He held it without much visible effort, though his muscles were tired and he still had several more rigorous hours to go. He would have some coffee after this. Take a minute to stretch out his arms and legs. Then there would be more work to do.

Life was about effort. Take your punishment like a man.

The thick canopy of trees gave way. His van suddenly burst into a clearing, where the dusky sky grew brighter and illuminated a scene straight out of a nightmare.

Yawning piles of sawdust stretched all the way up to the sky, still steaming from the compressed heat trapped in the middle and covered with a white film some people thought was dust, but was really a thin coating of fungus. To his left, ramshackle sheds with busted-out windows and teetering walls vainly attempted to shelter long conveyors lined with rusted belts and ending with giant saw blades. The teeth on the multiple blades appeared black in the fading light. Smeared with blood? Oil? It was anyone's guess.

This place had finally been closed down a few years ago. Too late. Tucked away in this backwoods shithole, the mill had already spent twenty years polluting streams, killing off surface vegetation, and doing far greater damage beneath the earth.

He'd seen the mill in action when he was younger. Watched workers attack tree trunks with gas-powered chain saws. No one wore protective eye gear. Few bothered with hard hats. Men strode around in loose flannel shirts, the excess material just waiting to get caught beneath the right hungry blade.

Coffee cups were tossed straight to the ground. Crumpled-up Coke cans formed an expanse of mini landmines. Old saw blades were yanked off the equipment and carelessly tossed aside. Walk around unaware and scratch up your pant leg. Walk around too unaware, and lose a limb.

That's the kind of place this was. And the mountains of sawdust had yet to spontaneously combust. Once that happened, there would be no hope for anything around here. Or anyone.

The stupid fucks. They destroyed the land, then called it quits, and had the gall to think that made things right.

The man got out of his van, reenergized by his outrage, and the bugs instantly swarmed his face. Mosquitoes, yellow flies, tiny gnats. They came en masse, attracted by the smell of fresh blood and salty sweat. The man waved his hand around his head but knew it was useless. Dusk was the hour for mosquitoes. And also for the brown bats, which were already swooping overhead and preparing to feast.

In the back of the van, the girl didn't stir. He'd administered 3.5 mg of Ativan four hours ago. She should be out for another two hours, if not four. That was important for the journey ahead.

First, he took care of himself. He donned a pair of blue coveralls. The material was a synthetic, thin but rubbery to the touch. As a general rule, he scorned unnatural fibers, but it was unavoidable here. The latest water test he'd done had revealed a pH level of 2.5; in other words, this water was so acidic, it would literally eat away cotton and peel away skin. Synthetic suit, it was.

Over his coveralls, the man donned a pair of canvas boots, then a thick pair of gloves. Around his waist went his care pack—extra water, saltine crackers, waterproof matches, a Swiss army knife, a handheld LED light, a compass, one extra loop of nylon rope, and two extra clamps.

Next, moving quickly, he turned his attention to the girl. This one was a brunette, not that it really mattered to him. She wore some kind of skimpy, yellow-flowered dress that did little to cover her long, tanned limbs. She looked like a runner, or some kind of athlete. Maybe that would help her in the days to come. Maybe it wouldn't.

He gritted his teeth, bent down, and hefted her unconscious form up over his shoulder. His arms screamed while his back groaned. She was not a heavy girl, but he was not a big man, and his body was already fatigued by forty-eight hours of intensive effort. Then he was standing, and the worst of the strain was over.

She got a suit of her own. For the entry. He dressed her the same way one might attend a doll. Flopping each limb into place. Tucking feet and hands where appropriate. Snapping the suit up tight.

Then he strapped her to the body board. At the last minute, he remembered her purse and the jug of water. Then he remembered her face, how close it would be to the acidic sludge, and pulled the hood as tightly as he could over her face.

He stood and the world went black.

What? Where? He needed to . . . He must . . .

He was standing in an old sawmill. He had a girl with him. He was outside his van.

The world spun again, black void threatening as he wobbled a little on his feet and clutched frantically at his temples. What? Where? He needed to . . . He must . . .

He was standing in an old sawmill. That's right. He had a girl with him . . . He rubbed his temples harder, trying to hold it together through a fresh burst of pain. Concentrate, man, focus. He was outside his van; he was wearing blue coveralls. He had his survival pack. The body board was already loaded with water; the girl was strapped on. Everything was all set.

Except that confused him even more. Why couldn't he remember getting it all set? What had happened?

The black holes, he realized faintly. They came more and more frequently these days. The future and the past, both slipping through his fingers with frightening speed. He was an educated man. Someone who prided himself on intelligence, strength, and control. But he, too, was part of nature's web. And nothing lived forever. Everything of beauty died.

Lately, he'd been dreaming so often of the flames.

The man reached down, attached his line to the body board, swung the rope over his shoulder and started to pull.

Seventeen minutes later, he had arrived at the opening of a small hole in the ground. Not many people would notice it, just another sinkhole in a state whose limestone foundation was more hole-riddled than Swiss cheese. This opening was special, though. The man had known it since his youth, and understood even back then its full potential.

First he had to fasten his rope around the thick trunk of a nearby tree, forming a rough belay. He stationed his feet for balance, then used the rope to carefully lower the body board down through the hole deep into the bowels of the earth. Ten minutes later, he heard the small splash of the board landing. He tied off one end of the rope around the tree, and rappelled down the other, also disappearing into the foul-smelling earth. He landed standing upright in knee-deep water. Fading light forty feet above. Endless darkness all around.

Most people never looked past the sawmill above. They didn't understand that in Virginia, there was often a whole other ecosystem far below.

He turned on his headlight, identified the cavern's narrow passageway to his right, and got on his hands and knees to crawl. The girl floated after him, the board's rope tied once more to the belt at his waist.

Within minutes the passageway shrank. He extended his narrow frame, body flattening carefully into the oily stream of rancid water. He was protected in synthetic shrink-wrap; he still swore he could feel the water lapping away at his skin, sluicing off his cells, eroding him down to his very bones. Soon the water would get into his brain, and then he would have no hope left. Ashes to ashes. Dust to dust.

The smells were richer now. The stifling decay of layers and layers of bat guano, now melted into an oozing morass that squished around his hands and knees. The sharp, pungent odor of sewage and waste. The deeper, more menacing smell of death.

He moved slowly, feeling his way even with the light. Bats startled easily and you didn't need a panicked, rabid creature flying at your face. Ditto the raccoons, though he'd be surprised if any of them could survive this passageway anymore. Most of what had once lived here had probably died years ago.

Now there was just this rancid water, corroding away the last of the limestone walls and spreading its slow, insidious death.

The body board bobbed along behind him, bumping him from time to time in the rear. And then, just when the ceiling was shrinking dangerously low, forcing his face closer and closer to that putrid water, the tunnel ended. The room opened up, and he and the girl spilled out into a vast, expansive cavern.

The man shot immediately to his feet, embarrassed by his own need to stand, but doing it nonetheless. He compulsively took giant gulps of air, his need for oxygen outweighing his apprehension of the smell. He looked down, and was genuinely surprised by how badly his hands were shaking.

He should be stronger than this. He should be tougher. Forty-eight hours without sleep, even he was starting to go.

He wasted another thirty seconds regaining his composure, then belatedly went to work on the rope at his waist. He was here, the worst of it was over, and he was aware once again of just how fast the clock was ticking.

He fetched the girl from the mini-stretcher. He laid her out on a ledge away from the dark running stream, and quickly stripped the coveralls from her body. Purse went beside her. Bottle of water as well.

Forty feet above, an eight-inch-diameter pipe formed a makeshift skylight in the ceiling. When daylight came, she would be greeted by a narrow shaft of light. He thought that gave her a sporting chance.

He retied the board to his waist, and ready now for his exit, gave the brunette one last glance.

She was propped up near a small pool of water. This water wasn't polluted like the stream. Not yet. It was replenished from the rain and put up a better fight.

This water rippled and surged with the promise of life. Things moved beneath the pitch-black surface. Things that lived and breathed and fought. Things that bit. Some things that slithered. And many things that wouldn't care for intruders in their home.

The girl was moaning again.

The man bent over. "Shhhh," he whispered in her ear. "You don't want to wake up just yet."

The water surged again. The man turned his back on the girl and left.

15

"She doesn't look very good," Rainie said.

"I know."

"What the hell happened to her eye? It looks like she's gone ten rounds with Tyson."

"Shotgun training would be my guess."

"She's definitely lost weight."

"It's not supposed to be easy."

"But you're worried about her. Come on, Quince. Give up the ghost. You'd like to go punch Watson's lights out. Pretty please. I'll hold him down for you."

Quincy sighed. He finally put down the case file he was reading—the homicide notes from the Georgia case years ago. These were just summary documents, of course. The original detective reports, evidence sheets, and activity logs probably took up enough boxes to fill a small family room. They both hated working off case summary reports—almost by definition, the documents were filled with erroneous assumptions and conclusions. Here, however, they had to make do.

The page Quincy currently had open was labeled "Profile: Atlanta Case #832." Rainie's hands itched reflexively. GBI's profile of the Eco-Killer, no doubt. She'd like to read that report herself, particularly after listening to that Georgian cop's take on things. But Quincy had grabbed the file first. He'd probably read it long into the night, pinching the bridge of his nose in that gesture which meant he was thinking too hard and giving himself a headache.

"If I say anything, she'll just get angry," he said now.

"That's because she's your daughter."

"Exactly. And my daughter hates for me to be involved in her life. My daughter believes pigs will fly before she'll accept help from me."

Rainie frowned at him. She was sitting Indian-style in the middle of the orange-covered bed. This was only her fourth time at Quantico and the place never failed to intimidate the crap out of her. The grounds practically screamed reputable-law-enforcement-agents-only. Even though she and Quincy had been together for six years, they were still given separate

628

rooms—they were unmarried, you know, and the Academy did have its sense of propriety.

Rainie knew the way the world worked. She would never have been allowed through those hallowed gates if she hadn't had Quincy to vouch for her. Not way back when, and not now. Thus, she could understand some of Kimberly's issues, having taken the long route to elite law enforcement herself.

"I don't think she's going to make it," Rainie said flatly. "She looks too haggard around the eyes. Like a dog that's been beat too many times."

"The training pushes you. It's meant to test your level of endurance."

"Oh, bullshit! You think Kimberly lacks endurance? My God, she held up even after a madman killed Bethie. She remained functional and alert when that same madman came after her. I was with her, remember. Kimberly has plenty of endurance. She doesn't need a bunch of numbnuts in suits to prove otherwise."

"I don't think Watson would care to be labeled a numbnut."

"Oh, now you're just pissing me off."

"Apparently." Quincy threw up his hands. He'd discarded his suit jacket after their meeting with Watson and Kaplan. Sequestered in his room, he'd even gone so far as to roll up the cuffs of his white dress shirt and loosen his tie. He still looked like an FBI agent, and Rainie had the overwhelming compulsion to fight with him, if only to mess him up a little. "What do you want me to do?" he asked.

"Stop being an agent."

"I am not an agent!"

"Oh, for the love of God. There is no agent more agent than you. I swear you have pin-striped ties encrypted into your DNA. When you die, the coffin is going to read Property of the FBI."

"Did you just think that up off the top of your head?"

"Yep, I'm on a roll. No changing the subject. Kimberly's in trouble. You've seen her, and you've seen how Watson is treating her. It's only a matter of time before things come to a head."

"Rainie . . . Not that you're going to want to hear this, but Watson is an experienced Academy supervisor. Maybe he has a point."

"What? Are you fucking mad?"

Quincy sighed deeply. "She disobeyed orders. Even if she had good reasons, she still disobeyed orders. Kimberly is a new agent. This is the life she chose, and the whole beginning of her career is going to be defined by doing what she's told. If she can't do that, maybe the FBI isn't the right organization for her."

"She found a body. When you were training here, how many bodies did you find? Uh huh. That's what I thought. She has the right to be a little rattled."

"Rainie, look at these crime-scene photos. You tell me. Who does this girl look like?"

Rainie grudgingly turned her gaze to the photos, currently spread out on the foot of the bed. "Mandy," she said without hesitation.

Quincy nodded somberly. "Of course she looks like Mandy. It's the first thing I noticed and the first thing you noticed. Yet Kimberly hasn't mentioned anything about it."

"If she so much as whispers that the victim reminds her of her dead sister, they'll cart her out of here in a straitjacket for sure."

"And yet the victim must remind her of her sister. Isn't that the whole point?"

Rainie scowled. He was leading her down some psychobabble trail. She could feel the trap closing in. "You're working the case," she countered.

"I've worked over three hundred homicides. I've had a bit more time to develop objectivity about these things."

"But you saw the resemblance."

"I did."

"Does it bother you, Quincy?"

"What? That a victim should look so much like Mandy, or that Mandy is still gone, and I never did a damn thing to help her?" His question was harsh. Rainie took that as an invitation to slide off the bed. He stiffened when she first touched his shoulders. She expected that. After all these years, they each still had their barriers and self-defenses. It didn't used to bother her so much. But lately it had been making her sad.

"You hurt for her," she whispered.

"For Kimberly? Of course I do. She's picked a hard path. It's just sometimes . . ." He blew out a breath.

"Go on."

"Kimberly wants to be tough. She wants to be strong. I understand that. After everything that happened to her, a desire for some level of invincibility is natural. And yet . . . does shooting a gun make you omnipotent, Rainie? Does pushing yourself to run six miles every day mean you'll never be a victim? Does engaging in every kind of physical combat imaginable mean you'll never lose?" He didn't wait for her answer; none was necessary. "Kimberly seems to honestly believe that if she can become an FBI agent, no one will ever hurt her again. Oh God, Rainie, it is so damn hard to watch your child repeat your own mistake."

Rainie slid her arms around his shoulder. She leaned her head against Quincy's chest. Then, because there were no words to comfort him, she went to the one topic that was always safe. Work. Dead bodies. A good, intriguing homicide case.

"Do you think the Georgian hunk is right?" she asked.

"The Georgian hunk?"

"I'm only thinking of Kimberly. I'm very altruistic that way. So, you grabbed the case file first. What do you think of his allegation that the Georgian Eco-Killer is now hunting Virginian prey?"

"I don't know yet," Quincy said reluctantly. His hand came up and rested on the back of her neck. After another moment, he stroked her hair. She closed her eyes, and thought for a moment that things might be all right.

"The Eco-Killer is an interesting case, remarkable almost more for what the investigators don't know about the killer than for what they do. For example, seven homicides later, the investigators have recovered no murder weapon, identified no primary murder scene, and not recovered a single bit of trace evidence such as hair, fiber, blood, or semen. In fact, the killer seems to have spent only the barest amount of time with each of the victims, limiting the opportunity for evidence transfer. He simply strikes, kills, and runs."

"An efficiency freak."

Quincy shrugged. "Most killers are driven by blood lust. They don't just want to kill, they want to savor their victim's pain and suffering. In contrast, this is the coldest string of murders I've ever seen. The UNSUB has little apparent interest in violence and yet, he is extraordinarily deadly."

"He's into gamesmanship," Rainie thought out loud. "For him the sport isn't the kill, but setting up the bodies, and establishing his riddles. Then he writes his notes, ensuring he'll receive credit for his crime."

"He writes the notes," Quincy agreed. "Giving his game an environmental slant. Now, do we believe this man really cares about the environment, or is this yet another aspect of his game? I don't know enough yet, but I'm fairly certain that even the notes are just another type of prop. The man is setting a stage. He is like the great Oz, hiding behind a curtain and pulling all the strings. But to what end? What does he really want—and what does he really get—out of doing all this? I don't have that answer yet."

"So what are the similarities between the Georgia case and this one?" Rainie prodded.

"Cause of death," Quincy said promptly. "There aren't too many serial predators who kill using prescription tranquilizers. At least not male killers."

"Women love poison," Rainie said knowingly.

"Exactly. Your dear friend Watson, however, also raised some good points. First, the Georgian Eco-Killer always dumped the first victim near a major road, where his 'map' per se could be easily found. Following that pattern, the victim could still be left on the Marine base, but should be near such roads as MCB-4 or MCB-3. A dirt jogging path isn't quite the same. Second, the stitched-up mouth bothers me. It shows an increased need for violence, postmortem mutilation of the victim, let alone the very obvious symbol of the victim keeping her mouth shut."

"Or the killer is engaging in a more dangerous game, as Special Agent McCormack theorizes."

"True. The new location, however, bothers me as well. I've only just glanced at the Georgia profile, but one of the main assumptions is that the man is local. His knowledge of certain areas is too intimate to be an outsider's. In fact, the very nature of his game is that of someone who lives in and loves his surroundings. That's not the kind of person who simply shifts to a whole new state."

"Maybe he felt the police were getting too close."

"It's possible. For his game to work in Virginia, however, he'd have to do his homework."

"What about the phone calls?" Rainie switched gears. "It seems more than coincidental that McCormack should start getting anonymous tips that the Eco-Killer would strike in Virginia right before the discovery of a new body. Seems to me the caller might know something."

"The anonymous tips are what make it interesting," Quincy agreed. He sighed again, then rubbed his temple. "Seems at the end of the day, we have six reasons why the cases shouldn't be related, and half a dozen reasons why they should. Now we need a tiebreaker." He looked at her. "You know what? We need to know the victim's ID. Right now, we have one body, which may or may not bear resemblance to another case. If, however, we had concrete evidence that *two girls* had been kidnapped . . ."

"Then it would definitely point to the Eco-Killer," Rainie filled in.

"Then I would definitely pay more attention to the Georgia case."

"Has Kaplan checked missing persons reports?"

"He has someone going through old files. No new cases, however, have opened up in the last twenty-four hours. At least not for a young woman."

"How sad," Rainie murmured. "To be kidnapped and murdered, and have no one even realize that you're gone yet."

"Most colleges are on break," Quincy said with a shrug. "If our victim is a student, the lack of a regular schedule might make it take longer for anyone to notice that she's disappeared."

"Maybe that's why there's no ID," Rainie said after a moment. "If we don't know who she is, we can't know for sure that she—or a companion—is missing. The Eco-Killer has bought himself some time."

Quincy eyed her speculatively. "But doesn't that work both ways?"

"He either is the Eco-Killer and doesn't want us to know it yet," she said slowly.

"Or someone has done their homework," Quincy concluded quietly. "Someone has committed murder, and now is seeking to cover his tracks by sending us off on a wild-goose chase."

"Where do you want to start?" she asked.

"We start where we always start. Close to home. Right here." His arms finally went around her waist. He drew her up against his chest. "Come on, Rainie," he murmured in her ear. "Tell me the truth. Haven't you always wanted to tear apart the FBI Academy?"

"You have no idea."

And then, a moment later: "I'm trying," he whispered.

"I know," she said, and closed her eyes against the fresh sting of tears.

16

Kimberly sat alone in her dorm room. Lucy had returned briefly, dumping one pile of books on the cluttered desk before scooping up the next.

"Wow, you look worse than you did this morning," she said by way of greeting.

"Been working on it all day," Kimberly assured her.

"Finding a corpse must be hard on a girl."

"So you heard."

"Everyone's heard, my dear. It's the hottest topic around. This your first corpse?"

"You mean other than my mother and sister?"

Lucy stilled in front of the desk. The silence grew long. "Well, I'm off to study group," she said finally. She turned, her expression gentle. "Want to come along, Kimberly? You know we don't mind."

"No," Kimberly said flatly.

And then Lucy was gone.

She should sleep. Supervisor Watson was right. Her nerves were frayed, the adrenaline rush gone and leaving her feeling empty. She wanted to tip over on the narrow bed. Slip into the blessed numbness of sleep.

She'd dream about Mandy. She'd dream about her mother. She wasn't sure which dream would hurt her worse.

She could find her father over at the Jefferson Dormitory. He would talk to her, he always did. But she knew already the look she'd see on his face. Slightly distracted, slightly puzzled. A man who had just started a terribly important assignment, and even as he listened to his daughter lament, the other half of his brain would be reshuffling crime-scene photos, murder books, investigator logs. Her father loved her. But she and Mandy had come to understand early on that he mostly belonged to the dead.

She couldn't stand the empty room. She couldn't stand the sound of footsteps in the hall. People meeting friends, sharing laughs, swapping stories, having a good time. Only Kimberly sat alone, the island she'd worked so hard to become.

She left the room, too. She took her knife and disappeared down the hall.

Outside it was hot. The dark, oppressive heat greeted her like a wall. Ten

P.M. and still this unbearably sticky. Tomorrow would be punishing for sure.

She slogged forward, feeling blotches of dark gray sweat bloom across the front of her T-shirt, while more moisture began trailing down the small of her back. Her breath came out in shallow pants, her lungs laboring to find oxygen in air that was 90 percent water.

She could still hear fading laughter. She turned away from it and headed toward the welcoming dark of the firing range. No one came out here this time of night. Well, almost no one.

The thought came only briefly, and then she knew just how much trouble she was in.

"Been waitin' for you," Special Agent Mac McCormack drawled softly, pushing away from the entrance to the range.

"You shouldn't have."

"I don't like to disappoint a pretty girl."

"Did you bring a shotgun? Well then, too bad."

He merely grinned at her, his teeth a flash of white in the dark. "I thought you'd spend more time with your father."

"Can't. He's working the case and I'm not allowed."

"Being family doesn't entitle you to some perks?"

"You mean like a sneak peek of homicide photos? I think not. My father is a professional. He takes his job seriously."

"Now, how many years of therapy has it taken you to say that in such a calm, clear voice?"

"More than most suspect," she admitted grudgingly.

"Come on, sugar. Let's take a seat." He headed out into the green field of the range without looking back. It amazed her how easy it was to follow him.

The grass was nice. Soft beneath her battered body. Cool against her bare, sweat-slicked legs. She lay back, with her knees pointed at the sky and her short, serrated hunting knife snug against the inside of her left leg. Mac lay down beside her. Close. His shoulder brushing hers. She found his proximity faintly shocking, but she didn't move away.

He'd showered since their meeting with Kaplan and Watson. He smelled like soap and some kind of spicy men's aftershave. She imagined that his hair was probably still damp. For that matter, his cheeks had appeared freshly shaven when he'd walked through the glow cast by the streetlight. Had he cleaned up for her? Would it matter if he had?

She liked the smell of his soap, she decided, and left it at that.

"Stars are out," he said conversationally.

"They do that at night."

"You noticed? Here I thought you driven new agent types were too busy for those kinds of things."

"In personal combat training, we get to spend a lot of time on our backs. It helps."

He reached over and brushed her cheek. The contact was so unexpected, she flinched.

"A blade of grass," he said calmly. "Stuck to your cheek. Don't worry, honey. I'm not gonna attack you. I know you're armed."

"And if I wasn't?"

"Why then, I'd roll you right here and now, of course. Being a testosterone-bound male who's prone to that kind of brutish behavior."

"I don't mean it that way."

"You don't like touching much, do you? I mean, biting, flipping and beating the bejesus out of me aside."

"I'm not . . . used to it. My family was never very demonstrative."

He seemed to consider that. "If you don't mind me saying, your father seems wound a bit tight."

"My father is wound *way* tight. And my mother came from an upper-class family. As you can imagine, holidays were a gay, frolicking time in our home. You wouldn't believe the boisterous outbreaks."

"My family's loud," he volunteered casually. "Not big, but definitely demonstrative. My father still grabs my mother around the waist and tries to lure her into dark corners. As an adult, I appreciate their relationship. As a kid . . . Hell, we were scared to death not to announce ourselves before walking down a darkened hall."

Kimberly smiled faintly. "You got an education?"

"Heavens, yes. It's sweet, though, I suppose. My father's a civil engineer who designs roads for the state. My mother teaches high school English. Who would've thought they'd be so happy?"

"Siblings?"

"One sister. Younger, of course. I terrorized her for most of our childhood. On the other hand, every time I fell asleep in the family room, she put makeup on my face and took pictures. So I guess it evens itself out. Plus, I'm the only man you'll ever meet who understands just how hard it is to remove waterproof mascara. And I guess I'll never run for political office. The photos alone would ruin me."

"What does she do now?"

"Marybeth's a kindergarten teacher, so in other words, she's tougher than most cops. Has gotta be to keep all those little critters in line. Maybe when they fall asleep, she puts makeup on their faces, too. I'm too scared to ask."

"You're the only police officer in your family."

"I have a cuz who's a fireman. That's pretty close."

She smiled again. "They sound like fun."

"They are," he agreed, and she heard the genuine affection in his voice. "I mean, they could still use some good training and all. But as families go, they're keepers. Do you miss your mother and sister?" he asked abruptly.

"Yes."

"Should I shut up?"

"Would you obey me if I said yes?"

"No. I suppose I need some training, too. Besides, the stars are out. You should always talk when you're lying beneath the stars."

"I hadn't heard that before," Kimberly said, but she turned her face up toward the night sky, feeling the hot air against her face, and it did make it easier. "My family wasn't happy. Not in the typical way. But we tried. I give us credit for that. We wanted to be happy, so we tried. I guess you could say we were earnest."

"Your parents divorced?"

"Eventually. When we were teens. But the problems were way before that. The usual cop stuff. My father had a demanding job, worked long hours. And my mom . . . She'd been raised expecting something different. She would've done well with a banker, I think. Or even a doctor; the hours would've been just as bad, but at least her husband would've held a title with a certain level of decorum. My father, on the other hand, was an FBI pro- filer. He dealt in death, *extreme* violent death each and every day. I don't think she ever got used to that. I don't think she ever stopped finding it dis- tasteful."

"It's a good job," Mac said quietly.

She turned toward him, finding herself surprisingly serious. "I think so. I was always proud of him. Even when he had to leave in the middle of birth- day parties or missed them altogether. His job sounded so larger-than-life to me. Like something a superhero would do. People got hurt. And my father went to save the day. I missed him, I'm sure I had tantrums, but mostly I remember feeling proud. My daddy was cool. For my sister, however, it was another story."

"Older or younger?"

"Mandy was older. She was also . . . different. High-strung. Sensitive. A little wild. I think my first memory of her is her being yelled at for breaking something. She struggled with our parents. I mean, really, truly struggled. They were so by-the-book and she was so color-outside-the-lines. And life was harder for her in other ways. She took things to heart too much. One harsh word and she was wounded for days. One wrong look and she'd be devastated. She had nightmares, was prone to crying jags and had genuine fits. My father's job terrified her. My parents' divorce shattered her. And adulthood didn't get much easier."

"She sounds intense."

"She was." For a moment, Kimberly was silent. "You know what gets to me, though? You know what's truly ironic?"

"What?"

"She needed us. She was exactly the kind of person that my father and I have sworn our lives to protect. She wasn't tough. She made bad choices. She drank too much, she dated the wrong men, she believed anyone's pack of lies. God, she desperately needed someone to save her from herself. And we didn't do it. I spent so much of my childhood resenting her. Crying, com- plaining Mandy who was always upset about something. Now, I just wonder why we didn't take better care of her. She was in our own family. How could we fail her so completely?"

Mac didn't say anything. He touched her cheek again. Gently. With his thumb. She felt the slow rasp of his work-roughened skin all the way down to her jaw line. It made her shiver. Then it made her want to close her eyes, and arch her back like a cat.

"Another blade of grass?" she whispered.

"No," he said softly.

She turned toward him then, knowing her eyes said too much, knowing she needed more armor, but helpless to find it now.

"They don't believe you," she said softly.

"I know." His fingers traced along her jaw, lingered at the curve of her ear.

"My father's good. Very good. But like all investigators, he's meticulous. He's going to start at the very beginning and have to work his way toward your conclusion. Maybe on another case it wouldn't matter. But if you're right, and there's another girl already out there . . ."

"Clock's ticking," Mac murmured. The rough pads of his fingers returned along her jaw, then feathered down her neck. She could feel her chest rising and falling faster. As if she were running once more through the woods. Was she running toward something this time, or was she still running away?

"You're very relaxed about all this," she said brusquely.

"The case? Not really." His fingers stopped moving. They rested at the base of her neck, his fingers bracing her collarbone and her skittering pulse. He was gazing at her with an intense look. A man about to kiss a woman? A cop obsessed with a difficult case? She was no good at this sort of thing. The Quincy women had a long history of being unlucky at love. In fact, the last man her mother and Mandy thought they had loved had killed them both. That was female intuition for you.

She wished suddenly that she didn't think of her family so much. She wished suddenly that she really were an island, that she could be born again without any attachments, without any past. What would her life have become if her family hadn't been murdered? Who would've Kimberly Quincy been then?

Kinder, softer, gentler? The kind of woman capable of kissing a handsome man under the stars? Maybe a woman actually capable of falling in love?

She turned her head away. Pulled her body away from his touch. It didn't matter anymore. She suddenly hurt too much to look him in the eye.

"You're going to work this, aren't you?" she asked, giving him her back.

"I did a little reading on Virginia this afternoon," he said conversationally, as if she hadn't just jerked away. "Did you know this state has over forty thousand square acres of beaches, mountains, rivers, lakes, bays, swamps, reservoirs, and caverns? We're talking several major mountain ranges offering over a thousand miles of hiking trails. Two million acres of public land. Then we have the Chesapeake Bay, which is the largest coastal estuary in the United States. Plus, four thousand caverns and several reservoirs that have been formed by flooding complete towns. You want rare and ecologically sensitive? Virginia has rare and ecologically sensitive. You want dangerous? Virginia has dangerous. In short, Virginia is perfect for Eco-Killer, and hell yes, I'm definitely gonna pursue a few things."

"You don't have jurisdiction."

"All's fair in love and war. I called my supervisor. We both believe this is the first solid lead we've had in months. If I take off from the National Academy to do a little sidebar exploration, he's not gonna cry any rivers. Besides, your father and NCIS are moving too slow. By the time they realize what we already know, the second girl will be long dead. I don't want that, Kimberly. After all these years, I'm tired of being too late."

"What will you do?"

"First thing tomorrow morning, I'm meeting with a botanist from the U.S. Geological Survey team. Then I'll take it from there."

"Why are you meeting a botanist? You don't have the leaf anymore."

"I don't have the original," he said quietly. "But I might have scanned a copy."

She turned sharply. "You copied evidence."

"Yep."

"What else?"

"Gonna run to Daddy?"

"You know me better than that!"

"I'm trying to."

"You really are obsessed with this, you know. You could be wrong. This case could have no bearing on the Eco-Killer or those girls in Georgia. You missed your man the first time. Now you see what you want to see."

"It's possible." He shrugged. "Does it matter? A girl is dead. A man did it. Whether he's my guy or someone else's guy, finding the son of a bitch will make the world a better place. Frankly, that's good enough for me."

Kimberly scowled. It was hard to argue with that kind of logic. She said abruptly, "I want to go with you."

"Watson will have your hide." Mac sat up, brushing the grass from his hands. "He'll kick you out so far so fast, it'll be days before you feel the bruise on your butt."

"I can take personal leave. I'll talk to one of the counselors. Plead emotional distress from finding a dead body."

"Ah honey, you tell them you got emotional distress from finding a corpse, and they'll kick you out for sure. This is the FBI Academy. You can't handle a corpse, you're in the wrong line of work."

"It's not his call. The counselor says yes, I get to go, simple as that."

"And once he learns what you're really doing?"

"I'm on leave. What I do in my personal time is my business. Watson has no authority over me."

"You haven't been in the FBI very long, have you, Kimberly?"

Kimberly's chin came up. She understood his point. She agreed with his point, which was why her heart was pounding so hard in her chest. Pursuing this case would earn her her first political enemy. Let alone a less-than-stellar start to her career. She'd waited twenty-six years to become an FBI agent. Funny, how easy it seemed to throw it all away now.

"Kimberly," Mac said abruptly as if reading her thoughts, "you know that this won't bring your mother or sister back, don't you? That no matter how many murderers you hunt down, none of it changes the fact that your family is still dead, and you still didn't save them in time?"

"I've been to their graves, Mac. I know how dead they are."

"And you're just a rookie," he continued relentlessly. "You know nothing about this guy, you're not even fully trained. Your efforts probably won't make one iota of difference. Think about that before you throw away your career."

"I want to go."

"Why?"

She finally smiled at him, though she knew the look must appear strained on her face. There was the million-dollar question. And honestly, there were so many answers she could give. That Watson had been right this morning, and nine weeks later she had no friendships or allegiances among her own classmates. In fact, the closest she'd come to feeling any loyalty was for a dead body she'd found in the woods.

Or that she did feel survivor's guilt, and she was tired of holidays spent in fields of white crosses. Or that she had a morbid need to chase after death, having once felt its fingers brush across the nape of her neck. Or that she was her father's daughter after all. No good with the living, desperately attached to the dead, particularly when the body bore such a startling resemblance to Mandy.

So many possible answers. She surprised herself then, by going with the one that was closest to the truth. "Because I want to."

Mac stared at her a heartbeat longer, then suddenly, finally, nodded in the dark. "All right. Six A.M. Meet me in the front of Jefferson. Bring hiking gear.

"And Kimberly," he added as they both rose. "Don't forget your Glock."

17

Albany, Georgia
1:36 A.M.
Temperature: 85 degrees

Nora Ray's mother was still watching TV. She slumped on their old brown sofa, wearing the same faded pink bathrobe she'd worn for the past three years. Her short dark hair stood up around her face, gray showing at the roots, where it would remain until Nora Ray's grandmother visited again and forcefully took her daughter in hand. Otherwise, Abigail Watts rarely moved from the sofa. She sat perfectly hunched, mouth slightly agape, eyes fixed straight ahead. Some people turned to booze, Nora Ray thought. Her mother had Nick@Nite.

Nora Ray still remembered the days when her mother had been beautiful. Abigail had risen at six every morning, fixing her hair in hot rollers and doing her makeup while her hair set. By the time Nora Ray and Mary Lynn made it downstairs for breakfast, their mother would be bustling around the kitchen in a nice floral dress, pouring coffee for their father, setting out cereal for them, and prattling away cheerfully until seven-oh-five on the dot, at which point she would grab her purse and head to work. She had been a secretary at a law firm back then. Not great money, but she'd enjoyed the job and the two partners who ran the place. Plus, it gave her an aura of prestige in the tiny blue-collar neighborhood where they lived. Working at a law firm . . . Now, that was respectable work.

Nora Ray's mother hadn't been to the office now in years. Nora Ray didn't even know if she'd ever officially quit. More likely she'd walked out one day after getting a call from the police, and she'd never been back since.

The lawyers had been nice about it. They'd volunteered their services for a trial that never happened in a case where the perpetrator was never caught. They kept Abigail on the payroll for a while. Then they put her on a leave of absence. And now? Nora Ray couldn't believe her mom still had a job after three years. No one was that nice. No one's life stayed frozen for that long a period of time.

Except, of course, for Nora Ray's family. They lived in a time warp. Mary Lynn's room, painted sunshine yellow and lined with blue ribbons and horse trophies, remained exactly the same day after day. The last pair of dirty jeans she'd tossed in the corner were still waiting for an eighteen-year-old girl to come home and throw them in the wash. Her hairbrush, filled with long strands of brunette hair, sat on top of her dresser. A tube of pink lip gloss was half-opened next to the brush. Ditto the tube of mascara.

And still taped to the mirror above the dresser was the letter from Albany State University. *We are proud to inform you that Mary Lynn Watts has been formally accepted into the freshman class of 2000 . . .*

Mary Lynn had wanted to study veterinary sciences. Someday she could work full-time saving the horses she loved so much. Nora Ray was going to become a lawyer. Then they would buy farms side by side in the country, where they could ride horses together every morning before reporting to their high-paying and no doubt highly rewarding jobs. That's what they had talked about that summer. Giggled about, really. Especially that last night, when it had been so friggin' hot, they had decided to head out for ice cream.

In the beginning, right after Nora Ray came home and Mary Lynn didn't, things had been different. People stopped by, for one thing. The women brought casseroles and cookies and pies. The men showed up with lawn mowers and hammers, wordlessly attending to small details around the house. Their little home had hummed with activity, everyone trying to be solicitous, everyone wanting to make sure that Nora Ray and her family were all right.

Her mother had still showered and put on clothes in those days. Bereft of a daughter, she at least clung to the skeletal fabric of everyday life. She got up, put her hair in rollers, and started the pot of coffee.

Her father had been the worst back then. Roaming from room to room while constantly flexing his big, work-callused hands, a dazed look in his eyes. He was the man who was supposed to be able to fix anything. He'd built their deck one summer. He did odd jobs around the neighborhood to help pay for Mary Lynn's horse camp. He painted their house like clockwork every three years and kept it the neatest one on the block.

Big Joe could do anything. Everyone said that. Until that day in July.

Eventually people stopped coming by so much. Food no longer magically appeared in the kitchen. Their lawn was no longer mowed every Sunday. Nora Ray's mom stopped getting dressed. And her father returned to his job at Home Depot, coming home every night to join her mother on the couch, where they would sit like zombies in front of a score of mindless comedies, the TV spraying their faces with brightly colored images deep into the night.

While weeds took over their lawn. And their front porch sagged with neglect. And Nora Ray learned how to cook her mother's casseroles while her own dreams of law school drifted further and further away.

People in the neighborhood whispered about them now. *That sad family in the sad little house on the corner. Did you hear what happened to their daughter? Well, let me tell you . . .*

Sometimes Nora Ray thought she should walk around with a scarlet letter attached to her clothes, like the woman in that book she'd read her senior year of high school. Yes, we're the family that lost a daughter. Yes, we're the ones who actually fell victim to violent crime. Yes, it could happen to you, too, so you're right, you should turn away when we walk too close and whisper behind our backs. Maybe murder is contagious, you know. It's found our house. Soon, it'll find yours.

She never said these things out loud, however. She couldn't. She was the last functioning member of her family. She had to hold it together. She had to pretend that one daughter could be enough.

Her mother's head was starting to bob now, in that way it did right before sleep. Her father had already called it a night. He had work in the morning and that made him somewhat more normal, in this strange little pattern they called their lives.

Abigail finally succumbed. Her head fell back. Her shoulders sank into the deep comfort of their overstuffed sofa, bought during happier times and meant for happier days.

And Nora Ray finally stepped into the room. She didn't turn off the TV. She knew better by now; the sudden absence of TV voices awakened her mother faster than any shrieking alarm. Instead, she merely took the remote from the pocket of her mother's faded bathrobe and slowly turned down the volume.

Her mother started to snore. Soft little wheezes of a woman who hadn't moved in months, yet remained exhausted beyond her years.

Nora Ray clenched her hands by her sides. She wanted to stroke her mother's face. She wanted to tell her everything would be all right. She wanted to plead for her real mother to come back to her because sometimes she didn't want to be the strong one. Sometimes, she wanted to be the one who curled up and cried.

She set the remote on the coffee table. Then she tiptoed back to her room, where the air-conditioning was permanently cranked to a frosty fifty-eight and a full pitcher of water sat by her bed at all times.

Nora Ray buried herself under the thick comfort of her bedcovers, but she still didn't fall immediately asleep.

She was thinking of Mary Lynn again. She was thinking of their last night, driving back from T.G.I. Friday's, and Mary Lynn chatting away merrily in the driver's seat.

"Uh oh," her sister was saying. "I think we just got a flat. Oh, wait. Good news. Some guy's pulled in behind us. Isn't that neat, Nora Ray? The world is just filled with good people."

The man was tired. Very, very tired. Shortly after two A.M. he completed his last chore and wearily called it a night. He returned the van to where it belonged, and though his muscles truly ached now, he took the time to wash the vehicle, inside and out, by the comforting glow of lantern light. He even crawled under the van and hosed down the undercarriage. Dirt could tell stories. Didn't he know.

Next he pulled out the dog carrier. He sponged it down with ammonia, the sharp, pungent scent stinging his senses back into hyperalertness, while also destroying any evidence of fingerprints.

Finally, he took inventory. He should wash down the aquarium, too, though what could it prove? That he once had a pet snake? No crime in that. Still, you didn't want to leave things to chance.

You didn't want to be one of those dumb fucks his father talked about, who couldn't find their assholes with a flashlight and their own two hands.

The world was spinning. He felt the gathering storm clouds in the back of his brain. When he got tired, the spells grew worse. The black holes grew to tremendous size, swallowing not just hours and minutes, but sometimes consuming entire days. He couldn't afford that now. He had to be sharp. He had to be alert.

He thought of his mother again and the sad look she wore every time she watched the sun die in the sky. Did she know the planet was dying? Did she understand even back then that anything that was beautiful could not belong long on this earth?

Or was she simply afraid to go back inside, where his father would be waiting with his quick temper and hamlike fists?

The man did not like these thoughts. He didn't want to play this game anymore. He jerked the aquarium from the inside of the van. He dumped its grass and twig matting into the woods. Then he dumped in half of a bottle of ammonia and went to work with his bare hands. He could feel the harsh chemical burn his skin.

Later the runoff from this little exercise would seep into a stream, and kill off algae, bacteria, and cute little fishes. Because he was no better, you know. No matter what he did, he was still a man who drove a car and bought a refrigerator and probably once kissed a girl who used a can of aerosol spray on her hair. Because that's what men did. Men killed. Men destroyed. Men beat their wives, abused their kids, and took a planet and warped it into their own twisted image.

His eyes were running now. Snot poured from his nose and his chest heaved until his breath came out in savage gasps. The harsh scent of ammonia, he thought. But he knew better. He was once again thinking of his mother's pale, lonely face.

He and his brother should have gone back inside with her. They could've walked through the door first, judged the mood, and if it came to it, taken their punishment like M-E-N. They didn't, though. Their father was home, and they ran away into the woods, where they lived like gods on pokeweed salad, wild raspberries, and tender fiddleheads.

They turned to the land for shelter, and tried not to think about what was happening back in one tiny cabin in the woods. At least that's what they'd done when they could.

The man turned off the hose. The van was washed, the aquarium cleansed, the whole project sanitized within an inch of its life. Forty-eight hours later, it was over.

He was tired again. Bone-deep weary in a way that people who had never killed could never appreciate. But it was over. Now, at long last, he was done.

He took his kill kit away with him. Later, he tucked it beneath his mattress before finally crawling into bed.

His head touched the pillow. He thought of what he had just done. High heels, blond hair, blue eyes, green dress, bound hands, dark hair, brown eyes, long legs, scratching nails, flashing white teeth.

The man closed his eyes. He slept the best he had in years.

18

Quincy jerked awake to the sound of the phone ringing. Instinct bred of so many other calls in the middle of so many other nights led him to reach automatically toward the nightstand. Then the ringing penetrated a second time, shrill and insistent, and he remembered that he was at the FBI Academy, staying in a dorm room, where the lone phone sat on the desk halfway across the room.

He moved quietly and quickly, but it was no longer necessary. Even as he cut off the third ring, Rainie was sitting up sleepily in the bed. Her long chestnut hair was tousled around her pale face, drawing attention to the striking angles of her cheeks and the long, bare column of her neck. God, she was lovely first thing in the morning. For that matter, she was lovely at the end of a long day. All these years later, day in, day out, she never failed to take his breath away.

He looked at her, and then, as happened too often these days, he felt a sharp pain in his chest. He turned away, cradling the phone between his shoulder and his ear.

"Pierce Quincy."

And then a moment later, "Are you sure? That's not what I meant— Kimberly . . . Well, if that's what you want to do. Kimberly . . ." Big sigh again. The beginning of a headache already building in his temples. "You're a grown adult, Kimberly. I respect that."

It didn't do him any good. His last surviving daughter had ended yesterday angry with him and had apparently started today even madder. She slammed down the phone. He returned his own receiver much more gently, trying not to notice how his hands shook. He had been trying to mend the bridge with his mercurial daughter for six years now. He hadn't made much progress yet.

In the beginning, Quincy had thought Kimberly simply needed time. After the intense episode of what happened to their family, of course she harbored a great deal of rage. He had been an FBI agent, a trained professional, and still he'd done nothing to save Bethie and Amanda. If Kimberly hated him, he couldn't blame her. For a long time, he had hated himself, too.

Now, however, as year advanced into year, and the raw ache of loss and failure began to subside, he wondered if it wasn't something more insidious than that. He and his daughter had gone through a harrowing experience. They had joined forces to outwit a psychopath as he'd hunted them down one by one. That kind of experience changed people. Changed relationships.

And it built associations. Perhaps Kimberly simply couldn't view him as a father anymore. A parent should be a safe harbor, a source of shelter amid turbulent times. Quincy was none of those things in his daughter's eyes. In fact, his presence was probably a constant reminder that violence often struck close to home. That real monsters didn't live under the bed. They could be very attractive, fully functioning members of society, and once they targeted you, not even a smart, strong, professionally trained father could make any difference.

It still amazed Quincy how easy it was to fail the ones you loved.

"Was that Kimberly?" Rainie asked from behind him. "What did she want?"

"She's leaving the Academy this morning. She talked one of the counselors into giving her a leave of absence for emotional distress."

"Kimberly?" Rainie's voice was incredulous. "Kimberly, who would walk barefoot through fire before asking for a pair of shoes, let alone a fire extinguisher? No way."

Quincy merely waited. It didn't take long. Rainie had always been exceptionally bright. She got it in the next instant.

"She's going to work the case!" she exclaimed suddenly. In contrast to his reaction, however, she threw back her head and laughed. "Well, what do you know. I told you the Georgian was a hunk!"

"If Supervisor Watson finds out," Quincy said seriously, "her career will be over."

"If Watson finds out, he'll simply be mad he didn't get to save the second girl first." Rainie bounded out of bed. "Well, what do you want to do?"

"Work," Quincy said flatly. "I want the ID on the victim."

"Yes, sir!"

"And maybe," he mused carefully, "it wouldn't hurt to pay a visit to the forensic linguist, Dr. Ennunzio."

Rainie regarded him in surprise. "Why, Pierce Quincy, are you beginning to believe in the Eco-Killer?"

"I don't know. But I definitely think that my daughter is much too involved. Let's work, Rainie. And let's work fast."

Kimberly and Mac drove toward Richmond mostly in silence. She learned that his taste in radio stations ran toward country music. In turn, she taught him that she didn't function well without a morning cup of coffee.

They had taken his car; the rented Toyota Camry was nicer than her ancient Mazda. Mac had thrown a backpack filled with supplies into the trunk. Kimberly had added hiking boots and a duffel bag filled with her sparse collection of clothes.

She'd retrieved her gun first thing this morning, turning in the plastic Crayola along with her handcuffs. She signed a few forms, relinquished her ID, and that was that. She was officially on leave from the FBI Academy. For the first time since she was about nine years old, she was not actively aspiring to be a federal agent.

She should feel anxious, guilt-stricken, and horrified, she thought. So many years of her life she was suddenly throwing away on a whim. As if she ever did anything on a whim. As if her life had ever held a hint of the whimsical.

And yet, she didn't feel horrible. No shortness of breath that would indicate an oncoming anxiety attack. No bunched muscles or pounding headache. In all honesty, she actually felt the lightest she had in weeks. Maybe, beneath her sleep-deprived haze, she was even a little giddy.

What that meant, she didn't want to know.

They made good time getting to Richmond. Mac handed her a printed-out e-mail, and she navigated to the offices of the U.S. Geological Survey team, which were located in an office park north of the city. First glance wasn't what Kimberly had expected. The office park, for one thing, was plunked down in the middle of suburban sprawl. They passed a community college, a housing development, and a local school. There were lovely sidewalks shaded by graceful trees, wide expanses of deep green yards, and brightly flowering pink and white crepe myrtle trees.

The USGS office building, too, was different from what she had pictured. One story of brick and glass. Newer. Lots of windows. Nicely landscaped with more crepe myrtle trees and God knows what kind of bushes. Definitely a far cry from the usual government décor of monochromatic malaise.

So a nice building in a nice place. Kimberly wondered if Mac knew that the FBI Richmond field office was literally right down the street.

She and Mac got out of the car, pushed their way through the heavy glass door and were immediately greeted by the waiting receptionist.

"Ray Lee Chee," Mac said. The receptionist smiled at them brightly, then led the way.

"He's a botanist?" Kimberly asked as she followed Mac down the wide, sunny hall.

"Geographer, actually."

"What's a geographer?"

"I think he works on maps."

"You're bringing our leaf to a *mapmaker*?"

"Genny knows him. He went to school with her brother or something like that. Apparently he has a background in botany and he said he could help." Mac shrugged. "I have no jurisdiction; it's not like I can order up any expert I want in the state."

The receptionist had arrived at an interior office. She gestured to the partially opened door, then turned back down the hall, leaving Kimberly alone with Mac, already wondering if this wasn't some kind of fool's errand.

"Mr. Chee?" Mac asked, poking his head through the doorway. A short, well-built Asian man promptly fired back his desk chair and popped up to greet them.

"Oh God, don't call me that. Ray, by all means, or I'll keep looking around for my father."

Ray pumped Mac's hand vigorously, then greeted Kimberly with the same enthusiasm. The geographer was younger than Kimberly would've thought, and definitely not a dried-out academic. He sported khaki shorts and a short-sleeved shirt made out of one of those micro-fibers favored by hikers for wicking the sweat from their bodies.

Now, he gestured them into his paper-jammed office, then bounced back into his chair with about four times the necessary energy. His biceps bulged even when sitting and his hands were moving a mile a minute around his desk, looking for God knows what.

"So Genny said you needed my help," Ray stated brightly.

"We're trying to identify a leaf. I understand you have some experience in that sort of thing."

"Spent my undergrad days studying botany," Ray said, "before I moved into geography. For that matter, I also studied zoology and for a brief stint in time, auto mechanics. Seemed kind of funky at the time. On the other hand, when our truck gets stuck out in the field, everyone's happy to have me along." He turned toward Kimberly. "Do you talk?"

"Not before coffee."

"You need some java? I brewed the world's strongest batch in the kitchenette just half an hour ago. Stuff will knock the ZZZs right out of you, while putting some hair on your chest." He held up both of his hands, which were trembling with caffeine jitters. "Want some?"

"Mmmm, I think I'll wait."

"Well, suit yourself, but after the first sixteen ounces or so, I'm telling you, it's not so bad." His dark gaze rebounded to Mac. "So where's the leaf?"

"Actually, we brought you a picture." Mac dug into his folder and pulled out the piece of paper.

"That's all you got? A *picture*?"

"It's a scanned image. Actual size. Front and back." Ray kept staring at him and finally Mac shrugged ruefully. "Sorry, man. It's all we got."

"A real leaf would be better, you know. I mean, *much* better. What's this for again?"

"It's a piece of evidence in a case."

"Like from a crime scene?" Ray's face brightened. "If I ID this, can it be used to catch the bad guy or locate a corpse? Like they do on *CSI*?"

"Absolutely," Mac assured him.

"Groovy." Ray accepted the paper with more enthusiasm. "A picture is definitely tougher, but I like a challenge. Let's see what you got."

He took out a magnifying glass and studied the image for a second. "Well, let's start with the basics. It's an angiosperm—to you, a broadleaf tree. Given the oval shape with pointed tip and coarse-tooth margins, it's most likely from the *Betula* family—some kind of birch." He looked up. "Where did you find this again?"

"I'm afraid I can't comment further on that subject."

Ray resumed staring at the picture. He frowned. "This is really all you've got? No bark, no flowers, no twig?"

"That's it."

"Well, then you also like a challenge." Ray's desk chair shot back. He jerked to a stop in front of the bookshelf across the way and rapidly skimmed titles. His fingers settled on a big volume labeled *Gray's Manual of Botany.* "In the good news/bad news department, birch is one of the larger tree families, with a number of species commonly found here in Virginia. If you're into history, the old Appalachian mountaineers used to make birch beer from the sap of black birch trees, which tastes a bit like wintergreen. They came close to harvesting all of the black birches in the mountains to make the stuff, then synthetic wintergreen oil was developed, and the mountaineers moved on to making moonshine. All's well that ends well, you know."

He shot back to his desk, propelling his chair as easily as a small automobile, while his fingers rapidly flipped through the thick index guide. Peering over his shoulder, Kimberly saw page after page of tree leaves, all richly photographed and documented with lists of words that appeared to be in Latin. Definitely not a light summer read.

"Okay, for starters we have *Betula lenta,* otherwise known as black birch, sweet birch, or cherry birch. Its leaves are approximately three to four inches long. Your picture is closer to two and a half inches long, but maybe our leaf isn't mature yet, so that's a possibility."

"Where are black birches found?" Mac asked.

"Oh, a little bit of everywhere. You can find them in the mountains of the western half of the state, or around parts of Chesapeake Bay close to streams. Does that work?"

"I don't know yet," Mac said. Now, he was also frowning. "Other options?"

"The *Betula lutea,* or yellow birch, which is found generally higher up in the mountains than the black birch. It's a significantly larger tree, however, growing up to eighty feet with five-inch leaves, so I'm going to guess that it's too big to be our suspect here. Let's see . . ." Ray rapidly flipped through the book.

"Okay, consider *Betula papyrifera,* or paper birch. Leaves also grow three inches in length, which is closer in size. It's also found in the mountains, generally in clear-cut or burned-out areas. Then there's *Betula nigra,* or river birch, which is found in low elevations along waterways or around streams, ponds, lakes, etc. It's also a smaller birch with leaves two to three inches long. So that's a possibility." He looked up at them sharply. "You don't have any catkins?"

"Cat what?"

"The flowers that are generally found with the leaves. In birches, they resemble long, conelike structures, dangling down from amid the leaves. Flower size varies dramatically, which would help narrow the scope. Better yet, would be a twig with bark. As you can guess from the names, black versus yellow versus paper, one of the key distinguishing features of birch is the color of the tree's bark."

"I only have a leaf," Mac said, then muttered under his breath, "because our guy also likes a challenge." He turned toward Kimberly, the tension building in his shoulders.

"He wouldn't use something common," she said quietly. "No compass, remember? So this time, the clues must narrow down a region. Or it's really not that much of a game."

"Good point." Mac turned back toward the geographer. "You said birches are commonly found in Virginia. Are there any that *aren't* common? Maybe a type that is rare or endangered?"

Ray's dark eyes brightened. He stroked his chin. "Not a bad question . . . Nope, this isn't going to help." He flipped the book shut, seemed to think for a second, then turned abruptly to his computer and swiftly hit a bunch of keys. "See, what you guys really need is a dendrologist. I'm just a lowly geographer who's spent some time dabbling with botany. A dendrologist, on the other hand . . ."

"Has a bigger name?" Kimberly asked.

"No, is a botanical expert on trees. See, I'm a generalist. Come on, ask me about a flower. I'm really good with flowers. Or ferns, for that matter. A dendrologist, on the other hand, could tell you anything you ever wanted to know about trees."

"My God, there is an ologist for everything," Kimberly muttered.

"You have no idea," Mac said.

"See, you guys have come to the Richmond field office. Here, we're mostly geographers and hydrologists. Most of us have other backgrounds as well—botany, biology, geology, etc., and we're happy to help you out, but maybe we're not as specific as you need. Now, up in Reston at our national headquarters, we got botanists, palynologists, geologists, karst geologists, you name it. That's where the big dawgs live."

"Where is Reston?" Mac asked.

"Two hours north of here."

"I don't have two hours."

"Suit yourself." Ray's fingers danced over his keyboard. "Then for the time-conscious researcher, we have the greatest marvel of the twentieth century. Ta dah! The Internet, where for every ology, there is almost always a website. Let's face it. Geeks love technology." He hit return, and sure enough, a website of the U.S. Department of Agriculture labeled Dendrology of Virginia appeared on the screen.

"As I live and breathe," Kimberly said.

"And how," Mac seconded.

"And we have a final suspect for your consideration," Ray announced. "Lady and gentleman, may I introduce *Betula populifolia,* otherwise known as gray birch. This smaller member of the birch family grows only thirty feet high, with leaves of approximately three inches in length. The bark may appear brown in color, but is in fact gray-white. It is also smooth, and not peeling, unlike the yellow birch and paper birch members of the family which, frankly, always look like they're sporting a bad case of bed head. The wood is light and soft, used mostly for pulpwood spools and fuel. Better yet, it is located in only one area of the state. Huh, well, here's the kicker. It doesn't say where that is."

Ray stopped, scrunching up his nose and wiggling it from side to side as he continued to study the screen. Mac hunkered down behind the geographer, his face taking on the intent expression Kimberly was coming to know so well.

"Are you saying this birch could be the one in our picture?"

"Could be."

"And it's found in only one spot in the entire state of Virginia?"

"That's what the dendrologists say."

"I need to know that spot." Mac paused a heartbeat. "*Now*."

"Mmm hmmm, mmm hmmm, mmm hmmm. Well, here's a thought." Ray tapped the computer screen with his pencil. "Look at the other ranges of distribution. The gray birch is common in New York, Pennsylvania, and New Jersey. All states north of us. Which means, this tree probably prefers cooler temperatures. So if it's growing somewhere in Virginia . . ."

"The mountains," Kimberly filled in.

He nodded. "Yeah. Now the question is, which range? Are we talking the Blue Ridge Mountains, the Shenandoah Mountains, the Appalachians? Hang on, I have an idea." His chair shot across the room again. He found a directory on top of his bookcase, flipped through several pages, grabbed a phone and made a call. "Kathy Levine, please. She's out? When do you expect her back? I'll leave a message." And in another moment, "Kath, hey, it's Ray Lee Chee from USGS. Got a question about gray birch. Where is it in the state? It's actually important, very Sherlock Holmes. When you get in, give me a buzz. We'll be waiting. Bye."

He hung up the phone, then met their expectant gazes. "Kathy's the botanist with Shenandoah National Park. She's more familiar with the trees in that area and if anyone knows about the gray birch, it's her. Unfortunately, she's out in the field right now."

"For how long?" Mac demanded to know.

"Four days."

"We don't have four days!"

Ray held up a hand. "Yeah, yeah, yeah. Kind of got that. Give her until around noon. Come lunch, she'll check messages, give me a call, and then I can give you a call. Noon's only four hours away."

"Four hours can be a long time," Mac said grimly.

"What can I say? It's not easy when you only have a picture of a leaf."

"I have a question," Kimberly spoke up. "From all of your various studies . . . Is there any connection between Virginia and Hawaii?"

"Virginia and Hawaii?"

"Yes."

"Huh. Hell if I know. From a plant perspective, I can't think of a thing. Hawaii's kind of tropical, you know. And Virginia isn't. Well, except for this week, of course. We're always prepared to make an exception."

"No other way they might be related?" Kimberly prodded.

Ray did the nose wiggle again. "You might ask a geologist. We have mountains, they have mountains. We have Chesapeake Bay with its multitude of barrier islands, which might be similar to their barrier islands. But from a flora and fauna perspective, I don't see a relationship."

"And where in this building might we find a geologist?"

"We don't have geologists, you'd have to go to Reston. Wait!" He read her expression and immediately held up a hand. "I know, I know, you don't have time for Reston. Okay . . . Jennifer York. She's one of our core samplers, and I believe she has a background in geology."

"Where's her office?"

"Other side of the building, third office on the left."

"Okay." She turned toward Mac, who was looking at her with a puzzled expression. "You heard the man," she said crisply, "let's go find a geologist."

19

"Why are we asking about Hawaii?" Mac asked thirty seconds later when they were back in the halls of the USGS building.

"Because the ME's assistant said the victim had a travel brochure for Hawaii in her purse."

He grabbed her arm and they both came to a sudden halt. Mac looked cool. She was already breathing hard and gazing with lethal intent at his fingers on her wrist.

"I don't recall you mentionin' that yesterday," he said ominously.

"I didn't think of it. The brochure was something the ME's assistant brought up in passing and I took it in kind. But then last night, I remembered what you said. That for some of the victims, the man put things in their purses—a business card, a cocktail napkin with a name. And that got me wondering."

Mac slowly released her. "Anything else you remembered last night?"

"Yes. I remembered to strap on my knife."

He grinned. "Where is it this time? Ankle? Inside of a thigh? I swear it's the first thing I thought when I saw you this morning. So few clothes and yet somewhere on that lean little body, I know there rests a three-inch blade. I swear, honey, I never met a woman who could make a man think of knives quite the way you do."

Mac leaned a little closer. He smelled of soap again. Clean, strong. Kimberly instantly took a small step back. Funny how it felt as if all the air had just been sucked from her lungs.

"If I'm a good boy," Mac murmured softly, "do I get to search you later? Or would you prefer it if I were bad?"

"Hey. Hey, hey, hey." Kimberly finally found her bearings, getting her hands up and placing them firmly between them. "I am not flirting with you!"

"Of course not."

"Now, what is *that* supposed to mean?"

"You're not the type for a casual social gesture, Kimberly. I know that. Nah, with you, I imagine it would be very serious." He nodded at her, his blue eyes suddenly somber and affecting her far more strongly than any of his teasing ever had. Then he was straightening up and turning back toward the hall. "So where's that geologist?"

He strode forward, and Kimberly had to scramble to follow suit.

Five minutes later Mac rapped on a closed door bearing the nameplate Jennifer York. The door almost immediately opened up.

"Yes?" a young woman asked. Like Ray Lee Chee, she was dressed casually—khaki shorts, white scooped-collar shirt, and heavy-duty hiking boots.

Mac flashed a smile, and went to work. "Jennifer York, I presume? Special Agent Mac McCormack, ma'am. And this here is . . . Special Investigator Quincy. We were just asking your associate Ray Lee Chee some questions relevant to a case, and he highly recommended you as an expert in the field of geology."

The woman blinked her eyes a few times. Her gaze had started on Mac's face, but now had drifted to the broad expanse of his chest. "Special Agent? As in police?"

"Yes, ma'am. We're working on a special situation, a kidnapping, if you will. We have a few items from the scene—tree leaves, rocks, etc.—that we need to identify to help find the victim. Could we take a moment of your time? It sure would be a big help."

Mac gave the woman one last charming smile, and she practically tripped over herself getting the door all the way open and inviting Mac inside. Briefly, she seemed to notice Kimberly was in tow, but then her gaze was all Mac all the time. Not that the man didn't have a way with women.

Inside the office, Jennifer York's workspace appeared very similar to Ray Lee Chee's—a modest arrangement of overstuffed bookshelves, crammed filing cabinets, and a utilitarian desk. Now she stood with one hand lightly touching her desk and the other supporting her lower back, which she had arched in a not-so-subtle attempt to emphasize her breasts.

"So," Kimberly spoke up curtly, finally earning York's attention. "We were wondering if there is any connection between Hawaii and Virginia."

"You mean the two states?"

"I believe they are states, yes. So are they related or what?"

The brunette stared at Kimberly a moment longer, then abruptly abandoned her feline pose, and took a seat in her desk chair. Now that they were on the subject of work, her expression had grown serious.

"Actually, from a geologist's perspective there is quite a connection. We often compare the Blue Ridge Mountains in Shenandoah National Park with the Hawaiian Islands—both were partially formed by flows of basaltic lava. Essentially, one billion years ago, what we now call the Blue Ridge Mountains were actually the Grenville Mountains, which we believe may have stretched from Newfoundland to Texas and may have reached as high as the present-day Himalayas. This mountain range eroded over time, however, until by six hundred million years ago it was little more than a series of rolling hills. Then, however, we had the Catoctin volcanics."

"A volcano?" Mac asked with surprise. "In Virginia?"

"More or less. A large rift opened up in the valley and basaltic magma from the earth's mantle seeped to the surface, flooding the valley and forming the Catoctin Formation, which you can view in the northern section of the park."

"The Catoctin Formation still exists?" Mac asked. "And its geology is similar to Hawaii's?"

"Yes, the Catoctin Formation still exists," Jennifer said, flashing him a warm smile. "The geology, however, isn't exact. The basalts in Hawaii are black, while the rocks in the Shenandoah National Park are dark green. Basically, a process called metamorphism caused the basalts in Shenandoah to recrystallize with new minerals, such as chlorite, epidote, and albite, which help give the rocks their greenish hue. In fact, we no longer call the rocks in Shenandoah basalts, but metabasalts, due to this alteration."

Mac turned toward Kimberly. She could read the question in his eyes. The victim had been found holding a rock. Had it been greenish in color? She couldn't remember. They hadn't gotten a good look at it and it had been one of the first things NCIS investigators had taken away.

"Are metabasalts rare in the park?" Mac asked York.

"Not at all. You can view them as road outcroppings as you drive from the northern entrance of the park all the way to Thornton Gap, then there's another good twenty-mile stretch from Stony Man to Swift Run Gap, then there's more all the way to the southern point of the park."

"Are there *any* kinds of rocks that are rare in the park?" Kimberly spoke up.

York had to think about it. "Well, the Shenandoah National Park actually involves *three* major types of bedrock. The metabasalts are found in the north and south, which we've discussed. But there are also siliciclasts, which are found in the southern section of the park or around Thornton Gap. Then we have the granites, which are in the central part of the park. The siliciclasts, which are sedimentary rocks containing abundant amounts of silica, probably have the smallest area of distribution. The granites probably have the most definable area, however, being bunched in the middle to north section of the park. Now, within each bedrock type, there are variances. For example, certain kinds of granites will have more of one mineral or another, depending on where they are found in the park. Same with the metabasalts and same with the siliciclasts."

"Not all rocks are created equal?" Mac asked.

"Exactly." She gave him another warm smile, a teacher bestowing praise on her favorite student. "Geologists analyze rocks all the time. Basically, you take a cross section of the rock sample and view it under a polarizing microscope. By breaking the rock down to its mineral components, you could pinpoint more precisely from where in the park it probably came. In some cases, in fact, the distribution range might be very small. Of course, we don't have that kind of equipment here, but if you had a rock, I'd be happy to make a few phone calls . . ."

"We don't exactly have a rock . . ."

She arched a brow. "No rock?"

"No." He added helpfully, "But we do have a travel brochure for Hawaii."

York blinked her eyes, obviously trying to follow that thought, then finally gave up. "Well, without an actual rock sample, I'm not sure what to tell you. Yes, there are lots of rocks in the Shenandoah National Park. And yes, some of them are similar to those found in Hawaii. But I don't know how to break things down for you any more than that. The wilderness area of the Shenandoah National Park encompasses nearly eighty thousand acres, you know. That's a lot of rock types and areas of geologic interest."

"Do you have a book or a rock guide we could take with us?" Kimberly asked. "You know, that way once we did have a sample, we could look up more information."

"It wouldn't be specific enough. With your naked eye, the best you would be able to determine was if the stone in question were basalt versus granite versus siliciclast. That would only cut your search area in half, leaving you with forty thousand acres. No, to truly analyze a rock, you need to be able to look at its mineral components through a microscope."

"Do you have a microscope we could borrow?" Kimberly attempted weakly.

"They cost a couple pennies. I think the U.S. government might notice."

"Darn government."

"Get the rock," York said. "Give me a call. I'd be very happy to help." Her gaze was once more locked on Mac.

"We'll try," Mac said diligently, but Kimberly knew he was just being polite. They would never have access to the rock found in the victim's hand; they were outsiders no longer privy to such helpful little tidbits as real evidence.

"One last question," Kimberly said. "Are there rattlesnakes in the Shenandoah National Park?"

York appeared surprised. "More than a few. Why do you ask?"

"Just checking. Guess I better put on a thicker pair of boots."

"Watch out for rocks," York advised. "Rattlers like to curl up in the nooks and crannies between boulders. Or even sleep out on the sun-warmed surface once it's dusk."

"Got it."

Mac shook the woman's hand. York gave him a dazzling smile, while managing to once more arch her back. Kimberly engaged in a significantly stiffer handshake, which is apparently what happened when you didn't have a Southern drawl—or Mac's muscled chest.

They made their way back to the front door, where the blue sky already stretched bright and hot beyond the glass. "That wasn't so good," Mac said, pausing before the entranceway. He seemed to be bracing himself for leaving the cool comfort of air-conditioning behind and bursting once more into the heat.

"We have a start," Kimberly said firmly. "All signs point to the Shenandoah National Park."

"Yes, all eighty thousand acres. You're right, we should find this girl in no time at all." He shook his head in disgust. "We need choppers. Hell, we need search-and-rescue, the National Guard, and about half a dozen dogs. This poor woman . . ."

"I know," Kimberly said quietly.

"It doesn't seem fair, does it? A kidnap victim deserves all the help in the world. And instead . . ."

"She's only going to get us."

He nodded and the lines of frustration etched into his dark face almost made her reach out her hand. She wondered who that sort of unsolicited contact would shock more—her or him?

"We need supplies," Mac said. "Then we'd better hit the road. It's a long drive to Shenandoah, particularly when we don't know where we're going yet."

"We're going to find her," Kimberly said.

"We need more information. Damn, why didn't I just take that rock?"

"Because that would've been crossing the line. The leaf had already been mishandled by the ME. The rock, on the other hand . . ."

"Has been properly bagged and tagged and even now is wasting away in some crime lab," Mac finished bitterly.

"We're going to find her," Kimberly said again.

He finally stilled in front of the glass door. His blue eyes were still dark, fired by frustration. For just a moment, however, the look on his face softened. "Earnest Kimberly," he whispered.

"Yes."

"I hope you're right." He glanced at his watch. "Ten A.M.," he said softly, then abruptly pushed through the heavy door. "And boy, is it getting hot."

Tina woke up slowly, becoming aware of two things at once: a deep, racking thirst that had left her tongue swollen and cottony in her mouth and the incessant sound of buzzing around her head.

She opened her eyes, but couldn't see a thing through the thick tangle of blond hair, now glued uncomfortably to her sweat-slicked face. She roughly pushed back the long strands, only to encounter a fuzzy black haze. And then, abruptly, she knew what that buzzing was.

Tina leapt to her feet, already waving her arms frantically while a scream built in her throat. Mosquitoes. She was covered, head to toe, with hundreds of swarming, buzzing, biting mosquitoes.

Malaria, she thought instantly. The West Nile Virus. Hell, the bubonic plague, as far as she was concerned. She had never seen so many bugs, fluttering in her hair, sinking their hungry mouths into her skin. Oh God, oh God, oh God.

Her feet landed in mud, her three-inch-high platform sandals immediately sinking into the watery marsh. She had a faint sensation of cool relief as the mud hit her toes, then she made the mistake of looking down and this time she did scream. Right there, slithering by her ankle in the muck, went a long black snake.

Tina scrambled quickly back onto the rock that had apparently been her perch. The mosquitoes swarmed hungrily. And now she could see other hunters as well. Yellow flies, gnats, buzzing creatures of all sorts and sizes. They swarmed her head and shoulders, seeking the unprotected skin of her throat, the corners of her mouth, and the whites of her eyes. Fresh welts rose on her ears, her eyelids, her cheeks. Her legs were covered in red marks, some still oozing fresh blood as more mosquitoes were drawn to the scent.

She started clapping her hands. Then she slapped them against her entire body.

"Die, die, die," she gasped. And they did. She felt plump, overfed bodies explode between her fingers, staining her palms with her own blood as she took out dozens. Then hundreds more insects swooped in to take their place, biting painfully at her tender skin.

She was crying now. She gasped for breath. Then in the middle of her frenzy, the inevitable happened. Her stomach rolled, she got down on her hands and knees, and then she vomited over the edge of the rock into the foul-smelling muck below.

Water. Green bile. Precious little food. Her stomach contracted anyway, her head dropping between her shoulders as she dry-heaved. The mosquitoes used the opportunity to swarm her shoulders, her elbows, her calves. She was being eaten alive, and there wasn't a thing she could do to save herself.

Minutes passed. The knot eased in her stomach. The cramping nausea released its hold on her bowels. Shakily, she straightened, brushing back her long, sweaty hair, and feeling new welts already raise up on her ears.

The mosquitoes danced in front of her eyes, seeking skin. She batted them away, but her movements were already halfhearted, the actions of a woman who realized she was no match for the enemy. She could kill hundreds of insects. A thousand would simply take their place. Oh God . . .

Her throat burned. Her skin felt as if it were on fire. She raised her trembling hands to her face and saw that they were also covered in red, angry bites. Then her gaze went all the way up to white-hot sky, where the sun was already starting to blaze overhead. The dog crate was gone. Instead, from all appearances she had been cast into some kind of swampy pit, fodder for insects, snakes, and God knows what.

"Good news," Tina whispered to herself. "He's not a sexually deranged pervert after all."

And then she started to laugh. And then she started to cry. And then she whispered in a voice probably heard only by the mosquitoes and snakes, "I'm so sorry, Ma. Oh God, somebody, get me out of here quick."

20

Quantico, Virginia
10:08 A.M.
Temperature: 91 degrees

At eight a.m., Special Agent Kaplan escorted Rainie and Quincy to the roped-off crime scene where the victim had been found yesterday morning. At eight-ten, Kaplan took off to attend to his own tasks for the day, leaving Rainie and Quincy alone. That was fine by Quincy. He liked to walk a scene unescorted, without the murmur of voices, incessant clicking of cameras, or the needling scratch of pencil on paper to divert his attention. Death inevitably took on a life of its own, and Quincy preferred the calm after the storm. When all the other investigators had left and he could be alone with his musings.

Rainie stood a good thirty feet away from him, walking soundlessly around the fringes of the forest. She was used to his ways by now, and worked as quietly as he did. They had been at this for two hours already, falling seamlessly into the usual grid pattern, slowly and methodically dissecting each inch of the roped-off area, and then, because even the best cops missed things, moving outside of the cordoned-off space, searching for what the others might have missed, for that one clue which would magically bring it all together. If such a thing really existed.

Underneath the relative shade of the thick oak trees, the heat hammered down on them relentlessly. They shared one bottle of water, then another, and were now almost done with the lukewarm third. Quincy's white dress shirt, sharply pressed just this morning, was now plastered against his chest while thin trickles of sweat beaded down his face. His fingers left damp stains on his small notepad while his pencil slid wetly between his fingers.

It was a brutal morning, serving as a brutal start to what would be no doubt an extremely brutal day. Was this what the killer wanted? Overheated law enforcement officers struggling to function in damp, unbearable weather that glued their uniforms to their bodies and robbed them of breath? Some killers picked extremely harsh or disgusting places to dump bodies because they relished the thought of homicide detectives picking through Dumpsters or wading through swamps. First they humiliated the victims. Then they reveled in the thought of what they could do to the police.

Quincy stopped and turned once more, frowning in spite of himself. He wanted to know this space. He wanted to *feel* this space. He wanted a glimpse into why, of all places on this nearly four-hundred-acre base, had the killer dumped the body *here*.

The area was sheltered, the thick canopy of trees making the path invisible at night. The path itself was wide enough for a car, but four tires would have definitely left at least a faint impression and there was none. No, their unidentified subject—UNSUB—had selected a spot half a mile from the road. And then he'd walked that half mile in pitch-black night while staggering beneath the awkward weight of a hundred-and-ten-pound body. Surely there were dozens of spots more accessible and less physically demanding.

So again: Why had their UNSUB chosen here?

Quincy was beginning to have some ideas. He'd bet Rainie would also have a few opinions on the subject.

"How are you making out?" Kaplan called out.

He was coming down the dirt path, looking fresher than they did, so wherever he'd been, it had had air-conditioning. Quincy found himself resentful already.

"Brought you bug spray," Kaplan said merrily.

"You're the king of men," Quincy assured him. "Now look behind you."

Kaplan obediently stopped and looked behind him. "I don't see anything."

"Exactly."

"Huh?"

"Look down," Rainie said impatiently, from twenty feet back. "Check out your footsteps."

Rainie had pulled her heavy chestnut hair back in a ponytail first thing this morning. It had come loose about an hour ago and was now plastered in sweaty tendrils against her neck. She looked wild, her hair curly with the humidity and her gray eyes nearly black with the heat. Having grown up on the Oregon coast with its relatively mild climate, Rainie absolutely loathed high heat and humidity. Quincy figured he had about another hour before she'd be driven to violence.

"There aren't any footsteps," Kaplan said.

"Exactly." Quincy sighed and finally pulled his attention away from the scene. "According to reports on the Weather Channel, this area received two inches of rain five days ago. And if you venture off the path into the woods, there are patches where the ground is still marshy and soft to the touch. The thick trees protect the dirt from baking in the sun, plus I don't think much can dry out given this humidity."

"But the path is solid."

"Yes. Apparently, nothing hard-packs soil quite like the daily grind of a few hundred pounding Marine and FBI trainees. The path is hard as a rock. It would take more than a two-hundred-pound person, plus a hundred-pound body, to dent it now."

Kaplan frowned at them both, still obviously confused. "I already said there weren't any footprints. We looked."

Quincy wanted to sigh again. He so preferred working with Rainie, who was now regarding the NCIS special agent with a fresh level of annoyance.

"If you simply walked off the road into the woods around here, what would happen?"

"The ground is still soft; you'd leave a footprint."

"So to a casual visitor, the woods are marshy?"

"Yeah, I guess."

"And what's thirty feet to my left?" Quincy asked crisply.

"The PT course."

"The paved PT course."

"Sure, the paved PT course."

Quincy looked at him. "If you were carrying a body into the woods, wouldn't you take the paved path? The one that offered you better footing? The one that would be guaranteed not to leave footprints, given the soft soil you see all around?"

"The wooded path has less traffic," Kaplan said slowly. "He's better hidden."

"According to the ME's report, the UNSUB probably dumped the body in the small hours of the morning. Given the late hour, the man's already well hidden. Why take the dirt path? Why risk footprints?"

"He's not very bright?" But Kaplan was no longer convinced.

Rainie shook her head impatiently, crossing over to them. "The UNSUB knew. He's been on this path. He knew the ground was hard and would protect him, while the wide scope makes it less likely he'd bump the body against a tree limb or accidentally leave a scrap of fabric on a twig. Face it, Kaplan. The UNSUB isn't some random guy. He knows this place. Hell, he's probably run this course sometime in the last five days."

Kaplan was clearly discouraged as they trudged back to the Academy.

"I spoke with the four Marines on duty Tuesday night," he reported. "They had nothing out of the ordinary. No unusual vehicles, no suspicious drivers. Only thing they could think of was that it was a particularly busy night. A bunch of the National Academy students had hightailed it for air-conditioned bars, so they had cars coming and going right up until two A.M. Everyone showed proper ID, however. Nothing stood out in their minds."

"Do they keep a log of who comes and goes?" Rainie asked, walking beside Quincy.

"No. All drivers have to show proper security passes, however. The Marine sentries may also ask for a license and the driver's final destination."

"What does a security pass look like?"

Kaplan gestured to Rainie's shirt, where a white plastic card dangled from her collar. "It looks like that, except in a variety of colors. Some are blue, some are white, some yellow. Each color indicates a certain level of clearance. A yellow card indicates an unescorted guest pass, someone who's allowed full access. We also have cards reading Escorted Guests, which means they wouldn't be allowed back onto the base without being in the company of the proper person. That sort of thing."

Rainie glanced down. "They don't look that complicated to me. Couldn't someone just swipe one?"

"You have to sign a badge in and out. And believe me, the FBI police keep tabs on that sort of thing. None of us would feel particularly good if just any

Tom, Dick, or Harry could swipe a card."

"Just asking," Rainie said mildly.

Kaplan scowled at her anyway. Their earlier conversation had obviously wounded his ego. "You can't steal a badge. You can't just walk onto this base. For God's sake, we take this kind of thing very seriously. Look, you're probably right. It probably is an insider. Which really depresses me, though I don't know why. If all the good guys were really good people, I wouldn't have a job, would I?"

"That's not an encouraging thought," Rainie said.

"Ma'am, it's the worst thought in the world." He glanced at Quincy. "You know, I've been thinking . . . Given the lack of sexual assault, and that the 'weapon,' so to speak, was a drug, shouldn't we be looking at women, too?"

"No," Quincy said.

"But women are the ones who predominantly kill with poison. And the lack of sexual assault bothers me. A guy doesn't just OD a woman and dump her body in the woods. Men are sexual predators. And did you see how this girl was dressed?"

Quincy drew up short. "The victim," he said curtly, "was wearing a short skirt, not uncommon for this time of year. To imply that a certain manner of dress invites sexual assault—"

"That's not what I was saying!" Kaplan interrupted immediately.

"It's not about sex for any predator," Quincy continued as if Kaplan hadn't spoken. "It's about power. We've had many serial killers who were not sexual-sadist predators. Berkowitz, for one, was strictly a triggerman, so to speak. He picked his victims, walked up to the car, opened fire on the couple, and walked away. Kaczynski was content to kill and maim long-distance. Even more recently, we had the Beltway Snipers, who held most of the East Coast in absolute terror by picking off victims from the trunk of their car. Murder isn't about sex. It's about power. And in this context, then, drugs make perfect sense, as drugs are weapons of control."

"Besides," Rainie spoke up, "there's no way a woman carried a dead body half a mile into the woods. We don't have that kind of upper-body strength."

They finally emerged from the relative comfort of the woods. Immediately, the sun struck them like a ball-peen hammer while waves of heat shimmered above the paved road.

"Holy Lord," Kaplan said. "And it's not even noon."

"It's going to be a hot one," Quincy murmured.

And Rainie said, "Fuck the Academy, I'm putting on shorts."

"One last thing," Kaplan said, holding up a hand. "Something you should both know."

Rainie halted with an impatient sigh. Quincy waited with a far more prescient sense of something significant about to break.

"We have the tox report back on the victim. Two drugs were found in her system. A small dose of ketamine, and a significantly larger dose—no doubt lethal dose—of the benzodiazepine, Ativan. In other words . . ."

"Special Agent McCormack listed them both last night," Quincy murmured.

"Yeah," Kaplan said slowly. "McCormack knew the drugs. Now how about that?"

21

Quantico, Virginia
11:48 A.M.
Temperature: 95 degrees

Mac drove until they'd left the concrete columns of Richmond behind them. He headed west on Interstate 64, where a towering line of dark green mountains stood out in vivid contrast to the bright blue sky and drew them steadily forward.

They stopped at Texaco for gas. Then they stopped at a Wal-Mart to cover the essentials: bug spray, first-aid kit, hiking socks, energy bars, chocolate bars, extra water bottles, and a whole case of water. Mac already had a compass, Swiss army knife, and waterproof matches in his backpack. They grabbed an extra set for Kimberly to carry, just in case.

When they returned to his rented Toyota, Mac discovered a message on his cell phone from Ray Lee Chee. The botanist, Kathy Levine, would meet them at Big Meadows Lodge in the Shenandoah National Park at one-thirty. Without a word, they started driving again.

Cities came and went. Major housing developments bloomed alongside the road, then slowly withered away. They headed deeper west, where the land opened up like an emerald sea and took Mac's breath away.

"God's country," his father would say. There wasn't much of this kind of land left.

As Kimberly navigated, they turned off the interstate for the rolling lanes of U.S. 15, leading to U.S. 33. They swept by vast fields, each dotted by a single redbrick ranch house with a fresh-painted white porch. They passed dairy farms, horse stables, vineyards, and agricultural spreads.

Outside the car, everything took on a green hue, a rolling patchwork of square fields seamed by groves of dark green trees. They passed horses and cows. They came upon tiny towns defined by run-down delis, old gas stations, and pristine Baptist churches. Then, in the blink of an eye, the towns disappeared and they headed deeper into the growing shade cast by a towering mountain range. Slowly but surely, they started to climb.

Kimberly had been quiet since their meeting with the geologist. Her visor was down, casting a shadow across the top half of her face and making it difficult to read her expression.

Mac was worried about her. She'd shown up bright and early this morning with the gaunt cheeks and feverish eyes of a woman who'd had little sleep. She wore linen trousers, topped with a white dress shirt and matching linen jacket. The outfit looked sharp and professional, but he suspected she'd chosen the long pants to hide her knife, and the jacket to cover the discreet bulge of the Glock strapped to her waist. In other words, she was a woman going to war.

He suspected she went to war a lot. He suspected that since the deaths of her mother and sister, life for her had essentially been one long battle. The thought pained him in a way he hadn't expected.

"It's beautiful," he said at last.

She finally shifted in her seat, giving him a brief glance before stretching out her legs. "Yes."

"You like the mountains? Or are you a city gal?"

She shook her head. "City gal. Technically speaking, I grew up in Alexandria, close to these mountains. But Alexandria functions more as a suburb of D.C. than Richmond. And let's just say my mother's interests ran more to the Smithsonian Institution than the Shenandoah Mountains. Then I went off to school in New York. You?"

"I love mountains. Hell, I love rivers, fields, orchards, streams, woods, you name it. I was lucky growing up. My grandparents—my mother's parents— own a hundred-acre peach orchard. As their kids married, they gifted each one with three acres of land to build a home; that way all the siblings could live close by. Basically, my sister and I grew up in booneyville, surrounded by a dozen cousins, and a ton of open space. Each day my mom would kick us out of the house, tell us not to die, and come home in time for dinner. So we did."

"You must have liked your cousins."

"Nah, we annoyed the snot out of each other. But that was half the fun. We made up games, we got into trouble. We basically ran around like heathens. And then at night," he slanted her a look, "we played board games."

"Your whole family? Every night?" Her voice was skeptical.

"Yep. We'd rotate around each aunt and uncle's house and off we'd go. My mom started it. She hates TV, thinks it rots the brain. The Boob Tube, she calls it. When I turned twelve, she threw ours out. I'm not sure my father's ever recovered from the loss, but after that we had to do something to pass the time."

"So you played games?"

"All the good ones. Monopoly, Scrabble, Yahtzee, Boggle, Life, and my personal favorite, Risk."

Kimberly raised a brow. "And who won?"

"I did, of course."

"I believe that," she said seriously. "You attempt this whole laid-back Southern routine, but deep down inside, you're a natural-born competitor. I can see it every time you talk about this case. You don't like to lose."

"The person who said there are no winners or losers obviously lost."

"I'm not disagreeing."

His lips curved. "I didn't think you would."

"My family didn't play board games," she volunteered finally. "We read books."

"Serious stuff or fun stuff?"

"Serious, of course. At least when my mother was watching. After lights out, however, Mandy used to sneak in copies of Sweet Valley High. We'd read them under the covers using a flashlight. Oh, we giggled ourselves sick."

"Sweet Valley High? And here I figured you for a Nancy Drew kind of gal."

"I liked Nancy, but Mandy was better at smuggling contraband, and she preferred Sweet Valley High. And booze for that matter, but that's another story."

"You rebel."

"We all have our moments. So." She turned toward him. "Big charming Southern man. You ever been in love?"

"Uh oh."

She stared at him intently, and he finally relented with a sigh. "Yeah. Once. One of my sister's friends. She set us up, we hit it off, and things went pretty well for a while."

"What happened?"

"I don't know."

"That's no kind of answer."

"Honey, coming from a man, that's the only kind of answer."

She resumed staring and he caved again. "I was probably an idiot. Rachel was a nice girl. Funny, athletic, sweet. She taught second grade and was really good with kids. I certainly could've done worse."

"So you ended it, broke your sister's best friend's heart?"

He shrugged. "More like I let it trickle out. Rachel was the kind of girl a guy should marry, then settle down and raise two point two kids. I wasn't there yet. You know how this job is. You get a call, you have to go. And God knows when you're comin' home. I had visions of her waiting more and more and smiling less and less. It didn't seem the thing to do."

"Do you miss her?"

"Honestly, I hadn't thought of her in years."

"Why? She sounds perfect."

Mac shot her an impatient glance. "Nobody's perfect, Kimberly, and if you must know, we did have a problem. A significant problem, in my mind. We never fought."

"You never fought?"

"Never. And a man and woman should fight. Frankly, they should have a good head-to-head battle about every six months, then make love until they break the box springs. At least that's my opinion. Your turn. What was his name?"

"I don't have a name."

"Honey, everyone's got a name. The boy you sat behind in math class. The college quarterback who got away. Your sister's boyfriend who you secretly wished was your own. Come on. Confession's good for the soul."

"And I still don't have a name. Honest. I've never been in love. I don't think I'm the type."

He frowned at her. "Everyone falls in love."

"That's not true," she countered immediately. "Love's not for everyone.

There are people who live their whole lives alone and are very happy that way. To fall in love . . . It involves giving. It involves weakening. I'm not very good at that."

Mac gave her a slow, lingering look. "Ah, honey, you obviously haven't met the right man yet."

Kimberly's cheeks grew red. She turned away from him and resumed staring out the window. The road was steep now; they'd officially hit the Blue Ridge Mountains and were now making the grinding climb through Swift Run Gap. They zigzagged around sharp corners, getting teasing glimpses of million-dollar views. Then they were up the side, cresting at twenty-four hundred feet and watching the world open up like a deep green blanket. Before them, green valleys plunged, gray granite soared, and blue sky stretched for as far as the eye could see.

"Wow," Kimberly said simply and Mac couldn't think of a better response.

He took the entrance into the Shenandoah National Park. He paid the fee and in turn they got a map of all the various lookout points. They headed north, toward Big Meadows, on Skyline Drive.

The going was slower here, the speed limit a steady 35 mph, which was just as well because suddenly there were a million things to see and not nearly enough time to look. Wild grass bordered the winding road, thickly dotted with yellow and white flowers, while deeper in the woods a vast array of ferns spread out like a thick green carpet. Towering oak trees and majestic beeches wove their branches overhead, breaking the sun into a dozen pieces of gold. A yellow butterfly darted in front of them. Kimberly gasped, and Mac turned just in time to see a mother and fawn cross the road behind them.

He spotted two yellow finches playing tag in a grove of pine trees. Then they were already upon the first viewing platform, where the trees gave way and half of Virginia once again opened up before them.

Mac pulled over. He was no neophyte to the great outdoors, but sometimes a man just had to sit and stare. He and Kimberly absorbed the panorama of emerald forest mixing with gray stone outcrops and brightly colored wildflowers. The Blue Ridge Mountains really knew how to put on a show.

"Do you think he's really an environmentalist?" Kimberly murmured quietly.

Mac didn't need to ask to know whom she meant. "I'm not sure. He certainly picks some great places."

"The planet is dying," she said softly. "Look over to the right. You can see patches of dead hemlocks, probably killed by the wooly adelgid, which is infesting so many of our forests. And while this range is protected as a national park, how long will the valley before us remain untouched? Someday, those fields will become subdivisions, while all of those distant trees will be turned into yet more strip malls to feed hungry consumers. Once upon a time, most of the U.S. looked like this. Now you have to drive hundreds of miles just to find this kind of beauty."

"Progress happens."

"That's nothing but an excuse."

"No," Mac said abruptly. "And yes. Everything changes. Things die. We probably should fear for our kids. But I still don't know what that has to do with why one man kills a bunch of innocent women. Maybe this guy *wants* to think he's different. Hell, maybe he does have some sort of conscience and it bothers him to kill for killing's sake. But the letters, the environmental talk . . . Personally, I think it's nothing but a bunch of bullshit designed to give the Eco-Killer permission to do what he really wants to do—kidnap and kill women."

"In psychology," Kimberly said, "we learn that there are many different reasons for why people behave certain ways. This applies to killers as well. Some killers are driven by ego, by their own overdeveloped id, which puts their needs first and refuses to accept limits on their behavior. It's the serial killer who kills because he likes to feel powerful. It's the stockbroker who murders his mistress after she threatens to tell his wife, because he honestly believes his own desire for security is more important than another person's life. It's the kid who pulls the trigger, just because he wants to."

"There's another kind of killer, though. The morality killer. That's the fanatic who walks into a synagogue and opens fire because he believes it is his duty. Or the person who shoots abortion doctors because she believes they are committing a sin. These people don't kill to satisfy their inner child, but because they believe such an act is right. Perhaps the Eco-Killer falls into the morality category."

Mac arched a brow. "So these are our choices? Immature whackos on the one hand and righteous whackos on the other?"

"Technically speaking."

"All right. You want psychobabble? I can play this game. I believe it was Freud who said everything we do communicates something about ourselves."

"You know Freud?"

"Hey, don't let the good looks fool you, honey. I have a brain in my head. So all right, according to Freud, the tie you pick, the ring you wear, the shirt you buy, all say something about you. Nothing is random, everything you do has intent. Fine, now let's look at what this guy does. He kidnaps women traveling in pairs. Always young females leaving a bar. Now why does he do that? Seems to me that the terrorist type of killer goes after people of a certain faith—but then will equally target man, woman, or child. The moral killer goes after the abortion doctor for his occupation, not for his sex. And yet then we got our guy again. Eight victims in Georgia, ten if you think he struck here, and always a young, college-aged girl leaving a bar. Now what does that communicate about him?"

"He doesn't like women," Kimberly answered softly. "Particularly women who drink."

"He hates them," Mac said flatly. "Loose women, fast women, I don't know how he categorizes them in his mind, but he hates women. I don't know why. Maybe he doesn't know why. Maybe he honestly believes this is about the environment. But if our guy was really about saving the world, then we should see some variety in his targets. We don't. He only goes after women. Period. And in my mind, that makes him just another garden-variety very dangerous whacko."

"You don't believe in profiling?"

"Kimberly, we've had a profile for four years. Ask that poor girl in the morgue if it's done a thing to help us yet."

"Bitter."

"Realistic," he countered. "This case isn't going to be solved in the back room by some guy in a suit. It's going to be solved out here, roaming these mountains, sweating buckets, and dodging rattlesnakes. Because that's what Eco-Killer wants. He hates women, but every time he sticks one in a dangerous location, he's also targeting *us*. Law enforcement officers, search-and-rescue workers—we're the ones who have to walk these hills and sweat this terrain. Don't think he doesn't know it."

"Have any search-and-rescue workers been hurt?"

"Hell, yes. In the Tallulah Gorge we had several falls and broken limbs. The cotton field caused two volunteers to succumb to heatstroke. Then we had a wonderful search along the Savannah River, where one guy tangled with a gator, and two people were bitten by cottonmouth snakes."

"Fatalities?" she asked sharply.

Mac looked back out at the vast, plunging terrain. He murmured, "Well, honey, not yet."

22

Shenandoah National Park, Virginia
1:44 P.M.
Temperature: 97 degrees

Kathy Levine was a petite, no-nonsense woman with short-cropped red hair and a dash of freckles across her nose. She greeted Mac and Kimberly briskly as they entered the glass-and-beam expanse of Big Meadows Lodge and beckoned them immediately toward a back office.

"Ray said you had a picture of a leaf. Not a real leaf, mind you, but a picture."

"Yes, ma'am." Mac dutifully provided the scanned image. Kathy plopped it down on the desk in front of her and snapped on a bright overhead light. It barely made a dent in a room already lit by an entire wall of sunshine.

"It could be a gray birch," the botanist said at last. "It would be better if you had the real leaf."

"Are you a dendrologist?" Kimberly asked curiously.

"No, but I know what's in my park." The woman snapped off the light and regarded them both frankly. "Are you two familiar with refugia?"

"Refugee what?" Mac said.

"That's what I thought. *Refugia* is a term for plants that exist as glacial relics in a climate where they no longer belong. Essentially, millions of years ago, this whole area was ice. But then the ice melted and certain plants got left behind. In most cases, those plants moved high up in the mountains, seeking the cool conditions they need to survive. Balsam fir and red cedar are both examples of refugia found in this park. And so is gray birch."

"Ray said it was only found in one area." Mac spoke up intently.

"Yes. Right outside the door. Let me get a map." The botanist climbed out of her chair and rifled the bookshelf along the wall. Then, she proceeded to unfold the largest map Kimberly had ever seen. It was labeled Geologic Map of Shenandoah County, and it was filled with enough streaks of bright purple, deep fuchsia, and neon orange to hurt a person's eyes.

"This is the geologic map which includes this section of the park. We are here." Levine plopped the massive spread of paper on the jumbled surface of the desk, and promptly tapped a lime-green spot near the bottom of the page. "Now, gray birch grows thickest in the swampy plateau across from the Big Meadows camp, but can also be found here and there in this whole one-mile area. So basically, if you're looking for the only gray birch in Virginia, you're standing in the middle of it."

"Wonderful," Mac murmured. "Now if only we were sure we were looking for gray birch. How populated is this area this time of year?"

"You mean campers? We have thirty or so people signed in at the
moment. Generally it would be more, but the heat has chased a lot away.
Also we get a fair number of day hikers and the like. Of course, in this
weather, we're probably getting mostly drive-throughs—people coming to
the park, but never leaving the air-conditioned comfort of their cars."

"Do guests have to sign in?"

"No."

"Do you have park rangers or any kind of monitors working the area?"

"We have enough personnel if trouble should come up, but we don't go
looking for it, if that's what you mean."

"So a person could come and go, and you'd never know he'd been here?"

"I would imagine most people come and go, and we never know they
were here."

"Damn."

"You want to tell me what this is about?" Levine nodded toward
Kimberly. "I can already tell she's armed. You might as well fill in the rest."

Mac seemed to consider it. He looked at Kimberly, but she didn't know
what to tell him. He might be out of his jurisdiction, but at least he was still
a special agent. As of six A.M. this morning she had become no one at all.

"We're working a case," Mac told Levine tersely. "We have reason to
believe this leaf may tie into the disappearance of a local girl. Find where the
leaf came from, and we'll find her."

"You're saying this girl may be somewhere in my park? Lost? In this kind
of heat?"

"It's a possibility."

Levine crossed her arms over her chest while regarding both of them
intently. "You know," she said at last, "right about now, I think I'd like to see
some ID."

Mac reached into his back pocket and pulled out his credentials.
Kimberly just stood there. She had nothing to show, nothing to say. For the
first time, the enormity of what she had done struck her. For all of her life,
she'd wanted to be one thing. And now?

She turned away from both of them. Through the windows, the bright
sunlight burned her eyes. She closed them tightly, trying to focus on the feel
of heat on her face. A girl was out there. A girl needed her.

And her mother was still dead and her sister was still dead. And Mac was
right after all. Nothing she did would change anything, so what was she
really trying to prove? That she could self-destruct as completely as Mandy?

Or that just once, she wanted to get something right. Just once, she
wanted to find the girl, save the day. Because anything had to be better than
this six-year ache.

"This says Georgia Bureau of Investigation," Levine was saying to Mac.

"Yes, ma'am."

"If my memory serves, we're still in Virginia."

"Yes, ma'am."

"Ray didn't ask you nearly enough questions now, did he?"

"Ray was very helpful in our investigation. We appreciate his efforts and are happy you were able to talk to us."

Levine wasn't fooled. She drew a bead on Kimberly. "I'm guessing you have no ID at all."

Kimberly turned back around. She kept her voice even. "No, I don't."

"Look, it's gotta be a good hundred degrees in the shade right now, and while I'm not a big fan of doing field work in this kind of heat, that's my lot in life. So you both had better start talking fast, because I'm not amused to be yanked from my federally required duties to talk to two wanna-be cops who seem to be way out of their jurisdiction."

"I am pursuing a case," Mac said crisply. "The killer started in Georgia, where he attacked eight girls. You wanna see photos, I can give you all your stomach can take. I have reason to believe he's now operating in Virginia. The FBI is involved, but by the time they figure out who did what to whom, this girl will probably have fed ten bears for a week. I, on the other hand, have been working this case for years. I know this man. And I have legitimate reason to believe that he has kidnapped a young woman and abandoned her all alone in the middle of your park. Yes, it's hot outside. Yes, she is lost. And no, I don't plan on standing idly by and waiting for a bunch of Feds to complete all the required paperwork. I plan on finding this girl, Ms. Levine, and Ms. Quincy has agreed to assist. So that's why we're here and that's what we're doing. And if that offends you, well, too bad. Because this girl probably is in your park, and boy oh boy, does she need some help."

Kathy Levine appeared troubled. "Do you have references?" she asked at last.

"I can give you the name of my supervisor in Georgia."

"He knows about this case?"

"He sent me here to pursue it."

"If I cooperate with you, what does that mean?"

"I have no jurisdiction, ma'am. Officially speaking, I can't ask you to do anything."

"But you think the girl might be here. For how long?"

"He would've abandoned her yesterday."

"It was nearly a hundred degrees yesterday," Levine said curtly.

"I know."

"Does she have gear?"

"He kidnaps women from bars. The best she has is her purse and her party clothes."

Levine blinked twice. "Sweet Jesus. And he's done this before?"

"Eight girls. So far, only one has survived. Today, I'd like to make that two."

"We have a search-and-rescue team for the park," Levine said briskly. "If . . . if you had strong reason to believe there was, say, a lost hiker in the Big Meadows area, and if you reported that lost hiker, I would have authority to call the team."

Mac stilled. The offer was both unexpected and desperately needed. A search-and-rescue team. Multiple people. Trained experts. In other words, the first genuine chance at success they'd had all day.

"Are you sure?" Mac asked sharply. "It could be a wild-goose chase. I could be wrong."

"Are you wrong often?"

"Not about this."

"Well, then . . ."

"I'd like to report a lost hiker," Mac said immediately.

And Kathy Levine said, "Let me make a call."

23

Quantico, Virginia
2:23 P.M.
Temperature: 99 degrees

Kaplan had scheduled a two-thirty meeting with Dr. Ennunzio to follow up on Mac's conversations with the forensic linguist. Rainie didn't think Kaplan believed Dr. Ennunzio was a link to Georgia's Eco-Killer, as much as he wanted to grill a new person about the various doings of Special Agent McCormack.

Still, she and Quincy followed gamely along. Kaplan had his questions, they would have theirs. Besides, the BSU offices would probably be only eighty degrees, and that sure as hell beat the places they'd been thus far.

The offices of the Behavioral Science Unit were located in the basement of the indoor firing ranges building. Rainie had only been there once before, but she always thought it was a little funny. Not just because people were literally firing weapons two floors above you, which should give anyone pause, but because the elevators going down to the highly esteemed BSU offices were tucked in an isolated corner next to the laundry room. Walk by bins of dirty linens and used flak vests. Go to work for the day.

In the basement, the elevator door opened to a wood-paneled lobby area, with corridors going off every which way. Here, visitors could sit on the leather sofa while admiring various posters advertising BSU projects. "Domestic Violence by Police Officers," declared one, promoting an upcoming seminar. "Suicide and Law Enforcement," said another. "Futuristics and Law Enforcement: The Millennium Conference," advertised a third.

When Rainie had first met Quincy seven years ago, he'd been conducting research for the BSU. His project of choice—developing a schema for the effective profiling of juvenile mass murderers. Never let it be said that the BSU researchers were a bunch of lightweights.

And just in case someone thought the group was without a sense of humor, a new addition had been included in the lineup of agent photographs adorning the wall. Last photo in the middle row—a lovingly framed headshot of an extraterrestrial. Complete with a cone-shaped head and big black eyes. Really, it was the best-looking photo of the bunch.

Kaplan took off down the middle corridor and Rainie and Quincy followed in his wake.

"Miss it?" Rainie whispered in Quincy's ear.

"Not in the least."

"It's never as dreary as I expect."

"Wait until you've spent an entire week working without any natural light."

"Whiner."

"Be nice, or I'll lock you in the bomb shelter."

"Promises, promises," Rainie murmured. Quincy squeezed her hand, the first contact he'd made with her all day.

From what Rainie could determine, the space down here was basically a large square, bisected by three rows of hallways sprouting narrow offices. Kaplan came to the last door of the middle row, knocked twice and a man promptly opened it as if he were expecting them. "Special Agent Kaplan?" he asked.

Rainie bit her lower lip just in time. Wow, she thought. A Quincy clone.

Dr. Ennunzio wore a trim-fitting navy blue suit with proper Republican-red tie. In his mid-forties, he had the lean build of an avid runner and the intense gaze of an academic who always took work home at night. His short-cropped hair was dark, but beginning to gray at the temples. His manner was direct, his expression slightly impatient, and Rainie already had a feeling he considered this meeting a waste of his very valuable time.

Kaplan made the introductions. Ennunzio shook Rainie's hand briefly, but paused with genuine sincerity in front of Quincy. Apparently, he was familiar with the former agent's work.

Rainie simply kept gazing from the linguist to Quincy, back to the linguist. Maybe it was an FBI hiring requirement, she thought. You must wear these suits and have eyes this intense to ride this ride. That could be.

Ennunzio gestured to his cramped office, much too small to hold four grown adults, then ushered them back down the hallway to an unused conference room.

"This used to be the director's office," he explained, his attention returning to Quincy. "Back in your day. Now it's a conference room, while the bigwigs are across the way. It's not so hard to find their new offices. Just follow all the posters for the *Silence of the Lambs*."

"Everyone loves Hollywood," Quincy murmured.

"Now then," Ennunzio said, taking a seat and placing a manila folder in front of him, "you had questions about Special Agent McCormack from the GBI?"

"Yes," Kaplan spoke up. "We understand you were supposed to meet with him."

"Tuesday afternoon. It didn't happen. I got held up at a conference in D.C., sponsored by the Forensic Linguistics Institute."

"A conference for linguists," Rainie muttered. "That had to be a blast."

"Actually it was quite fascinating," Ennunzio told her. "We had a special presentation on the anthrax envelopes sent to Senator Tom Daschle and Tom Brokaw. Were the envelopes sent by someone whose first language was English or Arabic? It's an extremely interesting analysis."

Rainie startled, intrigued in spite of herself. "Which one was it?"

"Almost certainly a native English speaker trying to impersonate an

Arabic speaker. We call that 'trick mail,' when the sender attempts certain devices to mislead the receiver. In this case, the definitive evidence is the seemingly random mix of uppercase and lowercase letters throughout the text on the envelope, as well as a mixing of large and small caps. While this is meant to appear sloppy and childlike—someone uncomfortable with proper English syntax—in fact, it indicates someone so comfortable with the Roman alphabet he can manipulate it at will. Otherwise, it would be difficult to construct such a varied combination of letter styles. And while the messages in the two envelopes are short and filled with misspellings, this is again an attempt to deceive. Short missives actually involve a very concise use of the English language and are consistent with someone of higher, not lower, education. All in all, it was a first-rate presentation."

"Okay," Rainie said. She looked at Kaplan helplessly.

"So you didn't actually see Special Agent McCormack on Tuesday?" Kaplan asked.

"No."

"But you had spoken to him before?"

"When Special Agent McCormack arrived at the National Academy, he stopped by my office asking if I would have time to consult on an old homicide case. He had copies of some letters that had been sent to the editor, and he wanted any information on them I could provide."

"Did he give you copies of the letters?" Quincy spoke up.

"He gave me what he had. Unfortunately the GBI was only able to recover the original document for the last letter, and frankly, there's not much I can do with published versions. The newspapers sanitize too much."

"You wanted to see if the guy also mixed small and large caps?" Rainie asked.

"Something like that. Look, I'll tell you the same thing I told Special Agent McCormack. Forensic linguistics is a broad field. As an expert, I'm trained to study language, syntax, spelling, grammar. I don't analyze penmanship per se—you need a handwriting expert for that—but how a document is prepared and presented provides context for my own analysis, so it is relevant. Now, within the field, we all have our own domains. Some linguists pride themselves on a sort of forensic profiling—you give them a document, and they can tell you the probable race, gender, age, education, and street address of who wrote it. I can do that to a certain degree, but my own subspecialty is authorship. You give me two samples of text and I can tell you if the person who wrote the threatening letter is the same person who wrote that second note to his mom."

"How do you do that?" Rainie quizzed him.

"In part, I look at format. Mostly, however, I'm looking at word choice, sentence structure, and repeated errors or phrases. Everyone has certain expressions they favor, and these phrases have a tendency to appear over and over again in their writings. Are you familiar with the cartoon sitcom *The Simpsons*?"

Rainie nodded.

"All right, if you were the chief of police in Springfield and you received a ransom note including repeated uses of the expression 'D'oh!,' you'd probably want to start your investigation with Homer Simpson. If, on the other hand, the letter contained the phrase 'Eat my shorts,' you'd be better off looking at the younger Simpson, Bart. All people have phrases they like to use. When writing text, they are even more likely to repeat these catch-phrases. The same goes for grammatical mistakes and spelling errors."

"And in the case of the Eco-Killer?" Quincy spoke up again.

"Not enough data points. Special Agent McCormack presented me with three copies and one original. With only one original, I can't compare penmanship, ink, or paper choice. In terms of content, all four letters contain the exact same message: 'Clock ticking . . . planet dying . . . animals weeping . . . rivers screaming. Can't you hear it? Heat kills . . .' Frankly, to compare authorship, I need additional material, say another letter you believe may have been written by the suspect, or a longer document. Are you familiar with Ted Kaczynski?"

"The Unabomber? Of course."

"That case was largely broken on the writings of Mr. Kaczynski. Not only did we have the writing on the packages he used to mail out his bombs, but we also had several notes he included in the packages, many letters he wrote to the press, and finally the manifesto he demanded be run in the papers. Even then, it wasn't a forensic linguist who made the connections, but Kaczynski's own brother. He recognized parts of the manifesto from his brother's letters to him. Without such an extensive amount of material to analyze, who knows if we ever would have identified the Unabomber?"

"But this guy hasn't given the police much to work with," Rainie said. "Isn't that unusual? I mean, according to your own example, once these guys get talking, they have a lot to say. But this guy is implying he's earnest about the environment, while on the other hand, he's pretty quiet on the subject."

"That is actually the one thing that jumped out at me," Ennunzio said, his gaze going to Quincy. "This is getting more into your domain than mine, but four short, identical messages are unusual. Once a killer makes contact with the press, or someone in authority, generally the communication becomes more expansive. I was a little surprised that by the last letter to the editor, at least, the message didn't include more."

Quincy nodded. "Communication by a killer with either the press or an officer in charge of the investigation is almost always about power. Sending letters and watching those messages be retold by the media gives certain subjects the same kind of vicarious thrill other killers experience when revisiting the scene of the crime or handling a souvenir from one of their victims. Killers will generally start small—an initial note or phone call—but once they know they have everyone's attention, the communication becomes about boasting, bragging, and constantly reasserting their sense of control. It's all part of their ego trip. This message . . ." Quincy frowned. "It's different."

"He distances himself from the act," Ennunzio said. "Notice the phrase, 'heat kills.' Not that he kills, that *heat* kills. It's as if he has nothing to do with it."

"Yet the message is filled with short phrases, which you said earlier indicates a higher level of intelligence."

"He's smart, but guilty," Ennunzio told them. "He doesn't want to kill, but feels driven to do it, and thus seeks to lay the blame elsewhere. Maybe that's why he hasn't written more. For him, the letters aren't about establishing power, but seeking absolution."

"There's another possibility," Quincy said shortly. "Berkowitz also wrote extensively to the press in an attempt to explain his crimes. Berkowitz, however, suffered from mental illness; he falls into a different category from the organized killer. Now, people suffering from some kind of mental incapacity such as delusions or schizophrenia—"

"Often repeat a phrase," Ennunzio filled in. "You also see that in stroke victims or people with brain tumors. They'll have anything from a word to a mantra they repeat over and over again."

"You're saying this guy is insane?" Rainie spoke up sharply.

"It's one possibility."

"But if he's nuts, how has he successfully eluded the police while kidnapping and killing eight women?"

"I didn't say he was stupid," Quincy countered mildly. "It's possible that he's still functional in many ways. People close to him, however, would know there was something 'not right' about him. He's probably a loner and ill at ease with others. It could help explain why he has spent so much time outdoors, and also why he employs an ambush style of attack. A Ted Bundy-style killer would rely on his social skills to smooth-talk his way inside a prey's defenses. This man knows he can't."

"This man builds elaborate riddles," Rainie said flatly. "He targets strangers, communicates with the press, and plays games with the police. That sounds like a good old-fashioned organized psychopath to me."

Kaplan held up a hand. "Okay, okay, okay. We're getting a little off track here. This so-called Eco-Killer is Georgia's problem. We're here about Special Agent McCormack."

"What about him?" Dr. Ennunzio asked with a frown.

"Do you think McCormack could've written these notes?"

"I don't know. You'd have to give me something else he's written. Why are you looking at Special Agent McCormack?"

"You haven't heard?"

"Heard what? I've been out of town at the conference. I haven't even had time to clear all my voice mail yet."

"A body was found yesterday," Kaplan said curtly. "Of a young girl. On the Marine PT course. We have reason to believe McCormack might be involved."

"There are elements of the case similar to the Eco-Killer," Rainie added, ignoring Kaplan's dark look. "Special Agent McCormack thinks the murder is the work of the Eco-Killer, starting over here in Virginia. Special Agent Kaplan thinks maybe McCormack is our guy, and merely staged the scene to match an old case."

"A body was found *here*? At Quantico? Yesterday?" Ennunzio appeared dazed.

"You should leave the bomb shelter every once in a while," Rainie told him.

"This is horrible!"

"I don't think the young girl enjoyed it much, either."

"No, you don't understand." Ennunzio was looking down at his notes wildly. "I did have a theory, one thing I was going to suggest to Special Agent McCormack if I ever got a chance. It was a long shot, but . . ."

"What?" Quincy asked intently. "Tell us."

"Special Agent McCormack mentioned in passing that he'd started getting phone calls about the case. Some anonymous tipster trying to help them out. He believed it might be someone close to the killer, a family member or spouse. I had another idea. Given that the letters to the editor were so brief, and that most killers expand their communication over time . . ."

"Oh no," Quincy said, closing his eyes and obviously tracking the thought. "If the UNSUB feels guilty, if he's dissociating himself from the act . . ."

"I wanted Special Agent McCormack to either tape those calls, or write down the conversations verbatim the minute he hangs up the phone," Ennunzio said grimly. "That way I could compare language from the caller with wording from the letters. You see, I don't think he's hearing from a family member. It's possible . . . Special Agent McCormack may be hearing from the killer himself."

24

Virginia
3:13 P.M.
Temperature: 98 degrees

Tina dreamt of fire. She was tied to a stake in the middle of a pile of kin-
dling, feeling the flames wick up her legs while the gathered crowd cheered.
"My baby," she screamed at them. "Don't hurt my baby!"

But no one cared. The people laughed. The fire lapped her flesh. Now it
seared her fingers, starting at the tips and racing up to her elbows. Then her
hair was ablaze, the flames licking her ears and singeing her eyelashes. The
heat gathered and built, forcing its way into her mouth and searing her
lungs. Her eyeballs melted. She felt them run down her face. Then the fire
was inside her eye sockets, greedily devouring her flesh, while her brains
began to boil and her face peeled back from her skull . . .

Tina awakened with a jolt. Her head flew up from the rock and she
became aware of two things at once. Her eyes were swollen shut and her skin
felt as if it were burning.

The mosquitoes still swarmed her head. Yellow flies, too. She batted at
them feebly. She had no blood left. They should leave her alone and seek
fresher prey, not some exhausted girl on the verge of dehydration. The bugs
didn't seem to care. She was bathed from head to toe in sweat, which apparently in the insect world made her a feast fit for kings.

Hot, so hot. The sun was directly overhead now. She could feel it beating
down on her, burning her bite-sensitive skin and parching her lips. Her
throat was swollen and dry. She could feel the skin on her arms and legs
shrinking beneath the harsh glare and pulling uncomfortably at her joints.
She was a piece of meat left too long in the sun. She was, quite literally, being
cured into a piece of human jerky.

You have to move. You have to do something.

Tina had heard the voice before, in the back of her mind. In the beginning, it had given her hope. Now, it just filled her with despair. She couldn't
move, she couldn't do anything. She was nothing but mosquito fodder and
if she moved off this rock, then she'd be snake fodder, too. She was sure of
it. Before her eyes had swollen shut from mosquito bites, she'd taken inventory as best she could. She was in some kind of open pit, with sides that
stretched out ten to fifteen feet, while the broad mouth yawned twenty feet
overhead at least. She had a rock. She had her purse. She had a one-gallon

jug of water the son of a bitch had probably thrown in just to toy with her.

That was it. Pit, rock, water. Only other thing around was the foul-smelling muck that oozed out from under her rocky perch. And no way was she stepping off her boulder into that slime. She'd seen things *move* in the marsh around her. Dark, slimy things she was certain would love to feast on human flesh. Things that genuinely frightened her.

Drink.

Can't. I won't have water, and then I'll die.

You are *dying. Drink.*

She groped around for the bottle of water. It too felt hot to the touch. She'd had a little when she'd first woken up, but then quickly recapped the precious supply. Her resources were limited. In her purse, she had a pack of gum and a package of six peanut-butter crackers. She also had a little Baggie filled with twelve saltines, the perks of being a pregnant woman.

Pregnant woman. She was supposed to be drinking at least eight glasses of water a day to help support the whole new infrastructure being built in her body. She should also be eating an extra three hundred calories a day, as well as getting plenty of rest. Nowhere in the preparing-for-parenthood book had it talked about surviving on three sips of water and a couple of crackers. How long could she go on like this? How long could her baby?

The thought both discouraged her and brought her strength. Her inner voice was right. She wasn't going to make it on this godforsaken rock in this godforsaken pit. She was already dying. She might as well put up a fight.

Tina worked grimly with her swollen fingers at the plastic cap of the water jug. At the last minute, it popped off wildly and went soaring somewhere in the muck. No matter. She brought the jug to her lips and drank greedily. The water was hot and tasted of cooked plastic. She downed it gratefully, each giant gulp soothing her rusty throat. Second turned into wonderful, indulgent second. At the last minute, she tore the jug from her lips, gasping for breath and already desperate for more.

Her thirst felt like a separate beast, freshly awakened and now ravenous.

"Crackers," she told herself firmly. "Salt is good."

She set the jug down carefully, feeling along the rock for a stable spot. Then she found her purse and after painful minutes fumbling with the zipper, got it open.

The mosquitoes had returned, attracted by the smell of fresh water. Yellow flies buzzed her lips, settling on the corners as if they'd sip the moisture straight from her mouth. She slapped savagely, and had the brief satisfaction of feeling plump insect bodies burst against her fingers. Then more flies were back, crawling on her lips, her eyes, the soft tissue of her inner ear, and she knew she had to let them go. Ignore the constant pricking bites, the awful, dreadful hum. Give up this battle, or most certainly lose the war.

Grimly, she set about searching her purse. Her fingers found the Baggie of saltines and drew them out. She counted out six. A dozen bites later, they were gone. The salty, dry texture immediately intensified her thirst.

Just one sip, she thought. To chase down the saltines. To soothe her pain, because oh God, the flies, the flies, the flies. They were everywhere, buzzing and biting, and the more she tried to ignore them the more they skittered across her skin and sank little teeth deep into her flesh. She wasn't going to make it after all. She was going to go insane and the least a crazy person could do was drink.

She reached for the bottle, then snatched back her hand. No, she'd had water. Not much, but enough. After all, she didn't know how long she'd been down here. Earlier, she'd screamed for a full hour without any luck. Best she could tell, the rat bastard had dropped her somewhere remote and isolated. If that was true, it was up to her. She had to be smart, stay calm. She had to think of a plan.

She rubbed her eyes. Bad idea. They immediately burned. Some of that water would feel so nice on her face. She could rinse out her eyes, maybe get them to crack open so she could see. Rinse off the sweat, then maybe the mosquitoes would finally leave her alone.

Stupid. Pipe dream. She was sweating down to her toes, her green sundress plastered to her skin and her underwear soaked straight through. She hadn't been this hot since she'd sat naked in a Swedish sauna. Rinsing her face would buy her respite for about two seconds. And then she'd be sweatsoaked and miserable again.

The key was to marshal her resources and use them sparingly.

She also had to get out of the sun. Find someplace shady and relatively cool for the day. Then she could make her escape at night.

She remembered the weather forecast now. Hot, working toward even hotter. Probably breaking triple digits by the end of the week. Not much time, especially if she was already feeling this exhausted.

She had to get moving. Get out of this pit, or die here.

Tina wasn't ready to die yet.

She used her fingers on her puffy eyelids, prying open the painful, swollen flesh. Some kind of thick liquid drained down her face. She held her eyelids open resolutely, permitting only a few short blinks.

In the beginning, nothing. And then . . . the goo cleared from her eyes and the world slowly came into focus. Bright, harsh, punishing.

Tina inspected her surroundings. Below her was some kind of thick, wet muck. Above her, fifteen to twenty feet overhead, was the mouth of the pit. And beyond that? She had no idea. She could see no signs of bushes, trees, or shrubs. Whatever was up there, however, it surely had to be better than what was down here.

She turned her inspection to the walls. Standing carefully on the edge of the boulder, she counted to three, then let her upper body fall forward. Her red, inflamed hands hit the surface hard. She felt a moment of stunning, cracking pain. Then she was there, feet on the boulder, the rest of her leaning against the side of the pit.

The side was cooler than she would've thought. Wet with something she didn't understand. Slippery. Like a rock covered with algae or mold. Tina wanted to yank back her hand in revulsion. Instead, she forced her fingers to spread, feeling around for handholds.

Not rock, she determined after a moment. The rough texture was too consistent, without any protruding knobs or zigzagging crevices. It was gravelly, lightly scraping her palms. Concrete, she realized abruptly. Oh my

God, she was in a man-made pit. The son of a bitch had dropped her into his own homemade hell!

Did that mean she was in a backyard? Her thoughts raced. Maybe some kind of residential area? If she could just climb up, then, find some way to the surface . . .

But if she was in a populated area, why hadn't someone responded to her screams? And what about the muck? That oozy, swampy mud, teeming with things she didn't want to know . . .

He probably had a place out in the country, or deep in the woods. Someplace far from civilization, where no one would ever be the wiser. That would make more sense, given his penchant for kidnapping young women.

But still, if she could climb out . . . Once on the surface she could run, hide, find a road, follow a stream. Even if she was deep in the middle of nowhere, up top she had a chance. It was more than she could say down here.

She resumed scouring the bumpy walls with her hands. Faster now. More determined. A moment later, she found it. A vine. Then another, and another. Some kind of invasive species, either seeking the mud or trying to escape. It didn't matter to her.

Tina wrapped three vines around her hand and gave them an experimental tug. They seemed strong and resilient. Maybe she could use them. Balance her feet against the wall and use the vines to pull her way up. Why not? She'd seen it dozens of times on TV.

Fired with purpose now, she got serious. She pushed herself back onto her rocky perch and examined her worldly goods. She needed her purse; it had food and who knows what else might come in handy. Easy enough. She slung it over her shoulder and tried not to wince as the leather rubbed against her sunburned flesh. The water was trickier. It didn't fit in her purse and she didn't think she could grip a gallon jug and the vines in the same hand.

Briefly, she considered drinking all of it. Why not? It would feel so good going down her throat. Wonderful and wet. And she was making a break for it. Escaping from this hell. If she got on top, she wouldn't need supplies anymore, would she?

Of course, she had no way of knowing that. She didn't even know what was up there. No, no more drinking. The water needed to go with her. Even if it was heavy and hot to the touch. It was the only supply she had.

Her dress. The material was thin and wispy. She could tear it into strips and use them to tie the jug to her purse. She reached down with both hands and yanked at her hem. The material immediately slid undamaged from her grip. Her fingers were swollen and refused to cooperate. She tried again and again, panting hard, working herself into a frenzy.

The damn material refused to tear. She needed scissors. Of all the things not to have in her purse.

She bit back a sob. Feeling defeated again as the mosquitoes welcomed her stillness by once more resuming to feed. She had to move, she had to do something!

Her bra. She could take that off and loop it through the gallon jug with the shoulder straps serving as a handle. Or better yet, she could wrap the bra around her purse strap and let the water hang from her purse. Then her hands would be free for climbing. Perfect.

She lifted the hem of her sundress and peeled it from her skin. The flies and mosquitoes instantly got excited. Fresh, white flesh. New, unbloodied areas. She tried not to think about it as she worked on removing her sweat-soaked bra. The nylon fabric was sticky to the touch. She grimaced and finally got it off with a sigh.

It seemed pure cruelty to yank on her dripping, stinky dress. It felt so much better to be naked in this heat, no uncomfortable fabric rubbing her raw, salty skin. The faintest of breezes wafting against her breasts, her back . . .

She gritted her teeth, and forced her dress back on, the fabric rolling and twisting uncooperatively as she wiggled. For one moment, her foot slipped on the rock. She teetered precariously, looking down at the oozing mud. She dropped down on the rock and held on tight.

Her heart hammered against her ribs. Oh, she wanted done with this. She wanted to go home. She wanted to see her mother. She wanted a wonderful Minnesotan winter, when she could run outside and fling herself into the deep white snow. She remembered how the flakes tasted on the tip of her tongue. The sensation of fresh ice crystals melting in her mouth. The delicate tickle of more flakes feathering across her eyelashes.

Was she crying now? It was so hard to know with all the sweat on her face and the flies encrusting the corners of her eyes.

"I love you, Ma," Tina whispered. And then she had to break off the thought before she definitely wept.

She looped her bra around the jug handle, fastened it around her purse and pushed it behind herself. The dragging weight of it was awkward, and the water sloshed up dangerously close to the uncapped top, but it was the best she could do. She had her supplies. Next.

She balanced on the rock, then grimly fell forward against the wall. Her hands scraped against the surface, catching her weight. Then she searched for vines. She found six. She wrapped three around each hand, feeling them bite into her sunburned hands. Time to grin and bear it.

Tina stepped out of her highly impractical shoes. One last deep breath. The sun beating down on her head. The sweat rolling down her cheeks. The bugs buzzing, buzzing, buzzing.

Tina pulled on the vines with both arms while simultaneously throwing her right foot at the wall. Her toes scrabbled for traction against the algae-slick surface, found a drier patch and dug in. On the count of three, she heaved up with her arms.

And simultaneously felt the vines give way. She was falling back, her leg already kicking back, trying to find her rocky perch. The water gallon jug swung wildly, further upsetting her balance. She wasn't going to make it, she was going to fall into the stinking muck.

Tina pushed desperately with her hands, releasing her panicked grip on the vines. She went careening back onto her rock. Windmilling, twisting, then suddenly, gratefully, collapsing down onto the stable surface. The water, water, water. Her hands frantically found the jug, still magically upright and holding the last of her precious supply.

She was back on her rock, she had some water, she was safe.

The vines collapsed into the muck below. As they did so, she noticed their edges. Cut clean halfway through. And then came the fluttering piece of white paper, as if loosened by the turbulence above.

Tina reached up a tired hand and felt the paper fall into her palm.

She drew it toward her.

It read: HEAT KILLS.

"You son of a bitch," Tina tried to scream, but her throat was too dry, the words coming out as a mere whisper. She licked her lips. It did no good. She hung her head tiredly, and felt the last of her strength leach from her body.

She needed more food. She needed more water. She needed a break from this desperate heat if she was ever going to survive. And now the bugs were back, the mosquitoes, the yellow flies, feasting, feasting, feasting.

"I'm not going to die here," she muttered resolutely, trying to summon some force of will. "Dammit, I won't do it."

But if she couldn't make it up out of the pit . . .

Very slowly, Tina's gaze went to the thick, slithering muck.

25

Shenandoah National Park, Virginia
4:25 P.M.
Temperature: 99 degrees

"The search area has been divided into ten different sections. Each team of two should analyze their section on the map, then work it in the standard grid pattern. In the good news department, since the hiker has been missing for only twenty-four hours, she shouldn't have wandered beyond a thirty-mile radius, giving us a fairly contained target for search. In the bad news department, this thirty-mile radius contains some of the harshest, steepest terrain in the entire park. Here's what you need to know:

"One, lost hikers inevitably head *down*. They're tired, they're fatigued and once they lose their sense of direction, they'll head down the mountain even when help lies just twenty feet away over the next hill. Two, hikers will also gravitate toward the sound of running water. Everyone knows how important water is, especially someone who is disoriented. If there is water in your section of the grid, check the areas around the streams carefully and follow them for as long as you can. Three, once off the groomed hiking trails, this is rough country. The underbrush is thick, the footing treacherous. Be on the lookout for upturned rocks, broken branches, and trampled underbrush. If this woman is still on the trails, chances are someone would've seen her by now. So most likely she's in the wild and we're going to have to do this the hard way."

Kathy Levine paused for a moment, gazing out somberly over the group of twenty search-and-rescue volunteers now gathered at Big Meadows Lodge. "It's hot out, people. Yeah, no kidding, you're thinking. But I mean it. In this kind of heat index, dehydration is a constant threat. The rule of thumb is that two quarts of water a day keeps dehydration away. Unfortunately, in these conditions your body can easily lose a *quart* of water per hour through your lungs and pores, so two quarts isn't going to cut it. Frankly, each person should carry two gallons of water, but since that weight would be prohibitive, we're requiring each rescue team to carry either water tablets or a water purification system. Then you can refill your water supply at the various streams you encounter along the way. *Don't drink untreated stream water*. Sure, the water looks clear and pretty up here, but most of it is contaminated by *Giardia lamblia*—a parasite which is guaranteed to give you a bad case of the seven-day trots. Drink often, but drink smart.

"Now, assuming that you stay properly hydrated, don't slip down a steep hillside, or stumble upon a sleeping bear, there are a few final things to keep in mind. For example, rattlesnakes. We have plenty. Every now and then, you'll come to a clear meadow with a pile of rocks from an old landslide. Looks like a terrific place to sit down. Don't. The snakes think so, too, and most of those rocks are their homes. Let's not argue with them. Second, we have hornets. They like to build nests in old hollows in the ground or in rotten logs. If you leave them alone, they'll leave you alone. If you step into a nest, however . . . might I recommend *not* running back to your partner. You'll only drag him into the mess and one of you will need to be able to hike back for help. Finally, we have stinging nettles. If you haven't ever seen one, they are about thigh-high with broad green leaves. If you boil them, they actually make a pretty good green to go with dinner. Walk into them, however, and welcome to nature's version of fiberglass. The prickers get immediately under the skin and emit a poison that remains long after the thistles are gone. It takes a good thirty to sixty minutes for the inflammation to subside and by then, you'll have renounced everything you once held dear.

"This park is beautiful. I've walked almost every inch of it in the last five years and I can't think of a more beautiful spot on earth. But nature also commands respect. We need to be focused. We need to move fast. But in these conditions, I also need each and every one of you to always be using your head. Our goal is to find one person, not lose any more. Any questions?" Levine paused. There were none. "Good," she said crisply. "Let's move. We have only four and a half hours of daylight left."

The group broke up, people finding their search partners and heading out of the lodge. Everyone had received their assignment, and most seemed to understand the drill. Mac and Kimberly were probably the biggest rookies of the bunch and Mac had done his fair share of search-and-rescue work by now. Kimberly, he could tell, was more uncomfortable. She had the gear, she had the fitness. But by her own admission, she'd never spent much time in the woods.

If what Kathy Levine had said was correct, this was going to be quite an adventure.

"What do you think she meant by the hornets?" Kimberly said now as they trudged out of the wonderfully air-conditioned lodge into the searing heat. "If the hornets build their nests in the ground and we're walking on the ground, how are we supposed to avoid them?"

"Look where you step," Mac said. He stopped, held up the map they'd been given, and worked on orienting it to their surroundings. They were officially Search Team D, assigned to search the three square miles of, logically enough, Search Area D.

"But if I'm looking at the ground, how am I supposed to look for a lost woman or broken branches or whatever?"

"It's just like driving. You look ahead ten feet to know what's coming, then gaze around all you want, then scope out the next ten feet. Look, glance, look, glance, look, glance. Okay, according to the map, we enter the trailhead there."

"I thought we weren't on a trail. Levine said we were in the 'rough country'—whatever the hell that means."

"We are," Mac said patiently. "But the first quarter of a mile is on a trail. Then we veer off into the wild underbelly of the beast."

"How will we know which way to go?"

"We chart and map usin' compass points. It'll be slow, but thorough."

Kimberly barely nodded. She was gazing nervously at the dark forest before them, carpeted in nine shades of green. Mac saw beauty. Kimberly, however, obviously saw something worse.

"Tell me again how often you've done this," she whispered.

"I assisted with two of the search operations in Georgia."

"You said people got hurt."

"Yep."

"You said he sets up scenarios like this, just to torture us."

"Yep."

"He's a real son of a bitch, isn't he?"

"Oh, yeah."

Kimberly nodded. She squared her shoulders, her chin coming up in that set he already knew so well. "All right," she said stiffly. "We're going to find this girl, we're going to save the day, and then we're going to walk out of this park so we can nail the bastard. Deal?"

"You are a woman after my own heart," Mac said soberly.

They pushed ahead into the thick, dark woods.

Footing was easy on the dirt trail. Steep, but manageable, with rocky ledges and worn tree roots forming a natural cascade of stairs. Shady, with the dense canopy of trees blocking out the sun. The heat and humidity, however, were harder to escape. Mac was already short of breath, his lungs laboring as they headed down the path. Within minutes, his face was drenched in sweat, and he could feel moisture beading uncomfortably between his shoulder blades, where his backpack pressed against his shirt. The sun was bad, but the humidity was their true enemy. It turned the high mountain woods from a shady reprieve to a steaming jungle where each footstep required hard physical effort and four hours of intense hiking would be about three hours too much.

Both Mac and Kimberly had changed clothes for the operation. Kimberly now wore khaki shorts and a short-sleeved cotton T-shirt, the casual outfit of an amateur day hiker. More experienced, Mac had donned nylon shorts and a quick-drying nylon top. As he began to sweat, the synthetic material wicked the moisture away from his body, allowing him a small degree of comfort. Kimberly's cotton T-shirt, on the other hand, was already plastered against her body. Soon, the shirt, as well as her shorts, would start to chafe her skin painfully. He wondered if she would complain, but already figured she wouldn't.

"Do you think she's still alive?" Kimberly asked tersely. Her breath also came out in short pants, but she was matching stride with stride. When called upon to perform, the lady didn't disappoint.

"I read a study once of search-and-rescue operations," Mac replied. "Of the fatalities, seventy-five percent died in the first forty-eight hours.

Assuming this girl was abandoned yesterday, that gives us another twenty-four hours to find her."

"What," *pant, pant,* "generally kills" *pant, pant,* "lost people?"

"Hypothermia. Or on a day like this, heatstroke. Basically, it's exposure that does a person in. Here's a fact for you: Did you know that children under the age of six have the highest survival rate when lost in the woods?"

Kimberly shook her head.

"Kids are better at listening to their instincts," Mac explained. "When they're tired, they sleep. When they're frightened, they seek shelter. Adults, on the other hand, are always convinced they can regain control. So rather than get out of the rain or the cold or the sun, they keep walking, determined that safety is just around the corner. It's exactly the wrong thing to do. Your odds are much better if you remain calm and stay in one place. After all, the average person can last up to five days with no water and up to a month without food. Wear yourself out walking, however, and you'll succumb to exposure, fall off a cliff, stumble into a bear's den, etc., etc. Next thing you know, the lost hiker's dead in forty-eight hours, when any old schmuck should be able to last a week."

Mac stopped abruptly. He looked at the map again, then his compass. "Hang on. Yep. We head off here."

Kimberly came to a halt beside him and he could feel her uneasiness immediately increase tenfold. There was no clearly marked trail in front of them. Instead, the earth opened up, then plummeted down, a tumbling mass of boulders, bushes, and grass. Fallen trees lay directly in their way, overgrown with shaggy moss and brilliant ferns. Jagged branches stuck out dangerously low, while some kind of thick green vine covered half the trees in sight.

The woods were dense, dark. Kathy Levine was right: they held secrets that were both beautiful and deadly.

"If we get separated," Mac said quietly, "just stay in one place and blow your whistle. I'll find you."

All the search-and-rescue operatives had been given shrill plastic whistles. One blow was to communicate between partners. Two blows meant a team had found the girl. Three shrills was the international call for distress.

Kimberly's gaze had gone to the ground. Mac could practically see her eyes scouring each rock and thicket for signs of rattlesnakes or hornets. Her hand now rested on the top of her left thigh. Where she had the knife strapped, he guessed, and immediately felt his gut tighten with a shot of good, old-fashioned male lust. He did not know why an armed woman should be so arousing, but man oh man, this one was.

"We're going to be fine," he said.

Kimberly finally looked at him. "Don't make promises you can't keep," she said. Then she stepped off the path into the wild underbrush.

Footing quickly grew rough. Twice Kimberly slipped and tumbled halfway down a steep slope. Long, thick grass offered little traction, even for her hiking boots, and rocks and tree roots stuck up in the damnedest places. If she looked down for obstacles, then a stray tree limb would catch her up high.

If she looked up high, she risked taking a fallen log in the shin. If she tried looking everywhere at once, she fell, a lot, regularly, and with generally painful, bloody results.

Within two hours, her legs wore a crisscross of scratches to match the ones still healing on her face. She avoided hornets, but blundered into a patch of poison ivy. She stopped running into dead logs, but twice twisted her ankles on slippery rocks.

All in all, she wasn't enjoying the woods much. She supposed it should be beautiful, but to her it wasn't. She felt the loneliness of this place, where the sound of your companion's footsteps was swallowed up by moss-covered rocks, and even knowing there was another search party within three miles, she didn't hear a peep. She felt the disorientation of the towering trees that blocked out the sun and made it difficult to get a sense of direction. The rough, undulating landscape meant they were often walking down to go up, or walking up to go down. Which way was north, south, east, west? Kimberly didn't know anymore, and that left her feeling anxious in a way she couldn't fully explain.

The immense size of the woods swallowed her up as effectively as any ocean. Now she was drowning in greenness, not sure how to get her head up, or which way to head for shore. She was a city girl who was way out of her league. And in a place like this, so much could go wrong without anyone ever finding your body.

She tried to focus on the missing woman to distract herself. If the girl had started the night at a bar, then she was probably wearing sandals. Had she gotten smart and ditched them right away? Kimberly had already slipped several times in hiking boots. Sandals would be impossible. Bare feet not great, but at least more manageable.

Where would she strike out for first? Head down is what Kathy Levine had said; lost hikers seek the easier path. In Kimberly's mind, this path wasn't that easy. Having to pick and choose for footing required slow, laborious work. Maybe it wasn't as aerobic as hiking up, but the muscles in her legs and butt were already screaming while her heart beat furiously.

Would the girl try to seek shelter? Someplace she could stay cool and not wear herself out? Mac had implied that staying put was the key. Be calm, in control, don't just wander around in a daze.

Kimberly looked around her, at the arching trees, the looming shadows, and the deep crevices with all their unknown inhabitants.

She bet the girl had started out at a dead run. She bet she'd torn through these bushes and trees, desperately seeking some sign of civilization. She'd probably screamed for hours, wearing herself hoarse with the need for human contact. And when night had fallen, when the woods had filled with the louder sounds of bigger beasts and buzzing insects . . .

The girl had probably run again. Tripped. Fallen. Maybe gone headfirst into a poison ivy patch or into a hornets' nest. And what would have happened to her then? Stung, terrorized, half-dressed, and lost in the dark?

She'd seek water, anything to cool her wounds. And because whatever lurked in the streams had to be less dangerous than the creatures that stalked the woods.

Kimberly halted abruptly, holding up a hand. "Do you hear it?" she asked Mac sharply.

"Water," Mac agreed. From his backpack, he retrieved his map. "There's a stream directly to the west."

"We should follow it. That's what Levine said, right? Hikers are drawn to water."

"Sounds like a plan to me."

Kimberly stepped left . . .

And her foot went totally out from under her. One moment she was on solid ground. The next, her leg shot out and she went careening butt-first down the slippery slope of grass. Her hip bounded over a rock. Her thigh scraped by a fallen log. Desperately she tried to get her hands beneath her, while vaguely she was aware of Mac shouting her name behind her.

"Kimberly!!!"

"Ahhhhhhhhhh." Thump. Thunk. Another dead log reared up ahead, and she slammed into it with all the grace of a rhino. Stars burst in front of her eyes. A buzzing roared through her ears. She was acutely aware of the rusty taste of blood in her mouth where she had bitten her tongue. And then, all at once, her body caught fire.

"Shit. Damn. Oh, what the hell!" She was on her feet, slapping at her arms and legs. It hurt, it hurt, it hurt, like a million little fire ants biting her skin again and again and again. She bolted out of the weeds and went scrambling back up the hillside, grabbing at tree limbs with her hands while churning up the grass with her feet.

She made it fifteen feet back up and not a single inch of it helped. Her skin burned. Her blood roared. She watched helplessly as her body suddenly bloomed with a bright red rash.

Mac finally came crashing to a halt in front of her. "Don't scratch, don't scratch, don't scratch."

"What the hell is it?" she cried frantically.

"Congratulations, honey, I think you just found the stinging nettles."

26

Quantico, Virginia
8:05 P.M.
Temperature: 98 degrees

"So what do we have?" Quincy asked. It was after eight o'clock now. He, Rainie, Special Agent Kaplan, and Supervisor Watson had taken over an unused classroom for their ad hoc meeting. No one looked particularly cheerful. For one thing, half of them were still wrung out from working the crime scene in this heat. For another, they had nothing to show for their fourteen-hour day.

"I think we still have to look harder at McCormack," Kaplan insisted. "In this business, you know there is no such thing as coincidence. And him being here at the same time one of his old cases heats up . . . That's too much coincidence for me."

"It was not coincidental, it was planned." Rainie spoke up in exasperation. Her opinion on this matter was clear, and now she shook her head in disgust at Kaplan. "You spoke to his boss. You know what McCormack said was true."

"People cover for their own."

"So the entire GBI is in on the crime? We've simply gone from coincidence to conspiracy theory."

Quincy held up his hand, attempting to cut off this argument before it got going. Again. "What about the ad?" he asked Kaplan.

"According to the Public Affairs Officer, the ad arrived yesterday, with instructions to run in today's paper. The *Quantico Sentry*, however, is a weekly paper. Next edition doesn't come out until this Friday. Besides, the officer didn't like the look of the ad. Seemed like code to him, maybe something drug related, so he passed it my way."

Kaplan pushed a photocopy of the ad in question across the table. It was a small, two-by-two-inch box, outlined with a black border and containing one block of text. The text read: Dear Editor, Clock ticking . . . planet dying . . . animals weeping . . . rivers screaming. Can't you hear it? Heat kills . . .

"Why an ad?" Watson spoke up.

"*Quantico Sentry* doesn't do letters to the editor."

"What are the rules for ad submissions?" Quincy asked.

Kaplan shrugged. "The newspaper is a civilian enterprise, published in cooperation with the Public Affairs Office here on the base, so it covers anything topical to the area. Lots of local merchants advertise, charities reach out, services for military personnel, etc. It's no different really from any other small, regional paper. Ads must be submitted typeset and with a payment. Otherwise, you're pretty much good to go."

"So our guy took the time to learn the submission requirements for an ad, but still didn't realize the paper wouldn't print it today?" Watson asked skeptically. "Doesn't seem too bright to me."

"He got what he wanted," Quincy said. "It's the next day, and we're reading his message."

"Pure chance," Watson said dismissively.

"No. This man does everything with a purpose. *Quantico Sentry* is the Corps' oldest newspaper. It's part of their tradition and pride. Putting his message in this paper is the same as dumping a body on the base. He's bringing his crime close to home. He's demanding our attention."

"It fits the pattern," Rainie said. "So far we have the same MO as with the Eco-Killer, and now we have the letter too. I'd say the next step is pretty obvious."

"And what would that be?" Watson asked.

"Call McCormack! Get him back in on this thing. He knows this guy better than we do. And, since there's probably another girl out there, maybe we ought to get some experts looking once more at the body, let alone those little details like the rattlesnake, leaf, and rock. Come on. As the ad says, the clock is ticking, and we've already wasted the entire day."

"I sent them to the lab," Kaplan said quietly.

"You did what?" Rainie asked incredulously.

"I sent the rock, the leaf, and, well, the various snake bits to the Norfolk crime lab."

"And what the hell is a crime lab going to do with them? Dust them for prints?"

"It's not a bad idea—"

"It's a fucking horrible idea! Weren't you listening to McCormack before? We've got to find the *girl!*"

"Hey!" Quincy's hand was up again, his voice loud and commanding across the table. Not that it did much good. Rainie was already half out of her chair, her hands fisted. And Kaplan appeared just as eager for a battle. It had been a long day. Hot, tiring, wearing. The kind of conditions that led to an increase in bar brawls, let alone a deterioration of cooperation in multi-jurisdictional homicide cases.

"We need to proceed along two tracks," Quincy continued firmly. "So shut up, sit down, and pay attention. Rainie's correct—we need to move quickly."

Rainie slowly sank back down into her chair. Kaplan, too, grudgingly gave him his attention.

"One, let's assume that perhaps this man is the Eco-Killer. Ep, ep, ep!" Kaplan was already opening his mouth to protest. Quincy gave him the same withering look he'd once used on junior agents, and the NCIS agent shut right up. "While we cannot be one hundred percent certain of this, the fact remains that we have a homicide that fits a pattern previously seen in Georgia. Given the similarities, we need to consider that another woman has also been abducted. If so, according to what happened in Georgia, we need to start approaching the evidence we've found on the body as pieces of a geographic puzzle." He looked at Kaplan.

"I can arrange for some experts in botany, biology, and geology to look at what we have," the special agent said grudgingly.

"Quickly," Rainie spoke up.

Kaplan gave her a look. "Yes, ma'am."

Rainie merely smiled at him.

Quincy took a deep breath. "Two," he said, "we need to explore some broader avenues. While I've read summaries of the Georgia case notes, it seems clear to me that they've never come close to knowing much about the killer. They generated a profile and a list of suppositions, none of which has ever been proven either way. I think we should start clean-slate, generating our own impressions based on *this* crime. For example, why plant the body on Quantico grounds? That seems clearly like a man who is making a statement against authority. He feels so invincible, he can operate even within the heart of America's elite law enforcement agency. Then we have the UNSUB's various letters to the editor, as well as his phone calls to Special Agent McCormack. Again this raises several questions. Is this an UNSUB seeking to reassert his feelings of power and control? Or is this a conflicted man, who is reaching out to law enforcement in the dim hope that he will be caught? Also, is the anonymous caller really our UNSUB, or someone else entirely?

"And there is a third motive we should also contemplate. That this killer's game is not targeted at either the Marines or the FBI, but rather, at Special Agent McCormack specifically."

"Oh, you have got to be kidding me," Kaplan grumbled.

Quincy gave the man his cool, hard stare. "Assume for a moment that the anonymous caller is the UNSUB. Through his comments, he brought Special Agent McCormack to Virginia. It stands to reason, then, that the UNSUB already had a plan of attack in mind for this area. And furthermore, as part of this plan, he knew of Special Agent McCormack's whereabouts and thus made sure to start the game here. The ad in the *Quantico Sentry* would fit this pattern. As of Friday, the paper would be distributed all over the base. Surely McCormack would get the hint."

Rainie appeared troubled. "That's getting out there," she said quietly.

"True. Killers rarely target a specific member of law enforcement. But stranger things have happened, and as the lead officer, McCormack was the most visible member of the Georgia task force. If the UNSUB *were* going to identify with a specific target, McCormack would be the logical one."

"So we have two options," Rainie murmured. "A garden-variety psychopath trying to mess with McCormack's head. Or a more troubled, guilt-stricken nut who's still murdering girls, but showing signs of remorse. Why doesn't either one of these theories help me sleep better at night?"

"Because either way, the man is deadly." Quincy turned toward Kaplan. "I assume you sent out the ad to the *Quantico Sentry* to be analyzed?"

"Tried," Kaplan said. "Not much to work with. Stamp and envelope are both self-adhesive, so no saliva. Latent found no prints on the paper, and the ad was typeset, so no handwriting."

"What about form of payment?"

"Cash. You're not supposed to send it through the mail, but apparently our killer is a trusting soul."

"Postmark?"

"Stafford."

"The town next door?"

"Yeah, sent yesterday. Local job all the way. Guy's in the area to murder a woman, might as well send his note, too."

Quincy raised a brow. "He's smart. Done his homework. Well, stationery is a good place to start. Dr. Ennunzio said that Georgia had sent him one original letter to the editor. I'd like you to turn over this ad to him as well. Perhaps that gives him two data points to consider."

Kaplan had to think about it. "He can have it for a week," he conceded at last. "Then I want it back at my lab."

"Your cooperation is duly noted," Quincy assured him.

There was a knock on the door. Quincy thinned his lips, frustrated by the intrusion when they were finally getting somewhere, but Kaplan was already climbing to his feet. "Probably one of my agents," he said by way of explanation. "I told him I'd be around here."

He opened the classroom door, and sure enough, a younger buzz-cut man entered the room. The agent was holding a piece of paper and his body practically thrummed with excitement.

"I thought you'd want to see this right away," the younger officer said immediately.

Kaplan took the paper, glanced at it, then looked up sharply. "Are you sure about this?"

"Yes, sir. Got it confirmed fifteen minutes ago."

"What?" Rainie was asking. Even Watson strained in his chair. Kaplan turned back to them slowly.

"We got an ID on the girl," he said, and his gaze went to Quincy. "It's not just like Georgia after all. Sweet Jesus, this is much, much worse."

"Water break."

"Soon."

"Kimberly, water break."

"I want to see what's around the next corner—"

"Honey, stop and drink some water, or I will tackle you."

Kimberly scowled at him. Mac's face remained resolute. He'd halted ten feet back, at a boulder jutting out from the stream they were following down the steep slope.

After three hours of hard hiking, half of her body was covered in a bright red rash—poison ivy, stinging nettles, take your pick. Her T-shirt was sweated through. Her shorts were drenched. Even her socks squished as she walked. Then there was the sodden skullcap that now passed as her hair.

In contrast, Mac stood with one knee bent comfortably on a large boulder.

His damp gray nylon shirt molded his impressive chest. His short dark hair was slicked back to better highlight his bronzed, chiseled face. He wasn't breathing hard. He didn't have a scratch on him. Three hours of brutal trekking later, the man looked like a damn L.L.Bean cover model.

"Bite me," Kimberly said, but she finally stopped and grudgingly dug out her water bottle. The water was tepid and tasted of plastic. It still felt good going down her throat. She was hot. Her chest heaved. Her legs trembled. She'd had easier times on the Marines' obstacle course.

"At least the heat keeps the ticks down," Mac said conversationally.

"What?"

"The ticks. They don't like it when it's this hot. Now if it were spring or fall . . ."

Kimberly gazed down frantically at her bare legs. Beneath the red rash, were any of her freckles moving? Blood-sucking parasites, that ought to top off the day . . . Then she registered the underlying humor in Mac's voice and looked up suspiciously.

"You're living dangerously," she growled.

He merely grinned. "Are you thinking of going for your knife? I've been waitin' all day."

"Not to put a damper on your male fantasies, but I'm sorry I wore the knife. It's rubbing off all the skin on my thigh and damn near killing me."

"Would you like to remove it? I could assist."

"Oh, for heaven's sake."

She turned away from him, swiping a hand through her short-cropped hair. Her palm came back wet and salty, disgusting even her. She must look like a wreck. And still he flirted with her. The man was insane.

Her gaze went to the sun. From this vantage point, she could just see it sinking low in the sky. Funny, it was easy to lose track of night around here. The trees already cast so much of the landscape into shadow, and it wasn't as if the temperature was magically cooling down. But the sun was definitely retreating, the hour growing late.

"Not much time," she murmured.

"No," he agreed, his voice now as somber as her own.

"We should get going." She bent to put her water bottle away. He stepped toward her and halted her hand with his own.

"You need to drink more."

"I just had water!"

"You're not drinking enough. You've only gone through a quart. You heard Kathy Levine. In these conditions you're probably sweating through at least that much an hour. Drink, Kimberly. It's important."

His fingers were still on her arm. Not gripping, certainly not bruising. She felt his touch anyway, more than she should. His fingertips were callused. His palm was damp, probably as sweaty as the rest of him, as the rest of her. She still didn't move away.

And for the first time . . .

She thought about moving closer. She thought about kissing him. He was the kind of man who would be very good at kissing. She imagined he would be slow and thorough. Kissing for him would be like flirting, a fun bit of foreplay he'd been practicing for most of his life.

And for her?

It would be desperate. She knew that without having to think why. It would be need and hope and anger. It would be a vain attempt to leave behind her own body, to break free of the relentless anxiety that shadowed every step she took. To forget for a moment that a young woman was lost out here, and she was trying so hard, but maybe she still wasn't good enough. She hadn't saved her sister. She hadn't saved her mother. Why did she think this time would be different?

She needed too much. She wanted too deeply. This man could laugh his way through life. While Kimberly would one day simply die trying.

Kimberly stepped away. After another moment, she brought her water bottle back up and took a long, deep swallow.

"Times like these," she said after drinking, "you should be able to push yourself harder."

Her tone was goading, but Mac merely arched a brow.

"You think I'm soft?"

She shrugged. "I think we're running out of daylight. I think we should be moving more, and talking less."

"Kimberly, what time is it?"

"A little after eight."

"And where are we?"

"Somewhere in our three-mile grid, I guess."

"Honey, we've been hiking *down* for three hours now. We're about to go down more, because like you, I also want to see what's around that next bend. Now, you want to tell me how we're going to complete our three-hour hike down *and* magically make it back up to base camp in the *one* hour of daylight we have left?"

"I . . . I don't know."

"It can't be done," he said flatly. "Come dark, we'll still be in these woods, plain and simple. Good news, according to my map, we're close to a trail due west. I figure we finish off this section of the stream, leave a marker, then find the trail before dark. Footing there will be better, and we can use my flashlight to pick our way back up. That way, it'll only be hard and danger-ous, versus downright foolhardy. Don't think I don't know how to push the envelope, honey. I've just had a few more years to perfect the act than you."

Kimberly studied him. Then, abruptly, she nodded. He was putting their lives at risk and, perversely, she liked him better for it.

"Good," she said, and hefted her pack. She turned down the streambed, calling out casually over her shoulder, "Old fart."

That got him crashing down behind her. It also put a smile on her face. It made her feel better all the way around the next bend, where they finally got their first lucky break.

Kimberly saw it first.

"Where are we?" she asked wildly.

"We're in our section, there shouldn't be any overlap . . ."

Kimberly pointed to the tree, with its freshly broken branch. And then she saw the crushed fern, followed by the flattened-down grass. She started walking faster, following the unmistakable signs of human passage as the coarse trail began to zigzag through the woods. It was wide. It was clearly marked. A single person, crashing down nearly out of control. Or perhaps even a man, doubled over from the weight of carrying a heavily drugged body.

"Mac," she said with barely contained excitement.

He was looking at the sun. "Kimberly," he said grimly. "Run."

She went careening down the path with Mac hot on her heels.

27

Tina hated the mud. It oozed and popped and smelled. It rippled and writhed with things she couldn't see and didn't want to know. It undulated slowly, like a living beast, just waiting for her to succumb.

She didn't have a choice. She was dangerously exhausted and dehydrated. Her skin burned from too much sun and too many bug bites. On the one hand, she felt as if her entire body were on fire. On the other hand, she had started shivering, her overheated skin breaking out incongruously with wave after wave of goose bumps.

She was dying; it was that simple. People were comprised of something like 70 percent water. Which made her a pond, now literally drying up from drought.

Curled up against the hot surface of the rock, she thought of her mom. Maybe she should've told her about the pregnancy. Sure, her mother would've been upset, but only because she personally knew how hard the life of a young, single mother could be. Once the shock wore off, she would've helped Tina, offered some support.

And it would've been something else, too. Bringing a little life into the world, seeing her baby's scrunched-up, squalling face. She could picture her and her mom crying together in the delivery room, exhausted and proud. She could see them picking out cute little baby clothes and fussing over midnight feedings. Maybe she'd have a girl, one more tough cookie to continue the family tradition. The three Krahns, ready to take over the world. Oh, the state of Minnesota had better look out.

She would've tried so hard to be a good mother. Maybe she wouldn't have succeeded, but she would've tried.

Tina finally turned her head, looking up at the sky. Through the slits of her swollen eyes, she could see the yawning blue canvas of her prison. The horizon seemed to be darkening now, the sun finally sinking from view and leaching away the white-hot glare. Funny, it didn't feel any cooler. The humidity was still a stifling wet blanket, as oppressive as the cloud of mosquitoes and yellow flies that continued to swarm her face.

Her head fell back down. She stared at her hand, inches from her face. She had open sores from scratching the hundreds of mosquito bites. Now, she watched a yellow fly land on her skin, dig into her open wounds, and lay a pile of tiny, shiny white eggs.

She was going to be sick. No, she couldn't be sick. It was an inefficient use of the little water she had left. She was going to throw up anyway. Not even dead yet and already being used for maggot bait. How much longer could she possibly go on like this? Her poor baby. Her poor mom.

And then, that calm, practical Minnesotan voice from the back of her head started speaking to her again: *You know what, girl? It's time to get tough. 'Cause you either do something now, or you really do get to forever hold your peace.*

Tina's gaze went to the oozing black mud.

Just do it, Tina. Be tough. Show the rat bastard what you're made of. Don't you dare go down without a fight.

She sat up. The world spun; the bile rose immediately in her throat. With a gagging cough, she choked it back down. Then, she pulled herself wearily to the edge of the boulder and gazed at the muck. Looks like pudding. Smells like . . .

No throwing up!

"All right," Tina whispered grimly. "I'll do it. Ready or not, here I come!"

She stuck her right foot in the muck. Something promptly slithered against her ankle, then darted away. She bit her lower lip to keep from screaming and forced her foot deeper into the muck. It felt like sliding her body into rotted-out guts. Warm, slimy, slightly chunky . . .

No throwing up!

She thrust her left foot into the ooze, saw the clear outline of a black snake slide away and this time she did scream, long, hoarsely, and helplessly. Because she was afraid and she hated this and oh God, why had this man done this to her? She'd never hurt anyone. She didn't deserve to be cast in a pit where she was baking alive while flies laid shiny white eggs into the deep sores of her skin.

And she was sorry for having sex now, and she was sorry for not taking better precautions, and she was sorry she had messed up her young life, but surely she didn't deserve this kind of torture. Surely she and her baby at least deserved a shot at making a better life.

The mosquitoes swarmed. She batted at them again and again, while standing mid-calf in the muck and gagging helplessly.

Drop down, Tina. It's like plunging into a cold pool. Just grit your teeth, and plunge into the muck. It's the only option you have left.

And then . . .

There, in the distance. She heard it again. A sound. Footsteps? No, no. Voices. Someone was around.

Tina jerked back her head to the mouth of the open pit. "Hey," she tried to scream, "hey, hey."

All that came out of her parched throat was the croak of a frog. The voices were fading. People were around, but walking away, she was sure of it.

Tina grabbed her half-empty gallon of water. She took giant, greedy gulps, desperate for help and careless of rationing. Then, with her newly lubricated throat, she threw back her head and screamed in earnest.

"Hey, hey. I'm down here! Someone, anyone! Oh please, come here . . ."

Kimberly was running. Her lungs were burning; a stitch had developed in her side. Still she powered down the slippery slope, crashing through thick brush, jumping over rotting logs, careening around boulders. She could hear the hot, heavy breathing of Mac, racing by her side.

It was a suicidal pace. They could twist an ankle, plummet over a ledge, crash into a tree, or suffer things that would be much, much worse.

But the sun was setting fast now, daylight slipping through their fingers to be replaced by a fiery dusk that shot the sky bloodred. And the path, so distinguishable only fifteen minutes ago, was already slipping into shadow, vanishing before their eyes.

Mac surged ahead. Kimberly put her head down and forced her shorter legs to keep up.

They came crashing down the heavily wooded slope into a sudden, broad clearing. Thorny bushes and tightly packed trees gave way to knee-high grass. The ground flattened out and footing eased up.

Kimberly didn't slow. She was still tearing forward at full throttle, trying to pick out the trail in the fading light, when she registered two things at once: the jagged tumble of hundreds of boulders off to her left and then, just fifteen feet up the pile, a startling strip of red. A skirt, her mind registered. And then . . . A human body. The girl!

They had found the girl!

Kimberly streaked toward the pile of rocks. Vaguely, she heard Mac yelling at her to stop. He grabbed at her wrist. She pulled away.

"It's her," she shouted back triumphantly, springing onto the pile. "Hey, hey you! Hello, hello, hello!"

Three sharp whistles sounded behind her. The international call of distress. Kimberly didn't understand why. They had found the girl. They had saved the day. She had been right to leave the Academy. She had finally done it.

Then the girl came fully into view and any bit of triumph Kimberly had felt burst like a proverbial bubble and left her halted dead in her tracks.

The streak of red was not a piece of brightly dyed cotton, but a pair of white shorts, now stained darkly with dried blood. The sprawling white limbs—not a young girl lying peacefully down to rest, but a bruised and bloated body, twisted beyond recognition. And then, as Kimberly watched in the dusky pall, she swore she saw one of the girl's limbs suddenly move.

The sound hit her all at once. A constant, building thrum. The deep vibration of dozens upon dozens of rattlesnakes.

"Kimberly," Mac said quietly from the ground behind her. "For the love of God, please don't move."

Kimberly couldn't even nod. She just stood there, perfectly frozen, while all around her, the shadows of the rocks uncurled into the shapes of snakes.

"The girl's dead," Kimberly said finally. Her voice sounded hoarse and faint, the tone of a woman already in shock. Mac eased closer to the boulders. By his third footstep, a fresh round of rattling shook the pile. He stopped instantly.

The sound seemed to be coming from everywhere. Ten, twenty, thirty different vipers. They seemed to be everywhere. Sweet Jesus, Mac thought, and reached back slowly for his gun.

"She must have been tired and dazed," Kimberly murmured. "Saw the rocks. Climbed up for a better view."

"I know."

"My God, I think they bit every inch of her body. I've never . . . I've never seen anything like it."

"Kimberly, I have my gun out. If something moves, I'm going to shoot it. Don't flinch."

"It won't work, Mac. There are too many of them."

"Shut up, Kimberly," he growled.

She turned her head toward him and actually smiled. "Now which one of us is being earnest?"

"Snakes don't like us any more than we like them. If you just remain calm and don't move, most of them will disappear back into the rocks. I've sounded the whistle; help will be here shortly."

"I almost died once. Did I ever tell you that? A man I thought I knew well. It turned out he was just using me to get to my father. He cornered Rainie and me in a hotel room. He held a gun to my head. There was nothing Rainie could do. I still remember just how the barrel felt. Not cold, but warm. Like living flesh. It's strange to feel so helpless. It's strange to be trapped in the arms of another human being and know he's going to take your life."

"You're not dead, Kimberly."

"No, my father surprised him. Shot him in the chest. Thirty seconds later, everything had changed and I was the one still alive, wearing his blood in my hair. And my father was telling me everything would be all right. It was nice of him to lie."

Mac didn't know what to say. Light was fading fast, the pile of boulders quickly becoming another world, filled with too much black.

"She never stood a chance," Kimberly murmured, her gaze returning to the girl's body. "Look at her in her shorts and silk blouse. She was dressed to have fun in a bar, not fend her way in a wilderness. It's beyond cruel."

"We're going to find him."

"Not until another girl is dead."

Mac closed his eyes. "Kimberly, the world's not as bad as you think."

"Of course not, Mac. It's worse."

He swallowed. He was losing her. He could feel Kimberly slide deeper into fatalism, a woman who had escaped death once and didn't expect to get that lucky again. He wanted to yell at her to buck up. And then he wanted to take her into his arms, and promise her everything would be all right.

She was right: when men tried to protect the people they cared about, they inevitably resorted to lies.

"Do you see the snakes?" he asked shortly.

"There's not enough light. They blend into the boulders."

"I don't hear them."

"No, they've fallen silent. Maybe they're tired. They've had a busy day."

Mac edged closer. He wasn't sure how near the old landslide he could get. He didn't hear any fresh rounds of rattling. He crept to within five feet, then took out his flashlight, flaring it over the pile of boulders. It was difficult to tell. Some rocks seemed clear. Others had bulging outlines that could very well be more rattlers.

"Do you think you can jump to me?" he asked Kimberly.

She was at least twenty feet away, at an awkward angle in the rock pile. Maybe if she bounded quickly from boulder to boulder . . .

"I'm tired," Kimberly whispered.

"I know, honey. I'm tired, too. But we need to get you off those rocks. I've sort of grown attached to your sunny smile and gentle disposition. Surely you wouldn't want to disappoint me now."

No answer.

"Kimberly," he said more sharply. "I need you to pay attention. You're strong, you're bright. Now, focus on how we're going to get out of this."

Her gaze went off in the distance. He saw her shoulders tremble. He didn't know what she thought about but, finally, she turned back to him. "Fire," she told him quietly.

"Fire?"

"Snakes do hate fire, right? Or have I watched too many Indiana Jones movies? If I make a torch, maybe I can use it to scare them away."

Mac moved fast. He wasn't an expert on snakes, but it sounded like a plan to him. He used his flashlight and quickly found a decent-sized fallen limb. "Ready?"

"Ready."

He lofted the branch into the air with an easy underhand. A moment later, he heard the small thump as she caught it in her hands. They both held their breath. A slight buzzing rattle, low and to the right.

"Stay still," Mac warned.

Kimberly dutifully froze and after several long minutes, the sound faded away.

"You need to get into your pack for the other supplies," Mac instructed. "If you have an extra pair of wool socks, wrap one around the end of the branch. Then you'll notice a small film canister in your front pocket. I added that. It contains three cotton balls dipped in Vaseline. They make an excellent fire starter. Just tuck them into the folds of the sock and hit 'em with a match."

He held the flashlight, illuminating her in its beam of light as she went to work. Her movements were slow and subdued, trying not to call attention to herself.

"I can't find my extra socks," she called back at last. "What about a T-shirt?"

"That'll do."

She had to set her pack down. Mac briefly lit up the ground beside her. It appeared free of snakes. She gingerly lowered her pack. Another hiss as the snakes sensed the disturbance and voiced their disapproval. She stilled again, straightening at the waist, and now Mac could see the fresh sheen of sweat on her brow.

"You're almost done," he told her.

"Sure." Her hands were shaking. She fumbled the stick briefly, nearly dropped it, and a fresh rattle, close and loud, reverberated through the dark. Mac watched Kimberly squeeze her eyes shut. He wondered if she was now remembering another truth about that day in the hotel room—that when the man had held a gun to her head, her first thought had been that she didn't want to die.

Come on, Kimberly, he willed her. *Come back to me.*

She got the T-shirt wrapped around the end of the stick. Then she tucked in the cotton balls. Then she found the matches. Her trembling hand held aloft the first small wooden match. The raspy sound of the tip scratching against the box. The match flared to life, she touched it to the cotton balls, and a torch was born in the night.

Immediately, the space around her blazed with fresh light, illuminating not one, but four coiled rattlers.

"Mac," Kimberly said clearly. "Get ready to catch."

She thrust the torch forward. The snakes hissed, then recoiled sharply from the flames, and Kimberly bolted off the first boulder. She bounded down, one, two, three, four, as the crevices came alive with slippery shapes tumbling off the boulders as the snakes sought to escape the flame. The rocks were alive, hissing, curling, rattling. Kimberly plunged through the writhing mess.

"Mac!" she yelled. She came catapulting off the final rock and crashed against his hard frame.

"Gotcha," he said, grabbing her shoulders and already removing the torch from her shaking hand.

For one moment, she just stood there, shell-shocked and dazed. Then, she collapsed against his chest and he held her more gratefully and desperately than he should.

"Mandy," Kimberly murmured. She began to cry.

28

Professionals arrived and took over the scene. Lanterns were brought in, along with battery-powered lights. Then volunteers, armed with sticks, served as emergency snake wranglers, while men wearing thick boots and heavy-duty pants waded onto the rock pile and removed the victim's body in a litter.

Kathy Levine stood by as Mac officially reported their latest find to the powers that be. As a national park, Shenandoah fell under FBI jurisdiction; Watson would have his case after all, and Mac and Kimberly would once again be relegated to the role of outsiders.

Kimberly didn't care. She sat alone on the sidewalk in front of Big Meadows Lodge, watching the emergency vehicles pile up in the parking lot. Ambulances and EMTs with no one to save. A fire department with no blaze to extinguish. Then finally, the ME's van, the only professional who would get to practice his trade tonight.

It was hot. Kimberly felt moisture roll down her face like tears. Or maybe she was still crying. It was hard to know. She felt empty in a way she'd never felt empty before. As if everything she had ever been had disappeared, been flushed down a drain. Without bones, her body would have no weight. Without skin, she would cease to have form. The wind would come, blow her away like a pile of burnt-out ash, and maybe it would be better that way.

More cars came and went. Exhausted search volunteers returned and headed for a makeshift canteen where they downed buckets of ice water, then sank their teeth into pulpy slices of orange. The EMTs treated them for minor cuts and slight sprains. Most people simply collapsed into the metal folding chairs, physically exhausted by the hike, and emotionally drained by a search that had ended with bitter disappointment.

Tomorrow all of this would be gone. The search-and-rescue volunteers would disperse back to their everyday lives, returning to mundane rituals and routine concerns. They would rejoin their families, hiking parties, fire departments.

And Kimberly? Would she go back to the Academy? Fire shotgun rounds at blank targets and pretend it made her tough? Or play dress-up in Hogan's Alley, dodging paint shells and matching wits with overpaid actors? She could pass the last round of tests, graduate to become a full-fledged agent, and go through the rest of her life pretending her career made her whole. Why not? It had worked for her father.

She wanted to lay her head down on the hard sidewalk bordering the parking lot. She wanted to melt into the cement until the world ceased to exist. She wanted to go back to a time when she did not know so much about violent death, or what dozens of rattlesnakes could do to the human body.

She had told Mac the truth earlier. She was tired. Six years' worth of sleepless, bone-weary nights. She wanted to close her eyes and never open them again. She wanted to disappear.

Footsteps grew closer. A shadow fell between her and the ambulance headlights. She looked up, and there was her father, striding across the parking lot in one of his impeccably tailored suits. His lean face was set. His dark eyes inscrutable. He bore down on her fiercely, a hard, dangerous man come to collect his own.

She didn't have the strength anymore to care.

"I'm fine," she started.

"Shut up," Quincy said roughly. He grabbed his daughter's shoulder. Then he shocked them both by pulling her roughly off the sidewalk and folding her into his embrace. He pressed his cheek against her hair. "My God, I have been so worried about you. When I got the call from Mac . . . Kimberly, you are killing me."

And then she shocked them both by bursting once more into tears. "We didn't make it. I thought for sure this time I would be right. But we were slow and she was dead. Oh God, Daddy, how can I always be too late?"

"Shhh . . ."

She pulled back until she could gaze into his hard-lined face. For so much of her childhood, he had been a cool, remote figure. She respected him, she admired him. She strove desperately for his praise. But he remained out of reach, a larger-than-life figure who was always rushing out the door to assist other families, and rarely around for his own. Now, it was suddenly, frantically important to her that he understand. "If I'd just known how to move faster. I have no experience in the mountains. How could I grow up around here and not know anything about the woods? I kept tripping and falling, Dad, and then I stumbled into the stinging nettles and God, *why couldn't I have moved faster?*"

"I know, sweetheart. I know."

"Mac was right after all. I wanted to save Mandy and Mom, and since I can't help them, I honestly thought saving this girl would make a difference. But they're still dead and she's still dead, and God, what is the point?"

"Kimberly, what happened to your mother and Mandy wasn't your fault—"

She wrenched away from him. Screaming now, her words carrying across the parking lot, but she was beyond noticing. "Stop saying that! You always say that! Of course it was my fault. I'm the one who trusted him. I'm the one who told him all about my family. Without me, he never would've known how to reach them. Without me, he never would've killed them! So stop lying to me, Dad. What happened to Mom and Mandy is exactly my fault. I just let you take the blame because I know it makes you feel better!"

"Stop it! You were only twenty. A young girl. You can't saddle yourself with this kind of guilt."

"Why not? You do."

"Then we're both idiots, all right? We're both idiots. What happened to your mom and Mandy . . . I would've died for them, Kimberly. Had I known, if I could've stopped it, I would've died for them." His breathing had grown harsh. She was shocked to see the glitter of tears in his eyes.

"I would've died, too," she whispered.

"Then we did the best we could, all we could. He was the enemy, Kimberly. *He* took their lives. And God help both of us, but sometimes the enemy is simply that good."

"I want them back."

"I know."

"I miss them all the time. Even Mandy."

"I know."

"Dad, I don't know why I'm still alive . . ."

"Because God took pity on me, Kimberly. Because without you, I think I would've gone insane."

He pulled her back into his arms. She sobbed against his chest, crying harder. And she could feel him crying, too, her father's tears falling onto her hair. Her stoic father, who didn't even cry at funerals.

"I wanted to save her so badly," Kimberly whispered.

"I know. It's not bad to care. Someday, that will be your strength."

"But it hurts. And now I have nothing left. The game is over, and the wrong person has won, and I don't know how to simply go home and wait for the next match. It's life and death. It shouldn't be this cavalier."

"It's not over, Kimberly."

"Of course it is. We didn't find the second girl. Now all we can do is wait."

"No. Not this time." Her father took a deep breath, then gently pulled away. He looked at her in the dark, breathless night, and his face was as sad as she'd ever seen it. "Kimberly," he said quietly. "I'm so sorry, sweetheart, but this time, there weren't just two girls. This time, the man took four."

Rainie was huffing badly by the time she made it down to the crime scene. Lanterns marked the trail, so the footing wasn't bad, but geez Louise, it was a ways down the mountain. And for the record, while it was now after midnight and the moon ruled the sky, apparently no one had bothered to tell the heat. She'd soaked through both her T-shirt and hiking shorts, ruining her third outfit of the day.

She hated this weather. She hated this place. She wanted to go home, and not to the high-rise co-op she shared with Quincy in downtown Manhattan, but home to Bakersville, Oregon. Where the fir trees grew to staggering heights, and a fresh ocean breeze blew off the water. Where people knew each other by first names, and even if it made it hard to escape the past, it also gave you an anchor in the present. Bakersville, where she'd had a town, a community, a place that felt like home . . .

The pang of longing struck hard and deep. As it had been doing so often these days. A ghost pain for the past. And it filled her with a restlessness she was having a harder and harder time trying to hide. Quincy could sense it, too. She caught him watching her sometimes with a question in his eyes. She wished she could give him an answer, but how could she, when she didn't have one herself?

Sometimes she ached for things she couldn't name. And sometimes, when she thought of how much she loved Quincy, it simply hurt her more.

She found Mac standing with a cluster of three people over by the body. The first guy appeared to be the Medical Examiner. Second guy had the look of an assistant. Third person was a woman with short red hair and lots of freckles. She was built like a firecracker, with the muscled legs and broad shoulders of a serious hiker. Not the ME's office. Probably leader of the search-and-rescue operations.

Thirty seconds later, Mac made the introductions, and Rainie was pleased to find out she was right. ME turned out to be Howard Weiss, his assistant was Dan Lansing, and the redhead was Kathy Levine, who had indeed organized the search.

Levine was still talking to the ME, so the three of them broke away, leaving Mac and Rainie standing over the partially wrapped body.

"Where's Quincy?" Mac asked.

"He said he needed to have a fatherly chat with Kimberly. I took one look at his face and decided not to argue."

"They fight a lot?"

"Only because they're too much alike." She shrugged. "Someday they'll figure that out."

"What about Kaplan and Watson? Are they gonna join the party, or are they not allowed off the base?"

"Not known yet. Watson has a full-time job at the Academy, so while the FBI is definitely assembling a team, it probably won't involve him personally. Kaplan, on the other hand, is lead investigator on the Quantico homicide. So he has plenty of time, but lacks jurisdiction. Given that he's a resourceful man, I figure in another hour or two, he'll crack that nut and show up with full NCIS entourage. Oh, aren't we the luckiest duckies in the whole wide world?"

She peered down into the black plastic body bag, the contents clearly lit by one of the generator-powered lights. "Whoa."

"Nearly two dozen puncture wounds," Mac said. "And countin'. Poor girl must've wandered right into the thick of things. After that, she never stood a chance."

"Her purse? The gallon of water?"

"No sign yet. We don't know where she was abandoned, though. In daylight, we can find her trail and backtrack. Probably discover her things along the way."

"Seems strange she'd drop the water."

He shrugged. "In this heat, a gallon of water is good for about two to four hours. She's been out here for at least twenty-four, so . . ."

"So even when the guy plays nice, he's still a total bastard." Rainie straightened. "Well, do you want the good news or the bad news first?"

Mac was silent for a moment. She could see fresh lines on his forehead, a gaunt set to his jaw. He'd been pushing himself hard and he looked it. Still, he didn't blink an eye. "If it's all the same, I think I'd like to start with the good news tonight."

"We might have a name." Rainie dug out her spiral notepad from her fanny pack and started flipping through. She glanced once more at the body. "Brunette, twenty years old, brown eyes, distinguishable by a birthmark on her upper left breast." She bent down, then paused, with a meaningful glance at Mac. He was already looking away. She approved. Some people handled bodies as if they were nothing more than dolls. Rainie had never liked that. This was a girl. She'd had a family, a life, people who deeply loved her. There was no need to disrespect her any more than necessary.

Gently, she lifted the top of the girl's blouse. She had to move her head to let in the light. Then she could see it clearly, the top edge just peeking out from beneath the edge of the girl's black satin bra—a dark brown clover-shaped birthmark.

"Yeah," Rainie said quietly. "It's Vivienne Benson. She was a student at Mary Washington College in Fredericksburg, spending the summer working for her uncle. He called her landlady yesterday when she didn't show up for work. Landlady went up to the apartment, found it empty, and the dog howling to be let out of its crate. She took pity on the poor beast, then called the police. According to her, it's not like Vivienne, or her roommate, Karen Clarence, to stay out all night. Particularly because of their dog, whom apparently they love madly."

"Karen is a blonde?"

"Actually, Karen's a brunette."

Mac immediately frowned. "The body we found at Quantico had blond hair."

"Yeah."

"It's not Karen Clarence?"

"No. Betsy Radison. Her brother made the ID just a few hours ago."

"Rainie, honey, I'm a little tired right now. Can you take pity on an exhausted GBI agent and start your story over in English?"

"I'd be delighted. Turns out the landlady is a real font of information. She was sitting out two nights ago, when Vivienne and Karen came downstairs to wait for their ride. According to her, Viv and Karen were picked up by two other friends from college, and the four of them were going to a bar in Stafford."

"The four of them?"

"Enter Betsy Radison and Tina Krahn, also living in Fredericksburg and taking some summer courses. All four girls went out Tuesday night in Betsy's Saab convertible. None has been seen since. Fredericksburg P.D. went into Betsy and Tina's apartment late tonight. All they could find were a dozen messages from Tina Krahn's mother on the answering machine. Apparently she didn't like her last conversation with her daughter. She's been frantically trying to reach Tina ever since."

"I gotta sit down," Mac said. He moved away from Vivienne Benson's body, found a tree stump and collapsed on the rough shape as if he'd abruptly lost all the strength in his legs. He ran a hand through his damp hair, then did it again and again. "He ambushed four girls at once," he said at last, trying out the words, feeling his way into the horrible concept. "Betsy Radison, he dumped at Quantico, Vivienne Benson he abandoned here. Which leaves us with Karen Clarence and Tina Krahn, who he may have taken . . . Goddamn . . . The gray birch leaf. I thought that was too easy for him. But of course. It wasn't an end. Just a strange beginning."

"Like Quincy said, serial killers have a tendency to escalate the violence of their crime."

"Did you find a letter to the editor?" he asked sharply.

"No letter. An ad in the *Quantico Sentry*."

"The Marines' newspaper?" Mac frowned. "The one distributed all over the base?"

"Yeah. We have the original of what was sent in, but it didn't give up much in the way of forensic evidence. Quincy had it turned over to Ennunzio to analyze the text."

"You got to meet with the forensic linguist? Hell, you *have* been busy."

"We try," Rainie said modestly. "You're going to see him again soon, too. Quincy's requested that Ennunzio join the case team. The two of them are working on a theory that your caller isn't an anonymous tipster, but the man himself. We're just not entirely sure why."

"He doesn't gloat. If I'm getting calls from the Eco-Killer, don't you think he'd want to take the credit?"

"Well, maybe and maybe not. One theory is that he feels guilty about what he's doing, so this is his roundabout way of getting you to stop him. Second theory, he's mentally incapacitated—hence his love of repeating the same message over and over again. Third, you're part of this game now, too, and he's luring you into the wild, just like he does with the girls. Look at the body, Mac. Can you be a hundred percent certain that wouldn't have been you?"

"It wasn't almost me," Mac said quietly. "It was almost Kimberly."

Rainie's expression became very gentle. "Yeah, and then he wins, too, right, Mac? Either way, he wins."

"Son of a bitch."

"Yeah."

"I'm getting too old for this shit, Rainie," he said. And then almost on cue, his phone rang.

29

Shenandoah National Park, Virginia
1:22 A.M.
Temperature: 89 degrees

"Special Agent McCormack."

"Heat kills."

"Shut the fuck up. You really think this is a game? We found your latest victim dead from two dozen rattlesnake bites. Does that make you feel good? Is feeding young girls to pit vipers how you get your jollies? You're nothing but a sick son of a bitch and I'm not talking to you anymore!"

Mac flipped his phone shut. He was mad. Madder than he'd ever been in his life. His heart thundered. He could hear the roar of blood in his ears. He wanted to do more than yell into a tiny phone. He wanted to find the man, and beat him into a bloody pulp.

Rainie was staring at him in mild shock. "While I am impressed, was that really a good idea?"

"Wait." His phone immediately rang again. He gave her a look. "Contacting the authorities is about exercising control, right? He's not gonna let it end on my terms. But that doesn't mean I can't make him work for it."

He flipped his phone open. "Now what?" he said. Good cop was definitely gone for the night.

"I'm only trying to help," the distorted voice echoed peevishly.

"You're a liar and a killer. And guess what, we know for a fact that makes you a bed wetter, too. So stop wasting my time, you little prick."

"I'm not a killer!"

"I got two bodies that say otherwise."

"He struck again? I thought . . . I thought you might have more time."

"Hey, buddy, stop the lies. I know you're him. You want to gloat? Is that what this is about? You drugged two young girls and then killed them. Yeah, you are just the biggest badass in town."

Rainie's eyes went wide. She shook her head furiously. She was right, of course. If the guy did want to boost his ego, it wasn't a good idea to egg him on.

"I am not the killer!" the voice protested shrilly, and then in the next instant, the voice grew an edge of its own. "I'm trying to help. You can either listen and learn, or continue this game on your own."

"Who are you?"

"He's getting angrier."

"No shit. Where are you calling from?"

"He's going to strike again. Soon. Maybe already."

Mac took a gamble. "He's already struck again. This time he didn't take two girls. This time, he took four. So what about it?"

A pause, as if the caller was genuinely surprised. "I didn't realize . . . I didn't think . . ."

"Why is he now in Virginia?"

"He grew up here."

"He's from Virginia?" Mac's voice picked up. He swapped concerned glances with Rainie.

"His first sixteen years," the caller replied.

"When did he move to Georgia?"

"I don't know. It's been . . . years. You have to understand. I don't think he really wants to hurt the victims. He wants them to figure it out. If they would just remain calm, be smart, show some strength—"

"For Christ's sake, they're only kids."

"So was he once."

Mac shook his head. The killer as a victim. He didn't want to hear this shit. "Listen, I have two dead girls and two more at risk. Give me his name, buddy. End this thing. You have it in your power. You can be the hero. Just give me his damn name."

"I can't."

"Then send it in the mail!"

"Did the first body lead you to the second?"

"Give me his goddamn name!"

"Then the second body will lead you to the third. Move quickly. I don't . . . I'm not even sure what he'll do next."

The signal went dead. Mac swore and hurled his phone into the brush. It spooked a scavenging raccoon and didn't do a thing to calm his temper. He wanted to run back up the mountainside. He wanted to plunge into an ice-cold stream. He wanted to throw back his head and howl at the moon. Then he wanted to swear every obscenity he'd ever learned as a child and collapse into a pile and weep.

He'd been working too long on this case to keep seeing so much death.

"Damn," he said at last. "Damn, damn, damn."

"He didn't give you a name."

"He swears he's not the killer. He swears he's just trying to help."

Rainie looked at the body. "Could've fooled me."

"No kidding." Mac sighed, straightening his shoulders and moving resolutely toward the body. "All four girls disappeared at once, from the same car?"

"That's what we're assuming."

"Then we don't have much time." He hunkered down, already pulling the black plastic body bag away from the girl.

"What are you doing?"

"Looking for clues. Because if the first girl led us to the second, then the second will lead us to the third."

"Ahh, shit," Rainie said.

"Yeah. You know what? Go find Kathy Levine. We're gonna need some help here. And a boatload of coffee."

"No rest for the weary?"

"Not tonight."

Nora Ray was dreaming again. She was in the happy place, the land of fantasy where her parents smiled and her dead dog danced, and she floated in a pool of cool, silky water, feeling it lap peacefully against her skin. She loved this place, longed to come here often.

She could listen to her parents laugh. Watch the pure blue sky, which never contained a red-hot sun. Feel the crystalline cleanness of pure water against her limbs.

She turned her head. She saw the door open. And without hesitation, she left the pool behind.

Mary Lynn was riding her horse. She drove Snowfall through miles of green pasture, racing through fields of wild daisies, and jumping fallen logs. She sat forward in the saddle, her body tight and compact like a jockey's, her hands light and steady on the reins. The horse soared. She soared with it. It was as if they were one.

Nora Ray crossed to the fence. Two other girls sat on the top rail. One blonde. One brunette.

"Do you know where we are?" the blonde asked Nora Ray.

"You're in my dream."

"Do we know you?" the brunette asked.

"I think we knew the same man."

"Will we get to ride the horse?" the brunette asked.

"I don't know."

"She's very good," said the blonde.

"There's never been anything my sister couldn't ride," Nora Ray replied proudly.

"I have a sister," said the brunette. "Will she dream of me?"

"Every night."

"That's very sad."

"I know."

"I wish there's something we could do."

"You're dead," Nora Ray said. "You can't do anything at all. Now, I think it's up to me."

Then her sister was gone, the pasture had vanished, and she was spiraling away from the pond long before she was ready. She woke up wide-eyed in her bed, her heart beating too fast and her hands knotted around her comforter.

Nora Ray sat up slowly. She poured herself a glass of water from the pitcher on her nightstand. She took a long drink and felt the cool liquid slide down her throat. Sometimes, she could still feel the salt building like rime around her mouth, coating her chin, covering her lips. She could remember the deep, unquenchable thirst that ran cell-deep, as the sun pounded and the salt built and she went mad with thirst. *Water, water everywhere, and not a drop to drink.*

She finished her glass of water now. Let the moisture linger on her lips, like dew on a rose. Then she left her room.

Her mother slept on the couch, her head crooked awkwardly to the side, while on the TV Lucille Ball crawled into a vat of grapes and gamely stomped away. In the neighboring bedroom, Nora Ray glimpsed her father, slumbering alone on the queen-sized bed.

The house was silent. It filled Nora Ray with a loneliness that threatened to cut her heart in two. Three years later, and no one had healed. Nothing was better. She could still remember the harsh grit of salt, leaching the last moisture from her body. She could remember her rage and confusion as the crabs nibbled on her toes. She could remember her simple desire to survive this hell and return to her family. If she could just see them again, slide into her parents' loving embrace . . .

Except her family had never returned to her. She had survived. They had not.

And now, two more girls in the pastureland of her dream. She knew what that meant. The heat had arrived on Sunday, and the shadowy man from her nightmares had resumed his lethal game.

The clock glowed nearly two A.M. She decided she didn't care. She picked up the phone and dialed the number she knew by heart. A moment later, she said, "I need to reach Special Agent McCormack. No, I don't want to leave a message. I need to see him. Quick."

Tina didn't dream. Her exhausted body had given out, and now she was collapsed in the mud in a sleep that bordered on unconsciousness. One arm still touched the boulder, a link to relative safety. The rest of her belonged to the muck. It oozed between her fingers, coated her hair, slithered up her throat.

Things came and went in the sucking muck. Some had no interest in prey quite that large. Some had no interest in a meal that wasn't already dead. Then, up above, a dark shadow lumbered along the path, stopping at the edge of the pit. A giant head peered down, dark eyes gleaming in the night. It smelled warm-blooded flesh, a fine, delectable meal that was just its size.

More sniffing. Two giant paws raked one side of the hole. The depth was too great, the terrain not manageable. The bear grunted, lumbered on. If the creature ever came up, it'd try again. Until then, there were other fine things to eat in the dark.

The man didn't sleep. Two A.M., he packed his bags. He had to move quickly now. He could feel the darkness gathering at the edges of his mind. Time was becoming more fluid, moments slipping through his fingers and disappearing into the abyss.

Pressure was growing in the back of his skull. He could feel it, a true physical presence at the top of his spine, with another tendril starting to press against the inner canal of his left ear. A tumor, he was pretty sure. He'd had one before, years ago when he'd had his first "episode" of vanishing time. Had it been only minutes he'd lost in the beginning? He couldn't even remember that anymore.

Time grew fluid, black holes took over his life. One tumor was removed. Another came back to eat his brain. It was probably the size of a grapefruit by now. Or maybe even a watermelon. Maybe his brain wasn't even his brain anymore, but a giant malignant mass of constantly dividing cells. He didn't doubt it. That would explain the bad dreams, the restless nights. It would explain why the fire came to him so often now, and made him do things he knew he shouldn't.

He found himself thinking of his mother more. Her pale face, her thin, hunched shoulders. He thought of his father, too, and the way he always strode through their tiny cabin in the woods.

"A man's gotta be tough, boys, a man's gotta be strong. Don't you listen to no government types, they just want to turn us into mealy-mouthed dependants who can't live without a federal handout. Not us boys. We got the land. We will always be strong, as long as we got the land."

Strong enough to beat his wife, abuse his kids and wring the neck of the family cat. Strong enough, and isolated enough, to live as he goddamned pleased, without even a neighbor to hear the screams.

The black storm clouds built, rolled, and roared. Now he was sitting tied to a chair, while his father took a strap to his brother, his mother washed the dishes, and his father told them both that next it would be their turn. Now he and his brother were huddled under the front porch, planning their big escape, while above their heads their mother wept and their father told her to go inside and wipe that goddamn blood off of her face. Now it was late at night and he and his brother were sneaking out the front door; at the last minute they turned, and saw their mother standing pale and silent in the moonlight. *Go,* her eyes told them. *Run away while you still can.* Her bruised cheeks were streaked with wordless tears. They crept back inside. And she clutched them to her breast as if they were the only hope she had left.

And he knew then that he hated his mother as much as he had ever loved her. And he knew then that she felt the same about him and his brother. They were the crabs stuck together in the bottom of a bucket, and pulling one another down so no one ever made it to freedom.

The man swayed on his feet. He felt the dark roll in, felt himself totter on the edge of the abyss . . . Time was slipping through his fingers.

The man turned. He drove his fist forcefully into the wall, and let the pain bring him back. The room came into focus. The dark spots cleared from his eyes. Better.

The man crossed to his dresser. He got out his gun.

He prepared for what must happen next.

30

Rainie and Mac were still working the victim's body when Quincy materialized before them. His gaze went from them to Kathy Levine, then back to them.

"She's one of us," Rainie said, as if he'd asked a question.

"Definitely?"

"Well, she risked ordering a search team based solely on Mac's hunch, and now she's picking rice out of a corpse's pocket. You tell us."

Quincy raised a brow and glanced at Levine again. "Rice?"

"Uncooked white," she said briskly. "Long grain. Then again, I'm a botanist, not a chef, so you may want a second opinion."

Quincy switched his attention to Mac, who was carefully going over the girl's left foot. "Why rice?"

"Damned if I know."

"Anything else?"

"She's wearing a necklace—some kind of vial filled with a clear fluid. That might be a hint. Then we got about nine different bits of leaves, four or five samples of dirt, half a dozen kinds of grass, some crushed flower petals, and a whole lotta blood." Mac gestured to a stack of evidence containers. "Help yourself to a sample. And good luck figuring out if it came from her hike through the woods or from him. This new strategy of his definitely puts a wrinkle in things. What'd you do with Kimberly?"

"Feds got her."

Three heads shot up. Quincy smiled grimly. "I believe there's been a change of plans."

"Quincy," Mac said curtly. "Tell me what the hell you're talking about."

Quincy didn't look at him directly. Instead, his gaze went to Rainie. "The FBI case team arrived. No Kaplan, no Watson. In fact, I don't recognize anyone on the team. They pulled in, spotted Kimberly, and immediately pulled her aside for questioning. I'm supposed to be waiting outside the lodge."

"Those assholes!" Rainie exploded. "First they want nothing to do with this. Now it's suddenly their party, and no one else is invited to play. What are they going to do? Start all over at this stage of the game?"

"I imagine they are going to do exactly that. The FBI can launch a pretty

714

good search, you know. They'll bring in computer operators, stenographers, dog handlers, search-and-rescue teams, topography experts, and recon pilots. Within twenty-four hours, they'll have a full ops center set up road-side, while planes search the surrounding areas with infrared photography and volunteers stand by to assist. It's not too shabby."

"Infrared photography is bullshit this time of year," Mac said tightly. "We tried it ourselves. Every damn boulder and wandering bear shows up as a hit. Not to mention deer also look roughly like humans in the still photos. We ended up with hundreds of targets and not a single one of them was ever the missing girl. Besides, that assumes the next victim is somewhere in these woods, and I already know she isn't. The man doesn't repeat an area, and the whole point of his game is to ramp up the challenge. The other girl is some-where far from here, and believe it or not, someplace even more dangerous."

"Judging from what I've seen so far, you're probably correct." Quincy turned around, looking back up the darkened path. "I give the new federal agents ten minutes before they arrive down here, and that delay is only because Kimberly promised to be unforthcoming with her answers. I know she's good at that." He grimaced, then turned back. "All right, for the next ten minutes at least, I'm part of this case and have authority over evidence. So, Ms. Levine, as a botanist, are any of these samples definitely out of place?"

"The rice," she said immediately.

"I'll take half."

"The vial with fluid, maybe. Though that could be a personal possession."

"Do we have an inventory of what any of the girls were last seen wearing?"

"No," answered Rainie.

Quincy mulled it over. "I'll take half the fluid."

Mac nodded, and immediately produced a glass vial from the evidence processing kit. Quincy noticed his hands were shaking slightly. Maybe fatigue. Maybe rage. Quincy knew from his own experience that it didn't really matter. Just as long as you got the job done.

"Why take only half the samples?" Levine asked.

"Because if I took the whole sample, something would be missing. The other agents might notice and ask, and then I might feel compelled to hand it over. If, on the other hand, nothing's obviously missing . . ."

"They'll never ask."

"And I'll never tell," Quincy said with a grim smile. "Now, what else?"

Levine gestured helplessly to the pile of bags. "I honestly don't know. Lighting's not great, I don't have a magnifying glass on me. Given the state of half of this stuff, I'd say she picked it up crashing through the under-brush. But without more time for analysis . . ."

"He generally leaves three to four clues," Mac said quietly.

"So we're missing something."

"Or he's making it harder," Rainie commented.

Mac shrugged. "I'd say the stack of false positives makes it hard enough."

Quincy glanced at his watch. "You have five minutes. Sort through, then go. Oh, and Rainie, love, better turn off your cell phone."

Mac had finished with the girl's foot and was moving up the body. He tilted back the girl's head, cracked open her mouth, then inserted a gloved finger into the abyss. "He's twice hidden something in a victim's throat," he said by way of explanation. He twisted his hand left, then right, then sighed and shook his head.

"I got something." Rainie looked up sharply. "Can I get some better light? I don't know if this is just bad dandruff or what."

Quincy adjusted his flashlight. Rainie parted the girl's hair. There appeared to be a fine powder dusted over the strands. As Rainie shook the victim's head, more residue fell onto the plastic bag she had laid beneath it.

Levine moved closer, catching some of the dust on her finger and sniffing experimentally. "I don't know. Not dandruff. Too gritty. Almost . . . I don't know."

"Take a sample," Quincy ordered tersely, his gaze returning to the path. There, he heard it again. Not far off anymore. The thump of descending footfalls.

"Rainie . . ." he murmured tightly.

She hastily scraped a small bit of the powder into a glass vial, corked it, and threw it in her fanny pack. Kathy added some of the rice; Mac had already claimed half of the fluid.

They were scrambling to their feet as Quincy moved toward Levine. "If they ask, you started working the scene under my orders. This is what you found, properly catalogued and waiting for them. As for me, last you knew, I was heading away from the scene. Trust me, you won't be lying."

The footsteps pounded closer. Quincy shook the botanist's hand. "Thank you," he told Kathy Levine.

"Good luck."

Quincy headed down the hillside and Rainie and Mac quickly followed suit. Levine watched as the darkness opened up, and then there was no one there at all.

"For the last time, how did you know to come to the park? What led you and Special Agent McCormack straight to Big Meadows and another girl's body?"

"You'd have to ask Special Agent McCormack about his reasoning. Personally, I was in the mood for a hike."

"So you just magically discovered the body? Your second corpse in twenty-four hours?"

"I guess I have a gift."

"Will you be asking for another hardship leave? Do you need more time to *grieve,* Ms. Quincy, in between finding all these dead bodies?"

Kimberly thinned her lips. They'd been at this for two hours now, she and Agent Tightass, who had introduced himself with a real name, though she'd long forgotten what it was. He'd thrust, she'd parry. He'd punch, she'd dodge. Neither one of them was having much fun, and in fact, given the late hour and lack of sleep, both of them were getting more than a little pissed.

"I want water," she said now.

"In a minute."

"I hiked five hours in nearly a hundred-degree heat. Give me water, or when I succumb to dehydration, I'll sue your ass, end your career, and keep you from ever having that fat government pension to fund your golden years. Are we clear?"

"Your attitude doesn't speak well for an aspiring agent," Tightass said curtly.

"Yeah, they didn't care for it much at the Academy either. Now I want my water."

Tightass was still scowling, obviously debating whether he should give in, when the door opened and Kimberly's father strode in. Funny, for the first time in years, she was genuinely happy to see him, and they'd only parted ways hours ago.

"The EMTs will see you now," Quincy said.

Kimberly blinked her eyes a few times, and then she got it. "Oh, thank God. My aching . . . everything."

"Wait a minute," Tightass started.

"My daughter has had a very long day. Not only has she been instrumental in finding a lost woman, but as you can tell by looking at her arms and legs, it was at great personal cost to herself."

Kimberly smiled at Tightass. It was true. She did look like hell. "I walked into a patch of stinging nettles," she volunteered cheerfully. "And some poison ivy. And about a dozen trees. Not to mention what I did to my ankles. Oh yeah, I need some medical attention."

"I have more questions," Tightass said tersely.

"When she's done being treated, I'm sure my daughter would be delighted to cooperate."

"She's not cooperating now!"

"Kimberly," her father said in a chastising tone.

She shrugged. "I'm tired, I'm hot, and I'm in pain. How am I supposed to think clearly when I've been denied water and proper medical attention?"

"Of course." Quincy was already crossing the room and helping her out of the metal folding chair. "Really, Agent, I know my daughter is a very strong young lady, but even you should know better than to question someone without first getting them proper treatment. I'm taking her straight to the EMTs. You can ask your questions again after that."

"I don't know—"

Quincy already had his right arm wrapped around Kimberly's waist, and his left hand holding her arm around his shoulder, as if she was in desperate need of support. "Come to the medic station in thirty minutes. I'm sure she'll be ready for you then."

Then Quincy and Kimberly were out the door, Quincy half bearing her weight and Kimberly managing a truly impressive limp.

In case Tightass was watching, Quincy took her straight to the first-aid station. And as long as she was there, Kimberly had some water, grabbed four orange slices, and then saw an EMT—for approximately thirty seconds. He gave her salve for her legs and arms, then she and Quincy were striding rapidly away from the station and into a remote section of the parking lot.

Rainie was waiting. So was Mac. They each had a vehicle.

"Get in the car," Quincy said. "We talk again on the road."

31

Shenandoah National Park, Virginia
3:16 A.M.
Temperature: 88 degrees

Mac followed Quincy's taillights, leading them away from the buzzing chaos of Big Meadows, and into the inky black of a winding road lit only by the moon and stars.

Kimberly didn't speak right away. Neither did Mac. She was tired again, but in a different sort of way now. This was the physical fatigue that came after a long, arduous journey and little sleep. She liked this kind of tired better. It was familiar to her. Almost comforting. She had always pushed her body hard and it had always recovered quickly. Her battered emotions, in contrast . . .

Mac reached over and took her hand. After another moment, she squeezed his fingers with her own.

"I could sure use some coffee," he said. "About four gallons."

"I could use a vacation. About four decades."

"How about a nice cool shower?"

"How about air-conditioning?"

"Fresh clothes."

"A soft bed."

"A giant platter of buttermilk biscuits smothered in gravy."

"A pitcher of ice water, topped with sliced lemon."

She sighed. He followed suit.

"We're not going to bed anytime soon, are we?" she asked quietly.

"Doesn't look it."

"What happened?"

"Not sure. Your father showed up, said an official FBI case team had arrived and that we were no longer invited to the party. Damn those Feds."

"They pulled Dad and Rainie off the case?" Kimberly was incredulous.

"Not yet. The fact that they both turned off their cell phones and made a quick getaway probably helped. But it looks like the Feds are trying to reinvent the wheel again, and even your father knows better. We worked with Kathy Levine to identify which items might be clues on the victim's body, then we took half the evidence. And now, just for the record, I believe we're officially AWOL. Did you really want to be an FBI agent, Kimberly? 'Cause after this . . ."

"Fuck the FBI. Now tell me the plan."

"We work with your father and Rainie. We see if we can't find the remaining two girls. Then we track down the son of a bitch who did this, and nail him to the wall."

"That's the nicest thing I've heard all night."

"Well," he said modestly. "I do try."

Shortly, Quincy's car turned in at one of the scenic vistas, and Mac followed suit. Given the hour, no other cars were around, and they were far enough off Skyline Drive to be invisible from the road. They all got out of the two vehicles and congregated around the hood of Mac's rental car.

The night still felt hot and heavy. Crickets buzzed and frogs croaked, but even those sounds were curiously subdued, as if everything were hushed and waiting. There should be heat lightning and thunder. There should be an impressive July thunderstorm, bringing cleansing rain and cooler temperatures. Instead, the heat wave pressed down on them, blanketing the world in stifling humidity and silencing half the creatures of the night.

Quincy had taken off his jacket, loosened his tie and rolled up his sleeves. "So we have three possible clues," he said by way of starting things off. "A vial of liquid, rice, and some kind of dust from the victim's hair. Any ideas?"

"Rice?" Kimberly asked sharply.

"Uncooked, white, long grain," Mac informed her. "At least that was Levine's best guess."

Kimberly shook her head. "That doesn't even make sense."

"He likes to make it harder," Mac said quietly. "Welcome to the rules of the game."

"How far away do you think the other two victims are?" Rainie spoke up. "If he's taken multiple victims, maybe the first victim speaks for all three. He's only one man after all, working with a limited amount of time to set this up."

Mac shrugged. "I can't be sure of this new format, of course. In Georgia, he definitely moved around a lot. We started at a state park famous for its granite gorge, then moved to cotton fields, then the banks of the Savannah River, and finally to the salt marshes on the coast. Four clearly diverse regions of the state. Here, however, you're right—he has some practical issues involved in placing bodies all over the state, particularly in twenty-four hours or less."

"The logistics of hauling multiple bodies are complicated," Quincy commented.

"Vehicle of choice is probably a cargo van. Gives him a place to stash kidnapped women, inject poison in their veins, and then haul them around. In this case, he'd also need plenty of room, given four victims."

"How did he manage to snatch four women at once?" Kimberly murmured. "You'd think at least one of them would put up a fight?"

"I doubt they had a chance. His favorite method of ambush is using a dart gun. He closes in on the car, darts the women with fast-acting ketamine, and they're drifting off to la-la land before anyone can protest. If another car drives by, he can pose as the designated driver with four passed-out passengers. Then, once the coast is clear, he loads the women into his van, ramps up the ketamine to keep them unconscious for as long as he needs, and he sets off for stage two of his master plan. He's not a flashy killer, but he certainly gets the job done."

They all nodded morosely. Yes, the man certainly got the job done.

"Rainie said you got a call again," Quincy said to Mac.

"At the scene. Caller swears he's not actually the killer, though. He got mad when I accused him of the crimes, swore he was just trying to help, and said he was sorry more girls had died. Not that he volunteered his name or the killer's name, mind you, but he still swears he's a stand-up guy."

"The caller's lying," Quincy said flatly.

"You think?"

"Consider the timing of both your recent calls. First one comes the night before the first victim is found—incidentally, right around the same time the killer must have been plotting his ambush, if he had not already taken the four girls. Then the second call comes tonight, when you're at the scene of the second victim. I believe that is what Special Agent Kaplan would consider a suspicious coincidence."

"You think the Eco-Killer's close?" Mac asked sharply.

"Killers like to watch. Why should this UNSUB be different? He's left a trail of breadcrumbs for us. Perhaps he also likes to note our progress." Quincy sighed, then squeezed the bridge of his nose. "Earlier, you said the GBI attempted several times to find the Eco-Killer. You tried tracing the drugs that were used. You did the standard victim profiling, you looked at veterinarians, campers, hikers, birdwatchers, all sorts of outdoorsmen."

"Yes."

"And you created a profile. It describes the killer as being male, white, above-average intelligence, but probably stuck in a menial job. Travels often, has limited social skills and is prone to fits of rage when frustrated."

"That's what the expert told us."

"Two things strike me," Quincy said. "One, I think the killer is even smarter than you think. By definition, his game forces your immediate attention and resources on finding the second victim—instead of pursuing him."

"Well, in the beginning, sure—"

"A trail grows cold, Mac. Every detective knows that. The more time has passed, the more difficult it is to find a suspect."

Mac nodded his head more grudgingly. "Yeah, okay."

"And second, we now know something very interesting that you didn't know before."

"Which is?"

"The man has access to the Marine base at Quantico. That narrows our suspect pool down to a relatively small group of people within the state of Virginia. And that's a lead we shouldn't squander."

"You think a Marine or an FBI agent did this?" Mac asked with a frown.

Quincy had a faraway look in his eye. "I don't know yet. But the emphasis on Quantico, the phone calls to you . . . There's something significant there. I just can't see it yet. Can you write down the conversation you had tonight? Word for word, all of the caller's comments? Dr. Ennunzio will want to see it."

"You think he'll still help us?" Kimberly spoke up.

"You assume he knows we've been taken off the case." Quincy shrugged. "He's a backroom academic; field agents never think to keep those kinds informed. They live in their world, the BSU lives in its own. Besides, we're going to need Dr. Ennunzio. So far, those letters and phone calls are the only direct link we have to the Eco-Killer. And that's important. If we're going to break this pattern, we must identify the UNSUB. Otherwise, we're only ever treating the symptoms, not the disease."

"You're not going to abandon the other two girls?" Mac asked sharply.

"I am," Quincy said calmly. "But you're not."

"Divide and conquer?" Rainie spoke up.

"Exactly. Mac and Kimberly, you work on finding the girls. Rainie and I will continue our pursuit of the man himself."

"That could be dangerous," Mac said quietly.

Quincy merely smiled. "That's why I'm taking Rainie with me. Let him just dare to tangle with her."

"Amen," Rainie said soberly.

"We could try the USGS again," Kimberly said. "Bring them the samples we have. I'm not sure what to make of the rice, but a hydrologist is a good start for the fluid."

Mac nodded thoughtfully. "They might know something about the rice. Maybe it's like the Hawaii connection. Wouldn't mean anything to a layman, but to the proper expert . . ."

"Where are those offices?" Quincy asked.

"Richmond."

"What time do they open?"

"Eight A.M."

Quincy glanced at his watch. "Well, good news, everyone. We can all grab a few hours' sleep after all."

They drove out of the park. They found a chain motel in one of the nearby towns and booked three rooms. Quincy and Rainie disappeared into their tiny quarters. Mac went into his. Kimberly went into hers.

The furniture was sparse and dingy. The bed was covered by a faded blue comforter and already had a crater in the middle from one too many guests. The air was motel air, stale, reeking of old cigarettes mixed with undertones of Windex.

It was a room. It had a bed. She could sleep.

Kimberly cranked the air-conditioning. She stripped off her sweat-soaked clothes, climbed into the shower and scrubbed her battered body. She shampooed her hair again and again, while trying to forget the rocks, the snakes, that poor girl's torturous death. She scrubbed and scrubbed. And she knew then that it would never be enough.

She was thinking of Mandy again. And of her mother. And of the girl found at Quantico. And of Vivienne Benson. Except the victims got all tangled in her mind. And sometimes the body in the Quantico woods bore

Mandy's face, and sometimes the girl in the rocks was actually Kimberly in disguise, and sometimes her mother was fleeing through the woods, trying to escape the Eco-Killer, when she had already been butchered by a madman six years before.

An investigator should have objectivity. An investigator should be dispassionate.

Kimberly finally got out of the shower. She pulled on a T-shirt. She used the dingy towel to wipe the steam from the mirror. And then she regarded her reflection. Pale, bruised face. Sunken cheeks. Bloodless lips. Oversized blue eyes.

Jesus. She looked too scared to be herself.

She almost lost it again. Her hands gripped the edge of the washbasin tightly. She sank her teeth in her lower lip and fought bitterly for some trace of sanity.

All of her life, she'd been focused. Shooting guns, reading homicide textbooks. She had genuinely found crime fascinating, sought it out as her father's daughter. All cases were puzzles to be solved. She wanted the challenge. Wear a badge. Save the world. Always be the one in control.

Tough, cool-as-a-cucumber Kimberly. She now felt her own mortality as a hollow spot deep in her stomach. And she knew she wasn't so tough anymore.

Twenty-six years old, all the defenses had finally been stripped away. Now here she was. A young, overwhelmed woman, who couldn't eat, couldn't sleep, and had a fear of snakes. Save the world? She couldn't even save herself.

She should just quit, let her father, Rainie, and Mac go at it alone. She'd already bailed from the Academy. What would it matter if she simply disappeared now? She could spend the rest of her life curled up in a closet, hands clasped around her knees. Who could blame her? She'd already lost half of her family, and almost been killed twice. If anyone was entitled to a nervous breakdown, surely it was Kimberly.

But then she started thinking of the two missing girls again. Mac had told her their names. Karen Clarence. Tina Krahn. Two young college students who'd simply wanted to hang out with friends on a hot Tuesday night.

Karen Clarence. Tina Krahn. Someone had to find them. Someone had to do something. And maybe she was her father's daughter after all, because she couldn't just walk away. She could quit the Academy, but she could not quit this case.

A knock sounded on the door. Kimberly's gaze came up slowly. She knew who had to be standing there. She should ignore him. She was already walking across the room.

She opened the door. Mac had obviously used the past thirty minutes to shower and shave.

"Hey," he said softly, and strode into her room.

"Mac, I'm too tired—"

"I know. I am, too." He took her arm and led her over to the bed. She followed only grudgingly. Maybe she did like the smell of his soap, but she also wished desperately to just be alone.

"Have I mentioned yet that I don't sleep well in strange motel rooms?" he asked.

"No."

"Have I mentioned that I think you look really good wearing just a T-shirt?"

"No."

"Have I mentioned how good I look wearing nothing at all?"

"No."

"Well, that's a shame, because it's all true. But you're tired and I'm tired, so this is all we're gonna do tonight." He sat on the bed and tried to pull her down with him. She, however, dug in her heels.

"I can't do this," she whispered.

He didn't force the issue. Instead, he reached up a large hand, and cradled her cheek. His blue eyes weren't laughing anymore. Instead, he studied her intently, his eyes dark, his expression somber. When he looked at her like this, she could barely breathe.

"You scared me tonight," he told her quietly. "When you were up on those rocks, surrounded by all those snakes, you scared me."

"I scared me, too."

"Do you think I'm toying with you, Kimberly?"

"I don't know."

"It bothers you, that I can flirt, that I can smile."

"Sometimes."

"Earnest Kimberly." His thumb stroked her cheek. "You are honestly the most beautiful woman I've ever met, and I don't know how to tell you that without you thinking it's just some kind of line."

She closed her eyes. "Don't."

"Would you like to hit me?" he murmured. "Would you like to yell and scream at the world, or maybe hurl your knife? I don't mind it when you're angry, honey. Anything's better than seeing you sad."

That did it. She sank down on the bed beside him, feeling something big and brittle give way in the middle of her chest. Was this weakening? Was this succumbing? She didn't know anymore. She didn't care. Suddenly, she wanted to press her head against the broad expanse of his chest. She wanted to wrap her arms tightly around his lean waist. She wanted his warmth all around her, his arms holding her close. She wanted his body above her body, demanding and taking and conquering. She wanted something fierce and fast, where she didn't have to think and didn't have to feel. She could simply be.

She would blame him for it all in the morning.

Her head came up. She brushed her lips over his, feeling his breath tickle her cheek and, being rewarded, his tremor. She kissed his jaw. Smooth. Square. She followed its line to his throat, where she could see his pulse pounding. His hands were on her waist, not moving. But she could feel his tension now, his body hard and tightly leashed with his effort at control.

She caught the fragrance of his soap again. Then the trace of the mint on his breath. The spicy tones of his aftershave on his freshly razored cheek. She faltered again. The elements were personal, powerful. Things he had done just for her that had no place in raw, meaningless sex.

She was going to cry again. Oh God, she hated this hard lump in her chest. She didn't want to be this creature anymore. She wanted to return to cold, logical Kimberly. Anything had to be better than to be this weepy all the time. Anything had to be better than to feel this much pain.

Mac's hands had moved. Now, they found her hair, gently feathering it back. Now his fingers ran from her temples all the way down to the taut lines of her neck.

"Shhh," he murmured. "Shhh," though she wasn't aware she'd ever made a sound.

"I don't know who I am anymore."

"You just need sleep, honey. It'll be better in the morning. Everything's better in the morning."

Mac pulled her down beside him. She fell without protest, feeling his arousal press hard against her hip. Now he would do something, she thought. But he didn't. He merely tucked her into the curve of his body, his chest hot against her back, his arms like steel bands around her waist.

"I don't like strange motel rooms, either," she said abruptly, and could almost see his grin against her hair. Then in another minute, she could tell he had drifted off.

Kimberly closed her eyes. She curled her fingers around Mac's arms. She slept the best she had in years.

32

Mac woke first, the tinny bleat of his cell phone penetrating his deep slumber. He had a moment of disorientation, trying to place the dimly lit room with its sagging bed and stale-smelling air. Then he registered Kimberly, still curled up soft and snug in the crook of his arm, and the rest of the evening came back to him.

He moved quickly now, not wanting to wake her. He slid his right arm from beneath her head, felt the resulting tingle shoot up from his elbow as various nerve endings fired to life, and swallowed a rueful curse. He shook out his hand, realizing now he didn't know where his phone was. He had a vague memory of throwing it across the room during the night. Frankly, given his recent treatment of his phone, it was a miracle it was working at all.

He dropped to the floor, scrambling on all fours until he finally came up with the palm-sized object. He flipped it open, just as it was ringing for the fourth time.

"Special Agent McCormack here." He glanced at the bed. Kimberly still hadn't stirred.

"Took you long enough," a distinctly male voice said.

Mac relaxed immediately. No more distorted voices to mess with his head. This was simply his boss, Special Agent in Charge Lee Grogen. "Been a long night," Mac replied.

"Successful?"

"Not especially." Mac filled in the details of the past twelve hours. Grogen listened without interruption.

"It's definitely him then?"

"No doubt in my mind. Of course, for an official opinion you'd have to consult the Feds. They probably think it's a terrorist act."

"You sound bitter, Mac."

"Three hours of sleep will do that to a guy. Now, best we can tell, we got two more girls out there. Pardon my French, but fuck the Feds. I have some leads, and I'm goin' after them."

"And I'm going to pretend I didn't hear that. In fact, I'm going to pretend we're talking about fishing." Grogen sighed. "Officially speaking, Mac,

725

there's nothing I can offer you. My boss can press their boss for cooperation, but given that it's the feebies . . ."

"We're frozen out."

"Probably. At least they'll refer to us one day—at the press conference when they announce their big catch, we'll be the local yokels who had a shot at the guy the first time around and couldn't get the job done. You know the drill."

"I can't give up," Mac said quietly.

"Don't let me come between a man and some fishing," Grogen said.

"Thank you, sir."

"We have another complication."

"Uh oh." Mac rubbed his hand over his face. He was already tired again and so far he'd only been awake ten minutes. "What's up?"

"Nora Ray Watts."

"Huh?"

"She called me in the middle of the night. She wants to talk to you. She claims she has information about the case and she'll only give it to you, in person. Mac, she knew two girls were dead."

"Has there been something in the papers?"

"Not a peep. Mac, *I* didn't even know two girls were dead until ten minutes ago when I called you. Frankly, I'm a little freaked out."

"He's contacted her," Mac murmured.

"It's possible."

"It's the only thing that makes sense. Writing his letters isn't enough anymore. Calling me is probably just frustrating him. Hell, I hope so. So now he's contacting a past victim . . . Son of a bitch!"

"What do you want to do?"

"I can't go back to Atlanta. I don't have time."

"I told Nora Ray you were out of town."

"And?"

"And she said she would come to you. In all honesty, Mac, I think that's what she wants."

Mac blinked his eyes, dumbfounded. After everything Nora Ray had been through. To drag her back into this mess. A civilian. A victim. "No," he said gruffly.

His supervisor was quiet.

"No way," Mac said again. "She doesn't deserve this. He messed with her life once already. Now it's time for her to be free of him, to heal and be with her family. Hell, to forget this ever happened."

"I don't think that's working for her."

"I can't protect her, Lee! I don't know where this guy is, I don't know where he's gonna strike next. It's a long story, but I've been working with a former FBI profiler, and he thinks the killer may be keeping tabs on us."

"I'll tell her that."

"Damn right!"

"And if she still wants to come?"

"She's a fool!"

"Mac, if she knows something, if she has a lead . . ."

Mac hung his head. He raked his hand through his hair. God, there were times he hated his job. "I can meet her at the airport in Richmond," he said at last. "Sooner versus later. Day's young and a lot can happen yet."

"I'll be in touch. And Mac—good luck fishing."

Mac flipped his phone shut. He rested his forehead against the cool silver shape. What a mess. He should go back to bed. Or at the very least, crawl back into a shower. When he got up the second time, maybe this day would make more sense.

But the fuzz was already clearing. He was thinking of water and rice, and obscure clues that had to lead to real and terrible places. They had been lucky to sleep at all last night. God knows when they'd sleep again.

He rose and crossed to the bed. Kimberly's arms were wrapped around her waist, her body held tightly together, as if she were protecting herself even when asleep. He sat down on the edge of the mattress. He touched the curve of her jaw with his thumb, then feathered back her short, dusty-blond hair. She didn't stir.

She looked more vulnerable in sleep, her fine features delicate and even a trace fragile. He didn't let the image fool him. A guy could spend years just working on learning the curve of her smile. And still, one day, she'd walk out the door and never look back. Probably think she'd done him a favor.

In her world, guys like him didn't fall for girls like her. Funny, 'cause in his world, he was already long gone.

He stroked his fingers down her arm and her eyes finally fluttered open.

"I'm sorry, sweetheart," he whispered.

"Did someone else die?"

"Not if we keep moving."

Kimberly sat up and, without another word, headed for the bathroom. He lay down on the bed and placed his hand on the spot still warm from the heat of her body. He could hear the sound of running water now, the rattle of old, rusty pipes. He thought again of yesterday, and the sight of Kimberly surrounded by dozens of rattlesnakes.

"I'm going to take better care of you," he vowed in the quiet of the room.

But he already wondered where the day would lead, and if that promise could be kept.

33

"Sure as hell looks like water to me."

Kimberly sighed with relief, while Mac visibly sagged against the wall of the tiny office. Neither of them had realized just how tensely they'd been awaiting that news until USGS hydrologist Brian Knowles had delivered it.

"Could it be holy water?" Kimberly asked.

Knowles shot her a look. "I don't exactly have a test for that. I'm just a mere government employee, you know, not the Pope."

"But can you help them out?" Ray Lee Chee prodded him. He'd personally brought Mac and Kimberly to Knowles's office just ten minutes earlier. Now he was perched on the edge of a gunmetal-gray filing cabinet, swinging his feet rhythmically.

Mac spoke up. "We'd like to be able to test the sample. Ideally, we need to trace it to a source such as a specific pond or stream or watering hole. Can you do that?"

Knowles yawned, rolled out one sleepy shoulder and seemed to consider it. He appeared to be in his mid-thirties, a good-looking guy with a thick head of woolly brown hair and the world's rattiest jeans. Like Ray Lee Chee, he appeared remarkably fit. Unlike the geographer, however, mornings weren't his thing. Brian Knowles looked as tired as Kimberly felt.

"Well," he said shortly, "we can test a water sample for all sorts of things: pH, dissolved oxygen, temperature, turbidity, salinity, nitrogen, ammonia, arsenic, bacteria . . . Then there's water hardness, tests for various inorganic constituents such as iron, manganese, and sulfates, as well as tests for various water pollutants. So testing, yeah, we can do that."

"Good, good," Mac said encouragingly.

"Just one hitch, though." Knowles spread his hands in a helpless gesture. "We're not out in the field, and you can't do squat with six drops of water."

Mac raised a startled brow. He glanced at Kimberly, who shrugged. "At least we brought you water," she commented. "We only gave Ray a picture of a leaf."

"Damn right. And I did good," Ray boasted. "So don't you ruin our track record now, Knowles. We keep this up, and maybe we can get our own TV show. You know, *Law and Order: U.S. Geological Survey Unit*. Think of the chicks, Brian. Think of the chicks."

Knowles, however, didn't appear convinced. He leaned back in his desk chair and locked his hands behind his head. "Look, I'm just being practical here. To get accurate results from any sort of water test, you need to be at the source, looking at the sample *in situ*. The minute you bottled up this water, a couple of things happened. One, you changed the temperature. Two, you removed it from its oxygen source, rendering a test for diffused oxygen useless. Three, the pH is going up from off-gas. Four, you may have contaminated the sample from the container itself, and five . . . Well, hell, I can't think of five at the moment, but let's just agree it's not good. Whatever I do to this sucker, the results are about as meaningful as a sixth toe—gives you something to look at, but doesn't do a damn thing."

"But we don't have a source," Mac reminded him curtly. "That's the whole damn point. This sample is what we've been given, the source is what we gotta find. Come on, surely there's something you can do."

Mac stared at the man with mute appeal. After another moment, Knowles caved with a sigh. "It won't be accurate," he warned.

"At this point, we'll take an educated guess."

"I don't know if I'd even call it that." But Knowles was fingering the glass tube bearing their precious sample. "You're sure you don't have more? I'd prefer about forty milliliters."

"The best I could do would be six more drops."

Knowles blinked. "Damn, whoever gave you this was definitely feeling stingy."

"He likes a challenge."

"No kidding. I don't suppose you're gonna tell me anything more about this case."

"Nope."

"Ah well, never hurts to ask." Knowles sighed again, sat up in his chair and stared intently at the sample. "Okay. It's possible to test for salinity. We just need enough water to cover the end of the probe. I could do pH, which also uses a meter. Of course, the probe on the pH meter can deposit a tiny amount of potassium chloride in a sample, raising the electrical conductivity and screwing the salinity test . . . So we do salinity first, I guess, then examine pH. As for mineral testing . . . Hell, I don't know if any of our test equipment is even calibrated for a sample this small. Bacteria tests . . . You have to run the water through a sieve, not sure that would do much here. Same with testing for plant matter." He looked up. "Salinity and pH it is then, though I'm telling you now, the sample size is too limited, the methodology flawed, and all the results will be too relative to draw any sort of accurate conclusions. Other than that, what the hell, I'm game. I've never worked a murder case before."

"Any information is helpful," Mac said grimly.

Knowles opened a drawer. He pulled out a small plastic box with a well-worn label that read Field Kit. He popped open the container and started pulling out handheld meters complete with long metal probes. "Salinity first," he murmured to himself, fiddled around, then stuck the probe in the water.

He didn't say anything right away. Just grunted a few times.

"What does a salinity test measure?" Kimberly asked. "If it's freshwater or salt water?"

"It can." Knowles glanced up at her. "Basically, I'm measuring the amount of microsiemens per centimeter in the water, which gives me an idea of the dissolved content. Water on its own has no electrical conductivity. But water that has a lot of salt or other dissolved minerals in it will have a higher level of conductivity. More microsiemens per centimeter. So, in a roundabout way, we're trying to tell where this water has been."

He looked at the meter, then pulled the probe from the sample. "All right. According to my handy dandy salinity meter, this water has a reading of fifteen thousand microsiemens per centimeter. So, bearing in mind all my earlier caveats, what does that tell us?"

They all looked at him blankly, and he generously filled in. "The water has good conductivity. Not high enough to be salt water, but there's a fair amount of dissolved content in this sample. Maybe minerals or ions. Something that conducts electricity better than water alone."

"The water is contaminated?" Mac asked hesitantly.

"The water is high in dissolved content," Knowles reiterated stubbornly. "At this moment, we can't conclude anything more than that. Now, the logical thing would be to run tests for various minerals, which might answer your question. But we can't do that, so let's try pH."

He set aside the first meter and inserted a second. He watched the meter, then frowned at it, then pulled out the tip and muttered, "Goddamn probe. Hang on a sec."

He wiped the tip. Blew on the tip. Then gave the whole thing a small whack with his hand. With a grunt of satisfaction, he finally returned the probe to the water. The second time didn't make him any happier.

"Well, shit on a stick, this is no good."

"What's wrong?" Kimberly asked.

"Sample must be too small for the probe, or my meter's out of whack. To believe this thing, the pH is three-point-eight, and that just ain't happening."

This time, he banged the probe twice against the desk. Then he tried again.

"What does three-point-eight mean?" Mac asked.

"Acidic. Very acidic. Eat-holes-in-your-clothes level of acidic. Basic is a perfect seven-point-oh. Most fish and algae need at least six-point-five to survive; snails, clams, and mussels require seven-point-oh; while insects, suckers, and carp can go as low as six. So when we're testing ponds and streams with any sort of aquatic life, generally we're at least in the sixes. Now, in Virginia, rainfall has a pH of four-point-two to four-point-five, so pure rainwater would test low, but we know this isn't pure rainwater thanks to the salinity test. Three-point-eight," he was still shaking his head. "That's ridiculous."

He glanced at the meter again, gave a final growl of disgust, and yanked out the probe.

"What's it saying?" Mac asked intently.

"Same garbage as before, three-point-eight. I'm sorry, but the sample has got to be too small. That's all there is to it."

"You're three for three." Kimberly spoke up quietly. "Three tests, three similar results. Maybe the water *is* that acidic."

"It doesn't make any sense, especially when you consider that any pH reading we're getting now is actually *higher* than the original pH at the source. Frankly, we just don't see pH readings below four-point-five. It doesn't happen. Well, except maybe in cases of acid mine drainage."

Mac straightened immediately. "Tell us about acid mine drainage."

"Not much to tell. Water spills out of the mine or goes through tailings of the mine, getting contaminated as it goes. The pH ends up extremely low, possibly in the twos."

"And that would be extremely rare? Something unusual in this state?"

Knowles gave Mac a look. "Buddy, there aren't many places in the *world* that have pH readings in the twos, let alone in the state of Virginia."

"Where is this mine?" Kimberly said urgently.

"You mean mines, *s* as in plural, as in coal mines. We're loaded with them."

"Where?"

"Southwestern Virginia mostly. There's a good seven counties, I think." Knowles was looking at Ray for confirmation. "Let's see . . . Dickenson, Lee, Russell, Scott. Hell, I'm never going to be able to do this off the top of my head; let me look 'em up." He pushed back toward his filing cabinet, gave Ray's legs a prodding shove, then rifled through some manila files.

"How big is the area?" Kimberly pressed him.

Knowles shrugged, then looked again at Ray. "Most of the southwestern corner of the state," Ray offered up. "It's not small, if that's what you mean."

"But the water probably came from there," Mac asserted.

"I will not say that," Knowles warned him. "Sample too small, results too subjective, too many variables beyond my control."

"But it is a strong possibility."

"*If* you accept that reading of three-point-eight to be correct, then *yes,* a mine would be a good place to look for this kind of contaminated water supply. The only other possible theory . . ." He stopped, chewed on his lower lip. "It's gotta be contamination of some kind," he muttered at last. "That's the only thing that could reduce the pH level so dramatically. Now, it could be from a mine. It could also be pollution from organic wastes. Basically, a large dose of biodegradable organic material gets in the water. Bacteria feed off the waste, bacterial population explodes, and now the bacteria consume oxygen faster than the algae or aquatic plants can replace it. *Badda bing, badda boom:* anything that needs oxygen to live—say, fish, insects, plants—dies, and anaerobic bacteria take over the water source; they're about the only thing that can live at pH that low."

"But you can't test it for bacteria, can you?" Kimberly quizzed him.

"Nah, sample's too small."

"Is . . . is there anything else you can do?"

"Well, I could *try* testing for minerals. We got a guy around here who's been squeezing water out of core samples going back thousands of years and running that stuff through the equipment. I know those water samples have gotta be small, but he's gotten some results. I don't know how good—"

"We'll take anything," Mac interrupted him.

"It's very important," Kimberly reiterated. "We need to narrow down this water to the smallest geographic region possible. Seven counties is a start, but seven miles would be better."

"Seven miles huh?" Knowles gave her a doubtful look. "Even if I did get lucky and identify a bunch of minerals . . . Well," he caught himself. "Then again, there are some key physiographic differences among the mine counties. A lot of sandstone and shale in some areas. Karst in others. So mineral results might help. Not seven miles, mind you, but I might be able to get you down to a county or two. I guess we'll find out."

"How long?" Mac pressed him.

"First I'm going to have to talk to the guy, figure out how to set up the equipment . . . I'd say give me a couple of days."

"I'll give you two hours."

"Say what?"

"Listen to me. Two women are missing. It's been nearly forty-eight hours now, and one woman is somewhere around that water. We either find her soon, or it won't much matter anymore."

Knowles's mouth was ajar. He looked pale and troubled at the news, then glanced at the tiny sample with a fresh distrust. "All right," he said abruptly. "Give me two hours."

"One last item." Mac's attention went to Ray Lee Chee. "We have one more sample we need tested. Problem is, we don't know what it is."

He held out the glass vial bearing the residue from the second victim's hair. Ray took it first, then handed it over to Knowles. Neither man knew what it was, but decided a palynologist would be their best bet—an expert in pollen. And they were in luck. One of the best in the state, Lloyd Armitage, was due in this afternoon for a team meeting.

"Anything else?" Ray asked.

"Rice," Kimberly said. "Uncooked long grain. Does that mean anything to either of you?"

That brought a fresh round of bemused looks. Knowles confessed he was a pasta man. Ray Lee Chee said he'd always hated to cook. But hey, they'd ask around.

And that was that. Knowles would attempt to test their water for mineral samples; Ray would inquire about rice; and Mac and Kimberly would hit the road.

"The leaf was easier," Kimberly said shortly, as they walked down the hall.

"That was probably the point." Mac pushed through the exterior door and led them back into the wall of heat. He glanced at his watch and Kimberly caught the gesture.

"Time?"

"Yep." They got into his car and headed for the airport.

34

Kimberly's first glimpse of Nora Ray Watts was not what she had expected. In her mind, she had pictured a young, deeply traumatized girl. Head bowed, shoulders hunched. She would wear nondescript clothes, trying desperately to blend in, while her furtive gaze would dash around the crowded airport, already seeking the source of some unnamed threat.

They'd handle the girl with kid gloves. Buy her a Coke, pick her brain for what she claimed to know about the Eco-Killer, then send her back to the relative safety of Atlanta. That's how these things were done, and frankly, they didn't have time to dick around.

Nora Ray Watts, however, had another plan in mind.

She strode down the middle of the airport terminal, with an old flowered bag slung over her shoulder. Her head was up, her shoulders square. She wore a pair of slim-fitting jeans, a wispy blue shirt over a white tank top, and a pair of heavy-duty hiking boots. Her long brown hair was pulled back into a ponytail, and she hadn't a shred of makeup on her face. She headed straight for them, and the other travelers immediately gave way.

Kimberly had two impressions at once. A young girl, grown up too fast, and a remote woman who now existed as an island in the sea of humanity. Then Kimberly wondered, with almost a sense of panic, if that's what people saw when they peered into her own face.

Nora Ray walked up and Kimberly looked away.

"Special Agent McCormack," she said gravely and shook Mac's outstretched hand.

He introduced Kimberly, and Nora Ray took her hand as well. The girl's grip was firm, but quick. Someone who didn't like touching.

"How was the flight?" Mac asked.

"Fine."

"How are your parents?"

"Fine."

"Uh huh. And what kind of story did you feed them about today?"

Nora Ray brought her chin up. "I told them I was going to spend a few days with an old college classmate in Atlanta. My father was happy I was going to see a friend. My mother was busy watching *Family Ties*."

"Lying's not good for the soul, little girl."

"No. And neither is fear. Shall we?"

She headed toward the food court, while Mac arched a brow.

"She's not your typical victim," Kimberly murmured as they fell in step behind the girl. Mac merely shrugged.

"She has a good family. Least she did before this."

In the food court, Mac and Kimberly got large cups of bitter coffee. Nora Ray purchased a soda and a banana muffin, which she then proceeded to pick at with her fingers as they sat at a small plastic table.

Mac didn't ask anything right away. Kimberly, too, took her time. Sipping the foul-tasting brew, looking around the Richmond airport as if she hadn't a care in the world. Nothing better to do than sit around in air-conditioned glory. Nothing more urgent today than getting that perfect cup of coffee. If only her heart hadn't been beating so hard in her chest. If only they all hadn't been so unbearably aware of the fleeting nature of time.

"I want to help," Nora Ray said abruptly. She'd finished destroying her muffin, and now she looked at them with a nervous, shaky expression. Closer to the young girl again, not so much the remote woman.

"My boss tells me you know something about the current situation," Mac said neutrally.

"He's at it again. Taking girls. Two are dead, aren't they?"

"How do you know that, honey?"

"Because I do."

"He call you?"

"No."

"Send you letters?"

"No." She stiffened her spine. Her voice grew stubborn. "You answer my question first. Are two more girls dead? Is he doing it again?"

Mac was silent, letting the moment drag out. Nora Ray's fingers returned to the bits of her muffin. She kneaded them back together, then tore them apart into a fresh round of small, doughy balls. But the girl was good. She outlasted both of them.

"Yeah," Mac said tersely. "Yeah, he's killing again."

The fire left her all at once. Nora Ray's shoulders slumped, her hands fell heavily on the table. "I knew it," she whispered. "I didn't want to know, I wanted to believe it was only a dream. But in my heart . . . In my heart I always knew. Poor girls. They never stood a chance."

Mac leaned forward. He folded his arms on the table and studied her intently. "Nora Ray, you have to start talking. How do you know these things?"

"You won't laugh?"

"After the last thirty-six hours, I don't have the strength left in me to smile."

Nora Ray's gaze flickered to Kimberly.

"I'm even more tired than he is," Kimberly told her. "So your secret's safe with us."

"I dreamt them."

"You *dreamt* them?"

"I dream of my sister all the time, you know. I never tell people. It would only upset them. But for years I've watched Mary Lynn. She's happy, I think. Wherever she is, there are fields and horses and plenty of sunshine. She doesn't see me; I don't know if I exist in her place. But I get to see her, from time to time, and I think she's doing all right. But then, a few days ago, another girl appeared. And last night, a second girl joined her on the fence. I think they're still figuring out that they're dead."

Mac's expression had gone blank. He rubbed one large hand over his face, then did it again and again. He doesn't know what to do, Kimberly realized. He doesn't know what to say. However either one of them had imagined this conversation going, this wasn't it.

"Are these girls aware of you?" Kimberly asked at last. "Do they talk to you?"

"Yes. One of them has a younger sister. She wanted to know if her sister would also dream about her at night."

"Can you describe the girls?"

Nora Ray rattled off two descriptions. They weren't exactly right, but neither were they wrong. A blonde, a brunette. People who claimed to have psychic ability often relied on generic descriptions to get your own imagination to fill in the blanks. Kimberly was feeling tired again.

"Do you see the man?" Mac asked Nora Ray sharply.

"No."

"You just dream of the girls?"

"Yes."

Mac spread his hands. "Nora Ray, I don't see how that helps us."

"I don't either," she admitted, her tone suddenly sodden and on the edge of tears. "But it's something, isn't it? I have a connection. Some kind of . . . I don't know what! But I'm seeing these girls. I know they died! I know they're hurt and confused and angry as hell at this man for what he did to them. Maybe I can use that. Maybe I can ask them more questions, get information on the killer, find out where he lives. I don't know. But it's something! I know it's something!"

Her voice broke off raggedly. Her hands were now compulsively mashing muffin bits into the tabletop. She squished the soft dough harder and harder with her thumbs. It appeared to be her last link to sanity.

Kimberly looked at Mac. He seemed sorry to have agreed to this meeting. She couldn't blame him.

"I appreciate you coming out and telling me this," he said at last, his tone grave.

"You're not sending me home."

"Nora Ray—"

"No. I can help! I don't know how yet. But I can help. If you're still looking, then I'm staying."

"Nora Ray, you're a civilian. Now, I'm in the middle of a formal police investigation. It's demanding and time-consuming and while I'm sure you mean well, your presence in fact will only slow me down, and—if you'll pardon my French—fuck things up. So go home. I'll call you when we've learned something."

"He's going to strike again. That last summer, he struck twice. He'll do the same now."

"Nora Ray, honey . . ." Mac spread his hands. He seemed to be searching for some way to get through to the girl, to make her understand the futility of her efforts. "The killer's already struck twice in a manner of speaking. This time, instead of taking two girls, he ambushed four. Now two are dead, two are missing, and so help me God, I can't keep sitting here and having this conversation. We are in the middle of serious business. Go home, Nora Ray. I'll be in touch."

Mac rose from the table. Kimberly took that as her cue to join him. But once again, Nora Ray did not conform to type. She also got up from the table, and this time her brown eyes held a bright, feverish light.

"That's it, then," the young girl breathed. "We're going to find the missing girls. That's why I'm seeing the first two in my dreams. I was meant to come. I was meant to help."

"Nora Ray—"

The girl cut him off with a firm shake of her head. "No. I'm twenty-one, I'm an adult. I've made my choice. I'm going with you, whether I have to follow you in a taxi or latch on to your trunk. You're in a hurry, so just nod yes and we can all get on with this. Three heads are better than two. You'll see."

"Get on that plane or I will call your parents."

"No. You look me in the eye and tell me that I'm wrong. Go on: Tell me you're one hundred percent certain I can't help. Because this man's been killing a long time, Special Agent McCormack. This man, he's been killing for years, and you *still haven't stopped him*. Given all that, maybe dreams aren't such a bad place to start."

Mac visibly faltered. As guilt trips went, the girl was good. And there was a nugget of truth to what she said. More than a few reputable police departments had brought in psychics and seers over the years. Detectives got to a point in a case where everything logical had been done. Timelines had been analyzed and overanalyzed. Evidence traced and retraced. And cops grew frustrated and trails grew cold and next thing they knew, the mad hatter on the other end of the phone saying *I've had a vision* was the best lead they'd gotten all year.

Kimberly found she was suddenly very into the idea of dreams and she'd only been working the case thirty-six hours. She couldn't imagine how Mac must feel after five brutal years. And now here they were. Two girls dead. Two girls missing. Clock ticking . . .

"You know the kind of terrain this man picks," Mac said at last.

Nora Ray hefted the pack by her side, then kicked out one hiking boot. "I came prepared."

"It's dangerous."

She merely smiled. "You don't have to tell me that."

"You were lucky three years ago."

"I know. I've practiced since then. Read survival books, studied nature, got in shape. You'd be amazed how much I know now. I might even be helpful to you."

"This isn't your battle to fight."

"It's my only battle to fight. My sister's never coming home, Special Agent McCormack. My family has fallen apart. I've spent three years shut inside a dead house, waiting for the day I'd magically stop being afraid. Well, you know what? It's never going to happen on its own. So I might as well be here."

"It's not a vendetta. We find him and you try to touch a hair on his head . . ."

"I'm a twenty-one-year-old girl, traveling with a pack that's been cleared by airport security. What do you think I'm going to do?"

Mac still looked very uncomfortable. He glanced at Kimberly. She shrugged. "You do attract a certain kind of woman," she told him.

"I'm changing my cologne," he said seriously.

"And until then?"

He sighed. Stared down the terminal. "Fine," he said suddenly, shortly. "What the hell. I'm illegal on this case. Kimberly's illegal on this case. What's one more member of unsanctioned personnel? Goddamn strangest investigation I've ever led. Know anything about rice?" he asked Nora Ray sharply.

"No."

"What about pollen?"

"It makes you go ah-choo."

He shook his head. "Grab your bag. We've got a lot more ground to cover and it's already getting late."

Nora Ray fell in step beside Kimberly as both of them scrambled to keep up with Mac's long, angry strides.

"Feel better?" Kimberly asked Nora Ray at last.

"No," the young girl answered. "Mostly, I feel afraid."

35

Quincy and Rainie drove to Quantico in silence. They did that a lot these days. Ate in silence, traveled in silence, shared a room in silence. Funny how Rainie hadn't noticed it much in the beginning. Maybe it had seemed like personable silence back then. Two people so comfortable with each other they no longer needed words. Now, it seemed more ominous. If silence was a noise, then this silence was the sharp crack of an iceberg, suddenly tearing apart in the middle of an ancient glacier field.

Rainie pressed her forehead against the warm glass of the passenger side window. She rubbed her temples unconsciously and wished she could get these thoughts out of her head.

Outside, the sun beat down relentlessly. Even with the AC cranked in the tiny rental car, she could feel the heat gathering just beyond the vents. Her bare legs were hot from sunbeams. She could already feel sweat trickle uncomfortably down her back.

"Thinking of Oregon?" Quincy asked abruptly. He was wearing his customary blue suit; jacket draped neatly in the backseat for now, but tie still knotted around his throat. She didn't know how he did it every morning.

"Not exactly." She straightened in her seat, stretching out her bare legs. She wore a fresh pair of khaki shorts and a white collared shirt that desperately needed ironing. No suits for her. Not even if they were returning to Quantico. The place wasn't her hallowed ground and they both knew it.

"You're thinking of Oregon a lot these days, aren't you?" Quincy asked again. She looked at him more carefully, surprised by his tenacity. His face was impossible to read. Dark eyes peering straight ahead. His lips set in a tight line. He was going for the neutral, psychologist-on-duty approach, she decided.

"Yeah," she said.

"It's been a long time. Nearly two years. Maybe after this, we should go there. To Oregon. Have a vacation."

"All right." Her voice came out thicker than she intended. Dammit, she had tears in her eyes.

He heard it, turned toward her and for the first time, she saw the full panic on his face. "Rainie . . ."

"I know."

"Have I done something wrong?"

"It's not you."

"I know I can be distant. I know I get a little lost in my work . . ."

"It's my work, too."

"But you're not happy, Rainie. It's not just today either. You haven't been happy in a long, long time."

"No." It shocked her to finally say it out loud, and in the next instant, she felt a curious sensation in the middle of her chest. Relief. She had gotten the word out. She had said it, had acknowledged the elephant that had been lurking in the room for a good six months now. Someone had to.

Quincy's gaze returned to the road. His hands flexed and unflexed on the wheel. "Is there something I can do?" he asked at last, already sounding more composed. That was his way, she knew. You could hit the man in the gut, and he'd merely square his shoulders. If you hurt his daughter, on the other hand, or threatened Rainie . . . That's when the gloves came off. That's when his dark eyes gleamed feral, and his runner's body fell into the stance of a long, lean weapon, and he emerged not as Quincy, top criminology researcher, but as Pierce, an extremely dangerous man.

That was only when you harmed someone he loved, however. He had never done much of anything to protect himself.

"I don't know," Rainie said bluntly.

"If you want to go to Oregon, I'll go to Oregon. If you need a break, we can take a break. If you need space, I'll give you space. If you need comfort, then just tell me and I'll pull over this car right now and take you into my arms. But you have to tell me something, Rainie, because I've been floating in the dark for months now, and I think I'm losing my mind."

"Quincy . . ."

"I would do anything to make you happy, Rainie."

And she said in a small voice, "I'm so sorry, Quincy, but I think I want a baby."

Kaplan was already waiting for them when they pulled into the parking lot outside the Jefferson Dormitory. He looked hot, tired, and already pissed as hell with the day.

"A little birdie told me I'm not supposed to be talking to you two," he said the moment they climbed out of their car. "Said I should deal only with some new guy, who's now heading the investigation."

Quincy shrugged mildly. "I haven't been notified of any change in staffing. Have you, Rainie?"

"Nope," she said. "Never heard a thing."

"That little birdie must be pulling your leg," Quincy told Kaplan.

Kaplan raised a brow. In a surprisingly quick move for a big guy, he swiped the cell phone clipped to Quincy's waist, eyed its lack of power, and grunted. "Smart. Well, as long as they're fucking their own people, welcome to my happy little club. I got a body, I still have jurisdiction, and I'm not giving it up."

"Amen," Quincy said. Rainie merely yawned.

Kaplan remained scowling. "So why do you want to reinterview my sentries? Think I couldn't possibly have gotten it right the first time?"

"No, but now we have new information on the suspect."

That seemed to appease the special agent. He shook out his shoulders, indicated for them to climb into his car, then headed back out onto the base. "Guys were out training this morning," Kaplan filled them in. "I had their CO pull them aside. Both should be waiting for us at the school. They're young, but good. If they know anything that can be of help, they'll tell you."

"Any more activity around here?"

"Dead bodies? Thankfully, no. Ads in the *Quantico Sentry*? None that has crossed anyone's desk. I met with Betsy Radison's parents late last night. That's been about it."

"Tough business," Quincy said quietly.

"Yeah, it is."

Kaplan turned into the cluster of buildings that marked Marine TBS— The Basic School. Sure enough, two young recruits sat to the side, dressed in jungle camo with hats pulled low to shield their faces and thick black utility belts strapped around their waists. Kaplan, Quincy, and Rainie climbed out of the car, and immediately the two snapped to attention.

Kaplan made the introductions, while the recruits held their rigid stance.

"This is civilian Pierce Quincy. He is going to ask you some questions regarding the night, fifteen of July. This is his partner, Lorraine Conner. She may also ask you questions regarding the same evening. You will answer all of their questions to the best of your ability. You will accord them the full respect and cooperation you would give any Marine officer requesting your assistance. Is that clear?"

"Sir, yes sir!"

Kaplan nodded at Quincy. "You may proceed."

Quincy raised a brow. The pomp and circumstance was a little extreme. Then again, Kaplan had taken a lot of hits recently. The FBI had forced him out of their world. Now he was showing off the power he still wielded in his.

Quincy approached the two Marines. "You were both on duty for the night shift, July fifteenth?"

"Sir, yes sir."

"Both of you stopped each vehicle and checked each driver for proper ID?"

"We stopped all incoming vehicles, sir!"

"Did you check passengers for proper identification?"

"All visitors to the base must show proper identification, sir!"

Quincy shot Rainie another dry look. She didn't dare meet his eye or she would start giggling or burst into tears or both. The morning had already taken on a surreal quality, and now it felt as if they were interviewing two trained seals.

"What kind of vehicles did you stop that night?" Quincy asked.

For the first time, no immediate answer was shouted forth. Both recruits were still staring straight ahead as procedure dictated, but it was clear they were confused.

Quincy tried again. "Special Agent Kaplan said you both reported heavy traffic that night."

"Sir, yes sir!" both Marines cried out promptly.

"The majority of this traffic seemed to be National Academy students returning to the dorms."

"Sir, yes sir!"

"Is it fair to say that these people mostly drove rental cars or their own personal vehicles? I would guess you saw a lot of small, nondescript automobiles."

"Sir, yes sir." Not quite as vehement, but still an affirmative.

"What about vans?" Quincy asked gently. "Particularly a cargo van arriving in the early morning hours?"

Quiet again. Both sentries wore a frown.

"We did see a few vans, sir," one finally reported.

"Did you happen to note these vehicles in your logs, or glance at the license plates?"

"No, sir."

Quincy's turn to frown. "Why not? I would think you'd see mostly cars coming and going off the base. A cargo van should be unusual."

"No, sir. Construction, sir."

Quincy looked blankly at Kaplan, who seemed to get it. "We have a number of projects active here on the base," the special agent explained. "New firing ranges, new labs, new admin buildings. It's been a busy summer, and most of those crews are driving vans or trucks. Hell, we've cleared guys on forklifts."

Quincy closed his eyes. Rainie could already see the anger building behind his deceptively quiet façade. The little details no one thought to mention in the beginning. The one little detail, of course, that could make all the difference in a case.

"You have a ton of construction personnel active on this base," Quincy said in a steely voice. His eyes opened. He looked straight at Kaplan. "And you never mentioned this before?"

Kaplan shifted uneasily. "Didn't come up."

"You have a murder on the base, and you don't think to mention that you have an abnormally high number of eighteen-to-thirty-five-year-old males engaged in transient, menial labor, in other words, men who fit the murderer's profile, passing through these gates?"

Now even the two Marine sentries were regarding Kaplan with interest. "Each and every person who receives authorization to enter this base must first pass security clearance," Kaplan replied evenly. "Yeah, I got a list of the names, and yeah, my people have been reviewing them. But we don't allow people with records on this base period—not as personnel, not as contractors, not as guests, and not as students. So it's a clean list."

"That's wonderful," Quincy said crisply. "Except for one thing, Special Agent Kaplan. Our UNSUB doesn't have a record—he hasn't been caught yet!"

Kaplan's face blazed red. He was definitely aware of the two sentries watching him, and he was definitely aware of Quincy's growing fury. But still he didn't back down. "We pulled the list. We analyzed the names. No one has a history of violence or a record of assault. In other words, there is nothing to indicate any one of those contractors should be pursued as a suspect. Unless, excuse me, you want me to start attacking any guy who drives a cargo van."

"It would be a start."

"It would be half the list!"

"Yes, but then how many of those people once lived in Georgia!"

Kaplan drew up short, blinked, and Quincy finally nodded in grim satisfaction. "A simple credit report, Special Agent. That's all you have to do. It'll give you previous addresses and we can identify anyone who also has ties to Georgia. And then we'd have a suspect list. Don't you think?"

"It . . . but . . . well . . . Yeah, okay."

"There are two more girls out there," Quincy said quietly. "And this UNSUB has gotten away with this for far too long."

"You don't know that he's really a member of the construction crews," Kaplan said stubbornly.

"No, but we should at least be asking these questions. You can't let the UNSUB control the game. Take it from me," Quincy's gaze had taken on a faraway look. "You have to take control, or you will lose. With these kinds of predators, it's all about gamesmanship. Winner takes all."

"I'll put my people on the list," Kaplan said. "Give us a few hours. Where will you be?"

"At the BSU, talking to Dr. Ennunzio."

"Has he learned anything from the ad?"

"I don't know. But let's hope he's been lucky. Because the rest of us certainly haven't."

36

Tina had gone native. Mud streaked her arms, her legs, her pretty green sundress. She had stinking ooze coating her face and neck, primordial slime squishing between her toes. Now she picked up another sticky handful and smeared it across her chest.

She remembered reading a book in high school, *Lord of the Flies*. According to one of the notations in the handy yellow Cliffs Notes, *Lord of the Flies* was really about a wet dream. Tina hadn't gotten that part. Mostly she remembered the stranded kids turning into little savages, first taking on wild boars, then taking on one another. The book possessed a fearful edgy quality that was also definitely sexy. So maybe it was about wet dreams after all. She couldn't tell if the guys in her class had read it with any more enthusiasm than they'd read the other literary classics.

But that wasn't really the point. The point was that Tina Krahn, knocked-up college student and madman's current plaything, was finally getting a real-life lesson in literature. Who said high school didn't teach you anything?

She started mucking up first thing this morning, the sun already climbing in the sky and threatening to fry her like a bug caught in the glare of a magnifying glass. The mud stank to high heaven, but it sure did feel good against her flesh. It went on cool and thick, coating her festering skin with a thick layer of protection not even the damn mosquitoes could penetrate. It filled her nostrils with a putrid, musky smell. And it made her head practically swim with relief.

The mud liked her. The mud would save her. The mud was her friend. Now she stared at the bubbling, popping mess and she wondered why she didn't eat a handful as well. Her water was gone. Crackers, too. Her stomach had a too-tight, pained feeling, like she was on the verge of the world's worst menstrual cramps. The baby was probably leaving her. She had been a bad mother, and now the baby wanted the mud, too.

Was she crying? It was so hard to tell, with the heavy weight of drying filth on her cheeks.

The mud was wet. It would feel so good sliding down her parched, ravenous throat. It would fill her stomach with a heavy, rotten mass. She could

743

stop digesting her stomach lining, and dine on dirt instead.

It would be so easy. Pick up another oozing handful. Slide it past her lips.

Delirious, the voice in the back of her brain whispered. The heat and dehydration had finally taken their toll. She had chills even in the burning heat. The world swam uneasily every time she moved. Sometimes she found herself laughing, though she didn't know why. Sometimes she sat and sobbed, though at least that made some kind of sense.

The sores on her arms and legs had started moving this morning. She had squeezed one scabbed-over mass between her fingers, then watched in horror as four white maggots popped out. Her flesh was rotting. The bugs had already moved in to dine. It wouldn't be much longer for her now.

She dreamt of water, of ice-cold streams rippling over her skin. She dreamt of nice restaurants with white linen tablecloths, where four tuxedoed waiters brought her an endless supply of frosty water glasses, filled to the brim. She would dine on seared steak and twice-baked potatoes covered in melted cheese. She would eat marinated artichoke hearts straight from the container, until olive oil dribbled down her chin.

She dreamt of a pale yellow nursery and a fuzzy head nestled at her breast.

She dreamt of her mother, attending her funeral and standing alone next to her grave.

If she closed her eyes, she could return to the world of her dreams. Let the maggots have her flesh. Let her body sink into the mud. Maybe when the end came, she wouldn't even know anymore. She would just slide away, taking her baby with her.

Tina's eyes popped open. She forced her head up. Struggled to her feet. The world spun again, and she leaned against the boulder.

No eating mud! No caving in. She was Tina Krahn and she was made of sterner stuff.

Her breath came out in feeble gasps, her chest heaving with effort to inhale the overheated, muggy air. She staggered toward one vine-covered wall, watching a snake dart out of her way, hissing at her as it passed. Then she was braced against the wall, the vines cool against her muddy cheek.

Her fingers patted the structure as if it were a good dog. Funny, the surface over here didn't feel like rough cement. In fact . . .

Tina pushed herself back. Her eyelids were terribly swollen; it was so hard to see. . . . She forced them wide with all of her might, while simultaneously pushing back the vines. Wood. This part of the rectangular pit was held up by wood. Railroad ties or something like that. Old, peeling railroad ties that were already rotting with age.

Frantically, she dug her fingers into one visible hole. She tugged hard, and felt the meat of the lumber start to give way. She needed more strength. Something harder, a tool.

A rock.

Then she was down on her hands and knees, once again digging in the mud while her eyes took on a feverish light. She would find a rock. She would gouge out the boards. And then she would climb out of this pit, just like Spider Man. She would get to the top, she would find coolness, find water, find tender green things to eat.

She, Tina Krahn, knocked-up college student and madman's current plaything, would finally be free.

Lloyd Armitage, USGS palynologist and Ray Lee Chee's new best friend, met them shortly after noon. Five minutes later, Mac, Kimberly, and Nora Ray were piling into a conference room Armitage had set up as his traveling lab. It was a strange entourage, Mac thought, but then this was a strange case. Kimberly looked bone-tired but alert, wearing that slightly edgy look he'd come to know so well. Nora Ray was much harder to read. Her face was blank, shut down. She'd made a big decision, he thought, now she was trying not to think about it.

"Ray Lee Chee says you're working some kind of homicide case," Armitage stated.

"We have evidence from a scene," Mac answered. "We need to trace it back to the original source. I'm afraid I can't tell you much more than that, other than whatever you have to tell us, we needed to have heard it yesterday."

Armitage, an older man with bushy hair and a thick brown beard, arched a curling eyebrow. "So that's how it is. Well, for the record, pollen analysis isn't as specific as botany. Most of my job is taking soil samples from various field sites. Then I use a little bit of hydrochloric acid and a little bit of hydrofluoric acid to break apart the minerals in the sediment. Next, I run everything through sieves, mix that with zinc chloride, then place it in a medical centrifuge until voilà, I have a nice little sample of pollen, fresh from the great outdoors—or from several thousand years ago, as the case might be. At that point, I can identify the general plant family that deposited the pollen, but *not* a specific species. For example, I can tell you the pollen is from locust, but not that it's from a bristly locust. Will that help?"

"I'm not sure what a locust is," Mac said. "So I guess whatever you discover, it'll be more than what we knew before."

Armitage seemed to accept that. He held out his hand and Mac gave him the sample.

"That's not pollen," the palynologist said immediately.

"You're sure?"

"Too big. Pollen is roughly five to two hundred microns or considerably smaller than the width of human air. This is closer to the size of sediment."

The palynologist didn't give up, however. He opened the glass vial, shook out a small section of the dusty residue onto a slide, then slid it under a microscope. "Huh," he said. Then "huh" again.

"It's organic," Armitage told them after another minute. "All one substance rather than a mix of various residues. Seems to be some kind of dust, but coarser." His bushy head popped up. "Where did you find this?"

"I'm afraid I can't tell you that."

"Are there other samples you found with it?"

"Water and uncooked rice."

"Rice? Why in heaven's name did you find rice?"

"That's the million-dollar question. Got any theories?"

Armitage frowned, wagged his eyebrows some more, then pursed his lips. "Tell me about the water. Have you brought it to a hydrologist?"

"Brian Knowles examined it this morning. It has an extremely low pH, three-point-eight, and high . . . salinity, I guess. It registers fifteen thousand microsiemens per centimeter, meaning there might be lots of minerals or ions present. Knowles believes it comes from a mine or was polluted by organic waste."

Armitage was nodding vigorously. "Yes, yes, he's thinking the coal counties, isn't he?"

"I think so."

"Brian's good. Close, just missed one thing." Lloyd slid out the slide and then did the totally unexpected by dabbing his index finger into the sample and touching it to his tongue. "It's unusually fine, that's the problem. In its coarser form, you would have recognized it yourself."

"You know what it is?" Mac asked sharply.

"Absolutely. It's sawdust. Not pollen at all, but finely ground wood."

"I don't get it," Kimberly said.

"Sawmill, my dear. In addition to coal mines, the southwestern part of the state also has a lot of timber industry. This sample is sawdust. And, if these samples are supposed to go together . . ."

"We hope so," Mac said.

"Then your water's pH is due to organic waste. See, if mill wastes are not disposed of properly, the organic matter leaches into a stream, where it leads to bacterial buildup, eventually suffocating all other life-forms. Has Brian tested the sample for bacteria yet?"

"The amount's too small."

"But the high salinity," Armitage was muttering. "Must be minerals of some kind. Pity he can't test it more."

"Wait a minute," Kimberly said intently. "You're saying this is from a mill, not a mine?"

"Well, I don't generally associate sawdust with coal mines. So yes, I'm going to say a lumber mill."

"But that could give you acidic water?"

"Contamination is contamination, my dear. And with a pH reading of three-point-eight, your water came from an extremely contaminated source."

"But Knowles indicated this water is at a crisis," Mac said. "Aren't mills regulated for how they dispose of waste?"

"In theory, yes. But then, there's a lot of lumber mills in this state and I wouldn't be surprised if some of the smaller, backwoods operations fall through the cracks."

Nora Ray had finally perked up. She was looking at the palynologist with interest. "What if it were a closed mill?" she asked quietly. "Some place shut down, abandoned." Her gaze flickered to Mac. "That would be his kind of place, you know. Remote and dangerous, like something from a B-grade horror movie."

"Oh, I'm sure there are plenty of abandoned mills in the state," Armitage said. "Particularly in the coal counties. That's not a very populated area.

And, frankly, not a bad location for a horror movie."

"How so?" Mac asked.

"It's an impoverished area. Very rural. People first moved out there to get their own land and be free from government. Then the coal mines opened and attracted hordes of cheap labor, looking to make a living. Unfortunately, farming, timber, or mining hasn't made anyone rich yet. Now you just have a broad expanse of bruised and battered land, housing a bruised and battered population. People still eke out a living, but it's a hard life and the communities look it."

"So we're back to seven counties," Mac murmured.

"That would be my guess."

"Nothing more you can tell us?"

"Not from a minute sample of sawdust."

"Shit." Seven counties. That just wasn't specific enough. Maybe if they'd started yesterday or the day before. Maybe if they had hundreds of searchers or what the hell, the entire National Guard. But three people, two of them not even in law enforcement . . .

"Mr. Armitage," Kimberly spoke up suddenly. "Do you have a computer we can use? One with Internet access."

"Sure, I have my laptop."

Kimberly was already up out of her chair. Her gaze went to Mac and he was startled by the light he now saw blazing in her eyes. "Remember how Ray Lee Chee said there was an ology for everything?" she asked excitedly. "Well, I'm about to put him to the test. Give me the names of the seven coal-producing counties and I think I can find our rice!"

37

Dr. Ennunzio was not in his office. A secretary promised to hunt him down, while Quincy and Rainie took a seat in the conference room. Quincy rifled through his files. Rainie stared at the wall. Periodically, sounds came from the hallway as various agents and admin assistants rushed by doing a day's work.

"It's not that simple," Quincy said abruptly.

Rainie finally looked at him. As always, she didn't need a segue to follow his line of thought. "I know."

"We're not exactly spring chickens. You're nearly forty, I'm pushing fifty-five. Even if we wanted to have kids, it doesn't mean it would happen."

"I've been thinking of adopting. There are a lot of children out there who need a family. In this country, in other countries. Maybe I could give a child a good home."

"It's a lot of work. Midnight feedings if you adopt an infant. Bonding issues if you adopt an older child. Children need the sun, the moon, and the stars at night. No more jetting around the world at the drop of a hat. No more dining at fine restaurants. You'd definitely have to cut back on work."

She was silent for a moment. Then she said, "Don't get me wrong, Quincy. I like the work that we do. But lately . . . it's not enough for me. We go from dead body to dead body, crime scene to crime scene. Catch a psychopath today, hunt a new one tomorrow. It's been six years, Quince. . . ." She looked down at the table. "If I do this, I'll quit the practice. I've waited too long to have a child not to do it right."

"But you're my partner," he protested without thinking.

"Consultants can be hired. Parents can't."

He turned away, then tiredly shook his head. He didn't know what to say. Perhaps it was only natural that someday she would want children. Rainie was younger than him, hadn't already weathered the domestic storm that had been his pathetic attempt at domestic bliss. Maternal instincts were natural, particularly for a woman her age who was bound to be hearing the steady beat of her own biological clock.

And for a moment, an image came to him. Rainie with a small bundle wrapped in her arms, cooing in that high-pitched voice everyone used with babies. Him, watching little feet and hands kick in the air. Catching that first giggle, seeing the first smile.

But the other images inevitably followed. Coming home late from work and realizing your child was already in bed—again. The urgent phone calls that pulled you away from piano recitals and school plays. The way a five-year-old could break your heart by saying, "It's okay, Daddy. I know you'll be there next time."

The way children grew too fast. The way they could die too young. The way parenthood started with so much promise, but one day tasted like ashes in your mouth.

And then he felt a hot, unexpected surge of anger toward Rainie. When he'd first met her, she'd said she never wanted marriage or kids. Her own childhood had been a dark, twisted tale, and she knew better than most to believe she could magically break the cycle. God knows, he'd asked her to marry him twice over the past six years, and each time she'd turned him down. "If it's not broke, don't fix it," she'd told him. And each time, though it had hurt a little, stung more than he'd expected, he'd taken her at her word.

But now she was changing the rules. Not enough to marry him, heaven forbid, but enough to want kids.

"I've already served my time," he said harshly.

"I know, Quincy." Her own voice was quiet, harder on him than if she had yelled. "I know you raised two girls and dealt with midnight feedings and adolescent angst and so much more. I know you're at the phase of your life where you're supposed to be looking forward to retirement, not your kid's first day of kindergarten. I thought I would be there, too. I honestly thought this would never be an issue. But then . . . Lately . . ." She gave a little shrug. "What can I say? Sometimes, even the best of us change our minds."

"I love you," he tried one last time.

"I love you, too," Rainie replied, and he thought she'd never looked so sad.

When Dr. Ennunzio finally strode into the room, the silence was definitely awkward and strained. He didn't seem to notice, however. He came to an abrupt halt, a stack of manila files bulging under his arm. "Up," he told them curtly. "Out. We're taking a walk."

Quincy was already climbing out of his chair. Confused, Rainie was slower to follow suit.

"You got a call," Quincy said to Ennunzio.

The agent shook his head warningly and looked up at the ceiling. Quincy got the message. Years ago, a BSU agent had spied on his fellow members of the FBI. Elaborate surveillance systems and audio devices were found snaking through the vast crawl space above the dropped ceiling. Better yet, when the FBI began to suspect espionage activity, they had responded by inserting their own surveillance devices and wiretaps to catch the man. In short, for a span of time—who knows how long—all the BSU agents were being watched by both the good guys and the bad. Nobody forgot those days easily.

Quincy and Rainie followed Ennunzio to the stairwell, where he swiped his security badge over the scanner, then led them up to the great outdoors.

"What the hell is going on?" the linguist asked the minute they were across the street from the building. Now their conversation was muffled by the steady sounds of gunfire.

"I'm not sure." Quincy held up his dead cell phone. "I've been a little out of touch."

Ennunzio shook his head. He looked decidedly frayed around the edges and not happy with how things had turned out. "I thought you guys were doing good. I thought by talking to you, I was assisting a major investigation. Not killing my own career."

"We are doing good. And I have every intention of catching this man."

"Things are heating up," Rainie told him. "We found another victim late last night. Everything matches the Eco-Killer's MO. Except this time he kidnapped four girls at once. Which means two more are out there, and if we're going to break this thing, we need to move fast."

"Damn," Ennunzio said tiredly. "After meeting with you guys, I was hoping . . . Well, what do you need from me?"

"Any luck with the newspaper ad?" Quincy asked.

"I sent the paper out to the lab, so I don't have results yet. Given that the ad was delivered already typeset inside an envelope with a computer-generated label, there's no handwriting to analyze. Perhaps we'll get lucky with paper choice and ink. As for the text, I don't have anything new to say. Author is most likely male and of above-average intelligence. I repeat the theory that we might be dealing with someone who is somehow mentally incapacitated. Maybe suffering from paranoia or otherwise impaired. Ritual is obviously extremely important to him. The process of killing is as satisfying as the killing itself. You know the rest of that as well as I do." Ennunzio looked at Quincy. "He'll never stop unless someone makes him."

Quincy nodded his head. The news discouraged him more than it should and abruptly he was tired of everything. Worrying about Kimberly. Worrying about Rainie. And wondering what it meant when talk of babies scared him more than talk of psychopaths.

"Special Agent McCormack received another call," Quincy said. "He was going to write down the conversation, but with everything that's happened, I don't think he's had the time."

"When was he contacted?"

"Late last night. When he was at the crime scene."

Ennunzio immediately looked troubled. "I don't like that."

"The UNSUB has a keen knack for timing."

"You think he's watching."

"As you said, he likes the process. For him, it's as important as the kill itself. We have a new theory." Quincy was watching Ennunzio's face very closely. "The UNSUB most likely uses a cargo van as his kill vehicle. We understand from Special Agent Kaplan that there is an unusually high number of vans coming and going off the base these days—they belong to various contractors doing construction work on the property."

Ennunzio squeezed his eyes shut. He was already nodding. "That would fit."

"Kaplan is now examining the list of workers for anyone with a previous address in Georgia. That may give us a name, but I think it's too late."

Ennunzio opened his eyes, staring at them both sharply.

"The UNSUB wanted Quantico, the UNSUB got Quantico, and now he doesn't need it anymore," Quincy continued. "The action is out in the field, and I think that's where we're going to have to go if we're to have any chance of finding him. So, Doctor, what do you know that you're not telling us yet?"

The forensic linguist appeared genuinely startled, then wary, then carefully composed. "I don't know why you say that."

"You're taking a lot of interest in this case."

"It's what I do."

"You've gone out of your way to focus on the caller, when in fact, you deal with notes."

"Linguistics is linguistics."

"We're accepting all theories," Quincy tried one last time. "Even the fuzzy, half-baked ones."

Ennunzio finally hesitated. "I don't know. There's just something about this . . . A feeling I get on occasion. But feelings are not facts, and in my line of work I should know better."

"Would it make a difference," Rainie said, "if we told you we had three more clues?"

"What are they?"

"Water. Some kind of residue. And some uncooked rice. We believe we can trace the water and residue. We haven't a clue about the rice."

Ennunzio was gazing at them now with a curious smile on his face. "Rice?"

"Uncooked long grain. What about it?"

"You said he favors dangerous terrain, correct? Unpopulated areas where there is little risk of his victims being found by accident? Oh, he is good, very, very good. . . ."

"What the hell do you know, Ennunzio?"

"I know I used to be a caver in my younger days. And now I know your UNSUB was, as well. Quick, we need to make a call!"

38

The sun was high in the sky. It baked Tina's little pit, until the mud flaked off her body to reveal tantalizing slices of burnt, festering skin, and the mosquitoes had themselves some lunch. Tina didn't care anymore. She barely felt the pain.

No more sweat. She didn't even have to pee and it had easily been over twelve hours. Nope, not even the tiniest drop of water could be squeezed from her body. Dehydration definitely severe now. She worked at her task, covered in goose bumps and shivering again and again from some deep, unnatural chill.

Rocks didn't work. Too large and bulky for prying away rotting wood. She'd remembered her purse and feverishly dumped out the contents in a jumbled pile on the center of the boulder. A metal nail file. Much better.

Now she gouged out slices of old railroad ties, desperately crafting footholds and handholds while the mosquitoes buzzed her face, the yellow flies bit her shoulders, and the world spun round and round and round.

Nail file dropped. She slithered to the ground. Panting hard. Her hand trembled. It took so much effort just to locate the file in the mud. Oh looky, another snake.

She would like to close her eyes now. She would like to sink back into the comforting stink of the muck. She would feel it slide across her hair, her cheek, her throat. She would part her lips and let it into her mouth.

Fight or die, fight or die, fight or die. It was all up to her, and it was getting so hard to know the difference.

Tina retrieved the nail file. She went back to work on the railroad ties, while the sun burned white-hot overhead.

"Where am I going? Right turn? Okay, now what? Wait, wait, you said right. No, you said left. Damn, give me a sec." Mac slammed the brakes, threw his rental car in reverse and jolted backward thirty feet on the old dirt road. Sitting beside him, Kimberly was trying desperately to find their location on a Virginia state map. Most of these old logging roads didn't seem to show up, however, and now he had Ray Lee Chee trying to guide him by cell phone over terrain that was as spotty as the phone connection.

"What? Say that again? Yeah, but I'm only hearing every fourth word. Bats? What's this about bats?"

"Cavers . . . rescue team . . . bats . . . on cars," Ray said.

"A batmobile?" Mac said, just as Kimberly yelled, "Look out!" He glanced up in time to see the giant tree fallen smack across the middle of the road.

He hit the brakes. In the backseat, Nora Ray went, "Oooomph."

"Everyone okay?"

Kimberly looked at Nora Ray, Nora Ray looked at Kimberly. Simultaneously, they both nodded. Mac gave up on the road for a second, and returned his attention to the cell phone.

"Ray, how close are we?"

". . . two . . . three . . . zzz."

"Miles?"

"Miles," Ray confirmed.

All right, forget the damn car, they could walk. "How's the team coming?" Mac asked. Ray was under strict orders to assemble the best people he could find for a down-and-dirty field team. Brian Knowles, the hydrologist, and Lloyd Armitage, the palynologist, were already on board. Now Ray was trying to round up a forensic geologist and a karst botanist. In theory, by the time Mac, Kimberly, and Nora Ray magically found and rescued victim number three, Ray's team would have arrived, ready to analyze the next round of clues and pinpoint victim number four. It was late in the game, but they were preparing to make up for lost time.

"Bats . . . cavers . . ." Ray said again.

"I can't hear you."

"Karst . . . volunteers . . . bats . . ."

"You have volunteer bats?"

"Search-and-rescue!" Ray exploded. "Cavern!"

"A volunteer group for search-and-rescue. Oh, in the cave!" Mac hadn't even thought that far ahead. Kimberly had searched the various county names combined with rice, and lo and behold, up had come an article on the Orndorff's Cavern. Apparently, it was home to an endangered isopod, a tiny white crustacean that's approximately a fourth of an inch long. To make a long story short, some politician had wanted to build an airport in the area, environmentalists had tried to block it using the Endangered Species Act, and the politician had replied that no way in damn hell would progress be halted by a grain of rice. And now the Orndorff's Cavern isopod had a cool nickname among karst specialists.

So they had a location. If they could find it, and if they could get the girl back out.

"Water . . . dangerous," Ray was saying on the other end of the phone. "Entrance difficult . . . Ropes . . . coveralls . . . lights."

"We need special equipment to access the cave," Mac translated. "Okay, so when will the search-and-rescue team arrive?"

"Making calls . . . different locations . . . Bats . . . on cars."

"Their cars will have bats?"

"Stickers!"

"Gotcha."

Mac popped open his car door and got out to survey the fallen tree. Kimberly was already out and walking its length. She glanced up at his approach and grimly shook her head. He saw her point. The tree trunk was a good three feet in diameter. It would take a four-wheel-drive vehicle, a chain saw, and a winch to move this sucker now. No way was it happening with a guy, two girls, and a Camry.

"We made the left turn," Mac said into the phone. "What do we do next?" This time he couldn't make out Ray's reply at all. Something about "smell the fungus." Mac looked around sourly. They were in the middle of soaring woods, deep into the heart of nowhere. Since turning off Interstate 81 forty minutes ago, they'd drifted into the westernmost part of the state, a thin peninsula wedged between Kentucky and North Carolina. Nothing around here but trees, fields, and double-wides. Last building they'd seen was a decrepit gas station fifteen miles back. It looked like it hadn't pumped a drop since 1968. Before that had been half a dozen mobile homes and one tiny Baptist church. Lloyd Armitage hadn't been kidding. Whatever better days had come to this part of the state had departed a long time ago.

Now it was strictly backwoods country, and Mac's cell phone reception would not be getting better anytime soon.

"I'll try you again at the scene," Mac said. Ray made some kind of reply, but Mac still couldn't hear him and finally snapped his phone shut.

"What do we do?" Nora Ray asked him.

"Now, we walk."

Actually, first they assembled gear. True to her word, Nora Ray had come prepared. From her travel bag, she pulled out a modest daypack, complete with dried food, first-aid kit, compass, Swiss army knife, and water filtration system. She also had waterproof matches and a small flashlight. She loaded up her gear; Kimberly and Mac attended to their own.

They had three gallons of water left. Mac thought of the condition the girl would probably be in, unglued his shirt from his torso for the fourth time in the last five minutes, and stuck all three gallons in his backpack. The weight was considerable, the nylon pack feeling like a son of a bitch as it dragged against his shoulders and pressed his shirt against his overheated skin.

Kimberly came over, removed one of the gallon jugs and stuck it in her own backpack. "Don't be an idiot," she told him, then hefted on her pack and clipped it around her hips.

"At least the trees are providing shade," Mac said.

"Now if only they'd soak up the wet. How far?"

"Couple of miles. I think."

Kimberly glanced at her watch again. "We'd better get moving." She sneaked a peek at Nora Ray, and Mac could read her thoughts. How hard could the civilian push it? They'd soon find out.

It was a surreal hike, Mac thought later. Moving down a thickly shaded logging road in the middle of a blistering afternoon. The sun seemed to chase them, peeking in and out of the trees as it dodged their footsteps and seared them with unrelenting beams of light.

Bugs came out in force. Mosquitoes the size of hummingbirds. Some kind of obnoxious fly with a vicious little bite. They were batting at their faces before they'd gone fifteen feet. At thirty feet, they stopped and got out the cans of bug repellent. A quarter of a mile later, they stopped again and sprayed each other down as if the stuff were gallons of cheap perfume.

It didn't make a difference. The flies swarmed, the sun burned and the humidity covered their bodies in never-ending rivulets of sweat. No one spoke. They just put one foot in front of the other and focused on walking.

Forty minutes later, Mac smelled it first. "What the hell is that?"

"Deet," Kimberly said grimly. "Or sweat. Take your pick."

"No, no, it's worse than that."

Nora Ray stopped. "It's like something rotten," she said. "Almost like . . . sewage."

Mac suddenly got it. What Ray Lee Chee had been trying to tell him on the phone. Smell the fungus. He picked up the pace. "Come on," he said. "We're almost there."

He started jogging now, Kimberly and Nora Ray hastily following suit. They crested the small rise of the hill, came down the other side, and then abruptly drew up short.

"Holy shit," Mac said.

"B-grade horror movie," Nora Ray murmured.

And Kimberly just shook her head.

Quincy was getting frustrated. He'd tried Kimberly's cell phone three or four times without success. Now he turned back to Ennunzio and Rainie.

"Do you know where this cave is?" he asked Ennunzio.

"Absolutely. It's in Lee County, a good three or four hours from here. But you can't just crash into this cavern as if it's one of the tourist hot spots from the Shenandoah Valley. To access Orndorff's Cavern, you need serious gear."

"Fine. Get the gear, then take us."

Ennunzio was silent for a moment. "Perhaps it's time to let the official case team know what's going on."

"Really? What do you think they'll do first, Doctor? Rescue the victim? Or call you in for a three-hour interview to corroborate every last detail of your story?"

The linguist saw his point. "I'll get my gear."

"What are we looking for?"

"Hell if I know. Some kind of cavern entrance. Maybe amid a pile of rocks, or a sinkhole at the base of a tree. I've never done any spelunking. Then again, how hard can it be to find the entrance to a cave?"

Pretty hard, it turned out. Mac had already been running around the sawmill for a good fifteen minutes. So had Kimberly and Nora Ray. They were probably all being stupid. The smell was the first kicker. The foul odor rose so thick in the heavy, humid air it stung their eyes and burned their throats. Mac was now holding an old T-shirt over his mouth, but even that didn't make much difference.

Next to the smell was the intense wall of heat rising from the same sky-high pile of sawdust. None of them had even recognized the wood residue at first. It had looked like a pile of white sand, or maybe dirt covered in snow. Ten minutes ago, Kimberly had gotten close enough to discern the truth. Fungus. The entire stinking, rotten pile was covered in some kind of fungus.

When Brian Knowles had guessed their water sample came from a site in crisis, he hadn't been kidding.

Now Mac leapt belatedly over one abandoned blade saw. He wove in and out of long, shed-style buildings with busted-out windows and sagging roof beams. The old conveyors still gleamed darkly in the shadows, complete with nasty-looking pikes used for skewering the wood as it was brought before the blade.

Litter covered the ground. Crumpled-up soda cans, discarded Styrofoam cups. Mac found a pile of old gasoline containers, probably used to fill up the handheld chain saws. He found another pile of old fluorescent lights. A faint popping sound was emitted from the debris field as some of the glass exploded from the heat of the sun.

He'd never seen anything like it. Strings of rusted barbed wire clawed at his legs. Abandoned saw blades lay hidden in the overgrown weeds, waiting to do far, far worse. This place was straight out of an environmentalist's nightmare. He was 100 percent sure their third girl had to be around here somewhere.

Kimberly came staggering around one of the broken-down sheds. She had tears streaming down her face from the stench. "Any luck?"

Mac shook his head.

She nodded and went careening on by, still looking for some hint of an underground cavern.

He came upon Nora Ray soon afterward. She'd stopped running around and was now standing in one place, her eyes closed, her hands spread by her sides.

"See anything?" he asked brusquely.

"No." She opened her eyes and seemed embarrassed to find him there. "I don't know . . . It's not like I'm a psychic or anything. I just have these dreams so I thought maybe if I closed my eyes . . ."

"Anything that works."

"But it's not working. Nothing's working. And that's so unbelievably frustrating. I mean, if she's in a cavern, well then, aren't we literally walking on top of her right now?"

"It's possible. Search-and-rescue isn't easy, Nora Ray. The Coast Guard passed back and forth over your spot five times before seeing your red shirt."

"I was lucky."

"You were smart. You hung in there. You kept trying."

"Do you think this girl is smart?"

"I don't know. But I'm willing to settle for lucky if that gets her home."

Nora Ray nodded. She resumed walking and Mac zigzagged through another abandoned building. Already past four o'clock. His heart was beating too fast, his face felt dangerously hot to the touch. They were pushing too hard for the conditions. Raising their core body temperatures to dangerous levels and going too long between drinks. This was no way to manage a rescue operation and yet he couldn't bring himself to stop.

Nora Ray was right; if the girl was in the cavern, they could literally be standing on top of her right now. So close, yet so far away.

Then, through the buzzing drone of the insects, he finally heard a welcome cry. It was Kimberly, somewhere off to the left.

"Hey, hey," she yelled. "I found something. Over here, quick!"

39

"Hello, hello? can you hear me?" Kimberly had found an eight-inch-wide duct sticking up through the ground like a section of stovepipe. She peered down the tube, trying to see where it led, but encountered only darkness. Next, she waved her hand over the top. Definitely a draft of cooler air coming up from somewhere. She tried dropping a small pebble. She never heard it land.

Mac was running over. Nora Ray as well. Kimberly leaned closer to the pipe, cupping her mouth to amplify her voice. "Is anyone down there?"

She lowered her ear to the mouth of the pipe. Did she hear movement? Sounds of something shifting way down in the dark, dank depths? It was hard to be sure.

"Hellooooooo!"

Mac finally drew up at her side. His hair was spiky with sweat, his shirt and shorts plastered to his skin. He dropped to his knees beside her and added his voice to the pipe.

"Is anyone down there? Karen Clarence? Tina Krahn? Are you in there?"

"She might be asleep," Kimberly murmured.

"Or unconscious."

"Are you sure that goes to the cavern?" Nora Ray asked.

Kimberly shrugged wearily. "As sure as I am about anything."

"But that can't be the entrance," Nora Ray said. "No one could fit down that hole."

"No, it can't be an entrance. Maybe it's an airhole, or a skylight. Someone at least took the time to engineer the pipe. That's gotta mean something."

"The cavern's big," Mac muttered. He tried the pebble trick and got the exact same results. "From the website it sounded as if it were several rooms connected by long tunnels, and some of the rooms are the size of small cathedrals. Maybe this pipe leads to one of those chambers, letting in some natural light."

"We need an entrance," Kimberly said.

"No kidding."

"I'll stay here and keep yelling. You and Nora Ray see if you can't find another opening. Maybe you'll hear my voice echoing through and that will help. Besides . . ." Kimberly faltered. "If one of the girls is down there, I don't want her to think we went away. I want her to know that we're coming. That it'll be over soon."

Mac nodded, giving her a look that was hard to read. He and Nora Ray resumed their frantic scouring of the woods. Kimberly got down on the dusty ground, placing her mouth next to the rusty pipe.

"This is Kimberly Quincy," she called. She wasn't sure what to say, so she started with the basics. "I'm with Special Agent Mac McCormack and Nora Ray Watts. We've come to help you. Can you hear me at all? I can't hear you. Maybe, if you're too weak to yell, you could try banging on something."

She waited. Nothing.

"Are you thirsty? We have water and food. We also have a blanket. I understand the caverns are cold, even this time of year. And boy, I bet you're sick to death of the dark."

She thought she heard something this time. She paused, holding her breath. A thud against the rocks? Or maybe a cold, frightened girl, trying to drag her body closer to the hole in the sky?

"A whole team is coming. Search-and-rescue specialists, karst specialists. They'll have all the proper gear to be able to get you out of there. And trust me, if you think it's cold down there, wait 'til you find out how hot it is up here. Must be a good hundred degrees in the shade. You'll be missing that cool hunk of rock in no time. But I bet you'll love seeing the sun again. And the trees and the sky and all the smiling faces of us rescue workers, who can't wait to meet you."

She was still talking. Rambling, really. Funny, her voice had grown thick.

"You don't need to be afraid. I know it's hard to be alone in the dark. But people are here now. We've been looking for you a long time. And we're going to go into the cavern, we're going to bring you back up to the light and then we're going to find the man who did this, so it never happens again."

Sounds now. Loud, startling noises like the crunch of gravel. Kimberly jerked her head up in excitement, then realized the noise wasn't coming from the stovepipe. Instead, she saw two dusty trucks pull in straight ahead. One had a sticker of a bat glued to the driver-side window.

A door banged open. A man sprang out, already running to the back, jerking down his tailgate, and tossing out gear.

"You the one that reported the lost caver?" the guy yelled over his shoulder. The second truck had already come to a halt and was now shedding two more men rushing for gear.

"Yes."

"Sorry for the delay. Would've been here sooner if not for that damn tree. What can you tell us of the missing caver?"

"We believe she's been abandoned in the cavern for at least forty-eight hours. She doesn't have proper gear, and was probably left with only a gallon of water."

The man drew up short. "Huh? You want to try that again?"

"She's not a caver," Kimberly said quietly. "She's just a girl, a victim of a violent crime."

"You're kiddin'?"

"No."

"Ah hell, I'm not sure I want to know anything more after that." The man turned to his two companions. "Bob, Ross, you catch that?"

"Girl, no gear, lost somewhere in the cavern. You don't want to know anything more." The two other men didn't even look at Kimberly. They were busy pulling on long johns in hundred-degree heat. Then they grabbed pairs of thick blue coveralls and jerked them on over the long underwear. Both men were sweating profusely. They didn't seem to notice.

"I'm Josh Shudt," the first guy said, coming over and belatedly shaking Kimberly's hand. "I wouldn't say I'm the leader of this group, but I'm probably as close as it gets. We have two others on the way, but given what you say, the three of us should probably head on in."

"Does this stovepipe go to the cave?"

"Yes, ma'am. It's a skylight in the main chamber right beneath your feet."

"I've been talking down it. I don't know if she can hear anything . . ."

"She probably appreciates that," Shudt said.

"Can I go with you?"

"You have any gear?"

"Just what I'm wearing."

"That's not gear. In a cave, it's fifty-five degrees every day of the year. Feels like a fucking refrigerator, and that's before you get into the water. To enter Orndorff's Cavern, we gotta descend forty feet by rope into knee-high water. Then we get to wiggle through thirty feet of watery tunnel that's 'bout twelve inches high. Good news is then we enter the main chamber, which has a forty-foot vault. Assuming, of course, we don't run into a rabid raccoon or a ring-necked snake."

"Snakes?" Kimberly asked weakly.

"Yes, ma'am. At least there are no bats. Orndorff's Cavern is dying, sad to say. And even if the bats had still found it an acceptable hibernaculum, this time of year they're out eating bugs. October through April, it's another story. Never a dull moment being a caver."

"I thought you guys were called spelunkers."

"No, ma'am. We're cavers. Cavers rescue spelunkers. So don't you worry. Just let us do our thing, and we'll find your missing person. She got a name?"

"Karen or Tina."

"She has two names?"

"We don't know which victim she is."

"Ah man, I really don't want to know more about your case. You do your thing. We'll do ours."

Shudt walked back to his pile of gear, snapping on his coveralls, while Mac and Nora Ray finally came running over. Everyone made curt introductions, then Mac, Kimberly, and Nora Ray were left standing awkwardly to the side while the three men finished suiting up, strapped on packs, then donned thick hiking boots and tough leather gloves.

They had piles of brightly colored rope among them. In deft movements they coiled up the various heavy-duty lengths, then looped them over their shoulders. They seemed to be down to final adjustments then, testing out multiple light sources, adjusting their hard hats. Finally Shudt grunted approval at each man's gear, returned to the back of his truck, and pulled out a long backboard.

For transporting the victim out of the cave. In case she couldn't walk on her own. Or in case she was dead.

Shudt looked over at Mac. "We could use a spotter to help man the ropes up top. Ever worked with a belay?"

"I've done some rock climbing."

"Then you're our man. Let's go."

Shudt turned one last time toward Kimberly.

"Keep talking down the pipe," he told her quietly. "You never know."

The men turned and walked into the woods. Kimberly sank back down to the ground. Nora Ray joined her in the dust.

"What do we say?" the girl murmured.

"What did you want to hear most?"

"That it was going to end. That I was going to be okay."

Kimberly thought about it a moment. Then she cupped her hands and leaned over the pipe. "Karen? Tina? This is Kimberly Quincy again. The search-and-rescue workers are on their way. Do you hear me? The tough part is over. Soon, we'll have you home to your family again. Soon, you'll be safe."

Tina had gouged as much as she could gouge. She had started at knee level, digging holes up as far as she could reach. Then, as an experiment, she'd crammed her muddy toes into the first two rough holes, gripped other ragged edges with her hands, and climbed up a whole two feet.

Her legs shook violently. She felt at once light as a feather and as heavy as an anchor. She would rocket to the top like a human spider. She would plummet to the ground and never get up again.

"Come on," she whispered through her parched, cracked lips. And then she started to climb.

Three feet up. Her arms now shook as violently as her legs and her stomach contracted with a painful cramp. She rested her head against the blanket of dense green vines, prayed not to throw up, and resumed climbing again.

Up toward the sun. Light as a feather. Be like Spiderman.

Six feet up, she came to an exhausted halt. No more handholds and she still didn't trust the vines. Awkwardly, she tried to support herself with her feet, straining up on her tiptoes as she reached above her head with her right hand and blindly dug in her nail file. The ancient wood crumbled beneath the fumbling metal and gave her fresh courage. She gouged wildly, already envisioning herself at the top.

Maybe she'd find a lake on the surface. A vast blue oasis. She would plunge in headfirst. She would float on tranquil waves. She would dive low, letting the water wash the mud from her hair. And then she would swim to the cool depths in the middle of her fantasy lake, and drink until her belly swelled like a balloon.

Then when she reached the other side, she would be greeted by a tuxe-doed waiter, bearing a silver platter piled with fluffy white towels.

She giggled out loud. Delirium didn't bother her so much anymore. It seemed the only chance of happiness she would get.

Wood rained down on her head. She was reminded of her task by the sudden, fierce pain in her overexerted arms. She explored the hole she'd made with her fingertips. She could curl her fingers into the rough opening. Time to move again. How did the old TV theme song go? Had to keep moving on up, to the top, where she would finally get a piece of the pie.

She painfully pulled her body up another step, her butt sticking out precariously, her arms shaking violently from her efforts. She moved four more excruciating inches. And then once more she was stuck.

Time for another hole. Her left arm ached too badly to bear her weight. She switched to hanging on with her right hand, while digging at the wood with her left. The motion felt awkward. She had no idea if she was working one spot, or carelessly ripping up the whole board. Too hard to look.

She clung to the wall with her trembly legs and worn-out arms. Soon she had the next hole done and it was time for another step. She made the mistake of looking up then, and almost wept.

The sky. So high above her. What, a good ten to fifteen feet? Her legs already ached, her arms burned. She didn't know how much longer she could do this and she had only made it eight feet. She had spidey hands and spidey feet, but she did not have spidey strength.

She just wanted her lake. She wanted to swim through those cool waves. She wanted to step out the other side and fall into her mother's arms, where she would weep piteously and apologize for anything she'd ever done.

God give her strength to climb this wall. God give her courage. Because her mother needed her and her baby needed her and, please God, she did not want to die like a rat in a trap. She did not want to die all alone.

One more hole, she told herself. Climb up, dig one more hole, and then you can return to the muck to rest.

So she made it one more hole. And then she made it another. And then she promised herself, through her labored breathing, that she just needed to do one more. Which turned into two more, then three more, until finally, she had gone ten or twelve feet up the wall.

And it was scary now. Definitely no looking down. Had to just keep pushing up, even if her shoulders felt curiously elastic, as if the joints had pulled apart and now dangled loosely. And she swayed sometimes, having to catch herself with her fingers which made her shoulders shriek and her arms burn and she cried out in pain, though her throat was so dry it came out more like a chirpy croak, a sandpaper sound of protest.

Moving on up. To the top. Gonna finally get a piece of the pie.

She was weeping with no tears. She was clinging desperately to rotted timber and fragile vines and trying hard not to think of what she was doing. She hurt beyond pain. She pushed herself beyond endurance.

She pictured her mother. She pictured her baby and she pushed and she pushed and she pushed.

Fifteen feet up. The top ledge so close she could finally see an overhang of bushy grass. Surface vegetation. Her parched mouth watered at the thought.

She stared too long. Forgot what she was doing. And her exhausted, dehydrated body finally gave out. Her hand reached up. Her fingers failed to connect.

And then she went backwards.

For a moment, she felt herself suspended in midair. She could see her arms and legs churning, like one of those silly cartoon creatures. Then reality reasserted itself. Gravity took over.

Tina plummeted down into the muck.

No scream this time. The mud swallowed her whole and after all these days, she did not protest.

Kimberly was still talking forty-five minutes later. She talked of water and food and warm sun. She talked of the weather and the baseball season and the birds in the sky. She talked of old friends and new friends and won't it be nice to meet in person?

She talked of holding on. She talked of never giving up. She talked of miracles and how they could happen if you willed them hard enough.

Then Mac came out of the woods. She took one look at his face and stopped talking.

Seventeen minutes later, they brought the body up.

40

Lee County, Virginia
7:53 P.M.
Temperature: 98 degrees

The sun started to descend, surfing bright orange waves of heat. Shadows grew longer, while it remained stifling hot. And in the abandoned sawmill, vehicles started to pile up.

First came more members of the cavers' search-and-rescue team. They finished hauling out the lifeless body of a young girl with short-cropped brown hair. Her yellow-flowered slip dress had been reduced to tatters by the acidic water. The fingernails on both of her hands were broken and ragged, as if at some point she'd clawed frantically at the hard dolomite walls.

The rest of her was blue and bloated; Josh Shudt and his men had found her body floating in the long tunnel that connected the cavern's sinkhole entrance to the main chamber. They'd pushed through to the cathedral room after pulling out her body. There, on a ledge, they'd found an empty gallon jug of water and a purse.

According to her driver's license, the victim's name was Karen Clarence, and just one week ago she had turned twenty-one.

It didn't take much to fill in the rest. The UNSUB had delivered the victim, most likely drugged and unconscious, to the main chamber. The stovepipe skylight forty feet above would've offered precious little light when the girl awoke. Enough to realize she had a shallow pond of relatively safe rainwater to her left and a stream of highly polluted, toxic water to her right. Maybe she stayed on the ledge for a while. Maybe she tried the small pond and promptly got bitten by its already stressed inhabitants—the white, eyeless crayfish, or the tiny, rice-sized isopods. Maybe she even encountered a ring-necked snake.

Either way, the girl had probably ended up wet. And once you got wet in an environment that's constantly fifty-five degrees, hypothermia's only a matter of time.

Shudt told them all a story of a caver who'd lasted two weeks lost in five miles of winding underground caverns. Of course, he'd been wearing proper gear and had a pack full of protein bars. He'd also been lost in a healthy cavern, where the water was not only safe to drink, but according to local lore, brought the drinker good luck.

Karen Clarence hadn't been so lucky. She'd managed not to brain her skull on a thick stalactite. She'd managed not to bruise a knee or sprain a wrist crawling in the dark amid the stalagmites. But at some point, she'd headed straight into the polluted stream. Water that acidic must have burned her skin, just as it promptly ate holes in her dress. Was she beyond caring at that point? Had the cold set in so deep, the burning liquid felt good against her flesh? Or had she simply been that determined? She would die sitting on the ledge. The shallow pond led nowhere. That left only the stream to guide her back to civilization.

Either way, she immersed herself in the stream, her clothes eroding, her face streaming with tears. She had followed the stream to the narrow tunnel. She had pushed her head and shoulders into that long, skinny space. And then she had died in the darkness there.

Ray Lee Chee showed up shortly after seven. With him came Brian Knowles, Lloyd Armitage, and Kathy Levine. They unloaded two Jeep Cherokees filled with field equipment, camping packs, and bins of books. Their mood in the beginning was giddy, bordering on festive. Then they saw the body.

They put down their field kits. They held a moment of silence for a girl they'd never met. Then, they got to work.

Thirty minutes later Rainie and Quincy arrived, bearing Ennunzio in tow. Nora Ray left the camp shortly thereafter. And Kimberly followed suit.

The nature experts had the clues. The law enforcement professionals had the body. She wasn't sure what was left for her to do.

She found Nora Ray sitting on a tree stump deeper in the woods. A fern sprouted green shoots nearby and Nora Ray was running her hands through the fronds.

"Long day," Kimberly said. She leaned against a nearby tree trunk.

"It's not over yet," Nora Ray said.

Kimberly smiled thinly. She'd forgotten—this girl was good. "Holding up?"

Nora Ray shrugged. "I guess. I've never seen a dead person before. I thought I would be more upset. But mostly I'm just . . . tired."

"It has the same effect on me."

Nora Ray finally looked up at her. "Why are you here?"

"In the woods? Anything's better than the sun."

"No. On this case, working with Special Agent McCormack. He said you were illegal, or something like that. Did you . . . Are you?"

"Oh. You mean, am I a relative of one of the victims?"

Nora Ray nodded soberly.

"No. Not this time." Kimberly slid down the tree trunk. The dirt felt cooler against her legs. It made it easier to talk. "Until two days ago, actually, I was a new agent at the FBI Academy. I was seven weeks from graduation, and while my supervisors will tell you I have trouble with authority figures, I think I would've made it in the end. I think I would've graduated."

"What happened?"

"I went for a run in the woods and I found a dead body. Betsy Radison. She was the one driving that night."

"She was the first?"

Kimberly nodded.

"And now we're finding her friends."

"One by one," Kimberly whispered softly.

"It doesn't seem fair."

"No, it's not meant to be fair. It's meant to be about one man. And our job is to catch him."

They both drifted off to silence again. There wasn't much sound in the woods. A faint breeze crinkling the damp, heavy trees. The distant rustle of a squirrel or bird, foraging in a pile of dead leaves.

"My parents must be worried by now," Nora Ray said abruptly. "My mom . . . Ever since what happened to my sister, she doesn't like me to be away for more than an hour. I'm supposed to check in by phone every thirty minutes. Then she can yell at me to come home."

"Parents aren't meant to outlive their children."

"And yet it happens all the time. Like you said, life isn't fair." Nora Ray jerked impatiently on the fern frond. "I'm twenty-one years old, you know. Frankly, I should be back at college. I should be planning a career, going on dates, drinking too hard some nights and studying diligently on others. I should be doing smart things and stupid things and all sorts of things to figure out my own life. Instead . . . My sister died, and my life went with her. No one in my house does anything anymore. We just . . . exist."

"Three years isn't that long. Maybe your family needs longer to make it through the stages of grief."

"Make it through?" Nora Ray's voice was incredulous. "We're not making it through. We haven't even started the process. Everything's stagnant. It's like my life has been cut in half. There's everything that was before that one night—college classes and a boyfriend and an upcoming party—and now there is everything after. Except *after* doesn't have any content. *After* is still an empty slate."

"You have your dreams," Kimberly said quietly.

Nora Ray immediately appeared troubled. "You think I'm making them up."

"No. I'm absolutely sure you dream of your sister. But some hold that dreams are the unconscious's way of working things out. If you're still dreaming of your sister, then maybe your unconscious has something to work out. Maybe your parents aren't the only ones who aren't over her yet."

"I don't like this conversation very much," Nora Ray said.

Kimberly merely shrugged. Nora Ray narrowed her eyes.

"What are you? Some kind of shrink?"

"I've studied psychology, but I'm not a shrink."

"So you've studied psychobabble and you've attended half of the FBI Academy. What does that make you?"

"Someone who also lost her sister. And her mother, too, for that matter." Kimberly smiled crookedly in the failing light. "Trump. In the contest of who has gotten dumped on more by life, I believe I just won."

Nora Ray had the good grace to appear ashamed. Her hand was back on the fern. Now she methodically picked off its fronds. "What happened?"

"Same old story. Bad man believes my father, an FBI profiler, ruined his life. Bad man decides to seek revenge by destroying my father's family. Bad man targets my older sister first—she is troubled and has never been a great judge of character. He kills her and makes it look like an accident. Then he uses everything she has told him to befriend my mother. Except my mother is smarter than he thinks. In the end, there is nothing accidental about her death. The blood spray goes on for seven rooms. Finally, bad man goes after me. Except my father gets him first. And now I've spent the last six years much like you—trying to figure out how to go on merrily living a life that's already been touched by too much death."

"Is that why you joined the FBI? So you could help others?"

"No. I joined the FBI so I could be heavily armed, and also help others."

Nora Ray nodded as if that made perfect sense. "And now you're going to catch the man who killed my sister. That's good. The FBI is lucky to have you."

"The FBI doesn't have me anymore."

"But you said you were halfway through training . . ."

"I took a personal leave to pursue this case, Nora Ray. The FBI Academy is not fond of that sort of thing. I'm not sure I'll ever be allowed back."

"I don't understand. You're going after a killer, you're trying to save people's lives. What more can they want from an agent?"

"Objectivity, professionalism, a clear understanding of the big picture, and an ability to make tough decisions. When I left the Academy, I did it to help one life. Staying, on the other hand, and completing my training, would have given me the opportunity to save hundreds. My supervisors are tiresome at times, but they aren't stupid."

"Then why did you do it?"

"Because Betsy Radison looked just like my sister, Mandy."

"Oh," Nora Ray said quietly.

"Oh," Kimberly agreed. She leaned her head back against the rough bark of the tree and sighed deeply. It felt better than she would've thought to say the words out loud. It felt good to finally confront the truth.

She had lied to Mac when she'd told him this wasn't about her family. She had lied to her father when she had told him she could handle things. But mostly, she had lied to herself. Young, passionate Kimberly, fighting valiantly for the underdog in a jurisdiction-mad case gone wrong. It sounded so good, but in fact, her decision to help Mac had had nothing to do with Betsy Radison, or the Eco-Killer or even her supervisor Mark Watson. All along, it had been about herself. Six years of grieving and growing and telling herself she was doing just fine, and all it had taken was one victim who looked slightly like Mandy for her to throw it all away. Her career, her dreams, her future. She hadn't even put up much of a fight.

Betsy Radison had died, and Kimberly had run back to the heavy burden of her past as if it were the ultimate comfort food. Why not? As long as she kept obsessing about her family's death, she'd never have to face the future. As long as she kept dwelling on her mother and Mandy, she would never have to define Kimberly. She had wondered what her life would've been like if her mother and sister had never died. In truth, her life could still be about whatever she wanted it to be. If she was that strong. If she was that smart. Maybe she could even fall in love. You never knew.

"What happens now?" Nora Ray asked softly.

"Short-term now, or long-term now?"

"Short-term now."

"Ray and the team from the USGS figure out the clues left with this victim. Then we try to find the fourth girl. And then we try to find the Eco-Killer and light up his ass."

Nora Ray nodded with satisfaction. "And long-term now?"

"Long-term now, you and I finally realize that none of it has made a difference. Your sister is still dead, my family is still gone, and we still have to get on with the rest of our lives. So we start seriously wading through the grief and seriously wading through the guilt and see if we can't make something out of this mess. Or we do nothing at all, and let a couple of killers take what little we have left."

"I don't like long-term now very much," Nora Ray said.

"I know," Kimberly said. "I'm a little worried about it myself."

41

The bats came out. In the inky hues of fading daylight, they glided gracefully among the trees, dive-bombing clusters of fireflies and scattering the flickering lights. The humidity was still unbearable, but with the sun low in the sky and the bats feasting silently overhead, dusk took on a peaceful, almost soothing feel.

When Kimberly was younger, she and her sister had loved to catch fireflies. They would run around their back lawn with Mason jars, trying desperately to capture the shooting darts of lights. Mandy had been horrible at it, but Kimberly had gotten pretty good. They'd sit around the patio table, trying to feed the fireflies stalks of fresh-cut grass or tender stems of dandelions. Then they'd let the flies go again; their mother didn't allow bugs in the house.

Now Kimberly sat in the circle they had formed around a Coleman lantern, her knee brushing Mac's, while Rainie and Quincy talked of contacting the local coroner. Ennunzio and Nora Ray sat across from Kimberly. Ray and his team remained off to one side, still working the body.

"We've done the best we can," Quincy was saying. "Now we need to notify the official case team."

"It'll only piss them off," Mac said.

"Why? Because we've moved the body, destroyed chain of custody for the evidence, and made the crime scene perfectly useless for basic investigative procedures?" Quincy regarded the younger man drolly. "Yes, I'm sure they will have a few thoughts on the subject."

"Saving a life always takes priority over preserving a scene," Mac insisted stubbornly.

"I'm not questioning what we did," Quincy said. "I'm simply trying to bring us back to reality. We found the body, we brought in professionals to analyze the clues, and now we need to start thinking about what should happen next. I certainly hope none of you is suggesting that we return the body to the cavern. Or worse, leave it unattended."

Everyone shifted uncomfortably. Quincy was right; none of them had thought that far ahead.

"You contact the official case team, and we'll spend the rest of the night in jail," Kimberly pointed out. "Which pretty much defeats the purpose of coming here in the first place."

"Agreed. I was thinking you and Mac should continue. Rainie and I will wait here for the proper authorities. Sooner or later, someone must face the music." His gaze rested on Rainie's face.

"If it's all the same," Ennunzio said, "I'd like to continue on with the others. I want to be around if Special Agent McCormack gets another call."

Mac glanced at the cell phone clipped to his waist and grimaced. "Fat chance, with the signal strength around here."

"As we get closer to civilization, however . . ."

"I'm going, too." Nora Ray was regarding Ennunzio steadily, as if daring the FBI agent to deny her.

"This is outside your responsibility," Quincy said. "In all honesty, Ms. Watts, the biggest help you could give this team right now is to go home. Your parents must be worried."

"My parents are worried even when I am home. No. I can help and I'm going to stay."

The tone of her voice was set and none of them had the energy left to argue. Instead, Kimberly turned to Ennunzio, regarding him curiously. "How did you know about this cave? I understand from Josh Shudt that Orndorff's Cavern isn't exactly a common cave for exploration."

"Not after what the mill did to it," Ennunzio said, "but twenty, thirty years ago, it used to be beautiful." He shrugged. "I grew up in this area. Spent my free time running wild among these mountains and caverns. It's been a long time now, but I like to think it'll come back to me. And maybe the little bits and pieces I remember can be of help. I hardly know the whole state, but I know this one corner of Virginia fairly well."

"Do you have any idea where he might have placed the fourth victim?" Quincy spoke up quietly, his eyes on Mac.

The special agent rolled out his shoulders, contemplating the question. "Let's see . . . he's done a Marine base, a national forest, and an underground cavern. So what do we have left? Chesapeake Bay rates high on the geological interest scale. I read about scuba diving in some reservoirs formed by flooding old mining towns—that's gotta float his boat. Then there are a variety of rivers—last time he liked the Savannah."

"There are two more major mountain ranges," Ennunzio considered, but Mac shook his head.

"He's done forests. He'll go for something different."

"What about the coastline?" Nora Ray asked. She was still staring at Ennunzio.

"Beaches around here are more populated than the Georgia coastline," Mac said. "It's possible, but I think he'll look for someplace more remote. We can check with Ray."

He waved his hand, and after a moment, the USGS man came over. Ray's face was pale and covered with a fine sheen of sweat. Now that he'd seen an actual body, working a murder case had clearly lost some of its appeal.

"Any luck?" Mac asked him.

"Some. It's hard to know what to look for on the girl . . . body . . . victim.

Body." He seemed to decide. "It, um, it was in the water for a bit, and who knows what that washed away. Kathy found some kind of crumpled leaf in a dress pocket. She's trying to extract it now without doing more damage; tissue tears easily when this wet. Also, Josh Shudt went in and checked the ledge for us. Lloyd's now working on some soil samples he took from the girl's . . . body's shoes. I'm trying to go through her purse, since you said he sometimes puts things there."

"Have you tried the back of the throat?"

"Nothing."

"I wonder about her stomach," Mac murmured. "With the first victim, the map, he was very inventive. I'm not sure how he would consider these next ones in line. Maybe we should consider cutting her open."

Nora Ray got up abruptly and moved away from the lantern light. Mac watched her go, but didn't apologize.

Ray Lee Chee had turned green. "You didn't, uh . . . you didn't mention anything like that before."

"We need the coroner," Quincy said.

"You can't ask a geologist to serve as ME," Rainie seconded.

"Oh good," Ray said. " 'Cause I think I'm gonna barf." He didn't though. He just turned in a dazed little circle, then returned to them even paler, but with his expression set. "Look, we've done about as much as we can here. Best bet is to find a hotel, hole up for a few hours with our equipment, and see what we can figure out. I know you're in a hurry, but if we gotta guarantee that we're not sending you off on a wild-goose chase, then we need a shot at doing this right."

"You're the boss," Mac said. "Pack up if that's what you'd like. Rainie and Quincy are going to remain here with the body. The rest of us will follow you."

Ray nodded gratefully, then returned to his team.

There didn't seem much more to say, or much more to do.

Quincy was looking up at the sky. "One more girl to go," he murmured. "And it's already dark."

Tina woke up to the sound of someone's whimper. It took her a moment to realize it was her own.

The world was black, refusing to come into focus. She almost panicked. Her eyes had swollen shut again or worse, she'd gone blind. Then she realized the black wasn't pitch black, but only the deep, purple shadows of night.

Hours had passed with her lying in the mud. Now she lifted one arm and attempted to move. Her whole body groaned. She could feel muscles tremble with effort. Her left hip ached, her ribs throbbed. For a moment, she didn't think anything was going to happen, then she finally rolled over in the mud. She got her arms beneath her for leverage, pushed up weakly, and staggered to her feet.

The world promptly spun. She staggered over to the pit wall, dragging her feet through the heavy muck and grasping desperately at the vines for support. She leaned too far left, then lurched too far right, then finally got her hands planted against the wall. Her stomach rolled and cramped. She bent in agony and tried not to think about what must be happening now.

She cried. She cried all alone in her pit, and it was all that she could do.

Things came back to her in bits and pieces. Her glorious attempt at being a human spider. Her not-so-glorious fall. She lifted her arms again. Tried out her legs and inspected for damage. Technically speaking at least, she was still in one piece.

She tried to take a step. Her right leg buckled and she immediately sank back into the mud. Gritting her teeth, she tried again, only to get the same results. Her legs were too weak. Her body had simply had enough.

So she lay with her head in the cool, soothing muck. She watched the slime ooze and pop inches from her face. And she decided maybe dying wouldn't be so bad after all.

If she could just get water . . . Her mouth, her throat, her shriveled stomach. Her parched, festering skin.

She stared at the mud a minute longer, then she staggered up onto her hands and knees.

She shouldn't . . . It would kill her. But did that matter anymore?

Spreading her fingers, she flattened them into the muck. The small indent instantly filled with putrid, stinking water.

Tina put down her head and drank like a dog.

42

Wytheville, Virginia
10:04 P.M.
Temperature: 94 degrees

Kimberly checked them into the tiny, roadside motel. Ray and his team got their rooms. Kimberly booked another for Nora Ray, plus one for Dr. Ennunzio. Then she reserved one room for her and Mac to share.

She couldn't meet his eyes when she returned to the car. She distributed keys, deliberately omitting him, which earned her a curious glance. Then she was busy unloading bags from the trunk. They needed a game plan. Ray would ring Mac or Kimberly's room when the team had a theory. They, in turn, would rouse the others. In the meantime, Mac had his cell phone on and seemed to be receiving a faint signal. Kimberly also turned hers on, in case her father needed her.

Nothing left to do now but grab a shower and snatch a few hours' sleep. Soon enough, they would all be up again.

Kimberly watched Nora Ray disappear behind the plain white door of the single-story structure. Then she watched as Dr. Ennunzio crossed the parking lot to his wing of the motel. She waited until he was gone from view before finally turning toward Mac.

"Here," she said. "I got us a room."

If he was surprised, he didn't say anything. He simply took the key from her trembling hand. Then he picked up their bags and carried them through the doorway.

Inside she almost lost her courage again. The room was too beige, too generic, too worn. It could've been any room in any motel in any part of the country, and for some reason that nearly broke her heart. Just once she wanted something more out of life than desperate attempts at happiness. They should go to a bed-and-breakfast. One of those places with rose-patterned wallpaper and red quilted comforters and a giant four-poster bed. Where you could sink deep into the mattress and sleep well past noon and forget the real world ever existed.

They didn't have that kind of luxury. She supposed she wouldn't have known what to do with it if she had.

Mac set their bags down at the foot of the bed. "Why don't you shower first," he suggested quietly. She nodded and disappeared gratefully into the solitude of the tiny bath.

She showered. First, hot and steamy to relax her tired muscles, then cool and crisp to eradicate all memories of the heat. She didn't cry this time. She didn't stand there with haunted images of her mother or sister. The worst of her grief had passed, and in some ways, she felt the most composed she'd been in weeks.

They had tried again. They had failed again. And soon, maybe in a day, maybe in an hour, they would try yet again. That's the way life worked. She could either quit now, or forge ahead, and for whatever reason, she wasn't the quitting type. So that was it, then. She had chosen her path. She would keep trying, and keep trying, even if some days it broke her heart.

She took her time drying off. She searched her small toiletry bag for the bottle of perfume she didn't own. She wondered if she should do something with her hair, or put makeup on her wan face. She wished she possessed even a bottle of lotion to smooth over her sun-battered skin.

But she wasn't that kind of girl. She didn't travel with those kinds of things.

She walked back into the bedroom with a threadbare white towel wrapped self-consciously around her breasts. Mac still didn't say anything. He merely grabbed his shaving kit and disappeared into the bathroom.

She put on a plain gray FBI T-shirt and waited as he showered.

It was pitch black outside now. Still hot, she imagined. Was that easier on a missing person than being someplace cold and dark? Or by now, was the girl delirious with her need for something cool and soothing against her overheated skin? It must seem like a ridiculous joke for the air to remain so hot, long after the sun had retreated from the sky.

Nora Ray had survived out there. She'd protected herself from the sun; she'd found a way to keep cool as endless day slipped into day. How small she must have felt, as she dug deeper into the marsh and waited for someone to find her in the vast line of a coastal horizon. She'd never given up hope, however. She'd never succumbed to panic. And in the end, she'd survived.

Only to lose sight of the victory in her grief for her sister. She had won the battle, then lost the war. It was such an easy thing to do.

The shower shut off. Kimberly heard the rake of metal as the shower curtain was pulled back. Her breathing grew uneven. She took a seat in the broken-down chair next to the TV. Her hands trembled on her thighs.

The sound of running water in the sink. A toothbrush sudsing across teeth. Now some fresh splashes. He was probably shaving.

Kimberly got up, paced the room. She had had final exams easier than this. She had held her first loaded firearm with less trepidation. Oh, how could this be so hard?

Then the door opened. Mac was standing there, freshly showered, freshly shaven, with just a towel wrapped around his lean, tanned waist.

"Hey, beautiful," he said softly. "Come here often?"

She crossed to him, placed her hands on his bare shoulders and it wasn't so difficult after all.

Nora Ray didn't sleep. Alone at last in the motel room, she plopped down in an old chair and contemplated her traveling bag. She knew what she needed to do. Funny, now that the moment was at hand, she was stalling. She was nervous.

She hadn't thought it would feel like this. She'd expected to be stronger, more triumphant. Instead, she was terrified.

She got up out of the chair, idly inspecting the room. The lumpy double bed. The cheap TV cabinet, covered in fresh nicks and ancient water rings. The TV itself, so old and small no one would even consider it worth stealing. She counted the cigarette burns in the carpet.

Three years was such a long time. She could be wrong, but she didn't think so. You didn't forget your last moments with your sister. Nor one man's voice saying, "You need some help, ladies?"

So now here she was. And now here he was. What was she going to do?

She crossed to her bag, unzipped the canvas top, reached in and pulled out the plastic Ziploc bag that passed as her toiletry kit. She hadn't lied to Mac. There wasn't much a young girl could get past airport security.

But there was something. In fact, she had learned it straight from him.

She pulled out the bottle of eyedrops. Then from the inside of her hiking boot, she found the long needle slipped between the sides of the rubber sole. It took her only a moment longer to retrieve the plastic syringe from her bottle of shampoo.

She assembled the needle first. And then, very carefully, she squeezed out the liquid from the bottle of Visine. Once the tiny bottle had contained genuine eyedrops, but she had replaced the contents just last week.

Now, it held ketamine. Fast acting. Powerful, and in the proper dosage, quite deadly.

The man was dreaming. He thrashed from side to side. Waved his hands and kicked his feet. He hated this dream, fought to bring himself back to waking. But the dream memory was stronger, sucking him back into the abyss.

He was at a funeral. The sun burned starkly overhead, an unbearably hot day in an unbearably hot graveyard, while the priest droned on and on at a service no one else had bothered to attend. His mother gripped his hand too tightly. Her only black dress—long-sleeved and woolen—was too heavy for this weather. She rocked from side to side, panting pitifully, while he and his younger brother fought to keep her standing.

It was finally done. The priest shut up. The coffin sank down. The sweaty gravedigger moved in, looking relieved to get his task under way.

They went home, and the man was grateful.

He used the last of the coal to light their oven when they returned to the cabin. The air was too stuffy for the heat, but without electricity, it was the only way to get supper on the table. Tomorrow he'd have to find wood to feed the stove. And tomorrow after that, he'd have to think of something else. That was okay. This was now, and he just wanted to get food on the table and see some color in his mother's cheeks.

His brother was waiting with a saucepan to heat broth.

They fed their mother wordlessly. Didn't take a drop for themselves, but spooned beef bouillon past her bloodless lips, while tearing up chunks of stale bread. Finally she sighed, and he thought the worst had passed.

"He's gone, Mama," he heard himself say. "Things will be better now. You'll see."

And then her bloodless face came up. Her lifeless eyes turned vibrant, snapping blue, and her cheeks filled with a color that was frightening to behold.

"Better? *Better?* You ungrateful little bastard! He put a roof over your head, he put food on the table. And what did he ever ask for in return? A little respect from his wife and kids? Was that too much, Frank? Was that really too goddamn much?"

"No, Mama," he tried to say, already frantically backing up from the table. His nervous gaze darted to his equally nervous brother. They had never seen her like this.

She rose from the table, too pale, too thin, too bony, and stalked her older son across the room.

"We have no food!"

"I know, Mama—"

"We have no money!"

"I know, Mama—"

"We will lose this house."

"No, Mama!"

But she would not be placated; closer she came and closer. And now he had backed up all the way across the room, his shoulders pressed against the wall.

"You are a bad boy, you are a filthy boy, you are a rotten, ungrateful, selfish little boy. What did I ever do to deserve a boy as bad as you!"

His brother was weeping. The broth grew cold on the table. And the manchild realized now that there truly was no escape. His father had gone. A new monster had already arisen to take his place.

The boy lowered his hands. He exposed his face. The first blow didn't even feel that bad, nothing like his father's. But his mother learned very quickly.

And he did nothing. He kept his hands at his sides. He let his mother beat him. Then he slid down, down, down to the hot, dusty floor while his mother went to get his father's belt.

"Run away," he told his brother. "Run now, while you still can."

But his brother was too terrified to move. And his mother was back soon enough, snapping the strip of leather through the air, and already getting a feel for its cutting hiss.

The man woke up harshly. His breathing was ragged, his eyes were wild. Where was he? What had happened? For a moment, he thought the black void had taken over completely. Then he got his bearings.

He was standing in the middle of a room. And in his hands, he held a box of matches, the first match already clutched between his fingers . . .

The man gently laid the matches back on the table. Then he quickly stepped away, grabbing at his head and trying to tell himself he wasn't yet insane.

He needed aspirin. He needed water, he needed something far more potent than that. Not yet, not yet, no time. His fingers clawed his rough-shaven cheeks, sinking into his temples as if through sheer force of will he could keep his skull from shattering apart.

He had to hold it together. Not much longer. Not much more time.

Helplessly, he found himself staring at the matches again. And then he knew what he must do. He retrieved the box from the table. He held the precious sticks in the palm of his hand, and he thought of things he had not thought of in a long, long time.

He thought of fire. He thought that all things of beauty must die. And then he allowed himself to remember that day in the cabin, and what had happened next.

43

Lee County, Virginia
1:24 A.M.
Temperature: 94 degrees

"This is the most irresponsible handling of a case I've ever seen in my life. It's inappropriate and, frankly, it's goddamn criminal! We lose this man, Quincy, and I swear to God I will spend the next two years making your life a living hell. I want you off this property as fast as you can drive. And don't bother heading back to Quantico. I know about your little chats with Special Agents Kaplan and Ennunzio. So much as step one foot onto Academy grounds, and I'll have you arrested at the gate. Your work on this case is over. As far as I'm concerned, your whole fucking career is over. Now get out of my sight."

Special Agent Harkoos finally wrapped up his tirade and stormed away. His navy-blue blazer hung limply in the heavy heat. His face, covered in sweat before he'd started yelling, was dripping. In other words, he looked about the same as the other FBI agents now swarming the abandoned sawmill.

"I don't think he likes you much," Rainie said to Quincy.

He turned toward her. "Be honest with me. Do I look that ridiculous in a navy blue suit?"

"Most of the time."

"Huh. The things you learn thirty years too late."

They started walking toward their car. Their light tones fooled neither of them. Harkoos's dressing-down had been thorough and honest. They were fired from the case, banned from the Academy, and once word of this disaster spread, probably finished as consultants in the tight, incestuous world of high-profile law enforcement investigations. Reputations were built in a lifetime, but ruined in only a matter of minutes.

Quincy had a hollow, sick feeling in his stomach, one he hadn't had in ages.

"When we catch the Eco-Killer, they'll quickly forget about this," Rainie offered.

"Perhaps."

"Irresponsible is only irresponsible if you fail. Succeed, however, and irresponsible quickly becomes merely unorthodox."

"True."

"Quincy, those guys had the same body and same evidence we did last night, and they weren't even in the area when you gave them a call. Frankly, if we hadn't gone off the deep end, that girl would still be floating in a cavern, and the fourth victim would be no closer to discovery. Harkoos is just mad because you beat him to the punch. There's nothing more embarrassing than being upstaged, especially by a bunch of outsiders."

Quincy stopped walking. "I'm sick of this," he said abruptly.

"Politics is never fun."

"No! I don't mean this damn case. Fuck this case. You're absolutely right. Failure today, hero tomorrow. It's always changing and none of it means a thing."

Rainie had stopped moving completely. He could see her pale face in the thin moonlight. He rarely swore, and the fact that he was driven to it now had her both fascinated and frightened.

"I don't want things to be like this between us, Rainie."

Her expression faltered. She looked down at the ground. "I know."

"You are the best thing that ever happened to me, and if I don't tell you that enough, then I am a total idiot."

"You're not a total idiot."

"I don't know about kids. I'll be honest: the very thought scares me to death. I was not a great father, Rainie. I'm still not a great father. But I am willing to talk about it. If this is what you really, truly want, then I can at least explore the notion."

"I want."

"All right, then you have to be honest with me. Is it only kids you want? Because I tried . . . I thought . . . Rainie, each time I've asked you to marry me, why have you never said yes?"

Her eyes filled with tears. "Because I thought you'd never stop asking. You're not the idiot, Quincy. It's me."

He felt the world spin again. He had thought . . . Had been so sure . . . "Does that mean . . ."

"You think you're scared of kids? Hell, Quince, I'm scared of everything. I'm scared of commitment and I'm scared of responsibility. I'm afraid I'll disappoint you and I'm afraid one day I'll physically harm my child. We all get a little older, but we never completely outgrow our past. And mine is looming behind me now, this big giant shadow I want so desperately to leave behind."

"Oh, Rainie . . ."

"I tell myself to be happy with what I've got. You, me, this is a good gig, better than anything I thought I'd have. And we do important work and meet important people, and hey, that's not bad for a woman who used to be a human punching bag. But . . . but I get so restless now. Maybe happiness is like a drug. You get a little, then you want a lot. I don't know, Quincy. I want so badly not to want so much, but I think I can't help it anymore. I want more you. I want more me. I want . . . kids and white picket fences and maybe tea cozies, except I'm not sure I know what a tea cozy is. Maybe you're frightened. But I'm pretty sure I've lost my mind."

"Rainie, you are the strongest, bravest woman I know."

"Oh, you're just saying that so I don't whoop your ass."

She kicked at the ground in disgust, and Quincy finally smiled. It amazed him how much better he already felt. The world had righted. His hands had steadied. It was as if a crushing weight he didn't even know he'd been carrying had suddenly been lifted off his chest.

This was not the time, he knew. This was not the place. But then he'd spent too much of his life waiting for perfect moments that had never come. And he knew better than most how fleeting opportunity could be. Life gave, but life also took away. He was older, wiser, and he didn't want any more regrets.

He went down on his knee, a crush of dirt and pine needles staining his suit. He took hold of Rainie's hands. She was crying openly now, tears streaming down her face, but she didn't pull away.

"Grow old with me, Rainie," he whispered. "We'll adopt some children. We'll cut back on cases, create a home, then do the fashionable thing and write our memoirs. I'll be terrified. You can help show me the way."

"I don't know if I'll be a good mother!"

"We'll learn together."

"I don't know if I'll be a good wife!"

"Rainie, I just need you to be you. And then I'm the happiest man in the world."

"Oh for God's sake, get up off the dirt." But she was clasping his hands with both of hers now, and crying harder, and since he wouldn't get up, she sank down to the ground with him. "We have to talk more."

"I know."

"I mean about something other than work!"

"I understand that, too."

"And you have to tell me when you're frightened, Quincy. I can't stand it when you pull away."

"I'll try."

"Okay."

"Okay?"

She sniffed. "I mean, better than okay. I mean yes, I'll marry you. What the hell. If we can catch a few killers, we oughtta be able to figure out this domestic thing."

"You would think so," Quincy agreed. He pulled her closer, wrapped his arms around her shoulders. He could feel her trembling now and understood for the first time that she was as nervous as he. It gave him strength. You didn't have to know all the answers. You just had to be brave enough to try.

"I love you, Rainie," he whispered in her ear.

"I love you, too."

She gripped him tighter and he kissed all the tears from her face.

The call came almost an hour later. They had made it back to I-81 and were heading north, seeking a more populated Virginia. They had both turned on their cell phones. No reason to dodge the FBI anymore and Quincy wanted to be ready when Kimberly and Mac had new information.

The caller wasn't Kimberly, however. It was Kaplan.

"I have some news from the name game," the special agent said.

"It's only fair to tell you, we've been officially removed from the case," Quincy replied.

"Well then, you didn't hear this from me. But I've had my people scouring every contractor with ties to Georgia in the past ten years. Good news, we got a few hits. Bad news, none of them panned out. Better news, then I expanded the search."

"Expanded?"

"I started looking at everyone on the whole damn base. Now we got lots of hits, but I thought there was one you should know about right away. Dr. Ennunzio. The linguist."

"He used to live in Georgia?"

"Worked there. A high-profile string of kidnappings that had him flying in and out of Atlanta for a good three years. Say 'ninety-eight to two thousand. Which would be . . .'"

"The same time the Eco-Killer started up his game. Dammit." Quincy smacked the wheel. He already had Kaplan on the phone, so he turned to Rainie. "Quick, dial Kimberly! Tell her it's Ennunzio, and get Nora Ray away from him quick!"

Kimberly wasn't sleeping. Sleeping would be the smart thing to do. Recharge while she had a chance. Catch some desperately needed shut-eye. But she didn't sleep.

She was tracing lines on Mac's bronzed shoulder with her index finger. Then she ran her fingers through the light smattering of hair on his chest. She couldn't get over the feel of him, his skin like warm satin to the touch.

He snored. She'd learned that right away. He was also unbearably hot and heavy. Twice he'd flung his large frame over, tossing one arm across her chest or over her hip in a highly proprietary manner. She thought she should break him of that habit, while finding it secretly endearing.

And then she suspected she was experiencing the same downward slide she'd witnessed in other women—they started out strong and independent with firm beliefs on how to manage men, then caved like spun sugar when Tall, Dark, and Handsome crooked his little finger.

Well, she wasn't going to cave, she decided. Not totally, anyway. She was going to demand her own side of the bed. Space where she could sprawl comfortably and sleep. Just as soon as she stopped tracing the ripple of his triceps, or the hard line of his jaw . . .

Now her fingers wandered down to his hip and were rewarded by a growing length against the juncture of her thighs.

Her phone rang. Her hand stilled. She swore a word nice young women probably weren't supposed to use in bed. Then she was frantically trying to kick off the tangle of sheets.

"I fucking hate cell phones," Mac said clearly.

"Cheater! You were awake."

"Delightfully so. Wanna punish me? I could use a good spanking."

"This had better be good," Kimberly declared, "or I'll break every microchip in this damn phone."

But they already knew it would be urgent. Given the early morning hour, it was probably Ray Lee Chee with news on the fourth victim. They'd had their reprieve. Now, time was up.

Kimberly flipped open the phone, already expecting the worst, and then was genuinely startled to hear Rainie's voice on the other end of the line.

"It's Ennunzio!" she said without preamble. "Where the hell are you?"

Kimberly rattled off the name of the motel and the exit number, still in shock.

"Get him secured," Rainie was saying. "We're on our way. And Kimberly—take care of Nora Ray."

The phone went click. Mac and Kimberly scrambled for clothes.

Dark out. Very hot. They pressed against the wall of the motel, working their way down to Ennunzio's room with weapons drawn and faces tense. They came to Nora Ray's room first. Kimberly knocked. No answer.

"Deep sleeper," Mac murmured.

"Don't we both wish."

They cut across the parking lot, moving now with anxious speed. Ennunzio's room was in the other wing of the L-shaped building. Door closed. Lights off. Kimberly pressed her ear against the door and listened. First nothing. Then, the sudden, crashing sound of furniture—or a body— being thrown around the room.

"Go, go, go!" Kimberly cried.

Mac heaved up a leg and kicked in the cheap wooden door. It snapped back, caught on the chain. He gave it one more thunderous whack, and the door ricocheted into the wall.

"Police, freeze!"

"Nora Ray, where are you?"

Kimberly and Mac rolled into the room, one taking high, another taking low. In the next instant, Kimberly's groping fingers snapped on the light.

In front of them, two people were clearly involved in a struggle. Chairs had been tossed, the bed destroyed, the TV toppled. But it was not Dr. Ennunzio bearing down on a frightened girl. It was Nora Ray who had the special agent, clad in just a pair of boxers, backed into a corner. Now she loomed over him, brandishing a giant, gleaming needle.

"Nora Ray!" Kimberly said in shock.

"He killed my sister."

"It wasn't me, it wasn't me. I swear to God!" Ennunzio pressed harder against the wall. "I think . . . I think it was my brother."

44

"You have to understand, I don't think he's well."

"Your brother may have kidnapped and killed over ten women. Being not well is the least of his problems!"

"I don't think he meant to hurt them—"

"Holy shit!" Mac drew up short. He was looming above Ennunzio, who was now slumped on the edge of his bed. Quincy and Rainie had arrived and guarded the door, while in the right-hand corner, Kimberly kept watch over Nora Ray. Kimberly had taken the girl's needle away. Hostility in the small room, however, remained sky-high. "You're the caller!"

Ennunzio bowed his head.

"What the hell? You've been playing me from the start!"

"I was not trying to play you. I've been trying to help—"

"You said the caller might be the killer. What was that all about?"

"I wanted you to take the calls more seriously. Honest to God, I've been trying very hard to assist, I just don't know much myself."

"You could've given me your brother's name."

"It wouldn't have done you any good. Frank Ennunzio doesn't exist. However he's living now, it's under an assumed name. Please, you have to understand, I haven't actually spoken to my brother in over thirty years."

That brought them all to attention. Mac frowned, not liking this newest bit of news. He crossed his arms over his chest and started to pace the tiny room.

"Maybe you should start from the beginning," Quincy said quietly.

Ennunzio tiredly nodded his head. "Five years ago, I started work on a case in Atlanta, a kidnapping involving a young doctor's child. I was called in to analyze notes being delivered to the house. While I was there, two girls from Georgia State University also vanished. I clipped the articles from the newspaper. At the time, I chalked it up to an investigative hunch. I was working a disappearance, here was another disappearance, you never knew. So I started to follow the case of the missing college girls as well. That summer and then the next summer, when two other girls also went missing during a heat wave.

"By now, I knew the case of the young girls had nothing to do with my own. I was dealing with what turned out to be a string of ransom cases. A very cool young man who worked at one of the more prominent country clubs was using his position to identify and stalk wealthy young families. It took us three years, but we finally identified him, in large part from his ransom notes.

"The heat-wave kidnappings, however, were an entirely different beast. The UNSUB always struck young, college-aged girls traveling in pairs. He'd leave one body next to a road and the second in some remote location. And he always sent a note to the press. Clock ticking . . . heat kills. I've remembered that note for a long, long time. It's not the sort of thing you forget."

Ennunzio's voice broke off. He stared down at the carpet, lost now in his own thoughts.

"What did your brother do?" Rainie spoke up quietly. "Tell us about Frank."

"Our father was a hard man."

"Some fathers are."

"He worked in the coal mines, not far from where we were today. It's an unforgiving life. Backbreaking labor by day. Brutal poverty by night. He was a very angry person."

"Angry people often become physical," Rainie commented.

Ennunzio finally looked up at her. "Yes. They do."

"Did your brother kill your father?"

"No. The mines got him first. Coal dust built up in my father's lungs, he started to cough, and then one day we didn't have to fear him anymore."

"Ennunzio, what did your brother *do*?"

"He killed our mother," Ennunzio whispered. "He killed the woman we had spent all of our childhood trying to protect."

His voice broke again. He didn't seem capable of looking at anyone anymore. Instead his shoulders sagged, his head fell forward, and on his lap he began to wring his hands.

"You have to understand . . . After the funeral, our mother went a little crazy. She started yelling at Frank that he was ungrateful, and next thing we both knew, she went at him with my father's belt. At first, Frank didn't do anything. He just lay there until he wore herself out. Until she was so exhausted from hitting him that she couldn't even lift her own arm. And then he got off the floor. He picked her up. So gently. I remember that clearly. He was only fourteen, but he was already big for his age and my mother was built like a bird. He cradled her in his arms, carried her to her room and laid her down on the bed.

"He told me to get out of the house. But I couldn't leave. I stood in the middle of the cabin, while he got down the oil lamps and started pouring the oil around the rooms. I think I knew then what he was going to do. My mother just watched. Lying on the bed, her chest still heaving. She didn't utter a word. Didn't even lift her head. He was going to kill her, maybe kill all of us, and I think she was grateful.

"He covered the cabin in oil. Then he went to our stove and dumped the burning coals onto the floor. The whole house went up with a single whoosh. It was an old wood cabin, dry from age, never burdened by insulation. Maybe the house was grateful, too; it had never been a very happy place. I don't know. I just remember my brother grabbing my hand. He pulled me through the door. Then we stood outside and watched our house burn. At the last minute, my mother started screaming. I swore I saw her standing right in the middle of those flames, her arms over her head, shrieking to high heaven. But there was nothing anyone could do for her by then. Nothing anyone could do for any one of us.

"My brother walked me to the road. He told me someone would be by soon. Then he said, 'Just remember, Davey. Heat kills.' He disappeared into the woods and I haven't seen or talked to my brother since. One week later, I was placed with a foster family in Richmond and that was that.

"When I turned eighteen, I returned to the area briefly. I wanted to visit my parents' headstone. I found a hole had been gouged into the marker, and inside I found a rolled-up piece of paper that read, 'Clock ticking . . . planet dying . . . animals weeping . . . rivers screaming. Can't you hear it? Heat kills.' I think that summarizes my brother's last thoughts on the subject."

"Everything must die?" Kimberly spoke up grimly.

"Everything of beauty." Ennunzio shrugged. "Don't ask me to explain it completely. Nature was both our refuge—where we went to escape our father—and our prison—the isolated area where no one could see what was really happening. My brother loved the woods, he hated the woods. He loved our father, he hated our father. And in the end, he loved my mother and he loathed her. For him, I think the lines are all blurred. He hates what he loves and loves what he hates and has himself tangled in a web he'll never escape."

"So he seeks heat," Quincy murmured, "which purifies."

"And uses nature, which both saved him and betrayed him," Rainie filled in. She turned troubled eyes toward Nora Ray. "And how did you end up in here? I thought you never knew who attacked you and your sister."

"Voice," Nora Ray said. "I remember . . . I recognized his voice. From when the man came walking up to our window and asked if we needed help."

"Did you see his face?"

"No."

"So the man you heard that night could've been Dr. Ennunzio, or it could've been his brother, or, in all honesty, it could've been anyone who sounds like either of them. Don't you think you should've mentioned this to one of us, before you came charging in with a syringe?"

Nora Ray stared at Rainie with hard eyes. "She wasn't your sister."

Rainie sighed. "So what are you going to do now, Nora Ray?"

"I don't know."

"Do you believe Dr. Ennunzio's story?"

"Do you?" asked the girl.

"I'm thinking about it. If we turn you loose, are you going to attack Dr. Ennunzio again?"

"I don't know." Her overbright gaze swung to Ennunzio. "So maybe it was your brother instead of you. You should still be ashamed of yourself! You're an FBI agent, you're supposed to be protecting people. Instead, you knew something about a killer and you said nothing."

"I had nothing to add, not a name, not a location—"

"You knew his past!"

"I didn't know his present. All I could do was watch and wait. And I swear, the minute I saw my brother's note suddenly resurface in a Virginia paper, I mailed a copy to the GBI. I wanted Special Agent McCormack involved. I did everything in my power to get the police's attention. Surely that must count for something—"

"Three girls are dead," Nora Ray spat out. "You tell me how valuable your efforts have been."

"If I could've been sure . . ." Ennunzio murmured.

"Coward," Nora Ray countered savagely and Ennunzio finally shut up.

Quincy took a deep breath. He regarded Rainie, Mac, and Kimberly. "So where does this leave us?"

"Still short one killer and still short one victim," Mac said. "Now we've got motive, but that's only going to help us at trial. Bottom line is that it's the middle of the night, scary hot, and another girl's still out there. So cough it up, Ennunzio. He's your brother. Start thinking like him."

The forensic linguist, however, merely shook his head. "I understood some of the clues in the beginning, only because I've also spent a lot of time outdoors. But the evidence you're seeing now—water samples, sediment, pollen. That's way over my head. You need the experts."

"Doesn't your brother have any favorite places?"

"We grew up dirt poor in the foothills of the Appalachian Mountains. The only favorite places we knew were the ones we could walk to."

"You knew the cave."

"Because I used to be into caving. And of all the places Frank's chosen, that's been the most local."

"So we should look at the Appalachian Mountains, stay in the area," Rainie spoke up.

Both Mac and Ennunzio, however, were shaking their heads.

"My brother's methodology may be influenced by the past," Ennunzio told them, "perhaps even triggered by the trauma of heat spells, but the places themselves aren't tied to our family. I didn't even know he lived in Georgia."

"Ennunzio's right," Mac said. "Whatever hang-ups got this guy started, he's moved beyond them now. He's sticking to his game plan, and that means diversity. Wherever we are now, the last girl will be the farthest point away."

"We need Ray's team," Kimberly said.

"I'll go check on them," Mac said.

But in the end, he didn't have to. Ray met him halfway across the parking lot, already on his way to Mac's room.

"We have a winner," the USGS worker said excitedly. "Lloyd's soil samples turned out to contain three kinds of pollen from three types of trees—bald cypress, tupelo gum, and red maple—while the crushed plant matter is actually a sorely abused log fern. The shoes were also covered in peat moss. Which could only mean . . ."

"We're going to DisneyLand?"

"Better. The Dismal Swamp."

Four A.M., the group made their decision to divide and conquer. Quincy, as elder statesman, once more inherited the responsibility of contacting the official FBI case team. He and Rainie also assumed watch over Nora Ray, whom nobody trusted alone.

The USGS team members were packing up their gear and loading up their vehicles. According to Kathy Levine's debriefing, the Dismal Swamp was six hundred square miles of bugs, poisonous snakes, black bears, and bobcats. Trees grew to stupendous sizes, while a dense underbrush of brier bushes and wild vines made sections of the swamp virtually impassable.

They needed water. They needed insect repellent. They needed machetes. In other words, they needed all the help they could get.

Mac and Kimberly had Ennunzio in the back of their car. They would follow Ray's team to the site. That gave them seven people to search an area that had daunted even George Washington. While the sun once again peeked over the horizon, and the mosquitoes started to swarm.

"Ready?" Mac asked Kimberly as he climbed into the car.

"Ready as I'm gonna get."

His gaze rested on Ennunzio in the rearview mirror. The agent was wearily rubbing his head; he looked like he had just aged twenty years. "Why didn't they arrest your brother after the fire?" Mac asked crisply.

"I don't think they ever found him."

"Did you tell anyone what happened?"

"Of course."

"Because you never hold back the truth."

"I'm a federal agent," Ennunzio said curtly. "I know what needs to be done."

"Good, because finding this next girl is only half the battle. After that we go after your brother, and we don't stop until we've found him."

"He'll never surrender. He's not the type to spend the rest of his life in a cage."

"Then you'd better be prepared," Mac said grimly, "because we're not the types to let him go."

45

Dismal Swamp, Virginia
6:33 A.M.
Temperature: 96 degrees

Her mother was yelling at her. "I sent you to college for an education. So you could make something of yourself. Well, you've certainly made something, now haven't you?"

Tina yelled back. "Woman, bring me a goddamn glass of water. And get those tuxedoed waiters out of here."

Then she sat down and watched the blue butterfly.

Water. Lakes. Ice-cold streams. Potato chips. Oh, she was hot, hot, hot. Skin on fire. She longed to peel it off in strips. Peel down to the bone and roll in the muck. Wouldn't that feel good?

The flesh on her forearm squirmed. She watched bloody sores ripple and ooze. Maggots. Horrible little white worms. Writhing under her flesh, feasting on meat. She should pull them out and pop them in her mouth. Would they taste like chicken?

Pretty blue butterfly. How it glided along the air. Dancing up, up, and away. She longed to dance like that. To dance and glide and soar. To drift off to the comforting shade of a giant beech tree . . . or lake . . . or cool mountain stream.

Itched. Her skin itched and itched. She scratched and scratched. Didn't make a difference. Hot, hot, hot. So thirsty. Sun, coming up. Going to burn, burn, burn. She would cry, but no moisture left. She slathered on the mud, flattened out puddles and sought desperately to wet her tongue.

Her mother was hollering at her again. *Now look at what you've done.* She didn't have the strength to yell back.

"I'm sorry," she whispered. Then she closed her eyes. She dreamt of deep Minnesotan winters. She dreamt of her mother holding out her arms to her. And she prayed the end would happen quick.

It took over two hours to drive due east to the swamp. The visitors' entrance was in North Carolina on the east side. Operating under the assumption that the killer would stick to the Virginian playing field, however, Kathy Levine led their little caravan to a hiking entrance in Virginia, on the west side. All three vehicles pulled into the dirt parking lot and Kathy, the official search-and-rescue member of their party, assumed command. First, she handed out whistles.

"Remember, three blasts signifies the international call for distress. Get in trouble, stay put, blow away, and we'll find you."

Next, she handed out maps. "I downloaded these from the Internet before we left the motel. As you can see, the Dismal Swamp is basically a rectangle. Unfortunately for us, it's a very large rectangle. Looking at only the Virginia half, we're still talking over a hundred thousand acres. That's going to be a bit much for seven people."

Mac took one of the maps. The printout showed a large, shadowed area, crisscrossed by a maze of lines. He followed the various markings with his finger. "What are these?"

"The dashed lines represent hiking and biking trails bisecting the swamp. The broader lines here are unpaved roads. The thin dark lines reveal the old canals, most hand-dug by slaves hundreds of years ago. When the water levels were higher, they would use the canals to harvest the cypress and juniper trees."

"And now?"

"Most of the canals are marshy messes. Not enough water for a canoe, but not dry enough to walk."

"What about the roads?"

"Wide, flat, grassy; you don't even need four-wheel drive." Levine already understood where he was going with this. She added, "Technically speaking, visitors aren't permitted to bring vehicles onto the roads, but as for what happens under the cover of night . . ."

Mac nodded. "Okay. So our guy needs to get an unconscious, hundred-and-twenty-pound body into the heart of the swamp. He'd want to take her someplace remote, where she wouldn't immediately be found by others. He'd need a road for access, however, because carrying a woman through a hundred thousand acres would be a bit much. Where does that leave us?"

They all studied the map. The marked hiking paths were fairly centralized, with a clear grid pattern occupying most of the west side of the swamp. Closest to them was a simple loop labeled a boardwalk trail. They immediately dismissed that as too touristy. Farther in lay the dark oval shadow of Lake Drummond, also highly populated with hiking trails, roads, and feeder ditches. Beyond the lake, however, moving farther east, north, and south, the map became a solid field of gray, only periodically bisected by old, unpaved roads. This is where the swamp became a lonely place.

"We need to drive in," Kimberly murmured. "Make it to the lake."

"Branch off from there," Mac agreed. He looked at Levine intently. "He wouldn't leave her by a road. Given the grid pattern, it would be too easy for her to walk out."

"True."

"He wouldn't use a canal either. Again, she could just follow it straight out of the swamp."

Kathy nodded silently.

"He took her into the wild," Mac concluded softly. "Probably in this northeastern quadrant, where the trees and thick underbrush are disorienting. Where the predator population is higher and that much more dangerous. Where she can scream all she wants and no one will hear a thing."

He fell silent for a moment. It was already so hot out this morning. Sweat trickled down their faces, staining their shirts. The air felt too heavy to breathe, making their hearts beat faster and their lungs labor harder, and it was barely sunrise. Conditions were harsh, bordering on brutal. What must the girl be going through, trapped here for over three days?

"Going there ourselves will be dangerous," Kathy said quietly. "We're talking brier thickets so dense in places you can't even hack your way through. One minute you might be walking on hard-packed earth; the next you'll have sunk down to your knees in sucking mud. You need to be on the lookout for bears and bobcats. Then there's the matter of cottonmouth snakes, copperhead snakes, and the canebrake rattler. Normally they keep to themselves. But once off the trails, we're intruding in their terrain, and they won't take it kindly."

"Canebrake rattler?" Kimberly spoke up nervously.

"Shorter than its cousin, with a thick, squat head that will scare the piggy out of you. Cottonmouth and copperhead will be around the wet, swampy patches. The canebrake rattler will prefer rocks and piles of dead leaves. Finally, we have the bugs. Mosquitoes, yellow flies, gnats, chiggers, and ticks . . . Most of the time, none of us considers the insect population. But the overwhelming swarms of mosquitoes and yellow flies are what help the Dismal Swamp to be considered one of the least hospitable places on earth."

"No kidding," Ray muttered darkly. He was already swatting at the air around his face. The first few mosquitoes had picked up their scent, and judging from the growing buzz in the air, the rest were on their way.

Ray and Brian dug in their packs for bug repellent, while the mood grew subdued. If the girl was in the wild lands of the swamp, then of course that's where they would go. No one liked it, but no one was arguing it either.

"Look," Kathy said tersely, "the biggest dangers today are dehydration and heatstroke. Everyone needs to be drinking at least one liter of water an hour. Filtered water is best, but in a pinch, you can drink the swamp water. It looks like something that's been used to wash dirty socks, but the water is actually unusually pure, preserved by the tannic acids in the bark of the juniper, gum, and cypress trees. As a matter of fact, they used to fill barrels with this water for long sea voyages. The habitat and water have changed some since then, but given today's temperatures . . ."

"Drink," Mac said.

"Yes, drink a lot. Liquids are your friends. Now, assume for a moment that we get lucky and find Tina alive: First priority with anyone suffering severe heatstroke and dehydration is to reduce core body temperature. Douse her with water. Massage her limbs to increase circulation. Give her water, but also plenty of salty snacks, or better yet a saline solution. Don't be surprised if she fights you. Victims of extreme heatstroke are often delusional and argumentative. She may be ranting and raving, she may seem perfectly lucid, then lash out at you the next instant. Don't try to reason with her. Get her down, and get her hydrated as fast and efficiently as you can. She can blame you for the bruised jaw later if need be. Other questions?"

No one had any. The mosquitoes were arriving in force now, buzzing their eyes, their ears, their mouths. Ray and Brian took some halfhearted swipes at the winged insects with their hands. The mosquitoes didn't seem to notice. They all doused with bug repellent. The mosquitoes didn't seem to mind that either.

Last-minute check of gear now. Everyone had water, first-aid kits, and whistles. Everyone had a map and plenty of bug spray. That was it, then. They loaded their packs back into their vehicles. Ray opened the gate to the main road leading to Lake Drummond. And one by one, they drove into the swamp.

"Scary place," Ennunzio murmured as the first dark, muddy canal appeared on their right and snaked ominously through the trees.

Mac and Kimberly didn't say anything at all.

Things grow bigger in a swamp. Kimberly ducked her head for the fourth time, trying to wind her way through the thick woods of twisted cypress trees and gargantuan junipers. Tree trunks grew wider than the span of her arms. Some leaves were bigger than her head. In other places, tree limbs and vines were so grossly intertwined, she had to take off her backpack to squeeze through the narrow space left between.

Sun was a distant memory now, flickering in a tree canopy far above. Instead, she, Mac, and Ennunzio walked through a silent, boggy hush. The spongy ground absorbed the sound of their footsteps, while the rich scent of overripe vegetation filled their nostrils and made them want to gag.

On a different day, in different circumstances, she supposed she would've found the swamp beautiful. Bright orange flowers from the trumpet vines dappled the swamp floor. Gorgeous blue butterflies appeared in the beams of sunlight, playing tag among the trees. Dozens of green and gold dragonflies darted along their path, offering delicate flashes of color amid the deepening gloom.

Mostly, however, Kimberly was aware of the danger. Piles of dried leaves bunched at the base of trees and made the perfect home for sleeping snakes. Predatory vines, the same thickness as her arm, bound trees in tight, suffocating coils. Then there were clearings, sections of the swamp that had been logged out decades ago, and now just worn, rounded tree stumps dotted the shadowed landscape like endless rows of miniature gravestones. The ground would be softer there, marshy and popping as toads and salamanders leapt out of their hiding places to escape the encroaching footsteps.

Things moved in the dark recesses of the swamp. Things Kimberly never saw but felt like whispers in the wind. Deer, bear, bobcat? She couldn't be sure. She just knew she jumped at the random, distant noises and was aware of the hair rising at the nape of her neck.

It had to be over a hundred degrees out. And still she battled a chill.

Mac led their little party. Then came Kimberly, then Ennunzio. Mac was trying to work a rough grid, sweeping between two unpaved roads. It had seemed like a good idea at the time. Thickets and dense trees often made passage impossible, however, so they started having to veer a little more to the right, then a little more to the left. They had to take this detour and then that detour. Mac had a compass. Maybe he knew where they were. From what Kimberly could tell, however, the swamp now owned them. They walked where it let them, passed where it let them pass. And increasingly, that path was taking them to a dark, decaying place, where the tree branches grew denser, and they had to round their shoulders to fit through the tight, cramped spaces.

They didn't speak much. They slogged their way through the hot, wet vines, searching for signs of broken twigs, scuffed ground, or bruised vegetation that might indicate recent human passage. They took turns issuing single blasts on their whistles or calling out Tina Krahn's name. Then they heaved themselves over giant, lightning-felled trees. Or wriggled between particularly large boulders. Or hacked their way futilely through dense, prickly thickets.

While they downed more and more of their precious supply of water. While their breathing became hard and panting, and their footsteps grew unsteady, and their arms started to tremble visibly from the heat.

Kimberly's mouth had gone dry, a sure sign she wasn't drinking enough water. She found herself stumbling more, having to catch herself on tree limbs and tangled brush. The sweat stung her eyes. The yellow flies constantly swarmed her face, trying to feast on the corners of her mouth or the tender flesh behind her ears.

She didn't even know how long they had been hiking anymore. It seemed as if she'd been in the steaming jungle forever, pushing her way through thick, wet leaves only to encounter another choking eternity of vines, briers, and bushes.

Then, all of a sudden, Mac held up his hand.

"Did you hear that?" he asked sharply.

Kimberly stopped, drew in a ragged gasp of air, and strained to hear: There, for just an instant. A voice in the wind.

Mac turned, his sweat-covered face at once triumphant and intent. "Where is that coming from?"

"Over there!" Kimberly cried, pointing to her right.

"No, I think it's more like over there," Mac said, pointing straight ahead. He frowned. "Damn trees; they're distorting the sound."

"Well, somewhere off in that direction."

"Let's go!"

Then, a new and sudden realization sucked the last of the moisture from Kimberly's mouth. "Mac," she said sharply. "Where is Ennunzio?"

46

Richmond, Virginia
11:41 A.M.
Temperature: 101 degrees

"I'm telling you, the fourth girl, Tina Krahn, has been abandoned some-where in the Dismal Swamp."

"And I'm telling you, you have absolutely no authority in this case."

"I know I have no authority!" Quincy started yelling, caught the outburst, and bitterly swallowed it back down. He had arrived at the FBI's Richmond field office just thirty minutes ago, seeking a meeting with Special Agent Harkoos. Harkoos wouldn't grant him permission to come to his office, but instead had grudgingly agreed to meet with him in a downstairs alcove. The blatant lack of courtesy was not lost on Quincy. "I'm not seeking authority," Quincy tried again. "I'm seeking help for a missing person."

"You tampered with evidence," Harkoos growled.

"I arrived late at the scene, the USGS personnel had already started ana-lyzing data, and there was nothing I could do."

"You could've forced them away until the real professionals arrived."

"They are experts in the field—"

"They are not trained forensic technicians—"

"They've identified three different sites!" Quincy was yelling again and about to start swearing, too. Really, the last twenty-four hours had been a banner day of emotional outbursts for him. He forced himself to take another deep breath. Time for logic, diplomacy, and calm rationality. Failing that, he'd have to kill the son of a bitch. "We need your help," he insisted.

"You fucked this case."

"This case was already fucked. Four girls missing, three now dead. Agent, we have one last shot at doing this right. One girl, in the middle of a hundred-thousand-acre swamp. Call in the rescue teams, find that girl, get the headlines. It really is that simple."

Special Agent Harkoos scowled. "I don't like you," he said, but his voice had lost its vehemence. Quincy had spoken the truth, and it was hard to argue with headlines. "You have behaved in an unorthodox manner which has put prosecuting this case in jeopardy," Harkoos grumbled. "Don't think I'm going to forget that."

"Call in the rescue teams, find that girl, get the headlines," Quincy repeated.

"The Dismal Swamp, huh? Is it as bad as its name sounds?"

"Most likely, yes."

"Shit." Harkoos dug out his cell phone. "Your people had better be right."

"My people," Quincy said tersely, "haven't been wrong yet."

Quincy had no sooner left the building to rejoin Rainie and Nora Ray at the car when his cell phone rang. It was Kaplan, calling from Quantico.

"Do you have Ennunzio in custody?" the special agent demanded to know.

"It's not him," Quincy said. "Try his brother."

"Brother?"

"According to Ennunzio, his older brother murdered their mom thirty years ago. Burned her to death. Ennunzio hasn't seen him since, but his brother once left a note at their parents' grave, bearing the same message as the notes now sent by the Eco-Killer."

"Quincy, according to Ennunzio's personnel records, he doesn't have a brother."

Quincy drew up short, frowning now as he stood beside Rainie. "Maybe he doesn't consider him family anymore. It's been thirty years. Their last time together was hardly a Kodak moment."

There was a pause. "I don't like this," Kaplan said. "Something's wrong. Look, I was calling because I just got off the phone with Ennunzio's secretary. Turns out, two years ago, he took a three-month leave of absence to have major surgery. The doctors removed a tumor in his brain. According to his secretary, Ennunzio started complaining of headaches again six months ago. She's been really worried about him."

"A tumor . . ."

"Now, you're the expert, but brain tumors can impact behavior, correct? Particularly ones growing in the right place . . ."

"The limbic system," Quincy murmured, closing his eyes and thinking fast. "In cases of brain trauma or tumors, you often see a marked change in behavior in the subject—increased irascibility, we call it. Normally mild-mannered people become violent, aggressive, use foul language."

"Maybe even go on a murder spree?"

"There have been some instances of mass murder," Quincy replied. "But something this cold and calculated . . . Then again, a tumor might trigger psychotic episodes, paving the way. Special Agent, are you at a computer? Can you look up the name David Ennunzio for me? Search birth and death records, Lee County, Virginia."

Rainie was watching him curiously now. Nora Ray as well. "Isn't David Dr. Ennunzio's first name?" Rainie whispered.

"That's what we all assumed."

"Assumed?" Her eyes widened and he knew she was getting it, too. Why should you never assume something when working an investigation? Because it made an ass out of you and me. Kaplan was already back on the line.

"According to the obits, David Joseph Ennunzio died July 14, 1972, at the age of thirteen. He was killed in a house fire along with his mother. They are survived by . . . Christ! Franklin George Ennunzio. Dr. Frank Ennunzio. Quincy, Ennunzio doesn't have a brother."

"He had a brother but he killed him. He killed his brother, his mother— hell, maybe he killed his father, too. Then he spent all these years covering it up and trying to forget. Until something else went even more wrong in his head."

"You have to get him in custody now!" Kaplan shouted.

And Quincy whispered, "I can't. He's in the Dismal Swamp. With my daughter."

The man knew what he must do. He was letting himself think again, remembering the old days and old ways. It hurt his head. Brought on raging bolts of pain. He staggered as he walked and clutched his temples.

But remembering brought him clarity, too. He thought of his mother, the look on her face as she lay so passively on the bed and watched him splatter lamp oil on the floor of their wooden shack. He thought of his younger brother, and how he'd cowered in the corner instead of bolting for safety.

No fighting from either of them. No protest. His father had beaten the resistance out of them over all those long, bloody years. Now, death came and they simply waited.

He had been weak thirty years ago. He had tossed the match, then out-run the flames. He had thought he would stay. He'd been so sure death was what he wanted, too. Then, at the last moment, he couldn't do it. He'd bro-ken from the fire's mesmerizing spell. He had dashed out the door. He had heard his mother's raw, angry screams. He had heard his brother's last piti-ful cries. Then he had run for the woods and begged the wilderness to save him.

Mother Nature was not that kind. He had been hungry and hot. He had spent weeks dazed and desperate with thirst. So finally he had emerged, walking into town, waiting to see what would happen next.

People had been kind. They fawned over him, hugged him, and fussed over this lone survivor of a tragic fate. How big and strong he must have been to survive in the woods all this time, they told him. What an amazing miracle he'd made it out of the house in time. God must surely favor him to show him such compassion.

They made him a hero; he was much too tired to protest.

But fire still found him in his dreams. He ignored it for years, wanting to be the proverbial phoenix rising from the ashes in a new and improved life. He worked hard and studied hard. He swore to himself he would do good. He would *be* good. As a child he had committed a horrible act. Now, as an adult, he would do better.

Maybe for a while it had worked. He'd been a good agent. He'd saved lives, worked important cases, advanced critical research. But then the pain started and the flames grew more mesmerizing in his dreams and he let the fire talk to him. He let it convince him to do things.

He had killed. Then he had begged the police to stop him. He had kid-napped girls. Then he'd left clues for someone else to save them. He hated himself; he serviced himself. He had sought redemption through work; he committed bigger sins in his personal life. In the end, he had been everything his family had raised him to be.

Everything of beauty betrayed you. Everything of beauty lied. All you could trust was the flame.

He ran around now, in the dark recesses of the swamp. He listened to the deer dash out of his way, the stealthy foxes race for cover. Somewhere in the leaves came an ominous rattle. He didn't care anymore.

His head throbbed, his body begged for rest. While his hands played with matches, raking them across the sulfur strips and letting them fall with hissing crackles into the bog.

Some matches were immediately squelched by muddy water. Others found dry patches of leaves. Still others found the nice, slow-burning peat.

He ran by the pit. He thought he heard a sound far below.

He dropped in another match just for her.

Everything of beauty must die. Everything, everyone, and him.

Mac and Kimberly were running now. They could hear frantic crashes in the underbrush, the pounding of footsteps that seemed to come from everywhere and nowhere. Someone was here. Ennunzio? His brother? The swamp had suddenly come alive, and Kimberly had her Glock out, holding it desperately with sweat-slicked hands.

"To the right," Mac said, low under his breath.

But almost immediately the sound came again, this time from their left.

"Woods are distorting it," Kimberly panted.

"We can't lose our bearings."

"Too late."

Kimberly's cell phone vibrated on her hip. She snatched it with her left hand, still holding her gun in her right, and trying to look everywhere at once. The trees swirled darkly around her, the woods closing in.

"Where's Ennunzio?" her father said in her ear.

"I don't know."

"There is no brother, Kimberly. He died thirty years ago in the fire. It's Ennunzio. It sounds as if he may have a brain tumor and has now experienced a psychotic break. You must consider him armed and dangerous."

"Dad," Kimberly said softly. "I smell fire."

Tina's head came up sharply. Her eyes were swollen shut again; she couldn't see, but her hearing was just fine. Noise. Lots of noise. Footsteps and panting and crackling underbrush. It was as if the swamp overhead had suddenly exploded with activity. Rescuers!

"Hello?" she tried weakly. Her voice came out as nothing more than a croak.

She swallowed, tried again, and got little better results.

Desperate now, she attempted to pull herself up. Her arms trembled violently, too exhausted to bear her weight. But then she heard a fresh pounding of footsteps and adrenaline surged through her veins. She heaved herself half upright, groping around vainly in the mud. Something squished between her fingers, something plopped by her hand.

She gave up on caution, and brought a big handful of muck to her mouth, sucking greedily at the mud. Moisture for her parched throat, lips. So close, so close, so close.

"Hello," she tried again. "Down here!"

Her voice was slightly louder now. Then she heard a faint pause, and sensed a presence suddenly close.

"Hello, hello, hello!"

"Clock ticking," a clear voice whispered from above. "Heat kills."

And the next thing Tina knew, she felt a sharp pain on her hand, as if a pair of fangs had finally found her flesh.

"Ow!" She slapped at her hand, feeling the heat of the flames. "Ow, ow, ow." She beat at the heat frantically, squashing the match into the mud. Son of a bitch. Now he was trying to burn her out!

That did it. Tina staggered to her feet. She raised her tired arms over her head, balling her hands into fists. Then she screamed at the top of her sandpaper-dry throat. "You come down here and face me, you bastard. Come on. Fight like a man!"

Her legs promptly collapsed beneath her. She lay there in the mud, dazed and panting. She heard more sounds, this time the man running away. Perversely, she missed him; it was the closest to a human connection she'd had in days.

Hey, she thought weakly. She smelled smoke.

Kimberly was blowing frantically on her whistle. Three sharp blasts. Mac was whistling, too. They could see smoke now directly ahead. They raced to the pile of leaves, kicking them open and stomping furiously on the burning embers.

More smoke spiraled from the left, while a sputtering sound came from the right. Kimberly blew futilely on her whistle. Mac, too.

Then they were off to the right and off to the left, dashing through the woods and desperately seeking out the dozens of burning piles.

"We need water."

"None left."

"Damp clothing?"

"Only what I'm wearing." Mac peeled off his soaked shirt and used it to smother a burning stump.

"It's Ennunzio. No brother. Has a brain tumor. Apparently has gone insane." Kimberly kicked frantically at yet another pile of smoldering leaves. Snakes? She didn't have time to worry about them anymore.

A fresh sound of rustling tree limbs came from their right. Kimberly jerked toward the noise, already raising her gun and trying to find a target. A deer raced by, followed swiftly by two more. For the first time, she became aware of the full activity around them. Squirrels scrambling up trees, birds taking to the air. Soon they would probably see otters, raccoons, and foxes, a desperate exodus of all creatures great and small.

"He hates what he loves and loves what he hates," Kimberly said grimly.

"They have the right idea. Two of us alone can't stop this. We have to think of bailing out."

But Kimberly was already running to a fresh batch of curling smoke. "Not yet."

"Kimberly . . ."

"Please, Mac, not yet."

She tore apart a rotting tree limb, stomping on the scattering flames. Mac tended to the next hot spot, then they both heard it at once. Yelling. Distant and rough.

"Hey . . . Down here! Somebody . . . Help."

"Tina," Kimberly breathed.

They ran toward her voice.

Kimberly nearly found Tina Krahn the hard way. One moment she was running forward, the next her right foot pedaled through open air. She staggered at the edge of the rectangular pit, frantically windmilling her arms until Mac grabbed her by the backpack and yanked her to firmer footing.

"I gotta start looking before I leap," she muttered.

Drenched in sweat and covered with soot, Mac managed a crooked smile. "And ruin your charm?"

They dropped down on their stomachs and gazed intently into the hole. The pit seemed quite large, maybe a ten-by-fifteen-foot area, at least twenty feet deep. It obviously wasn't new. Thick, tangled vines covered most of the walls, while beneath Kimberly's fingertips, she could feel old, half-rotted railroad ties. She didn't know who had built the pit, but given that slaves had been used to dredge most of the swamp, she had her theories as to why. Don't want to watch the help too much at night? Well, talk about restricted sleeping quarters . . .

"Hello!" she called down. "Tina?"

"Are you for real?" a feeble voice called back from the shadows. "You're not wearing a tuxedo, are you?"

"Noooo," Kimberly said slowly. She glanced at Mac. They were both thinking about what Kathy Levine had said. Heatstroke victims were often delusional.

The smell of smoke was growing thicker. Kimberly narrowed her eyes, still trying to pick out a human being below. Then she saw her. All the way down in the muck, curled tight against a boulder. The girl was covered head to toe in mud, blending in perfectly with her surroundings. Kimberly could just barely make out the flash of white teeth when Tina spoke.

"Water?" the girl croaked hopefully.

"We're going to get you out of there."

"I think I lost my baby," Tina whispered. "Please, don't tell my mom."

Kimberly closed her eyes. The words hurt her, one more casualty in a war they never should have had to fight.

"We're going to throw you a rope." Mac's voice was steady and calm.

"I can't . . . No Spiderman. Tired . . . So tired . . ."

"You go down," Mac murmured to Kimberly. "I'll haul up."

"We don't have a litter."

"Loop the end of the rope to form a swing. It's the best we can do."

Kimberly looked at his arms wordlessly. It would take a tremendous amount of strength to pull up a hundred pounds of deadweight, and Mac had been hiking for nearly three days straight, on virtually no sleep. But Mac merely shrugged. In his eyes she saw the truth. The smoke was thickening, the deadly fire taking hold. They didn't have many options left.

"I'm coming down," Kimberly called into the pit.

Mac pulled out the vinyl coil, worked a rough belay using a clamp around his waist, then gave her the go-ahead. She rappelled down slow and easy, trying not to recoil at the stench, or to think about what kind of things must be slithering in the muck.

At the bottom, she was startled by her first close-up view of the girl. Tina's bones stood out starkly. Her skin was shrink-wrapped around her frame in a macabre imitation of a living mummy. Her hair was wild and muddy, her eyes swollen shut. Even beneath the coating of mud, Kimberly could see giant sores oozing blood and pus. Was it her imagination, or did one of those sores just wiggle? The girl hadn't been lying. In her condition, she was never going to be able to climb up the pit walls on her own.

"It's very nice to meet you, Tina," Kimberly said briskly. "My name is Kimberly Quincy, and I've come to get you out of here."

"Water?" Tina whispered hopefully.

"Up top."

"So thirsty. Where's the lake?"

"I'm going to loop this rope. You need to sit in it like a swing. And then Special Agent McCormack up there is going to pull you up. If you can use your legs against the wall to assist him, that would be very helpful."

"Water?"

"All the water you want, Tina. You just have to make it to the top."

The girl nodded slowly, her head bobbing back and forth almost drunkenly. She seemed dazed and unfocused, on the edge of checking back out. Kimberly moved quickly, wrapping the rope around Tina's hips and getting it in place.

"Ready?" she called up.

"Ready," Mac replied, and Kimberly heard a new urgency in his voice. The fire was obviously sweeping closer.

"Tina," she said intently. "If you want that water, you gotta move. And I mean *now*."

She hefted the girl up, felt the slack immediately tighten in the rope. Tina seemed to half get it; her feet kicked weakly at the wall. A groan from up top. A heaving gasp as Mac began to pull.

"Water at the top, Tina. Water at the top."

Then Tina did something Kimberly didn't expect. From deep in her haze, she roused her tired limbs, stuck her feet in what appeared to be small gaps between the railroad ties and actually tried to help.

Up, up, up she went, climbing toward freedom. Up, up, up out of her dark hellhole.

And just for a moment, Kimberly felt something lighten in her chest. She stood there, watching this exhausted girl finally make it to safety and she felt a moment of satisfaction, of sublime peace. She had done good. She had gotten this one right.

Tina disappeared over the edge. Within seconds the rope was back down.

"*Move!*" Mac barked.

Kimberly grabbed the rope, spotted the toeholds and bolted for the top.

She crested the pit just in time to watch a wall of flames hit the trees and bear down upon them.

47

Dismal Swamp, Virginia
2:39 P.M.
Temperature: 103 degrees

"We need choppers, we need the manpower, we need help."

Quincy pulled up at the cluster of cars and spotted the thin columns of smoke darkening the bright blue sky. One, two, three—there had to be nearly a dozen of them. He turned back to the forestry official who was still barking orders into a radio.

"What the hell has happened?"

"Fire," the man said tersely.

"Where is my daughter?"

"Is she a hiker? Who is she with?"

"Dammit." Quincy spotted Ray Lee Chee staggering out of a vehicle and made a beeline for him, Rainie hot on his heels. "What happened?"

"Don't know. Drove into Lake Drummond to start the search. Next thing I know, I'm hearing whistle blasts and smelling smoke."

"Whistle blasts?"

"Three sharp blows, the international call of distress. Sounded from the northeast quadrant. I was headed in that direction, but man, the smoke got so thick so fast. Brian and I figured we'd better bug out while we still had the chance. We're not equipped with that kind of gear."

"And the others?"

"Saw Kathy and Lloyd headed toward their vehicle. Don't know about Kimberly, Mac, or that doctor dude."

"How do I get to Lake Drummond?"

Ray just looked at him, then at the clouds of smoke. "Now, sir, you don't."

Mac and Kimberly had Tina slung between them, one of her arms over each of their shoulders. The girl was a fighter, trying vainly to help them by moving her feet. But her body had been pushed beyond its limits days ago. The more she tried to run with them, the more she stumbled and careened sluggishly, throwing them all off balance.

The awkward motions were getting them nowhere and the fire was gaining fast.

"I got her," Mac said tersely.

"It's too much weight—"

"Shut up and help." He stopped and hunkered down. Tina wrapped her arms around his neck, Kimberly boosted the muddy girl up onto his back.

"Water," the girl croaked.

"When we're out of the woods," Mac promised. Neither of them had the heart to tell Tina that they had no water left. For that matter, if they didn't magically find their vehicle in about the next five minutes, all of the water in the world would make no difference.

They were off and running again. Kimberly had no sense of time or place. She was stumbling around trees, battling her way through choking underbrush. Smoke stung her eyes and made her cough. In the good news department, the bugs were gone. In the bad news department, she didn't know if she was heading north or south, east or west. The swamp had closed in on her and she'd long ago lost any sense of direction.

Mac seemed to know where he was going, however. He had a hard, lean look on his face, pushing himself forward and determined to take both of them with him.

A lumbering shape appeared to their left. Kimberly watched in awe as a full-grown black bear went running by not ten feet away. The big animal didn't spare them a glance, but kept on trucking. Next came deer, foxes, squirrels, and even some snakes. Everything was clearing out, and normal food-chain rules did not apply in the face of this far greater foe.

They ran, sweat streaming down their arms and legs. They ran faster, Tina beginning to mumble incoherently, her head lolling forward on Mac's shoulder. They ran harder, the smoke penetrating their lungs, making them all gasp.

They squeezed through a narrow space between two towering trees, rounded a large patch of thickets and came face-to-face with Ennunzio. He was on the ground, propped up against a tree trunk. He seemed unsurprised to see them burst through the roiling smoke.

"You shouldn't run from the flames," he murmured, and then Kimberly saw what was at his feet. A coiled nest of brown mottled skin. Two pinpricks of red showed on Ennunzio's calf where the rattler had bitten him.

"I shot him," he said, in reply to their unasked question. "But not before he got me. Just as well. Can't run anymore. Time to wait. Must take your punishment like a man. What do you think my father thought about, each time he heard us scream?"

His gaze went to the muddy shape on Mac's back. "Oh good, you found her. That's nice. Out of four girls, I was hoping you'd get at least one right."

Kimberly took a furious step forward and Ennunzio's hand immediately twitched by his side. He was holding his gun.

"You shouldn't run from the flames," he said sternly. "I tried it thirty years ago, and look what happened to me. Now sit. Stay a while. It only hurts for a short time."

"You're dying," Kimberly told him flatly.

"Aren't we all?"

"Not today. Look—sit here all you want. Die in your precious fire. But we're out of here."

She took another step, and Ennunzio immediately raised the gun.

"Stay," he said firmly and now she could see the light flaming in his eyes, a feverish, rabid glow. "You must die. It's the only way to find peace."

Kimberly pressed her lips into a thin, frustrated line. She shot a glance at Mac. He had a gun somewhere, but with his hands full trying to keep Tina on his back, he was in no position to do anything quickly or stealthily. Kimberly shot her gaze back to Ennunzio. This one was up to her.

"Who are you?" she asked. "Frank or David?"

"Frank. I've always been Frank." Ennunzio's lips curled weakly. "But do you want to hear something stupid? I tried to pretend in the beginning that it wasn't me. I tried to pretend the killer was Davey, come back to do all those terrible things, because I was big brother Frank and I'd gotten out and I wasn't going to be anything like my family. But of course it wasn't Davey. Davey got beat one too many times. Davey stopped having any hope. Davey, given a choice between running and dying, chose dying. So of course it could only be me, hunting down innocent girls. Once I had the tumor removed, I could see more clearly. I had done bad things. The fire had made me do it, and now I must stop. But then the pain came back and all I could dream of was bodies in the woods."

The smoke was growing thicker. It made Kimberly blink owlishly and become even more aware of the intense heat growing at her back. "If we fashioned a tourniquet above the bite, you could still live," Kimberly tried desperately. "You could walk out of this swamp, get yourself some anti-venom, and then get yourself some serious psychological help."

"But I don't want to live."

"I do."

"Why?"

"Because living is hope. Trying is hope. And because I come from a long line of people who have excelled at being earnest." Ennunzio's gaze had drifted to Mac. It was the opportunity she'd been waiting for. Choking back a harsh cough, Kimberly swiftly brought up her Glock and leveled it at Ennunzio's face. "Throw down your weapon, Frank. Let us pass, or you won't have to worry about your precious fire."

Ennunzio merely smiled. "Shoot me."

"Put down your weapon."

"Shoot me."

"Shoot your own goddamn self! I wasn't put on this earth to end your misery. I'm here to save a girl. Now we have her and we're getting out." The smoke was so thick now, Kimberly could barely see.

"No," Ennunzio said distinctly. "Move, and I'll shoot. The flames are coming. Now take your punishment like a man."

"You're a coward. Always taking your rage out on others, when all along you know who you truly hate the most is yourself."

"I saved lives."

"You killed your own family!"

"They wanted me to do it."

"Bullshit! They wanted help. Ever think who your brother could've been? I'm sure he would've done better than turn into a serial murderer who preyed on young girls."

"Davey was weak. Davey needed my protection."

"Davey needed his family and you took them away from him! It's always been about you, Ennunzio. Not what your brother needed, not what your mom needed and sure as hell not what the environment needed. You kill because you want to kill. Because killing makes you happy. And maybe that's why Davey stayed in the house that day. He already knew the truth—that of the whole family, you are the worst of the bunch."

Kimberly leaned forward. Ennunzio's face had turned a mottled shade of scarlet while his Glock trembled in his hand. The fire had grown dangerously close. She could smell the acrid odor of singeing hair. Not much time left. For him, for her, for any of them.

Kimberly took a deep breath. She waited, one, two, three. A popping sound came from the woods, an old tree trunk exploding. Ennunzio jerked his head toward the noise. And Kimberly descended upon him with a vengeance. Her foot connected with his hand, the Glock went flying out of his grasp. A second hard kick had him holding his gut. A third whipped his head around.

She was moving in for the kill, when she heard his rough laugh.

"Take it like a man," he cackled. "By God, boys, don't you waste your pathetic cries on me. Hold your chin up when I beat you. Square those shoulders. Look me in the eye, and take your punishment like a man." Ennunzio laughed again, a hollow sound that sent shivers up her spine.

His head came up. He peered straight at Kimberly. "Kill me," he said, very clearly. "Please. Make it quick."

Kimberly walked over. She picked up his gun. Then she threw it deep into the heart of the oncoming flames.

"No more excuses, Ennunzio. You want to die, you go do it yourself."

She turned back toward Mac and Tina. The fire was so close now, she could feel its heat on her face. But mostly she was aware of Mac, his calm blue eyes, his big strong body. His absolute faith that she could handle Ennunzio. And now his readiness to take her and Tina Krahn straight out of here.

Life was filled with choices, Kimberly thought. Living, dying, fighting, running, hoping, dreading, loving, hating. Existing in the past or living in the present. Kimberly looked at Mac, then looked at Tina, and she had no problem with her choices anymore.

"Let's go," she said crisply.

They started running. Ennunzio howled behind them. Or maybe he simply laughed. But the fire was moving fast now. The flames would no longer be denied.

The wall of fire descended, and one way or another, Ennunzio had his peace at last.

They found the car ten minutes later. Tina was piled into the backseat, Mac and Kimberly plunked down in the front. Then Mac had the keys out and the engine running and they were tearing down the flat, grassy road, dodging fleeing animals.

Kimberly heard a roar that sounded like an inferno, while overhead the skies filled with rescue choppers and forestry planes. The cavalry coming, bringing in professionals to fight the blaze and save what could be saved.

They tore out of the swamp, coming to a screeching halt in a parking lot now filled with vehicles.

Mac jumped out first. "Medical attention, quick, over here."

Then EMTs were working on Tina with water and cooling packs, while Quincy and Rainie were running across the parking lot toward Kimberly, and Mac was beating them both to the punch by taking her into his arms. She rested her head against his chest. He put his arms around her, and things finally felt safe.

Nora Ray appeared out of the crowd, moving toward Tina's side.

"Betsy?" Tina murmured weakly. "Viv? Karen?"

"They're happy that you're alive," Nora Ray said quietly, squatting down next to Tina's prostrate form.

"Are they okay?"

"They're happy that you're alive."

Tina understood then. She closed her eyes. "I want my mother," she said, and then she started to cry.

"You'll be okay," Nora Ray said. "You have to take it from me. A bad thing happened, but you survived it. You won."

"How do you know?"

"Because three years ago, the same man kidnapped me."

Tina finally stopped crying. She looked at Nora Ray through bloodshot eyes. "Do you know where they're going to take me?"

"I don't know, but I can stay with you if you'd like."

"Buddy system?" Tina whispered.

Nora Ray finally smiled. She squeezed Tina's hand and said, "Always."

Epilogue

Quantico, Virginia
10:13 A.M.
Temperature: 88 degrees

She was running, tearing through the woods at breakneck speed. Dangling leaves snatched at her hair, low branches tore at her face. She leapt fallen tree trunks, then threw herself full throttle at the fifteen-foot wall. Her hands found the rope, her feet scrabbled for footing. Up, up, up she went, heart pounding, lungs heaving, and throat gasping.

She crested the top, had an absolutely stellar view of the lush, green Virginia woods, then flipped herself down the other side. Tires coming up. Bing, bing, bing, she punched one foot through the center of each rubber mass. Then she was hunched over like a turtle, scrambling down a narrow metal pipe. Now out the other end, racing down the homestretch. Sun on her face. Wind in her hair.

Kimberly careened over the finish line, just as Mac clicked off the stopwatch and said, "Ah, honey, you call that a time? Hell, I know guys that go twice as fast."

Kimberly launched herself at his chest. He saw the attack coming and tried to brace his feet. She'd learned a new move in combat training just last week, however, and had him flat on his back in no time.

She was still breathing hard, sweat glistening across her face and dampening her navy blue FBI Academy T-shirt. For a change, however, she wore a smile.

"Where's the knife?" Mac murmured with a wicked gleam in his eyes.

"Don't you wish."

"Pretty please. I can insult you more, if you'd like."

"No way can you do that course twice as fast."

"Well, I might have been exaggerating." His hands were now on her bare legs, tracing lines from her ankles up to the hem of her nylon shorts. "But I'm at *least* two seconds faster."

"Upper body strength," Kimberly spat out. "Men have more and it comes in handy at the wall."

"Yep, ain't life unfair?" He rolled with a surprise move of his own, and now she was the one on the dirt and he was the one looming above. Trapped, she did the sensible thing; she lunged up, grabbed his shoulders and nailed him with a long, lingering kiss.

"Miss me?" he gasped three seconds later.

"No. Not much."

Other voices were coming from the woods now. More students, taking advantage of this beautiful Saturday to train. Mac got up grudgingly. Kimberly vaulted up with more energy, hastily wiping dirt and leaves from her hair. The students were almost in view now, about to top the wall. Mac and Kimberly bolted for the shelter of the neighboring woods.

"How's it going?" Mac asked as they drifted into the lush, green shade.

"Hanging in there."

He stopped, took her arm, and made her face him. "No, Kimberly. I mean for real. How is it going?"

She shrugged, wishing the sight of him didn't make her want to throw her arms around his waist or bury her head against his shoulder. Wishing the sight of him didn't make her feel so damn giddy. Life was still life, and these days, hers carried a lot of obligations.

"Some of the students aren't wild about my presence," she admitted at last. She had resumed her studies nearly a month ago. Some of the powers-that-be weren't wild about it, but Rainie had been right: everybody blamed a failure, nobody argued with a hero. Kimberly and Mac's dramatic rescue of Tina Krahn had been front-page news for nearly a week. When she'd called Mark Watson about returning to the Academy, he'd even gotten her her own room.

"Not easy being recycled?"

"No. I'm the outsider who showed up halfway through the school year. Worse, I'm an outsider with a reputation half want to challenge and the other half don't want to believe."

"Are they mean to you?" he asked soberly, thumb beneath her chin.

"Someone actually short-sheeted my bed. Oh my God, the horrors. I should write home to Daddy."

"Uh oh, what did you do in retaliation?" Mac asked immediately.

"I haven't decided yet."

"Oh dear."

She resumed walking. After a moment, he fell in step beside her. "I'm going to make it, Mac," she said seriously. "Five weeks to go, and I'm going to make it. And if some people don't like me, that's okay. Because others do, and I'm good at this job. With more experience, I'm going to be even better at the job. Why, someday I might even follow a direct order. Think of what the Bureau will do then."

"You'll be like a whole new secret weapon," Mac said with awe.

"Exactly." She nodded her head with pride. Then, not being stupid, she regarded him intently. "So why are you here, Mac? And don't tell me you missed my smile. I know you're a little too busy for social calls these days."

"It's always something, isn't it?"

"At the moment."

He sighed, looked as if he wished he could say something clever, then must've decided to get on with it. "They found Ennunzio's body."

"Good." It had taken weeks to completely annihilate the swamp fire. In the good-news department, crews had contained the blaze fairly quickly, limiting damage. In the bad-news department, the smoldering peat continued to flare up for nearly a month, requiring constant vigilance on the part of the U.S. Forestry Service.

During that time, volunteers worked the site, tending the woods and seeking some sign of Ennunzio's body. As week had grown into week, they had all started getting a little nervous, especially Kimberly.

"He made it farther than any of us would've guessed," Mac was saying now. "True to his natural ambivalence, he must have decided at the last minute that he wanted to live. He actually hiked a good mile with his bitten leg. Who even knows what got him in the end? The venom pumped into his heart, or the smoke, or the flames?"

"They do a postmortem?"

"Completed it yesterday. Kimberly, he didn't have a tumor."

She halted, blinked her eyes a few times, then had to run a hand through her hair. "Well, that figures, doesn't it," she murmured. "Guy's such a fuck-up, he's gotta blame his actions on everything but himself. His mother, his brother, and a medical condition he doesn't even have. Doesn't that take the cake?"

"For the record, he did have a tumor once," Mac said. "Doctors confirmed his operation two years ago to remove the mass. According to them, a tumor could affect someone's propensity for violence. I understand there was even a mass murderer in Texas who claimed his actions were caused by a tumor."

"Charles Whitman," Kimberly murmured. "Stabbed his mother to death, then murdered his wife, then climbed a clock tower at the University of Texas and opened fire on the population below. In the end, he killed eighteen people and wounded thirty others before being shot and killed himself. He left a note, didn't he? Said he wanted an autopsy performed because he was sure there was something physically wrong with him."

"Exactly. The autopsy revealed a small tumor in his hypothalamus, which some experts say could have contributed to his rampage, while others claim it could not. Who knows? Maybe Ennunzio liked that story. Maybe it made an impression upon him, especially when he found out he had a tumor himself. But there was no tumor this time, so once again, he was just giving himself an excuse."

"You had him nailed in the beginning," Kimberly said. "Why does the Eco-Killer target and murder young women? Because he wants to. Sometimes, it really is as simple as that."

"The guy did feel some level of guilt," Mac said with a shrug. "Hence leaving us clues to find the second girl. Hence contacting the police as an anonymous tipster and getting us all into the game. Hence his personal involvement as an FBI agent, keeping us on track. When he analyzed the letters, he described the author as someone who felt compelled to kill, but who also wanted to be stopped. Maybe that was his way of trying to explain himself to us."

Kimberly, however, vehemently shook her head. "Did he really want to help, Mac, or did he just want more people to hurt? This is the guy who started out hating his father, but actually killed his mother and brother. He targeted young women, but also set up hazardous conditions for the search-

and-rescue volunteers. I don't think he placed those anonymous phone calls because he wanted you to catch him. He was seeking to involve more people in his game. He obviously didn't mind collateral damage. And if he could have, he would've killed us in the swamp that day."

"You're probably right."

"I'm glad he's dead."

"Honey, I'm not so sad about it myself."

"Any sign of the girls' cars?" she asked.

"Funny you should mention it; we think we've found one."

"Where at?"

"In the Tallulah Gorge, camouflaged with netting, green paint, and a whole lotta leaves. We're revisiting the other sites now, to see if we'll find the victims' vehicles nearby. We also discovered Ennunzio's home base—he has a cabin in the woods not far from here. Very rustic, like an old hunting shack. In it, we found a cot, gallons of water, boxes of crackers, a tranquilizer gun, and tons of drugs. He really could've kept doing this for a very long time."

"Then I'm doubly glad he's dead. And Tina?"

"At home in Minnesota with her mom," Mac reported immediately. "I understand from Nora Ray that Tina had just discovered she was pregnant before the kidnapping. Unfortunately, she lost the baby and is taking it rather hard. But I hear her mother's been a pillar of strength and Tina's gonna spend the rest of the summer recuperating at home, then see what she wants to do. She lost her three best friends; I'm not sure exactly how you recover from something like that. She and Nora Ray seem to have grown close, however. Maybe they can help each other out. Nora Ray's talking of visiting her in a few weeks. Minnesota has cooler summers. Nora Ray likes that. Okay, your turn. How're your father and Rainie?"

"They're in Oregon. They're planning on doing absolutely nothing but stroll on beaches and play a little golf until my graduation in five weeks. I give my father two days, and he'll be working the first local homicide case he can find. The Oregon cops will never know what hit them."

"Have dead body, will travel?" Mac teased her.

"Something like that."

"And you?" His finger traced a slow, gentle line down her cheek. Then both his hands settled on her waist. "What are you going to do in five weeks?"

"I'm a new agent," Kimberly said quietly. Her hands had come up, resting on the hard curve of his arms. "We don't have much say in things. You get assigned where you get assigned."

"Can you list preferences?"

"We can. I said Atlanta might be nice. No reason, of course."

"No reason?" Mac's hands stroked up her sides, his thumbs feathering across her breasts.

"Okay, I have a little bit of a reason."

"When will you know?"

"Yesterday."

"You mean . . ."

She smiled, feeling a little bit ridiculous now, and ducked her head. "Yeah, I got lucky. Atlanta's a big field office and they needed a fair amount of agents. I guess I'm going to have to learn to talk with a drawl, and drink a lot of Coke."

"I want you to meet my family," Mac said immediately. He was holding her tighter now. She hadn't been 100 percent sure of what he would think. They had both been so busy lately, and you never knew . . .

But he was grinning. His blue eyes danced. He bobbed his head and nailed her with a second kiss. "Oh, this will be fun!"

"I'm bringing my knife," she warned weakly.

"My sister will be thrilled."

"I'm not trying to rush you. I know we'll both be very busy."

"Shut up and kiss me again."

"Mac . . ."

"You're beautiful, Kimberly, and I love you."

She barely knew what to say anymore. She took his hand. She whispered the words. She pressed her lips against his.

Then they walked together through the woods, with the wind sighing in the trees and the sun shining softly overhead.